THE SPIRIT OF THE CITY

She haunts the city's streets at night—just as she haunts my mind.

I know her now. She's like a rose bush grown old, gone wild; untrimmed, neglected for years, the thorns become sharper, more bitter; her foliage spreading, grown out of control, reaching high and wide, while the center chokes and dies. The blossoms that remain are just small now, hidden in the wild growth, memories of what they once were.

I know her now. She's the spirit that connects the notes of a tune—the silences in between the sounds; the resonance that lies under the lines I put down on a page. Not a ghost, but a spirit all the same: the city's heart and soul.

I don't wonder about her origin. I don't wonder whether she was here first, and the city grew around her, or if the city created her. She just is. . . .

I look for her on my rambles. She's all around me, of course, in every brick of every building, in every whisper of wind as it scurries down an empty street. She's a cab's lights at 3:00 A.M., a siren near dawn, a shuffling bag lady pushing a squeaky grocery cart, a dark-eyed cat sitting on a shadowed stoop.

She's all around me, but I can't find her. . . .

Sometimes I wish I'd never met her.

"An undoubted master of urban fantasy."—*Booklist*

Tor books by Charles de Lint

Dreams Underfoot
The Fair at Emain Macha
Into the Green
The Little Country
Moonheart
Spiritwalk

∿ · ACKNOWLEDGMENTS · ∿

Creative endeavors require inspiration and nurturing, and these stories are no exception. I'd like to take this opportunity to thank a few people who were important to the existence of this collection:

First and foremost, my wife MaryAnn, not only for her indefatigable work as first reader and editor, but also for her part in the genesis of many of the individual stories;

Terri Windling, for her ongoing support, both professionally and personally, especially with this cycle of stories, and for providing the collection's title, which was also the title of her 1992 one-woman art show at the Book Arts Gallery in Tucson, Arizona;

Kris Rusch and Dean Smith of Axolotl Press/Pulphouse Publishing, who were always asking for more stories and provided the first home for many of these;

And for all those other editors who gave me the opportunity to take a holiday from longer work to explore Newford's streets: Bruce Barber, Ellen Datlow, Gardner Dozois, Robert T. Garcia, Ed Gorman, Martin H. Greenberg, Cara Inks, Paul F. Olson, Jan and George O'Nale, Byron Preiss and David B. Silva.

∽· CONTENTS ·∽

Tread softly because you tread on my dreams.
　　　—W. B. YEATS, FROM "HE WISHES
　　　　FOR THE CLOTHS OF HEAVEN"

DREAMS UNDERFOOT

⌐• INTRODUCTION •⌐

The book you hold is neither a novel nor a simple gathering of short stories. Rather, it is a cycle of urban myths and dreams, of passions and sorrows, romance and farce woven together to create a tapestry of interconnected dramas, interconnected lives—the kind of magic to be found at the heart of any city, among any tightly knit community of friends. If the imaginary city of Newford is more mythic, more mysterious than the cities you have known, that may be only because you've not seen them through Charles de Lint's eyes, through the twilight dreams he weaves out of language and music. Here he spreads these dreams before us and bids us, in the words of Yeats's poem, to *tread softly,* for urban magic is fleeting and shy . . . and its touch is a transformation.

Joseph Campbell, Carl Jung, James Hillman, Louise-Marie von Franz and others have written eloquently and extensively about the importance of myth in our modern society, the need for tales rich in archetypal images to give coherence to fragmented modern lives. "Using archetypes and symbolic language,'' writes folklore scholar and author Jane Yolen, ''[fantasy tales] externalize for the listener conflicts and situations that cannot be spoken of or explained or as yet analyzed. They give substance to dreams . . . [and] lead us to the understanding of the deepest longings and most daring visions of humankind. The images from the ancients speak to us in modern tongue though we may not always grasp the 'meanings' consciously. Like dreams, the meanings slip away, leaving us shaken into new awarenesses. We are moved by them, even when—or perhaps *because*—we do not understand them on a conscious level. They are penumbral, partially lit, and it is the dark side that has the most power. So when the modern mythmaker, the writer of literary fairy tales, dares to touch the old magic and try to make it work in new ways, it must be done with the surest of touches.''

De Lint is one of those writers who mine this vein with a deft, sure touch. Readers new to his distinctive brand of ''urban fantasy'' might find his mix of ancient folklore motifs and contemporary urban characters somewhat startling—for ours is a society that loves to separate and classify, putting ''fantasy'' fiction on a shelf far away from books of ''realistic'' or ''mainstream'' fiction (despite the fact that the mainstream shelves include works of modern fantasy by foreign authors such as Calvino, Allende and Garcia Marquez). While American book distributors and critics continue to build up genre walls, writers like de Lint are quietly laboring to take them down again, brick by brick, story by story. Forget the labels. Forget the assumptions you make when you think of *fantasy,* or even *short story collections.* And then you will be able to fully enter the enchanted streets de Lint has created.

We enter Newford via the more familiar streets of Los Angeles, via the tales of Newford author Christy Riddell; and then de Lint leads us on to Newford itself, a North American city that might exist anywhere or nowhere, thousands of miles away or just past the next exit on the Interstate. Like any city, Newford has its posh districts, its slums, its day-life and night-life and the twilight between; but most of all it's the street people, the downtown people, that de Lint wants us to meet: the buskers and artists, punkers and gypsies, street walkers and wizards and runaway kids, people for whom magic is not just a supernatural visitation but a manifestation of the soul's deepest longings and a bright spark of hope lodged within a desperate heart. The greatest magic on the streets of Newford is the magic of community, of friendship and love, support and compassion—for these are the larger themes de Lint uses the bright symbols of folklore to address.

In Newford, *creation* is the supreme act of magic, whether that creation be a painting, a fiddle tune or a poem, an AIDS clinic or battered children's shelter, or one's own family and a harmonious way of life. By these acts we create magic in our own lives; by these acts, large and small, we reinvent the world. For de Lint, these acts are transformed into stories to nurture the growth of his Tree of Tales, which contains the collective stories of the world:

"The Tree of Tales," says de Lint's Conjure Man, "is an act of magic, an act of faith. Its existence becomes an affirmation of the power that the human spirit can have over its own destiny. The stories are just stories—they entertain, they make one laugh or cry—but if they have any worth they carry with them a deeper resonance that remains long after the final page is turned. . . ."

The interconnected stories of the Newford cycle are a particularly lovely new limb on that ancient tree, and one that shall grow and flower beyond the pages of this single book as de Lint continues to explore Newford's myriad streets.

In his own city of Ottawa, in Canada, Charles de Lint is a novelist, a poet, a fiddler, a flute-player, a painter, a critic and folklore scholar; but most of all he is a magician: the kind who makes magic with his multi-disciplined creativity, with the tools of myth, folklore and fantasy. "I think those of us who write fantasy," said fellow author Susan Cooper in her Newbery Award acceptance speech, "are dedicated to making impossible things seem likely, making dreams seem real. We are somewhere between the Abstract and Impressionist painters. Our writing is haunted by those parts of our experience which we do not understand, or even consciously remember. And if you, child or adult, are drawn to our work, your response comes from that same shadowy land. . . . I have been attempting definitions, but I am never really comfortable when writing about 'fantasy.' The label is so limiting. It seems to me that every work of art is a fantasy, every book or play, painting or piece of music, everything that is made, by craft and talent, out of somebody's imagination. We have all dreamed, and recorded our dreams as best we could."

In these pages, de Lint has recorded dreams: Jilly Coppercorn's and Geordie's, Sophie's and Christy's, Tallulah's and the dreams of Newford itself. There are dreams underfoot here, some fragile as spiders' webs, others solid as asphalt and brick-cobbled streets. As you walk into the heart of the city of Newford, remember: tread warily. Tread softly.

—Terri Windling
*(Co-editor of "The Year's Best
Fantasy" annual collection)*
Weaver's Cottage, Devon, 1992

UNCLE DOBBIN'S
⌐·PARROT FAIR·⌐

1

S HE WOULD SEE them in the twilight when the wind was
right, roly-poly shapes propelled by ocean breezes, turning end-over-end along the beach or down the alley behind
her house like errant beach balls granted a moment's freedom. Sometimes they would get caught up against a building
or stuck on a curb and then spindly little arms and legs
would unfold from their fat bodies until they could push
themselves free and go rolling with the wind again. Like
flotsam in a river, like tumbleweeds, only brightly colored in
primary reds and yellows and blues.

They seemed very solid until the wind died down. Then
she would watch them come apart the way morning mist will
when the sun burns it away, the bright colors turning to ragged ribbons that tattered smoke-like until they were completely gone.

Those were special nights, the evenings that the Balloon
Men came.

* * *

In the late sixties in Haight-Ashbury, she talked about them once. Incense lay thick in the air—two cones of jasmine burning on a battered windowsill. There was an old iron bed in the room, up on the third floor of a house that no one lived in except for runaways and street people. The mattress had rust-colored stains on it. The incense covered the room's musty smell. She'd lived in a form of self-imposed poverty back then, but it was all a part of the Summer of Love.

"I know what you mean, man," Greg Longman told her. "I've seen them."

He was wearing a dirty white T-shirt with a simple peace symbol on it and scuffed plastic thongs. Sticking up from the waist of his bell-bottomed jeans at a forty-five degree angle was a descant recorder. His long blonde hair was tied back with an elastic. His features were thin—an ascetic-looking face, thin and drawn-out from too much time on the streets with too little to eat, or from too much dope.

"They're like . . ." His hands moved as he spoke, trying to convey what he didn't feel words alone could say— a whole other language, she often thought, watching the long slender fingers weave through the air between them. ". . . they're just too much."

"You've really seen them?" she asked.

"Oh, yeah. Except not on the streets. They're floating high up in the air, y'know, like fat little kites."

It was such a relief to know that they were real.

" 'Course," Greg added, "I gotta do a lot of dope to clue in on 'em, man."

Ellen Brady laid her book aside. Leaning back, she flicked off the light behind her and stared out into the night. The memory had come back to her, so clear, so sharp, she could almost smell the incense, see Greg's hands move between them, little colored afterimage traces following each movement until he had more arms than Kali.

She wondered what had ever happened to the Balloon Men.

Long light-brown hair hung like a cape to her waist. Her parents were Irish—Munster O'Healys on her mother's side, and Bradys from Derry on her father's. There was a touch of Spanish blood in her mother's side of the family, which gave her skin its warm dark cast. The Bradys were pure Irish and it was from them that she got her big-boned frame. And something else. Her eyes were a clear grey—twilight eyes, her father had liked to tease her, eyes that could see beyond the here and now into somewhere else.

She hadn't needed drugs to see the Balloon Men.

Shifting in her wicker chair, she looked up and down the beach, but it was late and the wind wasn't coming in from the ocean. The book on her lap was a comforting weight and had, considering her present state of mind, an even more appropriate title. *How to Make the Wind Blow.* If only it *was* a tutor, she thought, instead of just a collection of odd stories.

The author's name was Christy Riddell, a reed-thin Scot with a head full of sudden fancies. His hair was like an unruly hedgerow nest and he was half a head shorter than she, but she could recall dancing with him in a garden one night and she hadn't had a more suitable partner since. She'd met him while visiting friends in a house out east that was as odd as any flight of his imagination. Long rambling halls connected a bewildering series of rooms, each more fascinating than the next. And the libraries. She'd lived in its libraries.

"When the wind is right," began the title story, the first story in the book, "the wise man isn't half so trusted as the fool."

Ellen could remember when it was still a story that was told without the benefit of pen and paper. A story that changed each time the words traveled from mouth to ear:

There was a gnome, or a gnomish sort of a man, named Long who lived under the pier at the end of Main Street. He had skin brown as dirt, eyes blue as a clear summer sky. He was thin, with a fat tummy and a long crooked nose, and he wore raggedy clothes that he found discarded on the beach and wore until they were threadbare. Sometimes he bundled his tangled hair up under a bright yellow cap. Other times he wove it into many braids festooned with colored beads and the discarded tabs from beer cans that he polished on his sleeve until they were bright and shiny.

Though he'd seem more odd than magical to anyone who happened to spy him out wandering the streets or along the beach, he did have two enchantments.

One was a pig that could see the wind and follow it anywhere. She was pink and fastidiously clean, big enough to ride to market—which Long sometimes did—and she could talk. Not pig-talk, or even pig-Latin, but plain English that anyone could understand if they took the time to listen. Her name changed from telling to telling, but by the time Long's story appeared in the book either she or Christy had settled on Brigwin.

Long's other enchantment was a piece of plain string with four complicated elf-knots tied in it—one to call up a wind from each of the four quarters. North and south. East and west. When he untied a knot, that wind would rise up and he'd ride Brigwin in its wake, sifting through the debris and pickings left behind for treasures or charms, though what Long considered a treasure, another might throw out, and what he might consider a charm, another might see as only an old button or a bit of tangled wool. He had a good business trading his findings to woodwives and witches and the like that he met at the market when midnight was past and gone, ordinary folk were in bed, and the beach towns belonged to those who hid by day, but walked the streets by night.

Ellen carried a piece of string in her pocket, with four complicated knots tied into it, but no matter how often she undid one, she still had to wait for her winds like anyone else. She knew that strings to catch and call up the wind were only real in stories, but she liked thinking that maybe, just once, a bit of magic could tiptoe out of a tale and step into the real world. Until that happened, she had to be content with what writers like Christy put to paper.

He called them mythistories, those odd little tales of his. They were the ghosts of fancies that he would track down from time to time and trap on paper. Oddities. Some charming, some grotesque. All of them enchanting. Foolishness, he liked to say, offered from one fool to others.

Ellen smiled. Oh, yes. But when the wind is right . . .

She'd never talked to Christy about the Balloon Men, but she didn't doubt that he knew them.

Leaning over the rail of the balcony, two stories above the walkway that ran the length of the beach, Christy's book held tight in one hand, she wished very hard to see those roly-poly figures one more time. The ocean beat its rhythm against the sand. A light breeze caught at her hair and twisted it into her face.

When the wind is right.

Something fluttered inside her, like wings unfolding, readying for flight. Rising from her chair, she set the book down on its wicker arm and went inside. Down the stairs and out the front door. She could feel a thrumming between her ears that had to be excitement moving blood more quickly through her veins, though it could have been the echo of a half-lost memory—a singing of small deep voices, rising up from diaphragms nestled in fat little bellies.

Perhaps the wind *was* right, she thought as she stepped out onto the walkway. A quarter moon peeked at her from above the oil rigs far out from the shore. She put her hand in the pocket of her cotton pants and wound the knotted string she found there around one finger. It was late, late for the Balloon Men to be rolling, but she didn't doubt that there was something waiting to greet her out on the street. Perhaps only memories. Perhaps a fancy that Christy hadn't trapped on a page yet.

There was only one way to find out.

2

Peregrin Laurie was as sharp-faced as a weasel—a narrow-shouldered thin whip of a teenager in jeans and a torn T-shirt. He sat in a doorway, knees up by his chin, a mane of spiked multi-colored hair standing straight up from his head in a two-inch Mohawk swath that ran down to the nape of his neck like a lizard's crest fringes. Wrapping his arms around bruised ribs, he held back tears as each breath he took made his chest burn.

Goddamn beach bums. The bastards had just about killed him and he had no one to blame but himself. Scuffing through a parking lot, he should have taken off when the car pulled up. But no. He had to be the poseur and hold his ground, giving them a long cool look as they came piling drunkenly out of the car. By the time he realized just how many of them there were and what they had planned for him, it was too late to run. He'd had to stand there then, heart hammering in his chest, and hope bravado'd see him through, because there was no way he could handle them all.

They didn't stop to chat. They just laid into him. He got a few licks in, but he knew it was hopeless. By the time he hit the pavement, all he could do was curl up into a tight ball and take their drunken kicks, cursing them with each fiery gasp of air he dragged into his lungs.

The booger waited until he was down and hurting before making its appearance. It came out from under the pier that ran by the parking lot, black and greasy, with hot eyes and a mouthful of barracuda teeth. If it hadn't hurt so much just to breathe, he would have laughed at the way his attackers backed away from the creature, eyes bulging as they rushed to their car. They took off, tires squealing, but not before the booger took a chunk of metal out of the rear fender with one swipe of a paw.

It came back to look at him—black nightmare head snuffling at him as he lifted his head and wiped the blood from his face, then moving away as he reached out a hand towards it. It smelled like a sewer and looked worse, a squat creature that had to have been scraped out of some monstrous nose, with eyes like hot coals in a smear of a face and a slick wet look to its skin. A booger, plain and simple. Only it was alive, clawed and toothed. Following him around ever since he'd run away. . . .

His parents were both burnouts from the sixties. They lived in West Hollywood and got more embarrassing the older he became. Take his name. Laurie was bad enough, but Peregrin . . . Lifted straight out of that *Lord of the Rings* book. An okay read, sure, but you don't use it to name your kid. Maybe he should just be thankful he didn't get stuck with Frodo or Bilbo. By the time he was old enough to start thinking for himself, he'd picked out his own name and wouldn't answer to anything but Reece. He'd gotten it out of some book, too, but at least it sounded cool. You needed all the cool you could get with parents like his.

His old man still had hair down to his ass. He wore wire-framed glasses and listened to shit on the stereo that sounded as burned-out as he looked. The old lady wasn't much better. Putting on weight like a whale, hair a frizzy brown, as long as the old man's, but usually hanging in a braid. Coming home late some nights, the whole house'd have the sweet smell of weed mixed with incense and they'd give him these goofy looks and talk about getting in touch with the cosmos and other spacey shit. When anybody came down on him for the way he looked, or for dropping out of school, all they said was let him do his own thing.

His own thing. Jesus. Give me a break. With that kind of crap to look forward to at home, who wouldn't take off first chance they got? Though wouldn't you know it, no sooner did he get free of them than the booger latched onto him, following him around, skulking in the shadows.

At first, Reece never got much of a look at the thing—just

glimpses out of the corner of his eyes—and that was more than enough. But sleeping on the beaches and in parks, some nights he'd wake with that sewer smell in his nostrils and catch something slipping out of sight, a dark wet shadow moving close to the ground. After a few weeks, it started to get bolder, sitting on its haunches a half-dozen yards from wherever he was bedding down, the hot coal eyes fixed on him.

Reece didn't know what it was or what it wanted. Was it looking out for him, or saving him up for its supper? Sometimes he thought, what with all the drugs his parents had done back in the sixties—good times for them, shit for him because he'd been born and that was when his troubles had started—he was sure that all those chemicals had fucked up his genes. Twisted something in his head so that he imagined he had this two-foot high, walking, grunting booger following him around.

Like the old man'd say. Bummer.

Sucker sure seemed real, though.

Reece held his hurt to himself, ignoring Ellen as she approached. When she stopped in front of him, he gave her a scowl.

"Are you okay?" she asked, leaning closer to look at him.

He gave her a withering glance. The long hair and jeans, flowered blouse. Just what he needed. Another sixties burnout.

"Why don't you just fuck off and die?" he said.

But Ellen looked past the tough pose to see the blood on his shirt, the bruising on his face that the shadows half-hid, the hurt he was trying so hard to pretend wasn't there.

"Where do you live?" she asked.

"What's it to you?"

Ignoring his scowl, she bent down and started to help him to his feet.

"Aw, fuck—" Reece began, but it was easier on his ribs to stand up than to fight her.

"Let's get you cleaned up," she said.

"Florence fucking Nightingale," he muttered, but she merely led him back the way she'd come.

From under the pier a wet shadow stirred at their departure. Reece's booger drew back lips that had the rubbery texture of an octopus' skin. Row on row of pointed teeth reflected back the light from the streetlights. Hate-hot eyes glimmered red. On silent leathery paws, the creature followed the slow-moving pair, grunting softly to itself, claws clicking on the pavement.

3

Bramley Dapple was the wizard in "A Week of Saturdays," the third story in Christy Riddell's *How to Make the Wind Blow*. He was a small wizened old man, spry as a kitten, thin as a reed, with features lined and brown as a dried fig. He wore a pair of wire-rimmed spectacles without prescription lenses that he polished incessantly, and he loved to talk.

"It doesn't matter what they believe," he was saying to his guest, "so much as what *you* believe."

He paused as the brown-skinned goblin who looked after his house came in with a tray of biscuits and tea. His name was Goon, a tallish creature at three-foot-four who wore the garb of an organ-grinder's monkey: striped black and yellow trousers, a red jacket with yellow trim, small black slippers, and a little green and yellow cap that pushed down an unruly mop of thin dark curly hair. Gangly limbs with a protruding tummy, puffed cheeks, a wide nose, and tiny black eyes added to his monkey-like appearance.

The wizard's guest observed Goon's entrance with a startled look, which pleased Bramley to no end.

"There," he said. "Goon proves my point."

"I beg your pardon?"

"We live in a consensual reality where things exist because we want them to exist. I believe in Goon, Goon believes in Goon, and you, presented with his undeniable presence, tea tray in hand, believe in Goon as well. Yet, if you were to listen to the world at large, Goon is nothing more than a figment of some fevered writer's imagination—a literary construct, an artistic representation of something that can't possibly exist in the world as we know it."

Goon gave Bramley a sour look, but the wizard's guest leaned forward, hand outstretched, and brushed the goblin's shoulder with a feather-light touch. Slowly she leaned back into the big armchair, cushions so comfortable they seemed to embrace her as she settled against them.

"So . . . anything we can imagine can exist?" she asked finally.

Goon turned his sour look on her now.

She was a student at the university where the wizard taught; third year, majoring in fine arts, and she had the look of an artist about her. There were old paint stains on her jeans and under her fingernails. Her hair was a thick tangle of brown hair, more unruly than Goon's curls. She had a smudge of a nose and thin puckering lips, workman's boots that stood by the door with a history of scuffs and stains written into their leather, thick woolen socks with a hole in the left heel, and one shirttail that had escaped the waist of her jeans. But her eyes were a pale, pale blue, clear and alert, for all the casualness of her attire.

Her name was Jilly Coppercorn.

Bramley shook his head. "It's not imagining. It's knowing that it exists—without one smidgen of doubt."

"Yes, but someone had to think him up for him to . . ." She hesitated as Goon's scowl deepened. "That is . . ."

Bramley continued to shake his head. "There is some semblance of order to things," he admitted, "for if the world was simply everyone's different conceptual universe mixed up together, we'd have nothing but chaos. It all relies on will, you see—to observe the changes, at any rate. Or the differences. The anomalies. Like Goon—oh, do stop scowling,'' he added to the goblin.

"The world as we have it," he went on to Jilly, "is here mostly because of habit. We've all agreed that certain things exist—we're taught as impressionable infants that this is a table and this is what it looks like, that's a tree out the window there, a dog looks and sounds just so. At the same time we're informed that Goon and his like don't exist, so we don't—or can't—see them."

"They're not made up?" Jilly asked.

This was too much for Goon. He set the tray down and gave her leg a pinch. Jilly jumped away from him, trying to back deeper into the chair as the goblin grinned, revealing two rows of decidedly nasty-looking teeth.

"Rather impolite," Bramley said, "but I suppose you do get the point?"

Jilly nodded quickly. Still grinning, Goon set about pouring their teas.

"So," Jilly asked, "how can someone . . . how can I see things as they really are?"

"Well, it's not that simple," the wizard told her. "First you have to know what it is that you're looking for—before you can find it, you see."

Ellen closed the book and leaned back in her own chair, thinking about that, about Balloon Men, about the young man lying in her bed. To know what you were looking for. Was that why when she went out hoping to find Balloon Men, she'd come home with Reece?

She got up and went to the bedroom door to look in at him. After much protesting, he'd finally let her clean his hurts and put him to bed. Claiming to be not the least bit hungry, he'd polished off a whole tin of soup and the better part of the loaf of sourdough bread that she had just bought that afternoon. Then, of course, he wasn't tired at all and promptly fell asleep the moment his head touched the pillow.

She shook her head, looking at him now. His rainbow Mohawk made it look as though she'd brought some hybrid creature into her home—part rooster, part boy, it lay in her bed snoring softly, hardly real. But definitely not a Balloon Man, she thought, looking at his thin torso under the sheets.

About to turn away, something at the window caught her eye. Frozen in place, she saw a dog-like face peering back at her from the other side of the pane—which was patently impossible since the bedroom was on the second floor and there was nothing to stand on outside that window. But impossible or not, that dog-like face with its coal-red eyes and a fierce grin of glimmering teeth was there all the same.

She stared at it, feeling sick as the moments ticked by. Hunger burned in those eyes. Anger. Unbridled hate. She couldn't move, not until it finally disappeared—sliding from sight, physically escaping rather than vanishing the way a hallucination should.

She leaned weakly against the doorjamb, a faint buzzing in her head. Not until she'd caught her breath did she go to the window, but of course there was nothing there. Consensual reality, Christy's wizard had called it. Things that exist because we want them to exist. But she knew that not even in a nightmare would she consider giving life to that monstrous head she'd seen staring back in at her from the night beyond her window.

Her gaze went to the sleeping boy in her bed. All that anger burning up inside him. Had she caught a glimpse of something that *he'd* given life to?

Ellen, she told herself as she backed out of the room, you're making entirely too much out of nothing. Except something had certainly seemed to be there. There was absolutely no question in her mind that *something* had been out there.

In the living room she looked down at Christy's book. Bramley Dapple's words skittered through her mind, chased by a feeling of . . . of strangeness that she couldn't shake. The wind, the night, finding Reece in that doorway. And now that thing in the window.

She went and poured herself a brandy before making her bed on the sofa, studiously avoiding looking at the windows. She knew she was being silly—she had to have imagined it—but there was a feeling in the air tonight, a sense of being on the edge of something vast and grey. One false step, and she'd plunge down into it. A void. A nightmare.

It took a second brandy before she fell asleep.

Outside, Reece's booger snuffled around the walls of the house, crawling up the side of the building from time to time to peer into this or that window. Something kept it from entering—some disturbance in the air that was like a wind, but not a wind at the same time. When it finally retreated, it was with the knowledge in what passed for its mind that time itself was the key. Hours and minutes would unlock whatever kept it presently at bay.

Barracuda teeth gleamed as the creature grinned. It could wait. Not long, but it could wait.

4

Ellen woke the next morning, stiff from a night spent on the sofa, and wondered what in God's name had possessed her to bring Reece home. Though on reflection, she realized, the whole night had proceeded with a certain surreal quality of which Reece had only been a small part. Rereading Christy's book. That horrific face at the window. And the Balloon Men—she hadn't thought of them in years.

Swinging her feet to the floor, she went out onto her balcony. There was a light fog hazing the air. Boogie-boarders were riding the waves close by the pier—only a handful of them now, but in an hour or so their numbers would have multiplied beyond count. Raking machines were cleaning the beach, their dull roar vying with the pounding of the tide. Men with metal detectors were patiently sifting through the debris the machines left behind before the trucks came to haul it away. Near the tide's edge a man was jogging backwards across the sand, sharply silhouetted against the ocean.

Nothing out of the ordinary. But returning inside she couldn't shake the feeling that there was someone in her head, something flying dark-winged across her inner terrain like a crow. When she went to wash up, she found its crow eyes staring back at her from the mirror. Wild eyes.

Shivering, she finished up quickly. By the time Reece woke she was sitting outside on the balcony in a sweatshirt and shorts, nursing a mug of coffee. The odd feeling of being possessed had mostly gone away and the night just past took on the fading quality of half-remembered dreams.

She looked up at his appearance, smiling at the way a night's sleep had rearranged the lizard crest fringes of his Mohawk. Some of it was pressed flat against his skull. Elsewhere, multi-colored tufts stood up at bizarre angles. His mouth was a sullen slash in a field of short beard stubble, but his eyes still had a sleepy look to them, softening his features.

"You do this a lot?" he asked, slouching into the other wicker chair on the balcony.

"What? Drink coffee in the morning?"

"Pick up strays."

"You looked like you needed help."

Reece nodded. "Right. We're all brothers and sisters on starship earth. I kinda figured you for a bleeding heart."

His harsh tone soured Ellen's humour. She felt the something that had watched her from the bathroom mirror flutter inside her and her thoughts returned to the previous night. Christy's wizard talking. *Things exist because we want them to exist.*

"After you fell asleep," she said, "I thought I saw something peering in through the bedroom window. . . ."

Her voice trailed off when she realized that she didn't quite know where she was going with that line of thought. But Reece sat up from his slouch, suddenly alert.

"What kind of something?" he asked.

Ellen tried to laugh it off. "A monster," she said with a smile. "Red-eyed and all teeth." She shrugged. "I was just having one of those nights."

"You *saw* it?" Reece demanded sharply enough to make Ellen sit up straighter as well.

"Well, I thought I saw something, but it was patently impossible so . . ." Again her voice trailed off. Reece had sunk back into his chair and was staring off towards the ocean.

"What . . . what was it?" Ellen asked.

"I call it a booger," he replied. "I don't know what the hell it is, but it's been following me ever since I took off from my parents' place. . . ."

The stories in Christy's book weren't all charming. There was one near the end called "Raw Eggs" about a man who had a *Ghostbusters*-like creature living in his fridge that fed on raw eggs. It pierced the shells with a needle-fine tooth, then sucked out the contents, leaving rows of empty eggshells behind. When the man got tired of replacing his eggs, the creature crawled out of the fridge one night, driven forth by hunger, and fed on the eyes of the man's family.

The man had always had a fear of going blind. He died at the end of the story, and the creature moved on to another household, more hungry than ever. . . .

Reece laid aside Christy Riddell's book and went looking for Ellen. He found her sitting on the beach, a big, loose T-shirt covering her bikini, her bare legs tucked under her. She was staring out to sea, past the waves breaking on the shore, past the swimmers, body-surfers and kids riding their boogie-boards, past the oil rigs to the horizon hidden in a haze in the far-off distance. He got a lot of weird stares as he scuffed his way across the sand to finally sit down beside her.

"They're just stories in that book, right?" he said finally.

"You tell me."

"Look. The booger it's—Christ, I don't know what it is. But it can't be real."

Ellen shrugged. "I was up getting some milk at John's earlier," she said, "and I overheard a couple of kids talking about some friends of theirs. Seems they were having some fun in the parking lot last night with a punker when something came at them from under the pier and tore off part of their bumper."

"Yeah, but—"

Ellen turned from the distant view to look at him. Her eyes held endless vistas in them and she felt the flutter of wings in her mind.

"I want to know how you did it," she said. "How you brought it to life."

"Look, lady. I don't—"

"It doesn't have to be a horror," she said fiercely. "It can be something good, too." She thought of the gnome that lived under the pier in Christy's story and her own Balloon Men. "I want to be able to see them again."

Their gazes locked. Reece saw a darkness behind Ellen's clear grey eyes, some wildness that reminded him of his booger in its intensity.

"I'd tell you if I knew," he said finally.

Ellen continued to study him, then slowly turned to look back across the waves. "Will it come to you tonight?" she asked.

"I don't kn—" Reece began, but Ellen turned to him again. At the look in her eyes, he nodded. "Yeah," he said then. "I guess it will."

"I want to be there when it does," she said.

Because if it was real, then it could all be real. If she could see the booger, if she could understand what animated it, if she could learn to really *see* and, as Christy's wizard had taught Jilly Coppercorn, *know* what she was looking for herself, then she could bring her own touch of wonder into the world. Her own magic.

She gripped Reece's arm. "Promise me you won't take off until I've had a chance to see it."

She had to be weirded-out, Reece thought. She didn't have the same kind of screws loose that his parents did, but she was gone all the same. Only, that book she'd had him read . . . it made a weird kind of sense. If you were going to accept that kind of shit as being possible, it might just work the way that book said it did. Weird, yeah. But when he thought of the booger itself . . .

"Promise me," she repeated.

He disengaged her fingers from his arm. "Sure," he said. "I got nowhere to go anyway."

5

They ate at The Green Pepper that night, a Mexican restaurant on Main Street. Reece studied his companion across the table, re-evaluating his earlier impressions of her. Her hair was up in a loose bun now and she wore a silky cream-colored blouse above a slim dark skirt. Mentally she was definitely a bit weird, but not a burnout like his parents. She looked like the kind of customer who shopped in the trendy galleries and boutiques on Melrose Avenue where his old lady worked, back home in West Hollywood. Half the people in the restaurant were probably wondering what the hell she was doing sitting here with a scuzz like him.

Ellen looked up and caught his gaze. A smile touched her lips. "The cook must be in a good mood," she said.

"What do you mean?"

"Well, I've heard that the worse mood he's in, the hotter he makes his sauces."

Reece tried to give her back a smile, but his heart wasn't in it. He wanted a beer, but they wouldn't serve him here because he was underage. He found himself wishing Ellen wasn't so much older than him, that he didn't look like such a freak sitting here with her. For the first time since he'd done his hair, he was embarrassed about the way he looked. He wanted to enjoy just sitting here with her instead of knowing that everyone was looking at him like he was some kind of geek.

"You okay?" Ellen asked.

"Yeah. Sure. Great food."

He pushed the remainder of his rice around on the plate with his fork. Yeah, he had no problems. Just no place to go, no place to fit in. Body aching from last night's beating. Woman sitting there across from him, looking tasty, but she was too old for him and there was something in her eyes that scared him a little. Not to mention a nightmare booger dogging his footsteps. Sure. Things were just rocking, mama.

He stole another glance at her, but she was looking away, out to the darkening street, wine glass raised to her mouth.

"That book your friend wrote," he said.

Her gaze shifted to his face and she put her glass down.

"It doesn't have anything like my booger in it," Reece continued. "I mean it's got some ugly stuff, but nothing just like the booger."

"No," Ellen replied. "But it's got to work the same way. We can see it because we believe it's there."

"So was it always there and we're just aware of it now? Or does it exist *because* we believe in it? Is it something that came out of us—out of me?"

"Like Uncle Dobbin's birds, you mean?"

Reece nodded, unaware of the flutter of dark wings that Ellen felt stir inside her.

"I don't know," she said softly.

* * *

"Uncle Dobbin's Parrot Fair" was the last story in Christy Riddell's book, the title coming from the name of the pet shop that Timothy James Dobbin owned in Santa Ana. It was a gathering place for every kind of bird, tame as well as wild. There were finches in cages and parrots with the run of the shop, not to mention everything from sparrows to crows and gulls crowding around outside.

In the story, T. J. Dobbin was a retired sailor with an interest in nineteenth-century poets, an old bearded tar with grizzled red hair and beetling brows who wore baggy blue cotton trousers and a white T-shirt as he worked in his store, cleaning the bird cages, feeding the parakeets, teaching the parrots words. Everybody called him Uncle Dobbin.

He had a sixteen-year-old assistant named Nori Wert who helped out on weekends. She had short blonde hair and a deep tan that she started working on as soon as school was out. To set it off she invariably wore white shorts and a tank-top. The only thing she liked better than the beach was the birds in Uncle Dobbin's shop, and that was because she knew their secret.

She didn't find out about them right away. It took a year or so of coming in and hanging around the shop and then another three weekends of working there before she finally approached Uncle Dobbin with what had been bothering her.

"I've been wondering," she said as she sat down on the edge of his cluttered desk at the back of the store. She fingered the world globe beside the blotter and gave it a desultory spin.

Uncle Dobbin raised his brow questioningly and continued to fill his pipe.

"It's the birds," she said. "We never sell any—at least not since I've started working here. People come in and they look around, but no one asks the price of anything, no one ever buys anything. I guess you could do most of your business during the week, but then why did you hire me?"

Uncle Dobbin looked down into the bowl of his pipe to

make sure the tobacco was tamped properly. "Because you like birds," he said before he lit a match. Smoke wreathed up towards the ceiling. A bright green parrot gave a squawk from where it was roosting nearby and turned its back on them.

"But you don't sell any of them, do you?" Being curious, she'd poked through his file cabinet to look at invoices and sales receipts to find that all he ever bought was birdfood and cages and the like, and he never sold a thing. At least no sales were recorded.

"Can't sell them."

"Why not?"

"They're not mine to sell."

Nori sighed. "Then whose are they?"

"Better you should ask what are they."

"Okay," Nori said, giving him an odd look. "I'll bite. What are they?"

"Magic."

Nori studied him for a moment and he returned her gaze steadily, giving no indication that he was teasing her. He puffed on his pipe, a serious look in his eyes, then took the pipe stem from his mouth. Setting the pipe carefully on the desk so that it wouldn't tip over, he leaned forward in his chair.

"People have magic," he said, "but most of them don't want it, or don't believe in it, or did once, but then forgot. So I take that magic and make it into birds until they want it back, or someone else can use it."

"Magic."

"That's right."

"Not birds."

Uncle Dobbin nodded.

"That's crazy," Nori said.

"Is it?"

He got up stiffly from his chair and stood in front of her with his hands outstretched towards her chest. Nori shrank back from him, figuring he'd flaked out and was going to cop a quick feel, but his hands paused just a few inches from her breasts. She felt a sudden pain inside—like a stitch in her side from running too hard, only it was deep in her chest. Right in her lungs. She looked down, eyes widening as a beak appeared poking out of her chest, followed by a parrot's head, its body and wings.

It was like one of the holograms at the Haunted House in Disneyland, for she could see right through it, then it grew solid once it was fully emerged. The pain stopped as the bird fluttered free, but she felt an empty aching inside. Uncle Dobbin caught the bird, and soothed it with a practiced touch, before letting it fly free. Numbly, Nori watched it wing across the store and settle down near the front window where it began to preen its feathers. The sense of loss inside grew stronger.

"That . . . it was in me . . . I . . ."

Uncle Dobbin made his way back to his chair and sat down, picking up his pipe once more.

"Magic," he said before he lit it.

"My . . . my magic . . . ?"

Uncle Dobbin nodded. "But not anymore. You didn't believe."

"But I didn't know!" she wailed.

"You got to earn it back now," Uncle Dobbin told her. "The side cages need cleaning."

Nori pressed her hands against her chest, then wrapped her arms around herself in a tight hug as though that would somehow ease the empty feeling inside her.

"E-earn it?" she said in a small voice, her gaze going from his face to the parrot that had come out of her chest and was now sitting by the front window. "By . . . by working here?"

Uncle Dobbin shook his head. "You already work here and I pay you for that, don't I?"

"But then how . . . ?"

"You've got to earn its trust. You've got to learn to believe in it again."

* * *

Ellen shook her head softly. Learn to believe, she thought. I've always believed. But maybe never hard enough. She glanced at her companion, then out to the street. It was almost completely dark now.

"Let's go walk on the beach," she said.

Reece nodded, following her outside after she'd paid the bill. The lemony smell of eucalyptus trees was strong in the air for a moment, then the stronger scent of the ocean winds stole it away.

6

They had the beach to themselves, though the pier was busy with strollers and people fishing. At the beach end of the long wooden structure, kids were hanging out, fooling around with bikes and skateboards. The soft boom of the tide drowned out the music of their ghetto blasters. The wind was cool with a salt tang as it came in from over the waves. In the distance, the oil rigs were lit up like Christmas trees.

Ellen took off her shoes. Carrying them in her tote bag, she walked in the wet sand by the water's edge. A raised lip of the beach hid the shorefront houses from their view as they walked south to the rocky spit that marked the beginning of the Naval Weapons Station.

"It's nice out here," Reece said finally. They hadn't spoken since leaving the restaurant.

Ellen nodded. "A lot different from L.A."

"Two different worlds."

Ellen gave him a considering glance. Ever since this afternoon, the sullen tone had left his voice. She listened now as he spoke of his parents and how he couldn't find a place for himself either in their world, nor that of his peers.

"You're pretty down on the sixties," she said when he was done.

Reece shrugged. He was barefoot now, too, the waves coming up to lick the bottom of his jeans where the two of them stood at the water's edge.

"They had some good ideas—people like my parents," he said, "but the way they want things to go . . . that only works if everyone agrees to live that way."

"That doesn't invalidate the things they believe in."

"No. But what we've got to deal with is the real world and you've got to take what you need if you want to survive in it."

Ellen sighed. "I suppose."

She looked back across the beach, but they were still alone. No one else out for a late walk across the sand. No booger. No Balloon Men. But something fluttered inside her, dark-winged. A longing as plain as what she heard in Reece's voice, though she was looking for magic and he was just looking for a way to fit in.

Hefting her tote bag, she tossed it onto the sand, out of the waves' reach. Reece gave her a curious look, then averted his gaze as she stepped out of her skirt.

"It's okay," she said, amused at his sudden sense of propriety. "I'm wearing my swimsuit."

By the time he turned back, her blouse and skirt had joined her tote bag on the beach and she was shaking loose her hair.

"Coming in?" she asked.

Reece simply stood and watched the sway of her hips as she headed for the water. Her swimsuit was white. In the poor light it was as though she wasn't wearing anything—the swimsuit looked like untanned skin. She dove cleanly into a wave, head bobbing up pale in the dark water when she surfaced.

"C'mon!" she called to him. "The water's fine, once you get in."

Reece hesitated. He'd wanted to go in this afternoon, but

hadn't had the nerve to bare his white skinny limbs in front of a beach full of serious tanners. Well, there was no one to see him now, he thought as he stripped down to his underwear.

The water hit him like a cold fist when he dove in after her and he came up gasping with shock. His body tingled, every pore stung alert. Ellen drifted further out, riding the waves easily. As he waded out to join her, a swell rose up and tumbled him back to shore in a spill of floundering arms and legs that scraped him against the sand.

"Either go under or over them," Ellen advised him as he started back out.

He wasn't much of a swimmer, but the water wasn't too deep except when a big wave came. He went under the next one and came up spluttering, but pleased with himself for not getting thrown up against the beach again.

"I love swimming at night," Ellen said as they drifted together.

Reece nodded. The water was surprisingly warm, too, once you were in it. You could lose all sense of time out here, just floating with the swells.

"You do this a lot?" he asked.

Ellen shook her head. "It's not that good an idea to do this alone. If the undertow got you, it'd pull you right out and no one would know."

Reece laid his head back in the water and looked up at the sky. Though they were less than an hour by the freeway out of downtown L.A., the sky was completely different here. It didn't have that glow from God-knows-how-many millions of lights. The stars seemed closer, too, or maybe it was that the sky seemed deeper.

He glanced over at Ellen. Their reason for being out here was forgotten. He wished he had the nerve to just sort of sidle up to her and put his arms around her, hold her close. She'd feel all slippery, but she'd feel good.

He paddled a little bit towards her, riding a swell up and then down again. The wave turned him slightly away from her. When he glanced back, he saw her staring wide-eyed at the shore. His gaze followed hers and then that cold he'd felt when he first entered the water returned in a numbing rush.

The booger was here.

It came snuffling over a rise in the beach, a squat dark shadow in the sand, greasy and slick as it beelined for their clothing. When it reached Ellen's tote bag, it buried its face in her skirt and blouse, then proceeded to rip them to shreds. Ellen's fingers caught his arm in a frightened grip. A wave came up, lifting his feet from the bottom. He kicked out frantically, afraid he was going to drown with her holding on to him like that, but the wave tossed them both in towards the shore.

The booger looked up, baring its barracuda teeth. The red coals of its eyes burned right into them both, pinning them there on the wet sand where the wave had left them. Leaving the ruin of Ellen's belongings in torn shreds, it moved slowly towards them.

"Re-Reece," Ellen said. She was pressed close to him, shivering.

Reece didn't have the time to appreciate the contact of her skin against his. He wanted to say, this is what you were looking for, lady, but things weren't so cut and dried now. Ellen wasn't some nameless cipher anymore—just a part of a crowd that he could sneer at—and she wasn't just something he had the hots for either. She was a person, just like him. An individual. Someone he could actually relate to.

"Can—can't you stop it?" Ellen cried.

The booger was getting close now. Its sewer reek was strong enough to drown out the salty tang of the ocean. It was like something had died there on the beach and was now getting up and coming for them.

Stop it? Reece thought. Maybe the thing had been created out of his frustrated anger, the way Ellen's friend made out it could happen in that book of his, but Reece knew as sure as shit that he didn't control the booger.

Another wave came down upon them and Reece pushed at

the sand so that it pulled them partway out from the shore on its way back out. Getting to his knees in the rimy water, he got in front of Ellen so that he was between her and the booger. Could the sucker swim?

The booger hesitated at the water's edge. It lifted its paws fastidiously from the wet sand like a cat crossing a damp lawn and relief went through Reece. When another wave came in, the booger backstepped quickly out of its reach.

Ellen was leaning against him, face near his as she peered over his shoulder.

"It can't handle the water," Reece said. He turned his face to hers when she didn't say anything. Her clear eyes were open wide, gaze fixed on the booger. "Ellen . . . ?" he began.

"I can't believe that it's really there," she said finally in a small voice.

"But you're the one—you said . . ." He drew a little away from her so that he could see her better.

"I know what I said," Ellen replied. She hugged herself, trembling at the stir of dark wings inside her. "It's just . . . I *wanted* to believe, but . . . wanting to and having it be real . . ." There was a pressure in the center of her chest now, like something inside pushing to get out. "I . . ."

The pain lanced sharp and sudden. She heard Reece gasp. Looking down, she saw what he had seen, a bird's head poking gossamer from between her breasts. It was a dark smudge against the white of her swimsuit, not one of Uncle Dobbin's parrots, but a crow's head, with eyes like the pair she'd seen looking back at her from the mirror. Her own magic, leaving her because she didn't believe. Because she couldn't believe, but—

It didn't make sense. She'd always believed. And now, with Reece's booger standing there on the shore, how could she help *but* believe?

The booger howled then, as though to underscore her thoughts. She looked to the shore and saw it stepping into the waves, crying out at the pain of the salt water on its flesh, but determined to get at them. To get at her. Reece's magic, given life. While her own magic . . . She pressed at the half-formed crow coming from her chest, trying to force it back in.

"I believe, I believe," she muttered through clenched teeth. But just like Uncle Dobbin's assistant in Christy's story, she could feel that swelling ache of loss rise up in her. She turned despairing eyes to Reece.

She didn't need a light to see the horror in his eyes—horror at the booger's approach, at the crow's head sticking out of her chest. But he didn't draw away from her. Instead, he reached out and caught hold of her shoulders.

"Stop fighting it!" he cried.

"But—"

He shot a glance shoreward. They were bracing themselves against the waves, but a large swell had just caught the booger and sent it howling back to shore in a tumble of limbs.

"It was your needing proof," he said. "Your needing to see the booger, to know that it's real—that's what's making you lose it. Stop trying so hard."

"I . . ."

But she knew he was right. She pulled free of him and looked towards the shore where the booger was struggling to its feet. The creature made rattling sounds deep in its throat as it started out for them again. It was hard, hard to do, but she let her hands fall free. The pain in her chest was a fire, the aching loss building to a crescendo. But she closed herself to it, closed her eyes, willed herself to stand relaxed.

Instead of fighting, she remembered. Balloon Men spinning down the beach. Christy's gnome, riding his pig along the pier. Bramley Dapple's advice. Goon pinching Jilly Coppercorn's leg. The thing that fed on eggs and eyeballs and, yes, Reece's booger too. Uncle Dobbin and his parrots and Nori Wert watching her magic fly free. And always the Balloon Men, tumbling end-over-end, across the beach, or down the alleyway behind her house. . . .

And the pain eased. The ache loosened, faded.

"Jesus," she heard Reece say softly.

She opened her eyes and looked to where he was looking. The booger had turned from the sea and was fleeing as a crowd of Balloon Men came bouncing down the shore, great round roly-poly shapes, turning end-over-end, laughing and giggling, a chorus of small deep voices. There was salt in her eyes and it wasn't from the ocean's brine. Her tears ran down her cheeks and she felt herself grinning like a fool.

The Balloon Men chased Reece's booger up one end of the beach and then back the other way until the creature finally made a stand. Howling, it waited for them to come, but before the first bouncing round shape reached it, the booger began to fade away.

Ellen turned to Reece and knew he had tears in his own eyes, but the good feeling was too strong for him to do anything but grin right back at her. The booger had died with the last of his anger. She reached out a hand to him and he took it in one of his own. Joined so, they made their way to the shore where they were surrounded by riotous Balloon Men until the bouncing shapes finally faded and then there were just the two of them standing there.

Ellen's heart beat fast. When Reece let go her hand, she touched her chest and felt a stir of dark wings inside her, only they were settling in now, no longer striving to fly free. The wind came in from the ocean still, but it wasn't the same wind that the Balloon Men rode.

"I guess it's not all bullshit," Reece said softly.

Ellen glanced at him.

He smiled as he explained. "Helping each other—getting along instead of fighting. Feels kind of good, you know?"

Ellen nodded. Her hand fell from her chest as the dark wings finally stilled.

"Your friend's story didn't say anything about crows," Reece said.

"Maybe we've all got different birds inside—different

magics.'' She looked out across the waves to where the oil rigs lit the horizon.

"There's a flock of wild parrots up around Santa Ana," Reece said.

"I've heard there's one up around San Pedro, too."

"Do you think . . . ?" Reece began, but he let his words trail off. The waves came in and wet their feet.

"I don't know," Ellen said. She looked over at her shredded clothes. "Come on. Let's get back to my place and warm up."

Reece laid his jacket over her shoulders. He put on his T-shirt and jeans, then helped her gather up what was left of her belongings.

"I didn't mean for this to happen," he said, bundling up the torn blouse and skirt. He looked up to where she was standing over him. "But I couldn't control the booger."

"Maybe we're not supposed to."

"But something like the booger . . ."

She gave his Mohawk a friendly ruffle. "I think it just means that we've got to be careful about what kind of vibes we put out."

Reece grimaced at her use of the word, but he nodded.

"It's either that," Ellen added, "or we let the magic fly free."

The same feathery stirring of wings that she felt moved in Reece. They both knew that that was something neither of them was likely to give up.

In Uncle Dobbin's Parrot Fair, Nori Wert turned away from the pair of cages that she'd been making ready.

"I guess we won't be needing these," she said.

Uncle Dobbin looked up from a slim collection of Victorian poetry and nodded. "You're learning fast," he said. He stuck the stem of his pipe in his mouth and fished about in his pocket for a match. "Maybe there's hope for you yet."

Nori felt her own magic stir inside her, back where it

should be, but she didn't say anything to him in case she had to go away, now that the lesson was learned. She was too happy here. Next to catching some rays, there wasn't anywhere she'd rather be.

⌒ · THE STONE DRUM · ⌒

There is no question that there is an unseen world. The problem is how far is it from midtown and how late is it open?
—ATTRIBUTED TO WOODY ALLEN

IT WAS JILLY Coppercorn who found the stone drum, late one afternoon.

She brought it around to Professor Dapple's rambling Tudor-styled house in the old quarter of Lower Crowsea that same evening, wrapped up in folds of brown paper and tied with twine. She rapped sharply on the Professor's door with the little brass lion's head knocker that always seemed to stare too intently at her, then stepped back as Olaf Goonasekara, Dapple's odd little housekeeper, flung the door open and glowered out at where she stood on the rickety porch.

"You," he grumbled.

"Me," she agreed, amicably. "Is Bramley in?"

"I'll see," he replied and shut the door.

Jilly sighed and sat down on one of the two worn rattan chairs that stood to the left of the door, her package bundled on her knee. A black and orange cat regarded her incuriously from the seat of the other chair, then turned to watch the progress of a woman walking her dachshund down the street.

Professor Dapple still taught a few classes at Butler U., but he wasn't nearly as involved with the curriculum as he had been when Jilly attended the university. There'd been some kind of a scandal—something about a Bishop, some old coins and the daughter of a Tarot reader—but Jilly had never quite got the story straight. The Professor was a jolly fellow—wizened like an old apple, but more active than many who were only half his apparent sixty years of age. He could talk and joke all night, incessantly polishing his wire-rimmed spectacles.

What he was doing with someone like Olaf Goonasekara as a housekeeper Jilly didn't know. It was true that Goon looked comical enough, what with his protruding stomach and puffed cheeks, the halo of unruly hair and his thin little arms and legs, reminding her of nothing so much as a pumpkin with twig limbs, or a monkey. His usual striped trousers, organ grinder's jacket and the little green and yellow cap he liked to wear, didn't help. Nor did the fact that he was barely four feet tall and that the Professor claimed he was a goblin and just called him Goon.

It didn't seem to allow Goon much dignity and Jilly would have understood his grumpiness, if she didn't know that he himself insisted on being called Goon and his wardrobe was entirely of his own choosing. Bramley hated Goon's sense of fashion—or rather, his lack thereof.

The door was flung open again and Jilly stood up to find Goon glowering at her once more.

"He's in," he said.

Jilly smiled. As if he'd actually had to go in and check.

They both stood there, Jilly on the porch and he in the doorway, until Jilly finally asked, "Can he see me?"

Giving an exaggerated sigh, Goon stepped aside to let her in.

"I suppose you'll want something to drink?" he asked as he followed her to the door of the Professor's study.

"Tea would be lovely."

"Hrumph."

Jilly watched him stalk off, then tapped a knuckle on the study's door and stepped into the room. Bramley lifted his gaze from a desk littered with tottering stacks of books and papers and grinned at her from between a gap in the towers of paper.

"I've been doing some research since you called," he said. He poked a finger at a book that Jilly couldn't see, then began to clean his glasses. "Fascinating stuff."

"And hello to you, too," Jilly said.

"Yes, of course. Did you know that the Kickaha had legends of a little people long before the Europeans ever settled this area?"

Jilly could never quite get used to Bramley's habit of starting conversations in the middle. She removed some magazines from a club chair and perched on the edge of its seat, her package clutched to her chest.

"What's that got to do with anything?" she asked.

Bramley looked surprised. "Why everything. We *are* still looking into the origins of this artifact of yours, aren't we?"

Jilly nodded. From her new position of vantage she could make out the book he'd been reading. *Underhill and Deeper Still,* a short story collection by Christy Riddell. Riddell made a living of retelling the odd stories that lie just under the skin of any large city. This particular one was a collection of urban legends of Old City and other subterranean fancies—not exactly the factual reference source she'd been hoping for.

Old City was real enough; that was where she'd found the drum this afternoon. But as for the rest of it—albino crocodile subway conductors, schools of dog-sized intelligent goldfish in the sewers, mutant rat debating societies and the like . . .

Old City was the original heart of Newford. It lay deep underneath the subway tunnels—dropped there in the late eighteen hundreds during the Great Quake. The present city, including its sewers and underground transportation tunnels, had been built above the ruins of the old one. There'd been talk in the early seventies of renovating the ruins as a tourist attraction—as had been done in Seattle—but Old City lay too far underground for easy access. After numerous studies on the project, the city council had decided that it simply wouldn't be cost efficient.

With that decision, Old City had rapidly gone from a potential tourist attraction to a home for skells—winos, bag ladies and the other homeless. Not to mention, if one was to believe Bramley and Riddell, bands of ill-mannered goblin-like creatures that Riddell called skookin—a word he'd stolen from old Scots which meant, variously, ugly, furtive and sullen.

Which, Jilly realized once when she thought about it, made it entirely appropriate that Bramley should claim Goon was related to them.

"You're not going to tell me it's a skookin artifact, are you?" she asked Bramley now.

"Too soon to say," he replied. He nodded at her parcel. "Can I see it?"

Jilly got up and brought it over to the desk, where Bramley made a great show of cutting the twine and unwrapping the paper. Jilly couldn't decide if he was pretending it was the unveiling of a new piece at the museum or his birthday. But then the drum was sitting on the desk, the mica and quartz veins in its stone catching the light from Bramley's desk lamp in a magical glitter, and she was swallowed up in the wonder of it again.

It was tube-shaped, standing about a foot high, with a seven-inch diameter at the top and five inches at the bottom. The top was smooth as the skin head of a drum. On the sides were what appeared to be the remnants of a bewildering flurry of designs. But what was most marvelous about it was that the stone was hollow. It weighed about the same as a fat hardcover book.

"Listen," Jilly said and gave the top of the drum a rap-a-tap-tap.

The stone responded with a quiet rhythm that resonated

eerily in the study. Unfortunately, Goon chose that moment to arrive in the doorway with a tray laden with tea mugs, tea pot and a platter of his homemade biscuits. At the sound of the drum, the tray fell from his hands. It hit the floor with a crash, spraying tea, milk, sugar, biscuits and bits of crockery every which way.

Jilly turned, her heartbeat double-timing in her chest, just in time to see an indescribable look cross over Goon's features. It might have been surprise, it might have been laughter, but it was gone too quickly for her to properly note. He merely stood in the doorway now, his usual glowering look on his face, and all Jilly was left with was a feeling of unaccountable guilt.

"I didn't mean . . ." Jilly began, but her voice trailed off.

"Bit of a mess," Bramley said.

"I'll get right to it," Goon said.

His small dark eyes centered their gaze on Jilly for too long a moment, then he turned away to fetch a broom and dustpan. When Jilly turned back to the desk, she found Bramley rubbing his hands together, face pressed close to the stone drum. He looked up at her over his glasses, grinning.

"Did you see?" he said. "Goon recognized it for what it is, straight off. It has to be a skookin artifact. Didn't like you meddling around with it either."

That was hardly the conclusion that Jilly would have come to on her own. It was the sudden and unexpected sound that had more than likely startled Goon—as it might have startled anyone who wasn't expecting it. That was the reasonable explanation, but she knew well enough that reasonable didn't necessarily always mean right. When she thought of that look that had passed over Goon's features, like a trough of surprise or mocking humor between two cresting glowers, she didn't know what to think, so she let herself get taken away by the Professor's enthusiasm, because . . . well, just what if . . . ?

By all of Christy Riddell's accounts, there wasn't a better candidate for skookin-dom than Bramley's housekeeper.

"What does it mean?" she asked.

Bramley shrugged and began to polish his glasses. Jilly was about to nudge him into making at least the pretense of a theory, but then she realized that the Professor had simply fallen silent because Goon was back to clean up the mess. She waited until Goon had made his retreat with the promise of putting on another pot of tea, before she leaned over Bramley's desk.

"Well?" she asked.

"Found it in Old City, did you?" he replied.

Jilly nodded.

"You know what they say about skookin treasure . . . ?"

They meaning he and Christy, Jilly thought, but she obligingly tried to remember that particular story from *Underhill and Deeper Still*. She had it after a moment. It was the one called "The Man with the Monkey" and had something to do with a stolen apple that was withered and moldy in Old City but became solid gold when it was brought above ground. At the end of the story, the man who'd stolen it from the skookin was found in little pieces scattered all over Fitzhenry Park. . . .

Jilly shivered.

"Now I remember why I don't like to read Christy's stuff," she said. "He can be so sweet on one page, and then on the next he's taking you on a tour through an abattoir."

"Just like life," Bramley said.

"Wonderful. So what are you saying?"

"They'll be wanting it back," Bramley said.

Jilly woke some time after midnight with the Professor's words ringing in her ears.

They'll be wanting it back.

She glanced at the stone drum where it sat on a crate by the window of her Yoors Street loft in Foxville. From where she lay on her Murphy bed, the streetlights coming in the window wove a haloing effect around the stone artifact. The drum glimmered with magic—or at least with a potential for magic. And there was something else in the air. A humming sound, like barely audible strains of music. The notes seemed disconnected, drifting randomly through the melody like dust motes dancing in a beam of sunlight, but there was still a melody present.

She sat up slowly. Pushing the quilt aside, she padded barefoot across the room. When she reached the drum, the change in perspective made the streetlight halo slide away; the drum's magic fled. It was just an odd stone artifact once more. She ran her finger along the smoothed indentations that covered the sides of the artifact, but didn't touch the top. It was still marvelous enough—a hollow stone, a mystery, a puzzle. But . . .

She remembered the odd almost-but-not-quite music she'd heard when she first woke, and cocked her ear, listening for it.

Nothing.

Outside, a light drizzle had wet the pavement, making Yoors Street glisten and sparkle with its sheen. She knelt down by the windowsill and leaned forward, looking out, feeling lonely. It'd be nice if Geordie were here, even if his brother did write those books that had the Professor so enamoured, but Geordie was out of town this week. Maybe she should get a cat or a dog—just something to keep her company when she got into one of these odd funks—but the problem with pets was that they tied you down. No more gallivanting about whenever and wherever you pleased. Not when the cat needed to be fed. Or the dog had to be walked.

Sighing, she started to turn from the window, then paused. A flicker of uneasiness stole up her spine as she looked more closely at what had caught her attention—there, across the street. Time dissolved into a pattern as random as that faint music she'd heard when she woke earlier. Minutes and seconds marched sideways; the hands of the old Coors clock on her wall stood still.

A figure leaned against the wall, there, just to one side of the display window of the Chinese groceteria across the street, a figure as much a patchwork as the disarray in the shop's window. Pumpkin head under a wide-brimmed hat. A larger pumpkin for the body with what looked like straw spilling out from between the buttons of its too-small jacket. Arms and legs as thin as broom handles. A wide slit for a mouth; eyes like the sharp yellow slits of a jack-o'-lantern with a candle burning inside.

A Halloween creature. And not alone.

There was another, there, in the mouth of that alleyway. A third clinging to the wall of the brownstone beside the groceteria. Four more on the rooftop directly across the street— pumpkinheads lined up along the parapet, all in a row.

Skookin, Jilly thought and she shivered with fear, remembering Christy Riddell's story.

Damn Christy for tracking the story down, and damn the Professor for reminding her of it. And damn the job that had sent her down into Old City in the first place to take photos for the background of the painting she was currently working on.

Because there shouldn't be any such thing as skookin. Because . . .

She blinked, then rubbed her eyes. Her gaze darted left and right, up and down, raking the street and the faces of buildings across the way.

Nothing.

No pumpkin goblins watching her loft.

The sound of her clock ticking the seconds away was suddenly loud in her ears. A taxi went by on the street below, spraying a fine sheet of water from its wheels. She waited for it to pass, then studied the street again.

There were no skookin.

Of course there wouldn't be, she told herself, trying to laugh at how she'd let her imagination run away with itself, but she couldn't muster up even the first hint of a smile. She looked at the drum, reached a hand towards it, then let her hand fall to her lap, the drum untouched. She turned her attention back to the street, watching it for long moments before she finally had to accept that there was nothing out there, that she had only peopled it with her own night fears.

Pushing herself up from the sill, she returned to bed and lay down again. The palm of her right hand itched a little, right where she'd managed to poke herself on a small nail or wood sliver while she was down in Old City. She scratched her hand and stared up at the ceiling, trying to go to sleep, but not expecting to have much luck. Surprisingly, she drifted off in moments.

And dreamed.

Of Bramley's study. Except the Professor wasn't ensconced behind his desk as usual. Instead, he was setting out a serving of tea for her and Goon, who had taken the Professor's place behind the tottering stacks of papers and books on the desk.

"Skookin," Goon said, when the Professor had finished serving them their tea and left the room. "They've never existed, of course."

Jilly nodded in agreement.

"Though in some ways," Goon went on, "they've always existed. In here—" He tapped his temple with a gnarly, very skookin-like finger. "In our imaginations."

"But—" Jilly began, wanting to tell him how she'd *seen* skookin, right out there on her very own street tonight, but Goon wasn't finished.

"And that's what makes them real," he said.

His head suddenly looked very much like a pumpkin. He leaned forward, eyes glittering as though a candle was burning there inside his head, flickering in the wind.

"And if they're real," he said.

His voice wound down alarmingly, as though it came from the spiraling groove of a spoken-word album that someone had slowed by dragging their finger along on the vinyl.

"Then. You're. In. A. Lot. Of—"

Jilly awoke with a start to find herself backed up against the frame of the head of her bed, her hands worrying and tangling her quilt into knots.

Just a dream. Cast off thoughts, tossed up by her subconscious. Nothing to worry about. Except . . .

She could finish the dream-Goon's statement.

If they were real . . .

Never mind being in trouble. If they were real, then she was doomed.

She didn't get any more sleep that night, and first thing the next morning, she went looking for help.

"Skookin," Meran said, trying hard not to laugh.

"Oh, I know what it sounds like," Jilly said, "but what can you do? Christy's books are Bramley's pet blind spot and if you listen to him long enough, he'll have you believing anything."

"But skookin," Meran repeated and this time she did giggle.

Jilly couldn't help but laugh with her.

Everything felt very different in the morning light— especially when she had someone to talk it over with whose head wasn't filled with Christy's stories.

They were sitting in Kathryn's Cafe—an hour or so after Jilly had found Meran Kelledy down by the Lake, sitting on the Pier and watching the early morning joggers run across the sand: yuppies from downtown, health-conscious gentry from the Beaches.

It was a short walk up Battersfield Road to where Kathryn's was nestled in the heart of Lower Crowsea. Like the area itself, with its narrow streets and old stone buildings, the cafe had an old world feel about it—from the dark wood paneling and hand-carved chair backs to the small round tables, with checkered tablecloths, fat glass condiment containers and straw-wrapped wine bottles used as candleholders. The music piped in over the house sound system was mostly along the lines of Telemann and Vivaldi, Kitaro and old Bob James albums. The waitresses wore cream-colored pinafores over flowerprint dresses.

But if the atmosphere was old world, the clientele were definitely contemporary. Situated so close to Butler U., Kathryn's had been a favorite haunt of the university's students since it first opened its doors in the mid-sixties as a coffee house. Though much had changed from those early days, there was still music played on its small stage on Friday and Saturday nights, as well as poetry recitations on Wednesdays and Sunday morning storytelling sessions.

Jilly and Meran sat by a window, coffee and homemade banana muffins set out on the table in front of them.

"Whatever were you *doing* down there anyway?" Meran asked. "It's not exactly the safest place to be wandering about."

Jilly nodded. The skells in Old City weren't all thin and wasted. Some were big and mean-looking, capable of anything—not really the sort of people Jilly should be around, because if something went wrong . . . well, she was the kind of woman for whom the word petite had been coined. She was small and slender—her tiny size only accentuated by the oversized clothing she tended to wear. Her brown hair was a thick tangle, her eyes the electric blue of sapphires.

She was too pretty and too small to be wandering about in places like Old City on her own.

"You know the band, No Nuns Here?" Jilly asked.

Meran nodded.

"I'm doing the cover painting for their first album," Jilly explained. "They wanted something moody for the background—sort of like the Tombs, but darker and grimmer—and I thought Old City would be the perfect place to get some reference shots."

"But to go there on your own . . ."

Jilly just shrugged. She was known to wander anywhere and everywhere, at any time of the night or day, camera or sketchbook in hand, often both.

Meran shook her head. Like most of Jilly's friends, she'd

long since given up trying to point out the dangers of carrying on the way Jilly did.

"So you found this drum," she said.

Jilly nodded. She looked down at the little scab on the palm of her hand. It itched like crazy, but she was determined not to open it again by scratching it.

"And now you want to . . . ?"

Jilly looked up. "Take it back. Only I'm scared to go there on my own. I thought maybe Cerin would come with me—for moral support, you know?"

"He's out of town," Meran said.

Meran and her husband made up the two halves of the Kelledys, a local traditional music duo that played coffee houses, festivals and colleges from one coast to the other. For years now, however, Newford had been their home base.

"He's teaching another of those harp workshops," Meran added.

Jilly did her best to hide her disappointment.

What she'd told Meran about "moral support" was only partly the reason she'd wanted their help because, more so than either Riddell's stories or Bramley's askew theories, the Kelledys were the closest thing to real magic that she could think of in Newford. There was an otherworldly air about the two of them that went beyond the glamour that seemed to always gather around people who became successful in their creative endeavors.

It wasn't something Jilly could put her finger on. It wasn't as though they went on and on about this sort of thing at the drop of a hat the way that Bramley did. Nor that they were responsible for anything more mysterious than the enchantment they awoke on stage when they were playing their instruments. It was just there. Something that gave the impression that they were aware of what lay beyond the here and now. That they could see things others couldn't; knew things that remained secret to anyone else.

Nobody even knew where they had come from; they'd just arrived in Newford a few years ago, speaking with accents that had rapidly vanished, and here they'd pretty well stayed ever since. Jilly had always privately supposed that if there was a place called Faerie, then that was from where they'd come, so when she woke up this morning, deciding she needed magical help, she'd gone looking for one or the other and found Meran. But now . . .

"Oh," she said.

Meran smiled.

"But that doesn't mean I can't try to help," she said.

Jilly sighed. Help with what? she had to ask herself. The more she thought about it, the sillier it all seemed. Skookin. Right. Maybe they held debating contests with Riddell's mutant rats.

"I think maybe I'm nuts," she said finally. "I mean, goblins living under the city . . . ?"

"I believe in the little people," Meran said. "We called them bodachs where I come from."

Jilly just looked at her.

"But you laughed when I talked about them," she said finally.

"I know—and I shouldn't have. It's just that whenever I hear that name that Christy's given them, I can't help myself. It's so silly."

"What I saw last night didn't feel silly," Jilly said.

If she'd actually seen anything. By this point—even with Meran's apparent belief—she wasn't sure what to think anymore.

"No," Meran said. "I suppose not. But—you're taking the drum back, so why are you so nervous?"

"The man in Christy's story returned the apple he stole," Jilly said, "and you know what happened to him. . . ."

"That's true," Meran said, frowning.

"I thought maybe Cerin could . . ." Jilly's voice trailed off.

A small smile touched Meran's lips. "Could do what?"

"Well, this is going to sound even sillier," Jilly admitted, "but I've always pictured him as sort of a wizard type."

Meran laughed. "He'd love to hear that. And what about me? Have I acquired wizardly status as well?"

"Not exactly. You always struck me as being an earth spirit—like you stepped out of an oak tree or something." Jilly blushed, feeling as though she was making even more of a fool of herself than ever, but now that she'd started, she felt she had to finish. "It's sort of like he learned magic, while you just are magic."

She glanced at her companion, looking for laughter, but Meran was regarding her gravely. And she did look like a dryad, Jilly thought, what with the green streaks in the long, nut-brown ringlets of her hair and her fey sort of Pre-Raphaelite beauty. Her eyes seemed to provide their own light, rather than take it in.

"Maybe I did step out of a tree one day," Meran said.

Jilly could feel her mouth forming a surprised "O," but then Meran laughed again.

"But probably I didn't," she said. Before Jilly could ask her about that "probably," Meran went on: "We'll need some sort of protection against them."

Jilly made her mind shift gears, from Meran's origins to the problem at hand.

"Like holy water or a cross?" she asked.

Her head filled with the plots of a hundred bad horror films, each of them clamoring for attention.

"No," Meran said. "Religious artifacts and trappings require faith—a belief in their potency that the skookin undoubtedly don't have. The only thing I know for certain that they can't abide is the truth."

"The truth?"

Meran nodded. "Tell them the truth—even if it's only historical facts and trivia—and they'll shun you as though you were carrying a plague."

"But what about after?" Jilly said. "After we've delivered the drum and they come looking for me? Do I have to walk around carrying a cassette machine spouting dates and facts for the rest of my life?"

"I hope not."

"But—"

"Patience," Meran replied. "Let me think about it for awhile."

Jilly sighed. She regarded her companion curiously as Meran took a sip of her coffee.

"You really believe in this stuff, don't you?" she said finally.

"Don't you?"

Jilly had to think about that for a moment.

"Last night I was scared," she said, "and I'm returning the drum because I'd rather be safe than sorry, but I'm still not sure."

Meran nodded understandingly, but, "Your coffee's getting cold," was all she had to say.

Meran let Jilly stay with her that night in the rambling old house where she and Cerin lived. Straddling the border between Lower Crowsea and Chinatown, it was a tall, gabled building surrounded by giant oak trees. There was a rounded tower in the front to the right of a long screen-enclosed porch, stables around the back, and a garden along the west side of the house that seemed to have been plucked straight from a postcard of the English countryside.

Jilly loved this area. The Kelledys' house was the easternmost of the stately estates that stood, row on row, along McKennitt Street, between Lee and Yoors. Whenever Jilly walked along this part of McKennitt, late at night when the streetcars were tucked away in their downtown station and there was next to no other traffic, she found it easy to imagine that the years had wound back to a bygone age when time moved at a different pace, when Newford's streets were cobblestoned and the vehicles that traversed them were horse-drawn, rather than horse-powered.

"You'll wear a hole in the glass if you keep staring through it so intently."

Jilly started. She turned long enough to acknowledge her

hostess's presence, then her gaze was dragged back to the window, to the shadows cast by the oaks as twilight stretched them across the lawn, to the long low wall that bordered the lawn, to the street beyond.

Still no skookin. Did that mean they didn't exist, or that they hadn't come out yet? Or maybe they just hadn't tracked her here to the Kelledys' house.

She started again as Meran laid a hand on her shoulder and gently turned her from the window.

"Who knows what you'll call to us, staring so," Meran said.

Her voice held the same light tone as it had when she'd made her earlier comment, but this time a certain sense of caution lay behind the words.

"If they come, I want to see them," Jilly said.

Meran nodded. "I understand. But remember this: the night's a magical time. The moon rules her hours, not the sun."

"What does that mean?"

"The moon likes secrets," Meran said. "And secret things. She lets mysteries bleed into her shadows and leaves us to ask whether they originated from otherworlds, or from our own imaginations."

"You're beginning to sound like Bramley," Jilly said. "Or Christy."

"Remember your Shakespeare," Meran said. " 'This fellow's wise enough to play the fool.' Did you ever think that perhaps their studied eccentricity protects them from sharper ridicule?"

"You mean all those things Christy writes about are *true*?"

"I didn't say that."

Jilly shook her head. "No. But you're talking in riddles just like a wizard out of some fairy tale. I never understood why they couldn't talk plainly."

"That's because some things can only be approached from the side. Secretively. Peripherally."

Whatever Jilly was about to say next, died stillborn. She pointed out the window to where the lawn was almost swallowed by shadows.

"Do . . ." She swallowed thickly, then tried again. "Do you see them?"

They were out there, flitting between the wall that bordered the Kelledys' property and those tall oaks that stood closer to the house. Shadow shapes. Fat, pumpkin-bodied and twig-limbed. There were more of them than there'd been last night. And they were bolder. Creeping right up towards the house. Threats burning in their candle-flicker eyes. Wide mouths open in jack-o'-lantern grins, revealing rows of pointed teeth.

One came sidling right up to the window, its face monstrous at such close proximity. Jilly couldn't move, couldn't even breathe. She remembered what Meran had said earlier—

they can't abide the truth

—but she couldn't frame a sentence, never mind a word, and her mind was filled with only a wild unreasoning panic. The creature reached out a hand towards the glass, clawed fingers extended. Jilly could feel a scream building up, deep inside her. In a moment that hand would come crashing through the window, shattering glass, clawing at her throat. And she couldn't move. All she could do was stare, stare as the claws reached for the glass, stare as it drew back to—

Something fell between the creature and the house—a swooping, shapeless thing. The creature danced back, saw that it was only the bough of one of the oak trees and was about to begin its approach once more, but the cries of its companions distracted it. Not until it turned its horrible gaze from her, did Jilly feel able to lift her own head.

She stared at the oaks. A sudden wind had sprung up, lashing the boughs about so that the tall trees appeared to be giants, flailing about their many-limbed arms like monstrous, agitated octopi. The creatures in the yard scattered and in moments they were gone—each and every one of them. The wind died down; the animated giants became just oak trees once more.

Jilly turned slowly from the window to find Meran pressed close beside her.

"Ugly, furtive and sullen," Meran said. "Perhaps Christy wasn't so far off in naming them."

"They . . . they're real, aren't they?" Jilly asked in a small voice.

Meran nodded. "And not at all like the bodachs of my homeland. Bodachs are mischievous and prone to trouble, but not like this. Those creatures were weaned on malevolence."

Jilly leaned weakly against the windowsill.

"What are we going to *do*?" she asked.

She scratched at her palm—the itch was worse than ever. Meran caught her hand, pulled it away. There was an unhappy look in her eyes when she lifted her gaze from the mark on Jilly's palm.

"Where did you get that?" she asked.

Jilly looked down at her palm. The scab was gone, but the skin was all dark around the puncture wound now—an ugly black discoloration that was twice the size of the original scab.

"I scratched myself," she said. "Down in Old City."

Meran shook her head. "No," she said. "They've marked you."

Jilly suddenly felt weak. Skookin were real. Mysterious winds rose to animate trees. And now she was marked?

She wasn't even sure what that meant, but she didn't like the sound of it. Not for a moment.

Her gaze went to the stone drum where it stood on Meran's mantel. She didn't think she'd ever hated an inanimate object so much before.

"Marked . . . me . . . ?" she asked.

"I've heard of this before," Meran said, her voice apologetic. She touched the mark on Jilly's palm. "This is like a . . . bounty."

"They really want to kill me, don't they?"

Jilly was surprised that her voice sounded as calm as it did. Inside she felt as though she was crumbling to little bits all over the place.

"Skookin are real," she went on, "and they're going to tear me up into little pieces—just like they did to the man in Christy's stupid story."

Meran gave her a sympathetic look.

"We have to go now," she said. "We have to go and confront them now, before . . ."

"Before what?"

Jilly's control over her voice was slipping. Her last word went shrieking up in pitch.

"Before they send something worse," Meran said.

Oh great, Jilly thought as she waited for Meran to change into clothing more suitable for the underground trek to Old City. Not only were skookin real, but there were worse things than those pumpkinhead creatures living down there under the city.

She slouched in one of the chairs by the mantelpiece, her back to the stone drum, and pretended that her nerves weren't all scraped raw, that she was just over visiting a friend for the evening and everything was just peachy, thank you. Surprisingly, by the time Meran returned, wearing jeans, sturdy walking shoes and a thick woolen shirt under a denim jacket, she did feel better.

"The bit with the trees," she asked as she rose from her chair. "Did you do that?"

Meran shook her head.

"But the wind likes me," she said. "Maybe it's because I play the flute."

And maybe it's because you're a dryad, Jilly thought, and the wind's got a thing about oak trees, but she let the thought go unspoken.

Meran fetched the long, narrow bag that held her flute and slung it over her shoulder.

"Ready?" she asked.

"No," Jilly said.

But she went and took the drum from the mantelpiece and joined Meran by the front door. Meran stuck a flashlight in the pocket of her jacket and handed another to Jilly, who thrust it into the pocket of the coat Meran was lending her. It was at least two sizes too big for her, which suited Jilly just fine.

Naturally, just to make the night complete, it started to rain before they got halfway down the walkway to McKennitt Street.

For safety's sake, city work crews had sealed up all the entrances to Old City in the mid-seventies—all the entrances of which the city was aware, at any rate. The street people of Newford's back lanes and allies knew of anywhere from a half-dozen to twenty others that could still be used, the number depending only on who was doing the bragging. The entrance to which Jilly led Meran was the most commonly known and used—a steel maintenance door that was situated two hundred yards or so down the east tracks of the Grasso Street subway station.

The door led into the city's sewer maintenance tunnels, but had long since been abandoned. Skells had broken the locking mechanism and the door stood continually ajar. Inside, time and weathering had worn down a connecting wall between the maintenance tunnels and what had once been the top floor of one of Old City's proud skyscrapers—an office complex that had towered some four stories above the city's streets before the quake dropped it into its present subterranean setting.

It was a good fifteen minute walk from the Kelledys' house to the Grasso Street station and Jilly plodded miserably through the rain at Meran's side for every block of it. Her sneakers were soaked and her hair plastered against her scalp. She carried the stone drum tucked under one arm and was very tempted to simply pitch it in front of a bus.

"This is crazy," Jilly said. "We're just giving ourselves up to them."

Meran shook her head. "No. We're confronting them of our own free will—there's a difference."

"That's just semantics. There won't be a difference in the results."

"That's where you're wrong."

They both turned at the sound of a new voice to find Goon standing in the doorway of a closed antique shop. His eyes glittered oddly in the poor light, reminding Jilly all too much of the skookin, and he didn't seem to be the least bit wet.

"What are *you* doing here?" Jilly demanded.

"You must always confront your fears," Goon said as though she hadn't spoke. "Then skulking monsters become merely unfamiliar shadows, thrown by a tree bough. Whispering voices are just the wind. The wild flare of panic is merely a burst of emotion, not a terror spell cast by some evil witch."

Meran nodded. "That's what Cerin would say. And that's what I mean to do. Confront them with a truth so bright that they won't dare come near us again."

Jilly held up her hand. The discoloration was spreading. It had grown from its pinprick inception, first to the size of a dime, now to that of a silver dollar.

"What about this?" she asked.

"There's always a price for meddling," Goon agreed. "Sometimes it's the simple curse of knowledge."

"There's always a price," Meran agreed.

Everybody always seemed to know more than she did these days, Jilly thought unhappily.

"You still haven't told me what you're doing here," she told Goon. "Skulking about and following us."

Goon smiled. "It seems to me, that you came upon me."

"You know what I mean."

"I have my own business in Old City tonight," he said. "And since we all have the same destination in mind, I thought perhaps you would appreciate the company."

Everything was wrong about this, Jilly thought. Goon was never nice to her. Goon was never nice to anyone.

"Yeah, well, you can just—" she began.

Meran laid a hand on Jilly's arm. "It's bad luck to turn away help when it's freely offered."

"But you don't know what he's like," Jilly said.

"Olaf and I have met before," Meran said.

Jilly caught the grimace on Goon's face at the use of his given name. It made him seem more himself, which, while not exactly comforting, was at least familiar. Then she looked at Meran. She thought of the wind outside the musician's house, driving away the skookin, the mystery that cloaked her which ran even deeper, perhaps, than that which Goon wore so easily. . . .

"Sometimes you just have to trust in people," Meran said, as though reading Jilly's mind.

Jilly sighed. She rubbed her itchy palm against her thigh, shifted the drum into a more comfortable position.

"Okay," she said. "So what're we waiting for?"

The few times Jilly had come down to Old City, she'd been cautious, perhaps even a little nervous, but never frightened. Tonight was different. It was always dark in Old City, but the darkness had never seemed so . . . so watchful before. There were always odd little sounds, but they had never seemed so furtive. Even with her companions—maybe because of them, she thought, thinking mostly of Goon—she felt very much alone in the eerie darkness.

Goon didn't appear to need the wobbly light of their flashlights to see his way and though he seemed content enough to simply follow them, Jilly couldn't shake the feeling that he was actually leading the way. They were soon in a part of the subterranean city that she'd never seen before.

There was less dust and dirt here. No litter, nor the remains of the skells' fires. No broken bottles, nor the piles of newspapers and ratty blanketing that served the skells as bedding. The buildings seemed in better repair. The air had a clean, dry smell to it, rather than the close, musty reek of refuse and human wastes that it carried closer to the entrance.

And there were no people.

From when they'd first stepped through the steel door in Grasso Street Station's east tunnel, she hadn't seen a bag lady or wino or any kind of skell, and that in itself was odd because they were always down here. But there was something sharing the darkness with them. Something watched them, marked their progress, followed with a barely discernible pad of sly footsteps in their wake and on either side.

The drum seemed warm against the skin of her hand. The blemish on her other palm prickled with itchiness. Her shoulder muscles were stiff with tension.

"Not far now," Goon said softly and Jilly suddenly understood what it meant to jump out of one's skin.

The beam of her flashlight made a wild arc across the faces of the buildings on either side of her as she started. Her heartbeat jumped into second gear.

"What do you see?" Meran asked, her voice calm.

The beam of her flashlight turned towards Goon and he pointed ahead.

"Turn off your flashlights," he said.

Oh sure, Jilly thought. Easy for you to say.

But she did so a moment after Meran had. The sudden darkness was so abrupt that Jilly thought she'd gone blind. But then she realized that it wasn't as black as it should be. Looking ahead to where Goon had pointed, she could see a faint glow seeping onto the street ahead of them. It was a little less than a half block away, the source of the light hidden behind the squatting bulk of a half-tumbled-down building.

"What could it . . . ?" Jilly started to say, but then the sounds began, and the rest of her words dried up in her throat.

It was supposed to be music, she realized after a few moments, but there was no discernible rhythm and while the sounds were blown or rasped or plucked from instruments, they searched in vain for a melody.

"It begins," Goon said.

He took the lead, hurrying them up to the corner of the street.

"What does?" Jilly wanted to know.

"The king appears—as he must once a moon. It's that or lose his throne."

Jilly wanted to know what he was talking about—better yet, *how* he knew what he was talking about—but she didn't have a chance. The discordant not-music scraped and squealed to a kind of crescendo. Suddenly they were surrounded by the capering forms of dozens of skookin that bumped them, thin long fingers tugging at their clothing. Jilly shrieked at the first touch. One of them tried to snatch the drum from her grip. She regained control of her nerves at the same time as she pulled the artifact free from the grasping fingers.

"1789," she said. "That's when the Bastille was stormed and the French Revolution began. Uh, 1807, slave trade was abolished in the British Empire. 1776, the Declaration of Independence was signed."

The skookin backed away from her, as did the others, hissing and spitting. The not-music continued, but its tones were softened.

"Let me see," Jilly went on. "Uh, 1981, the Argentines invade—I can't keep this up, Meran—the Falklands. 1715 . . . that was the year of the first Jacobite uprising."

She'd always been good with historical trivia—having a head for dates—but the more she concentrated on them right now, the further they seemed to slip away. The skookin were regarding her with malevolence, just waiting for her to falter.

"1978," she said. "Sandy Denny died, falling down some stairs. . . ."

She'd got that one from Geordie. The skookin took another step back and she stepped towards them, into the light, her eyes widening with shock. There was a small park there, vegetation dead, trees leafless and skeletal, shadows dancing from the light cast by a fire at either end of the open space. And it was teeming with skookin.

There seemed to be hundreds of the creatures. She could see some of the musicians who were making that awful din—holding their instruments as though they'd never played them before. They were gathered in a semi-circle around a dais made from slabs of pavement and building rubble. Standing on it was the weirdest looking skookin she'd seen yet. He was kind of withered and stood stiffly. His eyes flashed with a kind of dead, cold light. He had the grimmest look about him that she'd seen on any of them yet.

There was no way her little bits of history were going to be enough to keep back this crew. She turned to look at her companions. She couldn't see Goon, but Meran was tugging her flute free from its carrying bag.

What good was that going to do? Jilly wondered.

"It's another kind of truth," Meran said as she brought the instrument up to her lips.

The flute's clear tones echoed breathily along the street, cutting through the jangle of not-music like a glass knife through muddy water. Jilly held her breath. The music was so beautiful. The skookin cowered where they stood. Their cacophonic noise-making faltered, then fell silent.

No one moved.

For long moments, there was just the clear sound of Meran's flute, breathing a slow plaintive air that echoed and sang down the street, winding from one end of the park to the other.

Another kind of truth, Jilly remembered Meran saying just before she began to play. That's exactly what this music was, she realized. A kind of truth.

The flute-playing finally came to an achingly sweet finale and a hush fell in Old City. And then there was movement. Goon stepped from behind Jilly and walked through the still crowd of skookin to the dais where their king stood. He clambered up over the rubble until he was beside the king. He pulled a large clasp knife from the pocket of his coat. As he opened the blade, the skookin king made a jerky motion to get away, but Goon's knife hand moved too quickly.

He slashed and cut.

Now he's bloody done it, Jilly thought as the skookin king tumbled to the stones. But then she realized that Goon hadn't cut the king. He'd cut the air above the king. He'd cut the— her sudden realization only confused her more—strings holding him?

"What . . . ?" she said.

"Come," Meran said.

She tucked her flute under her arm and led Jilly towards the dais.

"This is your king," Goon was saying.

He reached down and pulled the limp form up by the fine-webbed strings that were attached to the king's arms and shoulders. The king dangled loosely under his strong grip—a broken marionette. A murmur rose from the crowd of skookin—part ugly, part wondering.

"The king is dead," Goon said. "He's been dead for moons. I wondered why Old City was closed to me this past half year, and now I know."

There was movement at the far end of the park—a fleeing figure. It had been the king's councilor, Goon told Jilly and Meran later. Some of the skookin made to chase him, but Goon called them back.

"Let him go," he said. "He won't return. We have other business at hand."

Meran had drawn Jilly right up to the foot of the dais and was gently pushing her forward.

"Go on," she said.

"Is he the king now?" Jilly asked.

Meran smiled and gave her another gentle push.

Jilly looked up. Goon seemed just like he always did when she saw him at Bramley's—grumpy and out of sorts. Maybe it's just his face, she told herself, trying to give herself courage. There were people who look grumpy no matter how happy they are. But the thought didn't help contain her shaking much as she slowly made her way up to where Goon stood.

"You have something of ours," Goon said.

His voice was grim. Christy's story lay all too clearly in Jilly's head. She swallowed dryly.

"Uh, I never meant . . ." she began, then simply handed over the drum.

Goon took it reverently, then snatched her other hand before she could draw away. Her palm flared with sharp pain—all the skin, from the base of her hand to the ends of her fingers, was black.

The curse, she thought. It's going to make my hand fall right off. I'm never going to paint again. . . .

Goon spat on her palm and the pain died as though it had never been. With wondering eyes, Jilly watched the blackness dry up and begin to flake away. Goon gave her hand a shake and the blemish scattered to fall to the ground. Her hand was completely unmarked.

"But . . . the curse," she said. "The bounty on my head. What about Christy's story . . . ?"

"Your curse is knowledge," Goon said.

"But . . . ?"

He turned away to face the crowd, drum in hand. As Jilly made her careful descent back to where Meran was waiting for her, Goon tapped his fingers against the head of the drum. An eerie rhythm started up—a real rhythm. When the skookin musicians began to play, they held their instruments properly and called up a sweet stately music to march across the back of the rhythm. It was a rich tapestry of sound, as different from Meran's solo flute as sunlight is from twilight, but it held its own power. Its own magic.

Goon led the playing with the rhythm he called up from the stone drum, led the music as though he'd always led it.

"He's really the king, isn't he?" Jilly whispered to her companion.

Meran nodded.

"So then what was he doing working for Bramley?"

"I don't know," Meran replied. "I suppose a king—or a king's son—can do pretty well what he wants just so long as he comes back here once a moon to fulfill his obligation as ruler."

"Do you think he'll go back to work for Bramley?"

"I know he will," Meran replied.

Jilly looked out at the crowd of skookin. They didn't seem at all threatening anymore. They just looked like little men—comical, with their tubby bodies and round heads and their little broomstick limbs—but men all the same. She listened to the music, felt its trueness and had to ask Meran why it didn't hurt them.

"Because it's their truth," Meran replied.

"But truth's just truth," Jilly protested. "Something's either true or it's not."

Meran just put her arm around Jilly's shoulder. A touch of a smile came to the corners of her mouth.

"It's time we went home," she said.

"I got off pretty lightly, didn't I?" Jilly said as they started back the way they'd come. "I mean, with the curse and all."

"Knowledge can be a terrible burden," Meran replied. "It's what some believe cast Adam and Eve from Eden."

"But that was a good thing, wasn't it?"

Meran nodded. "I think so. But it brought pain with it—pain we still feel to this day."

"I suppose."

"Come on," Meran said, as Jilly lagged a little to look back at the park.

Jilly quickened her step, but she carried the scene away with her. Goon and the stone drum. The crowd of skookin. The flickering light of their fires as it cast shadows over the Old City buildings.

And the music played on.

Professor Dapple had listened patiently to the story he'd been told, managing to keep from interrupting through at least half of the telling. Leaning back in his chair when it was done, he took off his glasses and began to needlessly polish them.

"It's going to be very good," he said finally.

Christy Riddell grinned from the club chair where he was sitting.

"But Jilly's not going to like it," Bramley went on. "You know how she feels about your stories."

"But she's the one who told me this one," Christy said.

Bramley rearranged his features to give the impression that he'd known this all along.

"Doesn't seem like much of a curse," he said, changing tack.

Christy raised his eyebrows. "What? To know that it's all real? To have to seriously consider every time she hears about some seemingly preposterous thing, that it might very well be true? To have to keep on guard with what she says so that people won't think she's gone off the deep end?"

"Is that how people look at us?" Bramley asked.

"What do you think?" Christy replied with a laugh.

Bramley hrumphed. He fidgeted with the papers on his desk, making more of a mess of them, rather than less.

"But Goon," he said, finally coming to the heart of what bothered him with what he'd been told. "It's like some re-telling of 'The King of the Cats,' isn't it? Are you really going to put that bit in?"

Christy nodded. "It's part of the story."

"I can't see Goon as a king of anything," Bramley said.

"And if he *is* a king, then what's he doing still working for me?"

"Which do you think would be better," Christy asked. "To be a king below, or a man above?"

Bramley didn't have an answer for that.

⌐• TIMESKIP •⌐

Every time it rains a ghost comes walking.

He goes up by the stately old houses that line Stanton Street, down Henratty Lane to where it leads into the narrow streets and crowded backalleys of Crowsea, and then back up Stanton again in an unvarying routine.

He wears a worn tweed suit—mostly browns and greys with a faint rosy touch of heather. A shapeless cap presses down his brown curls. His features give no true indication of his age, while his eyes are both innocent and wise. His face gleams in the rain, slick and wet as that of a living person. When he reaches the streetlamp in front of the old Hamill estate, he wipes his eyes with a brown hand. Then he fades away.

Samantha Rey knew it was true because she'd seen him.

More than once.

She saw him every time it rained.

"So, have you asked her out yet?" Jilly wanted to know.

We were sitting on a park bench, feeding pigeons the left-over crusts from our lunches. Jilly had worked with me at the post office, that Christmas they hired outside staff instead of letting the regular employees work the overtime, and we'd been friends ever since. These days she worked three nights a week as a waitress, while I made what I could busking on the Market with my father's old Czech fiddle.

Jilly was slender, with a thick tangle of brown hair and pale blue eyes, electric as sapphires. She had a penchant for loose clothing and fingerless gloves when she wasn't waitressing. There were times, when I met her on the streets in the evening, that I mistook her for a bag lady: skulking in an alleyway, gaze alternating between the sketchbook held in one hand and the faces of the people on the streets as they walked by. She had more sketches of me playing my fiddle than had any right to exist.

"She's never going to know how you feel until you talk to her about it," Jilly went on when I didn't answer.

"I know."

I'll make no bones about it: I was putting the make on Sam Rey and had been ever since she'd started to work at Gypsy Records half a year ago. I never much went in for the blonde California beach girl type, but Sam had a look all her own. She had some indefinable quality that went beyond her basic cheerleader appearance. Right. I can hear you already. Rationalizations of the North American libido. But it was true. I didn't just want Sam in my bed; I wanted to know we were going to have a future together. I wanted to grow old with her. I wanted to build up a lifetime of shared memories.

About the most Sam knew about all this was that I hung around and talked to her a lot at the record store.

"Look," Jilly said. "Just because she's pretty, doesn't mean she's having a perfect life or anything. Most guys look at someone like her and they won't even approach her because they're sure she's got men coming out of her ears. Well, it doesn't always work that way. For instance—" she touched her breastbone with a narrow hand and smiled "—consider yours truly."

I looked at her long fingers. Paint had dried under her nails.

"You've started a new canvas," I said.

"And you're changing the subject," she replied. "Come on, Geordie. What's the big deal? The most she can say is no."

"Well, yeah. But . . ."

"She intimidates you, doesn't she?"

I shook my head. "I talk to her all the time."

"Right. And that's why I've got to listen to your constant mooning over her." She gave me a sudden considering look, then grinned. "I'll tell you what, Geordie, me lad. Here's the bottom line: I'll give you twenty-four hours to ask her out. If you haven't got it together by then, I'll talk to her myself."

"Don't even joke about it."

"Twenty-four hours," Jilly said firmly. She looked at the chocolate-chip cookie in my hand. "Are you eating that?" she added in that certain tone of voice of hers that plainly said, all previous topics of conversation have been dealt with and completed. We are now changing topics.

So we did. But all the while we talked, I thought about going into the record store and asking Sam out, because if I didn't, Jilly would do it for me. Whatever else she might be, Jilly wasn't shy. Having her go in to plead my case would be as bad as having my mother do it for me. I'd never been able to show my face in there again.

Gypsy Records is on Williamson Street, one of the city's main arteries. It begins as Highway 14 outside the city, lined with a sprawl of fast food outlets, malls and warehouses. On its way downtown, it begins to replace the commercial properties with ever-increasing handfuls of residential blocks until it reaches the downtown core where shops and low-rise apartments mingle in gossiping crowds.

The store gets its name from John Butler, a short round-bellied man without a smidgen of Romany blood, who began his business out of the back of a hand-drawn cart that gypsied its way through the city's streets for years, always keeping just one step ahead of the municipal licensing board's agents. While it carries the usual best-sellers, the lifeblood of its sales are more obscure titles—imports and albums published by independent record labels. Albums, singles and compact discs of punk, traditional folk, jazz, heavy metal and alternative music line its shelves. Barring Sam, most of those who work there would look just as at home in the fashion pages of the most current British alternative fashion magazines.

Sam was wearing a blue cotton dress today, embroidered with silver threads. Her blonde hair was cut in a short shag on the top, hanging down past her shoulders at the back and sides. She was dealing with a defect when I came in. I don't know if the record in question worked or not, but the man returning it was definitely defective.

"It sounds like there's a radio broadcast right in the middle of the song," he was saying as he tapped the cover of the Pink Floyd album on the counter between them.

"It's supposed to be there," Sam explained. "It's *part* of the song." The tone of her voice told me that this conversation was going into its twelfth round or so.

"Well, I don't like it," the man told her. "When I buy an album of music, I expect to get just music on it."

"You still can't return it."

I worked in a record shop one Christmas—two years before the post office job. The best defect I got was from someone returning an in-concert album by Marcel Marceau. Each side had thirty minutes of silence, with applause at the end—I kid you not.

I browsed through the Celtic records while I waited for Sam to finish with her customer. I couldn't afford any of them, but I liked to see what was new. Blasting out of the store's speakers was the new Beastie Boys album. It sounded like a cross between heavy metal and bad rap and was about as appealing as being hit by a car. You couldn't deny its energy, though.

By the time Sam was free I'd located five records I would have bought in more flush times. Leaving them in the bin, I drifted over to the front cash just as the Beastie Boys' last cut ended. Sam replaced them with a tape of New Age piano music.

"What's the new Oyster Band like?" I asked.

Sam smiled. "It's terrific. My favorite cut's 'The Old Dance.' It's sort of an allegory based on Adam and Eve and the serpent that's got a great hook in the chorus. Telfer's fiddling just sort of skips ahead, pulling the rest of the song along."

That's what I like about alternative record stores like Gypsy's—the people working in them actually know something about what they're selling.

"Have you got an open copy?" I asked.

She nodded and turned to the bin of opened records behind her to find it. With her back to me, I couldn't get lost in those deep blue eyes of hers. I seized my opportunity and plunged ahead.

"Areyouworkingtonight — wouldyouliketogooutwithmesomewhere?"

I'd meant to be cool about it, except the words all blurred together as they left my throat. I could feel the flush start up the back of my neck as she turned and looked back at me with those baby blues.

"Say what?" she asked.

Before my throat closed up on me completely, I tried again, keeping it short. "Do you want to go out with me tonight?"

Standing there with the Oyster Band album in her hand, I thought she'd never looked better. Especially when she said, "I thought you'd never ask."

I put in a couple of hours of busking that afternoon, down in Crowsea's Market, the fiddle humming under my chin to the jingling rhythm of the coins that passersby threw into the case lying open in front of me. I came away with twenty-six dollars and change—not the best of days, but enough to buy a halfway decent dinner and a few beers.

I picked up Sam after she finished work and we ate at The Monkey Woman's Nest, a Mexican restaurant on Williamson just a couple of blocks down from Gypsy's. I still don't know how the place got its name. Ernestina Verdad, the Mexican woman who owns the place, looks like a showgirl and not one of her waitresses is even vaguely simian in appearance.

It started to rain as we were finishing our second beer, turning Williamson Street slick with neon reflections. Sam got a funny look on her face as she watched the rain through the window. Then she turned to me.

"Do you believe in ghosts?" she asked.

The serious look in her eyes stopped the half-assed joke that two beers brewed in the carbonated swirl of my mind. I never could hold my alcohol. I wasn't drunk, but I had a buzz on.

"I don't think so," I said carefully. "At least I've never seriously stopped to think about it."

"Come on," she said, getting up from the table. "I want to show you something."

I let her lead me out into the rain, though I didn't let her pay anything towards the meal. Tonight was my treat. Next time I'd be happy to let her do the honors.

"Every time it rains," she said, "a ghost comes walking down my street. . . ."

She told me the story as we walked down into Crowsea. The rain was light and I was enjoying it, swinging my fiddle case in my right hand, Sam hanging onto my left as though she'd always walked there. I felt like I was on top of the world, listening to her talk, feeling the pressure of her arm, the bump of her hip against mine.

She had an apartment on the third floor of an old brick and frame building on Stanton Street. It had a front porch that ran the length of the house, dormer windows—two in the front and back, one on each side—and a sloped mansard roof. We stood on the porch, out of the rain, which was coming down harder now. An orange and white tom was sleeping on the cushion of a white wicker chair by the door. He twitched a torn ear as we shared his shelter, but didn't bother to open his eyes. I could smell the mint that was growing up alongside the porch steps, sharp in the wet air.

Sam pointed down the street to where the yellow glare of a streetlamp glistened on the rain-slicked cobblestone walk that led to the Hamill estate. The Hamill house itself was separated from the street by a low wall and a dark expanse of lawn, bordered by the spreading boughs of huge oak trees.

"Watch the street," she said. "Just under the streetlight."

I looked, but I didn't see anything. The wind gusted suddenly, driving the rain in hard sheets along Stanton Street, and for a moment we lost all visibility. When it cleared, he was standing there, Sam's ghost, just like she'd told me. As he started down the street, Sam gave my arm a tug. I stowed my fiddle case under the tom's wicker chair, and we followed the ghost down Henratty Lane.

By the time he returned to the streetlight in front of the Hamill estate, I was ready to argue that Sam was mistaken. There was nothing in the least bit ghostly about the man we were following. When he returned up Henratty Lane, we had to duck into a doorway to let him pass. He never looked at us, but I could see the rain hitting him. I could hear the sound of his shoes on the pavement. He had to have come out of the walk that led up to the estate's house, at the same time as that sudden gust of wind-driven rain. It had been a simple coincidence, nothing more. But when he returned to the streetlight, he lifted a hand to wipe his face, and then he was gone. He just winked out of existence. There was no wind. No gust of rain. No place he could have gone. A ghost.

"Jesus," I said softly as I walked over to the pool of light cast by the streetlamp. There was nothing to see. But there had been a man there. I was sure of that much.

"We're soaked," Sam said. "Come on up to my place and I'll make us some coffee."

The coffee was great and the company was better. Sam had a small clothes drier in her kitchen. I sat in the living room in an oversized housecoat while my clothes tumbled and turned, the machine creating a vibration in the floorboards that I'm sure Sam's downstairs neighbors must have just loved. Sam had changed into a dark blue sweatsuit—she looked best in blue, I decided—and dried her hair while she was making the coffee. I'd prowled around her living room while she did, admiring her books, her huge record collection, her sound system, and the mantel above a working fireplace that was crammed with knickknacks.

All her furniture was the kind made for comfort—they crouched like sleeping animals about the room. Fat sofa in front of the fireplace, an old pair of matching easy chairs by the window. The bookcases, record cabinet, side tables and trim were all natural wood, polished to a shine with furniture oil.

We talked about a lot of things, sitting on the sofa, drinking our coffees, but mostly we talked about the ghost.

"Have you ever approached him?" I asked at one point.

Sam shook her head. "No. I just watch him walk. I've never even talked about him to anybody else." That made me feel good. "You know, I can't help but feel that he's waiting for something, or someone. Isn't that the way it usually works in ghost stories?"

"This isn't a ghost story," I said.

"But we didn't imagine it, did we? Not both of us at the same time?"

"I don't know."

But I knew someone who probably did. Jilly. She was into every sort of strange happening, taking all kinds of odd things seriously. I could remember her telling me that Bramley Dapple—one of her professors at Butler U. and a friend of my brother's—was really a wizard who had a brown-skinned goblin for a valet, but the best thing I remembered about her was her talking about that scene in Disney's *101 Dalmatians,* where the dogs are all howling to send a message across town, one dog sending it out, another picking it up and passing it along, all the way across town and out into the country.

"That's how they do it," she'd said. "Just like that."

And if you walked with her at night and a dog started to howl—if no other dog picked it up, then she'd pass it on. She could mimic any dog's bark or howl so perfectly it was uncanny. It could also be embarrassing, because she didn't care who was around or what kinds of looks she got. It was the message that had to be passed on that was important.

When I told Sam about Jilly, she smiled, but there wasn't any mockery in her smile. Emboldened, I related the ultimatum that Jilly had given me this afternoon.

Sam laughed aloud. "Jilly sounds like my kind of person," she said. "I'd like to meet her."

When it started to get late, I collected my clothes and changed in the bathroom. I didn't want to start anything, not yet, not this soon, and I knew that Sam felt the same way, though neither of us had spoken of it. She kissed me at the door, a long warm kiss that had me buzzing again.

"Come see me tomorrow?" she asked. "At the store?"

"Just try and keep me away," I replied.

I gave the old tom on the porch a pat and whistled all the way home to my own place on the other side of Crowsea.

Jilly's studio was its usual organized mess. It was an open loft-like affair that occupied half of the second floor of a four-story brown brick building on Yoors Street where Foxville's low rentals mingle with Crowsea's shops and older houses. One half of the studio was taken up with a Murphy bed that was never folded back into the wall, a pair of battered sofas, a small kitchenette, storage cabinets and a tiny box-like bathroom obviously designed with dwarves in mind.

Her easel stood in the other half of the studio, by the win-

dow where it could catch the morning sun. All around it
were stacks of sketchbooks, newspapers, unused canvases
and art books. Finished canvases leaned face front, five to
ten deep, against the back wall. Tubes of paint covered the
tops of old wooden orange crates—the new ones lying in
neat piles like logs by a fireplace, the used ones in a haphaz-
ard scatter, closer to hand. Brushes sat waiting to be used in
mason jars. Others were in liquid waiting to be cleaned. Still
more, their brushes stiff with dried paint, lay here and there
on the floor like discarded pick-up-sticks.

The room smelled of oil paint and turpentine. In the corner furthest from the window was a life-sized fabric mâché
sculpture of an artist at work that bore an uncanny likeness
to Jilly herself, complete with Walkman, one paintbrush in
hand, another sticking out of its mouth. When I got there that
morning, Jilly was at her new canvas, face scrunched up as
she concentrated. There was already paint in her hair. On the
windowsill behind her a small ghetto blaster was playing a
Bach fugue, the piano notes spilling across the room like a
light rain. Jilly looked up as I came in, a frown changing
liquidly into a smile as she took in the foolish look on my
face.

"I should have thought of this weeks ago," she said.
"You look like the cat who finally caught the mouse. Did
you have a good time?"

"The best."

Leaving my fiddle by the door, I moved around behind
her so that I could see what she was working on. Sketched
out on the white canvas was a Crowsea street scene. I recognized the corner—McKennitt and Lee. I'd played there from
time to time, mostly in the spring. Lately a rockabilly band
called the Broken Hearts had taken over the spot.

"Well?" Jilly prompted.

"Well what?"

"Aren't you going to give me all the lovely sordid details?"

I nodded at the painting. She'd already started to work in the background with oils.

"Are you putting in the Hearts?" I asked.

Jilly jabbed at me with her paintbrush, leaving a smudge the color of a Crowsea red brick tenement on my jean jacket.

"I'll thump you if you don't spill it all, Geordie, me lad. Just watch if I don't."

She was liable to do just that, so I sat down on the ledge behind her and talked while she painted. We shared a pot of her cowboy coffee, which was what Jilly called the foul brew she made from used coffee grounds. I took two spoons of sugar to my usual one, just to cut back on the bitter taste it left in my throat. Still, beggars couldn't be choosers. That morning I didn't even have used coffee grounds at my own place.

"I like ghost stories," she said when I was finished telling her about my evening. She'd finished roughing out the buildings by now and bent closer to the canvas to start working on some of the finer details before she lost the last of the morning light.

"Was it real?" I asked.

"That depends. Bramley says—"

"I know, I know," I said, breaking in.

If it wasn't Jilly telling me some weird story about him, it was my brother. What Jilly liked best about him was his theory of consensual reality, the idea that things exist *because* we agree that they exist.

"But think about it," Jilly went on. "Sam sees a ghost—maybe because she expects to see one—and you see the same ghost because you care about her, so you're willing to agree that there's one there where she says it will be."

"Say it's not that, then what could it be?"

"Any number of things. A timeslip—a bit of the past slipping into the present. It could be a restless spirit with unfinished business. From what you say Sam's told you, though, I'd guess that it's a case of a timeskip."

She turned to grin at me, which let me know that the word

was one of her own coining. I gave her a dutifully admiring look, then asked, "A what?"

"A timeskip. It's like a broken record, you know? It just keeps playing the same bit over and over again, only unlike the record it needs something specific to cue it in."

"Like rain."

"Exactly." She gave me a sudden sharp look. "This isn't for one of your brother's stories, is it?"

My brother Christy collects odd tales just like Jilly does, only he writes them down. I've heard some grand arguments between the two of them comparing the superior qualities of the oral versus written traditions.

"I haven't seen Christy in weeks," I said.

"All right, then."

"So how do you go about handling this sort of thing?" I asked. "Sam thinks he's waiting for something."

Jilly nodded. "For someone to lift the tone arm of time." At the pained look on my face, she added, "Well, have you got a better analogy?"

I admitted that I didn't. "But how do you do that? Do you just go over and talk to him, or grab him, or what?"

"Any and all might work. But you have to be careful about that kind of thing."

"How so?"

"Well," Jilly said, turning from the canvas to give me a serious look, "sometimes a ghost like that can drag you back to whenever it is that he's from and you'll be trapped in his time. Or you might end up taking his place in the timeskip."

"Lovely."

"Isn't it?" She went back to the painting. "What color's that sign Duffy has over his shop on McKennitt?" she asked.

I closed my eyes, trying to picture it, but all I could see was the face of last night's ghost, wet with rain.

It didn't rain again for a couple of weeks. They were good weeks. Sam and I spent the evenings and weekends together.

We went out a few times, twice with Jilly, once with a couple of Sam's friends. Jilly and Sam got along just as well as I'd thought they would—and why shouldn't they? They were both special people. I should know.

The morning it did rain it was Sam's day off from Gypsy's. The previous night was the first I'd stayed over all night. The first we made love. Waking up in the morning with her warm beside me was everything I thought it would be. She was sleepy-eyed and smiling, more than willing to nestle deep under the comforter while I saw about getting some coffee together.

When the rain started, we took our mugs into the living room and watched the street in front of the Hamill estate. A woman came by walking one of those fat white bull terriers that look like they're more pig than dog. The terrier didn't seem to mind the rain but the woman at the other end of the leash was less than pleased. She alternated between frowning at the clouds and tugging him along. About five minutes after the pair had rounded the corner, our ghost showed up, just winking into existence out of nowhere. Or out of a slip in time. One of Jilly's timeskips.

We watched him go through his routine. When he reached the streetlight and vanished again, Sam leaned her head against my shoulder. We were cozied up together in one of the big comfy chairs, feet on the windowsill.

"We should do something for him," she said.

"Remember what Jilly said," I reminded her.

Sam nodded. "But I don't think that he's out to hurt anybody. It's not like he's calling out to us or anything. He's just there, going through the same moves, time after time. The next time it rains . . ."

"What're we going to do?"

Sam shrugged. "Talk to him, maybe?"

I didn't see how that could cause any harm. Truth to tell, I was feeling sorry for the poor bugger myself.

"Why not?" I said.

About then Sam's hands got busy and I quickly lost interest in the ghost. I started to get up, but Sam held me down in the chair.

"Where are you going?" she asked.

"Well, I thought the bed would be more . . ."

"We've never done it in a chair before."

"There's a lot of places we haven't done it yet," I said.

Those deep blue eyes of hers, about five inches from my own, just about swallowed me.

"We've got all the time in the world," she said.

It's funny how you remember things like that later.

The next time it rained, Jilly was with us. The three of us were walking home from Your Second Home, a sleazy bar on the other side of Foxville where the band of a friend of Sam's was playing. None of us looked quite right for the bar when we walked in. Sam was still the perennial California beach girl, all blonde and curves in a pair of tight jeans and a white T-shirt, with a faded jean-jacket overtop. Jilly and I looked like the scruffs we were.

The bar was a place for serious drinking during the day, serving mostly unemployed blue-collar workers spending their welfare checks on a few hours of forgetfulness. By the time the band started around nine, though, the clientele underwent a drastic transformation. Scattered here and there through the crowd was the odd individual who still dressed for volume—all the colors turned up loud—but mostly we were outnumbered thirty-to-one by spike-haired punks in their black leathers and blue jeans. It was like being on the inside of a bruise.

The band was called the Wang Boys and ended up being pretty good—especially on their original numbers—if a bit loud. My ears were ringing when we finally left the place sometime after midnight. We were having a good time on the walk home. Jilly was in rare form, half-dancing on the street around us, singing the band's closing number, making up the words, turning the piece into a punk gospel number.

She kept bouncing around in front of us, skipping backwards as she tried to get us to sing along.

The rain started as a thin drizzle as were making our way through Crowsea's narrow streets. Sam's fingers tightened on my arm and Jilly stopped fooling around as we stepped into Henratty Lane, the rain coming down in earnest now. The ghost was just turning in the far end of the lane.

"Geordie," Sam said, her fingers tightening more.

I nodded. We brushed by Jilly and stepped up our pace, aiming to connect with the ghost before he made his turn and started back towards Stanton Street.

"This is not a good idea," Jilly warned us, hurrying to catch up. But by then it was too late.

We were right in front of the ghost. I could tell he didn't see Sam or me and I wanted to get out of his way before he walked right through us—I didn't relish the thought of having a ghost or a timeskip or whatever he was going through me. But Sam wouldn't move. She put out her hand, and as her fingers brushed the wet tweed of his jacket, everything changed.

The sense of vertigo was strong. Henratty Lane blurred. I had the feeling of time flipping by like the pages of a calendar in an old movie, except each page was a year, not a day. The sounds of the city around us—sounds we weren't normally aware of—were noticeable by their sudden absence. The ghost jumped at Sam's touch. There was a bewildered look in his eyes and he backed away. That sensation of vertigo and blurring returned until Sam caught him by the arm and everything settled down again. Quiet, except for the rain and a far-off voice that seemed to be calling my name.

"Don't be frightened," Sam said, keeping her grip on the ghost's arm. "We want to help you."

"You should not be here," he replied. His voice was stiff and a little formal. "You were only a dream—nothing more. Dreams are to be savoured and remembered, not walking the streets."

Underlying their voices I could still hear the faint sound of my own name being called. I tried to ignore it, concentrating on the ghost and our surroundings. The lane was clearer than I remembered it—no trash littered against the walls, no graffiti scrawled across the bricks. It seemed darker, too. It was almost possible to believe that we'd been pulled back into the past by the touch of the ghost.

I started to get nervous then, remembering what Jilly had told us. Into the past. What if we *were* in the past and we couldn't get out again? What if we got trapped in the same timeskip as the ghost and were doomed to follow his routine each time it rained?

Sam and the ghost were still talking but I could hardly hear what they were saying. I was thinking of Jilly. We'd brushed by her to reach the ghost, but she'd been right behind us. Yet when I looked back, there was no one there. I remembered that sound of my name, calling faintly across some great distance. I listened now, but heard only a vague unrecognizable sound. It took me long moments to realize that it was a dog barking.

I turned to Sam, tried to concentrate on what she was saying to the ghost. She was starting to pull away from him, but now it was his hand that held her arm. As I reached forward to pull her loose, the barking suddenly grew in volume—not one dog's voice, but those of hundreds, echoing across the years that separated us from our own time. Each year caught and sent on its own dog's voice, the sound building into a cacophonous chorus of yelps and barks and howls.

The ghost gave Sam's arm a sharp tug and I lost my grip on her, stumbling as the vertigo hit me again. I fell through the sound of all those barking dogs, through the blurring years, until I dropped to my knees on the wet cobblestones, my hands reaching for Sam. But Sam wasn't there.

"Geordie?"

It was Jilly, kneeling by my side, hand on my shoulder. She took my chin and turned my face to hers, but I pulled free.

"Sam!" I cried.

A gust of wind drove rain into my face, blinding me, but not before I saw that the lane was truly empty except for Jilly and me. Jilly, who'd mimicked the barking of dogs to draw us back through time. But only I'd returned. Sam and the ghost were both gone.

"Oh, Geordie," Jilly murmured as she held me close. "I'm so sorry."

I don't know if the ghost was ever seen again, but I saw Sam one more time after that night. I was with Jilly in Moore's Antiques in Lower Crowsea, flipping through a stack of old sepia-toned photographs, when a group shot of a family on their front porch stopped me cold. There, among the somber faces, was Sam. She looked different. Her hair was drawn back in a tight bun and she wore a plain unbecoming dark dress, but it was Sam all right. I turned the photograph over and read the photographer's date on the back. 1912.

Something of what I was feeling must have shown on my face, for Jilly came over from a basket of old earrings that she was looking through.

"What's the matter, Geordie, me lad?" she asked.

Then she saw the photograph in my hand. She had no trouble recognizing Sam either. I didn't have any money that day, but Jilly bought the picture and gave it to me. I keep it in my fiddle case.

I grow older each year, building up a lifetime of memories, only I've no Sam to share them with. But often when it rains, I go down to Stanton Street and stand under the street-light in front of the old Hamill estate. One day I know she'll be waiting there for me.

⌒• FREEWHEELING •⌒

There is apparently nothing that cannot happen.
                    —ATTRIBUTED TO MARK TWAIN

*There are three kinds of people: those who make things happen,
those who watch things happen, and those who wonder, "What
happened?"*

                              —MESSAGE FOUND INSIDE A
                              CHRISTMAS CRACKER

1

HE STOOD ON the rain-slick street, a pale fire burning behind his eyes. Nerve ends tingling, he watched them
go—a slow parade of riderless bicycles.

Ten-speeds and mountain bikes. Domesticated, urban. So
inbred that all they were was spoked wheels and emaciated
frames, mere skeletons of what their genetic ancestors had
been. They had never known freedom, never known joy;
only the weight of serious riders in slick, leather-seated
shorts, pedaling determinedly with their cycling shoes
strapped to the pedals, heads encased in crash helmets, fingerless gloves on the hands gripping the handles tightly.

He smiled and watched them go. Down the wet street,
wheels throwing up arcs of fine spray, metal frames glistening in the streetlights, reflector lights winking red.

The rain had plastered his hair slick against his head, his

clothes were sodden, but he paid no attention to personal discomfort. He thought instead of that fat-wheeled aboriginal one-speed that led them now. The maverick who'd come from who knows where to pilot his domesticated brothers and sisters away.

For a night's freedom. Perhaps for always.

The last of them were rounding the corner now. He lifted his right hand to wave goodbye. His left hand hung down by his leg, still holding the heavy-duty wire cutters by one handle, the black rubber grip making a ribbed pattern on the palm of his hand. By fences and on porches, up and down the street, locks had been cut, chains lay discarded, bicycles ran free.

He heard a siren approaching. Lifting his head, he licked the rain drops from his lips. Water got in his eyes, gathering in their corners. He squinted, enamored by the kaleidoscoping spray of lights this caused to appear behind his eyelids. There were omens in lights, he knew. And in the night sky, with its scattershot sweep of stars. So many lights . . . There were secrets waiting to unfold there, mysteries that required a voice to be freed.

Like the bicycles were freed by their maverick brother.

He could be that voice, if he only knew what to sing.

He was still watching the sky for signs when the police finally arrived.

"Let me go, boys, let me go. . . ."

The new Pogues album *If I Should Fall From Grace With God* was on the turntable. The title cut leaked from the sound system's speakers, one of which sat on a crate crowded with half-used paint tubes and tins of turpentine, the other perched on the windowsill, commanding a view of rainswept Yoors Street one floor below. The song was jauntier than one might expect from its subject matter while Shane MacGowan's voice was as rough as ever, chewing the words and spitting them out, rather than singing them.

It was an angry voice, Jilly decided as she hummed softly

along with the chorus. Even when it sang a tender song. But what could you expect from a group that had originally named itself Pogue Mahone—Irish Gaelic for "Kiss my ass"?

Angry and brash and vulgar. The band was all of that. But they were honest, too—painfully so, at times—and that was what brought Jilly back to their music, time and again. Because sometimes things just had to be said.

"I don't get this stuff," Sue remarked.

She'd been frowning over the lyrics that were printed on the album's inner sleeve. Leaning her head against the patched backrest of one of Jilly's two old sofas, she set the sleeve aside.

"I mean, music's supposed to make you feel good, isn't it?" she went on.

Jilly shook her head. "It's supposed to make you feel *something*—happy, sad, angry, whatever—just so long as it doesn't leave you brain-dead the way most Top Forty does. For me, music needs meaning to be worth my time—preferably something more than 'I want your body, babe,' if you know what I mean."

"You're beginning to develop a snooty attitude, Jilly."

"*Me?* To laugh, dahling."

Susan Ashworth was Jilly's uptown friend, as urbane as Jilly was scruffy. Sue's blonde hair was straight, hanging to just below her shoulders, where Jilly's was a riot of brown curls, made manageable tonight only by a clip that drew it all up to the top of her head before letting it fall free in the shape of something that resembled nothing so much as a disenchanted Mohawk. They were both in their twenties, slender and blue-eyed—the latter expected in a blonde; the electric blue of Jilly's eyes gave her, with her darker skin, a look of continual startlement. Where Sue wore just the right amount of makeup, Jilly could usually be counted on having a smudge of charcoal somewhere on her face and dried oil paint under her nails.

Sue worked for the city as an architect; she lived uptown

and her parents were from the Beaches, where it seemed you needed a permit just to be out on the sidewalks after eight in the evening—or at least that was the impression that the police patrols left when they stopped strangers to check their ID. She always had that upscale look of one who was just about to step out to a restaurant for cocktails and dinner.

Jilly's first love was art of a freer style than designing municipal necessities, but she usually paid her rent by waitressing and other odd jobs. She tended to wear baggy clothes—like the oversized white T-shirt and blue poplin lace-front pants she had on tonight—and always had a sketchbook close at hand.

Tonight it was on her lap as she sat propped up on her Murphy bed, toes in their ballet slippers tapping against one another in time to the music. The Pogues were playing an instrumental now—"Metropolis"—which sounded like a cross between a Celtic fiddle tune and the old "Dragnet" theme.

"They're really not for me," Sue went on. "I mean if the guy could sing, maybe, but—"

"It's the feeling that he puts into his voice that's important," Jilly said. "But this is an instrumental. He's not even—"

"Supposed to be singing. I know. Only—"

"If you'd just—"

The jangling of the phone sliced through their discussion. Because she was closer—and knew that Jilly would claim some old war wound or any excuse not to get up, now that she was lying down—Sue answered it. She listened for a long moment, an odd expression on her face, then slowly cradled the receiver.

"Wrong number?"

Sue shook her head. "No. It was someone named . . . uh, Zinc? He said that he's been captured by two Elvis Presleys disguised as police officers and would you please come and explain to them that he wasn't stealing bikes, he was just setting them free. Then he hung up."

"Oh, shit!" Jilly stuffed her sketchbook into her shoulderbag and got up.

"This makes sense to you?"

"Zinc's one of the street kids."

Sue rolled her eyes, but she got up as well. "Want me to bring my checkbook?"

"What for?"

"Bail. It's what you have to put up to spring somebody from jail. Don't you *ever* watch TV?"

Jilly shook her head. "What? And let the aliens monitor my brainwaves?"

"What scares me," Sue muttered as they left the loft and started down the stairs, "is that sometimes I don't think you're kidding."

"Who says I am?" Jilly said.

Sue shook her head. "I'm going to pretend I didn't hear that."

Jilly knew people from all over the city, in all walks of life. Socialites and bag ladies. Street kids and university profs. Nobody was too poor, or conversely, too rich for her to strike up a conversation with, no matter where they happened to meet, or under what circumstances. She'd met Detective Lou Fucceri, now of the Crowsea Precinct's General Investigations squad, when he was still a patrolman, walking the Stanton Street Combat Zone beat. He was the reason she'd survived the streets to become an artist instead of just one more statistic to add to all those others who hadn't been so lucky.

"Is it true?" Sue wanted to know as soon as the desk sergeant showed them into Lou's office. "The way you guys met?" Jilly had told her that she'd tried to take his picture one night and he'd arrested her for soliciting.

"You mean UFO-spotting in Butler U. Park?" he replied.

Sue sighed. "I should've known. I must be the only person who's maintained her sanity after meeting Jilly."

She sat down on one of the two wooden chairs that faced

Lou's desk in the small cubicle that passed for his office. There was room for a bookcase behind him, crowded with law books and file folders, and a brass coat rack from which hung a lightweight sports jacket. Lou sat at the desk, white shirt sleeves rolled halfway up to his elbows, top collar undone, black tie hanging loose.

His Italian heritage was very much present in the Mediterranean cast to his complexion, his dark brooding eyes and darker hair. As Jilly sat down in the chair Sue had left for her, he shook a cigarette free from a crumpled pack that he dug out from under the litter of files on his desk. He offered the cigarettes around, tossing the pack back down on the desk and lighting his own when there were no takers.

Jilly pulled her chair closer to the desk. "What did he do, Lou? Sue took the call, but I don't know if she got the message right."

"I *can* take a message," Sue began, but Jilly waved a hand in her direction. She wasn't in the mood for banter just now.

Lou blew a stream of blue-grey smoke towards the ceiling. "We've been having a lot of trouble with a bicycle theft ring operating in the city," he said. "They've hit the Beaches, which was bad enough, though with all the Mercedes and BMWs out there, I doubt they're going to miss their bikes a lot. But rich people like to complain, and now the gang's moved their operations into Crowsea."

Jilly nodded. "Where for a lot of people, a bicycle's the only way they *can* get around."

"You got it."

"So what does that have to do with Zinc?"

"The patrol car that picked him up found him standing in the middle of the street with a pair of heavy-duty wire cutters in his hand. The street'd been cleaned right out, Jilly. There wasn't a bike left on the block—just the cut locks and chains left behind."

"So where are the bikes?"

Lou shrugged. "Who knows. Probably in a Foxville chopshop having their serial numbers changed. Jilly, you've got to get Zinc to tell us who he was working with. Christ, they took off, leaving him to hold the bag. He doesn't owe them a thing now."

Jilly shook her head slowly. "This doesn't make any sense. Zinc's not the criminal kind."

"I'll tell you what doesn't make any sense," Lou said. "The kid himself. He's heading straight for the loonie bin with all his talk about Elvis clones and Venusian thought machines and feral fuck—" He glanced at Sue and covered up the profanity with a cough. "Feral bicycles leading the domesticated ones away."

"He said that?"

Lou nodded. "That's why he was clipping the locks—to set the bikes free so that they could follow their, and I quote, 'spiritual leader, home to the place of mystery.' "

"That's a new one," Jilly said.

"You're having me on—right?" Lou said. "That's all you can say? It's a new one? The Elvis clones are old hat now? Christ on a comet. Would you give me a break? Just get the kid to roll over and I'll make sure things go easy for him."

"Christ on a comet?" Sue repeated softly.

"C'mon, Lou," Jilly said. "How can I make Zinc tell you something he doesn't know? Maybe he found those wire cutters on the street—just before the patrol car came. For all we know he could—"

"He *said* he cut the locks."

The air went out of Jilly. "Right," she said. She slouched in her chair. "I forgot you'd said that."

"Maybe the bikes really did just go off on their own," Sue said.

Lou gave her a weary look, but Jilly sat up straighter. "I wonder," she began.

"Oh, for God's sake," Sue said. "I was only joking."

"I know you were," Jilly said. "But I've seen enough odd things in this world that I won't say anything's impossible anymore."

"The police department doesn't see things quite the same way," Lou told Jilly. The dryness of his tone wasn't lost on her.

"I know."

"I want these bike thieves, Jilly."

"Are you arresting Zinc?"

Lou shook his head. "I've got nothing to hold him on except for circumstantial evidence."

"I thought you said he admitted to cutting the locks," Sue said.

Jilly shot her a quick fierce look that plainly said, Don't make waves when he's giving us what we came for.

Lou nodded. "Yeah. He admitted to that. He also admitted to knowing a hobo who was really a spy from Pluto and asked why the patrolmen had traded in their white Vegas suits for uniforms. He wanted to hear them sing 'Heartbreak Hotel.' For next of kin he put down Bigfoot."

"*Gigantopithecus blacki,*" Jilly said.

Lou looked at her. "What?"

"Some guy at Washington State University's given Bigfoot a Latin name now. *Giganto*—"

Lou cut her off. "That's what I thought you said." He turned back to Sue. "So you see, his admitting to cutting the locks isn't really going to amount to much. Not when a lawyer with half a brain can get him off without even having to work up a sweat."

"Does that mean he's free to go then?" Jilly asked.

Lou nodded. "Yeah. He can go. But keep him out of trouble, Jilly. He's in here again, and I'm sending him straight to the Zeb for psychiatric testing. And try to convince him to come clean on this—okay? It's not just for me, it's for him too. We break this case and find out he's involved, nobody's going to go easy on him. We don't give out rain checks."

"Not even for dinner?" Jilly asked brightly, happy now that she knew Zinc was getting out.

"What do you mean?"

Jilly grabbed a pencil and paper from his desk and scrawled "Jilly Coppercorn owes Hotshot Lou one dinner, restaurant of her choice," and passed it over to him.

"I think they call this a bribe," he said.

"I call it keeping in touch with your friends," Jilly replied and gave him a big grin.

Lou glanced at Sue and rolled his eyes.

"Don't look at me like that," she said. "I'm the sane one here."

"You wish," Jilly told her.

Lou heaved himself to his feet with exaggerated weariness. "C'mon, let's get your friend out of here before he decides to sue us because we don't have our coffee flown in from the Twilight Zone," he said as he led the way down to the holding cells.

Zinc had the look of a street kid about two days away from a good meal. His jeans, T-shirt, and cotton jacket were ragged, but clean; his hair was a badly mown lawn, with tufts standing up here and there like exclamation points. The pupils of his dark brown eyes seemed too large for someone who never did drugs. He was seventeen, but acted half his age.

The only home he had was a squat in Upper Foxville that he shared with a couple of performance artists, so that was where Jilly and Sue took him in Sue's Mazda. The living space he shared with the artists was on the upper story of a deserted tenement where someone had put together a makeshift loft by the simple method of removing all the walls, leaving a large empty area cluttered only by support pillars and the squatters' belongings.

Lucia and Ursula were there when they arrived, practicing one of their pieces to the accompaniment of a ghetto blaster pumping out a mixture of electronic music and the sound of breaking glass at a barely audible volume. Lucia was wrapped in plastic and lying on the floor, her black hair spread out in an arc around her head. Every few moments one of her limbs would twitch, the plastic wrap stretching tight against her skin with the movement. Ursula crouched beside the blaster, chanting a poem that consisted only of the line, "There are no patterns." She'd shaved her head since the last time Jilly had seen her.

"What am I doing here?" Sue asked softly. She made no effort to keep the look of astonishment from her features.

"Seeing how the other half lives," Jilly said as she led the way across the loft to where Zinc's junkyard of belongings took up a good third of the available space.

"But just look at this stuff," Sue said. "And how did he get that in here?"

She pointed to a Volkswagen bug that was sitting up on blocks, missing only its wheels and front hood. Scattered all around it was a hodgepodge of metal scraps, old furniture, boxes filled with wiring and God only knew what.

"Piece by piece," Jilly told her.

"And then he reassembled it here?"

Jilly nodded.

"Okay. I'll bite. Why?"

"Why don't you ask him?"

Jilly grinned as Sue quickly shook her head. During the entire trip from the precinct station, Zinc had carefully explained his theory of the world to her, how the planet Earth was actually an asylum for insane aliens, and that was why nothing made sense.

Zinc followed the pair of them across the room, stopping only long enough to greet his squat-mates. "Hi, Luce. Hi, Urse."

Lucia never looked at him.

"There are no patterns," Ursula said.

Zinc nodded thoughtfully.

"Maybe there's a pattern in that," Sue offered.

"Don't start," Jilly said. She turned to Zinc. "Are you going to be all right?"

"You should've seen them go, Jill," Zinc said. "All shiny and wet, just whizzing down the street, heading for the hills."

"I'm sure it was really something, but you've got to promise me to stay off the streets for awhile. Will you do that, Zinc? At least until they catch this gang of bike thieves?"

"But there weren't any thieves. It's like I told Elvis Two, they left on their own."

Sue gave him an odd look. "Elvis too?"

"Don't ask," Jilly said. She touched Zinc's arm. "Just stay in for awhile—okay? Let the bikes take off on their own."

"But I like to watch them go."

"Do it as a favor to me, would you?"

"I'll try."

Jilly gave him a quick smile. "Thanks. Is there anything you need? Do you need money for some food?"

Zinc shook his head. Jilly gave him a quick kiss on the cheek and tousled the exclamation point hair tufts sticking up from his head.

"I'll drop by to see you tomorrow, then—okay?" At his nod, Jilly started back across the room. "C'mon, Sue," she said when her companion paused beside the tape machine where Ursula was still chanting.

"So what about this stock market stuff?" she asked the poet.

"There are no patterns," Ursula said.

"That's what I thought," Sue said, but then Jilly was tugging her arm.

"Couldn't resist, could you?" Jilly said.

Sue just grinned.

"Why do you humor him?" Sue asked when she pulled up in front of Jilly's loft.

"What makes you think I am?"

"I'm being serious, Jilly."

"So am I. He believes in what he's talking about. That's good enough for me."

"But all this stuff he goes on about . . . Elvis clones and insane aliens—"

"Don't forget animated bicycles."

Sue gave Jilly a pained look. "I'm not. That's just what I mean—it's all so crazy."

"What if it's not?"

Sue shook her head. "I can't buy it."

"It's not hurting anybody." Jilly leaned over and gave Sue a quick kiss on the cheek. "Gotta run. Thanks for everything."

"Maybe it's hurting him," Sue said as Jilly opened the door to get out. "Maybe it's closing the door on any chance he has of living a normal life. You know—opportunity comes knocking, but there's nobody home? He's not just eccentric, Jilly. He's crazy."

Jilly sighed. "His mother was a hooker, Sue. The reason he's a little flaky is her pimp threw him down two flights of stairs when he was six years old—not because Zinc did anything, or because his mother didn't trick enough johns that night, but just because the creep felt like doing it. That's what normal was for Zinc. He's happy now—a lot happier than when Social Services tried to put him in a foster home where they only wanted him for the support check they got once a month for taking him in. And a lot happier than he'd be in the Zeb, all doped up or sitting around in a padded cell whenever he tried to tell people about the things he sees.

"He's got his own life now. It's not much—not by your standards, maybe not even by mine, but it's his and I don't want anybody to take it away from him."

"But—"

"I know you mean well," Jilly said, "but things don't always work out the way we'd like them to. Nobody's got time for a kid like Zinc in Social Services. There he's just a statistic that they shuffle around with all the rest of their files and red tape. Out here on the street, we've got a system that works. We take care of our own. It's that simple. Doesn't matter if it's the Cat Lady, sleeping in an alleyway with a half dozen mangy toms, or Rude Ruthie, haranguing the commuters on the subway, we take care of each other."

"Utopia," Sue said.

A corner of Jilly's mouth twitched with the shadow of a humorless smile. "Yeah. I know. We've got a high asshole quotient, but what can you do? You try to get by—that's all. You just try to get by."

"I wish I could understand it better," Sue said.

"Don't worry about it. You're good people, but this just isn't your world. You can visit, but you wouldn't want to live in it, Sue."

"I guess."

Jilly started to add something more, but then just smiled encouragingly and got out of the car.

"See you Friday?" she asked, leaning in the door.

Sue nodded.

Jilly stood on the pavement and watched the Mazda until it turned the corner and its rear lights were lost from view, then she went upstairs to her apartment. The big room seemed too quiet and she felt too wound up to sleep, so she put a cassette in the tape player—Lynn Harrell playing a Schumann concerto—and started to prepare a new canvas to work on in the morning when the light would be better.

2

It was raining again, a soft drizzle that put a glistening sheen on the streets and lampposts, on porch handrails and street signs. Zinc stood in the shadows that had gathered in the mouth of an alleyway, his new pair of wire cutters a comfortable weight in his hand. His eyes sparked with reflected lights. His hair was damp against his scalp. He licked his lips, tasting mountains heights and distant forests within the drizzle's slightly metallic tang.

Jilly knew a lot about things that were, he thought, and things that might be, and she always meant well, but there was one thing she just couldn't get right. You didn't make art by capturing an image on paper, or canvas, or in stone. You didn't make it by writing down stories and poems. Music and dance came closest to what real art was—but only so long as you didn't try to record or film it. Musical notation was only so much dead ink on paper. Choreography was planning, not art.

You could only make art by setting it free. Anything else was just a memory, no matter how you stored it. On film or paper, sculpted or recorded.

Everything that existed, existed in a captured state. Animate or inanimate, everything wanted to be free.

That's what the lights said; that was their secret. Wild lights in the night skies, and domesticated lights, right here on the street, they all told the same tale. It was so plain to see when you knew *how* to look. Didn't neon and streetlights yearn to be starlight?

To be free.

He bent down and picked up a stone, smiling at the satisfying crack it made when it broke the glass protection of the streetlight, his grin widening as the light inside flickered, then died.

It was part of the secret now, part of the voices that spoke in the night sky.

Free.

Still smiling, he set out across the street to where a bicycle was chained to the railing of a porch.

"Let me tell you about art," he said to it as he mounted the stairs.

* * *

Psycho Puppies were playing at the YoMan on Gracie Street near the corner of Landis Avenue that Friday night. They weren't anywhere near as punkish as their name implied. If they had been, Jilly would never have been able to get Sue out to see them.

"I don't care if they damage themselves," she'd told Jilly the one and only time she'd gone out to one of the punk clubs further west on Gracie, "but I refuse to pay good money just to have someone spit at me and do their best to rupture my eardrums."

The Puppies were positively tame compared to how that punk band had been. Their music was loud, but melodic, and while there was an undercurrent of social conscience to their lyrics, you could dance to them as well. Jilly couldn't help but smile to see Sue stepping it up to a chorus of, "You can take my job, but you can't take me, ain't nobody gonna steal my dignity."

The crowd was an even mix of slumming uptowners, Crowsea artistes and the neighborhood kids from surrounding Foxville. Jilly and Sue danced with each other, not from lack of offers, but because they didn't want to feel obligated to any guy that night. Too many men felt that one dance entitled them to ownership—for the night, at least, if not forever—and neither of them felt like going through the ritual repartee that the whole business required.

Sue was on the right side of a bad relationship at the moment, while Jilly was simply eschewing relationships on general principal these days. Relationships required changes, and she wasn't ready for changes in her life just now. And besides, all the men she'd ever cared for were already taken and she didn't think it likely that she'd run into her own particular Prince Charming in a Foxville night club.

"I like this band," Sue confided to her when they took a break to finish the beers they'd ordered at the beginning of the set.

Jilly nodded, but she didn't have anything to say. A glance across the room caught a glimpse of a head with hair enough like Zinc's badly-mown lawn scalp to remind her that he hadn't been home when she'd dropped by his place on the way to the club tonight.

Don't be out setting bicycles free, Zinc, she thought.

"Hey, Tomas. Check this out."

There were two of them, one Anglo, one Hispanic, neither of them much more than a year or so older than Zinc. They both wore leather jackets and jeans, dark hair greased back in ducktails. The drizzle put a sheen on their jackets and hair. The Hispanic moved closer to see what his companion was pointing out.

Zinc had melted into the shadows at their approach. The streetlights that he had yet to free whispered, *careful, careful,* as they wrapped him in darkness, their electric light illuminating the pair on the street.

"Well, shit," the Hispanic said. "Somebody's doing our work for us."

As he picked up the lock that Zinc had just snipped, the chain holding the bike to the railing fell to the pavement with a clatter. Both teenagers froze, one checking out one end of the street, his companion the other.

" 'Scool," the Anglo said. "Nobody here but you, me and your cooties."

"Chew on a big one."

"I don't do myself, *puto.* "

"That's 'cos it's too small to find."

The pair of them laughed—a quick nervous sound that belied their bravado—then the Anglo wheeled the bike away from the railing.

"Hey, Bobby-o," the Hispanic said. "Got another one over here."

"Well, what're you waiting for, man? Wheel her down to the van."

They were setting bicycles free, Zinc realized—just like he was. He'd gotten almost all the way down the block, painstakingly snipping the shackle of each lock, before the pair had arrived.

Careful, careful, the streetlights were still whispering, but Zinc was already moving out of the shadows.

"Hi, guys," he said.

The teenagers froze, then the Anglo's gaze took in the wire cutters in Zinc's hand.

"Well, well," he said. "What've we got here? What're you doing on the night side of the street, kid?"

Before Zinc could reply, the sound of a siren cut the air. A lone siren, approaching fast.

The Chinese waitress looked great in her leather miniskirt and fishnet stockings. She wore a blood-red camisole tucked into the waist of the skirt which made her pale skin seem even paler. Her hair was the black of polished jet, pulled up in a loose bun that spilled stray strands across her neck and shoulders. Blue-black eye shadow made her dark eyes darker. Her lips were the same red as her camisole.

"How come she looks so good," Sue wanted to know, "when I'd just look like a tart if I dressed like that?"

"She's inscrutable," Jilly replied. "You're just obvious."

"How sweet of you to point that out," Sue said with a grin. She stood up from their table. "C'mon. Let's dance."

Jilly shook her head. "You go ahead. I'll sit this one out."

"Uh-uh. I'm not going out there alone."

"There's LaDonna," Jilly said, pointing out a girl they both knew. "Dance with her."

"Are you feeling all right, Jilly?"

"I'm fine—just a little pooped. Give me a chance to catch my breath."

But she wasn't all right, she thought as Sue crossed over to where LaDonna da Costa and her brother Pipo were sitting. Not when she had Zinc to worry about. If he was out there, cutting off the locks of more bicycles . . .

You're not his mother, she told herself. Except—

Out here on the streets we take care of our own.

That's what she'd told Sue. And maybe it wasn't true for a lot of people who hit the skids—the winos and the losers and the bag people who were just too screwed up to take care of themselves, little say look after anyone else—but it was true for her.

Someone like Zinc—he was an in-betweener. Most days he could take care of himself just fine, but there was a fey streak in him so that sometimes he carried a touch of the magic that ran wild in the streets, the magic that was loose late at night when the straights were in bed and the city belonged to the night people. That magic took up lodgings in people like Zinc. For a week. A day. An hour. Didn't matter if it was real or not, if it couldn't be measured or catalogued, it was real to them. It existed all the same.

Did that make it true?

Jilly shook her head. It wasn't her kind of question and it didn't matter anyway. Real or not, it could still be driving Zinc into breaking corporeal laws—the kind that'd have Lou breathing down his neck, real fast. The kind that'd put him in jail with a whole different kind of loser.

Zinc wouldn't last out a week inside.

Jilly got up from the table and headed across the dance floor to where Sue and LaDonna were jitterbugging to a tune that sounded as though Buddy Holly could have penned the melody, if not the words.

"Fuck this, man!" the Anglo said.

He threw down the bike and took off at a run, his companion right on his heels, scattering puddles with the impact of their boots. Zinc watched them go. There was a buzzing in the back of his head. The streetlights were telling him to run too, but he saw the bike lying there on the pavement like a wounded animal, one wheel spinning forlornly, and he couldn't just take off.

Bikes were like turtles. Turn 'em on their backs—or a

bike on its side—and they couldn't get up on their own again.

He tossed down the wire cutters and ran to the bike. Just as he was leaning it up against the railing from which the Anglo had taken it, a police cruiser came around the corner, skidding on the wet pavement, cherry light gyrating—screaming, *Run, run!* in its urgent high-pitched voice—headlights pinning Zinc where he stood.

Almost before the cruiser came to a halt, the passenger door popped open and a uniformed officer had stepped out. He drew his gun. Using the cruiser as a shield, he aimed across its roof at where Zinc was standing.

"Hold it right there, kid!" he shouted. "Don't even blink."

Zinc was privy to secrets. He could hear voices in lights. He knew that there was more to be seen in the world if you watched it from the corner of your eye than head on. It was a simple truth that every policeman he ever saw looked just like Elvis. But he hadn't survived all his years on the streets without protection.

He had a lucky charm. A little tin monkey pendant that had originally lived in a box of Crackerjacks—back when Crackerjacks had real prizes in them. Lucia had given it to him. He'd forgotten to bring it out with him the other night when the Elvises had taken him in. But he wasn't stupid. He'd remembered it tonight.

He reached into his pocket to get it out and wake its magic.

"You're just being silly," Sue said as they collected their jackets from their chairs.

"So humor me," Jilly asked.

"I'm coming, aren't I?"

Jilly nodded. She could hear the voice of Zinc's roommate Ursula in the back of her head—

There are no patterns.

—but she could feel one right now, growing tight as a drawn bowstring, humming with its urgency to be loosed.

"C'mon," she said, almost running from the club.

Police officer Mario Hidalgo was still a rookie—tonight was only the beginning of his third month of active duty—and while he'd drawn his sidearm before, he had yet to fire it in the line of duty. He had the makings of a good cop. He was steady, he was conscientious. The street hadn't had a chance to harden him yet, though it had already thrown him more than a couple of serious uglies in his first eight weeks of active duty.

But steady though he'd proved himself to be so far, when he saw the kid reaching into his pocket of his baggy jacket, Hidalgo had a single moment of unreasoning panic.

The kid's got a gun, that panic told him. The kid's going for a weapon.

One moment was all it took.

His finger was already tightening on the trigger of his regulation .38 as the kid's hand came out of his pocket. Hidalgo wanted to stop the pressure he was putting on the gun's trigger, but it was like there was a broken circuit between his brain and his hand.

The gun went off with a deafening roar.

Got it, Zinc thought as his fingers closed on the little tin monkey charm. Got my luck.

He started to take it out of his pocket, but then something hit him straight in the chest. It lifted him off his feet and threw him against the wall behind him with enough force to knock all the wind out of his lungs. There was a raw pain firing every one of his nerve ends. His hands opened and closed spastically, the charm falling out of his grip to hit the ground moments before his body slid down the wall to join it on the wet pavement.

Goodbye, goodbye, sweet friend, the streetlights cried.

He could sense the spin of the stars as they wheeled high

above the city streets, their voices joining the electric voices of the streetlights.

My turn to go free, he thought as a white tunnel opened in his mind. He could feel it draw him in, and then he was falling, falling, falling. . . .

"Goodbye. . . ." he said, thought he said, but no words came forth from between his lips.

Just a trickle of blood that mingled with the rain that now began to fall in earnest, as though it, too, was saying its own farewell.

All Jilly had to see was the red spinning cherries of the police cruisers to know where the pattern she'd felt in the club was taking her. There were a lot of cars here—cruisers and unmarked vehicles, an ambulance—all on official business, their presence coinciding with her business. She didn't see Lou approach until he laid his hand on her shoulder.

"You don't want to see," he told her.

Jilly never even looked at him. One moment he was holding her shoulder, the next she'd shrugged herself free of his grip and just kept on walking.

"Is it . . . is it Zinc?" Sue asked the detective.

Jilly didn't have to ask. She knew. Without being told. Without having to see the body.

An officer stepped in front of her to stop her, but Lou waved him aside. In her peripheral vision she saw another officer sitting inside a cruiser, weeping, but it didn't really register.

"I thought he had a gun," the policeman was saying as she went by. "Oh, Jesus. I thought the kid was going for a gun. . . ."

And then she was standing over Zinc's body, looking down at his slender frame, limbs flung awkwardly like those of a rag doll that had been tossed into a corner and forgotten. She knelt down at Zinc's side. Something glinted on the wet pavement. A small tin monkey charm. She picked it up, closed it tightly in her fist before anyone could see what she'd done.

"C'mon, Jilly," Lou said as he came up behind her. He helped her to her feet.

It didn't seem possible that anyone as vibrant—as *alive*—as Zinc had been could have any relation whatsoever with that empty shell of a body that lay there on the pavement.

As Lou led her away from the body, Jilly's tears finally came, welling up from her eyes to salt the rain on her cheek.

"He . . . he wasn't . . . stealing bikes, Lou. . . ." she said.

"It doesn't look good," Lou said.

Often when she'd been with Zinc, Jilly had had a sense of that magic that touched him. A feeling that even if she couldn't see the marvels he told her about, they still existed just beyond the reach of her sight.

That feeling should be gone now, she thought.

"He was just . . . setting them free," she said.

The magic should have died, when he died. But she felt, if she just looked hard enough, that she'd see him, riding a maverick bike at the head of a pack of riderless bicycles—metal frames glistening, reflector lights glinting red, wheels throwing up arcs of fine spray, as they went off down the wet street.

Around the corner and out of sight.

"Nice friends the kid had," a plainclothes detective who was standing near them said to the uniformed officer beside him. "Took off with just about every bike on the street and left him holding the bag."

Jilly didn't think so. Not this time.

This time they'd gone free.

THAT EXPLAINS
∽ · POLAND · ∾

1

MAYBE THAT EXPLAINS Poland.
Lori's mother used to say that. In the fullness of her Stalinism, the great hamster (as Lori called her) was convinced that every radical twitch to come from Poland and Solidarity was in fact inspired by the CIA, drug addicts, M&Ms, reruns of "The Honeymooners" ("To the moon, Alice!") . . . in fact, just about everything except the possibility of real dissension among the Polish people with their less than democratic regime. It got to the point where she was forever saying "That explains Poland!", regardless of how absurd or incomprehensible the connection.

It became a family joke—*a proposito* to any and all situations and shared by sundry and all, in and about the Snelling clan. You still don't get it?

Maybe you just had to be there.

2

"Listen to this: BIGFOOT SPIED IN UPPER FOXVILLE," Lori read from the Friday edition of *The Daily Journal.* "Bigfoot. Can you believe it? I mean, can you *believe* it?"

Ruth and I feigned indifference. We were used to Lori's outbursts by now and even though half the *clientela* in The Monkey Woman's Nest lifted their heads from whatever had been occupying them to look our way, we merely sipped our beer and looked out onto Williamson Street, watching the commuters hustle down into the subways or jockeying for position at the bus stop.

Lori was an eventful sort of a person. You could always count on something happening around her, with a ninety-nine percent chance that she'd been the catalyst. On a Friday afternoon, with the week's work behind us and two glorious days off ahead, we didn't need an event. Just a quiet moment and a few beers in *la Hora Frontera* before the streets woke up and the clubs opened their doors.

"Who's playing at Your Second Home this weekend?" Ruth asked.

I wasn't sure, but I had other plans anyway. "I was thinking of taking in that new Rob Lowe movie if it's still playing."

Ruth got a gleam in her eye. "He is *so* dreamy. Every time I see him I just want to take him home and—"

"Don't be such a pair of old poops," Lori interrupted. "This is important. It's history in the making. Just listen to what it says." She gave the paper a snap to keep our attention, which set off another round of lifting heads throughout the restaurant, and started to read.

"The recent sighting of a large, hairy, human-like creature in the back alleys of Upper Foxville has prompted Councilman Cohen to renew his demands

*for increased police patrols in that section of the city.
Eyewitness Barry Jack spotted the huge beast about
1 A.M. last night. He estimated it stood between seven
and eight feet tall and weighed about 300 to 400
pounds.''*

"Lori . . .''
"Let me finish.

'' *'While I doubt that the creature seen by Mr. Jack—
that a Bigfoot—exists,'* Cohen is quoted as saying, *'it
does emphasize the increased proliferation of tran-
sients and the homeless in this area of the city, a problem that the City Council is doing very little about,
despite continual requests by residents and this Council member.'*

"Right.'' Lori gave us a quick grin. "Well, *that's* stretching
a point way beyond *my* credibility.''
"Lori, what are you talking about?'' I asked.
"The way Cohen's dragging in this business of police patrols.'' She went back to the article.

"*Could such a creature exist? According to archaeol-
ogy professor Helmet Goddin of Butler University,
'Not in the city. Sightings of Bigfoot or the Sasquatch
are usually relegated to wilderness areas, a description that doesn't apply to Upper Foxville, regardless
of its resemblance to an archaeological dig.'*

"Which is just his way of saying the place is a disaster
area,'' Lori added. "No surprises there.''
She held up a hand before either Ruth or I could speak and
plunged on.

"*Goddin says that the Sasquatch possibly resulted
from some division in the homonid line, which evolved*

separately from humans. He speculates that they are 'more intelligent than apes . . . and apes can be very intelligent. If it does exist, then it is a very, very important biological and anthropological discovery.' "

Lori laid the paper down and sipped some of her beer. "So," she said as she set the glass back down precisely in its ring of condensation on the table. "What do you think?"

"Think about what?" Ruth asked.

Lori tapped the newspaper. "Of this." At our blank looks, she added, "It's something we can do this weekend. We can go hunting for Bigfoot in Upper Foxville."

I could tell from Ruth's expression that the idea had about as much appeal for her as it did for me. Spend the weekend crawling about the rubble of Upper Foxville and risk getting jumped by some junkie or hobo? No thanks.

Lori's studied Shotokan karate and could probably have held her own against Bruce Lee, but Ruth and I were just a couple of Crowsea punkettes, about as useful in a confrontation as a handful of wet noodles. And going into Upper Foxville to chase down some big *muchacho* who'd been mistaken for a Sasquatch was not my idea of fun. I'm way too young for suicide.

"Hunting?" I said. "With what?"

Lori pulled a small Instamatic from her purse. "With this, LaDonna. What else?"

I lifted my brows and looked to Ruth for help, but she was too busy laughing at the look on my face.

Right, I thought. Goodbye, Rob Lowe—it could've been *mucho primo.* Instead I'm going on a *gaza de grillos* with Crowsea's resident madwomen. Who said a weekend had to be boring?

3

I do a lot of thinking about decisions—not so much trying to make up my mind about something as just wondering, *¿que si?* Like if I hadn't decided to skip school that day with my brother Pipo and taken El Sub to the Pier, then I'd never have met Ruth. Ruth introduced me to Lori and Lori introduced me to more trouble than I could ever have gotten into on my own.

Not that I was a Little Miss Innocent before I met Lori. I looked like the kind of *muchacha* that your mother warned you not to hang around with. I liked my black jeans tight and my leather skirt short, but I wasn't a *puta* or anything. It was just for fun. The kind of trouble I got into was for staying out too late, or skipping school, or getting caught having a cigarette with the other girls behind the gym, or coming home with the smell of beer on my breath.

Little troubles. Ordinary ones.

The kind of trouble I got into with Lori was always *mucho* weird. Like the time we went looking for pirate treasure in the storm sewers under the Beaches—the ritzy area where Lori's parents lived before they got divorced. We were down there for hours, all dressed up in her father's spelunking gear, and just about drowned when it started to rain and the sewers filled up. Needless to say, her *papa* was *not* pleased at the mess we made of his gear.

And then there was the time that we hid in the washrooms at the Watley's Department Store downtown and spent the whole night trying on dresses, rearranging the mannequins, eating chocolates from the candy department. . . . If it had been just me on my own—coming from the barrios and all— I'd've ended up in jail. But being with Lori, her *papa* bailed us out and paid for the chocolates and one broken mannequin. We didn't do much for the rest of that summer except for gardening and odd jobs until we'd worked off what we owed him.

¿No muy loco? Verdad, we were only thirteen, and it was just the start. But that's all in the past. I'm grown up now— just turned twenty-one last week. Been on my own for four years, working steady. But I still wonder sometimes.

About decisions.

How different everything might have been if I hadn't done this, or if I *had* done that.

I've never been to Poland. I wonder what it's like.

4

"We'll set it up like a scavenger hunt," Lori said. She paused as the waitress brought another round—Heineken for Lori, Miller Lites for Ruth and I—then leaned forward, elbows on the table, the palms of her hands cupping her chin. "With a prize and everything."

"What kind of a prize?" Ruth wanted to know.

"Losers take the winner out for dinner to the restaurant of her choice."

"Hold everything," I said. "Are you saying we each go out by ourselves to try to snap a shot of this thing?"

I had visions of the three of us in Upper Foxville, each of us wandering along our own street, the deserted tenements on all sides, the only company being the bums, junkies and *cabrones* that hung out there.

"I don't want to end up as just another statistic," I said.

"Oh, come on. We're around there all the time, hitting the clubs. When's the last time you heard of any trouble?"

"Give me the paper and I'll tell you," I said, reaching for the *Journal.*

"You want to go at *night*?" Ruth asked.

"We go whenever we choose," Lori replied. "The first one with a genuine picture wins."

"I can just see the three of us disappearing in there," I said. " 'The lost women of Foxville flats.' "

"Beats being remembered as loose women," Lori said.

"We'd be just another urban legend."

Ruth nodded. "Like in one of Christy Riddell's stories."

I shook my head. "No thanks. He makes the unreal too real. Anyway, I was thinking more of that Brunvand guy with his choking Doberman and Mexican pets."

"Those are all just stories," Lori said, trying to sound like Christopher Lee. She came off like a bad Elvira. "This could be real."

"Do you *really* believe that?" I asked.

"No. But I think it'll be a bit of fun. Are you scared?"

"I'm sane, aren't I? Of course I'm scared."

"Oh, poop."

"That doesn't mean I'm not up for it."

I wondered if it wasn't too late to have my head examined. Did the hospital handle that kind of thing in their emergency ward?

"Good for you, LaDonna," Lori was saying. "What about you, Ruth?"

"Not at night."

"We'll get the jump on you."

"Not at night," she repeated.

"Not at night," I agreed.

Lori's eyes had that mad little gleam in them that let me know that we'd been had again. She'd never planned on going at night either.

"A toast," she said, raising her beer. "May the best woman win."

We clinked our mugs against each other's and made plans for the night while we finished our beer. I don't think anyone in the restaurant was sorry to see us go when we finally left. First up was the early show at the Oxford (you didn't really think I'd stand you up, did you, Rob?), then the last couple of sets at the Zorb, where the Fat Man Blues Band was playing, because Ruth was crazy about their bass player and Lori and I liked to egg her on.

5

By now you're probably thinking that we're just a bunch of airheads, out for laughs and not concerned with anything important. Well, it isn't true. I think about things all the time. Like how hanging around with Anglos so much has got me to the point where half the time I sound like one myself. I can hardly speak to my grandmother these days. I don't even think in Spanish anymore and it bothers me.

It's only in the barrio that I still speak it, but I don't go there much—just to visit the family on birthdays and holidays. I worked hard to get out, but sometimes when I'm in my apartment on Lee Street in Crowsea, sitting in the windowseat and looking out at the park, I wonder why. I've got a nice place there, a decent job, some good friends. But I don't have any roots. There's nothing connecting me to this part of the city.

I could vanish overnight (disappear in Upper Foxville on a *caza de grillos*), and it wouldn't cause much more than a ripple. Back home, the *abuelas* are *still* talking about how Donita's youngest girl moved to Crowsea and when was she going to settle down?

I don't really know anybody I can talk to about this kind of thing. Neither my Anglo friends nor my own people would understand. But I think about it. Not a lot, but I think about it. And about decisions. About all kinds of things.

Ruth says I think too much.

Lori just wonders why I'm always trying to explain Poland. You'd think I was her mother or something.

6

Saturday morning, bright and early, and only a little hungover, we got off the Yoors Street subway and followed the stairs up from the underground station to where they spat us out on the corner of Gracie Street and Yoors. Gracie Street's the *frontera* between Upper Foxville and Foxville proper. South of Gracie it's all low-rent apartment buildings and tenements, shabby old *viviendas* that manage to hang on to an old world feel, mostly because it's still families living here, just like it's been for a hundred years. The people take care of their neighborhood, no differently than their parents did before them.

North of Gracie a bunch of developers got together and planned to give the area a new facelift. I've seen the plans— condominiums, shopping malls, parks. Basically what they wanted to do was shove a high class suburb into the middle of the city. Only what happened was their backers pulled out while they were in the middle of leveling about a square mile of city blocks, so now the whole area's just a mess of empty buildings and rubble-strewn lots.

It's creepy, looking out on it from Gracie Street. It's like standing on the line of a map that divides civilization from no-man's-land. You almost expect some graffiti to say, ''Here there be dragons.'' And maybe they wouldn't be so far off. Because you can find dragons in Upper Foxville— the *muy malo* kind that ride chopped-down Harleys. The Devil's Dragon. Bikers making deals with their junkies. I think I'd prefer the kind that breathe fire.

I don't like the open spaces of rubble in Upper Foxville. My true self—the way I see me—is like an alley cat, crouching for shelter under a car, watching the world go by. I'm comfortable in Crowsea's narrow streets and alleyways. They're like the barrio where I got my street smarts. It's easy to duck away from trouble, to get lost in the shadows. To hang out and watch, but not be seen. Out there, in those desolate blocks north of Gracie, there's no place to hide, and too many places—all at the same time.

If that kind of thing bothered Lori, she sure wasn't showing it. She was all decked out in fatigues, hiking boots and a khaki-colored shoulderbag like she was in the Army Reserves and going out on maneuvers or something. Ruth was almost as bad, only she went to the other extreme. She was wearing baggy white cotton pants with a puffed sleeve blouse and a trendy vest, low-heeled sandals and a matching purse.

Me? That morning I dressed with survival in mind, not fashion. I had my yellow jeans and my red hightops, an old black Motorhead T-shirt and a scuffed leather jacket that I hoped would make me look tough. I had some of my hair up in a top-knot, the rest all *loco*, and went heavy on the makeup. My camera—a *barato* little Vitoret that I'd borrowed from Pipo last fall and still hadn't returned yet—was stuffed in a shapeless canvas shoulderbag. All I wanted to do was fit in.

Checking out the skateboarders and other kids already clogging up Gracie's sidewalks, I didn't think I was doing too bad a job. Especially when this little *muchacho* with a pink Mohawk came whipping over on his board and tried to put the moves on me. I felt like I was sixteen again.

"Well, I'm going straight up Yoors," Lori said. "Everybody got their cameras and some film?"

Ruth and I dutifully patted our purse and shoulderbag respectively.

"I guess I'll try the Tombs," I said.

It only took a week after the machines stopped pushing over the buildings for people to start dumping everything from old car parts to bags of trash in the blocks between Lanois and Flood north of MacNeil. People took to calling it the Tombs because of all the wrecked vehicles.

I'd had some time to think things through over a breakfast of black coffee this morning—a strangely lucid moment, considering the night before. I'd almost decided on getting my friend Izzy from the apartment downstairs to hide out in an ape suit somewhere in the rubble, and then it hit me. Lori probably had something similar planned. She'd have Ruth and I tramping around through the rubble, getting all hot and sweaty, and more than a little tense, and then she'd produce a photo of some friend of *hers* in an ape suit, snapped slightly out of focus as he was ducking into some run-down old building. It'd be good for a laugh and a free dinner and it was just the kind of stunt Lori'd pull. I mean, we could have been doing some serious shopping today. . . .

My new plan was to head out towards the Tombs, then work my way over to Yoors where I'd follow Lori and take my picture of her and her pal in his monkeysuit. *Mama* didn't raise any stupid kids, no matter what her neighbors thought.

So I gave them both a jaunty wave and set off down Gracie to where Lanois would take me north into the Tombs. Lori went up Yoors. Ruth was still standing by the stairs going down to the subway station by the time I lost sight of her, looking back through the crowds. My pink Mohawked admirer followed me until I turned up towards the Tombs, then he went whizzing back to his friends, expertly guiding his skateboard down the congested sidewalk like the pro he was. He couldn't have been more than thirteen.

7

When you're a *niña*—and maybe twenty-one is still being a kid to some people—it's not so weird to be worrying about who you are and how you're ever going to fit in. But then you're supposed to get a handle on things and by the time you're my age, you've got it all pretty well figured out. At least that's the impression I got when I was a *niña* and twenty-one looked like it was about as old as you ever wanted to get.

Verdad, I still don't know who I am or where I fit in. I stand in front of the mirror and the *muchacha* I see studying me just as carefully as I'm studying her *looks* older. But I don't feel any different from when I was fifteen.

So when does it happen?

Maybe it never does.

Maybe that explains Poland.

8

All things considered—I mean, this *was* Upper Foxville—it wasn't a bad day to be scuffling around in the Tombs. The sun was bright in a sky so blue it hurt to look at it. Good thing I hadn't forgotten my shades. Broken glass shimmered and gleamed in the light and crunched underfoot.

What's this thing people have for busting windows and bottles and the like? It seems like all you need is an unbroken piece of glass and rocks just sort of pop into people's hands. Of course it makes such an interesting sound when it breaks. And it gives you such a feeling of . . . oh, I don't know. Having *cojones*, I suppose. What's that song by Nick Lowe? "I Love the Sound of Breaking Glass." Not that I'm into that kind of thing—okay, at least not anymore. And better it be in a place like this than on the sidewalk or streets where people have to walk or go wheeling by on their bikes.

I was feeling pretty punky by the time I'd been in the Tombs for an hour or so. That always happens when I wear my leather jacket. I may not be a real *machona*—or at least not capable of violence, let's say—but the jacket makes me *feel* tough anyway. It says don't mess with me all over it. Not that there was anybody there to mess around with me.

I spotted a few dogs—feral, mangy-looking *perros* that kept their distance. The rat that surprised me as I came around a corner was a lot less forgiving about having its morning disturbed. It stood its ground until I pitched a rock at it, then it just sort of melted away, slinky and fast.

It was early for the junkies and other lowlifes that were out in full force come late afternoon, but the bag ladies were making their rounds, all bundled up in layers of coats and dresses, pushing their homes and belongings around in shopping carts or carrying it all about in plastic shopping bags. I passed winos, sleeping off last night's booze, and hoboes huddled around small fires, taking their time about waking up before they hit the streets of Foxville and Crowsea to panhandle the Saturday crowds. They gave me the creeps, staring at me like I didn't belong—fair enough, I guess, since I didn't—obviously thinking what the hell was I doing here? Would you believe looking for Bigfoot? Didn't think so.

Did I mention the smell? If you've ever been to a dump, you'll know what I mean. It's a sweet-sour cloying smell that gets into your clothes and hair and just hangs in there. You could get used to it, I guess—it stopped bothering me after the first fifteen minutes or so—but I wouldn't want to have to be sitting next to me on El Sub going home.

I guess I killed an hour or so before I worked my way west towards Yoors Street to look for Lori. It was kind of fun, playing Indian scout in the rubble. I got so involved in sneaking around that I almost ran right into them.

Them. Yeah, I was right. Lori was sitting on what was left of some building's front steps, sharing a beer with a guy named Byron Murphy. Near Byron's knee was a plastic shopping bag out of which spilled something that looked remarkably like a flat ape's arm. I mean the arm was flat, because it was part of a costume and there was nobody in it at the moment. Come to think of it, that *would* make it a flat ape, wouldn't it?

Byron worked at the sports clinic at Butler U. as a therapist. Like most of Lori's old boyfriends, he'd stayed her friend after they broke up. That kind of thing never happens to me. When I break up with a guy it usually involves various household objects flying through the air aimed for his head. You'd think I had a Latin temper or something.

I backed up quickly, but I shouldn't have worried. Neither of them had spotted me. I thought about trying to find Ruth, then realized that I'd have to wait until later to let her in on the joke. What I didn't want to do was miss getting this all down on film. Byron putting on the apesuit. The two of them setting up the shot. I wanted the whole thing. Maybe I could even sell my photos to *The Daily Journal*—"BIGFOOT HOAXERS CAUGHT IN THE ACT"—and really play the trick back on her.

Circling around them, I made my way to an old deserted brownstone and went in. After checking around first to make sure I was alone, I got comfortable by a window where I had a perfect view of Lori and Byron and settled down to wait.

Gotcha now, Lori.

9

The best kinds of practical jokes are those that backfire on whoever's playing the trick. Didn't you ever want to get a camera on Alan Funt and catch *him* looking silly for a change? I didn't get many opportunities to catch Lori—and don't think I haven't tried. (Remind me to tell you the story of the thirty-five pizzas and the priest sometime.) The trouble with Lori is that she doesn't think linearly or even in intuitive leaps. Her mind tends to move sideways in its thinking, which makes it hard to catch her out, since you haven't a clue what she's on about in the first place.

She gets it from her mother, I guess.

It might not explain Poland, but it says volumes about genetics.

10

I had to wait a half hour before they finally pulled the gorilla suit out of the bag. It didn't fit Byron all that well, but did an okay job from a distance. I figured Lori would put him in the shadows of the building on the other side of the street and move the camera a bit while she was taking her shot. Nothing's quite so effective as a slightly blurry, dark shot when you're dealing with whacko things like a Bigfoot or flying saucers.

Me, I was wishing for a telephoto lens and a decent camera, but I was pretty sure the Vitoret would work fine. We weren't talking high art here. Anyway, I could always have the prints blown up—and no, smart guy, I'm not talking about dynamite.

I got the whole thing on film. Byron putting on the costume. Lori posing him, taking her shots. Byron taking the costume off and stashing it away. The two of them leaving. All I wanted to do was lean out the window and shout, "Nya nya!", but I kept my mouth shut and let them go. Then, camera in hand, I left the building by the back, heading for the Tombs.

There were no steps, so I had to jump down a three-foot drop. I paused at the top to put away my camera, and then I froze.

Not twenty yards away, a huge figure in a bulky overcoat

and slouched down hat was shuffling through the rubble. Before I could duck away, the figure turned and I was looking straight into this hairy face.

I don't quite know how to describe him to you. You're not going to believe me anyway and words just don't quite do justice to the *feeling* of the moment.

He wasn't wearing anything under the overcoat and the sun was bright enough so that I could see he was covered with hair all over. It was a fine pelt—more like an ape's than a bear's—a rich dark brown that was glossy where it caught the sun. His feet were huge, his chest like a barrel, his arms like a weightlifter's. But his face . . . It was human, and it wasn't. It was like an ape's, but it wasn't. The nose was flat, but the cheekbones were delicate under the fine covering of hair. His lips were thin, chin square. And his eyes . . . They were a warm brown liquid color, full of smarts, no question about it. And they were looking straight at me, thinking about what kind of a threat I posed for him.

Let me tell you, my heart stopped dead in my chest. It was all a joke, right? Lori's gag that I was playing back on her. Except there *had* been that article in the newspaper, and right now I was staring at Bigfoot and there were no ifs, ands, or buts about it. I had my camera in my hand. All I had to do was lift it, snap a shot, and take off running.

But I thought about what it would mean if I did that. If there was a photo to *really* prove this guy existed, they'd be sending in teams to track him down. When they caught him, they'd keep him locked up, maybe dissect him to see what made him work. . . . Like everybody else, I've seen *E.T.*

I don't want to sound all mushy or anything, but there was something in those eyes that I didn't ever want to see locked away. I moved really slowly, putting the camera away in my bag, then I held my hands out to him so that he could see that I wasn't going to hurt him.

(Me hurt *him*—there's a laugh. The *size* of him . . .)

"You don't want to hang around this city too long," I told

him. ''If they catch you, nobody's going to be nice about it.''

I was surprised at how calm I sounded.

He didn't say anything. He just stood there, looking at me with those big browns of his. Then he grinned—proof positive, as if I needed it, that he wasn't some guy in a suit like Byron, because there was no way they'd made a mask yet that could move like his features did right then. His whole face was animated—filled with a big silly lopsided grin that made me grin right back when it reached his eyes. He tipped a hairy finger to the brim of his hat, and then he just sort of faded away into the rubble—as quick and smooth as the rat had earlier, but there was nothing sneaky or sly about the way he moved.

One minute he was there, grinning like a loon, and the next he was gone.

I sank down and sat in the doorway, my legs swinging in the space below, and looked at where he'd been. I guess I was there for awhile, just trying to take it all in. I remembered a time when I'd been camping with my brother and a couple of friends from the neighborhood. I woke early the first morning and stuck my head out of the tent to find myself face to face with a deer. We both held our breath for what seemed like hours. When I finally breathed, she took off like a shot, but left me with a warm feeling that stayed with me for the rest of that weekend.

That's kind of what I was feeling right now. Like I'd lucked into a peek at one of the big mysteries of the world and if I kept it to myself, then I'd always be a part of it. It'd be our secret. Something nobody could ever take away from me.

11

So we all survived our *casa de grillos* in Upper Foxville. Ruth had gotten bored walking around in the rubble and gone back to Gracie Street, where she'd spent the better part of the day hanging around with some graffiti artists that she'd met while she was waiting for us. I got my film processed at one of those one-hour places and we made Lori pay up with a fancy dinner for trying to pull another one over on us.

Some reporters were in the area too, we found out later, trying to do a follow-up on the piece in the *Journal* yesterday, but nobody came back with a photo of Bigfoot, except for me, and mine's just a snapshot sitting there in the back of my head where I can take it out from time to time whenever I'm feeling blue and looking for a good memory.

It's absurd when you think about it—Bigfoot wandering around in the city, poorly disguised in an oversized trenchcoat and battered slouch hat—but I like the idea of it. Maybe he was trying to figure out who he was and where he fit in. Maybe it was all a laugh for him too. Maybe he really was just this hairy *muchacho*, making do in the Tombs. I don't know. I just think of him and smile.

Maybe that explains Poland.

⌁ · ROMANO DROM · ⌁

The road leading to a goal does not separate you from the destination; it is essentially a part of it.

—ROMANY SAYING

A LIGHT FRIDAY night drizzle had left a glistening sheen on Yoors Street when Lorio Munn stepped out of the club. She hefted her guitar case and looked down at her running shoes with a frown. The door opened and closed behind her and Terry Dixon joined her on the sidewalk, carrying his bass.

"What's the problem?" he asked.

Lorio lifted a shoe to show him the hole in its sole. "It's going to be a wet walk."

"You want a lift? Jane's meeting me at the Fan—we can give you a lift home after, if you want."

"No. I'm not much in the mood for socializing tonight."

"Hey, come on. It was a great night. We packed the place."

"Yeah. But they weren't really listening."

"They were dancing, weren't they? All of a sudden, that's not enough? You used to complain that all they'd do is just sit there."

"I know. I like it when they dance. It's just—"

Terry caught her arm. Putting a finger to his lips, he nodded to a pair of women who were walking by, neither of whom noticed Lorio and Terry standing in the club's doorway. One of them was humming the chorus to the band's last number under her breath:

> *I don't need nobody staring at me,*
> *stripping me down with their 1-2-3,*
> *I got a right to my own dignity*
> *—who needs pornography?*

"Okay," Lorio said when the women had passed them. "So somebody's listening. But when I went to get our money, Slimy Ted—"

"Slimy Toad."

Lorio smiled briefly. "He told me I could make a few extra bucks if I'd go out with a couple of his friends who, quote, 'liked my moves,' unquote. What does that tell you?"

"That I ought to break his head."

"It means the people that I want to reach *aren't* listening."

"Maybe we should be singing louder?"

"Sure." Lorio shook her head. "Look, say hi to Jane for me, would you? Maybe I'll make it next time."

She watched him go, then set off in the opposite direction towards Stanton Street. Maybe she shouldn't be complaining. No Nuns Here was starting to get the decent gigs. *In the City* had run an article on them—even spent a paragraph or two on what was behind the band, instead of just dismissing what they were trying to say as post-punk jingoism like their one two-line review in *The Newford Star* had.

Oh, it was still very in to sing about women's rights, gay rights, *people*'s rights, for God's sake, but the band still got the "aren't you limiting yourselves?" thrown at them by people who should know better. Still, at least they were getting some attention and, more importantly, what they were trying to say was getting some attention. It might bore the pants off of Joe Average Jock—but that was just the person they were trying to reach. So where did you go? If they could only get a decent gig. A big one where they could really reach more—

She paused in mid-step, certain she'd heard a moan from the alleyway she was passing. As she peered into it, the sound was repeated. Definitely a moan. She looked up and down Yoors Street, but there was no one close to her.

"Hey!" she called softly into the alley. "Is there someone in there?"

She caught a glimpse of eyes, gleaming like a cat's caught in the headbeams of a car—just a shivery flash and they were gone. Animal's eyes. But the sound she'd heard had seemed human.

"Hey!"

Swallowing thickly, she edged into the alley, her guitar case held out in front of her. As she moved down its length, her eyes began to adjust to the poor light.

Why was she doing this? She had to be nuts.

The moan came a third time then and she saw what she took to be a small man lying in some refuse.

"Oh, jeez." She moved forward, fear forgotten. "Are you okay?"

She laid her guitar case down and knelt beside the figure, but when she reached out a hand to his shoulder, she touched fur instead of clothing. Muscles moved under her fingers—weakly, but enough to tell her that it wasn't a fur coat. She snatched back her hand as a broad face turned towards her.

She froze, looking into that face. The first thing she thought of were the orangutans in the Metro Zoo. The features had a simian cast with their close-set eyes, broad overhanging brow and protruding lower jaw. Reddish fur surrounded the face—the same fur that covered the creature's body.

It had to be a costume, she thought. Except it was too real. She began to back away.

"Help . . . me. . . ."

This *couldn't* be real.

"When they track me down again . . . this time . . . they will . . . they will kill me. . . ."

The gaze that met her own was cloudy with pain, but it wasn't an animal's. Intelligence lay in its depth, behind the pain. But this wasn't a man wearing a costume either.

"Who will?" she asked at last.

For the first time, the gaze appeared to really focus on her.

"You . . . you're a Gypsy," the creature said. *"Sarishan, Romani chi."*

Lorio shook her head, unable to accept what she was hearing.

"The blood's awfully thin," she said finally. "And I don't speak Romany."

Though she knew it to hear it and remembered the odd word. The last person to speak it in her presence had been her uncle Palko, but that was a long time ago now.

"You are strangely garbed," the creature said, "but I know a Gypsy when I see one."

Strangely garbed? Well, it all depended, Lorio thought.

Her long curly hair was dyed a black too deep to be natural and grew from a three-inch swatch down the center of her head. Light brown stubble grew on either side of the mohawk where the sides of her head had been shaved. She wore a brown leather bomber's jacket over a bright red and black Forties dress, net stockings, and her running shoes. A strand of plastic pearls hung around her neck. Six earrings, from a rhinestone stud to threaded beads, hung from her right ear. In her left lobe was a stud in the shape of an Anarchy symbol.

"My mother was a Gypsy," she said, "but my father—"

She shook her head. What was she doing? Arguing with a ragged bundle of orange fur did not make much bloody sense.

"Your people know the roads," the creature said. "The roads of this world and those roads beyond that bind the balance. You . . . you can help me. Take my place. The hound

caught me before—before I could complete my journey. The
boundaries grow thin . . . frail. You must—''

''I don't know what you're talking about,'' Lorio said.
''God, I don't even know what you are.''

''My name is Elderee and this time Mahail's hound did
its job too well. It will be back . . . once it scents my weak-
ness. . . .'' He coughed and Lorio stared at the blood speck-
ling the hand-like paw that went up to his mouth.

''Look, you shouldn't be talking. You need a doctor.''

Right. Maybe a vet would be more like it. She started to
take off her jacket to lay it over him, but Elderee reached out
and touched her arm.

''You need only walk it,'' he said. ''That's all it takes.
Walk it with intent. An old straight track . . . there for those
who know to see it. Like a Gypsy road—*un Romano drom*. It
will take you home.''

''How do you know where I live?''

And why, she asked herself, am I taking this all so
calmly? Probably because any minute she expected Steven
Spielberg to step out and say, ''Cut! That's a take.''

''Not where you live—but *home*. Where all roads meet.
Jacca calls it Lankelly—because of the sacred grove in the
heart of the valley—but I just think of it as the Wood.''

Lorio shook her head. ''This is a joke, right? You're just
wearing a . . . a costume, right? A really good one.''

''No, I—''

''Sure. It's almost Halloween. You were at a party and
you got mugged. The Gypsy bit was a good guess. I can handle this—no problem. Now we've got to get you to a hospital.''

''Too . . . too late. . . .''

''Jeez, don't fade out on me now. I can . . .''

Her voice trailed off as she realized that the man in the
monkey suit was looking behind her. She turned just in time
to see a dog-like creature materialize out of nowhere. It
came with a *whufft* of displaced air, bringing an unpleasant
reek in its wake. Crouching on powerful legs, it looked like a

cross between a hyena and a wolf, except for the protruding canines that Lorio had only seen in zoological texts on extinct species such as the saber-toothed tiger.

"Flee!" Elderee croaked. "You can't hope to face a polrech. . . ."

His warning came too late. With a rumbling growl that came from deep in its chest, the creature charged. Lorio didn't even stop to think of what she was doing. She just hoisted her guitar case and swung it in a flailing arc as hard as she could. The end of the case holding the body of her guitar struck the creature with such force that it snapped the beast's neck with an audible crack.

Lorio lost her hold on the case and it flew from her hands to land in a skidding crash well beyond the polrech that had dropped in its tracks. She stared at the dying creature, numb with fright. Adrenaline roared through her, bringing a buzz to her ears.

Saliva dripped from the creature's open mouth. The pavement of the alley smoked at its acidic touch. A pair of red fiery eyes glared at her. Taloned paws twitched, trying to reach her. When the light died in the creature's eyes, its shape wavered, then came apart, drifting away like smoke. A spark or two, like coals in a dying fire, hissed on the pavement, then there was nothing except for the small hole where the creature's saliva had pooled.

Lorio hugged herself to keep from shaking. Slowly she turned to look at her companion, but he lay very still now.

"Uh . . . Elderee?" she tried.

She moved forward, keeping half an eye on the alley behind her in case there were more of the hounds coming. Gingerly she touched Elderee. His eyes flickered open and something sparked between them, leaving Lorio momentarily dizzy. When her gaze cleared, she saw that the life-light was fading in his eyes now.

He had been holding his left arm across his lower torso. It fell free, revealing a gaping wound. Blood had matted in the fur around it. A queasy feeling started up in Lorio's stomach, but she forced it down. She tried to be calm. Something weird was going on—no doubt about that—but first things first.

"You must . . ." Elderee began in a weak voice.

"Uh-uh," Lorio interrupted. "You listen to me. You're hurt. I don't know what you are and I can't take you to a regular hospital, but you look enough like a . . . like an orangutan that the Zoo might take you in and hopefully patch you up. Now what I want you to do is keep your mouth shut and pretend you're an animal, okay? Otherwise they'll probably dissect you, just to see what makes you tick. We'll figure out how to get you out of the Zoo again when that problem comes up."

"But . . ."

"Take it easy. I'm going to get us a ride."

Without letting him reply, she bolted from the alleyway and ran down Yoors Street. She didn't know how she was going to explain this to Terry—she wasn't sure she could explain it to herself—but that didn't matter. First she had to get Elderee to a place where his injury could be treated. Everything else had to wait until then. The Fan loomed up on her left and she charged into the restaurant, ignoring the stares she was getting as she pushed her way to Terry and Jane's table.

"Lorio!" Terry said, looking up with a smile. "So you changed your—"

"No time to talk, Terry. I'm taking you up on that offer of a ride—only I need it right away."

"What's the big—"

"We're talking desperate here, Terry. Please?"

The bass player of No Nuns Here exchanged a glance with his girlfriend. Jane shrugged, so he dumped a handful of bills on the table and hurried out of the restaurant with her, trying to catch up to Lorio who was already running back to the alleyway where she'd left her monkeyman.

* * *

It was a twenty minute drive from downtown Newford to the Metro Zoo, and another twenty minutes back again. Terry pulled his Toyota over to the curb in front of Lorio's apartment building on Lee Street in Crowsea. She shared a second floor loft with a traditional musician named Angie Tichell in the old three-story brick building. The loft retained a consistent smell of Chinese food because of the ground floor that specialized in Mainland dishes.

Terry looked back between the bucket seats and studied Lorio for a moment.

"Are you going to be okay?" he asked.

Lorio nodded. "At least they took him in," she said.

They'd stayed in the Zoo parking lot long enough to be sure of that.

"I'm sure they'll do the best they can for him."

"But what if they can't help him? I mean, he *looks* like an orangutan, but what if he's too alien for them to help him?"

Terry had no answer for her. He'd been shocked enough to see the ape with its orange-red fur lying there in the alleyway, but when he'd heard it talk . . .

"Just what *is* he?" Jane asked.

Lorio wore a mournful expression. "I don't know." She sat there a moment longer, then stepped out of the car. "Thanks for the lift," she told Terry as he got her guitar out of the back for her. "I'll see you tomorrow night. You too, Jane," she added, leaning into the open window on the passenger's side of the car for a moment.

Jane touched her arm. "You take care of yourself," she said.

Lorio nodded. She stepped back as the Toyota pulled away and stood watching its taillights until it turned west on McKennitt and was lost from view. Turning, she faced the door to her building and wished her roommate wasn't away for the weekend. Being on her own in the loft tonight didn't hold very much appeal.

That's because you're scared, she chided herself. Don't be a baby. Just go to sleep.

She gave the night street one last look. A cab went by, but then the street was quiet again. No pedestrians at this time of night; everybody was sensibly in bed and asleep. The rain had stopped, the streetlights reflected in the puddles that it had left behind. Up and down the street the second floor windows were dark above the soft glow of the lit-up display windows of the stores on the ground floors.

Everything seemed normal. There wasn't even a hint that behind the facade there was another world that held talking monkeymen and bizarre dogs that appeared out of nowhere.

Sighing, Lorio squared her shoulders and went upstairs to bed, trying not to think about the weird turn the night had taken. She didn't have much luck.

She kept seeing that dog-like creature and worried about one finding its way into her apartment. Or to the Zoo where Elderee was. Then she worried about Elderee. When she finally nodded off, she fell into a fitful sleep, all too full of disturbing dreams.

At first she was in the alleyway again. For all that it was very real around her, there was a distancing sense, a feeling of dislocation in her being there. As she looked around, the pavement underfoot began to fracture. Cracks went up and down its length, then webbed the sides of the buildings. She started to back away onto Yoors Street when everything shattered like a piece of dropped glass.

Shards of the alley, like images reflected in a broken mirror, whirled and spun around her. When they settled down, drifting slowly around her like feathers after a pillow fight, she found herself on a roadway—more of a farmer's track, really—that stretched on to either horizon. On both sides of the track were rolling hills dotted with stands of trees.

"A pretty scene," a voice said from behind her. "Though not for long."

The man she saw, when she turned around, was a good head taller than her own five-four. His hair was black, his eyes glittery bright, his mouth an arrogant slash in a pale face. He was dressed all in browns and blacks, his clothing hanging in a poor fit from his too-thin frame.

"Who're—" Lorio began, but the man cut her off.

"This I claim for the Dark, while you—" he shook his head, taking in her hair, her clothes, with a disdainful look "—will be my gift to Mahail."

He made a motion towards her with his hand and sparks flew from his fingertips. She stumbled as the road dissolved under her and she began to drop through grey space. There was light far below her. In it was a writhing mass of tentacles that reached up for her from a dark heart of shadow. As she rushed down to meet it, the darkness resolved into a monstrous bloated shape with coal-eyes and a gaping maw.

It didn't take much speculation to realize that this thing had to be Mahail.

"Tell him Dorn sent you!" the pale-faced man cried after her.

She dropped like a bullet, straight for Mahail, her mouth open, but the scream dying before it left her throat. The monster's oozing tentacles snatched her out of the air. They squeezed her, shook her, held her up for inspection to one eye, then the other.

The soul studying her behind those eyes was like something dead. The air was filled with a reek of decay and rot. The tentacles tightened around her chest and lower torso, squeezing the breath from her as they brought her up to the monster's mouth. Slime covered her, burning and painful where it touched her bare skin. She flailed her arms, slapped at the creature's rubbery lips. The scream building up in her throat finally broke free, shrill and rattling and—

—it woke her to a tangle of bedclothes that were wrapped around her. Cold sweat covered her from head to toe.

She lay gasping, pushed aside the sheet and blankets, and stared up at the dark ceiling of her bedroom. Her heart beat a wild tattoo. Slowly the fear drained away.

Just a dream, she thought. That was all. Maybe the whole night had been just a dream. But as she finally drifted off again, she remembered Elderee's warm eyes and the long winding track of a road that went uphill and down, and this time she smiled and her sleep was dreamless.

The next day it all did seem like a dream. She checked the papers, tried the news on both TV and radio, but there was no mention of the Zoo acquiring a mysterious new animal. It wasn't until she called Terry to confirm that they *had* taken Elderee to the Zoo that she was willing to believe that she hadn't gone crazy. Things were weird, sure, but at least she hadn't totally lost it herself.

She spent the day in a state of anxiety that didn't go away until she got on stage at the club and No Nuns Here went into their first set. The chopping rhythms of the music, her guitar humming in her hands, her voice soaring over the blast of the instruments, let her escape that feeling of being lost. By the time they got to the last song of the night, she was filled with a crackling energy that let her rip through the song and make it not just a statement, but an anthem.

> *I hear your whistle when I cross the park,*
> *you make me nervous when I walk in the dark,*
> *but I won't listen—I won't scream,*
> *you won't find me in your magazines*
> *   'cos*
> *I don't need nobody staring at me,*
> *stripping me down with their 1-2-3. . . .*

The song ended with a thunderous chord that shook the stage underfoot. She helped pack up the gear once the crowd was gone, but left on her own, not even taking her guitar with her. Terry promised to drop it off on Sunday afternoon, but she only nodded and made her way out onto Yoors Street.

The sidewalks were crowded, overfilled with a strutting array of humanity from the trendy to punks to burnouts, everyone on their own personal course and all of them the same. They made the city come to life, but at the same time they drowned it with postures, and images like costumes. It was all artifice, lacking depth. Lorio turned to look at her own reflection in a store window. She was no different. Any meaning she meant to communicate was lost behind a shuffle of makeup, styling and pose.

Mahail fed on hearts, she thought, not knowing where the thought had come from. He fed on them and left the shells to walk around just like we walk around.

She turned from the window and made her way through the people to the alley where she'd found Elderee. Without a pause, she turned into it and walked straight to its end. There she stopped and looked back at the sidewalk she'd just left. Cars flickered by on the street beyond it. On the sidewalk itself, every size and shape of Yoors Street poseur walked by the mouth of the alley, leaving echoing spills of conversation or laughter in their wake. But here it was quiet, like a world apart. Here it was . . . different.

Your people know the roads. . . .

You need only walk it . . . with intent. . . .

She sighed. Maybe the Rom of old had known hidden roads, but nobody had taken the time to show her any—not even Palko. Besides, her Gypsy blood was thin, a matter of chance rather than upbringing, and these days there were as many Gypsies in business suits as there were those following the old ways. Gypsy magic was just something the Rom used to baffle the *Gaje,* the non-Gypsies. Magic itself was just parlor tricks. Except . . .

She remembered the polrech, appearing out of nowhere, dissolving into smoke when she'd killed it. And Elderee . . . like an orangutan, only he could talk.

Magic.

She moved closer to one side of the alley, studying the brick wall of the building there. This alleyway was the last place in the world that she would ever expect to find a marvel. The grime and the dirt, the plastic garbage bags torn open in their corners, the refuse heaped against the walls—

this wasn't the stuff of magic. Magic was Tolkien's Middle Earth. Cat Midhir's Borderlands. This was . . . She ran a hand down the side of the wall and looked at the smudge it left on her fingers. This was an armpit of the real world.

Turning, she faced the mouth of the alley again, only to find a tall figure standing there, watching her. Fear made her blood pump quicker through her veins and for the first time in her life she knew what it meant to have one's heart in one's mouth. She knew who this was.

"Dorn."

The name came out of her mouth in a spidery croak. The man's face was in shadow, but she could still see, no, sense his grin.

"I warned you not to involve yourself further in what doesn't concern you."

He'd warned her? Then she remembered the dream. The thought of his sending her that dream, of his being inside her head like that, made her skin crawl.

"You should not have come back," he said.

"You don't . . . you don't scare me," she said.

No. He terrified her. How could something she'd only dreamed be real? She took a step back and the heel of her shoe came up against a garbage bag.

"Elderee's road is *mine*," he said, moving closer. "*I* took it from him. *I* set the hound on him."

"You—"

"But I felt you drawing on its power, and then I knew you would try to take it from me."

"I think you're making a—"

"No mistake." He touched his chest. "I can *feel* the bond between you and that damned monkey. He gave it to you, didn't he? Heart's shadow, look at you!"

He stood very close to her now. A hand went up and flicked a finger against the stubble on the shaved part of her scalp. Lorio flinched at the touch, but couldn't seem to move away. She was weak with fear. Sparks flickered around Dorn's fingers. She stared at them with widening eyes.

"You're nothing better than an animal yourself," he told her.

Strangely enough, Lorio took comfort in that remark. She looked up into his eyes and saw that they were as dead as Mahail's had been in her nightmare. Nightmare. If Dorn was real, did that mean the road was too? Could she shatter this alleyway, as she had in her dream, to find the road lying underfoot—behind its facade?

An old straight track . . . there for those who know to see it.

Something sparked in his eyes. It wasn't until he spoke that Lorio realized it had been amusement.

"You don't know, do you?" he mocked. "You couldn't find a road if your life depended on it."

"I . . ."

"Let me show you."

Before she could do anything, he grabbed her, one hand on either lapel of her bomber's jacket, and slammed her against the wall of the alley. The impact knocked the breath out of her and brought tears to her eyes.

"Watch," he grinned, his face inches from hers.

He held her straight-armed and slowly turned from the wall. He made one full circuit, then dumped her on the ground. Lorio's legs gave away from under her and she tumbled to the dirt.

Dirt?

Slowly the realization settled in her. He'd taken her back into her dream.

The silence came to her first, a sudden cessation of all sound so that her breathing sounded ragged to her ears. Then she looked around. The city was gone. She was crouching on a dirt road, under a starry sky. The hills of her dream were on either side, the road running between them like a straight white ribbon.

Dorn grabbed a handful of her hair and hauled her to her feet. She blinked with the pain, eyes tearing, but as she turned slowly to face her captor she could feel something shift inside her. She had no more doubt that magic was real, that the road existed, that Elderee had offered her something precious beyond compare. There was no way she was going to let Dorn with his dead eyes take this from her.

On the heels of that realization, knowledge filled her like a flower sprouting from a seed in time-lapse photography. Eye to eye, mind to mind, Elderee had left that seed in her mind until something—the promise of this place, the magic of this road, her own understanding of it, perhaps—woke it and set it spinning through her.

There was not one road, but a countless number of them. They made a pattern that webbed not only her own world, but all worlds; not only her own time, but all times. They upheld a fragile balance between light and dark, order and chaos, while at the center of the web lay a sacred grove in that valley that Elderee had called Lankelly.

And I know how to get there, she realized.

I know that Wood. And it was home.

Her understanding of the roads and all they meant took only a moment to flash through her. In the same breath she knew that the magic that Elderee and others like him used was drawn from the pattern of the roads. A being like Dorn was a destroyer and gained his power from what he destroyed. It was a power that came quickly, draining as it ravaged, leaving the user hungry for more, while the power Elderee used worked in harmony with the pattern, built on it, drew from it, then gave back more than it took. It was a slower magic, but a more enduring one.

Dorn saw the understanding come into her eyes. Its suddenness, the depth of it filling her, shocked him. His grip on her hair slackened for a moment and Lorio brought her knee up into his groin. His hand dropped from her hair as he folded over.

Lorio stood over him, staring at his bent figure. She raised her hands and gold sparks flickered between her fingers. But she didn't need magic to deal with him. She brought doubled fists down on the nape of his neck and he sprawled face forward in the dirt. He turned pained eyes to her, hands scrabbling at the surface of the road. His magic glimmered dully between his fingers, but Lorio shook her head.

He wouldn't look at her. Instead he concentrated, brow furrowed, as he called up his magic. Whatever spell he was trying to work made the light between his fingers gleam more sharply. Lorio stepped quickly forward and stamped down hard on his hand. She was wearing boots tonight. Bones crunched under the impact of her heel.

"That's for Elderee," she said, her voice soft but grim.

Dorn bit back a scream and glared at her. He sat up and scuttled a few paces away, moving on two bent legs and one arm, sideways like a crab. When he stopped, he cradled his hurt hand against his chest.

Silently they faced each other. Dorn knew that she was stronger than he was at this moment. Her will was too focused, the cloak of knowledge that Elderee had given her was too powerful in its newness. She'd hurt him. Among humanoids, hands were needed to spark spells—fingers and voice. She'd effectively cut him off from the use of his own spells, from calling up a polrech, from anything he might have done to hurt her. In her eyes, he could see that she knew too.

She took a step towards him and he called up the one magic he could use, that which would take him from the road to safety in any one of the myriad worlds touched by the roads.

"There will be another time," he muttered, and then he was gone.

Displaced air *whuff*ed where he'd stood and Lorio found herself alone on the road.

She let out a long breath and looked around.

The road. The Chinese called it a dragon track. Alfred Watkins, in England, had discovered the old straight tracks there and called them leys. Secret ways, hidden roads. The Native Americans had them. African tribesmen and the aborigines of Australia. Even her own people had secret roads unknown to the non-Gypsy. In every culture, the wise people, the shamans and magicians and the outsiders knew these ways, and it made sense, didn't it? It was by following such roads that they could grow strong themselves.

But not like Dorn, she thought. Not the kind of strength that destroys, but rather the kind of strength that gives back more than it takes. Like . . . like playing on stage with No Nuns Here. Having something to say and putting it across as honestly as possible. When it worked, when something sparked between herself and the audience, a strength went back and forth between them, each of them feeding the other, the sensation so intense that she often came off the stage just vibrating.

Lorio smiled. She started to walk the road, giving herself to it as step followed step. She walked and a hum built up in her mind. Time went spilling down other corridors, leaving her to stride through a place where hours moved to a different step. The stars in their unfamiliar constellations wheeled above her. The landscape on either side of the road changed from hills to woodlands to deserts to mountainsides to seashores until she found herself back in the hills once more.

She paused there. A thrumming sensation filled her, giving her surroundings a sparkle. Rich scents filled her nostrils. The wind coming down from the hills was a sigh like a synthesizer, dreamy and distant. And underfoot, the road glimmered faintly as though in response to what she'd given it by walking its length.

There's no end to it, she realized. It just goes around and around. Sometimes it'll be longer, sometimes shorter. It just goes on. Because it wasn't where she was coming from, nor where she was going to that was important, but the road itself and how she walked it. And it would never be the same.

She ruffled through the knowledge that Elderee had planted in her and found a way to step off the road. But when she moved back into her own world, she didn't return to the alleyway where it had all begun. Instead she chose a different exit point and stepped towards it. The road and surrounding hills shimmered around her and then were gone.

It was more a room than a cage, the concrete floor and walls smelling strongly of disinfectant and the unmistakable odor of a zoo's monkey house. The only light came through the barred front of the cage, but it was enough for Lorio to see Elderee glance up at her sudden appearance. A look of fatherly pride came over his simian features. Lorio stood self-consciously in the middle of the floor for a long moment, then after a quick look around to make sure they were alone, she walked over to where Elderee lay, her boots scuffing quietly on the concrete.

"Hi," she said, crouching down beside him.

"Hello, yourself."

"How're you feeling?"

A faint smile touched his lips. "I've felt better."

"The doctors fixed you up?"

"Oh, yes. And a remarkable job they've done. I'm alive, am I not?" He paused, then laid a hand gently on her shoulder. "You found the road?"

Lorio smiled. "Along with everything else you stuck in my head. How did you do that?"

She didn't ask why. Having walked the road, she knew that someone had to assume his responsibility of it. He'd chosen her.

"I'll show you sometime—when I'm better. Did you go to the Wood?"

"No. I thought I'd save that for when I could go with you."

"Did you have any . . . trouble?"

Her dream of Mahail flashed into her mind. And Dorn's very real presence. The hounds that he could have called down on her if he hadn't been so sure of himself.

"Ah," Elderee said, catching the images. "Dorn. I wish I'd been there to see you deal with him."

"Are you reading my mind?"

"Only what you're projecting to me."

"Oh." Lorio settled down into a more comfortable position. "He folded pretty easily, didn't he? Just like the polrech that attacked us in the alley."

Elderee shrugged. "Dorn is a lesser evil. He could control one hound at a time, no more. But like most of his kind, he liked to think of himself as far more than he was. You did well. As for the polrech—you were simply stronger. And quicker."

Lorio flushed at the praise.

"And now?" Elderee asked. "What will you do?"

"Jeez, I . . . I don't know. Take care of your part of the road until you get better, I guess."

"I'm getting old," Elderee said. "I could use your help—even when I'm better. There are more of them—" he didn't need to name Mahail and his minions for Lorio to know whom he meant "—than there ever are of us. And there are many roads."

"We'll handle it," Lorio said, still buzzing from her time on the road. "No problem."

"It can be dangerous," Elderee warned, "if a polrech catches you unaware—or if you run into a pack of them. And there are others like Dorn—only stronger, fiercer. But," he added as Lorio's humor began to drain away, "there are good things, too. Wait until you see the monkey puzzle tree—there are more birds in it, and from stranger worlds, than you could ever imagine. And there are friends in the Wood that I'd like you to meet—Jacca and Mabena and . . ."

His voice began to drift a bit.

"You're wearing yourself out," Lorio said.

Elderee nodded.

"I'll come back and see you tomorrow night," she said. "You should rest now. There'll be time enough to meet all your friends and for us to get to know each other better later on."

She stood up and smiled down at him. Elderee's gaze lifted to meet hers.

"*Bahtalo drom,*" he said in Romany. Roughly translated it meant, follow a good road.

"I will," Lorio said. "Maybe not a Gypsy road, but a good road all the same."

"Not a Gypsy road? Then what are you?"

"Part Rom," Lorio replied with a grin. "But mostly just a punker."

Elderee shook his head. Lorio lifted a hand in farewell, then reached for and found the road that would take her home. She stepped onto it and disappeared. Elderee lay back with a contented smile on his lips and let sleep rise up to claim him once again.

⌒ · THE SACRED FIRE · ⌒

No one lives forever,
and dead men rise up never,
and even the longest river
winds somewhere safe to sea.
—FROM BRITISH FOLKLORE;
   COLLECTED BY STEPHEN GALLAGHER

THERE WERE TEN thousand maniacs on the radio—the band, not a bunch of lunatics; playing their latest single, Natalie Merchant's distinctive voice rising from the music like a soothing balm.

Trouble me. . . .

Sharing your problems . . . sometimes talking a thing through was enough to ease the burden. You didn't need to be a shrink to know it could work. You just had to find someone to listen to you.

Nicky Straw had tried talking. He'd try anything if it would work, but nothing did. There was only one way to deal with his problems and it took him a long time to accept that. But it was hard, because the job was never done. Every time he put one of them down, another of the freaks would come buzzing in his face like a fly on a corpse.

He was getting tired of fixing things. Tired of running. Tired of being on his own.

Trouble me. . . .

He could hear the music clearly from where he crouched

in the bushes. The boom box pumped out the song from one corner of the blanket on which she was sitting, reading a paperback edition of Christy Riddell's *How to Make the Wind Blow*. She even looked a little like Natalie Merchant. Same dark eyes, same dark hair; same slight build. Better taste in clothes, though. None of those thrift shop dresses and the like that made Merchant look like she was old before her time; just a nice white Butler U. T-shirt and a pair of bright yellow jogging shorts. White Reeboks with laces to match the shorts; a red headband.

The light was leaking from the sky. Be too dark to read soon. Maybe she'd get up and go.

Nicky sat back on his haunches. He shifted his weight from one leg to the other.

Maybe nothing would happen, but he didn't see things working out that way. Not with how his luck was running.

All bad.

Trouble me. . . .

I did, he thought. I tried. But it didn't work out, did it?

So now he was back to fixing things the only way he knew how.

Her name was Luann. Luann Somerson.

She'd picked him up in the Tombs—about as far from the green harbor of Fitzhenry Park as you could get in Newford. It was the lost part of the city—a wilderness of urban decay stolen back from the neon and glitter. Block on block of decaying tenements and run-down buildings. The kind of place to which the homeless gravitated, looking for squats; where the kids hung out to sneak beers and junkies made their deals, hands twitching as they exchanged rumpled bills for little packets of short-lived empyrean; where winos slept in doorways that reeked of puke and urine and the cops only went if they were on the take and meeting the moneyman.

It was also the kind of place where the freaks hid out, waiting for Lady Night to start her prowl. Waiting for dark. The freaks liked her shadows and he did too, because he could hide in them as well as they could. Maybe better. He was still alive, wasn't he?

He was looking for the freaks to show when Luann approached him, sitting with his back against the wall, right on the edge of the Tombs, watching the rush hour slow to a trickle on Gracie Street. He had his legs splayed out on the sidewalk in front of him, playing the drunk, the bum. Three-days' stubble, hair getting ragged, scruffy clothes, two dimes in his pocket—it wasn't hard to look the part. Commuters stepped over him or went around him, but nobody gave him a second glance. Their gazes just touched him, then slid on by. Until she showed up.

She stopped, then crouched down so that she wasn't standing over him. She looked too healthy and clean to be hanging around this part of town.

"You look like you could use a meal," she said.

"I suppose you're buying?"

She nodded.

Nicky just shook his head. "What? You like to live dangerously or something, lady? I could be anybody."

She nodded again, a half smile playing on her lips.

"Sure," she said. "Anybody at all. Except you're Nicky Straw. We used to take English 201 together, remember?"

He'd recognized her as well, just hoped she hadn't. The guy she remembered didn't exist anymore.

"I know about being down on your luck," she added when he didn't respond. "Believe me, I've been there."

You haven't been anywhere, he thought. You don't want to know about the places I've been.

"You're Luann Somerson," he said finally.

Again that smile. "Let me buy you a meal, Nicky."

He'd wanted to avoid this kind of a thing, but he supposed he'd known all along that he couldn't. This was what happened when the hunt took you into your hometown. You didn't disappear into the background like all the other bums. Someone was always there to remember.

Hey, Nicky. How's it going? How's the wife and that kid of yours?

Like they cared. Maybe he should just tell the truth for a change. You know those things we used to think were hiding in the closet when we were too young to know any better? Well, surprise. One night one of those monsters came out of the closet and chewed off their faces. . . .

"C'mon," Luann was saying.

She stood up, waiting for him. He gave it a heartbeat, then another. When he saw she wasn't going without him, he finally got to his feet.

"You do this a lot?" he asked.

She shook her head. "First time," she said.

All it took was one time. . . .

"I'm like everyone else," she said. "I pretend there's no one there, lying half-starved in the gutter, you know? But when I recognized you, I couldn't just walk by."

You should have, he thought.

His silence was making her nervous and she began to chatter as they headed slowly down Yoors Street.

"Why don't we just go back to my place?" she said. "It'll give you a chance to clean up. Chad—that's my ex— left some clothes behind that might fit you. . . ."

Her voice trailed off. She was embarrassed now, finally realizing how he must feel, having her see him like this.

"Uh . . ."

"That'd be great," he said, relenting.

He got that smile of hers as a reward. A man could get lost in its warmth, he thought. It'd feed a freak for a month.

"So this guy," he said. "Chad. He been gone long?"

The smile faltered.

"Three and a half weeks now," she said.

That explained a lot. Nothing made you forget your own troubles so much as running into someone who had them worse.

"Not too bright a guy, I guess," he said.

"That's . . . Thank you, Nicky. I guess I need to hear that kind of thing."

"Hey, I'm a bum. We've got nothing better to do than to think up nice things to say."

"You were never a bum, Nicky."

"Yeah. Well, things change."

She took the hint. As they walked on, she talked about the book she'd started reading last night instead.

It took them fifteen minutes or so to reach her apartment on McKennitt, right in the heart of Lower Crowsea. It was a walk-up with its own stairwell—a narrow, winding affair that started on the pavement by the entrance of a small Lebanese groceteria and then deposited you on a balcony overlooking the street.

Inside, the apartment had the look of a recent split-up. There was an amplifier on a wooden orange crate by the front window, but no turntable or speakers. The bookcase to the right of the window had gaps where apparently random volumes had been removed. A pair of rattan chairs with bright slipcovers stood in the middle of the room, but there were no end tables to go with them, nor a coffee table. She was making do with another orange crate, this one cluttered with magazines, a couple of plates stacked on top of each other and what looked like every coffee mug she owned squeezed into the remaining space. A small portable black-and-white Zenith TV stood at the base of the bookcase, alongside a portable cassette deck. There were a couple of rectangles on the wall where paintings had obviously been removed. A couple of weeks' worth of newspapers were in a pile on the floor by one of the chairs.

She started to apologize for the mess, then smiled and shrugged.

Nicky had to smile with her. Like he was going to complain about the place, looking like he did.

She showed him to the bathroom. By the time he came out again, showered and shaved, dressed in a pair of Chad's corduroys and a white linen shirt, both of which were at least a size too big, she had a salad on the tiny table in the kitchen, wine glasses out, the bottle waiting for him to open it, breaded pork chops and potatoes on the stove, still cooking.

Nicky's stomach grumbled at the rich smell that filled the air.

She talked a little about her failed marriage over dinner—sounding sad rather than bitter—but more about old times at the university. As she spoke, Nicky realized that the only thing they had shared back then had been that English class; still he let her ramble on about campus events he only half-remembered and people who'd meant nothing to him then and even less now.

But at least they hadn't been freaks.

He corrected himself. He hadn't been able to *recognize* the freaks among them back then.

"God, listen to me," Luann said suddenly.

They were finished with their meal and sitting in her living room having coffee. He'd been wrong; there were still two clean mugs in her cupboard.

"I am," he said.

She gave him that smile of hers again—this time it had a wistfulness about it.

"I know you are," she said. "It's just that all I've been talking about is myself. What about you, Nicky? What happened to you?"

"I . . ."

Where did he start? Which lie did he give her?

That was the one good thing about street people. They didn't ask questions. Whatever put you there, that was your business. But citizens always wanted whys and hows and wherefores.

As he hesitated, she seemed to realize her faux pas.

"I'm sorry," she said. "If you don't want to talk about it . . ."

"It's not that," Nicky told her. "It's just . . ."

"Hard to open up?"

Try impossible. But oddly enough, Nicky found himself

wanting to talk to her about it. To explain. To ease the burden. Even to warn her, because she was just the kind of person the freaks went for.

The fire inside her shimmered off her skin like a high voltage aura, sending shadows skittering. It was a bright shatter of light and a deep golden glow like honey, all at the same time. It sparked in her eyes; blazed when she smiled. Sooner or later it was going to draw a nest of the freaks to her, just as surely as a junkie could sniff out a fix.

"There's these . . . things," he said slowly. "They look enough like you or me to walk among us—especially at night—but they're . . . they're not human."

She got a puzzled look on her face which didn't surprise him in the least.

"They're freaks," he said. "I don't know what they are, or where they came from, but they're not natural. They feed on us, on our hopes and our dreams, on our vitality. They're like . . . I guess the best analogy would be that they're like vampires. Once they're on to you, you can't shake them. They'll keep after you until they've bled you dry."

Her puzzlement was turning to a mild alarm, but now that he'd started, Nicky was determined to tell it all through, right to the end.

"What," she began.

"What I do," he said, interrupting her, "is hunt them down."

The song by 10,000 Maniacs ended and the boom box's speakers offered up another to the fading day. Nicky couldn't name the band this time, but he was familiar with the song's punchy rhythm. The lead singer was talking about burning beds. . . .

Beside the machine, Luann put down her book and stretched.

Do it, Nicky thought. Get out of here. Now. While you still can.

Instead, she lay down on the blanket, hands behind her

head, and looked up into the darkening sky, listening to the music. Maybe she was looking for the first star of the night.

Something to wish upon.

The fire burned in her brighter than any star. Flaring and ebbing to the pulse of her thoughts.

Calling to the freaks.

Nicky's fingers clenched into fists. He made himself look away. But even closing his eyes, he couldn't ignore the fire. Its heat sparked the distance between them as though he lay beside her on the blanket, skin pressed to skin. His pulse drummed, twinning her heartbeat.

This was how the freaks felt. This was what they wanted, what they hungered for, what they fed on. This was what he denied them.

The spark of life.

The sacred fire.

He couldn't look away any longer. He had to see her one more time, her fire burning, burning . . .

He opened his eyes to find that the twilight had finally found Fitzhenry Park. And Luann—she was blazing like a bonfire in its dusky shadows.

"What do you mean, you hunt them down?" she asked.

"I kill them," Nicky told her.

"But—"

"Understand, they're not human. They just *look* like us, but their faces don't fit quite right and they wear our kind of a body like they've put on an unfamiliar suit of loose clothing."

He touched his borrowed shirt as he spoke. She just stared at him—all trace of that earlier smile gone. Fear lived in her eyes now.

That's it, he told himself. You've done enough. Get out of here.

But once started, he didn't seem to be able to stop. All the lonely years of the endless hunt came spilling out of him.

"They're out there in the night," he said. "That's when

they can get away with moving among us. When their shambling walk makes you think of drunks or some feeble old homeless bag lady—not of monsters. They're freaks and they live on the fire that makes us human.''

''The . . . the fire . . . ?''

He touched his chest.

''The one in here,'' he said. ''They're drawn to the ones whose fires burn the brightest,'' he added. ''Like yours does.''

She edged her chair back from the table, ready to bolt. Then he saw her realize that there was no place to bolt to. The knowledge sat there in her eyes, fanning the fear into an ever-more debilitating panic. Where was she going to go that he couldn't get to her first?

''I know what you're thinking,'' he said. ''If someone had come to me with this story before I . . . found out about them—''

(''Momma! Daddy!'' he could hear his daughter crying. ''The monsters are coming for me!''

Soothing her. Showing her that the closet was empty. But never thinking about the window and the fire escape outside it. Never thinking for a minute that the freaks would come in through the window and take them both when he was at work.

But that was before he'd known about the freaks, wasn't it?)

He looked down at the table and cleared his throat. There was pain in his eyes when his gaze lifted to meet hers again—pain as intense as her fear.

''If someone had told me,'' he went on, ''I'd have recommended him for the Zeb, too—just lock him up in a padded cell and throw away the key. But I don't think that way now. Because I can see them. I can recognize them. All it takes is one time and you'll never disbelieve again.

''And you'll never forget.''

''You . . . you just kill these people . . . ?'' she asked.

Her voice was tiny—no more than a whisper. Her mind

was tape looped around the one fact. She wasn't hearing anything else.

"I told you—they're not people," he began, then shook his head.

What was the point? What had he thought was going to happen? She'd go, yeah, right, and jump in to help him? Here, honey, let me hold the stake. Would you like another garlic clove in your lunch?

But they weren't vampires. He didn't know what they were, just that they were dangerous.

Freaks.

"They know about me," he said. "They've been hunting me for as long as I've been hunting them, but I move too fast for them. One day, though, I'll make a mistake and then they'll have me. It's that, or the cops'll pick me up and I wouldn't last the night in a cell. The freaks'd be on me so fast . . ."

He let his voice trail off. Her lower lip was trembling. Her eyes looked like those of some small panicked creature, caught in a trap, the hunter almost upon her.

"Maybe I should go," he said.

He rose from the table, pretending he didn't see the astonished relief in her eyes. He paused at the door that would let him out onto the balcony.

"I didn't mean to scare you," he said.

"I . . . you . . ."

He shook his head. "I should never have come."

"I . . ."

She still couldn't string two words together. Still didn't believe that she was getting out of this alive. He felt bad for unsettling her the way he had, but maybe it was for the best. Maybe she wouldn't bring any more strays home the way she had him. Maybe the freaks'd never get to her.

"Just think about this," he said, before he left. "What if I'm right?"

Then he stepped outside and closed the door behind him.

He could move fast when he had to—it was what had kept

him alive through all these years. By the time she reached her living room window, he was down the stairs and across the street, looking back at her from the darkened mouth of an alleyway nestled between a yuppie restaurant and a bookstore, both of which were closed. He could see her, studying the street, looking for him.

But she couldn't see him.

And that was the way he'd keep it.

He came out of the bushes, the mask of his face shifting and unsettled in the poor light. Luann was sitting up, fiddling with the dial on her boom box, flipping through the channels. She didn't hear him until he was almost upon her. When she turned, her face drained of color. She sprawled backwards in her attempt to escape and then could only lie there and stare, mouth working, but no sound coming out. He lunged for her—

But then Nicky was there. The hunting knife that he carried in a sheath under his shirt was in his hand, cutting edge up. He grabbed the freak by the back of his collar and hauled him around. Before the freak could make a move, Nicky rammed the knife home in the freak's stomach and ripped it up. Blood sprayed, showering them both.

He could hear Luann screaming. He could feel the freak jerking in his grip as he died. He could taste the freak's blood on his lips. But his mind was years and miles away, falling back and back to a small apartment where his wife and daughter had fallen prey to the monsters his daughter told him were living in the closet. . . .

The freak slipped from his grip and sprawled on the grass. The knife fell from Nicky's hand. He looked at Luann, finally focusing on her. She was on her knees, staring at him and the freak like they were both aliens.

"He . . . his face . . . he . . ."

She could barely speak.

"I can't do it anymore," he told her.

He was empty inside. Couldn't feel a thing. It was as

though all those years of hunting down the freaks had finally extinguished his own fire.

In the distance he could hear a siren. Someone must have seen what went down. Had to have been a citizen, because street people minded their own business, didn't matter what they saw.

"It ends here," he said.

He sat down beside the freak's corpse to wait for the police to arrive.

"For me, it ends here."

Late the following day, Luann was still in shock.

She'd finally escaped the endless barrage of questions from both the police and the press, only to find that being alone brought no relief. She kept seeing the face of the man who had attacked her. Had it really seemed to *shift* about like an ill-fitting mask, or had that just been something she'd seen as a result of the poor light and what Nicky had told her?

Their faces don't fit quite right. . . .

She couldn't get it out of her mind. The face. The blood. The police dragging Nicky away. And all those things he'd told her last night.

They're freaks. . . .

Crazy things.

They live on the fire that makes us human.

Words that seemed to well up out of some great pain he was carrying around inside him.

They're not human . . . they just look *like us. . . .*

A thump on her balcony had her jumping nervously out of her chair until she realized that it was just the paperboy tossing up today's newspaper. She didn't want to look at what *The Daily Journal* had to say, but couldn't seem to stop herself from going out to get it. She took the paper back inside and spread it out on her lap.

Naturally enough, the story had made the front page. There was a picture of her, looking washed out and stunned.

A shot of the corpse being taking away in a body bag. A head and shoulders shot of Nicky . . .

She stopped, her pulse doubling its tempo as the headline under Nicky's picture sank in.

"KILLER FOUND DEAD IN CELL—POLICE BAFFLED."

"No," she said.

They know about me.

She pushed the paper away from her until it fell to the floor. But Nicky's picture continued to look up at her from where the paper lay.

They've been hunting me.

None of what he'd told her could be true. It had just been the pitiful ravings of a very disturbed man.

I wouldn't last the night in a cell. The freaks'd be on me so fast . . .

But she'd known him once—a long time ago—and he'd been as normal as anybody then. Still, people changed. . . .

She picked up the paper and quickly scanned the story, looking for a reasonable explanation to put to rest the irrational fears that were reawakening her panic. But the police knew nothing. Nobody knew a thing.

"I suppose that at this point, only Nicky Straw knows what really happened," the police spokesman was quoted as saying.

Nicky and you, a small worried voice said in the back of Luann's mind.

She shook her head, unwilling to accept it.

They're drawn to the ones whose fires burn the brightest.

She looked to her window. Beyond its smudged panes, the night was gathering. Soon it would be dark. Soon it would be night. Light showed a long way in the dark; a bright light would show further.

The ones whose fires burn the brightest . . . like yours does.

"It . . . it wasn't true," she said, her voice ringing hollowly in the room. "None of it. Tell me it wasn't true, Nicky."

But Nicky was dead.

She let the paper fall again and rose to her feet, drifting across the room to the window like a ghost. She just didn't seem to feel connected to anything anymore.

It seemed oddly quiet on the street below. Less traffic than usual—both vehicular and pedestrian. There was a figure standing in front of the bookstore across the street, back to the window display, leaning against the glass. He seemed to be looking up at her window, but it was hard to tell because the brim of his hat cast a shadow on his face.

Once they're on to you, you can't shake them.

That man in the park. His face. Shifting. The skin seeming too loose.

They'll keep after you until they bleed you dry.

It wasn't real.

She turned from the window and shivered, hugging her arms around herself as she remembered what Nicky had said when he'd left the apartment last night.

What if I'm right?

She couldn't accept that. She looked back across the street, but the figure was gone. She listened for a footstep on the narrow, winding stairwell that led up to her balcony. Waited for the movement of a shadow across the window.

∿ · WINTER WAS HARD · ∿

I pretty much try to stay in a constant state of confusion just because of the expression it leaves on my face.

—JOHNNY DEPP

IT WAS THE coldest December since they'd first started keeping records at the turn of the century, though warmer, Jilly thought, than it must have been in the ice ages of the Pleistocene. The veracity of that extraneous bit of trivia gave her small comfort, for it did nothing to lessen the impact of the night's bitter weather. The wind shrieked through the tunnel-like streets created by the abandoned buildings of the Tombs, carrying with it a deep, arctic chill. It spun the granular snow into dervishing whirligigs that made it almost impossible to see at times and packed drifts up against the sides of the buildings and derelict cars.

Jilly felt like a little kid, bundled up in her boots and parka, with long johns under her jeans, a woolen cap pushing down her unruly curls and a long scarf wrapped about fifty times around her neck and face, cocooning her so completely that only her eyes peered out through a narrow slit. Turtle-like, she hunched her shoulders, trying to make her neck disappear into her parka, and stuffed her mittened hands deep in its pockets.

It didn't help. The wind bit through it all as though unhindered, and she just grew colder with each step she took as she plodded on through the deepening drifts. The work crews were already out with their carnival of flashing blue and amber lights, removing the snow on Gracie Street and Williamson, but here in the Tombs it would just lie where it fell until the spring melt. The only signs of humanity were the odd little trails that the derelicts and other inhabitants of the Tombs made as they went about their business, but even those were being swallowed by the storm.

Only fools or those who had no choice were out tonight. Jilly thought she should be counted among the latter, though Geordie had called her the former when she'd left the loft earlier in the evening.

"This is just craziness, Jilly," he'd said. "Look at the bloody weather."

"I've got to go. It's important."

"To you and the penguins, but nobody else."

Still, she'd had to come. It was the eve of the solstice, one year exactly since the gemmin went away, and she didn't feel as though she had any choice in the matter. She was driven to walk the Tombs tonight, never mind the storm. What sent her out from the warm comfort of her loft was like what Professor Dapple said they used to call a geas in the old days—something you just had to do.

So she left Geordie sitting on her Murphy bed, playing his new Copeland whistle, surrounded by finished and unfinished canvases and the rest of the clutter that her motley collection of possessions had created in the loft, and went out into the storm.

She didn't pause until she reached the mouth of the alley that ran along the south side of the old Clark Building. There, under the suspicious gaze of the building's snow-swept gargoyles, she hunched her back against the storm and pulled her scarf down a little, widening the eye-slit so that she could have a clearer look down the length of the alley. She could almost see Babe, leaning casually against the side of the old Buick that was still sitting there, dressed in her raggedy T-shirt, black body stocking and raincoat, Doc Martin's dark against the snow that lay underfoot. She could almost hear the high husky voices of the other gemmin, chanting an eerie version of a rap song that had been popular at the time.

She could almost—

But no. She blinked as the wind shifted, blinding her with snow. She saw only snow, heard only the wind. But in her memory . . .

By night they nested in one of those abandoned cars that could be found on any street or alley of the Tombs—a handful of gangly teenagers burrowed under blankets, burlap sacks and tattered jackets, bodies snugly fit into holes that seemed to have been chewed from the ragged upholstery. This morning they had built a fire in the trunk of the Buick, scavenging fuel from the buildings, and one of them was cooking their breakfast on the heated metal of its hood.

Babe was the oldest. She looked about seventeen—it was something in the way she carried herself—but otherwise had the same thin androgynous body as her companions. The other gemmin all had dark complexions and feminine features, but none of them had Babe's short mauve hair, nor her luminous violet eyes. The hair coloring of the others ran more to various shades of henna red; their eyes were mostly the same electric blue that Jilly's were.

That December had been as unnaturally warm as this one was cold, but Babe's open raincoat with the thin T-shirt and body stocking underneath still made Jilly pause with concern. There was such a thing as carrying fashion too far, she thought—had they never heard of pneumonia?—but then Babe lifted her head, her large violet eyes fixing their gaze as curiously on Jilly as Jilly's did on her. Concern fell by the wayside, shifting into a sense of frustration as Jilly realized that all she had in the pocket of her coat that day was a stub of charcoal and her sketchbook instead of the oils and canvas which was the only medium that could really do justice in capturing the startling picture Babe and her companions made.

For long moments none of them spoke. Babe watched her, a half-smile teasing one corner of her mouth. Behind her, the cook stood motionless, a makeshift spatula held negligently in a delicate hand. Eggs and bacon sizzled on the trunk hood in front of her, filling the air with their unmistakable aroma. The other gemmin peered up over the dash of the Buick, supporting their narrow chins on their folded arms.

All Jilly could do was look back. A kind of vertigo licked at the edges of her mind, making her feel as though she'd just stepped into one of her own paintings—the ones that made up her last show, an urban faerie series: twelve enormous canvases, all in oils, one for each month, each depicting a different kind of mythological being transposed from its traditional folkloric rural surroundings onto a cityscape.

Her vague dizziness wasn't caused by the promise of magic that seemed to decorate the moment with a sparkling sense of impossible possibilities as surely as the bacon filled the air with its come-hither smell. It was rather the unexpectedness of coming across a moment like this—in the Tombs, of all places, where winos and junkies were the norm.

It took her awhile to collect her thoughts.

"Interesting stove you've got there," she said finally.

Babe's brow furrowed for a moment, then cleared as a radiant smile first lifted the corners of her mouth, then put an infectious humor into those amazing eyes of hers.

"Interesting, yes," she said. Her voice had an accent Jilly couldn't place and an odd tonality that was at once both husky and high-pitched. "But we—" she frowned prettily, searching for what she wanted to say "—make do."

It was obvious to Jilly that English wasn't her first language. It was also obvious, the more Jilly looked, that while the girl and her companions weren't at all properly dressed for the weather, it really didn't seem to bother them. Even with the fire in the trunk of the Buick, and mild winter or not, they should still have been shivering, but she couldn't spot one goosebump.

"And you're not cold?" she asked.

"Cold is . . . ?" Babe began, frowning again, but before Jilly could elaborate, that dazzling smile returned. "No, we have comfort. Cold is no trouble for us. We like the winter; we like any weather."

Jilly couldn't help but laugh.

"I suppose you're all snow elves," she said, "so the cold doesn't bother you?"

"Not elves—but we are good neighbors. Would you like some breakfast?"

A year and three days later, the memory of that first meeting brought a touch of warmth to Jilly where she stood shivering in the mouth of the alleyway. Gemmin. She'd always liked the taste of words and that one had sounded just right for Babe and her companions. It reminded Jilly of gummy bears, thick cotton quilts and the sound that the bass strings of Geordie's fiddle made when he was playing a fast reel. It reminded her of tiny bunches of fresh violets, touched with dew, that still couldn't hope to match the incandescent hue of Babe's eyes.

She had met the gemmin at a perfect time. She was in need of something warm and happy just then, being on the wrong end of a three-month relationship with a guy who, throughout the time they'd been together, turned out to have been married all along. He wouldn't leave his wife, and Jilly had no taste to be someone's—anyone's—mistress, all of which had been discussed in increasingly raised voices in The Monkey Woman's Nest the last time she saw him. She'd been mortified when she realized that a whole restaurant full of people had been listening to their breaking-up argument, but unrepentant.

She missed Jeff—missed him desperately—but refused to listen to any of the subsequent phonecalls or answer any of the letters that had deluged her loft over the next couple of weeks, explaining how they could "work things out." She wasn't interested in working things out. It wasn't just the fact that he had a wife, but that he'd kept it from her. The thing she kept asking her friend Sue was: having been with him for all that time, how could she not have *known*?

So she wasn't a happy camper, traipsing aimlessly through the Tombs that day. Her normally high-spirited view of the world was overhung with gloominess and there was a sick feeling in the pit of her stomach that just wouldn't go away.

Until she met Babe and her friends.

Gemmin wasn't a name that they used; they had no name for themselves. It was Frank Hodgers who told Jilly what they were.

Breakfast with the gemmin on that long gone morning was . . . odd. Jilly sat behind the driver's wheel of the Buick, with the door propped open and her feet dangling outside. Babe sat on a steel drum set a few feet from the car, facing her. Four of the other gemmin were crowded in the back seat; the fifth was beside Jilly in the front, her back against the passenger's door. The eggs were tasty, flavored with herbs that Jilly couldn't recognize; the tea had a similarly odd tang about it. The bacon was fried to a perfect crisp. The toast was actually muffins, neatly sliced in two and toasted on coat hangers rebent into new shapes for that purpose.

The gemmin acted like they were having a picnic. When Jilly introduced herself, a chorus of odd names echoed back in reply: Nita, Emmie, Callio, Yoon, Purspie. And Babe.

"Babe?" Jilly repeated.

"It was a present—from Johnny Defalco."

Jilly had seen Defalco around and talked to him once or twice. He was a hash dealer who'd had himself a squat in the Clark Building up until the end of the summer when he'd made the mistake of selling to a narc and had to leave the city just one step ahead of a warrant. Somehow, she couldn't see him keeping company with this odd little gaggle of street girls. Defalco's taste seemed to run more to what her bouncer friend Percy called the three B's—bold, blonde and built—or at least it had whenever she'd seen him in the clubs.

"He gave all of you your names?" Jilly asked.

Babe shook her head. "He only ever saw me, and whenever he did, he'd say, 'Hey Babe, how're ya doin'?'"

Babe's speech patterns seemed to change the longer they talked, Jilly remembered thinking later. She no longer sounded like a foreigner struggling with the language; instead, the words came easily, sentences peppered with conjunctions and slang.

"We miss him," Purspie—or perhaps it was Nita—said. Except for Babe, Jilly was still having trouble telling them all apart.

"He talked in the dark." That was definitely Emmie—her voice was slightly higher than those of the others.

"He told stories to the walls," Babe explained, "and we'd creep close and listen to him."

"You've lived around here for awhile?" Jilly asked.

Yoon—or was it Callio?—nodded. "All our lives."

Jilly had to smile at the seriousness with which that line was delivered. As though, except for Babe, there was one of them older than thirteen.

She spent the rest of the morning with them, chatting, listening to their odd songs, sketching them whenever she could get them to sit still for longer than five seconds. Thanks goodness, she thought more than once as she bent over her sketchbook, for life drawing classes and Albert Choira, one of her art instructors at Butler U., who had instilled in her and every one of his students the ability to capture shape and form in just a few quick strokes of charcoal.

Her depression and the sick feeling in her stomach had gone away, and her heart didn't feel nearly so fragile anymore, but all too soon it was noon and time for her to go. She had Christmas presents to deliver at St. Vincent's Home for the Aged, where she did volunteer work twice a week. Some of her favorites were going to stay with family during the holidays and today would be her last chance to see them.

"We'll be going soon, too," Babe told her when Jilly explained she had to leave.

"Going?" Jilly repeated, feeling an odd tightness in her chest. It wasn't the same kind of a feeling that Jeff had left in her, but it was discomforting all the same.

Babe nodded. "When the moon's full, we'll sail away."

"Away, away, away," the others chorused.

There was something both sweet and sad in the way they half spoke, half chanted the words. The tightness in Jilly's chest grew more pronounced. She wanted to ask, Away to where?, but found herself only saying, "But you'll be here tomorrow?"

Babe lifted a delicate hand to push back the unruly curls that were forever falling in Jilly's eyes. There was something so maternal in the motion that it made Jilly wish she could just rest her head on Babe's breast, to be protected from all that was fierce and mean and dangerous in the world beyond the enfolding comfort that that motherly embrace would offer.

"We'll be here," Babe said.

Then, giggling like schoolgirls, the little band ran off through the ruins, leaving Jilly to stand alone on the deserted street. She felt giddy and lost, all at once. She wanted to run with them, imagining Babe as a kind of archetypal Peter Pan who could take her away to a place where she could be forever young. Then she shook her head, and headed back downtown to St. Vincent's.

She saved her visit with Frank for last, as she always did. He was sitting in a wheelchair by the small window in his room that overlooked the alley between St. Vincent's and the office building next door. It wasn't much of a view, but Frank never seemed to mind.

"I'd rather stare at a brick wall, anytime, than watch that damn TV in the lounge," he'd told Jilly more than once. "That's when things started to go wrong—with the invention of television. Wasn't till then that we found out there was so much wrong in the world.''

Jilly was one of those who preferred to know what was going on and try to do something about it, rather than pretend it wasn't happening and hoping that, by ignoring what was wrong, it would just go away. Truth was, Jilly had long ago learned, trouble never went away. It just got worse—unless you fixed it. But at eighty-seven, she felt that Frank was entitled to his opinions.

His face lit up when she came in the door. He was all lines and bones, as he liked to say; a skinny man, made almost cadaverous by age. His cheeks were hollowed, eyes sunken, torso collapsed in on itself. His skin was wrinkled and dry, his hair just a few white tufts around his ears. But whatever ruin the years had brought to his body, they hadn't managed to get even a fingerhold on his spirit. He could be cantankerous, but he was never bitter.

She'd first met him last spring. His son had died, and with nowhere else to go, he'd come to live at St. Vincent's. From the first afternoon that she met him in his room, he'd become one of her favorite people.

''You've got that look,'' he said after she'd kissed his cheek and sat down on the edge of his bed.

''What look?'' Jilly asked, pretending ignorance.

She often gave the impression of being in a constant state of confusion—which was what gave her her charm, Sue had told her more than once—but she knew that Frank wasn't referring to that. It was that strange occurrences tended to gather around her; mystery clung to her like burrs on an old sweater.

At one time when she was younger, she just collected folktales and odd stories, magical rumors and mythologies—much like Geordie's brother Christy did, although she never published them. She couldn't have explained why she was drawn to that kind of story; she just liked the idea of what they had to say. But then one day she discovered that there *was* an alternate reality, and her view of the world was forever changed.

It had felt like a curse at first, knowing that magic was real, but that if she spoke of it, people would think her mad. But the wonder it woke in her could never be considered a curse and she merely learned to be careful with whom she spoke. It was in her art that she allowed herself total freedom to express what she saw from the corner of her eye. An endless stream of faerie folk paraded from her easel and sketchbook, making new homes for themselves in back alleys and city parks, on the wharves down by the waterfront or in the twisty lanes of Lower Crowsea.

In that way, she and Frank were much alike. He'd been a writer once, but, "I've told all the tales I have to tell by now," he explained to Jilly when she asked him why he'd stopped. She disagreed, but knew that his arthritis was so bad that he could neither hold a pencil nor work a keyboard for any length of time.

"You've seen something magic," he said to her now.

"I have," she replied with a grin and told him of her morning.

"Show me your sketches," Frank said when she was done.

Jilly dutifully handed them over, apologizing for the rough state they were in until Frank told her to shush. He turned the pages of the sketchbook, studying each quick drawing carefully before going on to the next one.

"They're gemmin," he pronounced finally.

"I've never heard of them."

"Most people haven't. It was my grandmother who told me about them—she saw them one night, dancing in Fitzhenry Park—but I never did."

The wistfulness in his voice made Jilly want to stage a breakout from the old folk's home and carry him off to the Tombs to meet Babe, but she knew she couldn't. She couldn't even bring him home to her own loft for the holidays because he was too dependent on the care that he could only get here. She'd never even be able to carry him up the steep stairs to her loft.

"How do you know that they're gemmin and whatever *are* gemmin?" she asked.

Frank tapped the sketchbook. "I know they're gemmin because they look just like the way my gran described them to me. And didn't you say they had violet eyes?"

"But only Babe's got them."

Frank smiled, enjoying himself. "Do you know what violet's made up of?"

"Sure. Blue and red."

"Which, symbolically, stand for devotion and passion; blended into violet, they're a symbol of memory."

"That still doesn't explain anything."

"Gemmin are the spirits of place, just like hobs are spirits of a house. They're what make a place feel good and safeguard its positive memories. When they leave, that's when a place gets a haunted feeling. And then only the bad feelings are left—or no feelings, which is just about the same difference."

"So what makes them go?" Jilly asked, remembering what Babe had said earlier.

"Nasty things happening. In the old days, it might be a murder or a battle. Nowadays we can add pollution and the like to that list."

"But—"

"They store memories you see," Frank went on. "The one you call Babe is the oldest, so her eyes have turned violet."

"So," Jilly asked with a grin. "Does it make their hair go mauve, too?"

"Don't be impudent."

They talked some more about the gemmin, going back and forth between, "Were they really?" and "What else could they be?" until it was time for Frank's supper and Jilly had to go. But first she made him open his Christmas present. His eyes filmed when he saw the tiny painting of his old house that Jilly had done for him. Sitting on the stoop was a younger version of himself with a small faun standing jauntily behind him, elbow resting on his shoulder.

"Got something in my eye," he muttered as he brought his sleeve up to his eyes.

"I just wanted you to have this today, because I brought everybody else their presents," Jilly said, "but I'm coming back on Christmas—we'll do something fun. I'd come Christmas eve, but I've got to work at the restaurant that night."

Frank nodded. His tears were gone, but his eyes were still shiny.

"The solstice is coming," he said. "In two days."

Jilly nodded, but didn't say anything.

"That's when they'll be going," Frank explained. "The gemmin. The moon'll be full, just like Babe said. Solstices are like May Eve and Halloween—the borders between this world and others are thinnest then." He gave Jilly a sad smile. "Wouldn't I love to see them before they go."

Jilly thought quickly, but she still couldn't think of any way she could maneuver him into the Tombs in his chair. She couldn't even borrow Sue's car, because the streets there were too choked with rubble and refuse. So she picked up her sketchbook and put it on his lap.

"Keep this," she said.

Then she wheeled him off to the dining room, refusing to listen to his protests that he couldn't.

A sad smile touched Jilly's lips as she stood in the storm, remembering. She walked down the alleyway and ran her mittened hand along the windshield of the Buick, dislodging the snow that had gathered there. She tried the door, but it was rusted shut. A back window was open, so she crawled in through it, then clambered into the front seat, which was relatively free of snow.

It was warmer inside—probably because she was out of the wind. She sat looking out the windshield until the snow covered it again. It was like being in a cocoon, she thought. Protected. A person could almost imagine that the gemmin were still around, not yet ready to leave. And when they did, maybe they'd take her with them. . . .

A dreamy feeling stole over her and her eyes fluttered, grew heavy, then closed. Outside the wind continued to howl, driving the snow against the car; inside, Jilly slept, dreaming of the past.

The gemmin were waiting for her the day after she saw Frank, lounging around the abandoned Buick beside the old Clark Building. She wanted to talk to them about what they were and why they were going away and a hundred other things, but somehow she just never got around to any of it. She was too busy laughing at their antics and trying to capture their portraits with the pastels she'd brought that day. Once they all sang a long song that sounded like a cross between a traditional ballad and rap, but was in some foreign language that was both flutelike and gritty. Babe later explained that it was one of their traditional song cycles, a part of their oral tradition that kept alive the histories and genealogies of their people and the places where they lived.

Gemmin, Jilly thought. Storing memories. And then she was clearheaded long enough to ask if they would come with her to visit Frank.

Babe shook her head, honest regret in her luminous eyes.

"It's too far," she said.

"Too far, too far," the other gemmin chorused.

"From home," Babe explained.

"But," Jilly began, except she couldn't find the words for what she wanted to say.

There were people who just made other people feel good. Just being around them, made you feel better, creative, uplifted, happy. Geordie said that she was like that herself, though Jilly wasn't so sure of that. She tried to be, but she was subject to the same bad moods as anybody else, the same impatience with stupidity and ignorance which, parenthetically speaking, were to her mind the prime causes of all the world's ills.

The gemmin didn't seem to have those flaws. Even better, beyond that, there was magic about them. It lay thick in the air, filling your eyes and ears and nose and heart with its wild tang. Jilly desperately wanted Frank to share this with her, but when she tried to explain it to Babe, she just couldn't seem to make herself understood.

And then she realized the time and knew she had to go to work. Art was well and fine to feed the heart and mind, and so was magic, but if she wanted to pay the rent on the loft and have anything to eat next month—never mind the endless drain that art supplies made on her meager budget—she had to go.

As though sensing her imminent departure, the gemmin bounded around her in an abandoned display of wild monkeyshines, and then vanished like so many will-o'-the-wisps in among the snowy rubble of the Tombs, leaving her alone once again.

The next day was much the same, except that tonight was the night they were leaving. Babe never made mention of it, but the knowledge hung ever heavier on Jilly as the hours progressed, coloring her enjoyment of their company.

The gemmin had washed away most of the residue of her bad breakup with Jeff, and for that Jilly was grateful. She could look on it now with that kind of wistful remembering one held for high school romances, long past and distanced. But in its place they had left a sense of abandonment. They were going, would soon be gone, and the world would be that much the emptier for their departure.

Jilly tried to find words to express what she was feeling, but as had happened yesterday when she'd tried to explain Frank's need, she couldn't get the first one past her tongue.

And then again, it was time to go. The gemmin started acting wilder again, dancing and singing around her like a pack of mad imps, but before they could all vanish once more, Jilly caught Babe's arm. Don't go, don't go, she wanted to say, but all that came out was, "I . . . I don't . . . I want . . ."

Jilly, normally never at a loss for something to say, sighed with frustration.

"We won't be gone forever," Babe said, understanding Jilly's unspoken need. She touched a long delicate finger to her temple. "We'll always be with you in here, in your memories of us, and in here—" she tapped the pocket in Jilly's coat that held her sketchbook "—in your pictures. If you don't forget us, we'll never be gone."

"It . . . it won't be the same," Jilly said.

Babe smiled sadly. "Nothing is ever the same. That's why we must go now."

She ruffled Jilly's hair—again the motion was like one made by a mother, rather than someone who appeared to be a girl only half Jilly's age—then stepped back. The other gemmin approached, and touched her as well—featherlight fingers brushing against her arms, tousling her hair like a breeze—and then they all began their mad dancing and pirouetting like so many scruffy ballerinas.

Until they were gone.

Jilly thought she would just stay here, never mind going in to work, but somehow she couldn't face a second parting. Slowly, she headed south, towards Gracie Street and the subway that would take her to work. And oddly enough, though she was sad at their leaving, it wasn't the kind of sadness that hurt. It was the kind that was like a singing in the soul.

Frank died that night, on the winter solstice, but Jilly didn't find out until the next day. He died in his sleep, Jilly's painting propped up on the night table beside him, her sketchbook with her initial rough drawings of the gemmin in it held against his thin chest. On the first blank page after her sketches of the gemmin, in an awkward script that must have taken him hours to write, he'd left her a short note:

"I have to tell you this, Jilly. I never saw any real

magic—I just pretended that I did. I only knew it through the stories I got from my gran and from you. But I always believed. That's why I wrote all those stories when I was younger, because I wanted others to believe. I thought if enough of us did, if we learned to care again about the wild places from which we'd driven the magic away, then maybe it would return.

"I didn't think it ever would, but I'm going to open my window tonight and call to them. I'm going to ask them to take me with them when they go. I'm all used up—at least the man I am in this world is—but maybe in another world I'll have something to give. I hope they'll give me the chance.

"The faerie folk used to do that in the old days, you know. That was what a lot of the stories were about—people like us, going away, beyond the fields we know.

"If they take me, don't be sad, Jilly. I'll be waiting for you there."

The script was almost illegible by the time it got near the end, but Jilly managed to decipher it all. At the very end, he'd just signed the note with an "F" with a small flower drawn beside it. It looked an awful lot like a tiny violet, though maybe that was only because that was what Jilly wanted to see.

You saw real magic, she thought when she looked up from the sketchbook. You *were* real magic.

She gazed out the window of his room to where a soft snow was falling in the alley between St. Vincent's and the building next door. She hoped that on their way to wherever they'd gone, the gemmin had been able to include the tired and lonely spirit of one old man in their company.

Take care of him, Babe, she thought.

That Christmas was a quiet period in Jilly's life. She had gone to a church service for the first time since she was a child to attend the memorial service that St. Vincent's held for Frank. She and Geordie and a few of the staff of the home were the only ones in attendance. She missed Frank and found herself putting him in crowd scenes in the paintings she did over the holidays—Frank in the crowds, and the thin ghostly shapes of gemmin peering out from behind cornices and rooflines and the corners of alleyways.

Often when she went out on her night walks—after the restaurant was closed, when the city was half-asleep—she'd hear a singing in the quiet snow-muffled streets; not an audible singing, something she could hear with her ears, but one that only her heart and spirit could feel. Then she'd wonder if it was the voices of Frank and Babe and the others she heard, singing to her from the faraway, or that of other gemmin, not yet gone.

She never thought of Jeff, except with distance.

Life was subdued. A hiatus between storms. Just thinking of that time, usually brought her a sense of peace, if not completion. So why . . . remembering now . . . this time . . . ?

There was a ringing in her ears—sharp and loud, like thunderclaps erupting directly above her. She felt as though she was in an earthquake, her body being violently shaken. Everything felt topsy-turvy. There was no up and no down, just a sense of vertigo and endless spinning, a roar and whorl of shouting and shaking until—

She snapped her eyes open to find Geordie's worried features peering out at her from the circle that the fur of his parka hood made around his face. He was in the Buick with her, on the front seat beside her. It was his hands on her shoulders, shaking her; his voice that sounded like thunder in the confines of the Buick.

The Buick.

And then she remembered: walking in the Tombs, the storm, climbing into the car, falling asleep . . .

"Jesus, Jilly," Geordie was saying. He sat back from her, giving her a bit of space, but the worry hadn't left his features yet. "You really are nuts, aren't you? I mean, falling asleep out here. Didn't you ever hear of hypothermia?"

She could have died, Jilly realized. She could have just

slept on here until she froze to death and nobody'd know until the spring thaw, or until some poor homeless bugger crawled in to get out of the wind and found himself sharing space with Jilly, the Amazing Dead Woman.

She shivered, as much from dread as the storm's chill.

"How . . . how did you find me?" she asked.

Geordie shrugged. "God only knows. I got worried, the longer you were gone, until finally I couldn't stand it and had to come looking for you. It was like there was a nagging in the back of my head—sort of a Lassie kind of a thought, you know?"

Jilly had to smile at the analogy.

"Maybe I'm getting psychic—what do you think?" he asked.

"Finding me the way you did, maybe you are," Jilly said.

She sat up a little straighter, then realized that sometime during her sleep, she had unbuttoned her parka enough to stick a hand in under the coat. She pulled it out and both she and Geordie stared at what she held in her mittened hand.

It was a small violet flower, complete with roots.

"Jilly, where did you . . . ?" Geordie began, but then he shook his head. "Never mind. I don't want to know."

But Jilly knew. Tonight was the anniversary, after all. Babe or Frank, or maybe both of them, had come by as well.

If you don't forget us, we'll never be gone.

She hadn't.

And it looked like they hadn't either, because who else had left her this flower, and maybe sent Geordie out into the storm to find her? How else could he have lucked upon her the way he had with all those blocks upon blocks of the Tombs that he would have to search?

"Are you going to be okay?" Geordie asked.

Jilly stuck the plant back under her parka and nodded.

"Help me home, would you? I feel a little wobbly."

"You've got it."

"And Geordie?"

He looked at her, eyebrows raised.

"Thanks for coming out to look for me."

It was a long trek back to Jilly's loft, but this time the wind was helpful, rather than hindering. It rose up at their backs and hurried them along so that it seemed to only take them half the time it should have to return. While Jilly changed, Geordie made great steaming mugs of hot chocolate for both of them. They sat together on the old sofa by the window, Geordie in his usual rumpled sweater and old jeans, Jilly bundled up in two pairs of sweatpants, fingerless gloves and what seemed like a half-dozen shirts and socks.

Jilly told him her story of finding the gemmin, and how they went away. When she was done, Geordie just said, "Wow. We should tell Christy about them—he'd put them in one of his books."

"Yes, we should," Jilly said. "Maybe if more people knew about them, they wouldn't be so ready to go away."

"What about Mr. Hodgers?" Geordie asked. "Do you really think they took him away with them?"

Jilly looked at the newly potted flower on her windowsill. It stood jauntily in the dirt and looked an awful lot like a drawing in one of her sketchbooks that she hadn't drawn herself.

"I like to think so," she said. "I like to think that St. Vincent's was on the way to wherever they were going." She gave Geordie a smile, more sweet than bitter. "You couldn't see it to look at him," she added, "but Frank had violet eyes, too; he had all kinds of memories stored away in that old head of his—just like Babe did."

Her own eyes took on a distant look, as though she was looking into the faraway herself, through the gates of dream and beyond the fields we know.

"I like to think they're getting along just fine," she said.

⌐ · PITY THE MONSTERS · ⌐

We are standing in the storm of our own being.
　　　　　　　　　　　　—MICHAEL VENTURA

I WAS A beauty once,'' the old woman said. ''The neighbor-hood boys were forever standing outside my parents' home, hoping for a word, a smile, a kiss, as though somehow my unearned beauty gave me an intrinsic worth that far over-shadowed Emma's cleverness with her schoolwork, or Betsy's gift for music. It always seemed unfair to me. My value was based on an accident of birth; theirs was earned.''

The monster made no reply.

''I would have given anything to be clever or to have had some artistic ability,'' the old woman added. ''Those are as-sets with which a body can grow old.''

She drew her tattery shawl closer, hunching her thin shoulders against the cold. Her gaze went to her companion. The monster was looking at the blank expanse of wall above her head, eyes unfocused, scars almost invisible in the dim light.

''Yes, well,'' she said. ''I suppose we all have our own cross to bear. At least I have good memories to go with the bad.''

* * *

The snow was coming down so thickly that visibility had already become all but impossible. The fat wet flakes whirled and spun in dervishing clouds, clogging the sidewalks and streets, snarling traffic, making the simple act of walking an epic adventure. One could be anywhere, anywhen. The familiar was suddenly strange; the city transformed. The wind and the snow made even the commonest landmarks unrecognizable.

If she hadn't already been so bloody late, Harriet Pierson would have simply walked her mountain bike through the storm. She only lived a mile or so from the library and the trip wouldn't have taken *that* long by foot. But she was late, desperately late, and being sensible had never been her forte, so there she was, pedaling like a madwoman in her highest gear, the wheels skidding and sliding for purchase on the slippery street as she biked along the narrow passageway between the curb and the crawling traffic.

The so-called waterproof boots that she'd bought on sale last week were already soaked, as were the bottoms of her jeans. Her old camel hair coat was standing up to the cold, however, and her earmuffs kept her ears warm. The same couldn't be said for her hands and face. The wind bit straight through her thin woolen mittens, her cheeks were red with the cold, while her long, brown hair, bound up into a vague bun on the top of her head, was covered with an inch of snow that was already leaking its wet chill into her scalp.

Why did I move to this bloody country? she thought. It's too hot in the summer, too cold in the winter . . .

England looked very good right at that moment, but it hadn't always been so. England hadn't had Brian whom she'd met while on holiday here in Newford three years ago, Brian who'd been just as eager for her to come as she had been to emigrate, Brian who walked out on her not two months after she'd arrived and they had gotten an apartment together. She'd refused to go back. Deciding to make the best of her new homeland, she had stuck it out surprisingly well, not so much because she led such an ordered existence, as that she'd refused to run back home and have her mother tell her, ever so patronizingly, "Well, I told you so, dear."

She had a good job, if not a great one, a lovely little flat that was all her own, a fairly busy social life—that admittedly contained more friends than it did romantic interests—and liked everything about her new home. Except for the weather.

She turned off Yoors Street onto Kelly, navigating more by instinct than vision, and was just starting to congratulate herself on having completed her journey all in one piece, with time to spare, when a tall shape loomed suddenly up out of the whirling snow in front of her. Trying to avoid a collision, she turned the handlebars too quickly—and the wrong way.

Her front wheel hit the curb and she sailed over the handlebars, one more white airborne object defying gravity, except that unlike the lighter snowflakes with which she momentarily shared the sky, her weight brought her immediately down with a jarring impact against a heap of refuse that someone had set out in anticipation of tomorrow's garbage pickup.

She rose spluttering snow and staggered back towards her bike, disoriented, the suddenness of her accident not yet having sunk in. She knelt beside the bike and stared with dismay at the bent wheel frame. Then she remembered what had caused her to veer in the first place.

Her gaze went to the street, but then traveled up, and up, to the face of the tall shape that stood by the curb. The man was a giant. At five-one, Harriet wasn't tall, and perhaps it had something to do with her low perspective, but he seemed to be at least seven feet high. And yet it wasn't his size that brought the small gasp to her lips.

That face . . .

It was set in a squarish head which was itself perched on thick broad shoulders. The big nose was bent, the left eye was slightly higher than the right, the ears were like huge cauliflowers, the hairline high and square. Thick white scars crisscrossed his features, giving the impression that he'd been sewn together by some untalented seamstress who was too deep in her cups to do a proper job. An icon from an old horror movie flashed in Harriet's mind and she found herself looking for the bolts in the man's neck before she even knew what she was doing.

Of course they weren't there, but the size of the man and the way he was just standing there, staring at her, made Harriet unaccountably nervous as though this really was Victor Frankenstein's creation standing over her in the storm. She stood quickly, wanting to lessen the discrepancy of their heights. The sudden movement woke a wave of dizziness.

"I'm dreadfully sorry," she meant to say, but the words slurred, turning to mush in her mouth and what came out was, "Redfolly shurry."

Vertigo jellied her legs and made the street underfoot so wobbly that she couldn't keep her balance. The giant took a quick step towards her, huge hands outstretched, as a black wave swept over her and she pitched forward.

Bloody hell, she had time to think. I'm going all faint. . . .

Water bubbled merrily in the tin can that sat on the Coleman stove's burner. The old woman leaned forward and dropped in a tea bag, then moved the can from the heat with a mittened hand.

Only two more bags left, she thought.

She held her hands out to the stove and savored the warmth.

"I married for money, not love," she told her companion. "My Henry was not a handsome man."

The monster gaze focused and tracked down to her face.

"But I grew to love him. Not for his money, nor for the comfort of his home and the safety it offered to a young woman whose future, for all her beauty, looked to take her no further than the tenements in which she was born and bred."

The monster made a querulous noise, no more than a grunt, but the old woman could hear the question in it. They'd been together for so long that she could read him easily, without his needing to speak.

"It was for his kindness," she said.

Harriet woke to the cold. Shivering, she sat up to find herself in an unfamiliar room, enwrapped in a nest of blankets that carried a pungent, musty odor in their folds. The room itself appeared to be part of some abandoned building. The walls were unadorned except for their chipped paint and plaster and a cheerful bit of graffiti suggesting that the reader of it do something that Harriet didn't think was anatomically possible.

There were no furnishings at all. The only light came from a short, fat candle which sat on the windowsill in a puddle of cooled wax. Outside, the wind howled. In the room, in the building itself, all was still. But as she cocked her head to listen, she could just faintly make out a low murmur of conversation. It appeared to be a monologue, for it was simply one voice, droning on.

She remembered her accident and the seven-foot tall giant as though they were only something she'd experienced in a dream. The vague sense of dislocation she'd felt upon awakening had grown into a dreamy kind of muddled feeling. She was somewhat concerned over her whereabouts, but not in any sort of a pressing way. Her mind seemed to be in a fog.

Getting up, she hesitated for a moment, then wrapped one of the smelly blankets about her shoulders like a shawl against the cold and crossed the room to its one doorway. Stepping outside, she found herself in a hall as disrepaired and empty as the room she'd just quit. The murmuring voice led her down the length of the hall into what proved to be a foyer. Leaning against the last bit of wall, there where the hallway opened up into the larger space, she studied the odd scene before her.

Seven candles sat in their wax on wooden orange crates

that were arranged in a half circle around an old woman. She had her back to the wall, legs tucked up under what appeared to be a half-dozen skirts. A ratty shawl covered her grey hair and hung down over her shoulders. Her face was a spider-web of lines, all pinched and thin. Water steamed in a large tin can on a Coleman stove that stood on the floor in front of her. She had another, smaller tin can in her hand filled with, judging by the smell that filled the room, some kind of herbal tea. She was talking softly to no one that Harriet could see.

The old woman looked up just as Harriet was trying to decide how to approach her. The candlelight woke an odd glimmer in the woman's eyes, a reflective quality that reminded Harriet of a cat's gaze caught in a car's headbeams.

"And who are you, dear?" the woman asked.

"I . . . my name's Harriet. Harriet Pierson." She got the odd feeling that she should curtsy as she introduced herself.

"You may call me Flora," the old woman said. "My name's actually Anne Boddeker, but I prefer Flora."

Harriet nodded absently. Under the muddle of her thoughts, the first sharp wedge of concern was beginning to surface. She remembered taking a fall from her bike . . . had she hit her head?

"What am I doing here?" she asked.

The old woman's eyes twinkled with humor. "Now how would I know?"

"But . . ." The fuzz in Harriet's head seemed to thicken. She blinked a couple of times and then cleared her throat. "Where are we?" she tried.

"North of Gracie Street," Flora replied, "in that part of town that, I believe, people your age refer to as Squatland. I'm afraid I don't know the exact address. Vandals have played havoc with the street signs, as I'm sure you know, but I believe we're not far from the corner of Flood and MacNeil where I grew up."

Harriet's heart sank. She was in the Tombs, an area of Newford that had once been a developer's bright dream. The old, tired blocks of tenements, office buildings and factories were to be transformed into a yuppie paradise and work had already begun on tearing down the existing structures when a sudden lack of backing had left the developer scrambling for solvency. All that remained now of the bright dream was block upon block of abandoned buildings and rubble-strewn lots generally referred to as the Tombs. It was home to runaways, the homeless, derelicts, bikers, drug addicts and the like who squatted in its buildings.

It was also probably one of the most dangerous parts of Newford.

"I . . . how did I get here?" Harriet tried again.

"What do you remember?" Flora said.

"I was biking home from work," Harriet began and then proceeded to relate what she remembered of the storm, the giant who'd loomed up so suddenly out of the snow, her accident . . . "And then I suppose I must have fainted."

She lifted a hand to her head and searched about for a tender spot, but couldn't find a lump or a bruise.

"Did he speak to you?" Flora asked. "The . . . man who startled you?"

Harriet shook her head.

"Then it was Frank. He must have brought you here."

Harriet thought about what the old woman had just said.

"Does that mean there's more than one of him?" she asked. She had the feeling that her memory was playing tricks on her when she tried to call up the giant's scarred and misshapen features. She couldn't imagine there being more than one of him.

"In a way," Flora said.

"You're not being very clear."

"I'm sorry."

But she didn't appear to be, Harriet realized.

"So . . . he, this Frank . . . he's mute?" she asked.

"Terrible, isn't it?" Flora said. "A great big strapping lad like that."

Harriet nodded in agreement. "But that doesn't explain

what you meant by there being more than one of him. Does he have a brother?''

"He . . ." The old woman hesitated. "Perhaps you should ask him yourself."

"But you just said that he was a mute."

"I think he's down that hall," Flora said, ignoring Harriet. She pointed to a doorway opposite from the one that Harriet had used to enter the foyer. "That's usually where he goes to play."

Harriet stood there for a long moment, just looking at the old woman. Flora, Anne, whatever her name was—she was obviously senile. That had to explain her odd manner.

Harriet lifted her gaze to look in the direction Flora had pointed. Her thoughts still felt muddy. She found standing as long as she had been was far more tiring than it should have been and her tongue felt all fuzzy.

All she wanted to do was to go home. But if this *was* the Tombs, then she'd need directions. Perhaps even protection from some of the more feral characters who were said to inhabit these abandoned buildings. Unless, she thought glumly, this "Frank" was the danger himself. . . .

She looked back at Flora, but the old woman was ignoring her. Flora drew her shawl more tightly around her shoulders and took a sip of tea from her tin can.

Bother, Harriet thought and started across the foyer.

Halfway down the new hallway, she heard a child's voice singing softly. She couldn't make out the words until she'd reached the end of the hall where yet another candlelit room offered up a view of its bizarre occupant.

Frank was sitting cross-legged in the middle of the room, the contents of Harriet's purse scattered on the floor by his knees. Her purse itself had been tossed into a corner. Harriet would have backed right out of the room before Frank looked up except that she was frozen in place by the singing. The child's voice came from Frank's twisted lips—a high, impossibly sweet sound. It was a little girl's voice, singing a skipping song:

Frank and Harriet, sitting in a tree
K-I-S-S-I-N-G
First comes love, then comes marriage
Here comes Frank with a baby's carriage

Frank's features seemed more monstrous than ever with that sweet child's voice issuing from his throat. He tossed the contents of Harriet's wallet into the air, juggling them. Her ID, a credit card, some photos from back home, scraps of paper with addresses or phone numbers on them, paper money, her bank card . . . they did a fluttering fandango as he sang, the movement of his hands oddly graceful for all the scarred squat bulk of his fingers. Her makeup, keys and loose change were lined up in rows like toy soldiers on parade in front of him. A half-burned ten dollar bill lay beside a candle on the wooden crate to his right. On the crate to his left lay a dead cat, curled up as though it was only sleeping, but the glassy dead eyes and swollen tongue that pushed open its jaws gave lie to the pretense.

Harriet felt a scream build up in her throat. She tried to back away, but bumped into the wall. The child's voice went still and Frank looked up. Photos, paper money, paper scraps and all flittered down upon his knees. His gaze locked on hers.

For one moment, Harriet was sure it was a child's eyes that regarded her from that ruined face. They carried a look of pure, absolute innocence, utterly at odds with the misshapen flesh and scars that surrounded them. But then they changed, gaining a feral, dark intelligence.

Frank scattered the scraps of paper and money in front of him away with a sweep of his hands.

"Mine," he cried in a deep, booming voice. "Girl is mine!"

As he lurched to his feet, Harriet fled back the way she'd come.

* * *

"The hardest thing," the old woman said, "is watching everybody die. One by one, they all die: your parents, your friends, your family. . . ."

Her voice trailed off, rheumy eyes going sad. The monster merely regarded her.

"It was hardest when Julie died," she went on after a moment. There was a hitch in her voice as she spoke her daughter's name. "It's not right that parents should outlive their children." Her gaze settled on the monster's face. "But then you'll never know that particular pain, will you?"

The monster threw back his head and a soundless howl tore from his throat.

As Harriet ran back into the room where she'd left Flora, she saw that the old woman was gone. Her candles, the crates and stove remained. The tin can half full of tea sat warming on the edge of the stove, not quite on the lit burner.

Harriet looked back down the hall where Frank's shambling bulk stumbled towards her.

She had to get out of this place. Never mind the storm still howling outside the building, never mind the confusing maze of abandoned buildings and refuse-choked streets of the Tombs. She just had to—

"There you are," a voice said from directly behind her.

Harriet's heart skipped a beat. A sharp, small inadvertent squeak escaped her lips as she flung herself to one side and then backed quickly away from the shadows by the door from which the voice had come. When she realized it was only the old woman, she kept right on backing up. Whoever, whatever, Flora was, Harriet knew she wasn't a friend.

Frank shambled into the foyer then, the queer lopsided set of his gaze fixed hungrily upon her. Harriet's heartbeat kicked into double-time. Her throat went dry. The muscles of her chest tightened, squeezing her lungs so that she found it hard to breathe.

Oh god, she thought. Get out of here while you can.

But she couldn't seem to move. Her limbs were deadened weights and she was starting to feel faint again.

"Now, now," the old woman said. "Don't carry on so, Samson, or you'll frighten her to death."

The monster obediently stopped in the doorway, but his hungry gaze never left Harriet.

"Sam-samson?" Harriet asked in a weak voice.

"Oh, there's all sorts of bits and pieces of people inside that poor ugly head," Flora replied. "Comes from traumas he suffered as a child. He suffers from—what was it that Dr. Adams called him? Dissociation. I think, before the accident, the doctor had documented seventeen people inside him. Some are harmless, such as Frank and little Bessie. Others, like Samson, have an unfortunate capacity for violence when they can't have their way."

"Doctor?" Harriet asked. All she seemed capable of was catching a word from the woman's explanation and repeating it as a question.

"Yes, he was institutionalized as a young boy. The odd thing is that he's somewhat aware of all the different people living inside him. He thinks that when his father sewed him back together, he used parts of all sorts of different people to do so and those bits of alien skin and tissue took hold of his mind and borrowed parts of it for their own use."

"That . . ." Harriet cleared her throat. "That was the . . . accident?"

"Oh, it wasn't any accident," Flora said. "And don't let anyone try to tell you different. His father knew exactly what he was doing when he threw him through that plate glass window."

"But . . ."

"Of course, the father was too poor to be able to afford medical attention for the boy, so he patched him up on his own."

Harriet stared at the monstrous figure with growing horror.

"This . . . none of this can be true," she finally managed.

"It's all documented at the institution," Flora told her. "His father made a full confession before they locked him away. Poor Frank, though. It was too late to do anything to help him by that point, so he ended up being put away as well, for all that his only crime was the misfortune of being born the son of a lunatic."

Harriet tore her gaze from Frank's scarred features and turned to the old woman.

"How do you know all of this?" she asked.

"Why, I lived there as well," Flora said. "Didn't I tell you?"

"No. No, you didn't."

Flora shrugged. "It's old history. Mind you, when you get to be my age, everything's old history."

Harriet wanted to ask why Flora had been in the institution herself, but couldn't find the courage to do so. She wasn't even sure she *wanted* to know. But there was something she had no choice but to ask. She hugged her blanket closer around her, no longer even aware of its smell, but the chill that was in her bones didn't come from the cold.

"What happens now?" she said.

"I'm not sure I understand the question," Flora replied with a sly smile in her eyes that said she understood all too well.

Harriet pressed forward. "What happens to me?"

"Well, now," Flora said. She shot the monster an affectionate look. "Frank wants to start a family."

Harriet shook her head. "No," she said, her voice sounding weak and ineffectual even to her own ears. "No way."

"You don't exactly have a say in the matter, dear. It's not as though there's anyone coming to rescue you—not in this storm. And even if someone did come searching, where would they look? People disappear in this city all of the time. It's a sad, but unavoidable fact in these trying times that we've brought upon ourselves."

Harriet was still shaking her head.

"Oh, think of someone else for a change," the old woman

told her. "I know your type. You're filled with your own self-importance; the whole world revolves around you. It's a party here, an evening of dancing there, theatre, clubs, cabaret, with never a thought for those less fortunate. What would it hurt you to give a bit of love and affection to a poor, lonely monster?"

I've gone all demented, Harriet thought. All of this—the monster, the lunatic calm of the old woman—none of it was real. None of it *could* be real.

"Do you think he *likes* being this way?" Flora demanded.

Her voice grew sharp and the monster shifted nervously at the tone of her anger, the way a dog might bristle, catching its master's mood.

"It's got nothing to do with me," Harriet said, surprising herself that she could still find the courage to stand up for herself. "I'm not like you think I am and I had nothing to do with what happened to that—to Frank."

"It's got everything to do with you," the old woman replied. "It's got to do with caring and family and good Samaritanism and decency and long, lasting relationships."

"You can't force a person into something like that," Harriet argued.

Flora sighed. "Sometimes, in *these* times, it's the only way. There's a sickness abroad in the world, child; your denial of what's right and true is as much a cause as a symptom."

"You're the one that's sick!" Harriet cried.

She bolted for the building's front doors, praying they weren't locked. The monster was too far away and moved too slowly to stop her. The old woman was closer and quicker, but in her panic, Harriet found the strength to fling her bodily away. She raced for the glass doors that led out of the foyer and into the storm.

The wind almost drove her back inside when she finally got a door open, but she pressed against it, through the door and out onto the street. The whirling snow, driven by the mad, capricious wind, soon stole away all sense of direction, but she didn't dare stop. She plowed through drifts, blinded by the snow, head bent against the howling wind, determined to put as much distance between herself and what she fled.

Oh god, she thought at one point. My purse was back there. My ID. They know where I live. They can come and get me at home, or at work, anytime they want.

But mostly she fought the snow and wind. How long she fled through the blizzard, she had no way of knowing. It might have been an hour, it might have been the whole night. She was shaking with cold and fear when she stumbled to the ground one last time and couldn't get up.

She lay there, a delicious sense of warmth enveloping her. All she had to do was let go, she realized. Just let go and she could drift away into that dark, warm place that beckoned to her. She rolled over on her side and stared up into the white sky. Snow immediately filmed her face. She rubbed it away with her hand, already half-frozen with the cold.

She was ready to let go. She was ready to just give up the struggle, because she was only so strong and she'd given it her all, hadn't she? She—

A tall dark figure loomed up suddenly, towering over her. Snow blurred her sight so that it was only a shape, an outline, against the white.

No, she pleaded. Don't take me back. I'd rather die than go back.

As the figure bent down beside her, she found the strength to beat at it with her frozen hands.

"Easy now," a kind voice said, blocking her weak blows. "We'll get you out of here."

She stopped trying to fight. It wasn't the monster, but a policeman. Somehow, in her aimless flight, she'd wandered out of the Tombs.

"What are you doing out here?" the policeman said.

Monster, she wanted to say. There's a monster. It attacked me. But all that came out from her frozen lips was, "Muh . . . tacked me . . ."

"First we'll get you out of this weather," he told her, "then we'll deal with the man who assaulted you."

The hours that followed passed in a blur. She was in a hospital, being treated for frostbite. A detective interviewed her, calmly, patiently sifting through her mumbled replies for a description of what had happened to her, and then finally she was left alone.

At one point she came out of her dozing state and thought she saw two policemen standing at the end of her bed. She wasn't sure if they were actually present or not, but like Agatha Christie characters, gathered at the denouement of one of the great mystery writer's stories, their conversation conveniently filled in some details concerning her captors of which she hadn't been aware.

"Maybe it was before your time," one of the policemen was saying, "but that description she gave fits."

"No, I remember," the other replied. "They were residents in the Zeb's criminal ward and Cross killed their shrink during a power failure."

The first officer nodded. "I don't know which of them was worse: Cross with that monstrous face, or Boddeker."

"Poisoned her whole family, didn't she?"

"Yeah, but I remember seeing what Cross did to the shrink—just about tore the poor bastard in two."

"I heard that it was Boddeker who put him up to it. The poor geek doesn't have a mind of his own."

Vaguely, as though observing the action from a vast distance, Harriet could sense the first officer looking in her direction.

"She's lucky she's still alive," he added, looking back at his companion.

In the days that followed, researching old newspapers at the library, Harriet found out that all that the two men had said, or that she'd dreamed they had said, was true, but she couldn't absorb any of it at the moment. For now she just drifted away once more, entering a troubled sleep that was plagued with dreams of ghosts and monsters. The latter wore masks to hide the horror inside them, and they were the worst of all.

She woke much later, desperately needing to pee. It was still dark in her room. Outside she could hear the wind howling.

She fumbled her way into the bathroom and did her business, then stared into the mirror after she'd flushed. There was barely enough light for the mirror to show her reflection. What looked back at her from the glass was a ghostly face that she almost didn't recognize.

"Monsters," she said softly, not sure if what she felt was pity or fear, not sure if she recognized one in herself, or if it was just the old woman's lunatic calm still pointing an accusing finger.

She stared at that spectral reflection for a very long time before she finally went back to bed.

"We'll find you another," the old woman said.

Her tea had gone cold but she was too tired to relight the stove and make herself another cup. Her hands were folded on her lap, her gaze fixed on the tin can of cold water that still sat on the stove. A film of ice was forming on the water.

"You'll see," she added. "We'll find another, but this time we'll put her together ourselves, just the way your father did with you. We'll take a bit from one and a bit from another and we'll make you the perfect mate, just see if we don't. I always was a fair hand with a needle and thread, you know—a necessary quality for a wife in my time. Of course everything's different now, everything's changed. Sometimes I wonder why we bother to go on. . . ."

The monster stared out the window to where the snow still fell, quietly now, the blizzard having moved on, leaving only this calm memory of its storm winds in its wake. He gave no indication that he was listening to the old woman, but she went on talking all the same.

GHOSTS OF WIND
⌒·AND SHADOW·⌒

There may be great and undreamed of possibilities awaiting mankind; but because of our line of descent there are also queer limitations.

—CLARENCE DAY, FROM *THIS SIMIAN WORLD*

TUESDAY AND THURSDAY afternoons, from two to four, Meran Kelledy gave flute lessons at the Old Firehall on Lee Street which served as Lower Crowsea's community center. A small room in the basement was set aside for her at those times. The rest of the week it served as an office for the editor of *The Crowsea Times,* the monthly community newspaper.

The room always had a bit of a damp smell about it. The walls were bare except for two old posters: one sponsored a community rummage sale, now long past; the other was an advertisement for a Jilly Coppercorn one-woman show at the The Green Man Gallery featuring a reproduction of the firehall that had been taken from the artist's *In Lower Crowsea* series of street scenes. It, too, was long out of date.

Much of the room was taken up by a sturdy oak desk. A computer sat on its broad surface, always surrounded by a clutter of manuscripts waiting to be put on diskette, spot art, advertisements, sheets of Lettraset, glue sticks, pens, pencils, scratch pads and the like. Its printer was relegated to an apple crate on the floor. A large cork board in easy reach of the desk held a bewildering array of pinned-up slips of paper with almost indecipherable notes and appointments jotted on them. Post-its laureled the frame of the cork board and the sides of the computer like festive yellow decorations. A battered metal filing cabinet held back issues of the newspaper. On top of it was a vase with dried flowers—not so much an arrangement as a forgotten bouquet. One week of the month, the entire desk was covered with the current issue in progress in its various stages of layout.

It was not a room that appeared conducive to music, despite the presence of two small music stands taken from their storage spot behind the filing cabinet and set out in the open space between the desk and door along with a pair of straight-backed wooden chairs, salvaged twice a week from a closet down the hall. But music has its own enchantment and the first few notes of an old tune are all that it requires to transform any site into a place of magic, even if that location is no more than a windowless office cubicle in the Old Firehall's basement.

Meran taught an old style of flute-playing. Her instrument of choice was that enduring cousin of the silver transverse orchestral flute: a simpler wooden instrument, side-blown as well, though it lacked a lip plate to help direct the airstream; keyless with only six holes. It was popularly referred to as an Irish flute since it was used for the playing of traditional Irish and Scottish dance music and the plaintive slow airs native to those same countries, but it had relatives in most countries of the world as well as in baroque orchestras.

In one form or another, it was one of the first implements created by ancient people to give voice to the mysteries that words cannot encompass, but that they had a need to express; only the drum was older.

With her last student of the day just out the door, Meran began the ritual of cleaning her instrument in preparation to packing it away and going home herself. She separated the flute into its three parts, swabbing dry the inside of each piece with a piece of soft cotton attached to a flute-rod. As she was putting the instrument away in its case, she realized that there was a woman standing in the doorway, a hesitant presence, reluctant to disturb the ritual until Meran was ready to notice her.

"Mrs. Batterberry," Meran said. "I'm sorry. I didn't realize you were there."

The mother of her last student was in her late thirties, a striking, well-dressed woman whose attractiveness was undermined by an obvious lack of self-esteem.

"I hope I'm not intruding . . . ?"

"Not at all; I'm just packing up. Please have a seat."

Meran indicated the second chair, which Mrs. Batterberry's daughter had so recently vacated. The woman walked gingerly into the room and perched on the edge of the chair, handbag clutched in both hands. She looked for all the world like a bird that was ready at any moment to erupt into flight and be gone.

"How can I help you, Mrs. Batterberry?" Meran asked.

"Please, call me Anna."

"Anna it is."

Meran waited expectantly.

"I . . . it's about Lesli," Mrs. Batterberry finally began.

Meran nodded encouragingly. "She's doing very well. I think she has a real gift."

"Here perhaps, but . . . well, look at this."

Drawing a handful of folded papers from her handbag, she passed them over to Meran. There were about five sheets of neat, closely-written lines of what appeared to be a school essay. Meran recognized the handwriting as Lesli's. She read the teacher's remarks, written in red ink at the top of the first page—"Well written and imaginative, but the next time, please stick to the assigned topic"—then quickly scanned through the pages. The last two paragraphs bore rereading:

"The old gods and their magics did not dwindle away into murky memories of brownies and little fairies more at home in a Disney cartoon; rather, they changed. The coming of Christ and Christians actually freed them. They were no longer bound to people's expectations but could now become anything that they could imagine themselves to be.

"They are still here, walking among us. We just don't recognize them anymore."

Meran looked up from the paper. "It's quite evocative."

"The essay was supposed to be on one of the ethnic minorities of Newford," Mrs. Batterberry said.

"Then, to a believer in Faerie," Meran said with a smile, "Lesli's essay would seem most apropos."

"I'm sorry," Mrs. Batterberry said, "but I can't find any humor in this situation. This—" she indicated the essay "—it just makes me uncomfortable."

"No, I'm the one who's sorry," Meran said. "I didn't mean to make light of your worries, but I'm also afraid that I don't understand them."

Mrs. Batterberry looked more uncomfortable than ever. "It . . . it just seems so obvious. She must be involved with the occult, or drugs. Perhaps both."

"Just because of this essay?" Meran asked. She only just managed to keep the incredulity from her voice.

"Fairies and magic are all she ever talks about—or did talk about, I should say. We don't seem to have much luck communicating anymore."

Mrs. Batterberry fell silent then. Meran looked down at the essay, reading more of it as she waited for Lesli's mother to go on. After a few moments, she looked up to find Mrs. Batterberry regarding her hopefully.

Meran cleared her throat. "I'm not exactly sure why it is that you've come to me," she said finally.

"I was hoping you'd talk to her—to Lesli. She adores you. I'm sure she'd listen to you."

"And tell her what?"

"That this sort of thinking—" Mrs. Batterberry waved a hand in the general direction of the essay that Meran was holding "—is wrong."

"I'm not sure that I can—"

Before Meran could complete her sentence with "do that," Mrs. Batterberry reached over and gripped her hand.

"Please," the woman said. "I don't know where else to turn. She's going to be sixteen in a few days. Legally, she can live on her own then and I'm afraid she's just going to leave home if we can't get this settled. I won't have drugs or . . . or occult things in my house. But I . . ." Her eyes were suddenly swimming with unshed tears. "I don't want to lose her. . . ."

She drew back. From her handbag, she fished out a handkerchief which she used to dab at her eyes.

Meran sighed. "All right," she said. "Lesli has another lesson with me on Thursday—a makeup one for having missed one last week. I'll talk to her then, but I can't promise you anything."

Mrs. Batterberry looked embarrassed, but relieved. "I'm sure you'll be able to help."

Meran had no such assurances, but Lesli's mother was already on her feet and heading for the door, forestalling any attempt Meran might have tried to muster to back out of the situation. Mrs. Batterberry paused in the doorway and looked back.

"Thank you so much," she said, and then she was gone.

Meran stared sourly at the space Mrs. Batterberry had occupied.

"Well, isn't this just wonderful," she said.

From Lesli's diary, entry dated October 12th:

I saw another one today! It wasn't at all the same as the one I spied on the Common last week. That one was more like a wizened little monkey, dressed up like an Arthur Rackham leprechaun. If I'd told anybody about him, they'd say that it *was* just a dressed-up monkey, but we know better, don't we?

This is just so wonderful. I've always known they were there, of course. All around. But they were just hints, things

I'd see out of the corner of my eye, snatches of music or conversation that I'd hear in a park or the backyard, when no one else was around. But ever since Midsummer's Eve, I've actually been able to see them.

I feel like a birder, noting each new separate species I spot down here on your pages, but was there ever a birdwatcher that could claim to have seen the marvels I have? It's like, all of a sudden, I've finally learned how to *see*.

This one was at the Old Firehall of all places. I was having my weekly lesson with Meran—I get two this week because she was out of town last week. Anyway, we were playing my new tune—the one with the arpeggio bit in the second part that I'm supposed to be practicing but can't quite get the hang of. It's easy when Meran's playing along with me, but when I try to do it on my own, my fingers get all fumbly and I keep muddling up the middle D.

I seem to have gotten sidetracked. Where was I? Oh yes. We were playing "Touch Me If You Dare" and it really sounded nice with both of us playing. Meran just seemed to pull my playing along with hers until it got lost in her music and you couldn't tell which instrument was which, or even how many there were playing.

It was one of those perfect moments. I felt like I was in a trance or something. I had my eyes closed, but then I felt the air getting all thick. There was this weird sort of pressure on my skin, as though gravity had just doubled or something. I kept on playing, but I opened my eyes and that's when I saw her—hovering up behind Meran's shoulders.

She was the neatest thing I've ever seen—just the tiniest little faerie, ever so pretty, with gossamer wings that moved so quickly to keep her aloft that they were just a blur. They moved like a hummingbird's wings. She looked just like the faeries on a pair of earrings I got a few years ago at a stall in the Market—sort of a Mucha design and all delicate and airy. But she wasn't two-dimensional or just one color.

Her wings were like a rainbow blaze. Her hair was like honey, her skin a soft-burnished gold. She was wearing—

now don't blush, diary—nothing at all on top and just a gauzy skirt that seemed to be made of little leaves that kept changing colour, now sort of pink, now mauve, now bluish.

I was so surprised that I almost dropped my flute. I didn't—wouldn't that give Mom something to yell at me for if I broke it!—but I did muddle the tune. As soon as the music faltered—just like that, as though the only thing that was keeping her in this world was that tune—she disappeared.

I didn't pay a whole lot of attention to what Meran was saying for the rest of the lesson, but I don't think she noticed. I couldn't get the faerie out of my mind. I still can't. I wish Mom had been there to see her, or stupid old Mr. Allen. They couldn't say it was just my imagination then!

Of course they probably wouldn't have been able to see her anyway. That's the thing with magic. You've got to know it's still here, all around us, or it just stays invisible for you.

After my lesson, Mom went in to talk to Meran and made me wait in the car. She wouldn't say what they'd talked about, but she seemed to be in a way better mood than usual when she got back. God, I wish she wouldn't get so uptight.

"So," Cerin said finally, setting aside his book. Meran had been moping about the house for the whole of the hour since she'd gotten home from the Firehall. "Do you want to talk about it?"

"You'll just say I told you so."

"Told you so how?"

Meran sighed. "Oh, you know. How did you put it? 'The problem with teaching children is that you have to put up with their parents.' It was something like that."

Cerin joined her in the windowseat, where she'd been staring out at the garden. He looked out at the giant old oaks that surrounded the house and said nothing for a long moment. In the fading afternoon light, he could see little brown men scurrying about in the leaves like so many monkeys.

"But the kids are worth it," he said finally.

"I don't see you teaching children."

"There's just not many parents that can afford a harp for their prodigies."

"But still . . ."

"Still," he agreed. "You're perfectly right. I don't like dealing with their parents; never did. When I see children put into little boxes, their enthusiasms stifled . . . Everything gets regimented into what's proper and what's not, into recitals and passing examinations instead of just playing—" he began to mimic a hoity-toity voice "—I don't care if you want to play in a rock band, you'll learn what I tell you to learn. . . ."

His voice trailed off. In the back of his eyes, a dark light gleamed—not quite anger, more frustration.

"It makes you want to give them a good whack," Meran said.

"Exactly. So did you?"

Meran shook her head. "It wasn't like that, but it was almost as bad. No, maybe it was worse."

She told her husband about what Lesli's mother had asked of her, handing over the English essay when she was done so that he could read it for himself.

"This is quite good, isn't it?" he said when he reached the end.

Meran nodded. "But how can I tell Lesli that none of it's true when I know it is?"

"You can't."

Cerin laid the essay down on the windowsill and looked out at the oaks again. The twilight had crept up on the garden while they were talking. All the trees wore thick mantles of shadow now—poor recompense for the glorious cloaks of leaves that the season had stolen from them over the past few weeks. At the base of one fat trunk, the little monkeymen were roasting skewers of mushrooms and acorns over a small, almost smokeless fire.

"What about Anna Batterberry herself?" he asked. "Does she remember anything?"

Meran shook her head. "I don't think she even realizes that we've met before, that she changed but we never did. She's like most people; if it doesn't make sense, she'd rather convince herself that it simply never happened."

Cerin turned from the window to regard his wife.

"Perhaps the solution would be to remind her, then," he said.

"I don't think that's such a good idea. It'd probably do more harm than good. She's just not the right sort of person . . ."

Meran sighed again.

"But she could have been," Cerin said.

"Oh yes," Meran said, remembering. "She could have been. But it's too late for her now."

Cerin shook his head. "It's never too late."

From Lesli's diary, addendum to the entry dated October 12th:

I hate living in this house! I just hate it! How could she do this to me? It's bad enough that she never lets me so much as breathe without standing there behind me to determine that I'm not making a vulgar display of myself in the process, but this really isn't fair.

I suppose you're wondering what I'm talking about. Well, remember that essay I did on ethnic minorities for Mr. Allen? Mom got her hands on it and it's convinced her that I've turned into a Satan-worshipping drug fiend. The worst thing is that she gave it to Meran and now Meran's supposed to "have a talk with me to set me straight" on Thursday.

I just hate this. She had no right to do that. And how am I supposed to go to my lesson now? It's so embarrassing. Not to mention disappointing. I thought Meran would understand. I never thought she'd take Mom's side—not on something like this.

Meran's always seemed so special. It's not just that she

wears all those funky clothes and doesn't talk down to me
and looks just like one of those Pre-Raphaelite women, except that she's got those really neat green streaks in her hair.
She's just a great person. She makes playing music seem so
effortlessly magical and she's got all these really great stories about the origins of the tunes. When she talks about
things like where "The Gold Ring" came from, it's like she
really believes it was the faeries that gave that piper the tune
in exchange for the lost ring he returned to them. The way
she tells it, it's like she was there when it happened.

I feel like I've always known her. From the first time I
saw her, I felt like I was meeting an old friend. Sometimes I
think that she's magic herself—a kind of oak-tree faerie
princess who's just spending a few years living in the Fields
We Know before she goes back home to the magic place
where she really lives.

Why would someone like that involve themselves in my
mother's crusade against Faerie?

I guess I was just being naive. She's probably no different
from Mom or Mr. Allen and everybody else who doesn't believe. Well, I'm not going to any more stupid flute lessons,
that's for sure.

I hate living here. Anything'd be better.

Oh, why couldn't I just have been stolen by the faeries
when I was a baby? Then I'd *be* there and there'd just be
some changeling living here in my place. Mom could turn *it*
into a good little robot instead. Because that's all she wants.
She doesn't want a daughter who can think on her own, but a
boring, closed-minded junior model of herself. She should
have gotten a dog instead of having a kid. Dogs are easy to
train and they like being led around on a leash.

I wish Granny Nell was still alive. She would never, ever
have tried to tell me that I had to grow up and stop imagining
things. Everything seemed magic when she was around. It
was like she was magic—just like Meran. Sometimes when
Meran's playing her flute, I almost feel as though Granny

Nell's sitting there with us, just listening to the music with that sad wise smile of hers.

I know I was only five when she died, but lots of the time she seems more real to me than any of my relatives that are still alive. If she was still alive, I could be living with her right now and everything'd be really great.

Jeez, I miss her.

Anna Batterberry was in an anxious state when she pulled up in front of the Kelledy house on McKennitt Street. She checked the street number that hung beside the wrought-iron gate where the walkway met the sidewalk and compared it against the address she'd hurriedly scribbled down on a scrap of paper before leaving home. When she was sure that they were the same, she slipped out of the car and approached the gate.

Walking up to the house, the sound of her heels was loud on the walkway's flagstones. She frowned at the thick carpet of fallen oak leaves that covered the lawn. The Kelledys had better hurry in cleaning them up, she thought. The city work crews would only be collecting leaves for one more week and they had to be neatly bagged and sitting at the curb for them to do so. It was a shame that such a pretty estate wasn't treated better.

When she reached the porch, she spent a disorienting moment trying to find a doorbell, then realized that there was only the small brass door knocker in the middle of the door. It was shaped like a Cornish piskie.

The sight of it gave her a queer feeling. Where had she seen that before? In one of Lesli's books, she supposed.

Lesli.

At the thought of her daughter, she quickly reached for the knocker, but the door swung open before she could use it. Lesli's flute teacher stood in the open doorway and regarded her with a puzzled look.

"Anna," Meran said, her voice betraying her surprise. "Whatever are you—"

"It's Lesli," Anna said, interrupting. "She's . . . she . . ."

Her voice trailed off as what she could see of the house's interior behind Meran registered. A strange dissonance built up in her mind at the sight of the long hallway, paneled in dark wood, the thick Oriental carpet on the hardwood floor, the old photographs and prints that hung from the walls. It was when she focused on the burnished metal umbrella stand, which was, itself, in the shape of a partially-opened umbrella, and the sidetable on which stood a cast-iron, grinning gargoyle bereft of its roof gutter home, that the curious sense of familiarity she felt delved deep into the secret recesses of her mind and connected with a swell of long-forgotten memories.

She put out a hand against the doorjamb to steady herself as the flood rose up inside her. She saw her mother-in-law standing in that hallway with a kind of glow around her head. She was older than she'd been when Anna had married Peter, years older, her body wreathed in a golden Botticelli nimbus, that beatific smile on her lips, Meran Kelledy standing beside her, the two of them sharing some private joke, and all around them . . . presences seemed to slip and slide across one's vision.

No, she told herself. None of that was real. Not the golden glow, nor the flickering twig-thin figures that teased the mind from the corner of the eye.

But she'd thought she'd seen them. Once. More than once. Many times. Whenever she was with Helen Batterberry . . .

Walking in her mother-in-law's garden and hearing music, turning the corner of the house to see a trio of what she first took to be children, then realized were midgets, playing fiddle and flute and drum, the figures slipping away as they approached, winking out of existence, the music fading, but its echoes lingering on. In the mind. In memory. In dreams.

"Faerie," her mother-in-law explained to her, matter-of-factly.

Lesli as a toddler, playing with her invisible friends that could actually be *seen* when Helen Batterberry was in the room.

No. None of that was possible.

That was when she and Peter were going through a rough period in their marriage. Those sights, those strange ethereal beings, music played on absent instruments, they were all part and parcel of what she later realized had been a nervous breakdown. Her analyst had agreed.

But they'd seemed so real.

In the hospital room where her mother-in-law lay dying, her bed a clutter of strange creatures, tiny wizened men, small perfect women, all of them flickering in and out of sight, the wonder of their presences, the music of their voices, Lesli sitting wide-eyed by the bed as the courts of Faerie came to bid farewell to an old friend.

"Say you're going to live forever," Lesli had said to her grandmother.

"I will," the old woman replied. "But you have to remember me. You have to promise never to close your awareness to the Otherworld around you. If you do that, I'll never be far."

All nonsense.

But there in the hospital room, with the scratchy sound of the IVAC pump, the clean white walls, the incessant beep of the heart monitor, the antiseptic sting in the air, Anna could only shake her head.

"None . . . none of this is real. . . ." she said.

Her mother-in-law turned her head to look at her, an infinite sadness in her dark eyes.

"Maybe not for you," she said sadly, "but for those who will see, it will always be there."

And later, with Lesli at home, when just she and Peter were there, she remembered Meran coming into that hospital room, Meran and her husband, neither of them having aged since the first time Anna had seen them at her mother-in-law's house, years, oh now years ago. The four of them were there when Helen Batterberry died. She and Peter had bent their heads over the body at the moment of death, but the other two, the unaging musicians who claimed Faerie more silently, but as surely and subtly as ever Helen Batterberry had, stood at the window and watched the twilight grow across the hospital lawn as though they could see the old woman's spirit walking off into the night.

They didn't come to the funeral.

They—

She tried to push the memories aside, just as she had when the events had first occurred, but the flood was too strong. And worse, she knew they were true memories. Not the clouded rantings of a stressful mind suffering a mild breakdown.

Meran was speaking to her, but Anna couldn't hear what she was saying. She heard a vague, disturbing music that seemed to come from the ground underfoot. Small figures seemed to caper and dance in the corner of her eye, humming and buzzing like summer bees. Vertigo gripped her and she could feel herself falling. She realized that Meran was stepping forward to catch her, but by then the darkness had grown too seductive and she simply let herself fall into its welcoming depths.

From Lesli's diary, entry dated October 13th:

I've well and truly done it. I got up this morning and instead of my school books, I packed my flute and some clothes and you, of course, in my knapsack; and then I just left. I couldn't live there anymore. I just couldn't.

Nobody's going to miss me. Daddy's never home anyway and Mom won't be looking for me—she'll be looking for her idea of me and that person doesn't exist. The city's so big that they'll never find me.

I was kind of worried about where I was going to stay tonight, especially with the sky getting more and more overcast all day long, but I met this really neat girl in Fitzhenry Park this morning. Her name's Susan and even though she's just a year older than me, she lives with this guy in an apartment in Chinatown. She's gone to ask him if I can stay with them for a couple of days. His name's Paul. Susan says he's in his late twenties, but he doesn't act at all like an old guy. He's really neat and treats her like she's an adult, not a kid. She's his *girlfriend*!

I'm sitting in the park waiting for her to come back as I write this. I hope she doesn't take too long because there's some weird-looking people around here. This one guy sitting over by the War Memorial keeps giving me the eye like he's going to hit on me or something. He really gives me the creeps. He's got this kind of dark aura that flickers around him so I know he's bad news.

I know it's only been one morning since I left home, but I already feel different. It's like I was dragging around this huge weight and all of a sudden it's gone. I feel light as a feather. Of course, we all know what that weight was: neuro-mother.

Once I get settled in at Susan and Paul's, I'm going to go look for a job. Susan says Paul can get me some fake ID so that I can work in a club or something and make some real money. That's what Susan does. She said that there's been times when she's made fifty bucks in tips in just one night!

I've never met anyone like her before. It's hard to believe she's almost my age. When I compare the girls at school to her, they just seem like a bunch of kids. Susan dresses so cool, like she just stepped out of an MTV video. She's got short funky black hair, a leather jacket and jeans so tight I don't know how she gets into them. Her T-shirt's got this really cool picture of a Brian Froud faery on it that I'd never seen before.

When I asked her if she believes in Faerie, she just gave me this big grin and said, "I'll tell you, Lesli, I'll believe in anything that makes me feel good."

I think I'm going to like living with her.

* * *

When Anna Batterberry regained consciousness, it was to find herself inside that disturbingly familiar house. She lay on a soft, overstuffed sofa, surrounded by the crouching presences of far more pieces of comfortable-looking furniture than the room was really meant to hold. The room simply had a too-full look about it, aided and abetted by a bewildering array of knickknacks that ranged from dozens of tiny porcelain miniatures on the mantle, each depicting some anthropomorphized woodland creature playing a harp or a fiddle or a flute, to a life-sized fabric mâché sculpture of a grizzly-bear in top hat and tails that reared up in one corner of the room.

Every square inch of wall space appeared to be taken up with posters, framed photographs, prints and paintings. Old-fashioned curtains—the print was large dusky roses on a black background—stood guard on either side of a window seat. Underfoot was a thick carpet that had been woven into a semblance of the heavily-leafed yard outside.

The more she looked around herself, the more familiar it all looked. And the more her mind filled with memories that she'd spent so many years denying.

The sound of a footstep had her sitting up and half-turning to look behind the sofa at who—or maybe even, what—was approaching. It was only Meran. The movement brought back the vertigo and she lay down once more. Meran sat down on an ottoman that had been pulled up beside the sofa and laid a deliciously cool damp cloth against Anna's brow.

"You gave me a bit of a start," Meran said, "collapsing on my porch like that."

Anna had lost her ability to be polite. Forsaking small talk, she went straight for the heart of the matter.

"I've been here before," she said.

Meran nodded.

"With my mother-in-law—Helen Batterberry."

"Nell," Meran agreed. "She was a good friend."

"But why haven't I *remembered* that I'd met you before until today?"

Meran shrugged. "These things happen."

"No," Anna said. "People forget things, yes, but not like this. I didn't just meet you in passing, I knew you for years—from my last year in college when Peter first began dating me. You were at his parents' house the first time he took me home. I remember thinking how odd that you and Helen were such good friends, considering how much younger you were than her."

"Should age make a difference?" Meran asked.

"No. It's just . . . you haven't changed at all. You're still the same age."

"I know," Meran said.

"But . . ." Anna's bewilderment accentuated her nervous bird temperament. "How can that be possible?"

"You said something about Lesli when you first arrived," Meran said, changing the subject.

That was probably the only thing that could have drawn Anna away from the quagmire puzzle of agelessness and hidden music and twitchy shapes moving just beyond the grasp of her vision.

"She's run away from home," Anna said. "I went into her room to get something and found that she'd left all her schoolbooks just sitting on her desk. Then when I called the school, they told me that she'd never arrived. They were about to call me to ask if she was ill. Lesli never misses school, you know."

Meran nodded. She hadn't, but it fit with the image of the relationship between Lesli and her mother that was growing in her mind.

"Have you called the police?" she asked.

"As soon as I got off the phone. They told me it was a little early to start worrying—can you imagine that? The detective I spoke to said that he'd put out her description so that his officers would keep an eye out for her, but basically he told me that she must just be skipping school. Lesli would *never* do that."

"What does your husband say?"

"Peter doesn't know yet. He's on a business trip out east and I won't be able to talk to him until he calls me tonight. I don't even know what hotel he'll be staying in until he calls.'' Anna reached out with a bird-thin hand and gripped Meran's arm. "What am I going to *do*?"

"We could go looking for her ourselves."

Anna nodded eagerly at the suggestion, but then the futility of that course of action hit home.

"The city's so big," she said. "It's too big. How would we ever find her?"

"There is another way," Cerin said.

Anna started at the new voice. Meran removed the damp cloth from Anna's brow and moved back from the sofa so that Anna could sit up once more. She looked at the tall figure standing in the doorway, recognizing him as Meran's husband. She didn't remember him seeming quite so intimidating before.

"What . . . what way is that?" Anna said.

"You could ask for help from Faerie," Cerin told her.

"So—you're gonna be one of Paulie's girls?"

Lesli looked up from writing in her diary to find that the creepy guy by the War Memorial had sauntered over to stand beside her bench. Up close, he seemed even tougher than he had from a distance. His hair was slicked back on top, long at the back. He had three earrings in his left earlobe, one in the right. Dirty jeans were tucked into tall black cowboy boots, his white shirt was half open under his jean jacket. There was an oily look in his eyes that made her shiver.

She quickly shut the diary, keeping her place with a finger, and looked around hopefully to see if Susan was on her way back, but there was no sign of her new friend. Taking a deep breath, she gave him what she hoped was a look of appropriate streetwise bravado.

"I . . . I don't know what you're talking about," she said.

"I saw you talking to Susie," he said, sitting down beside her on the bench. "She's Paulie's recruiter."

Lesli started to get a bad feeling right about then. It wasn't just that this guy was so awful, but that she might have made a terrible misjudgment when it came to Susan.

"I think I should go," she said.

She started to get up, but he grabbed her arm. Off balance, she fell back onto the bench.

"Hey, look," he said. "I'm doing you a favor. Paulie's got ten or twelve girls in his string and he works them like they're dogs. You look like a nice kid. Do you really want to spend the next ten years peddling your ass for some homeboy who's gonna have you hooked on junk before the week's out?"

"I—"

"See, I run a clean shop. No drugs, nice clothes for the girls, nice apartment that you're gonna share with just one other girl, not a half dozen the way Paulie run his biz. My girls turn maybe two, three tricks a night and that's it. Paulie'll have you on the street nine, ten hours a pop, easy."

His voice was calm, easygoing, but Leslie had never been so scared before in her life.

"Please," she said. "You're making a mistake. I really have to go."

She tried to rise again, but he kept a hand on her shoulder so that she couldn't get up. His voice, so mild before, went hard.

"You go anywhere, babe, you're going with me," he said. "There are no other options. End of conversation."

He stood up and hauled her to her feet. His hand held her in a bruising grip. Her diary fell from her grip, and he let her pick it up and stuff it into her knapsack, but then he pulled her roughly away from the bench.

"You're hurting me!" she cried.

He leaned close to her, his mouth only inches from her ear.

"Keep that up," he warned her, "and you're really gonna find out what pain's all about. Now make nice. You're working for me now."

"I . . ."

"Repeat after me, sweet stuff: I'm Cutter's girl."

Tears welled in Lesli's eyes. She looked around the park, but nobody was paying any attention to what was happening to her. Cutter gave her a painful shake that made her teeth rattle.

"C'mon," he told her. "Say it."

He glared at her with the promise of worse to come in his eyes if she didn't start doing what he said. His grip tightened on her shoulder, fingers digging into the soft flesh of her upper arm.

"Say it!"

"I . . . I'm Cutter's . . . girl."

"See? That wasn't so hard."

He gave her another shove to start her moving again. She wanted desperately to break free of his hand and just run, but as he marched her across the park, she discovered that she was too scared to do anything but let him lead her away.

She'd never felt so helpless or alone in all her life. It made her feel ashamed.

"Please don't joke about this," Anna said in response to Cerin's suggestion that they turn to Faerie for help in finding Lesli.

"Yes," Meran agreed, though she wasn't speaking of jokes. "This isn't the time."

Cerin shook his head. "This seems a particularly appropriate time to me." He turned to Anna. "I don't like to involve myself in private quarrels, but since it's you that's come to us, I feel I have the right to ask you this: Why is it, do you think, that Lesli ran away in the first place?"

"What are you insinuating? That I'm not a good mother?"

"Hardly. I no longer know you well enough to make that sort of a judgment. Besides, it's not really any of my business, is it?"

"Cerin, please," Meran said.

A headache was starting up between Anna's temples.

"I don't understand," Anna said. "What is it that you're saying?"

"Meran and I loved Nell Batterberry," Cerin said. "I don't doubt that you held some affection for her as well, but I do know that you thought her a bit of a daft old woman. She told me once that after her husband—after Philip—died, you tried to convince Peter that she should be put in a home. Not in a home for the elderly, but for the, shall we say, gently mad?"

"But she—"

"Was full of stories that made no sense to you," Cerin said. "She heard and saw what others couldn't, though she had the gift that would allow such people to see into the invisible world of Faerie when they were in her presence. You saw into that world once, Anna. I don't think you ever forgave her for showing it to you."

"It . . . it wasn't real."

Cerin shrugged. "That's not really important at this moment. What's important is that, if I understand the situation correctly, you've been living in the fear that Lesli would grow up just as fey as her grandmother. And if this is so, your denying her belief in Faerie lies at the root of the troubles that the two of you share."

Anna looked to Meran for support, but Meran knew her husband too well and kept her own council. Having begun, Cerin wouldn't stop until he said everything he meant to.

"Why are you doing this to me?" Anna asked. "My daughter's run away. All of . . . all of this . . ." She waved a hand that was perhaps meant to take in just the conversation, perhaps the whole room. "It's not real. Little people and fairies and all the things my mother-in-law reveled in discussing just aren't real. She could make them *seem* real, I'll grant you that, but they could never exist."

"In your world," Cerin said.

"In the real world."

"They're not one and the same," Cerin told her.

Anna began to rise from the sofa. "I don't have to listen to any of this," she said. "My daughter's run away and I thought you might be able to help me. I didn't come here to be mocked."

"The only reason I've said anything at all," Cerin told her, "is for Lesli's sake. Meran talks about her all the time. She sounds like a wonderful, gifted child."

"She is."

"I hate the thought of her being forced into a box that doesn't fit her. Of having her wings cut off, her sight blinded, her hearing muted, her voice stilled."

"I'm not doing any such thing!" Anna cried.

"You just don't realize what you're doing," Cerin replied.

His voice was mild, but dark lights in the back of his eyes were flashing.

Meran realized it was time to intervene. She stepped between the two. Putting her back to her husband, she turned to face Anna.

"We'll find Lesli," she said.

"How? With *magic*?"

"It doesn't matter how. Just trust that we will. What you have to think of is of what you were telling me yesterday: her birthday's coming up in just a few days. Once she turns sixteen, so long as she can prove that she's capable of supporting herself, she can legally leave home and nothing you might do or say then can stop her."

"It's you, isn't it?" Anna cried. "You're the one who's been filling up her head with all these horrible fairy tales. I should never have let her take those lessons."

Her voice rose ever higher in pitch as she lunged forward, arms flailing. Meran slipped to one side, then reached out one quick hand. She pinched a nerve in Anna's neck and the woman suddenly went limp. Cerin caught her before she could fall and carried her back to the sofa.

"Now do you see what I mean about parents?" he said as he laid Anna down.

Meran gave him a mock-serious cuff on the back of his head.

"Go find Lesli," she said.

"But—"

"Or would you rather stay with Anna and continue your silly attempt at converting her when she wakes up again?"

"I'm on my way," Cerin told her and was out the door before she could change her mind.

Thunder cracked almost directly overhead as Cutter dragged Lesli into a brownstone just off Palm Street. The building stood in the heart of what was known as Newford's Combat Zone, a few square blocks of night clubs, strip joints and bars. It was a tough part of town with hookers on every corner, bikers cruising the streets on chopped-down Harleys, bums sleeping in doorways, winos sitting on the curbs, drinking cheap booze from bottles vaguely hidden in paper bags.

Cutter had an apartment on the top floor of the brownstone, three stories up from the street. If he hadn't told her that he lived here, Leslie would have thought that he'd taken her into an abandoned building. There was no furniture except a vinyl-topped table and two chairs in the dirty kitchen. A few mangy pillows were piled up against the wall in what she assumed was the living room.

He led her down to the room at the end of the long hall that ran the length of the apartment and pushed her inside. She lost her balance and went sprawling onto the mattress that lay in the middle of the floor. It smelled of mildew and, vaguely, of old urine. She scrambled away from it and crouched up against the far wall, clutching her knapsack against her chest.

"Now, you just relax, sweet stuff," Cutter told her. "Take things easy. I'm going out for a little while to find you a nice guy to ease you into the trade. I'd do it myself, but there's guys that want to be first with a kid as young and pretty as you are and I sure could use the bread they're willing to pay for the privilege.''

Lesli was prepared to beg him to let her go, but her throat was so tight she couldn't make a sound.

"Don't go away now," Cutter told her.

He chuckled at his own wit, then closed the door and locked it. Lesli didn't think she'd ever heard anything so final as the sound of that lock catching. She listened to Cutter's footsteps as they crossed the apartment, the sound of the front door closing, his footsteps receding on the stairs.

As soon as she was sure he was far enough away, she got up and ran to the door, trying it, just in case, but it really was locked and far too solid for her to have any hope of breaking through its panels. Of course there was no phone. She crossed the room to the window and forced it open. The window looked out on the side of another building, with an alleyway below. There was no fire escape outside the window and she was far too high up to think of trying to get down to the alley.

Thunder rumbled again, not quite overhead now, and it started to rain. She leaned by the window, resting her head on its sill. Tears sprang up in her eyes again.

"Please," she sniffed. "Please, somebody help me. . . ."

The rain coming in the window mingled with the tears that streaked her cheek.

Cerin began his search at the Batterberry house, which was in Ferryside, across the Stanton Street Bridge on the west side of the Kickaha River. As Anna Batterberry had remarked, the city was large. To find one teenage girl, hiding somewhere in the confounding labyrinth of its thousands of crisscrossing streets and avenues, was a daunting task, but Cerin was depending on help.

To anyone watching him, he must have appeared to be slightly mad. He wandered back and forth across the streets of Ferryside, stopping under trees to look up into their bare branches, hunkering down at the mouths of alleys or alongside hedges, apparently talking to himself. In truth, he was looking for the city's gossips:

Magpies and crows, sparrows and pigeons saw everything, but listening to their litanies of the day's events was like looking something up in an encyclopedia that was merely a confusing heap of loose pages, gathered together in a basket. All the information you wanted was there, but finding it would take more hours than there were in a day.

Cats were little better. They liked to keep most of what they knew to themselves, so what they did offer him was usually cryptic and sometimes even pointedly unhelpful. Cerin couldn't blame them; they were by nature secretive and, like much of Faerie, capricious.

The most ready to give him a hand were those little sprites commonly known as the flower faeries. They were the little winged spirits of the various trees and bushes, flowers and weeds, that grew tidily in parks and gardens, rioting only in the odd empty lot or wild place, such as the riverbanks that ran down under the Stanton Street Bridge to meet the water. Years ago, Cicely Mary Barker had catalogued any number of them in a loving series of books; more recently the Boston artist, Terri Windling, had taken up the task, specializing in the urban relations of those Barker had already noted.

It was late in the year for the little folk. Most of them were already tucked away in Faerie, sleeping through the winter, or else too busy with their harvests and other seasonal preoccupations to have paid any attention at all to what went on beyond the task at hand. But a few had seen the young girl who could sometimes see them. Meran's cousins were the most helpful. Their small pointed faces would regard Cerin gravely from under acorn caps as they pointed this way down one street, or that way down another.

It took time. The sky grew darker, and then still darker as the clouds thickened with an approaching storm, but slowly and surely, Cerin traced Lesli's passage over the Stanton Street Bridge all the way across town to Fitzhenry Park. It was just as he reached the bench where she'd been sitting that it began to rain.

There, from two of the wizened little monkey-like bodachs that lived in the park, he got the tale of how she'd been accosted and taken away.

"She didn't want to go, sir," said the one, adjusting the brim of his little cap against the rain.

All faerie knew Cerin, but it wasn't just for his bardic harping that they paid him the respect that they did. He was the husband of the oak king's daughter, she who could match them trick for trick and then some, and they'd long since learned to treat her, and those under her protection, with a wary deference.

"No sir, she didn't," added the other, "but he led her off all the same."

Cerin hunkered down beside the bench so that he wasn't towering over them.

"Where did he take her?" he asked.

The first bodach pointed to where two men were standing by the War Memorial, shoulders hunched against the rain, heads bent together as they spoke. One wore a thin raincoat over a suit; the other was dressed in denim jacket, jeans and cowboy boots. They appeared to be discussing a business transaction.

"You could ask him for yourself," the bodach said. "He's the one all in blue."

Cerin's gaze went to the pair and a hard look came over his features. If Meran had been there, she might have laid a hand on his arm, or spoken a calming word, to bank the dangerous fire that grew in behind his eyes. But she was at home, too far away for her quieting influence to be felt.

The bodachs scampered away as Cerin rose to his feet. By the War Memorial, the two men seemed to come to an agreement and left the park together. Cerin fell in behind them, the rain that slicked the pavement underfoot muffling his footsteps. His fingers twitched at his side, as though striking a harp's strings.

From the branches of the tree where they'd taken sanctuary, the bodachs thought they could hear the sound of a harp, its music echoing softly against the rhythm of the rain.

Anna came to once more just as Meran was returning from the kitchen with a pot of herb tea and a pair of mugs. Meran set the mugs and pot down on the table by the sofa and sat down beside Lesli's mother.

"How are you feeling?" she asked as she adjusted the cool cloth she'd laid upon Anna's brow earlier.

Anna's gaze flicked from left to right, over Meran's shoulder and down to the floor, as though tracking invisible presences. Meran tried to shoo away the inquisitive faerie, but it was a useless gesture. In this house, with Anna's presence to fuel their quenchless curiosity, it was like trying to catch the wind.

"I've made us some tea," Meran said. "It'll make you feel better."

Anna appeared docile now, her earlier anger fled as though it had never existed. Outside, rain pattered gently against the window panes. The face of a nosy hob was pressed against one lower pane, its breath clouding the glass, its large eyes glimmering with their own inner light.

"Can . . . can you make them go away?" Anna asked.

Meran shook her head. "But I can make you forget again."

"Forget." Anna's voice grew dreamy. "Is that what you did before? You made me forget?"

"No. You did that on your own. You didn't want to remember, so you simply forgot."

"And you . . . you didn't do a thing?"

"We do have a certain . . . aura," Meran admitted, "which accelerates the process. It's not even something we consciously work at. It just seems to happen when we're around those who'd rather not remember what they see."

"So I'll forget, but they'll all still be there?"

Meran nodded.

"I just won't be able to see them?"

"It'll be like it was before," Meran said.

"I . . . I don't think I like that. . . ."

Her voice slurred. Meran leaned forward with a worried expression. Anna seemed to regard her through blurring vision.

"I think I'm going . . . away . . . now. . . ." she said.

Her eyelids fluttered, then her head lolled to one side and she lay still. Meran called Anna's name and gave her a little shake, but there was no response. She put two fingers to Anna's throat and found her pulse. It was regular and strong, but try though she did, Meran couldn't rouse the woman.

Rising from the sofa, she went into the kitchen to phone for an ambulance. As she was dialing the number, she heard Cerin's harp begin to play by itself up in his study on the second floor.

Lesli's tears lasted until she thought she saw something moving in the rain on the other side of the window. It was a flicker of movement and color, just above the outside windowsill, as though a pigeon had come in for a wet landing, but it had moved with far more grace and deftness than any pigeon she'd ever seen. And that memory of color was all wrong, too. It hadn't been the blue/white/grey of a pigeon; it had been more like a butterfly—

doubtful, she thought, in the rain and this time of year

—or a hummingbird—

even more doubtful

—but then she remembered what the music had woken at her last flute lesson. She rubbed at her eyes with her sleeve to remove the blur of her tears and looked more closely into the rain. Face-on, she couldn't see anything, but as soon as she turned her head, there it was again, she could see it out of the corner of her eye, a dancing dervish of color and movement that flickered out of her line of sight as soon as she concentrated on it.

After a few moments, she turned from the window. She

gave the door a considering look and listened hard, but there was still no sound of Cutter's return.

Maybe, she thought, maybe magic can rescue me. . . .

She dug out her flute from her knapsack and quickly put the pieces together. Turning back to the window, she sat on her haunches and tried to start up a tune, but to no avail. She was still too nervous, her chest felt too tight, and she couldn't get the air to come up properly from her diaphragm.

She brought the flute down from her lip and laid it across her knees. Trying not to think of the locked door, of why it was locked and who would be coming through it, she steadied her breathing.

In, slowly now, hold it, let it out, slowly. And again.

She pretended she was with Meran, just the two of them in the basement of the Old Firehall. There. She could almost hear the tune that Meran was playing, except it sounded more like the bell-like tones of a harp than the breathy timbre of a wooden flute. But still, it was there for her to follow, a path marked out on a roadmap of music.

Lifting the flute back up to her lip, she blew again, a narrow channel of air going down into the mouth hole at an angle, all her fingers down, the low D note ringing in the empty room, a deep rich sound, resonant and full. She played it again, then caught the music she heard, that particular path laid out on the roadmap of all tunes that are or yet could be, and followed where it led.

It was easier to do than she would have thought possible, easier than at all those lessons with Meran. The music she followed seemed to allow her instrument to almost play itself. And as the tune woke from her flute, she fixed her gaze on the rain falling just outside the window where a flicker of color appeared, a spin of movement.

Please, she thought. Oh please . . .

And then it was there, hummingbird wings vibrating in the rain, sending incandescent sprays of water arcing away from their movement; the tiny naked upper torso, the lower wrapped in tiny leaves and vines; the dark hair gathered wetly against her miniature cheeks and neck; the eyes, tiny and timeless, watching her as she watched back and all the while, the music played.

Help me, she thought to that little hovering figure. Won't you please—

She had been oblivious to anything but the music and the tiny faerie outside in the rain. She hadn't heard the footsteps on the stairs, nor heard them crossing the apartment. But she heard the door open.

The tune faltered, the faerie flickered out of sight as though it had never been there. She brought the flute down from her lip and turned, her heart drumming wildly in her chest, but she refused to be scared. That's all guys like Cutter wanted. They wanted to see you scared of them. They wanted to be in control. But no more.

I'm not going to go without a fight, she thought. I'll break my flute over his stupid head. I'll . . .

The stranger standing in the doorway brought her train of thought to a scurrying halt. And then she realized that the harping she'd heard, the tune that had led her flute to join it, had grown in volume, rather than diminished.

"Who . . . who are you?" she asked.

Her hands had begun to perspire, making her flute slippery and hard to hold. The stranger had longer hair than Cutter. It was drawn back in a braid that hung down one side of his head and dangled halfway down his chest. He had a full beard and wore clothes that, though they were simple jeans, shirt and jacket, seemed to have a timeless cut to them, as though they could have been worn at any point in history and not seemed out of place. Meran dressed like that as well, she realized.

But it was his eyes that held her—not their startling brightness, but the fire that seemed to flicker in their depths, a rhythmic movement that seemed to keep time to the harping she heard.

"Have you come to . . . rescue me?" she found herself

asking before the stranger had time to reply to her first question.

"I'd think," he said, "with a spirit so brave as yours, that you'd simply rescue yourself."

Lesli shook her head. "I'm not really brave at all."

"Braver than you know, fluting here while a darkness stalked you through the storm. My name's Cerin Kelledy; I'm Meran's husband and I've come to take you home."

He waited for her to disassemble her flute and stow it away, then offered her a hand up from the floor. As she stood up, he took the knapsack and slung it over his shoulder and led her towards the door. The sound of the harping was very faint now, Lesli realized.

When they walked by the hall, she stopped in the doorway leading to the living room and looked at the two men that were huddled against the far wall, their eyes wild with terror. One was Cutter; the other a business man in suit and raincoat whom she'd never seen before. She hesitated, fingers tightening on Cerin's hand, as she turned to see what was frightening them so much. There was nothing at all in the spot that their frightened gazes were fixed upon.

"What . . . what's the matter with them?" she asked her companion. "What are they looking at?"

"Night fears," Cerin replied. "Somehow the darkness that lies in their hearts has given those fears substance and made them real."

The way he said "somehow" let Lesli know that he'd been responsible for what the two men were undergoing.

"Are they going to die?" she asked

She didn't think she was the first girl to fall prey to Cutter so she wasn't exactly feeling sorry for him at that point.

Cerin shook his head. "But they will always have the *sight*. Unless they change their ways, it will show them only the dark side of Faerie."

Lesli shivered.

"There are no happy endings," Cerin told her. "There are no real endings ever—happy or otherwise. We all have our own stories which are just a part of the one Story that binds both this world and Faerie. Sometimes we step into each others' stories—perhaps just for a few minutes, perhaps for years—and then we step out of them again. But all the while, the Story just goes on.''

That day, his explanation only served to confuse her.

From Lesli's diary, entry dated November 24th:

Nothing turned out the way I thought it would.

Something happened to Mom. Everybody tells me it's not my fault, but it happened when I ran away, so I can't help but feel that I'm to blame. Daddy says she had a nervous breakdown and that's why she's in the sanitarium. It happened to her before and it had been coming again for a long time. But that's not the way Mom tells it.

I go by to see her every day after school. Sometimes she's pretty spaced from the drugs they give her to keep her calm, but on one of her good days, she told me about Granny Nell and the Kelledys and Faerie. She says the world's just like I said it was in that essay I did for English. Faerie's real and it didn't go away; it just got freed from people's preconceptions of it and now it's just whatever it wants to be.

And that's what scares her.

She also thinks the Kelledys are some kind of earth spirits.

"I can't forget this time," she told me.

"But if you know," I asked her, "if you believe, then why are you in this place? Maybe I should be in here, too."

And you know what she told me? "I don't want to believe in any of it; it just makes me feel sick. But at the same time, I can't stop knowing it's all out there: every kind of magic being and nightmare. They're all real."

I remember thinking of Cutter and that other guy in his apartment and what Cerin said about them. Did that make my Mom a bad person? I couldn't believe that.

"But they're not *supposed* to be real," Mom said. "That's what's got me feeling so crazy. In a sane world, in the world that was the way I'd grown up believing it to be, that *wouldn't* be real. The Kelledys could fix it so that I'd forget again, but then I'd be back to going through life always feeling like there was something important that I couldn't remember. And that just leaves you with another kind of craziness—an ache that you can't explain and it doesn't ever go away. It's better this way, and my medicine keeps me from feeling too crazy.''

She looked away then, out the window of her room. I looked, too, and saw the little monkeyman that was crossing the lawn of the sanitarium, pulling a pig behind him. The pig had a load of gear on its back like it was a pack horse.

"Could you . . . could you ask the nurse to bring my medicine," Mom said.

I tried to tell her that all she had to do was accept it, but she wouldn't listen. She just kept asking for the nurse, so finally I went and got one.

I still think it's my fault.

I live with the Kelledys now. Daddy was going to send me away to a boarding school, because he felt that he couldn't be home enough to take care of me. I never really thought about it before, but when he said that, I realized that he didn't know me at all.

Meran offered to let me live at their place. I moved in on my birthday.

There's a book in their library—ha! There's like ten million books in there. But the one I'm thinking of is by a local writer, this guy named Christy Riddell.

In it, he talks about Faerie, how everybody just thinks of them as ghosts of wind and shadow.

"Faerie music is the wind," he says, "and their movement is the play of shadow cast by moonlight, or starlight, or no light at all. Faerie lives like a ghost beside us, but only the city remembers. But then the city never forgets anything."

I don't know if the Kelledys are part of that ghostliness. What I do know is that, seeing how they live for each other, how they care so much about each other, I find myself feeling more hopeful about things. My parents and I didn't so much not get along, as lack interest in each other. It got to the point where I figured that's how everybody was in the world, because I never knew any different.

So I'm trying harder with Mom. I don't talk about things she doesn't want to hear, but I don't stop believing in them either. Like Cerin said, we're just two threads of the Story. Sometimes we come together for awhile and sometimes we're apart. And no matter how much one or the other of us might want it to be different, both our stories are true.

But I can't stop wishing for a happy ending.

∽· THE CONJURE MAN ·∽

I do not think it had any friends, or mourners, except myself and a pair of owls.

—J. R. R. TOLKIEN, FROM THE INTRODUCTORY
NOTE TO *TREE AND LEAF*

You only see the tree by the light of the lamp. I wonder when you would ever see the lamp by the light of the tree.

—G. K. CHESTERTON, FROM
THE MAN WHO WAS THURSDAY

THE CONJURE MAN rode a red, old-fashioned bicycle with fat tires and only one, fixed gear. A wicker basket in front contained a small mongrel dog that seemed mostly terrier. Behind the seat, tied to the carrier, was a battered brown satchel that hid from prying eyes the sum total of all his worldly possessions.

What he had was not much, but he needed little. He was, after all, the conjure man, and what he didn't have, he could conjure for himself.

He was more stout than slim, with a long grizzled beard and a halo of frizzy grey hair that protruded from under his tall black hat like ivy tangled under an eave. Nesting in the hatband were a posy of dried wildflowers and three feathers: one white, from a swan; one black, from a crow; one brown, from an owl. His jacket was an exhilarating shade of blue, the color of the sky on a perfect summer's morning. Under it he wore a shirt that was as green as a fresh-cut lawn. His trousers were brown corduroy, patched with leather and plaid squares; his boots were a deep golden yellow, the color of buttercups past their prime.

His age was a puzzle, somewhere between fifty and seventy. Most people assumed he was one of the homeless—more colorful than most, and certainly more cheerful, but a derelict all the same—so the scent of apples that seemed to follow him was always a surprise, as was the good humor that walked hand in hand with a keen intelligence in his bright blue eyes. When he raised his head, hat brim lifting, and he met one's gaze, the impact of those eyes was a sudden shock, a diamond in the rough.

His name was John Windle, which could mean, if you were one to ascribe meaning to names, "favored of god" for his given name, while his surname was variously defined as "basket," "the red-winged thrush," or "to lose vigor and strength, to dwindle." They could all be true, for he led a charmed life; his mind was a treasure trove storing equal amounts of experience, rumor and history; he had a high clear singing voice; and though he wasn't tall—he stood five-ten in his boots—he had once been a much larger man.

"I was a giant once," he liked to explain, "when the world was young. But conjuring takes its toll. Now John's just an old man, pretty well all used up. Just like the world," he'd add with a sigh and a nod, bright eyes holding a tired sorrow. "Just like the world."

There were some things even the conjure man couldn't fix.

Living in the city, one grew used to its more outlandish characters, eventually noting them in passing with an almost familial affection: The pigeon lady in her faded Laura Ashley dresses with her shopping cart filled with sacks of birdseed and bread crumbs. Paperjack, the old black man with his Chinese fortune-teller and deft origami sculptures. The German cowboy who dressed like an extra from a spaghetti western and made long declamatory speeches in his native language to which no one listened.

And, of course, the conjure man.

Wendy St. James had seen him dozens of times—she lived and worked downtown, which was the conjure man's principle haunt—but she'd never actually spoken to him until one day in the fall when the trees were just beginning to change into their cheerful autumnal party dresses.

She was sitting on a bench on the Ferryside bank of the Kickaha River, a small, almost waif-like woman in jeans and a white T-shirt, with an unzipped brown leather bomber's jacket and hightops. In lieu of a purse, she had a small, worn knapsack sitting on the bench beside her and she was bent over a hardcover journal which she spent more time staring at than actually writing in. Her hair was thick and blonde, hanging down past her collar in a grown-out pageboy with a half-inch of dark roots showing. She was chewing on the end of her pen, worrying the plastic for inspiration.

It was a poem that had stopped her in mid-stroll and plunked her down on the bench. It had glimmered and shone in her head until she got out her journal and pen. Then it fled, as impossible to catch as a fading dream. The more she tried to recapture the impulse that had set her wanting to put pen to paper, the less it seemed to have ever existed in the first place. The annoying presence of three teenage boys clowning around on the lawn a half-dozen yards from where she sat didn't help at all.

She was giving them a dirty stare when she saw one of the boys pick up a stick and throw it into the wheel of the conjure man's bike as he came riding up on the park path that followed the river. The small dog in the bike's wicker basket jumped free, but the conjure man himself fell in a tangle of limbs and spinning wheels. The boys took off, laughing, the dog chasing them for a few feet, yapping shrilly, before it hurried back to where its master had fallen.

Wendy had already put down her journal and pen and reached the fallen man by the time the dog got back to its master's side.

"Are you okay?" Wendy asked the conjure man as she helped him untangle himself from the bike.

She'd taken a fall herself in the summer. The front wheel of her ten-speed struck a pebble, the bike wobbled dangerously and she'd grabbed at the brakes, but her fingers closed over the front ones first, and too hard. The back of the bike went up, flipping her right over the handlebars, and she'd had the worst headache for at least a week afterwards.

The conjure man didn't answer her immediately. His gaze followed the escaping boys.

"As you sow," he muttered.

Following his gaze, Wendy saw the boy who'd thrown the stick trip and go sprawling in the grass. An odd chill danced up her spine. The boy's tumble came so quickly on the heels of the conjure man's words, for a moment it felt to her as though he'd actually caused the boy's fall.

As you sow, so shall you reap.

She looked back at the conjure man, but he was sitting up now, fingering a tear in his corduroys, which already had a quiltwork of patches on them. He gave her a quick smile that traveled all the way up to his eyes and she found herself thinking of Santa Claus. The little dog pressed its nose up against the conjure man's hand, pushing it away from the tear. But the tear was gone.

It had just been a fold in the cloth, Wendy realized. That was all.

She helped the conjure man limp to her bench, then went back and got his bike. She righted it and wheeled it over to lean against the back of the bench before sitting down herself. The little dog leaped up onto the conjure man's lap.

"What a cute dog," Wendy said, giving it a pat. "What's her name?"

"Ginger," the conjure man replied as though it was so obvious that he couldn't understand her having to ask.

Wendy looked at the dog. Ginger's fur was as grey and grizzled as her master's beard without a hint of the spice's strong brown hue.

"But she's not at all brown," Wendy found herself saying.

The conjure man shook his head. "It's what she's made of—she's a gingerbread dog. Here." He plucked a hair from Ginger's back which made the dog start and give him a sour look. He offered the hair to Wendy. "Taste it."

Wendy grimaced. "I don't think so."

"Suit yourself," the conjure man said. He shrugged and popped the hair into his own mouth, chewing it with relish.

Oh boy, Wendy thought. She had a live one on her hands.

"Where do you think ginger comes from?" the conjure man asked her.

"What, do you mean your dog?"

"No, the spice."

Wendy shrugged. "I don't know. Some kind of plant, I suppose."

"And that's where you're wrong. They shave gingerbread dogs like our Ginger here and grind up the hair until all that's left is a powder that's ever so fine. Then they leave it out in the hot sun for a day and half—which is where it gets its brownish colour."

Wendy only just stopped herself from rolling her eyes. It was time to extract herself from this encounter, she realized. Well past the time. She'd done her bit to make sure he was all right and since the conjure man didn't seem any worse for the wear from his fall—

"Hey!" she said as he picked up her journal and started to leaf through it. "That's personal."

He fended off her reaching hand with his own and continued to look through it.

"Poetry," he said. "And lovely verses they are, too."

"Please . . ."

"Ever had any published?"

Wendy let her hand drop and leaned back against the bench with a sigh.

"Two collections," she said, adding, "and a few sales to some of the literary magazines."

Although, she corrected herself, "sales" was perhaps a misnomer since most of the magazines only paid in copies. And while she did have two collections in print, they were published by the East Street Press, a small local publisher, which meant the bookstores of Newford were probably the only places in the world where either of her books could be found.

"Romantic, but with a very optimistic flavor," the conjure man remarked as he continued to look through her journal where all her false starts and incomplete drafts were laid out for him to see. "None of that *Sturm und drang* of the earlier romantic era and more like Yeats' Celtic twilight or, what did Chesteron call it? *Mooreeffoc*—that queerness that comes when familiar things are seen from a new angle."

Wendy couldn't believe she was having this conversation. What was he? A renegade English professor living on the street like some hedgerow philosopher of old? It seemed absurd to be sitting here, listening to his discourse.

The conjure man turned to give her a charming smile. "Because that's our hope for the future, isn't it? That the imagination reaches beyond the present to glimpse not so much a sense of meaning in what lies all around us, but to let us simply see it in the first place?"

"I . . . I don't know what to say," Wendy replied.

Ginger had fallen asleep on his lap. He closed her journal and regarded her for a long moment, eyes impossibly blue and bright under the brim of his odd hat.

"John has something he wants to show you," he said.

Wendy blinked. "John?" she asked, looking around.

The conjure man tapped his chest. "John Windle is what those who know my name call me."

"Oh."

She found it odd how his speech shifted from that of a learned man to a much simpler idiom, even referring to himself in the third person. But then, if she stopped to consider it, everything about him was odd.

"What kind of something?" Wendy asked cautiously.

"It's not far."

Wendy looked at her watch. Her shift started at four, which was still a couple of hours away, so there was plenty of time. But she was fairly certain that interesting though her companion was, he wasn't at all the sort of person with whom she wanted to involve herself any more than she already had. The dichotomy between the nonsense and substance that peppered his conversation made her uncomfortable.

It wasn't so much that she thought him dangerous. She just felt as though she was walking on boggy ground that might at any minute dissolve into quicksand with a wrong turn. Despite hardly knowing him at all, she was already sure that listening to him would be full of the potential for wrong turns.

"I'm sorry," she said, "but I don't have the time."

"It's something that I think only you can, if not understand, then at least appreciate."

"I'm sure it's fascinating, whatever it is, but—"

"Come along, then," he said.

He handed her back her journal and stood up, dislodging Ginger, who leapt to the ground with a sharp yap of protest. Scooping the dog up, he returned her to the wicker basket that hung from his handlebars, then wheeled the bike in front of the bench where he stood waiting for Wendy.

Wendy opened her mouth to continue her protest, but then simply shrugged. Well, why not? He really didn't look at all dangerous and she'd just make sure that she stayed in public places.

She stuffed her journal back into her knapsack and then followed as he led the way south along the park path up to where the City Commission's lawns gave way to Butler University's common. She started to ask him how his leg felt, since he'd been limping before, but he walked at a quick, easy pace—that of someone half his apparent age—so she just assumed he hadn't been hurt that badly by his fall after all.

They crossed the common, eschewing the path now to walk straight across the lawn towards the G. Smithers Memorial Library, weaving their way in between islands of students involved in any number of activities, none of which included studying. When they reached the library, they followed its ivy hung walls to the rear of the building, where the conjure man stopped.

"There," he said, waving his arm in a gesture that took in the entire area behind the library. "What do you see?"

The view they had was of an open space of land backed by a number of other buildings. Having attended the university herself, Wendy recognized all three: the Student Center, the Science Building and one of the dorms, though she couldn't remember which one. The landscape enclosed by their various bulking presences had the look of recently having undergone a complete overhaul. All the lilacs and hawthorns had been cut back, brush and weeds were now just an uneven stubble of ground covering, there were clumps of raw dirt, scattered here and there, where trees had obviously been removed, and right in the middle was enormous stump.

It had been at least fifteen years since Wendy had had any reason to come here behind the library. But it was so different now. She found herself looking around with a "what's wrong with this picture?" caption floating in her mind. This had been a little cranny of wild wood when she'd attended Butler, hidden away from all the trimmed lawns and shrubbery that made the rest of the university so picturesque. But she could remember slipping back here, journal in hand, and sitting under that huge . . .

"It's all changed," she said slowly. "They cleaned out all the brush and cut down the oak tree. . . ."

Someone had once told her that this particular tree was—had been—a rarity. It had belonged to a species not native to North America—the *Quercus robur,* or common oak of Europe—and was supposed to be over four hundred years old, which made it older than the university, older than Newford itself.

"How could they just . . . cut it down . . . ?" she asked.

The conjure man jerked a thumb over his shoulder towards the library.

"Your man with the books had the work done—didn't like the shade it was throwing on his office. Didn't like to look out and see an untamed bit of the wild hidden in here disturbing his sense of order."

"The head librarian?" Wendy asked.

The conjure man just shrugged.

"But—didn't anyone complain? Surely the students . . ."

In her day there would have been protests. Students would have formed a human chain around the tree, refusing to let anyone near it. They would have camped out, day and night. They . . .

She looked at the stump and felt a tightness in her chest as though someone had wrapped her in wet leather that was now starting to dry out and shrink.

"That tree was John's friend," the conjure man said. "The last friend I ever had. She was ten thousand years old and they just cut her down."

Wendy gave him an odd look. Ten thousand years old? Were we exaggerating now or what?

"Her death is a symbol," the conjure man went on. "The world has no more time for stories."

"I'm not sure I follow you," Wendy said.

He turned to look at her, eyes glittering with a strange light under the dark brim of his hat.

"She was a Tree of Tales," he said. "There are very few of them left, just as there are very few of me. She held stories, all the stories the wind brought to her that were of any worth, and with each such story she heard, she grew."

"But there's always going to be stories," Wendy said, falling into the spirit of the conversation even if she didn't quite understand its relevance to the situation at hand. "There are more books being published today than there ever have been in the history of the world."

The conjure man gave her a sour frown and hooked his

thumb towards the library again. "Now you sound like him."

"But—"

"There's stories and then there's stories," he said, interrupting her. "The ones with any worth change your life forever, perhaps only in a small way, but once you've heard them, they are forever a part of you. You nurture them and pass them on and the giving only makes you feel better.

"The others are just words on a page."

"I know that," Wendy said.

And on some level she did, though it wasn't something she'd ever really stopped to think about. It was more an instinctive sort of knowledge that had always been present inside her, rising up into her awareness now as though called forth by the conjure man's words.

"It's all machines now," the conjure man went on. "It's a—what do they call it?—high-tech world. Fascinating, to be sure, but John thinks that it estranges many people, cheapens the human experience. There's no more room for the stories that matter, and that's wrong, for stories are a part of the language of dream—they grow not from one writer, but from a people. They become the voice of a country, or a race. Without them, people lose touch with themselves."

"You're talking about myths," Wendy said.

The conjure man shook his head. "Not specifically—not in the classical sense of the word. Such myths are only a part of the collective story that is harvested in a Tree of Tales. In a world as pessimistic as this has become, that collective story is all that's left to guide people through the encroaching dark. It serves to create a sense of options, the possibility of permanence out of nothing."

Wendy was really beginning to lose the thread of his argument now.

"What exactly is it that you're saying?" she asked.

"A Tree of Tales is an act of magic, of faith. It's existence becomes an affirmation of the power that the human spirit can have over its own destiny. The stories are just stories—

they entertain, they make one laugh or cry—but if they have any worth, they carry within them a deeper resonance that remains long after the final page is turned, or the storyteller has come to the end of her tale. Both aspects of the story are necessary for it to have any worth."

He was silent for a long moment, then added, "Otherwise the story goes on without you."

Wendy gave him a questioning look.

"Do you know what 'ever after' means?" he asked.

"I suppose."

"It's one bookend of a tale—the kind that begins with 'once upon a time.' It's the end of the story when everybody goes home. That's what they said at the end of the story John was in, but John wasn't paying attention, so he got left behind."

"I'm not sure I know what you're talking about," Wendy said.

Not sure? she thought. She was positive. It was all so much . . . well, not exactly nonsense, as queer. And unrelated to any working of the world with which she was familiar. But the oddest thing was that everything he said continued to pull a kind of tickle out from deep in her mind so that while she didn't completely understand him, some part of her did. Some part, hidden behind the person who took care of all the day-to-day business of her life, perhaps the same part of her that pulled a poem into the empty page where no words had ever existed before. The part of her that was a conjurer.

"John took care of the Tale of Trees," the conjure man went on. "Because John got left behind in his own story, he wanted to make sure that the stories themselves would at least live on. But one day he went wandering too far—just like he did when his story was ending—and when he got back she was gone. When he got back, they'd done *this* to her."

Wendy said nothing. For all that he was a comical figure in his bright clothes and with his Santa Claus air, there was nothing even faintly humorous about the sudden anguish in his voice.

"I'm sorry," she said.

And she was. Not just in sympathy with him, but because in her own way she'd loved that old oak tree as well. And—just like the conjure man, she supposed—she'd wandered away as well.

"Well then," the conjure man said. He rubbed a sleeve up against his nose and looked away from her. "John just wanted you to see."

He got on his bike and reached forward to tousle the fur around Ginger's ears. When he looked back to Wendy, his eyes glittered like tiny blue fires.

"I knew you'd understand," he said.

Before Wendy could respond, he pushed off and pedaled away, bumping across the uneven lawn to leave her standing alone in that once wild place that was now so dispiriting. But then she saw something stir in the middle of the broad stump.

At first it was no more than a small flicker in the air like a heat ripple. Wendy took a step forward, stopping when the flicker resolved into a tiny sapling. As she watched, it took on the slow stately dance of time-lapse photography: budded, unfurled leaves, grew taller, its growth like a rondo, a basic theme that brackets two completely separate tunes. Growth was the theme, while the tunes on either end began with the tiny sapling and ended with a full-grown oak tree as majestic as the behemoth that had originally stood there. When it reached its full height, light seemed to emanate from its trunk, from the roots underground, from each stalkless, broad saw-toothed leaf.

Wendy stared, wide-eyed, then stepped forward with an outstretched hand. As soon as her fingers touched the glowing tree, it came apart, drifting like mist until every trace of it was gone. Once more, all that remained was the stump of the original tree.

The vision, combined with the tightness in her chest and

the sadness the conjure man had left her, transformed itself into words that rolled across her mind, but she didn't write them down. All she could do was stand and look at the tree stump for a very long time, before she finally turned and walked away.

Kathryn's Cafe was on Battersfield Road in Lower Crowsea, not far from the university but across the river and far enough that Wendy had to hurry to make it to work on time. But it was as though a black hole had swallowed the two hours from when she'd met the conjure man to when her shift began. She was late getting to work—not by much, but she could see that Jilly had already taken orders from two tables that were supposed to be her responsibility.

She dashed into the restaurant's washroom and changed from her jeans into a short black skirt. She tucked her T-shirt in, pulled her hair back into a loose bun, then bustled out to stash her knapsack and pick up her order pad from the storage shelf behind the employee's coat rack.

"You're looking peaked," Jilly said as she finally got out into the dining area.

Jilly Coppercorn and Wendy were spiritual sisters and could almost pass as physical ones as well. Both women were small, with slender frames and attractive delicate features, though Jilly's hair was a dark curly brown—the same as Wendy's natural hair color. They both moonlighted as waitresses, saving their true energy for creative pursuits: Jilly for her art, Wendy her poetry.

Neither had known the other until they began to work at the restaurant together, but they'd become fast friends from the very first shift they shared.

"I'm feeling confused," Wendy said in response to Jilly's comment.

"You're confused? Check out table five—he's changed his mind three times since he first ordered. I'm going to stand here and wait five minutes before I give Frank his latest order, just in case he decides he wants to change it again.''

Wendy smiled. ''And then he'll complain about slow service and won't leave you much of a tip.''

''If he leaves one at all.''

Wendy laid a hand on Jilly's arm. ''Are you busy tonight?''

Jilly shook her head. ''What's up?''

''I need to talk to someone.''

''I'm yours to command,'' Jilly said. She made a little curtsy which had Wendy quickly stifle a giggle, then shifted her gaze to table five. ''Oh bother, he's signaling me again.''

''Give me his order,'' Wendy said. ''I'll take care of him.''

It was such a nice night that they just went around back of the restaurant when their shift was over. Walking the length of a short alley, they came out on small strip of lawn and made their way down to the river. There they sat on a stone wall, dangling their feet above the sluggish water. The night felt still. Through some trick of the air, the traffic on nearby Battersfield Road was no more than a distant murmur, as though there was more of a sound baffle between where they sat and the busy street than just the building that housed their workplace.

''Remember that time we went camping?'' Wendy said after they'd been sitting for awhile in a companionable silence. ''It was just me, you and LaDonna. We sat around the campfire telling ghost stories that first night.''

''Sure,'' Jilly said with a smile in her voice. ''You kept telling us ones by Robert Aickman and the like—they were all taken from books.''

''While you and LaDonna claimed that the ones you told were real and no matter how much I tried to get either of you to admit they weren't, you wouldn't.''

''But they were true,'' Jilly said.

Wendy thought of LaDonna telling them that she'd seen Bigfoot in the Tombs and Jilly's stories about a kind of earth spirit called a gemmin that she'd met in the same part of the city and of a race of goblin-like creatures living in the subterranean remains of the old city that lay beneath Newford's subway system.

She turned from the river to regard her friend. "Do you really believe those things you told me?"

Jilly nodded. "Of course I do. They're true." She paused a moment, leaning closer to Wendy as though trying to read her features in the gloom. "Why? What's happened, Wendy?"

"I think I just had my own close encounter of the weird kind this afternoon."

When Jilly said nothing, Wendy went on to tell her of her meeting with the conjure man earlier in the day.

"I mean, I know why he's called the conjure man," she finished up. "I've seen him pulling flowers out of people's ears and all those other stage tricks he does, but this was different. The whole time I was with him I kept feeling like there really was a kind of magic in the air, a *real* magic just sort of humming around him, and then when I saw the . . . I guess it was a vision of the tree . . .

"Well, I don't know what to think."

She'd been looking across the river while she spoke, gaze fixed on the darkness of the far bank. Now she turned to Jilly.

"Who is he?" she asked. "Or maybe I should be asking *what* is he?"

"I've always thought of him as a kind of anima," Jilly said. "A loose bit of myth that got left behind when all the others went on to wherever it is that myths go when we don't believe in them anymore."

"That's sort of what he said. But what does it mean? What is he really?"

Jilly shrugged. "Maybe what he is isn't so important as

that he is." At Wendy's puzzled look, she added, "I can't explain it any better. I . . . Look, it's like it's not so important that he is or isn't what he says he is, but *that* he says it. That he believes it."

"Why?"

"Because it's just like he told you," Jilly said. "People are losing touch with themselves and with each other. They need stories because they really are the only thing that brings us together. Gossip, anecdotes, jokes, stories—these are the things that we used to exchange with each other. It kept the lines of communication open, let us touch each other on a regular basis.

"That's what art's all about, too. My paintings and your poems, the books Christy writes, the music Geordie plays—they're all lines of communication. But they're harder to keep open now because it's so much easier for most people to relate to a TV set than it is to another person. They get all this data fed into them, but they don't know what to do with it anymore. When they talk to other people, it's all surface. How ya doing, what about the weather. The only opinions they have are those that they've gotten from people on the TV. They think they're informed, but all they're doing is repeating the views of talk show hosts and news commentators.

"They don't know how to listen to real people anymore."

"I know all that," Wendy said. "But what does any of it have to do with what the conjure man was showing me this afternoon?"

"I guess what I'm trying to say is that he validates an older kind of value, that's all."

"Okay, but what did he want from me?"

Jilly didn't say anything for a long time. She looked out across the river, her gaze caught by the same darkness as Wendy's had earlier when she was relating her afternoon encounter. Twice Wendy started to ask Jilly what she was thinking, but both times she forbore. Then finally Jilly turned to her.

"Maybe he wants you to plant a new tree," she said.

"But that's silly. I wouldn't know how to begin to go about something like that." Wendy sighed. "I don't even know if I believe in a Tree of Tales."

But then she remembered the feeling that had risen in her when the conjure man spoke to her, that sense of familiarity as though she was being reminded of something she already knew, rather than being told what she didn't. And then there was the vision of the tree . . .

She sighed again.

"Why me?" she asked.

Her words were directed almost to the night at large, rather than just her companion, but it was Jilly who replied. The night held its own counsel.

"I'm going to ask you something," Jilly said, "and I don't want you to think about the answer. Just tell me the first thing that comes to mind—okay?"

Wendy nodded uncertainly. "I guess."

"If you could be granted one wish—anything at all, no limits—what would you ask for?"

With the state the world was in at the moment, Wendy had no hesitation in answering: "World peace."

"Well, there you go," Jilly told her.

"I don't get it."

"You were asking why the conjure man picked you and there's your reason. Most people would have started out thinking of what they wanted for themselves. You know, tons of money, or to live forever—that kind of thing."

Wendy shook her head. "But he doesn't even know me."

Jilly got up and pulled Wendy to her feet.

"Come on," she said. "Let's go look at the tree."

"It's just a stump."

"Let's go anyway."

Wendy wasn't sure why she felt reluctant, but just as she had this afternoon, she allowed herself to be led back to the campus.

* * *

Nothing had changed, except that this time it was dark, which gave the scene, at least to Wendy's way of thinking, an even more desolate feeling.

Jilly was very quiet beside her. She stepped ahead of Wendy and crouched down beside the stump, running her hand along the top of it.

"I'd forgotten all about this place," she said softly.

That's right, Wendy thought. Jilly'd gone to Butler U. just as she had—around the same time, too, though they hadn't known each other then.

She crouched down beside Jilly, starting slightly when Jilly took her hand and laid it on the stump.

"Listen," Jilly said. "You can almost feel the whisper of a story . . . a last echo . . ."

Wendy shivered, though the night was mild. Jilly turned to her. At that moment, the starlight flickering in her companion's blue eyes reminded Wendy very much of the conjure man.

"You've got to do it," Jilly said. "You've got to plant a new tree. It wasn't just the conjure man choosing you—the tree chose you, too."

Wendy wasn't sure what was what anymore. It all seemed more than a little mad, yet as she listened to Jilly, she could almost believe in it all. But then that was one of Jilly's gifts: she could make the oddest thing seem normal. Wendy wasn't sure if you could call a thing like that a gift, but whatever it was, Jilly had it.

"Maybe we should get Christy to do it," she said. "After all, he's the story writer."

"Christy is a lovely man," Jilly said, "but sometimes he's far more concerned with how he says a thing, rather than with the story itself."

"Well, I'm not much better. I've been known to worry for hours over a stanza—or even just a line."

"For the sake of being clever?" Jilly asked.

"No. So that it's right."

Jilly raked her fingers through the short stubble of the weeds that passed for a lawn around the base of the oak stump. She found something and pressed it into Wendy's hand. Wendy didn't have to look at it to know that it was an acorn.

"You have to do it," Jilly said. "Plant a new Tree of Tales and feed it with stories. It's really up to you."

Wendy looked from the glow of her friend's eyes to the stump. She remembered her conversation with the conjure man and her vision of the tree. She closed her fingers around the acorn, feeling the press of the cap's bristles indent her skin.

Maybe it *was* up to her, she found herself thinking.

The poem that came to her that night after she left Jilly and got back to her little apartment in Ferryside, came all at once, fully formed and complete. The act of putting it to paper was a mere formality.

She sat by her window for a long time afterward, her journal on her lap, the acorn in her hand. She rolled it slowly back and forth on her palm. Finally, she laid both journal and acorn on the windowsill and went into her tiny kitchen. She rummaged around in the cupboard under the sink until she came up with an old flowerpot which she took into the backyard and filled with dirt—rich loam, as dark and mysterious as that indefinable place inside herself that was the source of the words that filled her poetry and had risen in recognition to the conjure man's words.

When she returned to the window, she put the pot between her knees. Tearing the new poem out of her journal, she wrapped the acorn up in it and buried it in the pot. She watered it until the surface of the dirt was slick with mud, then placed the flowerpot on her windowsill and went to bed.

That night she dreamed of Jilly's gemmin—slender earth spirits that appeared outside the old three-story building that housed her apartment and peered in at the flowerpot on the windowsill. In the morning, she got up and told the buried acorn her dream.

Autumn turned to winter and Wendy's life went pretty much the way it always had. She took turns working at the restaurant and on her poems, she saw her friends, she started a relationship with a fellow she met at a party in Jilly's loft, but it floundered after a month.

Life went on.

The only change was centered around the contents of the pot on her windowsill. As though the tiny green sprig that pushed up through the dark soil was her lover, every day she told it all the things that had happened to her and around her. Sometimes she read it her favorite stories from anthologies and collections, or interesting bits from magazines and newspapers. She badgered her friends for stories, sometimes passing them on, speaking to the tiny plant in a low, but animated voice, other times convincing her friends to come over and tell the stories themselves.

Except for Jilly, LaDonna and the two Riddell brothers, Geordie and Christy, most people thought she'd gone just a little daft. Nothing serious, mind you, but strange all the same.

Wendy didn't care.

Somewhere out in the world, there were other Trees of Tales, but they were few—if the conjure man was to be believed. And she believed him now. She had no proof, only faith, but oddly enough, faith seemed enough. But since she believed, she knew it was more important than ever that her charge should flourish.

With the coming of winter, there were less and less of the street people to be found. They were indoors, if they had such an option, or perhaps they migrated to warmer climes like the swallows. But Wendy still spied the more regular ones in their usual haunts. Paperjack had gone, but the pigeon lady still fed her charges every day, the German cowboy continued his bombastic monologues—though mostly on the subway platforms now. She saw the conjure man, too, but he was never near enough for her to get a chance to talk to him.

By the springtime, the sprig of green in the flowerpot grew into a sapling that stood almost a foot high. On warmer days, Wendy put the pot out on the backporch steps, where it could taste the air and catch the growing warmth of the afternoon sun. She still wasn't sure what she was going to do with it once it outgrew its pot.

But she had some ideas. There was a part of Fitzhenry Park called the Silenus Gardens that was dedicated to the poet Joshua Stanhold. She thought it might be appropriate to plant the sapling there.

One day in late April, she was leaning on the handlebars of her ten-speed in front of the public library in Lower Crowsea, admiring the yellow splash the daffodils made against the building's grey stone walls, when she sensed, more than saw, a red bicycle pull up onto the sidewalk behind her. She turned around to find herself looking into the conjure man's merry features.

"It's spring, isn't it just," the conjure man said. "A time to finally forget the cold and bluster and think of summer. John can feel the leaf buds stir, the flowers blossoming. There's a grand smile in the air for all the growing."

Wendy gave Ginger a pat, before letting her gaze meet the blue shock of his eyes.

"What about a Tree of Tales?" she asked. "Can you feel her growing?"

The conjure man gave her a wide smile. "Especially her." He paused to adjust the brim of his hat, then gave her a sly look. "Your man Stanhold," he added. "Now there was a fine poet—and a fine storyteller."

Wendy didn't bother to ask how he knew of her plan. She just returned the conjure man's smile and then asked, "Do you have a story to tell me?"

The conjure man polished one of the buttons of his bright blue jacket.

"I believe I do," he said. He patted the brown satchel that rode on his back carrier. "John has a thermos filled with the very best tea, right here in his bag. Why don't we find ourselves a comfortable place to sit and he'll tell you how he got this bicycle of his over a hot cuppa."

He started to pedal off down the street, without waiting for her response. Wendy stared after him, her gaze catching the little terrier, sitting erect in her basket and looking back at her.

There seemed to be a humming in the air that woke a kind of singing feeling in her chest. The wind rose up and caught her hair, pushing it playfully into her eyes. As she swept it back from her face with her hand, she thought of the sapling sitting in its pot on her back steps, thought of the wind, and knew that stories were already being harvested without the necessity of her having to pass them on.

But she wanted to hear them all the same.

Getting on her ten-speed, she hurried to catch up with the conjure man.

◟• SMALL DEATHS •◞

What unites us universally is our emotions, our feelings in the face of experience, and not necessarily the actual experiences themselves.

—ANAIS NIN

I FEEL LIKE I should know you.''
Zoe Brill looked up. The line was familiar, but it usually came only after she'd spoken—that was the down side of being an all-night DJ in a city with too many people awake and having nothing to do between midnight and dawn. Everybody felt they knew you, everybody was your friend. Most of the time that suited her fine, since she genuinely liked people, but as her mother used to tell her, every family has its black sheep. Sometimes it seemed that every one of them tended to gravitate to her at one point or another in their lives.

The man who'd paused by the cafe railing to speak to Zoe this evening reminded her of a fox. He had lean, pointy features, dark eyes, the corners of his lips constantly lifted in a sly smile, hair as red as her own, if not as long. Unlike her, he had a dark complexion, as though swimming somewhere back in the gene pool of his forebears was an Italian, an Arab, or a Native American. His self-assurance radiated a touch too shrill for Zoe's taste, but he seemed basically harmless. Just your average single male yuppie on the prowl, heading out for an evening in clubland—she could almost hear the Full Force–produced dance number kick up as a soundtrack to the moment. Move your body all night long.

He was well-dressed, as all Lotharios should be, casual, but with flair; she doubted there was a single item in his wardrobe worth under two hundred dollars. Maybe the socks.

"I think I'd remember if we'd met before," she said.

He ignored the wryness in her voice and took what she'd said as a compliment.

"Most people do," he agreed.

"Lucky them."

It was one of those rare, supernaturally perfect November evenings, warm with a light breeze, wedged in between a week of sub-zero temperatures with similar weather to follow. All up and down Lee Street, from one end of the Market to the other, the restaurants and cafes had opened their patios for one last outdoor fling.

"No, no," the man said, finally picking up on her lack of interest. "It's not like what you're thinking."

Zoe tapped a long finger lightly against the page of the opened book that lay on her table beside a glass of red wine.

"I'm kind of busy," she said. "Maybe some other time."

He leaned closer to read the running head at the top of the book's left-hand page: *Disappearing Through the Skylight.*

"That's by O. B. Hardison, isn't it?" he asked. "Didn't he also write *Entering the Maze*?"

Zoe gave a reluctant nod and upgraded her opinion of him. Fine. So he was a well-read single male yuppie on the prowl, but she still wasn't interested.

"Technology," he said, "is a perfect example of evolution, don't you think? Take the camera. If you compare present models to the best they had just thirty years ago, you can see—"

"Look," Zoe said. "This is all very interesting, and I don't mean to sound rude, but why don't you go hit on someone else? If I'd wanted company, I would've gone out with a friend."

He shook his head. "No, no. I told you, I'm not trying to pick you up." He put out his hand. "My name's Gordon Wolfe."

He gave her his name with the simple assurance inherent in his voice that it was impossible that she wouldn't recognize it.

Zoe ignored the hand. As an attractive woman living on her own in a city the size of Newford, she'd long ago acquired a highly developed sense of radar, a kind of mental dah-*dum,* dah-*dum* straight out of *Jaws,* that kicked in whenever that sixth sense hiding somewhere in her subconscious decided that the situation carried too much of a possibility of turning weird, or a little too intense.

Gordon Wolfe had done nothing yet, but the warning bell was sounding faintly in her mind.

"Then what do you want?" she asked.

He lifted his hand and ran it through his hair, the movement so casual it was as though he'd never been rebuffed. "I'm just trying to figure out why I feel like I should know you."

So they were back to that again.

"The world's full of mysteries," Zoe told him. "I guess that's just going to be another one."

She turned back to her book, but he didn't leave the railing. Looking up, she tried to catch the eye of the waiter, to let him know that she was being bothered, but naturally neither he nor the two waitresses were anywhere in sight. The patio held only the usual bohemian mix of Lower Crowsea's inhabitants and hangers-on—a well-stirred stew of actors, poets, artists, musicians and those who aspired, through their clothing or attitude, to be counted in that number. Sometimes it was all just a little too trendy.

She turned back to her unwelcome visitor who still stood on the other side of the cafe's railing.

"It's nothing personal," she began. "I just don't—"

"You shouldn't mock me," he said, cutting in. "I'm the bringer of small deaths." His dark eyes flashed. "Remember me the next time you die a little."

Then he turned and walked away, losing himself in among the crowd of pedestrians that filled the sidewalk on either side of Lee Street.

Zoe sighed. Why were they always drawn to her? The weird and the wacky. Why not the wonderful for a change? When was the last time a nice normal guy had tried to chat her up?

It wasn't as though she looked particularly exotic: skin a little too pale, perhaps, due to the same genes that had given her her shoulder-length red hair and green eyes, but certainly not the extreme vampiric pallor affected by so many fans of the various British Gothic bands that jostled for position on the album charts of college radio and independent record stores; clothing less thrift-shop than most of those with whom she shared the patio this evening: ankle-high black lace-up boots, dark stockings, a black dress that was somewhat tight and a little short, a faded jean jacket that was a couple of sizes too big.

Just your basic semi-hip working girl, relaxing over a glass of wine and a book before she had to head over to the studio. So where were all the nice semi-hip guys for her to meet?

She took a sip of her wine and went back to her book, but found herself unable to concentrate on what she was reading. Gordon Wolfe's parting shot kept intruding on the words that filled the page before her.

Remember me the next time you die a little.

She couldn't suppress the small shiver that slithered up her spine.

Congratulations, she thought to her now-absent irritant. You've succeeded in screwing up my evening anyway.

Paying her bill, she decided to go home and walk Rupert, then head in to work early. An electronic score with lots of deep, low bass notes echoed in her head as she went home,

Tangerine Dream crossed with B-movie horror themes. She kept thinking Wolfe was lurking about, following her home, although whenever she turned, there was no one there. She hated this mild anxiety he'd bestowed upon her like some spiteful parting gift.

Her relief at finally getting home to where Rupert waited for her far outweighed the dog's slobbery enthusiasm at the thought of going out for their evening ramble earlier than usual. Zoe took a long roundabout way to the station, letting Rupert's ingenuous affection work its magic. With the big galoot at her side, it was easy to put the bad taste of her encounter with Wolfe to rest.

An old Lovin' Spoonful song provided backdrop to the walk, bouncing and cheerful. It wasn't summer yet, but it was warmer than usual and Newford had always been a hot town.

The phone call came in during the fourth hour of her show, "Nightnoise." As usual, the music was an eclectic mix. An Italian aria by Kiri Te Kanawa was segueing into a cut by the New Age Celtic group from which the show had gotten its name, with Steve Earle's "The Hard Way" cued up next, when the yellow light on the studio's phone began to blink with an incoming call.

"Nightnoise," she said into the receiver. "Zoe B. here."

"Are we on the air?"

It was a man's voice—an unfamiliar voice, warm and friendly with just the vaguest undercurrent of tension

"I'm sorry," she said. "We don't take call-ins after three."

From one to three A.M. she took on-air calls for requests, commentaries, sometimes just to chat; during that time period she also conducted interviews, if she had any slated. Experience had proven that the real fruitcakes didn't come out of the woodwork until the show was into its fourth hour, creeping up on dawn.

"That's all right," her caller said. "It's you I wanted to talk to."

Zoe cradled the receiver between her shoulder and ear and checked the studio clock. As the instrumental she was playing ended, she brought up the beginning of the Steve Earle cut and began to cue up her next choice, Concrete Blonde's cover of a Leonard Cohen song from the *Pump Up the Volume* soundtrack.

"So talk," she said, shifting the receiver back to her hand.

She could almost feel the caller's hesitation. It happened a lot. They got up the nerve to make the call, but once they were connected, their mouths went dry and all their words turned to sand.

"What's your name?" she added, trying to make it easier on him.

"Bob."

"Not the one from *Twin Peaks* I hope."

"I'm sorry?"

Obviously not a David Lynch fan, Zoe thought.

"Nothing," she said. "What can I do for you tonight, Bob?" Maybe she'd make an exception, she thought, and added: "Did you have a special song you wanted me to play for you?"

"No, I . . . It's about Gordon."

Zoe went blank for a moment. The first Gordon that came to mind was Gordon Waller from the old UK band, Peter & Gordon, rapidly followed by rockabilly great Robert Gordon and then Jim Gordon, the drummer who'd played with everybody from Baez to Clapton, including a short stint with Bread.

"Gordon Wolfe," Bob said, filling in the blank for her. "You were talking to him earlier tonight on the patio of The Rusty Lion."

Zoe shivered. From his blanket beside the studio door, Rupert lifted his head and gave an anxious whine, sensing her distress.

"You . . ." she began. "How could you know? What were you doing, following me?"

"No. I was following him."

"Oh."

Recovering her equilibrium, Zoe glanced at the studio clock and cued up the first cut from her next set in the CD player, her fingers going through the procedure on automatic.

"Why?" she asked.

"Because he's dangerous."

He'd given her the creeps, Zoe remembered, but she hadn't really thought of him as dangerous—at least not until his parting shot.

Remember me the next time you die a little.

"Who is he?" she asked. "Better yet, who are you? Why are you following this Wolfe guy around?"

"That's not his real name," Bob said.

"Then what is?"

"I can't tell you."

"Why the hell not?"

"Not won't," Bob said quickly. "*Can't*. I don't know it myself. All I know is he's dangerous and you shouldn't have gotten him mad at you."

"Jesus," Zoe said. "I really need this." Her gaze flicked back to the studio clock; the Steve Earle cut was heading into its fade-out. "Hang on a sec, Bob. I've got to run some commercials."

She put him on hold and brought up the volume on her mike.

"That was Steve Earle," she said, "with the title cut from his latest album, and you're listening to Nightnoise on WKPN. Zoe B. here, spinning the tunes for all you night birds and birdettes. Coming up we've got a hot and heavy metal set, starting off with the classic 'Ace of Spades' by Motorhead. These are *not* new kids on the block, my friends. But first, oh yes, even at this time of night, a word from some sponsors."

She punched up the cassette with its minute of ads for this half hour and brought the volume down off her mike again. But when she turned back to the phone, the on-line light was dead. She tried it anyway, but Bob had hung up.

"Shit," she said. "Why are you doing this to me?"

Rupert looked up again, then got up from his blanket and padded across the floor to press his wet nose up against her hand. He was a cross between a golden lab and a German shepherd, seventy pounds of big-hearted mush.

"No, not you," she told him, taking his head in both of her hands and rubbing her nose against the tip of his muzzle. "You're Zoe's big baby, aren't you?"

The ads cassette ran its course and she brought up Motorhead. As she cued up the rest of the pieces for this set, she kept looking at the phone, but the on-line light stayed dead.

"Weird," Hilary Carlisle agreed. She brushed a stray lock of hair away from her face and gave Zoe a quick smile. "But par for the course, don't you think?"

"Thanks a lot."

"I didn't say you egged them on, but it seems to be the story of your life: put you in a roomful of strangers and you can almost guarantee that the most oddball guy there will be standing beside you within ten minutes. It's—" she grinned "—just a gift you have."

"Well, this guy's really given me a case of the creeps."

"Which one—Gordon or Bob?"

"Both of them, if you want the truth."

Hilary's smile faded. "This is really getting to you, isn't it?"

"I could've just forgotten my delightful encounter at The Rusty Lion if it hadn't been for the follow-up call."

"You think it's connected?"

"Well, of course it's connected."

"No, not like that," Hilary said. "I mean, do you think the two of them have worked this thing up together?"

That was just what Zoe had been thinking. She didn't really believe in coincidence. To her mind, there was always connections; they just weren't always that easy to work out.

"But what would be the point?" she asked.

"You've got me," Hilary said. "You can stay here with me for a few days if you like," she added.

They were sitting in the front room of Hilary's downstairs apartment which was in the front half of one of the old Tudor buildings on the south side of Stanton Street facing the estates. Hilary in this room always reminded Zoe of Mendelssohn's "Concerto in E Minor," a perfect dialogue between soloist and orchestra. Paintings, curtains, carpet and furniture all reflected Hilary's slightly askew worldview so that Impressionists hung side-by-side with paintings that seemed more the work of a camera; an antique sideboard housed a state-of-the-art stereo, glass shelves held old books; the curtains were dark antique flower prints, with sheers trimmed in lace, the carpet a riot of symmetrical designs and primary colors. The recamier on which Hilary was lounging had a glory of leaf and scrollwork in its wood; Zoe's club chair looked as though a bear had been hibernating in it.

Hilary herself was as tall as Zoe's five-ten, but where Zoe was more angular and big-boned, Hilary was all graceful lines with tanned skin that accentuated her blue eyes and the waterfall of her long straight blonde hair. She was dressed in white this morning, wearing a simple cotton shirt and trousers with the casual elegance of a model, and appeared, as she always did, as the perfect centerpiece to the room.

"I think I'll be okay," Zoe said. "Besides, I've always got Rupert to protect me."

At the sound of his name, Rupert lifted his head from the floor by Zoe's feet and gave her a quick, searching glance.

Hilary laughed. "Right. Like he isn't scared of his own shadow."

"He can't help being nervous. He's just—"

"I know. High-strung."

"Did I ever tell you how he jumped right—"

"Into the canal and saved Tommy's dog from drowning

when it fell in? Only about a hundred times since it happened."

Zoe's lips shaped a moue.

"Oh God," Hilary said, starting to laugh. "Don't pout. You know what it does to me when you pout."

Hilary was a talent scout for WEA Records. They'd met three years ago at a record launch party when Hilary had made a pass at her. Once they got past the fact that Zoe preferred men and wasn't planning on changing that preference, they discovered that they had far too much in common not to be good friends. But that didn't stop Hilary from occasionally teasing her, especially when Zoe was complaining about man troubles.

Such troubles were usually far simpler than the one currently in hand.

"What do you think he meant by small deaths?" Zoe asked. "The more I think of it, the more it gives me the creeps."

Hilary nodded. "Isn't sleep sometimes referred to as the little death?"

Zoe could hear Wolfe's voice in her head. *I'm the bringer of small deaths.*

"I don't think that's what he was talking about," she said.

"Maybe it's just his way of saying you're going to have bad dreams. You know, he freaks you out a little, makes you nervous, then bingo—he's a success."

"But why?"

"Creeps don't need reasons for what they do; that's why they're creeps."

Remember me the next time you die a little.

Zoe was back to shivering again.

"Maybe I will stay here," she said, "if you're sure I won't be in your way."

"Be in my way?" Hilary glanced at her watch. "I'm supposed to be at work right now—I've got a meeting in an hour—so you'll have the place to yourself."

"I just hope I can get to sleep."

"Do you want something to help you relax?"

"What, like a sleeping pill?"

Hilary shook her head. "I was thinking more along the lines of some hot milk."

"That'd be lovely."

Zoe didn't sleep well. It wasn't her own bed and the daytime street noises were different from the ones outside her own apartment, but it was mostly the constant replay of last night's two conversations that kept her turning restlessly from one side of the bed to the other. Finally, she just gave up and decided to face the day on less sleep than she normally needed.

She knew she'd been having bad dreams during the few times when she had managed to sleep, but couldn't remember one of them. Padding through the apartment in an oversize T-shirt, she found herself drawn to the front window. She peeked out through the curtains, gaze traveling up and down the length of Stanton Street. When she realized what she was doing—looking for a shock of red hair, dark eyes watching the house—she felt more irritable than ever.

She was not going to let it get to her, she decided. At least not anymore.

A shower woke her up, while breakfast and a long afternoon ramble with Rupert through the grounds of Butler University made her feel a little better, but by the time she got to work at a quarter to twelve that night and started to go through the station's library to collect the music she needed for the show, she was back to being tense and irritable. Halfway through the first hour of the show, she interrupted a Bobby Brown/Ice T/Living Colour set and brought up her voice mike.

"Here's a song for Gordon Wolfe," she said as she cued up an album cut by the local band No Nuns Here. "Memories are made of this, Wolfe."

The long wail of an electric guitar went out over the air waves, a primal screech as the high E string was fingered down around the fourteenth fret and pushed up past the G string, then the bass and drums caught and settled into a driving back beat. The wailing guitar broke into chunky bar chords as Lorio Munn's voice cut across the music like the punch of a fist.

> I don't want your love, baby
> So don't come on so sweet
> I don't need a man, baby
> Treats me like I'm meat
>
> I'm coming to your house, baby
> Coming to your door
> Gonna knock you down, right where you stand
> And stomp you on the floor

Zoe eyed the studio phone. She picked up the handset as soon as the on-line light began to flash. Which one was it going to be? she thought as she spoke into the phone.

"Nightnoise. Zoe B. here."

She kept the call off the air, just in case.

"What the hell do you think you're doing?"

Bingo. It was Bob.

"Tell me about small deaths," she said.

"I *told* you he was dangerous, but you just—"

"You'll get your chance to natter on," Zoe interrupted, "but first I want to know about these small deaths."

Silence on the line was the only reply.

"I don't hear a dial tone," she said, "so I know you're still there. Talk to me."

"I . . . Jesus," Bob said finally.

"Small deaths," Zoe repeated.

After another long hesitation, she heard Bob sigh. "They're those pivotal moments in a person's life that change it forever: a love affair gone wrong, not getting into the right post-graduate program, stealing a car on a dare and getting caught, that kind of thing. They're the moments that some people brood on forever; right now they could have the most successful marriage or career, but they can't stop thinking about the past, about what might have happened if things had gone differently.

"It sours their success, makes them bitter. And usually it leads to more small deaths: depression, stress, heavy drinking or drug use, abusing their spouse or children."

"What are you saying?" Zoe asked. "That a small death's like disappointment?"

"More like a pain, a sorrow, an anger. It doesn't have to be something you do to yourself. Maybe one of your parents died when you were just a kid, or you were abused as a child; that kind of trauma changes a person forever. You can't go through such an experience and grow up to be the same person you would have been without it."

"It sounds like you're just talking about life," Zoe said. "It's got its ups and its downs; to stay sane, you've got to take what it hands you. Ride the punches and maybe try to leave the place in a little better shape than it was before you got there."

What was *with* this conversation? Zoe thought as she was speaking.

As the No Nuns Here cut came to an end, she cued in a version of Carly Simon's "You're So Vain" by Faster Pussycat.

"Jesus," Bob said as the song went out over the air. "You really have a death wish, don't you?"

"Tell me about Gordon Wolfe."

The man's voice echoed in her mind as she spoke his name.

I'm the bringer of small deaths.

"What's he got to do with all of this?" she added.

Remember me the next time you die a little.

"He's a catalyst for bad luck," Bob said. "It's like, being in his company—just being in proximity to him—can bring on a small death. It's like . . . do you remember that character in the *L'il Abner* comic strip—the one who always had a cloud hanging over his head. What was his name?''

''I can't remember.''

''Everywhere he went he brought bad luck.''

''What about him?'' Zoe asked.

''Gordon Wolfe's like that, except you don't see the cloud. You don't get any warning at all. I guess the worst thing is that his effects are completely random—unless he happens to take a dislike to you. Then it's personal.''

''A serial killer of people's hopes,'' Zoe said, half jokingly.

''Exactly.''

''Oh, give me a break.''

''I'm trying to.''

''Yeah, right,'' Zoe said. ''You feed me a crock of shit and then expect me to—''

''I don't think he's human,'' Bob said then.

Zoe wasn't sure what she'd been expecting from this conversation—a confession, perhaps, or even just an apology, but it wasn't this.

''And I don't think you are either,'' he added.

''Oh, please.''

''Why else do you think he was so attracted to you? He recognized something in you—I'm sure of it.''

Wolfe's voice was back in her head.

I feel like I should know you.

''I think we've taken this about as far as it can go,'' Zoe said.

This time she was the one to cut the connection.

The phone's on-line light immediately lit up once more. She hesitated for a long moment, then brought the handset up to her ear.

''I am not bullshitting you,'' Bob said.

''Look, why don't you take it to the tabloids—they'd eat it up.''

''You don't think I've tried? I'd do anything to see him stopped.''

"Why?"

"Because the world's tough enough without having something like him wandering through it, randomly shooting down people's hopes. He's the father of fear. You know what fear stands for? Fuck Everything And Run. You want the whole world to be like that? People screw up their lives enough on their own; they don't need a . . . a *thing* like Wolfe to add to their grief."

The scariest thing, Zoe realized, was that he really sounded sincere.

"So what am I then?" she asked. "The mother of hope?"

"I don't know. But I think you scare *him*."

Zoe had to laugh. Wolfe had her so creeped out she hadn't even been able to go to her own apartment last night, and Bob thought she was the scary one?

"Look, could we meet somewhere?" Bob said.

"I don't think so."

"Somewhere public. Bring along a friend—bring a dozen friends. Face to face, I know I can make you understand."

Zoe thought about it.

"It's important," Bob said. "Look at it this way: if I'm a nut, you've got nothing to lose except some time. But if I'm right, then you'd really be—how did you put it?—leaving the world in a little better shape than it was before you got there. A lot better shape."

"Okay," Zoe said. "Tomorrow noon. I'll be at the main entrance of the Williamson Street Mall."

"Great." Zoe started to hang up, pausing when he added: "And Zoe, cool it with the on-air digs at Wolfe, would you? You don't want to see him pissed."

Zoe hung up.

"Your problem," Hilary said as the two of them sat on the edge of the indoor fountain just inside the main entrance of the Williamson Street Mall, "is that you keep expecting to find a man who's going to solve all of your problems for you."

"Of course. Why didn't I realize that was the problem?"

"You know," Hilary went on, ignoring Zoe's sarcasm. "Like who you are, where you're going, who you want to be."

Rupert sat on his haunches by Zoe's knee, head leaning in towards her as she absently played with the hair on the top of his head.

"So what're you saying?" she asked. "That I should be looking for a woman instead?"

Hilary shook her head. "You've got to find yourself first. Everything else'll follow."

"I'm not looking for a man."

"Right."

"Well, not actively. And besides, what's that got to do with anything?"

"Everything. You wouldn't be in this situation, you wouldn't have all these weird guys coming on to you, if you didn't exude a kind of confusion about your identity. People pick up on that kind of thing, even if the signals are just subliminal. Look at yourself: You're a nice normal-looking woman with terrific skin and hair and great posture. The loony squad shouldn't be hitting on you. Who's that actor you like so much?"

"Mel Gibson."

"Guys like him should be hitting on you. Or at least, guys like your idolized version of him. Who knows what Gibson's really like?"

Over an early breakfast, Zoe had laid out the whole story for her friend. Hilary had been skeptical about meeting with Bob, but when she realized that Zoe was going to keep the rendezvous, with or without her, she'd allowed herself to be talked into coming along. She'd left work early enough to return to her apartment to wake Zoe and then the two of them had taken the subway over to the Mall.

"You think this is all a waste of time, don't you?" Zoe said.

"Don't you?"

Zoe shrugged. A young security guard walked by and eyed the three of them, his gaze lingering longest on Rupert, but he didn't ask them to leave. Maybe he thought Rupert was a seeing-eye dog, Zoe thought. Maybe he just liked the look of Hilary. Most guys did.

Hilary glanced at her watch. "He's five minutes late. Want to bet he's a no-show?"

But Zoe wasn't listening to her. Her gaze was locked on the red-haired man who had just come in off the street.

"What's the matter?" Hilary asked.

"That's him—the red-haired guy."

"I thought you'd never met this Bob."

"I haven't," Zoe said. "That's Gordon Wolfe."

Or was it? Wolfe was still decked out like a highroller on the make, but there was something subtly different about him this afternoon. His carriage, his whole body language had changed.

Zoe was struck with a sudden insight. A long shiver went up her spine. It started out as a low thrum and climbed into a high-pitched, almost piercing note, like Mariah Carey running through all seven of her octaves.

"Hello, Zoe," Wolfe said as he joined them.

Zoe looked up at him, trying to find a physical difference. It was Wolfe, but it wasn't. The voice was the same as the one on the phone, but people could change their voices; a good actor could look like an entirely different person just through the use of his body language.

Wolfe glanced at Hilary, raising his eyebrows questioningly.

"You . . . you're Bob?" Zoe asked.

He nodded. "I know what you're thinking."

"You're twins?"

"It's a little more complicated than that." His gaze flicked to Hilary again. "How much does your friend know?"

"My name's Hilary and Zoe's pretty well filled me in on the whole sorry business."

"That's good."

Hilary shook her head. "No, it isn't. The whole thing sucks. Why don't just pack up your silly game and take it someplace else?"

Rupert stirred by Zoe's feet. The sharpness in Hilary's voice and Zoe's tension brought the rumbling start of a growl to his chest.

"I didn't start anything," Bob said. "Keep your anger for someone who deserves it."

"Like Wolfe," Zoe said.

Bob nodded.

"Your twin."

"It's more like he's my other half," Bob said. "We share the same body, except he doesn't know it. Only I'm aware of the relationship."

"Jesus, would you give us a break," Hilary said. "This is about as lame as that episode of—"

Zoe laid a hand on her friend's knee. "Wait a minute," she said. "You're saying Wolfe's a schizophrene?"

"I'm not sure if that's technically correct," Bob replied.

He sat down on the marble floor in front of them. It made for an incongruous image: an obviously well-heeled executive type sitting cross-legged on the floor like some panhandler.

"I just know that there's two of us in here," he added, touched a hand to his chest.

"You said you went to the tabloids with this story, didn't you?" Zoe asked.

"I tried."

"I can't believe that they weren't interested. When you think of the stuff that they do print . . ."

"Something . . . happened to every reporter I approached. I gave up after the third one."

"What kind of something?" Hilary asked.

Bob sighed. He lifted a hand and began to count on his fingers. "The first one's wife died in a freak traffic accident;

the second had a miscarriage; the third lost his job in disgrace.''

"That kind of thing just happens," Zoe said. "It's awful, but there's no way you or Wolfe could be to blame for any of it.''

"I'd like to believe you, but I know better.''

"Wait a sec," Hilary said. "This happened after you talked to these reporters? What's to stop something from happening to us?''

Zoe glanced at her. "I thought you didn't believe any of this.''

"I don't. Do you?''

Zoe just didn't know anymore. The whole thing sounded preposterous, but she couldn't shake the nagging possibility that he wasn't lying to her. It was the complete sincerity with which he—Bob, Wolfe, whatever his name was—spoke that had her mistrusting her logic. Somehow she just couldn't see that sincerity as being faked. She felt that she was too good a judge of character to be taken in so easily by an act, no matter how good; ludicrous as the situation was, she realized that she'd actually feel better if it was true. At least her judgment wouldn't be in question then.

Of course, if Bob was telling the truth, then that changed all the rules. The world could never be the same again.

"I don't know," she said finally.

"Yeah, well better safe than sorry," Hilary said. She turned her attention back to Bob. "Well?" she asked. "*Are we in danger?*''

"Not at the moment. Zoe negates Wolfe's abilities.''

"Whoa," Hilary said. "I can already see where this is going. You want her to be your shadow so that the big bad Wolfe won't hurt anybody else—right? Jesus, I've heard some lame pick-up lines in my time, but this beats them all, hands down.''

"That's not it at all," Bob said. "He can't hurt Zoe, that's true. And he's already tried. He's exerted tremendous amounts of time and energy since last night in making her life miserable and hasn't seen any success.''

"I don't know about that," Zoe said. "I haven't exactly been having a fun time since I ran into him last night.''

"What I'm worried about," Bob said, going on as though Zoe hadn't spoken, "is that he's now going to turn his attention on her friends.''

"Okay," Zoe said. "This has gone far enough. I'm going to the cops.''

"I'm not threatening you," Bob said as she started to stand up. "I'm just warning you.''

"It sounds like a threat to me, pal.''

"I've spent years looking for some way to stop Wolfe," Bob said. The desperation in his eyes held Zoe captive. "You're the first ray of hope I've found in all that time. He's scared of you.''

"Why? I'm nobody special.''

"I could give you a lecture on how we're all unique individuals, each important in his or her own way," Bob said, "but that's not what we're talking about here. What you are goes beyond that. In some ways, you and Wolfe are much the same, except where he brings pain into people's lives, you heal.''

Zoe shook her head. "Oh, please.''

"I don't think the world is the way we like to think it is," Bob went on. "I don't think it's one solid world, but many, thousands upon thousands of them—as many as there are people—because each person perceives the world in his or her own way; each lives in his or her own world. Sometimes they connect, for a moment, or more rarely, for a lifetime, but mostly we are alone, each living in our own world, suffering our small deaths.''

"This is stupid," Zoe said.

But she was still held captive by his sincerity. She heard a kind of mystical backdrop to what he was saying, a breathy sound that reminded her of an LP they had in the station's library of R. Carlos Nakai playing a traditional Native American flute.

"I believe you're an easy person to meet," Bob said. "The kind of person that people are drawn to talk to—especially by those who are confused, or hurt, or lost. You give them hope. You help them heal."

Zoe continued to shake her head. "I'm not any of that."

"I'm not so sure he's wrong," Hilary said.

Zoe gave her friend a sour look.

"Well, think about it," Hilary said. "The weird and the wacky are always drawn to you. And that show of yours. There's no way that Nightnoise should work—it's just too bizarre a mix. I can't see headbangers sitting through the opera you play, classical buffs putting up with rap, but they do. It's the most popular show in its time slot."

"Yeah, right. Like it's got so much competition at that hour of the night."

"That's just it," Hilary said. "It does have competition, but people still tune in to you."

"Not fifteen minutes ago, you were telling me that the reason I get all these weird people coming on to me is because I'm putting out confused vibes."

Hilary nodded. "I think I was wrong."

"Oh, for God's sake."

"You do help people," Hilary said. "I've seen some of your fan mail and then there's all of those people who are constantly calling in. You help them, Zoe. You really do."

This was just too much for Zoe.

"Why are you saying all of this?" she asked Hilary. "Can't you hear what it sounds like?"

"I know. It sounds ridiculous. But at the same time, I think it makes its own kind of sense. All those people are turning to you for help. I don't think they expect you to solve all of their problems; they just want that touch of hope that you give them."

"I think Wolfe's asking for your help, too," Bob said.

"Oh, really?" Zoe said. "And how am I supposed to do that? Find you and him a good shrink?"

"In the old days," Hilary said, "there were people who could drive out demons just by a laying on of the hands."

Zoe looked from Hilary to Bob and realized that they were both serious. A smartass remark was on the tip of her tongue, but this time she just let it die unspoken.

A surreal quality had taken hold of the afternoon, as though the Academy of St. Martin-in-the-Fields was playing Hendrix, or Captain Beefheart was doing a duet with Tiffany. The light in the Mall seemed incandescent. The air was hot on her skin, but she could feel a chill all the way down to the marrow of her bones.

I don't want this to be real, she realized.

But she knelt down in front of Bob and reached out her hands, laying a palm on either temple.

What now? she thought. Am I supposed to reel off some gibberish to make it sound like a genuine exorcism?

She felt so dumb, she—

The change caught her completely by surprise, stunning her thoughts and the ever-playing soundtrack that ran through her mind into silence. A tingle like static electricity built up in her fingers.

She was looking directly at Bob, but suddenly it seemed as though she was looking through him, directly into him, into the essence of him. It was flesh and blood that lay under her hands, but rainbowing swirls of light were all she could see. A small sound of wonder sighed from between her lips at the sight.

We're all made of light, she thought. Sounds and light, cells vibrating . . .

But when she looked more closely, she could see that under her hands the play of lights was threaded with discordances. As soon as she noticed them, the webwork of dark threads coalesced into a pebble-sized oval of shadow that fell through the swirl of lights, down, down, until it was gone. The rainbowing pattern of the lights was unblemished now, the lights faded, became flesh and bone and skin, and then she was just holding Bob's head in her hands once more.

The tingle left her fingers and she dropped her hands. Bob smiled at her.

"Thank you," he said.

That sense of sincerity remained, but it wasn't Bob's voice anymore. It was Wolfe's.

"Be careful," he added.

"What do you mean?" she asked.

"I was like you once."

"Like me how?"

"Just be careful," he said.

She tilted her head back as he rose to his feet, gaze tracking him as he walked away, across the marble floor and through the doors of the Mall. He didn't open the doors, he just stepped through the glass and steel out into the street and continued off across the pavement. A half-dozen yards from the entrance, he simply faded away like a video effect and was gone.

Zoe shook her head.

"No," she said softly. "I don't want to believe this."

"Believe what?" Hilary asked.

Zoe turned to look at her. "You didn't see what happened?"

"Happened where?"

"Bob."

"He's finally here?" Hilary looked around at the passersby. "I was so sure he was going to pull a no-show."

"No, he's not here," Zoe said. "He . . ."

Her voice trailed off as the realization hit home. She was on her own with this. What had happened? If she took it all at face value, she realized that meeting Wolfe *had* brought her a small death after all—the death of the world the way it had been to the way she now knew it to be. It was changed forever. *She* was changed forever. She carried a responsibility now of which she'd never been aware before.

Why didn't Hilary remember the encounter? Probably because it would have been the same small death for her as it had been for Zoe herself; her world would have been changed forever.

But I've negated that for her, Zoe thought. Just like I did for Wolfe, or Bob, or whoever he really was.

Her gaze dropped to the floor where he'd been sitting and saw a small black pebble lying on the marble. She hesitated for a moment, then reached over and picked it up. Her fingers tingled again and she watched in wonder as the pebble went from black, through grey, until it was a milky white.

"What've you got there?" Hilary asked.

Zoe shook her head. She closed her fingers around the small smooth stone, savoring its odd warmth.

"Nothing," she said. "Just a pebble."

She got up and sat beside Hilary again.

"Excuse me, miss?"

The security guard had returned and this time he wasn't ignoring Rupert.

"I'm sorry," he said, "but I'm afraid you'll have to take your dog outside. It's the mall management's rules."

"Yes," Zoe said. "Of course."

She gave him a quick smile which the guard returned with more warmth than Zoe thought was warranted. It was as though she'd propositioned him or something.

Jesus, she thought. Was she going to go through the rest of her life second-guessing every encounter she ever had? Does he know, does she? Life was tough enough without having to feel self-conscious every time she met somebody. Maybe this was what Wolfe had meant when he said that he had been just like her once. Maybe the pressure just got to be too much for him and it turned him from healing to hurting.

Just be careful.

It seemed possible. It seemed more than possible when she remembered the gratitude she'd seen in his eyes when he'd thanked her.

Beside her, Hilary looked at her watch. "We might as

well go," she said. "This whole thing's a washout. It's almost twelve-thirty. If he was going to come, he'd've been here by now."

Zoe nodded her head.

"See the thing is," Hilary said as they started for the door, Rupert walking in between them, "a guy like that can't face an actual confrontation. If you ask me, you're never going to hear from him again."

"I think you're right," Zoe said.

But there might be others, changing, already changed. She might become one of them herself if she wasn't—

just be

Her fingers tightened around the white pebble she'd picked up. She stuck it in the front pocket of her jeans as a token to remind her of what had happened to Wolfe, of how it could just as easily happen to her if she wasn't

—*careful.*

THE MOON IS DROWNING
⌒ · WHILE I SLEEP · ⌒

If you keep your mind sufficiently open, people will throw a lot of rubbish into it.

—WILLIAM A. ORTON

1

ONCE UPON A time there was what there was, and if nothing had happened there would be nothing to tell.

2

It was my father who told me that dreams want to be real. When you start to wake up, he said, they hang on and try to slip out into the waking world when you don't notice. Very strong dreams, he added, can almost do it; they can last for almost half a day, but not much longer.

I asked him if any ever made it. If any of the people our subconscious minds toss up and make real while we're sleeping had ever actually stolen out into this world from the dream world.

He knew of at least one that had, he said.

He had that kind of lost look in his eyes that made me think of my mother. He always looked like that when he talked about her, which wasn't often.

Who was it? I asked, hoping he'd dole out another little tidbit about my mother. Is it someone I know?

Even as I asked, I was wondering how he related my mother to a dream. He'd at least known her. I didn't have any memories, just imaginings. Dreams.

But he only shook his head. Not really, he told me. It happened a long time ago. But I often wondered, he added almost to himself, what did *she* dream of?

That was a long time ago and I don't know if he ever found out. If he did, he never told me. But lately I've been wondering about it. I think maybe they don't dream. I think that if they do, they get pulled back into the dream world.

And if we're not too careful, they can pull us back with them.

3

"I've been having the strangest dreams," Sophie Etoile said, more as an observation than a conversational opener.

She and Jilly Coppercorn had been enjoying a companionable silence while they sat on the stone river wall in the old part of Lower Crowsea's Market. The wall is by a small public courtyard, surrounded on three sides by old three-story brick and stone town houses, peaked with mansard roofs, the dormer windows thrusting out from the walls like hooded eyes with heavy brows. The buildings date back over a hundred years, leaning against each other like old friends too tired to talk, just taking comfort from each other's presence.

The cobblestoned streets that web out from the courtyard are narrow, too tight a fit for a car, even the small imported makes. They twist and turn, winding in and around the buildings more like back alleys than thoroughfares. If you have any sort of familiarity with the area you can maze your way by those lanes to find still smaller courtyards, hidden and private, and deeper still, secret gardens.

There are more cats in Old Market than anywhere else in Newford and the air smells different. Though it sits just a few blocks west of some of the city's principal thoroughfares, you can hardly hear the traffic, and you can't smell it at all. No exhaust, no refuse, no dead air. In Old Market it always seems to smell of fresh bread baking, cabbage soups, frying fish, roses and those tart, sharp-tasting apples that make the best strudels.

Sophie and Jilly were bookended by stairs going down to the Kickaha River on either side of them. Pale yellow light from the streetlamp behind them put a glow on their hair, haloing each with her own nimbus of light—Jilly's darker, all loose tangled curls, Sophie's a soft auburn, hanging in ringlets. They each had a similar slim build, though Sophie was somewhat bustier.

In the half-dark of the streetlamp's murky light, their small figures could almost be taken for each other, but when the light touched their features as they turned to talk to each other, Jilly could be seen to have the quick, clever features of a Rackham pixie, while Sophie's were softer, as though rendered by Rossetti or Burne-Jones.

Though similarly dressed with paint-stained smocks over loose T-shirts and baggy cotton pants, Sophie still managed to look tidy, while Jilly could never seem to help a slight tendency towards scruffiness. She was the only one of the two with paint in her hair.

''What sort of dreams?'' she asked.

It was almost four o'clock in the morning. The narrow

streets of Old Market lay empty and still about them, except for the odd prowling cat, and cats can be like the hint of a whisper when they want, ghosting and silent, invisible presences. The two women had been working at Sophie's studio on a joint painting, a collaboration that was going to combine Jilly's precise delicate work with Sophie's current penchant for bright flaring colors and loosely rendered figures.

Neither was sure the experiment would work, but they'd been enjoying themselves immensely with it, so it really didn't matter.

"Well, they're sort of serial," Sophie said. "You know, where you keep dreaming about the same place, the same people, the same events, except each night you're a little further along in the story."

Jilly gave her an envious look. "I've always wanted to have that kind of dream. Christy's had them. I think he told me that it's called lucid dreaming."

"They're anything but lucid," Sophie said. "If you ask me, they're downright strange."

"No, no. It just means that you know you're dreaming, *when* you're dreaming, and have some kind of control over what happens in the dream."

Sophie laughed. "I wish."

4

I'm wearing a long pleated skirt and one of those white cotton peasant blouses that's cut way too low in the bodice. I don't know why. I hate that kind of bodice. I keep feeling like I'm going to fall out whenever I bend over. Definitely designed by a man. Wendy likes to wear that kind of thing from time to time, but it's not for me.

Nor is going barefoot. Especially not here. I'm standing on a path, but it's muddy underfoot, all squishy between my toes. It's sort of nice in some ways, but I keep getting the feeling that something's going to sidle up to me, under the mud, and brush against my foot, so I don't want to move, but I don't want to just stand here either.

Everywhere I look it's all marsh. Low flat fens, with just the odd crack willow or alder trailing raggedy vines the way you see Spanish moss do in pictures of the Everglades, but this definitely isn't Florida. It feels more Englishy, if that makes sense.

I know if I step off the path I'll be in muck up to my knees.

I can see a dim kind of light off in the distance, way off the path. I'm attracted to it, the way any light in the darkness seems to call out, welcoming you, but I don't want to brave the deeper mud or the pools of still water that glimmer in the pale starlight.

It's all mud and reeds, cattails, bulrushes and swamp grass and I just want to be back home in bed, but I can't wake up. There's a funny smell in the air, a mix of things rotting and stagnant water. I feel like there's something horrible in the shadows under those strange overhung trees—especially the willows, the tall sharp leaves of sedge and water plantain growing thick around their trunks. It's like there are eyes watching me from all sides, dark misshapen heads floating frog-like in the water, only the eyes showing, staring. Quicks and bogles and dark things.

I hear something move in the tangle of bulrushes and bur-reeds just a few feet away. My heart's in my throat, but I move a little closer to see that it's only a bird caught in some kind of a net.

Hush, I tell it and move closer.

The bird gets frantic when I put my hand on the netting. It starts to peck at my fingers, but I keep talking softly to it until it finally settles down. The net's a mess of knots and tangles and I can't work too quickly because I don't want to hurt the bird.

You should leave him be, a voice says, and I turn to find an old woman standing on the path beside me. I don't know where she came from. Every time I lift one of my feet it makes this creepy sucking sound, but I never even heard her approach.

She looks like the wizened old crone in that painting Jilly did for Geordie when he got onto this kick of learning fiddle tunes with the word "hag" in the title: "The Hag in the Kiln," "Old Hag You Have Killed Me," "The Hag With the Money" and god knows how many more.

Just like in the painting, she's wizened and small and bent over and . . . dry. Like kindling, like the pages of an old book. Like she's almost all used up. Hair thin, body thinner. But then you look into her eyes and they're so alive it makes you feel a little dizzy.

Helping such as he will only bring you grief, she says.

I tell her that I can't just leave it.

She looks at me for a long moment, then shrugs. So be it, she says.

I wait a moment, but she doesn't seem to have anything else to say, so I go back to freeing the bird. But now, where a moment ago the netting was a hopeless tangle, it just seems to unknot itself as soon as I lay my hand on it. I'm careful when I put my fingers around the bird and pull it free. I get it out of the tangle and then toss it up in the air. It circles above me in the air, once, twice, three times, cawing. Then it flies away.

It's not safe here, the old lady says then.

I'd forgotten all about her. I get back onto the path, my legs smeared with smelly dark mud.

What do you mean? I ask her.

When the Moon still walked the sky, she says, why it was safe then. The dark things didn't like her light and fair fell over themselves to get away when she shone. But they're bold now, tricked and trapped her, they have, and no one's safe. Not you, not me. Best we were away.

Trapped her? I repeat like an echo. The moon?

She nods.

Where?

She points to the light I saw earlier, far out in the fens.

They've drowned her under the Black Snag, she says. I will show you.

She takes my hand before I realize what she's doing and pulls me through the rushes and reeds, the mud squishing awfully under my bare feet, but it doesn't seem to bother her at all. She stops when we're at the edge of some open water.

Watch now, she says.

She takes something from the pocket of her apron and tosses it into the water. It's like a small stone, or a pebble or something, and it enters the water without a sound, without making a ripple. Then the water starts to glow and a picture forms in the dim flickering light.

It's like we have a bird's eye view of the fens for a moment, then the focus comes in sharp on the edge of a big still pool, sentried by a huge dead willow. I don't know how I know it, because the light's still poor, but the mud's black around its shore. It almost swallows the pale wan glow coming up from out of the water.

Drowning, the old woman says. The moon is drowning.

I look down at the image that's formed on the surface and I see a woman floating there. Her hair's all spread out from her, drifting in the water like lily roots. There's a great big stone on top of her torso so she's only really visible from the breasts up. Her shoulders are slightly sloped, neck slender, with a swan's curve, but not so long. Her face is in repose, as though she's sleeping, but she's underwater, so I know she's dead.

She looks like me.

I turn to the old woman, but before I can say anything, there's movement all around us. Shadows pull away from trees, rise from the stagnant pools, change from vague blotches of darkness, into moving shapes, limbed and headed, pale eyes glowing with menace. The old woman pulls me back onto the path.

Wake quick! she cries.

She pinches my arm—hard, sharp. It really hurts. And then I'm sitting up in my bed.

5

"And did you have a bruise on your arm from where she pinched you?" Jilly asked.

Sophie shook her head and smiled. Trust Jilly. Who else was always looking for the magic in a situation?

"Of course not," she said. "It was just a dream."

"But . . ."

"Wait," Sophie said. "There's more."

Something suddenly hopped onto the wall between them and they both started, until they realized it was only a cat.

"Silly puss," Sophie said as it walked towards her and began to butt its head against her arm. She gave it a pat.

6

The next night I'm standing by my window, looking out at the street, when I hear movement behind me. I turn and it isn't my apartment any more. It's like the inside of an old barn, heaped up with straw in a big tidy pile against one wall. There's a lit lantern swinging from a low rafter beam, a dusty but pleasant smell in the air, a cow or maybe a horse making some kind of nickering sound in a stall at the far end.

And there's a guy standing there in the lantern light, a half dozen feet away from me, not doing anything, just looking at me. He's drop-down gorgeous. Not too thin, not too muscle-bound. A friendly open face with a wide smile and eyes to kill for—long moody lashes, and the irises are the color of violets. His hair's thick and dark, long in the back with a cowlick hanging down over his brow that I just want to reach out and brush back.

I'm sorry, he says. I didn't mean to startle you.

That's okay, I tell him.

And it is. I think maybe I'm already getting used to all the to-and-froing.

He smiles. My name's Jeck Crow, he says.

I don't know why, but all of a sudden I'm feeling a little weak in the knees. Ah, who am I kidding? I know why.

What are you doing here? he asks.

I tell him I was standing in my apartment, looking for the moon, but then I remembered that I'd just seen the last quarter a few nights ago and I wouldn't be able to see it tonight.

He nods. She's drowning, he says, and then I remember the old woman from last night.

I look out the window and see the fens are out there. It's dark and creepy and I can't see the distant glow of the woman drowned in the pool from here the way I could last night. I shiver and Jeck comes over all concerned. He's picked up a blanket that was hanging from one of the support beams and he lays it across my shoulders. He leaves his arm there, to keep it in place, and I don't mind. I just sort of lean into him, like we've always been together. It's weird. I'm feeling drowsy and safe and incredibly aroused, all at the same time.

He looks out the window with me, his hip against mine, the press of his arm on my shoulder a comfortable weight, his body radiating heat.

It used to be, he says, that she would walk every night until she grew so weak that her light was almost failing. Then she would leave the world to go to another, into Faerie, it's said, or at least to a place where the darkness doesn't hide quicks and bogles, and there she would rejuvenate herself for her return. We would have three nights of darkness, when evil owned the night, but then we'd see the glow of her lantern approaching and the haunts would flee her light and we could visit with one another again when the day's work was done.

He leans his head against mine, his voice going dreamy.

I remember my mam saying once, how the Moon lived another life in those three days. How time moves differently in Faerie so that what was a day for us, might be a month for her in that place.

He pauses, then adds, I wonder if they miss her in that other world.

I don't know what to say. But then I realize it's not the kind of conversation in which I have to say anything.

He turns to me, head lowering until we're looking straight into each other's eyes. I get lost in the violet and suddenly I'm in his arms and we're kissing. He guides me, step by sweet step, backward towards that heap of straw. We've got the blanket under us and this time I'm glad I'm wearing the long skirt and peasant blouse again, because they come off so easily.

His hands and his mouth are so gentle and they're all over me like moth wings brushing my skin. I don't know how to describe what he's doing to me. It isn't anything that other lovers haven't done to me before, but the way Jeck does it has me glowing, my skin all warm and tingling with this deep slow burn starting up deep between my legs and just firing up along every one of my nerve ends.

I can hear myself making moaning sounds and then he's inside me, his breathing heavy in my ear. All I can feel and smell is him. My hips are grinding against his and we're synched into this perfect rhythm and then I wake up in my own bed and I'm all tangled up in the sheets with my hand between my legs, finger tip right on the spot, moving back and forth and back and forth. . . .

7

Sophie fell silent.

"Steamy," Jilly said after a moment.

Sophie gave a little bit of an embarrassed laugh. "You're telling me. I get a little squirmy just thinking about it. And that night—I was still so fired up when I woke that I couldn't think straight. I just went ahead and finished and then lay there afterwards, completely spent. I couldn't even move."

"You know a guy named Jack Crow, don't you?" Jilly asked.

"Yeah, he's the one who's got that tattoo parlor down on Palm Street. I went out with him a couple of times, but—" Sophie shrugged "—you know. Things just didn't work out."

"That's right. You told me that all he ever wanted to do was to give you tattoos."

Sophie shook her head, remembering. "In private places so only he and I would know they were there. Boy."

The cat had fallen asleep, body sprawled out on her lap, head pressed tight up against her stomach. A deep resonant purr rose up from him. Sophie just hoped he didn't have fleas.

"But the guy in my dream was nothing like Jack," she said. "And besides, his name was Jeck."

"What kind of a name *is* that?"

"A dream name."

"So did you see him again—the next night?"

Sophie shook her head. "Though not from lack of interest on my part."

8

The third night I find myself in this one-room cottage out of a fairy tale. You know, there's dried herbs hanging everywhere, a big hearth considering the size of the place, with black iron pots and a kettle sitting on the hearth stones, thick hand-woven rugs underfoot, a small tidy little bed in one corner, a cloak hanging by the door, a rough set of a table and two chairs by a shuttered window.

The old lady is sitting on one of the chairs.

There you are, she says. I looked for you to come last night, but I couldn't find you.

I'm getting so used to this dreaming business by now that I'm not at all weirded out, just kind of accepting it all, but I am a little disappointed to find myself here, instead of in the barn.

I was with Jeck, I say and then she frowns, but she doesn't say anything.

Do you know him? I ask.

Too well.

Is there something wrong with him?

I'm feeling a little flushed, just talking about him. So far as I'm concerned, there's nothing wrong with him at all.

He's not trustworthy, the old lady finally says.

I shake my head. He seems to be just as upset about the drowned lady as you are. He told me all about her—how she used to go into Faerie and that kind of thing

She never went into Faerie.

Well then, where did she go?

The old lady shakes her head. Crows talk too much, she says and I can't tell if she means the birds, or a whole bunch of Jecks. Thinking about the latter gives me goosebumps. I can barely stay clear-headed around Jeck; a whole crowd of him would probably overload all my circuits and leave me lying on the floor like a little pool of jelly.

I don't tell the old lady any of this. Jeck inspired confidences, as much as sensuality; she does neither.

Will you help us? she says instead.

I sit down at the table with her and ask, Help with what?

The Moon, she says.

I shake my head. I don't understand. You mean the drowned lady in the pool?

Drowned, the old lady says, but not dead. Not yet.

I start to argue the point, but then realize where I am. It's a dream and anything can happen, right?

It needs you to break the bogles' spell, the old lady goes on.

Me? But—

Tomorrow night, go to sleep with a stone in your mouth and a hazel twig in your hands. Now mayhap, you'll find yourself back here, mayhap with your crow, but guard you don't say a word, not one word. Go out into the fen until you find a coffin, and on that coffin a candle, and then look sideways and you'll see that you're in the place I showed you yesternight.

She falls silent.

And then what am I supposed to do? I ask.

What needs to be done.

But—

I'm tired, she says.

She waves her hand at me and I'm back in my own bed again.

9

"And so?" Jilly asked. "Did you do it?"

"Would you have?"

"In a moment," Jilly said. She sidled closer along the wall until she was right beside Sophie and peered into her friend's face. "Oh don't tell me you didn't do it. Don't tell me that's the whole story."

"The whole thing just seemed silly," Sophie said.

"Oh, please!"

"Well, it did. It was all too oblique and riddlish. I know it was just a dream, so that it didn't have to make sense, but there was so much of a coherence to a lot of it that when it did get incomprehensible, it just didn't seem . . . oh, I don't know. Didn't seem fair, I suppose."

"But you *did* do it?"

Sophie finally relented.

"Yes," she said.

10

I go to sleep with a small smooth stone in my mouth and have the hardest time getting to sleep because I'm sure I'm going to swallow it during the night and choke. And I have the hazel twig as well, though I don't know what help either of them is going to be.

Hazel twig to ward you from quicks and bogles, I hear Jeck say. And the stone to remind you of your own world, of the difference between waking and dream, else you might find yourself sharing the Moon's fate.

We're standing on a sort of grassy knoll, an island of semi-solid ground, but the footing's still spongy. I start to say hello, but he puts his finger to his lips.

She's old, is Granny Weather, he says, and cranky, too, but there's more magic in one of her toenails than most of us will find in a lifetime.

I never really thought about his voice before. It's like velvet, soft and smooth, but not effeminate. It's too resonant for that.

He puts his hands on my shoulders and I feel like melting.

I close my eyes, lift my face to his, but he turns me around until I'm leaning against his back. He cups his hands around my breasts and kisses me on the nape of my neck. I lean back against him, but he lifts his mouth to my ear.

You must go, he says softly, his breath tickling the inside of my ear. Into the fens.

I pull free from his embrace and face him. I start to say, Why me? Why do I have to go alone? But before I can get a word out he has his hand across my mouth.

Trust Granny Weather, he says. And trust me. This is something only you can do. Whether you do it or not, is your choice. But if you mean to try tonight, you mustn't speak. You must go out into the fens and find her. They will tempt you and torment you, but you must ignore them, else they'll have you drowning too, under the Black Snag.

I look at him and I know he can see the need I have for him because in his eyes I can see the same need for me reflected in their violet depths.

I will wait for you, he says. If I can.

I don't like the sound of that. I don't like the sound of any of it, but I tell myself again, it's just a dream, so I finally nod. I start to turn away, but he catches hold of me for a last moment and kisses me. There's a hot rush of tongues touching, arms tight around each other, before he finally steps back.

I love the strength of you, he says.

I don't want to go, I want to change the rules of the dream, but I get this feeling that if I do, if I change one thing, everything'll change, and maybe he won't even exist in whatever comes along to replace it. So I lift my hand and run it along the side of his face, I take a long last drink of those deep violet eyes that just want to swallow me, then I get brave and turn away again.

And this time I go into the fens.

I'm nervous, but I guess that goes without saying. I look back, but I can't see Jeck anymore. I can just feel I'm being watched, and it's not by him. I clutch my little hazel twig tighter, roll the stone around from one side of my mouth to the other, and keep going.

It's not easy. I have to test each step to make sure I'm not just going to sink away forever into the muck. I start thinking of what you hear about dreams, how if you die in a dream, you die for real, that's why you always wake up just in time. Except for those people who die in their sleep, I guess.

I don't know how long I'm slogging through the muck. My arms and legs have dozens of little nicks and cuts—you never think of how sharp the edge of a reed can be until your skin slides across one. It's like a paper cut, sharp and quick, and it stings like hell. I don't suppose all the muck's doing the cuts much good either. The only thing I can be happy about is that there aren't any bugs.

Actually, there doesn't seem to be the sense of anything living at all in the fens, just me, on my own. But I know I'm not alone. It's like a word sitting on the tip of your tongue. I can't see or hear or sense anything, but I'm being watched.

I think of Jeck and Granny Weather, of what they say the darkness hides. Quicks and bogles and haunts.

After awhile I almost forget what I'm doing out here. I'm just stumbling along with a feeling of dread hanging over me that just won't go away. Bogbean and water mint leaves feel like cold wet fingers sliding along my legs. I hear the occasional flutter of wings, and sometimes a deep kind of sighing moan, but I never see anything.

I'm just about played out when suddenly I come up upon this tall rock under the biggest crack willow I've seen so far. The tree's dead, drooping leafless branches into the still water around the stone. The stone rises out of the water at a slant, the mud's all really black underfoot, the marsh is, if anything, even quieter here, expectant, almost, and I get the feeling like something—some*things* are closing in all around me.

I start to walk across the dark mud to the other side of the rock until I hit a certain vantage point. I stop when I can see that it's shaped like a big strange coffin and I remember what Granny Weather told me. I look for the candle and I see a tiny light flickering at the very top of the black stone, right where it's pushed up and snagged among the dangling branches of the dead willow. It's no brighter than a firefly's glow, but it burns steady.

I do what Granny Weather told me and look around myself using my peripheral vision. I don't see anything at first, but as I slowly turn towards the water, I catch just a hint of a glow in the water. I stop and then I wonder what to do. Is it still going to be there if I turn to face it?

Eventually, I move sideways towards it, always keeping it in the corner of my eye. The closer I get, the brighter it starts to glow, until I'm standing hip deep in the cold water, the mud sucking at my feet, and it's all around me, this dim eerie glowing. I look down into the water and I see my own face reflected back at me, but then I realize that it's not me I'm seeing, it's the drowned woman, the moon, trapped under the stone.

I stick my hazel twig down the bodice of my blouse and reach into the water. I have to bend down, the dark water licking at my shoulders and chin and smelling something awful, but I finally touch the woman's shoulder. Her skin's warm against my fingers and for some reason that makes me feel braver. I get a grip with one hand on her shoulder, then the other, and give a pull.

Nothing budges.

I try some more, moving a little deeper into the water. Finally I plunge my head under and get a really good hold, but she simply won't move. The rock's got her pressed down tight, and the willow's got the rock snagged, and dream or no dream, I'm not some kind of superwoman. I'm only so strong and I have to breathe.

I come up spluttering and choking on the foul water.

And then I hear the laughter.

I look up and there's these things all around the edge of the pool. Quicks and bogles and small monsters. All eyes and teeth and spindly black limbs and crooked hands with too many joints to the fingers. The tree is full of crows and their cawing adds to the mocking hubbub of sound.

First got one, now got two, a pair of voices chant. Boil her up in a tiddy stew.

I'm starting to shiver—not just because I'm scared, which I am, but because the water's so damn cold. The haunts just keep on laughing and making up these creepy little rhymes that mostly have to do with little stews and barbecues. And then suddenly, they all fall silent and these three figures come swinging down from the willow's boughs.

I don't know where they came from, they're just there all of a sudden. These aren't haunts, nor quicks nor bogles. They're men and they look all too familiar.

Ask for anything, one of them says, and it will be yours.

It's Jeck, I realize. Jeck talking to me, except the voice doesn't sound right. But it looks just like him. All three look like him.

I remember Granny Weather telling me that Jeck was untrustworthy, but then Jeck told me to trust her. And to trust him. Looking at these three Jecks, I don't know what to think anymore. My head starts to hurt and I just wish I could wake up.

You need only tell us what it is you want, one of the Jecks says, and we will give it to you. There should be no enmity between us. The woman is drowned. She is dead. You have come too late. There is nothing you can do for her now. But you can do something for yourself. Let us gift you with your heart's desire.

My heart's desire, I think.

I tell myself, again, it's just a dream, but I can't help the way I start thinking about what I'd ask for if I could really have anything I wanted, anything at all.

I look down into the water at the drowned woman and I think about my dad. He never liked to talk about my mother. It's like she was just a dream, he said once.

And maybe she was, I find myself thinking as my gaze

goes down into the water and I study the features of the drowned woman who looks so much like me. Maybe she was the Moon in this world and she came to ours to rejuvenate, but when the time came for her to go back, she didn't want to leave because she loved me and dad too much. Except she didn't have a choice.

So when she returned, she was weaker, instead of stronger like she was supposed to be, because she was so sad. And that's how the quicks and the bogles trapped her.

I laugh then. What I'm making up, as I stand here waist-deep in smelly dream water, is the classic abandoned child's scenario. They always figure that there was just a mix-up, that one day their real parents are going to show up and take them away to some place where everything's magical and loving and perfect.

I used to feel real guilty about my mother leaving us— that's something else that happens when you're just a kid in that kind of a situation. You just automatically feel guilty when something bad happens, like it's got to be your fault. But I got older. I learned to deal with it. I learned that I was a good person, that it hadn't been my fault, that my dad was a good person, too, and it wasn't his fault either.

I'd still like to know why my mother left us, but I came to understand that whatever the reasons were for her going, they had to do with her, not with us. Just like I know this is only a dream and the drowned woman might look like me, but that's just something I'm projecting onto her. I *want* her to be my mother. I want her having abandoned me and dad not to have been her fault either. I want to come to her rescue and bring us all back together again.

Except it isn't going to happen. Pretend and real just don't mix.

But it's tempting all the same. It's tempting to let it all play out. I know the haunts just want me to talk so that they can trap me as well, that they wouldn't follow through on any promise they made, but this is *my* dream. I can *make* them keep to their promise. All I have to do is say what I want.

And then I understand that it's all real after all. Not real in the sense that I can be physically harmed in this place, but real in that if I make a selfish choice, even if it's just in a dream, I'll still have to live with the fact of it when I wake up. It doesn't matter that I'm dreaming, I'll *still* have done it.

What the bogles are offering is my heart's desire, if I just leave the Moon to drown. But if I do that, I'm responsible for her death. She might not be real, but it doesn't change anything at all. It'll still mean that I'm willing to let someone die, just so I can have my own way.

I suck on the stone and move it back and forth from one cheek to the other. I reach down into my wet bodice and pluck out the hazel twig from where it got pushed down between my breasts. I lift a hand to my hair and brush it back from my face and then I look at those sham copies of my Jeck Crow and I smile at them.

My dream, I think. What I say goes.

I don't know if it's going to work, but I'm fed up with having everyone else decide what happens in my dream. I turn to the stone and I put my hands upon it, the hazel twig sticking out between the fingers of my right hand, and I give the stone a shove. There's this great big outcry among the quicks and bogles and haunts as the stone starts to topple over. I look down at the drowned woman and I see her eyes open, I see her smile, but then there's too much light and I'm blinded.

When my vision finally clears, I'm alone by the pool. There's a big fat full moon hanging in the sky, making the fens almost as bright as day. They've all fled, the monsters, the quicks and bogles and things. The dead willow's still full of crows, but as soon as I look up, they lift from the tree in an explosion of dark wings, a circling murder, cawing and crying, until they finally go away. The stone's lying on its side, half in the water, half out.

And I'm still dreaming.

I'm standing here, up to my waist in the smelly water, with a hazel twig in my hand and a stone in my mouth, and I stare up at that big full moon until it seems I can feel her light just singing through my veins. For a moment it's like being back in the barn with Jeck, I'm just on fire, but it's a different kind of fire, it burns away the darknesses that have gotten lodged in me over the years, just like they get lodged in everybody, and just for that moment, I'm solid light, innocent and newborn, a burning Midsummer fire in the shape of a woman.

And then I wake up, back home again.

I lie there in my bed and look out the window, but it's still the dark of the moon in our world. The streets are quiet outside, there's a hush over the whole city, and I'm lying here with a hazel twig in my hand, a stone in my mouth, pushed up into one cheek, and a warm burning glow deep inside.

I sit up and spit the stone out into my hand. I walk over to the window. I'm not in some magical dream now; I'm in the real world. I know the lighted moon glows with light borrowed from the sun. That she's still out there in the dark of the moon, we just can't see her tonight because the earth is between her and the sun.

Or maybe she's gone into some other world, to replenish her lantern before she begins her nightly trek across the sky once more.

I feel like I've learned something, but I'm not sure what. I'm not sure what any of it means.

11

"How can you say that?" Jilly said. "God, Sophie, it's so obvious. She really *was* your mother and you really *did* save her. As for Jeck, he was the bird you rescued in your first dream. Jeck *Crow*—don't you get it? One of the bad guys, only you won him over with an act of kindness. It all makes perfect sense."

Sophie slowly shook her head. "I suppose I'd like to believe that, too," she said, "but what we want and what really is aren't always the same thing."

"But what about Jeck? He'll be waiting for you. And Granny Weather? They both knew you were the Moon's daughter all along. It all means something."

Sophie sighed. She stroked the sleeping cat on her lap, imagining for a moment that it was the soft dark curls of a crow that could be a man, in a land that only existed in her dreams.

"I guess," she said, "it means I need a new boyfriend."

12

Jilly's a real sweetheart, and I love her dearly, but she's naive in some ways. Or maybe it's just that she wants to play the ingenue. She's always so ready to believe anything that anyone tells her, so long as it's magical.

Well, I believe in magic, too, but it's the magic that can turn a caterpillar into a butterfly, the natural wonder and beauty of the world that's all around me. I can't believe in some dreamland being real. I can't believe what Jilly now insists is true: that I've got faerie blood, because I'm the daughter of the Moon.

Though I have to admit that I'd like to.

* * *

I never do get to sleep that night. I prowl around the apartment, drinking coffee to keep me awake. I'm afraid to go to sleep, afraid I'll dream and that it'll all be real.

Or maybe that it won't.

When it starts to get light, I take a long cold shower, because I've been thinking about Jeck again. I guess if my making the wrong decision in a dream would've had ramifications in the waking world, then there's no reason that a rampaging libido shouldn't carry over as well.

I get dressed in some old clothes I haven't worn in years, just to try to recapture a more innocent time. White blouse, faded jeans, and hightops with this smoking jacket overtop that used to belong to my dad. It's made of burgundy velvet with black satin lapels. A black hat, with a flat top and a bit of a curl to its brim, completes the picture.

I look in the mirror and I feel like I'm auditioning to be a stage magician's assistant, but I don't much care.

As soon as the hour gets civilized, I head over to Christy Riddell's house. I'm knocking on his door at nine o'clock, but when he comes to let me in, he's all sleepy-eyed and disheveled and I realize that I should've given him another couple of hours. Too late for that now.

I just come right out with it. I tell him that Jilly said he knew all about lucid dreaming and what I want to know is, is any of it real—the place you dream of, the people you meet there?

He stands there in the doorway, blinking like an owl, but I guess he's used to stranger things, because after a moment he leans against the door jamb and asks me what I know about consensual reality.

It's where everything that we see around us only exists because we all agree it does, I say.

Well, maybe it's the same in a dream, he replies. If everyone in the dream agrees that what's around them is real, then why shouldn't it be?

I want to ask him about what my dad had to say about

dreams trying to escape into the waking world, but I decide I've already pushed my luck.

Thanks, I say.

He gives me a funny look. That's it? he asks.

I'll explain it some other time, I tell him.

Please do, he says without a whole lot of enthusiasm, then goes back inside.

When I get home, I go and lie down on the old sofa that's out on my balcony. I close my eyes. I'm still not so sure about any of this, but I figure it can't hurt to see if Jeck and I can't find ourselves one of those happily-ever-afters with which fairy tales usually end.

Who knows? Maybe I really am the daughter of the Moon. If not here, then someplace.

IN THE HOUSE
∽ · OF MY ENEMY · ∽

We have not inherited the earth from our fathers, we are borrowing it from our children.

—NATIVE AMERICAN SAYING

1

THE PAST SCAMPERS like an alleycat through the present, leaving the pawprints of memories scattered helter-skelter—here ink is smeared on a page, there lies an old photograph with a chewed corner, elsewhere still, a nest has been made of old newspapers, the headlines running one into the other to make strange declarations. There is no order to what we recall, the wheel of time follows no straight line as it turns in our heads. In the dark attics of our minds, all times mingle, sometimes literally.

I get so confused. I've been so many people; some I didn't like at all. I wonder that anyone could. Victim, hooker, junkie, liar, thief. But without them, I wouldn't be who I am today. I'm no one special, but I like who I am, lost childhood and all.

Did I have to be all those people to become the person I

am today? Are they still living inside me, hiding in some dark corner of my mind, waiting for me to slip and stumble and fall and give them life again?

I tell myself not to remember, but that's wrong, too. Not remembering makes them stronger.

2

The morning sun came in through the window of Jilly Coppercorn's loft, playing across the features of her guest. The girl was still asleep on the Murphy bed, sheets all tangled around her skinny limbs, pulled tight and smooth over the rounded swell of her abdomen. Sleep had gentled her features. Her hair clouded the pillow around her head. The soft morning sunlight gave her a Madonna quality, a nimbus of Botticelli purity that the harsher light of the later day would steal away once she woke.

She was fifteen years old. And eight months pregnant.

Jilly sat in the windowseat, feet propped up on the sill, sketchpad on her lap. She caught the scene in charcoal, smudging the lines with the pad of her middle finger to soften them. On the fire escape outside, a stray cat climbed up the last few metal steps until it was level with where she was sitting and gave a plaintive meow.

Jilly had been expecting the black and white tabby. She reached under her knees and picked up a small plastic margarine container filled with dried kibbles, which she set down on the fire escape in front of the cat. As the tabby contentedly crunched its breakfast, Jilly returned to her portrait.

"My name's Annie," her guest had told her last night when she stopped Jilly on Yoors Street just a few blocks south of the loft. "Could you spare some change? I really need to get some decent food. It's not so much for me. . . ."

She put her hand on the swell of her stomach as she spoke.

Jilly had looked at her, taking in the stringy hair, the ragged clothes, the unhealthy color of her complexion, the too-thin body that seemed barely capable of sustaining the girl herself, little say nourishing the child she carried.

"Are you all on your own?" Jilly asked.

The girl nodded.

Jilly put her arm around the girl's shoulder and steered her back to the loft. She let her take a shower while she cooked a meal, gave her a clean smock to wear, and tried not to be patronizing while she did it all.

The girl had lost enough dignity as it was and Jilly knew that dignity was almost as hard to recover as innocence. She knew all too well.

3

Stolen Childhood, by Sophie Etoile. Copperplate engraving. Five Coyotes Singing Studio, Newford, 1988.

A child in a ragged dress stands in front of a ramshackle farmhouse. In one hand she holds a doll—a stick with a ball stuck in one end and a skirt on the other. She wears a lost expression, holding the doll as though she doesn't quite know what to do with it.

A shadowed figure stands behind the screen door, watching her.

I guess I was around three years old when my oldest brother started molesting me. That'd make him eleven. He used to touch me down between my legs while my parents were out drinking or sobering up down in the kitchen. I tried to fight him off, but I didn't really know that what he was doing was wrong—even when he started to put his cock inside me.

I was eight when my mother walked in on one of his rapes and you know what she did? She walked right out again until my brother was finished and we both had our clothes on again. She waited until he'd left the room, then she came back in and started screaming at me.

"You little slut! Why are you doing this to your own brother?"

Like it was my fault. Like I *wanted* him to rape me. Like the three-year-old I was when he started molesting me had any idea about what he was doing.

I think my other brothers knew what was going on all along, but they never said anything about it—they didn't want to break that macho code-of-honor bullshit. When my dad found out about it, he beat the crap out of my brother, but in some ways it just got worse after that.

My brother didn't molest me anymore, but he'd glare at me all the time, like he was going to pay me back for the beating he got soon as he got a chance. My mother and my other brothers, every time I'd come into a room, they'd all just stop talking and look at me like I was some kind of bug.

I think at first my dad wanted to do something to help me, but in the end he really wasn't any better than my mother. I could see it in his eyes: he blamed me for it, too. He kept me at a distance, never came close to me anymore, never let me feel like I was normal.

He's the one who had me see a psychiatrist. I'd have to go and sit in his office all alone, just a little kid in this big leather chair. The psychiatrist would lean across his desk, all smiles and smarmy understanding, and try to get me to talk, but I never told him a thing. I didn't trust him. I'd already learned that I couldn't trust men. Couldn't trust women either, thanks to my mother. Her idea of working things out was to send me to confession, like the same God who let my brother rape me was now going to make everything okay so long as I owned up to seducing him in the first place.

What kind of a way is that for a kid to grow up?

4

"Forgive me, Father, for I have sinned. I let my brother . . ."

5

Jilly laid her sketchpad aside when her guest began to stir.
She swung her legs down so that they dangled from the windowsill, heels banging lightly against the wall, toes almost
touching the ground. She pushed an unruly lock of hair from
her brow, leaving behind a charcoal smudge on her temple.

Small and slender, with pixie features and a mass of curly
dark hair, she looked almost as young as the girl on her bed.
Jeans and sneakers, a dark T-shirt and an oversized peach-
colored smock only added to her air of slightness and youth.
But she was halfway through her thirties, her own teenage
years long gone; she could have been Annie's mother.

"What were you doing?" Annie asked as she sat up, tugging the sheets up around herself.

"Sketching you while you slept. I hope you don't mind."

"Can I see?"

Jilly passed the sketchpad over and watched Annie study
it. On the fire escape behind her, two more cats had joined
the black and white tabby at the margarine container. One
was an old alleycat, its left ear ragged and torn, ribs showing
like so many hills and valleys against the matted landscape
of its fur. The other belonged to an upstairs neighbor; it was
making its usual morning rounds.

"You made me look a lot better than I really am," Annie
said finally.

Jilly shook her head. "I only drew what was there."

"Yeah, right."

Jilly didn't bother to contradict her. The self-worth speech would keep.

"So is this how you make your living?" Annie asked.

"Pretty well. I do a little waitressing on the side."

"Beats being a hooker, I guess."

She gave Jilly a challenging look as she spoke, obviously anticipating a reaction.

Jilly only shrugged. "Tell me about it," she said.

Annie didn't say anything for a long moment. She looked down at the rough portrait with an unreadable expression, then finally met Jilly's gaze again.

"I've heard about you," she said. "On the street. Seems like everybody knows you. They say . . ."

Her voice trailed off.

Jilly smiled. "What do they say?"

"Oh, all kinds of stuff." She shrugged. "You know. That you used to live on the street, that you're kind of like a one-woman social service, but you don't lecture. And that you're—" she hesitated, looked away for a moment "—you know, a witch."

Jilly laughed. "A witch?"

That was a new one on her.

Annie waved a hand towards the wall across from the window where Jilly was sitting. Paintings leaned up against each other in untidy stacks. Above them, the wall held more, a careless gallery hung frame to frame to save space. They were part of Jilly's ongoing "Urban Faerie" series, realistic city scenes and characters to which were added the curious little denizens of lands which never were. Hobs and fairies, little elf men and goblins.

"They say you think all that stuff's real," Annie said.

"What do you think?"

When Annie gave her a "give me a break" look, Jilly just smiled again.

"How about some breakfast?" she asked to change the subject.

"Look," Annie said. "I really appreciate your taking me

in and feeding me and everything last night, but I don't want to be a freeloader.''

"One more meal's not freeloading."

Jilly pretended to pay no attention as Annie's pride fought with her baby's need.

"Well, if you're sure it's okay," Annie said hesitantly.

"I wouldn't have offered if it wasn't," Jilly said.

She dropped down from the windowsill and went across the loft to the kitchen corner. She normally didn't eat a big breakfast, but twenty minutes later they were both sitting down to fried eggs and bacon, home fries and toast, coffee for Jilly and herb tea for Annie.

"Got any plans for today?" Jilly asked as they were finishing up.

"Why?" Annie replied, immediately suspicious.

"I thought you might want to come visit a friend of mine."

"A social worker, right?"

The tone in her voice was the same as though she was talking about a cockroach or maggot.

Jilly shook her head. "More like a storefront counselor. Her name's Angelina Marceau. She runs that drop-in center on Grasso Street. It's privately funded, no political connections."

"I've heard of her. The Grasso Street Angel."

"You don't have to come," Jilly said, "but I know she'd like to meet you."

"I'm sure."

Jilly shrugged. When she started to clean up, Annie stopped her.

"Please," she said. "Let me do it."

Jilly retrieved her sketchpad from the bed and returned to the windowseat while Annie washed up. She was just adding the finishing touches to the rough portrait she'd started earlier when Annie came to sit on the edge of the Murphy bed.

"That painting on the easel," Annie said. "Is that something new you're working on?"

Jilly nodded.

"It's not like your other stuff at all."

"I'm part of an artist's group that calls itself the Five Coyotes Singing Studio," Jilly explained. "The actual studio's owned by a friend of mine named Sophie Etoile, but we all work in it from time to time. There's five of us, all women, and we're doing a group show with a theme of child abuse at the Green Man Gallery next month."

"And that painting's going to be in it?" Annie asked.

"It's one of three I'm doing for the show."

"What's that one called?"

" 'I Don't Know How To Laugh Anymore.' "

Annie put her hands on top of her swollen stomach.

"Me, neither," she said.

6

I Don't Know How to Laugh Anymore, *by Jilly Coppercorn. Oils and mixed media. Yoors Street Studio, Newford, 1991.*

A life-sized female subject leans against an inner city wall in the classic pose of a prostitute waiting for a customer. She wears high heels, a micro-miniskirt, tube-top and short jacket, with a purse slung over one shoulder, hanging against her hip from a narrow strap. Her hands are thrust into the pockets of her jacket. Her features are tired, the lost look of a junkie in her eyes undermining her attempt to appear sultry.

Near her feet, a condom is attached to the painting, stiffened with gesso.

The subject is thirteen years old.

I started running away from home when I was ten. The summer I turned eleven I managed to make it to Newford and lived on its streets for six months. I ate what I could find in the dumpsters behind the McDonald's and other fast food places on Williamson Street—there was nothing wrong with the food. It was just dried out from having been under the heating lamps for too long.

I spent those six months walking the streets all night. I was afraid to sleep when it was dark because I was just a kid and who knows what could've happened to me. At least being awake I could hide whenever I saw something that made me nervous. In the daytime I slept where I could—in parks, in the back seats of abandoned cars, wherever I didn't think I'd get caught. I tried to keep myself clean, washed up in restaurant bathrooms and at this gas bar on Yoors Street where the guy running the pumps took a liking to me. Paydays he'd spot me for lunch at the grill down the street.

I started drawing back then and for awhile I tried to hawk my pictures to the tourists down by the Pier, but the stuff wasn't all that good and I was drawing with pencils on foolscap or pages torn out of old school notebooks—not exactly the kind of art that looks good in a frame, if you know what I mean. I did a lot better panhandling and shoplifting.

I finally got busted trying to boost a tape deck from Kreiger's Stereo—it used to be where Gypsy Records is. Now it's out on the strip past the Tombs. I've always been small for my age, which didn't help when I tried to to convince the cops that I was older than I really was. I figured juvie would be better than going back to my parents' place, but it didn't work. My parents had a missing persons out on me, God knows why. It's not like they could've missed me.

But I didn't go back home. My mother didn't want me and my dad didn't argue, so I guess he didn't either. I figured that was great until I started making the rounds of foster homes, bouncing back and forth between them and the Home for Wayward Girls. It's just juvie with an old-fashioned name.

I guess there must be some good foster parents, but I never saw any. All mine ever wanted was to collect their check and treat me like I was a piece of shit unless my case worker was coming by for a visit. Then I got moved up from the mattress in the basement to one of their kids' rooms. The first time I tried to tell the worker what was going down, she didn't believe me and then my foster parents beat the crap out of me once she was gone. I didn't make that mistake again.

I was thirteen and in my fourth or fifth foster home when I got molested again. This time I didn't take any crap. I booted the old pervert in the balls and just took off out of there, back to Newford.

I was older and knew better now. Girls I talked to in juvie told me how to get around, who to trust and who was just out to peddle your ass.

See, I never planned on being a hooker. I don't know what I thought I'd do when I got to the city—I wasn't exactly thinking straight. Anyway, I ended up with this guy—Robert Carson. He was fifteen.

I met him in back of the Convention Center on the beach where all the kids used to all hang out in the summer and we ended up getting a room together on Grasso Street, near the high school. I was still pretty fucked up about getting physical with a guy but we ended up doing so many drugs—acid, MDA, coke, smack, you name it—that half the time I didn't know when he was putting it to me.

We ran out of money one day, rent was due, no food in the place, no dope, both of us too fucked up to panhandle, when Rob gets the big idea of selling my ass to bring in a little money. Well, I was screwed up, but not that screwed up. But then he got some guy to front him some smack and next thing I know I'm in this car with some guy I never saw before and he's expecting a blow job and I'm crying and all fucked up from the dope and then I'm doing it and standing out on the street corner where he's dumped me some ten minutes later with forty bucks in my hand and Rob's laughing, saying how we got it made, and all I can do is crouch on the sidewalk and puke, trying to get the taste of that guy's come out of my mouth.

So Rob thinks I'm being, like, so fucking weird—I mean, it's easy money, he tells me. Easy for him maybe. We have this big fight and then he hits me. Tells me if I don't get my ass out on the street and make some more money, he's going to do worse, like cut me.

My luck, I guess. Of all the guys to hang out with, I've got to pick one who suddenly realizes it's his ambition in life to be a pimp. Three years later he's running a string of five girls, but he lets me pay my respect—two grand which I got by skimming what I was paying him—and I'm out of the scene.

Except I'm not, because I'm still a junkie and I'm too fucked up to work, I've got no ID, I've got no skills except I can draw a little when I'm not fucked up on smack which is just about all the time. I start muling for a couple of dealers in Fitzhenry Park, just to get my fixes, and then one night I'm so out of it, I just collapse in a doorway of a pawn shop up on Perry Street.

I haven't eaten in, like, three days. I'm shaking because I need a fix so bad I can't see straight. I haven't washed in Christ knows how long, so I smell and the clothes I'm wearing are worse. I'm at the end of the line and I know it, when I hear footsteps coming down the street and I know it's the local cop on his beat, doing his rounds.

I try to crawl deeper into the shadows but the doorway's only so deep and the cop's coming closer and then he's standing there, blocking what little light the streetlamps were throwing and I know I'm screwed. But there's no way I'm going back into juvie or a foster home. I'm thinking of offering him a blow job to let me go—so far as the cops're concerned, hookers're just scum, but they'll take a freebie all the same—but I see something in this guy's face, when he turns his head and the streetlight touches it, that tells me he's an honest joe. A rookie, true blue, probably his first week on the beat and full of wanting to help everybody and I know for sure I'm screwed. With my luck running true, he's going to be the kind of guy who thinks social workers really want to help someone like me instead of playing bureaucratic mind-fuck games with my head.

I don't think I can take anymore.

I find myself wishing I had Rob's switchblade—the one he liked to push up against my face when he didn't think I was bringing in enough. I just want to cut something. The cop. Myself. I don't really give a fuck. I just want out.

He crouches down so he's kind of level with me, lying there scrunched up against the door, and says, "How bad is it?"

I just look at him like he's from another planet. How bad is it? Can it get any worse I wonder?

"I . . . I'm doing fine," I tell him.

He nods like we're discussing the weather. "What's your name?"

"Jilly," I say.

"Jilly what?"

"Uh. . . ."

I think of my parents, who've turned their backs on me. I think of juvie and foster homes. I look over his shoulder and there's a pair of billboards on the building behind him. One's advertising a suntan lotion—you know the one with the dog pulling the kid's pants down? I'll bet some old pervert thought that one up. The other's got the Jolly Green Giant himself selling vegetables. I pull a word from each ad and give it to the cop.

"Jilly Coppercorn."

"Think you can stand, Jilly?"

I'm thinking, If I could stand, would I be lying here? But I give it a try. He helps me the rest of the way up, supports me when I start to sway.

"So . . . so am I busted?" I ask him.

"Have you committed a crime?"

I don't know where the laugh comes from, but it falls out of my mouth all the same. There's no humor in it.

"Sure," I tell him. "I was born."

He sees my bag still lying on the ground. He picks it up while I lean against the wall and a bunch of my drawings fall out. He looks at them as he stuffs them back in the bag.

"Did you do those?"

I want to sneer at him, ask him why the fuck should he care, but I've got nothing left in me. It's all I can do to stand. So I tell him, yeah, they're mine.

"They're very good."

Right. I'm actually this fucking brilliant artist, slumming just to get material for my art.

"Do you have a place to stay?" he asks.

Whoops, did I read him wrong? Maybe he's planning to get me home, clean me up, and then put it to me.

"Jilly?" he asks when I don't answer.

Sure, I want to tell him. I've got my pick of the city's alleyways and doorways. I'm welcome wherever I go. World treats me like a fucking princess. But all I do is shake my head.

"I want to take you to see a friend of mine," he says.

I wonder how he can stand to touch me. I can't stand myself. I'm like a walking sewer. And now he wants to bring me to meet a friend?

"Am I busted?" I ask him again.

He shakes his head. I think of where I am, what I got ahead of me, then I just shrug. If I'm not busted, then whatever's he's got planned for me's got to be better. Who knows, maybe his friend'll front me with a fix to get me through the night.

"Okay," I tell him. "Whatever."

"C'mon," he says.

He puts an arm around my shoulder and steers me off down the street and that's how I met Lou Fucceri and his girlfriend, the Grasso Street Angel.

7

Jilly sat on the stoop of Angel's office on Grasso Street, watching the passersby. She had her sketchpad on her knee, but she hadn't opened it yet. Instead, she was amusing herself with one of her favorite pastimes: making up stories about the people walking by. The young woman with the child in a stroller, she was a princess in exile, disguising herself as a nanny in a far distant land until she could regain her rightful station in some suitably romantic dukedom in Europe. The old black man with the cane was a physicist studying the effects of Chaos theory in the Grasso Street traffic. The Hispanic girl on her skateboard was actually a mermaid, having exchanged the waves of her ocean for concrete.

She didn't turn around when she heard the door open behind her. There was a scuffle of sneakers on the stoop, then the sound of the door closing again. After a moment, Annie sat down beside her.

"How're you doing?" Jilly asked.

"It was weird."

"Good weird, or bad?" Jilly asked when Annie didn't go on. "Or just uncomfortable?"

"Good weird, I guess. She played the tape you did for her book. She said you knew, that you'd said it was okay."

Jilly nodded.

"I couldn't believe it was you. I mean, I recognized your voice and everything, but you sounded so different."

"I was just a kid," Jilly said. "A punky street kid."

"But look at you now."

"I'm nothing special," Jilly said, suddenly feeling self-conscious. She ran a hand through her hair. "Did Angel tell you about the sponsorship program?"

Annie nodded. "Sort of. She said you'd tell me more."

"What Angel does is coordinate a relationship between

kids that need help and people who want to help. It's different every time, because everybody's different. I didn't meet my sponsor for the longest time; he just put up the money while Angel was my contact. My lifeline, if you want to know the truth. I can't remember how many times I'd show up at her door and spend the night crying on her shoulder.''

"How did you get, you know, cleaned up?" Annie asked. Her voice was shy.

"The first thing is I went into detox. When I finally got out, my sponsor paid for my room and board at the Chelsea Arms while I went through an accelerated high school program. I told Angel I wanted to go on to college, so he cosigned my student loan and helped me out with my books and supplies and stuff. I was working by that point. I had part-time jobs at a couple of stores and with the Post Office, and then I started waitressing, but that kind of money doesn't go far—not when you're carrying a full course load.''

"When did you find out who your sponsor was?"

"When I graduated. He was at the ceremony.''

"Was it weird finally meeting him?"

Jilly laughed. "Yes and no. I'd already known him for years—he was my art history professor. We got along really well and he used to let me use the sunroom at the back of his house for a studio. Angel and Lou had shown him some of that bad art I'd been doing when I was still on the street and that's why he sponsored me—because he thought I had a lot of talent, he told me later. But he didn't want me to know it was him putting up the money because he thought it might affect our relationship at Butler U.'' She shook her head. "He said he *knew* I'd be going the first time Angel and Lou showed him the stuff I was doing.''

"It's sort of like a fairy tale, isn't it?" Annie said.

"I guess it is. I never thought of it that way.''

"And it really works, doesn't it?"

"If you want it to," Jilly said. "I'm not saying it's easy. There's ups and downs—lots more downs at the start.''

"How many kids make it?"

"This hasn't got anything to do with statistics," Jilly said. "You can only look at it on a person to person basis. But Angel's been doing this for a long, long time. You can trust her to do her best for you. She takes a lot of flak for what she does. Parents get mad at her because she won't tell them where their kids are. Social services says she's undermining their authority. She's been to jail twice on contempt of court charges because she wouldn't tell where some kid was."

"Even with her boyfriend being a cop?"

"That was a long time ago," Jilly said. "And it didn't work out. They're still friends but—Angel went through an awful bad time when she was a kid. That changes a person, no matter how much they learn to take control of their life. Angel's great with people, especially kids, and she's got a million friends, but she's not good at maintaining a personal relationship with a guy. When it comes down to the crunch, she just can't learn to trust them. As friends, sure, but not as lovers."

"She said something along the same lines about you," Annie said. "She said you were full of love, but it wasn't sexual or romantic so much as a general kindness towards everything and everybody."

"Yeah, well . . . I guess both Angel and I talk too much."

Annie hesitated for a few heartbeats, then said, "She also told me that you want to sponsor me."

Jilly nodded. "I'd like to."

"I don't get it."

"What's to get?"

"Well, I'm not like you or your professor friend. I'm not, you know, all that creative. I couldn't make something beautiful if my life depended on it. I'm not much good at anything."

Jilly shook her head. "That's not what it's about. Beauty isn't what you see on TV or in magazine ads or even necessarily in art galleries. It's a lot deeper and a lot simpler than that. It's realizing the goodness of things, it's leaving the world a little better than it was before you got here. It's appreciating the inspiration of the world around you and trying to inspire others.

"Sculptors, poets, painters, musicians—they're the traditional purveyors of Beauty. But it can as easily be created by a gardener, a farmer, a plumber, a careworker. It's the intent you put into your work, the pride you take in it—whatever it is."

"But still. . . . I really don't have anything to offer."

Annie's statement was all the more painful for Jilly because it held no self-pity, it was just a laying out of facts as Annie saw them.

"Giving birth is an act of Beauty," Jilly said.

"I don't even know if I want a kid. I . . . I don't know what I want. I don't know who I am."

She turned to Jilly. There seemed to be years of pain and confusion in her eyes, far more years than she had lived in the world. When had that pain begun? Jilly thought. Who could have done it to her, beautiful child that she must have been? Father, brother, uncle, family friend?

Jilly wanted to just reach out and hold her, but knew too well how the physical contact of comfort could too easily be misconstrued as an invasion of the private space an abused victim sometimes so desperately needed to maintain.

"I need help," Annie said softly. "I know that. But I don't want charity."

"Don't think of this sponsorship program as charity," Jilly said. "What Angel does is simply what we all should be doing all of the time—taking care of each other."

Annie sighed, but fell silent. Jilly didn't push it any further. They sat for awhile longer on the stoop while the world bustled by on Grasso Street.

"What was the hardest part?" Annie asked. "You know, when you first came off the street."

"Thinking of myself as normal."

8

Daddy's Home, by Isabelle Copley. Painted Wood. Adjani Farm, Wren Island, 1990.

The sculpture is three feet high, a flat rectangle of solid wood, standing on end with a child's face, upper torso and hands protruding from one side, as though the wood is gauze against which the subject is pressing.

The child wears a look of terror.

Annie's sleeping again. She needs the rest as much as she needs regular meals and the knowledge that she's got a safe place to stay. I took my Walkman out onto the fire escape and listened to a copy of the tape that Angel played for her today. I don't much recognize that kid either, but I know it's me.

It's funny, me talking about Angel, Angel talking about me, both of us knowing what the other needs, but neither able to help herself. I like to see my friends as couples. I like to see them in love with each other. But it's not the same for me.

Except who am I kidding? I want the same thing, but I just choke when a man gets too close to me. I can't let down that final barrier, I can't even tell them why.

Sophie says I expect them to just instinctively know. That I'm waiting for them to be understanding and caring without ever opening up to them. If I want them to follow the script I've got written out in my head, she says I have to let them in on it.

I know she's right, but I can't do anything about it.

I see a dog slink into the alleyway beside the building. He's skinny as a whippet, but he's just a mongrel that no one's taken care of for awhile. He's got dried blood on his shoulders, so I guess someone's been beating him.

I go down with some cat food in a bowl, but he won't

come near me, no matter how soothingly I call to him. I know he can smell the food, but he's more scared of me than he's hungry. Finally I just leave the bowl and go back up the fire escape. He waits until I'm sitting outside my window again before he goes up to the bowl. He wolfs the food down and then he takes off like he's done something wrong.

I guess that's the way I am when I meet a man I like. I'm really happy with him until he's nice to me, until he wants to kiss me and hold me, and then I just run off like I've done something wrong.

9

Annie woke while Jilly was starting dinner. She helped chop up vegetables for the vegetarian stew Jilly was making, then drifted over to the long worktable that ran along the back wall near Jilly's easel. She found a brochure for the Five Coyotes Singing Studio show in amongst the litter of paper, magazines, sketches and old paint brushes and brought it over to the kitchen table where she leafed through it while Jilly finished up the dinner preparations.

"Do you really think something like this is going to make a difference?" Annie asked after she'd read through the brochure.

"Depends on how big a difference you're talking about," Jilly said. "Sophie's arranged for a series of lectures to run in association with the show and she's also organized a couple of discussion evenings at the gallery where people who come to the show can talk to us—about their reactions to the show, about their feelings, maybe even share their own experiences if that's something that feels right to them at the time."

"Yeah, but what about the kids that this is all about?" Annie asked.

Jilly turned from the stove. Annie didn't look at all like a young expectant mother, glowing with her pregnancy. She just looked like a hurt and confused kid with a distended stomach, a kind of Ralph Steadman aura of frantic anxiety splattered around her.

"The way we see it," Jilly said, "is if only one kid gets spared the kind of hell we all went through, then the show'll be worth it."

"Yeah, but the only kind of people who are going to go to this kind of thing are those who already know about it. You're preaching to the converted."

"Maybe. But there'll be media coverage—in the papers for sure, maybe a spot on the news. That's where—if we're going to reach out and wake someone up—that's where it's going to happen."

"I suppose."

Annie flipped over the brochure and looked at the four photographs on the back.

"How come there isn't a picture of Sophie?" she asked.

"Cameras don't seem to work all that well around her," Jilly said. "It's like—" she smiled "—an enchantment."

The corner of Annie's mouth twitched in response.

"Tell me about, you know . . ." She pointed to Jilly's Urban Faerie paintings. "Magic. Enchanted stuff."

Jilly put the stew on low to simmer then fetched a sketchbook that held some of the preliminary pencil drawings for the finished paintings that were leaning up against the wall. The urban settings were barely realized—just rough outlines and shapes—but the faerie were painstakingly detailed.

As they flipped through the sketchbook, Jilly talked about where she'd done the sketches, what she'd seen, or more properly glimpsed, that led her to make the drawings she had.

"You've really seen all these . . . little magic people?" Annie asked.

Her tone of voice was incredulous, but Jilly could tell that she wanted to believe.

"Not all of them," Jilly said. "Some I've only imagined, but others . . . like this one." She pointed to a sketch that had been done in the Tombs where a number of fey figures were hanging out around an abandoned car, pre-Raphaelite features at odds with their raggedy clothing and setting. "They're real."

"But they could just be people. It's not like they're tiny or have wings like some of the others."

Jilly shrugged. "Maybe, but they weren't just people."

"Do you have to be magic yourself to see them?"

Jilly shook her head. "You just have to pay attention. If you don't you'll miss them, or see something else—something you expected to see rather than what was really there. Fairy voices become just the wind, a bodach, like this little man here—" she flipped to another page and pointed out a small gnomish figure the size of a cat, darting off a sidewalk "—scurrying across the street becomes just a piece of litter caught in the backwash of a bus."

"Pay attention," Annie repeated dubiously.

Jilly nodded. "Just like we have to pay attention to each other, or we miss the important things that are going on there as well."

Annie turned another page, but she didn't look at the drawing. Instead she studied Jilly's pixie features.

"You really, really believe in magic, don't you?" she said.

"I really, really do," Jilly told her. "But it's not something I just take on faith. For me, art is an act of magic. I pass on the spirits that I see—of people, of places, mysteries."

"So what if you're not an artist? Where's the magic then?"

"Life's an act of magic, too. Claire Hamill sings a line in one of her songs that really sums it up for me: 'If there's no magic, there's no meaning.' Without magic—or call it wonder, mystery, natural wisdom—nothing has any depth. It's all just surface. You know: what you see is what you get. I honestly believe there's more to everything than that, whether it's a Monet hanging in a gallery or some old vagrant sleeping in an alley."

"I don't know," Annie said. "I understand what you're saying, about people and things, but this other stuff—it sounds more like the kinds of things you see when you're tripping."

Jilly shook her head. "I've done drugs and I've seen Faerie. They're not the same."

She got up to stir the stew. When she sat down again, Annie had closed the sketchbook and was sitting with her hands flat against her stomach.

"Can you feel the baby?" Jilly asked.

Annie nodded.

"Have you thought about what you want to do?"

"I guess. I'm just not sure I even want to keep the baby."

"That's your decision," Jilly said. "Whatever you want to do, we'll stand by you. Either way we'll get you a place to stay. If you keep the baby and want to work, we'll see about arranging daycare. If you want to stay home with the baby, we'll work something out for that as well. That's what this sponsorship's all about. It's not us telling you what to do; we just want to help you be the person you were meant to be."

"I don't know if that's such a good person," Annie said.

"Don't think like that. It's not true."

Annie shrugged. "I guess I'm scared I'll do the same thing to my baby that my mother did to me. That's how it happens, doesn't it? My mom used to beat the crap out of me all the time, didn't matter if I did something wrong or not, and I'm just going to end up doing the same thing to my kid."

"You're only hurting yourself with that kind of thinking," Jilly said.

"But it *can* happen, can't it? Jesus, I . . . You know I've been gone from her for two years now, but I still feel like she's standing right next to me half the time, or waiting around the corner for me. It's like I'll never escape. When I lived at home, it was like I was living in the house of an enemy. But running away didn't change that. I still feel like that, except now it's like everybody's my enemy."

Jilly reached over and laid a hand on hers.

"Not everybody," she said. "You've got to believe that."

"It's hard not to."

"I know."

10

This Is Where We Dump Them, *by Meg Mullally. Tinted photograph. The Tombs, Newford, 1991.*

Two children sit on the stoop of one of the abandoned buildings in the Tombs. Their hair is matted, faces smudged, clothing dirty and ill-fitting. They look like turn-of-the-century Irish tinkers. There's litter all around them: torn garbage bags spewing their contents on the sidewalk, broken bottles, a rotting mattress on the street, half-crushed pop cans, soggy newspapers, used condoms.

The children are seven and thirteen, a boy and a girl. They have no home, no family. They only have each other.

The next month went by awfully fast. Annie stayed with me—it was what she wanted. Angel and I did get her a place, a one-bedroom on Landis that she's going to move into after she's had the baby. It's right behind the loft—you can see her back window from mine. But for now she's going to stay here with me.

She's really a great kid. No artistic leanings, but really bright. She could be anything she wants to be if she can just learn to deal with all the baggage her parents dumped on her.

She's kind of shy around Angel and some of my other friends—I guess they're all too old for her or something—

but she gets along really well with Sophie and me. Probably because, whenever you put Sophie and me together in the same room for more than two minutes, we just start giggling and acting about half our respective ages, which would make us, mentally at least, just a few years Annie's senior.

"You two could be sisters," Annie told me one day when we got back from Sophie's studio. "Her hair's lighter, and she's a little chestier, and she's *definitely* more organized than you are, but I get a real sense of family when I'm with the two of you. The way families are supposed to be."

"Even though Sophie's got faerie blood?" I asked her.

She thought I was joking.

"If she's got magic in her," Annie said, "then so do you. Maybe that's what makes you seem so much like sisters."

"I just pay attention to things," I told her. "That's all."

"Yeah, right."

The baby came right on schedule—three-thirty, Sunday morning. I probably would've panicked if Annie hadn't been doing enough of that for both of us. Instead I got on the phone, called Angel, and then saw about helping Annie get dressed.

The contractions were really close by the time Angel arrived with the car. But everything worked out fine. Jillian Sophia Mackle was born two hours and forty-five minutes later at the Newford General Hospital. Six pounds and five ounces of red-faced wonder. There were no complications.

Those came later.

11

The last week before the show was simple chaos. There seemed to be a hundred and one things that none of them had thought of, all of which had to be done at the last moment. And to make matters worse, Jilly still had one unfinished canvas haunting her by Friday night.

It stood on her easel, untitled, barely-sketched in images, still in monochrome. The colors eluded her. She knew what she wanted, but every time she stood before her easel, her mind went blank. She seemed to forget everything she'd ever known about art. The inner essence of the canvas rose up inside her like a ghost, so close she could almost touch it, but then fled daily, like a dream lost upon waking. The outside world intruded. A knock on the door. The ringing of the phone.

The show opened in exactly seven days.

Annie's baby was almost two weeks old. She was a happy, satisfied infant, the kind of baby that was forever making contented little gurgling sounds, as though talking to herself; she never cried. Annie herself was a nervous wreck.

"I'm scared," she told Jilly when she came over to the loft that afternoon. "Everything's going too well. I don't deserve it."

They were sitting at the kitchen table, the baby propped up on the Murphy bed between two pillows. Annie kept fidgeting. Finally she picked up a pencil and started drawing stick figures on pieces of paper.

"Don't say that," Jilly said. "Don't even think it."

"But it's true. Look at me. I'm not like you or Sophie. I'm not like Angel. What have I got to offer my baby? What's she going to have to look up to when she looks at me?"

"A kind, caring mother."

Annie shook her head. "I don't feel like that. I feel like

everything's sort of fuzzy and it's like pushing through cobwebs to just to make it through the day.''

"We'd better make an appointment with you to see a doctor.''

"Make it a shrink,'' Annie said. She continued to doodle, then looked down at what she was doing. "Look at this. It's just crap.''

Before Jilly could see, Annie swept the sheaf of papers to the floor.

"Oh, jeez,'' she said as they went fluttering all over the place. "I'm sorry. I didn't mean to do that.''

She got up before Jilly could and tossed the lot of them in the garbage container beside the stove. She stood there for a long moment, taking deep breaths, holding them, slowly letting them out.

"Annie . . . ?''

She turned as Jilly approached her. The glow of motherhood that had seemed to revitalize her in the month before the baby was born had slowly worn away. She was pale again. Wan. She looked so lost that all Jilly could do was put her arms around her and offer a wordless comfort.

"I'm sorry,'' Annie said against Jilly's hair. "I don't know what's going on. I just . . . I know I should be really happy, but I just feel scared and confused.'' She rubbed at her eyes with a knuckle. "God, listen to me. All it seems I can do is complain about my life.''

"It's not like you've had a great one,'' Jilly said.

"Yeah, but when I compare it to what it was like before I met you, it's like I moved up into heaven.''

"Why don't you stay here tonight?'' Jilly said.

Annie stepped back out of her arms. "Maybe I will—if you really don't mind . . . ?''

"I really don't mind.''

"Thanks.''

Annie glanced towards the bed, her gaze pausing on the clock on the wall above the stove.

"You're going to be late for work,'' she said.

"That's all right. I don't think I'll go in tonight."

Annie shook her head. "No, go on. You've told me how busy it gets on a Friday night."

Jilly still worked part-time at Kathryn's Cafe on Battersfield Road. She could just imagine what Wendy would say if she called in sick. There was no one else in town this weekend to take her shift, so that would leave Wendy working all the tables on her own.

"If you're sure," Jilly said.

"We'll be okay," Annie said. "Honestly."

She went over to the bed and picked up the baby, cradling her gently in her arms.

"Look at her," she said, almost to herself. "It's hard to believe something so beautiful came out of me." She turned to Jilly, adding before Jilly could speak, "That's a kind of magic all by itself, isn't it?"

"Maybe one of the best we can make," Jilly said.

12

How Can You Call This Love? *by Claudia Feder. Oils. Old Market Studio, Newford, 1990.*

A fat man sits on a bed in a cheap hotel room. He's removing his shirt. Through the ajar door of the bathroom behind him, a thin girl in bra and panties can be seen sitting on the toilet, shooting up.

She appears to be about fourteen.

I just pay attention to things, I told her. I guess that's why, when I got off my shift and came back to the loft, Annie was gone. Because I pay such good attention. The baby was still on the bed, lying between the pillows, sleeping. There was a note on the kitchen table:

I don't know what's wrong with me. I just keep wanting to hit something. I look at little Jilly and I

think about my mother and I get so scared. Take care
of her for me. Teach her magic.
*   Please don't hate me.*

I don't know how long I sat and stared at those sad, piteous words, tears streaming from my eyes.

I should never have gone to work. I should never have left her alone. She really thought she was just going to replay her own childhood. She told me, I don't know how many times she told me, but I just wasn't paying attention, was I?

Finally I got on the phone. I called Angel. I called Sophie. I called Lou Fucceri. I called everybody I could think of to go out and look for Annie. Angel was at the loft with me when we finally heard. I was the one who picked up the phone.

I heard what Lou said: "A patrolman brought her into the General not fifteen minutes ago, ODing on Christ knows what. She was just trying to self-destruct, is what he said. I'm sorry, Jilly. But she died before I got there."

I didn't say anything. I just passed the phone to Angel and went to sit on the bed. I held little Jilly in my arms and then I cried some more.

I was never joking about Sophie. She really does have faerie blood. It's something I can't explain, something we've never really talked about, something I just know and she's never denied. But she did promise me that she'd bless Annie's baby, just the way fairy godmothers would do it in all those old stories.

"I gave her the gift of a happy life," she told me later. "I never dreamed it wouldn't include Annie."

But that's the way it works in fairy tales, too, isn't it? Something always goes wrong, or there wouldn't be a story. You have to be strong, you have to earn your happily ever after.

Annie was strong enough to go away from her baby when she felt like all she could do was just lash out, but she wasn't strong enough to help herself. That was the awful gift her parents gave her.

I never finished that last painting in time for the show, but I found something to take its place. Something that said more to me in just a few rough lines than anything I've ever done.

I was about to throw out my garbage when I saw those crude little drawings that Annie had been doodling on my kitchen table the night she died. They were like the work of a child.

I framed one of them and hung it in the show.

"I guess we're five coyotes and one coyote ghost now," was all Sophie said when she saw what I had done.

13

In the House of My Enemy, *by Annie Mackle. Pencils. Yoors Street Studio, Newford, 1991.*

The images are crudely rendered. In a house that is merely a square with a triangle on top, are three stick figures, one plain, two with small "skirt" triangles to represent their gender. The two larger figures are beating the smaller one with what might be crooked sticks, or might be belts.

The small figure is cringing away.

14

In the visitor's book set out at the show, someone wrote: "I can never forgive those responsible for what's been done to us. I don't even want to try."

"Neither do I," Jilly said when she read it. "God help me, but neither do I."

BUT FOR THE GRACE
⌐·GO I ·⌐

*You can only predict things
after they've happened.*
—EUGENE IONESCO

I INHERITED TOMMY the same way I did the dogs. Found him wandering lost and alone, so I took him home. I've always taken in strays—maybe because a long time ago I used to hope that someone'd take me in. I grew out of that idea pretty fast.

Tommy's kind of like a pet, I guess, except he can talk. He doesn't make a whole lot of sense, but then I don't find what most people have to say makes much sense. At least Tommy's honest. What you see is what you get. No games, no hidden agendas. He's only Tommy, a big guy who wouldn't hurt you even if you took a stick to him. Likes to smile, likes to laugh—a regular guy. He's just a few bricks short of a load, is all. Hell, sometimes I figure all he's got is bricks sitting back in there behind his eyes.

I know what you're thinking. A guy like him should be in an institution, and I suppose you're right, except they pronounced him cured at the Zeb when they needed his bed for somebody whose family had money to pay for the space he was taking up and they're not exactly falling over themselves to get him back.

We live right in the middle of that part of Newford that some people call the Tombs and some call Squatland. It's the dead part of the city—a jungle of empty lots filled with trash and abandoned cars, gutted buildings and rubble. I've seen it described in the papers as a blight, a disgrace, a breeding ground for criminals and racial strife, though we've got every color you can think of living in here and we get along pretty well together, mostly because we just leave each other alone. And we're not so much criminals as losers.

Sitting in their fancy apartments and houses, with running water and electricity and no worry about where the next meal's coming from, the good citizens of Newford have got a lot of names and ways to describe this place and us, but those of us who actually live here just call it home. I think of it as one of those outlaw roosts like they used to have in the Old West—some little ramshackle town, way back in the badlands, where only the outlaws lived. Of course those guys like L'Amour and Short who wrote about places like that probably just made them up. I find that a lot of people have this thing about making crap romantic, the way they like to blur outlaws and heroes, the good with the bad.

I know that feeling all too well, but I broke the only pair of rose-colored glasses I had the chance to own a long time ago. Sometimes I pretend I'm here because I want to be, because it's the only place I can be free, because I'm judged by who I am and what I can do, not by how screwed up my family is and how dirt poor looked pretty good from the position we were in.

I'm not saying this part of town's pretty. I'm not even saying I like living here. We're all just putting in time, trying to make do. Every time I hear about some kid ODing, somebody getting knifed, somebody taking that long step off a building or wrapping their belt around their neck, I figure that's just one more of us who finally got out. It's a war zone in here, and just like in Vietnam, they either carry you out in a box, or you leave under your own steam carrying a piece of the place with you—a kind of cold shadow that sits inside your soul and has you waking up in a cold sweat some nights, or feeling closed in and crazy in your new work place, home, social life, whatever, for no good reason except that it's the Tombs calling to you, telling you that maybe you don't deserve what you've got now, reminding you of all those people you left behind who didn't get the break you did.

I don't know why we bother. Let's be honest. I don't know why *I* bother. I just don't know any better, I guess. Or maybe I'm just too damn stubborn to give up.

Angel—you know, the do-gooder who runs that program out of her Grasso Street office to get kids like me off the streets? She tells me I've got a nihilistic attitude. Once she explained what that meant, all I could do was laugh.

"Look at where I'm coming from," I told her. "What do you expect?"

"I can help you."

I just shook my head. "You want a piece of me, that's all, but I've got nothing left to give."

That's only partly true. See, I've got responsibilities, just like a regular citizen. I've got the dogs. And I've got Tommy. I was joking about calling him my pet. That's just what the bikers who're squatting down the street from us call him. I think of us all—me, the dogs and Tommy—as family. Or about as close to family as any of us are ever going to get. I can't leave, because what would they do without me? And who'd take the whole pack of us, which is the only way I'd go?

Tommy's got this thing about magazines, though he can't read a word. Me, I love to read. I've got thousands of books. I get them all from the dump bins in back of bookstores—you know, where they tear off the covers to get their money back for the ones they don't sell and just throw the book away? Never made any sense to me, but you won't catch me complaining.

I'm not that particular about what I read. I just like the stories. Danielle Steel or Dostoyevsky, Somerset Maugham or King—doesn't make much difference. Just so long as I can get away in the words.

But Tommy likes his magazines, and he likes them with his name on the cover—you know, the subscription sticker? There's two words he can read: Thomas and Flood. I know his first name's Tommy, because he knows that much and that's what he told me. I made up the last name. The building we live in is on Flood Street.

He likes *People* and *Us* and *Entertainment Weekly* and *Life* and stuff like that. Lots of pictures, not too many words. He gets me to cut out the pictures of the people and animals and ads and stuff he likes and then he plays with them like they were paper dolls. That's how he gets away, I guess. Whatever works.

Anyway, I've got a post office box down on Grasso Street near Angel's office and that's where I have the subscriptions sent. I go down once a week to pick them up—usually on Thursday afternoons. It's all a little more than I can afford—makes me work a little harder at my garbage picking, you know?—but what am I going to do? Cut him off from his only pleasure? People think I'm hard—when they don't just think I'm crazy—and maybe I am, but I'm not mean.

The thing about having a post office box is that you get some pretty interesting junk mail—well at least Tommy finds it interesting. I used to throw it out, but he came down with me to the box one time and got all weirded out when he saw me throwing it out so I bring most of it back now. He calls them his surprises. First thing he asks when I get back is, "Were there any surprises?"

I went in the Thursday this all started and gave the clerk my usual glare, hoping that one day he'll finally get the message, but he never does. He was the one who sicced Angel on me in the first place. Thought nineteen was too young to be a bag lady, pretty girl like me. Thought he could help.

I didn't bother to explain that I'd chosen to live this way. I've been living on my own since I was twelve. I don't sell my bod' and I don't do drugs. My clothes may be worn down and patched, but they're clean. I wash every day, which is more than I can say for some of the real citizens I pass by on the street. You can smell their B.O. a half block away. I look pretty regular except on garbage day when Tommy and I hit the streets with our shopping carts, the dogs all strung out around us like our own special honor guard.

There's nothing wrong with garbage picking. Where do you think all those fancy antique shops get most of their high-priced merchandise?

I do okay, without either Angel's help or his. He was probably just hard up for a girlfriend.

"How's it going, Maisie?" he asked when I came in, all friendly, like we're pals. I guess he got my name from the form I filled out when I rented the box.

I ignored him, like I always do, and gathered the week's pile up. It was a fairly thick stack—lots of surprises for Tommy. I took it all outside where Rexy was waiting for me. He's the smallest of the dogs, just a small little mutt with wiry brown hair and a real insecurity problem. He's the only one who comes everywhere with me because he just falls apart if I leave him at home.

I gave Rexy a quick pat, then sat on the curb, sorting through Tommy's surprises. If the junk mail doesn't have pictures, I toss it. I only want to carry so much of this crap back with me.

It was while I was going through the stack that this envelope fell out. I just sat and stared at it for the longest time. It looked like one of those ornate invitations they're always making a fuss over in the romance novels I read: almost square, the paper really thick and cream-colored, ornate lettering on the outside that was real high-class calligraphy, it was so pretty. But that wasn't what had me staring at it, unwilling to pick it up.

The lettering spelled out my name. Not the one I use, but my real name. Margaret. Maisie's just a diminutive of it that

I read about in this book about Scotland. That was all that was there, just ''Margaret,'' no surname. I never use one except for when the cops decide to roust the squatters in the Tombs, like they do from time to time—I think it's like some kind of training exercise for them—and then I use Flood, same as I gave Tommy.

I shot a glance back in through the glass doors because I figured it had to be from the postal clerk—who else knew me?—but he wasn't even looking at me. I sat and stared at it a little longer, but then I finally picked it up. I took out my pen knife and slit the envelope open, and carefully pulled out this card. All it said on it was, ''Allow the dark-robed access tonight and they will kill you.''

I didn't have a clue what it meant, but it gave me a royal case of the creeps. If it wasn't a joke—which I figured it had to be—then who were these black-robed and why would they want to kill me?

Every big city like this is really two worlds. You could say it's divided up between the haves and the have-nots, but it's not that simple. It's more like some people are citizens of the day and others of the night. Someone like me belongs to the night. Not because I'm bad, but because I'm invisible. People don't know I exist. They don't know and they don't care, except for Angel and the postal clerk, I guess.

But now someone did.

Unless it was a joke. I tried to laugh it off, but it just didn't work. I looked at the envelope again, checking it out for a return address, and that's when I realized something I should have noticed straightaway. The envelope didn't have my box number on it, it didn't have anything at all except for my name. So how the hell did it end up in my box? There was only one way.

I left Rexy guarding Tommy's mail—just to keep him occupied—and went back inside. When the clerk finished with the customer ahead of me, he gave me a big smile but I laid the envelope down on the counter between us and didn't smile back.

Actually, he's a pretty good-looking guy. He's got one of those flat-top haircuts—shaved sides, kinky black hair standing straight up on top. His skin's the color of coffee and he's got dark eyes with the longest lashes I ever saw on a guy. I could like him just fine, but the trouble is he's a regular citizen. It'd just never work out.

"How'd this get in my box?" I asked him. "All it's got is my name on it, no box number, no address, nothing."

He looked down at the envelope. "You found it in your box?"

I nodded.

"I didn't put it in there and I'm the one who sorts all the mail for the boxes."

"I still found it in there."

He picked it up and turned it over in his hands.

"This is really weird," he said.

"You into occult shit?" I asked him.

I was thinking of dark robes. The only people I ever saw wear them were priests or people dabbling in the occult.

He blinked with surprise. "What do you mean?"

"Nothing."

I grabbed the envelope back and headed back to where Rexy was waiting for me.

"Maisie!" the clerk called after me, but I just ignored him.

Great, I thought as I collected the mail Rexy'd been guarding for me. First Joe postal clerk's got a good Samaritan complex over me—probably fueled by his dick—now he's going downright weird. I wondered if he knew where I lived. I wondered if he knew about the dogs. I wondered about magicians in dark robes and whether he thought he had some kind of magic that was going to deal with the dogs and make me go all gooshy for him—just before he killed me.

The more I thought about it, the more screwed up I got. I wasn't so much scared as confused. And angry. How was I supposed to keep coming back to get Tommy's mail, knowing he was there? What would he put in the box next? A dead rat? It wasn't like I could complain to anybody. People like me, we don't have any rights.

Finally I just started for home, but I paused as I passed the door to Angel's office.

Angel's a little cool with me these days. She still says she wanted to help me, but she doesn't quite trust me anymore. It's not really her fault.

She had me in her office one time—I finally went, just to get her off my back—and we sat there for awhile, looking at each other, drinking this crappy coffee from the machine that someone donated to her a few years ago. I wouldn't have picked it up on a dare if I'd come across it on my rounds.

"What do you want from me?" I finally asked her.

"I'm just trying to understand you."

"There's nothing to understand. What you see is what I am. No more, no less."

"But why do you live the way you do?"

Understand, I admire what Angel does. She's helped a lot of kids that were in a really bad way and that's a good thing. Some people need help because they can't help themselves.

She's an attractive woman with a heart-shaped face, the kind of eyes that always look really warm and caring and long dark hair that seems to go on forever down her back. I always figured something really bad must have happened to her as a kid, for her to do what she does. It's not like she makes much of a living. I think the only thing she really and honestly cares about is helping people through this sponsorship program she's developed where straights put up money and time to help the down-and-outers get a second chance.

I don't need that kind of help. I'm never going to be much more than what I am, but that's okay. It beats what I had before I hit the streets.

I've told Angel all of this a dozen times, but she sat there behind her desk, looking at me with those sad eyes of hers, and I knew she wanted a piece of me, so I gave her one. I figured maybe she'd leave me alone then.

"I was in high school," I told her, "and there was this girl who wanted to get back at one of the teachers—a really nice guy named Mr. Hammond. He taught math. So she made up this story about how he'd molested her and the shit really hit the fan. He got suspended while the cops and the school board looked into the matter and all the time this girl's laughing her head off behind everybody's back, but looking real sad and screwed up whenever the cops and the social workers are talking to her.

"But I knew he didn't do it. I knew where she was, the night she said it happened, and it wasn't with Mr. Hammond. Now I wasn't exactly the best-liked kid in that school, and I knew what this girl's gang was going to do to me, but I went ahead and told the truth anyway.

"Things worked out pretty much the way I expected. I got the cold shoulder from everybody, but at least Mr. Hammond got his name cleared and his job back.

"One afternoon he asks me to see him after school and I figure it's to thank me for what I've done, so I go to his classroom. The building's pretty well empty and the scuff of my shoes in the hallway is the only sound I hear as I go to see him. I get to the math room and he takes me back into his office. Then he locks the door and he rapes me. Not just once, but over and over again. And you know what he says to me while he's doing it?

" 'Nobody's going to believe a thing you say,' he says, 'You try to talk about this and they're just going to laugh in your face.' "

I looked over at Angel and there were tears swimming in her eyes.

"And you know what?" I said. "I knew he was right. I was the one that cleared his name. There was *nobody* going to believe me and I didn't even try."

"Oh, Jesus," Angel said. "You poor kid."

"Don't take it so hard," I told her. "It's past history. Besides, it never really happened. I just made it up because I figured it was the kind of thing you wanted to hear.''

I'll give her this: she took it well. Didn't yell at me, didn't pitch me out onto the street. But you can see why maybe I'm not on her list of favorite people these days. On the other hand, she doesn't hold a grudge—I know that too.

I felt like a hypocrite going in to see her with this problem, but I didn't have anyone else to turn to. It's not like Tommy or the dogs could give me any advice. I hesitated for the longest moment in the doorway, but then she looked up and saw me standing there, so I went ahead in.

I took off my hat—it's this fedora that I actually bought new because it was just too cool to pass up. I wear it all the time, my light brown hair hanging down from it, long and straight, though not as long as Angel's. I like the way it looks with my jeans and sneakers and this cotton shirt I found at a rummage sale that only needed a tear fixed on one of its shirttails.

I know what you're thinking, but hey, I never said I wasn't vain. I may be a squatter, but I like to look my best. It gets me into places where they don't let in bums.

Anyway I took off my hat and slouched in the chair on this side of Angel's desk.

"Which one's that?" she asked, pointing to Rexy who was sitting outside by the door like the good little dog he is.

"Rexy."

"He can come in if you'd like."

I shook my head. "No. I'm not staying long. I just had this thing I wanted to ask you about. It's . . ."

I didn't know where to begin, but finally I just started in with finding the envelope. It got easier as I went along. That's one thing you got to hand to Angel—there's nobody can listen like she does. You take up *all* of her attention when you're talking to her. You never get the feeling she's thinking of something else, or of what she's going to say back to you, or anything like that.

Angel didn't speak for a long time after I was done. When

I stopped talking, she looked past me, out at the traffic going by on Grasso Street.

"Maisie," she said finally. "Have you ever heard the story of the boy who cried wolf?"

"Sure, but what's that got to do with—oh, I get it." I took out the envelope and slid it across the desk to her. "I didn't have to come in here," I added.

And I was wishing I hadn't, but Angel seemed to give herself a kind of mental shake. She opened the envelope and read the message, then her gaze came back to me.

"No," she said. "I'm glad you did. Do you want me to have a talk with Franklin?"

"Who's that?"

"The fellow behind the counter at the post office. I don't mind doing it, although I have to admit that it doesn't sound like the kind of thing he'd do."

So that was his name. Franklin. Franklin the creep.

I shrugged. "What good would that do? Even if he did do it—" and the odds looked good so far as I was concerned "—he's not going to admit to it."

"Maybe we can talk to his supervisor." She looked at her watch. "I think it's too late to do it today, but I can try first thing tomorrow morning."

Great. In the meantime, I could be dead.

Angel must have guessed what I was thinking, because she added, "Do you need a place to stay for tonight? Some place where you'll feel safe?"

I thought of Tommy and the dogs and shook my head.

"No, I'll be okay," I said as I collected my envelope and stuck it back in with Tommy's mail. "Thanks for, you know, listening and everything."

I waited for her to roll into some spiel about how she could do more, could get me off the street, that kind of thing, but it was like she was tuned right into my wavelength because she didn't say a word about any of that. She just knew, I guess, that I'd never come back if every time I talked to her that was all I could look forward to.

"Come see me tomorrow," was all she said as I got to my feet. "And Maisie?"

I paused in the doorway where Rexy was ready to start bouncing off my legs as if he hadn't seen me in weeks.

"Be careful," Angel added.

"I will."

I took a long route back to the squat, watching my back the whole time, but I never saw anybody that looked like he was following me, and not a single person in a dark robe. I almost laughed at myself by the time I got back. There were Tommy and the dogs, all sprawled out on the steps of our building until Rexy yelped and then the whole pack of them were racing down the street towards me.

Okay, big as he was, Tommy still couldn't hurt a flea even if his life depended on it and the dogs were all small and old and pretty well used up, but Franklin would still have to be crazy to think he could mess with us. He didn't *know* my family. You get a guy as big as Tommy and all those dogs . . . well, they just looked dangerous. What did I have to worry about?

The dogs were all over me then with Tommy right behind them. He grinned from ear to ear as I handed him his mail.

"Surprises!" he cried happily, in that weird high voice of his. "Maisie bring surprises!"

We went inside to our place up on the second floor. It's got this big open space that we use in the summer when we want the air to have a chance to move around. There's books everywhere. Tommy's got his own corner with his magazines and all the little cut-out people and stuff that he plays with. There's a couple of mismatched kitchen chairs and a card table. A kind of old cabinet that some hoboes helped me move up the one flight from the street holds our food and the Coleman stove I use for cooking.

We sleep on the mattresses over in another corner, the whole pack together, except for Chuckie. He's this old lab that likes to guard the doorway. I usually think he's crazy for doing so, but I wouldn't mind tonight. Chuckie can look real fierce when he wants to. There's a couple of chests by the bed area. I keep our clothes in one and dry kibbles for the dogs in another. They're pretty good scavengers, but I like to see that they're eating the right kind of food. I wouldn't want anything to happen to them. One thing I can't afford is vet bills.

First off I fed the dogs, then I made supper for Tommy and me—lentil soup with day-old buns I'd picked up behind a bakery in Crowsea. We'd been eating the soup for a few days, but we had to use it up because, with the spring finally here, it was getting too warm for food to keep. In the winter we've got smaller quarters down the hall, complete with a cast-iron stove that I salvaged from this place they were wrecking over in Foxville. Tommy and I pretty near killed ourselves hauling it back. One of the bikers helped us bring it upstairs.

We fell into our usual Thursday night ritual once we'd finished supper. After hauling down tomorrow's water from the tank I'd set up on the roof to catch rainwater, I lit the oil lamp, then Tommy and I sat down at the table and went through his new magazines and ads. Every time he'd point out something that he liked in a picture, I'd cut it out for him. I do a pretty tidy job, if I say so myself. Getting to be an old hand at it. By the time we finished, he had a big stack of new cut-out people and stuff for his games that he just had to go try out right away. I went and got the book I'd started this morning and brought it back to the table, but I couldn't read.

I could hear Tommy talking to his new little friends. The dogs shifting and moving about the way they do. Down the street a Harley kicked over and I listened to it go through the Tombs until it faded in the distance. Then there was only the sound of the wind outside the window.

I'd been able to keep that stupid envelope with its message out of my head just by staying busy, but now it was all I could think about. I looked out the window. It was barely eight, but it was dark already. The real long days of summer were still to come.

So is Franklin out there? I asked myself. Is he watching the building, scoping things out, getting ready to make his move? Maybe dressed up in some black robe, him and a bunch of his pals?

I didn't really believe it. I didn't know him, but like Angel had said, it didn't seem like him and I could believe it. He might bug me, being all friendly and wanting to play Pygmalion to my Eliza Doolittle, but I didn't think he had a mean streak in him.

So where *did* the damn message come from? What was it supposed to mean? And, here was the scary part: if it wasn't a joke, and if Franklin wasn't responsible for it, then who was?

I kept turning that around and around in my mind until my head felt like it was spinning. Everybody started picking up on my mood. The dogs became all anxious and when I walked near them got to whining and shrinking away like I was going to hit them. Tommy got the shakes and his little people started tearing and then he was crying and the dogs started in howling and I just wanted to get the hell out of there.

But I didn't. It took me a couple of hours to calm Tommy down and finally get him to fall asleep. I told him the story he likes the best, the one where this count from some place far away shows up and tells us that we're really his kids and he takes us away, dogs and all, to our real home where we all live happily ever after. Sometimes I use his little cut-outs to tell the story, but I didn't do that tonight. I didn't want to remind him of how a bunch'd gotten torn.

By the time Tommy was sleeping, the dogs had calmed down again and were sleeping too. I couldn't. I sat up all night worrying about that damned message, about what would happen to Tommy and the dogs if anything ever did happen to me, about all kinds of crap that I usually don't let myself think about.

Come the morning, I felt like I'd crawled up out of a sewer. You know what it's like when you pull an all-nighter? Your eyes have this burning behind them, you'd kill for a shower and everything seems a little on edge? I saw about getting breakfast for everyone, let the dogs out for a run, then I told Tommy I had to go back downtown.

"You don't go out today," I told him. "You understand? You don't go out and you don't let anybody in. You and the dogs play inside today, okay? Can you do that for Maisie?"

"Sure," Tommy said, like I was the one with bricks for brains. "No problem, Maisie."

God I love him.

I gave him a big hug and a kiss, patted each of the dogs, then headed back down to Grasso Street with Rexy. I was about half a block from Angel's office when the headlines of a newspaper outside a drugstore caught my eye. I stopped dead in my tracks and just stared at it. The words swam in my sight, headlines blurring with the subheadings. I picked up the paper and unfolded it so that I could see the whole front page, then I started reading from the top.

GRIERSON SLAIN BY SATANISTS.

DIRECTOR OF THE CITY'S NEW AIDS CLINIC FOUND DEAD IN FERRYSIDE GRAVEYARD AMID OCCULT PARAPHERNALIA.

POLICE BAFFLED.

MAYOR SAYS, 'THIS IS AN OUTRAGE.'

"Hey, this isn't a library, kid."

Rexy growled and I looked up to find the drugstore owner standing over me. I dug in my pocket until it coughed up a quarter, then handed it over to him. I took the paper over to the curb and sat down.

It was the picture that got to me. It looked like one of the buildings in the Tombs in which kids had been playing at ritual magic a few years ago. All the same kinds of candles and inverted pentacles and weird graffiti. Nobody squatted in that building anymore, though the kids hadn't been back for over a year. There was still something wrong about the

place, like the miasma of whatever the hell it was that they'd
been doing was still there, hanging on.

It was a place to give you the creeps. But this picture had
something worse. It had a body, covered up by a blanket,
right in the middle of it. The tombstones around it were all
scorched and in pieces, like someone had set off a bomb.
The police couldn't explain what had happened, except they
did say it hadn't been a bomb, because no one nearby had
heard a thing.

Pinpricks of dread went crawling up my spine as I reread
the first paragraph. The victim, Grierson. Her first name was
Margaret.

I folded the paper and got up, heading for the post office.
Franklin was alone behind the counter when I got inside.

"The woman who died last night," I said before he had a
chance to even say hello. "Margaret Grierson. The Director
of the AIDS Clinic. Did she have a box here?"

Franklin nodded. "It's terrible, isn't it? One of my friends
says the whole clinic's going to fall apart without her there
to run it. God, I hope it doesn't change anything. I know a
half-dozen people that are going to it."

I gave him a considering look. A half dozen friends? He
had this real sad look in his eyes, like . . . Jesus, I thought.
Was Franklin gay? Had he really been just making nice and
not trying to jump my bones?

I reached across the counter and put my hand on his arm.

"They won't let this screw it up," I told him. "The
clinic's too important."

The look of surprise in his face had me backing out the
door fast. What the hell was I doing?

"Maisie!" he cried.

I guess I felt like a bit of a shit for having misjudged him,
but all the same, I couldn't stick around. I followed my usual
rule of thumb when things get heavy or weird: I fled.

I just started wandering aimlessly, thinking about what I'd
learned. That message hadn't been for me, it had been for
Grierson. Margaret, yeah, but Margaret *Grierson,* not Flood.

Not me. Somehow it had gotten in the wrong box. I don't know who put it there, or how he knew what was going to happen last night before it happened, but whoever he was, he'd screwed up royally.

Better it had been me, I thought. Better a loser from the Tombs, than someone like Grierson who was really doing something worthwhile.

When I thought that, I realized something that I guess I'd always known, but I just didn't ever let myself think about. You get called a loser often enough and you start to believe it. I know I did. But it didn't have to be true.

I guess I had what they call an epiphany in some of the older books I've read. Everything came together and made sense—except for what I was doing with myself.

I unfolded the paper again. There was a picture of Grierson near the bottom—one of those shots they keep on file for important people and run whenever they haven't got anything else. It was cropped down from one that had been taken when she cut the ribbon at the new clinic a few months back. I remembered seeing it when they ran coverage of the ceremony.

"This isn't going to mean a whole lot to you," I told her picture, "but I'm sorry about what happened to you. Maybe it should've been me, but it wasn't. There's not much I can. do about that. But I can do something about the rest of *my* life."

I left the paper on a bench near a bus stop and walked back to Grasso Street to Angel's office. I sat down in the chair across from her desk, holding Rexy on my lap to give me courage, and I told her about Tommy and the dogs, about how they needed me and that was why I'd never wanted to take her up on her offers to help.

She shook her head sadly when I was done. She was looking a little weepy again—like she had when I told her that story before—but I was feeling a little weepy myself this time.

"Why didn't you tell me?" she asked.

I shrugged. "I guess I thought you'd take them away from me."

I surprised myself. I hadn't lied, or made a joke. Instead I'd told her the truth. It wasn't much, but it was a start.

"Oh, Maisie," she said. "We can work something out."

She came around the desk and I let her hold me. It's funny. I didn't mean to cry, but I did. And so did she. It felt good, having someone else be strong for a change. I haven't had someone be there for me since my grandma died in 1971, the year I turned eight. I hung in for a long time, all things considered, but the day that Mr. Hammond asked me to come see him after school was the day I finally gave up my nice little regulated slot as a citizen of the day and became a part of the night world instead.

I knew it wasn't going to be easy, trying to fit into the day world—I'd probably never fit in completely, and I don't think I'd want to. I also knew that I was going to have a lot of crap to go through and to put up with in the days to come, and maybe I'd regret the decision I'd made today, but right now it felt good to be back.

⌣ · BRIDGES · ⌣

S HE WATCHED THE taillights dwindle until, far down the
  dirt road, the car went around a curve. The two red dots
winked out and then she was alone.

Stones crunched underfoot as she shifted from one foot to
another, looking around herself. Trees, mostly cedar and
pine, crowded the narrow verge on either side. Above her,
the sky held too many stars, but for all their number, they
shed too little light. She was used to city streets and pavement, to neon and streetlights. Even in the 'burbs there was
always some manmade light.

The darkness and silence, the loneliness of the night as it
crouched in the trees, spooked her. It chipped at the veneer
of her streetsmart toughness. She was twenty miles out of
the city, up in the hills that backed onto the Kickaha Reserve. Attitude counted for nothing out here.

She didn't bother cursing Eddie. She conserved her breath
for the long walk back to the city, just hoping she wouldn't
run into some pickup truck full of redneck hillbillies who
might not be quite as ready to just cut her loose as Eddie had

when he realized he wasn't going to get his way. For too many men, no meant yes. And she'd heard stories about some of the good old boys who lived in these hills.

She didn't even hate Eddie, for all that he was eminently hateful. She saved that hatred for herself, for being so trusting when she knew—when she *knew*—how it always turned out.

"Stupid bloody cow," she muttered as she began to walk.

High school was where it had started.

She'd liked to party, she'd liked to have a good time, she hadn't seen anything wrong with making out because it was fun. Once you got a guy to slow down, sex was the best thing around.

She went with a lot of guys, but it took her a long time to realize just how many and that they only wanted one thing from her. She was slow on the uptake because she didn't see a problem until that night with Dave. Before that, she'd just seen herself as popular. She always had a date; someone was always ready to take her out and have some fun. The guy she'd gone out with on the weekend might ignore her the next Monday at school, but there was always someone else there, leaning up against her locker, asking her what was she doing tonight, so that she never really had time to think it through.

Never *wanted* to think it through, she'd realized in retrospect.

Until Dave wanted her to go to the drive-in that Saturday night.

"I'd rather go to the dance," she told him.

It was just a disco with a DJ, but she was in the mood for loud music and stepping out, not a movie. First Dave tried to convince her to go to the drive-in, then he said that if she wanted to go dancing, he knew some good clubs. She didn't know where the flash of insight came from—it just flared there inside her head, leaving a sick feeling in the pit of her stomach, a tightness in her chest.

"You don't want to be seen with me at the dance," she said.

"It's not that. It's just . . . well, all the guys . . ."

"Told you what? That I'm a cheap lay?"

"No, it's just, well . . ."

The knowing looks she got in the hall, the way guys would talk to her before they went out, but avoided her later—it all came together.

Jesus, how could she have been so stupid?

She got out of his car, which was still parked in front of her dad's house. Tears were burning the back of her eyes, but she refused to let them come. She never talked to Dave again. She swore that things were going to change.

It didn't matter that she didn't go out with another guy for her whole senior year; everyone still thought of her as the school tramp. Two months ago, she'd finally finished school. She didn't even wait to get her grades. With money she'd saved up through the years, she moved from her dad's place in the 'burbs to her own apartment in Lower Crowsea, got a job as a receptionist in an office on Yoors Street and was determined that things were going to be different. She had no history where she lived or where she worked; no one to snigger at her when she went down a hall.

It was a new start and it wasn't easy. She didn't have any friends, but then she hadn't really had any before either—she just hadn't had the time or good sense to realize that. But she was working on it now. She'd gotten to know Sandra who lived down the hall in her building, and they'd hung out together, watching videos or going to one of the bars in the Market—girls night out, men need not apply.

She liked having a girl for a friend. She hadn't had one since she lost her virginity just a few days before her fifteenth birthday and discovered that boys could make her feel really good in ways that a girl couldn't.

Besides Sandra, she was starting to get to know the people at work, too—which was where she met Eddie. He was the building's mail clerk, dropping off a bundle of mail on her desk every morning, hanging out for a couple of minutes, finally getting the courage up to ask her for a date. Her first one in a very long time.

He seemed like a nice guy, so she said yes. A friend of his was having a party at his cottage, not far from town. There'd be a bonfire on the beach, some people would be bringing their guitars and they'd sing old Buddy Holly and Beatles tunes. They'd barbecue hamburgers and hotdogs. It'd be fun.

Fifteen minutes ago, Eddie had pulled the car over to the side of the road. Killing the engine, he leaned back against the driver's door, gaze lingering on how her T-shirt molded to her chest. He gave her a goofy grin.

"Why are we stopping?" she'd asked, knowing it sounded dumb, knowing what was coming next.

"I was thinking," Eddie said. "We could have our private party."

"No thanks."

"Come on. Chuck said—"

"Chuck? Chuck who?"

"Anderson. He used to go to Mawson High with you."

A ghost from the past, rising to haunt her. She knew Chuck Anderson.

"He just moved into my building. We were talking and when I mentioned your name, he told me all about you. He said you liked to party."

"Well, he's full of shit. I think you'd better take me home."

"You don't have to play hard to get," Eddie said.

He started to reach for her, but her hand was quicker. It went into her purse and came out with a switchblade. She touched the release button and its blade came out of the handle with a wicked-sounding *snick*. Eddie moved back to his own side of the car.

"What the hell are you trying to prove?" he demanded.

"Just take me home."

"Screw you. Either you come across, or you walk."

She gave him a long hard stare, then nodded. "Then I walk."

The car's wheels spat gravel as soon as she was out, engine gunning as Eddie maneuvered a tight one-eighty. She closed up her knife and dropped it back into her purse as she watched the taillights recede.

Her legs were aching by the time she reached the covered bridge that crossed Stickers Creek just before it ran into the Kickaha River. She'd walked about three miles since Eddie had dumped her; only another seventeen to go.

Twice she'd hidden in the trees as a vehicle passed her. The first one had looked so innocent that she'd berated herself for not trying to thumb a ride. The second was a pickup with a couple of yahoos in it. One of them had tossed out a beer bottle that just missed hitting her—he hadn't known she was hiding in the cedars there and she was happy that it had stayed that way. Thankfully, she had let nervous caution overrule the desire to just get the hell out of here and home.

She sat down on this side of the bridge to rest. She couldn't see much of the quick-moving creek below her— just white tops that flashed in the starlight—but she could hear it. It was a soothing sound.

She thought about Eddie.

She should have been able to see it in him, shouldn't she? It wasn't as though she didn't know what to be looking out for.

And Chuck Anderson. Jesus.

What was the point in trying to make a new start when nobody gave you a break?

She sighed and rose to her feet. There was no sense in railing against it. The world wasn't fair, and that was that. But god it was lonely. How could you carry on, always by yourself? What was the *point*?

Her footsteps had a hollow ring as she walked across the covered bridge and she started to get spooked again. What if a car came, right *now*? There was nowhere to run to, nowhere to hide. Just the dusty insides of the covered bridge, its wood so old she was surprised it was still standing.

Halfway across she felt an odd dropping sensation in her stomach, like being in an elevator that was going down too quickly. Vertigo had her leaning against the wooden planks that sided the bridge. She knew a moment's panic—oh, Jesus, she was falling—but then the feeling went away and she could walk without feeling dizzy to the far end of the bridge.

She stepped outside and stopped dead in her tracks. Her earlier panic was mild in comparison to what she felt now as she stared ahead in disbelief.

Everything familiar was gone. Road, trees, hills—all gone. She wasn't in the same country anymore—wasn't in the country at all. A city like something out of an Escher painting lay spread out in front of her. Odd buildings, angles all awry, leaned against and pushed away from each other, all at the same time. Halfway up their lengths, there seemed to be a kind of vortal shift so that the top halves appeared to be reflections of the lower.

And then there were the bridges.

Everywhere she looked there were bridges. Bridges connecting the buildings, bridges connecting bridges, bridges that went nowhere, bridges that folded back on themselves so that you couldn't tell where they started or ended. Too many bridges to count.

She started to back up the way she'd come but got no further than two steps when a hand reached out of the shadows and pulled her forward. She flailed against her attacker who swung her about and then held her with her arms pinned against her body.

"Easy, easy," a male voice said in her ear.

It had a dry, dusty sound to it, like the kind you could imagine old books in a library's stacks have when they talk to each other late at night.

"Let me go, let me *GO*!" she cried.

Still holding her, her assailant walked her to the mouth of the covered bridge.

"Look," he said.

For a moment she was still too panicked to know what he was talking about. But then it registered. The bridge she'd walked across to get to this nightmare city no longer had a roadway. There was just empty space between its wooden walls now. If her captor hadn't grabbed her when he did, she would have fallen god knew how far.

She stopped struggling and he let her go. She moved gingerly away from the mouth of the covered bridge, then stopped again, not knowing where to go, what to do. Everywhere she looked there were weird tilting buildings and bridges.

It was impossible. None of this was happening, she decided. She'd fallen asleep on the other side of the bridge and was just dreaming all of this.

"Will you be all right?" her benefactor asked.

"I . . . I . . ."

She turned to look at him. The moonlight made him out to be a harmless-looking guy. He was dressed in faded jeans and an off-white flannel shirt, cowboy boots and a jean jacket. His hair was dark and short. It was hard to make out his features, except for his eyes. They seemed to take in the moonlight and then send it back out again, twice as bright.

Something about him calmed her—until she tried to speak.

"Whoareyou?" she asked. "WhatisthisplacehowdidI-gethere?"

As soon as the first question came out, a hundred others came clamoring into her mind, each demanding to be voiced, to be answered. She shut her mouth after the first few burst out in a breathless spurt, realizing that they would just feed the panic that she was only barely keeping in check.

She took a deep breath, then tried again.

"Thank you," she said. "For saving me."

"You're welcome."

Again that dry, dusty voice. But the air itself was dry, she realized. She could almost feel the moisture leaving her skin.

"Who are you?" she asked.

"You can call me Jack."

"My name's Moira—Moira Jones."

Jack inclined his head in a slight nod. "Are you all right now, Moira Jones?" he asked.

"I think so."

"Good, well—"

"Wait!" she cried, realizing that he was about to leave her. "What is this place? Why did you bring me here?"

He shook his head. "I didn't," he said. "No one comes to the City of Bridges unless it's their fate to do so. In that sense, you brought yourself."

"But . . . ?"

"I know. It's all strange and different. You don't know where to turn, who to trust."

There was the faintest hint of mockery under the dry tones of his voice.

"Something like that," Moira said.

. He seemed to consider her for the longest time.

"I don't know you," he said finally. "I don't know why you brought yourself here or where you come from. I don't know how, or even if, you'll ever find your way home again."

Bizarre though her situation was, oddly enough, Moira found herself adjusting to it far more quickly than she would have thought possible. It was almost like being in a dream where you just accept things as they come along, except she knew this wasn't a dream—just as she knew that she was getting the brush off.

"Listen," she said. "I appreciate your help a moment ago, but don't worry about me. I'll get by."

"What I do know, however," Jack went on as though she hadn't spoken, "is that this is a place for those who have no other place to go."

"What're you saying? That's it's some kind of a dead end place?"

The way her life was going, it sounded like it had been made for her.

"It's a forgotten place."

"Forgotten by who?"

"By the world in which it exists," Jack said.

"How can a place this weird be forgotten?" she asked.

Moira looked around at the bridges as she spoke. They were everywhere, of every size and shape and persuasion. One that looked like it belonged in a Japanese tea garden stood side by side with part of what had to be an interstate overpass, but somehow the latter didn't overshadow the former, although both their proportions were precise. She saw rope bridges, wooden bridges and old stone bridges like the Kelly Street Bridge that crossed the Kickaha River in that part of Newford called the Rosses.

She wondered if she'd ever see Newford again.

"The same way people forget their dreams," Jack replied. He touched her elbow, withdrawing his hand before she could take offense. "Come walk with me if you like. I've a previous appointment, but I can show you around a bit on the way."

Moira hesitated for a long moment, then fell into step beside him. They crossed a metal bridge, the heels of their boots ringing. Of course, she thought, they couldn't go anywhere without crossing a bridge. Bridges were the only kind of roads that existed in this place.

"Do you live here?" she asked.

Jack shook his head. "But I'm here a lot. I deal in possibilities and that's what bridges are in a way—not so much the ones that already exist to take you from one side of something to another, but the kind we build for ourselves."

"What are you talking about?"

"Say you want to be an artist—a painter, perhaps. The bridge you build between when you don't know which end of the brush to hold to when you're doing respected work can include studying under another artist, experimenting on your own, whatever. You build the bridge and it either takes you where you want it to, or it doesn't.''

"And if it doesn't?''

His teeth flashed in the moonlight. "Then you build another one and maybe another one until one of them does.''

Moira nodded as though she understood, all the while asking herself, what am I *doing* here?

"But this," he added, "is a place of failed dreams. Where bridges that go nowhere find their end.''

Wonderful, Moira thought. A forgotten place. A dead end.

They started across an ornate bridge, its upper chords were all filigreed metal, its roadway cobblestone. Two thirds of the way across, what she took to be a pile of rags shifted and sat up. It was a beggar with a tattered cloak wrapped around him or her—Moira couldn't tell the sex of the poor creature. It seemed to press closer against the railing as they came abreast of it.

"Cancer victim," Jack said, as they passed the figure. "Nothing left to live for, so she came here.''

Moira shivered. "Can't you—can't we do anything for her?''

"Nothing to be done for her," Jack replied.

The dusty tones of his voice made it impossible for her to decide if that was true, or if he just didn't care.

"But—''

"She wouldn't be here if there was," he said.

Wood underfoot now—a primitive bridge of rough timbers. The way Jack led her was a twisting path that seemed to take them back the way they'd come as much as forward. As they crossed an arched stone walkway, Moira heard a whimper. She paused and saw a child huddled up against a doorway below.

Jack stopped, waiting for her to catch up.

"There's a child," she began.

"You'll have to understand," Jack said, "that there's

nothing you can do for anyone here. They've long since given up Hope. They belong to Despair now.''

''Surely—''

''It's an abused child,'' Jack said. He glanced at his wrist watch. ''I've time. Go help it.''

''God, you're a cold fish.''

Jack tapped his watch. ''Time's slipping away.''

Moira was trapped between just wanting to tell him to shove off and her fear of being stuck in this place by herself. Jack wasn't much, but at least he seemed to know his way around.

''I'll be right back,'' she said.

She hurried back down the arched path and crossed a rickety wooden bridge to the doorway of the building. The child looked up at her approach, his whimpers muting as he pushed his face against his shoulder.

''There, there,'' Moira said. ''You're going to be okay.''

She moved forward, pausing when the child leapt to his feet, back against the wall. He held his hands out before him, warding her away.

''No one's going to hurt you.''

She took another step, and he started to scream.

''Don't cry!'' she said, continuing to move forward. ''I'm here to help you.''

The child bolted before she could reach him. He slipped under her arm and was off and away, leaving a wailing cry in his wake. Moira stared after him.

''You'll never catch him now,'' Jack called down from above.

She looked up at him. He was sitting on the edge of the arched walkway, legs dangling, heels tapping against the stonework.

''I wasn't going to hurt him,'' she said.

''He doesn't know that. I told you, the people here have long since given up hope. You can't help them—nobody can. They can't even help themselves anymore.''

''What are they doing here?''

Jack shrugged. "They've got to go somewhere, don't they?"

Moira made her way back to where he was waiting for her, anger clouding her features.

"Don't you even *care*?" she demanded.

His only reply was to start walking again. She hesitated for a long moment, then hurried to catch up. She walked with her arms wrapped around herself, but the chill she felt came from inside and it wouldn't go away.

They crossed bridges beyond her ability to count as they made their way into the central part of the city. From time to time they passed the odd streetlight, its dim glow making a feeble attempt to push back the shadows; in other places, the ghosts of flickering neon signs crackled and hissed more than they gave off light. In some ways the lighting made things worse for it revealed the city's general state of decay—cracked walls, rubbled streets, refuse wherever one turned.

Under one lamp post, she got a better look at her companion. His features were strong rather than handsome; none of the callousness she sensed in his voice was reflected in them. He caught her gaze and gave her a thin smile, but the humor in his eyes was more mocking than companionable.

They continued to pass by dejected and lost figures that hunched in the shadows, huddled against buildings, or bolted at their approach. Jack listed their despairs for her— AIDS victim, rape victim, abused wife, paraplegic—until Moira begged him to stop.

"I can't take anymore," she said.

"I'm sorry. I thought you wanted to know."

They went the rest of the way in silence, the bridges taking them higher and higher until they finally stood on the top of an enormous building that appeared to be the largest and most centrally placed of the city's structures. From its heights, the city was spread out around them on all sides.

It made for an eerie sight. Moira stepped back from the edge of the roof, away from the pull of vertigo that came creeping up the small of her back to whisper in her ear. She had only to step out, into the night sky, it told her. Step out and all her troubles would be forever eased.

At the sound of a footstep, she turned gratefully away from the disturbing view. A woman was walking towards them, pausing when she was a few paces away. Unlike the other inhabitants of the city, she gave the impression of being self-assured, of being in control of her destiny.

She had pale skin, and short spiky red hair. A half dozen silver earrings hung from one ear; the other had a small silver stud in the shape of a star. Like Jack, she was dressed casually: black jeans, black boots, white tank-top, a black leather jacket draped over one shoulder. And like Jack, her eyes, too, seemed like a reservoir for the moonlight.

"You're not alone," she said to Jack.

"I never am," Jack replied. "You know that. My sister, Diane," he added to Moira, then introduced her to Diane.

The woman remained silent, studying Moira with her moon-bright eyes until Moira couldn't help but fidget. The dreamlike quality of her situation was beginning to filter away. Once again a panicked feeling was making itself felt in the pit of her stomach.

"Why are you here?" Diane asked her finally.

Her voice had a different quality from her brother's. It was a warm, rounded sound that carried in it a sweet scent like that of cherry blossoms or rose buds. It took away Moira's panic, returning her once more to that sense of it all just being a dream.

"I . . . I don't know," she said. "I was just crossing a bridge on my way home and the next thing I knew I was . . . here. Wherever here is. I—look. I just want to go home. I don't want any of this to be real."

"It's very real," Diane said.

"Wonderful."

"She wants to help the unhappy," Jack offered, "but they just run away from her."

Moira shot him a dirty look.

"Do be still," Diane told him, frowning as she spoke. She returned her attention to Moira. "Why don't you go home?"

"I—I don't know *how* to. The bridge that brought me here . . . when I went to go back across it, its roadway was gone."

Diane nodded. "What has my brother told you?"

Nothing that made sense, Moira wanted to say, but she related what she remembered of her conversations with Jack.

"And do you despair?" Diane asked.

"I . . ."

Moira hesitated. She thought of the hopeless, dejected people she'd passed on the way to this rooftop.

"Not really, I guess. I mean, I'm not happy or anything, but . . ."

"You have hope? That things will get better for you?"

A flicker of faces passed through her mind. Ghosts from the distant and recent past. Boys from high school. Eddie. She heard Eddie's voice.

Either you come across, or you walk. . . .

She just wanted a normal life. She wanted to find something to enjoy in it. She wanted to find somebody she could have a good relationship with, she wanted to enjoy making love with him without worrying about people thinking she was a tramp. She wanted him to be there the next morning. She wanted there to be more to what they had than just a roll in the hay.

Right now, none of that seemed very possible.

"I don't know," she said finally. "I want it to. I'm not going to give up, but . . ."

Again, faces paraded before her—this time they belonged to those lost souls of the city. The despairing.

"I know there are people a lot worse off than I am," she said. "I'm not sick, I've got the use of my body and my mind. But I'm missing something, too. I don't know how it is for other people—maybe they feel the same and just handle it better—but I feel like there's a hole inside me that I just can't fill. I get so lonely . . .''

"You see," Jack said then. "She's mine."

Moira turned to him. "What are you talking about?"

It was Diane who answered. "He's laying claim to your unhappiness," she said.

Moira looked from one to the other. There was something going on here, some undercurrent, that she wasn't picking up on.

"What are you *talking* about?" she asked.

"This city is ours," Diane said. "My brother's and mine. We are two sides to the same coin. In most people, that coin lies with my face up, for you are an optimistic race. But optimism only carries some so far. When my brother's face lies looking skyward, all hope is gone."

Moira centered on the words, "you are an optimistic race," realizing from the way Diane spoke it was as though she and her brother weren't human. She looked away, across the cityscape of bridges and tilting buildings. It was a dreamscape—not exactly a nightmare, but not at all pleasant either. And she was trapped in it; trapped in a dream.

"Who are you people?" she asked. "I don't buy this 'Jack and Diane' bit—that's like out of that John Mellencamp song. Who are you *really?* What is this place?"

"I've already told you," Jack said.

"But you only gave her half the answer," Diane added. She turned to Moira. "We are Hope and Despair," she said. She touched a hand to her breast. "Because of your need for us, we are no longer mere allegory, but have shape and form. This is our city."

Moira shook her head. "Despair I can understand—this place reeks of it. But not Hope."

"Hope is what allows the strong to rise above their despair," Diane said. "It's what makes them strong. Not blind faith, not the certain knowledge that someone will step in and help them, but the understanding that through their own force of will they cannot merely survive, but succeed. Hope is what tempers that will and gives it the strength to carry on, no matter what the odds are ranked against them."

"Don't forget to tell her how too much hope will turn her into a lazy cow," her brother said.

Diane sighed, but didn't ignore him. "It's true," she said. "Too much hope can also be harmful. Remember this: Neither hope nor despair have power of their own; they can only provide the fuel that you will use to prevail or be defeated."

"Pop psychology," Moira muttered.

Diane smiled. "Yet, like old wives' tales, it has within it a kernel of truth, or why would it linger?"

"So what am I doing here?" Moira asked. "I never gave up. I'm still trying."

Diane looked at her brother. He shrugged his shoulders.

"I admit defeat," he said. "She is yours."

Diane shook her head. "No. She is her own. Let her go."

Jack turned to Moira, the look of a petulant child marring his strong features before they started to become hazy.

"You'll be back," he said. That dry voice was like a desert wind, its fine sand filling her heart with an aching forlornness. "Hope is sweet, I'll admit that readily, but once Despair has touched you, you can never be wholly free of its influence."

A hot flush ran through Moira. She reeled, dizzy, vision blurring, only half hearing what was being said. Her head was thick with a heavy buzz of pain.

But Hope is stronger.

Moira wasn't sure if she'd actually heard that, the sweet scent of blossoms clearing her heart of Despair's dust, or if it came from within herself—something she wanted—*had* to believe. But it overrode Despair's dry voice. She no longer fought the vertigo, but just let it take her away.

Moira was suddenly aware that she was on her hands and knees, with dirty wood under her. Where . . . ?

Then she remembered: Walking across the covered bridge. The city. Hope and Despair.

She sat back on her haunches and looked around herself. She was back in her own world. Back—if she'd ever even gone anywhere in the first place.

A sudden roaring filled her head. Lights blinded her as a car came rushing up on the far side of the bridge. She remembered Eddie, her fear of some redneck hillbillies, but there was nowhere to run to. The car screeched to a halt on the wood, a door opened. A man stepped out onto the roadway of the bridge and came towards her.

Backlit by the car's headbeams, he seemed huge—a monstrous shape. She wanted to bolt. She wanted to scream. She couldn't seem to move, not even enough to reach into her purse for her switchblade.

"Jesus!" the stranger said. "Are you okay?"

He was bent down beside her now, features pulled tight with concern.

She nodded slowly. "I just . . . felt dizzy, I guess."

"Here. Let me help you up."

She allowed him to do that. She let him walk her to his car. He opened up the passenger's door and she sank gratefully onto the seat. The man looked down to the end of the bridge by which she'd entered it what seemed like a lifetime ago.

"Did you have some car trouble?" the man asked.

"You could say that," she said. "The guy I was with dumped me from his car a few miles back."

"Are you hurt?"

She shook her head. "Just my feelings."

"Jesus. What a crappy thing to do."

"Yeah. Thanks for stopping."

"No problem. Can I give you a lift somewhere?"

Moira shook her head. "I'm going back to Newford. I think that's a little far out of your way."

"Well, I'm not just going to leave you here by yourself."

Before she could protest, he closed the door and went back around to the driver's side.

"Don't worry," he said as he got behind the wheel.

"After what you've been through, a guy'd have to be a real heel to—well, you know."

Moira had to smile. He actually seemed embarrassed.

"We'll just drive to the other side of the bridge and turn around and then—"

Moira touched his arm. She remembered what had happened the last time she'd tried to go through this bridge.

"Do me a favor, would you?" she asked. "Could you just back out instead?"

Her benefactor gave her a funny look, then shrugged. Putting the car into reverse, he started backing up. Moira held her breath until they were back out on the road again. There were pines and cedars pushing up against the verge, stars overhead. No weird city. No bridges.

She let out her breath.

"What's your name?" she asked as he maneuvered the car back and forth on the narrow road until he had its nose pointed towards Newford.

"John—John Fraser."

"My name's Moira."

"My grandmother's name was Moira," John said.

"Really?"

He nodded.

He seemed like a nice guy, Moira thought. Not the kind who'd try to pull anything funny.

The sweet scent of blossoms came to her for just a moment, then it was gone.

John's showing up so fortuitously as he had—that had to be Hope's doing, she decided. Maybe it was a freebie of good luck to make up for her brother's bad manners. Or maybe it was true: if you had a positive attitude, you had a better chance that things would work out.

"Thanks," she said. She wasn't sure if Hope could hear her, but she wanted to say it all the same.

"You're welcome," John said from beside her.

Moira glanced at him, then smiled.

"Yeah," she said. "You, too."

His puzzled look made her smile widen.

"What's so funny?" he asked.

She just shrugged and settled back into her seat. "It's a long weird story and you wouldn't believe me anyway."

"Try me."

"Maybe some other time," she said.

"I might just hold you to that," he said.

Moira surprised herself with the hope that maybe he would.

OUR LADY OF THE
~ • HARBOUR • ~

*People don't behave the way they should; they behave the way
they do.*

—JIM BEAUBIEN AND KAREN CAESAR

S HE SAT ON her rock, looking out over the lake, her back to
the city that reared up behind her in a bewildering array
of towers and lights. A half mile of water separated her island from Newford, but on a night such as this, with the
moon high and the water still as glass, the city might as well
have been on the other side of the planet.

Tonight, an essence of *Marchen* prevailed in the darkened
groves and on the moonlit lawns of the island.

For uncounted years before Diederick van Yoors first settled the area in the early part of the nineteenth century, the
native Kickaha called the island Myeengun. By the turn of
the century, it had become the playground of Newford's
wealthy, its bright facade first beginning to lose its luster
with the Great Depression when wealthy landowners could
no longer keep up their summer homes; by the end of the
Second World War it was an eyesore. It wasn't turned into a
park until the late 1950s. Today most people knew it only by
the anglicized translation of its Kickaha name: Wolf Island.

Matt Casey always thought of it as *her* island.

The cast bronze statue he regarded had originally stood in the garden of an expatriate Danish businessman's summer home, a faithful reproduction of the well-known figure that haunted the waterfront of the Dane's native Copenhagen. When the city expropriated the man's land for the park, he was generous enough to donate the statue, and so she sat now on the island, as she had for fifty years, looking out over the lake, motionless, always looking, the moonlight gleaming on her bronze features and slender form.

The sharp blast of a warning horn signaling the last ferry back to the city cut through the night's contemplative mood. Matt turned to look to the far side of the island where the ferry was docked. As he watched, the lights on the park's winding paths winked out, followed by those in the island's restaurant and the other buildings near the dock. The horn gave one last blast. Five minutes later, the ferry lurched away from the dock and began the final journey of the day back to Newford's harbour.

Now, except for a pair of security guards who, Matt knew, would spend the night watching TV and sleeping in the park's offices above the souvenir store, he had the island to himself. He turned back to look at the statue. It was still silent, still motionless, still watching the unfathomable waters of the lake.

He'd been here one afternoon and watched a bag lady feeding gulls with bits of bread that she probably should have kept for herself. The gulls here were all overfed. When the bread was all gone, she'd walked up to the statue.

"Our Lady of the Harbour," she'd said. "Bless me."

Then she'd made the sign of the cross, as though she was a Catholic stepping forward into the nave of her church. From one of her bulging shopping bags, she took out a small plastic flower and laid it on the stone by the statue's feet, then turned and walked away.

The flower was long gone, plucked by one of the cleaning crews no doubt, but the memory remained.

Matt moved closer to the statue, so close that he could have laid his palm against the cool metal of her flesh.

"Lady," he began, but he couldn't go on.

Matt Casey wasn't an easy man to like. He lived for one thing, and that was his music. About the only social intercourse he had was with the members of the various bands he had played in over the years, and even that was spotty. Nobody he ever played with seemed willing to just concentrate on the music; they always wanted to hang out together as though they were all friends, as though they were in some kind of social club.

Music took the place of people in his life. It was his friend and his lover, his confidant and his voice, his gossip and his comfort.

It was almost always so.

From his earliest years he suffered from an acute sense of xenophobia: everyone was a stranger to him. All were foreigners to the observer captured in the flesh, blood and bone of his body. It was not something he understood, in the sense that one might be aware of a problem one had; it was just the way he was. He could trust no one—perhaps because he had never learned to trust himself.

His fellow musicians thought of him as cold, aloof, cynical—descriptions that were completely at odds with the sensitivity of his singing and the warmth that lay at the heart of his music. The men he played with sometimes thought that all he needed was a friend, but his rebuffs to even the most casual overtures of friendship always cured such notions. The women he played with sometimes thought that all he needed was a lover, but though he slept with a few, the distance he maintained eventually cooled the ardor of even the most persistent.

Always, in the end, there was only the music. To all else, he was an outsider.

He grew up in the suburbs north of the city's center, part of a caring family. He had an older brother and two younger sisters, each of them outgoing and popular in their own way. Standing out in such contrast to them, even at an early age, his parents had sent him to a seemingly endless series of child specialists and psychologists, but no one could get through except for his music teachers—first in the school orchestra, then the private tutors that his parents were only too happy to provide for him.

They saw a future in music for him, but not the one he chose. They saw him studying music at a university, taken under the wing of some master whenever he finally settled on a chosen instrument, eventually playing concert halls, touring the world with famous orchestras. Instead he left home at sixteen. He turned his back on formal studies, but not on learning, and played in the streets. He traveled all over North America, then to Europe and the Middle East, finally returning home to busk on Newford's streets and play in her clubs.

Still the outsider; more so, perhaps, rather than less.

It wasn't that he was unfriendly; he simply remained uninvolved, animated only in the presence of other musicians and then only to discuss the esoterics of obscure lyrics and tunes and instruments, or to play. He never thought of himself as lonely, just as alone; never considered himself to be a social misfit or an outcast from the company of his fellow men, just an observer of the social dance to which most men and women knew the steps rather than one who would join them on the dance floor.

An outsider.

A gifted genius, undoubtedly, as any who heard him play would affirm, but an outsider all the same.

It was almost always so.

In the late seventies, the current band was Marrowbones and they had a weekend gig at a folk club in Lower Crowsea called Feeney's Kitchen—a popular hangout for those Butler University students who shunned disco and punk as well as the New Wave. The line-up was Matt on his usual

bouzouki and guitar and handling the vocals, Nicky Doyle
on fiddle, Johnny Ryan on tenor banjo, doubling on his classic Gibson mando-cello for song accompaniments, and
Matt's long-time musical associate Amy Scallan on Uillean
pipes and whistles.

They'd been playing together for a year and a half now
and the band had developed a big, tight sound that had recently brought in offers for them to tour the college and festival circuits right across the country.

But it'd never happen, Amy thought as she buckled on her
pipes in preparation for the selection of reels with which
they were going to end the first set of the evening.

The same thing was going to happen that always happened. It was already starting. She'd had to listen to Nicky
and Johnny going on about Matt earlier this afternoon when
the three of them had gotten together to jam with a couple of
other friends at The Harp. They couldn't deal with the dichotomy of Matt offstage and on. Fronting the band, Matt
projected the charming image of a friendly and outgoing
man that you couldn't help but want to get to know; offstage,
he was taciturn and withdrawn, uninterested in anything that
didn't deal with the music.

But that was Matt, she'd tried to explain. You couldn't
find a better singer or musician to play with and he had a
knack for giving even the simplest piece a knockout arrangement. Nobody said you had to like him.

But Nicky had only shaken his head, brown curls bobbing. "Your man's taking all the *craic* from playing in a
band."

Johnny nodded in agreement. "It's just not fun anymore.
He'll barely pass the time of day with you, but on stage he's
all bloody smiles and jokes. I don't know how you put up
with him."

Amy hadn't been able to come up with an explanation
then and looking across the stage now to where Matt was
raising his eyebrows to ask if she was ready, then winking
when she nodded back that she was, she couldn't explain it

any better. She'd just learned over the years that what they shared was the music—and the music was very good; if she wanted more, she had to look for it elsewhere.

She'd come to terms with it where most people wouldn't, or couldn't, but then there was very little in the world that ever fazed her.

Matt started a G-drone on his bouzouki. He leaned close to the mike, just a touch of a welcoming smile tugging the corner of his mouth as a handful of dancers, anticipating what was to come, stepped onto the tiny wooden dance floor in front of the stage. Amy gave him a handful of bars to lock in the tempo, then launched into the first high popping notes of "The Road West," the opening salvo in this set of reels.

She and Matt played the tune through twice on their own and room on the dance floor grew to such a premium that the dancers could do little more than jig in one spot. Their elbows and knees could barely jostle against one another.

It wasn't quite a sea of bobbing heads, Amy thought, looking down from the stage. More like a small lake, or even a puddle.

The analogy made her smile. She kicked in her pipe drones as the fiddle and tenor banjo joined in on "The Glen Allen." It was halfway through that second tune that she became aware of the young woman dancing directly in front of Matt's microphone.

She was small and slender, with hair that seemed to be made of spun gold and eyes such a deep blue that they glittered like sapphires in the light spilling from the stage. Her features reminded Amy of a fox—pointed and tight like a Rackham sprite, but no less attractive for all that.

The other dancers gave way like reeds before a wind, drawing back to allow her the room to swirl the skirt of her unbelted flowered dress, her tiny feet scissoring intricate steps in their black Chinese slippers. Her movements were at once sensual and innocent. Amy's first impression was that the young woman was a professional dancer, but as she watched more closely, she realized that the girl's fluidity and grace were more an inherent talent than a studied skill.

The dancer's gaze caught and held on Matt, no matter how her steps turned her about, her attention fixed and steady as though he had bewitched her, while Matt, to Amy's surprise, seemed just as entranced. When they kicked into "Sheehan's Reel," the third and final tune of the set, she almost thought Matt was going to leave the stage to dance with the girl.

"Again!" Matt cried out as they neared the usual end of the tune.

Amy didn't mind. She pumped the bellows of her pipes, long fingers dancing on the chanter, more than happy to play the piece all night if the dancer could keep up. But the tune unwound to its end, they ended with a flourish, and suddenly it was all over. The dance floor cleared, the girl was swallowed by the crowd.

When the applause died down, an odd sort of hush fell over the club. Amy unbuckled her pipes and looked over to see that Matt had already left the stage. She hadn't even seen him go. She tugged her chanter mike up to mouth level.

"We're, uh, going to take a short break, folks," she said into the mike. Her voice seemed to boom in the quiet. "Then," she added, "we'll be right back with some more music, so don't go away."

The patter bookending the tunes and songs was Matt's usual job. Since Amy didn't feel she had his natural stage charm, she just kept it simple.

There was another smatter of applause that she acknowledged with a smile. The house system came on, playing a Jackson Browne tune, and she turned to Nicky, who was putting his fiddle in its case.

"Where'd Matt go?" she asked.

He gave her a "who cares?" shrug. "Probably chasing that bird who was shaking her tush at him all through the last piece."

"I don't envy her," Johnny added.

Amy knew exactly what he meant. Over the past few months they'd all seen the fallout of casualties who gathered like moths around the bright flame of Matt's stage presence only to have their wings burnt with his indifference. He'd charm them in a club, sometimes sleep with them, but in the end, the only lover he kept was the music.

Amy knew all too well. There was a time . . .

She pushed the past away with a shake of her head. Putting a hand above her eyes to shade them from the lights, she scanned the crowd as the other two went to get themselves a beer but she couldn't spot either Matt or the girl. Her gaze settled on a black-haired Chinese woman sitting alone at at small table near the door and she smiled as the woman raised her hand in a wave. She'd forgotten that Lucia had arrived halfway through their first set—fashionably late, as always—and now that she thought about it, hadn't she seen the dancer come in about the same time? They might even have come in together.

Lucia Han was a performance artist based in Upper Foxville and an old friend of Amy's. When they'd first met, Amy had been told by too many people to be careful because Lucia was gay and would probably make a pass at her. Amy just ignored them. She had nothing against gays to begin with and she soon learned that the gossips' reasoning for their false assumption was just that Lucia only liked to work with other women. But as Lucia had explained to Amy once, "There's just not enough women involved in the arts and I want to support those who do make the plunge—at least if they're any good."

Amy understood perfectly. She often wished there were more women players in traditional music. She was sick to death of going to a music session where she wasn't known. All too often she'd be the only woman in a gathering of men and have to play rings around them on her pipes just to prove that she was as good as them. Irish men weren't exactly noted for their liberated standards.

Which didn't mean that either she or Lucia weren't fond

of the right sort of man. *"Au contraire,"* as Lucia would say in the phony Parisian accent she liked to affect, "I am liking them too much."

Amy made her way to the bar, where she ordered a beer on her tab, then took the brimming draught glass through the crowd to Lucia's table, trying to slosh as little of the foam as she could on her new jeans.

"Bet you thought I wouldn't come," Lucia said as Amy sat down with her stein relatively full. The only spillage had joined the stickiness of other people's spills that lay underfoot.

Lucia was older than Amy by at least six or seven years, putting her in her mid-thirties. She had her hair in a wild spiky do tonight—to match the torn white T-shirt and leather jeans, no doubt. The punk movement had barely begun to trickle across the Atlantic as yet, but it was obvious that Lucia was already an eager proponent. A strand of safety pins dangled from one earlobe; others held the tears of her T-shirt closed in strategic places.

"I don't even remember telling you about the gig," Amy said.

Lucia waved a negligent hand towards the small poster on the wall behind her that advertised the band's appearance at Feeney's Kitchen this weekend.

"But you are famous now, *ma cherie,*" she said. "How could I *not* know?" She dropped the accent to add, "You guys sound great."

"Thanks."

Amy looked at the tabletop. She set her stein down beside a glass of white wine, Lucia's cigarettes and matches and a half-filled ashtray. There was also an empty teacup with a small bright steel teapot on one side of it and a used tea bag on the lip of its saucer.

"Did you come alone?" she asked.

Lucia shook her head. "I brought a foundling—fresh from who really knows where. You probably noticed her and Matt making goo-goo eyes at each other all through the last piece you did.'' She brought a hand to her lips as soon as she'd made the last comment. ''Sorry. I forgot about the thing you used to have going with him.''

''Old history,'' Amy said. ''I've long since dealt with it. I don't know that Matt ever even knew anything existed between us, but I'm cool now.''

''It's for the better.''

''Definitely,'' Amy agreed.

''I should probably warn my little friend about him,'' Lucia said, ''but you know what they're like at that age— it'd just egg her on.''

''Who *is* your little friend? She moves like all she was born to do was dance.''

''She's something, isn't she? I met her on Wolf Island about a week ago, just before the last ferry—all wet and bedraggled like she'd fallen off a boat and been washed to shore. She wasn't wearing a stitch of clothing and I thought the worst, you know? Some asshole brought her out for a quick wham, bam, and then just dumped her.''

Lucia paused to light a cigarette.

''And?'' Amy asked.

Lucia shrugged, blowing out a wreath of blue-grey smoke. ''Seems she fell off a boat and took off her clothes so that they wouldn't drag her down while she swam to shore. Course, I got that from her later.''

Just then the door to the club opened behind Lucia and a gust of cool air caught the smoke from Lucia's cigarette, giving it a slow dervishing whirl. On the heels of the wind, Amy saw Matt and the girl walk in. They seemed to be in the middle of an animated discussion—or at least Matt was, so they had to be talking about music.

Amy felt the same slight twinge of jealousy watching him with the dancer as she did in the first few moments of every one of the short relationships that came about from some girl basically flinging herself at him halfway through a gig. Though perhaps ''relationship'' was too strong a word, since any sense of responsibility to a partner was inevitably one-sided.

The girl laughed at what he was saying—but it was a silent laugh. Her mouth was open, her eyes sparkled with a humored appreciation, but there was no sound. She began to move her hands in an intricate pattern that, Amy realized, was the American Sign Language used by deaf-mutes.

"Her problem right then," Lucia was saying, "was finding something to wear so that she could get into town. Luckily I was wearing my duster—you know, from when I was into my Sergio Leone phase—so she could cover herself up."

"She took off everything while she was in the water?" Amy asked, her gaze returning to her friend. "Even her underwear?"

"I guess. Unless she wasn't wearing any in the first place."

"Weird."

"I don't see you wearing a bra."

"You know what I meant," Amy said with a laugh.

Lucia nodded. "So anyway, she came on the ferry with me—I paid her fare—and then I brought her back to my place because it turned out she didn't have anywhere else to go. Doesn't know a soul in town. To be honest, I wasn't even sure she spoke English at first."

Amy looked over Lucia's shoulder to where Matt was answering whatever it was that the girl's hands had told him. Where had he learned sign language? she wondered. He'd never said anything about it before, but then she realized that for all the years she'd known him, she really didn't *know* much about him at all except that he was a brilliant musician and good in bed, related actions, perhaps, since she didn't doubt that they both were something he'd regard as a performance.

Meow, she thought.

"She's deaf-mute, isn't she?" she added aloud.

Lucia looked surprised. "Mute, but not deaf. How'd you know?"

"I'm watching her talk to Matt with her hands right now."

"She couldn't even do that when I first met her," Lucia said.

Amy returned her attention to Lucia once more. "What do you mean?"

"Well, I know sign language—I learned it when I worked at the Institute for the Deaf up on Gracie Street when I first got out of college—so when I realized she was mute, it was the first thing I tried. But she's not deaf—she just can't talk. She didn't even try to communicate at first. I thought she was in shock. She just sat beside me, looking out over the water, her eyes getting bigger and bigger as we approached the docks.

"When we caught a bus back to my place, it was like she'd never been in a city before. She just sat beside me all wide-eyed and then took my hand—not like she was scared, it was more like she just wanted to share the wonder of it all with me. It wasn't until we got back to my place that she asked for pen and paper." Lucia mimed the action as she spoke.

"It's all kind of mysterious, isn't it?" Amy said.

"I'll say. Anyway, her name's Katrina Ludvigsen and she's from one of those little towns on the Islands further down the lake—the ones just past the mouth of the Dulfer River, you know?"

Amy nodded.

"Her family came over from Norway originally," Lucia went on. "They were Lapps—as in Lapland—except she doesn't like to be called that. Her people call themselves Sami."

"I've heard about that," Amy said. "Referring to them as Lapps is a kind of insult."

"Exactly." Lucia took a final drag from her cigarette and butted it out in the ashtray. "Once she introduced herself, she asked me to teach her sign language. Would you believe she picked it up in *two* days?''

"I don't know," Amy said. "Is that fast?"

"Try *fantastique, ma cherie.*"

"So what's she doing here?"

Lucia shrugged. "She told me she was looking for a man—like, aren't we all, ha ha—only she didn't know his name, just that he lived in Newford. She just about had a fit when she spotted the picture of Matt in the poster for this gig."

"So she knows him from before."

"You tell me," Lucia said.

Amy shook her head. "Only Matt knows whatever it is that Matt knows."

"Katrina says she's twenty-two," Lucia went on, "but if you ask me, I think she's a lot younger. I'll bet she ran away from home—maybe even stowed away on some tourist's powerboat and jumped ship just outside the harbor because they were about to catch her and maybe take her back home."

"So what are you going to do about it?"

"Not a damn thing. She's a nice kid and besides," she added as Katrina and Matt walked by their table, heading for the bar, "I've got the feeling she's not even going to be my responsibility for much longer."

"Don't count on it," Amy said. "She'll be lucky if she lasts the night."

Although maybe not. Katrina *was* pretty, and she certainly could dance, so there was the musical connection, just as there had been with her.

Amy sighed. She didn't know why she got to feeling the way she did at times like this. She wouldn't even *want* to make a go at it with Matt again.

Lucia reached across the table and put her hand on Amy's, giving it a squeeze. "How're you handling this, Amy? I remember you were pretty messed up about him at one point."

"I can deal with it."

"Well—what's that line of yours? More power to your elbow then if you can, though I still can't figure out how you got past it enough to still be able to play with him."

Amy looked over to the bar where Matt was getting the girl a cup of tea. She wished the twinge of not so much jealousy, as hurt, would go away.

Patience, she told herself. She'd seen Matt with who knew how many women over the years, all of them crazy over him. The twinge only lasted for a little while—a reminder of a bad time, not the bad time itself. She was past that now.

Well, mostly.

"You just change your way of thinking about a person," she said after a few moments, trying to convince herself as much as Lucia. "You change what you need from them, your expectations. That's all."

"You make it sound easy."

Amy turned back to her friend. "It's not," she said in a quiet voice.

Lucia gave her hand a squeeze.

The girl was drunk on Matt, Amy realized. There was no other explanation for the way she was carrying on.

For the rest of the night, Amy could see Katrina sitting with Lucia at the back of the club, chin cupped in her hands as she listened to Matt sing. No, not just listening. She drank in the songs, swallowed them whole. And with every dance set they played, she was up on her feet at the front of the stage, the sinuous grace of her movement, the swirl and the lift and the rapid fire steps of her small feet capturing each tune to perfection.

Matt was obviously complimented by her attention—or at least whatever it was that he'd feel that would be close to flattered—and why not? Next to Lucia, she was the best looking woman in the club, and Lucia wasn't exactly sending out "available" signals, not dressed the way she was.

Matt and the girl talked between each set, filling up the twenty minutes or so of canned music and patron conversation with a forest of words, his spoken, hers signed, each of them oblivious to their surroundings, to everything except for each other.

Maybe Katrina will be the one, Amy thought.

Once she got past her own feelings, that was what she usually found herself hoping. Although Matt could be insensitive once he stepped off the stage, she still believed that all he really needed was someone to care about to turn him around. Nobody who put such heart into his music, could be completely empty inside. She was sure that he just needed someone—the right someone. It hadn't been her, fine. But somewhere there had to be a woman for him—a catalyst to take down the walls through which only his music dared forth to touch the world.

The way he'd been so attentive towards Katrina all night, Amy was sure he was going to take her home with him, but all he did was ask her out tomorrow.

Okay, she thought standing beside Lucia while Matt and Katrina "talked." That's a start and maybe a good one.

Katrina's hands moved in response to Matt's question.

"What's she saying?" Amy asked, leaning close to whisper to Lucia.

"Yes," Lucia translated. "Now she's asking him if they can ride the ferry."

"The one to Wolf Island?" Amy said. "That's where you found her."

"Whisht," Lucia told her.

"We'll do whatever you want," Matt was saying.

And then Katrina was gone, trailing after Lucia with a last lingering wave before the world outside the club swallowed her and the door closed behind the pair of them.

Matt and Amy returned to the stage to pack up their instruments.

"I was thinking of heading up to The Harp to see if there's a session on," Matt said. He looked around at the other three. "Anyone feel like coming?"

If there were enough musicians up for the music, Joe

Breen, the proprietor of The Harp, would lock the doors to the public after closing hours and just let the music flow until the last musician packed it in, acting no different on this side of the Atlantic than he had with the pub he'd run back home in Ireland.

Johnny shook his head. "I'm beat. It's straight to bed for me tonight."

"It's been a long night," Nicky agreed.

Nicky looked a little sullen, but Amy doubted that Matt even noticed. He just shrugged, then looked to her.

Well, and why not? she thought.

"I'll give it a go," she told him.

Saying their goodbyes to the other two outside the club, she and Matt walked north to the Rosses where The Harp stood in the shadow of the Kelly Street Bridge.

"Katrina seemed nice," Amy said after a few blocks.

"I suppose," he said. "A little intense, maybe."

"I think she's a little taken with you."

Matt nodded unself-consciously. "Maybe too much. But she sure can dance, can't she?"

"Like an angel," Amy agreed.

Conversation fell flat then, just as it always did.

"I got a new tune from Geordie this afternoon," Amy said finally. "He doesn't remember where he picked it up, but it fits onto the end of 'The Kilavel Jig' like it was born to it."

Matt's eyes brightened with interest. "What's it called?"

"He didn't know. It had some Gaelic title that he'd forgotten, but it's a lovely piece. In G-major, but the first part has a kind of a modal flavor so that it almost feels as though it's being played out of C. It'd be just lovely on the bouzouki."

The talk stayed on tunes the rest of the way to The Harp— safe ground. At one point Amy found herself remembering a gig they'd played a few months ago and the story that Matt had used to introduce a song called "Sure, All He Did Was Go" that they'd played that night.

"He couldn't help himself," Matt had said, speaking of the fiddler in the song who gave up everything he had to follow a tune. "Music can be a severe mistress, demanding and jealous, and don't you doubt it. Do her bidding and isn't it just like royalty that she'll be treating you, but turn your back on her and she can take back her gift as easily as it was given. Your man could find himself holding only the tattered ribbons of a tune and song ashes and that's the God's own truth. I've seen it happen."

And then he'd laughed, as though he'd been having the audience on, and they'd launched into the song, but Amy had seen more than laughter in Matt's eyes as he started to sing. She wondered then, as she wondered now, if he didn't half believe that little bit of superstition, picked up somewhere on his travels, God knew where.

Maybe that was the answer to the riddle that was Matt Casey: he thought he'd lose his gift of music if he gave his heart to another. Maybe he'd even written that song himself, for she'd surely never heard it before. Picked it up in Morocco, he'd told her once, from one of the Wild Geese, the many Irish-in-exile, but she wasn't so sure.

Did you write it? She was ready to ask him right now, but then they were at The Harp and there was old Joe Breen flinging open the door to welcome them in and the opportunity was gone.

Lucia put on a pot of tea when she and Katrina returned to the apartment. While they waited for it to steep, they sat on the legless sofa pushed up against one wall of the long open loft that took up the majority of the apartment's floor space.

There was a small bedroom and a smaller bathroom off this main room. The kitchen area was in one corner—a battered fridge, its paint peeling, a sink and a counter with a hot plate on it and storage cupboards underneath and a small wooden kitchen table with five mismatching chairs set around it.

A low coffee table made of a plank of wood set on two

apple crates crouched before the couch, laden with magazines and ashtrays. Along a far wall, three tall old mirrors
had been fastened to the wall with a twelve-foot long support
bar set out in front of them. The other walls were adorned
with posters of the various shows in which Lucia had performed. In two she had headlined—one a traditional ballet,
while the other had been a very outre multimedia event written and choreographed by a friend of hers.

When the tea was ready, Lucia brought the pot and two
cups over to the sofa and set them on a stack of magazines.
She poured Katrina a cup, then another for herself.

"So you found him," Lucia said as she returned to her
seat on the sofa.

Katrina nodded happily.

He's just the way I remember him, she signed.

"Where did you meet him?" Lucia asked.

Katrina gave a shy smile in response, then added, *Near my
home. He was playing music.*

The bright blue fire of her eyes grew unfocused as she
looked across the room, seeing not plaster walls and the
dance posters upon them, but the rough rocky shore of a
coastline that lay east of the city by the mouth of the Dulfer
River. She went into the past, and the past was like a dream.

She'd been underlake when the sound of his voice drew
her up from the cold and the dark, neither of which she felt
except as a kind of malaise in her spirit; up into the moonlight, bobbing in the white-capped waves; listening, *swallowing* that golden sound of strings and voice, and he so
handsome and all alone on the shore. And sad. She could
hear it in his song, feel the timbre of his loneliness in his
voice.

Always intrigued with the strange folk who moved on the
shore with their odd stumpy legs, this time she was utterly
smitten. She swam closer and laid her arms on a stone by the
shore, her head on her arms, to watch and listen.

It was his music that initially won her, for music had been
her first love. Each of her four sisters was prettier than the

next, and each had a voice that could charm moonlight from a stone, milk from a virgin, a ghost from the cold dark depths below, but her voice was better still, as golden as her hair and as rich and pure as the first larksong at dawn.

But if it was his music that first enchanted her, then he himself completed the spell. She longed to join her voice to his, to hold him and be held, but she never moved from her hiding place. One look at her, and he would be driven away, for he'd see only that which was scaled, and she had no soul, not as did those who walked ashore.

No soul, no soul. A heart that broke for want of him, but no immortal soul. That was the curse of the lake-born.

When he finally put away his instrument and walked further inland, up under the pines where she couldn't follow, she let the waves close over her head and returned to her home underlake.

For three nights she returned to the shore and for two of them he was there, his voice like honey against the beat of the waves that the wind pushed shoreward and she only loved him more. But on the fourth night, he didn't come, nor on the fifth night, nor the sixth, and she despaired, knowing he was gone, away in the wide world, lost to her forever.

Her family couldn't help her; there was no one to help her. She yearned to be rid of scales, to walk on shore, no matter the cost, just so that she could be with him, but as well ask the sun not rise, or the wind to cease its endless motion.

"No matter the cost," she whispered. Tears trailed down her cheek, a sorrowful tide that would not ebb.

"Maraghreen," the lake replied as the wind lifted one of its waves to break upon the land.

She lifted her head, looked over the white caps, to where the lake grew darker still as it crept under the cliffs into the hidden cave where the lake witch lived.

She was afraid, but she went. To Maraghreen. Who took her scales and gave her legs with a bitter potion that tasted of witch blood; satisfied her impossible need, but took Katrina's voice in payment.

"A week and a day," the lake witch told her before she took Katrina's voice. "You have only so long to win him and your immortal soul, or to foam you will return."

"But without my voice . . ." It was through song, she'd thought to win him, voices joined in a harmony so pure how could he help but love her? "Without it . . ."

"He must speak of his love first, or your soul will be forfeit."

"But without my voice . . ."

"You will have your body; that will need be enough."

So she drank the blood, bitter on her tongue; gained legs, and each step she took was fiery pain and would be so until she'd gained a soul; went in search of he who held her love, for whose love she had paid such a dear price. Surely he would speak the words to her before the seven days were past and gone?

"Penny for your thoughts," Lucia said.

Katrina only smiled and shook her head. She could tell no one. The words must come unbidden from him or all would be undone.

Matt was late picking Katrina up on Sunday. It was partly his own fault—he'd gotten caught up with a new song that he was learning from a tape a friend had sent him from Co. Cork and lost track of the time—and partly from trying to follow the Byzantine directions that Lucia had used to describe the route to her Upper Foxville apartment.

Katrina didn't seem to mind at all; she was just happy to see him, her hands said, moving as graceful in speech as the whole of her did when she danced.

You didn't bring your guitar, she signed.

"I've been playing it all day. I thought I'd leave it at home."

Your voice . . . your music. They are a gift.

"Yeah, well . . ."

He looked around the loft, recognizing a couple of the posters from having seen them around town before, pasted on subway walls or stuck in amongst the clutter of dozens of other ads in the front of restaurants and record stores. He'd never gone to any of the shows. Dance wasn't his thing, especially not modern dance or the performance art that Lucia was into. He'd seen a show of hers once. She'd spent fifteen minutes rolling back and forth across the stage, wrapped head to toe in old brown paper shopping bags to a soundtrack that consisted of water dripping for its rhythm, the hypnotic drone only occasionally broken by the sound of footsteps walking through broken glass.

Definitely not his thing.

Lucia was not his idea of what being creative was all about. In his head, he filed her type of artist under the general heading of lunatic fringe. Happily, she was out for the day.

"So," he said, "do you want to head out to the island?"

Katrina nodded. *But not just yet,* her hands added.

She smiled at him, long hair clouding down her back. She was wearing clothes borrowed from Lucia—cotton pants a touch too big and tied closed with a scarf through the belt loops, a T-shirt advertising a band that he'd never heard of and the same black Chinese slippers she'd been wearing last night.

"So what do you want—" he began.

Katrina took his hands before he could finish and placed them on her breasts. They were small and firm against his palms, her heartbeat echoing through the thin fabric, fluttering against his skin. Her own hands dropped to his groin, one gently cupping him through his jeans, the other pulling down the zipper.

She was gentle and loving, each motion innocent of artifice and certainly welcome, but she'd caught Matt off-guard.

"Look," he said, "are you sure you . . . ?"

She raised a hand, laying a finger against his lips. No words. Just touch. He grew hard, his penis uncomfortably bent in the confines of his jeans until she popped the top button and pulled it out. She put her small hand around it, fingers tight, hand moving slowly up and down. Speaking without words, her emotions laid bare before him.

Matt took his hands from her breasts and lifted the T-shirt over her head. He let it drop behind her as he enfolded her in an embrace. She was like liquid against him, a shimmer of movement and soft touches.

No words, he thought.

She was right. There was no need for words.

He let her lead him into Lucia's bedroom.

Afterwards, he felt so still inside it was though the world had stopped moving, time stalled, no one left but the two of them, wrapped up together, here in the dusky shadows that licked across the bed. He raised himself up on one elbow and looked down at her.

She seemed to be made of light. An unearthly radiance lay upon her pale skin like an angelic nimbus, except he doubted that any angel in heaven knew how to give and accept pleasure as she did. Not unless heaven was a very different place from the one he'd heard about in Sunday school.

There was a look in her eyes that promised him everything—not just bodily pleasures, but heart and soul—and for a moment he wanted to open up to her, to give to her what he gave his music, but then he felt something close up thick inside him. He found himself remembering a parting conversation he'd had with another woman. Darlene Flatt, born Darlene Johnston. Belying her stage name, she was an extraordinarily well-endowed singer in one of the local country bands. Partial to slow-dancing on sawdusted floors, bolo ties, fringed jackets and, for the longest time, to him.

"You're just a hollow man," she told him finally. "A sham. The only place you're alive is on stage, but let me tell you something, Matt, the whole world's a stage if you'd just open your eyes and see."

Maybe in Shakespeare's day, he thought, but not now, not here, not in this world. Here you only get hurt.

"If you gave a fraction of your commitment to music to another person, you'd be . . ."

He didn't know what Darlene thought he'd be because he tuned her out. Stepped behind the wall and followed the intricate turns of a song he was working on at the time until she finally got up and left his apartment.

Got up and left.

He swung his feet to the floor and looked for his clothes. Katrina caught his arm.

What's wrong? she signed. *What have I done?*

"Nothing," he said. "It's not you. It's not anything. It's just . . . I've just got to go, okay?"

Please, she signed. *Just tell me . . .*

But he turned away so that he couldn't see her words. Got dressed. Paused in the doorway of the bedroom, choking on words that tried to slip through the wall. Turned finally, and left. The room. The apartment. Her, crying.

Lucia found Katrina when she came home later, red-eyed and sitting on the sofa in just a T-shirt, staring out the window, unable or unwilling to explain what was wrong. So Lucia thought the worst.

"That sonuvabitch," she started. "He never even showed up, did he? I should have warned you about what a prick he can be."

But Katrina's hands said, *No. It wasn't his fault. I want too much.*

"He was here?" Lucia asked.

She nodded.

"And you had a fight?"

The shrug that came in response said, sort of, and then Katrina began to cry again. Lucia enfolded her in her arms. It was small, cold comfort, she knew, for she'd had her own time in that lonely place in which Katrina now found herself, but it was all Lucia had to offer.

* * *

Matt found himself on the ferry, crossing from the city over to Wolf Island, as though, by doing so, he was completing some unfinished ritual to which neither he nor Katrina had quite set the parameters. He stood at the rail on the upper deck with the wind in his face and let the words to long-dead ballads run through his mind so that he wouldn't have to think about people, about relationships, about complications, about Katrina.

But in the dusking sky and in the wake that trailed behind the ferry, and later on the island, in the shadows that crept across the lawn and in the tangle that branches made against the sky, he could see only her face. Not all the words to all the songs he knew could free him from the burden of guilt that clung to him like burrs gathered on a sweater while crossing an autumn field.

He stopped at the statue of the little mermaid, and of course even she had Katrina's face.

"I didn't ask to start anything," he told the statue, saying now what he should have said in Lucia's bedroom. "So why the hell do I have to feel so guilty?"

It was the old story, he realized. Everything, everybody wanted to lay claim to a piece of your soul. And if they couldn't have it, they made you pay for it in guilt.

"I'm not a hollow man," he told the statue, saying what he should have said to Darlene. "I just don't have what you want me to give."

The statue just looked out across the lake. The dusk stretched for long impossible moments, then the sun dropped completely behind the horizon and the lamps lit up along the island's pathways. Matt turned and walked back to where the ferry waited to return him to Newford.

He didn't see Katrina again for two days.

I'm sorry, was the first thing she said to him, her hands moving quickly before he could speak.

He stood in the hallway leading into Lucia's apartment, late on a Wednesday afternoon, not even sure what he was doing here. Apologizing. Explaining. Maybe just trying to understand.

"It wasn't your fault," he said. "It's just . . . everything happened too fast."

She nodded. *Do you want to come in?*

Matt regarded her. She was barefoot, framed by the doorway. The light behind her turned the flowered dress she was wearing into gossamer, highlighting the shape of her body under it. Her hair was the colour of soft gold. He remembered her lying on the bed, radiant in the afterglow of their lovemaking.

"Could we go out instead?" he said. "Just for a walk or something?"

Let me get my shoes.

He took her to the lakefront and they walked the length of the boardwalk and the Pier, and then, when the jostle of the crowds became too much, they made their way down to the sand and sat near the shoreline. For the most part, his voice, her hands, were still. When they did talk, it was to make up stories about the more colorful characters with whom they shared the beach, both using their hands to speak so that they wouldn't be overheard, laughing as each tried to outdo the other with an outrageous background for one person or another.

Where did you learn sign language? she asked him at one point.

My cousin's deaf, he replied, his hands growing more deft, remembering old patterns, the longer they spoke. *Our parents were pretty close and we all saw a lot of each other, so everybody in the family learned.*

They had dinner at Kathryn's Cafe. Afterwards, they went to the Owlnight, another of Newford's folk clubs, but this one was on the Butler University campus itself, in the Student Center. Garve MacCauley was doing a solo act, just guitar and gravely voice, mostly his own material.

You're much better, Katrina signed to Matt after the first few songs.

"Just different," he said.

Katrina only smiled and shook her head.

After the last set, he took her back to Upper Foxville and left her at Lucia's door with a chaste kiss.

Thursday evening they took in a play at the Standish, a small concert hall that divided its evenings between repertory theatre and music concerts. Katrina was entranced. She'd never seen live actors before, but then there was so much she didn't know about this new world in which she found herself and still more that she hadn't experienced in his company.

It was just past eleven by the time they got back to the apartment. Lucia had gone out, so they could have the place to themselves but when Katrina invited Matt in, he begged off. His confused mumble of an explanation made little sense. All Katrina knew was that the days were slipping away. Saturday night, the lake witch's deadline, was blurring all too close, all too fast.

When he bent to kiss her on the forehead as he had the night before, she lifted her head so that their lips met. The kiss lasted a long time, a tangle of tongues. She pressed in close to him, hands stroking his back, but he pulled away with a confused panic fluttering in his eyes.

Why do I frighten you? she wanted to ask, but she had already guessed that it wasn't just her. It was any close relationship. Responsibility frightened him and perhaps more to the point, he just didn't love her. Maybe he would, given time, but by then it would be too late. Days went by quickly; hours were simply a rush, one tumbling into the other.

She gave him a sad smile and let him go, listened to his footsteps in the stairwell, then slowly went into the apartment and closed the door behind her. Each step she took, as it always did since she stepped onto the land, was like small knives cutting through her feet. She remembered the freedom of the waves, of movement without pain, but she had turned her back on scales and water. For better or worse, she belonged on the land now.

But that night her dreams were of foam. It gathered against the craggy shore near her home as the wind drove the lake water onto the rocks. Her sisters swam nearby, weeping.

Late Friday afternoon, Amy and Lucia were sitting on a bench in Fitzhenry Park, watching the traffic go by on Palm Street. They'd been to the Y to swim laps and they each nursed a coffee now, bought from one of the vendors in the little parade of carts that set up along the sidewalk first thing every morning. The sky was overcast, with the scent of rain in the air, but for all the weather report's warnings, it had held off all day.

"So how's Katrina doing?" Amy asked.

An expression that was more puzzlement than a frown touched Lucia's features. She took a sip of her coffee then set it down on the bench between them and took out her cigarettes.

"Well, they started off rocky on Sunday," she said. "He left her crying."

"God, so soon?"

"It's not as bad as it sounds," Lucia said.

She got her cigarette lit and blew out a wreath of smoke. Amy coughed.

"Sorry," Lucia said. She moved the cigarette away.

"It's not the smoke," Amy told her, lifting a hand to rub her throat. "I've had a tickle in my throat all day. I just hope I'm not coming down with something." She took a sip of her coffee and wished she had a throat lozenge. "So what did happen?" she asked.

"He didn't show up for a couple of days, didn't call—well, I guess he wouldn't want to speak to me, would he?—but then he's been real nice ever since he did show up on Wednesday. Took her to see your friend MacCauley over at the Owlnight, the next night they went to that production of Lizzie's play that's running at the Standish and earlier today they were out just mooching around town, I guess."

"He really needs someone," Amy said.

"I suppose. But knowing your history with him, I don't know if I wish him on Katrina."

"But at least they're doing things. He's *talking* to her."

"Yeah, but then he told her today that he's going to be away this weekend."

"That's right. He canceled Saturday morning band practice because he's got a gig at that little bar in Hartnett's Point. What's the problem with that? That's his job. She must know that."

Lucia shrugged. "I just think he should've taken her with him when he left this afternoon."

Amy sighed in sympathy. "Matt's not big on bringing his current belle to a gig. I remember how it used to really piss me off when we were going together."

"Well, she's heartbroken that he didn't ask her to come along. I told her she should just go anyway—show up and meet him there; I even offered to lend her the money for the bus—but she thinks he'd get mad."

"I don't know. He seemed to like her dancing when we played at Feeney's last weekend." Amy paused. "Of course he'll just be doing songs on his own. There won't be anything for her to dance to."

"She likes his songs, too," Lucia said.

Amy thought of the intensity with which Katrina had listened to Matt's singing that night at Feeney's and she knew exactly why Matt hadn't asked Katrina along to the gig.

"Maybe she likes them too much," she said. "Matt puts a lot into his music, and you know how bloody brilliant he is, but he's pretty humble about it all at the same time. He probably thinks it'd freak him too much having her sitting there just kind of—" her shoulders lifted and fell "—I don't know, swallowing the songs."

"Well, I wish he'd given it a try all the same. I've got to help Sharon with some set decorations, so Katrina's going to be on her own all night, just moping about the apartment. I asked her to come along, but she didn't want to go out."

"I could drop by your place," Amy said.

Lucia grinned. "I thought you'd never offer."

Amy punched her lightly on the arm. "You set me up!"

"Has she still got it or what?" Lucia asked, blowing on her fingernails.

Amy laughed and they went through a quick little flurry of slapping at each other's hands until they were too giddy to continue. They both leaned back on the park bench.

"I bet I'll have a better time," Amy said after a moment. "I've helped Sharon before. If she's got anything organized at all, it'll only be because someone else did it."

Lucia nodded glumly. "Don't I know it."

Amy went home to change and have a bite to eat before she took the subway north to Upper Foxville. Looking in the mirror as she put on her makeup, she saw that she was looking awfully pale. Thinking about feeling sick made her throat tickle again and she coughed. She stopped for some lozenges at a drug store that was on her way. They helped her throat, but she felt a little light-headed now.

She should just go home, she thought, but she'd promised Lucia and she couldn't help but be sympathetic towards Katrina. She'd just stay a little while, that was all.

It was just going on nightfall when she reached Lucia's street. She paused at the corner, as she saw a small familiar figure step from the stoop of Lucia's building and head off the other way down the street. She almost called Katrina by name, but something stopped her. Curiosity got the better of her and she kept still, following along behind instead.

It was easy to keep track of her—Katrina's cloud of gold hair caught the light of every streetlamp she passed under and seemed to reflect a burnished glow up into the night. She led Amy down to MacNeil Street, turning west once she reached it. Her stride was both purposeful and wearied, but always graceful.

Poor kid, Amy thought.

More than once she started to hurry to catch up with Katrina, but then her curiosity would rise to the fore and she'd tell herself to be patient just a little longer. Since Katrina didn't know anyone in Newford—according to Lucia she didn't even know the city—Amy couldn't figure out where Katrina might be going.

Where MacNeil ended at Lee Street, Katrina crossed over and went down to the bank of the Kickaha River. She followed the riverbank southward, pausing only when she came near the Gracie Street Bridge. There the fenced-off ruins of the old L & B sawmill reared up in the darkness, ill-lit, drowning the riverbank with its shadow. It took up enough room that a person walking along the river by its chain-link fence would be almost invisible from any of the more peopled areas roundabout. Even across the river there were only empty warehouses.

Amy started to hurry again, struck by the sudden fear that Katrina meant to do herself harm. The river ran quicker here, rapiding over a descending shelf of broken stone slabs from where an old railway bridge had collapsed a few years ago. The city had cleared a channel through the debris, but that just made the river run more quickly through the narrower course. More than one person had drowned on this stretch of water—and not always by accident.

Matt's not worth it, she wanted to tell Katrina. *Nobody's worth it.*

Before she could reach Katrina, she came to an abrupt halt again. She stifled a cough that reared up in her throat and leaned against a fence post, suddenly dizzy. But it wasn't the escalating onset of a flu bug that had made her stop. Rather it was what she had spied, bobbing in the swift-moving water.

The light was bad, just a diffused glow from the streets a block or so over, but it was enough for her to make out four white shapes in the dark water. They each seemed as slender and graceful as Katrina, with the same spun gold hair, except theirs was cut short to their skulls, highlighting the fox-like shape of their features. They probably had, Amy thought, the same blue eyes, too.

What were they *doing* there?

Another wave of dizziness came over her. She slid down the side of the fence pole until she was crouched on the ground. She remembered thinking that this way she wouldn't have as far to fall if she fainted. Clutching the pole for support, she looked back to the river.

Katrina had moved closer to the shore and was holding her arms out to the women. As their shapes moved closer, Amy's heartbeat drummed into overtime for she realized that they had no legs. They were propelling themselves through the water with scaled fish tails. There was no mistaking the shape of them as the long tail fins broke the surface of the water.

Mermaids, Amy thought, no longer able to breathe. They were mermaids.

It wasn't possible. *How* could it be possible?

And what did it make Katrina?

The sight of them blurred. For a moment she was looking through a veil, then it was like looking through a double-paned window at an angle, images all duplicated and laid over each other.

She blinked hard. She started to lift her hand to rub at her eyes, but she was suddenly so weak it was all she could do to just crouch beside the pole and not tumble over into the weeds.

The women in the river drew closer as Katrina stepped to the very edge of the water. Katrina lifted her hair, then let it drop in a clouding fall. She pointed at the women.

"Cut away and gone," one of the women said.

"All gone."

"We gave it to Maraghreen."

"For you, sister."

"We traded, gold for silver."

Amy pressed her face against the pole as the mermaids spoke. Through her dizziness, their voices seemed preternaturally enhanced. They chorused, one beginning where another ended, words molten, bell-like, sweet as honey, and so very, very pure.

"She gave us this."

The foremost of the women in the river reached up out of the water. Something glimmered silver and bright in her hand. A knife.

"Pierce his heart."

"Bathe in his blood."

"Your legs will grow together once more."

"You'll come back to us."

"Oh, sister."

Katrina went down on her knees at the water's edge. She took the knife from the mermaid's hand and laid it gingerly on her lap.

"He doesn't love you."

"He will never love you."

The women all drew close. They reached out of the water, stroking Katrina's arms and her face with gentling hands.

"You must do it—before the first dawn light follows tomorrow night."

"Or foam you'll be."

"Sister, please."

"Return to those who love you."

Katrina bowed her head, making no response. One by one the women dove into the river deeps and were gone. From her hiding place, Amy tried to rise—she knew Katrina would be coming back soon, coming back this way, and she didn't want to be caught—but she couldn't manage it, even with the help of the pole beside her. Then Katrina stepped away from the river and walked towards her, the knife held gingerly in one hand.

As their gazes met, another wave of dizziness rose in Amy, this one a tsunami, and in its wake she felt the ground tremble underfoot, but it was only herself, tumbling into the dirt and weeds. She closed her eyes and let the darkness take her away.

*   *   *

It was late afternoon when Amy awoke on the sofa in Lucia's loft. Her surroundings and the wrong angle of the afternoon light left her disoriented and confused, but no longer feeling sick. It must have been one of those 24-hour viruses, she thought as she swung her legs to the floor, then leaned back against the sofa's cushions.

Lucia looked up from the magazine she was reading at the kitchen table. Laying it down she walked over and joined Amy on the sofa.

"I was *très* surprised to find you sleeping here when I got in last night," she said. "Katrina said you got sick, so she put you to bed on the sofa and slept on the floor herself. How're you feeling now, *ma cherie*?"

Amy worked through what Lucia had just said. None of it quite jibed with her own muddled memory of the previous evening.

"Okay . . . I guess," she said finally. She looked around the loft. "Where's Katrina?"

"She borrowed the bus money from me and went to Hartnett's Point after all. True love wins over all, *n'est-ce pas*?"

Amy thought of mermaids swimming in the Kickaha River, of Katrina kneeling by the water, of the silver knife.

"Oh, shit," she said.

"What's the matter?"

"I . . ."

Amy didn't know what to say. What she'd seen hadn't made any sense. She'd been sick, dizzy, probably delirious. But it had seemed so real.

Pierce his heart . . . bathe in his blood. . . .

She shook her head. None of it could have happened. There were no such things as mermaids. But what if there were? What if Katrina was carrying that silver knife as she made her way to Matt's gig? What if she did just what those . . . mermaids had told her . . .

You must do it—before the first dawn light that follows tomorrow night. . . .

What if—

Or foam you'll be . . .

—it was real?

She bent down and looked for her shoes, found them pressed up against one of the coffee table's crate supports. She put them on and rose from the sofa.

"I've got to go," she told Lucia.

"Go where? What's going on?"

"I don't know. I don't have time to explain. I'll tell you later."

Lucia followed her across the loft to the door. "Amy, you're acting really weird."

"I'm fine," Amy said. "Honest."

Though she still didn't feel quite normal. She was weak and didn't want to look in a mirror for fear of seeing the white ghost of her own face looking back at her. But she didn't feel that she had any choice.

If what she'd seen last night *had* been real . . .

Lucia shook her head uncertainly. "Are you sure you're—"

Amy paused long enough to give her friend a quick peck on the cheek, then she was out the door.

Borrowing a car was easy. Her brother Pete had two and was used to her sudden requests for transportational needs, relieved that he wasn't required to provide a chauffeur service along with it. She was on the road by seven, tooling west along the old lakeside highway in a gas-guzzling Chev, stopping for a meal at a truck stop that marked the halfway point and arriving at Harnett's Point just as Matt would be starting his first set.

She pulled in beside his VW van—a positive antique by now, she liked to tease him—and parked. The building that housed Murphy's Bar where Matt had his gig was a ramshackle affair, log walls here in back, plaster on cement walls in front. The bar sat on the edge of the point from which the village got its name, with a long pier out behind the building, running into the lake. The water around the pier was thick with moored boats.

She went around front to where the neon sign spelling the name of the bar crackled and spat an orange glow and stepped inside to the familiar sound of Matt singing Leon Rosselson's "World Turned Upside Down." The audience, surprisingly enough for a backwoods establishment such as this, was actually paying attention to the music. Amy thought that only a third of them were probably even aware of the socialist message the song espoused.

The patrons were evenly divided between the back-to-the-earth hippies who tended organic farms west of the village, all jeans and unbleached cotton, long hair and flower-print dresses; the locals who'd grown up in the area and would probably die here, heavier drinkers, also in jeans, but tending towards flannel shirts and baseball caps, T-shirts and work-boots; and then those cottagers who hadn't yet closed their places up for the year, a hodgepodge of golf shirts and cotton blends, short skirts and, yes, even one dark blue captain's cap, complete with braided rope trim.

She shaded her eyes and looked for Katrina, but didn't spot her. After a few moments, she got herself a beer from the bar and found a corner table to sit at that she shared with a pair of earth-mothers and a tall skinny man with drooping eyes and hair longer than that of either of his companions, pulled back into a ponytail that fell to his waist. They made introductions all around, then settled back into their chairs to listen to the music.

As Matt's set wound on, Amy began to wonder just exactly what it was that she was doing here. Even closing her eyes and concentrating, she could barely call up last night's fantastic images with any sort of clarity. What if the whole thing *had* just been a delirium? What if she'd made her way to Lucia's apartment only to pass out on the sofa and have dreamt it all?

Matt stopped by the table when he ended his set.

"What brings you up here, Scallan?" he asked.

She shrugged. "Just thought I'd check out how you do without the rest of us to keep you honest."

A touch of humor crinkled around his eyes. "So what's the verdict?"

"You're doing good." She introduced him to her companions, then asked, "Do you want to get a little air?"

He nodded and let her lead the way outside. They leaned against the back of somebody's Bronco and looked up and down the length of one of the village's two streets. This one cut north and south, from the bush down to the lake. The other was merely the highway as it cut through the village.

"So have you seen Katrina?" Amy asked.

Matt nodded. "Yeah, we walked around the Market for awhile yesterday afternoon."

"You mean, she's not up here?"

"Not so's I know."

Amy sighed. So much for her worries. But if Katrina hadn't borrowed the money from Lucia to come up here, then where *had* she gone?

"Why are you so concerned about Katrina?" Matt asked.

Amy started to make up some excuse, but then thought, screw it. One of them might as well be up front.

"I'm just worried about her."

Matt nodded. He kicked at the gravel underfoot, but didn't say anything.

"I know it's none of my business," Amy said.

"You're right. It's not." There was no rancor in Matt's voice. Just a kind of weariness.

"It's just that—"

"Look," he said, turning to Amy, "she seems nice, that's all. I think maybe we started out on the wrong foot, but I'm trying to fix that. For now, I just want to be her friend. If something else comes up later, okay. But I want to take it as it comes. Slowly. Is that so wrong?"

Amy shook her head. And then it struck her. For the first time that they weren't on stage together, or working out an arrangement, Matt actually seemed to focus on her. To listen to what she was saying, and answer honestly. Protective walls maybe not completely down, but there *was* a little breach in them.

"I think she loves you," Amy said.

Matt sighed. "It's kind of early for that—don't you think? I think it's more a kind of infatuation. She'll probably grow out of it just as fast as she fell into it."

"I don't know about that. Seems to me that if you're going to be at all fair, you'd be just a little bit more—"

"Don't talk to me about responsibility," Matt said, breaking in. "Just because someone falls in love with you, it doesn't mean you owe them anything. I've got no control over how other people feel about me—"

That's where you're wrong, Amy thought. If you'd just act more human, more like this . . .

"—and I'm sure not going to run my life by their feelings and schedules. I'm not trying to sound self-centered, I'm just trying to . . . I don't know. Protect my privacy."

"But if you don't give a little, how will you ever know what you might be missing?"

"Giving too much, too fast—that just leaves you open to being hurt."

"But—"

"Oh, shit," Matt said, glancing at his watch. "I've got another set to do." He pushed away from the Bronco. "Look, I'm sorry if I don't measure up to how people want me to be, but this is just the way I am."

Why didn't you open yourself up even this much while we were going out together? Amy wanted to ask. But all she did was nod and say, "I know."

"Are you coming in?"

She shook her head. "Not right away."

"Well, I've got—"

"I know." She waved him off. "Break a leg or whatever."

She moved away from the Bronco once he'd gone inside and crossed the parking lot, gravel crunching underfoot until she reached the grass verge. She followed it around to the lawn by the side of the building and down to the lakefront. There she stood, listening to the vague sound of Matt's voice and guitar as it carried through an open window. She looked at all the boats clustered around the pier. A splash drew her attention to the far end of the wooden walkway where a figure sat with its back to the shore having just thrown something into the lake.

Amy had one of those moments of utter clarity. She knew immediately that it was Katrina sitting there, feet dangling in the water, long hair clouding down her back, knew as well that it was the silver knife she'd thrown into the lake. Amy could almost see it, turning end on slow end as it sank in the water.

She hesitated for the space of a few long breaths, gaze tracking the surface of the lake for Katrina's sisters, then she slowly made her way down to the pier. Katrina turned at the sound of Amy's shoes on the wooden slats of the walkway. She nodded once, then looked back out over the lake.

Amy sat beside her. She hesitated again, then put her arm comfortingly around Katrina's small shoulders. They sat like that for a long time. The water lapped against the pilings below them. An owl called out from the woods to their left, a long mournful sound. A truck pulled into the bar's parking lot. Car doors slammed, voices rose in laughter, then disappeared into the bar.

Katrina stirred beside Amy. She began to move her hands, but Amy shook her head.

"I'm sorry," she said. "I can't understand what you're saying."

Katrina mimed steering, both hands raised up in front of her, fingers closed around an invisible steering wheel.

Amy nodded. "I drove up in my brother's car."

Katrina pointed to herself then to Amy and again mimed turning a steering wheel.

"You want me to drive you somewhere?"

Katrina nodded.

Amy looked back towards the bar. "What about Matt?"

Katrina shook her head. She put her hands together, eyes eloquent where her voice was silent. Please.

Amy looked at her for a long moment, then she slowly nodded. "Sure. I can give you a lift. Is there someplace specific you want to go?"

Katrina merely rose to her feet and started back down the pier towards shore. Once they were in the Chev, she pointed to the glove compartment.

"Go ahead," Amy said.

As she started the car, Katrina pulled out a handful of roadmaps. She sorted through them until she came to one that showed the whole north shore of the lake. She unfolded it and laid it on the dashboard between them and pointed to a spot west of Newford. Amy looked more closely. The place where Katrina had her finger was where the Dulfer River emptied into the lake. The tip of her small finger was placed directly on the lakeside campgrounds of the State Park there.

"Jesus," Amy said. "It'll take us all night to get there. We'll be lucky to make it before dawn."

As Katrina shrugged, Amy remembered what Katrina's sisters had said last night.

Before the first dawn light follows tomorrow night.

That was tonight. *This* morning.

Or foam you'll be.

She shivered and looked at Katrina.

"Tell me what's going on," she said. "Please, Katrina. Maybe I can help you."

Katrina just shook her head sadly. She mimed driving, hands around the invisible steering wheel again.

Amy sighed. She put the car in gear and pulled out of the parking lot. Katrina reached towards the radio, eyebrows raised quizzically. When Amy nodded, she turned it on and slowly wound through the stations until she got Newford's WKPN–FM. It was too early for Zoe B.'s "Nightnoise" show, so they listened to Mariah Carey, the Vaughan Brothers and the like as they followed the highway east.

Neither of them spoke as they drove; Katrina couldn't and Amy was just too depressed. She didn't know what was going on. She just felt as though she'd become trapped in a Greek tragedy. The storyline was already written, everything was predestined to a certain outcome and there was nothing she could do about it. Only Matt could have, if he'd loved Katrina, but she couldn't even blame him. You couldn't force a person to love somebody.

She didn't agree with his need to protect his privacy. Maybe it stopped him from being hurt, but it also stopped him from being alive. But he was right about one thing: he couldn't be held responsible for who chose to love him.

They crossed over the Dulfer River just as dawn was starting to pink the eastern horizon. When Amy pulled into the campgrounds, Katrina directed her down a narrow dirt road that led to the park's boat launch.

They had the place to themselves. Amy pulled up by the water and killed the engine. The pines stood silent around them when they got out of the car. There was birdsong, but it seemed strangely muted. Distant. As though heard through gauze.

Katrina lifted a hand and touched Amy's cheek, then walked towards the water. She headed to the left of the launching area where a series of broad flat rocks staircased down into the water. After a moment's hesitation, Amy followed after. She sat down beside Katrina, who was right by the edge of the water, arms wrapped around her knees.

"Katrina," she began. "Please tell me what's going on. I—"

She fussed in her purse, looking for pen and paper. She found the former, and pulled out her checkbook to use the back of a check as a writing surface.

"I want to help," she said, holding the pen and checkbook out to her companion.

Katrina regarded her for a long moment, a helpless look in her eyes, but finally she took the proffered items. She began to write on the back of one of the checks, but before she could hand it back to Amy, a wind rose up. The pine trees shivered, needles whispering against each other.

An electric tingle sparked across every inch of Amy's skin. The hairs at the nape of her neck prickled and goosebumps traveled up her arms. It was like that moment before a storm broke, when the air is so charged with ions that it seems anything might happen.

"What . . . ?" she began.

Her voice died in her throat as the air around them thickened. Shapes formed in the air, pale diffused airy shapes, slender and transparent. Their voices were like the sound of the wind in the pines.

"Come with us," they said, beckoning to Katrina.

"Be one with us."

"We can give you what you lack."

Katrina stared at the misty apparitions for the longest time. Then she let pen and checkbook fall to the rock and stood up, stretching her arms towards the airy figures. Her own body began to lose its definition. She was a spiderweb in the shape of a woman, gossamer, smoke and mist. Her clothing fell from her transparent form to fall into a tangle beside Amy.

And then she was gone. The wind died. The whisper stilled in the pines.

Amy stared open-mouthed at where Katrina had disappeared. All that lay on the rock were Katrina's clothes, the pen and the checkbook. Amy reached out towards the clothes. They were damp to the touch.

Or foam you'll be.

Amy looked up into the lightening sky. But Katrina hadn't just turned to foam, had she? Something had come and taken her away before that happened. If any of this had even been real at all. If she hadn't just lost it completely.

She heard weeping and lowered her gaze to the surface of the lake. There were four women's heads there, bobbing in the unruly water. Their hair was short, cropped close to their heads, untidily, as though cut with garden shears or a knife. Their eyes were red with tears. Each could have been Katrina's twin.

Seeing her gaze upon them, they sank beneath the waves, one by one, and then Amy was alone again. She swallowed thickly, then picked up her checkbook to read what Katrina had written before what could only have been angels came to take her away:

"Is this what having a soul means, to know such bittersweet pain? But still, I cherish the time I had. Those who live forever, who have no stake in the dance of death's inevitable approach, can never understand the sanctity of life."

It sounded stiff, like a quote, but then Amy realized she'd never heard how Katrina would speak, not the cadence of her voice, nor its timbre, nor her diction.

And now she never would.

The next day, Matt found Amy where her brother Pete said she was going. She was by the statue of the little mermaid on Wolf Island, just sitting on a bench and staring out at the lake. She looked haggard from a lack of sleep.

"What happened to you last night?" he asked.

She shrugged. "I decided to go for a drive."

Matt nodded as though he understood, though he didn't pretend to have a clue. The complexities that made up people's personalities were forever a mystery to him.

He sat down beside her.

"Have you seen Katrina?" he asked. "I went by Lucia's place looking for her, but she was acting all weird—" not unusual for Lucia, he added to himself "—and told me I should ask you."

"She's gone," Amy said. "Maybe back into the lake, maybe into the sky. I'm not really sure."

Matt just looked at her. "Come again?" he said finally.

So Amy told him about it all, of what she'd seen two nights ago by the old L & N sawmill, of what had happened last night.

"It's like in that legend about the little mermaid," she said as she finished up. She glanced at the statue beside them. "The real legend—not what you'd find in some kid's picturebook."

Matt shook his head. " 'The Little Mermaid' isn't a legend," he said. "It's just a story, made up by Hans Christian Andersen, like 'The Emperor's New Clothes' and 'The Ugly Duckling.' They sure as hell aren't real."

"I'm just telling you what I saw."

"Jesus, Amy. Will you listen to yourself?"

When she turned to face him, he saw real anguish in her features.

"I can't help it," she said. "It really happened."

Matt started to argue, but then he shook his head. He didn't know what had gotten into Amy to go on like this. He expected this kind of thing from Geordie's brother who made his living gussying up fantastical stories from nothing, but Amy?

"It looks like her, doesn't it?" Amy said.

Matt followed her gaze to the statue. He remembered the last time he'd been on the island, the night when he'd walked out on Katrina, when everything had looked like her. He got up from the bench and stepped closer. The statue's bronze features gleamed in the sunlight.

"Yeah," he said. "I guess it does."

Then he walked away.

He was pissed off with Amy for going on the way she had and brooded about her stupid story all the way back to the city. He had a copy of the Andersen Fairy Tales at home. When he got back to his apartment, he took it down from the shelf and read the story again.

"Aw, shit," he said as he closed the book.

It was just a story. Katrina would turn up. They'd all share a laugh at how Amy was having him on.

But Katrina didn't turn up. Not that day, nor the next, nor

by the end of the week. She'd vanished from his life as mysteriously as she'd come into it.

That's why I don't want to get involved with people, he wanted to tell Amy. Because they just walk out of your life if you don't do what they want you to do.

No way it had happened as Amy had said it did. But he found himself wondering about what it would be like to be without a soul, wondering if he even had one.

Friday of that week, he found himself back on the island, standing by the statue once again. There were a couple of tattered silk flowers on the stone at its base. He stared at the mermaid's features for a long time, then he went home and started to phone the members of Marrowbones.

"Well, I kind of thought this was coming," Amy said when he called to tell her that he was breaking up the band, "except I thought it'd be Johnny or Nicky quitting."

She was sitting in the windowseat of her apartment's bay window, back against one side, feet propped up against the other. She was feeling better than she had when she'd seen him on Sunday, but there was still a strangeness inside her. A lost feeling, a sense of the world having shifted underfoot and the rules being all changed.

"So what're you going to do?" she added when he didn't respond.

"Hit the road for awhile."

"Gigging, or just traveling?"

"Little of both, I guess."

There was another long pause and Amy wondered if he was waiting for her to ask if she could come. But she was really over him now. Had been for a long time. She wasn't looking to be anybody's psychiatrist, or mother. Or matchmaker.

"Well, see you then," he said.

"Bon voyage," Amy said.

She cradled the phone. She thought of how he had talked

with her the other night up at Hartnett's Point, opening up, actually *relating* to her. And now . . . She realized that the whole business with Katrina had just wound him up tighter than ever before.

Well, somebody else was going to have to work on those walls and she knew who it had to be. A guy named Matt Casey.

She looked out the window again.

"Good luck," she said.

Matt was gone for a year. When he came back, the first place he went to was Wolf Island. He stood out by the statue for a long time, not saying anything, just trying to sort out why he was here. He didn't have much luck, not that year, nor each subsequent year that he came. Finally, almost a decade after Katrina was gone—walked out of his life, turned into a puddle of lake water, went sailing through the air with angels, whatever—he decided to stay overnight, as though being alone in the dark would reveal something that was hidden from the day.

"Lady," he said, standing in front of the statue, drowned in the thick silence of the night.

He hadn't brought an offering for the statue—Our Lady of the Harbour, as the bag lady had called her. He was just here, looking for something that remained forever out of reach. He wasn't trying to understand Katrina or the story that Amy had told of her. Not anymore.

"Why am I so empty inside?" he asked.

"I can't believe you're going to play with him again," Lucia said when Amy told her about her new band, Johnny Jump Up.

Amy shrugged. "It'll just be the three of us—Geordie's going to be playing fiddle."

"But he hasn't changed at all. He's still so—cold."

"Not on stage."

"I suppose not," Lucia said. "I guess all he's got going for him is his music."

Amy nodded sadly.

"I know," she said.

⌐ • PAPERJACK • ⌐

*If you think education is
expensive, try ignorance.*
—DEREK BOK

CHURCHES AREN'T HAVENS of spiritual enlightenment;
they enclose the spirit. The way Jilly explains it, orga-
nizing Mystery tends to undermine its essence. I'm not so
sure I agree, but then I don't really know enough about it.
When it comes to things that can't be logically explained, I
take a step back and leave them to Jilly or my brother
Christy—they thrive on that kind of thing. If I had to describe myself as belonging to any church or mystical order,
it'd be one devoted to secular humanism. My concerns are
for real people and the here and now; the possible existence
of God, faeries, or some metaphysical Otherworld just
doesn't fit into my worldview.

Except . . .

You knew there'd be an "except," didn't you, or else
why would I be writing this down?

It's not like I don't have anything to say. I'm all for creative expression, but my medium's music. I'm not an artist
like Jilly, or a writer like Christy. But the kinds of things that
have been happening to me can't really be expressed in a

fiddle tune—no, that's not entirely true. I can express them, but the medium is such I can't be assured that, when I'm playing, listeners hear what I mean them to hear.

That's how it works with instrumental music, and it's probably why the best of it is so enduring: the listener takes away whatever he or she wants from it. Say the composer was trying to tell us about the aftermath of some great battle. When we hear it, the music might speak to us of a parent we've lost, a friend's struggle with some debilitating disease, a doe standing at the edge of a forest at twilight, or any of a thousand other unrelated things.

Realistic art like Jilly does—or at least it's realistically rendered; her subject matter's right out of some urban update of those Andrew Lang color-coded fairy tale books that most of us read when we were kids—and the collections of urban legends and stories that my brother writes don't have that same leeway. What goes down on the canvas or on paper, no matter how skillfully drawn or written, doesn't allow for much in the way of an alternate interpretation.

So that's why I'm writing this down: to lay it all out in black and white where maybe I can understand it myself.

For the past week, every afternoon after busking up by the Williamson Street Mall for the lunchtime crowds, I've packed up my fiddle case and headed across town to come here to St. Paul's Cathedral. Once I get here, I sit on the steps about halfway up, take out this notebook, and try to write. The trouble is, I haven't been able to figure out where to start.

I like it out here on the steps. I've played inside the cathedral—just once, for a friend's wedding. The wedding was okay, but I remember coming in on my own to test the acoustics an hour or so before the rehearsal; ever since then I've been a little unsure about how Jilly views this kind of place. My fiddling didn't feel enclosed. Instead the walls seemed to open the music right up; the cathedral gave the reel I was playing a stately grace—a spiritual grace—that it had never held for me before. I suppose it had more to do with the architect's design than the presence of God, still I could've played there all night only—

But I'm rambling again. I've filled a couple of pages now, which is more than I've done all week, except after just re-reading what I've written so far, I don't know if any of it's relevant.

Maybe I should just tell you about Paperjack. I don't know that it starts with him exactly, but it's probably as good a place as any to begin.

It was a glorious day, made all the more precious because the weather had been so weird that spring. One day I'd be bundled up in a jacket and scarf, cloth cap on my head, with fingerless gloves to keep the cold from my finger joints while I was out busking, the next I'd be in a T-shirt, breaking into a sweat just thinking about standing out on some street corner to play tunes.

There wasn't a cloud in the sky, the sun was halfway home from noon to the western horizon, and Jilly and I were just soaking up the rays on the steps of St. Paul's. I was slouched on the steps, leaning on one elbow, my fiddlecase propped up beside me, wishing I had worn shorts because my jeans felt like leaden weights on my legs. Sitting beside me, perched like a cat about to pounce on something terribly interesting that only it could see, Jilly was her usual scruffy self. There were flecks of paint on her loose cotton pants and her short-sleeved blouse, more under her fingernails, and still more half-lost in the tangles of her hair. She turned to look at me, her face miraculously untouched by her morning's work, and gave me one of her patented smiles.

"Did you ever wonder where he's from?" Jilly asked.

That was one of her favorite phrases: "Did you ever wonder . . . ?" It could take you from considering if and when fish slept, or why people look up when they're thinking, to more arcane questions about ghosts, little people living behind wallboards, and the like. And she loved guessing about people's origins. Sometimes when I was busking she'd tag along and sit by the wall at my back, sketching the people who were listening to me play. Invariably, she'd come up behind me and whisper in my ear—usually when I was in the middle of a complicated tune that needed all my attention—something along the lines of, "The guy in the polyester suit? Ten to one he rides a big chopper on the weekends, complete with a jean vest."

So I was used to it.

Today she wasn't picking out some nameless stranger from a crowd. Instead her attention was on Paperjack, sitting on the steps far enough below us that he couldn't hear what we were saying.

Paperjack had the darkest skin I'd ever seen on a man—an amazing ebony that seemed to swallow light. He was in his mid-sixties, I'd guess, short corkscrew hair all gone grey. The dark suits he wore were threadbare and out of fashion, but always clean. Under his suit jacket he usually wore a white T-shirt that flashed so brightly in the sun it almost hurt your eyes—just like his teeth did when he gave you that lopsided grin of his.

Nobody knew his real name and he never talked. I don't know if he was mute, or if he just didn't have anything to say, but the only sounds I ever heard him make were a chuckle or a laugh. People started calling him Paperjack because he worked an origami gig on the streets.

He was a master at folding paper into shapes. He kept a bag of different colored paper by his knee; people would pick their color and then tell him what they wanted, and he'd make it no cuts, just folding. And he could make anything. From simple flower and animal shapes to things so complex it didn't seem possible for him to capture their essence in a piece of folded paper. So far as I know, he'd never disappointed a single customer.

I'd seen some of the old men come down from Little Japan to sit and watch him work. They called him *sensei*, a term of respect that they didn't exactly bandy around.

But origami was only the most visible side of his gig. He

also told fortunes. He had one of those little folded paper Chinese fortune-telling devices that we all played around with when we were kids. You know the kind: you fold the corners in to the center, turn it over, then fold them in again. When you're done you can stick your index fingers and thumbs inside the little flaps of the folds and open it up so that it looks like a flower. You move your fingers back and forth, and it looks like the flower's talking to you.

Paperjack's fortune-teller was just like that. It had the names of four colors on the outside and eight different numbers inside. First you picked a color—say, red. The fortune-teller would seem to talk soundlessly as his fingers moved back and forth to spell the word, R-E-D, opening and closing until there'd be a choice from four of the numbers. Then you picked a number, and he counted it out until the fortune-teller was open with another or the same set of numbers revealed. Under the number you choose at that point was your fortune.

Paperjack didn't read it out—he just showed it to the person, then stowed the fortune-teller back into the inside pocket of his jacket from which he'd taken it earlier. I'd never had my fortune read by him, but Jilly'd had it done for her a whole bunch of times.

"The fortunes are always different," she told me once. "I sat behind him while he was doing one for a customer, and I read the fortune over her shoulder. When she'd paid him, I got mine done. I picked the same number she did, but when he opened it, there was a different fortune there."

"He's just got more than one of those paper fortune-tellers in his pocket," I said, but she shook her head.

"He never put it away," she said. "It was the same fortune-teller, the same number, but some time between the woman's reading and mine, it changed."

I knew there could be any number of logical explanations for how that could have happened, starting with plain sleight of hand, but I'd long ago given up continuing arguments with Jilly when it comes to that kind of thing.

Was Paperjack magic? Not in my book, at least not the way Jilly thought he was. But there was a magic about him, the magic that always hangs like an aura about someone who's as good an artist as Paperjack was. He also made me feel good. Around him, an overcast day didn't seem half so gloomy, and when the sun shone, it always seemed brighter. He just exuded a glad feeling that you couldn't help but pick up on. So in that sense, he was magic.

I'd also wondered where he'd come from, how he'd ended up on the street. Street people seemed pretty well evenly divided between those who had no choice but to be there, and those who chose to live there like I do. But even then there's a difference. I had a little apartment not far from Jilly's. I could get a job when I wanted one, usually in the winter when the busking was bad and club gigs were slow.

Not many street people have that choice, but I thought that Paperjack might be one of them.

"He's such an interesting guy," Jilly was saying.

I nodded.

"But I'm worried about him," she went on.

"How so?"

Jilly's brow wrinkled with a frown. "He seems to be getting thinner, and he doesn't get around as easily as he once did. You weren't here when he showed up today—he walked as though gravity had suddenly doubled its pull on him."

"Well, he's an old guy, Jilly."

"That's exactly it. Where does he live? Does he have someone to look out for him?"

That was Jilly for you. She had a heart as big as the city, with room in it for everyone and everything. She was forever taking in strays, be they dogs, cats, or people.

I'd been one of her strays once, but that was a long time ago.

"Maybe we should ask him," I said.

"He can't talk," she reminded me.

"Maybe he just doesn't *want* to talk."

Jilly shook her head. "I've tried a zillion times. He hears what I'm saying, and somehow he manages to answer with a smile or a raised eyebrow or whatever, but he doesn't talk." The wrinkles in her brow deepened until I wanted to reach over and smooth them out. "These days," she added, "he seems haunted to me."

If someone else had said that, I'd know that they meant Paperjack had something troubling him. With Jilly though, you often had to take that kind of a statement literally.

"Are we talking ghosts now?" I asked.

I tried to keep the skepticism out of my voice, but from the flash of disappointment that touched Jilly's eyes, I knew I hadn't done a very good job.

"Oh, Geordie," she said. "Why can't you just *believe* what happened to us?"

Here's one version of what happened that night, some three years ago now, to which Jilly was referring:

We saw a ghost. He stepped out of the past on a rainy night and stole away the woman I loved. At least that's the way I remember it. Except for Jilly, no one else does.

Her name was Samantha Rey. She worked at Gypsy Records and had an apartment on Stanton Street, except after that night, when the past came up to steal her away, no one at Gypsy Records remembered her anymore, and the landlady of her Stanton Street apartment had never heard of her. The ghost hadn't just stolen her, he'd stolen all memory of her existence.

All I had left of her was an old photograph that Jilly and I found in Moore's Antiques a little while later. It had a photographer's date on the back: 1912. It was Sam in the picture, Sam with a group of strangers standing on the front porch of some old house.

I remembered her, but she'd never existed. That's what I had to believe. Because nothing else made sense. I had all these feelings and memories of her, but they had to be what my brother called *jamais vu.* That's like *déjà vu,* except instead of having felt you'd been somewhere before, you remembered something that had never happened. I'd never heard the expression before—he got it from a David Morrell thriller that he'd been reading—but it had an authentic ring about it.

Jamais vu.

But Jilly remembered Sam, too.

Thinking about Sam always brought a tightness to my chest; it made my head hurt trying to figure it out. I felt as if I were betraying Sam by trying to convince myself she'd never existed, but I had to convince myself of that, because believing that it really *had* happened was even scarier. How do you live in a world where anything can happen?

"You'll get used to it," Jilly told me. "There's a whole invisible world out there, lying side by side with our own. Once you get a peek into it, the window doesn't close. You're always going to be *aware* of it."

"I don't want to be," I said.

She just shook her head. "You don't really get a lot of choice in this kind of thing," she said.

You always have a choice—that's what I believe. And I chose to not get caught up in some invisible world of ghosts and spirits and who knew what. But I still dreamed of Sam, as if she'd been real. I still kept her photo in my fiddlecase.

I could feel its presence right now, glimmering through the leather, whispering to me.

Remember me . . .

I couldn't forget. *Jamais vu.* But I wanted to.

Jilly scooted a little closer to me on the step and laid a hand on my knee.

"Denying it just makes things worse," she said, continuing an old ongoing argument that I don't think we'll ever resolve. "Until you accept that it really happened, the memory's always going to haunt you, undermining everything that makes you who you are."

"Haunted like Paperjack?" I asked, trying to turn the subject back onto more comfortable ground, or at least focus the attention onto someone other than myself. "Is that what you think's happened to him?"

Jilly sighed. "Memories can be just like ghosts," she said.

Didn't I know it.

I looked down the steps to where Paperjack had been sitting, but he was gone, and now a couple of pigeons were waddling across the steps. The wind blew a candy bar wrapper up against a riser. I laid my hand on Jilly's and gave it a squeeze, then picked up my fiddlecase and stood up.

"I've got to go," I told her.

"I didn't mean to upset you . . ."

"I know. I've just got to walk for a bit and think."

She didn't offer to accompany me and for that I was glad. Jilly was my best friend, but right then I had to be alone.

I went rambling; just let my feet just take me wherever they felt like going, south from St. Paul's and down Battersfield Road, all the way to the Pier, my fiddlecase banging against my thigh as I walked. When I got to the waterfront, I leaned up against the fieldstone wall where the Pier met the beach. I stood and watched the fishermen work their lines farther out over the lake. Fat gulls wheeled above, crying like they hadn't been fed in months. Down on the sand, a couple was having an animated discussion, but they were too far away for me to make out what they were arguing about. They looked like figures in some old silent movie; caricatures, their movements larger than life, rather than real people.

I don't know what I was thinking about; I was trying *not* to think, I suppose, but I wasn't having much luck. The arguing couple depressed me.

Hang on to what you've got, I wanted to tell them, but it wasn't any of my business. I thought about heading across town to Fitzhenry Park—there was a part of it called the Silenus Gardens filled with stone benches and statuary where I always felt better—when I spied a familiar figure sitting down by the river west of the Pier: Paperjack.

The Kickaha River was named after that branch of the Algonquin language family that originally lived in this area before the white men came and took it all away from them. All the tribe had left now was a reservation north of the city and this river named after them. The Kickaha had its source north of the reserve and cut through the city on its way to the lake. In this part of town it separated the business section and commercial waterfront from the Beaches where the money lives.

There are houses in the Beaches that make the old stately homes in Lower Crowsea look like tenements, but you can't see them from here. Looking west, all you see is green—first the City Commission's manicured lawns on either side of the river, then the treed hills that hide the homes of the wealthy from the rest of us plebes. On the waterfront itself are a couple of country clubs and the private beaches of the *really* wealthy whose estates back right onto the water.

Paperjack was sitting on this side of the river, doing I don't know what. From where I stood, I couldn't tell. He seemed to be just sitting there on the riverbank, watching the slow water move past. I watched him for awhile, then hoisted my fiddlecase from where I'd leaned it against the wall and hopped down to the sand. When I got to where he was sitting, he looked up and gave me an easy, welcoming grin, as if he'd been expecting me to show up.

Running into him like this was fate, Jilly would say. I'll stick to calling it coincidence. It's a big city, but it isn't that big.

Paperjack made a motion with his hand, indicating I should pull up a bit of lawn beside him. I hesitated for a moment—right up until then, I realized later, everything could have worked out differently. But I made the choice and sat beside him.

There was a low wall, right down by the water, with rushes and lilies growing up against it. Among the lilies was a family of ducks—mother and a paddling of ducklings—and that was what Paperjack had been watching. He had an empty plastic bag in his hand, and the breadcrumbs that remained in the bottom told me he'd been feeding the ducks until his bread ran out.

He made another motion with his hand, touching the bag, then pointing to the ducks.

I shook my head. "I wasn't planning on coming down," I said, "so I didn't bring anything to feed them."

He nodded, understanding.

We sat quietly awhile longer. The ducks finally gave up on us and paddled farther up the river, looking for better pickings. Once they were gone, Paperjack turned to me again. He laid his hand against his heart, then raised his eyebrows questioningly.

Looking at that slim black hand with its long narrow fingers lying against his dark suit, I marveled again at the sheer depth of his ebony coloring. Even with the bit of a tan I'd picked up busking the last few weeks, I felt absolutely pallid beside him. Then I lifted my gaze to his eyes. If his skin swallowed light, I knew where it went: into his eyes. They were dark, so dark you could barely tell the difference between pupil and cornea, but inside their darkness was a kind of glow—a shine that resonated inside me like the deep hum that comes from my fiddle's bass strings whenever I play one of those wild Shetland reels in A minor.

I suppose it's odd, describing something visual in terms of sound, but right then, right at that moment, I *heard* the shine of his eyes, singing inside me. And I understood immediately what he'd meant by his gesture.

"Yeah," I said. "I'm feeling a little low."

He touched his chest again, but it was a different, lighter gesture this time. I knew what that meant as well.

"There's not much anybody can do about it," I said.

Except Sam. She could come back. Or maybe if I just knew she'd been *real* . . . But that opened a whole other line of thinking that I wasn't sure I wanted to get into again. I wanted her to have been real, I wanted her to come back, but if I accepted that, I also had to accept that ghosts were real and that the past could sneak up and steal someone from the present, taking them back into a time that had already been and gone.

Paperjack took his fortune-telling device out of the breast pocket of his jacket and gave me a questioning look. I started to shake my head, but before I could think about what I was doing, I just said, "What the hell," and let him do his stuff.

I chose blue from the colors, because that was the closest to how I was feeling; he didn't have any colors like confused or lost or foolish. I watched his fingers move the paper to spell out the color, then chose four from the numbers, because that's how many strings my fiddle has. When his fingers stopped moving the second time, I picked seven for no particular reason at all.

He folded back the paper flap so I could read my fortune. All it said was: "Swallow the past."

I didn't get it. I thought it'd say something like that Bobby McFerrin song, "Don't Worry, Be Happy." What it did say didn't make any sense at all.

"I don't understand," I told Paperjack. "What's it supposed to mean?"

He just shrugged. Folding up the fortune-teller, he put it back in his pocket.

Swallow the past. Did that mean I was supposed to forget about it? Or . . . well, swallow could also mean believe or accept. Was that what he was trying to tell me? Was he echoing Jilly's argument?

I thought about that photo in my fiddlecase, and then an idea came to me. I don't know why I'd never thought of it before. I grabbed my fiddlecase and stood up.

"I . . ." I wanted to thank him, but somehow the words just escaped me. All that came out was, "I've gotta run."

But I could tell he understood my gratitude. I wasn't exactly sure what he'd done, except that that little message on his fortune-teller had put together a connection for me that I'd never seen before.

Fate, I could hear Jilly saying.

Paperjack smiled and waved me off.

I followed coincidence away from Paperjack and the riverbank and back up Battersfield Road to the Newford Public Library in Lower Crowsea.

Time does more than erode a riverbank or wear mountains down into tired hills. It takes the edge from our memories as well, overlaying everything with a soft focus so that it all blurs together. What really happened gets all jumbled up with the hopes and dreams we once had and what we wish had really happened. Did you ever run into someone you went to school with—someone you never really hung around with, but just passed in the halls, or had a class with—and they act like you were the best of buddies, because that's how they remember it? For that matter, maybe you *were* buddies, and it's you that's remembering it wrong. . . .

Starting some solid detective work on what happened to Sam took the blur from my memories and brought her back into focus for me. The concepts of ghosts or people disappearing into the past just got pushed to one side, and all I thought about was Sam and tracking her down; if not the Sam I had known, then the woman she'd become in the past.

My friend Amy Scallan works at the library. She's a tall, angular woman with russet hair and long fingers that would have stood her in good stead at a piano keyboard. Instead she took up the Uillean pipes, and we play together in an on-again, off-again band called Johnny Jump Up. Matt Casey, our third member, is the reason we're not that regular a band.

Matt's a brilliant bouzouki and guitar player and a fabulous singer, but he's not got much in the way of social skills, and he's way too cynical for my liking. Since he and I don't really get along well, it makes rehearsals kind of tense at times. On the other hand, I love playing with Amy. She's the kind of musician who has such a good time playing that you can't help but enjoy yourself as well. Whenever I think of Amy, the first image that always comes to mind is of her rangy frame folded around her pipes, right elbow moving back and forth on the bellows to fill the bag under her left arm, those long fingers just dancing on the chanter, foot tapping, head bobbing, a grin on her face.

She always makes sure that the gig goes well, and we have a lot of fun, so it balances out I guess.

I showed her the picture I had of Sam. There was a street number on the porch's support pillar to the right of the steps and enough of the house in the picture that I'd be able to match it up to the real thing. If I could find out what street it was on. If the house still existed.

"This could take forever," Amy said as she laid the photo down on the desk.

"I've got the time."

Amy laughed. "I suppose you do. I don't know how you do it, Geordie. Everyone else in the world has to bust their buns to make a living, but you just cruise on through."

"The trick's having a low overhead," I said.

Amy just rolled her eyes. She'd been to my apartment, and there wasn't much to see: a spare fiddle hanging on the wall with a couple of Jilly's paintings; some tune books with tattered covers and some changes of clothing; one of those old-fashioned record players that had the turntable and speakers all in one unit and a few albums leaning against the side of the apple crate it sat on; a couple of bows that desperately needed rehairing; the handful of used paperbacks I'd picked up for the week's reading from Duffy's Used Books over on Walker Street; and a little beat-up old cassette machine with a handful of tapes.

And that was it. I got by.

I waited at the desk while Amy got the books we needed. She came back with an armload. Most had Newford in the title, but a few also covered that period of time when the city was still called Yoors, after the Dutchman Diederick van Yoors, who first settled the area in the early 1800s. It got changed to Newford back around the turn of the century, so all that's left now to remind the city of its original founding father is a street name.

Setting the books down before me on the desk, Amy went off into the stacks to look for some more obscure titles. I didn't wait for her to get back, but went ahead and started flipping through the first book on the pile, looking carefully at the pictures.

I started off having a good time. There's a certain magic in old photos, especially when they're of the place where you grew up. They cast a spell over you. Dirt roads where now there was pavement, sided by office complexes. The old Brewster Theatre in its heyday—I remembered it as the place where I first saw Phil Ochs and Bob Dylan, and later all-night movie festivals, but the Williamson Street Mall stood there now. Boating parties on the river. Old City Hall—it was a youth hostel these days.

But my enthusiasm waned with the afternoon. By the time the library closed, I was no closer to getting a street name for the house in Sam's photo than I had been when I came in. Amy gave me a sympathetic "I told you so" look when we separated on the front steps of the library. I just told her I'd see her tomorrow.

I had something to eat at Kathryn's Cafe. I'd gone there hoping to see Jilly, only I'd forgotten it was her night off. I tried calling her when I'd finished eating, but she was out. So I took my fiddle over to the theatre district and worked the crowds waiting in line there for an hour or so before I headed off for home, my pockets heavy with change.

That night, just before I fell asleep, I felt like a hole sort of opened in the air above my bed. Lying there, I found myself touring Newford—just floating through its streets. Though the time was the present, there was no color. Everything appeared in the same sepia tones as in my photo of Sam.

I don't remember when I finally did fall asleep.

The next morning I was at the library right when it opened, carrying two cups of take-out coffee in a paper bag, one of which I offered to Amy when I got to her desk. Amy muttered something like, "when owls prowl the day, they shouldn't look so bloody cheerful about it," but she accepted the coffee and cleared a corner of her desk so that I could get back to the books.

In the photo I had of Sam there was just the edge of a bay window visible beside the porch, with fairly unique rounded gingerbread trim running off from either side of its keystone. I'd thought it would be the clue to tracking down the place. It looked almost familiar, but I was no longer sure if that was because I'd actually seen the house at some time, or it was just from looking at the photo so much.

Unfortunately, those details weren't helping at all.

"You know, there's no guarantee you're going to find a picture of the house you're looking for in those books," Amy said around mid-morning when she was taking her coffee break. "They didn't exactly go around taking pictures of everything."

I was at the last page of *Walks Through Old Crowsea*. Closing the book, I set it on the finished pile beside my chair and then leaned back, lacing my fingers behind my head. My shoulders were stiff from sitting hunched over a desk all morning.

"I know. I'm going to give Jack a call when I'm done here to see if I can borrow his bike this afternoon."

"You're going to pedal all around town looking for this house?"

"What else can I do?"

"There's always the archives at the main library."

I nodded, feeling depressed. It had seemed like such a good idea yesterday. It was still a good idea. I just hadn't realized how long it would take.

"Or you could go someplace like the Market and show the photo around to some of the older folks. Maybe one of them will remember the place."

"I suppose."

I picked up the next book, *The Architectural Heritage of Old Yoors,* and went back to work.

And there it was, on page thirty-eight. The house. There were three buildings in a row in the photo; the one I'd been looking for was the middle one. I checked the caption: "Grasso Street, circa 1920."

"I don't believe it," Amy said. I must have made some kind of a noise, because she was looking up at me from her own work. "You found it, didn't you?" she added.

"I think so. Have you got a magnifying glass?"

She passed it over, and I checked out the street number of the middle house. One-forty-two. The same as in my photo.

Amy took over then. She phoned a friend who worked in the land registry office. He called back a half hour later and gave us the name of the owner in 1912, when my photo had been taken: Edward Dickenson. The house had changed hands a number of times since the Dickensons had sold it in the forties.

We checked the phone book, but there were over a hundred Dickensons listed, twelve with just an initial "E" and one Ed. None of the addresses were on Grasso Street.

"Which makes sense," Amy said, "since they sold the place fifty years ago."

I wanted to run by that block on Grasso where the house was—I'd passed it I don't know how many times, and never paid much attention to it or any of its neighbors—but I needed more background on the Dickensons first. Amy showed me how to run the microfiche, and soon I was going through back issues of *The Newford Star* and *The Daily Journal,* concentrating on the local news sections and the gossip columns.

The first photo of Edward Dickenson that came up was in *The Daily Journal,* the June 21st, 1913, issue. He was standing with the Dean of Butler University at some opening ceremony. I compared him to the people with Sam in my photo and found him standing behind her to her left.

Now that I was on the right track, I began to work in a

kind of frenzy. I whipped through the microfiche, making notes of every mention of the Dickensons. Edward turned out to have been a stockbroker, one of the few who didn't lose his shirt in subsequent market crashes. Back then the money lived in Lower Crowsea, mostly on McKennitt, Grasso, and Stanton Streets. Edward made the papers about once a month—business deals, society galas, fund-raising events, political dinners, and the like. It wasn't until I hit the October 29, 1915, issue of *The Newford Star* that I had the wind knocked out of my sails.

It was the picture that got to me: Sam and a man who was no stranger. I'd seen him before. He was the ghost that had stepped out of the past and stolen her away. Under the photo was a caption announcing the engagement of Thomas Edward Dickenson, son of the well-known local businessman, to Samantha Rey.

In the picture of Sam that I had, Dickenson wasn't there with the rest of the people—he'd probably taken it. But here he was. Real. With Sam. I couldn't ignore it.

Back then they didn't have the technology to make a photograph lie.

There was a weird buzzing in my ears as that picture burned its imprint onto my retinas. It was hard to breathe, and my T-shirt suddenly seemed too tight.

I don't know what I'd been expecting, but I knew it wasn't this. I suppose I thought I'd track down the people in the picture and find out that the woman who looked like Sam was actually named Gertrude something-or-other, and she'd lived her whole life with that family. I didn't expect to find Sam. I didn't expect the ghost to have been real.

I was in a daze as I put away the microfiche and shut down the machine.

"Geordie?" Amy asked as I walked by her desk. "Are you okay?"

I remember nodding and muttering something about needing a break. I picked up my fiddle and headed for the front door. The next thing I remember is standing in front of the address on Grasso Street and looking at the Dickensons' house.

I had no idea who owned it now; I hadn't been paying much attention to Amy after she told me that the Dickensons had sold it. Someone had renovated it fairly recently, so it didn't look at all the same as in the photos, but under its trendy additions, I could see the lines of the old house.

I sat down on the curb with my fiddlecase across my knees and just stared at the building. The buzzing was back in my head. My shirt still felt too tight.

I didn't know what to do anymore, so I just sat there, trying to make sense out of what couldn't be reasoned away. I no longer had any doubt that Sam had been real, or that a ghost had stolen her away. The feeling of loss came back all over again, as if it had happened just now, not three years ago. And what scared me was, if she and the ghost were real, then what else might be?

I closed my eyes, and headlines of supermarket tabloids flashed across my eyes, a strobing flicker of bizarre images and words. That was the world Jilly lived in—one in which anything was possible. I didn't know if I could handle living in that kind of world. I needed rules and boundaries. Patterns.

It was a long time before I got up and headed for Kathryn's Cafe.

The first thing Jilly asked when I got in the door was, "Have you seen Paperjack?"

It took me a few moments to push back the clamor of my own thoughts to register what she'd asked. Finally I just shook my head.

"He wasn't at St. Paul's today," Jilly went on, "and he's always there, rain or shine, winter or summer. I didn't think he was looking well yesterday, and now . . ."

I tuned her out and took a seat at an empty table before I could fall down. That feeling of dislocation that had started up in me when I first saw Sam's photo in the microfiche kept coming and going in waves. It was cresting right now, and I found it hard to just sit in the chair, let alone listen to what Jilly was saying. I tuned her back in when the spaciness finally started to recede.

". . . heart attack, who would he call? He can't *speak*."

"I saw him yesterday," I said, surprised that my voice sounded so calm. "Around mid-afternoon. He seemed fine."

"He did?"

I nodded. "He was down by the Pier, sitting on the riverbank, feeding the ducks. He read my fortune."

"He *did*?"

"You're beginning to sound like a broken record, Jilly."

For some reason, I was starting to feel better. That sense of being on the verge of a panic attack faded and then disappeared completely. Jilly pulled up a chair and leaned across the table, elbows propped up, chin cupped in her hands.

"So tell me," she said. "What made you do it? What was your fortune?"

I told her everything that had happened since I had seen Paperjack. That sense of dislocation came and went again a few times while I talked, but mostly I was holding firm.

"Holy shit!" Jilly said when I was done.

She put her hand to her mouth and looked quickly around, but none of the customers seemed to have noticed. She reached a hand across the table and caught one of mine.

"So now you believe?" she asked.

"I don't have a whole lot of choice, do I?"

"What are you going to do?"

I shrugged. "What's to do? I found out what I needed to know—now I've got to learn to live with it and all the other baggage that comes with it."

Jilly didn't say anything for a long moment. She just held my hand and exuded comfort as only Jilly can.

"You could find her," she said finally.

"Who? Sam?"

"Who else?"

"She's probably—" I stumbled over the word dead and settled for "—not even alive anymore."

"Maybe not," Jilly said. "She'd definitely be old. But don't you think you should find out?"

"I . . ."

I wasn't sure I wanted to know. And if she were alive, I wasn't sure I wanted to meet her. What could we say to each other?

"Think about it, anyway," Jilly said.

That was Jilly; she never took no for an answer.

"I'm off at eight," she said. "Do you want to meet me then?"

"What's up?" I asked, halfheartedly.

"I thought maybe you'd help me find Paperjack."

I might as well, I thought. I was becoming a bit of an expert in tracking people down by this point. Maybe I should get a card printed: Geordie Riddell, Private Investigations and Fiddle Tunes.

"Sure," I told her.

"Great," Jilly said.

She bounced up from her seat as a couple of new customers came into the cafe. I ordered a coffee from her after she'd gotten them seated, then stared out the window at the traffic going by on Battersfield. I tried not to think of Sam— trapped in the past, making a new life for herself there—but I might as well have tried to jump to the moon.

By the time Jilly came off shift I was feeling almost myself again, but instead of being relieved, I had this great load of guilt hanging over me. It all centered around Sam and the ghost. I'd denied her once. Now I felt as though I was betraying her all over again. Knowing what I knew—the photo accompanying the engagement notice in that old issue of *The Newford Star* flashed across my mind—the way I was feeling at the moment didn't seem right. I felt too normal; and so the guilt.

"I don't get it," I said to Jilly as we walked down Battersfield towards the Pier. "This afternoon I was falling to pieces, but now I just feel . . ."

"Calm?"

"Yeah."

"That's because you've finally stopped fighting yourself and accepted that what you saw—what you remember—really happened. It was denial that was screwing you up."

She didn't add, "I told you so," but she didn't have to. It echoed in my head anyway, joining the rest of the guilt I was carrying around with me. If I'd only listened to her with an open mind, then . . . what?

I wouldn't be going through this all over again?

We crossed Lakeside Drive and made our way through the closed concession and souvenir stands to the beach. When we reached the Pier, I led her westward to where I'd last seen Paperjack, but he wasn't sitting by the river anymore. A lone duck regarded us hopefully, but neither of us had thought to bring any bread.

"So I track down Sam," I said, still more caught up in my personal quest than in looking for Paperjack. "If she's not dead, she'll be an old lady. If I find her—then what?"

"You'll complete the circle," Jilly said. She looked away from the river and faced me, her pixie features serious. "It's like the Kickaha say: everything is on a wheel. You stepped off the one that represents your relationship with Sam before it came full circle. Until you complete your turn on it, you'll never have peace of mind."

"When do you know you've come full circle?" I asked.

"You'll know."

She turned away before I could go on and started back towards the Pier. By day the place was crowded and full of noise, alive with tourists and people out relaxing, just looking to have a good time; by night, its occupancy was turned over to gangs of kids, fooling around on skateboards or simply hanging out, and the homeless: winos, bag ladies, hoboes, and the like.

Jilly worked the crowd, asking after Paperjack, while I

followed in her wake. Everybody knew him, or had seen him in the past week, but no one knew where he was now, or where he lived. We were about to give up and head over to Fitzhenry Park to start over again with the people hanging out there, when we heard the sound of a harmonica. It was playing the blues, a soft, mournful sound that drifted up from the beach.

We made for the nearest stairs and then walked back across the sand to find the Bossman sitting under the board-walk, hands cupped around his instrument, head bowed down, eyes closed. There was no one listening to him except us. The people with money to throw in his old cloth cap were having dinner now in the fancy restaurants across Lakeside Drive or over in the theatre district. He was just playing for himself.

When he was busking, he stuck to popular pieces—whatever was playing on the radio mixed with old show tunes, jazz favorites, and that kind of thing. The music that came from his harmonica now was pure magic. It trans-formed him, making him larger than life. The blues he played held all the world's sorrows in its long sliding notes and didn't so much change it, as make it bearable.

My fingers itched to pull out my fiddle and join him, but we hadn't come to jam. So we waited until he was done. The last note hung in the air for far longer than seemed possible, then he brought his hands away from his mouth and cradled the harmonica on his lap. He looked up at us from under drooping eyelids, the magic disappearing now that he'd stopped playing. He was just an old, homeless black man now, with the faint trace of a smile touching his lips.

"Hey, Jill—Geordie," he said. "What's doin'?"

"We're looking for Paperjack," Jilly told him.

The Bossman nodded. "Jack's the man for paperwork, all right."

"I've been worried about him," Jilly said. "About his health."

"You a doctor now, Jill?"

She shook her head.

"Anybody got a smoke?"

This time we both shook our heads.

From his pocket he pulled a half-smoked butt that he must have picked up off the boardwalk earlier, then lit it with a wooden match that he struck on the zipper of his jeans. He took a long drag and let it out so that the blue-grey smoke wreathed his head, studying us all the while.

"You care too much, you just get hurt," he said finally.

Jilly nodded. "I know. But I can't help it. Do you know where we can find him?"

"Well now. Come winter, he lives with a Mex family down in the Barrio."

"And in the summer?"

The Bossman shrugged. "I heard once he's got himself a camp up behind the Beaches."

"Thanks," Jilly said.

"He might not take to uninvited guests," the Bossman added. "Body gets himself an out-of-the-way squat like that, I'd think he be lookin' for privacy."

"I don't want to intrude," Jilly assured him. "I just want to make sure he's okay."

The Bossman nodded. "You're a stand-up kind of lady, Jill. I'll trust you to do what's right. I've been thinkin' old Jack's lookin' a little peaked myself. It's somethin' in his eyes—like just makin' do is gettin' to be a chore. But you take care, goin' back up in there. Some of the 'hoes, they're not real accommodatin' to havin' strangers on their turf."

"We'll be careful," Jilly said.

The Bossman gave us both another long, thoughtful look, then lifted his harmonica and started to play again. Its mournful sound followed us back up to the boardwalk and seemed to trail us all the way to Lakeside Drive where we walked across the bridge to get to the other side of the Kick-aha.

I don't know what Jilly was thinking about, but I was

going over what she'd told me earlier. I kept thinking about wheels and how they turned.

Once past the City Commission's lawns on the far side of the river, the land starts to climb. It's just a lot of rough scrub on this side of the hills that make up the Beaches and every summer some of the hoboes and other homeless people camp out in it. The cops roust them from time to time, but mostly they're left alone, and they keep to themselves.

Going in there I was more nervous than Jilly; I don't think she's scared of anything. The sun had gone down behind the hills, and while it was twilight in the city, here it was already dark. I know a lot of the street people and get along with them better than most—everyone likes a good fiddle tune— but some of them could look pretty rough, and I kept anticipating that we'd run into some big wild-eyed hillbilly who'd take exception to our being there.

Well, we did run into one, but—like ninety percent of the street people in Newford—he was somebody that Jilly knew. He seemed pleased, if a little surprised to find her here, grinning at us in the fading light. He was a tall, big-shouldered man, dressed in dirty jeans and a flannel shirt, with big hobnailed boots on his feet and a shock of red hair that fell to his neck and stood up on top of his head in matted tangles. His name, appropriately enough, was Red. The smell that emanated from him made me want to shift position until I was standing upwind.

He not only knew where Paperjack's camp was, but took us there, only Paperjack wasn't home.

The place had Paperjack stamped all over it. There was a neatly rolled bedroll pushed up against a knapsack which probably held his changes of clothing. We didn't check it out, because we weren't there to go through his stuff. Behind the pack was a food cooler with a Coleman stove sitting on top of it, and everywhere you could see small origami stars that hung from the tree branches. There must have been over a hundred of them. I felt as if I were standing in the middle of space with stars all around me.

Jilly left a note for Paperjack, then we followed Red back out to Lakeside Drive. He didn't wait for our thanks. He just drifted away as soon as we reached the mown lawns that bordered the bush.

We split up then. Jilly had work to do—some art for Newford's entertainment weekly, *In the City*—and I didn't feel like tagging along to watch her work at her studio. She took the subway, but I decided to walk. I was bone-tired by then, but the night was one of those perfect ones when the city seems to be smiling. You can't see the dirt or the grime for the sparkle over everything. After all I'd been through today, I didn't want to be cooped up inside anywhere. I just wanted to enjoy the night.

I remember thinking about how Sam would've loved to be out walking with me on a night like this—the old Sam I'd lost, not necessarily the one she'd become. I didn't know that Sam at all, and I still wasn't sure I wanted to, even if I could track her down.

When I reached St. Paul's, I paused by the steps. Even though it was a perfect night to be out walking, something drew me inside. I tried the door, and it opened soundlessly at my touch. I paused just inside the door, one hand resting on the back pew, when I heard a cough.

I froze, ready to take flight. I wasn't sure how churches worked. Maybe my creeping around here at this time of night was . . . I don't know, sacrilegious or something.

I looked up to the front and saw that someone was sitting in the foremost pew. The cough was repeated, and I started down the aisle.

Intuitively, I guess I knew I'd find him here. Why else had I come inside?

Paperjack nodded to me as I sat down beside him on the pew. I laid my fiddlecase by my feet and leaned back. I wanted to ask after his health, to tell him how worried Jill was about him, but my day caught up with me in a rush. Before I knew it, I was nodding off.

I knew I was dreaming when I heard the voice. I had to be dreaming, because there was only Paperjack and I sitting on the pew, and Paperjack was mute. But the voice had the sound that I'd always imagined Paperjack's would have if he could speak. It was like the movement of his fingers when he was folding origami—quick, but measured and certain. Resonant, like his finished paper sculptures that always seemed to have more substance to them than just their folds and shapes.

"No one in this world views it the same," the voice said. "I believe that is what amazes me the most about it. Each person has his or her own vision of the world, and whatever lies outside that worldview becomes invisible. The rich ignore the poor. The happy can't see those who are hurting."

"Paperjack . . . ?" I asked.

There was only silence in reply.

"I . . . I thought you couldn't talk."

"So a man who has nothing he wishes to articulate is considered mute," the voice went on as though I hadn't interrupted. "It makes me weary."

"Who . . . who are you?" I asked.

"A mirror into which no one will look. A fortune that remains forever unread. My time here is done."

The voice fell silent again.

"Paperjack?"

Still silence.

It was just a dream, I told myself. I tried to wake myself from it. I told myself that the pew was made of hard, unyielding wood, and far too uncomfortable to sleep on. And Paperjack needed help. I remembered the cough and Jilly's worries.

But I couldn't wake up.

"The giving itself is the gift," the voice said suddenly. It sounded as though it came from the back of the church, or even farther away. "The longer I remain here, the more I forget."

Then the voice went away for good. I lost it in a dreamless sleep.

I woke early, and all my muscles were stiff. My watch said it was ten to six. I had a moment's disorientation—where the hell *was* I?—and then I remembered. Paperjack. And the dream.

I sat up straighter in the pew, and something fell from my lap to the floor. A piece of folded paper. I bent stiffly to retrieve it, turning it over and over in my hands, holding it up to the dim grey light that was creeping in through the windows. It was one of Paperjack's Chinese fortune-tellers.

After awhile I fit my fingers into the folds of the paper and looked down at the colors. I chose blue, same as I had the last time, and spelled it out, my fingers moving the paper back and forth so that it looked like a flower speaking soundlessly to me. I picked numbers at random, then unfolded the flap to read what it had to say.

"The question is more important than the answer," it said.

I frowned, puzzling over it, then looked at what I would have gotten if I'd picked another number, but all the other folds were blank when I turned them over. I stared at it, then folded the whole thing back up and stuck it in my pocket. I was starting to get a serious case of the creeps.

Picking up my fiddlecase, I left St. Paul's and wandered over to Chinatown. I had breakfast in an all-night diner, sharing the place with a bunch of blue-collar workers who were all talking about some baseball game they'd watched the night before. I thought of calling Jilly, but knew that if she'd been working all night on that *In the City* assignment, she'd be crashed out now and wouldn't appreciate a phone call.

I dawdled over breakfast, then slowly made my way up to that part of Foxville that's called the Rosses. That's where the Irish immigrants all lived in the forties and fifties. The place started changing in the sixties when a lot of hippies who couldn't afford the rents in Crowsea moved in, and it changed again with a new wave of immigrants from Vietnam and the Caribbean in the following decades. But the area, for all its changes, was still called the Rosses. My apartment was in the heart of it, right where Kelly Street meets Lee and crosses the Kickaha River. It's two doors down from The Harp, the only real Irish pub in town, which makes it convenient for me to get to the Irish music sessions on Sunday afternoons.

My phone was ringing when I got home. I was half-expecting it to be Jilly, even though it was only going on eight, but found myself talking to a reporter from *The Daily Journal* instead. His name was Ian Begley, and it turned out he was a friend of Jilly's. She'd asked him to run down what information he could on the Dickensons in the paper's morgue.

"Old man Dickenson was the last real businessman of the family," Begley told me. "Their fortunes started to decline when his son Tom took over—he's the one who married the woman that Jilly said you were interested in tracking down. He died in 1976. I don't have an obit on his widow, but that doesn't necessarily mean she's still alive. If she moved out of town, the paper wouldn't have an obit for her unless the family put one in."

He told me a lot of other stuff, but I was only half listening. The business with Paperjack last night and the fortune-telling device this morning were still eating away at me. I did take down the address of Sam's granddaughter when it came up. Begley ran out of steam after another five minutes or so.

"You got enough there?" he asked.

I nodded, then realized he couldn't see me. "Yeah. Thanks a lot."

"Say hello to Jilly for me and tell her she owes me one."

After I hung up, I looked out the window for a long time. I

managed to shift gears from Paperjack to thinking about what Begley had told me, about wheels, about Sam. Finally I got up and took a shower and shaved. I put on my cleanest jeans and shirt and shrugged on a sports jacket that had seen better days before I bought it in a retro fashion shop. I thought about leaving my fiddle behind, but knew I'd feel naked without it—I couldn't remember the last time I'd gone somewhere without it. The leather handle felt comforting in my hand as I hefted the case and went out the door.

All the way over to the address Begley had given me I tried to think of what I was going to say when I met Sam's granddaughter. The truth would make me sound like I was crazy, but I couldn't seem to concoct a story that would make sense.

I remember wondering—where was my brother when I needed him? Christy was never at a loss for words, no matter what the situation.

It wasn't until I was standing on the sidewalk in front of the house that I decided to stick as close to the truth as I could—I was an old friend of her grandmother's, could she put me in touch with her?—and take it from there. But even my vague plans went out the door when I rang the bell and stood face-to-face with Sam's granddaughter.

Maybe you saw this coming, but it was the last thing I'd expected. The woman had Sam's hair, Sam's eyes, Sam's face . . . to all intents and purposes it *was* Sam standing there, looking at me with that vaguely uncertain expression that most of us wear when we open the door to a stranger standing on our steps.

My chest grew so tight I could barely breathe, and suddenly I could hear the sound of rain in my memory—it was always raining when Sam saw the ghost; it was raining the night he stole her away into the past.

Ghosts. *I* was looking at a ghost.

The woman's expression was starting to change, the uncertainty turning into nervousness. There was no recognition in her eyes. As she began to step back—in a moment she'd close the door in my face, probably call the cops—I found my voice. I knew what I was going to say—I was going to ask about her grandmother—but all that came out was her name: "Sam."

"Yes?" she said. She looked at me a little more carefully. "Do I know you?"

Jesus, even the name was the same.

A hundred thoughts were going through my head, but they all spiraled down into one mad hope: this was Sam. We could be together again. Then a child appeared behind the woman. She was a little girl no more than five, blonde-haired, blue-eyed, just like her mother—just like her *mother's* grandmother. Reality came crashing down around me.

This Sam wasn't the woman I knew. She was married, she had children, she had a life.

"I . . . I knew your grandmother," I said. "We were . . . we used to be friends."

It sounded so inane to my ears, almost crazy. What would her grandmother—a woman maybe three times my age if she was still alive—have to do with a guy like me?

The woman's gaze traveled down to my fiddlecase. "Is your name Geordie? Geordie Riddell?"

I blinked in surprise, then nodded slowly.

The woman smiled a little sadly, mostly with her eyes.

"Granny said you'd come by," she said. "She didn't know when, but she said you'd come by one day." She stepped away from the door, shooing her daughter down the hall. "Would you like to come in?"

"I . . . uh, sure."

She led me into a living room that was furnished in mismatched antiques that, taken all together, shouldn't have worked, but did. The little girl perched in a Morris chair and watched me curiously as I sat down and set my fiddlecase down by my feet. Her mother pushed back a stray lock with a mannerism so like Sam's that my chest tightened up even more.

"Would you like some coffee or tea?" she asked.

I shook my head. "I don't want to intrude. I . . ." Words escaped me again.

"You're not intruding," she said. She sat down on the couch in front of me, that sad look back in her eyes. "My grandmother died a few years ago—she'd moved to New England in the late seventies, and she died there in her sleep. Because she loved it so much, we buried her there in a small graveyard overlooking the sea."

I could see it in my mind as she spoke. I could hear the sound of the waves breaking on the shore below, the spray falling on the rocks like rain.

"She and I were very close, a lot closer than I ever felt to my mother." She gave me a rueful look. "You know how it is."

She didn't seem to be expecting a response, but I nodded anyway.

"When her estate was settled, most of her personal effects came to me. I . . ." She paused, then stood up. "Excuse me for a moment, would you?"

I nodded again. She'd looked sad, talking about Sam. I hoped that bringing it all up hadn't made her cry.

The little girl and I sat in silence, looking at each other until her mother returned. She was such a serious kid, her big eyes taking everything in; she sat quietly, not running around or acting up like most kids do when there's someone new in the house that they can show off to. I didn't think she was shy; she was just . . . well, ourious.

Her mother had a package wrapped in brown paper and twine in her hands when she came back. She sat down across from me again and laid the package on the table between us.

"Granny told me a story once," she said, "about her first and only real true love. It was an odd story, a kind of ghost story, about how she'd once lived in the future until grand-dad's love stole her away from her own time and brought her to his." She gave me an apologetic smile. "I knew it was just a story because, when I was growing up I'd met people she'd gone to school with, friends from her past before she met granddad. Besides, it was too much like some science fiction story.

"But it was true, wasn't it?"

I could only nod. I didn't understand how Sam and everything about her except my memories of her could vanish into the past, how she could have a whole new set of memories when she got back there, but I knew it was true.

I accepted it now, just as Jilly had been trying to get me to do for years. When I looked at Sam's granddaughter, I saw that she accepted it as well.

"When her effects were sent to me," she went on, "I found this package in them. It's addressed to you."

I had seen my name on it, written in a familiar hand. My own hand trembled as I reached over to pick it up.

"You don't have to open it now," she said.

I was grateful for that.

"I . . . I'd better go," I said and stood up. "Thank you for taking the time to see me."

That sad smile was back as she saw me to the door.

"I'm glad I got the chance to meet you," she said when I stepped out onto the porch.

I wasn't sure I could say the same. She looked so much like Sam, *sounded* so much like Sam, that it hurt.

"I don't think we'll be seeing each other again," she added.

No. She had her husband, her family. I had my ghosts.

"Thanks," I said again and started off down the walk, fiddlecase in one hand, the brown paper package in the other.

I didn't open the package until I was sitting in the Silenus Gardens in Fitzhenry Park, a place that always made me feel good; I figured I was going to need all the help I could get. Inside there was a book with a short letter. The book I recognized. It was the small J. M. Dent & Sons edition of Shakespeare's *A Midsummer Night's Dream* that I'd given Sam because I'd known it was one of her favorite stories.

There was nothing special about the edition, other than its size—it was small enough for her to carry around in her purse, which she did. The inscription I'd written to her was inside, but the book was far more worn than it had been when I'd first given it to her. I didn't have to open the book to remember that famous quotation from Puck's final lines:

> *If we shadows have offended,*
> *Think but this, and all is mended,*
> *That you have but slumber'd here,*
> *While these visions did appear.*
> *And this weak and idle theme,*
> *No more yielding but a dream . . .*

But it hadn't been a dream—not for me, and not for Sam. I set the book down beside me on the stone bench and un-folded the letter.

"Dear Geordie," it said. "I know you'll read this one day, and I hope you can forgive me for not seeing you in person, but I wanted you to remember me as I was, not as I've become. I've had a full and mostly happy life; you know my only regret. I can look back on our time together with the wisdom of an old woman now and truly know that all things have their time. Ours was short—too short, my heart—but we did have it.

"Who was it that said, 'better to have loved and lost, than never to have loved at all'? We loved and lost each other, but I would rather cherish the memory than rail against the un-fairness. I hope you will do the same."

I sat there and cried. I didn't care about the looks I was getting from people walking by, I just let it all out. Some of my tears were for what I'd lost, some were for Sam and her bravery, and some were for my own stupidity at denying her memory for so long.

I don't know how long I sat there like that, holding her letter, but the tears finally dried on my cheeks. I heard the scuff of feet on the path and wasn't surprised to look up and find Jilly standing in front of me.

"Oh Geordie, me lad," she said.

She sat down at my side and leaned against me. I can't tell you how comforting it was to have her there. I handed her the letter and book and sat quietly while she read the first and looked at the latter. Slowly she folded up the letter and slipped it inside the book.

"How do you feel now?" she asked finally. "Better or worse?"

"Both."

She raised her eyebrows in a silent question.

"Well, it's like what they say funerals are for," I tried to explain. "It gives you the chance to say goodbye, to settle things, like taking a—" I looked at her and managed to find a small smile "—final turn on a wheel. But I feel depressed about Sam. I know what we had was real, and I know how it felt for me, losing her. But I only had to deal with it for a few years. She carried it for a lifetime."

"Still, she carried on."

I nodded. "Thank god for that."

Neither of us spoke for awhile, but then I remembered Paperjack. I told her what I thought had happened last night, then showed her the fortune-telling device that he'd left with me in St. Paul's. She read my fortune with pursed lips and the start of a wrinkle on her forehead, but didn't seem particularly surprised by it.

"What do you think?" I asked her.

She shrugged. "Everybody makes the same mistake. Fortune-telling doesn't reveal the future; it mirrors the present. It resonates against what your subconscious already knows and hauls it up out of the darkness so that you can get a good look at it."

"I meant about Paperjack."

"I think he's gone—back to wherever it was that he came from."

She was beginning to exasperate me in that way that only she could.

"But who was he?" I asked. "No, better yet, *what* was he?"

"I don't know," Jilly said. "I just know it's like your fortune said. It's the questions we ask, the journey we take to get where we're going that's more important than the actual answer. It's good to have mysteries. It reminds us that there's more to the world than just making do and having a bit of fun."

I sighed, knowing I wasn't going to get much more sense out of her than that.

It wasn't until the next day that I made my way alone to Paperjack's camp in back of the Beaches. All his gear was gone, but the paper stars still hung from the trees. I wondered again about who he was. Some oracular spirit, a kind of guardian angel, drifting around, trying to help people see themselves? Or an old homeless black man with a gift for folding paper? I understood then that my fortune made a certain kind of sense, but I didn't entirely agree with it.

Still, in Sam's case, knowing the answer had brought me peace.

I took Paperjack's fortune-teller from my pocket and strung it with a piece of string I'd brought along for that purpose. Then I hung it on the branch of a tree so that it could swing there, in among all those paper stars, and I walked away.

⌒ · TALLULAH · ⌒

*Nothing is too wonderful
to be true.*
—MICHAEL FARADAY

FOR THE LONGEST time, I thought she was a ghost, but I know what she is now. She's come to mean everything to me; like a lifeline, she keeps me connected to reality, to this place and this time, by her very capriciousness.

I wish I'd never met her.

That's a lie, of course, but it comes easily to the tongue. It's a way to pretend that the ache she left behind in my heart doesn't hurt.

She calls herself Tallulah, but I know who she really is. A name can't begin to encompass the sum of all her parts. But that's the magic of names, isn't it? That the complex, contradictory individuals we are can be called up complete and whole in another mind through the simple sorcery of a name. And connected to the complete person we call up in our mind with the alchemy of their name comes all the baggage of memory: times you were together, the music you listened to this morning or that night, conversation and jokes and private moments—all the good and bad times you've shared.

Tally's name conjures up more than just that for me.

When the *gris-gris* of the memories that hold her stir in my mind, she guides me through the city's night like a totem does a shaman through Dreamtime. Everything familiar is changed; what she shows me goes under the skin, right to the marrow of the bone. I see a building and I know not only its shape and form, but its history. I can hear its breathing, I can almost read its thoughts.

It's the same for a street or a park, an abandoned car or some secret garden hidden behind a wall, a late night cafe or an empty lot. Each one has its story, its secret history, and Tally taught me how to read each one of them. Where once I guessed at those stories, chasing rumors of them like they were errant fireflies, now I know.

I'm not as good with people. Neither of us are. Tally, at least, has an excuse. But me . . .

I wish I'd never met her.

My brother Geordie is a busker—a street musician. He plays his fiddle on street corners or along the queues in the theatre district and makes a kind of magic with his music that words just can't describe. Listening to him play is like stepping into an old Irish or Scottish fairy tale. The slow airs call up haunted moors and lonely coastlines; the jigs and reels wake a fire in the soul that burns with the awesome wonder of bright stars on a cold night, or the familiar warmth of red coals glimmering in a friendly hearth.

The funny thing is, he's one of the most pragmatic people I know. For all the enchantment he can call up out of that old Czech fiddle of his, I'm the one with the fey streak in our family.

As far as I'm concerned, the only difference between fact and what most people call fiction is about fifteen pages in the dictionary. I've got such an open mind that Geordie says I've got a hole in it, but I've been that way for as long as I can remember. It's not so much that I'm gullible—though I've been called that and less charitable things in my time; it's more that I'm willing to just suspend my disbelief until whatever I'm considering has been thoroughly debunked to my satisfaction.

I first started collecting oddities and curiosities as I heard about them when I was in my teens, filling page after page of spiral-bound notebooks with little notes and jottings—neat inky scratches on the paper, each entry opening worlds of possibility for me whenever I reread them. I liked things to do with the city the best because that seemed the last place in the world where the delicate wonders that are magic should exist.

Truth to tell, a lot of what showed up in those notebooks leaned towards a darker side of the coin, but even that darkness had a light in it for me because it still stretched the realms of what was into a thousand variable what-might-be's. That was the real magic for me: the possibility that we only have to draw aside a veil to find the world a far more strange and wondrous place than its mundaneness allowed it could be.

It was my girlfriend back then—Katie Deren—who first convinced me to use my notebooks as the basis for stories. Katie was about as odd a bird as I was in those days. We'd sit around with the music of obscure groups like the Incredible String Band or Dr. Strangely Strange playing on the turntable and literally talk away whole nights about anything and everything. She had the strangest way of looking at things; everything had a soul for her, be it the majestic old oak tree that stood in her parents' back yard, or the old black iron kettle that she kept filled with dried weeds on the sill of her bedroom window.

We drifted apart, the way it happens with a lot of relationships at that age, but I kept the gift she'd woken in me: the stories.

I never expected to become a writer, but then I had no real expectations whatsoever as to what I was going to be when I "grew up." Sometimes I think I never did—grow up that is.

But I did get older. And I found I could make a living with my stories. I called them urban legends—independently of

Jan Harold Brunvand, who also makes a living collecting them. But he approaches them as a folklorist, cataloguing and comparing them, while I retell them in stories that I sell to magazines and then recycle into book collections.

I don't feel we're in any kind of competition with each other, but then I feel that way about all writers. There are as many stories to be told as there are people to tell them about; only the mean-spirited would consider there to be a competition at all. And Brunvand does such a wonderful job. The first time I read his *The Vanishing Hitchhiker,* I was completely smitten with his work and, like the hundreds of other correspondents Brunvand has, made a point of sending him items I thought he could use for his future books.

But I never wrote to him about Tally.

I do my writing at night—the later the better. I don't work in a study or an office and I don't use a typewriter or computer, at least not for my first drafts. What I like to do is go out into the night and just set up shop wherever it feels right: a park bench, the counter of some all-night diner, the stoop of St. Paul's Cathedral, the doorway of a closed junk shop on Grasso Street.

I still keep notebooks, but they're hardcover ones now. I write my stories in them as well. And though the stories owe their existence to the urban legends that give them their quirky spin, what they're really about is people: what makes them happy or sad. My themes are simple. They're about love and loss, honor and the responsibilities of friendship. And wonder . . . always wonder. As complex as people are individually, their drives are universal.

I've been told—so often I almost believe it myself—that I've got a real understanding of people. However strange the situations my characters find themselves in, the characters themselves seem very real to my readers. That makes me feel good, naturally enough, but I don't understand it because I don't feel that I know people very well at all.

I'm just not good with them.

I think it comes from being that odd bird when I was growing up. I was distanced from the concerns of my peers, I just couldn't get into so many of the things that they felt was important. The fault was partly the other kids—if you're different, you're fair game. You know how it can be. There are three kinds of kids: the ones that are the odd birds, the ones that pissed on them, and the ones that watched it happen.

It was partly my fault, too, because I ostracized them as much as they did me. I was always out of step; I didn't really care about belonging to this gang or that clique. A few years earlier and I'd have been a beatnik, a few years later, a hippie. I got into drugs before they were cool; found out they were messing up my head and got out of them when everybody else starting dropping acid and MDA and who knows what all.

What it boiled down to was that I had a lot of acquaintances, but very few friends. And even with the friends I did have, I always felt one step removed from the relationship, as though I was observing what was going on, taking notes, rather than just being there.

That hasn't changed much as I've grown older.

How that—let's call it aloofness, for lack of a better word—translated into this so-called gift for characterization in my fiction, I can't tell you. Maybe I put so much into the stories, I had nothing left over for real life. Maybe it's because each one of us, no matter how many or how close our connections to other people, remains in the end, irrevocably on his or her own, solitary islands separated by expanses of the world's sea, and I'm just more aware of it than others. Maybe I'm just missing the necessary circuit in my brain.

Tally changed all of that.

I wouldn't have thought it, the first time I saw her.

There's a section of the Market in Lower Crowsea, where it backs onto the Kickaha River, that's got a kind of Old World magic about it. The roads are too narrow for normal vehicular traffic, so most people go through on bicycles or by foot. The buildings lean close to each other over the cobblestoned streets that twist and wind in a confusion that not even the city's mapmakers have been able to unravel to anyone's satisfaction.

There are old shops back in there and some of them still have signage in Dutch dating back a hundred years. There are buildings tenanted by generations of the same families, little courtyards, secret gardens, any number of sly-eyed cats, old men playing dominoes and checkers and their gossiping wives, small gales of shrieking children by day, mysterious eddies of silence by night. It's a wonderful place, completely untouched by the yuppie renovation projects that took over the rest of the Market.

Right down by the river there's a public courtyard surrounded on all sides by three-story brick and stone town houses with mansard roofs and dormer windows. Late at night, the only manmade sound comes from the odd bit of traffic on the McKennitt Street Bridge a block or so south, the only light comes from the single streetlamp under which stands a bench made of cast iron and wooden slats. Not a light shines from the windows of the buildings that enclose it. When you sit on that bench, the river murmurs at your back and the streetlamp encloses you in a comforting embrace of warm yellow light.

It's one of my favorite places to write. I'll sit there with my notebook propped up on my lap and scribble away for hours, my only companion, more often than not, a tattered-eared tom sleeping on the bench beside me. I think he lives in one of the houses, though he could be a stray. He's there most times I come—not waiting for me. I'll sit down and start to work and after a half-hour or so he'll come sauntering out of the shadows, stopping a half-dozen times to lick this shoulder, that hind leg, before finally settling down beside me like he's been there all night.

He doesn't much care to be patted, but I'm usually too busy to pay that much attention to him anyway. Still, I enjoy his company. I'd miss him if he stopped coming.

I've wondered about his name sometimes. You know that old story where they talk about a cat having three names? There's the one we give them, the one they use among themselves and then the secret one that only they know.

I just call him Ben; I don't know what he calls himself. He could be the King of the Cats, for all I know.

He was sleeping on the bench beside me the night she showed up. He saw her first. Or maybe he heard her.

It was early autumn, a brisk night that followed one of those perfect crisp autumn days—clear skies, the sunshine bright on the turning leaves, a smell in the air of a change coming, the wheel of the seasons turning. I was bundled up in a flannel jacket and wore half-gloves to keep my hands from getting too cold as I wrote.

I looked up when Ben stirred beside me, fur bristling, slit-eyed gaze focused on the narrow mouth of an alleyway that cut like a tunnel through the town houses on the north side of the courtyard. I followed his gaze in time to see her step from the shadows.

She reminded me of Geordie's friend Jilly, the artist. She had the same slender frame and tangled hair, the same pixie face and wardrobe that made her look like she did all her clothes buying at a thrift shop. But she had a harder look than Jilly, a toughness that was reflected in the sharp lines that modified her features and in her gear: battered leather jacket, jeans stuffed into low-heeled black cowboy boots, hands in her pockets, a kind of leather carryall hanging by its strap from her shoulder.

She had a loose, confident gait as she crossed the court-yard, boot heels clicking on the cobblestones. The warm light from the streetlamp softened her features a little.

Beside me, Ben turned around a couple of times, a slow chase of his tail that had no enthusiasm to it, and settled back into sleep. She sat down on the bench, the cat between us, and dropped her carryall at her feet. Then she leaned back against the bench, legs stretched out in front of her, hands back in the pockets of her jeans, head turned to look at me.

"Some night, isn't it?" she said.

I was still trying to figure her out. I couldn't place her age. One moment she looked young enough to be a runaway and I waited for the inevitable request for spare change or a place to crash, the next she seemed around my age—late twenties, early thirties—and I didn't know what she might want. One thing people didn't do in the city, even in this part of it, was befriend strangers. Not at night. Especially not if you were young and as pretty as she was.

My lack of a response didn't seem to faze her in the least.

"What's your name?" she asked.

"Christy Riddell," I said. I hesitated for a moment, then reconciled myself to a conversation. "What's yours?" I added as I closed my notebook, leaving my pen inside it to keep my place.

"Tallulah."

Just that, the one name. Spoken with the brassy confidence of a Cher or a Madonna.

"You're kidding," I said.

Tallulah sounded like it should belong to a '20s flapper, not some punky street kid.

She gave me a smile that lit up her face, banishing the last trace of the harshness I'd seen in her features as she was walking up to the bench.

"No, really," she said. "But you can call me Tally."

The melody of the ridiculous refrain from that song by— was it Harry Belafonte?—came to mind, something about tallying bananas.

"What're you doing?" she asked.

"Writing."

"I can *see* that. I meant, what kind of writing?"

"I write stories," I told her.

I waited then for the inevitable questions: Have you ever been published? What name do you write under? Where do you get your ideas? Instead she turned away and looked up at the sky.

"I knew a poet once," she said. "He wanted to capture

his soul on a piece of paper—really capture it.'' She looked back at me. "But of course, you can't do that, can you? You can try, you can bleed honesty into your art until it feels like you've wrung your soul dry, but in the end, all you've created is a possible link between minds. An attempt at communication. If a soul can't be measured, then how can it be captured?''

I revised my opinion of her age. She might look young, but she spoke with too much experience couched in her words.

"What happened to him?'' I found myself asking. "Did he give up?''

She shrugged. "I don't know. He moved away.'' Her gaze left mine and turned skyward once more. "When they move away, they leave my life because I can't follow them.''

She mesmerized me—right from that first night. I sensed a portent in her casual appearance into my life, though a portent of what, I couldn't say.

"Did you ever want to?'' I asked her.

"Want to what?''

"Follow them.'' I remember, even then, how the plurality bothered me. I was jealous and I didn't even know of what.

She shook her head. "No. All I ever have is what they leave behind.''

Her voice seemed to diminish as she spoke. I wanted to reach out and touch her shoulder with my hand, to offer what comfort I could to ease the sudden malaise that appeared to have gripped her, but her moods, I came to learn, were mercurial. She sat up suddenly and stroked Ben until the motor of his purring filled the air with its resonance.

"Do you always write in places like this?'' she asked.

I nodded. "I like the night; I like the city at night. It doesn't seem to belong to anyone then. On a good night, it almost seems as if the stories write themselves. It's almost as though coming out here plugs me directly into the dark heart of the city night and all of its secrets come spilling from my pen.''

I stopped, suddenly embarrassed by what I'd said. It seemed too personal a disclosure for such short acquaintance. But she just gave me a low-watt version of her earlier smile.

''Doesn't that bother you?'' she asked.

''Does what bother me?''

''That perhaps what you're putting down on paper doesn't belong to you.''

''Does it ever?'' I replied. ''Isn't the very act of creation made up of setting a piece of yourself free?''

''What happens when there's no more pieces left?''

''That's what makes it special—I don't think you ever run out of the creative spark. Just doing it, replenishes the well. The more I work, the more ideas come to me. Whether they come from my subconscious or some outside source, isn't really relevant. What is relevant is what I put into it.''

''Even when it seems to write itself?''

''Maybe especially so.''

I was struck—not then, but later, remembering—by the odd intensity of the conversation. It wasn't a normal dialogue between strangers. We must have talked for three hours, never about ourselves, our histories, our pasts, but rather about what we were now, creating an intimacy that seemed surreal when I thought back on it the next day. Occasionally, there were lulls in the conversation, but they, too, seemed to add to the sense of bonding, like the comfortable silences that are only possible between good friends.

I could've kept right on talking, straight through the night until dawn, but she rose during one of those lulls.

''I have to go,'' she said, swinging the strap of her carryall onto her shoulder.

I knew a moment's panic. I didn't know her address or her phone number. All I had was her first name.

''When can I see you again?'' I asked.

"Have you ever been down to those old stone steps under the Kelly Street Bridge?"

I nodded. They dated back from when the river was used to haul goods from upland, down to the lake. The steps under the bridge were all that was left of an old dock that had serviced the Irish-owned inn called The Harp. The dock was long abandoned, but The Harp still stood. It was one of the oldest buildings in the city. Only the solid stone structures of the city's Dutch founding fathers, like the ones that encircled us, were older.

"I'll meet you there tomorrow night," she said. She took a few steps, then paused, adding, "Why don't you bring along one of your books?"

The smile she gave me, before she turned away again, was intoxicating. I watched her walk back across the courtyard, disappearing into the narrow mouth of the alleyway from which she'd first come. Her footsteps lingered on, an echoing tap-tap on the cobblestones, but then that too faded.

I think it was at that moment that I decided she was a ghost.

I didn't get much writing done over the next few weeks. She wouldn't—she said she couldn't—see me during the day, but she wouldn't say why. I've got such a head filled with fictions that I honestly thought it was because she was a ghost, or maybe a succubus or a vampire. The sexual attraction was certainly there. If she'd sprouted fangs one night, I'd probably just have bared my neck and let her feed. But she didn't, of course. Given a multiple-choice quiz, in the end I realized the correct answer was none of the above.

I was also sure that she was at least my own age, if not older. She was widely read and, like myself, had eclectic tastes that ranged from genre fiction to the classics. We talked for hours every night, progressed to walking hand in hand through our favorite parts of the benighted city and finally made love one night in a large, cozy sleeping bag in Fitzhenry Park.

She took me there on one of what we called our rambles and didn't say a word, just stripped down in the moonlight and then drew me down into the sweet harbor of her arms. Above us, I heard geese heading south as, later, I drifted into sleep. I remember thinking it was odd to hear them so late at night, but then what wasn't in the hours I spent with Tally?

I woke alone in the morning, the subject of some curiosity by a couple of old winos who casually watched me get dressed inside the bag as though they saw this kind of thing every morning.

Our times together blur in my mind now. It's hard for me to remember one night from another. But I have little fetish bundles of memory that stay whole and complete in my mind, the *gris-gris* that collected around her name in my mind, like my nervousness that second night under the Kelly Street Bridge, worried that she wouldn't show, and three nights later when, after not saying a word about the book of my stories I'd given her when we parted on the old stone steps under the bridge, she told me how much she'd liked them.

"These are my stories," she said as she handed the book back to me that night.

I'd run into possessive readers before, fans who laid claim to my work as their own private domain, who treated the characters in the stories as real people, or thought that I carried all sorts of hidden and secret knowledge in my head, just because of the magic and mystery that appeared in the tales I told. But I'd never had a reaction like Tally's before.

"They're about me," she said. "They're your stories, I can taste your presence in every word, but each of them's a piece of me, too."

I told her she could keep the book and the next night, I brought her copies of my other three collections, plus photocopies of the stories that had only appeared in magazines to date. I won't say it's because she liked the stories so much, that I came to love her; that would have happened anyway.

But her pleasure in them certainly didn't make me think any the less of her.

Another night she took a photograph out of her carryall and showed it to me. It was a picture of her, but she looked different, softer, not so much younger as not so tough. She wore her hair differently and had a flower print dress on; she was standing in sunlight.

"When . . . when was this taken?" I asked.

"In happier times."

Call me small-minded that my disappointment should show so plain, but it hurt that what were the happiest nights of my life, weren't the same for her.

She noticed my reaction—she was always quick with things like that—and laid a warm hand on mine.

"It's not you," she said. "I love our time together. It's the rest of my life that's not so happy."

Then be with me all the time, I wanted to tell her, but I already knew from experience that there was no talking about where she went when she left me, what she did, who she was. I was still thinking of ghosts, you see. I was afraid that some taboo lay upon her telling me, that if she spoke about it, if she told me where she was during the day, the spell would break and her spirit would be banished forever like in some hokey B-movie.

I wanted more than just the nights, I'll admit freely to that, but not enough to risk losing what I had. I was like the wife in "Bluebeard," except I refused to allow my curiosity to turn the key in the forbidden door. I could have followed her, but I didn't. And not just because I was afraid of her vanishing on me. It was because she trusted me not to.

We made love three times, all told, every time in that old sleeping bag of hers, each time in a different place, each morning I woke alone. I'd bring back her sleeping bag when we met that night and she'd smile to see its bulk rolled under my arm.

The morning after the first time, I realized that I was

changing; that she was changing me. It wasn't by anything she said or did, or rather it wasn't that she was making me change, but that our relationship was stealing away that sense of distancing I had carried with me through my life.

And she was changing, too. She still wore her jeans and leather jacket most of the time, but sometimes she appeared wearing a short dress under the jacket, warm leggings, small trim shoes instead of her boots. Her face kept its character, but the tension wasn't so noticeable anymore, the toughness had softened.

I'd been open with her from the very first night, more open than I'd ever been with friends I'd known for years. And that remained. But now it was starting to spill over to my other relationships. I found my brother and my friends were more comfortable with me, and I with them. None of them knew about Tally; so far as they knew I was still prowling the nocturnal streets of the city in search of inspiration. They didn't know that I wasn't writing, though Professor Dapple guessed.

I suppose it was because he always read my manuscripts before I sent them off. We had the same interests in the odd and the curious—it was what had drawn us together long before Jilly became his student, before he retired from the university. Everybody still thought of him as the Professor; it was hard not to.

He was a tiny wizened man with a shock of frizzy white hair and glasses who delighted in long conversations conducted over tea, or if the hour was appropriate, a good Irish whisky. At least once every couple of weeks the two of us would sit in his cozy study, he reading one of my stories while I read his latest article before it was sent off to some journal or other. When the third visit went by in which I didn't have a manuscript in hand, he finally broached the subject.

"You seem happy these days, Christy."

"I am."

He'd smiled. "So is it true what they say—an artist must suffer to produce good work?"

I hadn't quite caught on yet to what he was about.

"Neither of us believe that," I said.

"Then you must be in love."

"I . . ."

I didn't know what to say. An awful sinking feeling had settled in my stomach at his words. Lord knew, he was right, but for some reason, just as I knew I shouldn't follow Tally when she left me after our midnight trysts, I had this superstitious dread that if the world discovered our secret, she would no longer be a part of my life.

"There's nothing wrong with being in love," he said, mistaking my hesitation for embarrassment.

"It's not that," I began, knowing I had nowhere to go except a lie and I couldn't lie to the Professor.

"Never fear," he said. "You're allowed your privacy— and welcome to it, I might add. At my age, any relating of your escapades would simply make me jealous. But I worry about your writing."

"I haven't stopped," I told him. And then I had it. "I've been thinking of writing a novel."

That wasn't a lie. I was always thinking of writing a novel; I just doubted that I ever would. My creative process could easily work within the perimeters of short fiction, even a connected series of stories such as *The Red Crow* had turned out to be, but a novel was too massive an undertaking for me to understand, little say attempt. I had to have the whole of it in my head and to do so with anything much longer than a short novella was far too daunting a process for me to begin. I had discovered, to my disappointment because I did actually *want* to make the attempt, that the longer a piece of mine was, the less . . . substance it came to have. It was as though the sheer volume of a novel's wordage would somehow dissipate the strengths my work had to date.

My friends who did write novels told me I was just being a chickenshit; but then they had trouble with short fiction and avoided it like the plague. It was my firm belief that one should stick with what worked, though maybe that was just a way of rationalizing a failure.

"What sort of a novel?" the Professor asked, intrigued since he knew my feelings on the subject.

I gave what I hoped was a casual shrug.

"That's what I'm still trying to decide," I said, and then turned the conversation to other concerns.

But I was nervous leaving the Professor's house, as though the little I had said was enough to turn the key in the door that led into the hidden room I shouldn't enter. I sensed a weakening of the dam that kept the mystery of our trysts deep and safe. I feared for the floodgate opening and the rush of reality that would tear my ghostly lover away from me.

But as I've already said, she wasn't a ghost. No, something far stranger hid behind her facade of pixie face and tousled hair.

I've wondered before, and still do, how much of what happens to us we bring upon ourselves. Did my odd superstition concerning Tally drive her away, or was she already leaving before I ever said as much as I did to the Professor? Or was it mere coincidence that she said goodbye that same night?

I think of the carryall she'd had on her shoulder the first time we met and have wondered since if she wasn't already on her way then. Perhaps I had only interrupted a journey already begun.

"You know, don't you?" she said when I saw her that night.

Did synchronicity reach so far that we would part that night in that same courtyard by the river where we had first met?

"You know I have to go," she added when I said nothing.

I nodded. I did. What I didn't know was—

"Why?" I asked.

Her features seemed harder again—like they had been that first night. The softness that had grown as our relationship had was more memory than fact, her features seemed to be cut to the bone once more. Only her eyes still held a touch of warmth, as did her smile. A tough veneer masked the rest of her.

"It's because of how the city is used," she said. "It's because of hatred and spite and bigotry; it's because of homelessness and drugs and crime; it's because the green quiet places are so few while the dark terrors multiply; it's because what's old and comfortable and rounded must make way for what's new and sharp and brittle; it's because a mean spirit grips its streets and that meanness cuts inside me like a knife.

"It's changing me, Christy, and I don't want you to see what I will become. You wouldn't recognize me and I wouldn't want you to.

"That's why I have to go."

When she said go, I knew she meant she was leaving me, not the city.

"But—"

"You've helped me keep it all at bay, truly you have, but it's not enough. Neither of us have enough strength to hold that mean spirit at bay forever. What we have was stolen from the darkness. But it won't let us steal any more."

I started to speak, but she just laid her fingers across my lips. I saw that her sleeping bag was stuffed under the bench. She pulled it out and unrolled it on the cobblestones. I thought of the dark windows of the town houses looking into the courtyard. There could be a hundred gazes watching as she gently pulled me down onto the sleeping bag, but I didn't care.

I tried to stay awake. I lay beside her, propped up on an elbow and stroked her shoulder, her hair. I marveled at the softness of her skin, the silkiness of her hair. In repose, the harsh lines were gone from her face again. I wished that there was some way I could just keep all her unhappiness at bay, that I could stay awake and protect her forever, but sleep snuck up on me all the same and took me away.

Just as I went under, I thought I heard her say, "You'll know other lovers."

But not like her. Never like her.

When I woke the next morning, I was alone on the sleeping bag, except for Ben who lay purring on the bag where she had lain.

It was early, too early for anyone to be awake in any of the houses, but I wouldn't have cared. I stood naked in the frosty air and slowly got dressed. Ben protested when I shooed him off the sleeping bag and rolled it up.

The walk home, with the sleeping bag rolled up under my arm, was never so long.

No, Tally wasn't a ghost, though she haunts the city's streets at night—just as she haunts my mind.

I know her now. She's like a rose bush grown old, gone wild; untrimmed, neglected for years, the thorns become sharper, more bitter; her foliage spreading, grown out of control, reaching high and wide, while the center chokes and dies. The blossoms that remain are just small now, hidden in the wild growth, memories of what they once were.

I know her now. She's the spirit that connects the notes of a tune—the silences in between the sounds; the resonance that lies under the lines I put down on a page. Not a ghost, but a spirit all the same: the city's heart and soul.

I don't wonder about her origin. I don't wonder whether she was here first, and the city grew around her, or if the city created her. She just is.

Tallulah. Tally. A reckoning of accounts.

I think of the old traveling hawkers who called at private houses in the old days and sold their wares on the tally system—part payment on account, the other part due when they called again. Tallymen.

The payments owed her were long overdue, but we no

longer have the necessary coin to settle our accounts with her. So she changes; just as we change. I can remember a time when the city was a safer place, how when I was young, we never locked our doors and we knew every neighbor on our block. Kids growing up today wouldn't even know what I'm talking about; the people my own age have forgotten. The old folks remember, but who listens to them? Most of us wish that they didn't exist; that they'd just take care of themselves so that we can get on with our own lives.

Not all change is for the good.

I still go out on my rambles, most every night. I hope for a secret tryst, but all I do is write stories again. As the new work fills my notebooks, I've come to realize that the characters in my stories were so real because I really did want to get close to people, I really did want to know them. It was just easier to do it on paper, one step removed.

I'm trying to change that now.

I look for her on my rambles. She's all around me, of course, in every brick of every building, in every whisper of wind as it scurries down an empty street. She's a cab's lights at 3:00 A.M., a siren near dawn, a shuffling bag lady pushing a squeaky grocery cart, a dark-eyed cat sitting on a shadowed stoop.

She's all around me, but I can't find her. I'm sure I'd recognize her—

I don't want you to see what I will become.

—but I can't be sure. The city can be so many things. It's a place where the familiar can become strange with just the blink of an eye. And if I saw her—

You wouldn't recognize me and I wouldn't want you to.

—what would I do? If she could, she'd come to me, but that mean spirit still grips the streets. I see it in people's faces; I feel it in the coldness that's settled in their hearts. I don't think I would recognize her; I don't think I'd want to. I have the *gris-gris* of her memory in my mind; I have an old sleeping bag rolled up in a corner of my hall closet; I'm here if she needs me.

* * *

I have this fantasy that it's still not too late; that we can still drive that mean spirit away and keep it at bay. The city would be a better place to live in if we could and I think we owe it to her. I'm doing my part. I write about her—

They're about me. They're your stories, I can taste your presence in every word, but each of them's a piece of me, too.

—about her strange wonder and her magic and all. I write about how she changed me, how she taught me that getting close can hurt, but not getting close is an even lonelier hurt. I don't preach; I just tell the stories.

But I wish the ache would go away. Not the memories, not the *gris-gris* that keeps her real inside me, but the hurt. I could live without that hurt.

Sometimes I wish I'd never met her.

Maybe one day I'll believe that lie, but I hope not.

BESTSELLERS FROM TOR

☐ 51195-6 BREAKFAST AT WIMBLEDON $3.99
Jack Bickham Canada $4.99

☐ 52497-7 CRITICAL MASS $5.99
David Hagberg Canada $6.99

☐ 85202-9 ELVISSEY $12.95
Jack Womack Canada $16.95

☐ 51612-5 FALLEN IDOLS $4.99
Ralph Arnote Canada $5.99

☐ 51716-4 THE FOREVER KING $5.99
Molly Cochran & Warren Murphy Canada $6.99

☐ 50743-6 PEOPLE OF THE RIVER $5.99
Michael Gear & Kathleen O'Neal Gear Canada $6.99

☐ 51198-0 PREY $5.99
Ken Goddard Canada $6.99

☐ 50735-5 THE TRIKON DECEPTION $5.99
Ben Bova & Bill Pogue Canada $6.99

Buy them at your local bookstore or use this handy coupon:
Clip and mail this page with your order.

Publishers Book and Audio Mailing Service
P.O. Box 120159, Staten Island, NY 10312-0004

Please send me the book(s) I have checked above. I am enclosing $ _____
(Please add $1.50 for the first book, and $.50 for each additional book to cover postage and
handling. Send check or money order only—no CODs.)

Name _____
Address _____
City _____ State / Zip _____

Please allow six weeks for delivery. Prices subject to change without notice.

POPPY & RYE

BY Avi

SIMON AND SCHUSTER

SIMON AND SCHUSTER

This edition published in Great Britain by Simon & Schuster UK Ltd, 2005
First published in Great Britain in hardback, 2002,
and then in paperback, 2003 by Simon & Schuster UK Ltd.
A Viacom company

Copyright © Avi, 1998
Cover Illustration by Charles Fuge © 2005
Cover design by www.blacksheep-uk.com

1 3 5 7 9 10 8 6 4 2

Simon & Schuster UK Ltd
Africa House
64-78 Kingsway
London WC2B 6AH

A CIP catalogue record for this book is available from the British Library

ISBN 0-689-83719-4

Printed and bound in Great Britain by Cox & Wyman, Reading, Berkshire

For us

CONTENTS

I
Clover and Valerian

"Clover! Clover, love. You need to wake up! Something *awful* is happening."

Clover, a golden mouse, was small, round and fast asleep in a snug corner of her underground nest. Too sleepy to make sense of the words being spoken to her, she opened her silky black eyes, looked up, and gasped.

Was that Ragweed leaning over her? Ragweed was a particular favourite of her 63 children. He had gone east in search of adventures but had not been heard of for four months. Clover missed him terribly, and kept wishing he'd come back.

Her eyes focused. She could see more clearly now. "Valerian," she asked, "is that you?"

Valerian was Clover's husband. He was a long-faced, lanky, middle-aged golden mouse with shabby fur of orange hue and scruffy whiskers edged with grey. His face bore the fixed expression of being

perpetually overwhelmed without knowing quite what to do about it. At the moment his tail was whipping about in great agitation.

"Is something the matter with the children?" Clover asked. She had recently given birth to a new litter — her fourth that year — and was so tired, she hadn't ventured from the nest in more than a week.

"They're fine," Valerian assured her. "But Clover, you've got to see what I've discovered. You're not going to believe it."

"Can't you just tell me what it is?" Clover replied with a yawn. She never got enough sleep.

"Clover," Valerian whispered, "we're . . . we're in great danger."

A startled Clover looked about the nest where she and Valerian and all their children had made their home for six happy years. A small, deep and comfortable nest consisting of three chambers, each of its rooms was lined with milkweed fluff. There were a family room, a master bedroom, and the children's nursery, where 13 of the children were currently sleeping. The most recent litter — three in number and barely a week old — were still blind and without fur.

They were with Clover.

"Clover, love," Valerian urged, "please get up. It's *not* the children. But it will affect them. Badly."

With Clover, an appeal to family never failed. She forced herself up.

The two mice made their way up the entry hole to the ground surface. The long, twisting tunnel had a few storage rooms — one filled with nuts, another with dried berries, a third with seeds — built into the walls. Though Clover was, as usual, hungry, there was no time to eat.

When Valerian reached the ground's surface, he stuck his nose out of the entry hole, sniffed, then gazed about. Certain there were no foxes, wild cats or snakes, or any other danger about, he hauled himself out of the hole. Clover followed.

Tall, leafy trees, bushes, and brambles veiled the late summer sky, a sky aglow with the light of a full moon. The air was humid, the breeze soft. Barks and buzzes, grunts and chirps seemed to come from everywhere and nowhere all at once.

Valerian scampered down one of the many paths that radiated from the nest. When he took the

path that followed a steep decline, Clover knew they were heading for the Brook.

"The Brook," as the mice called it, meandered lazily between low, leafy banks. Water lilies floated on its wide, shallow surface. There, fireflies flashed, butterflies danced. Mosquitoes, like ancient instruments, droned. Water bugs skimmed. Cattails, standing tall, swayed to the rhythms of the night.

With nothing rough or dangerous about the Brook, the young mice loved to frolic about its banks. Rarely was the water more than six inches deep. Splendid to splash in. Fun to swim in. Sometimes the mice made rafts of bark chips and went boating. Indeed, it was the closeness of the Brook and its serenity that caused Clover and Valerian to build their nest and raise their family where they did.

That night everything was changed.

The water was muddier and deeper than it ever had been before. A full three feet of bare earth at the base of the pathway – the children's beach – had sunk beneath water. Lily pads and cattails were gone. No bugs teased the Brook's surface. Chips of wood floated here, there, everywhere.

"Look!" Valerian cried, in a hushed voice. He pointed downstream.

At first Clover didn't see it. Only gradually did she perceive the massive mound of sticks, twigs and logs that spread across the full width of the stream.

"Why . . . my goodness," she gasped. "It's a . . . *dam*! But . . . but why?"

Valerian pointed to the water's edge.

"What should I be looking at?" asked a puzzled Clover.

"The water," Valerian whispered. "Watch."

Clover stared until, with a shock, she jumped back. "Valerian," she cried, "the water is rising!"

"Exactly."

"But . . . if it keeps coming this fast, our home will be . . . flooded!"

Valerian nodded. "Clover, love, I'm afraid the whole neighbourhood is going under."

"But . . . but," Clover stammered, "who would do such a dreadful thing?"

"Take a gander out there," Valerian urged. This time he pointed across the water.

Clover stared. At first she thought she was

seeing nothing more than a floating brown lump of earth or wood. Then, with a start, she realised it was an animal swimming on the water's surface.

He was a large, portly fellow, with thick, glossy brown fur, a black nose, and two beady eyes. Two enormous buck teeth — brilliant orange in the light of the moon — stuck out from his mouth like chisels.

"A . . . *beaver!*" Clover exclaimed. Just to say the word brought understanding: Beavers had come and dammed the Brook.

As Clover and Valerian stared, the beaver saw them. Lifting his water-soaked head, he offered an immense, toothy smile.

"Bless my teeth and smooth my tail!" the beaver called out in a loud, raucous voice. "I do believe it's my new neighbours! Hey, pal! Evening, sweetheart! Tickled pink to meet up with you. The name is Caster P. Canad. But everybody calls me Cas. Hey," he added with another toothy grin, "you know what the philosopher says, 'A stranger is just a friend you haven't met.'

"As for me, I'm head of the construction company that's doing the work here. Canad and Co.

'Progress Without Pain,' that's our motto."

"But . . . but . . . you've . . . destroyed our brook," Clover managed to say.

"Easy does it, sweetheart, easy does it," Mr Canad boomed with insistent good nature. "Don't need to make a mountain out of a molehill, do we? Or for that matter," he added with a laugh that set his belly to shaking, "an ocean out of a puddle."

Without saying another word, Valerian and Clover turned and fled back up the path.

"Have a nice day!" the beaver shouted after them, though it was the middle of the night. "I mean that, sincerely!"

As the two mice dashed toward their nest, all Clover could think was, "Oh, Ragweed. Please, please come home. We need you! Where are you?"

2
Poppy and Ereth

It was cool in Dimwood Forest. Though the high canopy of trees, flecks of sunlight sprinkled the earth with spots of gold. But on the floor of the forest, inside a long, hollow, and decaying log, it was all stink and muck.

"Oh, skunk whizzle," mocked the old porcupine who lived in the log. "Who cares foot fungus about Ragweed's family? I bet they're nothing but nasty nose bumps."

Though his full name was Erethizon Dorsatum, the porcupine insisted on being called Ereth. Not the sweetest smelling of creatures, he had a flat face with a blunt, black nose and fierce, grizzled whiskers. Sharp quills covered him from head to tail.

He was talking to a deer mouse by the name of Poppy.

Though most of her fur was soft orange-brown, Poppy had pure white fur on her round,

gracefully plump belly. Her whiskers, which stuck straight out from her delicate pink nose, were quite full. Her toes were small and her tail was long. As for her ears, they were relatively large and dark, and from the right one hung an earring, nothing more than a purple plastic bead dangling from a tiny chain.

"Ereth," Poppy explained, "if something happened to a child of yours, wouldn't *you* want to hear about it?"

"Look here, slug-brain," the porcupine said with something close to anger, "I thought you liked living in my neighbourhood. Thought you were my friend. But if you want to trundle off, forget me, make new friends, start a new life, go ahead. I've got plenty of things to do."

"Like what?" Poppy asked.

"Eating," the porcupine growled. "And sleeping." With a rattle of quills Ereth moved off towards the far end of his log.

"Ereth," Poppy pleaded as she followed after him, "let me try to explain one more time. Ragweed was a golden mouse. He was like no one I'd ever met before. And when he came here, I fell in love with him."

"*Love!*" sneered Ereth. "You can put love in a wasp's nest and chew on it."

"But I *did* love him," Poppy insisted. "And we . . . we were going to get married."

"*Marriage!*" Ereth hooted. "Head for the toilet bowl and bring two plungers!"

"But then," Poppy continued patiently, "that owl, Mr Ocax, killed him and – "

"Poppy, stop! I've heard this slop a hundred times!"

"But all I want to do," an exasperated Poppy continued, "is tell Ragweed's parents what happened to him. Don't you think they should know? Besides, I want to give them this." She touched the earring. "So they'll have something to remember him by."

"Listen, swamp-mouth," Ereth said, "take my word. They don't care what happened to him. No more than I do. Wise up. You'd have to be mushroom mucus not to know that!"

"The thing is, Ereth," Poppy persisted, "the trip would be so much nicer if you came along. It'll be an adventure. We'll see the world."

"Oh, frozen frog pips!" Ereth cried. "I don't

want to see the world. I hate going places. I hate doing things. And I *like* being alone. Most of all, I'm sick and tired of hearing about Ragweed! So beat it!" The porcupine continued on towards the far end of his log.

A frustrated Poppy let out a sigh, tenderly fingered Ragweed's earring, then went to the open end of the log and gazed out at Dimwood Forest.

This forest of towering trees was her home. One moment it was dark, the next moment it was light. Usually serene, the forest often exploded with noisy life. Though Poppy loved the forest dearly, and would miss it, she felt a great need to make the journey.

Poppy had to acknowledge that there was no particular *reason* for Ereth to go. He had never met Ragweed. Besides, Poppy hardly knew where his home was. Ragweed had never offered much detail about it. "The Woodlands," he called his home area. He said it was a few miles west of Dimwood Forest.

His family nest, he had once told her, was on the banks of a brook. He referred to it as little more than "The Brook." "It's a decent spot, girl," Ragweed had told her. "But, know what I'm saying, like, yawn city. Totally. Nothing ever happens there."

"Tell me about your parents," Poppy had said to him.

"They're named Clover and Valerian," he said. "Pretty cool . . . for parents. But, hey, like, I needed to see the world. And I did, too."

"Did they give you permission to go?" Poppy asked, impressed with Ragweed's story. At the time not only had she not gone far from where her own family lived, she was certain her parents would never allow her to travel.

Ragweed laughed. "Nope, they weren't too chilled 'bout what I was doing. Particularly Clover, my old mouse. But girl, a mouse has to do what a mouse has to do."

"Will you ever go back?" Poppy wanted to know.

"Oh, sure, someday. And hey, dude, I'll take you there," Ragweed promised. "Bet you'll like my folks. They'll think you're way sweet."

"Why?"

"'Cause you're my special girl, girl!" Then — Poppy remembered — Ragweed had winked at her with a sense of his own saucy being.

But Ragweed had died. And Poppy wanted to tell his parents what had happened. Maybe, she mused, it was her way of saying a final goodbye to the mouse she had loved.

Still, to go all that distance alone would be quite an undertaking.

It was not that Poppy was frightened of the distance or of being alone. It was merely a question of wanting to go *with* someone. True, she had plenty of sisters and brothers — cousins, too, for that matter. Still, she could think of no better companion for an adventure than her best friend, Ereth. But now the porcupine had said no. Poppy sighed. There were moments she actually thought Ereth was jealous of Ragweed.

Then the notion struck Poppy that it was probably nothing more than Ereth feeling his age. How like Ereth to be so proud he wouldn't admit to such a thing. She wished she had not pushed him so.

Never mind. Poppy made up her mind: Since she wanted to go, she'd go alone.

Oh, well, she thought, I'm sure I'll meet *someone* interesting. Besides, once I get to Ragweed's brook it

should be pleasant and calm. Recalling his words about the Brook, Poppy smiled. I could use a little dullness in my life, she thought.

Poppy went back into the log to say good-bye to Ereth. He was at the far, smelly end, licking a hunk of salt as if it were a lollipop.

Trying to keep from inhaling too much, Poppy said, "Ereth, I wanted to say good-bye."

The porcupine offered up an indifferent grunt.

"And Ereth . . . I should apologise."

"What for?"

"Asking you to come."

Ereth paused in his licking and squinted angrily down at Poppy. "Why?"

"I should have remembered you're too old for such a trip."

The salt dropped from Ereth's paws with a clatter. "Too *what*? he gasped.

"Well, you know," Poppy said with care. "Elderly."

"Me? Old? Elderly?" the porcupine cried, quills bristling. "You twisted bee burp! I can do whatever I want. Where I want. When I want. Or are you

hankering to turn yourself into a busted bee bottom?"

"But, Ereth . . . "

"Look here, you pickle-tailed fur booger," he roared on, "I can keep up with you any day of the week. Night too, for that matter, you slippery spot of squirrel splat!"

"You mean you'll come with me?" Poppy cried, trying to keep from grinning.

"Blow your nose and fill a bucket!" Ereth screeched. "Can't you understand *anything*? Never mind me going with *you*. You're going with *me*!"

With that, Ereth burst past Poppy, moving so fast, so furiously, his quills combed her belly fur into 27 neat rows.

Poppy, laughing, ran after him.

3

Night Thoughts

Ereth moved along so fast Poppy had to race after him. Her cries of, "Hey, slow down! Wait for me!" were of no avail. Only when they reached the deepest part of Dimwood Forest did Ereth finally pause.

When Poppy caught up to him, the porcupine was calmly nibbling on some tender bits of bark which he had peeled from a tree.

It was a dusky place. The high trees kept the light out but not the heat. The air felt as thick as syrup and bore a smell of skunkweed and rotting mushrooms.

"What is this spot?" a panting Poppy asked, throwing herself down on the ground to rest. Though she had always known Dimwood Forest was big, she was beginning to fathom just how small a part of it she'd experienced.

"The forest," Ereth replied, smugly.

"Amazing," Poppy said, staring around.

"Now, look here," Ereth said, "where was it that you said we were going?"

Poppy, still breathing hard from her exertion, said, "It's called The Brook."

"Oh, fox flip," the porcupine growled. "There must be a million brooks in this forest! Are you saying that's the only name you have?"

"Ereth," Poppy said, "all Ragweed told me was it was west of the forest."

"Sticky roach toes," Ereth muttered. "According to that, it could be anywhere."

"No, it can't," Poppy pointed out. "It's not east. Or north. Or even south. It's *west*." She looked toward the sky. Though the sun was hidden behind heavy foliage, it was still possible to find its place in the sky. "Since it's afternoon," she said, "west must be that way."

"Fine," Ereth conceded. "But how are we supposed to know *which* brook it is?"

"Ereth," Poppy said, "we don't need to have all the answers, do we? Can't we just keep moving? We've got all the time we need."

"The faster we get there, the faster we get back," Ereth returned.

Poppy got up and started off, this time taking the lead. Ereth, muttering "Ragweed" under his breath, followed.

The two friends travelled side by side. Moving in a steady, westerly direction, speaking little, they did not stop until darkness came. They had not come upon one brook.

"I think we'd better find a place for the night," Poppy suggested. She was quite worn out.

"When I travel, I stay in trees," Ereth informed her.

"That's fine with me," Poppy assured him. "Pick out one you'd like."

"Can't be any tree, you know. Has to be comfortable."

"Fine."

"Right height."

"Good."

"And smell right."

"Just choose one, Ereth!" Poppy cried.

Constantly grumbling, Ereth lumbered about the forest floor, examining every tree he passed. Poppy followed, pausing now and again to nibble seeds when

she found them. It made little difference to her where she slept. As long as she was with Ereth, she was safe. Nobody wanted to mess with him or his quills.

The porcupine finally settled on a fat tamarack pine. Its branches were thick. Its smell was pungent.

Moving awkwardly from branch to branch, Ereth climbed. Poppy followed.

Halfway up the tree, Ereth came upon a particularly fat branch whose broad width at the point where it grew out of the main trunk made a platform. "I suppose this'll do," he said, and settled down.

"Mind if I snuggle in?" Poppy asked.

"*Snuggle,*" Ereth mocked. "Why don't you just say, 'mind if I lean on you?'"

"I prefer *snuggle,*" Poppy said with a grin. She settled herself between Ereth's front paws, curled up in a ball, and took a deep, relaxing breath.

Though the air was ripe with the sticky scent of pine, Poppy detected the smell of nearby blossoms. Loving flowers of any kind, she was happy.

The night was full of noises, too. She heard the soft, padded steps of animals, the slithering of snakes, the piping of frogs, the chirping of crickets. Now and

again leaves rustled in the breeze. The night is dancing, she thought.

The stars seemed so distant. How far, Poppy wondered, would she have to travel to reach one of them?

Letting slip a murmur of contentment, she nestled closer to Ereth. She was perfectly aware he was not the easiest of companions, but she loved him for the good, blunt friend he was. Besides, whether he meant it or not, he kept her mind off the sad part of this journey, the meeting with Ragweed's parents.

So far the trip was exactly what she had wanted. She could already sense her grief easing. She was convinced that once she saw Ragweed's parents and delivered her doleful news — and his earring — she would be able to return home and get on with her life. The thought soothed her. She began to drift off to sleep.

Ereth broke the silence. "Poppy," he growled, "when you tell Ragweed's parents what happened to him, I won't be around."

"Oh, why?" Poppy said with a yawn.

"Because it's just family fripple, that's why. I

hate all that rubbish."

"Ereth, you can do what you want."

"I do," Ereth said. "Always."

"Fine."

Poppy yawned again, and closed her eyes.

Then Ereth said, "It's all those stupid *feelings*. Porcupines get along without that drivel."

"Not *one* feeling?"

"For salt . . . maybe."

When Poppy made no response Ereth added, "It's better that way."

"How come?" Poppy asked sleepily.

"Oh, chipmunk cheese. It . . . just is."

Poppy was too tired to debate. Instead, she pondered what she might say to Ragweed's parents, wondering if they would blame her for his death. Yawning, she placed her tail under her nose, and was soon fast asleep.

Ereth stared into the dark. "This is dumb," he said to himself. "I never should have come. *Ragweed*," he sneered. "Nothing but Ragweed. Nothing but sugared mouse slops. Phooey!"

4

The Water Rises

The beavers built the dam higher. Inch by inch the water rose. It licked the low banks then swallowed them whole. It crept and crawled and poked into every crevice, filling them up. It trickled along animal paths and washed them away. It sank flowers and grasses and turned them into soup. It slid between bushes and trees and drowned them, root, leaf and branch. It made islands of low hills. It flooded nests. The water was unstoppable.

Though Clover and Valerian could observe the water rising with their own eyes, they found it hard to accept that their nest was doomed. After all, they had lived in one place for years. During that time how many storms had they weathered? How many droughts? How many cold winters? To all questions, the same answer: many.

"Why are the beavers doing this?" the children asked.

"Be fair," Valerian said with a catch in his throat and a harassed look on his face. "We don't own the Brook, do we? Don't you think the beavers have as much right to live here as we do?"

"But their pond is getting huge!" one of the children objected. "It's taking over everything!"

Valerian sighed. "Maybe I can talk to them."

So it was that Valerian — feeling apprehensive, trying to keep his grey whiskers neat — crept down to the shore of the newly created pond.

The old brook had been surrounded by many trees. The new pond was encircled by chewed-off and jagged stumps. The old brook had been tranquil. The new pond fairly rattled with beavers hard at work. Even as Valerian stood there he heard the sound of yet another tree cashing. He winced.

"Hello!" he called out across the pond. "Can I speak to someone?"

One of the beavers paused to look around. "Hey, old timer, what's up?"

"I'm fine, thank you," Valerian returned politely.

"Who are you?" the beaver asked.

"I . . . I live here."

"Do you? That's swell. What's happening, pal?"

"I'd like to speak to Mr Canad."

"Cas? He's probably busy, but I'll go check."

The beaver dived, leaving Valerian to pace nervously, tail waving in agitation.

Within moments Mr Canad burst up to the water's surface. "Hey, pal! Nice to see you again," he cried out. "Don't think I got your name."

"Valerian."

"Val. Right! What's up, pal?"

"Well, sir, it's this . . . pond you're building."

"Sight for sore eyes, isn't it?" the beaver boomed.

"Well, I was just wondering . . . how . . . I mean, no one *owns* the Brook. So, of course, naturally, we're obliged to share. But we . . . well, we were wondering just how . . . well . . . big you intended to make it."

"*Big?*" Mr Canad cried. "Tell you something, pal, you ain't seen nothing yet! Talking world-class pond here. The cat's pyjamas and meow all at once. Over the top! Premier league. The whole enchilada. Hey, pal, Canad and Co. don't *do* small."

"But," Valerian said plaintively, "if you make it too big . . . you'll drive us folk who live here . . . away."

"Look here, Pal," Mr Canad said, "I'm telling you, I'd be tickled pink to see you stay. You seem decent. Clean. Good manners. Not a troublemaker are you?"

"No, sir."

"Great! Glad to have you around! 'Progress Without Pain.' That's our slogan. But, if you have to move, well, hey, no problem. Have a great trip. *Bon voyage. Hasta la sweeta. Are revor.*"

"Can't we compromise?" Valerian pleaded. "So we can both stay?"

"Pal, I've put quality time into that question. Comes to this: beavers do what beavers do. There you are: Question in, answer out. Neat as a pin. Hey, nice talking to you, pal. Appreciate it. Really do. Have a nice day! I mean that, sincerely!" he cried, and dived beneath the water.

Valerian, more discouraged than when he went, returned to the nest.

"What did they say?" his children asked.

"We have to move."

So Valerian and Clover began a frantic search for another suitable home. It was not easy. In the best of times good nests were hard to find. Now they had waited too long. Many creatures — caught in the same predicament as they — were already gone. When the mice finally found an acceptable new home it was on a hill, cresting the ridge overlooking the new pond: a small, damp hole with a large, cold boulder for a roof.

The boulder was perched precariously atop the hill. As Valerian considered it, he worried that it wouldn't take much to set it rolling. That brought nightmarish visions of its tumbling away in the night, leaving his children exposed.

Clover sighed. "It'll have to do."

"I reckon it will," Valerian agreed, trying to hide his worries.

Neither one mentioned that fitting 13 children into one dank, chilly nest was going to be difficult.

Yet even after they had found their new quarters, they put off moving. It was too painful. Only when water began to trickle down their long entryway and make puddles in the middle of their

main room did they finally pack their belongings.

These belongings — already mildewed and sodden — were easy enough to gather and haul out of the tunnel. Much harder was the removal of their children.

"Do we *have* to move?" the first complained.

"But Mum!" said another. "What about my friends?"

"The water isn't *that* bad," said a third. "We can make rafts. Build a houseboat. Swim from room to room. Be great."

And a fourth: "Do you really, really, *really* promise we'll come back when the water goes down?"

"Dear, dear children," Clover said, trying unsuccessfully to keep back her tears, "we have to go."

Of those children who still lived at home, Rye was the eldest. Like all the golden mice, he had fur of an earthy orange colour, a tail that was not very long, small, round ears and youthful, downy whiskers. He did have a small notch in his right ear, but that was the result of a childhood accident.

Rye had never left home. He claimed he stayed behind to help his parents with the youngsters. Others

suggested it was because he enjoyed being the eldest — which he became once Ragweed had left.

"Rye," Valerian said, "take yourself and some of your siblings, and go and search out the rest of the family. Let them know your mother and I have moved to higher ground. Tell them where."

Rye's chest swelled with pride that it was he who had been called upon to inform his far-flung family about what was happening.

Thistle, his by-one-litter younger sister, squeaked, "Do we have to go to *everybody*?" She wasn't even sure how many brothers and sisters she had.

"Absolutely," Valerian insisted. "All 63."

"Now do hurry, Rye," Clover said. "It's urgent!"

Hearing the distress in their parents' voices, Rye, Thistle and a younger brother, Curleydock, sped off to do as they were told.

Later that day, the family moved. When the children were all out of the nest, Clover and Valerian took one last, lingering look about their old home. Side by side, she short and plump, he tall and thin, they held paws.

Suddenly, Clover said, "Valerian, what about Ragweed?"

"What about him?"

"Who's going to tell him where we've gone?"

Valerian pulled his whiskers. "Clover, love, I'd say that when and if Ragweed gets back he'll see for himself that things are changed. That's all."

"What do you mean *if*?" Clover asked tremulously.

"I'm just saying, if ever we had a clever child, it's Ragweed. He'll find us when he comes looking."

Clover and Valerian scampered out of the nest.

Within hours their old home was entirely under water.

5

Some Words Are Exchanged

The day after they moved, Rye, Thistle and Curleydock crouched beneath a tangle of blackberry bushes and looked out over the pond.

"There's one!" Rye hissed.

A fat beaver had climbed atop a particularly large mound of sticks in the pond not far from the dam. It was dumping and smoothing mud on the mound's surface.

"That's their main lodge," Rye said with authority, though it was Valerian who had informed him of that fact only the day before.

"How did they get into it?" Curleydock asked. As the family went Curleydock was on the small side, and rather plump like his mother.

"There's an underwater passageway," Rye said. "You have to swim deep to get in there."

"Cool," murmured Thistle. Tall and sleek, with swept back whiskers and narrow ears, she was a good

swimmer.

"It's not cool," Rye said sharply. "They have no right to come and just take over everything. Look what happened to our nest." He waved a paw over the water. "Gone. You call that cool?"

Thistle shrank down. "I was just saying the beavers' home is . . . *interesting*."

"Look!" Curleydock whispered.

Three beavers had surfaced near the shore. They tumbled and turned, smacking the water with their large, flat tails.

"Big, aren't they?" Thistle said, her voice full of awe.

"They look like they're having fun," Curleydock said wistfully.

"Fun!" Rye snarled under his breath. "I hate them! I'd like to show them some fun!"

"When Ragweed gets back, he'll do it," Curleydock said, "he's not afraid of anyone."

"Ragweed's gone," Rye snapped. "Besides," he went on, "who needs him? *I'm* not afraid of them."

Thistle stared at her elder brother with wide eyes. "You mean you'd . . . talk to them?"

"No big deal," Rye replied.

"Except Ragweed wouldn't *say* he would," Curleydock said, and tittered. "He'd just *do* it."

Rye felt hot. "So would I."

"Dare you," his brother goaded. "*Double* dare."

Rye, suddenly nervous, said, "I'll do it if you come with me."

"You first," Thistle replied.

Rye considered the beavers anew.

"See," Curleydock said. "I told you. You're no Ragweed."

Rye offered his brother a dirty look, then crawled out from under the berry bush. Wanting his heart not to beat so fast, he yanked his whiskers — he wished they were darker, stiffer — licked down the hair on his chest, then headed down towards the water, tail tucked between trembling legs.

Halfway to the pond, Rye halted. "You coming or not?" he called back, hoping he sounded cocky.

Thistle scampered back to her brother's side. The two looked back.

"Well?" Rye asked.

Curleydock crept forward.

The three mice inched to the water's edge near where the three beavers were playing. The beavers paid them no attention.

"Go on, tell them what you think," Curleydock said, giving Rye a little nudge. You know, the way Ragweed would."

Feeling he could not back down, a jittery Rye cupped his front paws around his mouth to make himself heard. "Hey you!" he shouted.

The beavers halted their play and looked about with dripping muzzles. "Were you speaking to us?" one of them asked.

"You're the only ones who dammed our brook, aren't you?"

The beavers exchanged looks. One of them paddled through the water until she was close to the mice.

Her orange front teeth were enormous. The three mice retreated a few steps.

"My name is Clara. Clara Canad. What's yours?"

"Rye."

"Is something bothering you, Rye?"

Rye took a deep breath. "You beavers just barged into our neighbourhood and . . . and . . . took over. Ruined the Brook! Ruined the land! Ruined our nest! You're thoughtless and greedy."

"Hey, buster," Clara retorted, "making a pond is progress."

"Progress?" Rye cried. "Progress for you, maybe. What about the rest of us? Who invited you here, anyway?"

"No one invited us," Clara replied. "Do you mice own this brook?"

"Well . . . no."

"Is there a sign posted, Reserved for Mice Only?"

"No, but . . ."

"And it's still a free country, isn't it?"

"I suppose . . ."

"Well, then, don't you think we've got the right to build our lodges here?"

"But it's *not* right!" a confused Rye cried. "You destroyed *our* nest!"

"Hey, sorry to hear it," Clara returned. "There's always a price to pay for progress."

"But who's paying that price?" Rye screamed. "*We are!* The ones who live here. You just flood, flood, flood!"

"I'd be more than happy to talk to you in a civil way," the beaver returned, "but if all you can do is rant and rave, I'd just as soon not listen." She turned about, and as she drew away she lifted her tail and brought it down hard and flat upon the water, sending out a great spray that thoroughly soaked the mice.

Sopping wet, the mice ran off. But not before Thistle stopped and shouted back at the beavers. "You just wait till my brother Ragweed comes home," she cried. "He'll fix you!"

6
Rye

The pond-side meeting with the beavers had infuriated and humiliated Rye. It wasn't only the beavers that had upset him. It was all that talk about his brother, Ragweed.

Rye loved his elder brother. A lot. Admired him. Looked up to him. But if Ragweed wasn't teasing Rye, he was lecturing him, telling him the best way to do something, saying Rye was doing something wrong. Rye chafed under such treatment. Despised it.

So there were times Rye was quite sure he hated Ragweed, too. It seemed that no matter what he did, his whole family — mother, father, brothers and sisters — was holding Ragweed up as the best. Rye was sure they were always comparing *him* to Ragweed. Unfavourably. As far as Rye was concerned, it wasn't fair. "I'm not Ragweed," he continually reminded them. "I'm me."

It didn't help that Rye and Ragweed looked so

much alike. Though a few months younger than Ragweed, Rye was just as long and thin, and had the same sharp, penetrating gaze and noble nose. The way most knew how to tell the brothers apart was that small notch in Rye's right ear.

But whereas Ragweed was blunt, even cocky, Rye was considered the more thoughtful mouse, something of a dreamer. "A romantic," Clover said, with a wistful shake of her head.

Rye often wandered nearby meadows, where he liked to fling himself under a flower and daydream of romantic adventures.

When he returned — flower in paw — and was asked what he'd done, he'd reply, "Oh, nothing. Some thinking, I suppose."

"But what were you thinking about?"

"Today? Oh, the sky, clouds and . . . flowers."

It was only when Ragweed left home that Rye came into his own. Now *he* was the eldest of the children at home. Now the younger ones looked up to *him*. Now his parents called upon *him* to do things. His opinion was asked. He was heard.

Yet, even as that happened, Rye feared things

would remain that way only until Ragweed returned. Hadn't Curleydock said as much when Rye tried to speak to the Beavers?

Hardly a wonder then that, as far as Rye was concerned, there were moments he hoped Ragweed would *not* come home. Of course he wouldn't *say* anything like that. The thought made him feel ashamed. It seemed unnatural, sinful.

So it was that after he shouted insults at the beavers and was splashed away for his efforts, Rye returned to the family's new nest in a deep sulk. To make things worse, no one seemed to understand why he was sulking.

"What's the matter with Rye?" One of his younger brothers asked Thistle.

"Just daydreaming"

"He's always daydreaming!"

Later that day Valerian called upon Rye to join him while he went to forage for food. A reluctant Rye heaved himself up and went along.

Father and son went out behind the boulder and took a path that led them to an old patch of sunflowers. The flowers had been planted years ago by

humans — or so the mice believed — and sunflowers had grown upon that spot ever since. The great, round, yellow blossoms, like so many tethered suns, nodded and bobbed. Even better — as far as the mice were concerned — it was a fine place for sunflower-seed gathering.

Rye and Valerian had gathered a fair pile of seeds when Valerian asked, "What's the problem, Rye? You seem a little droopy."

"Oh . . . never mind," Rye mumbled.

"You sure?"

"Well . . . yes." Rye, who always assumed no one would listen to him, found it hard to express himself. In that, he wished he *were* more like Ragweed. Ragweed always told everybody exactly what he was thinking.

Valerian sat down, leaned against a stump, put a blade of grass in his teeth, and adjusted his arms behind his head. "This business of the beavers, the Brook, and all they've done — it's upsetting. It is. Still, the family has done pretty well, considering. 'Course, your mother has been grand. Always is. You do know what a fine mother you have, don't you, son? Lovely

creature," he murmured. "Truly lovely."

"I suppose . . ." Rye said. He sat down next to his father.

"Truth is," Valerian continued with a rueful shake of his head, "it doesn't seem like there's much we can do. Beavers are big and powerful. They don't want to listen to us. I'm just hoping they stop building. Now of course —" Valerian's voice trailed off.

"Of course . . . what?" Rye asked.

Valerian threw the grass blade away and reached over to their seed pile. He looked it over, selected a seed, polished it against his chest, then took a bite.

"What?" Rye prompted.

"Oh," Valerian finally said, "your mother doesn't say, though it does slip out now and again. I'm fairly sure she thinks that when Ragweed comes home he'll solve everything." He contemplated the seed in his paws.

Rye stiffened. "Do *you* think so?" he asked, ready to bolt up and walk off.

"No," his father said. He took another bite of the seed and chewed thoughtfully.

"You don't?" said Rye, taken by surprise. "Why?"

Instead of answering, Valerian remained quiet and stared off into the distance. Now and again he nibbled at his seed.

"Well, son, it's a big world out there. Full of possibilities. Dangers. Your brother isn't shy. He likes getting into things. Seems to me, if he was coming back, well, he'd have done so by now." There was a tremor in his voice.

Shocked, Rye looked around. "Do . . . do you think something . . . happened to him?" he asked. Something in his world shifted.

At first Valerian only nodded. It took a moment for him to speak. "Don't know for sure, of course, do I?" There was another pause. "But well, I've got this . . . bad feeling."

"But . . . that would be awful," Rye said, gazing at his father's sad face. Yet hadn't he almost wished for it?

"Yep, it'd definitely be upsetting," his father said.

"Do you . . . do you think," Rye said, "I should go and look for him?"

"No," Valerian said. "Ragweed could be any-where. If he's coming back, he'll come in his own sweet time. Besides, we don't want you disappearing, too."

Rye hesitated before saying, "Why?"

"We need you, Rye," Valerian said. "We need you a lot."

Rye almost burst into tears of gratitude. But then he asked, "Does that mean that if . . . if Ragweed did come back, you . . . *wouldn't* need me?"

"Son," Valerian said, "all I'm saying is, I don't think Ragweed is coming back."

Rye, however, noticed that his father had not really answered his question: What would *Rye's* place be if Ragweed returned? Disappointed, he did not want to ask again. His thoughts were already too confused.

That night Rye could not sleep. Wedged in amidst his family in the one-room nest, he kept thinking about his talk with his father. What had happened to Ragweed? Would his brother come back? What would happen if he did? In particular, Rye won-dered what would happen to *him* if Ragweed came home? Would he be ignored again?

The more Rye thought about it, the more unappreciated he felt. He forgot how wonderful it had been when his father had talked to him mouse to mouse. Instead he thought, "Dad was telling me not to go off only because Ragweed is gone."

It was but a matter of moments before Rye was saying to himself, "Who pays attention to *me*?" He answered his own question quickly: "Nobody!"

Perhaps, he thought, it *would* be a good thing if he went off to look for Ragweed. When he found him, he'd tell his brother he was needed at home. Then Rye could go off and have his *own* adventures.

On the other paw, Rye mused, if he could not find Ragweed, but could discover what had happened to him, he could bring *that* news to his family. Not only could they be at rest with the matter, he could take his permanent place as the eldest child at home.

It was the middle of the night. The whole nest was asleep, except Rye. He got up quietly. There were no particular belongings he needed or wanted to take. Still, he thought it best to leave something to tell his parents where he was going. They might even think he was doing something brave as well as useful.

Finding a pale leaf, he wrote a good-bye note:

Dear Mum & Dad,
Farewell!
I've gone into the great world to search for Ragweed.
Fear not! I shall return!
Your devoted son,
Rye

Rye took a deep breath. The night was balmy, sweet with the smell of growing things. The moon appeared calm in a velvet black sky. The grass was soft beneath his toes. The whole world seemed full and ripe.

Rye's slim chest swelled with emotion. Oh, to have something important happen to *him* at last! Oh, to be noticed, to be told by someone, "Rye, how glad I am to see *you!*"

Yet was he, Rye kept wondering, doing the right thing by going? I'm doing it for the family, he told himself. It has nothing to do with me at all.

With that thought firmly embedded in his heart, Rye set off. He was heading due east.

Mr Caster P. Canad and Company

The beavers' lodge was a large, domed structure made of sticks and twigs, plastered over with mud. To get inside the lodge the beavers – just as Valerian had informed Rye – had to swim through an underwater tunnel.

Though a small vent hole at the top of the dome provided some fresh air, it was hot and humid inside the lodge. The light there came from the sporadic flashing light of fireflies, which the beavers had snared and brought into the lodge for just that purpose.

Standing at the far end of the lodge was Mr Caster P. Canad. Looking around, paws contentedly folded over his pot belly, he liked what he saw: 12 beavers, family all, sitting on their tails paying close attention to him. Wife, child, cousin, brother or sister, he treated them all with total equality. That is to say, he was everybody's boss. He offered up a ripe, toothy smile.

In one of Mr Canad's paws was a branch – a pointer. Next to him was a large sheet of bark, which he had attached to a wall. The bark bore a drawing of the new pond the beavers had created.

"All right then," Mr Canad began, tapping his stick against the drawing. "Here's where we've constructed the dam. Mighty fine dam, too, if I do say so myself. Yes, sir, when Canad and Co. builds a dam, we don't let the grass grow under our feet, do we?"

"Way to go, Cas," murmured a few of the beavers, slapping their tails down on the mud floor of the lodge by way of approval.

"Okay," Mr Canad continued, "every journey begins with a step. But it's plain as the nose on your face, we're going to build the biggest, best, most profitable pond in the whole country. Honest to goodness, as the day is long, take my word for it, we are. You know what the old philosopher said: 'If you can't see the forest for the trees, chew the trees down!'

"Okay. Good news and bad news. The good news is that so far we've done a fine job on the pond. Peachy keen-o job." Mr Canad tapped the map with his stick. "Bad news," he went on with a good natured

chuckle, "Rome wasn't built in a day, either."

"Which reminds me . . . Has anyone come up with a good name for this project? The locals call the brook, the Brook. Hey, dull as ditch water. Can't sell lodges by calling them the Brook. Far as I'm concerned, it doesn't hit the nail on the head."

"Hey, Cas," one of the beavers called out, "what about Wet Wonderland?"

"Or, Welcome Water World," suggested another.

"Mud Flats," offered a third.

To each suggestion Mr Canad offered up a toothy smile. "Fine, Fine," he said. "Keep those thinking caps on. Those names are A-OK. What we need, though, is something that hits folks square in the eye. Something strong. Dynamic. That goes over the top. Score's a bull's-eye. Is a hole in one. The whole ten yards. Out for the count. Grand slam. I'm telling you, straight from the heart, there's nothing I admire more than originality. As long as it fits the bill.

"So, sure as the sun rises in the morning, I put on my thinking cap and came up with – this should knock your front teeth cock-eyed – Canad's Happy Homes. Says it all, don't you know. Canad's Happy

Homes. Has a solid ring to it, wouldn't you say? The real plastic."

There was a general thumping of tails.

"Okay. We agree. From here on out, we call this project Canad's Happy Homes."

"Now," Mr Canad continued, using his stick to clarify his ideas, "with the dam built *here*, Canad's Happy Homes will extend its boundaries. Here. Here. Here. How do you like them wood chips?" He grinned, exposing his orange buck teeth to the fullest.

Tails thumped.

"As for lodges, we'll scatter them here, here, here. Plus a few more canals over here." Mr Canad pointed to different places on the bark.

"I know this is a lot of work. But don't forget the turtle, the hare, or the Alamo. We don't want to let the grass grow under our feet. Which is okay, except we want *water* under our feet. The more the better. If there's one thing I can tell you, Canad's Happy Homes will be *wet*.

"My loyal, hard-working company," Mr Canad continued, "we're the original eager beavers. Canad and Co. has never shied from hard work. Never will.

Yes, sir, if better ponds are to be built, Canad and Co. will build them! Any questions?"

One of the beavers raised a paw.

"Yes, Clara."

"I have received a complaint about what we're doing here. Rather rudely put, too, I'm afraid."

Mr Canad nodded sagely. "Hard to believe, sweetheart, but there are those who want life to go on the way it always has. Can't stand progress. Resist it.

"Okay. Let's be sensitive to these folks. Pity them. They don't understand they're sitting right smack bang in the middle of the future. So, be patient, but get on with the job. Be understanding, but don't give an inch. Keep saying Progress Without Pain, till they believe it. Anyway, little folks can't do much about us. Not by a long shot. Or a short one," he added with a chuckle.

"What if they make trouble?" asked one of the other beavers.

"Okay. I've been around the pond a few times. Talk is cheap. Actions speak louder than words. A flat whack of the old tail solves most problems. Hey! The bottom line is, we've got bigger bottoms."

The lodge rippled with laughter and a few tail slaps.

"All right then," Mr Canad concluded. "Don't have to remind you, there's work to be done. I'll be by your side. Don't want to hear about any beaver who isn't busy. Hang in there. Be fresh as a daisy. When the going gets tough, the tough gets going. And finally, from the bottom of my heart, and from the top, as well as the sides and also the middle, I want to say to you all, and I mean this, really, I do, with all my soul, honestly, *sincerely*, have a nice day!"

A Dance upon the Meadow

Poppy and Ereth continued travelling west. Though there were many trails from which to choose, there were no clear signs to follow. The best that Poppy could do was to keep them moving in a westerly direction. For Ereth, it was a point of pride to refuse to ask directions from anyone.

"But why?" Poppy wanted to know.

"Ask for directions and you're admitting you're helpless," the porcupine pronounced. "The only thing that matters is that I know my way back home."

When they did meet other mice, voles, a badger — once a deer and her fawn — it was Poppy who asked for advice. "We're looking for the Brook," she would say. "Do you have any idea where that might be?"

The other animals were more than obliging. When these fellow travellers knew where a brook was, they explained how to reach it. And Poppy and Ereth did find them: one or two large brooks, some three of

smaller size. But no golden mice were to be found.

"Ereth," Poppy finally said, "we don't seem to be getting any closer to where Ragweed said his family lived. Do you think he might have been confused about which way he came?"

"Probably," Ereth grumbled.

"I admit," Poppy confessed, "I'm beginning to wonder how much longer we should go on."

Ereth came to a quick stop. "Fine," he said. "Let's go home."

The anxiety in his voice caused Poppy to consider him thoughtfully. "You've been awfully quiet lately," she said. "Is something bothering you?"

"Oh, sparrow swit," Ereth barked. "Can't a fellow keep his thoughts to himself?"

"Of course he can."

"Look here, Poppy," the porcupine said, "I'm not used to being with others. How many times do I have to say it, I *like* being alone."

"That's fine," the mouse returned. "I was just wondering."

"Well, stop wondering, puzz ball."

"But the forest does seem to be thinning,"

Poppy pointed out. "Maybe we are closer to those woodlands."

Ereth looked about. "I prefer the dark," he said.

Poppy sighed. "I'm going on a bit more."

"Do what you want," Ereth growled.

By midday, with the trees thinning more and more and the sun beating down hard, it became too hot to travel. Ereth announced he needed a nap. Without even waiting for Poppy to reply, he rattled off the trail, found a shady spot in a tree, curled up in a ball, and went to sleep.

Poppy rolled over on her stomach, plucked a blade of grass, and chewed it meditatively.

Before her spread a small meadow. Surrounded on three sides by trees, it had a closed-in, secure feeling. The grasses were low, sprinkled about with flowers. She noticed yellow viola, forget-me-nots, and bluebells. There was a scarlet falsemallow and some lovely, lush poppies.

A black and orange butterfly came into view, fluttering its wings like a slow-motion dancer. Soon after a fat bumblebee, legs bulky with golden pollen, worked its way from flower to flower. A fast dancer, Poppy thought.

As Poppy looked on, something stirred within her. To her surprise, she felt lonely and empty yet full and content all at once. How, she wondered, could she feel such contradictions?

Then, as she watched a dragonfly dart by, she recalled that it had been a long time since she had danced. When she was young — a few months ago — she had thought a great deal about dancing. She had even wanted to be a dancer.

Sighing, she recollected that she never had danced with Ragweed. They had meant to. Now she felt the desire to dance again.

With a nervous glance up at Ereth to make sure he was sleeping, she got to her feet.

Poppy checked a second time to make sure her friend was asleep. She was in no mood to deal with the porcupine's teasing. When he didn't stir, she lifted her front paws as if to pluck the sun from the sky. Her tail began to wave to a steady beat. A miniature melody, halfway between a whistle and hum, rose to her throat. It was no particular tune, just *something* she made up then and there.

She took one step, and another, gliding

forward, pretending, wanting to be as graceful as possible. With every step her heart seemed to lighten.

Within moments Poppy was leaping about, skimming the surface of the field, bending and bowing, twirling and whirling, hardly thinking, aware mostly of the sun's warmth that caressed her fur, and the cool grasses that tickled her toes. Oh, how she loved to dance! Oh, how she loved life!

Almost overwhelmed with emotion, Poppy closed her eyes, spun, dipped, and danced some more. Then she opened her eyes. Standing before her was a mouse.

Poppy gasped. For one indescribable moment she thought it was Ragweed. The mouse before her had the same orange-coloured fur. His whiskers were fair. His tail was not very long. His ears were small and round. She almost cried, "Ragweed!" but could not find tongue to do it.

Then she noticed a small notch on this mouse's right ear. This was *not* Ragweed. Even so she stood there, transfixed, staring, heart pounding as fast as hummingbird wings.

For his part, the strange mouse stood absolutely still, gazing at Poppy as if in rhapsody.

When Poppy had opened her eyes she had been in the midst of a twirl, arms and paws extended before her, legs behind. As she gawked at the mouse before her she dared not move.

Now the strange mouse extended *his* paws. Without a word, he gently took Poppy's paws in his. At his touch Poppy felt a tingle ripple through her body. It was as if a feather had stroked her from her tail to her nose.

For a moment — a moment that felt like eternity — the two mice looked into each other's eyes.

He whispered, "May I dance with you?"

In answer, Poppy made the first move. It was not a movement away, or a retreat, but a small step to one side.

His paws in hers, the two mice moved in perfect rhythm. Round and round and paw-in-paw they danced upon the meadow. Eyes locked, whiskers sometimes brushing, they turned this way, that way, bobbing, bowing, soaring, in as graceful a duet as two mice ever had danced, could dance, would dance.

How much Poppy wanted to ask, "Who are you? What are you? Where do you come from?" She

could not. She had no voice or words capable of expressing what she felt. She only knew nothing bad was happening. Indeed, it was just the opposite. Something very fine was occurring, something grand, something *wonderful!*

Suddenly, Poppy slipped. Her paws jerked away from the stranger's paws and she fell back. The two mice continued to stare at one another.

The other mouse blushed, turned, and fled toward the west, disappearing amid the trees that surrounded the field.

A speechless Poppy stared after him, even as her questions returned: Who are you? What are you? Where do you come from? *Where are you going?* But the other mouse was gone. Poppy had no answers.

Overwhelmed, Poppy picked herself up from the ground. Half walking, half staggering, she made her way back to where Ereth had remained, asleep.

At the base of the tree she sat down and closed her eyes. Had it all been a dream? Or had something truly extraordinary occurred?

She was not sure.

The next thing Poppy felt was her shoulder

being rudely shaken. Simultaneously, she heard Ereth splutter into her ear, "Let's go, stink foot. The sooner we get to where we're going, the sooner we can get back home."

But what had happened to Rye? For it was Rye with whom Poppy had danced.

He had gone from the meadow in a stupor equal to Poppy's. As he went he paused now and again to look back longingly. "Who are you? What are you?" he asked the image of Poppy. "What is your name? Where do you hail from? Where will you go?" And why did he feel he had to go away, when in fact he wanted to go back and dance forever?

Rye also asked himself if the dance had been real or only a moment's fantasy.

So intent was he upon these questions that he completely forgot he was running away from home. When he did remember, he had already reached the entryway to the family nest under the boulder. "Oh, well," Rye said dreamily, "I might as well stay."

No one had noticed he had gone.

9

The Rain Falls

Poppy and Ereth trudged along in silence. With her mind taken up by thoughts of the mouse with whom she had danced, she was grateful for the quiet. How so very much like Ragweed he was! And yet — how different. While they looked alike, the stranger seemed softer, gentler than the bold, headstrong Ragweed she had known. Certainly this mouse was more romantic. Was he, Poppy kept wondering, a dream or not? If he was a dream, he was the best dream she'd ever had. Still, she hoped he was real.

If her dance partner had been real, how could she find him again? Of course it was impossible that he had been Ragweed. But the mouse clearly was a *golden* mouse. If there was one golden mouse in the area, perhaps there would be others. Did that mean she was nearing Ragweed's home?

As they walked, Poppy hummed the snippet of tune she had composed for her dance.

So preoccupied was Poppy by her musings that she failed to notice that Ereth was frowning and grumbling even more than usual.

"What's the noise?" he suddenly asked.

"It's me, humming."

"I'm in no mood for music."

"How come?"

"I . . . Oh, forget it."

Poppy paused to look at her friend closely. There was a look in his eyes she had never seen before. "Ereth," she said, suddenly alarmed. "What is it?"

Ereth looked a little sheepish. "I . . . well . . . bumblebee flunk. Never mind!"

Poppy offered a worried glance but chose to ask no more questions. In any case she preferred to think about her dance. Once again she began to hum her tune.

The two friends continued west. When on occasion they met others on the path — a mole, a water rat — Poppy asked if they had ever heard of the Brook. Much advice was offered, directions were given, and sure enough another brook was found. Small and calm, it was very much what Poppy imagined she was

looking for. To her disappointment no golden mice loved thereabout.

A resident otter did inform Poppy and Ereth that there was another pretty, shallow brook, no farther than two hills beyond, in "that" direction. The otter pointed due west.

"I bet we find the right one this time," Poppy, ever hopeful, said to Ereth as they started again.

Ereth grew even more gloomy.

Though the day had begun bright and clear, the sky had turned grey and cloudy, the air heavy. Tree tops flicked and bobbed in a humid breeze. Birds flew high and fast. Clearly, a storm was coming.

With a new urgency, Poppy and Ereth trudged toward the crest of the second hill.

"Maybe when we get to the top we'll see the brook that the otter mentioned," Poppy said.

"Soon as we get to the top of that hill," Ereth proclaimed, "I'm going back home."

"Why?"

"I'm sick of walking," the porcupine replied.

From the crest of the hill they looked down into a valley. At the very bottom was a pond.

"No brook," Ereth said with palpable relief. "Let's go home."

"Well, actually," Poppy pointed out, "there's a brook leading into the pond. And out of it."

Ereth muttered something unintelligible under his breath. Then he said, "It's going to rain."

"Ereth," Poppy said, "rain won't hurt us. I'm going to check that brook."

Even as they stood, drops began to fall. At first it came slowly, great plops of water. Then, while lightning crackled off to the distant north and thunder followed, a steady drizzle began to fall.

Ereth wheeled about and moved toward a clump of trees.

"Where are you going?" Poppy called.

"Where do you think, toad-wart? Out of the rain."

"Ereth, I want to explore that brook!"

"Buzzard traps," the porcupine muttered.

Poppy watched Ereth go. "Will you promise to stay there until I search a bit?" she called after him.

"I never promise anything."

"How will I know where you are?"

"Watch my tracks."

Poppy waited until Ereth reached a cottonwood tree and started to climb it. She noted its position then hurried down the path. By now the rain was falling steadily.

For his part, Ereth looked around, saw which way Poppy was going – down the other side of the hill – then curled himself into a tight ball and closed his eyes. "I never should have come," he muttered. "Ragweed. Nothing but Ragweed. I thought I was her best friend."

Poppy was approaching the pond. Halfway down the hill she could see that it had been created by beavers. At one end was a dam, and Poppy could even observe a number of beavers hard at work. Some were swimming upon the pond's surface. Others were labouring on lodges. A few were working on the main dam, building it higher.

At the far side of the pond, a particularly large, fat beaver was gnawing upon the trunk of an aspen tree. There was a sharp crack as the tree snapped and tumbled to earth, landing with a crash.

At the sound all the beavers in the pond looked

around. When they saw it was a tree that had fallen, they began to slap the pond's surface with their tails.

Poppy, standing in the rain, looking on, heard someone say, "Awful. Just awful."

She turned. Sitting beneath a large toadstool, protected from the rain, was a golden mouse.

Poppy's heart fluttered. For an instant she thought it was the one with whom she had danced. Then she saw that this mouse, though tall and thin, was a female.

"Hello," Poppy said.

The mouse looked beyond Poppy. "Oh, hi," she said. She sounded unhappy.

"Do you live around here?" Poppy asked.

"Yes."

"Are there . . . are there a lot of you around?" Poppy inquired. "I mean . . . *golden* mice."

The mouse looked down at herself as if she had never considered the question before. "I suppose."

"My name is Poppy," Poppy said. "I'm a deer mouse."

"My name is Thistle," said the other. "How come you're standing in the rain?"

"Oh, right. I am. May I join you?"

"Sure."

Poppy darted under the cover of the toadstool. Thistle, making room, asked, "Where are you from?"

"Back east. Over by Dimwood Forest."

"Never heard of it," Thistle said with polite indifference. She had turned back to stare down at the pond. Water dripped from around the edges of the toadstool like a tattered curtain.

"I hate beavers," Thistle said.

"Why?"

"When they made that pond they ruined everything for everybody. The Brook used to be so wonderful."

Poppy's heart gave a lurch. "Is that what you called it?" she asked, her voice faltering. "The Brook?"

Thistle nodded. "You wouldn't think it used to be so small and calm. Look at it now!" she said sadly. Then she added, "Our home was right on the banks of the Brook. No more. Flooded out. We had to move away. Because of them."

Poppy was trying to restrain her growing excitement.

"Thistle . . ." Poppy said nervously.

"What?"

"Does the name . . . *Ragweed* . . . mean anything to you?"

Thistle had been gazing mournfully down at the pond. At the name she whirled about. "*Ragweed!*" she cried. "That's my brother! Do you know him? Have you seen him? Have you any idea where he is? Is he coming back? I can't tell you how much we need him!"

Instead of answering Thistle's barrage of questions, Poppy asked one of her own, "Are your parents named Clover and Valerian?"

"How did you know? Ragweed must have told you. But that means you *do* know him. Oh, boy, you've got to see my parents. Our nest isn't far," she went on. "Come on. Please tell me about Ragweed. What's he doing? You don't know how much we miss him! Do you know when he's coming? We really need him to come back. I've got tons of brothers but Ragweed's the *best*."

Managing to push down her emotions, but speaking in a strained voice, Poppy said, "I think I'd better talk to your parents."

Thistle darted into the rain. "I'll take you. What did you say your name was?"

"Poppy."

"Poppy, you won't believe how glad my parents will be to see you!"

With Thistle looking over her shoulder to make sure Poppy was following, the two mice made their way through the rain along a path that led uphill from the pond. The farther they went, the more nervous Poppy became.

"It's just over here," Thistle kept calling.

They had come to a large boulder embedded in an outcropping of earth. A variety of shrubs and flowers rimmed the rock. In the rain they seemed shrunken and cold.

Poppy herself was thoroughly soaked as well as trembling. The wetness came from the rain but the trembling came from her emotions. Though Thistle was just as wet, she was too excited to notice Poppy's state.

"Just follow me," the young mouse said, darting along the base of the rock, then plunging into the small hole which was screened by some flowering rosecrown.

At the entry hole, Poppy paused to give herself strength. "Why did I ever want to do this?" she wondered.

Thistle popped back up out of the hole. "Come on!" she called, then plunged down the tunnel again. A reluctant Poppy followed at a slower pace. She could hear Thistle yell, "Mum! Dad! Everyone. Guess what? Someone's come with news about Ragweed!"

Full of dread, wishing the tunnel were a hundred miles long, Poppy crept the whole way. All the same, within moments she entered the nest.

In a glance Poppy saw the nest for what it was: a single, shabby room stuffed with golden mice. Golden mice tended to be bigger than deer mice, so Poppy's first sensation was not only that there were a lot of them, but that they all seemed quite large.

But Poppy had not the slightest doubt she was in the presence of Ragweed's family. The resemblance was uncanny. It was as if she were in a room full of familiar ghosts. She felt weak.

There were the two adults, Clover and Valerian, plus 11 children. The children ranged from fully grown young adults to squeaking infants, one of

which was being burped on Clover's shoulder.

When Poppy entered the nest the golden mice stared at her with twitching ears and wide eyes.

"This is Poppy," Thistle announced excitedly.

"How do," Valerian said, standing tall and thin, and fussing with his whiskers. There was a tremor in his voice.

Clover, very pale, said nothing. Her black eyes, open wide, just stared at Poppy. Her whiskers were shaking.

Thistle cried, "Poppy knows all about Ragweed, don't you?"

Poppy was so choked with emotion, it was all she could do to nod a response and gaze from face to face. Suddenly, she stopped. At the back of the pack was the mouse she had danced with. There was the same sweet, soft, noble face, the same right ear with a notch.

Their eyes met – and held. Poppy's heart fluttered. Grief, joy, relief, sadness – all mingled, but in such confusion she hardly knew *what* she felt.

She lowered her eyes.

Valerian, his voice husky, spoke out. "My dear

Miss mouse, *do* you have some news about our son, Ragweed?"

"Yes . . ." Poppy managed to say.

"What's . . . happened to him?" Clover blurted out. "When . . . when is he coming home?"

Poppy found it impossible to speak. Instead she sought out the face of her dancing partner. Once again their eyes met. How she wished he were not there. How she wished she were not going to say what she had to say.

"Please," she heard Clover beg as if from some distant place. "I really must know." As Clover spoke she stood up — infant still in her arms — and reached a paw to touch Valerian, as if she were in need of steadying. Her round, heavy body seemed uncertain on her stumpy legs.

Poppy turned back to Clover. "I'm afraid Ragweed . . ." The next word stuck. She could not speak the word. She had to force it out. "Ragweed is . . . dead," she finally said, her voice tiny.

Utter silence.

"*Dead?*" a small voice, a youngster's, echoed.

"Dead?" Clover repeated.

Poppy could only nod yes.

Valerian cleared his throat. "But . . . *how?*" he managed to ask.

"An owl killed him."

"An owl . . ." someone said. Then all was silence again.

Suddenly Clover sat down. "My own poor, sweet boy," she sobbed.

"Can you tell us more?" Valerian asked in a choked voice.

Poppy closed her eyes. When she opened them she sought out the face of the mouse with whom she had danced. When she found it, it was full of awful sadness. "We . . . we were . . . in love," Poppy said. "We were going to marry."

"Oh, my," Clover murmured, putting a paw to her trembling lips.

Valerian swallowed hard, cleared his throat and said, "Poppy . . . I . . . we thank you for coming and . . . telling us." He wiped a tear from one cheek, then the other.

"I thought you'd want to know," Poppy said softly. "That's why I came."

The golden mice stared at Poppy as if she had spoken a strange language. Clover, letting escape a small squeak, even as she stroked the baby she was holding, said, "It's a terrible thing to live beyond your own children."

With great effort Valerian drew himself up. "Poppy, it was generous of you to come so far to bring us . . . the news. You must be tired."

"I'm all right," Poppy said.

"You're welcome to stay with us as long as you like," he added. "This is not . . . where Ragweed was brought up. We've fallen on hard times. But . . . our nest is your nest."

"The beavers sank our nest," one of the young mice shouted. All the children began to talk at once.

"Poppy, I must ask you something . . ." Clover suddenly said. In an instant the nest became quiet again.

"Yes. Please," Poppy said.

"I hope you loved my son very much," Clover said.

Poppy did not answer right away. Instead, she looked down at her toes, then up and around, seeking

the face of the one with whom she had danced. He was gazing at her with a profound look of pain.

"*Did* you love him?" Clover pressed. The question seemed urgent.

"Yes," Poppy said, "I did. Very much."

"Oh, my dear . . ." Clover cried. Thrusting the baby she'd been holding into Valerian's paws, she rushed over to Poppy and gave her an engulfing hug. Poppy hugged her back. As she did, she saw, from the corner of an eye, the mouse she had danced with, his face awash with grief, rush past and fling himself up the tunnel.

10
Ereth Has Some Thoughts

Hunched on his perch in the cottonwood tree, Ereth stared gloomily at the falling rain. Lightning crackled overhead. Thunder rumbled. The world had become grey and sodden.

"I hate water," Ereth muttered, "I hate everything."

Again and again he wished he were back home in his smelly log in Dimwood Forest. It was dry there. It was quiet. He was alone. Nothing — no one — bothered him.

"Whatever made me come here?" he kept asking himself. "Poppy did. She forced me to come . . . Mouse frickets . . ." he muttered. "Double mouse frickets. *Quadruple* mouse frickets!"

From directly over his head, a pool of water that had collected in the fold of a leaf fell on his face.

"That's enough!" Ereth shouted with a furious shake of his head. "I'm going home!" Snarling and

hissing, he scrambled down the tree. Once on soggy ground, he paused. The storm appeared to be growing worse. The rain was falling harder and faster. If he went he would get soaked. Then a gust of wind shook the tree, causing a cascade of water to plop on his head. He moaned. If he stayed he would get soaked. Where was that foolish mouse? Why did he ever bother with her?

"If I go it will teach her a lesson. If I teach her a lesson she'll get upset with me," he told himself. "If she gets upset she'll scold me. Then I'll feel bad. Why should I care? She's just a friend. No," he corrected himself. "I have no friends. I don't want any friends. Poppy's just an acquaintance. A passer-by.

"Poppy!" he bellowed, "where are you? Why don't you come back? I need . . ." He bit off the rest of his sentence. "Spider spit," he swore out loud. "Sticky, slimy, sloppy, spider spit!"

Furious, he jumped out from under the tree, only to sink knee-deep in mud. Complaining bitterly, he shook his paws free. "Maybe Poppy's coming now," he thought. "I'll meet her halfway. Make her hurry. Tell her to stop all this drivel about Ragweed.

Ragweed . . ." He growled. "I *hate* Ragweed."

He tore down the path he had seen Poppy take. As he went the rain came down harder. Water poured over his face. He felt like a decaying mushroom. "Stupid storm!" he shouted.

He peered down the path. There appeared to be nothing before him but water, mist, mud, and more mud. The porcupine shivered violently, making his quills rattle like a bag of old bones.

"Better go back to that tree and wait for her there," he decided. "It was a little drier there."

He started off the way he had come, only to stop abruptly.

"This isn't right," he growled with rage. Spinning around, he lumbered in another direction, trying to catch the scent of his own tracks. It had vanished. The rain had washed it away.

Lost, increasingly frustrated, Ereth galloped first this way, then that in search of the cottonwood tree. "Duck dapple!" he shouted up at the clouds. "Dry up!" But the rain continued to fall.

Utterly wretched, Ereth peered through the gloom until he saw a clump of trees that he thought

would protect him.

He ran forward.

Reaching the trees was easy enough. But *which* tree should he climb? Confounded by his own anger, he rushed from one to another. The first was too small. The second was too thin.

Seven trees later he found one to his liking. The bark was rough. The foliage was thick. Frantic, Ereth clawed past the first layer of branches, the second, and the third. "This'll do," he muttered, moving towards a particularly large branch.

He reached it and squatted down, trying to make as tight a ball of himself as possible. Even so, the rain pelted him.

"Stupid mouse . . ." he mumbled. "No, she's not stupid. She's mean. What kind of friend would leave me in all this muck? She's abandoned me. Left me. When I'm her real friend. Her only friend. But no, all she thinks is about Ragweed. Who's *dead!* As for me, she keeps telling me I'm old. *Old!*" He shouted. "I'm not old! Don't I take care of her, help her, love . . ."

He stopped. "Love . . ." he muttered. "I don't love Poppy. I hate Poppy!" he shouted. "I hate love!"

Bursting with rage, the porcupine scrambled down from his tree and began to gallop as fast as he could. Where he was running he had no idea, no more than he knew if the water dripping from his cheeks was rain or . . . something else.

II

Mr Canad Makes Some Plans

It was still raining. In the middle of the pond, Mr Canad used his webbed feet to propel himself swiftly across the water with strong, steady strokes. There was something mighty fine about swimming, enough to make one fit as a fiddle.

Now and again he lifted his head and let the pattering rain soak him even more. "Bless my teeth and smooth my tail," he murmured. "I do love water!" Then he thought hard as to how best to express his feelings in words that had a real impact. Though it took some hard thinking, he worked it out. "The whole thing is," he decided, "it should only rain if it rains a lot."

When Mr Canad said the phrase out loud, biting off the last T with his large orange teeth, he enjoyed it so much he repeated it to himself: "It should only rain if it rains a lot – a lot.

"I must use that," he told himself. "Perhaps

during the next company meeting. They would appreciate it. They would."

With his strong paws Mr Canad pulled himself onto the bank, gave himself a shake – sending water in all directions – then turned to survey what had been achieved by the beavers' work.

In the little valley through which the Brook flowed there had been, in Mr Canad's mind, a dull, dreary landscape, with little to behold but a piddling stream without power or grandeur. It had no depth. Its banks were wasteful in their simple, sloping nature. Why, the water itself had no texture or colour. One could see through it!

Limpid lily pads and useless bulrushes had marred its lazy surface. The animals who had wasted their time on the banks – mice, voles, otters and toads – were insignificant. As far as Mr Canad was concerned, it had been a place where nothing important ever had or would happen. An utter waste.

But now, how different the beavers had made it! Every day the pond was growing wider, deeper, grander. It had taken on the vibrant colour of mud. It was a home for hearty, busy beavers who worked day and night.

"This," Mr Canad said to himself with genuine pride, "is *progress*." The portly beaver felt so good about it, he spelled the word out letter by letter: "P-R-O-G-R-E-S-S!"

And yet, Mr Canad had to confess, he was not fully satisfied. No, he was not. What he and his company had created was — he had to admit it — merely a pond.

Mind, he told himself, there was nothing wrong with a *pond*. A beaver who built a good pond had every reason to be pleased with himself. Yet even the word *pond* suggested smallness, a compactness of size which might be good enough for some, but not for the likes of Caster P. Canad and Co! Not only could they do better, they *should* do better. As Mr Canad saw things, it was not a pond that was needed but a *lake*.

The beaver cast his keen engineer's eye over the little valley. To achieve a lake they needed to build another dam higher up.

As he surveyed the little valley, he noticed a boulder perched on a hill. A large boulder, it was embedded in an outcropping of earth and stone. Flowers and shrubs shaded it. As Mr Canad perceived

it, the boulder was doing *nothing* but sitting there. But it could be providing the perfect anchor for a new dam. An immense dam! With a dam at that spot, a large lake could be created. It would be his crowning achievement, a monument to himself. Indeed, what could be a better name than Lake Canad? Mr Canad liked sound of it so much he said it a few times.

Then he reminded himself, with some gleeful rubbing of back feet, that it was time to stop dreaming. Time to get down to the nitty gritty. To grasp the nettle. To get into the trenches. To show the flag. To hit the road running.

But even as he watched and planned he saw a mouse creep out from under the boulder and rush away.

Mr Canad knew what that meant: Mice were living under the boulder. As far as he knew, these mice were the only ones left around the brook. Most of the other creatures had departed. How pleasing to know there had been no resistance. Surely these last mice would quickly see the hopelessness of resisting the future. But what if they did not?

He could swat them away. Mere nothings that

they were, squashing the mice would be easy, though the thought made Mr Canad uncomfortable. He was no bully. He just wanted progress. He wanted the world to appreciate him for the good he was doing. What he needed to do was find a way to convince the mice to leave — of their own accord. It would make him feel good. Nothing was more important than to make good their slogan, "Progress Without Pain."

Mr Canad dived back into the pond and made his way to the main lodge. When he came within five feet of it, he dived and swam underwater until he found the entrance.

Mr Canad went to his plans — laid out on bark — and began to draw in detail. The boulder here. The large new dam there. The lake . . . everywhere.

Then he mused, "If I can make a lake, well, bless my teeth and smooth my tail, why not an *ocean?*"

The thought made Mr Canad grin broadly. Then he said, "It should only rain if it rains a lot. On me."

Then he gave himself over to finding a way to convince those last few mice that they should move away.

12

In the Nest

In Clover and Valerian's nest under the boulder there was nothing but despair. Poppy's news of Ragweed's death had devastated the family. The coming of the beavers, the damming of the Brook, the creation of the pond, their change of homes, all of that had been difficult to accept. But the family had shared the notion – spoken and unspoken – that Ragweed would return and somehow, some way, sort things out. Poppy's tragic news made it perfectly clear that no such thing would happen.

Everything was now worse.

In one corner of the nest sat a disconsolate Clover, staring off into nothing that anyone else could see. From time to time she let forth a profoundly deep sigh and shifted her bulk – as if gathering her last breath in her chest. Though her black eyes were dry, they held such a weight of wretched pain, it alarmed her own children.

When a child brushed by — it always seemed like an accident but it happened often — Clover reached out and touched it gently. Sometimes she stroked it. But there was little life or spirit to her paw.

As for Valerian, though he was just as heart-broken as Clover, he spent his time and energy trying to comfort the children. "Your mother will be fine," he kept telling them. "She's just very sad. And it *is* sad."

The children did notice that now and again Valerian wiped his cheeks with the back of his paw, or blew his nose so loudly it sounded like the honking of a goose heading south. "Summer colds are stupid," he kept saying. No one pointed out that he had no cold before Poppy's news.

Those children who remembered Ragweed best sniffled, wept in corners, or exchanged reminiscences, trying, with little success, to keep their grief private or to keep a brave face.

Then they got it into their heads that it was their parents who needed to be consoled most. Not knowing what to say, they did what they thought was the next best thing: They did whatever they were asked to do and some things that they were not asked as well

— did them so fast they almost tripped over themselves in their desire to please. So they were constantly cleaning up, sweeping the entry hall, minding the infants, preparing meals — anything they could think of that might soothe their parents. Someone was always sweeping, straightening up, or burping babies . . . The result was a continual low hubbub that got on everybody's nerves.

If two of the youngest mice got into a scuffle — they didn't quite grasp what had happened — it was their elder brothers and sisters who stepped in and stifled the discord.

"Please," they whispered. "Clover is very sad." Or, "Valerian is crying." This so alarmed the youngsters that they sniffled and whimpered and clung to their parents more than ever.

As for Poppy, she hardly knew what to do or say. No one asked her to do anything. No one asked her to leave. On the contrary, they had assured her that she should stay. She was stared at a lot, as one who had a particular connection to Ragweed and his awful death and thus seemed extraordinary. Still, no one inquired about *her* feelings, *her* life. She felt as useless

as an extra tail.

She did find time to take Thistle aside, and ask, "Was I wrong, but didn't I see another brother here? He had a notch in his right ear. He was standing way in the back, behind you all. He seems to have rushed away."

"You must mean Rye," Thistle replied.

"Rye," Poppy repeated, grateful that at least she now had a name for the one with whom she had danced. "Where . . . where do you think he went?" she asked, sensing that she was blushing a little.

Thistle cocked her head to one side and considered Poppy. Then, in a matter-of-fact way, she said, "Rye's always a little weird."

"*Weird*? Why? How?"

"He gets sort of dreamy. You know, he goes off a lot by himself."

"Why . . . why do you think he ran off — this time?" Poppy wanted to know, though she had a fairly good idea.

"He's very emotional," Thistle said. "He loved Ragweed, but he sort of didn't, if you know what I mean."

"I don't think I do."

"A younger brother," Thistle whispered, as if that explained it all. Then she added, "You see, Ragweed wasn't big enough to admit Rye was better than he was at some things. He was always giving Rye a hard time. And Rye, he was, well, you know, envious that his brother was everybody's favourite."

"Do you think . . . Rye . . . will come back?"

Thistle shrugged. "Yeah, sure."

Poppy tried to make herself useful by tending to the children. She was not very good at it. Besides, they were inclined to stare at her as if she were odd. Being a deer mouse she was smaller than they, and her fur was a different colour.

For her own part Poppy knew perfectly well she was stalling, doing little except waiting for Rye's return. At the same time, the thought of his coming back made her nervous. She wasn't exactly sure what she felt. What would she say to him?

Poppy's thoughts were interrupted when Clover asked Valerian to bring her close.

"I need to ask you a little more about Ragweed," she said to Poppy.

"I'll tell you anything I know," Poppy said.

Clover and Valerian asked Poppy many questions. How had she met Ragweed? Where was this Dimwood Forest she had come from? Who and what was her family? Did she and Ragweed, in fact, marry?

Poppy told them all that had happened. How she had grown up with her own family on a farm at the edge of Dimwood Forest. How she had met and fallen in love with Ragweed only to be right there when the owl – a Mr Ocax – had killed him. She told them then how she had defeated this Mr Ocax. Finally, she told them of her own desire to bring them the news of their son.

As she told her tale, she kept looking out of the corner of her eye for Rye. The last thing she wanted was for him to show up and hear what she was saying.

"We need you to know," Valerian said, when Poppy was done, "that even though you didn't marry Ragweed we'd like to think of you as our daughter."

"We really do," Clover agreed with a catch in her voice.

"This isn't much of a home," Valerian went on,

"but it's all we have. You're welcome to stay, too."

"Thank you," Poppy returned. "I'm truly touched." She reached up and took off Ragweed's earring. "I brought this back for you," she said. "It was his. I thought you should have it."

She held out the earring. The purple bead seemed to glow. The little chain sparkled.

"Did he give it to you?" Clover asked.

"In a way," Poppy said.

"Ah," Clover said softly. "He wasn't wearing one when he left home. It must have something to do with the life he had with you."

"I have no idea where he got it," Poppy told them. "He had it on when I met him."

"Any notion what he did from the time he left here to the time he met you?" Valerian asked.

Poppy shook her head. "He never really said. But he did talk about his home fondly."

Clover held the earring in the palm of her paw, as if it were something magical. With a sigh she offered it to Valerian, who contemplated it, too.

Then Valerian handed it back to Poppy. "I think you should keep it."

Poppy looked to Clover. Clover nodded her agreement.

After a moment's hesitation, Poppy took the earring and fixed it back on her ear. "I'll stay a little while."

But Poppy knew she was only staying so she could speak to Rye. What had happened with Ragweed, she told herself, was the past. It was done. Finished. Complete. She would remember the past. But she would not live it. Instead she would wait for Rye.

But Rye did not return. Though no one seemed to be concerned, Poppy began to wonder if he would ever come back. She began to suspect — and fear — he would not.

What Happened to Rye?

As Rye had listened to Poppy speak about Ragweed, he hardly knew what to think. He felt humiliated. Ragweed was always getting in his way. He had done so when he was alive. Now he was doing so even after he had died.

And yet . . .

From the moment he had begun his dance on the meadow with this graceful mouse — this one named Poppy — he had fallen in love with her. He hoped — and thought — she felt something of the same for him. But now that she had discovered that he was Ragweed's brother — and admitted she loved Ragweed! — surely there was no hope for *him*.

And yet . . .

He found himself thinking that perhaps, now that Ragweed had died, Poppy might turn to him.

And yet . . .

Rye felt deeply ashamed of himself. How self-

centred and selfish he was! Such horrible thoughts! How low! How bad! Poppy would never be able to see anything decent in *him*.

But the very next moment he thought, "I'm not a bad mouse! I'm not!"

It was with these thoughts that Rye raced from the nest. He did not go far. He could not outrun his feelings. More importantly, he did not want to go from this deer mouse, this Poppy.

He found himself at the edge of the beavers' pond. It was raining steadily, monotonously. The world looked the way he felt, grey and sodden. Moreover, except for him, everything seemed immense. He was nothing but a small, bad, useless mouse.

Crouching down, consumed by the sensation that the whole world despised him, Rye shivered with wet and cold.

"Is there any place in this wide world for such a wretch as I?" He asked himself. Simultaneously, he darted a look over his shoulder to see if, just possible, someone — he dared not say who — had followed him. When he saw that no one had, he was angry he'd even checked.

A mournful Rye gazed down at the pond. A mist was rising off the water as if it were smouldering. A few beavers were hard at work. Suddenly Rye saw that the pond was much higher than it had been before.

Anger swept through him. How he *hated* the beavers. Yet there they were, making the dam higher, even as misery rained down on his head. Had they no feelings? Would they never stop?

As he looked on, Rye began to have an idea. If he could find some way to put an end to what the beavers were doing, might not he in some way redeem himself? Surely, if he kept them from building the dam higher, or — better yet — forced them to move away, he would become a hero to his family. He and he alone would defeat them! Why, even Poppy might see him as different from Ragweed then!

Rye surveyed the pond. The beavers' main lodge was not far from the dam. He remembered his father telling him that the way the beavers got into the lodge was by swimming through an underwater passage. If he could get into the lodge, he might . . . Actually, Rye was not at all sure what he might do. He

supposed he would think of *something* once in the lodge. The main thing was to get there. Surely he could do that. Like all his brothers and sisters, he was a good swimmer.

Rye raced down to the edge of the pond.

The beavers' dam was built where the Brook had narrowed out a V in the land. The dam — made of twigs, branches and logs plastered over with mud — was some 20 feet across and three feet wide. By going out along the dam he would be that much closer to the lodge.

But when Rye reached one end of the dam, a beaver was working on it. He had brought up a heap of mud and dumped it, and was now using his tail to smooth it down.

Though impatient, Rye bided his time. One whack of the beavers' tail — not to mention what he could do with his teeth — and Rye would be crushed.

The beaver on the dam gave some final pats to the mud, surveyed his work, uttered a few grunts, moved ponderously towards the edge of the dam, then dived into the water and swam away.

Rye crawled out upon the dam, his way

impeded by the twigs and branches which were criss-crossed and bent in all directions. By the time he got near the lodge he was caked with mud and bits of leaves.

Not caring how he looked, Rye crept down as close to the water as possible. There he hesitated. Then an image of Poppy rose in his mind's eye. If he could succeed, he would be a hero. Holding his nose with one paw, Rye jumped into the water, tail first.

He landed with a splat, momentarily floundered, then righted himself. Shaking his eyes and whiskers free of water, he began to swim towards the lodge.

Three feet from the lodge, he paused and began to tread water. He had reached the most difficult part: the entrance.

Suddenly he realised he had no notion where — other than underwater — the entry hole might be. It could be on the side he was, or opposite. He would have to try his luck.

Filling his lungs with air, he let himself drop down and began to swim underwater.

It had been grey on the water's surface. It was

much darker below. Before him the lodge loomed like a shadowy lump. It sat upon the bottom of the pond and rose up, a huge dome. Enormous. Impenetrable.

Stroking steadily, Rye pushed on, a trail of tiny bubbles escaping from his clenched mouth. Gradually, he began to make out what appeared to be a dark hole. Was that the entryway?

Lungs close to bursting, Rye had to make a decision. If he guessed wrong, he would drown. "At least I tried," he told himself. "Farewell, Poppy," he murmured. "Farewell, love. Farewell, world!"

Kicking hard, paws madly stroking the water, he propelled himself into the hole. The moment he did so everything turned as dark as a night without a moon.

Rye was no longer trying to get into the lodge. He was struggling to save his life. His strokes were wild, his kicks frenzied.

Unable to endure any more, he shot up — and found air. Gasping for breath, he waved his paws feebly to keep afloat and slowly moved towards a ledge of slippery mud. Reaching it, he clawed his way up, falling back a few times, finally heaving himself up

on the slimy shelf. Eyes shut, he lay there, coughing and spitting water.

He opened his eyes.

He was in the lodge. A few more feet away sat an enormous beaver. The beaver was looking right at him.

"Well, bless my teeth and smooth my tail," Mr Canad said with a smile full of orange teeth. "Glad you came, pal. A stranger is just a friend you haven't met. Hey, and I mean that, sincerely."

14
Ereth

Ereth ran among the trees. Heart pounding, quills rattling, he tried every dodge he knew to escape — as if some great beast were pursuing him — though this beast was his own feelings. He climbed trees. He threw himself behind bushes. It made no difference. He still felt miserable. When he found an old hollow log, he plunged into it. There, surrounded by the stench of pulpy rot and mouldering fungus, he crouched down and stared out at the rain but found no relief. Never had he felt so miserable.

Gradually the storm subsided. The rain ceased. Water dripped. A grey mist, clinging to the earth, slithered through the dark trees like forbidden thoughts.

Ereth crawled out of the log and shook himself. "Take hold of yourself," he muttered.

He headed back to the ridge in search of the cottonwood tree he had climbed when Poppy had left

him. This time he found it. But when he reached it and discovered she was not there, all his desperation returned.

"Where is she?" he muttered. "Why did she leave me? What kind of friend is she, anyway? Doesn't she know I need her? She should be here helping me!"

With that Ereth wheeled about and trundled down the path he had seen Poppy take. As he came down off the crest of the ridge he saw no sign of Poppy, only the pond where beavers were hard at work.

Ereth stared balefully at the beavers. They seemed to be working nicely together. At least they were smiling at one another. "A family," he snarled with contempt. "A *happy* family.

"Crabgrass up their snoots," Ereth snapped. "I'm going back to Dimwood Forest." With that he turned, galloped up the hill, and plunged among the trees again, quickly passing through them. The next moment he burst into an open area. Before him lay a sunken meadow filled with berry brambles and flowering vines.

Paying no particular mind to where he was

going, Ereth hurled himself into the most clotted part of the thicket.

It was a wild jumble, with plants growing so closely together he had to push and shove his way through the tangle of bushes. He was close to the middle when he was forced to stop. He could not move. His quills, caught in brambles and vines, held him fast. He was stuck.

Though he could not move, an exhausted Ereth was glad for the rest, glad for the quiet, glad he could not go anywhere.

"I'll stay here forever," he sighed. "Till I die. It's better that way. And it won't be long, either. Poppy was right. I'm old. Very old."

He closed his eyes and thought of home. He thought of Poppy. Momentarily, his anger rekindled. Then, grudgingly, he admitted to himself that it was he who had told her to go off by herself. Maybe her leaving him was — a little bit — his fault.

He sighed. The more he thought about her, the more he missed her. She was always so good-natured. Kind. And brave. His best friend. Perhaps he should find a way to tell her that. Someday.

With a shake of his head, he muttered, "Pickle piffle," and decided it would be better not to tell her anything. It wouldn't do. She might make fun of him. Tease him. Call him that horrid word, *old*, again. Still, he might find her a seed . . . or two. He could leave them where she might find them. As if by accident. Nothing more than that. If a porcupine didn't remain prickly what could he be? *Nothing.*

Ereth settled down, relieved that it was impossible for him to do anything but stay stuck. It was better that way. Much better. He didn't have to think. Or feel . . . anything. He would just die. That, he thought, will show her!

15

Rye in the Lodge

When Rye had swum into the lodge he was too exhausted to offer any resistance to Mr Canad. And by the time he did recover his strength, it was too late. The beaver had quickly constructed a cage of maple twigs and hard-packed mud, shovelled the exhausted mouse into it with his tail, then sealed the whole thing up. Rye was a prisoner.

"Well now, pal," Mr Canad said with his usual heartiness, "the name is Caster P. Canad. Feel free to call me Cas. What's your name?"

Rye, wretched, gazed mournfully up at the large beaver from behind the bars of his cage. "Rye," he said.

"Absolutely delighted to meet you, pal," Mr Canad enthused with a big grin. "Where do you live?"

"I used to live by the side of the Brook."

"Moved away, did you?"

Rye's eyes filled with angry tears. "You forced us to."

"Me? *Force* you? Not me. You could have stayed."

"We would have drowned."

"Hey, pal, that was your choice. Life isn't fair. No one promised you a rose garden. Take the good with the bad. The sweet with the sour. It all works out in the end." Mr Canad offered another toothy smile.

"Okay," he went on, "let's cut to the chase. What made you come here?"

Rye, glowering, looked up at the enormous beaver. "To get rid of you."

"Hey, pal, you are the violent type, aren't you? You make me nervous." The beaver grinned. "Where do you live now?"

"Up by a boulder."

"A boulder? That a fact? Exactly where?"

"On the ridge. Overlooking the pond."

Mr Canad's heart fluttered. "Not, by any chance, that boulder right on the ridge that's got a bunch of plants growing around it?"

"Yes," Rye answered.

"Well, bless my teeth and smooth my tail!" Mr Canad glowed. "There's a piece of luck. Do you live alone?"

"With my whole family."

"Your *whole* family!" the beaver said. "Better and better. Family man myself. I love families. This *is* a good day."

Mr Canad was thinking furiously: Here is a representative of that last mouse family. A violent type. He breaks in here. Okay. I'll use him to persuade them to move on their own. And it would keep my reputation for Progress Without Pain.

"Why is it a good day?" Rye demanded, becoming alarmed. "What are you going to do to my family?"

"Hey, pal," Mr Canad cried. "Nothing to worry about. I haven't the slightest intention of harming you or your family. You'll be as right as rain. All tip-top. As the day is long. I'm as straight as a ruler."

Rye, staring furiously at the large beaver, said, "How can you say that when you've ruined everything?"

"Not *everything*, pal," Mr Canad chortled. "The sun still shines, doesn't it? The moon glows? Admit it. Life goes on. We just changed a few things. Pal, when

you stop looking at things selfishly — when you see the big picture — you're going to have to agree that Caster P. Canad tells it like it is.

"But for now you're going to have to excuse me while I fetch my family. We need to have a meeting to decide what to do with you." With that Mr Canad plunged off the ledge and swam out of the lodge by way of the entry hole.

Alone and depressed, Rye sat within the cage and clutched the twig bars listlessly. He was much angrier at himself than he was at Mr Canad. Not only had he failed to do what he had set out to do, he was sure his capture would be hard for his parents. As for Poppy, when *she* learned what he'd done, Rye had little doubt she'd think him a fool. And she'd be right. He *was* a fool.

For a while Rye tried to break the bars of his cage. He rattled them. He chewed them. But they were made of maple wood, and were too hard to cut quickly. Then he attempted digging about in the mud that held the twigs to see if that might lead to escape. That, too, proved a failure. Mr Canad had packed it down hard. Rye had no choice but to wait and see

what the beavers did with him.

He did not have long to wait. Members of the Canad family came into the lodge and examined him.

"Isn't he nasty?" one said.

"What a little, puny fellow he is," another said.

"I wonder what he expected to do to us," a third said with a giggle. "He's so weak!"

Rye, sulking, shrank into a corner of his cage.

Mr Canad, standing next to the cage, called his company to order.

"Once in a blue moon," he began, "beavers find themselves placed to do great things. But if big things are to be done, Caster P. Canad and Co. will be the one to do them."

"Hear, hear!" murmured one of the beavers.

"Way to go, Cas," said another.

"All right, then," Mr Canad continued. "We're ready to move forward and expand Canad's Happy Homes into something grander. How about a lake?"

"Wow!"

"Fantastic!"

"Too cool!"

Beaming, Mr Canad went on. "'Course, we'll

call it Lake Canad. Here are the plans." He gestured toward the drawing on the bark.

"To make this lake, we'll need to put in a dam over by this boulder here. Turns out there's a mouse family living under that same boulder. Okay, we could just go ahead and build. They would be flooded out.

"But that's not our way, is it? Canad and Co. has a reputation for being sensitive. It's important to keep that notion afloat. We need those mice to leave on their own."

There was some beating of tails.

"Okay. How are we going to persuade these mice to move? No problem. Luck comes to those who work hard. Genius is 90 percent perspiration, ten percent inspiration. Good thing I've got the whole one hundred percent. Now, we have a visitor. A fine young mouse." Mr Canad rapped on the cage. "Goes by the name of Rye. Rye and his family live right under the boulder we've got the old eye on."

"Keep going, Cas," one of the beavers called out, beating his tail on the ground.

"Okay, I'm going to mosey on up and have a chat with these mice. Tell them that my pal here is . . .

visiting . . . with us. And," Mr Canad added with a toothy smile, "if they want to see him again, they'd better move on. Hey!" he said, grinning, "you know what they say: Walk softly but carry a big stick in your mouth."

"You said you wouldn't hurt me!" Rye cried out.

"Easy does it, pal. Not saying I *am* going to hurt you. Remember, you broke in here. You're the violent one. I'll just warn your folks that unless they make amends by moving away, they won't ever see you again. Get it? It's their free choice. And I mean that, sincerely."

As his family applauded wildly, Mr Canad grinned.

16
Poppy Hears Some News

It was quiet in the mouse nest. In one corner Clover tended to her three youngest children. Poppy was in another corner with the older ones, including Thistle and Curleydock, telling stories about Dimwood Forest. Valerian was in the middle of the room, surrounded by children, giving them seed lessons.

"Now this kind," he was saying, holding up a plump sunflower seed, "is particularly nourishing. And tasty. You never can go wrong with sunflower seeds. Rye and I know a particularly fine place to find them." He paused and looked around. "Hey, where is Rye?"

When none of the youngsters gave an answer, Valerian called out, "Anyone know where Rye is?"

Hearing the name, Poppy pricked up her ears and looked around, but said nothing. It was Thistle who called, "He went out."

"Do you know where?"

"No."

Valerian shrugged and resumed his lesson.

Poppy leaned over toward Thistle and whispered, "Do you think Rye will come back soon?"

"With Rye you never know. Poppy, please tell us some more about your forest." Thistle had grown very fond of Poppy.

Poppy talked but soon broke off. She could not concentrate. Thoughts of Rye crowded her mind. Besides, the warm, close underground air and the crowded conditions were beginning to bother her. "I think I need some fresh air," she announced.

Promising to return quickly, she made her way to the ground surface. The storm was over. Though dusk had fallen, the air had turned muggy. Poppy sat back against the boulder and looked out.

To the west a lush band of pink and purple layered the sky. Eastward a pale yellow moon had begun its climb. Fireflies punctuated the growing darkness with sparks of light, as if night itself had a bright pulse.

As Poppy remained sitting quietly, looking at nothing in particular, she thought of Ereth with a

pang. She had not returned to him. Then she reminded herself how unusually grumpy he'd been. She thought, too, of his repeated statements about his preference for being alone. Poppy decided she'd stay at the mouse nest for the night. Ereth could wait.

Putting her friend out of her mind, Poppy was glad to give herself over to thoughts of Rye. She wondered where he had gone. She had little doubt as to why he'd left the nest: It was her words about Ragweed, how she had loved him and had all but married him. The distress upon Rye's face as she told the tale was as easy to see as the sun in a cloudless sky.

And yet, Poppy mused, Ragweed *was* no more. To speculate about what might have been was useless. Poppy reminded herself that she had taken this trip as a way of bringing an end to that part of her life. That had been achieved. Even as she gently touched Ragweed's earring, aware how restless she was to start life anew.

In fact, she thought with a bolt of boldness, she knew she wanted to share the rest of her life with Rye.

Sighing, Poppy looked down towards the pond.

Even as she did, she saw a beaver haul himself out of the water, give himself a shake — sending a spray of water in all directions — then proceed to waddle clumsily uphill, right in her direction.

Poppy grew alarmed. She had never met a beaver before. Having heard angry accounts about them from the mice, she was not inclined to like them. She could see that, compared to her, they were enormous. Moreover, the approaching beaver's huge buck teeth — brilliant orange in colour — seemed positively fierce.

Dimly she recalled that beavers and mice were related, second cousins twice removed, or something like that. At the moment she didn't *feel* related, only very small.

The beaver drew near. He had a distinct musky smell.

Poppy, not sure what to do, glanced around to make sure that, just in case the beaver meant her harm, she wasn't trapped.

When they were about four feet apart, the beaver halted.

"How you doing, sweetheart? The name is

Caster P. Canad. All my friends call me Cas. As the philosopher said, a stranger is just a friend you haven't met. What's your name?"

"Poppy."

"Nice, sweetheart, very nice. You're just the one I wanted to talk to."

"*Me?*" Poppy said.

"You live under that boulder you're sitting against, don't you?"

"Well, not really," Poppy started to explain. "I've only just — "

"Hey, save your breath, sweetheart," Mr Canad interrupted. "I know all about it. You used to live somewhere else, and you've come up here recently."

"Actually . . ." Poppy tried to interject.

"Now, unless I'm holding the stick by the wrong end — and I rarely do — there's a mouse by the name of Rye who lives here, too. Did I hit the nail on the head?"

Poppy started. "Rye? Yes, he does live here."

"Good. I like coming to the point. I play hard-ball and call a spade a spade."

"Is something . . . the matter with Rye?" Poppy

stammered.

"Rye? The kid's as fit as a fiddle. Right as the rain. A-I okay," Mr. Canad assured her. "Except he broke into our lodge . . . "

"Broke in!"

"Hey, I'm giving it to you straight. You heard me right. He broke in where he had no business breaking in. I mean, a beaver's lodge is his castle. That Rye is head over heels in trouble."

"Trouble!" Poppy cried, unable to do more than echo what she was hearing. "What kind?"

"Off the cuff, shooting from the hip, taking the fast lane, I'd have to say Rye is violent. But don't worry, he's perfectly safe in a cage I built in my main lodge." He pointed to one of the mounds in the pond. "Right there."

"But . . . that's awful!" said Poppy, staring at the lodge.

"You took the words right out of my mouth. He shouldn't have done it," Mr Canad said. "Now, sweetheart, I'm talking on the up and up. We'd like to build a dam right here on this spot. Expand Canad's Happy Homes. Anchor it to that boulder. To make a

long story short, it would be better for everybody if you all moved. Do it in two shakes of a beaver's tail — with no fuss — and you'll see Rye again, no worse for wear."

"But . . . "

"'Course, if you don't move . . . "

"Then what?" Poppy cried.

"Look here, sweetheart, let's just say, I don't want to beat around the bush. It's a matter of life or death. The choice is all yours. This is a free country."

"But what if . . . we don't move?" Poppy cried.

"Well, sweetheart, I'll be honest with you: I hope that doesn't happen. Because, if you don't go, I'm afraid your pal will have met his Waterloo, sink or swim. Because your new home will be flooded, too. Some of your youngsters might drown. Naturally, that would upset my family so much — filled to the brim with anger, you know — I can't say *what* they might do to Rye. Hope I'm not boring you, but the decision is yours. Remember, we don't want to force anything on you.

"Anyway, nice talking with you, sweetheart. And have a nice day. I mean that, sincerely."

With that Mr Canad turned and began to waddle back down toward the pond.

Poppy, finding it hard to take in all she had heard, stared after him. Her first reaction was to go racing after the beaver, tell him what she thought of him, and make him release Rye instantly. But Mr Canad, as if knowing what Poppy was thinking, gave a great slap of his broad tail, sending out a resounding thump that shook the earth.

So instead Poppy remained where she was, watching the beaver go into the pond and swim off. Only then did she race down the entryway to Clover and Valerian's nest.

17

To Help Rye

"I've found out where Rye is!" Poppy shouted as she burst into the nest. "The beavers in the pond have caught him. They told me they won't let him go — or worse — unless you all move from this nest!"

The announcement brought stunned silence. It was followed by an eruption of squeaking, squealing, and talking. Clover put paws to either side of her head and cried, "It's too much!"

Valerian muttered, "I don't think I can take any more. No, I don't think I can." This seemed to give permission for the younger children to go out of control.

They raced around in circles, shouting, "It's too much. It's too much." Older children huddled in a corner and kept saying such things as, "This is so awful."

The chaos continued until Valerian, standing tall, cried, "Quiet, please."

The nest stilled.

"Poppy," Valerian said, "how do you know about this?"

Poppy repeated her conversation with Mr Canad, concluding with the beaver's threat that if the mice did not move, Rye would remain a captive. "Or, they might do worse," she said.

Clover opened her black eyes wide. "What do you mean . . . *worse?*" she asked.

"I think the beaver was threatening to . . . harm Rye."

"Now why," Valerian cried with exasperation, "did the boy have to go off and do such a thing?"

"I bet," Thistle injected boldly, "he just wanted to show everybody he was as good as Ragweed, that's why."

Thistle's comment made Poppy look down at her toes.

"That's great," Valerian exclaimed with a rare show of anger. "If that's what he intended then he's made things worse for himself *and* us."

Valerian's words threw the nest into another uproar. Everyone was talking at once and to no

particular purpose.

Clover's small, shrill voice rose above the clamour. "My dear family," she cried, "we can't take this kind of life any more. We need to find peace. I think we'd better move out of this area entirely and start over again. Let the beavers have the Brook."

Poppy hardly knew what to say, other than to feel that in some way she was responsible for what had happened. "But," she offered timidly, "isn't there *anything* we can . . . do?"

"*Do?*" Valerian returned, eyes full of anguish. "Poppy, I tried to compromise with them. They would have none of it. Clover's right. If we're to preserve this family, we've little choice."

"I'm sorry," Poppy murmured.

"Miss Poppy," Clover said, her voice shrill with tenseness, "you've been kind enough to come here and bring us the sad news about Ragweed. Rye is our problem. Not yours. You must let us handle things our own way."

"But Clover," Poppy replied as gently as she could, "I'm not sure that even if you do leave they'll let Rye go."

"But you said that Mr Canad promised he'd release Rye when we move," Clover cried. "What choice do we have but to trust them?"

"Clover is right," Valerian agreed. "It's the family we need to protect. There's little more to be said."

With that the mice began to scurry about, putting their possessions in order. It did not take long for Poppy to realise how much in the way, how much of an outsider, she was. Mortified, but not wishing to intrude any more than she already had, she crept from the nest.

Night had come. The moon's reflection lay upon the pond's surface like a tarnished spot of gold. Poppy could make out the islands and lodge tops, surrounded by dark water.

She thought about Rye. Just to think of him languishing in the beaver's lodge gave *her* pain. And longing. She sighed out loud.

"Don't worry," came a voice right behind her. "It's not your fault."

Poppy turned. It was Thistle. "You shouldn't take it personally," Thistle went on. "Our family has

been having a lousy summer."

"I know."

The two mice sat silently side by side.

"But I bet," Thistle said after a while, "I know why Rye did it."

"Do you?" Poppy said with some hesitation. "Why?"

"Poppy," Thistle asked shyly, "did you know Rye before you came here?"

"A little. How did you know?"

"Well . . ." Thistle said, too bashful to face Poppy directly, "it was when you were talking about Ragweed. When you first came. I noticed the way you two looked at each other. Rye acted as if he was going to die. You didn't look so great, either."

Poppy turned towards the pond and gazed at the big lodge. "Then it *is* my fault he's where he is," she said.

"Poppy . . . ?" Thistle said.

"What?"

"You didn't make Rye do it. He went on his own. He's not your responsibility. Don't do anything weird."

"I won't," Poppy replied.

"You all right?" Thistle asked, touching Poppy gently.

"Well, yes," Poppy replied. "I just need to be alone."

"Okay," the young mouse said, and she slipped back down into the nest.

Left to herself, Poppy allowed the darkness to give her solace. Without thinking about what she was doing, she meandered down to the pond.

"If only I could tell Rye that . . ." she paused. With a jolt, Poppy recalled that she had yet to have so much as *one* conversation with the mouse. And yet, and yet, she seemed to have had so many! It was so — extraordinary!

Poppy reminded herself that she didn't *need* to be with Rye. After all, she had spent her whole life — six months — without him. Yet she *wanted* to be with him. It was hard to sort out the difference.

When she reached the water's edge, Poppy gazed out at the beaver lodges, trying to recall in exactly which one Mr Canad had said Rye was being held. When she was sure she had located the right one she just stared

at it. Knowing she was a bit closer to Rye gave her comfort. She wished she were a good swimmer.

She meandered along the shore of the pond, looking for nothing in particular but hoping some idea would come. When she came upon a splinter of wood she picked it up and balanced it in her paws. "Make a good paddle," she mused.

The moment she had *that* thought, she knew exactly what she was looking for: a piece of wood to use as a raft. With it she could float over the pond and to Rye — somehow.

Clutching the would-be-paddle tightly, Poppy began a search. Near the stump of a chewed-down tree she found a thin, wide chip of wood. A raft.

Pushing and pulling, Poppy worked the wood chip to the water's edge, then set it afloat. The chip rode the water easily. Poppy leapt aboard. The chip wobbled but soon steadied itself. She was afloat.

18
To the Lodge

Using her wood splinter as a paddle, Poppy pushed off from the shore. The raft lurched erratically until she found a way to balance it. Then, from a kneeling position, she dipped the paddle into the dark waters and began to propel herself across the pond.

Repetitious cricket sounds tickled the air. From somewhere a fox barked. A night bird called. A frog croaked. Above, the spread of stars made Poppy think of a field of bright, scattered seeds. The moon seemed to be as adrift as she.

She gazed around, trying to get her bearings, trying to recall where the main lodge was. From the middle of the pond everything seemed different.

The moonlight did allow her to make out the humps of lodges as well as islands. They seemed all alike now. She had no idea which way to go.

Poppy paddled some more, moving farther over the pond. Knowing she had to land somewhere, she chose at random, and headed for one of the islands.

From out of the darkness she heard a splash. Coming unexpectedly, it made her jump. The next moment her raft began to rock wildly. Only by holding on tightly did she manage to keep from tumbling off.

When the waters calmed she strained to look through the darkness to determine what had caused the sound. She saw nothing. What if it were a beaver, Poppy wondered. Would it see her?

Dimly, she made out an island to her left. Its small size drew her. It would be easy to search. But after Poppy took a few more strokes, the little island seemed to have moved. Not quite believing what her eyes were telling her, Poppy stared hard. Sure enough, even as she looked, the island shifted again.

She gave a few more tentative paddle strokes. Suddenly the island moved and . . . raised its head. Poppy gasped. It was a beaver. She had almost paddled right into it.

Then to her right, there was another swell of water and a second beaver broke the pond's surface. Poppy was between them. It was the darkness that hid her.

"That you, Judy?" asked the newcomer.

"It's me," grunted the first. "Who's that?"

"Me. Joe."

"What you doing?"

"Taking a swim to cool off, the lodge is hot."

"Yeah. Hard to sleep. Hey, did you see that mouse?" Judy asked.

"The one Cas caught?" said the beaver named Joe. "I was sleeping right next to his cage. What about him?"

"What a pain," Judy said.

"If it were up to me, I'd just give him a swat with the old tail."

"Hey, you know Cas. Progress Without Pain."

"Right, sure," Joe said. "I'm going back."

"Okay."

"See you."

The beaver named Joe swam off. Poppy paddled after him as hard as she could.

Abruptly he dived beneath the water. Poppy waited and watched for him to resurface. When he didn't, she understood what had happened: the beaver must have gone into the lodge through an underwater passage.

She scrutinised the area. Sure enough, a large mound stuck out of the water nearby. She paddled until she bumped against it, then deftly leapt from her raft to the lodge. She made a grab for it, but the wood chip had already floated out of reach.

Resigned to being where she was, Poppy took a careful look around. The lodge was a mass of sticks, twigs, logs, leaves and vines, tightly woven together and cemented with mud. It made her think of an upside-down bird's nest.

Somewhere, inside, was Rye.

Her sense of urgency renewed, Poppy returned to the water's edge and wondered if she had the courage to swim down and find the lodge's entryway. When she reminded herself what a bad swimmer she was, she began to crawl about the lodge. She had to find a way to get in.

It was at the top of the lodge, while prying and poking amid the mud and sticks, that she discovered a hole. When she put her nose over it, she was certain she detected a flow of air — and the distinct smell of beaver — or at least of Mr Canad. A vent hole, perhaps.

Upon examining the hole closely, she found it was big enough for her to crawl through. Perhaps it could lead her inside. Nervous, she crept in, head first. The hole was pitch black and slimy, with a sickening stench of rotting mud. It was hard to hold on.

After going down a few inches she paused. How long is this hole? she asked herself. Will I be able to get out fast if I have to? What's going to be at the end of it? Do I really want to do this? She answered herself in one word: *Rye.* She had to get to Rye.

She went on. To keep from falling, she pressed her paws tightly against the slippery sides. Down she went. It seemed endless.

As it happened, she was concentrating so hard, she came to the end of the hole without realising she'd reached it. Catching herself just in time, she peered down into the lodge.

Such light as there was came from the occasional flashing glow of fireflies. At first Poppy thought she was looking at nothing but lumpy earth. Only gradually did she see that right below her was a room full of sleeping beavers. She gasped. There were so many! Some lay on their backs. Chins up, their

teeth seemed to glow like burning embers. Some beavers were flopped over others. Others lay on their bellies, tails occasionally flipping and flapping like loose flags. In their restless sleep they kept shifting about, moaning, grunting, and growling. It was as if a large mass of mud had come seethingly alive.

From her high perch Poppy searched about for the cage Mr Canad had spoken of, the one in which Rye was being held. She found it tucked away in a corner. She even thought she saw Rye, curled up in a ball, fast asleep.

How was she going to get down to him? She dared not jump. If she did, she'd land right in the midst of the beavers. That was a risk she did not want to take. Then she remembered something she'd seen on the lodge roof: vines. Perhaps she could lower herself down. But she'd have to work fast, before the beavers awoke.

Poppy clawed her way back to the lodge roof and searched for a vine. When she found two twisted about a stick she took the longest. Working fast, she tied one end of the vine to a stick, and taking its free end in her mouth, she crept back down the hole.

When she reached the end again she lowered the vine. It dangled free. But it was impossible to see exactly how far down the vine went. Was it too far or not far enough?

Poppy could not tell.

Why was she risking her life this way? she asked herself. The same answer came as before: *Rye.*

Taking a deep breath — her heart was beating madly — she grasped the vine tightly with her front paws, wrapped her rear legs and tail about it too, and headed down the vine, headfirst.

She reached the end. It was too short. She was dangling some 12 inches over the beavers. To go any farther she would have to drop — and land on a beaver's nose. The thought of it gave Poppy the shudders.

As she tried to make up her mind what to do, Poppy's shoulders began to ache painfully. She had to either let go or go back up. She looked up. The vent hole seemed a very long way up. She looked down. The beavers seemed enormous and powerful. What would they do to her if she dropped on them?

More and more nervous, her palms grew sweaty. She shifted her grip. The shifting made the

vine sway slightly. She tried to stop it but the swinging only increased. Suddenly she had an idea.

Carefully she turned about. Now she held the vine just with her paws. Her legs and tail dangled. Poppy began to pump her rear legs hard. It made the vine sway even more. Back and forth she swung until she was moving in a great arc — like a pendulum. With every swing her heart thumped.

When Poppy reached the highest point of arc — nearest to Rye — she let go. Out she sailed through the air, right over the sleeping beavers, until she landed with a *plop* in soft mud close to Rye's cage.

There she lay, panting, heart hammering, trying to recover her breath. Had she really done it? Almost afraid to look, she lifted her head. When she saw that she was beyond the beavers she took a deep sigh of relief. She turned towards the cage. There was nothing between her and it. The way was clear. Silently she crept forward and peered inside.

A firefly flashed. She saw Rye. He was curled up in a ball, fast asleep.

Poppy tried to reach through the bars to touch him. He was too far away.

"Rye!" she called softly. "Rye!"

Rye lifted a sleepy head and peered through the dark. It was by the light of a glowing firefly that he saw Poppy's face. Astonished, he squinted, unsure if what he was seeing was a dream or real.

But when Poppy said, "Oh, Rye, how glad I am to see *you!*" he knew she was the most real creature he had ever seen.

19
Poppy and Rye

Poppy and Rye gazed at one another by the light of firefly flashes.

He was quite sure he was looking at the most beautiful whiskers and pink nose he had ever seen upon any mouse with whom he was acquainted.

Poppy was sure Rye's face, covered as it was with delicate orange fur, was extraordinarily noble. What's more, he had altogether splendid ears, and the small notch in the right ear only added character.

"What," Rye said in a choked whisper, "are you doing here?"

"I came to see if you were all right."

"But . . . why?"

"Because . . . you . . . dance beautifully," Poppy replied, though it made her whiskers tremble to say it.

"Thank you. And . . . you dance as if . . . as if there were moonbeams in your toes!"

"And Rye . . . "

"What?"

"I did love Ragweed," Poppy said. "I'll never pretend I didn't. But he's . . . gone."

Rye hung his head. "I know."

"And Rye . . . you need to know. I never danced with him."

Rye looked up. His whiskers shook. "Poppy, you are the most kind, the most unselfish of mice," he whispered. "In fact, you are altogether *splendid!*"

For a moment neither spoke.

Then Poppy said, "Rye, why did you come here?"

"I wanted to do something about the beavers. To get rid of them. Somehow. Except . . . I didn't have a plan. The truth is . . . Poppy . . . I wanted to prove myself to . . . you. They caught me before I could do anything."

"Mr Canad told me you were being held captive," Poppy said. "He said if your family didn't move, he would keep you. Forever."

"Forever," Rye repeated dramatically. "But Poppy, it will have been worth it."

"Why?"

"Because . . . you came."

"But don't you want to get out?" Poppy asked.

"I'd like to, but I think I've made things much worse."

Poppy reached her paw through the bars and touched Rye's shoulder. "That you even tried seems brave to me," she said.

"Do you truly think so?"

"Yes. Just . . . maybe . . . well, too bold."

Rye took hold of Poppy's paw – which was resting on his shoulder – and kissed it. "What you said means more . . . more . . . than a life's supply of sunflower seeds," he murmured.

They looked at one another.

Then Rye said, "How did you get in here?"

"There's a hole in the roof. I crawled down a vine."

"You *are* amazing," he said.

Poppy blushed with pleasure.

Rye became alarmed. "But how are you going to get out?" he asked.

Poppy was about to say, "The same way," but even as she had the thought, she realised it would be

impossible for her to use the vine. It was dangling too high over the beavers for her to reach. "I'm not sure."

Rye said, "I swam in. Through an underwater tunnel. The way the beavers do. It's not too bad. You could go that way."

"I don't swim very well."

"Oh."

"Don't worry. I'll think of something."

Neither mouse spoke. Instead they looked at one another by the glow of the fireflies.

"Rye," Poppy said, suddenly becoming more brusque as she felt the urgency to leave, "have you tried chewing through these bars?"

"They're too tough."

Poppy tried for herself. She gave up quickly. "I see what you mean."

"I'm afraid," Rye said, "I really am going to stay here forever . . . I suppose I'll die of old age and . . . regret."

"Rye . . . "

"What?"

"Please, I know the bars are tough, but keep chewing on them. I'll find a way back to your family

nest. They need to know you're all right. And maybe if I get a longer vine, one that reaches the ground, we could get you out that way."

"Do . . . do you think so?"

"Maybe." She started to back away.

Rye, clinging to the twig bars called, "Poppy!"

"What?"

"I'm deeply moved that you came. But . . . maybe you shouldn't return. I don't want you to risk your life . . . for me."

"But Rye . . ." she said, taking a few more steps toward the cage.

"What?"

"I would . . . I would like to dance again."

"Oh, Poppy," Rye cried out. "So would I! With you!"

"*Shhh!*" Poppy cautioned as she backed away. Unable to take her eyes from Rye, she stumbled over a sleeping beaver's tail.

She stood still. Rye, looking on, was horrified. For a long moment, they dared not move. Finally, the beaver rolled away then settled down, never having awakened.

Poppy crept over to the far wall. The way was muddy. By pressing up against the wall she was able to skirt a large, sleeping beaver and come around to the edge of the water gate.

Once there she gazed into the murky water apprehensively, then looked around to see if there was any way to get up to the vine. It was impossible. She had no choice. Reluctantly she turned back to the water. The prospect of swimming caused her so much dread, she felt compelled to give herself a reassuring hug. Taking a deep breath, she jumped, hitting the water with a splash.

Across the lodge Mr Canad sat up and looked around. He had heard something. Taking a few sniffs, he detected a vague and unusual smell. He peered about but saw nothing except bulky beavers sleeping. All seemed perfectly normal. And yet — what was it he had heard?

He sniffed again. That time he detected the faint smell of . . . *mouse*! Could the mouse have escaped?

"Better safe than sorry," Mr Canad allowed and got up. Approaching Rye's cage, he peered through the

gloom. At first he couldn't see Rye, but by listening intently, he heard the sound of chewing.

He crept closer to the cage. Rye was at the back of the cage, gnawing on a bar.

Mr Canad broke into a toothy smile. "Well, bless my teeth and smooth my tail," he snorted. "You're trying to be a beaver!"

Rye, taken by surprise, looked up.

"Don't think you should try chewing your way out, pal," Mr Canad said. "We need you to stay."

Glowering, Rye said nothing.

"Just back away from those bars, pal. You don't want to cross over the line and force my paw. If I do something bad, it'll be your own fault."

Rye stepped away.

"Way to go, pal. Now, look," Mr Canad went on to say, "I think I'll catch my Z's here. For the next few days, anyway. Don't want to lock the barn door after the horses are gone."

Mr Canad was about to settle himself when he recalled the noise that had woken him. If this mouse was here, what was *that* sound? Now that he thought about it . . . could it have been a . . . splash?

He sat up and counted his beavers. All present and accounted for.

He did an inspection around the cage area. In the mud were Poppy's prints.

"You've had a visitor!" the beaver suddenly exclaimed. "Haven't you?"

"Leave me alone!" Rye cried.

"Never mind," said Mr Canad. "One picture is worth a thousand words. One of your pals was here."

The beaver scrutinised the lodge intently. By a firefly flash he caught sight of the vine dangling from the lodge roof. Mr Canad grunted. "The vent hole."

He lumbered across the lodge floor and ripped the vine down. "Better plaster some mud over that hole," he thought. "I can always make some other holes – and hide them. Don't want any mice in the ointment."

20

Poppy

The coldness of the water — its utter darkness — shocked Poppy. Not only did she not move, she didn't know which way *to* move. Instead, she sank, spiralling down. Unless she did something quickly, she would drown.

She began to thrash wildly. Her frenzy got her nowhere. Still sinking, she tried to think herself into calmness, succeeding just enough to move her legs and arms in unison. Within moments she bumped against some twigs. She grabbed hold.

Her breath was giving out. Letting go of the twigs, she clawed frantically upward and forward, hoping she was clear of the lodge.

Like a cork popping from a bottle, Poppy burst upon the pond's surface. Splashing frantically, she gulped great drafts of air into her hungry lungs.

She looked up. Through water-logged eyes she saw blurry bits of light. At first she thought they were

fireflies. Then she realised she was seeing stars. Never before had stars seemed so beautiful. She was out of the lodge.

Now, however, she had to get to the shore. She doubted her ability to swim. Flailing, she tried to make some sense of where she was. She did see what appeared to be other lodges. She wanted to avoid them.

As she floundered, she felt a bump on her head. Ready to defend herself, she whirled. It was only a chip of wood. Eagerly, she held on. It kept her afloat.

Clinging to the chip, Poppy kicked vigorously. She began to move forward.

Her progress was slow. Her energy was ebbing. Now and again she rested her head on the wood chip. She forced herself to think of Rye, caged in the beaver's lodge. "At least I'm free," she chided herself and resumed kicking.

Twenty minutes later she came to a lurching halt. In a daze she looked up. Land rose before her. She had reached the shore.

A weary Poppy stumbled out of the water. Once on land she gave herself a vigorous shake,

ridding herself of what felt like a ton of water. Much lighter, she lay down on the ground and cradled her head in her paws. Only then did she allow herself to feel the full depth of her exhaustion. Never again, she vowed, would she go into water.

As she lay there she thought of the imprisoned Rye and reviewed her plan. She would get another vine — longer than the one she had just used — and drop it down the vent hole. She would go down again, and somehow get Rye out of the cage. Then the two of them would climb out. There was no other way, and she wanted it to happen quickly.

Poppy hurried up the hill.

By the time she reached the boulder, the pink glow of sunlight had begun to bloom upon the eastern horizon. Birds began to twitter madly. It was as if a night of silence had been too much to bear, and there was a desperate need to make up for lost time.

She considered the pond. As Poppy watched, a swarm of beavers emerged from the lodge where she knew Rye was being held. She studied them with intense anger. They were so large and powerful. And those teeth and huge tails . . .

She hurried into the nest.

The mice were astir, but moving about as though weighted by great burdens. No one looked up or around. Talk was minimal. Little tasks were being performed with minute attention. The family was preparing to move.

"I'm back," Poppy announced.

The mice paused in their work and looked around.

"Ah, Poppy," Valerian said sadly, "I thought you had left us."

"Not at all. I went to see Rye."

"Rye!"

"How'd you do that?" Curleydock called out.

Poppy told how she got into the beavers' lodge, and of her subsequent visit with Rye. "He's not happy," she told them, "but he's all right."

"But . . . why did he even go there?" Clover asked.

"He wanted to do something about the beavers."

"And did he?"

"No."

Valerian's tail waved in agitation. "Why that mouse must always be trying to prove himself I can't begin to imagine. And now, a prisoner, held for a ransom, the ransom being our moving away. Well, we're trying to go as quickly as we can."

"I do have a plan to free him," Poppy offered.

The nest became very still.

"Miss Poppy," Valerian said, drawing himself up and speaking sombrely, "ever since you came to our nest, you've been telling and doing some remarkable things. We don't doubt you are an exceptional creature. Perhaps living quietly and simply by the Brook, we've become a tad shy of difficulty. No doubt the beavers have unnerved us, too. But the truth is," Valerian concluded, "it would be better if we just gave in."

"Won't you even listen to my plan?"

Valerian sighed, "I guess we can. You just mustn't expect us to do anything."

As Rye's family stared at her with dull eyes and twitching ears, an uncomfortable Poppy stood in the middle of the nest. She felt some anger. These mice had been generous when she told them of Ragweed's death. Now that she was suggesting they *do* something

to keep Rye from dying, they were not so hospitable.

"I got into the beavers' main lodge," she told them anew, "by using a vent hole and a vine to drop down inside. Unfortunately, Rye and I couldn't break his cage. I need more teeth or paws. I'll need a few of you to join me when I return to the lodge with a longer vine."

"Go into the beavers' lodge?" cried an alarmed mouse.

"Right. The way I did."

"Wouldn't that be dangerous?" called another. "Those beavers are so big. A swat of their tails —"

"And what about those teeth . . ." still another said. "One bite and . . . good-bye."

Poppy held up a paw to still the objections. "I have a friend. A best friend. He came with me here from Dimwood Forest."

"Another mouse?" asked one of the youngsters.

"He's a porcupine. His name is Ereth. Porcupine quills are very sharp. My friend is always losing his. I'll get some. When we go into the lodge we'll each carry a quill to defend ourselves."

"One quill against all those beavers?" asked another.

"Exactly."

"Where is this friend of yours?" someone asked.

"Waiting for me up beyond the ridge."

Valerian cleared his throat. "Poppy, how many of us do you propose it will take to get Rye out?"

"There's me, of course," she replied. "But I'll need at least a couple of others."

No one spoke.

It was Clover who said, "Poppy, perhaps you could get Rye out. But what about the beavers? They'll simply go on building. What will happen to the rest of us?"

"I'm not sure," Poppy admitted. "But I must free Rye."

"My dear," Clover said, "I do wish I could believe your plan would be helpful. I truly do. But, no, I . . . can't." She turned to Valerian. "Do you?" she asked.

Valerian gazed at his feet. "It seems terribly risky," he said gloomily. He looked up. "And it certainly will create greater danger for the rest of us."

No one spoke. Then, speaking gently, Poppy

said, "But, as I understand it, you've not resisted them at all."

Once again there was silence.

Valerian cleared his throat. "Poppy," he said, "since this matter concerns the family I think we need to talk this over. Privately."

"All right," Poppy said, trying to hide her disappointment. "I'll go where my friend is waiting, gather up some quills, and bring them back. When I do, you can tell me what you'd like to do."

"I think that would be best," Valerian agreed.

An angry Poppy ran up the entryway, took one more look down at the pond and the lodge where she knew Rye was being kept, then hurried up toward the ridge.

She had no trouble finding the cottonwood where she had seen Ereth go. But the porcupine was nowhere in sight.

Ereth Has More Thoughts

Deep within the thicket, unable to move, Ereth was thinking hard:

"I probably shouldn't be so hard on Poppy. She's only a mouse. Small. Helpless. Talks a lot. Jabbers. Too cheerful most of the time. Nothing but squirrel sludge and buzzard belch.

"But then, she doesn't know the world. Not like I do. She needs protecting. Actually, there's no one around who can protect her better than me. I've done it before. I could do it again. I know the world. Know how it works. Not that she appreciates me. What was it she said about me . . . *old*.

"I'm not old. Maybe I *look* old . . . but inside, where it counts . . . I'm young. Young as her. Younger! I'm good-looking too — in my way. Fine set of quills. And I'm clever. Very clever.

"I wonder what she thinks of me. Really thinks. Wonder if she likes me. Really likes me. The

way I . . . like . . . her. I suppose, in a way, I do like her. A lot. I can . . . allow that.

"Point is, I could do a lot for her. More than she could guess. Show her the world. Teach her the way it works.

"Now, with her being off on her own I'm always worried about her. But with me around, she'd never be in danger.

"I wonder if — just suppose — if she would, well . . . all she ever talks about is . . . love . . . and that Ragweed. What did he know about love? Or her for that matter. She told me he loved her. *Love.* Young folk think they're the only ones who love. Pish! Nothing but slug splat stew and weasel jam.

"Still, if she wanted me to — as a favour — I could love her. She'd probably like that. If she'd give me the chance.

"Wonder what she'd say if I hinted at it. Or suggest it. I mean, maybe I could say — I . . . love you — well, once. Not too loudly. A little bit. Just so she knew. I wouldn't have to say it again.

"She'd like that. Then we could get married. There would be talk. She being young. Me . . . older.

We wouldn't care. Not us. She's got a mind of her own. So have I.

"I bet she'll be thrilled. I'm big. Powerful. Sharp. Could give her lots of advice. She's a good listener. And it'll be good to have someone young around that old smelly log of mine. She could clean it up. A bit. A small bit. Not too much. Yes, she'd like it. Yes, soon as I see her again, I'll tell her. Sort of. Some way . . . "

So ran Ereth's thoughts, stuck as he was, deep within the thicket.

22
Poppy Makes Up Her Mind

Though Poppy waited at the tree, Ereth did not return. Knowing how unpredictable her friend was, she kept asking herself how long she should wait. After all, she had been with the mice longer than she'd planned. That certainly would have irritated the old porcupine.

She began to think he'd done what he'd threatened to all along — trundled back to Dimwood Forest. Yet Poppy was quite aware her friend might be doing no more than taking a nap in a nearby log.

Normally, Poppy would not have minded waiting. But she kept worrying that if she were going to save Rye, she had to act swiftly.

Having nothing better to do, she searched about the base of the cottonwood tree for some of Ereth's quills to take back to the nest. When she failed to find any, she became fretful. The thought of sneaking into the beavers' lodge without the protection of quills was something she did not relish.

Having no quills set off a nervous train of doubts in Poppy's mind. Would she be able to get into the lodge again? Was Rye's cage breakable? What if she or he got hurt? Would they be able to use the vine to get out of the lodge? And what if freeing Rye *did* bring greater harm to the rest of his family? Maybe Valerian and Clover were right. Maybe it all *was* too dangerous.

The more Poppy thought, the more doubts she had about her plan.

Suddenly Poppy felt an intense desire to race back to Dimwood Forest and hide. There she would be safe and secure in the world she knew and loved best. It was bitter-sweet to recall that when she began this trip, she had been looking forward to a time of calm. Perhaps Ereth was right. Perhaps it was better to be alone.

And yet she had fallen in love with Rye. Moreover, she had promised to help him. How could she abandon him? She could not, no more than she could abandon her feelings.

Too agitated to wait any longer for Ereth, Poppy hurried down the hill and crept back into the nest. It was very crowded. Some 50 and more mice

were there, most of whom she had not seen before.

She caught hold of Thistle. "What's happening?" Poppy asked.

"It's the rest of our family," Thistle explained. "Valerian asked them to come hear about your plan."

"Are they for it or against it?" Poppy asked.

"They can't make up their minds," Thistle confided. "Poppy, I think we should do it — as long as we have quills to defend ourselves."

"Thistle," Poppy confided, "I couldn't get the quills."

Thistle blanched. "You couldn't?"

"My friend, the porcupine, has disappeared."

"Does that mean we can't rescue Rye?" Thistle asked with dismay.

Poppy, feeling she had failed the young mouse, hardly knew what to say. "I'm not sure," she replied.

Valerian approached. "Poppy, I sent word to the rest of the family about what you want to do," he informed her. "It's so important I felt everyone should be involved in the decision.

"Attention, please!" he cried.

The mice hushed.

"For those who don't know her yet," Valerian said by way of introduction, "this is Poppy. She comes to us from out east. She was a special friend of Ragweed's. That makes her a good friend of ours."

To this there were murmurs of assent.

"You've heard what's happened to Rye and what choice we've been given," Valerian continued. "Move off somewhere — and, hopefully, have Rye freed — or try to save Rye on our own, and take our chances with the beavers.

"To be honest with you, your mother and I think it'd be best to move on. Poppy here wants to rescue Rye. Since this concerns the whole family, we thought it'd be wise for you to hear her for yourselves."

Once again Poppy found herself facing a world of grave, golden faces. Momentarily she thought of sharing her anxieties, but feared that if the mice knew how nervous she was, they would never give her help. Instead, she simply explained her plan for freeing Rye.

"Did you get those quills?" someone asked when she was done.

"I'm afraid not."

A nervous twitter passed over the family.

"I do need some volunteers," Poppy said, almost timidly.

Curleydock shyly lifted a paw. "I'll . . . go," he offered.

"Me, too," Thistle joined in.

"What about the rest of you?" Poppy asked. "Can I have your approval?"

Valerian cleared his throat. "Poppy, if you don't mind waiting outside, I think it would be easier for us to make up our minds."

It was a discouraged Poppy who left the nest.

Once above ground she gazed down at the pond and the lodge where she knew Rye was being kept. "Think of it," she told herself, "as just another kind of dance."

Thistle and Curleydock emerged from the nest. Poppy looked at them expectantly.

Thistle said, "They think you're making a mistake, but they won't keep you from trying. They're going to move. So we're on our own."

Poppy considered her young friends. "Please,"

she said to them, "you're very brave to volunteer. But it will be hard. Maybe impossible. I won't think less of you if you change your minds."

"No way," Thistle said with a stubbornness that made Poppy recall Ragweed. "We're going with you."

Curleydock nodded in agreement.

"All right then," Poppy said briskly as she tried to stir up her own energy. "The first thing we need to do is get a long piece of vine. Any idea where we can get one?"

The young mice exchanged looks. "Maybe, up by the berry thicket," Curleydock suggested.

With Curleydock leading the way, the three mice scampered up the hill. A short run brought them up and over the ridge. On the far side they went down into a sunny hollow. Before them lay an overgrown thicket of berry bushes and flowering honeysuckle vines. The air was filled with sweetness.

"We should be able to get a honeysuckle vine there," Thistle said. "They're long and tough."

The three mice were soon deep within the thicket. Cool and moist, it was perfumed by the almost overpowering, sticky-sweet scent of berries.

"How about this vine?" Curleydock asked. He was yanking on a green strand that twisted high over their heads and out of sight.

"It really needs to be long and strong," Poppy urged. "It has to get us into the lodge and out."

"This one looks okay," Thistle called from another spot.

She was joined by the others.

"Haul it in," Poppy said. While the other two worked to untangle the vine, she chewed through its roots. Then they began to pull.

"It's stuck," Thistle announced.

"Must be tied around something," Curleydock agreed.

No matter how hard the three pulled, the vine would not come.

"We can follow it along," Poppy suggested.

Curleydock was up front. Thistle was in the middle. Poppy came behind. As they followed the vine they became increasingly spread out, losing sight of one another.

Suddenly, from deep within the thicket, there was a frantic call from Curleydock. "Help!" he cried.

"Hurry! Fast!"

Poppy and Thistle dropped the vine and charged forward. Curleydock was crouched down in terror.

Looming over him was Ereth.

"Ereth!" Poppy cried.

"Poppy," Ereth snapped, "you simple smudge of a slimy slug! Where have you been?"

Poppy grinned. "I've been busy. But I've been looking for you. What are you doing here?"

"Never mind. Just get me out of here. I'm stuck." He pulled back and forth but his quills continued to hold him fast.

"Ereth," Poppy said, "this is Thistle and Curleydock. They're brother and sister to Ragweed."

"Ragweed," Ereth said. "I'm sick of talk about Ragweed. Just get me out. I need to talk to you."

"What about?"

"Just get me out!"

Poppy turned to Curleydock and Thistle. They had been looking on in great puzzlement. "It's all right," she told them. "He's perfectly harmless."

"Bee butter!" Ereth roared. "I am not harmless! I have a terrible temper. I say dreadful things. I'm a

selfish old coot who does what he wants when he wants and doesn't care what anyone else wants."

"He's really good," Poppy said.

"Don't listen to her. I'm bad!" Ereth screamed.

Nonetheless the three mice set to work chewing away at the vines that had ensnared Ereth. Even as they did, the impatient porcupine tossed and pulled, trying to free himself. Finally, with a snap, he broke loose.

"Now," Ereth said, "tell those friends of yours to disappear. I have something important to tell you."

"I'm sure they could listen — "

"It's private, mush-head!"

Poppy looked to Thistle and Curleydock, who, understanding, scampered off.

"I've got something to tell you, too," Poppy said when they were gone.

"You have to listen to me first," Ereth insisted. "What I've been thinking is . . ." He stopped, suddenly bashful and tongue-tied.

"What is it?"

"It's just that . . . what I think is . . . Now, see here, Poppy . . . I . . . wish . . . I wish . . . I had a piece

of salt! Tell me what you wanted to say first."

"Are you sure?"

"Push the belch button and run a bath! I just said so, didn't I?"

"Well, then," said Poppy, blushing with pleasure. "Ereth . . . I've fallen in love."

"You . . . *what*?" Ereth whispered, aghast.

"Fallen in love."

"With . . . whom?" Ereth asked. He was trembling with emotion.

Poppy smiled. "I know it must seem strange, but you see, I met . . . well, actually, he's Ragweed's brother. His name is Rye and he's . . . But what's the matter?"

"Thief! Crook!" Ereth yelled. "I'll skewer him! Whack him! Mash him! Turn him into skunk gunk."

"Ereth! What are you talking about?"

"You just think I'm too old," the porcupine ranted, rearing up and down as though bitten by ants. "Too stupid! Too big. Too sour. Too . . . me!" Abruptly he whirled around and began to rush away.

"But that's not true," Poppy called after him. "It's not. And what did you want to tell me?"

"Forget it," Ereth called back. "I'm leaving."

"Where are you going?"

"To Dimwood Forest, pickle seed!" he cried.

"Ereth!" Poppy called after him. "Please don't go. I need you!"

"You're on your own, traitor!" the porcupine shouted as he tore from view.

With great puzzlement Poppy gazed after him. Something was surely the matter with her friend. With a sigh, she wished she understood him better.

She glanced around. To her great relief she saw that in his fury Ereth had dropped some quills. She gathered them up and hurried to find Thistle and Curleydock.

The Rescue Begins

"How do we get to the lodge?" Curleydock asked after Poppy had given him and Thistle a lesson in the use of the quills. "We can swim. Can you?"

"Not really," Poppy admitted. "When I went to the lodge before I floated on a wood chip."

"The beavers leave all kinds of chips around," Thistle said. "I'm sure we could find one big enough to carry the three of us."

The trio crept down to the edge of the pond. A few beavers were about, working.

"Don't let them see us," Poppy warned.

Squatting down, the mice attempted to hide behind bushes. Only when Poppy was sure they were unnoticed did she and the others scout about in search of a chip.

Thistle found one near a recently chewed stump. All agreed the thin, square flake would be large enough to carry the three of them.

Quickly, they dragged it behind a bush and hid it, then searched out wood bits to use as paddles. Then they returned to the top of the hill.

"Better get some rest," Poppy suggested. "As soon as it gets dark we'll go."

As far as she was concerned all was ready.

But the mice *had* been observed. Clara Canad saw them sniffing about the edges of the pond. Suspicious, she had watched intently, but was not certain what the mice were doing.

She reported what she'd seen to Mr Canad. "What do you think?" she asked him.

"Don't know," he replied. "Don't want to make a mountain out of a mouse hill. Still, you might have a point. Give them an inch, these mice take a mile."

"The mice I saw were looking for something."

"What do you think it was?" Mr Canad asked.

"I'm not sure. Did you block that vent hole?"

"Piece of cake."

"Did you make another?"

"Needle in a haystack. But look here,

sweetheart, the less trouble, the better. We've been coasting along easy. We don't want to slip on banana peels now. So if you want to keep on watch, as far as I'm concerned, that's icing on the cake."

With that, Mr Canad swam away.

"Well, I don't like it," Clara said to herself. "I'm going to patrol the pond tonight."

The farewells Thistle and Curleydock made to their family that night were brief and painful. The elder mice tried to be kind but could do little to hide their apprehension.

For their part the youngsters tried to appear bold, but felt only uneasy.

Poppy, uncomfortable with the family's disapproval, kept away entirely.

It was dark when the three mice went down to the pond. The vine hung in a coil around Poppy's neck like a lifebelt.

Once they located the wood chip they had hidden, they pushed it into the water then jumped on. In moments they were afloat, moving slowly towards

the lodge.

The three mice knelt on the wood chip and paddled steadily. Thistle and Curleydock were up front. Poppy was in the rear. Now and again she stood tall and peered into the dark, trying to keep them on course. The beavers' main lodge, though visible, was distant. "To the left," she called. "To the right." Thistle and Curleydock shifted their paddles accordingly.

Other than normal night sounds, all was quiet. The moon kept slipping in and out behind clouds. A breeze from the north had begun to blow, bringing early hints of the autumn yet to come. It made the pond surface choppy.

Thistle's whispered voice broke through the dark. "I think I heard something."

The mice stopped paddling. Poppy's ears twitched. She was not sure, but she too had caught a faint, splashing sound off to her left. The noise, however, did not return.

"I think we're all right," she called, keeping her voice low. The three resumed their paddling.

As they approached the lodge, Curleydock whispered, "Is that it?"

"I'm pretty sure," Poppy replied.

"Which side should we aim for?" Thistle wanted to know.

"It doesn't matter," Poppy said. "We'll be crawling to the vent hole on top. Let's go. Keep your voices low."

They dipped their paddles and moved forward again. Even as they did, a great swell of water lifted their raft, causing it to slide back as if it were rolling down a hill.

The next moment, Clara Canad, orange teeth glowing, rose up before them.

"I thought I heard something," she barked. "What are you doing here? What are you trying to do?"

"Back paddle!" Poppy yelled frantically and plunged her oar deep into the water as if she could scoop them clear. Thistle tried, too, but with no more success. Worse, when she hauled back the strain was so great her paddle snapped in two. Curleydock, working frantically, only stirred the foaming waters.

With the raft rocking wildly, Thistle slipped. She did manage to hang on by the tips of her paws,

but her hold was precarious. Curleydock, seeing her danger, attempted to reach for her, but lost his step on the listing raft and flipped over her head into the water.

"Curleydock!" Thistle screamed. She twisted to see where he had gone. He had vanished.

Clara, meanwhile, swung herself completely around, and lifted her tail.

"Look out!" Poppy cried.

Poppy saw Thistle attempt to draw her quill. It caused her to lose her grip. She fell back into the water and disappeared.

As the beaver's tail struck, Poppy clung to the raft. The tail hit the raft's front end, causing it to flip up and over like a catapult, flinging Poppy into the air.

As she flew she spread her legs wide, landing in the water on her belly with a splosh. Stunned, she lay facedown in the water. It was the vine, still around her neck, which kept her from drowning.

Clara looked around. Seeing Poppy facedown in the water, she assumed she was dead. As for the other two mice, she did not see them at all. She was sure they, too, had perished.

With a satisfied grunt, the beaver dived beneath the water and headed for the entryway to the lodge.

Poppy, regaining consciousness, looked up. Giving her head a shake, she spat out water and called, "Thistle! Curleydock!" Her voice was weak. There was no reply.

She looked about. The beavers' lodge rose up before her. Giving a few feeble kicks, she moved close enough to reach out and grab hold of some of its branches. When she pulled at them, she came up against it. There she rested some more until her wind was completely restored. Only then did she crawl out of the water and onto the lodge. Turning, she gazed back over the pond.

"Thistle!" she called again. "Curleydock!"

She thought she heard an answering cry, but when it did not repeat itself, she was sure her young friends had drowned.

Drenched and forlorn, Poppy sat down, toying with the circle of vine by her side. Suddenly, she reached for her quill. It, too, was gone. That meant she had no way to defend herself. Everything bad that could have happened, had.

What she should do, she told herself, was to go back and inform Valerian and Clover of what had occurred. The mere thought of it made her groan. Why did she always have to bring bad news? It was all too ghastly.

The next moment she realised that going back was not possible. Her raft was gone. She couldn't swim to shore. There was little choice but to press on and attempt to save Rye – somehow.

Poppy hefted the circle of vine. Though heavy, she flung it back over her neck then began to climb the side of the lodge.

As she went she began to cry. Why did Ragweed have to die? Why did Rye have to run away? Why did Ereth and Clover and Valerian have to be angry with her? Why did Thistle and Curleydock have to drown? Was everything her fault? It was all too much.

Despite her anguish, Poppy continued up the side of the lodge. It was a hard climb. Her own distress, the rough nature of the lodge's construction, her sense of failure, all conspired to make the going difficult. Even so she kept climbing constantly,

slipping, banging her head, her knees. Her paws grew
raw. More than once she had to stop and regain her
breath as well as her composure. But up she went,
crawling on, over, under, and around twigs, sticks, and
logs, all the while slipping and sliding over mud that
stuck to her like glue. Sometimes the agony of it all
made her whimper.

And then, when she finally reached the top, she
could not find the vent hole. She could hardly believe
it. Back and forth over the top she crawled. All she
found was mud and more mud. Something was wrong,
altered.

Gradually, Poppy began to grasp what must
have happened. When she had visited Rye she had left
the vine dangling from the vent hole. The beavers must
have discovered what she'd done and covered the hole
with mud. If that was true — and it certainly seemed
to be so — then, short of swimming, there was no way
for her to get into the lodge.

Feeling defeated and alone, Poppy sat atop the
lodge. Ereth had fled back to Dimwood. Thistle and
Curleydock were gone, presumably drowned. Rye was
imprisoned. Rye! How close he was. How impossible

to reach! Her whole plan was a disaster.

Poppy lay back and stared up at the few stars peeking out now and again from behind drifting clouds. I might as well be up there for all I can do, she thought.

Exhaustion – fuelled by sorrow and defeat – took hold. She kept telling herself she mustn't sleep, that she must do something. But her fatigue, mixed with her melancholy state, proved too powerful. She nodded off.

24
Valerian and Clover

Though the packing of the nest had been completed, Valerian and Clover decided to wait for the morning to make their move. Without saying so, both were reluctant to go farther away from Rye, Thistle and Curleydock. In any case, it was night and the children were asleep. Better not to disturb them.

Sitting side by side, paw in paw, the two mice stared up at the moon, which kept slipping behind the scudding clouds. Lifting their noses and sniffing at the breeze, they gazed down towards the pond and the lodge where they knew Rye was being held.

"I wonder where Poppy and the children are now," Valerian mused.

"I just hope they're all right," Clover said.

"That Poppy is a tough one, love," Valerian said, trying to sound more reassuring than he felt. "I didn't think going was a good idea, but if anyone can get Rye out and come back safe, I suppose she can."

"And here we sit," she said.

Valerian nodded.

Suddenly Clover sighed. "Oh, Valerian," she whispered, "when I saw the faces of the family, it made me think how much I love them all. It isn't wrong to want to protect them, is it?"

"I don't think so," Valerian replied kindly. "I feel that way myself."

For a moment they were quiet.

Then Clover sighed. "Valerian, how long have we been together?" she asked.

"Six years."

"Such a long time," Clover said. "And a good time. A good life. So many children. Good children. Mostly. They come. They go. And here we are. Sometimes, Valerian, it seems the only difference in us is that you're greyer, I'm fatter, and we're both a lot more tired."

"You're still my love, Clover," Valerian murmured, giving her paw a gentle squeeze.

"Valerian . . ." Clover said, as if she hadn't heard, "I suppose sometimes it takes an outsider to see what we can't see for ourselves. I've been thinking

about what Poppy said. What she said is true: I haven't put up much resistance to the beavers. I've been too . . . fearful that some of us would get hurt . . . or worse. But sitting here, with you, looking on, I . . . "

She faltered, took a deep breath. With a painful catch in her throat, she said, "Valerian . . . Poppy was right. We can't just accept what these beavers are doing to us. It'll only get worse. Valerian, I just wish we could do something. *Anything.*"

Having spoken, Clover buried her face in Valerian's shoulder and began to weep.

Valerian patted her gently. Then he said, "Well, love, what do you have in mind?"

"That's just it," she whispered between sobs. "I don't know. But why," she cried, "did those beavers have to build that dam?" She hid her face again.

Valerian gazed down at the dam. Then he shifted about, looked at the boulder, then down at the dam, then the boulder again. "Maybe . . ." he said softly, "what we should do is . . . bust it."

Taken aback, Clover looked up. *"Bust their dam?"* she cried in astonishment.

"Look here," Valerian continued. "Maybe we

had no right to say they couldn't come here and build. It wasn't our brook. But they've taken over. Taken everything. If we busted that dam," Valerian continued, "the pond water would drain away. All the animals could use the Brook again. The way we did before."

"But we're *mice*, Valerian!" Clover squeaked. "We're small. It's huge. They're huge. How could we do anything big like that?"

Valerian looked all around. Then, nodding, he said, "I'll tell you how . . . by using the boulder we've been living under. Always seemed to me it might topple on its own. Well, listen here, love, suppose we dig around it and under it. Get it loose. Then, well, give it a shove. Let it roll down the hill so that it hits the beavers' dam smack on. I bet you a pile of acorns it'd punch out a pretty big hole. The water would drain right out."

"But . . ." Clover said, quite flabbergasted, "how could you get it to go the right way?"

Valerian studied the boulder, the hill, then the pond anew. "Let's say we made a kind of ditch right in front of it. Sort of a chute. Of course, we'd have to

aim it right at the dam. If we did it properly it couldn't miss."

Clover stared at her husband with wide-eyed admiration. "Valerian, do . . . do you think we really could do that?"

Valerian was getting more and more excited. "We've got the whole family around, haven't we? If everybody pitched in, worked hard, I think we could do it. But we'd have to do it right away. By dawn. Once we start, those beavers will figure out what we're doing."

"I'd want to work, too," Clover assured him. "One of us could be in charge of digging around the boulder. The other could make that ditch."

"Right!" Valerian cried. "But, like I said, we better do it right away."

"But what about Rye, Thistle and Curleydock? And Poppy?"

"Can't see how it'd do them any harm. Might even make things easier for them. And if it works, maybe the beavers will go away," he added, with new determination in his voice. "Forever."

Clover looked at him. Suddenly she cried, "Oh,

Valerian, I'm so glad it's you I love. I truly am!" And she threw her paws about him and gave him a tight hug, which he returned.

The next moment the two went rushing down into their nest. "Everybody up! Everybody up! There's work to do!"

The family having been roused, Valerian and Clover told them of the plan. Sensing their parents' enthusiasm, all the children pitched in eagerly.

In quick time, under Clover's direction, some 30 golden mice were scraping earth away from around the boulder. Though their paws were small and could carry but a little at a time, they attacked the task with great determination. The dirt began to fly.

Simultaneously, directly in front of the boulder and aimed right at the dam, Valerian and his crew marked out the ditch.

Valerian had but one worry: Could they do it all fast enough?

Inside the Lodge

Atop the beavers' lodge, Poppy woke with a start. How long had she slept? She stood tall and looked east. There was a faint hint of dawn. It made her heart lurch. With the coming of dawn she was sure the beavers would awaken. When they did, she would lose whatever chance she had to free Rye. A great deal of time already had been lost.

She scrambled to the top of the lodge where she thought the vent hole had been. As before, all she found was mud. This time, however, she was desperate. Putting the vine ring aside, she clawed at the mud. While heavy and thick, it was capable of being dug. Poppy began to hack at it.

Gradually, a hole emerged. The more she worked, the more her energy was restored. She worked harder. Unexpectedly, she broke through. A scent of beaver wafted up. It made her almost shout with joy. She had uncovered the vent hole. The mud had been

plastered over – and poorly at that.

Working fast now, Poppy dug out the vent hole to its fullest. Done, she sat back, breathless with her efforts. Now there was nothing to prevent her from at least trying to get to Rye, force open his cage, and free him. Then she recalled that one of the reasons she had wanted Thistle and Curleydock to join her was to help with the bars. There was nothing to do but go on. She and Rye would have to get him free on their own.

Feeling almost reckless now, Poppy tied one end of the vine to a stick, took the free end in her mouth, and crept into the vent hole.

Even though she had made her way through the hole before, this time the way seemed longer. Moreover, some of the mud from the top had fallen in. she was constantly scraping it away and pushing it behind her.

Down she went. When she finally reached the end, she peered into the lodge. To her horror, the beavers were not sleeping. They were having a meeting.

Mr Canad was standing before his family. Next to him was his daughter, Clara. With great glee, she was telling them what had happened out on the pond.

"I don't think any of them survived," she said with pride. "And it only took one smack of the old tail."

The other beavers beat their own tails against the ground. Even Mr Canad joined in.

"Okay, folks, I just went out to check for myself. Clara did a great job, but if seeing is believing, the mice up on the hill are up to no good around that boulder. That's where we're going to put in a new dam.

"What Clara discovered suggests they've got something up their sleeves. Maybe they're trying to pull the wool over our eyes. Okay, I say it's time we pulled out all the stops. End our kid-glove treatment. Teach the whole kit and caboodle a trick or two. Knock the spots off them. Playtime's over.

"Let's get up there and give them a few what-fors. Level the playing field with our tails. Do I have any volunteers?"

There was an enthusiastic chorus of yea-sayers.

"Good!" Mr Canad enthused. "Let's hit the water running. I'll lead you myself."

"Don't you think we should post some guards around by the waterway entry?" Clara asked. "Just in case they try something funny again."

"Good thinking, sweetheart. You're a chip off the old block. And for a beaver, you can't do better than that! We'll leave some guards here. Just in case."

High in the vent hole, Poppy heard it all. Although she was relieved the beavers were going, she worried about what was happening up by the nest.

She watched as the beavers scrambled out of the lodge. Soon only two remained.

It had been Poppy's intention to crawl down the vine — just as she had done on her previous visit. Then, the beavers all had been asleep. This time, the two beavers who stayed in the lodge were not just awake, one of them went over to the cage where Rye was being kept.

"What are you doing?" called the other beaver.

"Just checking to make sure this guy's secure."

"Is he?"

"Certainly is."

The two beavers waddled away from the cage and lay down near the lodge's water entry to guard it.

Poppy watched them intently. Their backs were to her.

In the dimness — the fireflies were not very

active – Poppy was sure she saw Rye. He was curled up in a tight ball at the far end of the cage. Even as she watched him, he got up and crept to one of the back bars. There he crouched. If she was seeing clearly, he was gnawing on one of them.

Just to see Rye working made Poppy's heart swell with love. Her doubts melted away. Together – somehow – they would get him out of the cage and to freedom. Her pulse quickened.

After giving a yank to the vine to make sure it would hold fast, Poppy began to lower it slowly. As she did, she kept her eyes on the two beavers. If they saw what she was doing, all was lost. She barely dared to breathe.

Inch by inch the vine dropped.

One of the beavers swung about and used a rear leg to scratch himself vigorously. Poppy froze. But the beaver's face was so scrunched up – he seemed to be enjoying his scratching – he gave no sign that he noticed anything unusual.

Poppy lowered the vine some more. She was pretty sure she had guessed its length properly, that it would touch the floor. She was wrong. Even when she

had lowered the vine as far as possible, it hung off the ground by a distance — as best Poppy could reckon — twice her full height when she stood tall. At first dismayed, she decided it did not matter. It was — it had to be — close enough.

The next step would be harder. It was time for her to go down. Head first or tail first? She glanced over at the beavers. They were paying no attention. Best to go tail first. If the need came, heading up would be easier and faster than backing up.

After wiping her sweaty paws on her fur, Poppy grasped the vine and began her descent by letting herself drop in a series of small jerks.

The moment she left the vent hole in the ceiling, the vine began to sway. The farther she went, the greater the sway. It made her dizzy, then nauseated. She knew then she should have come down headfirst like the last time.

Squeezing her eyes shut, Poppy continued down. Moving with her eyes closed gave her a panicky feeling — far worse than the dizziness. She opened them in haste and hung there. The vine swayed. Her dizziness increased. Gritting her teeth, she made herself go on.

As she moved, she kept looking around at the beavers. They had remained quite still. It was just as she reached the halfway point that they showed signs of activity.

One of them got up and arched his back. Then he turned fully around. Poppy almost fainted with fright. But the beaver turned back around and resumed guarding the entryway. Never had Poppy felt so glad to be so small.

Poppy struggled to suppress her anxiety and move faster. A little calmer, she continued down.

She had reached the vine's end. Now she was dangling above the floor. There she hung, swaying back and forth, her heart beating madly. After taking one more look at the beavers, she released her grip and dropped to the floor.

The second she landed, she crouched down into as tight a ball as she could. Then, with great care, she lifted her head to check what the beavers were doing. They had not noticed her.

With a burst she sprang up and darted to the cage. "Rye," she called in a whisper even as she clung to the bars.

Rye looked up. "Poppy!" he gasped and fell back.

"*Shhh!*" she warned.

"You are always such a wonderful surprise," he said.

In spite of herself, Poppy grinned.

"Poppy . . . ?"

"Yes?"

"I've . . . I've been working on a poem about you. Would you like to hear it? It goes,

"Hail, sweet mouse of shape divine!
Who pledged her heart and tail to me
And mine . . . "

"Rye," Poppy interrupted, "it sounds beautiful, but there's no time for that now. We need to get you out of here, fast."

"I'm all for that," Rye agreed. "I've been working away on this bar, too. It is awfully tough. Almost as hard as writing a good poem. And they do watch me. But I did make some progress. Poem and bar. Maybe the two of us can do the rest. The bar, that is."

"Show me where."

"Here." He went to the back of the cage. Poppy, on the outside, followed him. "This one."

Poppy looked at the twig. It was gnawed almost halfway through.

"Makes my teeth sore," Rye said.

"If you gripped from above," Poppy suggested, "and I held on from below, and we pulled in opposite directions, it might give."

"We can try."

The two mice did what Poppy suggested.

"Pull!" Rye urged. The two yanked. There was some give but not enough.

"Again," Rye said.

The twig splintered with a sudden snap. While it did not break completely in two, it had been pulled wide enough to allow Rye to squeeze through. He popped out and gave Poppy a hug. She returned it.

"Do you want to hear the rest of the poem?" he asked.

"Let's get out of here first."

"Of course. How silly of me. How did you come in?"

"The vent hole and another vine. A much longer one. Come on."

With Poppy in the lead, the two mice crept across the floor of the lodge.

As they went Poppy kept darting glances at the beavers.

Rye, following Poppy, kept thinking, "Isn't she amazing. Isn't she something."

They were halfway to the vine when one of the beavers turned, looked at them, saw what had happened and cried, "Mice on the loose!"

26

The Battle of the Boulder

What had happened to Thistle and Curleydock?

When Thistle, under attack from the beaver, lost her grip on the raft, she let herself sink below the water's surface. A good swimmer, she had the sense to move fast and far away from the tumbled raft as well as the beaver. For as long as her lungs allowed her to, she swam underwater. Then she rose to the surface and cried out, "Curleydock! Poppy!"

There was no reply. And it was too dark to see anything.

Terribly distressed, Thistle swam about in circles, in search of her companions. She was still searching when she heard a faint splash.

"Who's that?" she called.

"It's me. Curleydock! Who's that?"

"Thistle."

"Where are you?"

"Here. Keep talking. Try to swim towards me.

I'll try to move towards you."

The two met in the middle of the pond.

"Where's Poppy?" was the first thing Curleydock said.

"I hoped she'd be with you."

"I didn't see what happened to her."

"Do you think she's all right?" asked Thistle.

"I don't know."

"Listen!"

There came what sounded like a faint cry.

"Here we are!" Thistle called back loudly.

"*Shhh!* A beaver might hear you."

In any case, there was no response.

"Curleydock?"

"What?"

"Poppy said she wasn't that good a swimmer."

"Do . . . do you think . . ." Curleydock stammered, "do you think she . . . drowned?"

Instead of replying, Thistle said, "We'd better get back to the land."

"Which way?"

Thistle tried to gauge their place. "I think that way is closest." She pointed the way with her nose.

The two mice swam steadily. Neither spoke until they reached the shore. As soon as they got out they both looked back over the pond.

"Do you see anything?" Thistle said.

"No."

"What are we going to tell Dad and Mum?"

"Better just say what happened," Curleydock replied.

"What do you think . . . did happen?"

"She must have . . . drowned."

Thistle shook her head.

Curleydock said, "She said she couldn't swim. And we didn't hear her, did we?"

"Maybe she got to the lodge anyway."

"Thistle, even if she did, she said she needed us to get Rye out."

"But . . . then . . . what'll happen to Rye?"

There was no answer.

Suddenly Thistle said, "Curleydock, Mum and Dad were moving tonight. We don't know where they went."

"Maybe they left a note."

The two mice ran up the hill.

There was pale light — but no sun yet — upon the eastern horizon when an exhausted Thistle and Curleydock, full of their awful news, reached the hilltop. To their complete surprise, they saw the entire family working in a frenzy. Half were labouring in the ditch before the boulder. The others were toiling about the boulder's base, hauling away dirt as fast as they could. Most of the earth around the boulder already had been removed. To Thistle and Curleydock's eyes the boulder appeared to be resting on absolutely nothing.

"Dad!" Curleydock called.

Valerian turned. His mouth opened with surprise. "Why . . . what are you two doing here? Did you free Rye? Where's Poppy?"

"Dad," Thistle said, "we were getting close to the beaver's lodge — on a raft — when one of the beavers discovered us."

"No!"

"Then we got whacked with a tail," Curleydock continued. "The raft went over. But we're . . . Thistle and I . . . we're good swimmers."

"You mean . . . Poppy . . . ?"

"We're not sure, but . . . drowned, probably."

Valerian, mouth agape, struggled to control his emotions. Turning away, he gazed at the boulder, the ditch, the pond.

"Dad," Thistle asked, "what's everybody doing?"

Valerian explained as best he could.

"You're going to smash the dam?" Curleydock exclaimed when he heard the plan.

"We're trying. But I think I'd better talk to your mother. Tell her the news." He hurried away.

Clover, to oversee her part of the digging, had established herself — with her three youngest — just behind the large stone.

The moment Valerian appeared, she bolted up. "What is it? Something has happened. I can see it in your face."

"It's Thistle and Curleydock — "

Clover shut her eyes.

"They were going to the lodge on a wood chip when a beaver turned them over."

"Valerian . . . the children . . . what happened to them?"

"Thistle and Curleydock got back. They're good swimmers. But it's Poppy. They don't know what happened to her."

"Then they never reached . . . Rye?"

"No."

"Valerian!"

"Clover," Valerian asked, "what do you think we should do?"

Clover dipped her head, swallowed hard, then looked up. "Valerian, you said it before: Poppy's a clever mouse. Maybe she's all right. Maybe she isn't. But I still think we have to get that boulder going down the ditch as we planned. We have to do . . . *something*."

"But Clover, if Rye's still in the lodge . . . it might make things worse."

The two mice stared at each other.

"Valerian," Clover said in a whisper, struggling to remain dry eyed, "I still think we have to try. *I do*."

"I guess you're right," Valerian returned grimly. "The ditch is pretty much done. How soon can we push the boulder down?"

Clover, burping one of the babies, said, "We only need to dig a little more and then — "

Whatever Clover was about to say was cut off by a shout on the other side of the hill. "Beavers!" came the cry. "The beavers are attacking!"

"Oh, my goodness! Work as fast as you can!" Valerian urged Clover. "We'll try to hold them off." He gave Clover a quick hug, then tore around to the front of the boulder to see what was happening.

Thirteen beavers had waddled out of the pond. Arrayed all in a row, dripping wet, they were whacking their broad tails on the earth, making an awful racket. Their teeth, side by side, looked like an orange picket fence.

In the middle of the line was Mr Canad, peering up at the boulder. Now that the mice's work had progressed so far, he was able to grasp what it was the mice were attempting.

"Great balls of fire!" he raged. "They're going to topple that boulder. If it comes down, it'll hit the dam. It's unfair! It's wrong-headed! It's a matter of life or death!"

Up he reared. "For the honour of Canad's Happy Homes," he bawled, "we've got to draw the line somewhere. Give me a dam or give me death! Go the

whole hog! Go for broke! Fight tooth and tail! Charge!" As one, the beavers began to waddle up the hill.

The mice, taken by surprise, stopped work on the boulder and the ditch. Too terrified to do anything, they simply stared at the advancing line of beavers.

Valerian rushed down. "Defend yourselves!" he cried. "If only for a few minutes. That's what we need."

Galvanised, the mice scrambled in all directions, running and tripping over themselves as they gathered up sticks, pebbles and clods of dirt.

"Hold your fire," Valerian cried. "Wait till you can see the gap between their teeth."

The beavers, beating their tails, pressed up the hill. Their sheer bulk was enough to frighten away some of the mice.

Curleydock, unable to restrain himself, charged down the hill with a mud ball in either paw. "Come on," he called. "Don't stand there. Attack!"

Thistle, armed with a pointed stick, was the first to join him.

As soon as he was in throwing range, Curleydock chucked his mud balls at the beavers. When these balls bounced harmlessly off the beavers' pelts, he gathered up more and threw them.

Unfazed, the beavers continued their advance. "Be warned!" Mr Canad bawled up at the mice. "We don't intend to let anything happen to that boulder!"

Valerian, meanwhile, was in a frenzy, organising his sons, daughters and grandchildren into three brigades.

"When I give the word," he told them, "the first group will follow me. Go after one beaver at a time. It's the only way. You other two groups, attack when you think it's time. Now, chins up, whiskers straight, noses aquiver! Let's show them what mice can do!"

Brandishing a twig, he dashed down the hill, his offspring trailing close behind.

Thistle and Curleydock were off on their own, poking and pricking a beaver's feet with twigs. Maddened, the beaver spun about, lowering his tail shield. Brother and sister pressed their attack relentlessly. The beaver turned and fled back to the pond.

Meanwhile, Valerian and his pack of mice surrounded another beaver. They pelted her with mud balls, then followed up with a stick attack. The beaver responded by grabbing at them, snatching them up and flinging them off to one side. She also began to flail about with her tail, smashing down indiscriminately.

The mice, some hurt, retreated.

But even as they did, the second wave of mice – 15 strong and squeaking madly – swarmed down the hill. "Mice to the fore! Mice to the fore!" they cried in unison. So furious was their onslaught – with sticks, pebbles and mud balls – the attack of the beavers faltered. When one of the mice managed to shove a stick up a beaver's nose, the beaver turned and scampered back towards the pond.

Mr Canad reared up to block his way. "How dare you retreat," he cried, shoving the frightened beaver back up the hill. "They're only mice. Beavers never retreat! We have not yet begun to fight! Rally round the flag! Don't give up the ship. Remember Canad's Happy Homes. You're fighting for the honour and glory of me!"

A third wave of mice, emboldened by the success of the first two groups, poured down the hill in a great wave, squealing, "Mice and freedom! Mice and freedom!" at the top of their lungs. Too excited to stay organised, they struck out at any beaver that was near.

Dazed but unhurt, they shook themselves up, then hurled themselves back into the fray. WHACK! WHACK! went Mr Canad's tail. The mice danced away.

The mice did manage to dent the beavers' onslaught. Each beaver — surrounded by mice — was forced into fighting alone. But though the mice attacked and attacked again, the beavers gradually moved up the hill. Despite their stubborn resistance, the mice were forced into retreat. It was not a rout, but their strength was beginning to ebb.

Valerian, who was engaged with a particularly large beaver, had been knocked down twice. Each time he picked himself up, he cast an eye towards the top of the hill. When he saw that Clover and the other mice were still feverishly digging around the boulder, he threw himself back into the fray.

Clover, who kept looking from the frantic

digging around the boulder to the equally frantic battle below, finally shouted, "We're ready!" down to Valerian.

Valerian, who had just been brushed back, staggered up, heard the call. "Mice to the boulder!" he bellowed. "Mice to the boulder!"

The mice began an orderly retreat. But the beavers, sensing success, pressed harder, gnashing their orange teeth and smacking their tails down indiscriminately. "Drive them away!" Mr Canad shouted. "Show no mercy! Flatten them! Turn them into lily pads!"

The attack worked. The mice began to scatter. Once dispersed, they grew panicky. They started to race in all directions. Now their orderly retreat became a rout.

"Swat them!" Mr Canad cried. "Crush them! Flatten them out!"

Valerian raced towards the boulder. A blow from Mr Canad sent him backwards. Spinning about in corkscrew fashion, he collapsed to his knees, stunned.

Mr Canad reared up and beat his chest. "We

have them!" he cried triumphantly. "Strike while the iron is hot. Hit them where it hurts. Winning isn't everything, it's the only thing!"

Suddenly, from up behind the boulder came a great shout: "What the mice mollies is going on here? Where's Poppy? Get out of my way, fur face! Hit the road, tooth brain."

There was the sound of a slap, and a beaver — his nose a pincushion of quills — let forth a shriek, and began to bolt down the hill.

"Who's in charge here?" Ereth yelled. "Where's that seed brain, Poppy? Get out of my way, waffle tail!" WHACK! Another beaver went scrambling down the hill. "Beat it, buck tooth!"

Thistle approached him. "You are good. Just like Poppy said."

"Don't call me good, you furry inch of tail leavings. Just tell me what's going on. What's all this ruckus? Who are you, chisel mouth?" he demanded.

"The name is Caster P. Canad. But please, just call me Cas. We can be friends. You know what the philosopher said, A stranger is just someone you haven't met. I mean that, sin — "

"Don't tell me I'm your friend, buster!" Ereth interrupted with a roar. "I'm nobody's friend!" With that he slapped Mr Canad hard, right across the face, with his quill-covered tail. For a moment, Mr Canad, nose bristling with quills, could do no more than stare at Ereth with shock, horror and pain. Then he turned and fled down the hill towards the pond. Seeing their leader in a humiliating retreat, the rest of the beavers quickly lost heart and followed.

"Tumble the boulder!" Valerian cried. "Hurry!"

Regrouping, the mice raced up to the top of the hill. Some 40 of them, including Clover, dug their rear toes into the earth and placed their front paws against the boulder.

"Push!" Clover cried.

The boulder trembled.

"Push!" she cried again.

The boulder shook. It moved. It began to roll forward. Quickly it gathered speed and momentum until, to the high, shrill cheers of the mice, the boulder plopped into Valerian's ditch. Then, still rolling, it began to hurtle down the hill, moving faster and faster.

Plummeting, it struck a stone, which caused the boulder to bounce high into the air, over the heads of the astonished and retreating beavers. When it came down, it struck the dam.

There was a tremendous THUMP! Followed by absolute silence. The silence was broken by a sudden gurgling noise – the sound of the pond water emptying through the breach in the dam.

Neither beavers nor mice spoke. They could only stare.

It was Ereth who broke the profound silence by asking, "Where the busted bat bung is that Poppy, anyway?"

27

Inside the Lodge (continued)

When the first beaver cried out a warning that Rye was escaping, the second one spun about.

"Run!" Poppy cried and headed straight for the vine. Rye tore after her.

Poppy reached the vine first. She made a flying leap, grabbed it, swung wildly, steadied, then began to haul herself paw over paw until she made herself stop and see where Rye was.

To her horror she saw that Rye had not reached the vine. Moreover, one of the beavers had got to the centre of the lodge first and was blocking his way. The other beaver, meanwhile, was circling behind him.

"There's one behind you!" Poppy called.

Rye spun about, saw the beaver, and darted towards the side of the lodge.

Meanwhile the beaver just below the vine stood up and tried to grab Poppy.

Scrambling higher, she managed to elude the

beaver's claws. The beaver responded by grabbing hold of the vine and yanking, pulling it all down, including Poppy.

Down Poppy plummeted, landing with a thump on the soft floor of the lodge where she lay, dazed.

The vine, as it fell, dropped around the beaver. When the beaver tried to get rid of it, he became thoroughly entangled.

Rye, watching Poppy fall, gasped. Though the other beaver was coming right at him, he made a U-turn and shot back towards her. The beaver pursuing him was thrown off. She swiped at him but missed.

Rye approached the first beaver. Realising that he was still enmeshed in the vine, Rye ran forward and reached Poppy's side.

Poppy struggled woozily to get up.

Rye helped her. "Come on!" he cried, and led her back towards the broken cage.

The beaver entangled in the vine tore free. He hurried to where the other beaver was. Together they went after the mice, certain they had them cornered. Moving carefully, not wishing to miss their chance,

they slowed down and began to creep forward.

"Are you all right?" Rye asked Poppy. He was whispering.

"I think so."

"What should we do?"

Poppy twisted around. The beavers were approaching. "I'll act as if I'm hurt," she said, her voice low but urgent.

"Why?"

"Let them get close to us, then we'll race off."

"Which direction?"

"Doesn't matter."

"Poppy, they'll trap us. It would be better if we split, you right, me left. We'll meet at the water entry. We can swim from there."

"Rye," Poppy cried, "I *can't* swim. I was lucky the first time."

"Don't worry. I'll be with you."

"Rye . . . "

"There's no other way out," Rye insisted. "I'll be with you. The vine is down."

"But . . . "

"Here they come!"

The two mice approached the back wall. There they turned and waited. Poppy, keeping a wary eye, rubbed a leg as if it hurt. Rye acted as if he were tending to his friend.

The beavers advanced, sweeping wide to prevent any escape.

"Is your head clear?" Rye whispered to Poppy. "Can you do it?"

"I think so. But Rye, swimming . . . "

"*Shhh!* Here they come."

As the beavers advanced, Rye and Poppy pressed their backs against the wall.

"Don't try to escape!" one of the beavers called. "Just slip into the cage. Both of you. If you do, we won't hurt you." They lumbered forward.

Just as they were about to grab the mice, Rye shouted, "Go!" The two mice tore off in opposite directions.

The beavers, taken by surprise, lunged forward, but missed.

Rye and Poppy, racing in separate paths, reached the far side of the wall. They cut across to the shelf that hung out over the waterway.

Rye was ready to dive in. Poppy held back. Rye looked behind. The beavers, furious at being tricked again but seeing where the mice were perched, galloped across the centre of the lodge in pursuit.

"Jump in!" Rye called.

"I can't," Poppy cried. "I'll drown. I know I will."

"You must."

Poppy braced herself, ready to do what she knew she had to do.

Suddenly, from outside the lodge there was a great THUMP. The entire lodge shook.

Both mice and beavers stopped and looked around.

"What was that?" Rye asked, dazed.

"I'm not sure," Poppy replied, equally startled.

The next moment there was a great gurgling sound. Poppy and Rye looked down into the water entry. To their astonishment the water was draining swiftly away. Nothing was left but mud.

"The water's gone!" Poppy called.

She jumped off the shelf and landed in the mud and sprinted down the tunnel.

Rye followed.

When the beavers reached the shelf, they looked with amazement at the empty waterway. "Come on! You heard what Cas said, 'Hit the water running.'"

"But it's mud!"

"They'll get away."

The beavers leapt. Bigger and heavier than the mice, they sank deep into the mud. "Help! Help!" they cried. But the more they struggled, the more they sank. They dared not move, but could only wait and watch the mice scamper off to freedom.

28
Farewells

With the dam broken, the Brook soon resumed its calm, meandering state. The water cleared, the waterlogged banks dried. Almost overnight new, green shoots sprang up. Lilies quickly re-established themselves. Once again butterflies and dragonflies danced lazily over the languid mirror surface.

The beavers retreated far up the Brook. No one saw anything more of them — not their teeth, their tails, or their dams — or heard their thoughts.

Within a week, Poppy and Rye were married by the mice's old nest, which, after it had dried out, had been reclaimed by Valerian and Clover.

It was Valerian and Clover who, according to mouse custom, performed the marriage ceremony. Thistle and Curleydock held a canopy of wildflowers over their heads — another mouse tradition. The rest of the mouse family were in full attendance, giggling and laughing, squeaking and chatting, endlessly talking

among themselves. As part of the ceremony Rye read all 32 stanzas of his poem in praise of Poppy.

She was charmed.

Before the wedding took place, Poppy went to ask Ereth to be "best porcupine." The old fellow — who had retreated to a clump of trees beyond the ridge — refused with surly indignation.

"I'd rather wait here," he grumbled.

"It would mean so much to me if you were there," Poppy pressed.

"It would mean more to me if you *weren't* there," Ereth retorted.

Poppy considered him carefully. "Ereth, you never told me what you wanted to say back in the thicket."

"Forget it," he muttered.

"Ereth," she said, "I know you don't want me to say it, but you really are the greatest and sweetest of porcupines. And the ultimate best friend to have come back."

"I only came because I couldn't find my way home to Dimwood Forest," Ereth sneered. "I needed to get you to get me back home."

"But you did do good," Poppy insisted. "If you hadn't come, the beavers would have won."

"Beavers . . ." Ereth grumbled. "Bunch of furry-faced chisels."

"Well," Poppy said, "I still wish you'd come to the wedding." And before Ereth knew what she was doing, she went up to him and kissed him on the nose.

"Mouse mush . . ." Ereth muttered. As Poppy went away he started to rub the kiss away, but suddenly changed his mind. Instead, he sat for a long while, cross-eyed, staring at his nose.

Once the marriage ceremony was over, Rye announced that he and his bride would be leaving the woodlands and going to Dimwood Forest to Poppy's home. The couple invited the family to visit as often as possible, and promised to return when they could.

Poppy made her own good-bye. "I have loved two of your sons," she told Valerian and Clover. "What fine parents you are. We can only hope to do the same."

They all hugged one another — with such a large family it took a long time — and then, side-by-side, Rye and Poppy hurried up the hill.

Ereth was waiting.

"Did you get stuck together?" he asked sourly.

"It was a beautiful ceremony," Poppy said. "I would have loved you to have been there."

"*Love*," Ereth sneered. "The less said about all that slop, the better. Come on. Let's go home."

They started off. Early on, however, they came to the meadow where Poppy and Rye had first met, and danced.

Rye looked at Poppy. Poppy looked at Rye. They did not need to say a word. They held up their paws and began to dance upon the meadow. They dipped, they jumped, they swayed, they twirled and whirled.

Ereth, keeping his distance, watched from afar. Though he tried to hide it, the old porcupine allowed himself a small, hidden smile — and a tear. Catching himself, he frowned and turned his back on the dancers. "*Love*," he complained bitterly. "Nothing but slug splat stew and toad jam. Piffle!"

But — Ereth never did wash his nose.

ABOUT THE AUTHOR

Avi was born in 1937 in the city of New York. His twin sister gave him this name when they were about a year old, and it stuck.

He has written over forty-five highly acclaimed books for children. The gripping thriller *The Christmas Rat* was his first book for Simon & Schuster. *Poppy and Rye* is the second book of his celebrated Dimwood Forest Chronicles; also available are *Poppy, Ereth's Birthday* and *Ragweed*.

THE DIMWOOD CHRONICLES

ERETH'S BIRTHDAY

It's Ereth the prickly porcupine's birthday, and he's
certain his friend Poppy is planning a big surprise for
him. But when it seems she's forgotten all about him,
Ereth huffily decides to treat himself on his special day
instead.

Journeying deep into Dimwood Forest, he's on the search
for his favourite food – salt! But many dangers await the
grizzled old porcupine. He must survive a snowstorm,
hunters and an attack by a sly pine marten named Marty
– as well as a spell of parenthood!

Whatever else Ereth's birthday may be, it's certainly one
to remember...

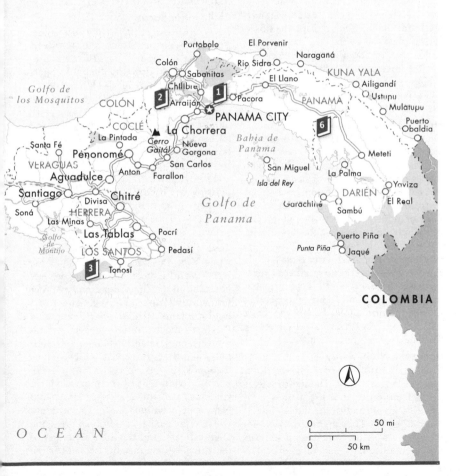

Caribbean Sea

Golfo de los Mosquitos

Portobelo
Colón
Sabanitas
Chilibre
El Porvenir
Río Sidra
Naraganá
KUNA YALA
El Llano
Ailigandí
Ustupu
Mulatupu
Puerto Obaldía

COLÓN
2 Arraiján
1 Pacora
PANAMA
★ PANAMA CITY
La Chorrera
6

COCLÉ
La Pintada
Cerro Gaital
Nueva Gorgona
San Carlos
Farallón
Bahía de Panamá
Meteti

Santa Fé
Penonomé
Antón
Isla del Rey
San Miguel
La Palma

VERAGUAS
Aguadulce
Santiago
Divisa
Chitré
Golfo de Panamá
Garachiné
Sambú
DARIÉN
Yaviza
El Real

Soná
HERRERA
Las Minas
Golfo de Montijo
Las Tablas
Pocrí
Pedasí
Puerto Piña
Punta Piña
Jaqué

LOS SANTOS
3 Tonosí

COLOMBIA

OCEAN

0   50 mi
0   50 km

TOP EXPERIENCES

Encounter the Big Ditch

In it, on it, over it, through it, next to it. There's a good reason that Panama's most-visited tourist attraction is its namesake canal, one of the world's remarkable engineering achievements. Take a full or partial transit of the waterway and imagine you're one of the canal pilots. (If you were your ship's captain, you'd be required to turn control of your vessel over to one of the facility's staff as it navigates the canal.) Or head for the observation platform at the Miraflores Locks and watch astoundingly huge ships rise or drop several feet with the water level in a few seconds. It's all the more amazing when you consider the canal's construction took place a century ago.

Stroll the Casco Viejo

One of the New World's best-preserved colonial quarters is a pastel patchwork of ancient churches, convents, shops, and homes on the west side of Panama City. The latticework balconies and brick streets evoke old New Orleans, without Mardi Gras or Bourbon Street, though . . . just a lovingly restored neighborhood with 300-year-old atmosphere to soak up. One caveat: The old quarter is reasonably safe by day—several government offices are based here in the old buildings—but less so at night, and the neighborhood's lodging options consist of only very basic backpackers' digs. Get out of Dodge by the time the sun goes down.

Dance the Night Away

You'll never run out of things to do at night in Panama City. The metropolis is rarely mentioned on a list of the hemisphere's great nighttime cities, but it deserves to be. The capital really comes into its own as the sun sets on the torrid afternoon and evening takes over. The country's best selection of restaurants holds court here, thanks to a variety of immigrants who have brought their cuisines from back home. After-dinner diversions are still limited in the arts, but there are lively casinos, and an exceptionally lively bar and dance scene fills in the gap, running the spectrum from conversing over a quiet drink to shaking your stuff to the latest Latin rhythms.

Chill Out in Bocas

Look up "laid back" in the dictionary. You just might see a picture of northeast Panama's Bocas del Toro. (Five minutes here and you'll drop the "del Toro" part of the name like everybody else does.) "Funky" is the term that gets bandied about to describe Bocas town, with almost no cars but lots of bicycles, and its brightly colored, wooden Caribbean houses that echo Jamaica. Deciding what to order for dinner at one of the many good restaurants here is the most pressing decision you'll have to make all day, but if the town starts to get too hectic, grab a water taxi to one of the neighboring palm-strewn islands in the archipelago.

Cavort with the Kuna

Kuna Yala, the homeland of one of the New World's most captivating indigenous cultures, strings along on Panama's northeast Caribbean coast. The Kuna hold the land deed to what is arguably Panama's most stunning scenery: white-sand beaches, coconut palms, and 300-plus islands off the coast. As clichéd as it sounds, as you emerge from the small plane or climb out of the motor launch, you'll feel as if you've stepped into an old *National Geographic* photo. You no doubt will find the colorful traditional dress, the dugout boats, and the intricate crafts of the Kuna fascinating, but remember the

cardinal rule of travel here: You accept the Kuna on their terms. It is *never* the other way around. But it's all the more reason a visit to Kuna Yala is Panama's signature cultural experience.

Find Your Perfect Beach

Where else in the Americas can you travel coast to coast in under an hour? With some 1,500 miles of coastline on both Pacific and Caribbean and with no spot in the country being more than 50 miles from the coast, Panama is its beaches—every chapter in this book encompasses some—and the folks here know their strands of sand. You'll find an incredible variety from which to choose. The Pacific coast west of Panama City and the Pearl Islands draw the biggest crowds with their ease of weekend access, good sand, and rising number of resorts. The central Caribbean coast means darker sand, and wetter weather, but lower prices. Farther afield, no photo can truly capture the postcard-perfect vistas of the beaches in Kuna Yala, Bocas del Toro, and Chiriquí. Go ahead and explore. Find your favorite beach. It might even be one not covered in this book.

Celebrate Folklore

There's that segment of the Miss Universe pageant where the contestants parade down the walkway in the traditional costumes from their countries. Miss Panama will don a frilly, lacy, full white dress that evokes the Azuero peninsula, the cradle of the country's traditional culture. Crafts and tradition live on in the towns, small and not so small, of this first part of Panama to be colonized by Spain. Any given weekend, some town here is celebrating a festival, usually its patron saint's day, with processions, music, and food. "*¡Venga!*" you'll be told as you stand watching

timidly on the edge of the crowd. "Come join us!" It's no wonder the region occupies a special place in the hearts of Panamanians; you just might leave with the same affection in yours.

Navigate Nature

Panama isn't just a human ethnic melting pot. As the narrow isthmus connecting the Americas, it's a cauldron of biodiversity too. Birders' eyes glaze over at the mention of more than 900 bird species that reside in Panama, around 100 being part-year migratory residents only. To add to the country's growing appeal as a nature destination, you don't need to trek hours over horrendous dirt roads to find Panama at its natural best as is so frequently the case in neighboring Costa Rica. The U.S. military preserved the former Canal Zone in reasonably pristine shape during the almost-century-long occupation, meaning nature sits just outside the capital, looking little different than it did when Spanish explorers crossed the land. You can be back in your high-rise city hotel that evening if you so choose. (It's actually possible to do birding at 2, relax in the hotel spa at 5, and have dinner at 7.) But the early bird catches the worm, and the early visitor sights the wildlife, so you don't need to flee back to civilization so quickly: Make it an overnight at Barro Colorado or Soberanía National Park. Farther out in the hinterlands, Chagres National Park, Bocas del Toro, the slopes of the Barú volcano, and the wild and wooly Darién offer ample wildlife-viewing opportunities.

WHAT'S NEW

New Ecotourism Ventures

Panama has cemented its eco-credentials with terrific nature excursions, most an easy day trip from the capital. Newest among these is the Panama Rainforest Discovery Center, adjoining Parque Nacional Soberanía, with an observation tower and solar-powered visitor center. The center will expand by the end of 2010 to include a walkway along treetop suspension bridges. The new Museo de la Biodiversidad (Museum of Biodiversity), designed by Frank Gehry, may open in Panama City in 2010.

No Smoking

Panama went smoke-free in mid-2008. Lighting up is prohibited in all businesses, including restaurants and bars. Fines are stiff, and compliance is good.

A Burgeoning Skyline

Panama City does not sit astride an earthquake fault, making it unique among Central American capitals. The sky can be the limit for building height here as a result, and each time you return, you'll see something new in the city skyline. Though not to be the city's tallest structure, the name most familiar to Americans will be the Trump Ocean Club, commissioned by The Donald himself. The 68-story tower might be mistaken for a giant sailboat moored at Punta Pacífica. Can the capital sustain and support such a building boom? Only time will tell.

A Bigger, Better Canal

"Post-Panamax" has become the watchword in world shipping, and authorities here have taken notice. With one in 14 of the world's ships now too big to use the Panama Canal, work has shifted into high gear on its expansion to avoid the facility's future irrelevance to even that small fraction of the world's fleet. A $5.2-billion project is underway to construct a larger set of locks with completion scheduled for 2014 in time for the canal's centennial.

A Place to Retire

Panama continues to win rave revues as a retirement destination. In 2009, the magazine *International Living* ranked Panama the world's number-one locale to retire. *Modern Maturity*, a publication of AARP (formerly the American Association of Retired Persons), had fingered highland Boquete as one of the world's ideal retirement places in 2001, and its successor publication, *AARP, the Magazine*, has touted Panama's benefits since then. The government here offers an active program of incentives to foreign retirees, including easy residency requirements and tax breaks on imported household goods. Might you be among the growing number of visitors each year who make the leap in status from tourist to resident?

A New President

U.S.-educated business leader Ricardo Martinelli assumed the presidency in mid-2009. The new chief executive, born in 1952 and a veteran of posts in previous administrations, gets high marks for his pro-business and anti-corruption stances. Most look with optimism at his ability to preside over the expanding economy of the country that *Forbes* magazine called "Monaco with Bananas" in a 2008 issue. Martinelli has pledged to continue support for Panama's growing tourism industry in the form of investment incentives and infrastructure development. Despite the worldwide economic downturn, the country's visitor numbers keep growing. Panama projects it will hit the magic two-million mark in 2010.

FREQUENTLY ASKED QUESTIONS

Is it safe to visit Panama? Panama does have a few trouble spots: poorer neighborhoods in the capital (we shade those on our Panama City maps), the city of Colón (other than the Colón 2000 cruise port, the free zone, the train station, and the hotels we list), and the border area with Colombia in the Darién. Standard travel precautions serve you well for the rest of the country, though. Most visitors have a hassle-free trip here.

How do I travel the Panama Canal? Many cruise lines offer itineraries that include a canal crossing but you miss out on the country itself because ships continue on their merry way and often don't actually call at a port in Panama. If you're already on the ground here, two companies in the capital offer full (whole-day) or partial (half-day) transits, both guided, of the canal. Plan your schedule carefully: partial transits run a few days each month; coast-to-coast excursions run only once or twice a month.

Pacific or Caribbean: Which coast do I choose? You can't go wrong with either shore, but distances are so short, you can easily incorporate both coastlines into a visit to Panama. If you are in the center of the country, a snazzy new highway zips you across the isthmus from Panama City to Colón in just 45 minutes. A squiggly land mass, a few mountains, and prevailing winds give the Caribbean side more rain, but myriad fans of Bocas del Toro, Portobelo, and Kuna Yala don't seem to mind.

I'm not much for hot weather. Are there parts of Panama that don't swelter? Most of this lowland country is hot year-round, but you'll be amazed at what a few hundred feet of altitude can do to cool things off. Try Boquete, Volcán, or Cerro Punta in Chiriquí province; Santa Fe in Veraguas province; El Valle de Antón, a couple of hours west of Panama City; or Cerro Azul, northeast of the capital. All live up to their "perpetual springtime" billings, with Boquete and El Valle de Antón, in particular, drawing substantial populations of foreign residents. Even in low-elevation areas, evenings are delightful once the sun starts to go down.

How do I change my money into balboas? No need to. Panama's currency is the U.S. dollar, which Panamanians call the *balboa,* named for explorer Vasco Nuñez de Balboa who "discovered" the Pacific Ocean and claimed it for Spain. No matter how you see prices written (*B.* or *$* plus the number), the dollar has been legal tender here since independence, except for seven days in 1941 when Panama issued balboa banknotes. The country does mint its own coins, the same size and value as their U.S. counterparts, and both types circulate freely here.

Where can I buy a Panama hat? That would be Ecuador. Teddy Roosevelt wore one of the wide-brimmed white hats when he came here to inspect canal construction, and the apparel became forever associated with Panama, much to Ecuador's chagrin. Any such headwear you do find for sale here should be labeled GENUINE PANAMA HAT MADE IN ECUADOR. You'll find some cheaper, though well-made hand woven headwear crafted on the Azuero Peninsula, but it has a tighter weave than the Ecuadoran product.

For more help on trip planning, see the Travel Smart chapter.

QUINTESSENTIAL PANAMA

The Big Ditch

A century has passed since its completion, but the Panama Canal remains an impressive feat of engineering, not to mention a simply inspiring sight. There are various spots from which you can admire the ""Big Ditch,"" and watching a giant cargo ship float under the Bridge of the Americas or slide into a massive lock is an unforgettable experience. The best way to appreciate it, however, is on one of the regular transit tours, which take you through locks and the canal's narrowest stretch. The canal's forests are home to plenty of wildlife, so you can also get onto its waters on a nature tour, such as the trip to Barro Colorado Nature Monument, or by fishing for the peacock bass that inhabit its depths.

Wild Things

Panama has an amazing array of wildlife and is a remarkably easy place to experience the diversity of tropical nature. Its capital, Panama City, lies near some of the world's most accessible rain forest, with several parks that you can reach in less than an hour from downtown. In fact, you can see keel-billed toucans, blue-headed parrots, and several simian species within city limits. The eastern province of the Darién is even wilder, home to such rare animals as harpy eagles, jaguars, and four types of macaw. And the country's coastal waters are comparably diverse, with hundreds of fish species, sea turtles, spotted dolphins, and humpback whales.

Idyllic Isles

Panamanian waters hold more than 1,600 islands, ranging from vast Isla del Rey to tiny cays topped with a few palm trees, like the castaway isles depicted in comics. The closest islands to Panama City are historic Isla Taboga and Isla Contadora, a mere 20-minute flight away from the city, which has a dozen beaches and nearby isles that were featured on "Survivor Pearl Islands." To the northeast are the San Blas Islands, home of the fascinating Kuna Indians, with white-sand cays ringed by coral reefs. The Bocas del Toro Archipelago, to the west, has comparable island scenery and marine life, and better accommodations. Less accessible Isla Iguana, Isla de Coiba, and the private archipelago of Islas Secas have some of the best diving in the eastern Pacific, plus great beaches. To leave Panama without visiting at least one island would be criminal; actually you could feasibly spend your entire trip island hopping.

Cultural Cornucopia

Panama is a human rainbow. Though the indigenous peoples represent only 6% of the population, the country's Kuna, Emberá, Wounaan, and Ngöbe-Buglé Indians have fascinating traditions that they happily share with visitors. The folk music and dances of the Latino majority are on display at colorful rural festivals and several Panama City venues all year long. Meanwhile, the country's European, African, Middle Eastern, and Asian immigrants ensure that you'll find a rich variety of cuisines and interesting neighborhoods to explore just about everywhere you go.

IF YOU LIKE

Adventure Sports

The options for enjoying Panama's great outdoors range from hiking through the cloud forest to paddling down a white-water river. The country's world-class fishing, surfing, diving, and bird-watching draw plenty of people focused on just one activity, but Panama is also a great destination for travelers who want to dabble in several adventure sports.

Rafting. The Chagres and Chiriquí Viejo Rivers have exciting white-water rafting routes that pass through pristine rain forest. From June to December they are complemented by half a dozen smaller rivers near Boquete.

Hiking. Panama's hiking options range from short walks into the rain forest near Panama City to longer hikes though the mountains above El Valle de Antón, Boquete, or Cerro Punta, to a two-week trek through the jungles of the Darién.

Surfing. With dozens of surf spots on two oceans, Panama has waves most of the year. Expert-only reef breaks are the norm, but a handful of beach breaks are good for neophytes too. Try Playa Venado, Playa Santa Catalina, Morro Negrito, Bocas del Toro, and Isla Grande.

Kayaking. Sit-on-top kayaks are available at many lodges for exploring reefs and mangroves, but serious kayakers can join tours by the outfitter Xtrop to paddle the lower Chagres River, the Panama Canal's Pacific entrance, or the San Blas Islands.

Horseback Riding. Equestrian tours can take you through the mountain forests of Cerro Azul, El Valle de Antón, Boquete, Volcán, or Cerro Punta, the tropical dry forests of the Azuero Peninsula, or the rain forest of Bocas del Toro.

History

The site of the first Spanish colony on the American mainland, Panama has remnants of five centuries of European influence, including ancient fortresses, a dozen colonial churches, and indigenous cultures that have hardly changed since Columbus sailed down the country's coast.

Panama Viejo. The ruins of Panama's first city—founded almost five centuries ago, and sacked by the pirate Henry Morgan in 1671—evoke the nation's start as a trade center.

Casco Viejo. Panama City's historic quarter holds an enchanting mix of colonial churches, abandoned monasteries, 19th-century buildings, and timeless plazas that are perfect for a drink, or meal.

Portobelo. Together with nearby Fuerte San Lorenzo, these colonial fortresses hemmed by jungle and perched over aquamarine waters are stunning reminders of the days when pirates cruised the Caribbean in search of booty.

The Azuero Peninsula. With their colonial churches, timeless plazas, and adobe homes, the Azuero Peninsula's older towns are time capsules where the past comes alive during religious holidays and folk festivals.

The Canal. The Panama Canal's creation only a century ago was a historic event that is celebrated by displays in the visitor center at Miraflores Locks and murals in the Canal Administration Building.

Nature Lodges

With more than 960 bird species, 9,000 kinds of flowering plants, and such rare animals as tapirs and ocelots, Panama is a great place for nature lovers. And there's no better way to experience that wildlife

than a stay at a nature lodge, where you can bird-watch from your porch or bed.

Cana Field Station. Nestled in Parque Nacional Darién, this remote and rustic lodge is surrounded by jungle that is home to more than 400 bird species and an array of other wildlife, making it the best place in Panama to see animals.

Canopy Tower. This refurbished radar station in Parque Nacional Soberanía has good bird-watching from the restaurant, the rooftop deck, and every room. Expert guides and daily hikes help guests see as much as possible, whereas the property's sister Canopy Lodge, in El Valle de Antón, provides more comfort in a gorgeous setting.

Sierra Llorona. Surrounded by a 500-acre private nature reserve traversed by miles of trails, this small, affordable lodge has more than 200 bird species, various types of monkeys, and other wildlife on the property.

Finca Lerida. Rooms on this coffee farm at the edge of Parque Nacional Volcán Barú are very near a cloud forest where guests regularly see resplendent quetzals, emerald toucanets, and hundreds of other birds.

La Loma Jungle Lodge. With just three open-air bungalows inside the rain forest on Isla Bastamentos, in Bocas del Toro, this intimate lodge provides constant exposure to nature.

Los Quetzales Lodge. Cabins inside the cloud forest here feature amazing views and bird-watching, whereas guests at the main lodge can choose from hikes in two national parks.

Diving

With two oceans, 1,600 islands, and countless acres of coral, Panama is a world-class dive destination. Its Caribbean reefs and wrecks are adorned with dozens of sponge and coral species and a mind-boggling array of fish and invertebrates. But the Pacific has the country's most spectacular dives, with schools of big fish, manta rays, sharks, and other marine creatures.

Isla de Coiba. Protected within a vast national park, Coiba is surrounded by the country's best diving, with immense reefs, submerged pinnacles, and legions of fish. Explore it on one-week dive cruises or shorter trips from Play Santa Catalina.

Isla Iguana. An inexpensive alternative to Coiba, this protected island off the coast of the Azuero Peninsula is encircled by a 100-acre coral reef inhabited by more than 350 fish species.

Islas Secas. This remote archipelago in the Gulf of Chiriquí has extensive reefs teeming with marine life that can be explored from the exclusive resort on the islands, or on day trips from Boca Chica.

Bocas del Toro. With plenty of coral reefs and several dive shops, this popular Caribbean archipelago is perfect for scuba divers and snorkeling enthusiasts alike.

Kuna Yala. Though scuba diving is prohibited in Kuna Yala, the province has impressive reefs, especially at the Cayos Holandeses, which can be visited on cruises with San Blas Sailing.

The Canal. Scuba Panama offers a unique dive in the Panama Canal, where steam shovels and trains used to dig it lie submerged in the murky depths.

National Parks
and Activities

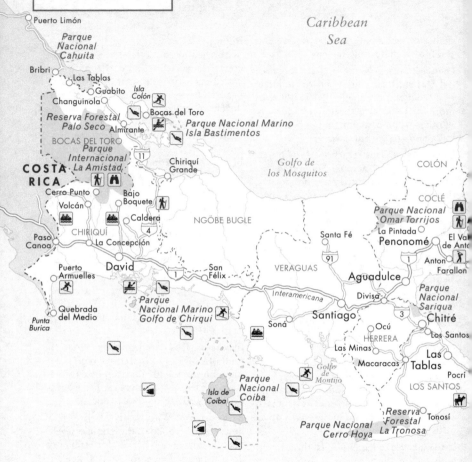

Puerto Limón

Parque Nacional Cahuita

Caribbean Sea

Bribri

Las Tablas

Guabito

Isla Colón

Changuinola

Bocas del Toro

Reserva Forestal Palo Seco

Almirante

Parque Nacional Marino Isla Bastimentos

BOCAS DEL TORO

Parque Internacional La Amistad

11

Chiriquí Grande

Golfo de los Mosquitos

COLÓN

COSTA RICA

Cerro Punto

Bajo Boquete

COCLÉ

Parque Nacional Omar Torrijos

Volcán

Caldera

4

NGÖBE BUGLÉ

La Pintada

Penonomé

El Va de Anto

Paso Canoa

CHIRIQUÍ

La Concepción

Santa Fé

91

Antón

Farallón

David

San Félix

VERAGUAS

Aguadulce

Puerto Armuelles

Parque Nacional Marino Golfo de Chiriquí

1

Interamericana

Divisa

3

Parque Nacional Sariqua

Chitré

Quebrada del Medio

Soná

Santiago

Ocú

HERRERA

Los Santos

Punta Burica

Golfo de Montijo

Las Minas

Macaracas

Las Tablas

Pocrí

Isla de Coiba

Parque Nacional Coiba

LOS SANTOS

Reserva Forestal La Tronosa

Tonosí

Parque Nacional Cerro Hoya

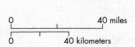

0   40 miles

0   40 kilometers

Portobelo
Parque
Nacional
Portobelo
Colón
Sabanitas
2
Chilibre
Gamboa
Pacora
Arraiján
La Chorrera

El Porvenir
Carti Suitupo
Burbayar
Rio Sidra
Parque
Nacional
Chagres
El Llano
Chepo
1

Naraganá
KUNA YALA
Ailigandí
Ustupu
Mulatupu

Panama City
PANAMA
Interamericana

Puerto
Obaldia

Cerro
Gaitál
Bahia de Panama
Nueva Gorgona
Playa Coronado
San Carlos

San Miguel
Isla
del Rey
Isla
San José

Meteti
DARIÉN
La Palma
Garachiné
Sambú
El Real
Yaviza

Golfo de Panama

Pedasí

Punta Piña
Jaqué
Puerto
Piña
Parque
Nacional
Darién

COLOMBIA

PACIFIC
OCEAN

KEY	
🦅	Bird watching
🤿	Diving
🎣	Fishing
🏌	Golf
🥾	Hiking
🐴	Horseback riding
🛶	Kayaking
🚣	Rafting
🏄	Surfing

PANAMANIAN CUISINE

Not all food south of the Río Grande is Mexican even though we Americans tend to anticipate that it will be. Although Panama does have plenty of Mexican restaurants, the food here is definitely not known for its spice; however, the country does have a distinct cuisine, which reflects its own peculiar ethnic mix and geography.

As the self-described "crossroads of the world," cosmopolitan Panama City has been a magnet for immigrants who have brought their cuisines here for the past century. While there are few types of food you can't find here, Chinese, Italian, Greek, and American restaurants dominate the ethnic-restaurant scene in the city, with a smaller selection of Peruvian, Argentine, Japanese, and Middle Eastern eateries among our favorites.

Outside Panama City, lunch is usually the big meal of the day, whether at home or in a restaurant, and it is almost always a good value at mom-and-pop eateries. Your best bet is usually a hearty, filling combination meal called a *casado,* meaning "married." It consists of a main dish—usually beef, chicken, pork— accompanied by rice, black beans, and cabbage. An upscale restaurant makes use of the casado concept for lunch but makes it all sound a bit more highbrow—more expensive too—calling its prix-fixe menu the *plato ejecutivo* ("executive plate").

The heart and soul of Panamanian gastronomy lie in the provinces, however—no surprise there—and sampling a few signature local dishes can be a highlight of your trip here. You'll find a more ample selection of *típico* food in rural areas. Searching for the country"s signature *carimañola* in the capital might be akin to asking for corn fritters in New York.

So what are carimañolas exactly? One of Panama's signature dishes consists of yucca, ground and boiled and made into a dumpling, or fritter, and filled with minced beef or chicken and pieces of boiled egg. Carimañolas are a Panamanian breakfast staple.

Sancocho is the other dish that has "Panama" written all over it, though you will also find it on Dominican menus. This chicken and yucca soup—some cooks make it thick enough that it qualifies more as a stew than a soup—is flavored with *culantro.* (Think "cilantro," but slightly more aromatic; it's a common flavoring used all over Central America.) As with your grandmother's chicken soup, sancocho is reputed to be good for whatever ails you. (Many swear by its supposed anti-hangover properties.) It can also be a surprisingly cooling dish to eat on a sweltering day. (We'll credit the culantro for its cooling effect.)

Several countries in the region, most notably Cuba, claim the descriptively named *ropa vieja* ("old clothes") as their own. As with putting on old clothing, a Panamanian cook uses whatever is available and left over in the kitchen to spice up a dish that is, at its most basic, shredded flank steak with rice and tomato sauce. (Ropa vieja is one of the few exceptions to the "Panamanian cuisine is not spicy" adage.)

Panamanian cooks make a variation on Mexican *tamales*—the singular is *tamal*— with a filling of chicken, peas, onions, and cornmeal boiled inside tied plantain leaves. Tamales are a cinch to reheat and serve—you eat the filling but not the leaves, and certainly not the string— making them a popular, convenient food to prepare in batches in advance and serve at Christmastime. Some cooks here make what they call a *tamal de olla* ("tamal in the pan"), with the same ingredients, but not wrapped in leaves and served immediately.

Also easy to prepare in advance and, thus, a staple for any holiday, are *empanadas.* Every Latin American country claims its own variation on this recipe. Panamanian cooks make semi-circular empanadas with a filling of ground beef and cheese fried in dough and served as appetizers. Caribbean cooks often add plantain to the filling.

Accompaniments to a meal are many. *Almojábana,* a corn flour bead, is a staple, as are *patacones,* green plantains fried golden brown and salted and pounded into crispy chips. Panamanians sometimes prepare patacones with breadfruit, but plantains are the hands-down favorite here. *Hojaldras* make a tasty side dish to any breakfast. When made sweet and sprinkled with powered sugar, you'll liken this Panamanian fry bread to doughnuts, but they are just as often prepared with ham and cheese too.

Since the country has some 1,500 miles of coastline, seafood is a naturally popular staple. (What else would you expect in a nation whose name means "abundance of fish"?) Corvina, a white sea bass, figures prominently into the cuisine here. It frequently shows up as the main ingredient in *ceviche (*sometimes spelled cebiche or *seviche,* among several spelling variations). Whatever the cubed pieces of fish or seafood used—shrimp and octopus are less common here—ceviche, Panamanian style, is marinated in lime juice, with onion and celery and sometimes hot pepper. It is served chilled as an appetizer. (Latino groceries in the United States frequently stock imported Panamanian ceviche, worth a pre- or post-trip sampling.)

Hearty Panamanian food gets washed down by some distinctive beverages, too. *Seco* gets distilled from sugarcane. Smooth it is not; "firewater" might be a better description for the drink. Its kick is most commonly tempered with milk in a popular beverage drunk chilled in the provinces called *seco con leche.* On the other hand, flavorful *chicheme,* does go down very easily, as you would expect of a blend of milk, cornmeal, cinnamon, and vanilla. Beverages don't come more basic than the ubiquitous Panamanian *pipa.* Poke a hole in an unripe coconut, stick in a straw, and you have a refreshing drink of coconut juice. Roadside stands everywhere sell them.

GREAT ITINERARIES

CANAL AND ISLANDS

The quintessential weeklong Panama itinerary takes in the country's capital, its famous canal, and gives you a taste of the adventure that awaits in the interior and on the outlying islands. With some judicious planning, you'll also have a taste of beach life and an introduction to one of the most important indigenous cultures of the region in just seven days, though spending a full week in Panama will require you to take a trip of nine days if you include your travel time; keep that in mind when planning your vacation. Happily, you can fly nonstop to Panama from several different cities in the U.S., and it"s a relatively short five-hour flight from New York or Chicago, slightly less from Dallas or Houston, slightly more from Los Angeles. If you have more time, there's plenty more to see, and a two-week itinerary would enable you to branch out and travel beyond central Panama to more far-flung parts of the country, such as Chiriquí or Bocas del Toro.

2 Days: Panama City and Canal

Base yourself in the capital for the first three days of your trip. Use taxis while in the city since they are much cheaper than renting a car, even if you are taking short trips to the outskirts of town (the Miraflores Locks, for instance). Start early with a partial transit tour of the Panama Canal, then spend the afternoon and evening exploring the Casco Viejo, which has several good restaurants. If you don't want to do a partial transit, then just head up to the Miraflores Locks and spend some quality time in the observation lounge there to get a feel for the Canal. Start Day 2 with a bird-watching excursion in the rain forest of Parque Natural Metropolitano or Parque National Soberanía, then check out city sights such as the Museo Antropológico, Esclusas Miraflores, Mi Pueblito, or Balboa. Calzada de Amador is a great place for sunset cocktails or dinner.

1 Day: Railway and Caribbean

Get up early on Day 3 to take the Panama Railroad to Colón so you can spend the day exploring the country's Caribbean coast, fortresses, rain forest, or beaches of Portobelo or San Lorenzo before returning to Panama City. The trip takes only an hour each way, but the schedule is aimed at commuters, so there's just one departure per day from each direction; you"ll leave Panama City at 7:15 and return at 5:15, but you'll have plenty of time to see all there is to see in and around Portobelo, where you go on a prearranged tour or hire a private taxi at the Colón 2000 cruise pier (don't take a taxi at the Colón train station; rather, take the shuttle to the cruise pier and get a taxi or rent a car there). You can also overnight on the Caribbean side (there are some decent hotels in Colón), but you'll need more time for travel on Day 4.

2 Days: Hills and Forests

After three days of history and city touring, it's time to enjoy a bit more of the country's natural environment. More active travelers may prefer to head to El Valle de Antón for bird-watching, hiking, biking, or horseback riding; there are several excellent lodging choices in this region of the Cordillera Central, where you can sleep in comfort and eat in style. You could also combine a night at Sierra Llorona or Burbayar lodge (both in the highlands northeast of Panama City) with a visit to an Emberá Indian village. Either of these options takes you to a cooler and higher climate than the capital, where

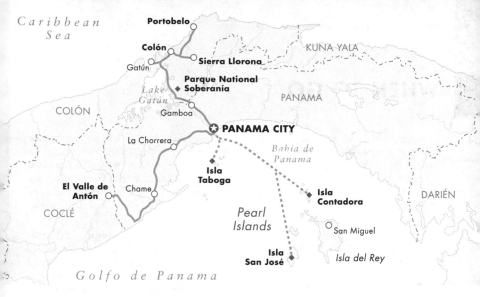

you'll enjoy the mountain air and a wide variety of outdoor pursuits. Another option (albeit a more predictable one) would involve spending your two days at the Gamboa Rainforest Resort, which is less than an hour north of Panama City by taxi; this option is rather expensive but provides several choices for activities, including the popular rain-forest aerial tram and trips onto Lago Gatún.

2 Days: Island Adventures

Some of the country's best beaches are on its islands, and three of the most accessible are in the Pearl Islands chain south of Panama City, all easily reachable on short flights (or in one case a ferry) from the city. Isla Taboga is a short 60-minute ferry ride from the Amador Causeway, and, though it's a popular day-trip destination for residents of the capital, there are also some small hotels where you can spend the night to enjoy the beaches at leisure. Alternatively, you could fly to Isla Contadora or Isla San José, two of the lovely Pearl Islands and top off your trip with sun, sea, and sand. Both are a short flight from Panama City (less than half an hour) and offer some of the country's best beaches. Isla Contadora is the more developed of the two, and it's a popular resort island with a range of activities as

LOGISTICS

■ Canal transit tours are not offered every day of the week.

■ In Colón, arrange a pick-up in advance through a tour company or take a shuttle to Colón 2000 (these shuttles always meet the Panama Railway trains), and rent a car or hire a taxi there.

■ Renting a car is the best option for El Valley de Antón, two hours west of Panama City. Lodges closer to Panama City can be reached by taxi (including the Gamboa Rainforest Resort) or may provide transportation.

■ From Panama City there are two daily flights to Isla Contadora, one flight to Isla San José most days, and two or three daily ferries to Isla Taboga.

well as good, small hotels. Isla San José is more distant and more remote (it's privately owned and has only one expensive resort). Sportfishing, snorkeling, or diving are good choices for more active travelers in the Pearl Islands.

WHEN TO GO

Most people head to Panama during the dry season, usually from December to May, but your choice depends on your interests. Bird-watching is best from October to March, when northern migrants boost the native population. In fact, it"s easier to see all wildlife during the dry months, because the forest foliage thins. The fishing is best from January to March, though Pacific sailfish run from April to July, and there are plenty of fish biting from July to January. The surf is best from June to December in the Pacific, whereas the Caribbean gets more waves between November and March, and some swells in July and August. The best months for white-water rafting and kayaking are June to December, when you have half a dozen rivers to choose from, but Panama"s two best can be navigated from June to March. Scuba diving varies according to the region. The Caribbean's best diving conditions are between August and November, though March and April can also be good. The Gulf of Panama and Azuero Peninsula have better visibility from June to December, but the trade winds make the sea progressively colder and murkier there from December through to May. Those winds have less of an impact on the Gulf of Chiriquí and Isla de Coiba, where the diving is best from December to July, after which large swells can decrease visibility and complicate diving.

Panama City is a fun place to visit any time of year, but the dry months are nicest. Jazz fans will want to be there in late January, when the city celebrates its annual jazz festival, but travelers interested in folk music and dance can track down a folk festival in the Azuero Peninsula just about any time of year. Hotels often fill up between Christmas and Easter, and it"s especially hard to find a room outside Panama City when Panamanians go on vacation—around New Year"s, Carnaval week, and Easter week. The holidays are bad times to go to the beach, but they hardly affect Kuna Yala and the Darién.

Climate

Panama is an unmistakably tropical country, where the temperature fluctuates between 70°F and 90°F year-round, and humidity is usually about eighty percent. The country experiences two seasons: dry, from late December to May, and rainy from early May to December. January through April are the sunniest months for most of the country, with the exception of Bocas del Toro province, which gets plenty of rain in December and January. The sunniest months in Bocas del Toro are March, September, and October. The Darién gets more rain than the central and western provinces, and has a slightly shorter dry season. The mountain valleys of Boquete, Bambito, and Cerro Punta experience strong winds, mist, and low temperatures from December to mid-February, making March and April the nicest months there. Panama experiences a partial dry season in July and August, when it can go days without raining. You can count on downpours just about every afternoon in May, June, October, and November, when it sometimes rains for days on end.

ON THE CALENDAR

1

	New Year's, Carnaval, and Holy Week are the holidays that have Panamanians flocking to the beaches and mountains, and folk festivals take place nearly every month on the Azuero Peninsula. Check the Panama Tourism Bureau's Web site (⊕ *www.visitpanama.com*) for exact dates.
DRY SEASON Jan.	The **Panama Jazz Festival** (⊕ *www.panamajazzfestival.com*) brings together international and local artists for a concert series in Panama City's historic Casco Viejo in late January.
Late Feb.–early Mar.	**Carnaval** is celebrated throughout Panama, but the most spectacular parades take place in Panama City and Las Tablas, on the Azuero Peninsula.
Apr.	The **Desfile Mil Polleras** *(Thousand Polleras Parade)* (☎ 526–7000 ⊕ *www.milpolleras.pa*) takes place in downtown Panama City on the last Sunday in April. It features lots of folk-music floats and women in *polleras* (embroidered dresses).
WET SEASON Late May–Early June	**Corpus Christi** is a colorful celebration in La Villa de Los Santos and nearby towns, featuring dances by *los diablitos* (little devils), groups of men in red and black costumes and elaborate papier-mâché masks.
June	The **Festival de Manito,** one of the country's most important folk festivals, is held in the tiny town of Ocú, in the heart of the Azuero Peninsula, during the last week in June.
July	The **Festival de la Pollera** is celebrated in the town of Las Tablas, on the Azuero Peninsula, July 20–23, with folk music, dancing, a parade, and plenty of women in *polleras*.
Aug.	The **Fundación de Panama la Vieja** (☎ 226–8915 ⊕ *www.panamaviejo.org*) celebrates the founding of Panama Viejo with a ceremony and folk dances in the ruins on August 15.
Sept.	The **Festival Nacional de la Mejorana** (⊕ *www.festivalnacionaldelamejorana.com*), held during the third week of September in tiny Gauraré, on the Azuero Peninsula, is dedicated to folk music played on a tiny guitar called *la mejorana.*
Nov.	The **Día de la Independencia** celebrates the country's independence from Spain in 1821 with parades and drumming.

Panama City

WORD OF MOUTH

"I enjoyed Panama City. Pleasant (and cheap) bars and restaurants. I was comfortable there, unlike how I felt in San Jose, Costa Rica."

—JeanH

"[I]f you happen to be on Amador Causeway stop in the [new Biodiversity] museum's administrative office (the old Officer's Club on Ft. Amador). It is right next to the work site. They can show you the models, which are fabulous. It will be a most extraordinary museum when open."

—cmcfong

By David
Dudenhoefer
Updated by
Sean Mattson

Panama City is an incredibly diverse and hospitable place, with an assortment of urban and natural environments to please just about any taste. Founded nearly five centuries ago, the city is steeped in history, yet much of it is remarkably modern. The baroque facades of the city's old quarter appear frozen in time, while the area around Punta Paitilla (Paitilla Point) is positively vaulting into the 21st century, with gleaming skyscrapers towering over the waterfront.

The city can feel schizophrenic, changing personality as you move from one neighborhood to another. That could be said of many a metropolis, but Panama City's diversity is disproportionate to its size. Though its metropolitan area has just over one million inhabitants, Panama City is home to races, religions, and cultures from around the world, reflected in its various Christian churches and synagogues, plus a mosque and a Hindu temple—not to mention its many restaurants. Whereas the high-rises of Punta Paitilla and the Área Bancária (banking district) create a skyline more impressive than that of Miami, the brick streets and balconies of the Casco Viejo evoke the French Quarter of New Orleans. The tree-lined boulevards of Balboa—built by the U.S. government between 1905 and 1920—are a pleasant mixture of early-20th-century American architecture and exuberant tropical vegetation. The islands reached by the nearby Calzada Amador (Amador Causeway)—a man-made causeway that stretches 2 mi into the Pacific—have brand-new bars and restaurants, plus a yacht-packed marina. The best part? All these neighborhoods lie within 15 minutes of one another (traffic permitting, of course).

The city's proximity to tropical nature is astounding, with significant patches of forest protected within city limits on Cerro Ancón (Ancón Hill) and in Parque Metropolitano, and the national parks of Camino de Cruces and Soberanía just to the northwest of town. You could spend a morning hiking through the rain forest of the Parque Metropolitano to see parrots and toucans, then watch pelicans dive into the sea while sipping a sunset drink at one of Amador Causeway's restaurants. There are plenty of spots in and around the city that offer views of the ocean or the Panama Canal, and those views include massive ships anchored offshore or plying the interoceanic waterway.

An impressive array of restaurants, an abundance of shops and handicraft markets, and a vibrant nightlife scene round out Panama City's charm. This is good news for travelers, since the city is Panama's transportation hub, which makes overnights here unavoidable. All international flights arrive at Panama City's Tocumen Airport (airport code PTY), which is 25 km (16 mi) east of the city; domestic flights and buses depart from the neighborhood of Albrook, just west of downtown. ⚠ The city can also serve as a base for an array of day trips, including

Panama Canal transit tours, a boat ride to Isla Taboga, a trip on the Panama Canal Railway, a day at the colonial fortresses of Portobelo, or hikes through various rain-forest reserves.

The downside of Panama City is that its colorful contrasts include all the ugly aspects of urban life in the developing world. It has its fair share of slums, including several around must-see Casco Viejo. Traffic is often downright terrible, and the ocean along its coast is very polluted. Brand-new SUVs waiting at stoplights are solicited by people selling oranges and car accessories. Crime is a problem in some neighborhoods. Be sure to use your common sense and be careful where you walk around, especially at night. The city as a whole, though, is quite safe, especially the downtown area, where you'll find its bustling hotels, restaurants, and bars.

ORIENTATION AND PLANNING

GETTING ORIENTED

Panama City is a sprawling urban area, stretching for 10 km (6 mi) along the Bahía de Panamá (Bay of Panama) on the Pacific Coast and several miles into the sultry hinterland. The good thing for visitors is that most of its attractions and accommodations are within a few miles of one another in the city's southwest corner, near the Panama Canal's Pacific entrance. The eastern edge of the canal's entrance—because Panama snakes west to east, the canal runs north from the Pacific to the Atlantic—is defined by the former American Canal Zone, which includes the Calzada Amador (the breakwater connecting several islands to the mainland) and the neighborhoods of Balboa, Ancón, and Albrook. To the east of Balboa stands Cerro Ancón, a forested hill topped by a big Panamanian flag that is a landmark visible from most of the city. To the east of Cerro Ancón is the busy Avenida de los Mártires, which was once on the border between the Canal Zone and Panama City. To the east of that former border lie the slums of Chorrillo and Santa Ana, both of which should be avoided; the Plaza Cinco de Mayo (where the country's congress is located); and the Avenida Central pedestrian mall, which runs southeastward into the historic Casco Viejo.

Avenida Balboa, one of the city's main east-west routes, runs along the Bay of Panama between the Casco Viejo and modern Paitilla Point. It runs through an attractive waterfront promenade called the Cinta Costera, a 3.5-km (2.2-mi) lineal park with a monument to Balboa. The neighborhood along its western half is a bit sketchy, so you should only stroll the Cinta Costera to the east of the Balboa monument. Avenida Balboa ends at Punta Paitilla, with its Multicentro shopping mall, skyscrapers, and private hospitals. There it branches into the Corredor Sur, an expressway to the international airport, and the inland Vía Israel, which eventually turns into Avenida Cincuentenario, and leads to the ruins of Panamá Viejo.

TOP REASONS TO GO

The Panama Canal. With a length of 50 mi, the interoceanic canal is literally Panama's biggest attraction. Whatever your reasons for traveling to Panama, the canal is simply a must-see; there are half a dozen spots in or near the capital from which to admire it. The Calzada Amador, the Balboa Yacht Club, the scenic overlook on the east side of the Bridge of the Americas, and the visitor center at Miraflores Locks all offer impressive vistas of the ""big ditch,"" which you can experience more closely on a transit tour or on one of the nature tours of Gatún Lake.

Casco Viejo. The balconies, brick streets, and quiet plazas of the historic Casco Viejo have a European air, and the neighborhood's ancient churches and monasteries stand as testimony to the country's rich colonial history. After decades of neglect, the old quarter is finally undergoing a renaissance. The neighborhood also has some of the city's nicest restaurants and bars, which makes it a must-visit, even if only for dinner followed by a stroll and a nightcap.

Rain Forests. Panama City lies near some of the most accessible rain forests in the world, with jungle trails a short drive from most hotels. Parque Natural Metropolitano, within the city limits, is home to more than 200 bird species. Within Parque Nacional Soberanía, and the highland forests of Cerro Azul and Altos de Campana, live such animals as the keel-billed toucan and howler monkey.

The Calzada Amador. The Amador Causeway provides a great escape from the cement and traffic of downtown Panama City. Stretching 2 mi (3 km) into the Pacific to connect three islands to the mainland, the causeway has panoramic views of the city's skyline, the canal's Pacific entrance, and the Bay of Panama, as well as an excellent selection of restaurants, bars, and diversions—all of them cooled by ocean breezes.

Day Trips. Panama City is the perfect base for day trips into the wild that can leave you sweaty, muddy, or sunburned but get you back to your hotel in time to clean up for a delicious three-course meal. In addition to boat trips on the Panama Canal or wildlife watching on Gatún Lake, you can hike into the forests of various national parks. Parque Nacional Chagres has Emberá Indian villages and white-water rafting, and day trips to the island of Isla Taboga or the Caribbean fortresses of Portobelo combine history with beach time. All in all, there are enough day-trip options to keep you busy for a week.

The main eastbound street to the north of Avenida Balboa is Avenida Justo Arosemena, which runs east from Plaza Cinco de Mayo and flows into Calle 50 (Cincuenta) (also called Calle Nicanor de Obarrio). The main westbound route is Vía España, a busy boulevard lined with banks and shopping centers that curves south to become the Avenida Central, which in turn becomes a pedestrian mall at Plaza Cinco de Mayo, after which it curves eastward to become the main avenue in the Casco Viejo.

PANAMA CITY PLANNER

GETTING HERE AND AROUND

BY AIR

All international flights land at Panama City's Aeropuerto Internacional de Tocumen (PTY), 26 km (16 mi) northeast of Panama City. Panama has two domestic airlines. Aeroperlas flies to approximately 11 destinations in the country, while Air Panama flies to about two dozen destinations and has the country's youngest fleet of aircraft. Both fly out of Aeropuerto Marcos A. Gelabert for the same prices—between $100 and $200 round-trip—which vary according to the destination.

BY BUS

If you don't mind the heat, cramped seating, and having to watch your wallet, the local buses (converted Blue Bird school buses) are a cheap (25¢) way to get around the city. Most have wild paint jobs, and each bus has its destination and route painted broadly across the windshield. The word to remember when you want to get off is *parada* (stop). You pay your fare as you get off. All buses pass by the massive Terminal de Buses in Albrook, where you can catch buses to almost everywhere else in the city and the country. Buses to the Miraflores Locks, Summit Zoo, and Gamboa leave hourly from the SACA terminal, one block north of Plaza Cinco de Mayo.

BY CAR

Driving a car in Panama City is not an undertaking for the meek, but renting a car is an excellent way to explore the surrounding countryside. Rentals usually cost $40 to $50 per day, whereas four-wheel-drive vehicles cost $60 to $90. All the big car-rental companies have one or more offices in the city and at the airports.

Car-Rental Agencies Avis (☎ *238–4056*). **Budget** (☎ *263–8777*). **Dollar** (☎ *270–0355*). **Hertz** (☎ *260–2111*). **National** (☎ *265–3333*). **Thrifty** (☎ *204–9555*).

BY TAXI

Taxis in Panama City are all independently owned, tend to be smaller cars, and don't have meters. The city is divided into zones, the flat fare for one person being $1, to which they add a quarter each time you cross into another zone, plus a quarter for each additional person, though those extra quarters are sometimes generously added on. Fares also increase about 20% after 10 PM and on Sundays. A short trip should cost about $1.50 for two people, whereas a trip to the domestic airport in Albrook or the Calzada Amador can run $3–$5, and the trip to Tocumen International Airport should cost $20. Tips are not expected. You will be charged double, or several times the standard rate, by the taxi drivers who wait outside hotels, but their cars are usually standard size, and drivers are likely to speak some English. Flagging a cab in the street is widely considered to be safe. If you're alone, you may be expected to share a taxi, a common practice in Panama, as is sitting in the passenger seat next to the driver.

Panamataxi Turismo provides personal transportation and various cultural tours for individuals and small groups.

Contacts **Panamataxi Turismo** (☏ *264-1078 or 6480-1078* ⊕ *www. panamataxi.com*).

WHEN TO GO

Because Panama City has the country's only international airport and is the transportation hub for domestic flights and buses, you may return here several times during your trip. This means you can explore the capital bit by bit over the course of your stay in the country.

Unlike the rest of the country, Panama City hardly has a low season, since the bulk of its visitors are business travelers. Most tourists head here during the dry season, from December to May; this is when the city's hotels are packed. Carnaval, around mid-February, is a fun time to be in the capital, since that long weekend is celebrated with parades and lots of partying. The city is fairly quiet during Easter week, on the other hand, since businesses close from Thursday to Easter Sunday and every resident who can leaves town. The Mil Polleras parade, held on the last Sunday of April, is a celebration worth catching, with lots of folk music and women in *polleras*, elaborately embroidered dresses. November 3 and 28 are independence days, from Colombia and Spain respectively. They are noisy dates to be in town, since every high school has a drum corps that marches in the parades. In fact, late October and November is a noisy time of year, because those drummers spend much of it practicing for the big parades.

May, June, and September through November are the rainiest months in Panama City, though most of that rain falls in the afternoon or evening. The rains let up a bit in July and August, which is a good time to visit, since you have to share the place with fewer tourists than during the dry season.

SAFETY

Most of the city is safe for walking, even at night, especially Vía España, El Cangrejo, the Área Bancária, and Paitilla, where the bulk of the city's hotels and restaurants are located. The Casco Viejo and Avenida Central pedestrian mall are safe by day, but after dark you should limit your wandering to the area around Plaza Bolívar and Plaza Francia, which is where all the restaurants and bars are. Even during the day you should leave most valuables and money in your hotel safe. At night you should travel to and from the Casco Viejo only by taxi or rental car, but by day walking there from Plaza Cinco de Mayo on Avenida Central is fine. You don't need a map or a Geiger counter to realize when you're headed into a bad neighborhood, though some areas look more dangerous than they actually are. If you're on foot and feel any apprehension about where you've ended up, flag down the first taxi, even if it has another passenger in it, and go someplace you know is safe. Between 11 AM and 3 PM the heat is usually oppressive, so serious strolling should be limited to the morning and evening hours. ⚠ **Areas that should be avoided at all hours are El Chorrillo and Santa Ana, just west of the Casco Viejo; the southwestern half of Caledonia, including the Avenida Balboa west of the Balboa Monument; and Curundú, just to the west of Caledonia.**

RESTAURANTS

Don't plan on losing weight in Panama City. There are simply too many good restaurants, and a cuisine selection that pretty much spans the globe, from Indian and Italian to Lebanese and Panamanian (needless to say). The city has some inventive chefs who do an excellent job of combining local ingredients with farther-flung culinary traditions; the results make for some remarkable dining at reasonable prices.

The seafood tends to be quite fresh, which shouldn't come as a surprise, since the word "*Panama*" means " "abundance of fish," " and it's relatively inexpensive, with the exception of lobster and crab. Pastas and pizzas are also affordable, but the best beef is imported from the United States and can be more expensive. A typical entrée at an expensive restaurant runs about $15, whereas a main dish at a less expensive eatery averages around $7. It's customary to tip at least 10%, but some restaurants automatically add a 10% *servicio* charge, so be sure to have a good look at the check. Service can be slow, especially in the more economical restaurants, and it's rarely delivered with a smile.

Many restaurants close Sundays, and many close for a couple of hours between lunch and dinner, especially in Casco Viejo. Reservations are required only at the best restaurants. Jackets and ties aren't necessary, but don't wear shorts and sandals unless the restaurant is outdoors.

HOTELS

Panama City has an extensive selection of hotels, yet there is often a shortage of rooms at everything but the budget levels, which means you'll want to reserve well ahead of time, especially for the December–May dry season. If you travel off-season, or reserve through the Web sites of the big hotels, you should be able to get rooms for considerably less than the rack rate. The city's best hotels are quite nice and varied enough in what they offer to suit most tastes, but some can suffer from poor service. Nevertheless, travelers on a budget can find a variety of comfortable accommodations for less than $100, including hotels with swimming pools and Internet. All hotels listed in this chapter have private bathrooms with hot water, air-conditioning, telephone, and cable TV.

WHAT IT COSTS IN U.S. DOLLARS					
	¢	$	$$	$$$	$$$$
Restaurants	under $5	$5–$10	$10–$15	$15–$20	over $22
Hotels	under $50	$50–$100	$100–$160	$160–$220	over $220

Restaurant prices are per person for a main course at dinner. Hotel prices are for two people in a standard double room, excluding service and 10% tax.

ESSENTIALS

ATMS

Cash machines aren't as ubiquitous in Panama City as they are in Miami or New York, but almost. You can find ATMs in the lobbies of the biggest hotels, gas stations with convenience stores, pharmacies, supermarkets, and the city's abundant banks. Banks that have a lot of ATMs

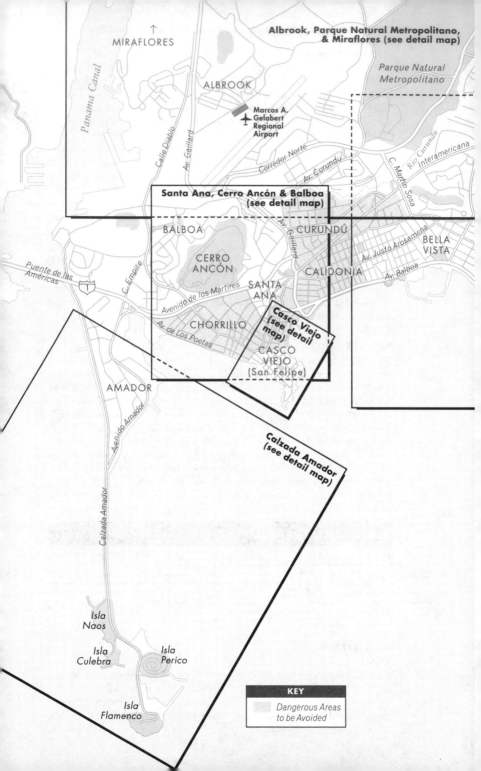

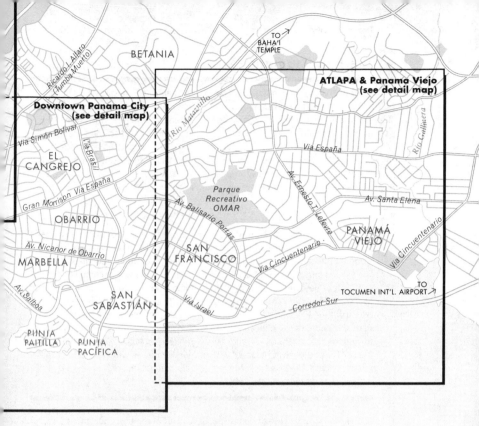

BETANIA

TO →
BAHA'I
TEMPLE

**ATLAPA & Panama Viejo
(see detail map)**

Ricardo J. Alfaro
(Tumba Muerto)

Río Matasnillo

Río Cabuya

**Downtown Panama City
(see detail map)**

Vía Simón Bolívar

Vía Brasil

EL
CANGREJO

Vía España

Av. Ernesto T. Lefevre

Av. Santa Elena

Gran Morrison Vía España

Parque
Recreativo
OMAR

Av. Balisario Porras

OBARRIO

PANAMÁ
VIEJO

Vía Cincuentenario

Av. Nicanor de Obarrio

SAN
FRANCISCO

MARBELLA

Vía Cincuentenario

Av. Balboa

SAN
SABASTIÁN

Vía Israel

TO
TOCUMEN INT'L. AIRPORT →

Corredor Sur

PUNTA
PAITILLA

PUNTA
PACÍFICA

Bahía de Panama

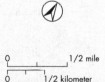

0 _____ 1/2 mile
0 _____ 1/2 kilometer

*PACIFIC
OCEAN*

Panama City

The Panamanians

You won't spend long in Panama City before realizing that it is home to an extremely varied populace. Thanks to the canal and the country's commercial importance, immigrants flock here from around the world. A walk through one of the city's busy streets will prove just how diverse its residents are.

The majority of Panamanians are mestizo, which refers to the mixture of European and native Panamanian blood that began with the conquest. The second-largest group of residents is of African descent, some of whose ancestors arrived in Panama as slaves, others whose ancestors came from Barbados and other Caribbean islands to work on the canal and stayed. About 10% of the country's population is of direct European descent, a group that includes descendants of Spanish conquistadors, seamen who have settled here, and former American "Zonians" who stayed on when the canal became Panamanian. The capital is also home to significant numbers of Sephardic and Ashkenazi Jews, Arabs from various nations, Chinese, and East Indians, who together control much of the city's retail and wholesale sectors.

Descendants of the original Panamanians, on the other hand, represent 10% of the national population, and most of them live in comarcas, or indigenous territories. There are plenty of native Panamanians working in the city, though; you're bound to spot Kuna women, who sell their molas (patchwork fabric pictures) and other handicrafts, as you explore the capital's neighborhoods.

scattered around the city include BAC and Banistmo. Debit cards and credit cards from U.S., Canadian, and European banks should work in all Panamanian ATMs, but there is usually an additional charge for international transactions of $3. The maximum permitted amount per withdrawal is $500.

TOURS

Panama City has a plethora of tour companies, all of which offer tours of the city, canal, and nearby parks, but not all of them have guides of the same caliber, and few have true naturalist guides. The premier ecotourism company is **Ancon Expeditions,** but the comparable **Ecocircuitos** also has good guides and environmentally friendly policies. One of the oldest companies is **Pesantez Tours,** which has some good naturalist guides but concentrates on more traditional tours. The problems with such established companies is that their best guides are often reserved by the top U.S. companies, which hire them to run their Panama tours, so independent tourists may end up with newer, less experienced guides. Smaller, newer companies that can often provide a more customized service include **Panoramic Panama** and **Advantage Panama,** which specializes in bird-watching and nature. Other established tour operators that offer some unique day trips are **Margo Tours, Futura Travel,** and **Aventuras Panama,** a white-water outfitter that also offers hiking, and visits to Emberá Indian communities in Chagres National Park.

EXPLORING TIPS

Panama City is a pretty hassle-free place to explore on your own: many people speak English, the U.S. dollar is legal tender, and there are ATMs, restaurants, pharmacies, shops, and taxis just about everywhere. You can explore some areas on foot, though distances between neighborhoods make public transportation necessary for many trips. If you ever feel uneasy about a location or situation and there aren't any police around, just flag down a taxi, which are abundant and widely considered to be safe. If you have a medical problem, go to Hospital Punta Pacífica, the best private clinic in the city. It also has a dental clinic.

It's best to get rolling early, take a long break around lunch (when the weather is hottest), and head back into the street when the heat begins to subside. If you're here during the rainy season, you can expect downpours every afternoon: the best thing to do when it starts to pour is find a restaurant and have a cup of coffee or a drink. Rest your feet until the deluge subsides, which is usually within 20 minutes. Keep in mind that most, though not all, museums are closed on Monday. The most convenient COTEL, or post office, is on the lower floor of the Plaza Concordia mall, on Vía España. Farmacia Arrocha has a dozen large pharmacies scattered around the city, and the ones near the big hotels are open 24 hours. ⚠ **The folks at the Autoridad de Tourismo Panama (ATP) office on the corner of Vía España and Calle Ricardo Arias can answer basic questions.**

National police (☎ 104). **Fire department** (☎ 103). **Ambulance** (Hospital Punta Pacífica ☎ 204–8180).

COTEL (post office) (✉ Plaza Concordia No. 121, Vía España El Cangrejo ☎ 512–6232). **ATP Tourist Information Offices** (✉ Vía España and Calle Ricardo Arias, El Cangrejo ☎ 526–7000). **Farmacia Arrocha** (✉ Calle 49 Este at Vía EspañaÁrea Bancária ☎ 360–4000 ✉ Av. Balboa Punta Paitilla ☎ 360–4000). **Hospital Punta Pacífica** (✉ Boulevard Pacífica y Vía Punta Darién Punta Pacífica ☎ 204–8000).

Tour Companies Advantage Panama (✉ Llanos de Curundú No. 2006, Curundú ☎ 6676–2466 ⊕ www.advantagepanama.com). **Ancon Expeditions** (✉ Calle Elvira Mendez, Edificio El Dorado No. 3, Área Bancária ☎ 269–9415 ⊕ www.anconexpeditions.com). **Aventuras Panama** (✉ Calle El Parcial, 1½ blocks west of Transistmica, Edif. Celina Of. J, El Dorado ☎ 260–0044 ⊕ www.aventuraspanama.com). **Eco Circuitos Panama** (✉ Country Inn & Suites, Calles Amador and Pelícano, Balboa ☎ 314–0068 ⊕ www.ecocircuitos.com). **Futura Travel** (✉ Centro Comercial Camino de Cruces, El Dorado ☎ 360–2030 ⊕ www.extremepanama.com). **Margo Tours** (✉ Centro Comercial Plaza Paitilla, local 36, Paitilla ☎ 302–0390 ⊕ www.margotours.com). **Panoramic Panama** (✉ Quarry Heights, casa #35, Cerro Ancón ☎ 314–1417 ⊕ www. panoramicpanama.com). **Pesantez Tours** (✉ Plaza Balboa oficina #2, Punta Paitilla ☎ 223–5374 ⊕ www.pesantez-tours.com).

VISITOR INFORMATION

The **Autoridad de Turismo Panama** (*ATP* ⊠ *Calle Ricardo Arias, across from Hotel Continental, Área Bancária* ☎ *526–7000* ⊕ *www.visitpanama. com*) has a decent Web page and a small information office, together with the Policía de Turismo, at Vía España and Calle Ricardo Arias, where they answer basic questions and hand out brochures.

EXPLORING PANAMA CITY

CASCO VIEJO

Panama City's charming historic quarter is known as the Casco Viejo, (pronounced CAS-coh Bee-EH-hoh), which translates as "old shell." It's spread over a small point in the city's southeast corner, where timeless streets and plazas are complemented by views of a modern skyline and the Bahía de Panamá. The Casco Viejo's narrow brick streets, wrought-iron balconies, and intricate cornices evoke visions of Panama's glorious history as a major trade center. A stroll here offers opportunities to admire a beautiful mix of Spanish colonial, neoclassical, and art nouveau architecture. And though most of its buildings are in a lamentable state of neglect, and the neighborhood is predominantly poor, it is a lively and colorful place, where soccer balls bounce off the walls of 300-year-old churches and radios blare Latin music.

While it's hardly the safest neighborhood in Panama City, Casco Viejo really shouldn't be missed. The streets tend to be busy on weekdays and weekend afternoons, when government workers and Panamanians head here in large numbers, and the area is always patrolled by tourism police, who work out of a station behind the Teatro Nacional. Take basic travelers' precautions, and don't wander around after dark.

TIMING AND PRECAUTIONS

The Casco Viejo is best explored on foot, though due to the intensity of the tropical heat, you should do your walking either first thing in the morning or late in the afternoon. Three o'clock in the afternoon is a great time to stroll around, when you can enjoy the evening light at Plaza Francia, have a drink on Plaza Bolívar, then dine at a nearby restaurant. Give yourself at least 2½ hours to tour this neighborhood, and more if you plan to shop and explore all the museums. Unfortunately, the area's museums have very little information in English.

Casco Viejo is predominantly poor, but it isn't as dangerous as it looks. Nevertheless, precautions should be taken: leave jewelry and valuables in your hotel safe, don't bring or show heaps of money, and be discreet with camera or video equipment. The crime problem is not so much in Casco Viejo but in the adjacent neighborhoods, so you shouldn't stray from the areas covered in the walking tour. At night you'll want to limit your wandering to the area around Plaza Francia, Plaza Bolívar, and Plaza Catedral.

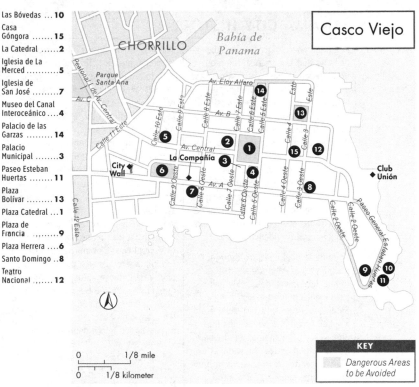

2

```
0        1/8 mile
0        1/8 kilometer
```

KEY
Dangerous Areas to be Avoided

WHAT TO SEE

10 **Las Bóvedas.** The arched chambers in the wall on the eastern side of Plaza Francia, which originally formed part of the city's battlements, served various purposes during the colonial era, from storage chambers to dungeons. Dating from the late 1600s, when the city was relocated to what is now Casco Viejo, the Bóvedas were abandoned for centuries. In the 1980s the Panama Tourist Board initiated the renovation of the cells, two of which house a sad, musty art gallery managed by the Instituto Nacional de Cultura. Three cells hold a French restaurant called Las Bóvedas, which also has tables on the plaza where you can enjoy drinks in the afternoon and live jazz on Friday nights. ✉ *Plaza Francia, Calle 1, Casco Viejo* ☎ *501–4034* ✉ *Free.*

15 **Casa Góngora.** Built by Captain Pablo Góngora in the late 18th century, this Spanish colonial house was restored by the mayor's office at the beginning of the 21st century to serve as a cultural center. It usually has an art exhibit and is worth popping into just to admire the restored architecture and woodwork. Free jazz concerts are on offer on Wednesday nights at 8 PM; check ahead, as there's occasionally a Friday night bolero concert as well. ✉ *Calle 4 and Av. Central, Casco Viejo* ☎ *506–5836* ✉ *Free* ☉ *Tues.–Sun. 10–6.*

PANAMA CITY HISTORY

In 1519, Panama City became the first city that the Spanish founded on the Pacific Coast of the Americas, and its Pacific orientation coupled with its location on a narrow isthmus led to a prosperous future. Only a decade earlier, Vasco Nuñez de Balboa had discovered a new ocean he'd dubbed "Pacific." Exploration of the Pacific Ocean was fairly limited, but in 1532 Francisco Pizarro sailed south to what is now Peru and conquered the Inca Empire, which had a treasure trove of gold and silver and a network of productive mines.

En route to Spain, Pizarro brought his plunder to Panama, and the former fishing village quickly gained prominence in the Spanish colonies. South American gold and silver were shipped to what is now called Panamá Viejo (Old Panama), from where it was carried across the isthmus on mule trains and river boats, and then loaded onto galleons for the trip across the Atlantic. Those same galleons carried European goods for the southern colonies, which crossed the isthmus in the other direction. Panama City grew rich, with cobblestone streets, mansions, and churches with altars covered in stolen gold, but that wealth soon attracted the attention of pirates. In 1671 the city was attacked and completely destroyed by the English pirate Henry Morgan (hence the ruins of Panamá Viejo). Two years later the city relocated to a small peninsula, now Casco Viejo, which was deemed easier to defend. Though it was fortified, the Spanish monarchy changed the shipping route, sending its gold through the Strait of Magellan instead.

With the departure of the Spanish fleet, many merchants abandoned the city, which slipped into a prolonged depression. The colonies won their independence from Spain in 1821, and Panama became a province of Colombia, but nothing improved until the 1850s. In response to the California Gold Rush, an American company built a railroad across the isthmus as part of a steamship route between the eastern and western costs of the United States that was used between 1855 and 1869. The enterprise was not only a boon to Panama's economy, it also marked the first of several waves of immigration of foreign laborers, which included the city's first Chinese immigrants. The inauguration of the U.S. Transcontinental Railroad in 1869 made the Panama route obsolete, and the city again slipped into a depression, but was revived in 1880 by the French, led by Ferdinand de Lesseps, who orchestrated the first attempt to build an interoceanic canal. Though de Lesseps's efforts failed within a decade, they had a lasting effect on the city's Casco Viejo, which the French completely refurbished.

Modern Panama City's development began with the arrival of the United States, which helped the country gain independence from Colombia, then demanded a 10-mi-wide slice of the isthmus. The Canal Zone was an American colony fenced off for most of the 20th century, but in accordance with the Panama Canal treaties, signed by Jimmy Carter and Omar Torrijos in 1977, it has since reverted to Panamanian control. The inauguration of the canal in 1914 led to the birth of a significant service sector in Panama City, which has only expanded of late.

2 **La Catedral** *(Catedral de Nuestra Señora de la Asunción)*. Built between 1688 and 1796, Panama City's stately cathedral survived an earthquake almost one hundred years later. The interior is rather bleak, but for the marble altar, made in 1884, beautiful stained glass, and a few religious paintings. The stone facade, flanked by painted bell towers, is quite impressive, especially when lit at night, with its many niches filled with small statues. The bell towers are decorated with mother-of-pearl from the Pearl Islands, and the bells in the left tower were salvaged from the city's first cathedral, in Panamá Viejo. ✉ *Av. Central and Calle 7, Casco Viejo* ☎ *No phone* ◔ *Open for Masses.*

5 **Iglesia de La Merced** *(Mercy Church)*. One of the oldest structures in the Casco Viejo, La Merced's timeworn, baroque facade was actually removed from a church of the same name in Panamá Viejo and reconstructed here, stone by stone, in 1680. Flanked by white bell towers and tiny chapels that are now abandoned, it's a charming sight, especially in late-afternoon light. The interior was destroyed by fires and rebuilt in the early 20th century, when some bad decisions were made, such as covering massive cement pillars with bathroom tiles. ✉ *Calle 9 and Av. Central, Casco Viejo* ☎ *No phone* ◔ *Mon.–Fri. 6:30–12 and 2–7, Sat. 4–7, Sun. 6:30–12 and 5–7.*

7 ★ **Iglesia de San José** *(Saint Joseph's Church)*. This church is an exact replica of the temple of the same name in Panamá Viejo. It is the sanctuary of the country's famous golden altar, the most valuable object to survive pirate Henry Morgan's razing of the old city. According to legend, a wily priest painted the altar with mud to discourage its theft. Not only did Morgan refrain from pilfering it, but the priest even managed to extract a donation from the pirate. The ornate baroque altar is made of carved mahogany covered with gold leaf. It is the only real attraction of the small church, though it does have several other wooden altars and a couple of lovely stained-glass windows. ✉ *Av. A at Calle 8, Casco Viejo* ☎ *No phone* ✉ *Free* ◔ *Mon.–Sat. 9–5, Sun. 8–12:30 and 5–6:30.*

4 **Museo del Canal Interoceánico** *(Interoceanic Canal Museum)*. Once the only museum dedicated to the Panama Canal, the Museo del Canal Interoceánico has been put to shame by the visitors' center at Miraflores Locks. The museum is packed with artifacts, paintings, photographs, and videos about the Panama Canal, but, unfortunately, the information is only in Spanish. There are English-speaking guides available, but you must call the day before to reserve one. Though the building was constructed in 1875 to be the Gran Hotel, it soon became the offices of the Compagnie Universelle du Canal Interoceanique, the French company that made the first attempt to dig a canal in Panama. After that effort went bust, the building became government property, and before being converted to a museum in the 1990s it was the central post office. ✉ *Plaza Catedral, Casco Viejo* ☎ *228–6231* ✉ *$2, children 75¢, tour guide $5* ◔ *Tues.–Sun. 9–5.*

14 ★ **Palacio de las Garzas** *(Palacio Presidential)*. The neoclassical lines of the stunning, white presidential palace stand out against the Casco Viejo's skyline. Originally built in the 17th century by an official of the Spanish crown, the palace was a customs house for a while, and passed through various mutations before being renovated to its current shape in 1922, under the administration of Belisario Porras. President Porras also started the tradition of keeping pet herons, or egrets, in the fountain of the building's front courtyard, which led to its popular name: ""Palace of the Egrets."" Because the building houses the president's offices and is surrounded by ministries, security is tight in the area, though nothing compared to the White House. During the day the guards may let you peek into the palace's Moorish foyer at its avian inhabitants, one great egret and two African cranes, but calling ahead for a free tour is a safer bet. Tours are held Tuesday to Friday, and require at least a week's notice ✉ *Av. Alfaro, 2 blocks north of Plaza Mayor, Casco Viejo* ☎ *527–9656.*

❸ **Palacio Municipal** *(City Hall).* The city council now meets in this stately white building, but it was originally built, in 1910, as the seat of the country's legislature (which grew too large for it and moved to its current home on Plaza Cinco de Mayo). It replaced a colonial palace that had stood at the same spot for nearly three centuries. On the third floor is the **Museo de la Historia de Panamá**, which traces the country's history from the explorations of Christopher Columbus to the present day. ■**TIP➜** As with the Museo del Canal Interoceánico, next door, the history museum's information is all in Spanish, but the admission is low enough that it is worth paying just to have a look inside the building. ✉ *Plaza Catedral, Casco Viejo* ☎ *228–6231* 💲 *$1* ⊙ *Weekdays 8–4.*

⓫ **Paseo Esteban Huertas.** This promenade built atop the old city's outer wall
★ is named for one of Panama's independence leaders. It stretches around the eastern edge of the point at the Casco Viejo's southern tip. From the Paseo you can admire views of the Bay of Panama, the Amador Causeway, the Bridge of the Americas, the tenements of El Chorrillo, and ships awaiting passage through the canal. As it passes behind the Instituto Nacional de Cultura, the Paseo is shaded by a bougainvillea canopy where Kuna women sell handicrafts and couples cuddle on the benches. It's amazing to see the modern skyline across the bay: the new city viewed from the old city. ✉ *Plaza Francia, between the stairway at the back of the plaza and Calle 1, Casco Viejo* ☎ *No phone* 💲 *Free* ⊙ *Always.*

⓭ **Plaza Bolívar.** A small plaza surrounded by 19th-century architecture,
Fodor's Choice this is one of the Casco Viejo's most pleasant spots, especially at night,
★ when people gather at its various cafés for drinks and dinner. It's centered around a monument to the Venezuelan general Simón Bolívar, the ""Liberator of Latin America,"" with decorative friezes marking events of his life and an Andean condor perched above him. In 1926 Bolívar organized a meeting of independence with leaders from all over Latin America in the Franciscan monastery in front of the plaza, which in the end, he was unable to attend. The hall in which the meeting took place, next to the Iglesia de San Francisco, holds a small museum called **Salón Bolívar** (✉ *Calle 3, Plaza Bolívar, Casco Viejo* ☎ *228–9594* 💲 *$1* ⊙ *Tues.–Sat. 9–4*). The original San Francisco Church was destroyed by fire in the 18th century and restored twice in the 20th century. The church is only open for Mass on Sunday evening, and the former monastery is now occupied by a Catholic school. Across the plaza from it,

on the corner of Avenida B and Calle 4, is the smaller church, the Iglesia de San Felipe de Neri, which was recently restored but only opens two days a year—on Good Friday and the saint's feast day, May 26. The Hotel Colombia, across the street from it, was one of the country's best when it opened its doors in 1937, but it fell into neglect during the late 20th century until it was renovated in the 1990s and converted to luxury apartments. The restaurant on the ground floor is a good spot for a drink or snack. ⊠ *Av. B between Calles 3 and 4, Casco Viejo.*

① **Plaza Catedral.** The city's main square is also known as Plaza Mayor and
★ Plaza de la Independencia, since the country's independence from both Spain and Colombia were celebrated here. Busts of Panama's founding fathers are scattered around the plaza, at the center of which is a large gazebo. The plaza is surrounded by historic buildings such as the Palacio Municipal, the Museo del Canal Interoceánico, and the Hotel Central, which once held the city's best accommodations but is now abandoned and awaits renovation. Plaza Catedral is shaded by some large *tabebuia* trees, which are ablaze with pink blossoms during the dry months, when the plaza is sometimes the site of weekend concerts. ⊠ *Av. Central between Calles 5 and 7, Casco Viejo.*

⑨ **Plaza de Francia.** Designed by Leonardo de Villanueva, this walled plaza
🦋 at the southern tip of the Casco Viejo peninsula is dedicated to the
Fodor's Choice French effort to build the canal, and the thousands who perished in
★ the process. An obelisk towers over the monument at the end of the plaza, where a dozen marble plaques recount the arduous task. Busts of Ferdinand de Lesseps and his lieutenants gaze across the plaza at the French Embassy—the large baby-blue building to the north of it. Next to them is a bust of Dr. Carlos Finlay, a Cuban physician who later discovered that yellow fever, which killed thousands during the French effort, originated from a mosquito bite—information that prompted the American campaign to eradicate mosquitoes from the area before they began digging. The plaza itself is a pleasant spot shaded by poinciana trees, which carry bright-orange blossoms during the rainy months. At the front of the plaza is a statue of Pablo Arosemena, one of Panama's founding fathers and one of its first presidents. The infamous dungeons of Las Bóvedas line one side of the plaza, and next door stands a large white building that was once the city's main courthouse but now houses the Instituto Nacional de Cultura (National Culture Institute) ⊠ *Bottom of Av. Central, near the tip, Casco Viejo.*

⑥ **Plaza Herrera.** This large plaza a block off the Avenida Central has seen much better days, as is apparent from the faded facades of the buildings that surround it. At the center of the plaza is a statue of local hero General Tomás Herrera, looking rather regal on horseback. Herrera fought in South America's wars for independence from Spain and later led Panama's first attempt to gain independence from Colombia, in 1840. The plaza lies next to a poorer section of the city, but you ought to cross it and have a look at the remaining chunk of the ancient wall that once enclosed the Casco Viejo, called the Baluarte de la Mano de Tigre (Tiger's Hand Bulwark), which stands just west of the plaza. ⊠ *Av. A and Calle 9, Casco Viejo.*

8 Santo Domingo. A catastrophic fire ruined this 17th-century church and Dominican monastery centuries ago. What's left at the entrance is the Arco Chato, or flat arch, a relatively precarious structure that served as proof that the country was not subject to earthquakes, tipping the scales in favor of Panama over Nicaragua for the construction of the transoceanic canal. The arch finally collapsed in 2003, without the help of an earthquake, but the city fathers considered it such an important landmark that they had it rebuilt. ⊠ *Av. A at Calle 3, Casco Viejo.*

NEED A BREAK? Exploring Casco Viejo's narrow streets can be a hot and exhausting affair, which makes the gourmet ice-cream shop of **Gran Clement** (⊠ *Av. Central and Calle 3* ☎ *228–0737*) an almost obligatory stop. Located in the ground floor of a restored mansion one block west of the Policía de Turismo station, the shop serves a wide assortment of ice creams including ginger, coconut, passion fruit, and mango. Gran Clement is also open at night, and until 9:30 PM on weekends.

12 Teatro Nacional *(National Theater).* The interior of this theater is truly posh, with ceiling murals, gold balconies, and glittering chandeliers—a little bit of Europe in the heart of old Panama City. After serving as a convent and, later, an army barracks, the building was remodeled by Italian architect Genaro Ruggieri in 1908. Paintings inside by Panamanian artist Roberto Lewis depict Panama's history via Greek mythology. Check the local papers so see whether the national symphony orchestra is playing here while you're in town, as attending a concert is the best way to experience the building. ⊠ *Av. B and Calle 3, Casco Viejo* ☎ *262–3525* ⊠ *$1* ⊙ *Mon.–Fri. 9:30–5:30.*

SANTA ANA, CERRO ANCÓN, AND BALBOA

For the better part of the 20th century, the area to the west of Casco Viejo held the border between the American Canal Zone and Panama City proper, and it continues to be an area of stark contrasts. The busy Avenida de Los Mártires (which separates the neighborhoods of El Chorrillo and Santa Ana from Cerro Ancón (Ancón Hill) was once lined with a chain-link fence, and the martyrs it was named for were Panamanian students killed during demonstrations against American control of the zone in 1964. To the west of that busy avenue, which leads to the Bridge of the Americas and the other side of the canal, rises the verdure and stately buildings of the former Canal Zone, whereas the area to the east of it is dominated by slums. Aside from Casco Viejo, the only areas to the east of that avenue that are worth visiting are Santa Ana's **Avenida Central** pedestrian mall and the area around **Plaza Cinco de Mayo,** at the pedestrian mall's northern end. A few blocks to the east of Plaza Cinco de Mayo is the **Museo Afroantillano,** but since it's in a rather sketchy neighborhood you may want to take a taxi there. Another option is to cross the Avenida de los Mártires near Plaza Cinco de Mayo, just south of the Palacio Legislativo, and explore the eastern side of Cerro Ancón, where you'll find the **Museo de Arte Contemporáneo,** a block to your left, and the offices of the **Smithsonian Tropical Research Institute** perched on a ridge to your right. **Mi Pueblito** is several blocks

TALE OF TWO CITIES

For the better part of the 20th century, this city was actually two cities—one American and one Panamanian—separated by walls and fences. When the newly created nation of Panama ceded a strip of its territory to the United States for the construction of the canal, a border was drawn along the edge of what was then the tiny capital. As that city grew, it soon found itself squeezed between the American Canal Zone and the Pacific Ocean, which led to a cramped urban core that sprawled eastward and suffered serious traffic problems. The Americans, on the other hand, had more than enough room; the U.S. government built orderly towns and military bases where tropical trees shaded sidewalks and vast expanses of rain forest were left intact. To house the thousands of laborers who flocked to the country to build the canal, the Americans built hundreds of wooden tenement houses on the Panamanian side of the border; though they have been largely replaced by cement buildings, most remain slums to this day.

Although the fences were dismantled following the signing of the Panama Canal Treaties in 1977, the border remains quite visible to this day in areas such as the Avenida de los Mártires, where the greenery and stately buildings of Cerro Ancón stand to the west and the crowded streets and buildings of El Chorrillo and Santa Ana lie to the east. Since the last American properties were handed over to Panama on January 31, 1999, the country has begun integrating the former Canal Zone into the city, building new roads and allowing some development, but strict zoning will likely ensure that the former Canal Zone retains its green areas and distinctive ambience.

south of the Museo de Arte—consider taking a taxi there. Also cab it to **Balboa,** which lies to the west of Cerro Ancón, about a mile over the hill from the Museo de Arte. There you'll want to be sure to visit the **Edificio de la Administración del Canal** (Panama Canal Administration Building), which overlooks Balboa from a ridge.

TIMING AND PRECAUTIONS

As with most of Panama City, you are better off exploring these areas in the morning or late afternoon, since the middle of the day is simply too hot for hoofing it. There is no reason to visit any of these areas at night. Whereas Balboa and Cerro Ancón are perfectly safe, you'll want to avoid the neighborhoods that flank the Avenida Central pedestrian mall and to the north and east of Plaza Cinco de Mayo.

WHAT TO SEE

7 Balboa. The heart of the former Canal Zone is quite a switch from the rest of Panama City, with its wide tree-shaded lawns and stately old buildings. It sometimes feels like a bit of a ghost town, especially after you spend time on the busy streets of Panama City proper, but it's an enjoyable, green area. You may spot toucans and *agoutis* (large jungle rodents) near the Panama Canal Administration Building; the Friday's restaurant behind the Balboa Yacht Club has a front-row view of the canal and Bridge of the Americas. Balboa also has Panama City's biggest

DAY-TRIPPING FROM THE CAPITAL

Panama City is the perfect base for an array of half- and full-day trips; enough even to fill a week or more. All of these excursions are to areas covered in "The Canal and Central Panama" chapter, and many of them can also be overnight trips. There are about a dozen day-trip options for exploring the canal and surrounding rain forest, which is protected within several national parks that you can explore on your own or with a guide on a bird-watching or hiking tour. The canal is best experienced on a transit tour, which takes you through the series of locks and Gaillard Cut, but you can also get onto the water on one of several nature tours on Lago Gatún. One of the best nature tours on Gatún Lake is the Smithsonian Tropical Research Institute's day tour to the island of **Barro Colorado** (⇨ *Barro Colorado Nature Monument in "The Canal and Central Panama"),* one of the world's oldest nature reserves, which is an excellent place to see wildlife. A 30- to 40-minute drive, taxi ride, or bus trip northwest from Panama City will bring you to trails that wind into the forests of **Parque Nacional Soberanía,** a vast rain-forest reserve that is home to more than 400 bird species and an array of mammals that ranges from timid tapirs to tiny tamarins. At **Gamboa,** which lies between the park and the canal, it is easy to spot wildlife on the grounds of the Gamboa Rainforest Resort, which has a rain-forest tram and an excellent restaurant, Los Lagartos, on the Chagres River, the perfect spot for lunch amidst nature (⇨ *Parque Nacional Soberanía, or Gamboa, in "The Canal and Central Panama").*

For a fascinating day trip, ride the **Panama Canal Railway** through the forests and lakes that line the canal to the Caribbean port of Colón and spend the day exploring either the rain forests around the colonial fort of **San Lorenzo** or the colonial fortresses, beaches, and forest of **Portobelo,** a trip that can be done independently or on a tour (⇨ *Panama Canal Railway, San Lorenzo, and Portobelo in The Canal and Central Panama).* There are several options for exploring nearby **Parque Nacional Chagres,** which include hiking in Cerro Azul, white-water rafting on the Chagres River, or a trip to one of several Emberá Indian communities within the park (⇨ *Parque Nacional Chagres in "The Canal and Central Panama").*

The beaches of the Central Pacific Coast can be visited on day trips, but note that most of them require a good deal of driving, which is why many Panamanians head to the nearby island of **Isla Taboga** on weekends. Historic Isla Taboga is a great day trip, since it has a small but lovely beach, and the boat trip there, which passes dozens of moored ships, is quicker and more pleasant than driving to the coastal beaches. (⇨ *Isla Taboga in "The Canal and Central Panama").* For a real treat, consider **Isla Contadora,** one of the Pearl Islands, because it has more and nicer beaches than Taboga. It is usually visited on overnight trips, but since there are relatively inexpensive flights to the island most mornings and afternoons, you could easily visit it on a day trip (⇨ *Isla Taboga in "The Canal and Central Panama").*

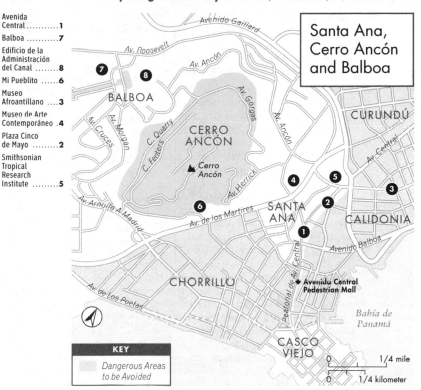

Santa Ana, Cerro Ancón and Balboa

2

handicraft market, in the former gym of the local YMCA, called the
Centro Artesanal Antiguo YMCA. ⊠ *Av. Arnulfo Arias and Av. Amador, Balboa* ☎ *211–0100.*

8 **★** **Edificio de la Administración del Canal** *(Panama Canal Administration
Building).* Well worth a stop is this impressive structure set atop a
ridge with a dramatic view of Balboa and the canal—a site chosen by
the canal's chief engineer, George W. Goethals. The building, designed
by New York architect Austin W. Lord, was inaugurated in 1914, one
month before the SS *Ancon* became the first ship to navigate the canal.
Since it holds the offices of the people in charge of running the canal,
most of the building is off-limits to tourists, but you can enter its lovely
rotunda and admire the historic murals of the canal's construction. The
murals were painted by William B. Van Ingen, who also created murals
for the U.S. Library of Congress and the Philadelphia Mint. They're
quite dramatic, and capture the monumental nature of the canal's construction in a style that is part Norman Rockwell, part Frederic Edwin
Church. The rotunda also houses busts of the three canal visionaries:
Spain's King Carlos V, who first pondered the possibility in the 16th
century; the Frenchman Ferdinand de Lesseps, who led the first attempt
to dig it; and President Theodore Roosevelt, who launched the successful construction effort. The doors at the back of the rotunda are locked,

but if you walk around the building you'll be treated to a view of the neat lawns and tree-lined boulevards of Balboa. ⊠ *Calle Gorgas, Balboa* ☎ *272–7602* ⊙ *Daily 6–6.*

6 ☪ ★ **Mi Pueblito.** It's touristy, but this hillside re-creation of rural Panama is worth a stop, especially if you won't be traveling to other parts of the country. The main attraction is a small replica of a 19th-century rural town square, similar to those in many Azuero Peninsula towns, such as Parita. The collection of faux-adobe buildings is actually quite picturesque, and the plaza comes to life on Sunday afternoons (starting around 1 or 2 PM), when it becomes the stage for a free folk-dance performance. You can also visit the traditional Panamanian restaurant on the plaza, the small museum dedicated to the *pollera* (an intricately stitched dress), and the obligatory souvenir shops. Next door is a re-creation of a Caribbean town that bears some resemblance to Bocas del Toro. On Saturday evenings Kuna dancers perform for tips in a tiny reproduction of a Kuna village above it. A trail through the forest leads to the re-creation of typical Emberá home. ⊠ *Off Av. de los Mártires and Calle Jorge Wilbert, Cerro Ancón* ☎ *506–5724 or 506–5725* ☞ *Free* ⊙ *Tues.–Sun. 9–9.*

> **AVENIDA CENTRAL**
>
> The city's Central Avenue is closed to traffic for about half of a mile between Casco Viejo and Plaza Cinco de Mayo; the resulting pedestrian mall is a great place for people watching and shopping. The bigger stores that line it sell some clothing items for as little as $1. Smaller stores employ aggressive salesmen who stand in front clapping and coaxing passersby inside. Though the pedestrian mall is busy and well patrolled by police, the side streets head into neighborhoods that you should avoid.

3 **Museo Afroantillano** *(Afro-Antillean Museum).* Three blocks northeast of Plaza Cinco de Mayo, in the midst of a rough neighborhood, stands a simple wooden museum dedicated to the tens of thousands of West Indian workers who supplied the bulk of the labor for the canal's construction. The West Indians, mostly Barbadians and Jamaicans, did the toughest, most dangerous jobs, but were paid in silver, while the Americans were paid in gold. A disproportionate number of them died during canal construction; the survivors and their descendents have made important contributions to Panamanian culture. The museum has period furniture and historic photos. ⚠ **You'll want to take a taxi here; consider asking the taxi to wait for you while you visit the museum.** ⊠ *Av. Justo Arosemena and Calle 24 Este, Santa Ana* ☎ *501–4130* ☞ *$1* ⊙ *Tues.–Sat. 9:30–3:30.*

4 **Museo de Arte Contemporáneo.** Panama's modern art museum, housed in a two-story white building on the edge of Cerro Ancón, is managed by a local foundation. Though the country isn't known for its modern art, it does have some excellent painters, some of whose work is in the museum's permanent collections. The museum also hosts temporary exhibitions for local artists, some better than others. ⊠ *Calle San Blas and Av. de los Mártires, Cerro Ancón* ☎ *262–8012* ☞ *$3* ⊙ *Tues.–Sun. 9–5.*

CONCRETE JUNGLE

Massive tropical trees shade Panama City's parks and streets, exuberant foliage grows right to the edge of the metropolis, and there are significant patches of forest protected within its city limits, namely on Cerro Ancón and in Parque Metropolitano. Even in parts of the Área Bancária and El Cangrejo, where most hotels and restaurants are located, parakeets fly overhead by day and tree frogs sing through the night. Of even more interest to nature lovers, though, is the vast swath of wilderness that stretches northwest from the city's edge all the way across the country to the Caribbean coast, which can be explored in nearby Soberanía National Park, Barro Colorado Nature Monument, or Chagres National Park. There are trails into the jungle just 10 to 30 minutes from most hotels, making Panama City one of the easiest places in the world to experience tropical nature. The most dangerous part of exploring one of those nature reserves is the drive there; however, you should hire a guide or join a tour to get the most out of your time in the rain forest.

② **Plaza Cinco de Mayo.** A tiny expanse on the north end of the Avenida Central pedestrian mall, this plaza has several notable landmarks nearby. To the northeast of the plaza stands a large brown building that was once a train station and later housed the country's anthropological museum, which was recently moved to a new home near the Parque Metropolitano. Just behind it on Avenida 4 Sur is a small handicraft market called the **Mercado de Buhonería** that few people visit, so you can score some good deals there. On the other side of the Avenida Central, behind a large monument, is the **Palacio Legislativo** (Legislative Palace), Panama's Congress, which opens to the public for some legislative sessions, but is hardly worth the visit. Across Calle 9 de Enero from the Palacio Legislativo is the Saca Bus Station, where buses depart for Miraflores Locks and Gamboa. The areas to the north and east of the Plaza should be avoided. Plan to arrive at and leave Plaza Cinco de Mayo in a taxi or bus. ⊠ *Av. Central, Santa Ana.*

❺ **Smithsonian Tropical Research Institute.** Spread over a ridge on the north side of Cerro Ancón and lined by trees, the home office of the Smithsonian Tropical Research Institute (STRI), known as the Earl S. Tupper Center, has offices, meeting halls, a large library, a bookstore, and a café. A branch of the Washington, D.C.–based Smithsonian Institution, the STRI has half a dozen research stations in Panama, the most famous of which is on Barro Colorado Island. The institute also coordinates scientific studies in various other tropical countries. Most people head to the Tupper Center to pay for their tour to Barro Colorado Island or to shop at the bookstore, which has an excellent selection of natural history titles, as well as souvenirs. The library has an extensive collection of literature on the tropics and is open to the general public, Panamanian and foreign. ⊠ *Av. Roosevelt, Cerro Ancón* ☎ *228–8000* ⊙ *Mon.–Fri. 9–5, Tues. 8–5, Sat. 9–12 (library); Mon. –Fri. 10–4:30 (bookstore).*

OFF THE BEATEN PATH

The rain forest that covers most of Cerro Ancón is a remarkably vibrant natural oasis in the midst of the city. The best area to see wildlife is on the trails to the **Cerro Ancón Summit**, which is topped by radio towers and a big Panamanian flag. The best way to ascend the hill is on a trail that starts high on its western slope, in the luxuriant residential neighborhood of Quarry Heights, above Balboa. Turn right at the offices of ANCON, Panama's biggest environmental group, and continue past several apartment buildings and the B&B La Estancia until you come upon a stairway on your left, which is the trailhead. The hike takes about 20 minutes each way, and is best done early in the morning or late in the afternoon, when you are likely to see animals such as the keel-billed toucan, squirrel cuckoo, and Geoffrey's tamarind—Panama's smallest simian. If you have a taxi drop you off at the trailhead (ask the driver to take you to the "Oficinas de ANCON" in Quarry Heights), you can hike down the other side of the hill to Mi Pueblito, where you should be able to flag a cab. ⊠ *Quarry Heights, 400 meters south of ANCON, Cerro Ancón.*

CALZADA AMADOR

The Calzada Amador (Amador Causeway) is the place to go when you tire of the city's cement and traffic jams. The sprawling views and refreshing breezes coming off the ocean seem a world apart from the hustle and bustle of Panama City, yet this oasis is less than 20 minutes from most downtown hotels. Located directly to the southeast of Balboa, the Calzada was originally constructed as a breakwater, when the canal's builders were looking for places to deposit the trainloads of debris that the digging produced. The resulting causeway, which is topped with a palm-lined road and promenade, stretches almost 2 mi (3 km) into the Pacific Ocean to connect the mainland to three islands: **Isla Naos, Isla Perico,** and **Isla Flamenco.** The causeway and islands have views of the canal's Pacific entrance, the city's gleaming skyline, Isla Taboga, and the dozens of ships that anchor offshore on any given day. Flocks of pelicans and magnificent frigate birds can often be seen on the forested islands. Long a popular destination for Panamanians, the Calzada has become busier than ever in recent years, thanks to the construction of several shopping centers with dozens of bars and restaurants and even hotels on the islands. The city's residents flock here on Sundays and holidays, when traffic on the two-lane road creeps along and the promenade fills with joggers, bikers, and roller skaters.

TIMING AND PRECAUTIONS

The Calzada Amador is a great spot to visit at just about any time of day, as long as it isn't raining, but the late afternoon is especially delightful, when you can watch the sunset illuminate the city's skyline. The restaurants on the islands serve lunch and dinner, some of them until quite late, and the bars on Isla Perico rock till the predawn hours on weekends. During the day, be sure to use sunscreen and a hat, since sunburn is the biggest danger here. There are a couple of small beaches on Isla Naos, but swimming in the ocean is not recommended until the government completes Panama City's sewage system.

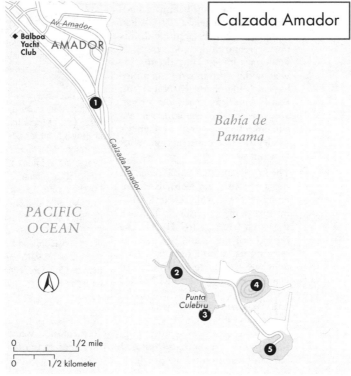

WHAT TO SEE

The mainland of Amador, a former U.S. Army base in the midst of slow redevelopment, is a rather desolate area with an abundance of parking lots and rundown military housing. Toward its southern tip stands the ornate Figali Convention Center, the site of occasional conventions and concerts, next to which is a hotel and condominium development. To the south of the convention center is a large open-air restaurant called Las Pencas, where you can rent bicycles, tandems, tricycles, and other pedal-powered vehicles for cruising on the nearby causeway.

NEED A BREAK?

Behind Pencas Restaurant, on the mainland at the entrance to Calzada Amador, **Bicicletas Moses** (☏ 211–3671 *restaurant, call and ask for bicicletas* ⊙ *Mon. –Fri. 10–8, Sat. 9–8, Sun. 8–8*) rents an array of bikes, including kids' sizes. One hour for an individual mountain bike costs $3 or up to $15 for a six-seater.

❶ The triangle of land where the Causeway begins is the site of the forthcoming **Museo de la Biodiversidad** (Museum of Biodiversity). Also called "Panama: Bridge of Life," the museum was designed by the American architect Frank O. Gehry, famous for the Guggenheim Museum in Bilbao, Spain, and the pavilion at Chicago's Millennium Park. The museum was originally due to open in 2009 but at this writing had fallen considerably behind schedule; it may open in late 2010. When completed, it will feature exhibits on the remarkable biodiversity of Panama's forests and oceans, as well as the isthmus's role as a biological bridge between North and South America. In the meantime, you can stop by the construction site and have a look at Gehry's model and the construction work in progress.

> ## WILD BUSES
>
> Panama City's buses are a sight to behold. They are all privately owned Blue Bird school buses, short on legroom and hot and stuffy, but what they lack in comfort, they make up for in pizzazz. Most of them have snazzy air-brush paint jobs, featuring lightning bolts, flames, cartoon characters, women's names, or a portrait of a famous person—usually a Latin American singer or *telenovela* star. They are called diablos rojos, or red devils, for their predominant color and drivers' disposition, and the thrill of riding one is worth well more than the 25¢ fare. Mind your wallet if the bus is crowded.

② The first island that you'll reach on the causeway, **Isla Naos**, is dominated by the marine research laboratories of the Smithsonian Tropical Research Institute (STRI). On the far side of the island are various restaurants, a large marina, which is where you catch the ferry to Isla Taboga, and the STRI Marine Exhibition Center on Punta Culebra. The dirt road that leads to the marina and Punta Culebra is on the right just in front of Mi Ranchito, one of the Causeway's most popular restaurants, which has a high thatch roof. Just south of Mi Ranchito is a small strip mall with several bars and restaurants, one of which has a swimming pool that costs just a few dollars to use.

③ Though it doesn't compare to the aquariums of other major cities, the **Centro de Exhibiciones Marinas** (Marine Exhibition Center) is worth a stop. It was created by the scientists and educators at the STRI and is located on a lovely, undeveloped point with examples of several ecosystems: beach, mangrove forest, rocky coast, and tropical forest. A series of signs leads visitors on a self-guided tour. There are several small tanks with fish and sea turtles, as well as pools with sea stars, sea cucumbers, and other marine creatures that kids can handle. The spyglasses are great for watching ships on the adjacent canal. ■TIP→ **Be sure to go out to the lookout on the end of the rocky point.** ⊠ *Punta Culebra, Isla Naos, Calzada Amador* ☎ *212–8793* ✉ *$2, children 50¢* ☉ *Tues.–Fri. 1–5, weekends 10–6.*

NEED A BREAK?

Al Tambor de la Alegría (⊠ *Brisas del Amador, Calzada de Amador* ☎ *314–3369 or 314–3380*) is one of the more popular Isla Perico restaurants. It presents a nightly folk-dancing spectacle.

④ The second island on the causeway, **Isla Perico**, is a popular nightspot, since its long strip mall, Brisas de Amador, holds an array of restaurants and bars, including some with terraces that face the canal's Pacific entrance, so you can watch the ships passing. The bars in Brisas de Amador are the causeway's most popular nightspots, so on weekends that mall stays busy until the wee hours. ⊠ *Calzada Amador.*

⑤ The Amador Causeway ends at **Isla Flamenco**, which has two shopping centers and an assortment of restaurants. The Flamenco Marina is a popular mooring spot for yachts and fishing boats; it's the disembarkation point for cruise-ship passengers, most of whom board tour buses. Several restaurants and bars overlook the marina, which also has a great view of the city's skyline, making it a popular destination night and day. ⊠ *Calzada Amador.*

ALBROOK, PARQUE NATURAL METROPOLITANO, AND MIRAFLORES

The area to the north of Balboa, which was also part of the American Canal Zone, has undergone considerable development since being handed over. The former U.S. Army airfield of Albrook is now Panama City's domestic airport, Aeropuerto Marcos A. Gelabert; next to that are Albrook Mall and the city's impressive bus terminal, the Terminal de Transporte Terrestre, which is simply called "La Terminal" by locals. To the northeast of Albrook is a large swath of rain forest protected within **Parque Natural Metropolitano**, which is home to more than 227 bird species. To the west of the park is the country's anthropological museum, **Museo Antropológico Reina Torres de Araúz**. The former military bases and canal-worker housing to the north of Albrook have gotten some new shopping centers, but remain largely the same as they were during the American tenure, though many people have expanded and modified their homes. The former army base of Clayton is now called the Ciudad del Saber, or City of Knowledge; many of its buildings are occupied by international organizations. Across the road is the first set of locks on the Pacific side of the canal, the **Esclusas de Miraflores** (Miraflores Locks), an area that is much more visitor-friendly than it was when the canal was U.S. property. The Panamanian administration has built a state-of-the-art visitor center and museum, making it among the most popular places to visit in Panama City. From there the road follows the canal northwest through the rain forest of Soberanía National Park to the small canal port and community of Gamboa, where it ends.

TIMING AND PRECAUTIONS

You should visit Parque Natural Metropolitano as early in the day as you can, or late in the afternoon, since those are the times when birds and other animals are most active. Bring insect repellent with you, stay on the trails, and watch your footing, since there are poisonous snakes in these areas. You could visit the Museo Antropológico immediately afterward, or anytime before 4 PM, except weekends, when the museum is closed. The visitor center at Miraflores Locks is open seven days a week; it's air-conditioned, so it is one of the few places in Panama City that you can comfortably visit in the late morning or early afternoon. ■ TIP→ Though the visitor center closes at 5 pm, the restaurant on its second floor is open until 10:30; it's a fun place to dine, as the canal is actually busier at night than during the day.

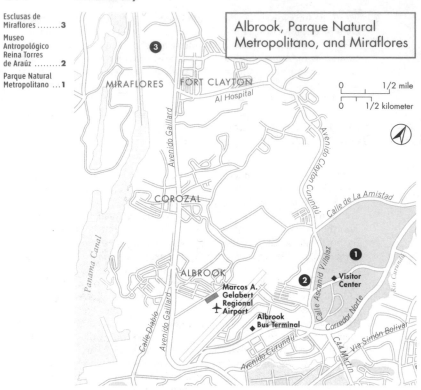

Albrook, Parque Natural
Metropolitano, and Miraflores

WHAT TO SEE

3 **Esclusas de Miraflores** *(Miraflores Locks)*. The four-story visitor cen-
Fodor's Choice ter next to these double locks provides a front-row view of massive
★ ships passing through the lock chambers. It also houses an excellent
museum about the canal's history, engineering, daily operations, and
environmental demands. Because most of the canal lies at 85 feet above
sea level, each ship that passes through has to be raised to that level
with three locks as they enter it, and brought back to sea level with
three locks on the other end. Miraflores has two levels of locks, which
move vessels between Pacific sea level and Miraflores Lake, a man-
made stretch of water between Miraflores Locks and the Pedro Miguel
Locks. Due to the proximity to Panama City, these locks have long been
the preferred place to visit the canal, but the visitor center has made it
even more popular.

There are observation decks on the ground and fourth floors of the massive cement building, from which you can watch vessels move through
the locks, as a bilingual narrator explains the process and provides
information about each ship, including the toll they paid to use the
canal. The museum contains an excellent combination of historic relics,
photographs, videos, models, and even a simulator of a ship passing
through the locks. There is also a gift shop, a snack bar, and a restaurant

on the second floor called Restaurante Miraflores, which has an excellent view from a few tables and a decent, though pricey, kitchen. While the canal is busier at night, the largest ships pass during the day. You can call at 9 AM the day before your visit to ask what time the largest ships are due through the locks. ✉ *Road to Gamboa, across from Ciudad del Saber, Clayton* ☎276–8617 ☜*$8, children $5; deck only $5, children $3* ⊙ *Daily 9–5.*

2 ❷ **Museo Antropológico Reina Torres de Araúz** *(Reina Torres de Araúz Anthropological Museum).* After decades of being on display in a former railway station, the government's collection of pre-Columbian artifacts is now housed in a spacious building just down the road from the Parque Natural Metropolitano visitor center. The museum is named for Panama's pioneering anthropologist, Reina Torres de Araúz, who first opened this and a half-dozen other museums in the country, and it includes a display on her life's work. The museum's main exhibits feature artifacts from various cultures dating back thousands of years. Its relatively small collection consists of stone statues, painted ceramics, and gold jewelry, including exquisite bells, and pendants in the shape of frogs, eagles, and other creatures. There is also information about the country's pre-Columbian inhabitants and current indigenous groups. ✉ *Av. Ascanio Villalaz, next to Esso station, Altos de Curundú* ☎*501–4743* ☜*free* ⊙ *Mon.–Fri. 8–4.*

❶ ℭ ★ **Parque Natural Metropolitano** *(Metropolitan Natural Park).* A mere 10-minute drive from downtown, this 655-acre expanse of protected wilderness is an excellent and remarkably convenient place to experience the flora and fauna of Panama's tropical rain forest. Its forest is home to 227 bird species ranging from migrant Baltimore orioles to keel-billed toucans. Five well-marked trails, covering a total of about 4.8 km (3 mi), range from a climb to the park's highest point to a fairly flat loop. On any given morning of hiking you may spot such spectacular birds as a gray-headed chachalaca, a collared aracari, a mealy parrot, or a red-legged honeycreeper. The park is also home to 45 mammal species, so keep an eye out for a sloth hanging from a branch or a dark brown agouti, which is a large jungle rodent. Keep your ears perked for tamarins, tiny monkeys that sound like birds.

There is a visitor center near the southern end of the park, next to El Roble and Los Caobas trails, where the nonprofit organization that administers the park collects the admission fee and sells cold drinks, snacks, and nature books. ■TIP➜ This is the best place to begin your exploration of the park, since you can pick up a simple map; El Roble and Los Caobas connect to form an easy loop through the forest behind the visitor center.

Across the street from the visitor center is a shorter loop called Sendero Los Momótides. Serious hikers may want to explore the Mono Titi and La Cieneguita trails, which head into the forest from the road about 1 km north of the visitor center and connect to each other to form a loop through the park's most precipitous terrain. The Smithsonian Tropical Research Institute (STRI) has a construction crane in the middle of the forest near the Mono Titi trail that is used to study life in the forest canopy, which is where the greatest diversity of flora and fauna is found. El Roble connects with La Cieneguita, so you can hike the northern loop and then continue through the forest to the visitor center; the total distance of that hike is 3½ km (2 mi).

If you reach the park in a taxi, you may want to have them pick you up a few hours later; otherwise you could flag a cab down on the road that runs through the middle of the park, Avenida Juan Pablo II, which is fairly busy. Be sure to bring water, insect repellent, and binoculars, and be careful where you put your feet and hands, since the park does have poisonous snakes, biting insects, and spiny plants. The park is open dawn to dusk, though the visitor's center doesn't open until 8 AM. ⊠ *Av. Juan Pablo II, Altos de Curundú* ☎ *232–5552* ⊕ *www.parquemetropolitano.org* 🖾 *$2, children 50¢* ⊙ *Daily dawn to dusk.*

OFF THE BEATEN PATH

Perched atop a forested hill 11 km (7 mi) north of the city is **Baha'i House of Worship** one of the world's seven Baha'i temples. The Baha'i believe that all the world's religions are separate manifestations of a single religious process, which culminated with the appearance of their founder, Bahà'u'llàh, who preached about a new global society. Most Baha'i temples are in Asia. Panama's temple is simple but also quite lovely, with a white dome surrounded by tropical foliage (from the air, it resembles a giant egg). It was designed by the British architect Peter Tillotson. It is open to everyone for prayer, meditation, and subdued exploring. Men should wear long pants, and women long pants or long skirts. ⊠ *Transístmica, near Centro Comercial Milla Ocho San Isidro* ☎ *231–6909 or 231–1137* ⊕ *www.parquemetropolitano.org* 🖾 *Free* ⊙ *Daily 9–6.*

DOWNTOWN PANAMA CITY

The area northeast of the old city, stretching from the neighborhoods of El Cangrejo to Punta Paitilla, is where you'll find most of the city's office towers, banks, hotels, restaurants, and shops. As Panama City's economy grew and diversified during the 20th century, those who had money abandoned Casco Viejo and built homes in new neighborhoods to the northeast; apartment buildings and office towers soon followed. Many of Panama City's best hotels and restaurants are clustered in **El Cangrejo,** which lies just west of busy **Vía España** and is dominated by **El Panamá,** the city's original luxury hotel, which covers a small hill there. Just to the east of El Cangrejo is the **Área Bancária** (Banking Area), which stretches southeast to Calle 50 (Calle Nicanor de Obarrio), another of the city's main arteries. A few hotels and a good selection of restaurants are scattered through the Área Bancária, amidst the gleaming towers of international banks. A few blocks to the southeast of Calle 50 is **Avenida Balboa,** another of the city's major thoroughfares, which curves along the coast between the Casco Viejo and Punta Paitilla. Between Calle 50 and Avenida Balboa you'll find the neighborhoods of Bella Vista and Marbella, which hold an interesting mix of tree-lined streets, apartment towers, aging mansions, and modern shopping centers. Just to the east of Marbella is Punta Paitilla, a small point packed with skyscrapers.

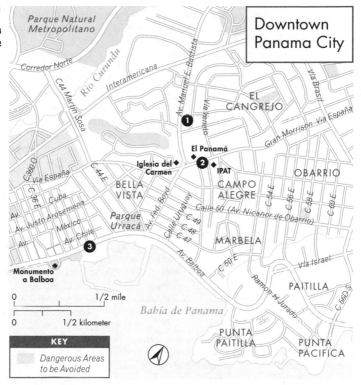

**Downtown
Panama City**

KEY

*Dangerous Areas
to be Avoided*

TIMING AND PRECAUTIONS
The downtown area is very safe to explore, although you should be careful crossing its main streets, especially during rush hour. Avenida Balboa is best strolled in the morning or evening; it skirts some rough neighborhoods to the west of the Balboa Monument, so stick to the stretch between the Monument and Punta Paitilla.

WHAT TO SEE
① **Área Bancária** *(Banking Area).* Narrow streets shaded by leafy tropical trees make the city's financial district a pleasant area to explore, especially at night when it is cooler and there is less traffic. Together with El Cangrejo, which lies across the Vía España from it, the Área Bancária holds a critical mass of hotels, restaurants, and other services that make it an almost obligatory stop for travelers. You'll find the city's highest concentration of bars and restaurants, however, in the area around **Calle Uruguay** (Calle 48), just to the south of the Área Bancária, between Calle 50 (Nicanor de Obarrio) and Avenida Balboa. Panama City's busiest area on weekend nights, Calle Uruguay, is a fun place to head any night but Sunday and is within walking distance of most hotels. ⊠ *Between Vía España and Calle 50.*

③ **La Cinta Costera.** One of the city's main attractions, the busy waterfront
★ boulevard Avenida Balboa and the linear park running alongside is

lined with palm trees and features great views of the Bay of Panama and Casco Viejo. The sidewalk that runs along the bay and the park wedged between the avenue is a popular strolling and jogging route. To the west of the Miramar towers and the Yacht Club is a small park with a monument to Vasco Nuñez de Balboa, who, after trudging through the rain forests of the Darién in 1501 became the first European to set eyes on the Pacific Ocean. That gleaming white **Monumento a Balboa** is topped by a steel sculpture of the conquistador gazing out at the Pacific. The statue was a gift to the Panamanian people from Spain's King Alfonso XIII in 1924. Do most of your walking to the east of the Monumento: if you can do it around high tide, all the better. Unfortunately, the big problem with the Cinta Costera is that Panama City's raw sewage pours into the bay from a series of pipes just below it, which is especially noxious when the tide is out. The government is finally building the city's long-overdue sewage system, which will take years to complete. ⊠ *Av. Balboa, Marbella.*

❷ Vía España. An extension of the Avenida Central, this busy one-way street is lined with shopping centers and office towers for the better part of a mile. Long an important commercial strip, the Vía España's star has faded a bit in recent years, due to the opening of several big malls in other neighborhoods. Nevertheless, it remains one of the city's busiest streets, and since it pretty much bisects the main hotel and restaurant district, you may risk your life crossing it. Thankfully, there is a pedestrian bridge just to the north of **Vía Veneto,** a crowded side street that runs west from Vía España to an array of hotels, restaurants, and shops. Several blocks to the southwest, where Vía España intersects with Avenida Federico Boyd, stands the pale and conspicuous **Iglesia del Carmen,** a Gothic-style church with high spires built in 1947. To the south of that church, the Vía España quickly loses its glitz.

ATLAPA AND PANAMÁ VIEJO

The coast to the east of Punta Paitilla has a growing supply of condominium towers, but just behind them lie residential neighborhoods where houses and smaller apartments are being mowed over in Panama City's waning construction boom. The area has only two spots of interest to travelers: **ATLAPA**, the city's original convention center, and the ruins of **Panamá Viejo,** which was the original city. That historic site consists of little more than a museum and a collection of stone walls, but it provides a vague idea of what the colonial city looked like and how its inhabitants lived.

TIMING AND PRECAUTIONS

As with any outdoor attraction in often-sweltering Panama City, it's best to visit Panamá Viejo first thing in the morning or later in the afternoon, though you need to get to the museum by 4 PM. Though the ruins are patrolled by tourism police on mountain bikes, the surrounding neighborhoods are less tourist-friendly, so don't wander too far from the main road—Vía Cincuentenaria—and the Plaza Mayor.

NO SWIMMING!

Viewed at night, the Bay of Panama looks very romantic; by day, however, you'll notice that the water is extremely murky. All it takes is a quick stroll (and, if you dare, a quick sniff) at low tide along the Cinta Costera—the waterfront park and promenade on Avenida Balboa—to understand the extent of the city's sewage-treatment problems: for centuries, the capital's raw sewage has been dumped directly into the ocean. Add to that neighboring municipalities such as San Miguelito and Pedregal, and you've got nearly one million toilet owners polluting this bay. It's amazing that there are still any fish along the coast, but there are plenty, as the flocks of pelicans attest. The only good news is that the government has finally started to fix the problem. The cost of modernizing the city's sewage system and building treatment plants has been calculated at more than $350 million; it will take years to finish the job. Our fingers are crossed that it'll happen in an organized and speedy manner.

WHAT TO SEE

1 Panamá Viejo (*Old Panama*). Crumbling ruins are all that's left of Old Panama (sometimes called Panamá la Vieja), the country's first major Spanish settlement, which was destroyed by pirate Henry Morgan in 1671.

Panamá Viejo was founded in 1519 by the conquistador Pedroarias Dávila. Built on the site of an indigenous village that had existed for centuries, the city soon became a busy colonial outpost. Expeditions to explore the Pacific coast of South America left from here. When Francisco Pizarro conquered the Incan empire, the copious gold and silver he stole arrived in Panamá Viejo, where it was loaded onto mules and taken across the isthmus to Spain-bound ships. For the next 150 years Panamá Viejo was a vital link between Spain and the gold and silver mines of South America. Year after year, ships came and went; mule trains carried precious metals to Panama's Caribbean coast and returned with Spanish goods bound for the southern colonies. The city's merchants, royal envoys, and priests accumulated enough gold to make a pirate drool. At the time of Morgan's attack, Panamá Viejo had a handful of convents and churches, one hospital, markets, and luxurious mansions. The fires started during the pirate attack reduced much of the city to ashes within days.

The paucity of the remaining ruins is not due entirely to the pirates' looting and burning: the Spanish spent years dismantling buildings after they decided to rebuild their city, now known as Casco Viejo, on the peninsula to the southwest, which was deemed easier to defend against attack. The Spanish carried everything that could be moved to the new city, including the stone blocks that are today the walls of the city's current cathedral and the facade of the Iglesia de la Merced. Panamá Viejo is part of all city tours, which can be a good way to visit the site, if you get a knowledgeable guide. There are also sometimes guides at the Plaza Mayor who provide free information in Spanish.

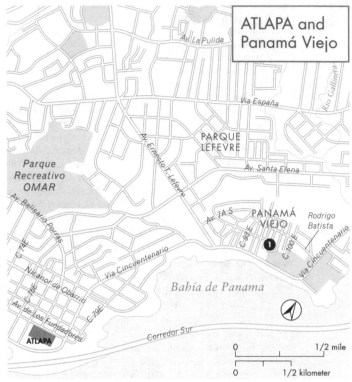

ATLAPA and Panamá Viejo

The collections of walls that you'll pass between the Visitor Center and the Plaza Mayor are all that remain of several convents, the bishop's palace, and the San Juan de Dios Hospital. The Plaza Mayor is approximately 1 km from the visitor center, so you may want to drive, or take a cab, instead of walking through the ruins, especially between 11 AM and 3 PM, when it can be especially hot.

A trip to Panamá Viejo is best begun at the **Centro de Visitantes** (*Visitor Center*)—a large building on the right as you enter Panamá Viejo on Vía Cincuentenaria, which is how most people get there. From ATLAPA, that street heads inland for 2 km through a residential neighborhood before arriving at the ruins, which are on the coast. Once you see the ocean again, look for the two-story visitor center on your right. It holds a large museum that chronicles the site's evolution from an indigenous village to one of the wealthiest cities in the Western Hemisphere. Works on display include indigenous pottery made centuries before the arrival of the Spanish, relics of the colonial era, and a model of what the city looked like shortly before Morgan's attack. Keep that model in mind as you explore the site, since you need a good dose of imagination to evoke the city that was once home to between 7,000 and 10,000 people from the rubble that remains of it. ⊠ *Vía Cincuentenaria, 2 km* *east of ATLAPA, Panamá Viejo* ☎ *226–1757 for Visitor Center* 🖥 *$3 museum, $4 for ruins, $6 for both* ⊙ *Tues.–Sun. 9–5*

Vía Cincuentenaria curves to the left in front of what was once the city's **Plaza Mayor** (*Main Plaza*), a simple cobbled square backed by a stone tower that is the only part of Panamá Viejo that has undergone any significant renovation. If you have previously paid admission at the Visitor Center, then you will need to show that ticket, or you can buy a separate ticket to enter the plaza alone. Climb the metal staircase inside the **Torre de la Catedral** (Cathedral Tower)—the former bell tower of Panama's original cathedral—for a view of the surrounding ruins. The structure just south of the tower was once the city hall; walls to the north and east are all that remains of homes, a church, and a convent. The extensive ruins are shaded by tropical trees, which attract plenty of birds, so the nature and scenery are as much of an attraction as the ancient walls. ⊠ *Av. Cincuentenario, about 3 km (2 mi) east of ATLAPA, Panamá Viejo* ☎ *226–8915* ⊕ *www.panamaviejo.org* 🖥 *Tower and ruins $4; Plaza Mayor and visitor center $6* ⊙ *Daily 9–5.*

Just to the south of the Plaza Mayor is the **Mercado de Artesanía** (*Craft Market*), where dozens of independent vendors sell their wares from separate shops and stands. You can buy many traditional crafts here, including Emberá baskets and Kuna-made molas. Prices vary, and there are some good buys, but you can get better prices in Portobelo, for example. The market also has decent public restrooms (for a small fee). ⊠ *Av. Cincuentenaria, just south of plaza Panamá Viejo* ☎ *No phone.* ⊙ *Daily 9:30–5:30.*

WHERE TO EAT

It's not quite New York or London, but Panama City's restaurant scene is pretty impressive for a city of its size. Panamanians like to eat out, and enough of them have incomes that allow for regular dining on the town, which has resulted in a growing cadre of excellent restaurants. The city is also quite cosmopolitan, which means the cuisine selection can take you right around the globe. Many of the best restaurants are clustered in parts of the Casco Viejo, El Cangrejo, and Área Bancária, the last two of which happen to be where most of the best hotels are. The area around Calle Uruguay, just south of the banking district, has a number of good restaurants, though it is better known for its bar scene. Java junkies will rejoice over the fact that you can get a good cup of coffee just about anywhere here; even the inexpensive restaurants usually grind their own beans and make every cup to order with espresso machines.

CASCO VIEJO

The old quarter has some of Panama City's best restaurants, and the ambience is spectacular to boot. The only problem is that it is relatively far from the hotels, so you'll have to take a taxi there and back. The good news is that from most hotels the ride is quick and inexpensive. And because the evening is a great time to explore that charming area and hang out on Plaza Bolívar, you may want to dine there several

Morgan's Fury

The countless pounds of gold and silver that crossed Panama in the 16th to 17th centuries made it the target of many a pirate, but none of them stole as much—or caused as much damage—as the legendary Henry Morgan. In 1668 the Welsh privateer captured Panama's Caribbean port of Portobelo and held it until the Spanish paid him a hefty ransom, which came in addition to what he had already plundered there. Though that adventure and previous piracy made Morgan a rich man, he still coveted the big prize—Panamá Viejo, a target most Caribbean corsairs considered too remote to capture.

In 1671 Morgan assembled an army of some 1,500 men of various nationalities and sailed to Panama's Caribbean coast with 36 vessels. He began by attacking Fort San Lorenzo, which guarded the mouth of the Chagres River from a high promontory; despite its imposing location, he managed to capture it with little trouble. From there he and his team traveled upriver in smaller boats and marched through the jungle on the Camino de Cruces to Panamá Viejo, where his troops managed to defeat a Spanish infantry of comparable strength by attacking the unfortified city from two sides.

What ensued were days of looting and pillaging that resulted in a fire that consumed much of the city's buildings. Morgan and his men took everything of value that they could find, even torturing people to learn where they'd hidden their money. They did miss out on one treasure, though: the famous golden altar that now sits in the Casco Viejo's Iglesia de San José. Legend has it that a clever priest covered the altar with mud to disguise it before the pirates arrived.

Morgan and his men needed 200 mules to carry their booty back to his boats on the Chagres River. When they reached Fort San Lorenzo, they rested before sailing to Jamaica, but story goes that Morgan slipped off in the night with the lion's share of the booty. Upon arriving in Jamaica, the pirate was informed that he had violated a peace treaty recently signed by England and Spain, and he was shipped to London. He was able to convince the English authorities that he hadn't heard about the treaty, and he received no punishment greater than having to give the state its share of his booty. Two years later Morgan was knighted, and the following year he was appointed Lieutenant Governor of Jamaica. He spent the rest of his years living quite comfortably on that Caribbean island, dabbling in politics, and as might be expected of a former pirate, drinking inordinate amounts of rum.

nights. The neighborhood's restaurants are definitely worth the trip.
■TIP→ **Many restaurants here close between lunch and dinner, so call ahead if you expect to dine in the mid-afternoon.**

$$
ECLECTIC
Fodor's Choice
★

✕ **Café René.** After managing Manolo Caracol for years, René opened his own place, while following Manolo's popular formula of offering a set menu that changes daily and consists of about a dozen items served in five or six courses. The difference is a more intimate setting, more Caribbean influence and less seafood in the cuisine, and the fact that René is almost always there, making sure his guests are happy. The small restaurant is in a historic building on the northwest corner of Plaza Catedral, with a high ceiling and white walls that are invariably decorated with the work of local artists. There are also several tables on the sidewalk with cathedral views. The dining experience is a sort of culinary journey, in which fresh dishes appear every time you complete a course, and you happily chew your way forward, toward a light dessert. Simpler, inexpensive lunches are an alternative to René's seemingly endless dinners. ⊠ *Plaza Catedral, Calle Pedro J. Sossa, Casco Viejo* ☎ *262–3487* ⚓ *Reservations essential* ☰ *MC, V* ☉ *Closed Sun.*

$–$$
ITALIAN
★

✕ **Ego y Narcisco.** These twin restaurants have tables on Plaza Bolívar, overlooking the Iglesia de San Francisco's illuminated facade, which makes it one of Panama City's most charming dinner spots. If you can't handle the heat, though, you can always move into one of the dim dining rooms in the historic building across the street. Separate in name and interior settings only, the restaurants now share a single menu and kitchen. From the original menu of Narciso, which was predominantly Italian cuisine with Latin American influences, you can still order stuffed ravioli with a spicy Peruvian chicken stew called *ají de gallina*. There are plenty of fresh pastas, as well as a few seafood and meat dishes. From the former menu of Ego, you can still order seafood carpaccio, Peruvian *ceviche* (fish "cooked" with lime juice), and *mini brochetas*: try the breaded pork option with sesame seeds and tamarind sauce. Those *tapas* and the gorgeous setting make this a good spot for a cocktails and appetizers even if you dine elsewhere. ⊠ *Calle 3 on Plaza Bolívar, Casco Viejo* ☎ *262–2045* ☰ *AE, MC, V.*

$$
MEDITERRANEAN
★

✕ **Manolo Caracol.** Owned by Spaniard Manolo Maduño and named after one of his country's great flamenco singers, this restaurant-cum-art gallery in a restored colonial building behind the Teatro Nacional is dedicated to the joy of dining and the art of cooking. Each night they offer only one set menu consisting of 10 to 12 items served in five or six courses. All you need to do is choose your beverage—perhaps a beer or a Spanish wine—and wait for the succession of succulent surprises that the waiters will deliver as you scrape each plate clean. Meals tend to be strong on seafood, but there are always a couple of meat dishes, and you can ask for less seafood. Manolo's is for people who like to eat big, so if you're a light eater you should head elsewhere, or come for lunch. With its tin buckets of fresh fruit, eclectic shrine to the Virgin Mary, and ancient, whitewashed walls hung with modern art, it's a charming spot to spend a few hours, which is how long dinner will take, especially when Manolo is there working the crowd. However, it can get noisy on weekend nights, when it can be hard to carry on a conversation, and it can get awfully hot at the tables near the cooking area, which is in the central back part of the dining area. ⊠ *Av. Central and Calle 3, Casco Viejo* ☎ *228–4640* ☰ *AE, MC, V.*

$$–$$$
LATIN AMERICAN
★

✕ **Mostaza.** Nestled in a restored colonial building across the street from the ruins of Santo Domingo, Mostaza offers a cozy and delicious dining experience in the heart of the historic quarter. Start with a drink on the plaza, then move into one of the two narrow dining rooms, one of which has a centuries-old exposed stone wall. The Argentine and Panamanian owners are usually in the kitchen, preparing an eclectic

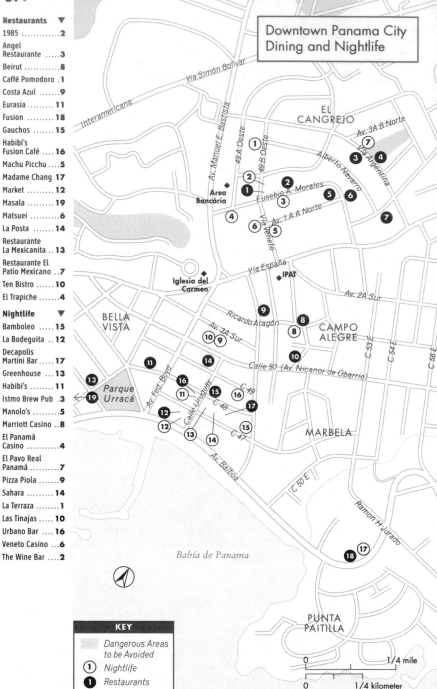

Downtown Panama City
Dining and Nightlife

EL CANGREJO

Via Simón Bolívar

Interamericana

Av. 3A B Norte

Via Argentina

Alberto Navarro

Eusebio A. Morales

Area Bancária

Av. 1 A A Norte

Via Veneto

Via España

IPAT

Iglesia del Carmen

Av. 2A Sur

Ricardo Aragón

BELLA VISTA

Av. 3A Sur

CAMPO ALEGRE

Calle 50 (Av. Nicanor de Obarrio)

Parque Urracá

Av. Fed. Boyd

Calle Uruguay

C. 49

C. 48

C. 47

MARBELA

Av. Balboa

C 50 E

Ramon H. Jurado

Bahía de Panama

PUNTA PAITILLA

KEY

Dangerous Areas
to be Avoided

① Nightlife

● Restaurants

0   1/4 mile

0   1/4 kilometer

2

mix of local seafood and meat dishes that range from *lenguado* (sole) in a mushroom sauce to pork tenderloin in a *maracuya* (passion fruit) sauce. They offer some inventive fresh pastas, such as seafood ravioli in a vodka salmon sauce, and *langostinos* (prawns) sautéed with Gran Marnier, but meat lovers will want to try the classic Argentine *bife de chorizo* (a thick cut of tenderloin) with *chimichurri*, an olive oil, garlic, and parsley sauce. ⊠ *Av. A and Calle 3, Casco Viejo* ☎ *228–3341* ▭ *MC, V* ⊘ *Closed Mon. No lunch weekends.*

$$$–$$$$
MEDITERRANEAN
★

✕ **S'cena.** One of Panama City's most popular restaurants, S'cena sits above one of its most popular bars, Platea, which makes it a busy spot on weekend nights. The city's hip and affluent flock here for Mediterranean classics such as paella and original dishes such as *langosta en salsa mediterránea* (lobster in almond sauce), *filete a los tres hongos* (filet mignon with portobello, shiitake, and cremini mushrooms), and *atún rojo* (grilled tuna marinated in a cherry-soy sauce). It occupies the second floor of a restored colonial-era building, with patches of exposed stone walls and historic photos and paintings by local artists hanging on the plastered stretches. S'cena's location between Plaza Francia and Plaza Bolívar makes it a good spot to have lunch before, or dinner after, exploring the Casco Viejo. It is also well worth the taxi trip, and if you have a late dinner there on a Thursday or Saturday, you can step downstairs afterward for the live music. ⊠ *Calle 1, Casco Viejo* ☎ *228–4011* ▭ *MC, V, AE* ⊘ *Bar closed Sun.*

SANTA ANA, CERRO ANCÓN AND BALBOA

Most of the restaurants in this area are low-budget cafeterias and fast-food outlets, though there are a couple of good lunch spots here that can be a convenient option for a meal while sightseeing.

$–$$
LATIN AMERICAN

✕ **El Rincón de Meche.** Overlooking the picture-perfect church and plaza of Mi Pueblito, this typical Panamanian restaurant occupies a copy of a turn-of-the-century adobe building, with beamed ceilings and colorful Carnaval masks hanging on the walls. The only anachronisms are the ceiling fans, the stereo playing Panamanian folk music, and the sound of traffic on nearby Avenida de los Mártires. Nevertheless, the setting is quite pleasant, and the ample menu includes typical Panamanian fare, from *arroz con pollo* (chicken and rice) to *cazuela de mariscos* (seafood stew). The views from tables on the covered terrace and second-floor porch are quite nice, if you can live without the ceiling fans. It's a good spot to be on Sunday afternoons, when there is a free folk-dancing performance on the plaza. ⊠ *Mi Pueblito, Cerro Ancón* ☎ *314–1427* ▭ *MC, V* ⊘ *Closed Mon.*

$
PIZZA

✕ **Ristorante Pizzeria Napoli.** If you're in the area of the Avenida Central pedestrian mall or Plaza Cinco de Mayo around lunchtime and you want to grab a quick, inexpensive pizza, pop into this historic restaurant down the street from the Avenida de los Mártires. It hasn't been redecorated since it opened in 1962, nor have the prices changed a lot—a small pepperoni pizza is just $3. The various pasta, meat, and seafood dishes won't run you a whole lot more, but pizza is the best bet here. ⊠ *Calle Estudiante, across from Instituto Nacional, Santa Ana* ☎ *262–2448* ▭ *V, MC* ⊘ *Closed Tues.*

CALZADA AMADOR

The best thing about eating on the Amador Causeway is that you usually get an ocean view with your meal. A great place for lunch, the Causeway is also a popular dinner destination, and its restaurants tend to serve food pretty late.

$$–$$$ ✕ **Alberto's.** The best tables here are across the drive from the main res-
ITALIAN taurant, overlooking the Flamenco Marina and the city skyline beyond,
★ but they are also the first ones to fill up. The other options are to sit on the large covered terrace, cooled by ceiling fans, or in the air-conditioned dining room. The food here is the best on the Causeway, but the service can be leisurely, especially if you sit by the marina. The menu has something for everyone, though seafood is definitely the best choice. You can start with *duo de mar* (corvina and lobster in béchamel sauce), or *mero* (grouper) carpaccio, and move on to pizza, salmon ravioli in a creamy tomato sauce, *corvina al cartucho* (sea bass and julienne vegetables broiled in tinfoil), or *langostinos provençal* (prawns sautéed with fine herbs and tomatoes). You may want to walk around the island a few times before visiting their Italian ice cream shop. ✉ *Edificio Fuerte Amador, Isla Flamenco, Calzada Amador* ✆ *Apdo. 11531-081, El Dorado* ☎ *314–1134* ▭ *AE, MC, V.*

$$–$$$ ✕ **Café Barko.** The correct spelling is *barco*, but "boats" are a common
SEAFOOD theme at this large restaurant in the Flamenco Shopping Plaza, with one room that is designed to resemble the deck of a Spanish galleon. The nicest place to sit is on the front deck under a thatch roof, in the middle of which is the trunk of a *gumbo-limbo* tree. Unfortunately, a parking lot takes up most of the view. The specialties are from the surrounding sea, such as grilled fresh tuna topped with sesame seeds and bean sprouts, and ceviche barko, lemon-marinated raw fish with coconut milk. Those familiar with the restaurant's old menu can still order now-removed specialties like *pulpo al coco isleño* (octopus in a ginger and coconut sauce). You can also feast on paella and steaks. The wine list has nearly 90 vintages from around the world. On Thursday nights there's a free folk-dancing show (reserve a table ahead). ✉ *Isla Flamenco, Calzada Amador* ☎ *314–0000* ▭ *MC, V, AE.*

$ ✕ **Kayuco.** This collection of simple tables shaded by umbrellas at the
SEAFOOD edge of the Flamenco Marina is the place to go for inexpensive sea-
☾ food or a cold drink with a view. The food is basic but good—the Panamanian version of bar food—with dishes such as ceviche, chicken fingers, whole fried snapper, all served with *yuca* (fried cassava root) or *patacones* (plantain slices that have been fried and smashed). The relaxed atmosphere and low prices are a winning combination, and the place is usually packed. The proximity to the water and lovely view of the Panama City skyline are best enjoyed at sunset. ✉ *Isla Flamenco, Calzada de Amador* ☎ *314–1998* ▭ *MC, V.*

$–$$ ✕ **Mi Ranchito.** Topped by a giant thatch roof that has become an Ama-
LATIN AMERICAN dor Causeway landmark, this popular restaurant is almost an obliga-
☾ tory stop, if only for a drink, for its excellent view of the city skyline.
★ It is also one of the best places in town for Panamanian food, such as *carimañolas* (fried yucca dumplings stuffed with ground beef), *camarones a la criolla* (shrimp in a tomato and onion sauce), and *pescado*

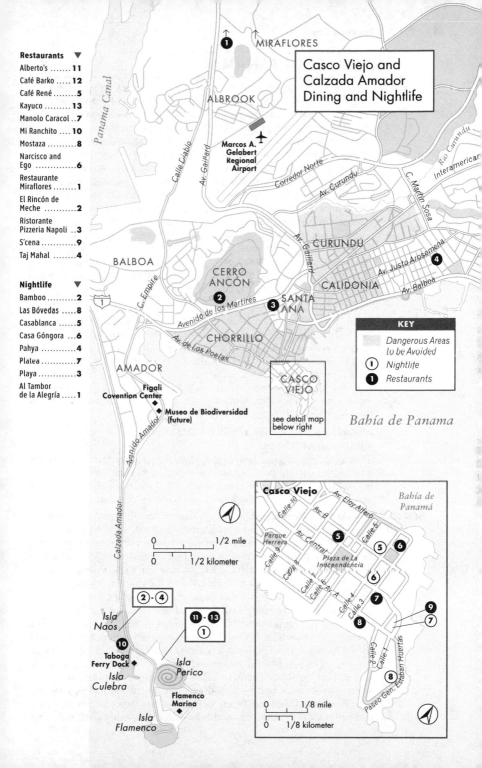

Restaurants ▼

Alberto's **11**
Café Barko **12**
Café René **5**
Kayuco **13**
Manolo Caracol .. **7**
Mi Ranchito **10**
Mostaza **8**
Narcisco and
Ego **6**
Restaurante
Miraflores **1**
El Rincón de
Meche **2**
Ristorante
Pizzeria Napoli .. **3**
S'cena **9**
Taj Mahal **4**

Nightlife ▼

Bamboo **2**
Las Bóvedas **8**
Casablanca **5**
Casa Góngora ... **6**
Pahya **4**
Platea **7**
Playa **3**
Al Tambor
de la Alegría **1**

Casco Viejo and
Calzada Amador
Dining and Nightlife

MIRAFLORES

Panama Canal

ALBROOK

Marcos A.
Gelabert
Regional
Airport

Corredor Norte

Av. Curundu

Río Curundu

C. Martín Sosa

Interamericar

Calle Diablo

Av. Gaillard

CURUNDU

Av. Gaillard

Av. Justo Arosemena

BALBOA

C. Empire

CERRO
ANCÓN

SANTA
ANA

CALIDONIA

Av. Balboa

Avenido de los Martires

CHORRILLO

KEY

Dangerous Areas
to be Avoided

① Nightlife

❶ Restaurants

Av. de los Poetas

AMADOR

Figali
Covention Center

Museo de Biodiversidad
(future)

CASCO
VIEJO

see detail map
below right

Bahía de Panama

Avenida Amador

Calzada Amador

N

0   1/2 mile
0   1/2 kilometer

②-④

⑪-⑬
①

Isla
Naos

❿

Taboga
Ferry Dock

Isla
Culebra

Isla
Perico

Flamenco
Marina

Isla
Flamenco

Casco Viejo

Bahía de
Panamá

Calle 10

Av. Eloy Alfaro

Av. B

Parque
Herrera

Av. Central

Calle 6

❺

❺ ❻

Calle 8

Plaza de La
Independencia

❻

Calle 9

Av. A

❼

Calle 4

Calle 3

❽

❾
❼

Calle 2

Calle 1

Paseo Gen. Esteban Huertas

❽

0   1/8 mile
0   1/8 kilometer

SERVICE IN PANAMA

Surprisingly enough, despite that fact that the service sector drives Panama's economy, few Panamanians follow the credo of ""service with a smile."" With the exception of the best hotels, it's not unusual for a receptionist to ignore you for the first minute or check you in as if she were doing you a favor. Upon arriving at most restaurants, you'll just look silly as you stand around waiting to be seated. Seat yourself. You will often have to call to your servers to get them to clear plates, get you another beer, or bring the check. In the worst-case scenario, you have to get up and look for them. Don't take it personally—it's the Panamanian way. The influx of foreign investment in tourism is slowly instilling a culture of service, but it is thus far spotty, at best. The flip side of the indifferent service workers are the aggressive salesmen, who clap and shout, and try to steer passersby into shops, or the hustlers and taxi drivers who hang outside some of the big hotels and greet you with ""Hello, friend,"" or ""Amigo,"" as the beginning of a pitch intended to get some of your dollars into their pockets.

entero (a whole fried small snapper). Our favorite is *corvina al ajillo* (sea bass smothered in a garlic sauce), though a hungry party of two can't go wrong with a *mixto de mariscos al ajillo* (a mix of seafood sautéed in the same sauce). They also serve great *batidos* (frozen fruit drinks) made from papaya, melon, and *piña* (pineapple). At night you can enjoy the live music, often traditional Panamanian; follow suit when those around you switch from batidos to rum. ⊠ *Isla Naos, Calzada Amador* ☎ *228–0116* ⊟ *AE, MC, V.*

ALBROOK, PARQUE METROPOLITANO AND MIRAFLORES

Though Albrook has a few restaurants, there's only one place worth making the trip out to this area for a meal, and that is the restaurant in the Miraflores Visitor Center, which offers an incomparable view of massive ships sliding through the locks to complement its menu.

$$$–$$$$
ECLECTIC
★

✕ **Restaurante Miraflores.** The big attractions here, literally, are the ships that make their careful way through the locks directly in front of the restaurant. Located on the second floor of the visitor center at Miraflores Locks, this eatery has glass walls that take advantage of its unique view. A fascinating sight by day, the locks are perhaps more impressive at night, when the area is well lighted and the canal at its busiest. The restaurant is run by the Hotel El Panamá, which has a good reputation, though the kitchen definitely plays second fiddle to the view. The eclectic menu runs the gamut from "Caribe scallops" (deep fried in a coconut batter), "San Blas Islands Crab" (king crab mixed with peach palm and served in its shell), to rabbit in a mustard sauce. It isn't cheap, and you can expect to pay $10 for a taxi back to your hotel, but the setting is incomparable—if you can get a table with a view. You can't see much from indoor tables and the half-dozen balcony tables with a view are usually reserved, and often empty. If the waiters won't let you sit there, just order a drink at the bar and take it to the balcony until the party with the reservation arrives. Reserve at least a day in advance and you might get a seat with a view. Preference, however, is given to visitors sent by partner hotels. ⊠ *Miraflores Visitor Center, 2nd fl., Clayton* ☎ *232-3120* ▱ *AE, MC, V.*

DOWNTOWN PANAMA CITY

This area is safe to walk around, and many of its restaurants are within walking distance of the big hotels. Not only does the downtown area have the highest concentration of restaurants, it also has the greatest variety of cuisines and prices. There are also plenty of bars for a pre-dinner cocktail.

$$$–$$$$

SPANISH

✕ **Angel Restaurante.** The most elegant of the city's Spanish restaurants, Angel has a dining room decorated with antiques and original art, as well as a few photos of the owner receiving awards for his cooking. The cuisine is Spanish with some French influence, with dishes such as *cordero chilidrón* (lamb sautéed in tomato sauce) and *conejo deshuesado* (rabbit in a garlic sauce). It's located on quiet, tree-lined Vía Argentina, a short walk from most El Cangrejo hotels. Dress up a bit if you dine here. ⊠ *Vía Argentina No. 6868, El Cangrejo* ☎ *263-6411* ▱ *AE, MC, V* ☾ *Closed Sun.*

$–$$

MIDDLE EASTERN

★

✕ **Beirut.** The interior of this Lebanese restaurant goes a bit overboard, with faux-stone columns and murals of Roman ruins, but the food is consistently good, and the waitstaff is attentive. The extensive menu goes beyond the Middle East to include dishes such as grilled salmon and pizzas, but the best bets are the Lebanese dishes, which include an array of starters such as *falafel* (fried garbanzo balls), *baba ghanoush* (roasted eggplant), and a dozen salads that can make for an inexpensive, light meal. It's a good choice for vegetarians. Be sure to order some fresh flat bread to go with your meal. There is usually Arabic music playing, and there is a collection of hookahs for smoking in the back room, or on the patio, which is a nice place to eat at night, as long as it isn't full of hookah smokers. The owners also have a restaurant on the Amador Causeway. ⊠ *Calles 52 and Ricardo Arias, across from Panama Marriott Hotel, Área Bancária* ☎ *214-3815* ▱ *AE, MC, V.*

$–$$

ITALIAN

Fodor's Choice

★

✕ **Caffé Pomodoro.** The best thing about this popular Italian restaurant in the Hotel Las Vegas is the large interior patio, with its tropical trees, potted plants, and palms decorated with swirling Christmas lights. At breakfast and lunch it feels like a jungle oasis in the heart of the city, with birds singing in the branches above. The food is a close second, with eight varieties of homemade pastas served with a dozen different sauces, a variety of broiled meat and seafood dishes, personal pizzas, and focaccia sandwiches, all at very reasonable prices. For dessert, choose from chocolate cheesecake, tiramisu, and other treats. There's often a guitarist playing at dinnertime, and the Wine Bar next door has acoustic Latin music until late. ⊠ *Vía Veneto and Calle Eusebio A. Morales, El Cangrejo* ✉ *Apdo. 0834-963, Plaza Concordia, Panama City, Panama* ☎ *269-5836* ▱ *MC, V.*

$

LATIN AMERICAN

✕ **Costa Azul.** A bit of an institution, this large, 24-hour restaurant half a block south of the Vía España is where locals head for a good meal at a reasonable price. The decor in the large, bright restaurant is functional, and the service can be slow when it's busy, but the terrace in front is a good place for people watching. The menu ranges from Panamanian classics such as *bistec a la criolla* (steak in a tomato sauce) to Spanish dishes such as *corvina a la vasca* (sea bass in a shrimp and clam sauce). An extensive list of daily specials printed on a piece of paper inserted into the menu is usually the best option, both in terms of price and freshness. They also make about 40 different *emparedados* (sandwiches), including the classic *Cubano* with salami, ham, roast beef, cheese, and toppings. ⊠ *Calle Ricardo Arias, between Hotel Continental and Panama Marriott, Área Bancária* ☎ 269–0409.

$–$$
LATIN AMERICAN

✗ **El Trapiche.** El Trapiche is one of the best places for traditional Panamanian food, thanks to its convenient location and the quality of its cuisine. The menu includes all the local favorites, from *ropa vieja* (stewed beef, but literally "old clothes") to *cazuelo de mariscos* (seafood stew) and *sancocho* (chicken soup). They serve inexpensive set lunches, and typical Panamanian breakfasts, which include *bistec encebollado* (skirt steak smothered in onions), *tortillas* (thick deep-fried corn patties), and *carimañolas*. The decor is appropriately folksy, with a terra-cotta floor, Carnaval masks and other handicrafts hanging on the walls, and a barrel-tile awning over the front terrace, at the end of which is the old *trapiche* (traditional sugarcane press) for which the place is named. ⊠ *Vía Argentina, 2 blocks off Vía España, El Cangrejo* ☎ 269–4353 ⊟ *AE, MC, V.*

$$$–$$$$
ECLECTIC
Fodor's Choice
★

✗ **Eurasia.** One of the city's most attractive restaurants, Eurasia has several dining rooms with high ceilings and walls hung with paintings by Latin American artists. It occupies the second floor of an elegant former home surrounded by condominium towers and has a small tropical garden in back that seems a world apart from the traffic of nearby Avenida Balboa. Owners Gloria and Kim Young offer a soothing ambience and an innovative mix of Asian and French cuisine, with dishes that range from veal chops in a mushroom sauce to duck in a pineapple-plum sauce. They also have some enticing seafood creations, such as prawns in a tamarind and coconut sauce, sea bass with Chinese parsley and pumpkin puree, and grouper in seafood tomato sauce au gratin. You'll walk by a well-stocked pastry table laden with yummy cakes as you enter the dining room; they should inspire you to save room for dessert. Three-course executive lunches are a good deal, include a glass of wine, and are an excellent excuse to take a break from the heat and hustle of the surrounding city. ⊠ *Calle 48, just east of Parque Urraca, Bella Vista* ⊄ *Apdo. 6-4396, El Dorado, Panama City, Panama* ☎ 264–7859 ⊟ *AE, MC, V.*

$$$–$$$$
ECLECTIC
★

✗ **Fusion.** The central dining area of this trendy restaurant in the Decapolis Hotel looks like something out of a Hollywood adventure movie, dominated by a 20-foot bust reminiscent of the statues on Easter Island. If that's a bit too much for you, look for a table in one of the other dining nooks, where the artistic decor includes giant vases and a wall of TVs broadcasting simultaneous images. The menu matches the atmosphere with originality and is true to the restaurant's name in its inventive mix of Continental, Asian, and Latin American cuisines. You can start your dinner with the likes of spring rolls with a sweet chili sauce or saffron-cream-spiked seared scallops, then dive into some shrimp and vegetables in a coconut curry, lamb chops with a sweet and spicy sauce, or grouper and shrimp ravioli. ✉ *In Hotel Decapolis, Av. Balboa next to Multicentro, Paitilla* ☎ *215–5000* ▤ *AE, MC, V.*

$$$–$$$$

ARGENTINE

✗ **Gauchos.** This Argentine restaurant in a Spanish-style house on Calle Uruguay is for serious carnivores who like their steaks big, tender, and juicy. The meat is flown in from the United States, but the cuts are mostly Argentine, such as the *bife de chorizo,* a thick sirloin cut, or the *filete en trozo,* a 16-ounce slice of filet mignon. They are served with *chimichuri,* whereas salads and sides, such as a baked potato, are à la carte. The restaurant also serves *corvina, langostinos,* and a dozen salads, but the real attraction here is the beef. Big windows surround the kitchen, so you can watch cooks slap slabs of meat onto the grill, or you can admire the cowhides, black-and-white photos, and paintings of *gauchos* (Argentine cowboys) that adorn the walls. ✉ *Calle Uruguay and Calle 48, Bella Vista* ☎ *263–4469* ▤ *AE, MC, V.*

$–$$

MIDDLE EASTERN

✗ **Habibi's Fusion Cafe.** Habibi's menu has a Middle Eastern core, but it draws from other Mediterranean and global influences. The offerings include good falafel and shish kebabs, but you can also get pizzas, pastas, *arañitas* (breaded baby octopuses), and even Cajun chicken. The dining room bears some semblance to a sultan's tent, with its white ceiling canopy, whereas the bar is very modern and cozy, with hardwoods, armchairs, and giant windows. The large, covered terrace is a happening spot on weekend nights, when it sits at the epicenter of the Calle Uruguay party scene. ✉ *Calle Uruguay and Calle 48, Bella Vista* ☎ *264–3647* ▤ *AE, MC, V.*

$$$–$$$$

LATIN AMERICAN

Fodor's Choice

★

✗ **La Posta.** The ambience in this elegant, refurbished house just off Calle Uruguay is classic Caribbean, with ceiling fans spinning over the cane chairs, white tablecloths, colorful tile floors, potted palms, and an abundance of young waiters in white *guayaberas* (traditional pocketed tops). There is usually Cuban music playing, and the shiny hardwood bar stretching down one end of the dining room is the perfect place to sip a *mojito.* La Posta is the work of New York restaurateur David Henesy, who ran the popular La Vitrola in Cartagena, Colombia, for years before opening what has become one of Panama City's hottest restaurants. His menu is an innovative mix of Latin American flavors with a bit of European flair thrown in for good measure. The menu changes regularly, but you can check its current and seasonal offerings at the restaurant's Web site. Reserve a table in the back, overlooking the small, tropical garden. ✉ *Calle 49 and Calle Uruguay, Marbella* ☐ *Apdo. 0832-0833, W. T. C., Panama City, Panama* ☎ *269–1076* ⊕ *www.lapostapanama.com* ▤ *AE, MC, V.*

$–$$

PERUVIAN

✗ **Machu Picchu.** This popular Peruvian restaurant named after that country's famous Inca ruins occupies an unassuming house a short walk from the hotels of El Cangrejo. Its relatively small dining room, decorated with paintings of Peruvian landscapes and colorful woven

2

tablecloths, is often packed with Panamanians at night. The food they come for is traditional Peruvian, with a few inventions such as *corvina Hiroshima* (sea bass in a shrimp, bell pepper, ginger sauce) and *langostinos gratinados* (prawns au gratin). You can't go wrong with such Peruvian classics as ceviche, *ají de gallina* (chicken in a chili-cream sauce), *seco de res* (Peruvian stewed beef), and *sudado de mero* (grouper in a spicy soup). Be careful how you apply the *ají* hot sauce; it's practically caustic. ⊠ *Calle Eusebio A Morales No. 16, El Cangrejo* ☎ *264–9308* 🖃 *AE, MC, V.*

$$–$$$

CHINESE

★

✕**Madame Chang.** The city's most elegant Chinese restaurant, Madame Chang has forgone the traditional red and gold of its competitors for a peach and beige decor. The long dining room is decorated with Oriental art. There really is a Madame Chang—Sui Mee Chang—though her children run the restaurant now. They serve traditional Cantonese cuisine (with a few exceptions) and local ingredients such as *róbalo* (snook) steamed with ginger and green onions, or corvina with mustard leaves. You can also sink your teeth into Peking-style barbecued pork ribs, and roast duck. Visiting celebrities often dine here. ⊠ *Calle 48, Bella Vista* ☎ *269–1313* 🖃 *AE, MC, V.*

$$$–$$$$

STEAK

✕**Market.** This casual steak house on busy Calle Uruguay, with cement floors and a corrugated metal roof, is an appropriate place to sink your teeth into anything from a cheeseburger to a rib eye. You can get only Omaha beef here, which isn't cheap, nor is it very exotic for American travelers, but if you've got to have a burger, this is the place to go, and it's a much cheaper alternative to the steaks. You can also get such American classics as a Cobb salad and sides of macaroni and cheese, which are no doubt novelties for their predominantly Panamanian clientele. For something more exciting, try a Cajun-rubbed sirloin or salmon *grille beurre d'hôtel*. There's an extensive wine selection. ⊠ *Calle Uruguay and Calle 47, Bella Vista* ☎ *226–9401* 🖃 *MC, V.*

$$

INDIAN

★

✕**Masala.** Panama City's best Indian restaurant is also one of your surest bets for going vegetarian in a town short on options for herbivores. The shrine behind the bar shows a traditionally dressed Indian woman making the gesture meaning welcome, and owners Koreena Bajwa and César Marín certainly make guests feel that way. Their authentic north Indian cuisine is served in cozy, colorfully decorated dining rooms, which include an area for shoeless dining on the floor on plush cushions where you might just see a client snoozing after eating too much. The chef was trained by Bajwa's father, who perfected the culinary arts of Rajasthan while serving in the Royal Indian Air Force. Just about any of the dozens of vegetarian, chicken, and lamb options on the menu are guaranteed to make your taste buds smile. A great nonmeat option is the *thali*, a plate that includes four hefty samplers including beans or lentils and a yogurt-based dish. Appetizer *gosht tikki* (potatoes stuffed with minced lamb in yogurt sauce) is a favorite, as is the main course chicken tikka masala, which goes well with white rice and roti bread. The attentive servers will ask you how spicy you'd like your dish—on a scale from one to five, with anything over three reserved only for the most valiant. This increasingly popular restaurant is on the small side, so it would be a good idea to make a reservation for dinner. ⊠ *Justo*

Arosemena between Calles 44 and 45, Bella Vista ☎ *225–0105* ▭ *MC, V, AE, DC* ⚠ *Reservations essential* ⊗ *Closed Sun.*

$$–$$$ ✕**Matsuei.** Panama City's original Japanese restaurant has been oper-
JAPANESE ated and owned by the Matsufuji family for three decades, and they have maintained a loyal clientele in the face of burgeoning competition. The small restaurant has a very traditional feel, with simple pine tables and chairs separated by shoji screens, but the roll selections are quite innovative. For some, they could be too innovative, considering such inventions as the "rasta roll," and the "rock & roll." Nonetheless, you can get rolls for every taste, and the sushi and sashimi are very fresh. The menu also includes an array of hot dishes including tempura, teri-yaki, and teppanyaki. ⊠ *Av. Eusebio A. Morales 12-A, El Cangrejo* ☎ *264–9562* ▭ *AE, DC, MC, V* ⊗ *No lunch Sun.*

$$–$$$ ✕**1985.** Named for the year it opened, this restaurant holds the strange
FRENCH distinction of occupying the only building in Panama City that resem-bles a Swiss chalet. The owner, chef Willy Dingelman, trained in Lau-sanne then moved to Panama on a lark three decades ago, only to end up developing a small restaurant and wine-importing empire. The menu is consequently complemented by an excellent wine cellar. When President Ricardo Martinelli was on the campaign trail, Dingelman promised he'd share a $15,000 bottle if he won the election; there's a photo of the post-election moment on the wall at the entrance. Ding-elman's original Swiss restaurant, called the Rincón Suizo, used to be next door; it's now a dining room in the back of 1985—two menus under one roof. The decor is a bit of this and a bit of that, with a clut-tered collection of chairs and couches in the long entrance, but people come here for the consistently good food at reasonable prices. Come hungry for chicken *cordon bleu*, chicken tarragon, lobster, tenderloin in green peppercorn sauce, raclette, bratwurst, or *Zürcher Geschnetzeltes* (veal chunks in a mushroom cream sauce). It is no coincidence that the large parking lot is often full on weeknights. A pianist performs most nights. ⊠ *Calle Eusebio A. Morales, in front of Sevilla Suites hotel, El Cangrejo* ☎ *263–8541* ▭ *AE, MC, V.*

$$–$$$ ✕**Restaurante El Patio Mexicano.** This place is a feast for the eyes. Every
MEXICAN surface seems to be painted a different bright color, and the walls are decorated with a collection of Mexican handicrafts that includes som-breros, angels, wooden statues, tin stars, ceramic suns, and a small collection of *calacas* (skeleton statues made for the Day of the Dead). Owners Juan Manuel and Laura Uribe, who hail from Guadalajara, have assembled what amounts to a museum of Mexican handicrafts, and their menu is a comparable celebration of the country's varied cui-sine. While they produce acceptable standards, including fajitas, enchi-ladas, and tacos, they earn kudos for dishes such as *estofado de puerco* (pork in a spicy sauce), *mole poblano* (chicken in a chili-chocolate sauce), *langostinos mayab* (prawns in a cheese sauce), and the hearty *mujer dormido* (sleeping woman), which includes a marinated steak, a quesadilla, and rice and beans. ⊠ *Calle Guatemala and Calle Alberto Navarro, El Cangrejo* ⊗ *Apdo. 6-3035, El Dorado* ☎ *263–5684* ▭ *AE, MC, V* ⊗ *Closed Mon.*

¢–$ ✕ **Restaurante La Mexicanita.** This unassuming Mexican eatery on the
MEXICAN   corner of Parque Urracá recently moved from its longtime home on
busy Calle 50 but remains a mom-and-pop place that still has the same
staff, menu, and, to a certain degree, clientele it has had for years.
Tortillas and chips are house-made, and guacamole is whipped up to
order. There's a fairly standard lineup of Tex-Mex entrées that includes
soft tacos, enchiladas, burritos, tostadas, and a combo platter called
the "Especial La Mexicanita." Wash it down with a Mexican beer,
margarita, or *horchata* (a sweet, cinnamony drink). The ambience is
"nothin' fancy," limited to a few, time-faded posters of Guadalajara-
area destinations in western Mexico on the walls. ⊠ *Calle 45, Bella
Vista* ☎ *225–1685* ▤ *AE, MC, V* ۞ *Closed Mon.*

$$$–$$$$ ✕ **Ten Bistro.** This trendy, eclectic bistro in the ground floor of the Hotel
ECLECTIC   De Ville is owned by Chef Fabién Migny, one of the founders of Eurasia.
Fodor's Choice   Ten's menu is similar to Eurasia's in its blending of French and Asian
★   traditions, but the decor is something completely different. The rounded
white walls, orange lights, abundant candles, and bird-of-paradise flow-
ers suspended over the tables in giant test tubes, together with the beat
of the house music, provide a very 21st-century ambience. You may
start with saffron crab soup in a puff pastry, or dip some prawn spring
rolls into a tropical sauce. The main fare ranges from grouper poached
in coconut milk to beef tenderloin Indochine—with Chinese mushrooms
and mustard leaves, served with potato tempura. The name refers to the
fact that many main courses cost just $10, though some dishes are con-
siderably more expensive. The desserts are decadent, so be sure to save
room. ⊠ *Hotel De Ville, Calle Beatriz Miranda, Área Bancária* ❍ *Apdo.
0832-0172 W.T.C.* ☎ *213–8250* ▤ *MC, V* ۞ *No lunch Sun.*

ATLAPA AND PANAMÁ VIEJO
Though slightly out of the way from most hotels, the following eateries
are good alternatives to dining at the Sheraton and convenient spots for
a meal either just before or after visiting Panamá Viejo.

$$$–$$$$ ✕ **Golden Unicorn.** Hidden on the fourth floor of the Evergreen Build-
CHINESE   ing, down the street from the Sheraton Hotel, this popular spot has a
★   spacious dining room decorated in gold and brown, with walls of win-
dows that provide views of the ATLAPA Convention Center and the
ocean beyond it. A Cantonese restaurant that serves some Mandarin
and Szechuan dishes, the Golden Unicorn is popular with Chinese fami-
lies, who gather around its large round tables and order enough dishes
to fill the lazy Susan. The menu is as long as a novella, and is written
in Spanish and Chinese, which can be a challenge. You can't go wrong
with dishes such as *robalo al vapor con salsa de frijol negro* (steamed
snook in a black bean sauce), *pollo salteado con setas* (sautéed chicken
and seta mushrooms), *pato salteado con piña y jengibre* (sautéed duck
with pineapple and ginger), *langostinos Yau Pau* (prawns with mini
vegetables), or spicy Szechuan *camarones* (shrimp). They also serve
dim sum, the traditional Chinese breakfast, starting at 8 AM. ⊠ *Edificio
Evergreen, 4th floor, ATLAPA* ☎ *226–3838* ▤ *AE, MC, V.*

$$–$$$ ✕ **Parrillada Jimmy.** Jimmy is Greek, but there is very little Greek food
LATIN AMERICAN   on the menu here. If he'd opened his restaurant in Chicago instead
★   of Panama City, it would no doubt be called Jimmy's Grill, which is

basically what the name means in Spanish. Its big draws are such local favorites as sizzling steaks, chicken, prawns, and octopus, all served with a green salad and baked potato or fries. You can also get a good *corvina al ajillo* (sea bass scampi), or *sancocho* (Panama's national dish, chicken soup with tropical tubers). It's a big place, with lots of windows, red-tile floors, and a large terrace overlooking busy Vía Cincuentenaria, but it still manages to get packed on weekends. ⊠ *Vía Cincuentenaria, behind ATLAPA Convention Center, ATLAPA* ☎ *Apdo. 0816-04699, Panama City* ☎ *226–1870* ⊟ *AE, MC, V.*

WHERE TO STAY

Panama City has a good hotel selection, with plenty of variety for tastes and budgets. There are various large hotels scattered around the city, but the majority of the upper- and middle-range hotels are clustered in El Cangrejo and parts of the Área Bancária. There are also some decent budget hotels to the southwest of there, between Bella Vista and the northern end of Caledonia. For a quieter alternative, head to the Cerro Ancón and Amador. Demand has outpaced supply in recent years, so reserve your room well ahead of time, especially if your trip is during high season. In contrast, there are plenty of rooms available during the low season and some hotels halve the rack rate this time of year.

CASCO VIEJO

For the moment, the only lodging options in the Casco Viejo are budget hotels, fit only for backpackers, and apartment rentals, which are an excellent option for those who want to experience life in the city's colorful historic quarter.

Half a dozen fully equipped apartments in beautifully restored Casco Viejo buildings can be rented through **Casco Viejo Living** (☎ *6602–0590* ⊕ *vielkaquezada@yahoo.com*), a small rental service run by Vielka Quezada. She can set you up with a two-bedroom apartment at $250, or a shared rental of a two-bedroom apartment for $125. Rentals include breakfast and daily maid service.

SANTA ANA, CERRO ANCÓN, AND BALBOA

$$ 🏨 **Country Inn & Suites Panama Canal.** The lobby of this American chain
★ hotel, with its fireplace and checkered armchairs, more resembles rural Pennsylvania than Panama, but historic photos of the canal's construction adorn the hallways, and the view from the pool and guest rooms of the Big Ditch's Pacific entrance is unmistakable. This is the best-situated hotel with a Panama Canal view, which, together with the peace and quiet that comes with its out-of-town location, is the reason to stay here. The rooms are standard size with tile floors, colorful quilts, and sliding-glass doors that open onto a balcony. There is, however, a big difference between the various views, so be sure to pay the extra money for a view of the canal or you'll end up contemplating the hotel's parking lot. The canal view is partially obstructed by a large tree on the right side of the hotel, so get into a room in the left, or south wing, preferably one with a number between 300 and 313, or 200 and 215. It's a short drive to downtown, and minutes to the restaurants, nightlife, and

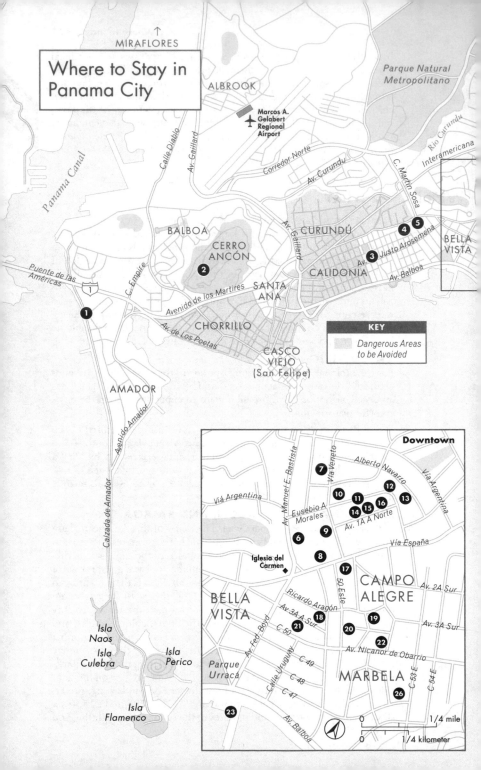

2

ocean views of the Calzada Amador. **Pros:** great canal views from some rooms; peaceful; good rates. **Cons:** far from downtown; "garden views" disappointing. ✉ *Calles Amador and Pelícano, Balboa* ☎ *211–4500; 888/201–1746 in the U.S.* ⊕ *www.countryinns.com* 🛏 *101 rooms, 58 suites* ⚭ *In-room: safe, refrigerator (some), Wi-Fi. In-hotel: restaurant, room service, tennis court, pool, gym, bicycles, laundry facilities, Wi-Fi, parking (free)* ☰ *AE, MC, V* ⊙ *BP.*

$

Fodor's Choice

★

🖽 **La Estancia.** One of the city's only bed-and-breakfasts, La Estancia is the perfect spot for nature lovers or anyone who wants to avoid the noise and crowds downtown, since it sits at the edge of the forest that covers the top of Ancón Hill (Cerro Ancón). The breakfast area and common lounges include long balconies that overlook a strip of forest where you might see tamarins, tanagers, and toucans. The trail to the summit of Cerro Ancón starts just up the road, so it is the perfect spot from which to make that hike first thing in the morning. The owners, Gustavo and Tammy Liu, have a small travel agency; they can set up day trips, or tours of the country but are also happy to offer friendly advice. The tile-floor rooms are small and simple. Because the hotel used to be an apartment building for the U.S. Army, the bathrooms of a few rooms are across the hall. There are also two suites that are full apartments with kitchens and balconies (these are the only rooms with TVs). Most guests hang out in the common areas, where complimentary breakfast is served, and which have wicker furniture, balconies, Wi-Fi, and a self-service bar. **Pros:** quiet; surrounded by nature; friendly, helpful owners and staff. **Cons:** rooms small; some bathrooms across the hall. ✉ *Quarry Heights, Casa No. 35; 50 yards south of ANCON office, Cerro Ancón* ✆ *Apdo. 0832-01705 W.T.C., Panama City, Panama* ☎ *314–1417* ⊕ *www.bedandbreakfastpanama.com* 🛏 *15 rooms, 2 suites* ⚭ *In-room: kitchen (some), no TV (some). In-hotel: public Wi-Fi, parking (free)* ☰ *MC, V* ⊙ *BP.*

DOWNTOWN PANAMA CITY

Panama City's critical mass of accommodations is found in this amalgam of neighborhoods that extends from Bella Vista to Punta Paitilla. Many of them are found near the intersection of Vía España and Vía Veneto, the heart of El Cangrejo. Several are scattered through the Área Bancária, the city's financial district, just to the east of El Cangrejo, and a few more are on the coast, near where Avenida Balboa terminates at Punta Paitilla. This area is safe for walking and is sprinkled with restaurants, nightlife, shops, and other diversions.

$$$$

★

🖽 **The Bristol.** Designed with an English manor in mind, the Bristol is gorgeous and classy, much like a European boutique hotel. Its selling points include a convenient location in the Área Bancária, personalized service, and attention to detail. This carries through to the rooms, with high ceilings, handsome hardwood furniture, original artwork adorning the walls, and a marble bathroom. The beds are sumptuous. Services include a 24-hour concierge, room service, and coffee or tea delivered with your wake-up call. There is a gorgeous bar downstairs with polished hardwoods and windows overlooking lush atriums. The restaurant next door, Las Barandas, is run by one of the country's most famous chefs, Cuquita, whose nouveau Panamanian menu includes

Asian and European touches. **Pros:** excellent service; good location; good restaurant. **Cons:** expensive; no pool. ✉ *Av. Aquilino de la Guardia, between Calle 50 and Vía España, Área Bancária* ☎ *264–0000, 800/323–7500 in the U.S.* ⊕ *www.thebristol.com* ✑ *44 rooms, 12 suites* ⚘ *In-room: safe, DVD, Wi-Fi. In-hotel: restaurants, room service, bar, gym, laundry service, parking (free)* ▭ *AE, MC, V* ☉|*BP.*

2

$ ⊞ **Coral Suites.** Like the other small "suite" hotels in El Cangrejo, Coral
★ Suites is a good deal, offering tiny apartments with many of the same amenities you get at the luxury hotels for about half the price. It is similar to Suites Ambassador next door but has smaller rooms. The hotel's rooms have tile floors and are well furnished, with a pullout bed in the sofa, a small bathroom, and all the necessary appliances. There is a small, blue-tile pool on the roof, an exercise room, and laundry facilities. The location on quiet Calle D near the restaurants and nightlife of El Cangrejo is a big part of the attraction of this economical hotel. The rates drop for stays longer than a week. **Pros:** affordable; lots of amenities; great location. **Cons:** pool is small. ✉ *Calle D, half a block east of Vía Veneto, El Cangrejo* ☎ *269–3898* ⊕ *www.coralsuites.net* ✑ *62 rooms* ⚘ *In-room: safe, kitchen, refrigerator, Wi-Fi. In-hotel: pool, gym, laundry facilities, parking (free)* ▭ *AE, MC, V* ☉| *BP.*

$$$$ ⊞ **Crowne Plaza.** Though it doesn't have a lot of personality, this large hotel has a good location and bright, spacious rooms. There is nothing about the rooms that would indicate that you are in Panama, aside from the view of such nearby landmarks as the Iglesia del Carmen and the Hotel El Panamá, but they are comfortable and well-equipped. The bar and restaurant, just off the lobby, are a bit cramped, without a window between them, but there are plenty of other bars, restaurants, and casinos within walking distance. The hotel also has a small pool in the corner of a deck off the fourth floor, near which is a small gym. The rack rate here is among the city's highest, but you can expect to pay a fraction of it at any time but the peak holidays. Check the hotel's Web site for special rates. **Pros:** good location; friendly staff; free airport shuttle. **Cons:** can be noisy; small pool; small public areas. ✉ *Av. Manuel Espinosa Batista and Vía España, El Cangrejo* ☎ *206–5555* ⊕ *www.cppanama.com* ✑ *114 rooms, 36 suites* ⚘ *In-room: safe, Wi-Fi. In-hotel: restaurant, room service, bar, pool, gym, spa, laundry service, parking (free)* ▭ *AE, DC, MC, V* ☉| *BP.*

$$$–$$$$ ⊞ **DeVille.** One of the city's few boutique hotels, the DeVille has a British
★ ambience, despite its French name and restaurant, and is considerably less expensive than the competition in that category, at least on weekends when the rack rate drops by $100. It clearly caters to the business traveler, for lack of a pool and other facilities, but plenty of vacationers stay here. Rooms are elegant, if a bit dark, since some of them overlook the wall of a nearby building. They have an eclectic mix of elegant Asian- and French-style furnishings, and the beds are heaped with fluffy goose-down pillows and have Egyptian cotton sheets. Bathrooms have Italian marble and roomy showers. Large desks with broadband Internet, the small business center behind the lobby, and a largely peaceful atmosphere make this a good choice if you've work to do. The restaurant, 10 Bistro, is one of the city's best, serving innovative French-Asian

fusion cuisine. **Pros:** handsome rooms; good location; great restaurant. **Cons:** no pool or gym. ✉ *Av. Beatriz Cabal, near Calle 50 Este, Área Bancária* ☎ *206–3100* ⊕ *www.devillehotel.com.pa* ⚡ *33 rooms* ⅁ *In-room: safe, Internet, Wi-Fi. In-hotel: restaurant, bar, laundry service, Wi-Fi, parking (free)* ▤ *AE, MC, V* ℔ *BP.*

$–$$ ▣ **The Executive.** This well-situated hotel is perfect for a business traveler on a budget, or any traveler looking for a good deal. Its 15 stories of carpeted rooms offer less space than the luxury hotels, and they have a very 1960s feel, but they are comfortable and equipped with one or two queen beds and all the amenities the big guys offer, for less money. Rooms have small balconies, and the hotel is perched on a hill, which gives it a great view of the city and sea beyond, but because of a design flaw, most rooms face the other direction. Each room has a large desk and Internet access. There's also a large business center and an exercise room on the roof. The tiny pool next to the lobby is quite possibly Panama City's smallest. The lobby bar and 24-hour coffee shop have a tropical feel, with wicker furniture and bright colors; the coffee shop is a popular Sunday breakfast spot with locals. **Pros:** conveniently located and affordable. **Cons:** small pool; not a ton of ambience. ✉ *Calle 52 and Calle Aquilino de la Guardia, Área Bancária* ☎ *265–8011* ⊕ *www. executivehotel-panama.com* ⚡ *96 rooms* ⅁ *In-room: safe, refrigerator, Internet. In-hotel: restaurant, room service, bar, pool, gym, laundry service, Wi-Fi, parking (free)* ▤ *AE, MC, V* ℔ *BP.*

¢   ▣ **Hotel California.** This place on the Vía España, a short hike from the restaurants of El Cangrejo and the Área Bancária, has long been popular with budget travelers, thanks to its spacious, bright, and clean rooms. It is usually full. It also has a problem: it lies on busy Vía España, which means it is quite noisy by day and is near the bad side of town, as the guayabera-wearing guard with the Terminator 2 shotgun at the entrance attests. Rooms in back are quieter—ask for a room with a number ending in 1, 2, 3, or 4—but there's no complete escape from the honking. As the night wears on, things get quieter. The hotel has an exercise room and a small restaurant that serves acceptable lunch specials. It is a short hike, or taxi trip, from the ample restaurant and nightlife selections of El Cangrejo, the Área Bancária, or Calle Uruguay. **Pros:** crisp, cheap and clean. **Cons:** busy and noisy during the day; sketchy neighborhood ✉ *Vía España and Calle 43 E, Bella Vista* ☎ *263–7736* ⊕ *www.hotelcaliforniapanama.com* ⚡ *60 rooms* ⅁ *In-hotel: restaurant, bar, laundry service, Wi-Fi* ▤ *AE, MC, V* ℔ *EP.*

¢   ▣ **Hotel Costa Inn.** This budget hotel is away from the main restaurant and bar areas, but it offers some good perks. Among its attractions are a rooftop pool and sundeck with an ocean view, free pickup at the domestic airport or bus station, free daily shuttles to the international airport, mini refrigerators, and free wireless Internet access. Its main problem is its location on busy Avenida Perú, one of the city's main bus routes, which means it can be noisy during the day. Be sure to get a room in the back of the building, preferably on the fourth or fifth floor. Rooms vary in size and design but most have pastel walls, tiled floors, and small bathrooms. Suites, which cost $20 more, are bigger, and have more amenities—rooms 509, 508, 601, and 607 are the best ones, since they have ocean views. There's a small restaurant, a bar, and a tour company on the ground floor. The pool deck is a good place for a sunset cocktail. **Pros:** friendly staff; pool; lots of freebies. **Cons:** noisy; mediocre rooms. ⊠ *Av. Peru and Calle 39, Bella Vista* ☎ *227–1522* 🛏 *99 rooms* 🔁 *In-room: Wi-Fi, refrigerator. In-hotel: restaurant, room service, bar, pool, laundry service, Internet terminal, parking (free)* ☰ *AE, MC, V* ᵀᴼᴵ *CP.*

$$$ 🔲 **Hotel El Panamá.** Known simply as "El Panamá," the city's venerable
🕓 and first luxury hotel once hosted every VIP who passed through town. Its star has since faded, and the design is a bit dated, but the expansive complex covering a small hill behind the Vía España is well maintained and quite pleasant. The spacious, open-air lobby has a very tropical feel, with polished floors, wicker furniture, and potted palms. Behind it lies a large pool surrounded by a wide deck, palm trees, gardens, and an open-air restaurant. Standard rooms in a nine-story building are big enough to play handball in—if it weren't for the queen beds, large desks, and other furniture—and their picture windows provide views of the banking district. "Cabañas" in two-story buildings along the pool area are brighter, slightly quieter rooms just steps away from the water, which makes them a good option for families. The open-air, poolside grill is a pleasant spot for dinner, but there are plenty of other dining, nightlife, and shopping options a short walk from the hotel. The hotel's location in the heart of busy El Cangrejo is a big part of the attraction, whereas the in-house shopping arcade and airline counters add to the convenience. **Pros:** big pool; big rooms; good location. **Cons:** some traffic noise; spotty service. ⊠ *Vía España and Vía Veneto, El Cangrejo* ☎ *216–9000* ⊕ *www.elpanama.com* 🛏 *113 rooms, 17 suites* 🔁 *In-room: safe, Wi-Fi. In-hotel: 2 restaurants, room service, bars, pool, laundry service, parking (free)* ☰ *AE, MC, V, DC* ᵀᴼᴵ *BP.*

¢–$ 🔲 **Hotel El Parador.** A relatively new addition to El Cangrejo's hotel selection, El Parador offers comfortable, though basic, rooms in an excellent location—this is the place for travelers on a tight budget who still want to be in the heart of things. Its smallish rooms are well furnished and have tiny, curved balconies with views of the surrounding apartment buildings and restaurants. The view from the swimming pool and deck atop this seven-story building is impressive—a full skyscraper panorama with glimpses of the sea. There is a small restaurant next to the lobby that offers room service, but you can get better food nearby, since the hotel is surrounded by good restaurants and is a short walk from both Vía España and Vía Veneto. The Parador is popular with Panamanians because it's a bargain, but the service is mediocre, and if the receptionist smiles, consider it a miracle. Still, it's often full. **Pros:** central location; pool; inexpensive. **Cons:** small rooms; indifferent staff; busy street. ⊠ *Calle Eusebio A. Morales, across from Martin Fierro, El Cangrejo* ☎ *214–4586* ⊕ *www.hotelparadorpanama.com* 🛏 *85 rooms* 🔁 *In-hotel: restaurant, room service, pool, laundry service, Internet terminal, parking (free)* ☰ *AE, MC, V* ᵀᴼᴵ *CP.*

¢–$ 🔲 **Hotel Marbella.** The attraction of this small hotel on tranquil Calle D, in the heart of El Cangrejo, is that it offers clean, affordable rooms in one of the nicest areas of the city, steps away from an array of restaurants, nightlife, shops, and services. The rooms are nothing special, slightly cramped, but comfortable with either one queen bed or a double plus a single, and such basic amenities as a small TV (cable), telephone, and a tiny desk. The brightest ones are at the front of the building. There is a tiny ""business center"" that offers Internet access and a small restaurant. **Pros:** great location; quiet; inexpensive. **Cons:** small rooms; indifferent staff; no pool. ⊠ *Calle D, half a block east of Vía Veneto, El Cangrejo* ☎ *263–2220* ⊕ *www.hmarbella.com* ⇨ *84 rooms* ☖ *In-hotel: restaurant, room service, laundry service, Internet terminal, parking (free)* ⊟ *AE, MC, V* ⦿*I EP.*

¢ ▦ **Hotel Milán.** With surprisingly inexpensive rooms near some of the
★ best restaurants in El Cangrejo, the Hotel Milán is one of the city's best options for budget travelers, especially considering its 25% discount if you pay cash. The rooms are nothing to write home about, but they are as big and well-equipped as those in hotels that charge twice as much. The hotel is consequently often full. Rooms have either a queen bed or a double plus a single, and some have small tables and chairs while others have a sofa. Spacious suites have a king-size bed and a bathtub, and cost just $10 more. There is a restaurant and free Internet access downstairs, and the hotel is a short walk from both Vía España and Vía Veneto. **Pros:** great location; inexpensive. **Cons:** no pool; indifferent staff. ⊠ *Calle Eusebio A. Morales No. 31, El Cangrejo* ☎ *263–6130* ⇨ *53 rooms* ☖ *In-room: safe. In-hotel: restaurant, room service, laundry service, Internet terminal, parking (free)* ⊟ *MC, V, DC, AE* ⦿*I EP.*

$ ▦ **Hotel Roma Plaza.** Located on busy Avenida Justo Arosemena, one block south of historic Parque Belisario Porras, which is surrounded by government buildings, the Roma is away from the main hotel and restaurant areas but is closer to the Casco Viejo, Balboa, and the Amador Causeway. It is pretty self-sufficient, with a small shop, the 24-hour Rainforest Café, travel services, exercise room, and a rooftop pool. The rooms aren't going to win any decorating awards, but they are clean, with shiny white-tile floors. Those in front are quite bright, but can be noisy by day, though things quiet down at night. They have some interior rooms that are much quieter, but they lack windows, which can be disconcerting. The rooftop pool has a nice view of the bay and Casco Viejo. **Pros:** good value; pool; restaurant. **Cons:** far from most other hotels and restaurants. ⊠ *Av. Justo Arosemena and Calle 33, Bella Vista* ☎ *227–3844* ⊕ *www.hotelromaplaza.net* ⇨ *133 rooms* ☖ *In-hotel: restaurant, room service, pool, laundry service, Internet terminal, parking (free)* ⊟ *AE, MC, V* ⦿*I BP.*

$$$$ ▦ **InterContinental Miramar.** No hotel in Panama City can top the Mira-
★ mar's view. Every room in this 25-story tower on the waterfront ends in a wall of windows with views of the Bay of Panama, the skyscrapers of nearby Punta Paitilla, the Casco Viejo, and the islands of the Amador Causeway. It is just as spectacular at night, when the lights of dozens of ships anchored offshore shine against the sea. The higher the floor, the more breathtaking the view. Once you pry your eyes from that panorama, you'll see that the rooms themselves are nicely decorated in earth tones, with hints of art nouveau in the wooden furniture and antique

prints of tropical flora on the wall. The top five floors hold executive rooms and suites, which share a lounge and a small pool on the 21st floor. George W. Bush once stayed in the Royal Suite. There is a bar on the fifth floor and a spacious restaurant near the lobby that serves a finger-licking complimentary breakfast buffet. It overlooks a large pool with a bridge, islands, tropical gardens, and artificial waterfall, surrounded by plenty of spots to soak up the sun. Step out onto Avenida Balboa, one of the city's most beautiful streets, and you can stroll down to the Balboa monument or to the shopping, restaurants, and nightlife of nearby Calle Uruguay and Punta Paitilla—but only after a careful crossing of the madly busy street, so be sure to walk a couple blocks east past Parque Urracá where a stoplight crosswalk was under construction at this writing. **Pros:** amazing view; good location; great pool. **Cons:** expensive, hemmed in by the Cinta Costera. ⊠ *Miramar Plaza, Av. Balboa at Av. Federico Boyd, Bella Vista* ✆ *Apdo. 816-2009* ☎ *206–8888* ⊕ *www.miramarpanama.com* ⤶ *165 rooms, 20 suites* ♿ *In-room: safe, Wi-Fi. In-hotel: restaurant, room service, bar, tennis court, pool, laundry service, parking (free)* ▭ *AE, MC, V* ℠*BP.*

$ ▧ **Las Huacas Hotel and Suites.** Rooms in this former apartment building
★   are spacious and anything but bland, thanks to their bright colors and murals depicting tropical wildlife. But this hotel's greatest assets are its location on a quiet side street just blocks away from El Cangrejo's busy Vía Veneto and its reasonable rates. The bright, comfortable rooms have kitchenettes with breakfast bar separated from the bedrooms by a half wall, high ceilings, and smallish bathrooms with interesting mosaic or stone showers. Some rooms have balconies, but because the building is squeezed between two apartment towers, only those in front have decent views. A complimentary breakfast buffet is served in Café Bijaos, a colorful restaurant behind the hotel that also serves inexpensive lunch specials and a mix of Panamanian and Continental cuisine. **Pros:** big rooms; great location; friendly staff. **Cons:** no pool; no gym. ⊠ *Calle 49, 1½ blocks north of Salsa's Bar and Grill, El Cangrejo* ✆ *Apdo. 0819-12496* ☎ *213–2222* ⊕ *www.lashuacashotel.com* ⤶ *33 rooms* ♿ *In-room: kitchen, refrigerator, Wi-Fi. In-hotel: restaurant, laundry service, parking (free)* ▭ *AE, MC, V* ℠*BP.*

$ ▧ **Las Vegas Hotel Suites.** El Cangrejo's original "suite" hotel recently concluded a painstakingly long renovation, and rooms now have new tile floors and furniture. The hotel is a good deal, especially for families or for long stays. Spacious studios have one or two queen beds, while suites have separate bedrooms, full kitchens, and a dining-living area. The hotel has free Internet access, laundry facilities, a small exercise room, and a covered deck on the roof with a great view; alas, there's no swimming pool. The popular Italian restaurant in the hotel's garden courtyard is a charming spot for a meal or drink, and it is mere steps away from El Cangrejo's varied nightlife and dining options. The problem is that the hotel sits at a busy intersection, and the street noise disturbs the peace and quiet of the day, and well into the night on weekends. **Pros:** central location; spacious rooms; great restaurant. **Cons:** noisy; no pool. ⊠ *Vía Veneto and Calle Eusebio A. Morales, El Cangrejo* ☎ *300–2020* ⊕ *www.lasvegaspanama.com* ⤶ *50 suites, 30 studios*

     ♿ *In-room: kitchen (some), Wi-Fi. In-hotel: restaurant, bar, gym, laundry facilities, public Wi-Fi, parking (free)* ☱, *MC, V* ⧖ *EP.*

$$$$
Fodor's Choice
★

⊞ **Panama Marriott Hotel.** Enter the ground floor of this sleek, 20-story tower in the heart of the banking district and you'll find yourself in an immaculate, airy lobby with high arches, marble floors, and leafy plants. The spacious rooms are equally attractive, with high ceilings, a hardwood desk, a couch and table, TV hidden in a cabinet, and a marble bathroom. The big windows have either impressive views of the sea through the office-tower jungle, or disappointing views of the skyscraper next door. The top-four executive floors share a lounge where complimentary breakfast and cocktail hour are served. There is a full-service gym and a small pool area hemmed by tropical foliage on the second floor. The expansive lobby has all the services of a small village: a large restaurant that specializes in buffets, an elegant lobby bar, airline and car-rental offices, a business center, a gift shop, a café, and a sports bar that serves a damn good burger. There's even a two-story casino next door, and the tree-lined streets that surround the hotel hold plenty more bars and restaurants. **Pros:** good location; friendly staff; spacious rooms; some great views. **Cons:** small pool; some obstructed views. ⊠ *Calle 52 and Calle Ricardo Arias, Área Bancária* ✆ *Apdo. 832-0498, W. T. C., Panama City, Panama* ☎ *210–9100; 888/236–2427 in the U.S.* ⊕ *www.marriott.com* ⇝ *290 rooms, 8 suites* ♿ *In-room: safe, Internet. In-hotel: 3 restaurants, room service, bars, pool, gym, laundry service, Wi-Fi, parking (free)* ☱ *AE, MC, V* ⧖ *EP.*

$
★

⊞ **Plaza Paitilla Inn.** Standing amidst the condominiums of Paitilla Point, this round, 19-story tower was no doubt a giant when it opened in the 1970s, but it is now a bit of a dwarf in Panama City's increasingly vertical skyline. Still, when you're on one of its upper floors peering across the bay, you feel like you're on top of the world. About half the rooms in this hotel have gorgeous views of the tower-lined Bay of Panama, Casco Viejo, and the Causeway. The views aren't quite as spectacular as those of the nearby Hotel Miramar, but they are a fraction of the price. The carpeted, wedge-shaped rooms have curved walls of windows but rather small bathrooms. Though they've been recently refurbished, you would think they could have come up with something better than the gold-trimmed wood furniture. Each room has a small desk, an armchair and table, and most of the same appliances that the luxury hotels offer. The only Internet access is in the business center. The circular pool has an ocean view. The hotel is on a quiet street just steps away from Avenida Balboa, various restaurants, and the Multicentro shopping mall. The refurbishers missed some parts of the lobby and grounds, which show their age, and you'll want to take meals other than breakfast elsewhere, but the ocean views from the upper floors here are priceless, and the rates quite reasonable. **Pros:** half of the rooms have great views; low rates; quiet neighborhood. **Cons:** half of the rooms have mediocre views; some dog-eared areas. ⊠ *Vía Italia at Av. Balboa, Punta Paitilla* ✆ *Apdo. 0816-06579, Zona 5* ☎ *208–0600* ⊕ *www.plazapaitillainn. com* ⇝ *255 rooms* ♿ *In-room: safe. In-hotel: restaurant, room service, bar, pool, laundry service, parking (free)* ☱ *AE, MC, V* ⧖ *EP.*

$$$ ⊡ **Radisson Decapolis.** Some hotels were clearly designed for business
Fodor's Choice travelers, but this ultramodern, 29-story high-rise is a party hotel. Con-
★ sider the fact that guests are given a $20 voucher for the hotel's bars
upon check-in, and that the lobby borders a large lounge that is often
packed with people sipping martinis to the pulsating beat of house
music. The hotel has a business center and executive floors, but the
atmosphere is definitely more conducive to non-business pursuits. The
rooms are quite mod, with white-tile floors, splashes of bright green and
orange, giant photos, and walls of windows with city views. Rooms on
the west side of the building have knockout ocean views through the
skyscrapers; those on the east side overlook cement. The hotel's trendy
restaurant, Fusion, serves an eclectic menu in what may be the city's
wildest ambience: round windows on the high ceiling allow guests to
look up into the hotel's pool. An elevated walkway connects the hotel's
lobby with the Multicentro shopping mall, which has a large casino,
movie theater, and Hard Rock Cafe. **Pros:** hip; some great views; good
restaurant; near shops and entertainment. **Cons:** some mediocre views;
small pool. ⊠ *Av. Balboa, next to Multicentro, Paitilla* ⏏ *Apdo. 0833-
0293* ☎ *215–5000; 888/201–1718 in the U.S.* ⊕ *www.radisson.com/
panamacitypan* ⇶ *240 rooms* ♿ *In-room: safe, refrigerator, Wi-Fi. In-
hotel: 3 restaurants, room service, bars, pool, gym, spa, laundry service,
Wi-Fi, parking (free)* ☰ *AE, MC, V* ⑩ *BP.*

$$$ ⊡ **Riande Continental.** Renovation and expansion have added a touch of
pizzazz to this hotel, one of the city's older luxury accommodations, but
the updates didn't completely strip it of kitsch. The rambling, wood-
paneled lobby has shops and a small, rounded bar that holds the pieces
of a giant Wurlitzer organ that was played each evening for decades
but has thankfully been retired. It overlooks a courtyard with a small,
round pool that turns into a fountain at night. The hotel is a 14-story,
L-shaped building on busy Vía España, which means street noise can be
a problem, but it is within walking distance of an array of shops, restaurants, and offices. Be sure to get a room with a pool view, to avoid the
traffic symphony. The bright rooms are conservatively furnished, with a
small desk, table, and chairs; they're decorated with prints of an English
fox hunt, of all things. There's a business center, a 24-hour casino, a
coffee shop, and an upscale restaurant, Rendezvous, which serves traditional Panamanian food. **Pros:** central location; friendly staff. **Cons:**
street noise; average rooms. ⊠ *Vía España and Calle Ricardo Arias,El
Cangrejo* ☎ *366–7700* ⊕ *www.hotelesriande.com* ⇶ *317 rooms, 44
suites* ♿ *In-room: safe, Wi-Fi. In-hotel: restaurant, room service, bar,
pool, gym, laundry service, parking (free)* ☰ *AE, MC, V* ⑩ *BP.*

$ ⊡ **Sevilla Suites.** This is one of several midrange hotels in El Cangrejo that
offer many of the same amenities as the luxury hotels on a smaller scale.
Sevilla Suites' rooms are well-stocked kitchenettes and have lots of amenities but are slightly smaller than the nearby competition, and they're
on a street that is pretty busy on weekdays. While all rooms have shiny
tile floors, kitchenettes, tables, chairs, and couches, the standard "Junior
Suites" are a bit cramped. Executive suites have separate bedrooms, and
a sofa with a foldout bed, which makes them well worth the extra $10.
There is a small pool, exercise room, and laundry room on the roof.

Rates include a Continental breakfast and free wireless Internet, and they drop for stays of one week or more. **Pros:** lots of amenities; good location. **Cons:** spotty service. ⊠ *Av. Eusebio Morales, east of Hotel Las Vegas, El Cangrejo* ☎ *213–0016* ⊕ *www.sevillasuites.com* ⤴ *44 rooms* ⟐ *In-room: safe, kitchen, refrigerator, DVD, Wi-Fi. In-hotel: pool, gym, laundry facilities, parking (free)* ⊟ *AE, MC, V* ⦿ *CP.*

$$$ 🖭 **Sheraton Four Points.** This comfortable hotel around the corner from busy Calle 53 is located near Punta Paitilla in Panama's World Trade Center. Its small, curved lobby has a shiny marble floor and a sunken bar in the corner with a large saltwater aquarium and live piano music most evenings. In the mezzanine is a business center and a small sports bar–restaurant that serves a mix of Panamanian and international dishes. Above it are a spa, gym, pool, and tennis court. The bright rooms are carpeted and tastefully decorated with a hardwood desk, a couch and coffee table, and paintings by Panamanian artists. **Pros:** attractive; friendly staff; near shopping mall. **Cons:** away from most restaurants and nightlife. ⊠ *Calle 53 and Av. 5 B Sur, World Trade Center, Marbella* ☎ *265–3636; 800/368–7764 in the U.S.* ⊕ *www.starwoodhotels.com* ⤴ *112 rooms, 16 suites* ⟐ *In-room: safe, Wi-Fi. In-hotel: restaurant, room service, bar, tennis court, pool, gym, spa, laundry service, parking (free)* ⊟ *AE, MC, V, D* ⦿ *BP.*

$ 🖭 **Suites Ambassador.** Most rooms in this small, friendly hotel are
★ extremely spacious, with a bedroom and a separate living room with a kitchenette, a couch, and a table with chairs for meals. They are actually small apartments, and the management will add extra beds for families. Rooms this size cost much more elsewhere, and the Ambassador is conveniently located on one of El Cangrejo's quieter streets, a short walk away from a dozen restaurants and the hustle and bustle of Vía Veneto. There are also some ""studios,"" with the kitchenette and bed packed into one large room, but those aren't much cheaper than the suites, so they're hardly a bargain. There is a small pool and sundeck on the roof, a workout room, and coin laundry. Internet access is free, as is the Continental breakfast served in a small lounge off the lobby, next to which is a room with computers for guest use. The hotel caters to long-term guests with discounted weekly rates. **Pros:** big suites; great location; friendly staff; lots of amenities. **Cons:** small pool. ⊠ *Calle D, half a block east of Vía Veneto, El Cangrejo* ⌂ *Apdo. 0816-01662* ☎ *263–7274* ⊕ *www.suitesambassador.com.pa* ⤴ *31 suites, 8 studios* ⟐ *In-room: safe, kitchen, refrigerator, Wi-Fi. In-hotel: pool, gym, laundry facilities, Internet terminal, parking (free)* ⊟ *AE, MC, V* ⦿ *CP.*

¢–$ 🖭 **Tower House Suites.** Located on a quiet side street in the banking district, this yellow cement tower has an attractive, though hot, open-air lobby, and a pool that is larger than those of some of the city's most expensive hotels. The rooms are much bigger than most in this price range, with separate areas that hold tables and chairs and a single bed. Rooms could use a fresh coat of paint and more diligent cleaning, but the place is a bargain. Through some architectural error, rooms here overlook the apartment buildings across the street, whereas they would have ocean views if the hotel were oriented in the other direction. Junior suites, at the end of each floor, have partial ocean views, cross ventilation, and kitchenettes for a few dollars more than standards. Complimentary breakfast is served in a large restaurant off the lobby, and the restaurants and nightlife of the Área Bancária and Calle Uruguay are within walking distance. Pros: inexpensive; good location; big pool. Cons: timeworn rooms; no views. ⊠ *Calle 51, No. 36, Área Bancária* ☎ *269–2244* ⤴ *40 rooms and 2 junior suites* ⚓ *In-room: refrigerator. In-hotel: restaurant, pool, Internet terminal, parking (free)* ⊟ *AE, MC, V* ⏀ *BP.*

2

$$$ 🏨 **Veneto Hotel and Casino.** The Veneto's massive marquee, plastered with flashing colored lights, is Panama City's answer to Las Vegas. It has become the epicenter of El Cangrejo's vibrant nightlife; on weekends its large entrance is a place of constant movement, as Panamanians and tourists flock to its popular casino and bars. The hotel is consequently a great place for people who like to party, and it's probably not the atmosphere that families and nature lovers are looking for. Nevertheless, the guest rooms, which are on floors 8 to 17, are surprisingly staid, and could well be another hotel entirely, if you didn't have to walk through the lobby to get to them. Those spacious rooms are carpeted, with either two queens or a king-size bed, a marble-topped desk and dresser, and a large marble bathroom. They are well equipped and have large windows with good views, especially those on the south side of the building, which glimpse the sea between office towers. The large pool and spa and gym are also relatively quiet, and the hotel has a small business center and an executive floor. The vast lobby has a peculiarly small check-in desk; it has an attractive lobby bar, a gift shop, an Italian restaurant, and a steak house, though you'll eat better at many of the restaurants in the surrounding neighborhood; escalators lead up to the even bigger casino. Pros: centrally located; hopping casino; good views. Cons: lobby may be too busy for some; indifferent service; definitely not a family-friendly atmosphere. ⊠ *Vía Veneto and Av. Eusebio A. Morales, El Cangrejo* ☎ *340–8888; 800/531–2034 in the U.S.* ⊕ *www. venetocasino.com* ⤴ *300 rooms, 26 suites* ⚓ *In-room: safe, Wi-Fi. In-hotel: 2 restaurants, room service, bars, pool, gym, spa, laundry service, public Wi-Fi, parking (free)* ⊟ *MC, V, AE* ⏀ *EP.*

SAN FRANCISCO

The predominantly residential neighborhood of San Francisco offers a decent supply of restaurants and one large hotel, the Sheraton, which is next door to the ATLAPA Convention Center.

$$$ 🏨 **Sheraton Panama.** One of the city's original luxury hotels, the Sheraton has had various names over the years, and has hosted numerous heads of state, including King Juan Carlos of Spain and Fidel Castro, who apparently went to the laundry to shake hands with the workers. It is now one of many luxury hotels but remains one of the best, in no small part thanks to the spaciousness of its public areas. The lobby is designed to resemble a colonial courtyard, surrounded by wooden balconies, with a central fountain and exuberant orchid displays. It spills into a gallery of shops with an excellent café. The pool area is also quite expansive, with gardens and tall coconut palms. The nearby health club is one of the city's best, and overlooking the pool is a 24-hour restaurant, next to which is the Italian restaurant Il Crostini. Guest rooms are quite chic but

Fodor's Choice
★

SPAS TO RELAX IN

Travelers are all too often tempted to *go, go, go,* but it's important to remember why we go on vacation—to relax. And the professionals at the country's abundant spas are trained to help you do just that. Spas at most Panama City hotels are open to nonguests; there are also spas near some of the country's beaches and in the mountains, so you'll have plenty of opportunities to rejuvenate during your travels.

CITY SPAS

One of Panama City's best spas is located on the fourth floor of the **Radisson Decapolis** (✉ *Av. Balboa, next to Multicentro, Paitilla* ☎ *215–5000* ⊕ *www.radisson.com/panamacitypan*). If the treatments there don't leave you sufficiently relaxed, you can always top them off with a martini at the hotel's trendy lobby bar. The flashy **Veneto Hotel and Casino** (✉ *Vía Veneto and Av. Eusebio A. MoralesEl Cangrejo* ☎ *340–8888* ⊕ *www.venetocasino.com*), on busy Vía Veneto, may seem like the last place you'd go to escape the hustle and bustle, but the large spa on the hotel's seventh floor is actually a very tranquil spot. The **Sheraton Panama** (✉ *Vía Israel and Calle 77, San Francisco* ☎ *305–5100* ⊕ *www.sheratonpanama.com.pa*), next to the ATLAPA convention center on the east end of town, has a small but pleasant spa next to its swimming pool. The serene **Sheraton Four Points** (✉ *World Trade Center, Paitilla* ☎ *265–3636* ⊕ *www.starwoodhotels.com*) has a small spa. The **Intercontinental Playa Bonita Resort and Spa** (✉ *Playa Kobbe* ☎ *211–8600* ⊕ *www.playabonitapanama.com*), on the beach 8 km (5 mi) from Panama City, has a large spa offering an array of treatments for guests.

SPAS OUTSIDE OF PANAMA CITY

The **Gamboa Rainforest Resort** (✉ *Gamboa* ☎ *314–9000* ⊕ *www.gamboaresort.com*) has a complete spa just steps away from the jungle. **Los Mandarinos** (✉ *El Valle de Antón* ☎ *983–6645* ⊕ *www.losmandarinos.com*) is an attractive hotel and spa at the edge of the forest El Valle de Antón and offers a long list of treatments ranging from massages to antiaging therapies. **La Posada Ecológica del Cerro la Vieja** (✉ *Chiguirí Arriba, Coclé* ☎ *983–8900* ⊕ *www.posadalavieja.com*), an eco-lodge in the mountains 30 km north of Penonomé, has a small, inexpensive spa with a wonderful forest view. In the western mountain town of Boquete, the historic **Panamonte Inn** (✉ *Boquete* ☎ *720–1324* ⊕ *www.panamonteinnandspa.com*) has a spa that offers massage and various beauty treatments. There is a small spa in the mountain town of Cerro Punta at **Los Quetzales Lodge** (✉ *Cerro Punta, Chiriquí* ☎ *771–2291* ⊕ *www.losquetzales.com*) that has a spa offering massage and various beauty treatments. **Esthetic Island Relax** (✉ *Calle 10, Av. G, Bocas del Toro* ☎ *6688–4303*) is a small spa near the beaches and coral reefs of Bocas del Toro that provides various massages and skin treatments.

on the dark side, with stained-wood furniture, marble-top tables, and lots of beige and brown in the carpet and walls. There is nothing about them that is terribly Panamanian, but they are well equipped, with large desks, three phones, and a plasma TV screen perched on the wall. The executive floor has a lounge with great view of the ocean, where complimentary breakfast is served. **Pros:** spacious; quiet; nice pool; friendly staff; quick trip to the airport. **Cons:** far from many attractions; low shower heads. ⊠ *Vía Israel and Calle 77, next to ATLAPA convention center, San Francisco* ⌖ *Apdo. 0819-05896, Panama City, Panama* ☎ *305–5100; 800/325–3535 in the U.S.* ⊕ *www.sheratonpanama.com. pa* ⟿ *342 rooms, 19 suites* ⌂ *In-room: safe, Wi-Fi. In-hotel: 2 restaurants, room service, bar, tennis courts, pool, gym, spa, laundry service, Wi-Fi, parking (free)* ⊟ *AE, MC, V* ⏀ *EP.*

NIGHTLIFE AND THE ARTS

There is plenty to do in Panama City once the sun sets, though it is much more of a party town than a cradle of the arts. Because it is so hot by day, the night is an especially inviting time to explore the city. The entertainment and nightlife centers are Casco Viejo, Calzada Amador, El Cangrejo, and the Calle Uruguay area. The entertainment tends more toward high culture in Casco Viejo, with its Teatro Nacional and several jazz venues, while the scene in the other areas is more about casinos, dining, and dancing the night away.

THE ARTS

Panama may be a commercial center, but its arts scene is lacking. There are a few small theaters downtown and occasional dance or classical music performances in Casco Viejo. The most popular arts attractions for tourists are the folk-dancing performances offered by several restaurants, and jazz or Latin music played at various bars and nightclubs. The Teatro Nacional hosts occasional concerts and performances by local and international artists that can be a wonderful way to experience that historic venue. For information on concerts, plays, and other performances, check out the listings in the free tourist newspaper called *The Visitor* or the ATP Web site (⊕ *www.visitpanama.com*).

FOLK DANCING

Panamanians love their folk dancing, which forms an important part of regional festivals and other major celebrations. The typical folk dances have their roots in popular Spanish dances of the 18th century, but there are also African and indigenous influences in the dances performed on certain holidays or in certain regions. The country's major indigenous groups also have their dances, though they are quite simple compared to the African and Spanish traditions. Several restaurants in the capital offer folk-dancing performances with dinner that combine the country's varied dance traditions.

You can enjoy a free folk-dancing performance at **Mi Pueblito** (⊠ *Off Av. de los Mártires and Calle Jorge Wilbert, Cerro Ancón* ☎ *506–5724 or 506–5725*) on Sunday afternoons, around 2 PM, which makes it a good place to head for lunch. A group of young Kuna dancers performs for tips in front of the nearby reproduction of a Kuna village on Saturdays and Sundays around 4 PM.

Al Tambor de la Alegría (⊠ *Brisas del Amador, Calzada Amador* ☎ *314–3369*) is a newer place on the second floor of the Brisas de Amador shopping center, on Isla Perico, near the end of the Amador Causeway, that serves traditional Panamanian food and offers a dance show that relates the country's history. Shows are Wednesday through Saturday at 9 PM and cost $5, with no minimum consumption at the restaurant. This is the only performance offered on Wednesday night, and it is a big show on an elevated stage, though it's a bit schmaltzy. The restaurant is not attractive, but the food is good.

Café Barko (⊠ *Isla Flamenco, Calzada Amador* ☎ *314–0000*) is a good seafood restaurant in the shopping center at the back of Isla Flamenco, at the end of the Amador Causeway, which offers a free folk-dancing show with dinner on Thursday nights.

Las Tinajas (⊠ *Calle 51, No. 22, near Av. Federico Boyd, Área Bancária* ☎ *269–3840*) is an attractive Panamanian restaurant that offers the city's original folk-dancing show at a convenient location in the banking district every Tuesday, Thursday, Friday, and Saturday night. The hour-long show starts at 9 PM and costs $5—plus you need to consume $10 of food and drink. You should reserve several days ahead of time and get there early to choose a good table, since the stage is at the center of the room and not all tables have great views.

JAZZ

Panama has long had a jazz scene, especially in the Caribbean port of Colón, but its best musicians have always moved abroad. The city's prodigal son is Danilo Pérez, a celebrated pianist who has played with the best and lives in the States. Other notable Panamanian jazz musicians have included saxophonist Maurice Smith, who played with everyone from Charlie Mingus to Dizzy Gillespie, and pianist Victor Boa. Some very good musicians live in the city, though some of them have to play salsa and other popular genres to survive. The best time for jazz fans to visit the city is late January, during the Panama Jazz Festival, which features concerts by international stars in the beautiful Casco Viejo. For information on the next festival, check the Web site (⊕ *www.panamajazzfestival.com*). Jazz fans do, however, have several opportunities per week to hear good music in the city throughout the rest of the year.

Casa Góngora (⊠ *Calle 9 and Av. Central, Casco Viejo* ☎ *506–5836*), a small cultural center in the Casco Viejo, offers free jazz concerts Wednesday nights at 7 PM, though sometimes the music is a Latin genre such as bolero or trova.

The bar at the French restaurant **Las Bóvedas** (⊠ *Plaza Francia, Casco Viejo* ☎ *228–8068*) has live jazz from the Colón tradition on Friday nights with a mellower atmosphere than the Latin vibe at nearby Platea, and they play early, starting around 7 PM.

Platea (⊠ *Calle 1, in front of the old Club Union, Casco Viejo* ☎ *228–4011*), the Casco Viejo's most popular night spot, offers Latin jazz on

Thursday nights with great ambience in the ground floor of a restored colonial building.

THEATER

Panama City has a small theater scene, but since most plays are in Spanish, they tend to be of little interest to tourists. There is, however, one group that performs plays in English, and attending a play in Panama is a lot cheaper than Broadway; tickets usually cost $10.

The Ancón Theater Guild (☎ 212–0060 ⊕ www.anconguild.com), which has been producing plays for more than 50 years, presents comedies and the occasional drama in English on Thursday, Friday, and Saturday nights at 8 PM in the Ancón Theater, next to the Judicial Police headquarters on Cerro Ancón.

Teatro La Cuadra (⊠ Calle D, near Vía Argentina, El Cangrejo ☎ 214–3695 ⊕ www.teatroquadra.com) is the city's best venue for Spanish-language theater and is conveniently located in El Cangrejo.

NIGHTLIFE

Panama City is a party town, no doubt about it. The city's after-dark offerings range from a quiet drink on historic Plaza Bolivar, to dancing till dawn at one of the clubs on Calle Uruguay, with plenty of options in between. While there are bars everywhere, nightlife is concentrated in the Casco Viejo, Calzada Amador, El Cangrejo, and Calle Uruguay, though there are also a few nice spots in the Área Bancária and near Punta Paitilla.

While the Casco Viejo has several spots for quiet drinks, the neighborhood's most popular club, Platea, rocks till the wee hours on weekends. The Calzada Amador offers something for everything, from a quiet beer and a snack to throbbing techno bars that could be in Fort Lauderdale, all of it surrounded by lovely ocean views. The streets around Calle Uruguay are packed on weekends, when a predominantly young crowd fills its abundant bars and dance clubs, but it also has a few spots for a quiet drink. There are a few night spots in the Área Bancária, whereas across the Vía España, in El Cangrejo, the options range from massive casinos to street-side cafés perfect for people-watching. The big attraction in Paitilla is the martini lounge in the Hotel Decapolis, but the area also has various other late-night spots.

There are half a dozen strip clubs, locally called "nightclubs," scattered between the Área Bancária and El Cangrejo. They have traditionally catered to business travelers but are becoming a bit of a tourist attraction in their own right. Prostitution is legal in Panama, but street-walking is not, so the world's oldest profession is based in the city's nightclubs and massage parlors. Those places all advertise in the free tourist publications *The Visitor* and *Focus Panama*.

BARS AND MUSIC
CASCO VIEJO

Casablanca (⊠ Calle 4 on Plaza Bolívar, Casco Viejo ☎ 212–0040), on the ground floor of the old Hotel Colombia, has tables on beautiful Plaza Bolívar, which is a great spot for a quiet drink and conversation.

Fodor's Choice   **Ego** (⊠ *Calle 3 on Plaza Bolívar, Casco Viejo* ☎ *262–2045*) is a tapas
★   restaurant with tables on Plaza Bolívar, most of which overlook the
illuminated facade of the Iglesia de San Francisco, making it one of the
city's most romantic spots for a drink.

Las Bóvedas (⊠ *Plaza Francia, Casco Viejo* ☎ *501–4034*), the French
restaurant on Plaza Francia, has tables on the plaza and a bar inside
one of the Bóvedas that features live jazz on Friday nights.

EL CANGREJO

Istmo Brew Pub (⊠ *Calle Eusebio Morales east of Vía Veneto, El Cangrejo*
☎ *265–5077*), across the street from the Las Vegas Hotel Suites, serves
several mediocre and overpriced home brews, as well as the city's best
selection of imported beers. It's a popular spot, with seating out front
and inside, pool tables, a bar, and pop music blasting. Sample the beers
before ordering a house brew.

El Pavo Real Panamá (⊠ *Vía Argentina and Calle José Martí, across street
from Angel Restaurante El Cangrejo* ☎ *269–0504*) is an attractive
British-style pub on a quiet street around the corner from the Panama
Marriott's casino. It has a pool table, serves fish-and-chips and other
bar food, and has live music, mostly rock, on weekends.

La Terraza (⊠ *Vía Veneto, half a block south of Calle Eusebio Morales,
El Cangrejo* ☎ *264–5822*) is a below-street-level bar that's a popular
watering hole for expat gringos and Panamanians alike. They serve
burgers and other bar food, play rock music, and sometimes have live
bands.

Manolo's (⊠ *Vía Veneto and Calle D, El Cangrejo* ☎ *269–4514*) is a
café and restaurant on busy Vía Veneto with a wraparound terrace
cooled by ceiling fans that is a great place for people-watching, a quiet
drink, a late-night snack, or a cheap bite to eat like an emparedado,
or sandwich.

The Wine Bar (⊠ *Calle Eusebio Morales east of Vía Veneto, El Cangrejo*
☎ *265–4701*), located on the ground floor of the Las Vegas Hotel Suites,
has live, mellow Latin music most nights, mostly duos or one musician,
and serves good pizza and other snacks till late.

ÁREA BANCÁRIA

Pizza Piola (⊠ *Calle 51, half a block up from The Bristol, Área Bancária*
☎ *263–4668*) is a small Argentine restaurant that offers tango nights on
Thursdays, starting with a class at 8 PM, and Argentine folk dancing on
Friday nights, on a small terrace in front.

CALLE URUGUAY

The **Greenhouse** (⊠ *Calle Uruguay, between Calles 47 and 48, Bella Vista*
☎ *269–6846*) is one of the few places in the Calle Uruguay area where
you can get a quiet drink on weekends. Seating is amidst the foliage on
the front patio or inside the low-lit bar. They also serve a good selection
of sandwiches, wraps, and salads.

Habibi's (⊠ *Calle 48 and Calle Uruguay, Bella Vista* ☎ *264–3647*) is
mainly a restaurant, but its covered terrace is also a great spot for a late-
night drink on weekends, since it sits at the center of the Calle Uruguay
action. Food is served till late.

Sahara (⊠ *Calle 48 and Calle Uruguay, Bella Vista* ☎ *214–8284*) is a massive bar with seating on a front terrace or inside, where there are a couple of pool tables. They sometimes have live rock bands, and reggae nights on Wednesdays.

Urbano Bar (⊠ *Calle 48, above Palms restaurant, Bella Vista* ☎ *265–7256*), located on the second floor above trendy Palms restaurant, near Calle Uruguay, is an otherworldly nightspot that is utterly 21st century. Think George Jetson on LSD.

PUNTA PAITILLA

★ **Decapolis Martini Bar** (⊠ *Av. Balboa next to Multicentro, Paitilla* ☎ *215–5000*), a large lounge located in the chic Hotel Decapolis, is a very hot spot, with DJs spinning house music and martinis being consumed in dangerous quantities.

CALZADA AMADOR

★ **Bamboo** (⊠ *Zona Viva, behind Figali Convention Center, Calzada Amador* ☎ *314–3337 or 6675–2714*), an open-air bar under a giant thatch roof, is one of the most popular spots in Zona Viva, a Treasure Island–like playground for young adults where much of the causeway's nightclub scene was recently relocated. The bar also has an enclosed air-conditioned lounge.

Kayuco (⊠ *Isla Flamenco, Calzada Amador* ☎ *314–1998*) is a popular open-air bar and restaurant overlooking the marina on Isla Flamenco, with a great view of the city's skyline. It's one of the only spots on the causeway for a drink by the water, and they serve fried seafood and other snacks into the wee hours.

The Wine Bar (⊠ *Isla Perico, Brisas de Amador shopping center* ☎ *314–3340*), is a franchise of the successful spot in El Cangrejo, with the same concept: a laid-back atmosphere with live Latin music, good food and wine, and service well into the wee hours.

CASINOS

Gambling is a popular pastime in Panama City, and there are casinos all over the place, ranging from fancy to seedy. The nicest by far are located in, or next to, the city's big hotels, namely the Panama Marriott, Veneto, and El Panamá, but few of the people who frequent them are guests. Panama City has a lot of gambling addicts.

El Panamá (⊠ *Vía Veneto and Calle Eusebio Morales, El Cangrejo* ☎ *213–1274*) has a large Fiesta Casino behind it that is popular with Panamanians. It includes a Salsas Sports Bar and a restaurant, and often has live music.

The **Panama Marriott** (⊠ *Calle 52 and Calle Ricardo Arias, Área Bancária* ☎ *210–9100*) has a two-story casino next door that is quite popular with locals. It often has live music and sometimes hosts concerts by the country's most popular groups.

The **Veneto Hotel and Casino** (⊠ *Vía Veneto and Calle Eusebio Morales, El Cangrejo* ☎ *340–8888*) has the city's biggest and most popular casino, which includes a sports bar, craps and poker, and a sea of slot machines. Expect music and young Panamanians who simply come to party.

CLOSE UP

Panama, Musica

Considering that Panama has long been a crossroads for people and goods, it's hardly surprising that the country is home to an array of musical styles. While traveling here, you are likely to hear such Panamanian music as *pindín* and *cantadera,* as well as such internationally popular genres as salsa, merengue, soca, and reggaetón. Commerce and immigration have long connected Panama to musical traditions from far-flung places. Witness the resulting musical mélange for yourself by surfing the radio in the capital, spending an evening at one of the city's dance clubs, or simply by walking up and down the streets catching snatches of music that seep out of homes and apartments.

Panama's current musical panorama has its roots in the mixing of Spanish, African, and indigenous traditions centuries ago, which resulted in the development of the country's folk music. Panamanian musicians have also excelled in genres from other countries, such as jazz, calypso, and salsa. However, most Panamanians are especially fond of the country's home-grown music, namely *cantadera, mejorana, música foclórica,* and *pindín.*

Mejorana is a Panamanian music that was developed on the Azuero Peninsula and can now be heard mostly at folk festivals and cultural celebrations. It is played on a five-string guitar called the *mejoranera,* and usually accompanies folk dancing. *Cantadera* is a popular music form evocative of flamenco; it consists of an improvisational exchange between a guitarist and singer, with a consistent rhythm. The guitarist performs a simple chord progression punctuated by more complex melodic improvisations called *torrentes,* and the singer accompanies him with a series of *décimas,* traditional ten-line poems that often have comic endings.

Folk dances are accompanied by what is simply called *música foclórica,* or folk music, which is similar to the *vallenato* of Colombia, a country of which Panama was a part for nearly a century. That rhythmic music is performed by groups with an accordion, different types of drums, and a *churuca*—a serrated gourd or metal cylinder that is scraped with a stick. During the twentieth century *música foclórica* gave birth to a more popular form known as *pindín:* a lyric-driven, danceable music in which the accordion is accompanied by an electric guitar and bass, and the percussion includes a drum set. Pindín is the music that many rural Panamanians party, dance, and live to, but it's also popular in the city, where you're likely to hear it in taxis and in bars and restaurants, and you can try dancing to it yourself. Pindín has its share of well-known stars, such as Dorindo Cárdenas, Victor Vergara, and the siblings Samy y Sandra Sandoval. In Panama City pindín has traditionally shared the airwaves with salsa and other Caribbean dance music. A child of the Cuban *son* (sound), salsa was largely developed in New York during the 1960s and '70s, but it has been popular in Panama from day one. The country has produced some excellent salsa musicians, the most famous of whom is singer and composer Ruben Blades, who is currently Panama's minister of tourism. He has also acted in dozens of Hollywood movies and TV shows, is known for using salsa to tell stories or to address social

and political issues. His most popular song, "Pedro Navaja," about a criminal, is based on the song "Mack the Knife" and is one of the greatest hits in the history of salsa.

Panama also has a strong tradition of jazz, especially in the Caribbean port of Colón, where big bands reigned in the 1940s and '50s. The country has produced some excellent jazz musicians, among them pianist Victor Boa, singer Barbara Wilson, and pianist Danilo Pérez. Pérez was instrumental in the creation of the Panama Jazz Festival (⊕ *www.panamajazzfestival. com*), a weeklong celebration that brings together international and local musicians in late January.

The thousands of Afro-Caribbean workers who settled in Panama after completion of the canal made the country home to Antillean music, such as *mento, calypso,* and *soca.* The Afro-Caribbean connection has more recently resulted in Panamanian versions of *reggaetón,* the Latin American response to Jamaican dance-hall, which mutated out of reggae in the 1980s as a response to American rap music. Panama has produced a few international reggaetón stars over the years, among them El General and Nando Boom, and for better or worse, reggaetón could well replace both pindín and salsa as Panama's most popular music.

DANCE CLUBS

The city's dance clubs play a broad mix of music, including American pop, salsa, merengue, reggaetón, and the popular Panamanian music called *pindín*. Cover charges run between $3 and $10, and sometimes include a drink. There are many clubs in the Calle Uruguay area, but they go out of fashion with the whims of the local college-age crew, and often close, remodel, and reopen with different names in a span of months.

CASCO VIEJO

Fodor's Choice
★ **Platea** (⊠ *Calle 1, in front of the old Club Union, Casco Viejo* ☎ *228–4011*), the popular bar underneath S'cena restaurant, may not have much of a dance floor, but the club books hot salsa bands and is packed most Friday and Saturday nights, when people dance in the aisles or wherever else there's room. The bartenders and waiters, dressed in black with Panama hats, are part of the show, as they juggle bottles and dance while delivering *mojitos* and Cuba libres.

CALLE URUGUAY

★ **Bamboleo** (⊠ *Calle 48, 1 block east of Calle Uruguay, Bella Vista* ☎ *390–5905*) is a popular dance club with an unreasonably small dance floor. It specializes in Latin music—salsa, merengue, reggaetón, and Panama's popular pindín.

La Bodeguita (⊠ *Calle Uruguay, half a block north of Av. Balboa, Bella Vista* ☎ *213–2153*), inspired by the famous Havana bar of the same name, sometimes has live bands and always has Cuban or another Latin music playing. It gets packed on weekends, when it closes around 5 AM.

CALZADA AMADOR

Pahyá (⊠ *Zona Viva nightclub area, behind Figali Convention Center, Calzada Amador* ☎ *263–0104*) is a fairly popular, modern dance club where they play a lot of reggaetón, as well as other Latin and pop music, and is one of a dozen hot spots in the relatively new nightclub area of Zona Viva.

SHOPPING

Panama City has more shopping options than you can shake a credit card at. Because of the country's role as an international port, manufactured goods from all over the world are cheaper in Panama than just about anywhere else in the hemisphere, and merchants from South and Central America regularly travel here to shop, though they tend to do their business in the Colón Free Zone. Even people who go to Panama on vacation end up filling the old suitcase with new toys, but American tourists will find that the U.S. megastores often beat the local prices for cameras and other electronic goods—plus the stores back home are more convenient in terms of warranties. Clothing, on the other hand, is dirt-cheap in Panama. The Avenida Central pedestrian mall is lined with massive clothing stores that sell imported shirts and blouses for as little as a few dollars, though most of the styles cater to Latin American tastes. Busy Vía Veneto, in El Cangrejo, has several decent souvenir and

T-shirt shops. The city also has several modern malls, where the selection ranges from the cheap stuff to name brands.

Panama also produces some lovely handicrafts. The famous Panama hat is misnamed since it originated in Ecuador, but it has been associated with Panama since Teddy Roosevelt was photographed wearing one when he traveled to the country to check on canal construction. Panama does, however, produce some handwoven hats, mostly in the provinces around the Azuero Peninsula, though they are stiffer than the Panama hat, and have dark brown patterns woven into them. Both Panamanian hats and imported Panama hats are available at souvenir shops and handicraft markets around the city.

The most popular Panamanian handicraft is the *mola,* a fabric picture sewn by Kuna women and worn on their blouses as part of their traditional dress. They are lovely framed, and the Kuna incorporate them into shirts, blouses, bags, and other items. The Kuna are also known for their bead bracelets and necklaces, as well as simple jewelry made from seeds and shells. The Emberá and Wounaan also make some fine handicrafts. The men carve animal figures out of dark cocobolo wood and the seed of a rain-forest palm called tagua, which is known as "vegetal ivory." The women weave attractive rattan baskets, bowls, and platters, which can take weeks to complete, and are consequently expensive. The Ngöbe-Buglé Indians are known for their colorful dresses and jute shoulder bags, which can serve as shopping bags or purses. They also create intricate bead necklaces called *chaquiras.*

HANDICRAFT MARKETS
Even if you're not interested in buying, take a walk around one of the city's various handicraft markets, all of which are open daily from 9 to 6. The rows of stalls filled with native handicrafts are great places to browse and learn a bit about the local cultures.

The city's biggest and nicest craft market occupies what was once the gym of the Balboa YMCA, which is why it is called the **Centro Artesanal Antiguo YMCA** (✉ *Av. Arnulfo Arias and Av. Amador, Balboa* ☎ *211–0100*). The spacious building holds dozens of stands, each with a different owner and selection. Wares range from kitsch to native handicrafts, and include molas sewn into bags, shirts, glasses cases, and pot holders, plus embroidered blouses, jewelry, handwoven hats, and plenty of work by the Emberá and Wounaan Indians of the Darién province.

A good place to shop for molas is the **Centro Municipal de Artesanías Panameñas** (✉ *Av. Arnulfo Arias, three blocks up from old YMCA, Balboa* ☎ *211–3924*), a small market where most of the stands are owned by Kuna women, who are often sewing molas as they wait for customers. They also sell *chaquiras,* bags, hammocks, dresses, framed butterflies, T-shirts, and other souvenirs.

The **Mercado de Artesanía de Panamá Viejo** (✉ *Vía Cincuentenaria, Panamá Viejo* ☎ *No phone*), next to the old cathedral tower at Panamá Viejo, is a two-story cement building packed with small shops and stalls selling everything for indigenous handicrafts—many shop owners are indigenous—to woven hats, Carnaval masks, and other works of mestizo artisans in the country's interior. A number of Kuna families

BOOKSHOPS

Panama City doesn't have a great selection of books in English, but it may be easier to find some titles on the local culture and tropical nature here.

The country's most successful book retailer is **El Hombre de la Mancha** (✉ *Calle 52 and Av. Federico Boyd, one block south of Vía España, Área Bancária* ☎ *263–6218*), which sells books in Spanish and English and has smaller outlets in the Albrook Airport, on Isla Flamenco, and in the Multicentro and Multiplaza shopping malls.

The department store **Gran Morrison** (✉ *Vía España across from Plaza Concordia, Área Bancária* ☎ *202–0031*) has a convenient location near El Cangrejo, a small selection of books on Panama, and a souvenir section.

Hibiscus (✉ *Calle 4 between Plaza Bolívar and Casa Góngora, Casco Viejo* ☎ *228–5698*) is an attractive little bookstore and café in the heart of the Casco Viejo that also sells some souvenirs.

The bookstore at the **Smithsonian Tropical Research Institute** (✉ *Av. Roosevelt, Cerro Ancón* ☎ *228–6231*) is a good stop for nature lovers, since it as an excellent selection of books on tropical flora and fauna, as well as postcards, posters, T-shirts, and other souvenirs.

have simple stalls on the second floor, which is a good place to shop for *molas*.

Masks, hammocks, and other handicrafts tend to be relatively inexpensive at the **Mercado de Buhonería** (✉ *Av. 4 at Av. B, Santa Ana* ☎ *No phone*), a small market behind the old train station, just east of Plaza Cinco de Mayo, that receives few visitors. If you visit the Avenida Central pedestrian mall, you should definitely stop by here.

HANDICRAFT SHOPS

Though the selections are never as impressive as those of the handicraft markets, the city's handicraft shops tend to have more convenient locations. **Flory Saltzman Molas** (✉ *Vía Veneto, by entrance to Hotel El Panamá, El Cangrejo* ☎ *223–6963*) has the country's biggest *mola* collection—thousands of those colorful creations divided by theme and quality, and stacked to the ceiling. Flory's daughter, Lynne, is usually there in the afternoons, and she is happy to explain the significance of the designs and their role in Kuna culture. The quality of their collection varies greatly, and the good ones tend to cost considerably more than the Kuna vendors charge on the streets or in the markets, though the quality is considerably higher.

Galería Arte Indígena (✉ *Calle 1, No. 844, Casco Viejo* ☎ *228–9557*), just down the street from Plaza Francia, has an extensive selection of indigenous handicrafts, such as Emberá baskets, animal figures carved from *tagua* palm seeds, decorated gourds, hammocks, Panama hats (imported from Ecuador), and T-shirts.

JEWELRY

Most of Panama's jewelry shops specialize in flashy, gold-plated stuff that you could pick up in any major city, but there are a couple of shops worth checking out.

The **Museo de la Esmeralda** (✉ *Calle Pedro J. Sossa on Plaza Catedral, Casco Viejo* ☎ *262–1665*) is a small, cheesy museum about emerald mining that is an excuse to get people in to look at their emerald jewelry. It is owned by a Colombian company that has its own mines and factories, so the quality and prices are good, but the designs aren't going to win any awards.

Reprosa (✉ *Av. A and Calle 4, Art Deco Building, Casco Viejo* ☎ *271–0033* ✉ *Av. Samuel Lewis and Calle 54, Obarrio* ☎ *269–0457*) sells elegant jewelry based on reproductions of pre-Columbian gold pieces and Spanish coins, as well as interesting modern designs in silver and high-quality indigenous *chaquira* beadwork, *cocobolo* wood carvings, paintings, and the obligatory *molas*. They have a shop in Obarrio, which is near El Cangrejo and the Área Bancária, and one in the heart of the Casco Viejo that closes Monday.

MALLS

Panama City has several modern shopping malls and the more traditional Avenida Central.

Albrook Mall (✉ *In front of Terminal de Buses, Albrook* ☎ *303–6333*) is the people's mall, with more discount stores than the malls downtown. That, combined with its convenient location between the city's massive bus terminal and Albrook Airport, makes it the busiest mall.

The **Avenida Central pedestrian mall** (✉ *Between Plaza Santa Ana and Plaza Cinco de Mayo, Santa Ana*) is lined with shops selling imported electronics, jewelry, fabrics, and clothing. A stroll down this busy street can be quite entertaining, even if you don't buy anything. But avoid the side streets and this area at night.

Multicentro (✉ *Av. Balboa, Punta Paitilla* ☎ *208–2500*), a modern, four-story mall, holds dozens of shops, as well as a movie theater, food court, and casino at a convenient location across from Punta Paitilla.

Multiplaza (✉ *Vía Israel, San Francisco* ☎ *302–5380*) is a large mall just east of Punta Paitilla that has dozens of shops, ranging from Tiffany & Co. to Payless ShoeSource, a movie theater, and a small food court.

SOUVENIR SHOPS

Artesanías Panamá Bahía (✉ *Vía Veneto, El Cangrejo* ☎ *399–9012*) sells a mix of Panamanian and Ecuadoran souvenirs, including an ample selection of Panama hats, from a convenient location on Busy Vía Veneto.

La Ronda (✉ *Calle 1 and Plaza Francia, Casco Viejo* ☎ *211–1001*) is an attractive little shop in a historic building near Plaza Francia that sells a mix of handicrafts and souvenirs: *molas,* Carnaval masks, wood carvings, paintings, Panama hats, and assorted knickknacks.

SPORTS AND THE OUTDOORS

Thanks to its proximity to forest, canal, and ocean, Panama City offers plenty of options for enjoying the outdoors, which include hiking in the world's largest chunk of urban rain forest, biking down the causeway, navigating the Panama Canal, and white-water rafting in the jungle.

BEACHES

Because of the silt that the Panama Canal dumps into the ocean and the sewage from Panama City, the beaches near the city are not recommended for swimming. Some of the country's nicest Pacific beaches are on **Isla Contadora**, a 20-minute flight from the city, which is usually visited as an overnight trip but is an easy day trip because there are flights to the island in the morning and afternoon (⇨ *Isla Contadora in Canal and Central Panama chapter*). The clearest water near Panama City is found on **Isla Taboga**, a 60-minute ferry ride from the Calzada Amador, which is a popular day trip (⇨ *Isla Taboga in Canal and Central Panama chapter*). The closest beach to Panama City is **Playa Bonita** (Playa Kobbe*)*, which is 8 km (5 mi) southwest of the city, on the other side of the canal. It is the site of the massive, expensive Intercontinental Playa Bonita Resort, and the only option there for nonguests is to have lunch at the hotel's beachfront restaurant, Pelícano, though you need to reserve the day before, and you can't use the pool (⇨ *Isla Taboga in Canal and Central Panama chapter*). **Playa Veracruz**, 16 km (10 mi) southwest of the city, is a wide, gray public beach lined with a few open-air restaurants where you can get an inexpensive beer and fish lunch.

BIKING

Though there are several good mountain-biking routes near the city, no tour operators currently offer guided bike tours. You can, however, rent bikes near the beginning of the Calzada Amador, which is a wonderful, easy ride out to the islands. If you're feeling energetic, you could also explore nearby Balboa and Cerro Ancón by bike; both are safe, and Cerro Ancón has plenty of shade. Be careful, however, not to take Avenida Arnulfo Arias past the busy Avenida de los Mártires, across which are the slums of El Chorrillo.

Bicicletas Moses (✉ *Behind Las Pencas, entrance to Calzada Amador* ☎ *211–3671* rents an array of bikes for riding on the causeway. The shop is open Monday through Friday from 10 to 8, Saturday from 9 to 8, and Sunday from 8 to 8.

Fodor's Choice **Eco Circuitos Panama** (✉ *Country Inn & Suites, Calles Amador and Pelí-
★ cano, Balboa* ☎ *314–0068* ⊕ *www.ecocircuitos.com*) rents mountain bikes at its office in the Country Inn & Suites Panama Canal, which is equidistant from Balboa and the Amador Causeway.

BIRD-WATCHING

Panama City has world-class bird-watching as close as the **Parque Natural Metropolitano,** which is home to more than 200 avian species and is less than 15 minutes from most hotels. There are several spots in nearby **Parque Nacional Soberanía,** which has more than 400 bird species, all within 40 minutes of downtown, including **Pipeline Road,** where the Panama Audubon Society has held several world-record Christmas bird counts (⇨ *Parque Nacional Soberanía in Canal and Central Panama chapter*). Unless you're an expert, you're best off going with an experienced birding guide. Several local tour companies can set you up with a private guide or can book you onto an existing trip, which is less expensive. You may need to call several companies to find a trip for your dates, though.

Advantage Panama (✉ *Llanos de Curundú No. 2006, Curundú* ☎ *6676–2466* ✪ *www.advantagepanama.com*) is a small nature tourism company that offers early-morning tours of Parque Natural Metropolitano and day trips to Parque Nacional Soberanía. The company can also arrange custom, reasonably priced trips to other areas.

Fodor's Choice ★ **Ancon Expeditions** (✉ *Calle Elvira Mendez, Edificio El Dorado No. 3, Área Bancária* ☎ *269–9415* ✪ *www.anconexpeditions.com*) has excellent birding guides and offers day tours to the main protected areas near the capital, including exploration of the forest canopy of Parque Natural Metropolitano using a modified construction crane, a great boat trip on Gatún Lake, and a birding tour in Darién.

Eco Circuitos Panama (✉ *Country Inn & Suites, Calles Amador and Pelícano, Balboa* ☎ *314–0068* ✪ *www.ecocircuitos.com*) offers several half- and full-day birding trips out of the capital.

The **Panama Audubon Society** (✉ *Casa #2006-B, Altos de Curundú* ☎ *232–5977* ✪ *www.panamaaudubon.org*) runs occasional, inexpensive bird walks and overnight excursions that require a bit of self-sufficiency but can be a great way to meet locals.

Panoramic Panama (✉ *Quarry Heights, Casa #35, Cerro Ancón* ☎ *314–1417* ✪ *www.panoramicpanama.com*) is a small company that can set up customized birding trips.

Pesantez Tours (✉ *Plaza Balboa Oficina #2, Punta Paitilla* ☎ *223–5374* ✪ *www.pesantez-tours.com*), one of the country's biggest tour operators, offers a half-day bird-watching trip to Parque Nacional Soberanía.

The **Smithsonian Tropical Research Institute (STRI)** (✉ *Tupper Center, Av. Roosevelt, Cerro Ancón* ☎ *228–8000* ✪ *www.stri.org*) offers full-day trips to Barro Colorado Island that combine bird-watching with general information on tropical ecology, but they usually need to be booked well ahead of time.

CANAL TOURS

While the canal is impressive when admired from any of the city's various viewing points, there's nothing quite like getting onto the water and navigating it amidst the giant cargo ships. People spend thousands of dollars on cruises that include a canal crossing, but you can have the same experience for $100 to $160 and spend the night in a spacious hotel room. Two companies offer partial transit tours, which travel through the canal's Pacific locks and Gaillard Cut, and occasional full transits, which take you from one ocean to the other. All transits are accompanied by an expert bilingual guide. Full transits include a Continental breakfast and a simple lunch. Partial transits travel between the islands at the end of the Amador Causeway and the port of Gamboa, on Gatún Lake, a trip that lasts 4–5 hours. They take place every

Saturday during the low season, and Thursday, Friday, and Saturday from January through April. Full transits take place once or twice a month and last 8–9 hours. Either trip is an unforgettable experience, fit for travelers of all ages.

Canal Bay Tours (⊠ *Bahía Balboa Building, next to Nunciatura Punta Paitilla* ☎ *209–2009* ⊕ *www.canalandbaytours.com*) offers partial and full transit tours on one of two ships: the 115-foot *Fantasía del Mar,* which has air-conditioned cabins and a large upper deck, and the 85-foot *Isla Morada,* which has one large covered deck. Partial transits cost $115 for adults and $55 for children; full transits, $165 adults and $75 children.

Pacific Marine Tours (⊠ *Villa Porras and Calle Belén, No. 106, San Francisco* ☎ *226–8917* ⊕ *www.pmatours.net*) runs canal transits on the 119-foot *Pacific Queen,* a comfortable ship with air-conditioned cabins and two large decks. Partial transits cost $115 for adults and $65 for children; full transits, $165 adults and $75 children.

GOLF

The **Summit Golf Resort** (⊠ *20 km [12 mi] northwest of town on road to Gamboa* ☎ *232–4653* ⊕ *www.summitgolfpanama.com*) has an 18-hole, par-72 championship course designed by Jeff Myers that is hemmed by the rain forest of Camino de Cruces National Park. It's just 30 minutes from most hotels, and the course is open to nonmembers. Greens fees are $126 on weekdays and $184 on weekends, golf cart included, and club rentals cost $47.

HIKING

The hiking options in and around Panama range from the 40-minute trek to the top of Cerro Ancón to more demanding expeditions into the vast lowland forest of Parque Nacional Soberanía and the mountains of Parque Nacional Altos de Campana. The **Parque Natural Metropolitano** has five well-marked trails covering a total of about 3 mi, which range from flat stretches to a steep road up to a viewpoint. **Parque Nacional Soberanía** has several trails ranging from the historic **Camino de Cruces** to the shorter **Sendero el Charco,** which is on the right after Summit Botanical Gardens and Zoo (⇨ *Parque Nacional Soberanía in Canal and Central Panama chapter).* The mountains of Cerro Azul and Parque Nacional Altos de Campana, which lie less than an hour to the east and west of the city respectively, also have hiking trails as well as panoramic views, and some flora and fauna different from what you'll see in the lowland forests around the city (⇨ *Cerro Azul, or Parque Nacional Altos de Campana in Canal and Central Panama chapter).*

Advantage Panama (⊠ *Llanos de Curundú No. 2006, Curundú* ☎ *6676–2466* ⊕ *www.advantagepanama.com*) can arrange custom tours for hiking enthusiasts.

Eco Circuitos Panama (⊠ *Country Inn & Suites, Calles Amador and Pelícano, Balboa* ☎ *314–0068* ⊕ *www.ecocircuitos.com*) offers hiking tours to Parque Metropolitano and Parque Nacional Soberanía.

Futura Travel (⊠ *Centro Comercial Camino de Cruces, El Dorado* ☎ *360–2030 or 6674–6050* ⊕ *www.panamatraveltours.com*) runs a hiking tour to the summit of Cerro de La Cruz in Parque Nacional Altos de Campana.

HORSEBACK RIDING

Margo Tours (✉ *Centro Comercial Plaza Paitilla local 36 Paitilla* ☎ *302–0390* ⊕ *www.margotours.com*) offers half-day horseback-riding tours through the pastures and forest of the Haras Orillac Ranch, in the mountains of Cerro Azul, just 40 minutes east of downtown.

SPORTFISHING

The Bay of Panama has good sportfishing, but the best fishing is around and beyond the Pearl Islands, which are best fished out of **Isla Contadora** or **Isla San José**, each of which is a short flight from the city (⇨ *Isla Contadora or Isla San José in Canal and Central Panama chapter*). Day charters are available out of Panama City and usually head to the area around Isla Otoque and Isla Bono, which are about 90 minutes southwest of the city. You have a chance of hooking mackerel, jack, tuna, roosterfish, or wahoo in that area (billfish are less common there than in other parts of the country). A closer, less expensive option is light-tackle fishing for snook and peacock bass in **Gatún Lake,** the vast man-made lake in the middle of the Panama Canal. The lake is full of South American peacock bass, which fight like a smallmouth bass but can reach 8–10 pounds (⇨ *Lago Gatún in Canal and Central Panama chapter*).

♻ **Margo Tours** (✉ *Centro Comercial Plaza Paitilla, local 36 Paitilla* ☎ *302–0390* ⊕ *www.pmatours.net*) offers a one-week tour that combines bass fishing on Gatún Lake with a day of ocean fishing with sightseeing in Panama City.

Pacific Marine Tours (✉ *Villa Porras and Calle Belén, No. 106, San Francisco* ☎ *226–8917* ⊕ *www.pmatours.net*) can arrange deep-sea fishing charters in the Bay of Panama.

Panama Canal Fishing (☎ *315–1905 or 6678–2653 or 6909–1501* ⊕ *www.panamacanalfishing.com*) is the premier operator for freshwater fishing on Gatún Lake. It runs fishing charters for serious anglers and families on a Hurricane Fundeck with two swivel chairs on the bow and usually hooks 20 or 30 fish per day. Trips also include wildlife observation and views of giant ships on the canal. An all-inclusive day of fishing for two people costs $395 and $20 per extra angler, up to six.

Panama Fishing and Catching (☎ *6622–0212 or 6505–9553* ⊕ *www.panamafishingandcatching.com*) offers bass and snook fishing on Gatún Lake ($450); snook, snapper, and tarpon fishing on the Bayano River ($490); and deep-sea fishing charters in the Bay of Panama ($600–$2,000 per day), with rates varying according to boat size.

WHITE-WATER RAFTING

Aventuras Panama (✉ *Calle El Parcial 1½ blocks west of Transístmica, Edif. Celma Of. 3* ☎ *260–0044* ⊕ *www.aventuraspanama.com*) runs white-water rafting trips on the Chagres River (Class II–III), which flows through the rain forests of Chagres National Park (⇨ *Parque Nacional Chagres in Canal and Central Panama chapter*). The full-day trip requires no previous rafting experience and provides access to impressive tropical nature. It begins with a long drive down rough dirt roads into the heart of the national park, where you begin a five-hour river trip that includes a picnic lunch, and ends at Madden Lake. The trip is available from May to late March; it lasts 11–12 hours and costs $165 per person. Also on offer is a shorter, more exhilarating trip on the Mamoní River (Class III–IV), which flows through an agricultural area and includes a portage around a waterfall. That trip is available from May to March and takes about eight hours, about half of which is spent on the river, and costs $125.

The Canal and Central Panama

By David
Dudenhoefer
Updated by
Jeffrey Van
Fleet

The Panama Canal bisects the country just to the west of Panama City, which enjoys excellent views of the monumental waterway. Between the canal and the rain forest that covers its islands, banks, and adjacent national parks, there is enough to see and do to fill several days.

Central Panama stretches out from the canal across three provinces and into two oceans to comprise everything from the mountains of the Cordillera Central to the west, to the jungles around Bayano Lake east of the canal, and from the coral reefs of the Caribbean coast in the north to the beaches of the Pearl Islands in the Bahía de Panamá (Bay of Panama) in the south. Much of the region can be visited on day trips from Panama City, but the hotels in gorgeous natural settings outside the city will make you want to do some overnights. You could easily limit your entire vacation to Central Panama; the region holds most of the nation's history and nearly all the things that draw people to the country—beaches, reefs, islands, mountains, rain forests, indigenous cultures, and, of course, the Panama Canal. Within hours of Panama City, in many cases a fraction of an hour, you can enjoy bird-watching, sportfishing, hiking, golf, scuba diving, white-water rafting, horseback riding, whale watching, or lazing on a palm-lined beach.

The Panama Canal can be explored from Panama City, Gamboa, or Colón, and its attractions range from the wildlife of Barro Colorado Island to the feisty peacock bass that abound in Gatún Lake. The coast on either side of the canal's Caribbean entrance offers the remains of colonial fortresses hemmed by jungle, half a dozen beaches, and mile upon mile of coral reef, most of it between 90 minutes and three hours from Panama City. The mountains to the east of the canal hold flora and fauna that you won't find in the forests that flank it, plus there are indigenous Emberá villages and a white-water rafting route on the Chagres River. The Pacific islands offer idyllic beaches, a little history, good sportfishing, decent dive sites, and seasonal whale watching, all within an hour of the capital by boat or plane. The coast to the southwest of Panama City also has some nice beaches, whereas the nearby highland refuge of El Valle presents exuberant landscapes populated by a multitude of birds and an ample selection of outdoor activities.

ORIENTATION AND PLANNING

ORIENTATION

Central Panama includes most destinations within a three-hour drive from Panama City, plus the islands to the southeast (within an hour of the city by boat or plane). Most of the region's attractions can be visited on day trips from the capital, but a few spots require overnights. Calle Omar Torrijos leads north from Panama City's Balboa neighborhood

TOP REASONS TO GO

The Panama Canal. History, technology, and nature combine like nowhere else in the world at the Panama Canal. The most popular way to explore is by taking the weekly transit tours that ply its waters between the Calzada Amador (Amador Causeway) and Gamboa. You can get a different perspective on one of the nature or fishing tours available out of Gamboa, or by staying at the Meliá resort, near Colón.

The Rain Forest. Central Panama has some of the most accessible rain forest in the world, with roads, trails, and waterways leading into wilderness that's home to hundreds of bird species and other animals. Tropical nature can be experienced to the fullest in the forests along the canal, in the mountains to the east and west of it, or along the Caribbean coast.

The Oceans. With the Caribbean and Pacific just 50 mi apart at the canal, you can bathe or skin-dive in two oceans on the same day. The Caribbean coast has miles of coral reef, whereas the Pacific islands lie near good fishing, dive spots, and seasonal whale watching.

The Islands. Panama's best beaches are on its islands, and Central Panama has isles where the sand is lined by coconut palms or thick jungle. These range from funky Isla Grande, a short boat ride from the Caribbean coast, to historic Isla Taboga, to the uninhabited isles of the Pearl Archipelago, where three seasons of *Survivor* were based.

The Mountains. The hills of Central Panama are considerably lower than those in the country's western provinces, but they still provide a refreshing respite from the lowland heat, and their lush forests are home to hundreds of bird species.

to the canal's Pacific locks, Summit, and Gamboa. The Corredor Norte connects to the Autopista Alfredo Motta, which leads to Sabanitas—where the road east to Portobelo and Isla Grande begins—and Colón. The Corredor Sur, which begins near Panama City's Punta Paitilla, flows into the eastbound Carretera Interamericana (Inter-American Highway, or CA1) just before Tocumen Airport, near which left turns lead to Cerro Azul. The westbound Carretera Interamericana is reached by taking Avenida de los Mártires over the Bridge of the Americas, near which left turns lead to Kobbe and Veracruz beaches. After that, it becomes a two-lane highway heading west around Chorrera and over the mountains to the Central Pacific beaches and El Valle de Antón, one to two hours from the city by car. The Pacific islands of Islas Taboga, Contadora, and San José are reached by daily ferries or flights.

PLANNING

WHEN TO GO

Most of the canal and Central Pacific sites lie within 30 minutes to two hours of Panama City, so if you're based there, plenty of attractions can be visited on a spare morning or afternoon; others are amenable to spending an extra night or two. The best time to explore the area is the

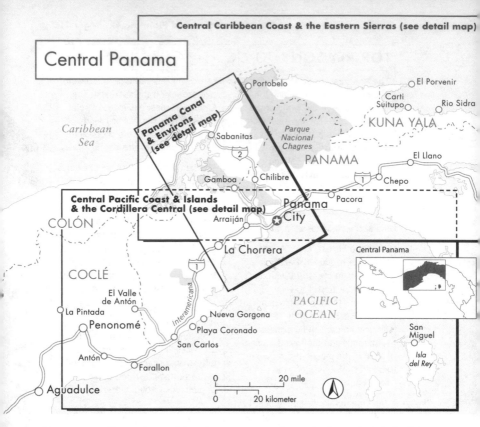

Central Panama

Panama Canal & Environs (see detail map)

Central Pacific Coast & Islands & the Cordillera Central (see detail map)

Caribbean Sea

Portobelo

El Porvenir

Carti Suitupo

Rio Sidra

KUNA YALA

Sabanitas

Parque Nacional Chagres

PANAMA

El Llano

Gamboa

Chilibre

Chepo

Pacora

Panama City

Arraiján

COLÓN

La Chorrera

Central Panama

COCLÉ

El Valle de Antón

La Pintada

Penonomé

Nueva Gorgona

PACIFIC OCEAN

San Miguel

Playa Coronado

Antón

San Carlos

Isla del Rey

Farallon

Aguadulce

Interamericana

0   20 mile

0   20 kilometer

December to May dry season, or when rains let up in July and August. Note that Panamanians generally travel between Christmas and New Year's, during the weekend of Carnaval in mid-February, or during Easter week; hotels fill up quickly at these times, and you will need to reserve rooms well in advance. Colorful Congo dances are performed in Portobelo for New Year's, Carnaval, and the Festival de Diablos y Congos (which takes place shortly after Carnaval).

GETTING HERE AND AROUND

You can visit most of the Central Pacific's sites on your own, but you have to join tours to do the canal transit, trips on Gatún Lake, tours of the indigenous communities, and white-water rafting in Chagres National Park. You can reach Summit, Parque Nacional Soberanía, and Gamboa by bus or taxi, but you should rent a car to explore more distant areas such as the Cerro Azul and most Pacific beaches. Tours or hotel transfers are available to most of those areas. Portobelo, Isla Grande, and El Valle de Antón are easy to reach on public buses, but you'll get there quicker in a car. The Panama Canal Railway is an interesting trip, but the downside is getting dumped in a dangerous part of Colón, which is why most people take the train as part of a tour that meets them at the Colón train station and takes them to nearby sites.

A BIT OF HISTORY

Nearly all Panama's history took place here in Central Panama, a region sometimes a mere 50 mi across. This was a vital link between Spain and its mineral-rich South American colonies; for centuries, Andean gold and silver crossed the isthmus via mule on a jungle road called the Camino Real. After pirate attacks on the Caribbean port Nombre de Dios, the Spanish moved the port to safer Portobelo, and the new Camino de las Cruces was built. But further attacks forced Spain to ship around Cape Horn instead, and Panama was eventually absorbed as a province of Colombia.

In 1849, tens of thousands of would-be millionaires joined the California Gold Rush. Before the Transcontinental Railroad sped up land travel across the United States, most people traveled to California by sea, first via Nicaragua's San Juan River and later through Panama. The American-built Panama Railroad, inaugurated in 1855, ran between Panama City and the new port, Aspinwall (now Colón). After the U.S. rail route started service in 1869, though, the Panama Railroad's heyday and the region's importance both hit a downturn.

Within a decade Ferdinand de Lesseps, of Suez Canal fame, acquired the rights from Colombia to dig an interoceanic canal here. His French company started work in 1882, but mismanagement and disease—some 20,000 workers died—caused the barely begun project to be abandoned in 1889. You can still see part of their effort to the west of the Gatún Locks.

When Colombia rejected a proposal by the United States to finish the job, President Theodore Roosevelt helped foment an independence movement, complete with U.S. battleship backup, that helped the Panamanians declare independence in 1903. A new treaty ceded a 10-mi-wide strip of land to the Americans, where the Canal would be constructed, and gave the U.S. military the right to intervene whenever U.S. interests were threatened.

For the next six decades the Canal Zone was an affluent guarded enclave ensuring American influence in the region. Republican 2008 presidential candidate John McCain was born here while his parents were posted to the Canal Zone. But by the middle of the 20th century, protests became frequent, one resulting in several student deaths. In the 1970s Panamanian General Omar Torrijos launched a successful international campaign to get the United States to negotiate, and the subsequent Torrijos-Carter treaties of 1977 mapped out the ultimate transfer of the Canal to Panama on December 31, 1999 (though not before the United States invaded in 1989 to firm up a democracy).

Since the handover, the Panamanian government has facilitated private investment, such as Panama Railway rehabilitation and the construction of hotels and housing while maintaining forests and historic structures. Following a nationwide referendum, the Panama Canal Authority has begun construction of a third set of locks, which will allow larger ships to transit the canal and launch a new era for the country and international shipping. Completion is slated for 2014, in time for the canal's centennial.

BY AIR

The domestic airlines Aeroperlas and Air Panama both have daily 25-minute flights to Isla Contadora. Aeroperlas flies every morning and evening; Air Panama flies every morning except Sunday, and Friday and Sunday evenings. Only Air Panama flies to Isla San José, an hour from Panama City; flights are every morning except Sunday, and Friday and Sunday evenings. All flights are from Panama City's Tocumen airport.

Contacts Aeroperlas (☎ 315–7500 ⊕ www.aeroperlas.com). **Air Panama** (☎ 316–9000 ⊕ www.flyairpanama.com).

BY BOAT

Barcos Calypso Taboga (✉ Marina Isla Naos ☎ 314–1730) has a daily ferry service from Panama City to Isla Taboga departing from the Marina on Isla Naos, on the Amador Causeway, Monday, Wednesday, and Friday at 8:30 and 3, Tuesday and Thursday at 8:30 only, and weekends and holidays at 8, 10:30, and 4. The ferry departs from Taboga from the pier on the west end of town Monday, Wednesday, and Friday at 9:30 and 4:30, Tuesday and Thursday at 4:30 only, and weekends and holidays at 9, 3, and 5. On weekends and holidays, arrive 30 minutes before departure to buy your ticket.

BY BUS

Buses to the Miraflores Locks, Summit, most of the trails into Parque Nacional Soberanía, and Gamboa depart from the **Terminal de Buses SACA** (✉ Calle 9 de Enero, Plaza Cinco de Mayo, Panama City ☎ No phone), just to the north of Plaza Cinco de Mayo, every 60 to 90 minutes; the trip takes 30 to 40 minutes.

All regional buses depart from the massive **Terminal de Transporte de Albrook** (✉ Av. Gaillard, Albrook, Panama City ☎ 232–5803). Buses to Colón and Sabanitas, where you get off to catch the bus to Portobelo and Isla Grande, depart every 20 minutes, and the trip takes 90 minutes. Buses to Penonomé and Santiago, which depart every 30 minutes, will drop you off at the entrances to the Pacific beaches, though most of them are a long hike from the highway. Buses to El Valle de Antón depart every 30 minutes.

BY CAR

Renting a car is an easy way to visit many of the Central Pacific sites, since there are paved roads to just about everything but the islands. Cars can be rented in Panama City and Colón. Rentals usually cost $40 to $50 per day, whereas 4WD vehicles cost $60 to $70. All major car-rental companies have offices in Panama City (⇨ Essentials, in "Panama City" chapter); only Budget and Hertz have offices in Colón, both in the secure confines of the Colón 2000 complex.

Contacts Budget (✉ Colón 2000, Colón ☎ 441–7161). **Hertz** (✉ Colón 2000, Colón ☎ 441–3272).

BY TRAIN

The Panama Canal Railway's commuter train to Colón departs from the train station in Panama City weekdays at 7:15 AM and departs from Colón at 5:15 PM. The trip costs $22 one way, $44 round-trip.

Train Station Information **Atlantic Passenger Station** (✉ *Calle Mt. Hope, Mt Hope, Colón* ☏ *No phone*). **Panama Canal Railway** (☏ *317–6070*). **Corozal Passenger Station** (✉ *Calle Corozal, Corozal, Panama City* ☏ *317–6070*).

RESTAURANTS

Though Central Panama's restaurant selection is neither as impressive nor as varied as Panama City's, the region has some excellent dining options, which include charming spots and impressive scenery. Rather than unforgettable food,

you're likely to enjoy good food in unforgettable settings, which include the ocean views on the Caribbean coast and Pacific Islands and Chagres River views in Gamboa.

HOTELS

The accommodations in Central Panama range from basic cement rooms to wonderful bungalows in stunning natural surroundings. The region includes some world-class nature lodges, where you can wake up to a full-service resort surrounded by rain forest, all-inclusive beach resorts where the bars stay open well past midnight, or homey B&Bs a short walk from the beach or forest. Even in the cheapest hotels you can expect a private bathroom and air-conditioning. While several more remote hotels nominally accept credit cards, sometimes the only way to pay with plastic is in advance via their Web sites rather than at the hotel at checkout. Smaller mom-and-pop places that do take credit cards might offer a slight discount if you pay in cash. Most hotels can book area tours for you, but tour companies will generally expect payment in cash. ■ TIP➔ You can sometimes save a bundle (occasionally upward of $100) at some of the more expensive hotels and resorts by booking via their Web sites, especially for midweek or off-season stays.

WHAT IT COSTS					
	¢	$	$$	$$$	$$$$
Restaurants	under $5	$5–$10	$10–$15	$15–$20	over $20
Hotels	under $50	$50–$100	$100–$160	$160–$220	over $220

Restaurant prices are per person for a main course at dinner. Hotel prices are for two people in a standard double room, excluding service and 10% tax.

ESSENTIALS

EMERGENCIES

Ambulance service can be slow in rural areas. There are clinics in some of the rural communities, but they are good for nothing more than first aid. If you suffer an accident or have medical problems, get to the Hospital Punta Pacífica or Centro Médico Paitilla in Panama City as soon as possible.

Emergency Services **Ambulance** (☎ *263–4522 Alerta;* 228–8127 *Cruz Roja*).
Fire department (☎ *103*). **National police** (☎ *104*).

MONEY

Credit cards are widely accepted in this region, except for at the smaller restaurants and hotels. ATM distribution is less uniform outside of Panama City, so it is often a good idea to stock up on cash before exploring the Central Pacific's rural reaches. The only ATMs near the Caribbean Coast's attractions are in and around Colón, whereas the eastern sierras and Pacific islands have no ATMs, so get cash before driving east or boarding the ferry or plane to Islas Taboga, Contadora, or San José. There are ATMs in the Albrook Airport terminal and at the Brisas de Amador shopping center, near the Taboga ferry dock, as well as in the lobby of the Gamboa Rainforest Resort, the Gatún Locks, and in the Super 99 supermarket in Colón 2000. To the west of Panama City, you can find ATMs in the Rey Supermarket at the entrance to Coronado, one block north of the Royal Decameron Beach Resort, in the lobby of the Playa Blanca Resort, on the Avenida Principal of El Valle, and at various banks in Penonomé, near Cerro de la Vieja.

SAFETY

There are certainly safety issues in Colón. When hiking through the forest, always be careful where you put your hand and your feet, since there are poisonous snakes and stinging insects. If you slip on a muddy trail in the rain forest, which happens quite frequently, resist the temptation to grab the nearest branch, because palms with spiny trunks are relatively common. If there are big waves at a beach you visit, don't go in unless you are an expert swimmer, since waves can create dangerous currents. The sun intensity at these latitudes means sunscreen and a brimmed hat are musts.

TOURS

Most of the major tour operators in Panama City *(Chapter 2 for details about these companies and their tours)*⇨ offer half- or full-day trips to attractions in this region, including the Panama Canal, trails in Parque Nacional Soberanía and Emberá villages in Parque Nacional Chagres. **Xtreme Adventures,** in Farallón, offers an array of outdoor and marine activities in the Coronado and Playa Blanca areas, including scuba diving, snorkeling, surfing, and sportfishing.

Contacts Xtreme Adventures (✉ *Playa Coronado, Farallón* ☎ *993–2823*).

THE PANAMA CANAL AND ENVIRONS

The Panama Canal stretches 80 km (50 mi) across one of the narrowest parts of the isthmus to connect the Pacific Ocean and the Caribbean Sea. For much of that route it's bordered by tropical wilderness. About half of the waterway is made up of Lago Gatún (Gatún Lake), an enormous artificial lake created by damming the Río Chagres (Chagres River). In addition to forming an integral part of the waterway, the lake is notable for its sportfishing and for the wildlife of its islands and the surrounding mainland.

As much an attraction as the canal itself are the forests that line it, which for decades were protected within the Canal Zone, a 10-mi-wide strip of land that was U.S. property until the Torrijos-Carter treaties took effect. The Panamanian government has turned most of the former Canal Zone forests into national parks, whereas most of the former U.S. infrastructure, including the Summit golf course and most buildings, has been privatized. Some of the former U.S. communities have become part of Panama City, while others, such as Gamboa, stand apart. The national parks have become increasingly important tourist attractions, and trails into the wilderness of Parque Nacional Soberanía and Monumento Natural Barro Colorado make the former Canal Zone one of the best places in the world to visit a tropical rain forest.

THE PANAMA CANAL

Panama's biggest attraction and most famous landmark, the Panama Canal stretches 80 km (50 mi) from the edge of Panama City to the Caribbean port of Colón, and a paved road follows its route between the islands of the Amador Causeway and the inland port of Gamboa. The most interesting spot for viewing the canal is the visitor center at the Miraflores Locks (⇨ *Esclusas de Miraflores in Chapter 2)*. North of Miraflores the road to Gamboa heads inland but still passes a couple of spots with canal vistas, namely the Pedro Miguel Locks and the one-way bridge over the Chagres River. The bridge (and Gamboa in general) offers front-row views of the big ships as they pass though the canal; it's one of the waterway's narrowest spots. The Panama Canal Railway train to Colón continues north from Gamboa past other vantage points, which is much of that trip's draw. Two other spots with impressive views are the monument erected by the country's Chinese community on the Bridge of the Americas" western side, and the Esclusas de Gatún (Gatún Locks), 10 km (6 mi) south of Colón. But nothing matches the experience of getting out onto the water, which can be done on a canal transit tour *(⇨ Canal Transits, below)* or on a nature tour or fishing trip on Gatún Lake *(⇨ Gamboa, below)*.

GETTING HERE AND AROUND

Since the Panama Canal runs along the western edge of Panama City, there are various spots within the metropolitan area from which to admire it (⇨ *Chapter 2)*. A taxi should charge $15 to Miraflores Locks and $25 to Gamboa. Buses to Gamboa depart from the SACSA station near Plaza Cinco de Mayo about every hour *(⇨ Gamboa, below)* and can drop you off at Miraflores Locks.

EN ROUTE The on-ramp to the **Puente Centenario** (Centennial Bridge) veers off the highway just before Summit. The bridge opened in 2005, crossing the Gaillard Cut and easing traffic congestion on the 1962 Puente de las Américas (Bridge of the Americas) at Panama City, 15 km (9 mi) south. The bridge bypasses the capital entirely for drivers coming from the west. (The two structures are the only permanent crossings over the Panama Canal.) The total span logs in at 1,052 meters (3,451 ft), longer than was needed at the time, but built with future (and now-begun) expansion of the canal in mind. The bridge's cables look delicate, and

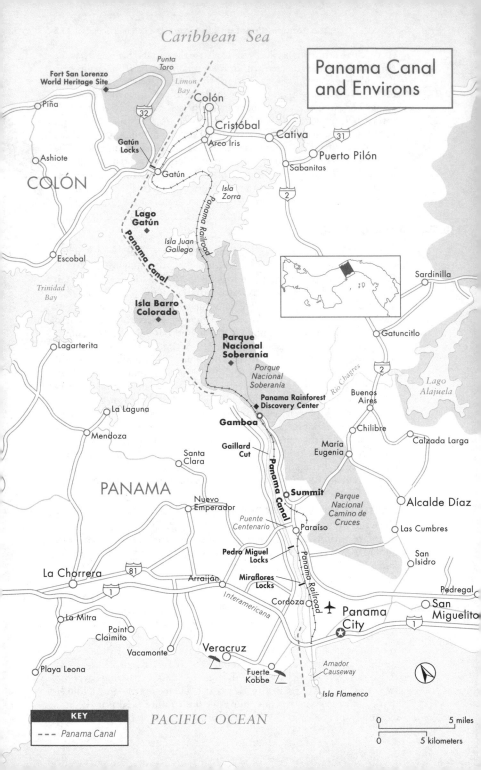

that's part of the beauty of the cable-stayed design, but the span handily and sturdily carries six lanes of traffic over the canal.

SUMMIT

20 km (12 mi) northwest of Panama City.

A short drive from the city, past Camino de Cruces National Park, this former American enclave consists of a golf course and a combination botanical garden and zoo. The course at **Summit Golf & Resort** (⇨ below) was created by the U.S. government in 1930 for canal workers and military personnel, but it was redesigned by Jeffery Myers in 1999 and is now a private club that's open to tourists.

The pastoral **Cementerio Francés** (French Cemetery) sits on the left side of the road just before Summit and serves as a testament to the human toll once taken by grand construction projects. Hundreds of crosses line a hill in this pretty cemetery and mark the resting place of a fraction of the 20,000 workers who died during France's brief attempt to construct a canal across the isthmus.

About a mile northwest of Summit Golf & Resort is **Parque Natural Summit** *(Jardín Botánico Summit, or Summit Botanical Garden)*, a large garden and zoo surrounded by rain forest. Started in 1923 as a U.S. government project to reproduce tropical plants with economic potential, it evolved into a botanical garden and a zoo in the 1960s. The gardens and surrounding forest hold thousands of species, but the focus is on about 150 species of ornamental, fruit, and hardwood trees from around the world that were once raised here. These range from coffee and cinnamon to the more unusual candle tree and cannonball tree. The zoo is home to 40 native animal species, most of them in cages that are depressingly small, though a few have decent quarters. Stars include jaguars, ocelots, all six of the country's monkey species, several macaw species, and the harpy eagle, Panama's national bird. A neat thing about Summit is that most of the animals exhibited in the zoo are also found in the surrounding forest, so you may spot parrots, toucans, and *agoutis* (large rodents) not only in cages, but in the wild as well. ⊠ *22 km (13 mi) northwest of downtown on road to Gamboa* ☎ *232–4854* ⊕ *www.summitpanama.org* ⊠ *$1* ◷ *Daily 9–5.*

GETTING HERE AND AROUND
Summit is an easy drive from Panama City. Follow the signs from Avenida Balboa or Avenida Central to Albrook, veer right at the traffic circle, and follow the Gaillard road 20 km (12 mi) to the Summit Golf & Resort entrance on the right. Less than a mile after that, turn left onto the road to Gamboa (after passing under a railroad bridge), and look for the Parque Natural Summit on your right. A taxi from Panama City should charge $10–$15 to drop you there. SACSA buses leave from the station two blocks east of Plaza Cinco de Mayo every hour or so on weekdays and every two hours on weekends.

WHERE TO STAY

$$$ ⚏ **Radisson Summit Hotel Panama Canal.** The chain's newest entry into Panama opened in the autumn of 2009 and revolves mostly around one of the country's premier golf courses. Your fellow guests here will likely all be golfers, but if you are a golf widow(er), never fear: You're smack-dab in the middle of an area with a ton of interesting things to do. Rooms are standard, dependable chain fare and overlook—what else?—the golf course. **Pros:** golf course; friendly staff. **Cons:** little to do at hotel if you don't golf. ⊠ *Paraíso, 20 km (12 mi) northwest of Panama City on road to Gamboa ☎232–4472, 800/395–7046 in U.S. and Canada ⊕ www.radisson.com ⇆ 103 rooms ⚒ In-room: safe, Wi-Fi. In-hotel: restaurant, room service, bar, golf course, pool, gym, laundry service, Internet terminal, parking (no fee)* ▭ *MC, V* ⚏ *BP.*

SPORTS AND THE OUTDOORS

The **Summit Golf & Resort** (⊠ *20 km [12 mi] northwest of Panama City on road to Gamboa ☎232–4653 ⊕ www.summitgolfpanama.com*) has an 18-hole, par-72 championship course designed by Jeff Myers that is hemmed by the rain forest of Camino de Cruces National Park. It is just 30 minutes from most hotels in Panama City, and the course is open to nonmembers. Greens fees are $120 on weekdays and $150 on weekends, golf cart included. Club rentals are $15–$45, depending on quality.

PARQUE NACIONAL SOBERANÍA

★ One of the planet's most accessible rain-forest reserves, **Parque Nacional Soberanía** (*Soberanía National Park*) comprises 19,341 hectares (48,000 acres) of lowland rain forest along the canal's eastern edge that is home to everything from howler monkeys to chestnut-mandible toucans. Long preserved as part of the U.S. Canal Zone, Soberanía was declared a national park, after being returned to Panama, as part of an effort to protect the canal's watershed. Trails into its wilderness can be reached by public bus, taxi, or by driving the mere 25 km (15 mi) from downtown Panama City. Those trails wind past the trunks and buttress roots of massive kapok and strangler fig trees and the twisted stalks of lianas dangling from their high branches. Though visitors can expect to see only a small sampling of its wildlife, the park is home to more than 500 bird species and more than 100 different mammals, including such endangered species as the elusive jaguar and the ocelot.

If you hike some of the park's trails (⇨ *Hiking, below*), you run a good chance of seeing white-faced capuchin monkeys, tamandua anteaters, raccoon-like *coatimundi*, or the large rodents called agouti. You may also see iridescent blue morpho butterflies, green iguanas, leafcutter ants, and other interesting critters. On any given morning here you might see dozens of spectacular birds, such as red-lored parrots, collared aracaris, violaceous trogons, and purple-throated fruit crows. From November to April the native bird population is augmented by the dozens of migrant species that winter in the park, among them the scarlet tanager, Kentucky warbler, and Louisiana water thrush. It is the combination of native and migrant bird species, plus the ocean birds along the nearby canal, that have enabled the Panama Audubon Society to set the Christmas bird count world record for two decades straight. ✉ *Ranger station on Carretera Gamboa, 25 km (15 mi) northwest of Panama City* 🖆 *Free* ⊙ *Daily 8–5.*

GETTING HERE AND AROUND

Soberanía is an easy drive from Panama City and is reached by following the same route for Summit and Gamboa. Shortly after the Summit Golf Resort the road passes under the railroad and comes to an intersection where a left turn will put you on the road to Gamboa and most of the park's trails. If you want to hike the Camino Cruces trail you should head straight at that intersection, toward Chilibre, and drive 6 km (3½ mi) to a parking area with picnic tables on your left, behind which is the trail. Turn left for the Plantation Road, which is on the right 3 km (1½ mi) past the Parque Natural Summit, at the entrance to the Canopy Tower. The dirt Plantation Road heads left from that entrance road almost immediately. The Sendero Los Charcos is on the right 2 km after the Plantation Road. The Pipeline Road begins in Gamboa, at the end of the main road, past the dredging division and town. A taxi should charge $15–$20 to drop you off at any of these trails. All but the Camino de Cruces trail can be reached via SACSA buses to Gamboa, which depart every hour or 90 minutes and will stop wherever you ask.

WHERE TO STAY

$$$ 🏨 **Canopy Tower Ecolodge.** Occupying a former U.S. Army radar tower
★ topped by a giant yellow ball, the Canopy Tower is perched on Semaphore Hill in the heart of Soberanía National Park, where it affords an amazing view of the rain forest. The innovative lodge is dedicated to serious bird-watchers and nature lovers with views of the forest canopy from every room and daily guided hikes. Rooms are small and basic, with cement floors, painted metal walls, ceiling fans, and tiny bathrooms, but they have big windows with views of the lower canopy—they are on the third floor—where there are often birds flitting about. Amenities such as air-conditioning have been forgone as part of the lodge's commitment to keeping its environmental impact as low as possible. Suites are roomier, with hammocks and decent-sized bathrooms, but people tend to spend most of their time in the forest or on the fourth floor, which holds a dining room and a lounge with a small natural-history library, and has walls of windows that let you look right into the forest canopy. The best view is from the rooftop deck,

Building the Panama Canal

Nearly a century after its completion, the Panama Canal remains an
impressive feat of engineering. It took
the U.S. government more than a
decade and $352 million to dig the
""'Big Ditch,'"" but its inauguration was
the culmination of a human drama
that spanned centuries and claimed
thousands of lives. As early as 1524,
King Carlos V of Spain envisioned
an interoceanic canal, and he had
Panama surveyed for routes where it
might be dug, though it soon became
clear that the task was too great to
attempt. It wasn't until 1880 that the
French tried to make that dream a
reality, but the job turned out to be
tougher than they'd imagined. The
Frenchman Ferdinand de Lesseps,
who'd recently overseen construction of the Suez Canal, intended to
build a sea-level canal similar to the
Suez, which would have been almost
impossible given the mountain range
running through Panama. But a different obstacle thwarted the French
enterprise: Panama's swampy, tropical
environment. More than 20,000 workers died of tropical diseases during
the French attempt, which together
with mismanagement of funds drove
the project bankrupt by 1889.

The United States, whose canal-
building enterprise was spearheaded
by President Theodore Roosevelt, purchased the French rights for $40 mil-
lion, and went to work in 1904. Using
recent advances in medical knowledge,
the Americans began their canal effort
with a sanitation campaign led by Dr.
William Gorgas that included draining
of swamps and puddles, construction
of potable water systems, and other
efforts to combat disease. Another
improvement over the French strategy
was the decision to build locks and

create a lake 85 feet above sea level.
For the biggest construction effort
since the building of the Great Wall of
China, tens of thousands of laborers
were brought in from the Caribbean
islands, Asia, and Europe to supple-
ment the local workforce. Some 6,000
workers lost their lives to disease and
accidents during the American effort,
which, when added to deaths during
the French attempt, is more than 500
lives lost for each mile of canal.

The most difficult and dangerous
stretch of the canal to complete
was Gaillard Cut through the rocky
continental divide. Thousands of workers spent seven years blasting and
digging through that natural barrier,
which consumed most of the 61 million pounds of dynamite detonated
during canal construction. The countless tons of rock removed were used
to build the Amador Causeway and to
fill in swamps that line much of the
coast of the capital.

By the time the SS *Ancon* became
the first ship to transit the Panama
Canal in August 15, 1914, numerous
records and engineering innovations
had been accomplished. One of the
biggest tasks was the damming of the
Chagres River with the Gatún Dam, a

massive earthen wall 1½ mi long and nearly a mile thick. It was the largest dam in the world when built, and the reservoir it created, Gatún Lake, was the largest man-made lake. The six sets of locks, which work like liquid elevators that raise and lower ships the 85 feet between Gatún Lake and the sea, were major engineering feats. Each lock chamber is 1,000 feet long and 110 feet wide—measurements that have governed shipbuilding ever since and gave the industry the term "Panamax"—and water flows in and out of them by gravity, so there are no pumps. Fears that the canal would fall into disrepair with the changing of the guard at the turn of the millennium never materialized, and experts have credited Panama for its forward-thinking administration and maintenance of the facility. Panama has also made the canal more tourist-friendly than it ever was during U.S. administration, a boon to you, dear visitor, as you view it in action. A $5.2-billion construction of new pairs of locks to complement Miraflores and Gatún began in 2007 and will allow larger post-Panamax ships, now 7 percent of the world's shipping fleet, to use the canal. As the canal approaches its 100th birthday, it remains an innovative and vital link in the global economy, and a monument to the ingenuity and industriousness of the people who built it.

CANAL FACTS

■ More than 14,000 vessels under the flags of some 70 countries use the canal each year.

■ Canal administration requires captains to turn over control of their ships to canal pilots for the duration of the transit.

■ A boat traveling from New York to San Francisco saves 7,872 mi by using the Panama Canal instead of going around Cape Horn.

■ Most ships take 8–10 hours to traverse the canal, but the U.S. Navy hydrofoil *Pegasus* has the record for the fastest transit at 2 hours and 41 minutes.

■ Each of the canal's locks is 1,000 feet long and 110 feet wide, dimensions that have governed shipbuilding since the canal's completion in 1914. The massive Panamax ships that move most cargo through the canal are designed to carry as much as possible while still fitting into the locks.

■ For each large ship that passes through the canal, 52 million gallons of fresh water are used by six locks, and more than one billion gallons of water flow from the canal into the sea every day. (It's a good thing the canal was built in a rain forest.)

■ The highest toll for Panama Canal passage was $331,200, paid by the cruise ship Disney Magic on May 16, 2008, though that record may have been broken by the time you read this.

■ The lowest toll on record was the $0.36 paid by Richard Halliburton, who swam the canal in 1928. Halliburton's record is safe for posterity, since tolls have risen considerably since then.

■ Shipping companies may reserve transit slots up to one year in advance and must do so a minimum of four days ahead. Tolls—it's cash only, no credit—must be paid prior to arrival.

3

CANAL TRANSITS

While the canal is impressive when admired from any of Panama City's various viewing points, there's nothing quite like getting onto the water and navigating it amidst the giant cargo ships. People spend thousands of dollars on cruises that include a canal crossing, but you can have the same experience for $100 to $200 and be free to spend the night in a spacious hotel room. Two companies offer partial transit tours, which travel through the canal's Pacific locks and Gaillard Cut, and full transits, which take you from one ocean to the other. All transits are accompanied by an expert guide who tells a bit of the canal's history, and include a continental breakfast, and, on full transits, a cold box lunch. Partial transits travel between the island marinas on the Amador Causeway and the port of Gamboa, on Gatún Lake, a trip that lasts four to five hours. They take place every Saturday, May–December, and on Thursday, Friday, and Saturday during the January–April high season. Full transits take place once or twice a month and last eight or nine hours.

■ TIP→ Departure times are fixed, but finishing times can be only approximate; the Panama Canal Authority always gives priority to larger cargo and cruise ships. Either trip is an unforgettable experience, suitable for travelers of all ages.

Canal Bay Tours (⊠ Bahia Balboa Building, next to Nunciatura, Punta Paitilla ☎ 209–2009 ⊕ www. canalandbaytours.com) offers partial and full transit tours on one of two ships: the 115-foot *Fantasía del Mar*, which has air-conditioned cabins and a large upper deck, and the 85-foot *Isla Morada*, which has one large covered deck. Partial transits are $115, full transits are $165. The company also operates a Friday-evening partial transit for $115. **Panama Marine Adventures** (⊠ Villa Porras and Calle Belén, no. 106, San Francisco ☎ 226–8917 ⊕ www.pmatours. net) runs canal transits on the 119-foot *Pacific Queen*, a comfortable ship with air-conditioned cabins and two large decks. Partial transits are $115, full transits are $165.

just above the forest canopy, where you can watch birds and climbing animals and see portions of the canal and of Panama City's skyline. Three meals and one nature tour per day are included in the price. **Pros:** constant exposure to nature; excellent guides; good food. **Cons:** basic rooms; lots of stairs; expensive. ⊠ *Carretera Gamboa, 25 km (15 mi) northwest of Panama City* ⌂ *Apdo. 0832-2701, W.T.C.* ☎ *264–5720; 800/930–3397 in the U.S.* ⊕ *www.canopytower.com* ⟳ *10 rooms, 2 suites* ⊘ *In-room: no a/c, no phone. In-hotel: restaurant, no-smoking rooms* ⊟ *AE, MC, V* ⫶⊙⫶ *FAP.*

SPORTS AND THE OUTDOORS
BIRD-WATCHING

Fodor's Choice
★ Soberanía has world-class bird-watching, especially from November to April, when the northern migrants boost the local population. Unless you're an expert, though, you're really better off joining a tour or hiring a guide through one of Panama City's nature-tour operators. Guests at the **Canopy Tower Ecolodge** (⇨ *above*) enjoy almost nonstop

Interoceanic Jungle

An almost continuous belt of forest stretches between the Pacific Ocean and the Caribbean Sea in Central Panama, where separate swaths of wilderness extend to the northwest and north of Panama City. That invaluable tropical nature is sequestered within a half-dozen national parks and other protected areas that are home to more than half of the country's bird species, five kinds of monkeys, the world's largest rodent (the capybara), and such endangered animals as the jaguar, tapir, and harpy eagle. One reason for the diversity is that though the interoceanic wilderness is relatively continuous, it is by no means homogenous, since the altitudes in the region range from sea level to more than 3,000 feet, and it rains twice as much per year in some of the Caribbean forests as it does in the forests near Panama City, less than 50 mi away. The combination of varied weather and topography provides niches for an amazing diversity of flora and fauna for such a small area.

Aside from the canal area, the only other place in Panama, or Central America, where the forest cover stretches from the Pacific to the Caribbean is in remote Darién Province, which is difficult and expensive to explore. But there are dozens of places and ways that you can explore the varied tropical wilderness of the canal area, ranging from an early morning bird-watching tour in the forests near Panama City to a one-week hiking expedition on the route of the historic Camino Real, offered by Ancon Expeditions (⇨ *Hiking in Parque Nacional Chagres, below*).

You can take a taxi or bus to Parque Nacional Soberanía and hike one of its trails; take one of several boat tours to the islands and forested shores of Gatún Lake; drive an hour to the mountain forests of Cerro Azul or Sierra Llorona; take a day trip to Barro Colorado, San Lorenzo, or Portobelo; raft down the Chagres River; or zip through forests of Soberanía on the Panama Canal Railway. But experiencing the flora and fauna can also be as effortless as looking out the window at nature lodges such as the Canopy Tower, Gamboa Rainforest Resort, and Sierra Llorona Lodge.

birding and daily tours led by the lodge's resident guides. **Ancon Expeditions** (☎ *269–9415* ⊕ *www.anconexpeditions.com*) has excellent guides that can take you bird-watching on Pipeline Road or on Gatún Lake. **Advantage Panama** (☎ *6676–2466* ⊕ *www.advantagepanama.com*) has a day trip to Soberanía that combines a forest hike with a boat trip on Gatún Lake. **Eco Circuitos Panama** (☎ *314–0068* ⊕ *www.ecocircuitos. com*) has a Soberanía birding tour that starts with a hike and ends with a boat trip. **Pesantez Tours** (☎ *366–9100* ⊕ *www.pesantez-tours. com*) runs a half-day tour to Soberanía. Colón-based **Nattur Panama** (☎ *442–1340* ⊕ *www.achiotecoturismo.com*) can put together à la carte birding tours of Soberanía.

HIKING AND BIKING

Soberanía's natural treasures can be discovered along miles and miles of trails and roads, whereas the western edge of the park can be explored on boat tours through local companies. The park also protects a significant portion of the old **Camino de las Cruces,** a cobbled road built by the Spanish that connected old Panama City with a small port on the Chagres River, near modern-day Gamboa. It's more than 10 km (6 mi) long and intersects with the Plantation Road before reaching the river, but you don't have to hike far to find cobbled patches that were restored a couple of decades ago.

The **Plantation Road** is a dirt road that heads east into the forest from the road to Gamboa for about 4 mi, to where it connects to the Camino de Cruces. That wide trail follows a creek called the Río Chico Masambi, and it's a great place to see waterbirds and forest birds. Two kilometers (1 mi) past the entrance to the Canopy Tower is the **Sendero el Charco** (Pool Footpath), which forms a loop through the forest to the east of the road to Gamboa. The *charco* (pool) refers to a man-made pond near the beginning of the trail that was created by damming a stream. The trail follows that stream part of the way, which means you may spot waterbirds such as tiger herons, in addition to such forest birds as toucans and *chachalacas*. It is one of the park's most popular trails because it's a loop, it's short (less than a kilometer), and it's flat enough to be an easy hike.

The park's most famous trail is the **Camino del Oleoducto** (Pipeline Road), a paved road that follows an oil pipeline for 17 km (11 mi) into the forest parallel to the canal. One of the country's premier bird-watching spots, it is here that the Panama Audubon Society has had record-breaking Christmas bird counts year after year. The Pipeline Road is a great place to see trogons (five species have been logged there), motmots, forest falcons, and other bird species as well as monkeys, tamandua anteaters, and agoutis. You can hike on your own, but you'll see and learn more if you take a bird-watching tour.

Aventuras Panama (☏ 260–0044 ⊕ *www.aventuraspanama.com*) leads mountain-biking excursions through Soberanía for $95. The moderately rugged route covers 15 km (9 mi), beginning in Summit and taking in the Camino de Cruces and Coco Plantation.**Panama Pete Adventures** (☏ 231–1438 ⊕ *www.panamapeteadventurs.com*) leads 14-km (8 mi) mountain-biking excursions through Soberanía and birding hikes on the Camino de Cruces within the park. Either excursion costs $68.

GAMBOA

32 km (20 mi) northwest of Panama City.

Though it lies a mere 40 minutes from downtown Panama City, the tiny community of Gamboa feels remote, no doubt due to the fact that it is surrounded by exuberant tropical nature. Its location on the north bank of the flooded Chagres River, nestled between the Panama Canal and rain forest of Soberanía National Park, makes Gamboa a world-class bird-watching destination and the departure point for boat trips on Lago Gatún. It is also a great place to stroll, have lunch amid nature, or kick back and admire the impressive tropical scenery. It is home to a massive nature resort that offers enough diversions to fill several days, but Gamboa's proximity to the capital also makes it a convenient day-trip from Panama City.

CRAZY WEATHER

Because Panama lies just north of the equator, the temperature tends to swing between warm and torrid, with the exception of the western mountains where it can actually get cold at night. In any region, though, there's more temperature variation in a day than through the course of a year. The temperature in the lowlands tends to be slightly cool at daybreak, miserable at noon, and bearable again once the sun starts to set, whether it's December or July. The only seasons are rainy (May–December) and dry (January–April). But the rainy season is not constant, since it rains considerably less in July and August. There is also plenty of regional variation, with much more rain falling along the Caribbean side of the country than the Pacific. In fact, though they are a mere 50 mi apart, Colón gets nearly twice as much rain as Panama City, though most of it falls at night.

3

The town of Gamboa was built by Uncle Sam in the early 20th century to house workers at the Panama Canal dredging division, which is based here. The town's tiny port is full of canal maintenance equipment, but it's also the point of departure for the daily boat to Barro Colorado Island and for Pacific-bound partial canal transits. Private yachts sometimes spend a night near the port on the way through the canal, and a simple marina on the other side of the Chagres River holds the boats of local fishermen and tour companies that take groups onto the canal for wildlife watching along the forest's edge.

Over the years, biologists and bird-watchers have come to realize that Gamboa's combination of forests and wetlands make it home to an inordinate diversity of birds. The Panama Audubon Society has set world records for Christmas bird counts year after year on the **Camino del Oleoducto** (Pipeline Road), which heads into Parque Nacional Soberanía on the northwest end of town. That trail is the main destination for day visitors, but you can also see plenty of wildlife from the roads around town and the banks of the Chagres River.

The massive **Gamboa Rainforest Resort** (⇨ *below*), just east of town, is spread over a ridge with a panoramic view of the Chagres River. The resort has a 340-acre forest reserve that is contiguous with Soberanía National Park, within which is an aerial tram, a small orchid collection, a butterfly farm, an aquarium, and a serpentarium. The resort also has its own marina on the Chagres River; near it is the riverside restaurant Los Lagartos, which is a great spot for lunch and wildlife watching even if you don't stay at the hotel. The resort's owner even convinced a small indigenous Emberá community who were living in nearby Chagres National Park to rebuild their village across the Chagres River from the hotel, where they now receive tourists. (Realize the setup is artificial; it can't compare to a visit to an Emberá community in the Darién.)

The Gamboa Rainforest Resort has its own tour company, **Gamboa Tours** (☎ *314–9000, Ext. 8158* ⊕ *www.gamboatours.com*), which offers a day tour to nonguests that includes the aerial tram, a wildlife-watching tour on Lago Gatún and Monkey Island, and lunch, for $90. The 1.2-km (¾-mi) tram, unfortunately, does not run early in the morning or late in the afternoon, when the best wildlife-spotting opportunities would take place. No matter: it's a novel ride. The tram shuts down for maintenance for a couple of weeks each year, usually in May.

Just beyond Gamboa, adjacent to the Parque Nacional Soberanía and near the start of the Pipeline Road, lies the **Panama Rainforest Discovery Center,** one of the country's newest tourist attractions. The center, operated by the local Eugene Eisenmann Avian Wildlife Foundation, is still a work in progress at this writing. Its centerpiece is a 32-meter (105-ft) steel observation tower giving ample opportunity for observation of life in the rain-forest canopy. Three other decks are positioned at about each of the quarter-way marks. A solar-powered visitors' center contains exhibits about avian life in the Panamanian rain forest. Leading from the visitors' center is 1.1 km (2/3 mi) of hiking trails. The early bird catches the worm, as the saying goes, and the early visitor has the best birding opportunities. Capacity is limited to 25 visitors at a time during the peak viewing hours before 10 AM and to 50 people for the rest of the day, making advance reservations a good idea. On schedule for completion by late 2010 is an expansion of the facility to include treetop-walkway suspension bridges and an expanded visitor's center. ⊠ *3 km (2 mi) northwest of Gamboa* ☎ *314–9386, 264–6266 in Panama City* ⊕ *www.pipelineroad.org* ⊠ *$15, $20 before 10* AM ⊗ *Daily 6–4*

GETTING HERE AND AROUND

Gamboa is an easy 40-minute drive from Panama City. Follow the signs from Avenida Balboa or Avenida Central to Albrook, veer right at the traffic circle and follow that road north, into the forest. Shortly after driving under a railroad bridge, turn left and stay on that road all the way to the one-way bridge over the Chagres River. Turn right just after the bridge for the Rainforest Resort and Los Lagartos restaurant, or continue straight ahead for the Pipeline Road. A taxi from Panama City should charge $15–$20 to drop you off here. SACSA buses depart from the station two blocks east of Plaza Cinco de Mayo in Panama City approximately every hour from 5 AM to 6:30 PM weekdays and approximately every two hours on weekends.

WHERE TO EAT AND STAY

$ ✕ **Los Lagartos.** Built out over the Chagres River, this open-air restaurant
LATIN AMERICAN   at the Gamboa Rainforest Resort is a great place to see turtles, fish,
★   crocodiles, and waterfowl feeding in the hyacinth-laden water. If you travel with binoculars, you'll definitely want to bring them here, so that you can watch wildlife while you wait for your lunch. A small buffet is frequently available, but the à la carte selection is usually a better deal, with choices such as peacock bass in a mustard sauce, grouper topped with an avocado sauce and cheese, or the hearty, spicy fisherman's stew. Lighter items include Caesar salad, hamburgers, and quesadillas. It isn't Panama's best food, but it's good, and the view of the forest-hemmed Chagres River populated with grebes, jacanas, and mangrove swallows

is worth the trip out here even if you have only a cup of tea. ✉ *Carretera Gamboa, right after bridge over Chagres River* ☎ *314–9000* ✆ *Apdo. 0816-02009, Panama City* ▤ *AE, MC, V* ⊗ *Closed Mon.*

$$–$$$$ 🏨 **Gamboa Rainforest Resort.** The panorama of the forested Chagres
☯ River valley through the lobby windows here is so captivating that it
★ takes you a while to notice the bright, airy lobby itself; life-size crane sculptures hang overhead and a stream cascades through a three-story tropical atrium, flowing into a swimming pool below. Spacious rooms have wicker furniture, hammocks, and tropical-flower bedspreads, but it's the balcony views that make them special. Junior suites, with two additional queen beds in a loft, work well for families. Garden views are disappointing—stick with rooms with numbers in the 100s. The historic "villas" cost considerably less, but they lack the view and suffer severe mildew problems. Activities include bird-watching, the aerial tram, a boat trip to Monkey Island, kayaking, and fishing. Both restaurants serve good food with a great view—El Corotu offers buffets and à la carte; the more upscale Chagres River View serves three-course prix-fixe dinners for $35. **Pros:** amazing views; wildlife; ample facilities and diversions. **Cons:** massive; rather expensive; guides are mediocre. ✉ *Carretera Gamboa, 32 km (19 mi) northwest of Panama City* ☎ *314–9000; 206–8888 in Panama City, 877/800–1690 in the U.S.* ⊕ *www.gamboaresort.com* ✆ *Apdo. 0816-02009, Panama City* 🛏 *160 rooms, 4 suites, 48 villas* ♿ *In-room: safe, Internet. In-hotel: 3 restaurants, bars, room service, bars, tennis courts, pool, gym, spa, water sports, laundry service, public Wi-Fi, no-smoking rooms* ▤ *AE, MC, V* ⦿ *BP.*

NIGHTLIFE AND THE ARTS

If you are staying at Gamboa Rainforest resort and just want a quiet drink, head to the Monkey Bar, behind the reception area in the lobby.

The **Discoteca Capybara** (✉ *Carretera Gamboa, 32 km (19 mi) northwest of Panama City* ☎ *314–9000*), in the basement of the Gamboa Rainforest Resort, opens on Friday and Saturday night.

SPORTS AND THE OUTDOORS
BIRD-WATCHING

All the big nature tour operators offer bird-watching tours on Pipeline Road (⇨ *Parque Nacional Soberanía, above*).

Guests at the Gamboa Rainforest Resort can book a morning of bird-watching on nearby Pipeline Road with **Gamboa Tours** (☎ *314–9000 Ext. 8158* ⊕ *www.gamboatours.com*), which will have them in the national park by 7 AM.

HIKING

Gamboa Tours (☎ *314–9000 Ext. 8158* ⊕ *www.gamboatours.com*) has a three-hour hiking tour on the historic Camino de Cruces, which ends on the other side of the Chagres River from the Gamboa Rainforest Resort—it's an excellent trip for seeing wildlife.

SPORTFISHING

☯ Gatún Lake is full of peacock bass and also has snook and tarpon, adding up to excellent sportfishing. Charters depart from Gamboa's two marinas, and anglers may hook as many as 20 or 30 peacock bass before returning in the afternoon. **Panama Canal Fishing** (☎ *315–1905 or 6699–0507* ⊕ *www.panamacanalfishing. com*) is the best operator for fishing on Gatún Lake. An all-inclusive day of fishing on the Hurricane Fundeck with swivel chairs on the bow costs $260. **Gamboa Tours** (☎ *314–9000 Ext. 8158* ⊕ *www.gamboatours. com*) offers full-day bass-fishing charters for up to three people for $263.

LAGO GATÚN (GATÚN LAKE)

Covering about 163 square mi, an area about the size of the island nation Barbados, Gatún Lake extends northwest from Parque Nacional Soberanía to the locks of Gatún, just south of Colón. The lake was created when the U.S. government dammed the Chagres River, between 1907 and 1910, so that boats could cross the isthmus at 85 feet above sea level. By creating the lake, the United States saved decades of digging that a sea-level canal would have required. It took several years for the rain to fill the convoluted valleys, turning hilltops into islands and killing much forest (some trunks still tower over the water nearly a century later). When it was completed, Gatún Lake was the largest man-made lake in the world. The canal route winds through its northern half, past several forest-covered islands (the largest is Barro Colorado, one of the world's first biological reserves). To the north of Barro Colorado are the Islas Brujas and Islas Tigres, which together hold a primate refuge—visitors aren't allowed. The lake itself is home to crocodiles—forego swimming here—manatees, and peacock bass, a species introduced from South America and popular with fishermen. Fishing charters for bass, snook, and tarpon are out of Gamboa Rainforest Resort (⇨ *above*).

GETTING HERE AND AROUND

Aside from seeing the entire canal on a complete transit tour, you can see a bit of the lake during the boat trip to Barro Colorado, or on one of the nature tours or sportfishing charters that leave from the marinas at Gamboa and the Meliá Resort, near Colón. You can also see parts of it from the Panama Railway.

ISLA BARRO COLORADO

55 km (34 mi) northwest of Panama City, in the Panama Canal.

Fodor'sChoice ★ The island of Barro Colorado in Lago Gatún is a former hilltop that became an island when the Río Chagres was dammed during construction of the Panama Canal. It covers 1,500 hectares (3,700 acres) of virgin rain forest and forms part of the Barro Colorado Nature Monument, which includes five peninsulas on the mainland and protects an area several times that size. The reserve is home for more than 400 species of birds, 225 ant species, and 122 mammal species, including collared peccaries, ocelots, coatis, and five kinds of monkeys. Its forest has 1,200 plant species—more than are found in all of Europe—ranging from delicate orchids to massive strangler fig trees.

In 1923 the island was declared a biological reserve and a tropical research station was built there; it is now the oldest such facility in the

THE HARPY EAGLE

The harpy eagle, Panama's national bird, is an impressive creature, with a beak the size of a jackknife, talons as long as a grizzly bear's claws, and a plumed crest evoking a war bonnet. It is one of the world's largest and most powerful raptors, with a wingspan of almost 6½ feet, and can tear a full-grown monkey out of a treetop with one swoop. Since pre-Columbian times the bird has maintained a mythical stature among the region's indigenous peoples, and you can see gold eagle figures displayed at the anthropological museum in Panama City. But because it is perched at the top of a food chain in an endangered ecosystem, the harpy is threatened in most of its range.

The harpy (*Harpia harpyja*) was once common from southeast Mexico to northern Argentina, but hunting and deforestation have practically wiped the species out north of Panama and are steadily reducing its numbers in South America. Panama still has a significant number of harpies—hundreds, perhaps—thanks to the work of conservation groups and governmental protection of vast expanses of rain forest. Harpies require large areas of forest to survive because their prey is relatively scarce; accordingly, deforestation hits them hard. They also have a low

reproductive rate, mating only once every two years, when they build a life-raft-size nest atop a large *kapok* or *quipo* tree—the tallest trees in the rain forest—and spend the next year raising one chick. The U.S. conservation group Peregrine Fund (⊕ www. peregrinefund.org) is working to save the harpy eagle in Panama by breeding captive birds on loan from zoos—they remove eggs so that the females lay more—then releasing young birds into the wild. The organization also runs an educational program for people in rural communities where the raptors live.

Panama is one of the countries where you are most likely to see the elusive harpy eagle. They are most common in the eastern Darién Province, but have been spotted in Soberanía, Chagres, and other central parks. If you are lucky enough to encounter a perched harpy, you may be able to get pretty close, because the birds generally don't fear people and are curious, which unfortunately works to the advantage of poachers. One place you are guaranteed to spot a harpy eagle is Parque Natural Summit, the botanical garden and zoo north of Panama City, which has captive birds and an excellent display about them.

world. The island is administered by the Smithsonian Tropical Research Institute (STRI), which facilitates research by 200 or so visiting scientists and students per year and runs several weekly educational tours. Those tours are not only one of the most informative introductions to tropical ecology you can get in Panama, they are excellent opportunities to see wildlife; after decades of living in a protected area full of scientists, the animals are hardly afraid of people. STRI also operates much smaller facilities for visitors at Bocas del Toro and the Calzada de Amador in Panama City.

Barro Colorado can be visited on full-day tours run by the **Smithsonian Tropical Research Institute (STRI)** (⊠ *Av. Roosevelt, Cerro Ancón,*

Panama City ☎ *212–8951* ⊕ *www.stri.org*) Tuesday, Wednesday, Friday, Saturday, and Sunday. The $70 tour is well worth the money, since the English-speaking guides do an excellent job of pointing out flora and fauna and explaining the rain forest's complex ecology. Lunch in the research station's cafeteria and boat transportation to and from Gamboa are included. Tours tend to fill up months ahead, so fill out the form on the STRI Web site and reserve your trip as early as possible. Reservations that haven't been paid for a week before the tour will be canceled; to join one at the last minute, it's worth calling Tamara Castillo at the STRI office and asking whether there is space on a tour (there often is). In this case, you have to pay at least one day in advance. Bring your passport, tour receipt, bottled water, binoculars, and a poncho or raincoat (May–December). Wear long pants, hiking shoes, and socks to protect against chiggers. Be in decent shape, since the tour includes several hours of hiking on trails that are steep in places and can be slippery; children under 10 are not allowed. You can reserve and pay for tours at the STRI's Tupper Center in Panama City weekdays from 8 to 2.

GETTING HERE AND AROUND
Barro Colorado can only be visited on tours run by the Smithsonian Tropical Research Institute *(*⇨ *above)*. Tours leave from the STRI pier in Gamboa at 7 AM on weekdays and 7:45 on weekends. The pier is down a gravel road on the left after the dredging division and is best reached from Panama City by taxi ($15–$20).

THE CENTRAL CARIBBEAN COAST

Coral reefs, rain forests, colonial ruins, and a predominant Afro-Caribbean culture make Panama's Caribbean coast a fascinating place to visit. People from Panama City head to the Costa Arriba, the coast northeast of Colón, to enjoy its beaches and feast on fresh lobster, conch, or king crab. Scuba divers flock to Portobelo, a colonial town guarded by ancient fortresses and surrounded by rain forest, but the diving is even better to the northeast of there. The bird-watching is excellent around the colonial fortress of San Lorenzo and on Sierra Llorona, but is also quite good at Portobelo.

COLÓN

79 km (49 mi) northwest of Panama City.

The provincial capital of Colón, beside the canal's Atlantic entrance, has clearly seen better days, as the architecture of its older buildings attests. Its predominantly Afro-Caribbean population has long had a vibrant musical scene, and in the late 19th and early 20th centuries Colón, named for the Spanish-language surname of Christopher Columbus, was a relatively prosperous town. But "Aspinwall"—generations of Canal Zone residents knew the city only by its American name—spent the second half of the 20th century in steady decay, and things have only gotten worse in the 21st century. For the most part, the city is a giant slum, with unemployment at 15% to 20% and crime on the rise.

THE PANAMA CANAL RAILWAY

The original Panama Railway was completed in 1855 in response to the 1849 California Gold Rush, since it was a safer and quicker way for people to travel between the East and West coasts of the United States than risking the trip through Indian country. That railroad took five years to build and cost $6.5 million, but it transported millions of passengers and more than $700 million worth of gold from California during the next decade. (Fares and freight originally were charged in gold.) When the U.S. government began work on the Panama Canal it moved the railway to its current route, as parts of the original route were flooded. The railway was given to the government of Panama in the 1980s, and in 1998 a consortium of American companies signed a 50-year concession to operate it, completely refurbishing it and connecting it to new container ports on either side of the canal. Transporting containers between ships in the two oceans is now the railway's main activity.

The one-hour trip on the **Panama Canal Railway** (⊠ *Av. Omar Torrijos, Corozal, Panama City* ☎ *317–6070* ⊕ *www.panarail.com*) from Corozal, just north of Albrook, to the Caribbean city of Colón, offers an interesting perspective on the rain forests of Soberanía National Park

and the wetlands along Gatún Lake. The railway primarily moves freight, but it has a commuter service on weekdays that departs from Panama City at 7:15 AM (returning from Colón at 5:15 PM, and costs $22 each way. Tourists ride in one of five air-conditioned cars (soon to be six) with curved windows on the roof that let you see the foliage overhead. The best views are from the left side of the train, and though the train moves too fast to see much wildlife, you may spot toucans, herons, and black snail kites flying over the lake. The downside: the trip passes a garbage dump and industrial zone near the end, and leaves you just outside the slums of Colón at 8:15 AM, which is why you may want to take the trip as part of a tour that picks you up in Colón and takes you to either San Lorenzo or Portobelo. It is possible to do the trip on your own, in which case you should board one of the shuttle vans that await the train in Colón and have them take you to the Colón 2000 (pronounced coh-*loan* dose-*mill*) cruise-ship port, where you can pick up a rental car and drive to Portobelo, or hire a taxi for the day ($80–$100). The trains leave promptly, and it is complicated to pre-purchase tickets, so get to the station by 7 AM to buy your tickets.

⚠ **Travelers who explore Colón on foot are simply asking to be mugged,** and the route between the train station and the bus terminal is especially notorious; do all your traveling in a taxi, rental car, or on a guided tour. If you do the Panama Railway trip on your own without a tour company, take one of the shuttle vans to the Colón 2000 (pronounced coh-*loan* dose-*mill*) cruise-ship terminal, where you can rent a car or hire a taxi to see the sights near town. The Espinar neighborhood 10 km (6 mi) to the south, in the former U.S. Canal Zone, is a tranquil area that holds the Meliá Hotel and can serve as a base to visit Gatún Locks, San Lorenzo, and Portobelo.

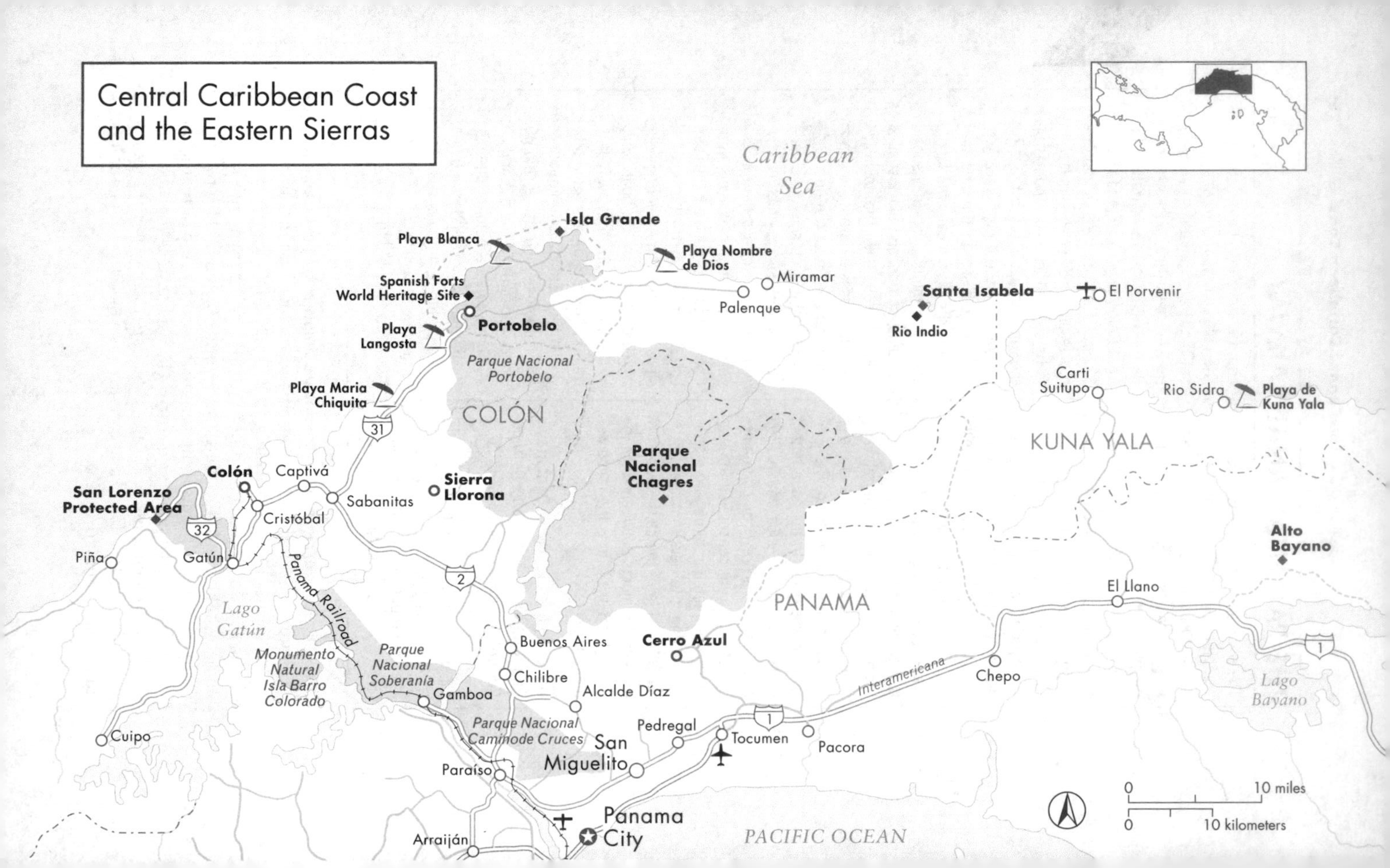
Central Caribbean Coast
and the Eastern Sierras
Caribbean
Sea
Isla Grande
Playa Blanca
Playa Nombre
de Dios
Miramar
Palenque
Spanish Forts
World Heritage Site
Portobelo
Santa Isabela
Rio Indio
El Porvenir
Playa
Langosta
Parque Nacional
Portobelo
Playa Maria
Chiquita
31
COLÓN
Carti
Suitupo
Rio Sidra
Playa de
Kuna Yala
KUNA YALA
Parque
Nacional
Chagres
Colón
Captivá
Sierra
Llorona
San Lorenzo
Protected Area
Sabanitas
Cristóbal
32
Alto
Bayano
Piña
Gatún
Panama Railroad
2
El Llano
PANAMA
Lago
Gatún
Buenos Aires
Cerro Azul
Monumento
Natural
Isla Barro
Colorado
Parque
Nacional
Soberanía
Chilibre
1
Chepo
Interamericana
Lago
Bayano
Alcalde Díaz
Gamboa
Parque Nacional
Caminode Cruces
Pedregal
1
Cuipo
San
Miguelito
Tocumen
Pacora
Paraíso
0
10 miles
Panama
City
0
10 kilometers
PACIFIC OCEAN
Arraiján

Two blocks from the Zona Libre is the city's cruise-ship port, **Colón 2000**, which is basically a two-story strip mall next to the dock where ships tie up and passengers load onto buses for day trips. It has a supermarket, restaurants, two rental-car offices, and English-speaking taxi drivers who can take you on sightseeing excursions ($70–$100 for a full day). A second terminal opened in 2008 and became the home port for Royal Caribbean's *Enchantment of the Seas*, with the Panamanian government aggressively courting other cruise companies to set up shop here too. ✉ *Calle El Paseo Gorgas* ☎ *447–3197* ⊕ *www.colon2000.com.*

Twelve kilometers (7 mi) south of Colón are the **Esclusas de Gatún** *(Gatún Locks)* a triple-lock complex that's nearly a mile long and raises and lowers ships the 85 feet between sea level and Gatún Lake. There's a small viewing platform at the locks and a simple visitor center that's nothing compared to the center at Miraflores Locks. However, the sheer magnitude of the Gatún Locks—they are the canal's largest—is impressive, especially when packed with ships. You have to cross the locks on a swinging bridge to get to San Lorenzo and the **Represa Gatún** (Gatún Dam) which holds the water in Gatún Lake. At 1½ mi long, it was the largest dam in the world when it was built, a title it held for several decades. Get there by taking the first left after crossing the locks. *12 km (7 mi) south of Colón* ☎ *Free* ☉ *Daily 8–4.*

Many South American merchants go to Colón to shop at the **Zona Libre de Colón** (Colón Free Zone), which handles about $6 million worth of wholesale and retail sales per year. Northern visitors likely won't be wowed by the prices and won't recognize the brand names here. It is also downright ugly. If you do visit, remember that this is a free port. Your purchases must be exported. The Zona Libre delivers what you buy for pick-up upon your departure at Tocumen International Airport. Allow a minimum of two days for the arrangements. *Calle 13 and Avenida Roosevelt* ⊕ *www.zonalibredecolon.com.pa* ☉ *Weekdays 8–5.*

GETTING HERE AND AROUND

The easiest way to get to Colón from Panama City is to take the Panama Canal Railway commuter train that departs from Panama City at 7:15 AM and returns at 5:15 PM. If you start your railway journey in Colón, you will need to purchase tickets from the conductor. Buses depart from Panama City's Albrook Terminal de Buses every 20 minutes, and the trip takes 90 minutes to two hours. Get directly into a

---

CONGO DANCING

One of the main cultural attractions of the Central Caribbean Coast are **congos**, dances developed in escaped-slave communities of the 15th through 18th centuries. One is a parody of Spanish officials marching while devils and witch doctors dance around them; the music is thoroughly African. Common on the patron saints' days of many coastal towns, congo is most prominent in Portobelo on January 31, March 20, or during a festival shortly after Carnaval. The Panama Tourist Bureau (ATP) Web site (www.visitpanama.com) has exact dates.

taxi upon arrival at either the train or bus station; both are in unsafe neighborhoods. ⚠ **Take only licensed taxis in Colón—the license plate and number on the door should match. Robberies have been committed by unofficial cabbies.** You can rent a car at the Colón 2000 cruise center. A spiffy, four-lane toll highway ($4) opened in 2009 and puts Colón a 40-minute drive from Panama City. Take the Corredor Norte to the Autopista Alfredo Motta. If you are headed for the Meliá Panama Canal, Gatún Locks, or San Lorenzo, bypass Colón and turn left at the Super 99, or the Centro Comercial Cuatro Altos, about 8 km (5 mi) before Colón, and follow the signs to Residencial Espinar for the hotel, and Esclusas de Gatún for the locks.

Contacts Budget (✉ *Colón 2000* ☎ *441–7161*). **Hertz** (✉ *Colón 2000* ☎ *441– 3272*). **Panama Canal Railway** (☎ *317–6070*). **Terminal de Bus de Colón** (✉ *Av. Balboa and Calle Terminal* ☎ *441–4044*).

WHERE TO STAY

¢ $ 🏨 **Harbor Inn.** In the Canal Zone neighborhood of Espinar, Harbor Inn offers safety, tranquility, and access to good bird-watching at a low price. The rooms are pretty basic, with tile floors and small desks. The restaurant serves fish, burgers, and other light fare; you can eat at the nearby Meliá hotel, too, which also offers various tours of Gatún Lake. **Pros:** inexpensive; quiet; natural area. **Cons:** mediocre rooms and restaurant. ✉ *Calle Principal, Res. Espinar* ☎ *470–0640* ⊕ *www. harborinnpanama.com* ↩ *24 rooms, 3 suites* ⚬ *In-room: no phone, Wi-Fi. In-hotel: restaurant, bar, laundry service, Internet terminal, parking (free), no-smoking rooms* ⊟ *AE, MC, V* ⦿ *CP.*

$$$ 🏨 **Meliá Panama Canal.** Perched on a lush peninsula 10 km (6 mi) south
☾   of Colón and overlooking Lago Gatún, the Meliá occupies buildings that were once the School of the Americas, a controversial U.S. training academy for Latin American military officers. It now promotes nothing more insidious than sportfishing, bird-watching, and lounging by the pool, which is surrounded by a lawn hemmed by tropical foliage. The hotel's interior is grand, with an Old Spain motif, handsome wooden furniture, stained-glass windows, and a four-story atrium in the lobby. Rooms have picture windows, large bathrooms with tubs, and are decorated with hand-painted tiles. A casino and business center are on-site. The steak house has views of the illuminated jungle and often offers poolside barbecues. If you get a discount rate on the resort's Web site, this can be a decent base for a night or two. **Pros:** quiet; safe; natural environment; outdoor diversions. **Cons:** erratic service; grounds can be overrun with cruise-ship passengers. ✉ *End of Calle Principal, Res. Espinar* ☎ *470–1100; 888/956–3542 in the U.S. and Canada* ⊕ *www. solmelia.com* ↩ *285 rooms* ⚬ *In-room: refrigerator, room service, safe, Wi-Fi. In-hotel: 2 restaurants, bars, tennis courts, pool, gym, water sports, laundry service, Internet terminal, parking (free), no-smoking rooms* ⊟ *MC, V* ⦿ *BP.*

$$$ 🏨 **Radisson Colón 2000.** If you come to this part of Panama on busi
☾   ness, this is your best option. Despite the name, this hotel sits inside the Zona Libre rather than the Colón 2000 cruise port, which is two blocks away, but the vistas of the port and its attendant hubbub can be enjoyed from your balcony. Your fellow guests will likely be Latin

American business travelers, who have come to make wholesale Free Zone purchases. All in all, it's a safe, standard, dependable entry from the Radisson chain with good business services and enormous buffet breakfasts. **Pros:** quiet; safe; business amenities. **Cons:** facilities can be overrun with cruise-ship passengers when ships are in port. ☒ *Paseo Gorgas, Calle 13* ☎ *446–2000, 800/395–7046 in the U.S. and Canada* ⊕ *www.radisson.com* ➦ *70 rooms, 32 suites* ⚭ *In-room: refrigerator, safe, Wi-Fi. In-hotel: restaurant, room service, bar, tennis courts, pool, gym, laundry service, Internet terminal, parking (free), no-smoking rooms* ▭ *MC, V* ◎| *BP.*

SPORTS AND THE OUTDOORS
SPORTFISHING
The **Meliá Panama Canal** (☒ *Calle Principal, Res. Espinar* ☎ *470–1100* ⊕ *www.solmelia.com*) runs inexpensive fishing tours ($35) on Gatún Lake that are open to nonguests. The fishing gear is basic, but you can be pretty much guaranteed that you'll catch some peacock bass. The hotel also offers bird-watching and night tours on the lake for a minimum of four people.

SAN LORENZO PROTECTED AREA

40 km (25 mi) west of Colón.

For information about San Lorenzo's park, fort, tours, and accommodations, visit ⊕ www.achiotecoturismo.com and ⊕ www.sanlorenzo.org.pa.

Perched on a cliff overlooking the mouth of the Chagres River are the ruins of the ancient Spanish **Fuerte San Lorenzo** *(San Lorenzo Fort)*, destroyed by pirate Henry Morgan in 1671 and rebuilt shortly after, then bombarded a century later. The Spaniards built Fort San Lorenzo in 1595 in an effort to protect the South American gold they were shipping down the Chagres River, which was first carried along the Camino de Cruces from Panamá Viejo. The gold was then shipped up the coast to the fortified city of Portobelo, where it was stored until the Spanish armada arrived to carry it to Spain. The fortress's commanding position and abundant cannons weren't enough of a deterrent for Morgan, whose men managed to shoot flaming arrows into the fort, causing a fire that set off stored gunpowder and forced the Spanish troops to surrender. Morgan then led his men up the river and across the isthmus to sack Panamá Viejo.

In the 1980s UNESCO restored the fort to its current condition, which is pretty sparse—it hardly compares to the extensive colonial ruins of Portobelo. Nevertheless, the setting is gorgeous, and the view from that promontory of the blue-green Caribbean, the coast, and the vast jungle behind it is breathtaking. ⚠ **Be careful walking around the edge outside the fort; there are some treacherous precipices, and guardrails are almost nonexistent. One visitor did have a fatal fall several years ago.** ☒ *23 km (14 mi) northwest of Gatún Locks* ☎ *No phone* ⊠ *Free* ☉ *Daily 8–4.*

The wilderness just behind the Fuerte San Lorenzo is part of **Parque Nacional San Lorenzo**, a 23,843-acre (9,653-hectare) protected area that includes rain forest, wetlands, rivers, and coastline. For decades this was the U.S. Army's jungle training area, where tens of thousands of troops trained for warfare in the tropics. The army used parts of the park as a bombing range, and there may still be unexploded ordnance in its interior, though far from the roads and fortress. Today the park is the haunt of bird-watchers, who hope to focus their binoculars on some of the more than 400 bird species. Mammalian residents include spider monkey, armadillo, tamarin, and coati mundi. The lush forest here gets nearly twice as much rain as Panama City, and it doesn't lose as much of its foliage during the dry season. Most of that rain falls at night, so mornings are often sunny, even during the rainy season.

The most famous bird-watching area in Parque Nacional San Lorenzo is the **Achiote Road** (Camino a Achiote), which is about 25 km (15 mi) south of the fort. To reach it, turn left after crossing the locks and drive 15 km (9 mi) south. Members of the Panama Audubon Society once counted 340 bird species in one day on the Achiote Road during their Christmas bird count. Achiote is an excellent place to observe the massive hawk and vulture migration in October and March. The community of Achiote, about 4 km (2½ mi) northwest of the park on the Achiote Road, has trained birding guides and a visitor center with rustic accommodations. ⌧ *15 km (9 mi) west of Gatún Locks* ☏ *6664–2339* ▢ *Free* ☉ *Daily 8–4.*

GETTING HERE AND AROUND

It usually takes two hours to drive to San Lorenzo from Panama City and 40 minutes from Colón, if it doesn't take too long to cross the Gatún Locks. Follow directions for Colón, but turn left at the Centro Comercial Cuatro Altos, 8 km (5 mi) before Colón, and follow the signs to Esclusas de Gatún. After crossing the locks, veer right and drive 12 km (7 mi) to Fort Sherman. Turn left onto a dirt road after the entrance to Fort Sherman and drive another 11 km (6 mi) to the fort. The Achiote Road is reached by turning left after crossing the locks and driving 12 km (7 mi)—over the Gatún Dam—to the second road on the right. The town of Achiote is 10 km (6 mi) up that dirt road.

SPORTS AND THE OUTDOORS
BIRD-WATCHING
Members of the small community of Achiote operate a rural-tourism operation, **Achiote Natural** (☏ 6664–2339) with knowledgeable birding guides to Parque Nacional San Lorenzo. **Advantage Panama** (☏ 6676–2466 ⊕ *www.advantagepanama.com*), in Panama City, runs a full-day tour to San Lorenzo with the option of returning by train. Panama City–based operator **Ancon Expeditions** (☏ 269–9415 ⊕ *www. anconexpeditions.com*) can send you to Colón on the train, pick you up at the station, and drive you straight to San Lorenzo for bird-watching and exploring the fortress. The tour operator at the **Meliá Panama Canal** (⌧ *Calle Principal, Residencial Espinar, Colón* ☏ *470–1100* ⊕ *www. solmelia.com*) runs half-day trips to San Lorenzo. Colón-based **Nattur Panama** (☏ 442–1340 ⊕ *www.natturpanama.com*) can put together à la carte birding tours of San Lorenzo.

PORTOBELO

★ *99 km (62 mi) north of Panama City; 48 km (30 mi) northeast of Colón.*

Portobelo has an odd mix of colonial fortresses, clear waters, and lushly forested hills that help to explain why Christopher Columbus named it "beautiful port" in 1502 during his fourth and final voyage to the Americas. However, today's ugly little town of cement-block houses crowded higgledy-piggledy amid the ancient walls belies the name, not to mention the lovely setting. Nevertheless, Portobelo contains some of Panama's most interesting colonial ruins, with rusty cannons still lying in wait for an enemy assault, and is a UNESCO World Heritage Site, together with San Lorenzo. Depending on your timing, you can also see congo dancing or the annual Festival del Cristo Negro (⇨ *Black Christ Festival, below*). Between the turquoise sea, jungle, coral reefs (great for scuba diving or snorkeling), and beaches, you may feel like a castaway.

Once the sister city of Panamá Viejo, Portobelo was an affluent trading center during the 17th century, when countless tons of Spanish treasure passed through its customs house, and shiploads of European goods were unloaded on their way to South America. The Spaniards moved their Atlantic port in Panama from Nombre de Dios to Portobelo in 1597, since the deep bay was deemed an easier place to defend against pirates, who had raided Nombre de Dios repeatedly. During the next two centuries Portobelo was one of the most important ports in the Caribbean. Gold from South America was stored here after crossing the isthmus via the Camino de Cruces and Chagres River, awaiting semi-annual *ferias,* or trade fairs, in which a fleet of galleons and merchant ships loaded with European goods arrived for several weeks of business and revelry before sailing home laden with gold and silver. That wealth attracted pirates, who repeatedly attacked Portobelo, despite the Spanish fortresses flanking the entrance to the bay and a larger fortress near the customs house. After a century and a half of attacks, Spain began shipping its South American gold around Cape Horn in 1740, marking the end of Portobelo's ferias, and turning the town into an insignificant Caribbean port. What remains today is a mix of historic and tacky, twentieth-century structures surrounded by spectacular natural scenery that looks much the same as it did in Columbus's day.

You can explore Portobelo's historic sites in a couple of hours, which leaves plenty of time for outdoor diversions. Several beaches in the area are worth visiting, half a dozen diving and snorkeling spots are nearby, and the bird-watching is good, too.

The forested hills that rise up behind the bay are part of **Parque Nacional Portobelo** *(Portobelo National Park),* a vast marine and rain-forest reserve contiguous with Chagres National Park. Though several towns lie within the park, and much of its lowlands were deforested years ago, its inaccessible mountains are covered with dense forest that holds plenty of flora and fauna. Extending from offshore coral reefs up to the cloud forest atop 3,212-foot Cerro Brujo, the park comprises an array of ecosystems and is rich in biodiversity. While the coastal area is home to everything from ospreys to sea turtles, the mountains house spider monkeys, brocket deer, harpy eagles, and an array of other endangered wildlife. There is no proper park entrance, but you can explore patches of its forested coast and mangrove estuaries on boat trips from Portobelo, when you might see birds such as the ringed kingfisher and fasciated tiger heron.

Portobelo's largest and most impressive fort is **Fuerte San Jerónimo,** at the end of the bay, which is surrounded by the "modern" town. It was built in the 1600s but was destroyed by Vernon and rebuilt to its current state in 1758. Its large interior courtyard was once a parade ground, but it is now the venue for all annual celebrations involving congo dancers, including New Year's, Carnaval, the Festival de Diablos y Congos (shortly after Carnaval), and the town's patron saint's day (March 20).

Fuerte San Fernando, one of three Spanish forts you can visit at Portobelo, is surrounded by forest and is a good place to see birds. It lies directly across the bay from Batería Santiago, on the left as you drive toward town, a large structure with cannons pointed at the entrance to the bay. The youngest of Portobelo's forts, Batería Santiago was built in the 1860s, after Vernon's fateful attack (⇨ *"Pirates of the Caribbean"*). The thick walls are coral, which was cut from the platform reefs that line the coast. Coral was more abundant and easier to cut than the igneous rock found inland, so the Spanish used it for most construction in Portobelo. ■**TIP→ Local boatmen who are usually sitting near the dock next to Batería Santiago can take you across the bay to explore Fuerte San Fernando for $3.** They also offer transportation to several local beaches, as well as a trip into the estuary at the end of the bay. ⊠ *Surrounding Portobelo* ☎ *448–2165 or 442–8348* ☎ *Free* ۞ *24 hrs.*

One block east of the Real Aduana is the **Iglesia de San Felipe,** a large white church dating from 1814 that's home to the country's most venerated religious figure: the **Cristo Negro** (Black Christ). According to legend, that statue of a dark-skinned Jesus carrying a cross arrived in Portobelo in the 17th century on a Spanish ship bound for Cartagena, Colombia. Each time the ship tried to leave, it encountered storms and had to return to port, convincing the captain to leave the statue in Portobelo. Another legend has it that in the midst of a cholera epidemic in 1821 parishioners prayed to the Cristo Negro, and the community was spared. The statue spends most of the year to the left of the church's altar, but once a year it's paraded through town in the Festival del Cristo Negro (⇨ *below)*. Each year the Cristo Negro is clothed in a new purple robe, donated by somebody who's earned the honor. Many of the robes that have been created for the statue over the past century are on display in the Museo del Cristo Negro (Black Christ Museum) in the Iglesia de San Juan, a smaller, 17th-century church next to the Iglesia de San Felipe. ⊠ *Calle Principal* ☎ *No phone* ☎ *$1* ۞ *Weekdays 8–4, weekends 8:30–3.*

Near the entrance to Fuerte San Jerónimo is the **Real Aduana** *(Royal Customs House)*, where servants of the Spanish crown made sure that the king and queen got their cut from every ingot that rolled through town.

Built in 1630, the Real Aduana was damaged during pirate attacks and then destroyed by an earthquake in 1882, only to be rebuilt in 1998. It is an interesting example of colonial architecture—note the carved coral columns on the ground floor—and it houses a simple museum with some old coins, cannonballs, and displays on Panamanian folklore. ✉ *Calle de la Aduana* ☎ *No phone* 💰 *$1* ⏰ *Tues.–Sat. 9–4, weekends 8:30–3.*

GETTING HERE AND AROUND

Portobelo is a two-hour drive from Panama City and a mere 40 minutes from Colón. To drive there from Panama City, follow the directions to Colón but turn right after 60 km (37 mi), at the town of Sabanitas; from there it's 39 km (24 mi) to Portobelo. From Colón, head south toward Panama City for 15 km (9 mi) and turn left at Sabanitas. To get there by bus, take one of the Colón buses that depart from the Albrook bus terminal every 20 minutes and ask the driver to drop you off in Sabanitas, at the turnoff for Portobelo and Isla Grande. There, catch one of the buses to Portobelo, which pass every hour. There is no reason to go to Colón on your way to Portobelo, unless you take the Panama Canal Railway, in which case hire a taxi or rent a car and drive to Portobelo to avoid hanging out at the Colón bus terminal.

> **FESTIVAL DEL CRISTO NEGRO**
>
> Every October 21, tens of thousands of pilgrims walk or drive to Portobelo to venerate the Iglesia de San Felipe's Black Christ statue. Celebrations begin with an evening mass, followed by a very long procession led by people carrying the statue. Many devotees wear purple robes like the Cristo Negro's; some of them even crawl the last stretch to the church. While it attracts the devout, it's also a party, with drinking and less-than-pious behavior. The road to Portobelo becomes a giant traffic jam (take a boat from a dive center down the road), and ultimately the town is trashed.

WHERE TO EAT AND STAY

$$
SEAFOOD
✕ **Restaurante Los Cañones.** This rambling restaurant with tables among palm trees and Caribbean views is one of Panama's most attractive lunch spots. Unfortunately, the food and service fall short of the setting, but not so far that you'd want to scratch it from your list. In good weather, dine at tables edging the sea surrounded by dark boulders and lush foliage. The other option is the open-air restaurant, decorated with shells, buoys, and driftwood, with a decent view of the bay and forested hills. House specialties include *pescado entero* (whole fried red snapper), *langosta al ajillo* (lobster scampi), and *centolla al jengibre* (king crab in a ginger sauce). ✉ *2 km (1 mi) before Portobelo on left* ☎ *448–2980* ═ *No credit cards* ⏰ *Closes at 7 PM.*

¢–$
🏨 **Coco Plum Ecolodge.** This place has a great location on the water, but the rooms are set back from the sea in an uninspiring cement building. The owners have tried to compensate with a colorful, playful decor, and satellite TV, but rooms are still dark, and tiny bathrooms have plastic showerheads with the heating element inside them—common in the rest of Central America but a rarity in Panama. Common areas are more appealing: the thatched platform on the dock and the second-floor

PIRATES OF THE CARIBBEAN

It has been said that a third of the world's gold passed through Portobelo during the 17th century, and that wealth attracted plenty of pirates. Even before the Spanish founded a town there, the bay of Portobelo was a popular spot for pirates and buccaneers to rest or hide from Spanish galleons. The English navigator and privateer Sir Frances Drake, famous for circumnavigating the globe and capturing many a Spanish treasure, died of dysentery when anchored near the bay in 1596. Legend has it that Drake's men buried him at sea in a lead coffin near what is now known as Drake Island, just east of Portobelo (though why the pirate would have been traveling with a lead coffin begs questioning).

Spanish authorities established the town in Portobelo a year after Drake's demise, and the bay soon turned from a pirates' resting spot to a target. William Parker was the first to attack the Spanish enclave in 1602; he captured significant booty

and set a dangerous precedent. Henry Morgan captured the city in 1668 and held it for two weeks, until the Spanish government paid him a hefty ransom. During the interim he tortured prisoners and filled his ships with booty. Morgan was followed by the likes of John Coxon, Edward Cook, and other pirates and privateers. None of them matched Morgan's haul, or his treachery, but together they stole copiously and instilled terror in the local population.

English Admiral Edward Vernon attacked Portobelo with six ships and 2,500 men in 1739, managing to capture the city and destroy its fortresses. Soon afterward, Spain began shipping most of its South American riches around Cape Horn, and Portobelo slipped into obscurity. Only in recent years have foreigners begun descending on the ancient port in growing numbers. The treasures that attract today aren't gold and silver, but rather historic monuments and tropical nature.

lounge on the water, with a pool table. Sporting attractions include an on-site dive center, trips to nearby beaches, snorkeling tours, and hikes to a waterfall in the national park. The restaurant ($-$$), Las Anclas, makes up for its lack of a view with inventive dishes like *langostinos en salsa de piña y jengibre* (prawns in a pineapple-ginger sauce) or *cazuela de mariscos,* a seafood stew in coconut milk. **Pros:** natural setting; outdoor activities. **Cons:** small; dark rooms. ⊠ *5 km (3 mi) before Portobelo on left* ☎ *448–2102* ⊕ *www.cocoplum-panama.com* ↻ *8 rooms* ⚲ *In-room: no phone. In-hotel: restaurant, bar, diving, no-smoking rooms* ⊟ *No credit cards* ❑ *EP.*

¢-$ 🛏 **Scuba Portobelo.** A dive resort owned by Panama's biggest dive company, Scuba Panama, this small place has the best rooms in the Portobelo area, but since it works mostly with tour groups booked out of Panama City, it skimps on services. Accommodations range from dorm rooms to bungalows; the second-floor "single" rooms—small, but bright and colorful, with ocean views and narrow balconies—are nice for couples. Free-standing *cabañas* (bungalows) are considerably bigger and cost just $10 more. Large trees shade the ample grounds, and there's a gazebo atop some boulders over the water. The resort has a full dive center with inexpensive trips like snorkeling to Isla Mogotes. The tiny, open-air restaurant serves breakfast and a limited seafood-heavy menu, but there's better food down the road. Rates are slightly lower during the week. Pros: great location; inexpensive; scuba diving and snorkeling. Cons: rooms basic; limited service; little privacy. ⊠ *6 km (3 mi) before Portobelo on left* ☎ *448–2147* ⊕ *www.scubapanama.com* ⇱ *6 rooms, 5 cabañas* ⚸ *In-room: no phone, no TV. In-hotel: restaurant, diving, no-smoking rooms* ▤ *AE, MC, V* ⍩ *EP.*

SPORTS AND THE OUTDOORS

BEACHES
The easiest beach to visit in the vicinity of Portobelo is **Playa Langosta**, which is about 8 km (5 mi) south of Portobelo. You may have that dark-gray beach to yourself during the week, but on weekends and holidays it is usually packed with visitors from Colón and Panama City. There are more isolated beaches to the east of Portobelo that are accessible only by sea; boatmen who hang out at the docks next to the Batería Santiago and Fuerte San Jerónimo can take you to one for $20–$30 round-trip.

About 20 minutes east of Portobelo by boat, **Playa Huertas** is a long beach backed by tropical vegetation and a good place for swimming.

Playa Blanca is a small, white-sand beach about 30 minutes by boat east of Portobelo. It has the nicest sand of any beach in the area but is backed by pasture and homes.

BIRD-WATCHING
The bird-watching is quite good at the edge of town and around the ruins. Bird-watchers may want to hire one of the boatmen who hang out around the docks near Batería Santiago and Fuerte San Jerónimo to take them into the estuary behind town, which should cost $20.

HIKING
Salvaventura (☎ *442–1042*) is a small company, started by José Malet, that offers guided hikes into Portobelo National Park, including one to a small waterfall. Guides don't speak much English, though.

SCUBA DIVING AND SNORKELING
Miles of coral reefs awash in rainbows of underwater wildlife lie within the northern reaches of **Portobelo National Park,** and dive centers on the road to Portobelo provide easy access to those marine wonders. Though they've suffered some damage from fishermen and erosion, the reefs in the Portobelo area consist of nearly 50 coral species and are inhabited by more than 250 fish species. The underwater fauna ranges from moray eels to colorful butterfly fish, damselfish, trumpet fish, and other reef dwellers. Popular spots include Buffet Reef, a plane wreck, a shipwreck, and the distant Escribano Bank, east of Isla Grande. Visibility varies according to the sea conditions, but tends to be low from December to April, when high seas can hamper dives. The best conditions are between September and December. Most boat dives cost less than $50, and snorkeling equipment rentals are a mere $10 per day. PADI certification courses are also available.

Panama Divers (✉ *Coco Plum Ecolodge, 5 km [3 mi] before Portobelo on left* ☎ *314–0817* ⊕ *www.panamadivers.com*) a small American-owned company, offers various boat dives, tours, and courses. **Scuba Portobelo** (✉ *6 km [3 mi] before Portobelo on the left* ☎ *448–2147 or 261–3841* ⊕ *www.scubapanama.com*) is a dive center owned by Scuba Panama, the country's oldest dive operator.

ISLA GRANDE

10- to 20-min boat trip from La Guaira; 25 km (16 mi) east of Portobelo.

Lushly forested hills, palm fronds swaying in the breeze, and glistening aquamarine waters give Isla Grande an idyllic, tropical ambience, but its scarcity of beaches (it has just one decent beach) and crowded, cement-block town make it less attractive than some of the country's other coastal destinations. It's comparable to Bocas del Toro, though smaller and with fewer things to do. It's popular mostly for its proximity to Panama City—just over a two-hour drive—but don't sacrifice precious time in Bocas, Kuna Yala, or the Pearl archipelago for Isla Grande.

The island sits just a few hundred meters off the coast in front of the fishing town of **La Guaira,** a 30-minute drive east of Portobelo. Isla Grande (Big Island) is a misnomer, as the island is just 3 mi long. The funky little Afro-Caribbean community along its southern shore has neither roads nor addresses, people come and go by boat, and it takes less than 30 minutes to walk from one end of the island to the other. Most of the island is quite precipitous, and hills covered with dense foliage rise up just behind town, thus visits are generally confined to the town, the small beach on the island's western tip ($3 entrance fee), or the north-shore bay where Bananas Village Resort is located.

A nicer beach with better snorkeling can be found on **Isla Mamey** (⇨ *Sports and the Outdoors, below),* a short boat trip away. The main activity on Isla Grande, aside from eating and drinking, is scuba diving. Though the reefs here are in bad shape, they have a good variety of fish and other marine life. There are, however, dozens of dive spots within 20 to 60 minutes from the island by boat, including healthy coral reefs, caves, and shipwrecks.

On weekend and holidays Isla Grande can get crowded, which in Panama means noise and littering. During the week it's a ghost town, and it's sometimes tough to find a meal. About 1,000 people live on the island, surviving on a mix of fishing, farming on the mainland, and tourism. Despite their relative dependence on tourism, the people of Isla Grande are not terribly friendly. But they do a good job of preparing lobster and other local seafood. Ask at the restaurants in town if they have *fufu,* a seafood soup made with coconut milk, plantains, and jungle tubers such as *ñame.*

GETTING HERE AND AROUND

To drive to Isla Grande, follow the directions for Portobelo, but continue through town and veer left at the intersection just after it, following the signs to La Guaria. Buses to La Guaira, the departure point for Isla Grande, leave Sabanitas and Portobelo every hour from 8 to 5. Boatmen are usually waiting at the dock in La Guaira; they charge $2 for the 10-minute trip to the island and $5 to Bananas Village Resort.

WHERE TO STAY

$$$ ⊞ **Bananas Village Resort.** Nestled on the north side of the island in a
☾ private cove surrounded by jungle, Bananas is Isla Grande's best hotel
★ by far. Bright, spacious rooms are in two-story buildings between the gardens and the forest. The ocean views from the hammocks on their balconies alone make the trip worthwhile. Suites, built out over the water, have a more impressive view for just $15 more. Apart from the caged birds, the only disappointment is the tiny beach, which is atop a coral platform, so the water is shallow. A swimming area at the end of the property has a dock and a nearby open-air bar. The use of kayaks and snorkeling equipment is included in the rates, as are volleyball, Ping-Pong, and a saltwater pool. Excursions such as a boat trip to Isla Mamey are extra. Guests arrive and depart by water, but you can also hike the 30-minute cement trail through the forest to town. The open-air restaurant ($–$$$$) serves fresh seafood, pastas, paella, and steaks, with an ocean view. **Pros:** good views; quiet; lots of diversions; kid-friendly. **Cons:** inconsistent service; relatively expensive tours. ⊠ *North side of Isla Grande* ☎ *448–2252, 263–9510 in Panama City* ⊕ *www.bananasresort.com* ➦ *36 rooms* ☖ *In-room: no phone, safe, refrigerator (some), DVD (some). In-hotel: restaurant, bar, pool, beachfront, water sports, no-smoking rooms, parking (no fee)* ⊟ *AE, D, DC, MC, V* ◎❘ *BP.*

$ ⊞ **Sister Moon.** These rustic wooden bungalows perched along a steep hillside east of town have great views of the sea and mainland but cheap mattresses and no hot water. They feature colorful tile bathrooms and other artistic touches. The higher ones are more private and have the best views. The open-air restaurant next to a small saltwater pool and stone deck is a great place to hang out and watch the waves crash against the rocks below. This is the closest hotel to the surf break but the farthest from the town beach. The hotel offers numerous multiday, Web-only promotions. **Pros:** great ocean view; quiet. **Cons:** rooms rustic and small; far from beach. ⊠ *Isla Grande, east of town* ☎ *448–2182 or 236–9489* ⊕ *www.hotelsistermoon.com* ➦ *17 bungalows* ☖ *In-room: no a/c, no phone, no TV. In-hotel: restaurant, bar, pool, Internet terminal, some pets allowed, no-smoking rooms* ⊟ *MC, V* ◎❘ *BP.*

¢ ⊞ **Villa en Sueño.** Rooms in this brightly painted hotel in the heart of town are in two cement buildings behind the restaurant of the same name. They are simple but clean, with cold-water showers, decent beds, and shared porches with hammocks overlooking a small lawn lined with lush gardens. The restaurant in front has an ocean view and is one of the better places to eat in town. The on-site store rents snorkeling equipment and can arrange boat tours. On weekends and holidays the hotel can get pretty crowded, since the hotel rents picnic areas on the grounds, but it's usually dead during the week. **Pros:** central location; near beach; boat tours available; inexpensive. **Cons:** rooms very basic; little privacy; can be noisy. ⊠ *Isla Grande, in front of cross* ☎ *448–2964* ✉ *villaen@cwpanama.net* ➦ *16 rooms* ☖ *In-room: no*

3

phone, no TV. In-hotel: restaurant, water sports, no-smoking rooms
⊟ *AE, MC, V* ⏸|⊚| *EP.*

SPORTS AND THE OUTDOORS

BEACHES

The island has only one decent beach, on the grounds of the dilapidated
Hotel Isla Grande west of town, which charges nonguests $3. The
advantage is that it is less crowded on weekends, and there is always
a cold beer nearby. The nicest beach in the area is on **Isla Mamey,** an
excursion offered by the hotels and boatmen.

SCUBA DIVING AND SNORKELING

Isla Grande is surrounded by reefs, but the coral is in bad shape. The
best snorkeling is off the island's north side, near the Bananas Village
Resort. You'll find healthier coral and more fish at **Isla Mamey,** a popular excursion, or farther out on the fringe reefs. Local barrier reefs are
home to hundreds of fish and invertebrate species, including barracudas,
nurse sharks, and spotted eagle rays. There are also several shipwrecks
in the area, one of which dates from the 16th century.

Diving conditions are best during the rainy season, especially from
September to December.

The **Isla Grande Dive Center** (☎ *6501–4374 or 232–6994* ⊕ *www.*
buceoenpanama.com), next to the town dock, offers snorkeling trips
to Isla Mamey and other nearby islands, and scuba diving at more than
two dozen spots for reasonable prices. If the seas are calm, you can
arrange (more expensive) dives at the Escribano Bank—a long coral
reef to the east with some of the best coral formations on the Caribbean coast.

SURFING

There is a surf break on the east end island—a left reef break at El
Faro—though it's often flat. When it pumps, it is an intermediate to
expert spot, since it breaks over a mix of rock and coral. You are most
likely to find good waves there between December and April.

SANTA ISABELA

44 km (27 mi) east of Isla Grande, 26 km (16 mi) west of El Porvenir
(Kuna Yala).

To the east of the Isla Grande the coast becomes wilder, and the ocean
more pristine. Nestled in a remote cove about two-thirds of the way
between Isla Grande and the Kuna enclave of El Porvenir (⇨ *Chapter 6*),
is one of the country's best eco-lodges, Coral Lodge, which provides
access to miles of coral reefs that few divers have seen. Those reefs,
known as the Escribano Bank, hold giant sea fans, staghorn and elk-
horn coral, colorful sponges, legions of parrot fish, moray eels, and
several sea turtle species. The lodge is near the fishing village of Santa
Isabela, which is 16 km (10 mi) from the nearest road, in Miramar, and
29 km (18 mi) by water from the island of El Porvenir, which is reached
by daily plane flights. Coral Lodge thus allows you to experience the
beauty and culture of the Kuna Yala (of the San Blas Islands) without
having to stay in the rustic Kuna-run lodges.

WHERE TO STAY

$$$$ ⊡ **Coral Lodge.** Though not really in the San Blas Islands (which is in
Fodor's Choice Kuna Yala), Coral Lodge is the hotel most closely associated with Pan-
★ ama's best-known indigenous territory. The idyllic cove here is the stuff
of tropical fantasies: emerald waters washing over coral reefs and a
golden beach backed by jungle. Miles from the nearest road, halfway
between El Porvenir and the village of Miramar, this remote eco-lodge
combines constant exposure to nature with such creature comforts as
air-conditioning and excellent food. Spacious, octagonal bungalows
stand over the water atop coral platforms, with waves washing beneath
them. A ladder from the wraparound balcony lets you climb into the
crystalline sea whenever you feel the urge, and the view of the lagoon
and coast is hypnotic. The bungalows are wonderfully designed, with
high thatched roofs, cane furniture, and Indonesian art. A walkway
connects them to a small beach, the pool, and an open-air restaurant
over the water. Snorkeling equipment and kayaks are included in the
rates; scuba diving, horseback riding, and rain-forest trips are extra. It's
quite expensive, but rather than luxury, the Coral Lodge offers exposure
to pristine nature with more comfort and better food than you'll get in
Kuna Yala proper (⇨ *Porvenir in Chapter 6*), which can be visited as
a half-day trip. **Pros:** gorgeous scenery; excellent scuba diving; kayaking; good food; friendly. **Cons:** expensive; no-see-ums a problem in
rainy season; boat rides rough in dry season. ⊠ *Santa Isabela, 25 km
(16 mi) west of Porvenir by sea* ☎ *832–0795, or 232–0200 in Panama
City Apdo. 0843-02518, Balboa, Panama* ⊕ *www.corallodge.com* ⇦ *8
bungalows* ⚥ *In-room: no phone, no TV. In-hotel: 2 restaurants, bar,
pool, beachfront, diving, water sports, Internet terminal, no kids under
10, no-smoking rooms* ⊟ *MC, V* ⎮⊙⎮ *FAP.*

THE EASTERN SIERRAS

A large mass of mountains rises up to the northeast of the waterway,
and most of the rain that falls on it provides the water used by the
canal's locks. The Panamanian government has consequently protected
that vast watershed within Parque Nacional Chagres. Chagres is contiguous with Portobelo National Park—the relatively small Sierra Llorona defines the border between the two parks—and its southern border
runs through a collection of hills known as Cerro Azul, which is the
closest highland area to Panama City. To the east of Parque Nacional
Chagres, the Serranía de San Blas stretches eastward toward Colombia. That long, narrow mountain range defines the southern border of
the *comarca*—or autonomous indigenous territory—of Kuna Yala. The
area to the south of it is known as Alto Bayano, and contains the vast
Lago Bayano, a hydroelectric reservoir created in the 1970s.

SIERRA LLORONA

80 km (50 mi) north of Panama City, 22 km (14 mi) southeast of Colón.

Sierra Llorona is a small but steep mountain range east of Gatún Lake and southwest of Portobelo that spends much of the year enveloped in clouds, and the abundant waterfalls that result from that rain are the origin of the range's name, which translates as "crybaby sierra." The sierra stretches southwestward from Portobelo and Chagres national parks to a sparsely populated area where you'll find the family-run Sierra Llorona Lodge, on a 500-acre private reserve that is home to hundreds of bird species and an array of other wildlife. The lodge is well worth spending a night or two at, but day visitors get lunch and a local guide for $35.

GETTING HERE AND AROUND

It's an easy one-hour drive to Sierra Llorona from Panama City. Follow directions for Colón and turn right shortly before Sabanitas, at a sign for Santa Arriba and Sierra Llorona, from where it's a 4½ km (3 mi) drive up a narrow, windy road. In the rainy season a four-wheel-drive vehicle is recommended for the last stretch. The Sierra Llorona Lodge has detailed instructions on its Web site and can pick guests up in either Panama City or Colón.

WHERE TO STAY

$$ ⊡ **Sierra Llorona Panama Lodge.** Birdsong is the Muzak at the Sierra Llo-
★ rona Lodge, where the chirping plays from sunup to sundown, and the gardens are visited by an array of winged creatures from snowy-bellied hummingbirds to clay-colored robins. The lodge is surrounded by 500 acres of protected rain forest that can be explored on 6 km (4 mi) of trails, but many visitors are happy to sit in the garden and wait for the birds to come to them. The lodge is simple but comfortable, with rooms in the old family home and a nearby wooden building that has small balconies overlooking the woods. Rooms at the ends of that building are brighter, though all are quite spacious. Rooms in the house are farther from the forest, but the bright suite on the second floor, with a Jacuzzi, is worth the extra $20. The restaurant serves a set menu, which changes daily. A local guide, who speaks very little English, is included in the rates, but if you want a bilingual birding guide, you'll need to request one when you reserve and pay extra. Massages can be arranged a day in advance. The lodge is a short drive up narrow country roads from the Transístmica (the lodge's Web site has driving directions). The lodge can provide transportation from either Panama City or Colón. **Pros:** good bird-watching; forest; hiking. **Cons:** service inconsistent. ⊠ *Santa Rita Arriba, 4½ km (3 mi) east of Transístmica* ☎ *442–8104* ⊕ *www. sierrallorona.com* ⌁ *7 rooms, 1 suite* ⅋ *In-room: no a/c, no phone, no TV. In-hotel: restaurant, bar, bicycles, laundry service, Internet terminal, no-smoking rooms* ⊟ *MC, V* ⅏ *BP.*

PARQUE NACIONAL CHAGRES (CHAGRES NATIONAL PARK)

40 km (24 mi) north of Panama City.

The mountains to the northeast of the canal form a vast watershed that feeds the Chagres River, which was one of the country's principal waterways until it was damned to create the canal, and is now the source of nearly half of the water used in the locks. To protect the forests that help water percolate into the ground and keep the river running through the dry season, the Panamanian government declared the entire watershed a national park in 1985. It is one of the country's largest parks, covering more than 320,000 acres, and it holds an array of ecosystems and expanses of inaccessible wilderness that is home to spider monkeys, harpy eagles, toucans, tapirs, and other endangered species. The park's northern border, defined by Sierra Llorona, and its southern extreme, in Cerro Azul, are the easiest areas to visit, thanks to paved roads. Most people visit the national park on day tours from Panama City to one of several Emberá villages, but you can see more of its forests on a white-water rafting trip down the Chagres River or by hiking on the trails of Cerro Azul.

All the major tour operators in Panama City offer day trips to **Emberá villages** in the park (⇨ *"Tours," in Panama City Essentials, Chapter 2*). Visiting the villages—relocated here from Alto Bayano three decades ago, when their land was flooded by a hydroelectric project—is an interesting cultural experience, but most itineraries aren't great for seeing wildlife. The Emberá's traditional territory stretches from eastern Panama to northwest Colombia, but the relocated communities live much as their relatives to the east do, in thatched huts with elevated floors and scant walls. Years of exposure to Western society and religion have led most people in the Chagres communities to wear clothes, but they switch to traditional dress when they know a tour is coming. The men wear loincloths and women wrap themselves in bright-color cloth skirts and no tops, sometimes covering their breasts with large necklaces. Men and women often paint their upper bodies with a dye made from mixing the sap of the *jagua* fruit with ashes. The tours are a bit of a show, but they provide an interesting introduction to Emberá culture. (However, if you will be traveling to the Darién or Alto Bayano, you can get a more authentic, if less picturesque, Emberá experience there.) Tours usually include demonstrations of how the Emberá live, a traditional dance, handicraft sales, and optional painting of visitors' arms with *jagua*. (Note the *jagua* tattoos take more than a week to wash off.) The community that receives the most visitors is Parara Puru, because it is accessible year-round. The town of San Juan de Pequiní, farther up river, can be difficult to reach in the dry season, but it is a less scripted trip that includes some exposure to nature. The best trip for nature lovers and adventurers is to Emberá Drua, which only the small companies book, since it entails a boat trip deeper into the park and a tough hike. For those who are up to the hike, this is the most authentic village trip in the Chagres area. ⊠ *Transístmica, Km. 40* ☎ *500–0080* ✆ *Free* ☉ *Daily 8–5.*

GETTING HERE AND AROUND

The only part of Parque Nacional Chagres that you can easily visit on your own is the Cerro Azul area (⇨ *below*). To get deeper into the park, you have to take a tour.

SPORTS AND THE OUTDOORS

HIKING

Serious hikers can trek deep into the jungles of Parque Nacional Chagres by following the old **Camino Real** across the mountains to the Caribbean coast. Spanish colonists built the ""Royal Road"" in the 16th century to carry gold and other goods between Panamá Viejo and the Caribbean port of Nombre de Dios, and most of that route remains surrounded by lush rain forest. Weeklong trips organized by **Ancon Expeditions** (☎ 269–9415 ⊕ *www.anconexpeditions.com*) include visits to colonial ruins and an Emberá village and several nights in tent camps in the national park, plus lots of exposure to tropical nature.

WHITE-WATER RAFTING

Aventuras Panama (☎ 260–0044 ⊕ *www.aventuraspanama.com*) runs white-water rafting trips on the Chagres River (class II–III), which flows through the heart of Parque Nacional Chagres. The full-day trip requires no previous rafting experience. It begins with a long drive down dirt roads deep into the national park, followed by a five-hour river trip that includes a picnic lunch. The trip is available only from May to late March; it lasts 11 to 12 hours and costs $165.

SHOPPING

A big part of a visit to an Emberá village is the opportunity to buy authentic indigenous handicrafts from the artisans themselves. Among the items usually sold are tightly woven baskets and platters, and animal figures carved from *tagua* palm seeds, or *cocobolo* wood. The baskets are much more expensive if you buy them in craft markets in Panama City.

CERRO AZUL

45 km (27 mi) northeast of Panama City.

This highland retreat a short drive east of Panama City offers a bit of relief from the heat, plus hiking trails and some birds than you won't find in the canal area. The altitude is close to 3,000 feet above sea level, and when there is a breeze it can be pleasantly cool; you may even need a light jacket if you spend the night. Cerro Azul translates as ""blue hill,"" but the predominant color here is green, since the northern half of these mountains is draped in a blanket of lush forest protected within Parque Nacional Chagres, and the area along the roadways is dominated by Honduran pines that were planted after a U.S. company deforested the hills to create pasture decades ago. The tiny community of Cerro Azul is next to a small lake completely surrounded by homes and fences.

GETTING HERE AND AROUND

It takes less than an hour to drive to Cerro Azul from downtown Panama City. Take the Corredor Sur to Tocumen Airport, turn left before the airport onto the Interamericana (CA1), following the signs to Chepo, and turn left again a few kilometers later, after the Super Xtra. The road will soon begin to climb, passing a large horse statue and some lovely views of Panama City before reaching the small collection of homes and restaurants around the lake that marks the center of Cerro Azul. The entrance to Los Nubes, where Casa de Campo is located, is on the left about a kilometer after the lake, and the entrance to Altos de Cerro Azul is on the left after that. You should be able to hire a taxi to take you to Cerro Azul for $10 to $15 per hour. To arrive by bus, catch an eastbound city bus with 4 DE DICIEMBRÉ on its windshield (on Calle 50), and get off at the terminal behind the Super Xtra, where buses leave for Cerro Azul every 30 minutes.

WHERE TO EAT AND STAY

$ ✕ **La Posada de Ferhisse.** Perched on a hill across the street from the lake,
LATIN AMERICAN this simple open-air restaurant is the best place to have lunch in Cerro Azul. The menu is predominantly Panamanian, with a few twists, such as the *colombo de pollo* (chicken in a mild curry sauce) and *chilindrín de cordero* (lamb in a tomato and beer sauce). There is a pool below the restaurant that is open to the public for a small fee, and next to that are a few basic, inexpensive rooms for rent. ⊠ *Calle Principal, on right* ☎ 297–0197 ☰ *MC, V.*

¢ 🛏 **Cabañas Turismaru.** This is the best option for travelers on a tight budget. Rooms are in cement duplexes with high ceilings, colorful paint jobs, sparse furnishings, and small porches with hammocks. Most overlook the pool, but those in the back—rooms 11 and 12—view some of the verdure and are quieter. There is a small playground, and a restaurant above the lobby serves basic Panamanian fare. **Pros:** inexpensive. **Cons:** very basic. ⊠ *Calle Prinicipal, across from lake* ☎ 297–0213 ⬑ *12 rooms* ⚹ *In-room: no a/c, no phone. In-hotel: restaurant, pool, laundry service, no-smoking rooms* ☰ *No credit cards* ⦿| *EP.*

$–$$ 🛏 **Hostal Casa de Campo.** Nestled among tall trees in the quiet residential neighborhood of Los Nubes, this small inn is a good spot to relax or watch some birds, but its rooms are a mixed bag. The nicest ones are in the main house—a former vacation home that has been decorated with a pleasant mix of antiques, wicker furniture, and an eclectic collection of art. The Hiedra and Geranios rooms share a large balcony with a hammock, table, and chairs. The bright suite, Orquídeas, is the nicest room of all, with a king bed, plus two singles on request. The other rooms tend to be dark and a bit musty, especially the newer cabañas in the back, which have stone walls and open onto wide covered terraces. In front of the restaurant are a small pool and a Jacuzzi, with a large barbecue that is fired up for weekend lunches. Spa services and yoga are available with reservations, but Panama City's many spas are much better options. Casa de Campo isn't all it could be, but it is nevertheless a tranquil, pleasant spot. The hotel does offer numerous Web-only promotions. **Pros:** natural surroundings; nice decor; transport from Panama City. **Cons:** some rooms dark; untidy. ⊠ *Urbanización Los*

Nubes (turn left after lake) ☎297–0067, 226—0074 *in Panama City* ⊕ *www.panamacasadecampo.com* ⇨ *11 rooms, 4 cabanas* ⚊ *In-room: no a/c, no phone. In-hotel: restaurant, bar, pool, laundry service, nosmoking rooms* ⊟ *MC, V* ⊙*EP.*

SPORTS AND THE OUTDOORS

HIKING

The most accessible hiking trails into the forests of Chagres National Park are beyond the town of Cerro Azul in a large housing development called **Altos de Cerro Azul** (⊠ *Entrance on left a few km after lake* ☎ *279–7189*), owned by the Melo corporation, a Panamanian conglomerate. However, because it is a private, guarded development, you should call ahead to get the name of a salesperson to give the guard, even if you don't look at real estate.

Several kilometers after entering Altos de Cerro Azul, there is a small waterfall on the right called **Cascada el Vigia.** Continue on for several kilometers more to a road on the left called El Valle de Alcanzar. Turn left onto it and drive to the end to the entrance to the **Sendero el Patriarca,** a trail that heads about 5 km (3 mi) into the forest to a massive mahogany tree called the Patriarch. If that seems like too long a hike, you can take a shorter trail called **Sendero Romeo y Julieta** that branches off Sendero El Patriarca after about 1 km, and leads to two small lakes another kilometer deeper into the forest. To access a third trail, **Sendero Cantar,** which makes a 2-km (1½-mi) loop through the forest, continue straight at the intersection with El Valle de Alcanzar, and stay on the main road to the far end of the development, veer right after a small lake, and follow Calle Andora to the end. If you get lost, ask somebody to point you in the direction of El Mirador. The dirt road that leaves Calle Andora on the left shortly before the trailhead leads to the **Mirador Vistamar,** a scenic overlook atop a small hill from which you can see most of Parque Nacional Chagres on a clear day, including the forested peaks of Cerro Jefe and Cerro Brewster, and Sierra Llorona in the distance. ■**TIP**➜ **You should head to the Mirador first, because the earlier you get there, the clearer the view will be.**

HORSEBACK RIDING

Margo Tours (☎ *302–0390* ⊕ *www.margotours.com*) offers half-day horseback-riding tours through the pastures and forest of the Haras Orillac Ranch, on the slopes of Cerro Azul.

ALTO BAYANO

100 km (60 mi) northeast of Panama City.

The Alto Bayano region is dominated by a large reservoir called Lago Bayano, which is surrounded by pastureland, and forests clinging to the upper slopes of the *serranías* (mountain ranges) to the north and south. There are various Emberá villages on the rivers that flow into the lake, and a dirt track heads north from it to the autonomous indigenous territory, or *comarca,* of Kuna Yala, which holds vast expanses of rain forest.

The road that heads north to Kuna Yala, known as the Llano-Cartí Road, leads to the private nature reserve of **Burbayar** (⇨ *Where to Stay, below)*, which offers access to lush forests that are home to ocelots, night monkeys, dozens of snakes and frog species, and hundreds of bird species.

The indigenous community of **Unión Emberá**, on the Río Majé in the southeast corner of Lago Bayano, receives a tiny fraction of the visitors that the Emberá communities in Parque Nacional Chagres do. To visit, you can hire a boat (about $50) at the bridge where the Interamericana crosses a sliver of Bayano Lake. The Burbayar nature reserve organizes visits to Unión Emberá as an add-on to overnights at the lodge. An interesting addition to a trip here is a bit of spelunking in La Cueva del Tigre (⇨ *Sports and the Outdoors, below)*.

GETTING HERE AND AROUND

Alto Bayano lies 100 km (60 mi) east of Panama City, which is reached by driving east on the Corredor Sur and turning left onto the Interamericana (CA1) right before Tocumen Airport. Transportation to and from Burbayar Lodge is included for guests.

WHERE TO STAY

$$$$ ★ 🏨 **Burbayar Lodge.** Perched on a ridge on the western end of the Serranía de San Blas, surrounded by the forests of the eponymous 150-acre private reserve, Burbayar was created by and for nature lovers. Its cabins overlook the treetops, where you might spot collared *aracaris*, brown-hooded parrots, or any of the other 320 bird species found in the area. Rare specimens such as the speckled ant shrike and broad-billed sapayoa draw serious birders, but all guests enjoy the abundant hummingbirds, howler monkeys, and other jungle denizens. Nearly 20 km (12 mi) of trails wind through the adjacent forest, which borders the *comarca* Kuna Yala. A day hike takes you to a 220-foot waterfall deep in the jungle. Rooms are comfortably rustic, with thatched roofs, varnished wood, small bathrooms, and balconies with forest views. Meals are served family-style on the porch of the main house and are included in the rates along with a guide, equipment, and transport to and from Panama City. The owner, Ignacio Ruiz, has taken pains to make Burbayar as environmentally friendly as possible. **Pros:** small; surrounded by forest; hiking. **Cons:** rustic rooms. ✉ *Camino Llano-Cartí, Km 15* ☎ *390–6674* ⊕ *www.burbayar.com* ➾ *7 rooms, none with bath* ⚲ *In-room: no a/c, no phone, no TV In-hotel: restaurant, no-smoking rooms* ⊟ *No credit cards* ⦙⦙ *FAP.*

SPORTS AND THE OUTDOORS

SPELUNKING

La Cueva del Tigre *(Jaguar's Cave)* is a large cave with a stream running through it on the southern shore of Bayano Lake. You'll need a good flashlight and a set of clothes and shoes that can get wet to explore the cave, which has waterfalls inside it. Boats can be hired (about $50) at the bridge where the Inter-American Highway crosses Bayano Lake—ask them to take you to the village of Pueblo Nuevo de Bayano; from there you can have locals point you in the direction of the cave.

THE CENTRAL PACIFIC ISLANDS

The Gulf of Panama holds more than a dozen islands and countless rocky islets, which include Isla Taboga, a mere 20 km (12 mi) south of Panama City, and the Archipelago de las Perlas (Pearl Islands), which are scattered across the gulf between 60 and 90 km (about 40 to 60 mi) southeast of the city. Isla Taboga has a historic town lined with vacation homes, whereas the Pearl Islands remain largely undeveloped, with a few fishing villages and vast expanses of rain forest. Only two of the Pearl Islands currently have hotels: Isla Contadora, which has several, as well as dozens of homes, and Isla San José, which has the eco-resort of Hacienda del Mar. The aquamarine waters that wash against the islands hold varied and abundant marine life, especially the sea south of Isla San José, so there are opportunities for sportfishing, scuba diving, and whale watching to complement the beaches.

The islands were inhabited well before the Spaniards arrived in Panama, as petroglyphs found on some of them attest. Isla Taboga became a Spanish stronghold from the start due to its deep bay, ideal for mooring ships close to shore. The Spanish conquistador Francisco Pizarro defeated the indigenous leader of the Pearl Islands, King Toe, in 1515. Pizarro stole plenty of pearls from Toe's people, and the Spanish government continued to exploit the archipelago's pearl beds for the next two centuries, first with indigenous labor, and later, with African slaves, after disease decimated the indigenous population. Overexploitation exhausted the pearl supply in the 19th century, and since then the archipelago's inhabitants have survived on fishing, tourism, and building vacation homes.

Because the Pearl Archipelago is so extensive, its islands were often the haunt of pirates, who used them as bases from which to attack Spanish galleons carrying South American gold to Panama during the 16th and 17th centuries. More recently, the archipelago has been exploited by a new breed of opportunist: the producers of the *Survivor* reality television series, who have based three seasons here (2003, 2004, and 2006). Modern-day invaders have discovered that the islands' true treasures are their beaches and ocean views, and their hotel supply will likely expand in the near future.

ISLA TABOGA

20 km (12 mi) south of Panama City.

A pleasant 60-minute ferry ride from the Amador Causeway takes you far from the traffic jams of Panama City to the tranquil isle of Taboga, which has a lovely beach, clear waters, and a funky little fishing village. Since the island lies so close to the city, most people visit on day trips, but it does have hotels and is worth an overnight.

Dominated by two large hills, Isla Taboga is known as the "Island of Flowers" for the abundant gardens of its small town, **San Pedro,** spread along the steep hillside of its eastern shore. One of the country's oldest towns, San Pedro was founded in 1524, though its whitewashed church is the only surviving structure from the colonial era; folks here

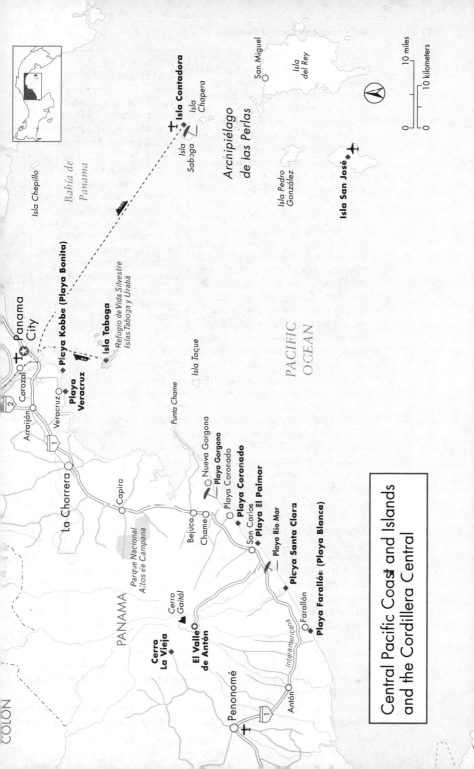

Central Pacific Coast and Islands
and the Cordillera Central

claim it is the second-oldest still-operating church in the Americas. The conquistador Francisco Pizarro embarked from Taboga in 1530 on his voyage to crush the Inca Empire, and it remained an important port until the 20th century. Because of the extreme variation of Panama's Pacific tides, ships were unable to moor near the coast of Panama, so the deep bay on Taboga's eastern shore was the perfect alternative. The Spanish built a fortress on Taboga in an attempt to defend the bay from pirates, the Pacific Steamship Company was based there during the 19th century, and the French built a sanatorium on the island during their attempt to build a canal. Upon completion of the canal, with its various docks and marinas, Taboga became what

> ## TABOGA'S LOSS, TAHITI'S GAIN
>
> Near Isla Taboga's central plaza stand the ruins of a colonial-era house where French painter Paul Gauguin lived for three months in 1887. The island's beauty captivated the artist, but, try as he might, Gauguin could not scrape together the funds to buy property here. Discouraged, he returned to mainland Panama where he took a construction job on the French team's 1880s efforts to construct a canal. Unable to take the trying working conditions, he lasted two weeks. Gauguin continued westward to Tahiti, and the rest, as they say, is history.

it is today, a sleepy fishing village that wakes up on weekends and holidays, when visitors from the capital arrive en masse.

Though it has a few historic buildings and ruins in the area of the church, San Pedro is mostly made up of the humble abodes of fishermen and the weekend homes of families from Panama City, which occupy most of the waterfront. There are few vehicles on the island, and most of its streets resemble extra-wide sidewalks. The main road runs along the town beach, Playa Honda, which lines a small bay holding dozens of fishing boats. Many of the bougainvillea-lined streets pass shrines to the Virgen del Carmen, considered the protector of fishermen throughout Latin America, who is celebrated every July 16 here.

Isla Taboga's main attractions are its two beaches: **Playa Honda,** the beach in front of town, and **Playa Restinga,** a spit of sand that connects Taboga with the tiny island of El Morro, just north of town. At low- or mid-tide, Playa Restinga is a gorgeous swath of golden sand flanked by calm waters, but at high tide it almost completely disappears. It's often packed on weekends and holidays, when the radios and screaming kids can be a bit too much, but it is practically deserted on most weekdays. For years Playa Restinga was accessible only via the Hotel Taboga, which was demolished in 2005, but a resort planned for that site could eventually restrict access to it. Playa Honda, the beach in front of town, is unfortunately unattractive, a bit rocky, and dirty—you are as likely to see vultures on it as seagulls—though it does retain a bit of sand at high tide. ⚠ San Pedro's sewage flows untreated into the bay, so **swimming at Playa Honda, or even on the south side of Playa Restinga, is not recommended.**

Aside from swimming and sunbathing, Taboga's outdoor options include snorkeling around El Morro, hiking, fishing, or a boat trip around the island. Trails lead to the island's two highest points: Cerro de la Cruz, a hill south of town that is topped with a 20-foot cross, and Cerro Vigia, the mountain behind town. A **wildlife refuge** covers the western half of Isla Taboga and the nearby island of Urabá, which is the best dive spot in the area. One of the best parts of going to Isla Taboga is actually the trip itself, since the ferry passes dozens of massive ships and provides great views of the islands and the city.

The **traditional celebrations** on Isla Taboga are on June 29, when the local parishioners celebrate San Pedro's day, and July 16, when the Virgen del Carmen is celebrated with a procession through town and a boat caravan around the island. Taboga is truly a bedroom community of Panama City, and it consequently has no pharmacy, and only a very small clinic. △ **There is no ATM on Taboga, so stock up on cash before heading there**—Isla Perico near the ferry dock on the Amador Causeway has ATMs.

GETTING HERE AND AROUND

Barcos Calypso Taboga (✉ *Marina Isla Naos* ☎ *314–1730*) has a daily ferry service to Taboga departing from the marina on Isla Naos, on the Amador Causeway. The trip takes one hour. The ferry leaves Monday, Wednesday, and Friday at 8:30 and 3; Tuesday and Thursday at 8:30 only; and weekends and holidays at 8, 10:30, and 4. The ferry departs from Taboga from the pier on the west end of town Monday, Wednesday, and Friday at 9:30 and 4:30; Tuesday and Thursday at 4:30; and weekends and holidays at 9, 3, and 5. △ **On weekends and holidays you should arrive 30 minutes before departure to buy your ticket.**

WHERE TO STAY

$-$$$ ▢ **Cerrito Tropical.** Perched at the top of a steep hill at the edge of the forest, this two-story apartment rental has good views, especially from the second-floor balcony. The Canadian owners have two apartments, which are a great deal for two couples or a family, but they can also be split and rented separately, with use of a full kitchen. The rooms are in the back and lack views, but they are spacious, with ceiling fans, private baths, and tiny TVs. People tend to spend most of their time on the wide terraces, which have a hammock, table, and chairs, so they can enjoy the ocean views. **Pros:** great views; quiet. **Cons:** far from beach; steep hike from the ferry. ✉ *6 blocks south of ferry dock* ☎ *390–8999* ⊕ *www.cerritotropicalpanama.com* ⟿ *5 rooms* ⟡ *In-room: DVD, no phone, Wi-Fi. In-hotel: laundry service, no smoking rooms* ▤ *No credit cards* ⟋ *CP*.

¢ ▢ **Cool Hostal.** Isla Taboga's backpacker option, this tiny hostel has two private rooms with two single beds each, as well as a small dorm. In a quiet, shady compound steps from the ferry dock and Playa Restinga, the hostel has a picnic table out front and a kitchen available to guests. **Pros:** cheap; quiet; near beach. **Cons:** small beds; foam mattresses; shared bath. ✉ *Uphill from ferry dock* ☎ *6596–2545* ✍ *luisveron@ hotmail.com* ⟿ *2 rooms, 1 dorm, none with private bath* ⟡ *In-room: no a/c, no phone, kitchen, no TV. In-hotel: laundry service, no-smoking rooms* ▤ *No credit cards* ⟋ *CP*.

$　⚏ **Hotel Vereda Tropical.** Isla Taboga's best hotel, the Vereda Tropical is perched on the hillside overlooking the Bay of Panama. Its best rooms share a view of the town's fishing fleet, cargo ships, and Panama City, which is almost as impressive at night, when the ship lights glow against the dark sea. Rooms have high ceilings, fans, Guatemalan-made bedspreads, and small bathrooms with colorful tile. The best rooms have French doors that open onto Juliet balconies with ocean views—well worth the extra money, since the cheapest rooms overlook rooftops and can be noisy. You may want to eat at the restaurant ($–$$) even if you don't stay here; it's the best kitchen on the island, and the terrace view is gorgeous. The eclectic menu includes a good pizza selection, pastas with a choice of about a dozen sauces, lobster served various ways, curried prawns, and *paella.* The house specialty is *corvina* (sea bass) in a coconut milk–passion fruit sauce. **Pros:** great views; good restaurant; short walk to beach. **Cons:** staff not friendly; some noise. ⊠ *100 meters south of ferry dock* ☎ *250–2154* ⊕ *www.veredatropicalhotel.com* ⇗ *10 rooms* ⌂ *In-room: no a/c (some), no phone. In-hotel: restaurant, laundry service, Internet terminal, no-smoking rooms* ⊟ *MC, V* ⑩| *CP.*

SPORTS AND THE OUTDOORS
HIKING
Hiking up one of Isla Taboga's two hills is an invigorating effort rewarded by amazing views. The easiest hike is to the top of **Cerro de La Cruz,** the smaller hill south of town that is topped by a 20-foot cross. You reach the trail by following the main street south along the coast and all the way through town until it becomes a dirt road; look for the footpath heading up the hill to the left. Since the hill is almost completely deforested, wear a hat and use sunblock. If you stay on the dirt road, it will take you to the top of **Cerro Vigia,** the highest point on the island, at 1,200 feet. There is a lookout point on the summit, which has the remains of a U.S. Army spotlight installation built during World War II. A nicer, though steeper, trail to the top of Cerro Vigia heads through the forest above town. To take that route, go up the street next to Restaurant Acuario, follow the trail into the forest, and when you reach the three crosses follow the road to the summit. ⚠ **Either hike should be done early in the morning or later in the afternoon,** since it is simply too hot in the middle of the day for such exertion.

SNORKELING
The snorkeling is pretty good around El Morro, where the visibility is best when the tide is coming in. Serious divers head to Isla Urubá, a protected island just south of Taboga.

The **Hotel Vereda Tropical** (☎ *470–1100* ⊕ *www.veredatropicalhotel.com*) rents snorkeling equipment to guests for $8 and can arrange a boat ride around the island for $50 that includes snorkeling at Isla Urubá. Taboga lacks a dive center, but the Panama City–based operator **Scuba Panama** (☎ *261–3841* ⊕ *www.scubapanama.com*) can arrange diving around Taboga.

ISLA CONTADORA

70 km (43 mi) southeast of Panama City.

The resort island of Contadora, a mere 20 minutes from Panama City by plane, has some of the country's best beaches. More than a dozen swaths of ivory sand backed by exuberant foliage line Contadora's perimeter, and they lie within walking distance of accommodations to fit any budget. It is a small island, covering less than a square mile, but it can serve as a base for day trips to nearby isles with deserted beaches and snorkeling sites, as well as deep-sea fishing, scuba diving, and whale watching. There is enough to see and do on Isla Contadora to fill several days, and if all you're looking for in Panama is sun, sea, and sand, you could easily spend a week there.

The Pearl Archipelago's indigenous inhabitants undoubtedly had another name for Contadora, but its current name, which translates as "counting isle," was given to it nearly five centuries ago, when it held the offices of the Spanish crown's pearl-diving enterprise. The island was deserted for years after the pearl harvest diminished. Contadora gained its current status as a resort isle in the 1970s, when wealthy Panamanians began to buy coastal property here. The government then built the massive Hotel Contadora—now closed and undergoing some type of renovation, although nobody seems sure just *what* its future reincarnation will be—and the island developed a healthy weekend party scene. The island's most famous temporary resident was the deposed Shah of Iran on the heels of the Tehran embassy takeover in 1979, who spent some of his last days on the island. Contadora's star faded a bit in the 1980s and '90s, and it isn't quite the haunt of the glitterati it once was. The island has recently undergone a renaissance, with the construction of new accommodations and condominiums and can now be a fun, mid-range place for a vacation.

The island's tiny town center is just to the west of the airstrip, next to which sits its largest resort hotel. Nearly everything to the west is residential. A series of narrow roads winds through the forests that cover most of the island to the stately vacation homes scattered along its coastline, and an inland neighborhood that has some smaller houses. Interestingly, the mansions tend to be Panamanian vacation homes, whereas the more humble abodes tend to belong to foreigners, many of them permanent residents. In the center of the island are a soccer field, a pond, and a small church, to the north lies Playa Ejecutiva, and to the south Playa Cacique, two of the island's nicest beaches. Contadora is small enough to walk everywhere, but given the midday heat you may want to rent a golf cart or scooter to get around.

Isla Contadora's main attraction is its selection of beaches, and it has a baker's dozen to choose from, plus those of nearby islands. As idyllic as its beaches may be, there is actually a good bit more to do at Isla Contadora. As you explore the island, you may spot white-tailed deer, agoutis (large brown rodents), and any of dozens of bird species, especially the abundant pelicans. There is decent snorkeling around its many rocky points, though you'll find even better snorkeling at several nearby islands. Though the water is warm most of the year, high winds from

December to April can cool it down significantly. Taking a boat trip to some of the surrounding islands is an excellent way to spend a morning or afternoon, and from June to December, you may see humpback whales on those trips. Captain Marco of Las Perlas Fishing Charters (see ⇨ *Sportfishing in Sports and Outdoor Activities, below*) offers popular half-day trips to nearby islands for just $35 per person.

Isla Mogo Mogo *(Isla Pájaros)*, 4 mi south of Contadora, on the other side of Isla Chapera, has a sugar-sand beach in a deep cove where snorkelers may find sea stars. Tiny **Isla Boyarena**, just to the south, has a pale sandbar that becomes a beach at low tide.

Isla Pacheca, 3 mi north of Contadora, has a lovely white-sand beach and a brown pelican rookery where about 8,000 birds nest, whereas the nearby islets of Pachequilla and Bartolomé have good scuba-diving and snorkeling spots.

GETTING HERE AND AROUND

Panama's domestic airlines, Aeroperlas and Air Panama, have daily flights to Contadora (OTD) from Aeropuerto Marcos A. Gelabert, commonly called Aeropuerto Albrook. The flight takes 25 minutes, and round-trip tickets cost around $100.

Contacts Aeroperlas (☎ *250–4026 in Contadora* ⊕ *www.aeroperlas. com*) has flights to and from Contadora every morning and evening, with extra flights on weekends. **Air Panama** (☎ *250–4009 in Contadora* ⊕ *www.flyairpanama.com*) has a morning flight to and from Contadora daily except Sunday, and evening flights on Fridays and Sundays.

WHERE TO EAT AND STAY

$$$$
SWISS

✕ **El Suizo.** Contadora's best (and most expensive) restaurant offers dishes that you would expect to find at a good restaurant in Switzerland—the chef and owner is Swiss—with some local touches. The ample menu includes beef tenderloin, prawns Provençal, and fish of the day prepared various ways, such as with herbs and butter or smothered in hollandaise sauce. The restaurant is a rustic, open-air affair under a thatch roof with a view of what was once the island's golf course and is now a pasture for its deer herd. ⊠ *On hill between Punta Galeón and Contadora Pearl Island hotels* ☎ *6560–3824* ▤ *MC, V.*

$–$$

▦ **Contadora Island Inn.** This small B&B sits in a quiet residential neighborhood, a 10-minute walk from the beach. Occupying adjacent ranch houses with decks and a thatched *rancho* overlooking the forest in back, the rooms don't offer a lot of privacy, but they are bright, clean, and share ample common areas, such as the small TV lounge, front porch, and back deck. Guests can use the kitchen, but the best room, Frigata Magnífica, has its own kitchen. The friendly, helpful owners and staff rent bicycles and scooters, and can book day-trips. **Pros:** affordable; quiet; clean. **Cons:** not on the beach. ⊠ *Paseo Urraca* ☎ *6699–4614* ⊕ *www.contadoraislandinn.com* ⤴ *9 rooms* ♿ *In-room: kitchen (some), no phone, safe, no TV. In-hotel: bicycles, laundry service, airport shuttle, no-smoking rooms* ▤ *MC, V* ⚫ *BP.*

$–$$
Fodor's Choice
★

▦ **Perla Real Inn.** This attractive B&B was designed to resemble a Spanish mission, and the owners have paid great attention to the details, importing hand-painted tiles and sinks and getting a local carpenter to make replicas of furniture in southern California missions. The bright rooms have high ceilings with fans and are tastefully decorated with ceramics and fine Mexican carpets. Suites are double the size, with kitchens and breakfast bars, and cost only $35 more. Rooms open onto a courtyard with a fountain, where the complimentary breakfast is served. The only drawback is that the inn isn't on a beach—it is in a residential neighborhood a 10-minute walk from Playas Cacique and Ejecutiva. Nevertheless, it's quiet, comfortable, and provides the personalized attention that the big resorts don't offer. The owner and manager can arrange day tours, provide free snorkeling equipment, and will rent you a golf cart at a discount. **Pros:** tasteful; friendly; nice rooms. **Cons:** not on the beach. ⊠ *Paseo Urraca 50* ⌂ *Apdo. 0843-03073, Balboa* ☎ *250–4095, 949/228–8851 in North America* ⊕ *www.perlareal.com* ⇨ *4 rooms, 2 suites, 1 villa* ♿ *In-room: no phone, kitchen (some), refrigerator (some), no TV, Wi-Fi. In-hotel: laundry service, airport shuttle, no-smoking rooms* ☰ *MC, V* ⦿ *CP.*

$$ **Punta Galeón Resort.** Spread along a rocky point that juts into the Pacific on the north side of the island, the Hotel Punta Galeón has a wide wooden boardwalk around its perimeter with captivating views of the surrounding sea and waves crashing against the rocks below. Just behind that boardwalk is a series of low, white-stucco buildings with barrel-tile roofs that hold the well-equipped guest rooms, each with a terrace with a view of the ocean through the foliage. Rooms have a very tropical feel, thanks to bright colors, shells decorating the mirrors, and the scenery visible through the picture window. The grounds and large poolside deck are shaded by huge trees. The open-air restaurant ($-$$) has sea views and is one of the nicer spots to eat on the island, specializing in fresh seafood such as *corvina al ajillo* (sea bass in a garlic sauce) and *camarones* (shrimp) served half a dozen ways, though they also offer a few meat and vegetarian dishes. **Pros:** great views; attractive rooms; beach; good restaurant. **Cons:** low ceilings; terraces not private. ⊠ *North of airstrip, next to Playa Galeón* ☎ *214–7869 or 250–1220* ⊕ *www.puntagaleonhotel.com* ⇨ *48 rooms* ♿ *In-room: safe. In-hotel: 2 restaurants, bar, pool, beachfront, water sports, laundry service, public Wi-Fi, Internet terminal, no-smoking rooms* ☰ *MC, V* ⦿ *EP.*

$-$$ **Villa Romántica.** You can't top this small hotel's location, on a ridge
★   just above stunning Playa Cacique, which means all the rooms are just steps away from the beige sand and turquoise waters. The friendly Austrian owner converted these *vacation home* into this hotel several years ago, making some questionable interior decorating decisions in the process. The giant hearts and bas-relief Grecian nudes on the walls of rooms and the shiny polyester bedspreads may be too much for some travelers. Rooms are quite varied. The Hawaii 1 and 2 rooms, on the bottom floor of the main building, have king-size beds, sliding-glass doors, and ocean views. The Panama and Castle rooms are similar but less private. Two "Panorama" rooms in the top floor have smaller gable windows with nice views, but they share a bathroom. The "Romantic" rooms, with heart motifs, overlook the gardens and mini-golf course, but the suite next door has an ocean-view balcony and a round water bed worthy of real swingers. The restaurant ($$–$$$$) is over the beach

and has a good menu that ranges from the traditional chateaubriand and chicken cordon bleu to fish of the day—usually mahimahi—served with a selection of sauces. Pros: beachfront; good restaurant; friendly owner. Cons: some tacky decor. ⊠ *Playa Cacique, 200 meters southwest of church* ☎ *250–4067* ⊕ *www.villa-romantica.com* ⤶ *14 rooms, 9 with bath, 1 suite* ⚷ *In-room: no phone, safe, Wi-Fi. In-hotel: restaurant, bar, beachfront, laundry service, no-smoking rooms* ⊟ *AE, MC, V* ⦿ *BP.*

SPORTS AND THE OUTDOORS

BEACHES

Because the Pacific tides are so extreme, beaches change considerably through the course of the day; what is a wide swath of sand at low tide is reduced to a sliver at high tide. Regardless of whether there's a large resort hotel present (as is the case with Playa Larga, albeit an abandoned one), all beaches in Panama are public property, so you can use any of them, no matter what hotel you stay in. You may have to pay or buy something in order to use a hotel's beach umbrellas and chairs, but the sand is always free.

★ **Playa Cacique,** on the south side of the island, is its loveliest beach, with pale sand backed by tropical trees and vacation homes and Isla Chapera visible across the turquoise waters. If you walk west on Playa Cacique and around a small bluff, you'll come upon a smaller beach called **Playa Camarón.**

★ One of Contadora's quietest beaches is **Playa Ejecutiva,** a few hundred yards north of the church and soccer field, which is backed by a small forest and has attractive thatched structures where the owners of the nearby homes have occasional beach parties.

Playa Galeón, just to the north of the airstrip and east of Punta Galeón, is a small beach in a deep bay that is used by the guests at the Hotel Punta Galeón, so it can also get crowded during high season. It is a good swimming beach and has decent snorkeling along the rocks of nearby Punta Galeón.

Contadora's longest beach, **Playa Larga,** stretches along the island's eastern end, in front of the now-closed Hotel Contadora. It is a lovely strip of ivory sand, backed by coconut palms and Indian almond trees, but its presence in front of an abandoned hotel gives it a forlorn feel. Things may pick up again if the hotel is ever reborn. There's no guarantee that that will happen soon.

Hidden in the island's southeast corner, at the end of the road that runs east from Hotel Villa Romantica, is **Playa Suecas,** Contadora's officially sanctioned nude beach—be sure to use plenty of sunscreen on those pale parts!

SCUBA DIVING

The reefs around Contadora have much less coral than you find in the Caribbean or the western Pacific, but you can see a lot of fish there, some of which gather in big schools. Isla Pachequilla, a small island near Isla Pacheco, is one of the area's best dive spots, with an array of reef fish, as well as rays, moray eels, white-tipped reef sharks, and large schools of jacks. The only problem is visibility, which averages 15 to 30 feet, but sometimes tops 45 feet, especially from June to August, though there is less marine life in the area then. The best diving is in December and January, when there is decent visibility and large numbers of fish; visibility is low from February to April.

Coral Dreams (✉ *Main road, across from airstrip* ☎ *6536–1776* ⊕ *www. coral-dreams.com*) offers scuba diving at various dive spots, as well as certification courses and snorkeling excursions.

The utilitarian-named **Glass Bottom Boat** (☎ *6750–5640*) offers you just that with two options: a one-hour tour ($20) encircles Isla Contadora, and a three-hour tour ($35) takes in Contadora and five of the nearby islands.

3

SPORTFISHING

The fishing around Contadora is quite good, which means you can go out for half a day and stand a decent chance of hooking something. The most common fish in the area are dolphin, jack, tuna, wahoo, roosterfish, and—in deeper water—snapper and grouper. Anglers sometimes hook sailfish and marlin in the area, but if it's billfish you're after, you'll want to head for the waters south of Isla Del Rey, which requires a full-day charter.

Captain Marco at **Las Perlas Fishing Charters** (☎ *6689–4916 or 6605– 5057*) has a 26-foot boat with one engine for $250 per half day and $500 per full day, and a 33-foot open-hulled boat with twin 200-hp engines for $450 per half day and $800 for a full day. Rods, tackle, snacks, and beverages are included.

ISLA SAN JOSÉ

90 km (54 mi) southeast of Panama City.

The southernmost island of the Pearl Archipelago, Isla San José is a remote, 14,000-acre isle that is almost completely covered with rain forest and lined with dozens of pristine beaches fronted by pristine blue waters. Its lush forests are home to white-tailed deer, tamandu anteater, keel-billed toucan, four species of macaw, and thousands of feral pigs. The ocean that surrounds it teems with an even greater diversity of life, and if you snorkel around the rocky islets off its coast you may see snapper, stingrays, parrot fish, and moorish idol. From June to September you may also spot humpback whales offshore. Head out for some fishing near Isla Galera, 25 mi to the east, and you stand the chance of hooking Pacific sailfish and tuna upwards of 100 pounds. The only wildlife that you won't be able to see are the sand fleas (aka "no-see-ums"), which can be a plague when the winds die down during the rainy season and are the only drawback of an otherwise enchanting isle.

This is the island that Air Panama built: it belongs to airline owner George Novey. Its only true development is his idyllic Hacienda del Mar, a nature lodge that covers a point on the island's western coast. The U.S. Army used the island as a training ground and bombing range during World War II; there is unexploded ordnance in its forests, though apparently, not near Hacienda del Mar. Nevertheless, it's not a place you want to go bushwhacking, nor would you need to, since you can see plenty of wildlife from the roads and beaches, or even from the porch of your bungalow.

GETTING HERE AND AROUND

Air Panama (☎ 316–9000 ⊕ *www.flyairpanama.com*) has morning flights to and from Isla San José (ISJ) daily except Sunday, and evening flights on Friday and Sunday. The hotel sometimes schedules Air Panama charter flights for other days during the dry season.

WHERE TO STAY

$$$$
★
🏨 **Hacienda del Mar.** Perched on a point overlooking the sea, Hacienda del Mar enjoys breathtaking views of the waves crashing against the surrounding islets, an adjacent beach, and forested coastline. Its comfortably rustic bungalows with large balconies that take advantage of the views are nestled in the forest along the ridge. Cane walls, wood ceilings, and hand-carved furniture are harmonious with the surroundings, though the decorations that adorn the walls are an odd mix of Panamanian handicrafts and New England kitsch. VIP suites have full ocean views, and are quite spacious; smaller junior suites are more private and set back from the point—only No. 14 overlooks the sea. The airy second-floor restaurant ($$–$$$$) has a wide balcony with the best view on the property. The menu is strong on seafood, such as paella and lobster thermidor, and fish of the day (usually mahimahi). The round, stone pool is set at the edge of the point. The dark, air-conditioned bar has the hotel's only TV, plus foosball and pool tables. The hotel rents kayaks and snorkeling equipment, and tours include bird-watching, sportfishing, jet skiing, and mountain biking. **Pros:** gorgeous surroundings; outdoor activities; good food; friendly staff. **Cons:** expensive; sand fleas; disappointing breakfast. ☎ 832–0214, 269–6613 *in Panama City, 866/433–5627 in the U.S.* ⊕ *www.haciendadelmar. net* ⇄ *17 bungalows, 2 suites* ⚟ *In-room: no phone, safe, refrigerator (some), no TV. In-hotel: restaurant, bar, pool, beachfront, water sports, laundry service, no-smoking rooms* ▤ *AE, DC, MC, V* �🍴 *BP.*

SPORTS AND THE OUTDOORS

BEACHES

The most visited beach on the island is **Playa Arenosa**, an attractive stretch of dark-beige sand just to the north of Hacienda del Mar. The Indian Almond trees that rise up behind that beach are often populated by macaws, and the rocks that surround the adjacent point are an excellent area for snorkeling at high tide. The hotel has a beach house where they provide chairs and umbrellas, and rent kayaks and snorkeling equipment.

SPORTFISHING

The sea southeast of Isla San José has some of Panama's best fishing, since the continental shelf ends nearby. Pacific sailfish and blue and black marlin ply those waters most of the year, but they are tough to catch. Anglers are more likely to get amberjack, tuna, dolphin, wahoo, roosterfish, and mackerel. Fishing charters cost $400 to $750 for a half day, which is usually enough to catch some fish, though billfish are always more of a challenge.

THE CENTRAL PACIFIC COAST

The Central Pacific Coast has Panama's most popular beaches, but it does not have its best strands of sand, nearly all of which are on islands. Due to the organic matter that washes out of the rivermouths along the coast, its beaches tend to have gray or salt-and-pepper sand. Also, the land behind most coastal beaches is almost completely deforested, so they lack the natural settings of the beaches on Isla Contadora or the islands of other regions. Strong tides make for terrific surfing, but risky swimming here, too. But no matter: their convenient location, all less than two hours from the capital make them favorite weekend destinations for city folk. (You'll have most of them to yourself if you visit during the week, especially during the May–November off-season.)

The Central Pacific beaches range from Coronado, lined with vacation homes and with little access for tourists, to Farallón (aka Playa Blanca), which has the country's largest resort. Several of the region's beaches attract devoted surfers but are backed by dingy towns with low-budget cement-box accommodations blocks from the beach. Though the Central Pacific beaches are geographically close to Panama City, it actually takes longer to reach most of them than it does to visit the Pacific islands, and in some cases, the Caribbean coast. But if you're a surfer or golfer, they're worth the trip.

PLAYA KOBBE (PLAYA BONITA)

7 km (4 mi) southwest of Panama City.

With 2 km (1 mi) of beige sand washed by relatively clear waters and surrounded by tropical forest, Playa Kobbe is a lovely spot. It is also the closest beach to Panama City, a mere 20 minutes from downtown by car, which could be a problem considering that all the city's sewage goes straight into the sea. Nevertheless, the water off Kobbe Beach *looks* clean, and the Intercontinental hotel management claims that lab tests have deemed the water perfectly safe for swimming. Its proximity to Panama City means it should be a popular weekend spot for the capital's residents, but since 2006, it has been dominated by the massive Intercontinental Playa Bonita Resort & Spa. Since the resort owns all the land around the beach and restricts access to it, it is for all practical purposes private, even though under Panamanian law all beaches are public property. The name Playa Bonita (beautiful beach) is a PR invention, but given the resort's stature and plans for a housing development there, it will probably replace Playa Kobbe, named for the one-time U.S. military base here, as the beach's official moniker.

GETTING HERE AND AROUND

To drive to Kobbe from Panama City, take the Avenida de los Mártires to the Bridge of the Americas and take the first exit after crossing the canal, turning left and following the signs to the Intercontinental Playa Bonita Resort. A taxi from Panama City should cost $20 to $25.

WHERE TO STAY

$$$$
☾
★

⊞ **Intercontinental Playa Bonita Resort & Spa.** It would be hard not to be impressed by this resort's vast lobby, with its polished marble floor, soaring arches, and giant wall of windows providing a panoramic view of the gardens, pool, beach, and blue Pacific. The hotel's design mixes Panamanian and Mediterranean motifs—white walls, orchid displays, Spanish tiles, and Grecian domes—that work together surprisingly well. Its 300 guest rooms are in a series of gleaming white five-story buildings that spread out to the east and west of the lobby like the wings of a giant seagull. They are equipped with the amenities you would expect to find at any luxury hotel, and have large balconies with ocean views. The beach is lined with coconut palms, behind which are two restaurants and a bar, several pools, volleyball courts, kayaks, and four-poster beds for massages. The hotel's vast spa is one of the best in the country. **Pros:** nice beachfront; facilities; spa; close to Panama City. **Cons:** massive and impersonal resort; ocean could be polluted; polyester sheets. ⊠ *7 km (4 mi) southwest of Panama City* ☎ *211–8600; 877/800–1690 in the U.S.* ⊕ *www.playabonitapanama.com* ⇋ *283 rooms, 27 suites* ⚭ *In-room: DVD, safe, refrigerator, Wi-Fi. In-hotel: 3 restaurants, room service, bars, pools, gym, spa, beachfront, water sports, laundry service, public Wi-Fi, parking (free), no-smoking rooms* ⊟ *AE, MC, V* ⊚ *BP.*

PLAYA VERACRUZ

15 km (9 mi) southwest of Panama City.

Panamanians who want to hit the beach but can't make the long drive over the mountains west of La Chorrera to the Central Pacific's nicest beaches usually pop over the canal to Playa Veracruz. It is a working-class beach, with no hotels and only rustic restaurants called *fondas*. On weekends its long stretch of light-brown sand can get pretty busy with families, groups of young people, and an array of vendors, but during the week you can practically have the beach to yourself. The beach is long and good for strolling, and at low tide you can walk out the spit of sand at the end of the beach to Isla Venado—a tiny, forested island. ⚠ **Head back to Panama City by the time the sun sets—there have been muggings on the beach at night.**

GETTING HERE AND AROUND

To drive to Playa Veracruz from Panama City, take Avenida de los Mártires to the Bridge of the Americas, turn off at the second exit after crossing the canal (Farfán and Veracruz), and follow the road around the abandoned airport to the beach. Buses to Veracruz depart from the Terminal de Buses hourly on weekends. If you go by taxi, you'll want to hire it for your entire trip ($10 to $15 per hour) to avoid getting stranded there.

▌ OFF THE
BEATEN
PATH

Though **Parque Nacional Altos de Campana** lies just north of the Carretera Interamericana, a mere 50 km (31 mi) west of Panama City, few people take the time to check out its exuberant forests and breathtaking views. The first national park created in Panama, Altos de Campana protects patches of cloud forest on the peaks of a steep and severely defor-ested mountain ridge to the southwest of La Chorrera. An excellent destination for hikers, thanks to its refreshingly cool climate—the park sits 400—850 meters (1,300—2,800 feet) above sea level—and 3 km (2 mi) of trails, Altos de Campana is also home to some interesting birds, such as slaty ant wrens, orange-bellied trogons, and hummingbirds not found in the forests around the canal. The summits of Cerro Campana and Cerro de la Cruz, in particular, have dramatic mountain scenery and amazing views of the Pacific Ocean. You can take a tour, but to visit the park on your own take the Carretera Interamericana 47 km (29 mi) west from Panama City, turn right 5 km (3 mi) after Capira, and drive another 5 km (3 mi) up a serpentine paved road to the ranger station; 3 km (2 mi) beyond that are the radio towers where the trails begin. ⚠ You'll need a 4WD vehicle with high clearance to drive the rough final few kilometers. ⊠ *52 km (32 mi) west of Panama City* ☏ *232-7223* ⊠ *$3.50* ☾ *Daily 7–5.*

Panama City–based **Futura Travel** (☏ *360–2030* ⊕ *www.extremepanama. com*) offers half-day hiking tours to Altos de Campana that include an ascent of Cerro de La Cruz.

PLAYA CORONADO

84 km (52 mi) southwest of Panama City.

From the capital, this is the closest decent Central Pacific beach. Playa Coronado began to develop as a weekend destination for wealthy Panamanians decades ago, and today the coast is almost completely lined with condos and weekend homes, leaving very few spots for nonresidents to get onto the beach. The sand here is pale gray with swaths of fine black dirt running through it, which gives it a sort of marbled appearance, and though the beach gets some waves it is usually safe for swimming. The big attraction is an 18-hole golf course designed by Tom and George Fazio, which is part of the Hotel Coronado *(below)* ⇨ . One of the country's best golf destinations, the resort is not fancy but spacious, with plentiful green areas. It gets packed with Panamanian families on weekends and holidays, but is practically dead most weekdays. Foreign tourists are always a minority here, which makes it a good place to experience the real Panama.

If you are in Playa Coronado on a Saturday, be sure to catch the horse and folklore show, which is free with dinner at **Estribo de Plata** (⊠ *Calle Principal, on left before resort* ☏ *240–4444*), a restaurant at an equestrian center in town that specializes in grilled meat.

GETTING HERE AND AROUND

There is no public transportation to Coronado, but the Hotel Coronado provides a shuttle for guests from Panama City for $30, with a two-passenger minimum. It is also an easy drive; take the Carretera Interamericana west from Panama City one hour, and look for the turnoff next to a large shopping center on the left, just after the town of Chame. You'll have to stop at a guardhouse, then look for the golf resort on the left. For Hotel Gaviota, head all the way to where the road veers left, after a tiny supermarket and turn right onto Paseo George Smith.

WHERE TO EAT AND STAY

The huge 24-hour **Supermercado El Rey** (⊠ *Centro Comercial Coronado* ☎ *240–1247*) makes a good place to stock up on food supplies. Just look for the tall sign; it's visible from everywhere.

$$

LATIN AMERICAN

✗ **El Rincón del Chef.** In a pleasant, colonial-style shopping plaza on the road to Coronado, this Panamanian restaurant belongs to Fernando Paredes, who was the executive chef at the nearby golf resort for years before starting his own place. He changes his menu daily, but it always offers a good mix of meat and seafood dishes with predominantly Panamanian preparation with international inspiration. There is invariably *corvina* (sea bass), *langostinos* (prawns), and other seafood served with sauces that range from mushroom to mango. He also serves (rather expensive) grilled USDA-certified beef. The building is right out of the 19th century, with terra-cotta floors, ocher walls, and ceiling fans hung from the high wooden beams beneath the barrel-tile roof. ⊠ *Beginning of road to Coronado, on right* ☎ *240–1941* ▭ *MC, V.*

$$$$
✪

▦ **Hotel Coronado.** Red-tile roofs, archways, beamed ceilings, and painted tiles reflect a hacienda architectural style at this rambling complex that is both a hotel and a country club—it was also the Pacific coast's first resort. As the name suggests, the main attractions are an 18-hole, par-72 golf course and the nearby beach club, which rents kayaks and Jet Skis. The resort also has an equestrian center, and its extensive, landscaped grounds feature several tennis courts, an Olympic-size pool, Jacuzzis, and a spa. Spacious guest rooms are in a series of two-story buildings scattered around ample grounds with common gardens, porches, and lawns. All rooms are suites with high ceilings and master bedrooms that can be separated from the living room and have wicker furniture, sofa beds, and big windows with views of the golf course or gardens. "Royal suites" have two bedrooms, two bathrooms, and a large balcony. "Residential suites" have full kitchens to boot. The gourmet restaurant upstairs serves dinner only, the spacious open-air restaurant by the pool is known for its Sunday lunch buffet. The beach is nearly a kilometer (½-mi) away from the rooms and greens, though sporadic transportation shuttles guests there. **Pros:** golf course; spacious rooms; ample facilities. **Cons:** not on a beach; very busy on weekends. ⊠ *Playa Coronado, Calle Principal, left at Brigada de Bomberos* ☎ *264–3134; 866/465–3207 in the U.S.* ⊕ *www.coronadoresort. com* ➷ *78 suites* ⚉ *In-room: safe (some), kitchen (some), refrigerator (some), Wi-Fi (some). In-hotel: 4 restaurants, bars, golf course, tennis courts, pools, gym, spa, beachfront, water sports, children's programs (ages 4–10), laundry service, public Wi-Fi, parking (free), no-smoking rooms* ▭ *AE, DC, MC, V* ⊙ *EP.*

$
▦ **Hotel Gaviota.** This small hotel and day resort at the west end of Playa Coronado sits behind one of the widest parts of the beach, next to a river mouth, which keeps the water murky here during the rainy months. Its large restaurant, pool, and lawn strewn with picnic areas cater to crowds of Panamanians on weekends and holidays, when you can get a $15 day pass that includes lunch, a welcome cocktail, and use of the beach and facilities. The guest rooms are in several buildings set back from the beach, and while they won't win any design awards,

they are clean and comfortable, with red-tile floors, wicker furniture, kitchenettes, and covered terraces furnished with plastic chairs and tables. To get here, drive to the end of the main road and turn right at the market. **Pros:** clean; covered terraces. **Cons:** murky water in rainy season; crowded on weekends. ✉ *Playa Coronado, end of Paseo George Smith* ☎ *240–4526 or 224–9056 in Panama City* ⊕ *www. hotelgaviotapanama.com* 🛏 *10 rooms* ⚴ *In-room: no phone, kitchen, refrigerator. In-hotel: restaurant, bar, pool, beachfront, parking (free), no-smoking rooms* ☰ *MC, V* ⦿ *EP, FAP.*

SPORTS AND THE OUTDOORS
GOLF
The **Hotel Coronado** (☎ 240–3137 ⊕ *www.coronadoresort.com*) has an 18-hole, par-72 golf course designed by Tom and George Fazio, which makes it a popular destination for golfers. The course is also open to nonguests, who sometimes drive the hour west of Panama City for a day of golf. The greens fee for 18 holes is $125, which includes golf-cart rental and lunch. The hotel also rent clubs and has a par-27, 9-hole executive course that is better for beginners and younger golfers. Bilingual golf pros hold classes for golfers of all ages and skill levels.

SHOPPING
The **Centro Artesanal de Coronado** (✉ *Road to Playa Coronado, on right* ☎ 240-1168) has a collection of tiny shops in what resembles the central square of a traditional Panamanian village. Each building holds several small shops selling different Panamanian handicrafts, such as hammocks, hats, and jewelry, as well as beachwear. None of the shops accepts credit cards.

PLAYA EL PALMAR

93 km (58 mi) southwest of Panama City.

With one of the less attractive beaches on the Central Pacific coast, tiny Playa El Palmar is a mecca for surfers, since it has one of the country's most accessible surf breaks and reasonably priced accommodations. Non-surfers have no reason to stop at El Palmar, and should keep driving to Playa Santa Clara, which has a wider, whiter beach and nicer accommodations.

GETTING HERE AND AROUND
To drive to Playa El Palmar, take the Carretera Interamericana west from Panama City for about 90 minutes and look for the entrance on the left after San Carlos. El Palmar is one of the few beaches that you can reach by public transportation. Buses to any of the destinations farther west—Penonomé, Aguadulce, Santiago, or Chitré—can drop you off across the highway from the entrance. From there it is a quarter-mile walk to the beach. Those buses depart from the Terminal de Buses in Albrook every 20 or 30 minutes.

WHERE TO STAY
¢–$ 🏨 **Palmar Surf Camp.** The best spot for surfers, around the corner from the breaks, this place has rooms in a two-story building set back from the beach, though close enough to hear the crashing of the waves

when the surf is up. Rooms are air-conditioned, with small bathrooms and either one queen or two single beds. Two suites at the end of the building have kitchenettes, and three beds each. Rooms cost $10 less during the week, which is the best time to come if you want to surf without a crowd. Basic meals and cold beers are available beneath a thatch roof just behind the beach. The hotel rents surfboards and kayaks and gives surfing lessons. Pros: activities; near beach; small camping area. Cons: crowded on weekends; unattractive beach. ⊠ *Playa El Palmar, just before end of road* ☎ *240–8004* ✐ *palmarsurfcamp@yahoo.com* ⇝ *8 rooms, 2 suites* ♿ *In-room: no phone. In-hotel: restaurant, pool, beachfront, parking (free), no-smoking rooms* ⊟ *No credit cards* ⼌ *EP.*

BREEZES PANAMA
Breezes Panama ($$$$: ☎ *877/273-3937* ⊕ *www.breezes. com*), a new 300-room all-inclusive resort in Santa Clara, opened in October 2009. Because the resort could not be visited before publication of this edition, we are unable to offer a full review, but the brand-new hotel does offer a very different kind of accommodation choice in Santa Clara. It is also SuperClubs' first all-inclusive resort in Panama.

SPORTS AND THE OUTDOORS

SURFING

Waves are the only reason to come to Playa El Palmar, which has two breaks. The beach break has lefts and rights, and can be ridden at any size by surfers with any level of experience, though it tends to close out at lower tides. The right point break nearby is for experienced surfers only, since the wave breaks over a stone platform, and it is only rideable when the tide is high and the swell is big. El Palmar can get crowded on weekends and holidays, especially during the dry season, but the surf is best in the rainy season, when you may have the break to yourself on weekdays.

PLAYA SANTA CLARA

112 km (69 mi) southwest of Panama City.

Playa Santa Clara, one of the Central Pacific coast's nicest beaches, with plenty of pale sand and good water for swimming, lies just east of Farallón (Playa Blanca). Santa Clara's hotels have always been comparatively small and catered mostly to Panamanians, but a new all-inclusive Breezes resort promises to change the face of this quiet community. On the western end of the beach is the tiny fishing village of Santa Clara, where dozens of small boats are anchored offshore, and visible from the beach is **Isla Farallón**, a giant, pale rock that has decent snorkeling around it.

GETTING HERE AND AROUND

To drive to Playa Santa Clara, take the Carretera Interamericana (CA1) west from Panama City for about 90 minutes and look for the entrance on the left at Santa Clara.

WHERE TO STAY

¢–$ ⊞ **Cabañas Las Veraneras.** Although a rambling restaurant ($) on the
★ beach is the primary business here, you can also take advantage of
economical accommodations. Four rustic rooms above the restaurant,
with high thatch roofs and tiny bathrooms, are right on the beach, but
unfortunately the restaurant blasts music day and night. Two-story
bungalows perched along the ridge behind the restaurant have ocean
views and are quieter, though you'll still hear the music on weekend
nights. Each has a double bed downstairs and three singles in the loft,
and a small porch with hammocks. The quietest rooms are behind the
ridge in cement buildings, with air-conditioning, cable TV, and terraces
that view a small forest. A large pool nearby is surrounded by a lawn
and a small bar open on weekends. The restaurant serves a wide variety
of Panamanian food, from *corvina con camarones* (sea bass in shrimp
sauce) to *churrasco,* grilled strip sirloin. **Pros:** on beach, inexpensive,
nice pool. **Cons:** mediocre rooms, crowded and loud on weekends/
holidays. ⊠ *Playa Santa Clara, 2 km south of CA1, veer right at Y, end
of road* ☎ *993–3313* ⟳ *27 rooms* ♿ *In-room: no a/c (some), no phone.
In-hotel: restaurant, bar, beachfront, parking (free), no-smoking rooms*
☰ *AE, MC, V* ⍟*EP.*

¢ ⊞ **Hotel Vida Abundante.** Set back about 1 km from the beach, this small,
☺ American-owned hotel offers Santa Clara's most economical rooms and
is a quiet, Christian alternative to the party atmosphere that dominates
the beach on weekends. The hotel's anti-partying policy is posted in
every room, and Bible scriptures have been written on the walls with
markers. The rooms themselves are simple but clean, ranging from
small doubles with one queen bed to larger rooms with two or three
beds in a house that has a kitchen guests can use. **Pros:** quiet; pool.
Cons: no restaurant; far from beach; no booze allowed. ⊠ *Playa Santa
Clara, 1 km south of CA1, bear right at Y and turn right at end of road*
☎ *202–1347* ⟳ *9 rooms* ♿ *In-room: no phone, no TV. In-hotel: pool,
parking (free), no-smoking rooms* ☰ *AE, MC, V* ⍟*EP.*

$$–$$$ ⊞ **Las Sirenas.** Families frequent Las Sirenas because each bungalow can
☺ sleep four to six people, albeit some on the foam cushions that serve as
couches by day, and because it is on a quiet stretch of beach. The nicest
of these cement cottages are on a ridge and have great ocean views past
the palm trees, bougainvillea, and other foliage. Decorated in yellow
and blue, the bungalows have high ceilings, an air-conditioned bedroom, a well-stocked kitchen, breakfast bar, living room with fans, and
a big front terrace with a table, chairs, hammock, and grill. Those down
the hill, on the beach, are slightly smaller and not as bright, but they
are mere steps from the sea; the bungalows share a lawn with common
grills and a playground. There are restaurants down the road, but this
place was designed for people who want to do their own cooking. The
shopping center at the entrance to Coronado has a supermarket. **Pros:**
nice beach; spacious bungalows. **Cons:** no pool; no restaurant. ⊠ *Playa
Santa Clara, 2 km south of CA1, bear left at Y and turn right at end of
road* ☎ *993–3235* ⊕ *www.lasirenas.com* ⟳ *10 rooms* ♿ *In-room: no
phone, safe, kitchen, refrigerator, Wi-Fi. In-hotel: beachfront, parking
(free), no-smoking rooms* ☰ *MC, V* ⍟*EP.*

PLAYA FARALLÓN (PLAYA BLANCA)

115 km (71 mi) southwest of Panama City.

For years, few people visited the long stretch of white beach between the fishing villages of Santa Clara and Farallón because it lay beneath a military base used by Panama's national guard. Access to the area was restricted. The base saw heavy fighting during the 1989 U.S. invasion, and for much of the 1990s its buildings, pockmarked with bullet holes, were slowly being covered with jungle. Everything changed at the beginning of the 21st century, when the Colombian hotel chain Decameron opened a massive resort here and began promoting it as "Playa Blanca" (White Beach). Panamanians still use the Farallón *(fahr-ah-YOHN)* name. Now the area has an 18-hole golf course, a growing number of condos, a second all-inclusive resort on the other side of the Farallón River, a third under construction at this writing, and others on the drawing board.

GETTING HERE AND AROUND

To drive to Playa Blanca, take the Carretera Interamericana west from Panama City for about 90 minutes and look for the hotel entrances on the left after Santa Clara—the entrance to the Playa Blanca Beach Resort is 2 km (1 mi) after the entrance to the Royal Decameron and Tucán Country Club; they are well marked. Both resorts provide shuttle services from Tocumen Airport and Panama City hotels for $32.

WHERE TO STAY

$$$ 🏨 **Playa Blanca Beach Resort.** With fewer than a quarter the number of rooms as the nearby Royal Decameron, Playa Blanca is definitely the lesser beach resort, though it is less a case of "size matters" than of design and location. The resort's Grecian-style white buildings are surrounded by grounds that were clearly bulldozed clean before construction began, because there is little shade to be found outside of the thatch-roof structures that surround the pools. The beach has swaths of black in its white sand, and because the hotel is next to a river mouth, the ocean is often murky here. The bright and spacious rooms are well furnished with wicker furniture and have a balcony or terrace; most overlook the pool or grounds—the few that have ocean views are worth the additional $20. Shows are performed nightly by the pool, and there are a tiny discotheque, a gift shop, and an aquatic center that provides free kayaks and pedal boats and sells an array of tours. **Pros:** on the beach; nice rooms; low-season discounts. **Cons:** murky sea; mediocre food; surrounded by construction sites. ☎ *993–2912 or 888/790–5264* ⊕ *www.playablancaresort.com* ⟳ *219 rooms, 3 suites* & *In-room: safe, Wi-Fi. In-hotel: 5 restaurants, bars, tennis court, pools, beachfront, water sports, children's programs (ages 4–12), laundry service, Internet terminal, parking (free), no-smoking rooms* ☰ *AE, D, DC, MC, V* ⎮◎⎮ *AI.*

$$$$ 🏨 **Royal Decameron Beach Resort.** This rambling vacation city is one of
☾ Panama's most attractive beach hotels and, hands down, its largest
★ resort. Its 1,100 rooms are in 50 four-story buildings scattered along 2 km of beach. Sidewalks and narrow roadways cruised by shuttle buses wind their way between those units through luxuriant grounds

shaded by massive tropical trees, which also hold six pools, 10 restaurants, eight bars, a game room, gym, aquatic center, and legions of beach chairs. The rooms have large bathrooms and balconies or terraces. Few have ocean views—those that do cost more and are worth it. Meal options range from massive buffets to restaurants specializing in seafood, Japanese, Thai, and Italian cusine, but none of the food is very memorable. Nor are the nightly shows, performed in an amphitheater below the main restaurant, in which dancers bedazzle vacationers with loud music and lots of hip shaking. The myriad daytime activities include kayaking, paddle-boating, windsurfing, horseback riding, tennis, and volleyball. For a small fee you can rent Jet Skis, play golf, fish, go diving or snorkeling around nearby Farallón Island, or rejuvenate at the spa. Reserve early, since the hotel often fills up. **Pros:** nice beach and grounds; lots of activities; good Web rates. **Cons:** mass tourism; mediocre food; lots of lines. ☎ *993–2255; 214–3535; 800/279–3718 in U.S.* 🌐 *www.decameron.com* *1,040 rooms, 60 junior suites* *In-room: safe, refrigerator (some). In-hotel: 10 restaurants, bars, tennis courts, pools, gym, spa, beachfront, water sports, children's programs (ages 4–12), laundry service, Internet terminal, parking (free), no-smoking rooms* *AE, DC, MC, V* *AI.*

RIP-CURRENT KNOW-HOW

Though Central Pacific beaches are usually safe for swimming, rip currents (riptides) are a danger on any beach with waves. Even the strongest swimmer can't fight these currents, but almost anyone can escape one. Swim parallel to shore until you feel that you are no longer heading out to sea, then head toward shore. Rip currents aren't wide, and it is always possible to swim out of them; however, you may be far from shore by the time you do, so don't waste energy swimming against the current. Only swim toward shore when you are free of the rip current.

SPORTS AND THE OUTDOORS

GOLF

The Royal Decameron Beach Resort's **Mantaraya Golf Club** (☎ *986–1915* 🌐 *www.decameron.com*) has an 18-hole, par-72 golf course designed by Randall Thompson that lies just inland from the hotel. Greens fees for 18 holes are $35 weekdays and $60 weekends and holidays. Greens fees for nine holes are $25 weekdays and $40 weekends. Cart rental costs $11 for nine holes and $22 for 18. Club rentals range from $15 to $25, according to their condition.

WATER SPORTS

Farallón-based **Xtreme Adventures** (☎ *993–2823* 🌐 *www.extremetours-panama.com*) offers all manner of guided beachy activities here and at adjoining Playa Coronado, including horseback riding, jet skiing, parasailing, and waterskiing.

THE CORDILLERA CENTRAL

Mountains rise up to the north of the Central Pacific coast, offering a refreshing alternative to the hot and deforested lowlands a short drive from the beaches. The massif to the southwest of Panama City, an extinct volcano that was in eruption 5 million years ago, forms the eastern extreme of the Cordillera Central, the country's longest mountain range. On the eastern slope of that verdant mountain is Parque Nacional Altos de Campana; its western slope holds Cerro de la Vieja. The highest point of the range is Cerro Gaital, a forested hill more than 3,500 feet above sea level that towers over El Valle de Antón, the ancient volcano's crater. Both Cerro de la Vieja and El Valle de Antón are cool and verdant refuges where you can take a break from the lowland heat, explore the mountain forests, and do a bit of bird-watching and hiking. El Valle is a well-established destination with an array of hotels and restaurants, but Cerro la Vieja, to the northeast of Penonomé, has just one eco-lodge.

EL VALLE DE ANTÓN

125 km (78 mi) southwest of Panama City; 28 km (17 mi) north of Las Uvas: the turnoff from Carretera Interamericana.

A serpentine road winds north from the Carretera Interamericana between Playa Coronado and Playa Farallón to a small, lush mountain valley and the town that is sheltered in it, both called El Valle de Antón, commonly referred to as El Valle (The Valley). That verdant valley has a refreshing climate, an abundance of trees and birds, and an array of outdoor activities. Thanks to its altitude of approximately 2,000 feet above sea level, the temperature in El Valle usually hovers in the 70sF, and at night it often dips down into the 60s, which means you may need a light jacket. El Valle has long been a popular weekend and holiday destination for Panama City's wealthier citizens, and the roads to the north and south of its Avenida Principal are lined with comfortable vacation homes with large lawns and gardens. In fact, one of those streets is called Calle de los Milionarios (millionaires' row).

Avenida Principal belies the beauty of El Valle's remote corners, resembling the main drag of any Panamanian town, with ugly Chinese-owned supermarkets and other uninspiring cement-block structures. The attractions for travelers are the flora and fauna of the protected forests north and west of town center, the varied hiking, mountain-biking, and horseback-riding routes, and the colorful crafts market, which is especially lively on weekends. Since El Valle has long been popular with Panamanian tourists, it has developed some touted but tepid attractions that can be skipped, such as its tiny hot springs, Pozos Termales, and the "square trees," or *arboles cuadrados,* behind the old Hotel Campestre.

Bowl-shaped El Valle was the crater of a volcano that went extinct millions of years ago. This is apparent when you view it from the *mirador* (lookout point) on the right as the road begins its descent into town—a worthwhile stop. The former crater's walls have eroded into a series of steep ridges that are covered with either luxuriant vegetation or the pale-green pasture that has replaced it. El Valle's volcanic soil has long made it an important vegetable-farming area, but as outsiders bought up the land on the valley's floor, the farming and ranching moved to its periphery, to the detriment of the native forests. Thankfully, large tracts of wilderness have been protected in the Cerro Gaital Natural Monument and adjacent Chorro el Macho Ecological Reserve.

NORTH AND WEST OF TOWN

★ El Valle's northern edge is protected within the 827-acre (335-hectare) nature reserve **Monumento Natural Cerro Gaital** *(Cerro Gaital Natural Monument)*, which covers the hills of Cerro Gaital, Cerro Pajita, and Cerro Caracoral. Cerro Gaital is a steep, forest-draped hill that towers over the valley's northern edge, rising to a summit of more than 3,500 feet above sea level. The lush wilderness that covers it is home to more than 300 bird species, including such spectacular creatures as the red-legged honeycreeper, bay-headed tanager, and blue-crowned motmot. It also protects the habitat of the rare golden toad (*Atelopus zeteki*), which has been virtually wiped out in the wild by a fungal disease during the past decade. The bird-watching is best along the edges of that protected area, since its lush foliage provides too many hiding places for those feathered creatures. The areas around El Nispero, Los Mandarinos hotel, and the old Hotel Campestre are excellent for bird-watching. The trail to Cerro Gaital's summit is on the right just west of Los Mandarinos, and the hike up and back takes two to three hours, depending on how much bird-watching you do. It requires good shoes and decent physical condition and is best done with a guide. Even if you don't make it to the summit, you should try to climb up to the mirador (lookout point), part of the way up, which provides a panoramic vista of the valley, the Pacific coast, and, on a clear morning, the Caribbean coast. ✉ *Take right off Av. Principal at Supermercado Hong Kong, left after 1.2 km, trail on right after entrance to Los Mandarinos* ☎ *No phone* 💰 *$3.50* ⊙ *Daily 6–6.*

⟳ El Valle's most user-friendly forest experience is available at the small, **Fodor's Choice** private **Refugio Ecológico del Chorro Macho** *(Chorro el Macho Ecological ★ Reserve)*, west of Cerro Gaital. The reserve has well-kept trails, walking sticks, and the option of hiring a guide at the gate. It belongs to Raúl Arias, who also owns the adjacent Canopy Lodge, and it contains one of El Valle's major landmarks, **El Chorro Macho**, a 115-foot cascade surrounded by lush foliage. You're not allowed to swim beneath the

---

LEGEND OF THE SLEEPING INDIAN GIRL

The partially forested ridge on the valley's far western edge is said to resemble the profile of a sleeping woman, and is known locally as the **India Dormida** ("sleeping Indian girl"). Legend has it that the daughter of Chief Urraca, who led local resistance to Spanish colonization, fell in love with a conquistador, thus betraying her people and the indigenous warrior who loved her. When the brave committed suicide by throwing himself off a precipice, the girl wandered into the forest and died of grief; her spirit entered the mountain, which now has her form.

3

waterfall, but there is a lovely swimming pool fed by river water to the left upon entering the reserve, so bring your bathing suit and a towel. Enter the gate to the left of the main entrance to reach the pool. The refuge has a tour called **Canopy Adventure** *(⇨ Sports and Outdoors, below)*, which can take you flying through the treetops and over the waterfall on zip lines strung between platforms high in trees. Most visitors are happy simply to explore the trails that loop through the lush forest past the waterfall and over a small suspension bridge that spans a rocky stream. ⊠ *2½ km (1½ mi) northwest of church, at west end of Av. Principal, on left* ☎ *983–6547* ✉ *$2.50, guided hike $25* ⊙ *Daily 8–5.*

A short drive to the west of the Mercado, at the end of a rough road and trail, is a simple remnant of El Valle's pre-Columbian culture called **Piedra Pintada**, a 15-foot boulder, the underside of which is covered with a bizarre collection of ancient petroglyphs. To get there, turn right at the end of the Avenida Principal and left onto the second road after the bridge, then drive to the end of that road, where a foot path heads to the nearby boulder. Kids sometimes hang out around the rock and explain the significance of the petroglyphs to visitors in Spanish, in hopes of extracting a tip. ⚠ **Cars left at the trailhead have been broken into, so don't leave any valuables in your vehicle, and leave the doors unlocked to avoid broken windows.** ⊠ *End of Calle La Pintada* ☎ *No phone* ✉ *Free* ⊙ *24 hrs.*

IN TOWN

Ell Valle's town center is basically the area west of the market, where you will find the library and the town church, **Iglesia de San José**, which is more a reference point than a sight to see. ⊠ *Av. Princpal, on left two blocks after Mercado* ☎ *No phone* ✉ *Free* ⊙ *Sun. 10–2.*

★   One traditional tourist attraction that you will definitely want to check out is the **Mercado**, an open–air bazaar under a high red roof on the left side of the Avenida Principal, two blocks before the church. The market is most interesting on weekends, especially Sunday mornings, when vendors and shoppers arrive from far and wide. Locals go to the market to buy fresh fruit, vegetables, baked goods, and plants. Handicrafts sold here include the *sombrero pintao* (a traditional straw hat), handmade jewelry, soapstone sculptures, and knickknacks such as the various renditions of El Valle's emblematic golden toad. Even if you don't want to buy anything, it's worth checking out, since it is a colorful, festive affair. The shops just to the east of the market have a comparable, if not better, selection of handicrafts. Most Panama City tour operators offer a day trip—a long day trip—to the market on Sundays. Consider basing yourself out here for a couple of days instead if you can. ⊠ *Av. Princpal, on left two blocks before church* ☎ *No phone* ✉ *Free* ⊙ *Daily 8–6.*

On the other side of an attractive garden to the left of Iglesia de San José is a tiny museum, **Museo del Valle**, which, together with the church, is only open on Sunday. Its meager collection includes some religious statues and pre-Columbian ceramic pieces. ⊠ *Av. Princpal, next to Iglesia San José* ☎ *No phone* ✉ *Free* ⊙ *Sun. 10–2.*

☾ **El Nispero,** a private zoo and plant nursery, is a good place to take the kids, even though most of the animals are in lamentably small cages. The zoo covers nearly 7 acres at the foot of Cerro Gaital and is one of the only places you can see the extremely rare golden toad, which has been wiped out in the wild by a fungal disease. Those attractive little yellow-and-black anurans—often mistakenly called frogs—are on display at the **El Valle Amphibian Research Center,** funded by several U.S. zoos. Biologists at the center are studying the fungus that is killing the species (*Batrachochytrium dendrobatidis*), while facilitating the toad's reproduction in a fungus-free environment. The zoo has many other Panamanian species that you are unlikely to see in the wild, such as endangered ocelots and margays (spotted felines), collared peccaries (wild pigs), white-faced capuchin monkeys, tapirs, toucans, parrots, and various macaw species. Exotic species such as Asian golden pheasants and white peacocks run the grounds. Most of the animals at El Nispero are former pets that were donated to the zoo or confiscated from their owners by government authorities. The tapirs, for example, belonged to former dictator Manuel Noriega. ⊠ *Calle Carlos Arosemena, 1½ km (1 mi) north of Av. Principal* ☎ *983–6142* 💲 *$2* ☺ *Daily 8–5.*

☾ A small but educational menagerie can be found at the **Sorpentario Maravillas Tropicales** (*Tropical Wonders Serpentarium*), an exhibit of a dozen snake species, frogs, iguanas, tarantulas, and scorpions a couple of blocks north of the Avenida Principal. It belongs to Mario Urriola, one of the valley's top nature guides, who is often on hand to tell about the creatures on display. ⊠ *Off Calle Rana Dorada* ☎ *6569–2676* 💲 *$2* ☺ *Daily 8–7.*

GETTING HERE AND AROUND

El Valle is 125 km (75 mi) southwest from Panama City, about two hours by car, on good roads. To drive, take the Carretera Interamericana west for 98 km (59 mi) to Las Uvas, where you turn right and drive 28 km (17 mi) north on a narrow, winding road. Buses to El Valle depart from the Terminal de Buses in Albrook every hour and cost $4, but they take almost three hours. Taxis hang out at the Mercado during the day, and charge $1–$2 for most trips within the valley.

WHERE TO EAT

¢   ✕ **Bruchetta.** This small Italian restaurant in the corner of what was once
ITALIAN   the town gas station has a small covered terrace where you can watch the townsfolk roll by. The food is usually quite good, with an ample selection of salads, half a dozen different bruschetta, plenty of pastas, corvina (sea bass), salmon, beef tenderloin, and other meats. You can sit in the tiny dining room if it's too cool at night, but the TV is usually blasting there. Service can be slow when it's full. The sister restaurant, Pizzeria Pinocchio's (open Thursday–Sunday), in the same building, serves good, inexpensive pizza. ⊠ *Av. Principal, 200 meters past market on right* ☎ *983–6603* 🚫 *No credit cards* ☺ *Closed Mon. and Tues.*

$$ ✕ **La Casa de Lourdes.** After years of running one of Panama City's most
ECLECTIC   popular restaurants, Golosinas, Lourdes Fabrega de Ward built this
Fodor's Choice   elegant place across from her retirement home so that she wouldn't
★   get bored. It now seems unlikely that she will ever retire, since former

Golosinas clients and a growing list of new fans pack the place on weekends, drawn by Lourdes' inventive menu and the magical ambience of her Tuscan-style *casa*. Meals are served on a back terrace with views of a garden and nearby Cerro Gaital framed by high columns, arches, and an elegant lap pool. It is truly a house, and you enter through a spacious living room with couches, a piano, and family photos. The menu changes, but is likely to include *yucca* (cassava) croquets with a Thai sauce, blackened *corvina* (sea bass) with a tamarind sauce, and the *Cassoulet de Lulu,* a stew of white beans, lamb, duck, pork, and sausages. Save room for desserts such as the Heart Attack: a chocolate sundae atop a chocolate cake. This place is so special that people have been known to helicopter in from Panama City for lunch. Reservations are essential on weekends, a good idea at other times. ⊠ *Calle El Ciclo, behind Hotel Los Mandarinos, 1.2 km north and 800 meters west of Supermercado Hong Kong La Casa de Lourdes, Calle El Ciclo, detrás del Hotel Los Mandarinos, El Valle de Antón, Cocle, Panama* ☎ *983–6450* ▤ *MC, V.*

$ ✕ **La Niña Delia.** The high, thatch roof on the left side of the Avenida
LATIN AMERICAN   Principal as you roll into town marks this spot for inexpensive Panamanian food. Its open-air dining area is rustic by design, with a hedge of foliage around the edges and woven hats and baskets hanging from the wood columns. Meals include traditional Panamanian breakfast and such favorites as *langostinos a la criolla* (prawns in a tomato sauce) and *lechón* (pork roast), but you can also get some international dishes, such as *pollo al limón* (lemon chicken) and filet mignon. The pastas should be avoided. Some of the cheapest rooms in town are rented in the building next door. ⊠ *Av. Principal, on left 600 meters past Texaco station* ☎ *983–1610* ▤ *No credit cards.*

WHERE TO STAY

$ ⛺ **Cabañas de Colores.** A short walk from the center of town, these four cement bungalows offer a good option to travelers on a budget. The bungalows occupy what was once the owner's backyard and surround a tiny playground, benches, and hammocks. They're a bit cramped but colorful, with kitchenettes and one or two bedrooms. The furniture is a bit dog-eared, but the Colombian owner is nice, and the location is conveniently central but relatively quiet. **Pros:** friendly owner; central location; garden; inexpensive. **Cons:** small bungalows; time-worn furniture. ⊠ *Calle El Gaital, 100 meters north of Av. Principal* ☎ *983–6613* ⇗ *4 bungalows* ⚐ *In-room: no a/c, no phone, kitchen, refrigerator. In-hotel: laundry service, parking (free), no-smoking rooms* ▤ *No credit cards* ⎰⎱ *EP.*

$$$$ ⛺ **Canopy Lodge.** Nestled in the forest overlooking the boulder-strewn
Fodor'sChoice   Guayabo River, this lovely lodge is dedicated to nature in all its glory.
★   Its attractions are honeycreepers, euphonias, hummingbirds, and the other 300 bird species found in the surrounding forest. The sister lodge of the Canopy Tower, near Panama City (you get a deal on weeklong packages that combine the two lodges), this place is more attractive and comfortable. Its bright, spacious rooms in a two-story cement building open onto wide balconies that overlook the river and forest. They have two queen beds, sliding screens, and ceiling fans; corner "suites" have

king beds and lots of windows. Meals are served family-style in an airy restaurant-lounge with a self-service bar. There is a good natural-history library, but not one TV to be found. Though rates are steep, they include tours led by an expert guide, three meals, and wine with dinner. There is a minimum two-night stay, which is what you need to appreciate this place. **Pros:** gorgeous setting; nice rooms; abundant birds; guide; good food; friendly; quiet. **Cons:** expensive; two-night minimum; set meals. ⊠ *2 km past church on road to El Chorro Macho Apdo. 0832-2701 W.T.C., Panama City, Rep. of Panama* ☎ *264–5720; 983–6837; 800/930–3397 in the U.S.* ⊕ *www.canopylodge.com* ⋑ *12 rooms* ⌂ *In-room: no a/c, no phone, safe, no TV. In-hotel: restaurant, laundry service, parking (free), no-smoking rooms* ⊟ *AE, MC, V* ⦿ *FAP.*

¢ ▦ **Don Pepe.** In a three-story building on Avenida Principal, with a crafts shop and restaurant on the ground floor, this hotel has centrally located, basic accommodation for budget travelers. Rooms are big, with tile floors, fans, so-so beds, and small bathrooms. Get one in back to avoid the street noise; corner rooms have more windows. The restaurant serves decent, inexpensive Panamanian fare and is one of the first places to open in the morning and last to close at night. **Pros:** inexpensive; big rooms; restaurant; bike rentals. **Cons:** on busy street; zero decor. ⊠ *Av. Principal, half a block before market* ☎ *983–6425 hoteldonpepe@hotmail.com* ⋑ *21 rooms* ⌂ *In-room: no a/c, no phone. In-hotel: restaurant, bicycles, laundry service, Internet terminal, parking (free), no-smoking rooms* ⊟ *MC, V* ⦿ *EP.*

$–$$ ▦ **The Golden Frog Inn.** One of the best deals in El Valle, this attractive
Fodor's Choice B&B near Cerro Gaital has bright rooms surrounded by 2½ acres of
★ gardens and lovely views. Built by a retired sea captain, it now belongs to another captain, Larry Thormahlen, and his wife, Becky, who make a stay here that much more enjoyable. On their extra-big front porch, with tables, chairs, and hammocks, they serve complimentary breakfasts and a glass of wine during social hour, when guests gather to watch the sunset. Another perk is the small pool surrounded by a stone deck and abundant flowers. Rooms in back have tile floors, wood ceilings, and varied views. The cheapest have two single beds, the slightly larger No. 6 has a queen bed and more windows and is nestled against the forest. The spacious "suites" have big windows, high ceilings, and private patios, and they don't cost much more; Suite 3 looks out over the India Dormida. Massages or breakfast can be arranged in your room. Guests can use a small kitchen by the pool. Rates include a glass of wine in the evening. **Pros:** friendly owners; pool; lovely grounds; great views; quiet. **Cons:** no bar or restaurant; 2 km from town. ⊠ *1½ km (1 mi) north of Texaco Station, dirt road on right Pa. 527948, Miami, FL 33152* ☎ *983–6117* ⊕ *www.goldenfroginn.com* ⋑ *6 rooms* ⌂ *In-room: no a/c, no phone, no TV. In-hotel: pool, laundry service, public Wi-Fi, parking (free), no-smoking rooms* ⊟ *No credit cards* ⦿ *BP.*

$–$$ ▦ **Los Capitanes.** This friendly little hotel on the northern side of the valley is owned by a retired German sea captain, who is usually there to offer advice on what to do during your stay. It is one of El Valle's older hotels but is well maintained, with verdant grounds bordered by a stream in back. Rooms are rather simple, with red-cement floor and white-stucco walls, cane furniture, and corrugated metal ceilings. The nicest standard rooms are on the left in the back, since they have small terraces from which you can admire Cerro Gaital. Family suites are spacious, semicircular structures with bedroom lofts, lots of furniture (including rocking chairs), and wraparound balconies with great views. The octagonal restaurant ($–$$) serves good German and Panamanian dishes. The owner extends the Panamanian senior discount to tourists, which is unusual, and a full meal plan is an option. **Pros:** nice grounds; views; friendly owner; good price. **Cons:** average rooms; some rooms are dark. ⊠ *Calle El Ciclo, 0.7 km north of Supermercado Hong Kong* ☎ *983–6080* ⊕ *www.los-capitanes.com* ⤶ *11 rooms, 4 suites* ⚴ *In-room: no a/c, no phone, refrigerator (some). In-hotel: restaurant, room service, bar, bicycles, laundry service, parking (free), no-smoking rooms* ☰ *MC, V* ⦿ *BP.*

$$–$$$ ⊞ **Los Mandarinos.** Like the Casa de Lourdes restaurant next door, this
★ small hotel and spa are built in the Tuscan style—stone and stucco walls, barrel-tile roofs—which the Panamanian owner fell in love with during an Italian vacation. The style is not entirely incongruous in highland El Valle, but the architects went overboard on the small Tuscan windows, which shortchange guests on the views. Spring for a superior room or a suite, either of which has a balcony and big windows. The hotel sits at the foot of Cerro Gaital, just steps away from the trail that leads to its summit, and is the perfect spot for morning walks and bird-watching. All rooms have high ceilings, paintings by Panama's best artists, and the same amenities provided by any of the country's top hotels. If you can afford it, the Gaital Suite has the best view, and the Honeymoon Suite, overlooking the valley, is a close second. The spa has an array of treatments and a Jacuzzi and sundeck on the roof. The hotel offers discounts for stays of four nights. **Pros:** great location; excellent restaurant; well-equipped rooms; friendly staff. **Cons:** standard "executive" rooms lack views. ⊠ *Calle El Ciclo* ☎ *983–6645* ⊕ *www.losmandarinos.com* ⤶ *30 rooms, 5 suites* ⚴ *In-room: safe, kitchen (some), refrigerator, Wi-Fi. In-hotel: restaurant, bar, pool, spa, laundry service, public Wi-Fi, parking (free), no-smoking rooms* ☰ *MC, V* ⦿ *BP.*

$–$$ ⊞ **Park Eden.** This lovely collection of houses and rooms surrounded by
☾ manicured gardens, great trees, and a babbling brook is one of El Valle's
★ more pleasant spots. Owners Lionel and Monica Alemán transformed their vacation home into a B&B upon retiring, and the accommodations are certainly homey, with frilled curtains and bedspreads, knickknacks, and cement ducks on the lawn. Ideal for families is either the two-bedroom Linda Vista cottage with a full kitchen, gas grill, fold-out couch, and an adjacent room with a bunk bed, or the suites with three beds. Two rooms in the back of the original home are less expensive: Limoneros, a yellow room, has a lovely private terrace, and the very pink Ma Vie En Rose has a slightly smaller patio. The policy here is to pamper, as is apparent in the sumptuous breakfasts, dinners, and attention provided by the charming, bilingual owners. **Pros:** friendly owners; nice gardens. **Cons:** far from center of town. ⊠ *Calle Espave, 100 meters south of Rincón Vallero* ☎ *983–6167* ⊕ *www.parkeden. com* ⤶ *6 rooms, 2 suites, 1 cottage* ⚴ *In-room: no a/c (some), DVD*

(some) no phone, kitchen (some), refrigerator (some), no TV (some). In-hotel: bicycles, laundry service, public Wi-Fi, parking (free), no-smoking rooms ⊟ AE, MC, V ⧖ BP.

$–$$ ⊡ **Rincón Vallero.** The main reason to come here is for the open-air res-
Ⓒ taurant ($–$$), a wonderful spot, like something out of a fairy tale, with stone floors, lots of plants, a fish pond, and a stream running through it. The selection ranges from traditional Panamanian *sancocho* (chicken soup with tropical tubers) to chicken cordon bleu and filet mignon. Rooms are just okay. Those in the back, open onto a small yard and garden with a playhouse, swing set, and a tiny pool and Jacuzzi surrounded by a stone terrace. They are a bit cramped and dark, with low, beamed ceilings, but are equipped with such amenities as DVD players and minibars. The suites and junior suites are considerably nicer, with high cane ceilings and big bathrooms. **Pros:** charming restaurant and gardens; nice suites; kid-friendly. **Cons:** standard rooms cramped and dark, low ceilings; down rough roads. ⊠ *Calle Espave, southern end of valley, 1 km from main road; turn left after bridge and veer right at Y ☎ 983–6175, 264–9119 in Panama City ⊕ www.hotelrinconvallero. com ⇢ 13 rooms, 4 suites ⚲ In-room: safe, DVD. In-hotel: restaurant, room service, pool, laundry service, parking (free), no-smoking rooms ⊟ MC, V ⧖ BP.*

SPORTS AND THE OUTDOORS

BIKING

Mountain biking is a great way to explore El Valle's side roads, which become rutted, dirt tracks the farther you get from the center of town. Good riding areas include the trail behind the old Hotel Campestre and the dirt roads west of the church. **Don Pepe** (⊠ *Av. Principal, half a block before market* ☎ 983–6425) rents mountain bikes for $3 per hour and $10 per day.

BIRD-WATCHING

From tiny green hermits to elegant swallow-tailed kites, a remarkable diversity of birds inhabits El Valle's sky and forests. More than 350 bird species have been spotted in the area—compared with 426 species in all of Canada. The best viewing season is October to March, when northern migrants such as the yellow warbler and northern waterthrush boost El Valle's bird diversity. The migrants are especially common in the gardens of the valley's hotels and homes, whereas the forests of Cerro Gaital and surroundings hold such tropical species as the tody motmot and sun bittern. El Valle's avian rainbow includes five kinds of toucans, six parrot species, and 25 hummingbird species. Though you can only hope to see a fraction of those birds, your chances will be greatly increased if you hire an experienced guide.

Guests at the **Canopy Lodge** (☎ 264–5720 ⊕ www.canopylodge.com) enjoy the services of Danilo Rodríguez, who has been birding in El Valle for 15 years. El Valle's most experienced guide is **Mario Bernal** (☎ 6693–8213), who has written a guide to the birds of El Valle. But he is often on the road with a group for Ancon Expeditions. The most popular nature guide in El Valle is **Mario Urriola** (☎ 6569–2676), a biologist who regularly leads visitors on hikes and birding tours, and whose rates are surprisingly inexpensive.

CANOPY TOUR

Adventure seekers will want to try the **Canopy Adventure** (☎ 983–6547 ⊕ *www.canopytower.com*), an installation affiliated with the Canopy Tower Ecolodge in Parque Nacional Soberanía. It takes you—you're strapped in with a very secure harness—flying through the forest canopy and over a 115-foot waterfall via zip-line cables strung between four platforms high in trees. The tour ($53) is in the **Refugio Ecológico del Chorro Macho**, a private reserve a few kilometers northwest of El Valle. This is more adrenaline rush than nature tour, though you do pass through some gorgeous rain forest scenery. The tour takes about 90 minutes and begins with a 30-minute hike to the first platform.

HIKING

El Valle has enough hiking routes to keep you trekking for days. ■ **TIP→** Hikes are best done early in the morning, when the air is clearer and the birds are more active. One of the best hiking trips in El Valle is the two- to three-hour hike up **Cerro Gaital**, which passes through lush forest and includes a mirador (lookout point) affording a view of the valley, the Pacific coast, and, on clear days, the Caribbean coast. There is also a trail around the back of Cerro Gaital that begins just behind the Hotel Campestre, which lacks the scenic views but passes through forest.

Another impressive view of El Valle is the one from the **Monte de la Cruz**, a deforested mountain ridge topped by a cement cross on the northwest end of the valley. It is reached by heading up the road to El Chorro Macho until it becomes a dirt road that ascends the slope as a series of switchbacks.

The popular hiking route up and along the **India Dormida** ridge on the western end of the valley combines treks through patches of forest with scenic views. The trail up the ridge is reached by heading west of town, turning right after the baseball stadium, and left again at the first road.

Because El Valle's trails are not well marked, you should hire a guide for these hikes. Any of El Valle's hotels can set you up with a hiking guide. Nature guide **Mario Urriola** (☎ 6569–2676) is a bilingual biologist who regularly leads small groups up Cerro Gaital, the India Dormida, and other hiking routes.

HORSEBACK RIDING

An inexpensive horseback adventure is available from **Alquiler de Caballos Mitzila** (✉ *Calle El Hato* ☎ 6646–5813), across from the small church on Calle El Hato, a few blocks before the Hotel Campestre. A horse costs $5 per hour, and each group has to pay an additional $5 per hour for the guide. The most popular ride is around the back of Cerro Gaital, a loop that takes about four hours to complete, though you can also ride for an hour and then come back on the same route. Neither the owner, Mitzila, nor her guides speak English, so have your hotel receptionist make the arrangements.

SHOPPING

A handicrafts selection to rival that at the nearby Mercado is available at **Artesanía Don Pedro** (✉ *Av. Prinicpal, on left 1 block before Mercado* ☎ 983–6425), open seven days a week.

El Valle is known for its Sunday-morning handicrafts market at the **Mercado** (⊠ *Av. Prinicpal, on left two blocks before church* ☎ *No phone*), a festive affair that brings together vendors and shoppers from far and wide.

CERRO LA VIEJA

32 km (20 mi) northeast of Penonomé, 176 km (109 mi) southwest of Panama City.

To the west of El Valle, on the road from Penenomé to Churuquita Grande, stands the impressive forested hill of Cerro la Vieja, with thick foliage clinging to its rocky face. The area around that peak holds a mix of farms and patches of forest, and it has been experiencing a slight ecological recovery in recent years, as local farmers allow regrowth in areas that were deforested decades ago. This is in no small part thanks to the efforts of Alfonso Jaen, who owns the Posada Ecológico Cerro la Vieja, one of the country's first eco-lodges. Guides at that lodge lead visitors through the surrounding countryside, to the summit of Cerro la Vieja, or all the way to El Valle. Because Cerro La Vieja is in a valley between the country's Pacific and Atlantic slopes, it gets more rain than the nearby Pacific lowlands, and thus stays greener during the dry season. It is also home to a good variety of birds, since it lies within the range of Pacific and Caribbean species. Travelers who prefer to take it easy may want to dedicate their stay to the Posada Ecológico's small spa.

GETTING HERE AND AROUND

The drive from Panama City to Cerro la Vieja takes about two and a half hours. Drive 144 km (89 mi) west on the Carretera Interamericana to Penonomé, and take the first entrance, which veers right after the Hotel Dos Continentes. Turn right again at the second street and follow the signs to Churuquita Grande and Tambo, for 32 km (20 mi).

WHERE TO STAY

$ ⊞ **Posada Ecológica Cerro de la Vieja.** The view of Cerro la Vieja from the
★ restaurant, spa, and rooms at this small eco-lodge alone is worth the trip there—the bird-watching, hiking, and inexpensive spa therapies are icing on the cake. The *posada* is perched on a hilltop directly in front of Cerro de la Vieja, with rooms in various buildings spread along the slope amid trees and gardens that attract an array of birds. "Premier" rooms are well worth the top dollar, since they are bright and spacious and have small balconies with hammocks and views. ""Superior"" rooms just below them are similar but not as bright and have less spectacular views. ""Standards,"" in back are even darker and overlook the forest. The panorama is best appreciated from the restaurant, which has a wall of windows and the spa below it. A lounge next door has pool and Ping-Pong tables, couches, and the hotel's only TV. The lodge offers eight inexpensive guided hikes, most of which can be done on a mule for slightly more money. The Trinidad Spa has a sauna, a hot tub with a view, and affordable massages and beauty treatments. **Pros:** amazing views; nature; hiking; spa. **Cons:** standard rooms lack view. ⊠ *Chiguirí, 32 km (20 mi) northeast of Penonomé on road to Churuquita Grande*

THE GOLDEN TOAD

El Valle has long been synonymous with a bright yellow amphibian with black spots called the golden toad (*Atelopus zeteki*), which, along with the harpy eagle, is one of Panama's emblematic animals. The beautiful toads were revered by the area's pre-Columbian inhabitants, who crafted frog-shaped jewelry and ceramic wares. The fascination continues, and you're likely to see images of golden toads on brochures, T-shirts, and an array of knickknacks. Where you won't see them, however, is in El Valle's forests, where they were fairly abundant as recently as the 1980s. The population of the golden toad, which exists only in Panama's Cordillera Central, has plummeted in recent years, due to the spread of a chytrid fungus (*Batrachochytrium dendrobatidis*) that covers the frogs' skin until they suffocate. Scientists have consequently captured toads in the wild and sequestered them in fungus-free environments, such as in the Amphibian Conservation Center at El Nispero zoo, which is one of the only places you can see the golden toad today.

Amphibian populations have declined throughout the mountains of Central America, and around the world, in recent decades, causing considerable alarm in the scientific community. Several scientists who studied climate changes in the Costa Rican mountain community of Monteverde, where another golden toad species went extinct in the 1990s, published a report in the prestigious journal *Nature* claiming that seasonal drought conditions resulting from global warming have weakened frogs' immune systems and made them more susceptible to diseases such as the chytrid fungus. Other scientists studying the fungal disease say that it is working its way eastward through Panama, and worry that tourists may transport the spores. Consequently, if you hike in the forests in western or central Panama you should, before traveling to the eastern half of the country, wash your hiking boots with soap and water and then alcohol to kill any fungus.

☎ *983–8900 or 269–8698* ⊕ *www.posadaecologica.com* ⇤ *18 rooms* ⧉ *In-room: no a/c (some), no phone, no TV. In-hotel: restaurant, bar, spa, laundry service, public Wi-Fi, parking (free), no-smoking rooms* ⊟ *MC, V* ⊚ *BP.*

SPORTS AND THE OUTDOORS
HIKING
Hiking is the specialty at the **Posada Ecológica Cerro de la Vieja** (☎ *983– 8900* ⊕ *www.posadaecologica.com*), where guests choose from eight different guided hikes ranging from the three-hour climb to the summit of Cerro la Vieja to full-day treks deep into the mountains. After the Cerro la Vieja ascent, the most popular hike is the three-hour trek to Tavidá Waterfall and nearby petroglyphs.

The Azuero Peninsula and Veraguas

WORD OF MOUTH

"[W]e drove through the Azuero Peninsula and stayed in the small town of Pedasí. We stayed in a lovely small hotel, Casa Margarita, which was recently opened by Americans who are relocating to Panama. It is a tiny town with your basic main street a few blocks long, but there appears to be lots of development in this area. While you are not very close to Panama City (about 5 hours' drive), you are near other cities such as Las Tablas and Chitré, which aren't generally touristy, except very popular for Carnival.

—hamlet

By David
Dudenhoefer
Updated by
Sean Mattson

The Azuero Peninsula and Veraguas constitute the other Panama, or perhaps, the real Panama. This was one of the first areas of the country to be colonized by Spain, and the colonial churches and squares of its historic towns provide perfect backdrops for its frequent folk festivals and religious celebrations. Before the Europeans arrived, the area had well-established indigenous societies, remnants of which can be seen today in museums, local ceramic work, and elements of Panamanian folk music. The region's predominant culture and race is now *mestizo*, a mixture of European and indigenous, whereas the economy is dominated by cattle ranching, a livelihood introduced by Spaniards centuries ago.

Panamanians flock to the Azuero Peninsula for Carnaval and other celebrations, but tourists have largely ignored it—those who do come are usually bound for some of Panama's best surfing beaches. Those beaches are neither as attractive nor as accessible as strands in Central Panama or Bocas del Toro, and are less of a draw for the nonsurfing traveler. Nor does the region have lush forests—centuries of colonization have left it predominantly deforested. There are, however, some patches of rare tropical dry forest here, whereas Isla Iguana and Isla de Coiba are surrounded by phenomenal marine life.

The peninsula is Panama's driest region and is consequently a good place to head during the rainy months, when conditions are optimal for surfing and skin diving. It is always an excellent destination for travelers with a keen interest in culture, especially during festival times, and it is the place to go to stray from the beaten path.

ORIENTATION AND PLANNING

ORIENTATION

The Azuero region is usually reached by driving west from Panama City on the Carretera Interamericana (CA1), though it can be easily visited on a drive from Central Panama or the western province of Chiriquí. From the Interamericana, roads head south into the Azuero Peninsula and to Santa Catalina.

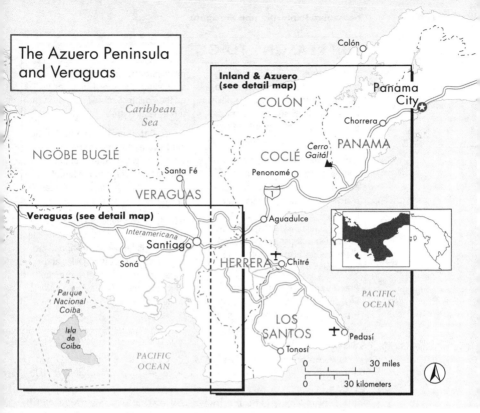

The Azuero Peninsula and Veraguas

Inland & Azuero (see detail map)

Veraguas (see detail map)

Caribbean Sea

Colón

Panama City

NGÖBE BUGLÉ

COLÓN

Chorrera

Santa Fé

COCLÉ

Cerro Gaitál

PANAMA

VERAGUAS

Penonomé

Interamericana

Santiago

Aguadulce

Soná

HERRERA

Chitré

Parque Nacional Coiba

PACIFIC OCEAN

Isla de Coiba

LOS SANTOS

Pedasí

PACIFIC OCEAN

Tonosí

0   30 miles

0   30 kilometers

PLANNING

WHEN TO GO

Most tourists visit during the December–May dry season, but because this is Panama's driest region, you can also head here in the rainy months and expect less rain than you'll get elsewhere. Serious surfers go to playas Venao and Santa Catalina between May and January when the waves are biggest and the ocean warmer. The rainy months are also the best time for skin-diving trips to Isla Iguana or Isla de Coiba. Deep-sea fishing is best from January to April, though winds can be problematic. Keep in mind that the peninsula's hotels get packed during Carnaval in mid- to late-February or early March, but it's a fun time to be here.

GETTING HERE AND AROUND

BY AIR

The domestic airline Air Panama has charter flights to Chitré and Pedasí. Flights depart from Panama City's Albrook Airport (⇨ Chapter 2), from Chitré's **Aeropuerto Capitan Alonso Valderrama** (⊠ Road to Playa El Agallito, Chitré ☎ 996–4432), and from Pedasí from an airstrip east of town on the road to Playa el Bajadero.

Contacts Air Panama (☎ 316–9000 or 316–9023 ⊕ www.flyairpanama.com)

TOP REASONS TO GO

Folk Festival. From Guararé's relatively tranquil Mejorana Festival to the unrepentant revelry of Carnaval, the Azuero Peninsula's frequent celebrations are great opportunities to experience the area's vibrant culture.

Isla Iguana. One of the oldest and best-developed coral reefs in Panama's Pacific waters and a lovely beach can be found at this small, protected island a short trip from Pedasí. Scuba divers may encounter more than 200 fish species found there, but it's also a great trip for sunbathers.

Playa Venao. One of Panama's best surf spots, Playa Venao has the added attraction of being near patches of tropical dry forest, good snorkeling, and sportfishing, as well as the country's most important sea-turtle nesting area.

Santa Catalina. This laid-back fishing town at the end of the road is synonymous with great surf, but it is also the gateway to excellent diving and good sportfishing and a nice place to get away from it all.

Isla de Coiba. One of Central America's best Pacific dive spots, Isla de Coiba is known for its abundant sharks, vast schools of jacks, and varied reef fish. It is a remote and wild spot that rewards those who make the trip with spectacular natural beauty.

BY BOAT
Various companies offer cruises to Isla de Coiba departing from David, in Chiriquí Province (⇨ *Isla de Coiba, above, and David, in Chapter 5*).

BY CAR
This region is best explored by car. All of this region's towns can be reached in a standard vehicle except for Parque Nacional El Copé and Playa Santa Catalina, which are better explored by truck or four-wheel drive. Cars can be rented in Chitré and Santiago.

Car-Rental Agencies Budget (✉ *Via Carmelo Spadafora, Chitré* ☎ *996–0027; 263–8777 reservations* ✉ *Hotel Galerias, Carretera Interamericana, Santiago* ☎ *998–1731; 263–8777 reservations*). **Hertz** (✉ *Aeropuerto Capitan Alonso Valderrama, Chitré* ☎ *996–2256; 301–2611 reservations*).

RESTAURANTS
The region's dining options are quite limited, but there are a few excellent restaurants, and plenty of mediocre ones. Seafood—especially fresh tuna—is put to great use at the few quality restaurants.

HOTELS
The Azuero region is short on quality hotels and has nothing even resembling a resort. There are plenty of cheap backpacker places and a few charming inns that take advantage of the surrounding nature. Hotel prices in the peninsula's towns double during Carnaval, when you should reserve at least a month in advance, and they all increase about 50% for New Year's and Easter week.

WHAT IT COSTS IN U.S. DOLLARS				
¢	$	$$	$$$	$$$$
Restaurants	under $5	$5–$10	$10–$15	$15–$20	over $20
Hotels	under $50	$50–$100	$100–$160	$160–$220	over $220

Restaurant prices are per person for a main course at dinner. Hotel prices are for two people in a standard double room, excluding service and 10% tax.

ESSENTIALS
EMERGENCIES
As far as medical care goes, this is one of Panama's more isolated regions, with local clinics and hospitals below the international standards of Panama City's major clinics. From most regions of the Azuero Peninsula, if you have health problems you'll want to head to Chitré Veraguas. From Santa Catalina, you should head to Santiago. Some emergency numbers are different for these two regions.

Pharmacies tend to open from 8 AM until between 7 and 9 PM. If you need medication late at night, go to the provincial hospital.

Emergency Services National police (☎ 996-4333 in Herrera, 966-8824 in Los Santos provinces and 970-3403 in Veraguas Province; or national police emergency line 104). **Fire department** (☎ 103). **Ambulance (Red Cross)** (☎ 996-1465 in Chitré; 958-7979 in Veraguas).

MONEY
ATMs that accept international credit and debit cards can be found at the branches of major banks in Chitré, Las Tablas, Pedasí, and Santiago. The closest ATMs to Playa Venao or Santa Catalina are at the Banco Nacional in Pedasí or Soná.

SAFETY
Most of this region's beaches get big waves, and some have rocks, which can be very dangerous. When hiking through the forest, always be careful where you put your hand, since many of the dry forest plants have thorns, and there are many creatures that bite or sting.

VISITOR INFORMATION
Arena (just north of Chitré), Pedasí, and Santiago have **ATP** offices, open weekdays 7:30–3:30.

Contacts ATP (✉ Av. Circunvalación in front of industrial park, Arena ☎ 974-4532 ✉ Carretera Nacional, north end of town, Pedasí ☎ 995-2339 ✉ Av. Central, Santiago ☎ 998-3929).

INLAND

The Carretera Interamericana crosses Panama to the north of the Azuero Peninsula, skirting the towns of Penonomé and Santiago, and passing a couple of quick stops that offer introductions to the region's history. Parque Arqueológico El Caño and Natá are just off the highway, making them worthwhile cultural pit stops if you're driving.

PARQUE ARQUEOLÓGICO EL CAÑO

27 km (17 mi) west of Penonomé, 171 km (106 mi) west of Panama City.

One of only two archaeological sites in Panama that are open to the public, El Caño illustrates why so little remains of the country's pre-Columbian jewelry and artwork. The looting of historic treasures in Panama began with the Spanish conquest and continues today, as grave diggers called *huaqueros* raid pre-Columbian sites and sell what they find to private collectors. At El Caño in the 1920s, American adventurer Hyatt Verrill removed 1,000-plus-year-old sculpted figures topping pillars and shipped them to U.S. museums, along with the ceramic pieces and gold jewelry that his crew found at the site. Today a circle of stone slabs is all that's left of the pillars. To make matters worse, most of the valuable pieces held in the site's small museum were stolen in the 1990s—quite possibly by corrupt government officials. The site's museum consequently doesn't have much to see, but the excavated burial pit nearby is worth a look. ⊠ *3 km (2 mi) north of Carretera Interamericana, veer left at El Caño church* ☎ *987–9352* ⊠ *$1* ☉ *Tues.–Sat. 9–noon and 1–4, Sun. 9–1.*

GETTING HERE AND AROUND

To drive to El Caño from Panama City, head west on the Carretera Interamericana for 171 km (106 mi) and look for the turnoff on the right 27 km (17 mi) after Penonomé.

NATÁ

36 km (22 mi) west of Penonomé, 180 km (112 mi) west of Panama City.

★ One of Panama's oldest inhabited towns, Natá (officially Natá de los Caballeros) has a lovely central plaza with a restored colonial church, and is worth a quick stop on the drive to the Azuero Peninsula or Santa Catalina. Founded in 1522, Natá was a key Spanish outpost in a region dominated by Indian chiefs who organized stiff resistance to colonization. *Caballeros* (knights) were sent to pacify the Indians and construct a Christian enclave here in 1522.

The most impressive of Natá's buildings is the ancient **Basílica Menor Santiago Apóstol**, with its high bell tower and wide facade. One of Panama's oldest functioning churches, it was built in the 17th century, and it holds eight colonial altars under its hardwood roof. The church is open only for Mass.

GETTING HERE AND AROUND

To drive to Natá from Panama City, head west on the Carretera Interamericana for 180 km (112 mi) and look for the turnoff on the left 36 km (22 mi) after Penonomé.

OFF THE BEATEN PATH

Parque Nacional El Copé, also known as Parque Nacional Omar Torrijos, was created after the Panamanian strongman died when his plane crashed into a mountain here in 1981. Together with the contiguous Parque Nacional Santa Fe, El Copé protects a vast expanse of forest

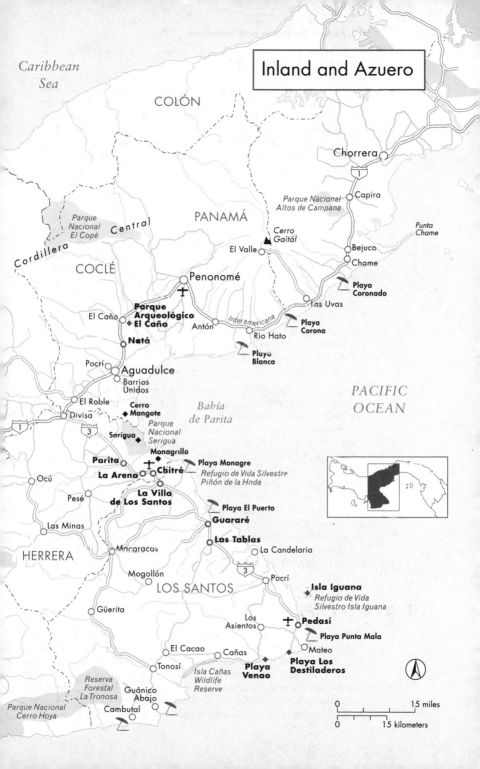

Inland and Azuero

Caribbean Sea

COLÓN

PANAMÁ

Parque Nacional El Copé

Cordillera Central

COCLÉ

Parque Nacional Altos de Campana

Chorrera

Capira

Cerro Gaitál

El Valle

Bejuco

Chame

Punta Chame

Penonomé

Playa Coronado

Parque Arqueológico El Caño

El Caño

Las Uvas

Antón

Interamericana

Playa Corona

Río Hato

Natá

Playa Blanca

Pocrí

Aguadulce

Barrios Unidos

Bahía de Parita

PACIFIC OCEAN

El Roble

Divisa

Cerro Mangote

Parque Nacional Sarigua

Sarigua

Monagrillo

Parita

La Arena

Chitré

Playa Monagre

Refugio de Vida Silvestre Piñón de la Hnda

Ocú

Pesé

La Villa de Los Santos

Playa El Puerto

Las Minas

Guararé

HERRERA

Macaracas

Las Tablas

La Candelaria

Mogollón

LOS SANTOS

Pocrí

Güerita

Isla Iguana

Refugio de Vida Silvestre Isla Iguana

Los Asientos

Pedasí

El Cacao

Cañas

Playa Punta Mala

Tonosí

Isla Cañas Wildlife Reserve

Mateo

Playa Venao

Playa Los Destiladeros

Reserva Forestal La Tronosa

Güánico Abajo

Parque Nacional Cerro Hoya

Cambutal

0   15 miles

0   15 kilometers

A BIT OF HISTORY

While Panama City grew rich from the transport of treasures to and from distant lands between the 16th and 18th centuries, Veraguas and the Azuero Peninsula developed economies based on agriculture and ranching, which have endured the booms and busts of Central Panama. The region had complex indigenous societies when the Spanish conquistadors arrived, as the pre-Columbian ceramic and gold work found here attests. The region's Indians resisted Spanish colonization for the first half of the 16th century, but conquistadors persisted, bolstered by the lure of gold in the mountains. After defeating the local chiefs, the Spaniards brought in African slaves to work the gold mines and founded towns such as Parita and La Villa

de Los Santos to grow food for the mining communities. The Spaniards mined out the region's major gold deposits by the 17th century, but the lowland communities continued to produce meat and produce for Panama City, and cottage industries producing such traditional goods as straw hats and ceramic wares remain to this day.

Recent centuries have seen the expansion of pastureland at the cost of the region's forests, first as a result of the population boost while the Panama Canal was built, and later when the country began exporting beef. The region's people have consequently become as synonymous with deforestation as they are with folklore.

along the Cordillera Central that provides a refuge for such rare endangered animals as the jaguar, tapir, and harpy eagle. Bird-watchers make the long, rough drive up to El Copé to look for such rare species as the red-fronted parrolet and the umbrella bird. The park's misty forests extend from the Pacific slope of the continental divide over to the Caribbean slope, which means it can rain here any time of year—the reason for its vast array of wildlife. Views of the Caribbean forest are amazing, and from the lookout point above the ranger station you can see both the Pacific and Atlantic oceans on a clear morning. The park has several well-marked hiking trails, a small camping area, and a rustic cabin that you can rent for $5. Several families rent rooms in the town of Barrigón, a 60-minute hike from the park. The road to the park is a rough, 4WD—track for the last 7 km (4 mi). Bring warm clothes if you overnight here—it cools off considerably. ⊠ *50 km (31 mi) west of Penonomé via El Copé and Barrigón* ☎ *997–7538* ⊠*$5* ⊙ *Daily 8–4.*

THE AZUERO PENINSULA

The Azuero Peninsula is sometimes called Panama's cultural cradle, due to the folk music and dance performed at its frequent festivals. The relatively dry region is covered with cattle ranches and dotted with tranquil agricultural towns where families chat on the porches of adobe houses and historic churches overlook tidy central plazas. The peninsula is known for maintaining traditions from the colonial era, when Spanish and indigenous customs were melded. These traditions include everything from folk music and dancing to the exquisite, hand-stitched *polleras* (elaborate embroidered dresses) and ubiquitous straw hats. Festivals—ideal opportunities to experience the region's folklore—are celebrated just about every month here.

Deforestation for farming and ranching has been rampant on the peninsula, and little remains of the original wilderness. Nevertheless, the roads are lined with gumbo limbo and Madera negro trees, and streams and gullies are shaded by kapok, guanacaste, and other tropical trees that provide homes for howler monkeys, iguanas, and birds. The long coast holds many beaches, the nicest of which are Playa Venao and the small beach on Isla Iguana, which also protects coral reefs. In addition to its main towns of Chitré, La Villa De Los Santos, Las Tablas, and Pedasí, Azuero has some picturesque villages that are worth checking out, such as Parita and—deep in the peninsula's interior—Pesé, Las Minas, and Ocú.

4

PARITA

240 km (149 mi) southwest of Panama City, 12 km (7 mi) north of Chitré.

★ One of the most picturesque and best-preserved colonial towns in the peninsula, Parita is just off the Carretera Nacional—the main road into the peninsula—which makes stopping here to admire its lovely central plaza and shady streets practically obligatory. Founded in 1566, it was the first Spanish settlement in the Azuero Peninsula, and it soon became one of the principal suppliers of food for the gold mines in the Cordillera Central. The grassy plaza that lies in front of that church is surrounded by long, colorful adobe homes with barrel-tile roofs. Parita's only monument is its colonial church, the 17th-century **Iglesia de Santo Domingo de Guzmán,** two blocks west of the Carretera Nacional. It holds some elaborately carved wooden altars and statues dating from the 18th century but is usually closed.

GETTING HERE AND AROUND

To reach Parita, and the Azuero Peninsula, drive west from Panama City on the Carretera Interamericana 215 km (129 mi) to the well-marked intersection at Divisa, where you turn south onto the Carretera Nacional. The entrance to Parita is on the right 25 km (16 mi) south of Divisa. You can also take a taxi there from nearby Chitré for $5–7.

LA ARENA

250 km (155 mi) southwest of Panama City, 10 km (6 mi) south of Parita.

This small, traditional town has been producing pottery since colonial times—and perhaps earlier. Much of the ceramic work replicates pre-Columbian designs, though the local artisans also produce more modern pieces. The town is most famous for its traditional *tinajas,* ceramic jugs or pots used to store water, which make lovely vases but are tough to get home in one piece. The Carretera Nacional runs right through

La Arena 2 km (1 mi) before Chitré, and the traffic slows here since the street is lined with shops and pedestrians.

GETTING HERE AND AROUND

To drive to La Arena from Panama City, follow directions for Parita and continue 15 km (9 mi) beyond. It's a five-minute taxi ride ($2–3) or 15-minute bus trip (25¢) from Chitré to La Arena.

SHOPPING

Shopping is what La Arena is all about, and most of the shops line the Carretera Nacional. At the center of town is a two-story building called the **Mercado de Artesanías** (⊠ *Carretera Nacional, on left if headed toward Chitré* ☎ *No phone*) that holds the stands of various vendors. In addition to ceramics, you'll find hammocks, Carnaval masks, straw hats, and more.

Some of the most traditional ceramic work is available at **Cerámica Calderón** (⊠ *Carretera Nacional, on left* ☎ 974–4946).

CHITRÉ

252 km (156 mi) southwest of Panama City, 37 km (23 mi) south of Divisa.

Chitré is a rambling town with a compact center that includes a lovely 18th-century church and the region's best museum. Those sites can be visited in an hour's time, but because it has the peninsula's best hotels outside of the beaches on the southern coast, Chitré can be a convenient base from which to visit the area's traditional towns, such as nearby La Villa de los Santos, Parita, Las Minas, Ocú, and Pesé. It's also the capital of Herrera Province and the principal commercial and administrative center for the Azuero Peninsula.

Chitré's only landmark to speak of is the lovely **Catedral de San Juan Bautista** (⊠ *Calle Aminta Burgos de Amado* ☎ *No phone*), which was inaugurated in 1910 but was built in the colonial style and has an attractive hardwood interior and stained-glass windows. The area around the cathedral is perfect for an afternoon stroll and a cool drink at one of the nearby restaurants.

Several blocks northwest of the cathedral is a white neoclassical building that holds the provincial museum, which is surprisingly good. The **Museo de Herrera** features pre-Columbian artifacts found in the area, some of which are more than 1,000 years old. There is also a replica of a chief's burial site that was discovered during the colonial era and well chronicled before being looted. Its exhibits on local folklore include Carnaval masks, traditional musical instruments such as the mejorana, and lovely embroidered polleras. Unfortunately, the information is all in Spanish. ⊠ *Calle Manuel María Correa and Av. Julio Arjona* ☎ 996–0077 🖅 $1 ☉ *Tues.–Sat. 8:30–4.*

GETTING HERE AND AROUND

Via car, head west from Panama City on the Carretera Interamericana 215 km (133 mi) to the well-marked intersection at Divisa; turn south onto the Carretera Nacional. Chitré is 37 km (23 mi) south of Divisa, and the Carretera Nacional continues south of it to nearby La Villa de

FOLK FESTIVALS

Check ⊕ www.visitpanama.com for current information.

JANUARY

The first days of January are marked by the **Reyes Magos** celebration in Macaracas, southwest of Chitré. **Patron saint days:** Ocú, January 17–20; Guararé, January 21; La Enea (just north of Las Tablas), January 30.

FEBRUARY

Las Trancas, between Las Tablas and Pedasí, is known for its **Festival de la Candelaria**, a religious celebration with folk music and dance on February 2. Las Tablas is famous for its **Carnaval** festivities (⇨ *Las Tablas, below*), but Chitré, Parita, Ocú, La Villa de Los Santos, and Pedasí also have notable celebrations.

MARCH AND APRIL

Rum-producing Pesé, southwest of Chitré, celebrates the **Festival de la Caña (Sugar Cane Festival)** in March (dates vary). **Semana Santa** is especially picturesque in La Villa de Los Santos, Pesé, and La Arena. The country-fair-like **Feria de Azuero** is held the last week in April in La Villa Los Santos. **Patron saint days:** San José (south of Las Tablas), March 19.

MAY AND JUNE

Corpus Christi, which falls in May or June, is celebrated in La Villa de Los Santos with dances by *los diablitos* (the little devils; ⇨ *Devilish Celebrations, below*). The **Festival de Manito**, a major folk music and dance event, is held in Ocú the last week of June. **Patron saint days:** Chitré, June 24; La Arena, June 29; Monagrillo (just north of Chitré), June 30.

JULY AND AUGUST

Las Tablas's **Festival de la Pollera**, July 21–23, features folk music, dancing, parades, and women in embroidered dresses. Parita celebrates its **foundation day** on August 18. Las Minas comes alive at the end of August for the **Festival de la Flor del Espiritu Santo. Patron saint days:** Las Tablas, July 20; Guararé, July 16; Parita, July 26–August 8; Tonosí, August 18.

SEPTEMBER AND OCTOBER

The **founding of Macaracas**, a small town southwest of Chitré, is fêted on September 12. The folk-music **Festival de la Mejorana** (⇨ *Guararé, below*) takes place the third weekend of September. La Villa de Los Santos, La Arena, and other towns celebrate **Semanas del Campesino** during various weeks from August to October.

NOVEMBER AND DECEMBER

The **founding of Chitré** is celebrated on October 19. La Villa de Los Santos celebrates **El Primer Grito de la Independencia** with folk music and dance on November 10. **Patron saint days:** Pedasí, November 25; Las Minas, December 4.

Los Santos, Las Tablas, and Pedasí. Buses to Chitré depart from Panama City's Albrook Terminal every 30 minutes; the trip is four to five hours. Air Panama has charter service to Chitré's small airport from Panama City's Albrook Airport. Chitré is the only town in the Azuero Peninsula where you can rent a car.

CLOSE UP

Folklore Fanatics

The Azuero Peninsula has been called Panama's cultural cradle, but its rich cultural heritage is by no means dormant, like some babe who's been rocked to sleep—rather, it is wide awake and impatiently awaiting the next folk festival. In these seemingly somnolent ranching towns, folk music and dancing aren't mere cultural artifacts, they are the way people celebrate life. And there are plenty of folks in the region who celebrate as often as possible.

Panama is a land of many cultures. You may experience indigenous or Afro-Caribbean folklore elsewhere in Panama, but the predominant culture in the Azuero Peninsula is *mestizo*, the mixture of European and indigenous races and traditions, which happens to be the folk tradition with which the majority of Panamanians identify. The mestizo culture is consequently considered the national culture, and you may see it on display throughout the country, but because the Azuero Peninsula was one of the first regions to be colonized, and has been a bit of a backwater since the colonial era, it has maintained more of the old traditions.

The best way to experience Panama's rich cultural heritage is to attend one of the Azuero Peninsula's frequent *ferias*, or festivals, of which there are usually a couple every month. These celebrations range from relatively solemn religious feasts in which icons are paraded through town to the pagan antics of *los diablitos* (the little devils) that animate the streets during Corpus Christi, but they invariably include plenty of folk music and dancing.

The frequency of folkloric celebrations in the Azuero Peninsula means that there should be one that coincides with your vacation, and this chapter has an extensive list of them. But because some celebrations change dates from year to year, you should check the Web site of the **Panama Tourist Bureau (ATP)** (⊕ *www.visitpanama.com*) for up-to-date information on fairs and festivals. Those with a keen interest in the subject should also check out the site **Folklore Panama Típico** (⊕ *www.folklore.panamatipico.com*).

Before you go exploring the world of Panamanian folklore, however, you should be familiar with its basic components:

Pollera. Panama's national dress, the *pollera* is a derivation of formal dresses worn by Spanish women in centuries of yore. Consisting of a white blouse and dress with elaborate embroidery, often in red or blue thread, they can take months to sew, and consequently can cost thousands of dollars. They also are often worn with thousands of dollars in gold jewelry. The best opportunity for admiring polleras is during the Festival de la Pollera in Las Tablas in late July.

Sombrero Pintao. The real Panama hat, these tightly woven straw hats have dark brown patterns woven into them, hence their name, which translates as "painted hat." They are national dress as well, since the majority of men in the countryside wear them everywhere but in church and bed. They are as practical as the pollera is extravagant, since they save necks and faces from being toasted by the tropical sun.

4

Música Folclórica. The pulse of any traditional celebration, this rhythmic acoustic music is performed by small groups with an accordion, two different types of drums, and a *churuca*— a serrated gourd or metal cylinder that is scraped with a stick. It is the music that most folk dances are performed to, with the exception of the *mejorana*, a more subdued kind of folk music played on a five-string guitar called the *guitarra mejoranera* and accompanied by different folk dances. *Tamborito*, on the other hand, is a drum-based music accompanied by a call and response similar to that of traditional African music.

Máscaras. Masks form an important part of Carnaval and Corpus Christi celebrations, but Panamanian devil masks have evolved significantly in recent decades. The traditional Panamanian devil mask bears some resemblance to the masks of Chinese New Year parades, and are similar to those used in the Peruvian highlands. Some of the most colorful characters of Panamanian folklore are *los*

diablitos (the little devils), who dance in the streets of La Villa de Los Santos during Corpus Christi celebrations. Those pagan characters wear diabolical papier-mâché masks and red-and-black striped jump suits. They often carry inflated, dried cow bladders, which they hit with sticks while emitting long, guttural shouts. To witness a group of men performing this ritual is to get an idea of just how seriously Panamanians take their folklore.

WHERE TO EAT AND STAY

$ ✗ **Restaurante DKDAS.** This small, open-air eatery at the edge of town is

LATIN AMERICAN one of Chitré's most popular restaurants. It is often packed with locals, who head there for inexpensive seafood and grilled meat, such as *filet de res pimienta* (fillet in a pepper sauce) or *langostinos al ajillo* (prawns sautéed with garlic). Everything is served no-frills in a long, bright dining room lined with ferns, and there are usually a couple of TVs blasting. The name is pronounced *day*-ka-das. ⊠ *Vía Circunvalación, half a block north of Hotel Hong Kong* ☎ *996–3339* ☐ *MC, V.*

$ 🔟 **Hotel Guaycanes.** Chitré's best hotel is west of town and bears some

☾ resemblance to an American motel. Ample grounds include a small pool, a small park with an artificial lake, and a playground. Rooms, in two-story buildings, are bright, with nice wood furniture and cable TV, but bathrooms are cramped and the mattresses are soft. Second-floor rooms, with small balconies and views of the grounds, are the nicest. A large casino near the parking lot is popular with locals. The attractive, open-air restaurant ($) serves a wide selection of food, from the traditional *arroz con pollo* (rice with chicken) to *corvina thai* (sea bass in a spicy coconut sauce). **Pros:** quiet; spacious grounds; decent restaurant. **Cons:** small bathrooms; taxi needed to get to town center. ⊠ *Vía Circunvaluación* ☎ *996–9758* ⊕ *www.losguayacanes.com* ⤺ *56 rooms, 8 suites* ☾ *In-hotel: restaurant, room service, bar, tennis courts, pool, gym, laundry service, public Wi-Fi, no-smoking rooms* ☐ *AE, MC, V* 🍽 *BP.*

¢ 🔟 **Hotel Rex.** Near the cathedral and a short walk from the museum,

☾ shops, and restaurants, this older hotel is the best option for budget travelers, or anyone who prefers to stay in the heart of town. The rooms are rudimentary but have cable TV and air-conditioning—those on the top floor are brighter. There's a small Internet café by the lobby as well as a common terrace with a view of the Plaza Central and cathedral. The El Mesón restaurant (¢–$) downstairs serves decent Panamanian and international fare, and its café seating in front is perfect for people-watching. **Pros:** central location; good restaurant. **Cons:** basic rooms. ⊠ *Calle Malitón Martín* ☎ *996–4310* ⤺ *32 rooms* ☾ *In-hotel: restaurant, laundry service, Internet, Wi-Fi, no-smoking rooms* ☐ *AE, MC, V* 🍽 *BP.*

LA VILLA DE LOS SANTOS

256 km (159 mi) southwest of Panama City, 4 km (2 mi) south of Chitré.

Just across the muddy Río La Villa from Chitré is La Villa de Los Santos, which is considerably smaller than its neighbor but more historically significant. When it was founded in 1569 it was one of just two Spanish outposts in an area dominated by hostile Indians. That indigenous population was highly developed, as excavations at the nearby burial site of Cerro Juan Díaz have established, but they were no match for Spanish swords or the old-world diseases.

La Villa's claim to fame in Panama is that it was the first community to express support for Simón Bolívar's South American revolution against Spain. People in the region were fed up with Spanish exploitation, but

CLOSE UP

Traditional Towns

Chitré is the perfect base from which to explore the peninsula's interior, where narrow roads wind between traditional agricultural towns with adobe homes and ancient churches. The tiny communities of Las Minas, Pesé, and Ocú become packed during annual folk festivals, but for most of the year they are somnolent villages that seem hardly touched by the hand of time. You can drive a loop through the most interesting towns in a matter of hours, heading first to Pesé, then to Las Minas, and north to Ocú, where you can continue north to the Carretera Interamericana just west of Divisa, and back to Chitré. The easiest town to visit is **Pesé**, 22 km (14 mi) west of Chitré, which is surrounded by a sea of sugarcane, used by the town's one industry, the rum distillery that produces Seco Herrerano, Panama's most popular booze. The rocket fuel powers the region's folk festivals and keeps its AA chapters running. Witness large quantities being consumed during Pesé's annual Festival de la Caña (Sugar Cane Festival) in March. Thirty-two kilometers (20 mi) southwest of Pesé in the mountains is **Las Minas**, a gold-mining community during the colonial era and now the site of traditional celebrations during the first days of September and on December 4. From Las Minas it's a rough 21-km (13-mi) drive north to **Ocú**, a more developed town that hosts the annual Festival de Manito that attracts musicians and dancers from across the region.

4

the politicians in the administrative center of Natá were pro-Spain, and they repressed La Villa's independence movement. The town's most powerful families consequently sent a letter directly to Bolívar on November 10, 1821, expressing their desire to join his recently liberated state of Gran Colombia (modern-day Colombia, Ecuador, and Venezuela). Several weeks later Panama declared its independence from Spain. The drafting of that letter, known as *el Primer Grito de la Independencia*, (the First Shout of Independence), is celebrated every November 10 on La Villa's central plaza with speeches and folk dancing.

Three blocks east of the Carretera Nacional, La Villa's central Plaza Simón Bolívar is surrounded by colonial- and republican-era buildings, the most impressive of which is the town's church. The **Iglesia de San Atanasio** (⊠ *Calle José Vallarino* ☎ *No phone*), completed in 1773, holds various treasures of colonial art, including a massive mahogany altar covered with gold leaf and nine smaller altars. The church also has an ornate mahogany archway and a large statue of Christ that is paraded through the streets during Semana Santa.

The famous letter to Simón Bolívar was drafted in 1821 in the white-washed colonial building across from the plaza, now the **Museo de la Nacionalidad** *(Nationhood Museum)*. The colonial-era furniture and sad collection of pre-Columbian pottery within are hardly worth the entrance fee, but the well-preserved building, with its ancient hand-hewn rafters, adobe walls, and terra-cotta floors, certainly is. ⊠ *Calle José Vallarino* ☎ *966–8192* ⊠ *$1* ☉ *Tues.–Sat. 8–4, Sun. 9–noon.*

DEVILISH CELEBRATIONS

The Christian holiday of Corpus Christi takes place on a Thursday in either May or June—62 days after Holy Thursday—and has been observed in Europe since the 13th century, but no town celebrates it like La Villa de Los Santos. Despite the fact that its name translates as Village of the Saints, the town celebrates Corpus Christi with traditional dances performed by *los diablitos* (little devils)—men in red and black costumes and demonic papier-mâché masks. Those pagan characters dominate 10 days of ancient rituals and modern revelry that begin the Wednesday before Corpus Christi and culminate with concerts that attract people from across Panama.

The pagan activities peak eight days after the mass of Corpus Christi, when diablitos dance in the streets and groups of adolescents in masks run around trying to scare people. The adult diablitos, who are usually accompanied by musicians, carry inflated, dried cow bladders that they bang with sticks while emitting bizarre groans. Groups of them may go from house to house performing their dances, though rather than candy they're given shots of rum. Though the masks were traditionally made of wood and first had indigenous, then Chinese motifs—Panama has had a Chinese population since the mid-19th century—they are increasingly influenced by the monsters of Hollywood movies.

GETTING HERE AND AROUND

La Villa de Los Santos lies to the east of the Carretera Nacional (Route 2) 4 km (2½ mi) south of Chitré. Driving directions are the same as those for Chitré, only you continue past town and drive over the Río La Villa. The 10-minute taxi trip from Chitré costs $2 or less.

GUARARÉ

277 km (172 mi) southwest of Panama City, 21 km (13 mi) south of Chitré.

It would be quite possible to miss the tiny town of Guararé as you drive from Chitré to Las Tablas. September 24 is the town's patron-saint day, with masses and other activities. Other than during that festival, there is little reason to stop in Guararé.

Though it's a sleepy spot most of the year, the town plaza wakes up during the last week of September, when it hosts the **Festival de la Mejorana**, which attracts fans of folk music from around the country. The festival was founded in the 1940s by a local scholar to celebrate and promote the preservation of *la mejorana*, a traditional genre of Panamanian music that is played on a small five-string guitar called the *guitarra mejoranera* (or simply a *mejorana*) and usually accompanied by folk dances. It's less of a party scene than Carnaval or Corpus Christi.

GETTING HERE AND AROUND

Most of Guararé lies to the east of the Carretera Nacional, just north of Las Tablas, which is served by buses that depart from Panama City's Albrook Terminal every 30 minutes. Driving directions are the same as those for Chitré, from which you continue south for another 21 km (13 mi).

LAS TABLAS

282 km (175 mi) southwest of Panama City, 30 km (19 mi) south of Chitré.

Though it has fewer than 9,000 inhabitants, Las Tablas is the main commercial center for the southern Azuero Peninsula. Its Carnaval celebrations and its annual Festival de la Pollera (July 21–23) are famous throughout Panama. The latter features folk music, dancing, and the election of a pollera-wearing queen. Though it was founded in the late 17th century, Las Tablas has few historic monuments.

> ## A LOCAL SPECIALTY
>
> Las Tablas, Guararé, and the nearby town of La Enea are known for producing some of the country's best *polleras*, the delicately embroidered dresses that are Panama's national costume and worn primarily during folk festivals. They take months to make, which is why they sell for thousands of dollars.

Carnaval transforms the normally quiet town of Las Tablas into a wild and colorful place for several days. Locals spend the better part of the year preparing for the four days of competitive events. The town is divided into the Calle Arriba (Upper Street) and Calle Abajo (Lower Street), and each elects its own queen and organizes competing parades. Adding to the festivities are strolling bands called *murgas*, folk-dance performances, fireworks, and water trucks that douse overheated revelers by day. Hotel prices double during Carnaval; reserve at least a month in advance.

West of Parque Porras is **La Iglesia Santa Librada** (✉ *Calle 8 de Noviembre and Av. Belisario Porras* ☎ *No phone*), which has an attractive hardwood interior and an impressive gilt altar with an image of the town's patron saint—the Santa Librada. It is the focus of a major pilgrimage every July 20, just before the annual pollera festival.

The town is the birthplace of Belisario Porras, one of the founders of the Panamanian republic, who served three presidential terms. The **Museo Belisario Porras** (✉ *Av. Belisario Porras at Parque Porras* ☎ *994–6326* ✉ *50¢* ☉ *Mon.–Sat. 8–4*), across from the central plaza (Parque Porras) is his former home and holds a small collection of memorabilia from his life.

GETTING HERE AND AROUND

Las Tablas lies 26 km (16 mi) south of Chitré via the Carretera Nacional (Route 3), which runs right through the middle of town, turning left (east) at the end of Parque Porras. It takes about four hours to drive to Las Tablas from Panama City; buses, which depart from Panama City's Albrook Terminal every 30 minutes, take five hours.

WHERE TO EAT AND STAY

$ ✕ **El Caserón.** This large, bright restaurant on a quiet corner several
LATIN AMERICAN blocks east of the central plaza has long been considered the best in Las
Tablas, but that doesn't necessarily say much. They have an extensive
menu that includes pizza and Chinese, both of which should be avoided.
The best bets are the seafood, such as corvina *al ajillo* (in a garlic sauce)
and inexpensive *langostinos* (prawns) or *langosta* (lobster), either of
which costs less than $10. If you want meat, order a *filete*, or perhaps
pollo con almendras (chicken breast with almonds, mushrooms, and
ginger). ✉ *Av. Moises Espino and Calle Agustin Batista* ☎ *994–6066*
◻ *No credit cards.*

¢ ⚙ **Hotel Piamonte.** Formerly Hotel Manolo, this is one of Las Tablas's
older hotels. Basic second-floor rooms have tile floors, small bathrooms,
and TVs. Most have small windows that open onto the central hallway,
so opt for either inexpensive "junior suites," with views of the street,
or the quieter and brighter rooms at the back. Popular with locals, the
large restaurant (¢–$) serves Chinese and Panamanian food; you're bet-
ter off ordering the latter, such as corvina *a la plancha* (sautéed), arroz
con pollo, or *filete a la parrilla* (grilled tenderloin). **Pros:** inexpensive;
central location. **Cons:** rooms are nothing special. ✉ *Carretera Nacional, 1 block east of park* ☎ *923–1603* ⇢ *16 rooms* ⚑ *In-hotel: restaurant, laundry service, Wi-Fi, no-smoking rooms* ◻ *AE, MC, V* ⛄ *EP.*

PEDASÍ

*324 km (201 mi) southwest of Panama City, 42 km (26 mi) south of
Las Tablas.*

Little Pedasí may make Chitré and Las Tablas look like cities, but it is
the tourist center of the Azuero Peninsula due to its proximity to Isla
Iguana and Playa Venao. A quiet ranching community with plentiful
gardens and a few adobe homes among cement-block buildings, Pedasí
is the birthplace of Mireya Moscoso, Panama's only female president
(1999–2004). She did a lot for her hometown, which now has a large
branch of the Banco Nacional, a refurbished central plaza, and a street
sign on every corner.

For travelers, Pedasí is a good place to sleep, eat, or hit the bank before
heading elsewhere. The Carretera Nacional runs right through town,
where it is called Avenida Central. Pedasí has a few small hotels and
a couple of grocery stores that offer your last chance for stocking up
before heading farther down the peninsula.

The nicest beaches on the mainland around Pedasí are Playa Los Destiladeros, 10 km (6 mi) to the south, and Playa Venao, 35 km (22 mi)
to the southwest *(both below)*⇢ .

GETTING HERE AND AROUND

Pedasí lies 74 km (46 mi) south of Chitré via the Carretera Nacional. It
takes a little over an hour to drive there. Buses that depart from Panama
City's Terminal de Buses every 40 minutes can take four to five hours.
Air Panama offers charter service to Pedasí.

WHERE TO EAT AND STAY

¢ **Pasta e Vino.** Simple but freshly made Italian fare is on the daily menu at
ITALIAN this cozy Italian restaurant run by a couple from northern Italy. Several
favorites regularly appear on the menu, including spaghetti, lasagna,
and ravioli with various fillings. The finest dining spot in Pedasí also
has a decent wine list. The only drawback is the town's open-air watering hole is right next door, and the locals can get a little boisterous.
⊠ *Camino a Playa el Toro, a few blocks from town plaza* ☎ *6695–2689*
⊟ *No credit cards* ☼ *No lunch. Closed Mon.*

¢ ✘ **Restauante Angela.** This small restaurant serves decent Panamanian
LATIN AMERICAN fare at dirt-cheap prices, but its best asset is the covered terrace. Popular
standards on the short menu might include *carne guisada* (stewed beef),
sopa de mariscos (seafood soup), and *pescado al ajillo* (fish of the day
with garlic). For a typical Panamanian breakfast, try *bistec encebollado*
(skirt steak smothered in onions) or *hojaldre* (deep-fried bread). ⊠ *Av.
Central at Calle Estudiante* ☎ *995–2207* ⊟ *No credit cards.*

¢ ☷ **Casa Margarita.** This restored santeño-style house, with its red-tile
roof and wooden awnings, is Pedasí's best lodging. Wood furnishings,
comfortable beds, and welcoming owners make this small bed-and-
breakfast an ideal base for sportfishing day trips or exploring the southern, more isolated, parts of the peninsula. A shared balcony, hardwood
floors, and a small library round off the fine restoration job. Fishing
tours and private dinners, prepared by the house chef, can be arranged.
Pros: comfortable and affordable base for exploring the region. **Cons:**
small rooms. ⊠ *Carretera Nacional, downtown near exit to Playa
Venao* ☎ *995–2898* ⊕ *www.pedasihotel.com* ⇆ *5 rooms* ⅃ *In-room:
Wi-Fi. In-hotel: 1 restaurant, laundry service, free parking, no-smoking
rooms.* ⊟ *AE, MC, V* ⲓⲟⲓ*BP.*

$ ☷ **Dim's Hostal.** This simple two-story house in the heart of town is
Pedasí's best spot for travelers on a tight budget. The rooms are rustic
but nicely decorated. Aside from the owner's hospitality, this place's
best asset is the round, thatched *rancho* in back where complimentary
breakfast is served and where guests can hang out during the day in
hammocks and chairs in the shade of mango trees. Guests can use
the adjacent kitchen. **Pros:** friendly owner; central location. **Cons:**
very basic rooms; some street noise. ⊠ *Av. Central at Calle Estudiante* ☎ *995–2303* ⇆ *7 rooms* ⅃ *In-hotel: laundry service, Internet, no-
smoking rooms* ⊟ *No credit cards* ⲓⲟⲓ*BP.*

SPORTS AND THE OUTDOORS
DIVING AND SNORKELING

For excellent scuba diving and snorkeling, head to Isla Iguana, a 30-min-
ute boat trip from Playa El Arenal, just east of town. *For more information on diving see the Isla Iguana and Playa Venao sections, below.*

Buzos de Azuero (⊠ *Carretera Nacional, north of town* ☎ *995–2894*
⊕ *www.dive-n-fishpanama.com*) arranges fishing and scuba-diving
trips.

SPORTFISHING

The ocean east and south of the Azuero Peninsula has rich fishing waters, and Pedasí is a good place for relatively inexpensive fishing charters. The area is known for its abundant tuna, but it also has plenty of roosterfish, wahoo, dolphinfish, amberjack, and occasional billfish. **Buzos de Azuero** (✉ *Carretera Nacional, north of town, Pedasí* ☎ *995–2894* ⊕ *www.dive-n-fishpanama.com*) offers a 27-foot boat with twin motors and fishing equipment for up to six people for $500 per day.

ISLA IGUANA

11 km (7 mi) northeast of Pedasí.

Fodor'sChoice
★
With the only white-sand beach on the Azuero Peninsula and excellent snorkeling and scuba diving less than an hour from Pedasí, Isla Iguana is the Azuero Peninsula's top natural attraction. Less than 1 km long, the island is covered with coconut palms and other tropical vegetation and has two beaches: immaculate **Playa El Cirial**, nearly 250 meters (800 feet) in length, and the tiny Playita del Faro, on the other side of the island's thin middle. The largest coral reef in the Gulf of Panama, at nearly 99 acres, surrounds Isla Iguana. The reef is composed of 14 coral species; some colonies are more than 800 years old. More than 200 species of invertebrates and at least 350 fish species, including parrot fish, black-and white-tipped reef sharks, puffer fish, and 16 eel species inhabit the reef. The island itself is inhabited by crabs and black iguanas and has a rookery used by more than 5,000 magnificent frigate birds. Both island and reef are protected within the **Reserva de Vida Silvestre Isla Iguana**.

Considering Isla Iguana's natural treasures, it's hard to believe that the U.S. Air Force used the island as a bombing range during World War II. Some unexploded bombs were detonated when it became a wildlife refuge. ⚠ **There may be still-unexploded shells buried in the sand, so stick to the trail when crossing the island between beaches.** In the middle of the trail is a lighthouse with views of the bomb craters.

The **National Environment Authority** (*ANAM*; ⊕ *www.islaiguana.com*) charges a $10 admission fee to visit the island; you can camp next to the ANAM station for $10. Fishing is prohibited in the reserve, as is removing anything from the reef or island. For more information, go to the Web site of the nonprofit Fundación Isla Iguana.

GETTING HERE AND AROUND

Isla Iguana is reached from Playa El Arenal, a beach just east of Pedasí, via a 20- to 30-minute boat ride, which can be arranged by Buzos de Azuero (⇨ *below*).

SPORTS AND THE OUTDOORS
SCUBA DIVING AND SNORKELING

Isla Iguana is a great place for snorkeling—the reef begins just a short swim from the island's beaches—and also has plenty for scuba divers to explore. Visibility is best—and waters are calmest and warmest—from April to December. From January through March, strong winds can make boating dangerous and the water quite cool.

Azuero's Tropical Dry Forest

Centuries ago, this region was largely covered with tropical dry forest, but that wilderness has been reduced to tiny remnants everywhere but in the mountains of the Azuero Peninsula's remote southwest corner and on Isla de Coiba. That endangered ecosystem is different from what you'll find in central and eastern Panama, or along the Caribbean coast. It is less diverse than the country's more humid forests, because fewer plants can endure the region's severe dry season, but it contains some species that you won't find in other parts of the country, such as the rare painted parakeet and the endemic Veraguan mango hummingbird.

The Azuero Peninsula is Panama's driest region and gets virtually no rain from December to May, when the pastures turn brown and most trees drop their foliage. From May to December, however, Pacific storms regularly drench the peninsula, and the trees burst into lush foliage.

The region's marked seasons make it easier to grow many food crops and maintain pasture, which appealed to Spanish colonists. They cut significant forest during the colonial era, but it wasn't until after World War II, when international banks promoted ranching in Latin America to meet the growing demand for hamburgers in the United States, that deforestation became rampant in the region. In the 1980s the Panamanian government finally began protecting the region's dwindling forests, but by then its original wilderness had receded to tiny remnants.

The region's remaining tropical dry-forest patches hold some interesting flora and fauna. Kapok, gumbo limbo, and spiny cedar trees are common here, and in the dry season you may see the rose and yellow flowers of the Tabebuia trees, or various orchid species. You may also catch sight of riverside wrens, brown jays, black iguanas, or howler monkeys in the branches of those trees. While Panama's underfunded National Environment Authority (ANAM) struggles to enforce the laws governing the protected areas on the western side of the Azuero Peninsula, organizations and landowners in its eastern half are focusing on ecological restoration, reforesting former pastureland, and protecting existing forest.

Buzos de Azuero (✉ *Carretera Nacional, north of town, Pedasí* ☎ 995–2894 ⊕ *www.dive-n-fishpanama.com*), arranges day trips from Pedasí for snorkeling or scuba diving. The company also rents snorkeling gear for $10, scuba gear with two tanks from $85, including a guide and transportation, and can arrange a boat to the island for up to six people for about $130.

PLAYA LOS DESTILADEROS

334 km (208 mi) southwest of Panama City, 10 km (6 mi) south of Pedasí.

This beach in the Azuero Peninsula's southeast corner isn't the region's nicest, given its dark sand and abundant rocks, but it has the peninsula's two best hotels. It is an attractive enough spot, with a swath of brown sand backed by hills covered with a mix of pastures, patches of forest, and scattered vacation homes. Rough seas often make for dangerous swimming here at high tide, but at low tide offshore rocks tend to break the force of the waves, creating some small pools for safe swimming. The best beach for swimming in the area is **Puerto Escondido,** a few miles north. Los Destiladeros is the most comfortable and expensive base for trips to Isla Iguana and Playa Venao, thanks to the two good hotels. The surrounding countryside is excellent for walking or horseback riding.

GETTING HERE AND AROUND

By car, follow the Carretera Nacional through Pedasí, and turn left 3 km (2 mi) south of town. That road quickly loses its pavement but is in good condition for the entire 7 km (4 mi) to the beach. Air Panama has charter service to Pedasí, and the hotels at Los Destiladeros can arrange an airport pickup.

WHERE TO STAY

$$-$$$
Fodor's Choice
★

Posada Los Destiladeros. This funky little lodge right on Playa Desiladeros has tropical gardens and views of the surf breaking over the rocks. The central wooden restaurant ($$) with a terrace and sea views, serves good French cuisine, mostly fresh seafood, on its ever-changing prix-fixe menu. Rooms, surrounding the gardens, a shallow pool, and several sun decks, are nature-inspired, with plenty of bamboo, terra-cotta, stonework, wooden sinks, high sloping ceilings, and terraces. The nicest rooms are the Virginia and the smaller Bouboulina on the beach. The spacious, thatched A-frames in back (Itzania and Ariel) are also nice, though more rustic. Less-expensive rooms behind the restaurant are a bit dark. The posada also sells real estate. Pros: gorgeous views; nice rooms; good food. Cons: the cheapest rooms are pretty dark. ⊠ *On beach, left at end of Rd.* 🖀🖀 *995–2771 or 6673–9262* ⊕ *www.panamabambu.net* ↝ *12 rooms* ⚹ *In-room: kitchen (some), no A/C (some). In-hotel: public Wi-Fi, parking (free), no-smoking rooms* ☰ *No credit cards* †◎† *CP.*

$$$-$$$$
★

Villa Camilla. On a forested ridge overlooking the ocean, this palatial boutique hotel—built as a showcase for the adjacent residential community—blurs the lines between nature and dwelling, with earth-toned polished cement, varnished hardwoods, tropical foliage, and abundant birdsong. Spacious guest rooms have high ceilings, large bathrooms, and modern amenities. Prix-fixe meals ($$$) are served either by the pool or in the dining room-cum-library. (A full meal plan is $50 per person per day.) The hotel is a five-minute walk from the beach. The main drawback is that the management seems to be more concerned with selling real estate than catering to vacationers. Pros: gorgeous design; great views; good food. Cons: weekend rates nearly double midweek rates; the resort is really built to sell real estate. ⊠ *On right before beach* 🖀 *232–0171 or 6678–8555* ⊕ *www.azueros.com* ↝ *3 rooms, 4 suites* ⚹ *In-room: no phone, safe. In-hotel: restaurant, pool, beachfront, public Wi-Fi, no-smoking rooms* ☰ *MC, V* †◎† *EP.*

SPORTS AND THE OUTDOORS

ECOTOURISM

Ecocircuitos (☎ 314–0068 ⊕ *www.ecocircuitos.com*) has a one-week luxury tour to the Azuero Peninsula that includes several nights at Villa Camilla.

HORSEBACK RIDING

The hills around Playa Destiladero hold a mix of pasture, patches of tropical dry forest, and stunning ocean views, which make the area perfect for horseback riding. Both **Villa Camilla** and the **Posada Los Destiladeros** rent horses to their guests. Ride first thing in the morning or in the late afternoon to see birds.

PLAYA VENAO (*PLAYA VENADO*)

4

358 km (222 mi) southwest of Panama City, 34 km (21 mi) southwest of Pedasí.

Fodor'sChoice
★
Long a mecca for surfers, the 2-mi-long pale-brown Playa Venao, in a deep, half-moon bay surrounded by largely deforested hills, has some of Panama's most consistent surf, and what could be the country's best beach break. The center of the beach is consistently pounded by surf, creating dangerous swimming conditions, but the western and eastern extremes are protected within the curved ends of the bay and thus have calm water, especially the eastern end. Other outdoor options include snorkeling, horseback riding, fishing, or a trip to the turtle-nesting beaches of Isla Cañas (most hotels can arrange trips here).

Playa Venao is off the beaten track, with no stores, ATMs, or phone lines (and limited cell-phone coverage)—which means you need to leave messages or e-mail reservations well ahead of time—and only one hotel accepts credit cards. All services are in Pedasí. About a mile west of the beach's first entrance is the main entrance, next to a colorful bus stop, which is where you'll find the surf break and an open-air restaurant, Jardín Vista Hermosa. On holidays and dry-season weekends there is usually a small tent city on the beach near the surf break. Campers use the restaurant's bathrooms and showers for a small fee. ⚠ **If there are waves, this area can develop dangerous rip currents, so don't swim there if the sea is rough.** There is another, steep entrance to the beach on Playa Venao's western end, a safe place to swim. A few kilometers to the west of Playa Madroño, which itself is west of Playa Venao, is the town of Cañas, where boats embark to cross the estuary to Isla Cañas.

About 4 km (2½ mi) before Playa Venao on the road from Pedasí (on the left) is the tiny fishing community of **El Ciruelo**, the embarkation point for local sportfishing charters and snorkeling trips.

A couple of kilometers west of El Ciruelo is the **Laboratorio Achotines** (☎ 995–8166 ⊕ *www.iattc.org*), a research center where biologists are studying the reproductive cycles of yellowfin tuna. You can visit its 130-acre protected tropical dry forest, where you might see monkeys and other wildlife, by reserving at least one day in advance; guided tours, however, are not available.

Fodor's Choice Just past the Laboratorio Achotines, in a bay east of Playa Venao, is
★ lovely **La Playita**, a safe swimming beach with the area's best snorkeling along its rocky edges. Though a "resort" on the beach rents a few
rooms, most people visit La Playita on day trips. It has a decent restaurant, and it gets packed during the holidays.

Just west of La Playita, the first entrance to Playa Venao on the left leads
to Villa Marina, the best swimming area, protected behind forested **El
Morro** island. At low tide you can walk out to the island.

GETTING HERE AND AROUND
By car, follow the Carretera Nacional through Pedasí and drive south-
west on a windy road for 34 km (21 mi). There is regular bus service to
Venao from Pedasí, and taxis in Pedasí will make the 20-minute trip for
$15. Air Panama has chartered flights from Panama City to Pedasí.

WHERE TO STAY
¢–$ 🏨 **Eco Venao.** This laid-back lodge up the hill from Playa Venao is part
★ of a project to reforest 300 acres of pastureland and hillsides, funded
in part by tourism earnings. It is largely self-service, with kitchens and
no restaurant (groceries are in Pedasí). Three gorgeous houses with
high ceilings, polished cement walls, and lovely woodwork—made from
fallen trees—are perched on ridges with great views. Each house has two
bedrooms with private bathrooms and a kitchen and living room. You
can rent a house, or just one room. Rustic, thatch-roof *cabañas* (cabins)
in the forest share a small bathhouse. They have one double bed, fans,
mosquito nets, and a loft with a mattress. Even cheaper are tiny doubles
behind the dorm, with shared bathrooms. The lodge rents surfboards,
kayaks, and snorkeling equipment and can arrange horseback riding
or hiking tours. Pros: great views; lovely design; eco-friendly. Cons: no
restaurant; not on the beach. ⊠ *Playa Venao, on right after bus stop*
🕿 *832–0530* ⊕ *www.venao.com* ☞ *2 rooms, 2 cabins, 3 houses* ♿ *In-
room: no a/c (some), no phone, kitchen (some), no TV, Wi-Fi. In-hotel:
water sports* ☰ *MC, V* ⫯❘ *EP.*

$ 🏨 **La Playita Resort.** With dinosaur statues decorating the lawn, pet
☺ macaws flying about, and temperamental emus wandering the grounds,
★ La Playita is certainly unique. Owner Lester Knight may be eccentric,
but while his neighbors chop trees down, he plants them, and most of
his 15-acre property is covered with forest. The beige beach is in a deep,
protected bay, making it perfect for swimming and snorkeling. Overlooking the beach is a large, thatched restaurant specializing in fresh
seafood, such as *corvina al ajillo* (sea bass with garlic) and *langostinos
a la criolla* (prawns in a tomato sauce). Rooms, in two cement buildings set back from the beach, are simple, with tile floors, nice woodwork, and small terraces with hammocks. Rooms 1 and 2 are the most
private. Although you'll have the place to yourself most weekdays,
on weekends between Christmas and Easter you'll share it with more
than 100 often-boisterous Panamanian day visitors. Be sure to ask for
room-cleaning service, which is included but only on request. At this
writing, an additional 10 rooms are under construction. Pros: great
beach and forest; friendly; good food. Cons: packed most weekends and
holidays; emus are sometimes aggressive; slight barnyard smell from

free-range chickens. ✉ *La Playita,*
2 km (1 mi) east of Playa Venao
☎ *996-6727 or 6639–2968* ⊕ *www.*
playitaresort.com 📠 *5 rooms* ♿ *In-*
room: no phone, no TV. In-hotel: 2
restaurants, bar, beachfront, water
sports, no-smoking rooms ▤ *No*
credit cards 🍴 *BP.*

$ ⛺ **Sereia do Mar.** Perched above the
sea in the fishing village just east
of Playa Venao, this is a convenient
hotel for anglers but also a decent
base for surfers and those interested
in other activities. Simple rooms
have high ceilings, red-tile floors,
and two queen beds each. They
open onto a long covered terrace

> **WHAT'S IN A NAME?**
>
> Playa Venao appears as Playa
> Venado on some maps and signs.
> *Venado* is Spanish for deer, which
> is what the beach was named for,
> but the Panamanian pronunciation
> is vehn-*ow*, thus Venao has come
> to be accepted as the name of
> the beach. Unfortunately, the deer
> for which the beach was named
> were hunted nearly to extinction.
> Reforestation projects have led
> to the occasional deer sighting in
> recent years.

with hammocks and chairs and ocean views, where breakfast is served.
There is a rustic bar under a thatch roof next door. **Pros:** reasonable
rates; nice views; sportfishing. **Cons:** no restaurant, no Internet, no cell
phone signal. ✉ *El Ciruelo, 4 km (2½ mi) east of Playa Venao* ☎ *6523–*
8758 or 6524–9421 ⊕ *www.sereiadomar.net* ✉ *neni_panama@hotmail.*
com 📠 *4 rooms* ♿ *In-room: no phone, no TV. In-hotel: bar, water*
sports, public Wi-Fi, no-smoking rooms ▤ *No credit cards* 🍴 *BP.*

$$ ⛺ **Villa Marina.** At the eastern end of Playa Venao—the safest swim-
ming area—this colonial-hacienda-inspired lodge is on a 160-acre
ranch. Older rooms have high ceilings and porticos with hammocks
overlooking a small courtyard with a fountain. Newer rooms are bright
and spacious and have ocean views but are less attractive. Prix-fixe
meals ($$) are served family-style in a traditional ranch house or on
the porch with a view of the sea. The hotel has great potential but falls
short on many details. Nevertheless, it's the only place in Playa Venao
that takes credit cards or that has Internet or satellite TV. Horseback
riding, fishing, and hiking trips can be arranged. **Pros:** beachfront location; nice design; friendly. **Cons:** loosely managed. ✉ *First entrance to*
Playa Venao ☎ *202–9044* 📠 *9 rooms* ♿ *In-room: no phone, safe. In-*
hotel: restaurant, bar, pool, beachfront, water sports, public Wi-Fi,
no-smoking rooms ▤ *MC, V* 🍴 *CP.*

SPORTS AND THE OUTDOORS
DIVING AND SNORKELING
The coast and islets around Playa Venao hold rocky reefs with sparse
coral formations that are frequented by an array of fish. The **Islas Frailes,**
two islets to the south of Playa Venao, have more, and bigger, fish.
From June to October you may also see humpback whales in the sea
south of Playa Venao.

Experienced divers can arrange boat dives at Islas Frailes with **Buzos
de Azuero** (✉ *Calle Principal, Pedasí* ☎ *995–2894* ⊕ *www.dive-n-*
fishpanama.com). The boat to Islas Frailes costs $100.

La Playita Resort (☎ 996–6727 or 6639–2968 ⊕ www.playitaresort.com) rents snorkeling equipment for exploring the deep bay it sits on.

The hotel **Sereia do Mar** (✉ El Ciruelo ☎ 6523–8758) rents snorkeling equipment and can provide transportation to nearby Isla La Monja, which is a good skin-diving spot when the sea is calm.

HORSEBACK RIDING
The hills around Playa Venao have some excellent horseback routes.

Eco Venao (☎ 832–0530) has a horseback tour of their vast property.

Villa Marina (☎ 202–9044) offers horseback riding on the beach or on the surrounding ranch.

SPORTFISHING
It is no coincidence that the Inter-American Tropical Tuna Commission has its research center next to Playa Venao. The ocean here holds plenty of tuna, as well as dolphinfish, roosterfish, wahoo, and other sport fish. Some of the area's best fishing is around the **Islas Frailes**, just to the south of Playa Venao.

Pedasí-based **Buzos de Azuero** (✉ Calle Principal, north of town, Pedasí ☎ 995–2405 ⊕ www.dive-n-fishpanama.com) charters a 27-foot boat with twin motors with fishing gear for up to six people for $500 per day.

Relatively inexpensive ($30 per hour) inshore fishing is available at **La Playita Resort** (☎ 996–6727 or 6639–2968 ⊕ www.playitaresort.com), but the resort has only a 16-foot boat with a 40-hp motor, so you won't be able to go out far on a rough day.

Sportfishing charters can be arranged through the hotel **Sereia do Mar** (✉ El Ciruelo ☎ 6524–9421 ✎ pimplisurf@yahoo.com). A day of fishing in the hotel's 30-foot boat with twin 70-hp motors costs $400.

SURFING
If you've got the time, and a 4WD vehicle, you can drive to **Playa Cambutal**, south of Tonosí, about 90 minutes from Playa Venao, which has point breaks and beach breaks. Waves are often bigger than at Playa Venado—and great when the swell gets overhead.

When Playa Venao is crowded, or at lower tides, you can drive a couple of miles to the west, over the ridge, and hike 20 minutes to **Playa Madroño**, a left beach break that is best near low to medium tide and tends to be bigger than Playa Venao.

Playa Venao is one of the country's most popular surfing spots. It is one of the few good beach breaks in the country—popular with experts and novices alike. On weekends and holidays it's crowded, but it's usually not bad during the week. Breaks are a good mix of lefts and rights, but the waves are only decent from mid- to high tide and below six feet—beyond that they close out. The surf tends to be good here from March to November, though it's best from August through October. Eco Venao and La Playita Resort rent surfboards.

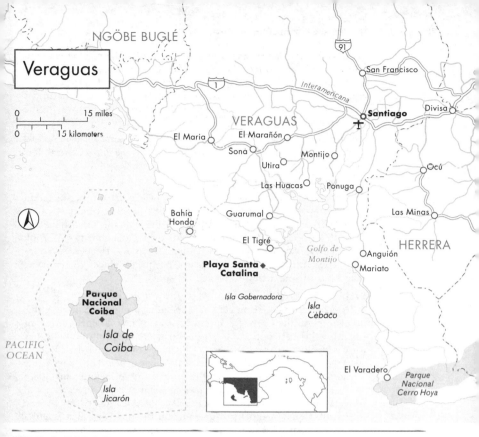

VERAGUAS

The only Panamanian province with coastline on both oceans, Veraguas was named by Christopher Columbus, who sailed along its Caribbean coast on his fourth voyage to the Americas. The name is likely a contraction of *verdes aguas* (green waters), referring to the coastal jungle reflected in the sea. Traveling along the province's coast or islands during the rainy season, you may experience that green-water effect.

Few tourists visit Veraguas, and those who do head for its remote Pacific coast and Isla de Coiba for world-class scuba diving and surfing. Playa Santa Catalina, which has one of the country's best surf breaks, is currently the only spot in the province with any semblance of a tourist industry, catering primarily to surfers on tight budgets. Santa Catalina and Isla de Coiba are well off the beaten track.

SANTIAGO

250 km (155 mi) southwest of Panama City, 190 km (118 mi) east of David.

The provincial capital, Santiago is usually nothing more than a pit stop between Panama City and the westernmost province of Chiriquí, Playa Santa Catalina, or Isla de Coiba. With a population of 27,000,

Santiago is little more than a large town, but as the commercial and administrative center for a large ranching and farming area, it's considered one of Panama's principal cities. Though founded in the colonial era, Santiago has very little historic architecture and lacks charm. Its main street, Avenida Central, runs southwest from the highway to the Plaza Central.

An attractive, white, 19th-century church, the **Catedral Santiago Apóstol** (⊠ *North side of plaza* ☏ *No phone*), dominates the Plaza Central. It is the focus of a small religious festival the last week of July.

GETTING HERE AND AROUND
To drive to Santiago from Panama City, head west on the Carretera Interamericana 250 km (155 mi), and look for the Avenida Central on the left. The road to Playa Santa Catalina is on the left at the Plaza Central. Direct buses to Santiago depart from Panama City's Albrook Terminal every hour and take four hours. Buses also run every 90 minutes between Santiago and David, in Chiriquí Province. You can also take a bus to Soná from Albrook.

WHERE TO STAY
$ ⊡ **Hotel La Hacienda.** If you get stuck spending a night in Santiago, this large hotel on the Carretera Interamericana a few kilometers west of town is your best option. The two-story, white-stucco building has tile floors, lots of wide arches, and a large interior garden. Rooms are bright and decorated with colorful Mexican art. They have cable TV and small bathrooms, and the hotel's ample facilities include a nice pool, a playground, and a bar. The restaurant ($) serves a mix of Mexican and Panamanian dishes. **Pros:** reasonable rates; decent rooms; nice pool. **Cons:** mediocre restaurant; on the highway. ⊠ Carretera Interamericana, *3 km (2 mi) west of Santiago, Uvito exit* ☏ *958–8580* 🖷 *958–8579* ⇥ *56 rooms* 🛆 *In-hotel: restaurant, room service, bar, pool, Internet, Wi-Fi, no-smoking rooms* ▭ *AE, MC, V* ⦿ *EP.*

■ OFF THE BEATEN PATH
If you've got an hour to spare, consider making the 20-minute drive north to the tiny town of San Francisco, known for the colonial art in its historic church, the **Iglesia de San Francisco de Asis.** Built in the early 1700s, that stout stone structure doesn't look like much from the outside, but it holds some lovely baroque altars. San Francisco was one of the first Spanish settlements in western Panama, and played an important role in their struggle to subjugate the Indians and convert them to Christianity. By 1756 the town had a population of 2,277, which is about how many people live there today. It was largely indigenous artisans that built the eight altars with local hardwoods, under the supervision of Franciscan monks. The ornate main altar, which consists of more than 400 pieces of colorfully painted tropical cedar, is an impressive example of colonial art. The road to San Francisco (and, ultimately, Santa Fe) heads north from the Carretera Interamericana just west of the turnoff for Avenida Central and is paved for the entire 17 km (11 mi).

PLAYA SANTA CATALINA

360 km (223 mi) southwest of Panama City, 110 km (68 mi) southwest of Santiago.

Fodor's Choice
★
Literally at the end of the road, the tiny fishing village of Santa Catalina sits near some of the best surfing spots in the country and is the closest port to Isla de Coiba, Panama's top dive destination. For years, the only people who visited Playa Santa Catalina were adventurous surfers who made the long trip here on rough roads and slept in rustic rooms for the pleasure of riding La Punta, a right point break. The roads and accommodations are better now, and two dive centers have opened. For the moment, Santa Catalina remains a quiet beach town with little to offer other than ocean views through the palm fronds, friendly locals, cheap seafood, and amazing surf and diving.

Santa Catalina virtually shuts down in early fall, with some businesses closed in September or October. Call businesses you wish to plan to visit in advance if you go this time of year. The town's limited night scene is hampered by a fairly well-respected 10 PM closing time for bars and restaurants, which is only flaunted during the busiest times of year like Easter. Most of the area's dirt roads are passable in a basic car, but a truck or 4x4 is a safer bet.

GETTING HERE AND AROUND

It takes about six hours to drive to Santa Catalina from Panama City, driving west on the Carretera Interamericana to Santiago, and then southwest, via Soná, the 110 km (68 mi) to Playa Santa Catalina. In Santiago, turn left at the church and follow the signs to Soná, which is 50 km (31 mi) southwest of Santiago. The turnoff for Santa Catalina is shortly before Soná, by the Shell gas station. From there, it is another 45 km (28 mi) to the village of El Tigre, where you have to make another left, and at the next town, Hicaco, turn right at the police station. The main road ends at the beach, but the Punta Brava Lodge and other hotels are up a rough dirt road on the left before the beach.

WHERE TO EAT AND STAY

¢–$$
LATIN AMERICAN
★
✕ **Jamming Pizza.** Surprisingly good pizza is served at this small, Italian-owned open-air restaurant a short walk from the beach. The thin pies baked in a wood-burning brick oven would be popular in Panama City, but they taste that much better served at the edge of civilization. On holidays and dry-season weekends the place can get packed, and it stays open late as locals and visitors top off their dinners with cold beers and good music. ⊠ *Road to El Estero, first right* ☎ *No phone* 🚫 *No credit cards.*

¢–$
ITALIAN
✕ **Pinguino Cafe.** Smack at the end of the main road to Santa Catalina, this beachside restaurant has a fine selection of seafood and Italian dishes, with recipes for pollo a la scalopina and filete de pescado a la mediterránea taken straight from the cookbook of the Italian owner's mother. With a great sunset view of the bay at Playa Santa Catalina, finer dining in a more sandals-optional location won't be found. ⊠ *End of Carretera Nacional, right side facing the beach* ☎ *No phone* 🚫 *No credit cards.*

$ ⌖ **La Buena Vida.** Charming fauna-themed villas showcase the U.S. owners' attention to detail at this small lodge. The Gecko Villa, for example, comes complete with tiled geckos in the shower and bedroom, the latter's eyes functioning as bed lights. In the middle of Santa Catalina's "downtown," La Buena Vida has a vegetarian restaurant ($) that is open for breakfast and lunch. The owners also run the adjacent hostel Boarders Haven, which, due to its small size, can easily be rented in full by a small group of budget travelers seeking a bit of privacy. **Pros:** central location close to dive shops, beach, and restaurants. **Cons:** often booked full. ⊠ *Carretera Nacional, on left in front of school* ☎ *6635–1895* ∰ *www.labuenavida.biz* ⇴ *3 rooms* ☾ *In-room: refrigerator, no TV (some), Wi-Fi. In-hotel: restaurant, no-smoking rooms* ▭ *No credit cards* �𐃏 *EP.*

¢   ⌖ **Hotel Hibiscus Garden.** Ten kilometers before Santa Catalina is this simple but comfortable and affordable lodge at Playa Lagartero on the Gulf of Montijo. Rustically accented rooms employ driftwood and local resources creatively; each has a patio with hammock. There's a shared kitchen for guests to use. The German-owned hotel runs birding tours along a nearby river and horseback rides on the long, virtually abandoned beach, which is named for the small alligators, or lagartos, that populate the area's rivers. **Pros:** relaxed location. **Cons:** many mosquitoes on beach. ⊠ *Playa Lagartero, entrance off Carretera Nacional, 10 km northeast of Santa Catalina* ☎ *6615–6097* ∰ *www.hibiscusgarden.com* ⇴ *7 rooms* ☾ *In-room: no TV. In-hotel: restaurant, beachfront, Internet, free parking, no-smoking rooms* ▭ *No credit cards* ⌯ *EP.*

¢   ⌖ **Oasis Surf Camp.** This rustic, Italian-owned lodge is right on Playa Santa Catalina, amid the coconut palms and mere steps from the surf. Most rooms are basically cement boxes with beds, a fan, and a bathroom with a cold-water shower—the additional $10 for air-conditioning and hot water is well worth it. But you can hear the waves and the rustling of palm fronds at night, and when you step out your door you're on the beach. A nearby open-air restaurant ($–$$) serves three meals a day and becomes a bar at night. Surfing lessons are given on the nearby beach break—the only place in Santa Catalina where novices can surf without risking their lives. The lodge rents boards. Camping is allowed for a small fee, and it's a zoo during the holidays. **Pros:** on the beach; laid-back atmosphere; good food. **Cons:** very basic rooms; you have to wade through or cross in an adequate vehicle a shallow river to reach property. ⊠ *Playa Catalina* ☎ *6588–7077* ∰ *www.oasissurfcamp.com* ⇴ *10 rooms* ☾ *In-room: no a/c (some), no phone, no TV. In-hotel: restaurant, water sports, no-smoking rooms* ▭ *No credit cards* ⌯ *EP.*

SPORTS AND THE OUTDOORS
SCUBA DIVING AND SNORKELING

Playa Santa Catalina is the closest embarkation point to Isla de Coiba *(below)*⇨ , which has Panama's best scuba diving, but there are numerous other spots nearby. Visibility and sea conditions can change from one day to the next, but in general the diving is better during the rainy season than during the dry season. Many of the dive spots around Isla de Coiba require ocean-diving experience, but some closer to town are appropriate for novices or for snorkeling. Within an hour of Santa Catalina are dive sites such as **Punta Pargo** and **Palo Grande,** where you might see moray eels, parrot fish, various types of puffers, and big schools of jacks, among other things. If you can afford a trip to Isla de Coiba, 90 minutes away by boat, you can expect to see an even greater variety and amount of marine life, including lots of sharks and, with luck, manta rays, or whale sharks. Isla de Coiba is best done as an overnight.

Coiba Dive Center (✉ *Calle Principal, on right before beach* ☎ *6009–4169* ⊕ *www.coibadivecenter.com*) offers a variety of similar professional services.

Scuba Coiba (✉ *Calle Principal, on left before beach* ☎ *202–2171* ⊕ *www. scubacoiba.com*), Santa Catalina's first dive center, was started in 2003 by Austrian expat Herbie Sunk. The company offers boat dives at dozens of spots near Santa Catalina and multiday trips to Isla de Coiba with overnights in the ANAM cabins there. They also offer PADI certification courses and snorkeling/beach trips to other nearby islands as well.

SURFING

An excellent alternative to the coastal breaks is **Isla Cebaco**, a 90-minute boat ride from Santa Catalina, which has both a beach break and point break. Those breaks are usually noticeably bigger than at Santa Catalina. The trip there costs $15 to $30.

Santa Catalina's legendary point break, known simply as **La Punta**, is one of the country's best. The waves break over a rock platform in front of a point just east of town, forming both lefts and rights, though the rights are more hollow and longer. It is best surfed from mid- to high tide and usually needs a four- to five-foot swell to break. When a good swell rolls in, the faces can get as big as 15 to 20 feet.

An alternative to La Punta that can be surfed at low to mid-tide is the nearby beach break at **Playa Santa Catalina**, which is usually smaller and less treacherous than the point break, so it is better for surfers who are out of practice.

If La Punta is too small or crowded, you can hike 30 minutes west of town, past the beach, to another point called **Punta Brava**, where a fast left tubes over a rocky bottom. The waves here are often bigger than at La Punta, but it can only be surfed from low to mid-tide.

Panama Surf Tours (☎ *6671–7777* ⊕ *www.panamasurftours.com*), run by longtime resident Kenny Myers, has a rustic lodge near the break and offers five- and eight-day guided surfing packages that include transportation to and from Playa Santa Catalina and a guide. The company also offers lessons and surf tours in other parts of Panama.

PARQUE NACIONAL COIBA

50 km (31 mi) southwest of Santa Catalina.

Fodor's Choice ★ Remote and wild, Panama's largest island has the country's best scuba diving, world-class fishing, and palm-lined beaches. About 80% of the island is covered with tropical dry forest, home to an array of wildlife, including the scarlet macaw. But it is the ocean that holds the big attractions: Parque Nacional Coiba is one of the world's largest marine parks, not to mention a UNESCO World Heritage Site.

For the better part of the 20th century, however, Isla de Coiba was a penal colony, where as many as 3,000 criminals once toiled on farms carved out of the dry forest, growing food for the country's entire prison system. The Panamanian government declared the island a national park in 1991, but it took more than a decade to relocate the prisoners. In 2004 the prison was finally shut down, and the park was significantly expanded to include nine more islands, 28 islets, and vast expanses of ocean to the north and south of Coiba. Parque Nacional Coiba now protects 667,493 acres of sea and islands, of which Isla de Coiba constitutes about 120,000 acres.

The marine life of the park is as impressive as that of the Galapagos. The extensive and healthy reefs are home to comical frog fish, sleek rays, and massive groupers. The national park holds more than 4,000 acres of reef, composed of two-dozen different types of coral, and is home to 760 fish species. The park's waters are also visited by 22 species of whale and dolphin, including killer whales and humpback whales, which are fairly common there from July to September.

The wildlife on Coiba doesn't compare to that on the Galapagos, but its forests are home to howler monkeys, agoutis (large rodents), and 150 bird species, including the endemic Coiba spinetail, the rare crested eagle, and the country's biggest population of endangered scarlet macaws. Several trails wind through the island's forests; the **Sendero de los Monos** (Monkey Trail), a short boat trip from the ranger station, is the most popular. The island's extensive mangrove swamps are inhabited by crocodiles, and sea turtles nest on some beaches from April to September. The most popular beach in the park is on the tiny **Granito de Oro** (Gold Nugget) island, where white sand is backed by lush foliage, and good snorkeling lies a short swim away. It's a popular stop with small cruise ships from December to May, so local tour operators often avoid it during those months.

Options for visiting Isla de Coiba range from a day trip out of Playa Santa Catalina to one-week tours, or cruises that include lodging on a ship, or in the National Environment Authority (ANAM) accommodations ($20 per bed; five beds per building) in air-conditioned cement buildings near the ranger station. There is a communal kitchen; you have to bring your food. There is also space for 15 campers ($10 per two-person tent). Reserve at least a month ahead of time during the dry season. ☎ 998–4271 or 998–0615 ✉ $20.

GETTING HERE AND AROUND

Most people visit Isla de Coiba on fishing, diving, or nature tours offered by the companies listed above. It is possible to organize your own trip, in which case you would hire a boat in Playa Santa Catalina. Most fishermen there charge about $200 for a day trip to Isla de Coiba, and more if they must stay overnight on the island.

SPORTS AND THE OUTDOORS
SCUBA DIVING AND SNORKELING

Isla de Coiba has Panama's best scuba diving, and some of the best diving in Central America, with vast reefs inhabited by hundreds of species and jaw-dropping schools of fish. On any given dive there you may see spotted eagle rays, white-tip reef sharks, sea turtles, giant snapper and grouper, moray eels, stargazers, frog fish, pipefish, angelfish, and Moorish idols. The reefs hold plenty of invertebrates, whereas offshore pinnacles attract big schools of jacks, Pacific spadefish, and other species.

Among the park's best dive spots are **Santa Cruz,** a vast coral garden teeming with reef fish; **Mali Mali,** a submerged rock formation that is a cleaning station for large fish; **La Viuda,** a massive rock between Islas de Coiba and Canales that attracts major schools of fish; and **Frijoles,** submerged rocks where divers often see sharks, large eels, and manta rays. Many of the dive spots around Isla de Coiba require a bit of ocean-diving experience, but there are also dive spots that are appropriate for novices and good snorkeling areas. Visibility can change from one day to the next, but in general it is better during the rainy season, when it averages 70 feet and the sea is warmer. Surface water temperatures average in the low 80s, but thermoclines in the depths can be in the mid-70s, and upwelling from February to April brings colder water and lower visibility—down to 20 feet—but more fish.

Ecocircuitos (☎ 314–0068 ⊕ www.ecocircuitos.com), based in Panama City, has a one-week snorkeling and hiking tour to Isla de Coiba with overnights in the ANAM cabins and in Santa Catalina.

The **M/V** (☎ 866/924–2837 in U.S. ⊕ www.coralstar.com) Coral Star, a 115-foot yacht based in David, has one-week cruises to Isla de Coiba and surroundings that can include sportfishing, skin diving, snorkeling, and sea kayaking.

Panama Divers (☎ 314–0817 or 448–2293 ⊕ www.panamadivers. com) offers relatively inexpensive diving tours to Isla de Coiba for small groups that include overnights in the ANAM cabins. **Scuba Coiba** (☎ 202–2171 ⊕ www.scubacoiba.com), in Santa Catalina, are the local experts, offering boat dives at dozens of spots in the park on trips with overnights in the ANAM cabins.

SPORTFISHING

Catch-and-release fishing is permitted inside Coiba National Park, but the fishing is just as good outside the park. Blue marlin, black marlin, and Pacific sailfish run here in significant numbers from December to April, with January to March being the peak months. The area also holds legions of wahoo, dolphin (mahimahi), and tuna, which often run bigger than 200 pounds. The fishing is less spectacular from April to December, but there are still plenty of roosterfish, mackerel, amberjack, snapper, and grouper. Some of the area's best fishing is around **Isla Montousa** and the **Hannibal Banks,** which are 65 to 80 km (40 to 50 mi) west of Isla de Coiba. The sea south of **Isla Jicarón** and **Isla Jicarita,** 10 km (7 mi) south of Isla de Coiba, also has good fishing.

Captain Tom Yust's **Coiba Adventure Sportfishing** (☏ *999–8108; 800/800–0907 in the U.S.* ⊕ *www.coibadventure.com*) runs fishing tours of the waters around Isla de Coiba on a 31-foot Bertram, or a Mako 221, with overnights at the ANAM cabins. Tom also offers free-diving underwater photography tours.

The **M/V *Coral Star*** (☏ *866/924–2837 in the U.S.* ⊕ *www.coralstar.com*) is a 115-foot ship that runs Saturday-to-Saturday cruises to Isla de Coiba and surroundings with sportfishing from 22-foot launches.

Panama Yacht Tours (☏ *263–5044* ⊕ *www.panamayachtours.com*), based in Panama City, offers fishing tours to the waters around Isla de Coiba with overnighters at the ANAM cabins or land-based overnighters at better lodges.

Pesca Panama (☏ *6614–5850; 800/946–3473 in the U.S.* ⊕ *www. pescapanama.com*) offers one-week fishing tours to the waters west of Isla de Coiba with overnights on a barge near David.

Chiriquí Province

WORD OF MOUTH

"The Boquete and Volcán areas give you the best of the mountain activities, and the Gulf of Chiriquí gives you the best of the ocean activities. You can get a boat to tool around the islands from Pedregal (a few minutes from David) or Boca Chica (about an hour from David, but then closer to open ocean boating)."

—flimoncelli

By David
Dudenhoefer
Updated by
Marlise Kast

Panama's southwest province of Chiriquí contains the country's most varied scenery. Landscapes that evoke different continents—from the alpine peak of Volcán Barú to the palm-lined beaches of Parque Nacional Golfo de Chiriquí—lie mere hours apart. The diverse environments provide conditions for world-class sportfishing, bird-watching, scuba diving, river rafting, horseback riding, hiking, and surfing, making Chiriquí an ideal destination for nature lovers.

The Cordillera de Talamanca, which extends from Costa Rica into Panama, defines northern Chiriquí. Lush cloud forest covers its upper slopes, and the valleys that flank Volcán Barú—an extinct volcano and Panama's highest peak—have cool mountain climates and unforgettable scenery. Those valleys hold the towns of Boquete, Bambito, and Cerro Punta, which are popular with bird-watchers, rafters, and hikers, and have captivating landscapes and charming restaurants and inns.

The lowlands to the south of the Cordillera are less impressive—hot and almost completely deforested—and become brown and dusty in the dry season. To the south lies the Golfo de Chiriquí, with dozens of pristine islands and countless acres of coral reef awash with rainbows of marine life. Those waters also offer world-class surfing and sportfishing that few have sampled. The tiny fishing port of Boca Chica provides convenient access to the gulf's treasures, whereas the isolated lodges of Cala Mia, Islas Secas, and Moro Negrito are in the gulf itself.

Chiricanos, or residents of Chiriquí, fly their red-and-green provincial flag with more vigor than they do the national banner. The province's population is almost as varied as its landscapes; the majority is *mestizo*—a mix of European and indigenous bloodlines—with a sprinkling of Asian immigrants.

The Ngöbe (aka "Guaymí"), the country's largest indigenous group, has been in this region since long before Chiriquí or Panama existed. Though most Ngöbe live in the tribe's *comarca* (autonomous indigenous territory) northeast of Chiriquí, you find them in Boquete, Cerro Punta, and David. Ngöbe women are recognizable by their colorful traditional dresses.

ORIENTATION AND PLANNING

ORIENTATION

Most travelers arrive by plane in the provincial capital of David. Centrally located in the lowlands, it is no more than two hours from most of Chiriquí's attractions. The Carretera Interamericana (CA1) skirts David's northern edge, as a four-lane highway lined with gas stations,

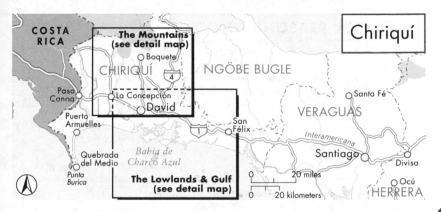

5

shopping plazas, and fast-food restaurants. It becomes a two-lane road east of town, where it leads to the town of Chiriquí and to the turn-off for Boca Chica, the gateway to Parque Nacional Marino Golfo de Chiriquí. A 30-minute drive southwest of David takes you to Playa Barqueta; a 40-minute drive north takes you to Boquete. Concepción is a short drive west of David on CA1, and there the road veers north to Volcán, Bambito, and Cerro Punta. The first of these communities is near the base of Barú Volcano; the latter two are nestled along that mountain's western slope. If you continue west on CA1, you'll reach the border with Costa Rica at Paso Canoa in 15 minutes.

PLANNING

WHEN TO GO

The December-to-May dry season is the most popular time to visit Chiriquí since days tend to be sunny in the lowlands. From December to March the valleys of Cerro Punta and Boquete can be cool and windy and may get light rain. Here trade winds push clouds over the mountains creating a misty condition known as *bajareque*. In March and April the mountain valleys are warm and sunny, whereas the low lands become increasingly dry and brown. It rains just about every day from May to mid-July, but from mid-July to mid-September you can get several sunny days in a row. Again, from mid-September to mid-December it rains almost daily. Boquete's Feria de Flores, the annual flower festival, is the third week of January and includes folk dancing and indigenous handicrafts but also excessive drinking and blasting music. You'll find the town's Expo Orquideas in mid-April is more pleasant. The water in the Golfo de Chiriquí is clearest for scuba diving and snorkeling from December to July, whereas the surf is best from July to December.

GETTING HERE AND AROUND
BY AIR

The easiest way to reach Chiriquí is by plane. There are half a dozen daily flights between Panama City and David's Aeropuerto Enrique Malek. Aeroperlas and Air Panama have daily flights between Panama

TOP REASONS TO GO

Misty Mountains. The upper slopes of the Cordillera de Talamanca are draped with lush cloud forest and are usually enveloped in mist. Much of that forest is protected within La Amistad and Barú Volcano National Parks, home to a wealth of wildlife, which can be explored via hiking trails.

Teeming Sea. The Golfo de Chiriquí is home to an amazing array of fish, ranging from colorful king angelfish to the mighty black marlin, making the province an ideal destination for scuba divers and sport fishers alike.

Birds in the Bush. The mountains of Chiriquí are a must-visit for birdwatchers since they hold species found nowhere else in Panama, such as the resplendent quetzal and long-tailed silky flycatcher. From November to April, northern migrants push the bird count to more than 500 species.

Pristine Islands. Between Parque Nacional Marino Golfo de Chiriquí and the Islas Secas, the sea here brims with uninhabited islands: think palm-lined beaches, crystalline waters, and coral reefs a short swim from shore.

Farming Communities. The mountain communities of Boquete, Bambito, and Cerro Punta are surrounded by gorgeous scenery and are distinguished by charming wooden houses, exuberant flower gardens, cozy restaurants, and hotels that combine all of the above.

City and David. Aeroperlas has one flight between David and Bocas del Toro on weekdays. Air Panama has direct flights between David and San José, Costa Rica, three days a week.

Contacts Aeroperlas (☎ 315–7500 or 721–1230 ⊕ www.aeroperlas.com). **Aeropuerto Enrique Malek** (✉ Av. Reed Gray, 5 km [3 mi] south of town ☎ 721–1072). **Air Panama** (☎ 316–9000 or 721–0841 ⊕ www.flyairpanama. com).

BY BUS

Padafont has hourly buses between Panama City's Albrook Terminal and David from 6 AM to 8 PM and direct buses at 10:45 PM and midnight. The trip takes about eight hours, with a meal stop in Santiago. Small buses to Boquete, Volcán, Cerro Punta, and Paso Canoa (the border post with Costa Rica), depart every 20–30 minutes during the day. International bus company, Ticabus, makes daily trips from David to San José at 4 AM and 4 PM. Once you are in the area, there is frequent bus service to the mountain towns.

Contacts Padafont (☎ 774–2974). **Terminal de Buses** (Piquera✉ Av. del Estudiante, just east of where Av. Obaldía and Av. 2 Este intersect, east side of town, David).**Ticabus** (☎ 507/314–6385 ⊕ www.ticabus.com).

BY CAR

A car is the best way to explore Chiriquí as roads are in good repair and relatively well marked. Most major rental companies have offices in David. Avenida Obaldía heads straight north out of David to Boquete, no turns required. All other areas are reached via the Carretera

Interamericana (CA1), which skirts David to the north and east. To reach CA1 from David's airport, turn left onto Avenida Reed Gray, then left onto Calle F Sur at the police station, 1½ km north of which you'll reach the two-lane CA1. All rental agencies in David offer 4WD vehicles as well as less expensive standards (sufficient for most trips).

Car-Rental Agencies Alamo (✉ *Enrique Malek Airport, David* ☎ *721–0101 or 236–5777*). **Avis** (✉ *Enrique Malek Airport, David* ☎ *721–0884 or 278–9444*). **Budget** (✉ *Enrique Malek Airport, David* ☎ *715–5597 or 263–8777*). **Hertz** (✉ *Av. 20, at Calle F Sur, David* ☎ *775–8471 or 301–2611*). **National** (✉ *Enrique Malek Airport, David* ☎ *721–0974 or 265–2222*). **Thrifty** (✉ *Enrique Malek Airport, David* ☎ *721–2477 or 204–9555*).

BY TAXI

Although driving is the easiest way to explore the spread-out mountain regions, especially around Boquete, it isn't obligatory. In fact, if you want to hike the Sendero los Quetzales, it's best to hire a taxi in Cerro Punta to take you to the trailhead. It only takes about 90 minutes to drive from David to Boca Chica. If you spend a few nights there, you may want to have your hotel arrange a taxi transfer from David.

RESTAURANTS

You can get a good meal almost anywhere in the province, but Boquete has its best restaurant selection. The specialty in the mountains is local farm-raised trout, but because the Gulf of Chiriquí has such great fishing, seafood is also a good bet. Chiriquí is cattle country, so you'll also find plenty of beef on the menu. While not as tender as corn-fed beef, the fillets and sirloins are quite good.

HOTELS

Accommodations in Chiriquí range from Boquete's affordable B&Bs to the luxurious eco-lodge on the Islas Secas, where the rates are twice those of any other hotel in the country. The province has some of Panama's best small lodges, many surrounded by tropical nature.

WHAT IT COSTS					
	¢	$	$$	$$$	$$$$
Restaurants	Under $5	$5–$10	$10–$15	$15–$20	over $20
Hotels	under $50	$50–$100	$100–$160	$160–$220	over $220

Restaurant prices are per person for a main course at dinner. Hotel prices are for two people in a standard double room, excluding service and 10% tax.

ESSENTIALS
EMERGENCIES

If you have a medical emergency in Chiriquí, head straight to David, which has a modern hospital. Boquete and Volcán have ambulances, and there are police stations in every town.

Emergency Services Ambulance (☎ *775–4221 in David; 720–1356 in Boquete; 771–4283 in Volcán*). **Fire** (☎ *103*). **Police** (☎ *104*).

A BIT OF HISTORY

Chiriquí remained the realm of indigenous chiefdoms for most of the colonial era, although conquistadors first visited the region in the 16th century, founding a few outposts that were soon abandoned or destroyed. According to Spanish chroniclers, the region was divided among various indigenous ethnicities, which conquistadors collectively dubbed the Guaymí—a name that persists to this day. Though they founded David and a few neighboring towns in the early 17th century, the Spaniards remained a minority in the region until the 19th century. They introduced cattle early in the conquest. As ranching took hold, the area's forests receded, and the Indians retreated into the mountains they now call home. The trend continues to this day; pasture is the province's predominant landscape.

Originally considered part of Veraguas, the province of Chiriquí wasn't created until 1849, when it had just 16,000 inhabitants. Because nearly all the buildings were made of wood or adobe, hardly a structure survives from the colonial era. Chiriquí didn't really start to grow till the late 19th and early 20th centuries, when ranches and banana and sugar plantations completely covered the lowlands. European immigrants then began moving into the mountain valleys, where they took advantage of the rich volcanic soil to produce coffee, fruit, and vegetables. With agricultural expansion, indigenous territory shrank. The majority of Chiriquí's Indians now live in the mountains in what was once the province's northeast corner, though many also work on farms in Boquete and Cerro Punta. The 21st century brought a real-estate boom as foreigners were drawn to the mountain valleys' spring-like climate and to the beautiful coast.

INTERNET

Most hotels in the region have Internet access for guests; some even have Wi-Fi. If yours doesn't, there's usually an Internet café nearby.

MONEY MATTERS

There are ATMs all over David, in front of banks and in the big supermarkets, pharmacies, and gas stations, though they tend to be concentrated around the central plaza and along the Interamericana. There are also ATMs at the banks in the centers of Boquete and Volcán.

SAFETY

Aside from the usual dangers associated with scuba diving and surfing, the province's biggest health concerns are sunburn and hypothermia on the heights of Volcán Barú. If you hike to the summit of Barú, take warm, waterproof clothing, even in the dry season, since the weather can change radically near the peak within an hour. If you get wet and the temperature plummets, hypothermia can be a danger.

VISITOR INFORMATION

People at the ATP's regional office (open weekdays 8:30–4:30) in David are amiable but not very helpful. The CEFATI Visitor Center (open daily 9–3:30), on the southern end of Boquete, does a better job.

Tourist Information ATP (✉ *Av. Domingo Díaz, across from Cable and Wireless, David* ☎ *775–4120* ⊕ *www.chiriqui.org*). **CEFATI** (✉ *Av. Central, 1 km [½ mi] south of town* ☎ *720–4060* ⊕ *boquete.chiriqui.org*).

THE LOWLANDS AND GULF

The torrid lowlands that spread out around David are almost all pasture, and the small towns there are home to the province's traditional Chiricano cowboy culture. You'll drive past these towns on your way to the more attractive valleys or beaches, but there is little reason to stop in any of them. The vast Golfo de Chiriquí holds dozens of islands, coral reefs, world-class surf breaks and sportfishing. Although David can serve as a base for gulf trips, it's more easily explored from Boca Chica, Boca Brava, the Islas Secas, or Moro Negrito.

DAVID

440 km (274 mi) west of Panama City, 53 km (33 mi) east of Paso Canoa.

With almost 80,000 inhabitants, this provincial capital is Panama's second-largest city, yet it has almost nothing to offer travelers. With its businesses scattered indiscriminately among the residential community, the expansive town has absolutely no zoning and an equal amount of charm. However, David is the commercial and administrative center for a province of about 370,000 and consequently has plenty of banks, car-rental agencies, and other services. Many shops are concentrated in the streets and avenues around its central plaza; newer shopping centers line the roads around its periphery.

David is a grid of *avenidas* running north–south, and *calles* running east–west. Avenida Central and Calle Central cross near the heart of town; the rest of the calles are lettered (Calle A, etc.), followed by either Norte or Sur (North or South), whereas the avenidas are numbered and Este or Oeste (East or West). A recent administration changed many street names, but locals still use the old ones.

Though founded in the 17th century, David has almost no historic buildings or attractions. Add oppressive heat and you have enough reasons to avoid David. Since it's the regional transportation hub, however, many visitors must spend a night here at the beginning or end of their time in Chiriquí. It also serves as a departure point for scuba-diving or sportfishing excursions, and can be a convenient base for hiking the Sendero Los Quetzales because you can bus to Cerro Punta in the morning, hike to Boquete, and bus back to David in the evening.

If you're in Chiriquí during the third week of March you can check out the **Feria Internacional de David**. It's like a county fair with lots of cows and commercial exhibits, plus folk music and dancing.

The central plaza, **Parque Cervantes**, was renovated in 2007 but is surrounded by some uninspiring architecture, including the very unattractive **Iglesia de la Sagrada Familia,** built in the early 20th century.

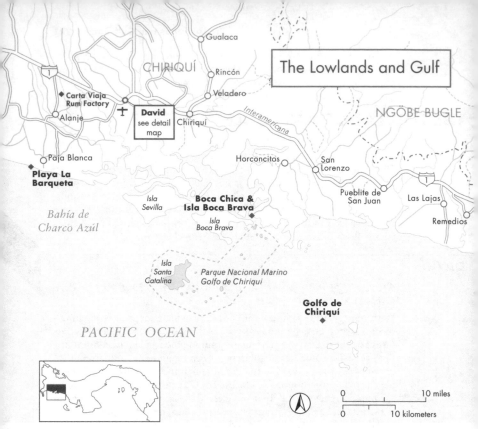

GETTING HERE AND AROUND

The 440-km (274-mi) drive between David and Panama City takes six to seven hours—an easy trip on the Carretera Interamericana (CA1) that can be done in a day. However, because there are plenty of flights and rental-car companies in David, it isn't worth doing unless you visit the Azuero Peninsula or Santa Catalina en route, since the scenery consists primarily of pastures and unattractive towns.

Domestic airlines Aeroperlas and Air Panama have half a dozen flights a day between David and Panama City. There is a flight between David and Bocas del Toro most mornings for under $50 one-way; and Air Panama has three flights a week between David and San José, Costa Rica.

Buses between David and Panama City depart hourly during the day, and direct, overnight buses depart at 10:45 PM and midnight. The trip usually takes eight hours, with a meal stop in Santiago. A couple of buses depart each morning for the nine-hour trip to San José, Costa Rica, which is a rough way to spend a day. From David, buses depart every 20 minutes for the 53-km (33-mi) trip to Paso Canoas, the Costa Rica border post, where hourly buses leave for Golfito. Buses also depart from David for Boquete or Cerro Punta every 30 minutes.

WHERE TO EAT

$ ✕ **Bernard's.** You don't even have
ECLECTIC to leave David's airport to find
a decent meal. This small café,
located on the second floor of the
main terminal, offers a hodgepodge
of cuisines ranging from Thai and
Panamanian to Indian and Mediterranean. The owner is Iranian expat
Bernard Bahary, who introduces
himself to just about every traveler
who walks through the door. His
famed breakfasts habitually lure
locals, who head to the airport
for Bernard's fruit waffles, curry
omelets, or Panamanian breakfasts
of eggs, tostadas, cheese, and fries. The lunch menu features pasta, burgers, and delicious desserts such as bread pudding à la mode. ✉ *Dole-
guita, Aeropuerto de David, David* ☎ *6751–5028* ⊕ *MC, V* ⊗ *Closed
Sun. No dinner.*

$–$$ ✕ **Pizzería Gran Hotel Nacional.** This simple restaurant serves 17 variet-
ITALIAN ies of good pizza, as well as mediocre pastas, many meat and seafood
dishes, and inexpensive, three-course lunch specials. The decor is limited
to vibrant tablecloths and tacky art, but the place is clean, bright, and
air-conditioned. ✉ *Gran Hotel Nacional, Calle Pérez Balladares (Calle
Central) at Av. 9 de Enero (Av. Central)* ☎ *775–1042* ▤ *AE, MC, V.*

¢–$$ ✕ **Restaurante Steakhouse.** Located at the edge of town across from the
CHINESE *estadio* (stadium), this popular spot is worth the $2 taxi ride to get
there. It's a Chinese restaurant, but true to the name, the extensive
menu includes lots of grilled items. The spacious dining room has a
high ceiling, huge chandeliers, big Chinese prints on the walls, and a
flat-screen TV. Locals pack in to feast on *chiau jiam ja* (spicy shrimp
in fried noodles), *king tung* (pork ribs with sweet-and-sour sauce), and
langosta estilo cantonés (lobster medallions stir-fried with vegetables).
✉ *Calle Alberto Osorio at Av. 7 Oeste* ☎ *775–8490* ▤ *MC, V.*

WHERE TO STAY

$ ▦ **Gran Hotel Nacional.** The best hotel in town, this 1950s two-story
complex with a colonial Spanish motif was remodeled in the 1990s.
Rooms are spacious, but the decor is dated. Front rooms have views
of the large trees that shade the parking area; rooms near the lobby
have Wi-Fi. The small pool area's gardens and lawn may be the most
pleasant spots in David. The hotel also boasts an in-house movie the-
ater and casino. Its three restaurants include a pizzeria (⇨ *above*) and
the open-air Barbacoa, which serves a small dinner selection of meat
and seafood. **Pros:** pool; spacious rooms; central location; decent res-
taurants. **Cons:** surly receptionists; rooms facing the street have poor
views. ✉ *Calle Pérez Balladares (Calle Central) and Av. 9 de Enero (Av.
Central)* ☎ *775–2221* 🖷 *775–7729* ⊕ *www.hotelnacionalpanama.com*
🛏 *112 rooms, 5 suites* ⚭ *In-room: safe. In-hotel: 3 restaurants, room*

TAKE A DIP

If the heat in David is too much,
head to **Balenario Mojagua**, a
popular river swimming hole with
a small waterfall and tropical
foliage. It can be busy on week-
ends and holidays when *pindín*
or *reggaetón* music blasts from
the open-air bar but tends to be
dead at other times. ✉ *Road to
Boquete, 4 km (2 mi) north of
David* ☎ *No phone* 🗮 *$1* ⊗ *Daily
9–6.*

5

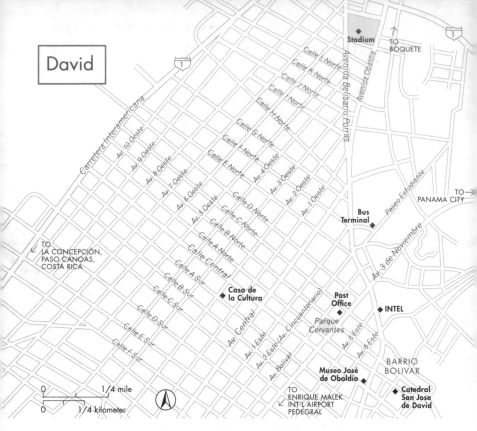

service, bar, pool, laundry service, Wi-Fi, parking (free), no-smoking rooms ▤ *AE, MC, V* ⦿| *EP.*

¢–$ ⛨ **Hotel Castilla.** This three-story building located kitty-corner from Parque Cervantes has basic rooms with good beds and small desks at reasonable prices. Interior rooms are dark, but corner junior suites have big windows and private balconies, albeit overlooking busy streets. This place is nothing fancy but is well located and a good value. **Pros:** central location; competitive rates. **Cons:** interior rooms dark; junior suites can be noisy. ⊠ *Calle Aristides Romero (Calle A Norte) at Calle Bolívar (Calle 3 Este)* ☎ *774–5260* ⊕ *castilladavi@cwpanama.net* ⬚ *62 rooms, 6 suites* ♿ *In-room: refrigerator (some). In-hotel: restaurant, laundry service, Internet terminal, parking (free), no-smoking rooms* ▤ *AE, MC, V* ⦿| *EP.*

$$ ⛨ **Hotel Puerta del Sol.** Just a five-minute drive from David's Enrique Malek Airport, this clean hotel has rooms that can sleep up to four people, each with cable TV and private bath. Air-conditioning and tile floors keep rooms cool, but don't expect much in the way of decor or views. Curtains and bedding clash horribly with the brightly patterned wallpaper, and most rooms overlook tin roofs or busy streets. For the price, however, the spacious rooms are still a bargain. Panamanian and Spanish dishes are served in the downstairs restaurant, as is the buffet that's offered Sundays and holidays. As one of David's newest hotels,

it is also one of the few with underground parking and an elevator.
Pros: clean hotel; centrally located.
Cons: poor views; Wi-Fi access limited to one hour per day. ⊠ *Between Av. 3 and Calle Central* ☎ *774-8422* ⊕ *www.hotelpuertadelsol.com.pa* ⋙ *80 rooms, 6 suites* ⚷ *In-room:*

WHEN TO DIVE

The best diving is from December to July, after which you may get either decent conditions or rough seas that decrease visibility.

refrigerator (some), Wi-Fi. In-hotel: restaurant, room service, bar, laundry service, Internet terminal, safe, parking (free), no-smoking rooms ⊟ *AE, MC, V* ☉ *EP.*

NIGHTLIFE AND THE ARTS
The **Cine Alhambra** (⊠ *Gran Hotel Nacional, Calle Pérez Balladares [Calle Central] and Av. 9 de Enero [Av. Central]* ☎ *774–7887*), David's main movie theater, is part of the Hotel Nacional.

The **Fiesta Casino** (⊠ *Calle Pérez Balladares [Calle Central] and Av. 9 de Enero [Av. Central]* ☎ *775–6667*), across the street from the Hotel Nacional, is a popular, though smoky, spot that includes a small sports bar called Salsa Bar.

SPORTS AND THE OUTDOORS
HIKING
★ David is a convenient base from which to hike the **Sendero Los Quetzales** (⤷ *Cerro Punta, below*), an all-day adventure through the cloud forest on the north slope of Volcán Barú. The country's highest peak, it is located between the mountain valleys of Cerro Punta and Boquete. Watch for the rare, resplendent quetzal and dozens of other birds. Bring sunblock, plenty of water, food, and warm, waterproof clothing, since it can get quite cool on the trail, and is often raining, when David is hot and sunny. **Tours with David-based guide Yania Massiel de Bradford** (☎ *775–9649 or 6709–8204*) **include transportation from David to Cerro Punta, a guided hike (three to four hours) to Boquete, and transportation back to David, all for $30 to $65, depending on the number of hikers.**

SCUBA DIVING AND SNORKELING
The excellent dive spots around Islas Ladrones and Islas Secas (⤷ *Golfo de Chiriquí, below*) are two hours from David, and within just one hour are the islands of the Parque Nacional Marino Golfo de Chiriquí (⤷ *box, below*), with decent diving and snorkeling.

Day trips to the spots in the Gulf of Chiriquí with **Scuba Charters** (☎ *938–0007*) depart from Pedregal Marina, 10 minutes south of David, as do overnight excursions to Isla Coiba (⤷ *chapter 4*).

SPORTFISHING
The Gulf of Chiriquí has great fishing within hours of David's Pedregal Marina. Cast for amberjack, mackerel, tuna, wahoo, roosterfish, and seasonal billfish.

The **M/V Coral Star** (☎ *866/924–2837 in U.S.* ⊕ *www.coralstar.com*), a 115-foot live-aboard, runs weeklong fishing cruises to the Gulf of Chiriquí and Isla Coiba.

Pesca Panama (☎ *6614–5850 in Panama; 800/946–3473 in the U.S.* ⊕ *www.pescapanama.com*) has one-week fishing tours west of the Golfo de Chiriquí with overnights on a barge or day charters out of Pedregal on 27-foot boats.

PLAYA LA BARQUETA

26 km (16 mi) southwest of David.

Playa La Barquete, the closest beach to David, is a long ribbon of dark-gray sand that's popular with local surfers. The area behind the beach is deforested, and the sea is often murky due to a nearby mangrove estuary. Nonetheless, it's a pleasant spot to spend a day or two. La Barqueta has the province's only beach resort and several vacation homes and condos, but most of the beach is backed by scrubby vegetation; you can stroll for miles without seeing a soul (except during holidays). The beach is public, but a day pass ($10) from the resort, Hotel Las Olas, includes pool, gym, and bar access. There are also several simple restaurants—especially Las Garzas, Miramar, and Rancho La Costena—west of Hotel Las Olas (not part of the resort) with inexpensive Panamanian fare. ⚠ **La Barqueta's sand can get hot enough to burn your feet. If the sea is rough there's a risk of rip currents, so don't go in any farther than waist-deep.**

Five sea-turtle species nest on Playa la Barqueta, and 14 km (8½ mi) of the beach's eastern half is within the **Refugio de Vida Silvestre Playa de la Barqueta Agrícola** (*Playa La Barqueta Agricultural Wildlife Refuge* ☎ *6716–8301 or 6524–9421*). From June to November, olive ridley, hawksbill, loggerhead, and green sea turtles nest on the beach; massive leatherback turtles and olive ridleys nest from November to March. The marine reptiles crawl onto the beach at night and bury their eggs in the sand; two months later eggs hatch and baby turtles dig their way out and scurry to the sea. The best time to look for nesting turtles is high tide, preferably when the moon is a mere crescent, though you may find hatchlings on the beach any afternoon from August to January. To look for nesting turtles, you must pay an admission fee ($5) and get a permit during the day at the Ranger Station just east of the Las Olas Beach Resort.

GETTING HERE AND AROUND

The 26-km (16-mi) drive southwest from David to Playa La Barqueta has a few turns, but they are all well marked with signs for Las Olas. Take Avenida 9 de Enero south, across Calle F Sur, and follow the signs. Every two hours, buses leave for Playa La Barqueta from the main bus terminal in David.

WHERE TO STAY

$$$ ⊞ **Las Brisas Del Mar.** The land that once served as a cattle plantation now holds 42 modern vacation rentals that overlook the Pacific Ocean. With all the amenities of home, these three-bedroom condos have fully-equipped kitchens, large living rooms, dining areas, and sliding glass doors that open onto furnished terraces. Ideal for families or long-term stays, each unit has a washer and dryer, walk-in closets, vaulted ceilings, granite countertops, and modern furnishings. Since the property

is under the same ownership as Las Olas Resort, guests of Las Brisas are given maid service and access to neighboring pools, tennis courts, restaurants, and a spa at the resort. Request a third-floor condo for the best view. **Pros:** spacious; great ocean views; access to nearby resort amenities. **Cons:** 3-night minimum stay; construction at nearby housing development can be annoying. ⊠ *Playa La Barqueta* ☏ *772–3000* ⊕ *www.lasolasresort.com* ⬥ *42 3-bedroom condos* ⚲ *In-room: kitchen, DVD, Wi-Fi (some), laundry facilities. In-hotel: restaurant, room service, bar, tennis courts, pools, gym, spa, beachfront, water sports, laundry service, Internet terminal, Wi-Fi, parking (free), no-smoking rooms* ⊟ *AE, MC, V* ☻ *EP.*

$$$ ⊞ **Las Olas Beach Resort.** One of only two hotels on Playa La Barqueta, this small beach resort has ample diversions, including four pools, massages, and surfing lessons, as well as volleyball and tennis courts, boogie boards, and horseback riding. Second-floor rooms have the best views, but ground-floor rooms are just steps away from the surf. Rooms are modestly sized with one king or two queen beds. Las Olas can also be a base for sportfishing or scuba-diving charters, white-water rafting, or day trips to Cerro Punta and Boquete. The hotel has two boats for rent as well as kayaks for paddling through 9 km of protected mangroves. Discount rates outside of high season can be a bargain. **Pros:** beachfront; wildlife refuge; ample facilities. **Cons:** mediocre beach; can be dead during low season. ⊠ *Playa La Barqueta* ☏ *772–3000* ⊕ *www. lasolasresort.com* ⬥ *48 rooms* ⚲ *In-room: safe, Internet. In-hotel: 2 restaurants, room service, bar, pools, gym, tennis courts, beachfront, water sports, laundry service, Internet terminal, no-smoking rooms* ⊟ *AE, MC, V* ⊧ *EP.*

SPORTS AND THE OUTDOORS
SURFING
Playa La Barqueta has the best surf near David, with various beach breaks.Serious surfers will want to go west of La Barqueta to **Playa Sandía,** due south of Santo Tomás, which has a beach break and a long right in front of the estuary at the west end of the beach.

Few surfers get to isolated **Punta Burica,** a three-hour trip down the beach south from Puerto Armuelles. It's accessible only at low tide and with a 4WD vehicle.

A rustic, American-owned lodge called the **Mono Feliz** (⊠ *Punta Burica* ☏ *6595–0388 or 6574–4386* ⊕ *monofeliz@hotmail.com*) offers inexpensive lodging and basic meals in Punta Burica.

BOCA CHICA AND ISLA BOCA BRAVA

54 km (32 mi) southeast of David.

Long a sleepy fishing port at the end of a bone-rattling road, Boca Chica now has a paved road and a small selection of hotels that serve the islands of Parque Nacional Marino Golfo de Chiriquí. The town is on a peninsula overlooking the nearby island of Boca Brava. Together, Boca Chica and Isla Boca Brava define the eastern edge of a mangrove estuary that extends all the way to Playa La Barqueta.

Isla Boca Brava, across the channel from Boca Chica, is mostly covered with forest and is home to howler monkeys, but neither the island nor the mainland has nice beaches, and the ocean is usually murky because of the estuary. The attractions are beyond Boca Brava on the uninhabited islands of the Parque Nacional Marino Golfo de Chiriquí (⇨ *below*), a 40-minute boat ride away. Beyond them lie world-class sportfishing and diving around the Islas Ladrones and Islas Secas.

GETTING HERE AND AROUND

The Panama Big Game Fishing Club and Cala Mia have boat transport (60 minutes) for guests from Pedregal. It's more expensive than by land, but more pleasant and takes half the time. It takes about 90 minutes to drive from David to Boca Chica; go east on the Carretera Interamericana (CA1) for 39 km (24 mi), then turn right at the intersection for Horconcitos. From David's airport, turn left onto Avenida Reed Gray, then left onto Calle F Sur at the police station, and right onto the Interamericana. Follow the signs in Horconcitos, after which the road improves. Most hotels arrange transfers from the David airport.

WHERE TO STAY

$$$
Fodor's Choice
★
⊞ **Cala Mia.** Bungalows at this Boca Brava eco-lodge are tastefully decorated and have terraces with couches, hammocks, and tree-shrouded water views. The restaurant ($$) at the end of the point has walls of windows and specializes in fresh seafood and vegetables from the hotel's organic farm. Three-course dinners change nightly. A suspension bridge leads to an islet with a massage and yoga gazebo. Activities include sea kayaking, excursions to nearby islands, snorkeling, scuba diving, and horseback riding. Ocean-view bungalows are better ventilated than bay-view ones. Electricity is solar (meaning no a/c), garbage is recycled or composted for farm use, and 5% of income goes to projects for indigenous communities. **Pros:** gorgeous design and location; trips to islands; natural food; friendly staff. **Cons:** isolated; no-see-ums can be a problem. ⊠ *Isla Boca Brava* ☎ *6747–0011* ☏ *0448 Entrega General, Horconcito, David, Chiriquí* ⊕ *www.boutiquehotelcalamia.com* ⋟ *11 bungalows* ⚿ *In-room: no a/c, safe, no TV. In-hotel: restaurant, Wi-Fi, bar, pool, beachfront, water sports, laundry service, no-smoking rooms* ▤ *MC, V, AE* ⊢◉⊣ *BP.*

$$
⊞ **Gone Fishing.** Though fishing is an option here, this is really a waterfront hotel that offers various activities. The name reflects the attitude of the owners, Bruce and Donna, who retired to Boca Chica from south Florida. Spacious, well-equipped rooms have private balconies and are decorated with themed murals. It's popular with families and has ample grounds, a large pool, and a lively common area open to the public. Bruce's boats are docked below for his next fishing trip, but he'll take you island hopping and can arrange scuba diving. Meals are served on a wide terrace with a view. **Pros:** great view; nice pool. **Cons:** bugs can be a problem; loud noise from common areas. ⊠ *Boca Chica, on left before town* ☎ *851-0104* ⊕ *www.gonefishingpanama.com* ⋟ *5 rooms* ⚿ *In-room: no phone, no TV (some). In-hotel: restaurant, bar, pool, water sports, laundry service, Wi-Fi, no-smoking rooms* ▤ *MC, V* ⊢◉⊣ *EP.*

¢
⊞ **Hotel Boca Brava.** Across the channel from Boca Chica, this backpacker's lodge belongs to a retired German architect, though you wouldn't

guess it from the uninspiring white rooms with foam mattresses on cement platforms. Rooms are scattered around the forested grounds. The best have a/c, TV, and glimpses of the ocean. Four without a/c cost half as much and share a bathhouse. The three-level restaurant at the end of the point serves a good selection of seafood and meat and can get busy on weekends; however, the kitchen closes early. The lodge rents kayaks and snorkeling equipment and has island excursions. The nearest beach is a mile away via a forest trail. **Pros:** inexpensive; decent restaurant. **Cons:** very basic rooms; bugs can be a problem; smoky environment; hotel constantly under repair. ⊠ *Isla Boca Brava* ☏ *851-0017* ⤳ *14 rooms* ⚷ *In-room: no a/c (some), no phone, no TV (some). In-hotel: restaurant, bar, Wi-Fi, water sports* ▤ *No credit cards.*

$$$$ 🖫 **Panama Big Game Fishing Club.** This small lodge on Boca Brava, just across the channel from Boca Chica, is all about sportfishing. Customized three- to six-day packages include daily fishing, all meals and beverages, and in-country transportation. You can access the waters around the Islas Ladrones, Islas Montuosos, and the Hannibal Bank for some of Panama's best fishing. Accommodations are in two- to six-person cement bungalows nestled in the rain forest. Meals are served family-style in a circular building at the top of the hill, decorated with the obligatory mounted fish. **Pros:** small and intimate setting; great fishing; good food. **Cons:** no pool; nothing for nonfishers; bugs can be a problem; four-night minimum. ⊠ *Isla Boca Brava* ☏ *6674–4824; 866/281–1225 in the U.S.* ⊕ *www.panamabiggamefishingclub.com* ⤳ *4 bungalows* ⚷ *In-room: no phone. In-hotel: restaurants, bar, laundry service, public Wi-Fi, no-smoking rooms* ▤ *AE, MC, V* ⏰*FAP.*

$$ 🖫 **Seagull Cove Lodge.** This hillside hotel belongs to a charming Spanish-
★ Italian couple; the decor is Mediterranean with its arched doorways, terra-cotta flooring, and manicured gardens. The spotless bungalows have high ceilings, hand-painted ceramic sinks, and barrel-tile roofs. They come with satellite TV and other modern amenities, but their best selling points are the terrace views of the forest and bay. There is a tiny pool, and a long stairway leads past the bungalows to a sliver of beach and a dock where you can leave for island trips. The open-air restaurant ($$–$$$$) has the best view on the property, serving light lunches and delightful dinners ranging from grilled tenderloin to shrimp pasta. **Pros:** great views of the bay; clean property; good food; friendly service. **Cons:** steep stairs; small grounds; bugs can be a problem. ⊠ *Boca Chica, on left just before town* ☏ *851–0036, 786–735 1475 in the U.S.* ⊕ *www.seagullcovelodge.com* ⤳ *5 bungalows* ⚷ *In-room: no phone, safe. In hotel: Wi-Fi, restaurant, bar, pool, water sports, laundry service, no kids under 10, no-smoking rooms* ▤ *MC, V* ⏰*EP.*

SPORTS AND THE OUTDOORS
SCUBA DIVING AND SNORKELING
Boca Chica is the most convenient base for scuba-diving and snorkeling trips to Parque Nacional Marino Golfo de Chiriquí *(below)* ⇨ and to Islas Ladrones and Islas Secas *(⇨ below).*

Master diver Carlos Spragge at **Buzos Boca Brava** (⊠ *Boca Chica* ☏ *775–3185 or 6600–6191* ⊕ *www.scubadiving-panama.com*) offers day trips to either the Islas Ladrones or Islas Secas. Overnight trips with lodging on board can combine both islands or can include Isla Coiba (⇨ *chapter 4*).

SPORTFISHING
The Gulf has superb fishing, especially around the Islas Montuosos and Hannibal Bank. The best fishing is for black marlin and sailfish from January to April. Find huge yellowfin tuna from March to May; dolphin (the fish, not the mammal) abound from November to January. From July to January it's roosterfish and wahoo; catch amberjacks, mackerel, snapper, and grouper year-round.

Panama Big Game Fishing Club (⇨ *Where to Stay, above*) includes daily fishing trips to the gulf's best spots in their rates. **Gone Fishing** (⇨ *Where to Stay, above*) offers deep-sea charters or less-expensive inshore fishing that start at $700.

GOLFO DE CHIRIQUÍ ISLANDS

The vast Gulf of Chiriquí holds dozens of uninhabited islands surrounded by healthy coral formations and excellent conditions for surfing, diving, and fishing. You can base yourself in the Boca Chica/Boca Brava area (⇨ *above*) to explore these islands, but there are also two gulf-island resorts that provide more immediate access. Isla Ensenada, in the gulf's northeast corner, is near five of the country's best and most remote breaks, accessed from the Morro Negrito Surf Camp. The beautiful, remote **Islas Secas** (Dry Islands), a 16-isle archipelago 35 km (21 mi) from the coast, has one luxury eco-lodge but can be visited from Boca Chica or Boca Brava. On the southern edge of the gulf are the **Islas Ladrones,** with fantastic scuba diving and angling.

The 14,740 hectares (36,400 acres) of the **Parque Nacional Marino Golfo de Chiriquí** (*Chiriquí Marine National Park*) include more than 20 islands—all but one of which are uninhabited. The islands' beaches are the nicest in Chiriquí Province, with pale sand, clear waters, tropical dry forest, and colorful reef fish just a shell's toss from shore. The loveliest are the palm-lined strands of **Isla Parida** (the largest in the archipelago), **Isla San José, Isla Gamez,** and **Isla Bolaños,** where the sand is snow-white. Various species of sea turtle nest on the islands' beaches, and the water holds hundreds of species including lobsters, moray eels, and schools of parrot fish. You may also see frigate birds, brown pelicans, and green iguanas. Dolphins sometimes cruise the park's waters, and from August to October you may spot humpback whales. There are no lodging facilities; visit on day trips from Boca Chica, 30 to 60 minutes away, depending on the island. ⊠ *12 km (7 mi) southwest of Boca Chica* 🕾 *774–6671 or 774–6671* 🖃 *$3.50* ⊙ *Daily 8–6.*

GETTING HERE AND AROUND
Transportation to Golfo de Chiriquí lodges is provided by the lodges. The Parque Nacional Marino Golfo de Chiriquí, Islas Secas, and Islas Ladrones can be visited on day trips from Boca Chica and Boca Brava via boat.

WHERE TO STAY

$$$$ ⚏ **Islas Secas Resort.** Constant exposure to the bounties of nature, gour-
Fodor's Choice met food, spa services, and other pampering are what you get at this
★ all-inclusive luxury eco-lodge on the Islas Secas. To limit environmental
impact, accommodations are in seven spacious *yurts* (round tents of
Mongolian origin), with a hot-water bath, minibar, and other amenities that run on solar power and propane. Walking paths, made from
washed-up coral and seashells, wind past lush jungle and towering
palms to the dining area where meals are served in an open-air restaurant overlooking a cove. Snorkeling, scuba diving, surfing, whale
watching, use of catamarans and kayaks, and light-tackle fishing are
included, as are meals and drinks; deep-sea fishing and spa services are
extra. Popular with honeymooners is the casita that can be reached only
by kayak during high tide. Typically there are no more than 14 guests
and 14 staff members on the island at any given time. The downside is
rates are more than double those of any other hotel in Panama. To reach
this island paradise, you can either fly directly from Panama City to
the resort's landing strip, which takes one hour, or you can take a commercial flight to David and travel two hours by boat. Since the resort's
owner purchased the entire 16-isle archipelago, there are no plans to
develop the pristine islands that surround Isla Secas. New owners are
considering converting the yurts to more permanent units at this writing, but the resort will still remain eco-sensitive. **Pros:** gorgeous, remote
location; excellent scuba diving; high-end sports equipment; gourmet
food. **Cons:** extremely expensive; hard to get to; may be closed during rainy season. ⊠ *Islas Secas* ☎ *805/729–2737 in the U.S.* ⊕ *www.*
islassecas.com ⌨ *7 rooms* ⚠ *In-room: no a/c, no phone, safe, no TV. In-*
hotel: restaurant, spa, beachfront, diving, water sports, laundry service,
spa, Internet terminal, no-smoking rooms ⊟ *AE, MC, V* ❘○❘ *FAP.*

$$$ ⚏ **Morro Negrito Surf Camp.** California surfer Steve Thompson built this
basic lodge on a coastal island in the gulf's northeast corner, near 10
excellent breaks that are usually ridden only by the two-dozen surfers
the camp accommodates. The lodge rents boards ($15–25 per day)
and provides transportation to nearby breaks and also offers inshore
fishing, snorkeling, hiking, bird-watching, yoga, and massages. A one-
week stay is usually required, but if you are in the area and e-mail the
resort, you might be accommodated for as few as two nights. Rooms
have tile floors, basic beds with mosquito nets, and fans. Hearty meals
are served family style, and there's a small bar, a Ping-Pong table, horse-
shoes, basketball, hammocks, and terrace swings made from broken
surfboards. Since the focus is on surfing here, the decor and amenities
are not a priority. The camp has low environmental impact—solar and
wind energy, recycling—and supports a local student scholarship fund,
but there's only electricity at night when the generator is on. **Pros:** great
waves with few surfers. **Cons:** basic rooms; shared bathrooms; cold-
water showers; bugs can be a problem. ⊠ *Isla Ensenada* ☎ *832–2831;*
760/632–8014 in U.S. ⊕ *www.panamasurfcamp.com* ⌨ *12 rooms, 1*
with bath ⚠ *In-room: no a/c, no phone, no TV. In-hotel: restaurant,*
water sports, laundry service, Internet terminal, no-smoking rooms
⊟ *MC, V* ❘○❘ *FAP.*

5

SPORTS AND THE OUTDOORS
SCUBA DIVING AND SNORKELING

The Islas Secas and Islas Ladrones are surrounded by more than 50 excellent dive sites, with visibility averaging 70 feet and healthy coral formations surrounded by hundreds of fish species and comparable invertebrate diversity. You might see various species of sea stars and angelfish, elegant Moorish idols, frog fish, and sea turtles. The best time to dive is during dry season when you can see up to 30 species of shark and eel.

The **Islas Secas Resort** (⇨ *above*) lies in the middle of the archipelago's coral gardens, and daily scuba dives and snorkeling are included in the rates. Those islands can also be visited on day trips from the Morro Negrito Surf Camp or the Boca Chica/Boca Brava lodges.

Buzos Boca Brava (☎ *775–3185 or 6600–6191* ⊕ *www.scubadiving-panama.com*) offers day trips and overnights to the Islas Secas out of Boca Chica that start at $150.

SURFING

The Golfo de Chiriquí has some undervisited, remote surf breaks. Surfing is best from June to December when waves consistently break overhead, and faces sometimes reach 20 feet; there are often four- to five-foot swells during the dry season, too.

The most convenient wave for guests at the Morro Negrito Surf Camp is **Emily**, a left that breaks over the reef right in front of the camp.

Advanced surfers enjoy the rush of **Nestles**, a big reef break in front of Isla Silva de Afuera.

The most impressive wave in the gulf is called **The Point**, a tubular reef break that has surfers booking several weeks at the Morro Negrito Surf Camp year after year.

The Sandbar, a long break that has both lefts and rights, is popular with intermediate surfers and beginners. Intermediate and advanced surfers enjoy **P Land**, a left reef break on Isla Silva de Afuera, year-round.

THE MOUNTAINS

Nestled in the Cordillera de Talamanca, which towers along the province's northern edge, are the lush mountain valleys of Boquete, Cerro Punta, and Bambito, each with unique scenery. To the east of Boquete a road winds over the Cordillera near Lago Fortuna, an area that also has excellent hiking and amazing vistas. The mountain range's upper slopes are covered with lush cloud forest, which is kept wet by the mist that the trade winds regularly push over the continental divide. That mist not only keeps the landscape green, it creates the perfect conditions for rainbows, commonly sighted during the afternoon. Mountain streams feed half a dozen rafting rivers in the Cordillera, and its abundant forests are excellent areas for bird-watching, hiking, horseback riding, or canopy tours. All travelers can enjoy the area's captivating beauty, abundant flowers, and charming restaurants and inns.

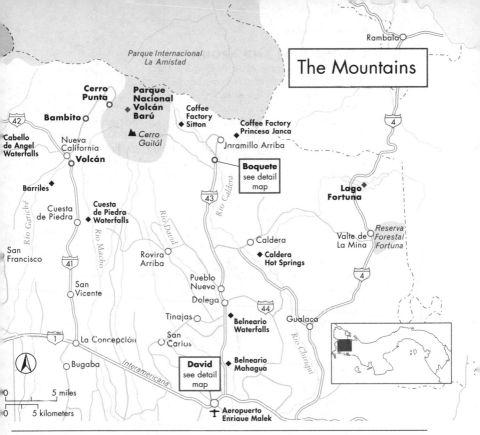

BOUQUETE

★ *38 km (24 mi) north of David.*

This pleasant town sits at 3,878 feet above sea level in the always spring-like valley of the Río Caldera. The surrounding mountains are covered with forest and shade coffee farms, where coffee bushes grow amidst tropical trees. It's superb for bird-watching, and the roads and trails can be explored on foot, horseback, mountain bike, or four wheels.

Though the surrounding countryside holds most of Boquete's attractions, the town itself is quite appealing, with tidy wooden houses and prolific flower gardens. Fewer than 30,000 people live here, most of them scattered around the valley. The town center is thus sparsely populated, with a simple *parque central* (central park), officially the Parque de las Madres, surrounded by shops, the town hall, and roads lined with patches of pink impatiens and the pale trumpet-like flowers of the Datura, also known as jimson weed or devil's trumpet. Streams meander through town, and the Río Caldera flows through a wide swath of boulders along its eastern edge.

GETTING HERE AND AROUND

It's an easy 45-minute drive to Boquete from David, where you follow Avenida Obaldía north across the highway and continue straight. From David's airport, turn left onto Avenida Reed Gray, then left onto Calle F Sur at the police station and right onto the two-lane Interamericana (CA1). Get into the left lane and watch for the turnoff for Boquete. Buses depart from David's terminal on Avenida del Estudiante every 30 minutes and take 60–90 minutes to reach Boquete. From Boquete, catch the bus to David on Avenida Central anywhere south of the parque central. The trip costs $2. If you bus from Cerro Punta, Paso Canoas, or Bocas del Toro, you'll need to change to the Boquete bus in David.

Boquete's local transportation is via vans that depart regularly from Avenida Central just north of the parque central for either the Alto Quiel/Bajo Mono loop or the Alto Lino/Palo Alto loop. They pick up and drop off passengers anywhere en route for $1. Taxis wait around the parque central and charge $1–$5 for valley trips.

Contacts Boquete Shuttle Service (☎ 720–1635) runs direct transfers between hotels in Boquete and David's airport for $15.

Daniel Higgins (☎ 6617–0570) is an English-speaking driver who'll take you to David, Boca Chica, or Cerro Punta. He can also drive you to or from Almirante, the gateway to Bocas del Toro, for $150; it's a beautiful four-hour drive.

WHAT TO SEE

Unlike most Panamanian towns, Boquete was settled by European and North American immigrants at the beginning of the 20th century. This lineage is apparent in everything from the architecture to the faces of many residents. There are also plenty of Ngöbe Indians in Boquete who migrate there from the northeast of Chiriquí to work in the orange and coffee harvests. Recently the valley has become popular with U.S. retirees, drawn by the climate and beauty of the area.

6 ★ **Bajo Mono Road.** The road, near San Ramón, leads to the trailhead for the **Sendero Los Quetzales** (⇨ *Cerro Punta, below*), which winds its way through the forest between Cerro Punta and Boquete. Start that hike in Cerro Punta, though; it's all uphill from Boquete. Head to Bajo Mono to look for quetzals and hundreds of other bird species; the best area for bird-watching is the beginning of the Sendero Los Quetzales, above the Alto Chiquero ranger station. Two other good hiking trails head off of the Bajo Mono road: the **Sendero Culebra,** on the right 1½ km (1 mi) up the road to Alto Chiquero, and **Pipeline Road,** a gravel track on the left that leads to a canyon and waterfall.

4 **Café Ruiz.** The Ruiz family has been growing coffee in Boquete since the late 1800s, and their coffee-roasting and packaging plant just south of Mi Jardín Es Su Jardín offers a 15-minute tour that includes a taste of the coffee on sale here. A full three-hour tour visits the family farm and processing plant in the mountains above town. Because it has plenty of trees and uses few chemicals, the farm is a good place to see birds. Do the tour in the morning between October and May, during harvest. Reserve a tour by phone or via the Web site. ⊠ *Av. Central, ½ km (¼ mi)* *south of park, on right, Boquete* ☎ *720–1000* ⊕ *www.caferuiz.com* 📧 *Plant tour $9, full tour $30* ⊗ *Mon.–Sat. 8–12 and 1–4.*

❶ **CEFATI Information Center.** If you're driving, stop at the town's official visitor center, on the right as you climb the hill into town. The center offers free information on local sights and services, but the main reason to stop is to admire the view of the Boquete Valley. The building also has a small café and gift shop. ⚠ **Beware of any businesses that advertise themselves as a "Tourist Center" or "Visitor Center" near the main park on Avenida Central. Unlike CEFATI, they operate solely on commission and generally steer travelers toward operations for which they can increase service rates. Additionally, their information and prices are not always reliable.** ✉ *Av. Central, 1 km (½ mi) south of the town center, Boquete* ☎ *720–4060* ⊗ *Daily 8–3:30.*

❷ **Feria.** Two blocks east of Boquete's parque central are the fairgrounds where the Feria de las Flores y del Café (Flower and Coffee Fair) is held for 10 days in mid-January, and the smaller Expo Orquídeas (Orchid Fair) is held in mid-April. During the interim, the fairgrounds are open to anyone who wants to admire the flower beds. ✉ *Follow Calle 4 Sur, along park's southern side, go over bridge across Río Caldera, Feria on east side of bridge,Boquete.*

❺ **Finca Lérida.** On the eastern slope of Volcán Barú, at an altitude of 4,800
Fodor's Choice feet above sea level, one coffee farm encompasses nearly 263 hectares
★ (650 acres) of bird-filled cloud forest. The farm is recommended in *A Guide to the Birds of Panama* as the place to see quetzals, and you're practically guaranteed to see them here from February to June. You may also see silver-throated tangers, collared trogons, clorophonias, and about 150 other bird species. The farm's resident guide can take you along its 10 km (6 mi) of hiking trails, one of which leads to a small waterfall, or you can explore them on your own. The guide is invaluable if you're looking for quetzals. If owner John Collins is available, you can get a coffee tour from a native English speaker who grew up on the farm. The farm has a great view and a moderately priced restaurant that serves Panamanian food, homemade desserts, and fresh-roasted coffee. ✉ *7 km (4 mi) northwest of second Y, via Callejón Seco, Alto Quiel* ☎ *720–2285* ⊕ *www.fincalerida.com* 📧 *$10, coffee tour $25, guided hike or bird-watching $65* ⊗ *Daily 7–8.*

❼ **Kotowa Estate.** In the hills of Palo Alto, this coffee farm has belonged to the MacIntyre family for three generations. The MacIntyres produce one of Boquete's best coffees and own a small chain of coffee shops. The farm still has the original coffee mill from 1920. Today the Kotowa Estate is recognized for its innovation such as burning coffee bean husks for fuel. A Dutch couple, Hans and Terry van der Vooren, runs tours here that provide a close look at the cultivation, harvest, and processing of coffee. Go during the October-to-May harvest and reserve for the tour a day in advance for free transport from your hotel. ✉ *Palo Alto* ☎ *720–3852 or 6634–4698* ⊕ *www.coffeeadventures.net* 📧 *Tour $29* ⊗ *Tour daily at 9* AM *by reservation.*

Volcán Barú. The region's main landmark is the country's highest mountain, a dormant volcano that towers over the valley's western edge.

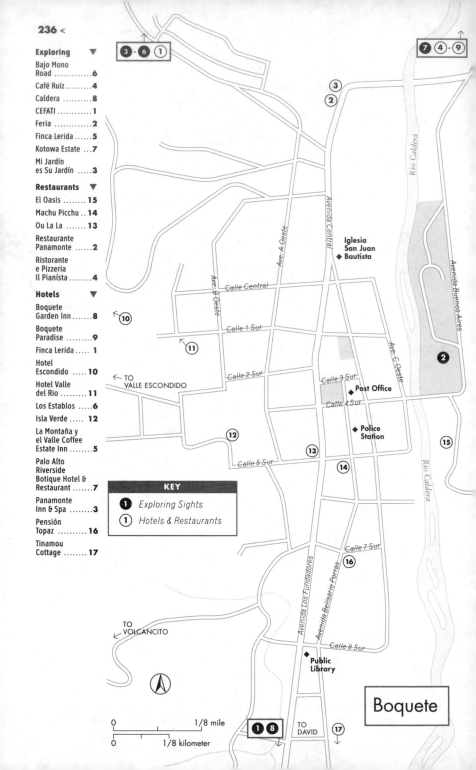

KEY

① Exploring Sights

① Hotels & Restaurants

Iglesia
San Juan
◆ Bautista

◆ Post Office

◆ Police
Station

TO
VALLE ESCONDIDO

TO
VOLCANCITO

◆ Public
Library

Rio Caldera

Avenida Central

Avenida Buenos Aires

Ave. A Oeste

Ave. B Oeste

Ave. C Oeste

Calle Central

Calle 1 Sur

Calle 2 Sur

Calle 3 Sur

Calle 4 Sur

Calle 5 Sur

Calle 7 Sur

Calle 8 Sur

Avenida Los Fundadores

Avenida Belisario Porras

TO
DAVID

Boquete

0 — 1/8 mile

0 — 1/8 kilometer

Much of Volcán Barú's green mantle of cloud forest is protected within Parque Nacional Volcán Barú. The rough road to Barú's summit begins just west of Boquete's commercial center across from the church, but its forests can also be explored on trails in the nearby areas of Alto Quiel, Bajo Mono, and Sendero los Quetzales. When starting from the Boquete trailhead, the ascent generally takes five to seven hours, followed by a three- to five-hour return trip. Climbers should take their time to avoid altitude sickness. SINAPROC (Civil Defense Rescue Group) requests that individual travelers who plan to climb Volcán Barú register with them before leaving (SINAPROC is located across from Edificio Don Vidal near the bridge to the fairgrounds). ✛ *From downtown Boquete, follow the road 10 km (6.5 mi) toward the ANAM (National Environment Authority) ranger station that guards the entrance to the national park. The last stretch of the road is bumpy, so only those with 4WD vehicles should attempt the 20-minute drive. Park at the ranger station and continue on foot, 14 km (8.5 mi) to the summit.* ✉ *$3.*

3 **Mi Jardín Es Su Jardín** *(My Garden Is Your Garden)*. A few blocks north of the parque central, Avenida Central veers left at a Y in the road. Just past the Y is a garden surrounding an eccentric Panamanian's vacation home. Cement paths wind past vibrant flower beds and bizarre statues of animals and cartoon characters, which make this place a minor monument to kitsch. ✉ *Av. Central ½ km (¼ mi) north of park, on right, Boquete* ☎ *No phone* ✉ *Free* ☉ *Daily 9–5.*

OFF THE BEATEN PATH

Half an hour south of Boquete is the small village of **Caldera**, known for its hot springs (Los Pazos) and pre-Columbian petroglyphs. Los Pazos is next to the Caldera River, at the end of a rough road on the right after town, which requires 4WD. Before the turnoff for Los Pozos is the Piedra Pintada (Painted Rock), behind the Jardín La Fortuna, a large boulder with pre-Columbian petroglyphs scrawled into its side. Both sites can be visited on a tour offered by Boquete's bird-watching and hiking guides.

WHERE TO EAT

$$$ ✕ **El Oasis.** Perched on the banks of Caldera River, this pleasant restau-
INTERNATIONAL rant serves international dishes prepared by a former Panamonte chef, Belisario Torres. The smoked trout and pasta with prawns are delicious, but it is the rack of lamb in a mint and rosemary crust that is a local favorite. For a romantic dinner, the fireside gazebo has the best view. A more social setting can be found at the bar, appropriately named "La Roca" (The Rock) for a boulder that washed onto the property during a rainstorm in 1970; the boulder remains. Live music is often presented here, making it is a great place to enjoy a glass of wine or the richly decadent triple mousse dessert. Lighter fare of soups, salads, and sandwiches are also on the menu. ✉ *From Av. Central, cross over Caldera River bridge, 50 meters to the right, Boquete* ☎ *720–1586* ⊕ *www. oasisboquete.com* ⚫ ▭ *MC, V.*

¢–$ ✕ **La Casona Mexicana.** Owned by a local woman who lived in Mexico
MEXICAN for many years, this open-air restaurant on the south end of town serves a decent selection of Aztec taste treats. The menu ranges from such Tex-Mex classics as burritos, soft tacos, fajitas, enchiladas, and *flautas* (deep-fried tacos) to more original items such as *pechuga Michoacán*

5

The Quetzal and the Cloud Forest

Some people travel to Boquete specifically to see a resplendent quetzal (*Pharomachrus mocinno*), and if you're lucky enough to spot a male quetzal in flight, its iridescent colors flashing and long tail feathers streaming behind it, you'll quickly understand why. The resplendent quetzal is one of the world's most beautiful birds, a flying jewel with an emerald-green back and wings, ruby-red belly, and golden-green crest. Though a mature bird stands just 14 inches tall, male quetzals have two- to three-foot tail feathers that float behind them as they fly, giving the impression of an airborne snake, or a tiny dragon. Quetzals, which live only in cloud forests from western Panama to southern Mexico, occupied an important place in ancient Maya and Aztec cosmology. The Aztecs associated the bird with Quetzalcoatl, one of their most important deities, who was known as the Plumed Serpent. The chiefs of those cultures wore headdresses of quetzal tail feathers—Montezuma's is on display in Mexico City's anthropology museum—but the feathers were plucked from live birds that were then released, since it was a crime to kill a quetzal in those pre-Columbian societies.

The quetzal is the national bird of Guatemala, where the currency is named for it, but destruction of its cloud forest habitat has made the bird extremely rare there. Quetzals abound in the forests above Boquete, which is one of the best places in the world to see the bird. That said, it is not easy to see a quetzal, since they spend most of their time sitting on branches in the shade of the cloud forest, where their green feathers blend in perfectly with the lush surroundings.

You will consequently want to hire a local birding guide who can take you to spots where they commonly feed, or reproduce during the February to June nesting season.

In January the quetzal's slightly melancholy song becomes more common in the forests above Boquete, as the mating season begins. Female quetzals aren't as spectacular as males and look more like trogons—the quetzal is a member of the trogon family—since they lack the long tail feathers and crimson breast. Interestingly, the females have black beaks, whereas the males' beaks are light brown. The females' lack of adornment doesn't discourage males from courting them energetically. Lucky is the birdwatcher who witnesses the aerial mating dance that males perform for females, flying high and then plummeting in front of them, iridescent tail feathers streaming behind.

Once a match is made, the quetzal couple digs or finds a cavity in a rotting tree trunk and she lays two pale blue eggs, which they take turns incubating for several weeks. They guard their nest tirelessly, since various animals prey on quetzal eggs and chicks, especially the emerald toucanet, a common cloud-forest bird. Quetzals feed their chicks insects, frogs, lizards, and fruit, but the primary food for adults is *aguacatillo*, the pecan-size fruit of several trees in the avocado family. Those fruits have very large pits that are too big to pass through the quetzal's digestive tract—they can barely get them past their beaks—so the birds simply keep the fruit in their stomach for awhile, digesting the pulp, and then vomit the seed up, often far from the tree it came from.

5

The quetzal thus distributes aguaca tillo seeds around the forest, so the bird and tree are interdependent, which leads biologists to believe they evolved together. As destruction of the region's cloud forests continues, and climate change leaves many cloud-forest regions drier than they should be, the quetzal and the agaucatillo tree are increasingly endangered. Thanks to the amount of protected cloud forest around Boquete, though, both species should remain abundant there for many years, hopefully generations.

Even if you have little interest in bird-watching, taking a tour to Finca Lérida or one of the other spots above Boquete where quetzals are common, is highly recommended. Though you may not catch a glimpse of the legendary resplendent quetzal, you're bound to see dozens of other spectacular birds, and the quetzal's cloud-forest habitat is a magically beautiful ecosystem. If you travel to Cana, in Panama's eastern Darién Province,

you may be fortunate enough to also see a golden-headed quetzal, which is native to South America but is found in the mountains of the Darién. Such a quetzal double-header is only possible in Panama, and is just one of the countless examples of why this country is such an amazing place for nature lovers.

(chicken breast in an orange sauce). The food itself isn't spicy, but hot sauce is offered on the side. The restaurant's stucco walls are painted wild colors and decorated with a few Mexican souvenirs. ⊠ *Av. Central, 1 block south of Texaco gas station, Boquete* ☎ *720–1274* ▤ *MC, V.*

$–$$
PERUVIAN

✕ **Machu Picchu.** The local branch of Panama City's most popular Peruvian chain serves the same selection of spicy delicacies. The dining room is a bit plain, despite paintings of Peruvian landscapes and colorful woven tablecloths, but you can't go wrong with such classics as ceviche, *ají de gallina* (chicken in a chili cream sauce), *seco de res* (Peruvian stewed beef), and *sudado de mero* (grouper in a spicy soup). Be careful with their *ají* hot sauce; it's practically caustic. ⊠ *Av. Belisario Porras, behind Banco Nacional, Boquete* ☎ *720–1502* ▤ *AE, MC, V.*

$–$$$
FRENCH
★

✕ **Ou La La.** Five minutes' drive north of Boquete's town center, this small restaurant fills up with people who appreciate good food even though it doesn't have the best ambience. The Bordeaux-trained chef, Cristophe Giroud, serves traditional French cuisine, including escargots, pâté, and chicken Cordon Bleu. The delicacies also include fresh trout *en papillote,* shrimp flambé with bourbon, and lobster medallions and tomatoes au gratin. The menu, (handwritten on an easel) changes weekly but always features a variety of meat and seafood dishes. Couples may want to try the $45 three-course meal and bottle of wine for two. ⊠ *Los Naranjos, five minutes north of park, Los Naranjos* ☎ *6661–7838* ▤ *No credit cards* ⊗ *Closed Thurs. No lunch.*

$–$$
ECLECTIC

✕ **Palo Alto Riverside Restaurant.** This place's greatest selling point is its view of the Palo Alto River and the forest beyond it. If the weather is nice, you may want to sit outside near the riverbank, though the spacious walls of windows also let you enjoy the scenery from inside. The food is tasty and inventive, though service can be slow. Starters range from seafood crêpes and creamy chicken soup to spicy-sour butterfly shrimp on a nest of wontons. Entrées worth sinking your teeth into include steamed trout in a black-bean sauce, tenderloin with a Cognac-and-green-pepper sauce, baby back ribs, and steamed salmon with a caviar-hollandaise sauce. ⊠ *Right at first Y north of town, left after bridge, then 1½ km (1 mi) on left, Palo Alto* ☎ *720–1076* ▤ *MC, V.*

$–$$
LATIN AMERICAN
Fodor's Choice
★

✕ **Restaurante Panamonte.** Though Boquete's first hotel now faces stiff competition, its charming restaurant remains one of the best in town, if not the country. Inventive dishes based on traditional Panamanian cuisine include pumpkin soup, shrimp-and-plantain croquettes, mountain trout sautéed with almonds, and grilled beef tenderloin topped with a three-pepper sauce. It's served in a historic European atmosphere that's hardly changed over the past century. Sunday breakfast is popular. ⊠ *Panamonte Inn and Spa, right at first Y north of town, on left, Boquete* ☎ *720–1324* ✆ *Apdo. 0413-00086, Boquete, Chiriquí* ▤ *AE, MC, V*

$–$$
ITALIAN
★

✕ **Ristorante e Pizzería Il Pianista.** There is something European about the stone building that houses this restaurant a short drive northeast of town, and Chef Giovanni Santoro completes the illusion with his authentic Italian cuisine. The small dining room is on the ground floor overlooking a stream surrounded by trees and impatiens; an outdoor patio sits beside a small waterfall. The menu includes fresh pastas such as vegetable lasagna and fettuccine *del Chef* (with prawn-and-mushroom cream sauce) or *napolitano* (with tomato-clam sauce). Other specialties include *trucha al forno* (trout baked with tomatoes and mushrooms) and *calamares rellenos* (squid stuffed with tomatoes, cheese, and pine nuts). You can also build your own pizza or calzone or grab a pizza to go. ✉ *Right at first Y north of town, left after the bridge, 3½ km (2 mi) north on right, Arco Iris* ☎720–2728 ♍ *Giovanni Santoro, Entrega General, Boquete, Chiriquí* ▭ *No credit cards* ⊘ *Closed Mon. and Oct.*

A GOOD DRIVE

Just north of Café Ruiz there's a second Y in Avenida Central. The right fork heads to the farms and scenic overlooks of Alto Lino, looping back to Boquete via Palo Alto. Veer left there to reach yet another Y that marks the beginning of a second, longer loop (30 minutes) that winds through the farming areas of Alto Quiel, Bajo Mono, and San Ramón, passing forest and more great views. Both loops are well worth driving.

5

WHERE TO STAY

Hotels in Boquete don't have air-conditioning—the town's springlike climate makes it unnecessary. Theft has been a problem at some Boquete hotels, so lock your valuables in a safe if you can.

$ ★ ▦ **Boquete Garden Inn.** As the name suggests, this small hotel's grounds hold plenty of flowers, as well as trees, a few boulders, and a nature path. The most pleasant area is behind the rooms, along the Río Palo Alto, where a gazebo bar overlooks the swift-running waters and forest beyond. Guests gather here nightly for cocktail hour at 6 PM—the first beer or wine is on the house. Rooms, named after flowers, are decorated with exotic local art and have small windows (set in bare stucco walls) that give a glimpse of the surrounding greenery. They have kitchenettes in a corner, humidifiers, and most have a double bed plus a single or a bunk bed. Included in the rate is "breakfast with the birds," an excellent opportunity to photograph Boquete's hummingbirds. The staff will arrange day trips. **Pros:** lovely grounds on river; friendly staff; spacious rooms; good value. **Cons:** limited views, no-see-ums can be a problem. ✉ *Right at first Y north of town, 1½ km (1 mi) north of bridge over Río Caldera, Palo Alto* ☎720–2376 ⊕ *www.boquetegardeninn.com* ⇘ *10 rooms* ⚐ *In-room: no phone, safe, kitchen (some), refrigerator. In-hotel: laundry service, bar, Wi-Fi* ▭ *MC, V* ◉|CP.

$–$$ ▦ **Boquete Paradise.** This small collection of two story buildings has lush gardens, tall trees, and the rocky Río Palo Alto nearby. Rooms are ideal for couples, with one queen and a roll-out bed; suites with several beds and full kitchens work well for families. All rooms have a cluttering array of appliances, and their decor is a bit tacky—lots of gold and shiny polyester—but they open onto enclosed terraces with great views of the surrounding verdure. Second-floor rooms have high ceilings and the best views. There are several patios in the gardens and a gas grill for guest use. **Pros:** lush grounds; great views; nice terraces; good value. **Cons:** rooms a bit cluttered; decor is tacky. ✉ *Left at first Y, 2½ km (1½ mi) north of bridge, on left, Palo Alto* ☎720–2278 or 720–2554 ⊕ *www.panamatropicalvacations.com* ⇘ *8 rooms, 3 suites*

♿ *In-room: no a/c, no phone, refrigerator, Wi-Fi. In-hotel: laundry service, no-smoking rooms* ☰ *MC, V* ⦿| *BP.*

$–$$$ ▦ **Finca Lérida.** This working coffee farm on the eastern slope of Volcán Barú above Boquete has almost 650 acres of bird-replete cloud forest. The hotel has a resident nature guide and offers bird-watching tours. Rooms are either in the newer mountainside eco-lodge or in the original farmhouse B&B. Eco-lodge rooms are bright and spacious with hardwood floors, high, sloping ceilings, one king or two queen beds, and picture windows with panoramic views, but immediate surroundings are a bit bare. They share a large lounge with a fireplace, self-service bar, and library. The small restaurant has views and serves hearty lunches and dinners. B&B rooms are smaller, older, and less expensive but have character, and the house is surrounded by big trees and gardens—great for bird-watching. Kids under 10 aren't allowed in the B&B. **Pros:** gorgeous views of the cloud forest; guided bird-watching and coffee tours. **Cons:** eco-lodge lacks greenery nearby; hotel is isolated. ⊠ *7 km (4 mi) northwest of Av. Central, turn left at second Y, entrance on left, Callejón Seco, Alto Quiel* ☎ *720–2285* ✉ *Apdo. 0413-00146, Boquete, Chiriquí* ⊕ *www.fincalerida.com* ⌨ *16 rooms* ♿ *In-room: no a/c, no phone, no TV. In-hotel: restaurant, bar, laundry service, Internet terminal, no-smoking rooms* ☰ *AE, MC, V* ⦿| *EP.*

$$–$$$ ▦ **Hotel Isla Verde.** Three minutes from the center of town, this garden property has six spacious "roundhouses" and two enchanting suites. Marking the hotel's entrance is an A-frame building that houses the lobby, not to mention the owner and her friendly golden retriever. Stone pathways wind past a cluster of citrus trees to the brightly painted lodges, each outfitted with a private bath, kitchen, and hammock, as well as cable TV and Wi-Fi. Roundhouses, influenced by ancient Indian architecture, can sleep between four and six people but lack the large balconies of the suites. The Mariposa suite has by far the best view and design. Centering the property is a purple dome where breakfast is served daily (guests can place food orders the evening before and have it ready at a specific time). Pampering can be had in the small spa where massages and facials are available. **Pros:** on the river; creative design; beautiful gardens. **Cons:** Lobby often smells of wet dog; minimal parking spaces; inconsistent water temperature in the showers. ⊠ *Turn left at Calle 5 intersection at Delta Gas, follow the road two blocks up the hill on the right, Boquete* ☎ *720–2533* ⊕ *www.islaverdepanama.com* ⌨ *6 rooms, 2 suites* ♿ *In-room: no a/c, no phone, kitchen, Wi-Fi. In-hotel: restaurant, spa, laundry service, Wi-Fi, parking (free)* ☰ *AE, V* ⦿| *EP.*

$$
Fodor's Choice
★   ▦ **La Montaña y el Valle Coffee Estate Inn.** These charming bungalows on a six-acre shade coffee farm offer peace, privacy, plentiful birdlife and one of Boquete's best views. Each unit has a kitchenette, sitting room with dining table, and large bedrooms. Big windows and ample balconies with lounge chairs frame Volcán Barú and the valley below. Footpaths and benches dot the tropical gardens, which are filled with coffee plants and forest patches that are home to 130 avian species. You can have a delicious three-course dinner ($$-$$$$) ranging from roasted duck to grilled fish served by candlelight in your bungalow, though you need to order in the morning. Each fridge is stocked with

homemade breads and fresh-roasted coffee to accompany the fruit baskets for do-it-yourself breakfasts. Canadian owners Barry and Jane sell crafts, coffee, and coffee liqueur, all made in-house. The main building has a small library, computer and lounge area where guests can plan the next leg of their trip with help from the friendly owners. Terrace massages can be arranged upon request. Reserve well ahead of time. **Pros:** great views; lovely grounds; helpful owners; gourmet dinners. **Cons:** often full; two-night minimum stay; no kids. ✉ *1½ km (1 mi) northeast of town; right at first Y, first right north of bridge, just past El Explorador, Jaramillo Arriba* ☎ *720–2211* ⚘ *Apdo. 0143-00014, Boquete, Chiriquí* ⊕ *www.coffeeestateinn.com* ⇱ *3 bungalows* ♿ *In-room: no a/c, no phone, kitchen, Wi-Fi. In-hotel: room service, laundry service, Internet terminal, no kids under 14, no-smoking rooms* ☰ *MC, V* ⦿ *CP.*

$$–$$$$ ⌂ **Los Establos.** This small, Spanish-style inn with a stirring view of Volcán Barú started out as a horse stable, hence its name, and each room is named after a horse. Standard rooms are nicely decorated in Spanish villa style with terra-cotta tile flooring and gold satin bedding. They have high, canopy-draped ceilings, wrought-iron lamps, rattan and wooden furniture, and small terraces overlooking the coffee bushes. Only the Solita room and the suites have volcano views, since the breakfast room–bar takes up most of that side of the building. Double-size suites on the second floor have great views but are much more expensive. Rates include beer and wine in the evening. The 12-acre grounds have a wide lawn and a coffee farm. **Pros:** volcano view from some rooms; nice decor; ample grounds; lovely lounge and porch. **Cons:** most standard rooms lack views; fairly expensive; caged parrots squawk in early morning; echoing hallways. ✉ *2 km (1 mi) northeast of town, right at first Y north of town, left after bridge, then first right, Jaramillo Arriba* ☎ *720–2685* ⊕ *www.losestablos.net* ⇱ *5 rooms, 2 suites* ♿ *In-room: no a/c, safe, TV, DVD, Wi-Fi. In-hotel: restaurant, bar, laundry service, Internet terminal, no kids under 14, no-smoking rooms* ☰ *AE, MC, V* ⦿ *BP.*

$$$ ⌂ **Palo Alto Riverside Boutique Hotel.** This large yellow house with a wide front lawn looks like something you'd expect to see in New England. It contains six luxurious suites and a cozy lounge with a stone fireplace. The hotel is decorated with Panamanian art and offers views of the Río Palo Alto. Elegant guest rooms have high ceilings and handsome hardwood furniture, one king or two queen beds with Egyptian cotton linens, and amenities such as satellite TV and a boom box. A few rooms also have lofts with two single beds. Only the Master and Bonsai suites have river views, but there is a stone terrace overlooking the river where you can eat breakfast. The Palo Alto Riverside Restaurant *(⇨ above)* is next door. **Pros:** luxurious rooms; lovely lounge; nice riverside location; great restaurant. **Cons:** grounds a bit barren; service inconsistent. ✉ *Right at first Y north of town, left after bridge, then 1½ km (1 mi) on the left, Palo Alto* ☎ *720–1076* ⊕ *www.paloaltoriverside.com* ⇱ *5 suites, 1 master suite* ♿ *In-room: refrigerator, DVD, Wi-Fi. In-hotel: restaurant, bar, laundry service, public Wi-Fi, no-smoking rooms* ☰ *AE, MC, V* ⦿ *CP.*

5

$–$$ ⊞ **Panamonte Inn and Spa.** Opened in 1914, the Panamonte was long
Fodor's Choice   Boquete's only tourist hotel, and over the decades it has hosted the
★   likes of Teddy Roosevelt, Charles Lindbergh, and Ingrid Bergman. You
haven't been to Boquete unless you at least stop by the restaurant ($–$$)
(⇨ *above*) and wander the hotel's charming gardens. The honeymoon
suite and Quetzal I room are bright and pleasant, but some standard
rooms are cramped, and the Fresal annex has historic mustiness. The
newer Garden Terrace Rooms offer more room and privacy and have
front porches with furniture handcrafted by local artisans. The fireside
lounge is a great spot to hang out, and the hotel has a wellness spa,
which opened in 2009, and can arrange day tours. Panamonte's latest
venture is a cooking school at the nearby home of the executive chef/
owner, Charlie Collins. **Pros:** charming; timeless; nice gardens; great
restaurant and bar. **Cons:** some rooms are small, musty, or both; near
a busy road. ⊠ *Right at first Y north of town, on left, Boquete* ☎ *720–
1324* ⊕ *www.panamonteinnandspa.com* ⇨ *36 rooms, 5 suites, 8 garden terraces, 1 apartment* ঌ *In-room: safe, Wi-Fi. In-hotel: restaurant,
bar, spa, laundry service, public Wi-Fi, no-smoking rooms* ⊟ *AE, MC,
V* ⎮⊙⎮ *EP.*

¢   ⊞ **Pensión Topaz.** This colorful, German-owned lodge near the parque
central has several different room types, not to mention one of Boquete's
few swimming pools. The brightest rooms are in a two-story cement
building behind the house; the biggest ones are across from the tiny
pool, in a low building with a covered terrace. They're all clean, well
decorated, and have firm beds. A couple of tiny, dirt-cheap single rooms
share a bathroom. Hearty breakfasts are a few dollars extra. The large
garden, play area, and volleyball court make this a popular choice
for families. **Pros:** swimming pool; nice rooms; good value. **Cons:** big
rooms a bit dark. ⊠ *Calle 6 Sur and Av. Belisario Porras, behind Texaco
station, Boquete* ☎ *720–1005* ⇨ *7 rooms, 6 with bath* ঌ *In-room: no
a/c, no phone, no TV. In-hotel: pool, no-smoking rooms* ⊟ *No credit
cards* ⎮⊙⎮ *EP.*

$–$$$ ⊞ **Tinamou Cottage Jungle Lodge.** Bird-watchers will love this jungle para-
★   dise run by a Dutch couple, Terry and Hans van der Vooren. Although
it may lack the amenities of a full-service hotel, each of the lodge's cot-
tages is privately situated in a dense forest where monkeys, sloths, and
plenty of birds can be found. Within the 25-acre property are horses,
creeks, trails, waterfalls, and a small coffee farm. Charming two bed-
rooms cottages have a living room and kitchen and are decorated with
colonial style furniture including rocking chairs and four-poster beds
with European duvets; the studio cottage is smaller and similarly deco-
rated. Hardwood floors and exposed beam ceilings show craftsman-
ship in design. Breakfast is delivered to the cottages, where guests can
admire the ocean view from a private terrace. In addition to the B&B,
the couple owns Coffee Adventures, a tour company specializing in
bird-watching and Kotowa Coffee tours. **Pros:** jungle setting; knowl-
edgeable owners; good beds; organized tours. **Cons:** No restaurant;
one-hour walk from town; low water pressure; poor road to the prop-
erty. ⊠ *Near the school, 300 meters up the road on the right, Jaramillo
Abajo* ☎ *720–3852* ⊕ *www.coffeeadventures.net* ⇨ *1 studio cottage, 2*

2-bedroom cottages ⚓ *In-room: no a/c, kitchen, DVD, Wi-Fi. In-hotel: parking (free), no kids under 8, no-smoking rooms* ▭ *MC, V* ☺ *BP.*

$$ 🔲 **Valle Del Rio Inn.** Opened in 2008, this hotel takes pride in reflect-
☺ ing the "great American chain hotels" with comforts like digital TV, Wi-Fi, coffee makers, and minibars in the rooms. But it is the Euro-pean décor that makes this place so stunningly beautiful. Standard rooms have marble bathrooms, hardwood floors, white linens, and satin curtains that frame mountain views from wrought-iron balconies. On the river's edge is a large terrace where meals are served from the hotel's wine bar and Italian bistro, Café Pomodoro. A play area and enclosed trampoline make this a popular hotel with families. **Pros:** great showers; authentic Italian cuisine; on the river. **Cons:** steep parking lot; nearby construction. ⊠ *Calle Costarica, on the right just before Valle Escondido, Bajo Boquete* ☎ *720–2525* ⊕ *www.valledelrioboquete.com* 🛏 *25 rooms, 3 suites* ⚓ *In-room: no a/c (some), safe, kitchen (some), refrigerator, Wi-Fi. In-hotel: restaurant, room service, bar, gym, spa, laundry facilities, Internet terminal, Wi-Fi, parking (free) no-smoking rooms* ▭ *MC, V* ☺ *BP.*

$$$$ 🔲 **Valle Escondido.** The main attractions of this lavish resort are its 9-hole golf course and luxury spa. The property itself is set inside a gated com-munity where Panama's wealthy zip around on golf carts and reside in Spanish villas that resemble the hotel. Rooms here have a patio overlooking either the river or fairway and are built around ponds and a replica of a 17th-century Spanish pueblo. Less extravagant than the lobby, rooms have dark furnishings, tile floors, flat-screen TVs, and ceiling fans. All the expected amenities are available, as well as a few extras including a beauty center, indoor pool, steam room, and rac-quetball court. Local tours and activities can be arranged by the hotel staff. The resort's Latin restaurant, Sabor Escondido, is by reservation only, and the dress code (collared shirts only) is strictly enforced. **Pros:** good food, reasonably priced spa treatments; excellent amenities. **Cons:** gaudy decor; gated security entrance sometimes has a long line; rooms may smell musty during rainy season. ⊠ *At the top of Calle Costarica, just beyond Valle Del Rio Inn, entrance through private gate, Valle Escondido* ☎ *720–2454 or 720–2893* ⊕ *www.valleescondido.biz* 🛏 *36 rooms, 3 suites* ⚓ *In-room: no a/c, safe, DVD, Wi-Fi. In-hotel: 2 restau-rants, bar, golf course, tennis courts, pools, gym, spa, laundry service, Wi-Fi, parking (free), no-smoking rooms* ▭ *AE, MC, V* ☺ ⦿ *CP.*

NIGHTLIFE AND THE ARTS

The most pleasant place in Boquete for a quiet cocktail is the bar in the **Panamonte Inn and Spa** (⊠ *Right at first Y north of town, on left, Boquete* ☎ *720–1324*), which has a terrace hemmed by gardens, a big fireplace, and lots of couches and cane chairs.

The hip crowd hangs at **Zanzibar** (⊠ *Av. Central, 2 blocks north of church, Boquete* ☎ *No phone*), an attractive lounge with an odd African decor and comfy chairs.

5

SPORTS AND THE OUTDOORS
BIRD-WATCHING

Boquete is a bird-watcher's heaven, and its avian diversity tops 400 species during the dry season. The mountain forests shelter emerald toucanet, collared redstart, sulfur-winged parakeet, a dozen hummingbird species, and the resplendent quetzal. Even the gardens of homes and hotels offer decent birding; they're the best places to see migrant birds wintering in Boquete, from the Tennessee warbler to the Baltimore oriole. The less accessible upper slopes of Volcán Barú are home to rare species like the volcano junco and volcano hummingbird.

One of the best places to see the quetzal and other cloud-forest birds is **Finca Lérida** (⇨ *above*), a short drive north of town in Alto Quiel. Another good place to see quetzal is along the **Bajo Mono Road** just up the road from Finca Lérida. One great birding area that few people get to is **Finca El Oasis**, above the ANAM (National Environment Authority) ranger station on the road to the summit of Volcán Barú, a 90-minute drive from Boquete on a rough, 4WD-only road, which has plenty of quetzals and others. Quetzals are hard to spot, and bird-watching in general is difficult in a cloud-forest environment. Even experienced birders should hire a local guide, at least for the first day.

Santiago (Chago) Caballero (☎ 6626–2200) is considered the best birding guide in Boquete, and can practically guarantee you'll see quetzal from February to June, when they nest. Santiago's son is the resident guide at Finca Lérida.

Hans and Terry van der Vooren (☎ 720–3852 *or* 6634–4698), who run coffee tours at the Kotowa Estate, also offer bird-watching and hiking tours.

HIKING

★ Boquete is a great place for hiking, with countless farm roads and footpaths in and around the valley.

The **Bajo Mono** area, near Alto Quiel, has shorter trails into the park that can be explored in a matter of hours. The **Pipeline Road,** a dirt track that heads off the main road to the left, leads into a forested canyon with a waterfall. The **Sendero Culebra** trailhead is on the right from the road to Alto Chiquiero about 1.4 km from the Bajo Mono road.

The most popular hike is the 9-km (5-mi) **Sendero Los Quetzales** (⇨ *Cerro Punta, below*). The forest here is a breeding area for quetzal and holds many other birds and animals. It's best to go from Cerro to Boquete, since the reverse trip is completely uphill. For a day trip from Boquete, pay someone to drive you to El Respingo and pick you up at Alto Chiquero four hours later or to drop off your 4WD vehicle at Alto Chiquero.

The summit hike to **Volcán Barú** in Parque Nacional Volcán Barú (⇨ *below*) is more demanding than the Sendero Los Quetzales, as it's uphill and very steep. You can drive your 4WD vehicle to, or arrange for a ride to and from, the ANAM ranger station, 14 km (8½ mi) from the summit. Above this point, the road is so rough that only high-suspension trucks can ascend it. Some people begin hiking around midnight in order to reach the summit at sunrise, when you might see both the

Atlantic and Pacific oceans, weather permitting. (You can always see the Pacific.) Bring at least three liters of water, snacks, sunblock, a hat, and warm, waterproof clothing. ⚠ **The weather can change drastically within minutes near the top, where it freezes regularly during the dry season—hypothermia is a real risk if you're caught in a storm.**

GUIDES AND OUTFITTERS
Aventurist (✉ *Plaza Los Establos, Av. Central, Boquete* ☎ *720–1635* ⊕ *www.aventurist.com*), which owns Boquete Tree Trek, has a three-hour hike ($30) to see waterfalls and wildlife in its private reserve.

Feliciano González (☎ *6624–9940 or 6632–8645* ⊕ *www.geocities.com/boquete_tours*) has been guiding hikers through Boquete's mountains for two decades. In addition to tours of the Sendero Los Quetzales and to the summit of Volcán Barú, he leads a six-hour hike on the Sendero El Pianista through primary forest along the continental divide. Tours are $20–$50 per person.

Daniel Higgins (☎ *6617–0570*) regularly drops people and cars off for the hike in Sendero Los Quetzales.

HORSEBACK RIDING

There are some excellent horseback-riding routes in the mountains around Boquete that include panoramic views and exposure to abundant birdlife. Eduardo Cano at **Boquete Tours** (☎ *720–1750*) can arrange inexpensive horseback tours, as well as guided hikes down the Sendero Los Quetzales or a Volcán Barú ascent.

MOUNTAIN BIKING

Aventurist (*Boquete Tree Trek* ✉ *Plaza Los Establos, Av. Central, Boquete* ☎ *720–1635* ⊕ *www.aventurist.com*) runs a three-hour bike tour ($30) through the mountains north of Boquete that is mostly downhill.

WHITE-WATER RAFTING

Chiriquí has Panama's best white-water rafting, with many rivers to choose from during the rainy season (June–November). ■**TIP→** **Only one river—Río Chiriquí Viejo—is navigable during the December–May dry season.**

The **Río Chiriquí Viejo** is considered Panama's best white-water river; it churns its way through pristine rain forest and an impressive canyon. Of its two rafting routes, the harder is the Class III–IV Palón section, which requires previous experience and can become too dangerous to navigate during the rainiest months. The easier, Class II–III Sabo section is good for beginners. Chiriquí Viejo is a three-hour drive from Boquete each way, which makes for a long day. Unfortunately, it's threatened by government plans to dam it for a hydroelectric project. The **Río Estí** is a Class II–III river fit for beginners that is closer to Boquete (a 90-minute drive) and doubles as a good wildlife-watching trip. The **Río Chiriquí** is a fun Class III river with one Class IV rapids; it's a 90-minute drive from Boquete and appropriate for beginners. The **Río Gariche** is one of several Class II–III rivers near Boquete and is a great trip for seeing wildlife. The **Río Dolega** is a fun Class II–III river near Boquete and suitable for beginners.

Boquete Outdoor Adventures (✉ *Plaza Los Establos at Av. Central, Boquete* ☎ *720–2284* ⊕ *www.boqueteoutdooradventures.com* offers multisport trips that combine rafting, kayaking, island tours, hiking, and tree trekking.

Chiriquí River Rafting (✉ *Av. Central, across from park, Boquete* ☎ *720–1505* ⊕ *www.panama-rafting.com*), founded in the 1990s by Hector Sanchez, makes safety and eco-friendliness a priority. The company offers trips on all area rivers ($85–$105); the Río Chiriquí Viejo trip is the most expensive.

Panama Rafters (✉ *Plaza Los Establos at Av. Central, Boquete* ☎ *720–2712* ⊕ *www.panamarafters.com*) is a small, American-owned company that only runs rafting trips on the Chiriquí Viejo; trips cost $75–$90, depending on the section and include transportation, lunch, river shoes, and towels. The company also offers kayaking trips on other rivers.

ZIP-LINE TOURS

A canopy tour involves gliding along cables (to which you're attached via a harness), strung between platforms in the high branches of tropical trees. It gives both the sensation of flying through the treetops and a bird's-eye view of the cloud forest. **Boquete Tree Trek** (✉ *Plaza Los Establos, Av. Central, Boquete* ☎ *720–1635* ⊕ *www.aventurist.com*) has trained guides that provide instruction and accompany groups through the tour ($60), which lasts about five hours. Prohibited from canopy tours are children under six and anyone weighing more than 250 pounds.

SHOPPING

The small shop at **CEFATI** (✉ *Av. Central, 1 km (½ mi) south of town, Boquete* ☎ *720–4060*) has a good selection of indigenous handicrafts such as Emberá woven bowls and Ngöbe *chácaras* (colorful woven jute bags).

Folklórica (✉ *Av. Central, 2 blocks north of church, Boquete* ☎ *720–2368*) has an eclectic mix of antiques, ceramics, jewelry, and handicrafts.

Souvenirs Cacique (✉ *Av. Central, at park, Boquete* ☎ *720-2217*) sells everything from handicrafts to T-shirts.

PARQUE NACIONAL VOLCÁN BARÚ

★ Towering 11,450 feet above sea level, Barú Volcano is literally Chiriquí's biggest attraction, and Panama's highest peak to boot. The massive dormant volcano is visible from David and is the predominant landmark in Boquete and Volcán, but Bambito and Cerro Punta are tucked so tightly into its slopes that you can hardly see it from there. The upper slopes, summit, and northern side of the volcano are protected within Barú Volcano National Park, which covers more than 14,000 hectares (35,000 acres) and extends northward to connect with the larger Parque Internacional La Amistad. The vast expanse of protected wilderness is home to everything from cougars to howler monkeys and more than 250 bird species. You might see white hawks, black guans, violet sabrewings, sulphur-winged parakeets, resplendent quetzals, and rare three-wattled bellbirds in the park's cloud forests. The volcano's craggy summit, on the other hand, is covered with a scrubby high-altitude ecosystem known as *páramo,* a collection of shrubs and grasses common in the Andes. There you may spot the rare volcano junco, a small gray bird that lives on the highest peaks of the Cordillera de Talamanca. The summit is also topped by radio towers and a cement bunker, and unfortunately many of its boulders are covered with graffiti.

Several paths penetrate the park's wilderness, including two trails to the summit. The main road to the summit begins in Boquete, across from the church, and is paved for the first 7 km (4 mi), where it passes a series of homes and farms and then becomes increasingly rough and rocky. You pay the park fee at the ANAM ranger station 15 km (9 mi) from town, which takes about 90 minutes to reach in a 4WD vehicle. Park your vehicle at the station, since the road above it can only be ascended in trucks with super-high suspension. From here it's a steep 14-km (8½ mi) hike to the summit. The other trail to the summit begins 7 km (4 mi) north of Volcán and ascends the volcano's more deforested western slope, a grueling trek only recommended for serious athletes. Another popular trail into the park is the **Sendero Los Quetzales** (⇨ *Cerro Punta, below),* which has excellent bird-watching.

For information about hiking in Parque Nacional Volcán Barú, see ⇨ *Hiking in Boquete, above.* ☎ 774–6671 or 775–3163 🖃 $5

GETTING HERE AND AROUND

You can drive to the park's entrances in a 4WD vehicle or hire a 4WD taxi to drop you off and pick you up.

VOLCÁN

60 km (36 mi) northwest of David, 16 km (10 mi) south of Cerro Punta.

A breezy little town, Volcán has the best view of Volcán Barú, several miles northeast. The town, also known as Hato de Volcán, is a dreary succession of restaurants, banks, and other businesses spread along a north-south route, from which roads to east and west lead to residential areas. This is where residents of Bambito and Cerro Punta come to shop and pay bills. As you drive north from the Interamericana the road descends onto a plain and heads into the center of Volcán, where the town's one stoplight marks the right turn for Bambito and Cerro Punta; the road continues northwest to Río Sereno.

Bambito and Cerro Punta are more attractive and have the area's best hotels, so there is little reason to stay in Volcán except that it's much warmer than Cerro Punta, which can get cool at night between December and March. It is also a convenient jumping-off point for summiting Barú Volcano via the southern route or bird-watching at Finca Hartmann. This is an ideal base for white-water rafting on the Río Chiriquí Viejo, since you can join rafting trips in Concepción, 33 km (21 mi) south.

One of Panama's most important archaeological sites and its most visitor-friendly by far, **Sitio Barriles** *(Barrels Site)* is a collection of abandoned digs and pre-Columbian artifacts on a private farm 6 km (3½ mi) south of Volcán. The site was discovered in 1947 by the farm's owner, who found cylindrical stone carvings that resembled barrels. Subsequent digs unearthed hundreds of artifacts, the most important of which have been taken to other museums, although many are displayed in the small on-site museum. Sitio Barriles was the main town of an agricultural society that farmed the surrounding plains from AD 300 to 600, though archaeologists know very little about their culture. They left behind an interesting collection of volcanic-stone carvings, ceramic wares, tools, jewelry, and other artifacts. The farm's current owners, José Luis and Edna Landau, manage it under an agreement with the National Culture Institute. Edna, who speaks some English, usually leads visitors on a 45-minute tour. The turnoff for Sitio Barriles is west of the road to Bambito, on the left one block after the road to the airstrip, and is marked Cazán. ⊠ *Road to Cazán, 6 km (3½ mi) south of Volcán* ☎ *6607–5438 or 6575–1828* ☒ *$6* ⊙ *Daily 8–5.*

La Torcaza Estate, a large coffee farm near the Lagunas de Volcán, gives a coffee tour of the farming and processing of their high-quality beans that ends with a cupping. Do the tour during the October–March harvest. They also offer horseback-riding tours of the farm and nearby lakes. ⊠ *Vía Aeropuerto, 2 km (1 mi) south of Volcán* ☎ *771–4306 www.estatecafe.com* ☒ *$10* ⊙ *Mon.–Sat. 8–noon and 1–5; tours by appointment or upon arrival.*

Lagunas de Volcán, two protected lakes with adjacent forest near Volcán's old airstrip, are visited by a mix of migratory and native birds, making this a decent stop for bird-watchers. You may spot grebe, purple gallinule, or, during the dry season, migrants such as the black-and-white warbler. **Western Wind Ventures** (☎ *771–5049 or 6775–0118*) runs canoeing and bird-watching tours of the lakes. Though the lakes are just 2 km (1 mi) south of town, the road gets quite rough as you approach them, so you'll need 4WD or you'll have to hike the last stretch. ⊠ *Vía Aeropuerto, 2 km (1 mi) south of Volcán, turn left at Agroquímicos Volcán* ☎ *775–2055* ⊙ *Daily 6–6.*

■ OFF THE BEATEN PATH

Down the hill from the village of Cuesta de Piedra is the narrow canyon of the **Río Macho de Monte,** which has several small waterfalls that flow into a boulder-strewn river. The canyon's walls are draped with lush foliage where you might spot birds from dozens of species, such as the squirrel cuckoo, torrent tyrannulet, and riverside wren. Even if you aren't into birds, it's worth popping down for the scenery. The canyon belongs to the country's electrical company, which has built catwalks into it, facilitating exploration. The path is on the right after the guard-house, just down the hill from the tiny town of Cuesta de Piedra, 20 km (12 mi) north of Concepción on the road to Volcán. You can hire a guide in Volcán to take you to the waterfalls or simply inquire at Restaurant Porvenir, on the right at the entrance to Cuesta de Piedra, whether there is anyone available to lead you to the Macho del Monte.

GETTING HERE AND AROUND

Because Volcán's attractions are so spread out, it's best to drive there. From David, head west 22 km (14 mi) on the CA1 to Concepción, where you turn right after the Shell station and drive north 33 km (21 mi) through the mountains to Volcán. Buses depart from David's terminal for Volcán ($2) every 30 minutes during the day.

WHERE TO EAT AND STAY

$$$

Fodor's Choice

★

ITALIAN

✕ **Il Forno.** Authentic Italian recipes, handed down from generations, are what you'll get from Chef Joseph Mattina, who first migrated from Italy to New Jersey and finally to Panama. Joseph still duplicates the dishes once prepared by his grandfather from Salerno. It might be a challenge, but try not to fill up on the warm baked breads served with roasted garlic and olive oil. On the menu you'll find veal, salmon, chicken, pork, and, of course, brick-oven pizzas. His pastas are all named after women, like "Pasta a la Jessie" served with a bacon and tomato cream sauce. The menu also features lighter options like spinach salad with candied almonds and apples. Adding to the dining experience is the pleasant atmosphere created by wooden tables, a wine room, opera music, and the smell of garlic wafting from the kitchen. ⊠ ¼ *mile past the turnoff for Cerra Punta on the road to Volcán; turn left after Romeros. Il Forno is the second building on the right next to Hotel California* ☎ *771–5731* ⌐ *Cash only* ☉ *Closed Mon–Wed.*

$

🛏 **Hotel Dos Ríos.** Volcán's biggest hotel, the Dos Ríos is an original two-story wooden building fronted by a newer cabinlike lobby. The L-shaped structure encloses a lush yard with a playground and stone footbridge over a stream. Most rooms have wooden floors, a TV, armoire, desk, and chandeliers that suspend over floral-printed beds. The "suites," with lime and tangerine hues, are the nicest rooms with lots of light and small balconies looking onto the gardens and Volcán Barú. The cement casitas are cramped and dark but sleep three. A restaurant in front serves Italian cuisine; the bar next door is a bit ugly but is next to the river and has large windows with volcano views. **Pros:** best in town; good views; beautiful garden pathways. **Cons:** bar open only in high season; most rooms mediocre. ⊠ *Road to Río Sereno, 2½ km (1½ mi) north of turnoff for Bambito* ☎ *771–4271* ⊕ *www. dosrios.com.pa* ⌐ *17 rooms, 3 bungalows* ⎣ *In-room: no a/c. In-hotel: restaurant, bar, laundry service, Internet terminal, no-smoking rooms* ▭ *AE, MC, V* 🍴 *CP.*

SPORTS AND THE OUTDOORS

HIKING

Volcán is a popular departure point for summit hikes of **Volcán Barú** (⇨ *Parque Nacional Volcán Barú, above)* via the southern route, though the Hotel Bambito is just as close to that trailhead. Though not a technical climb, that trail is more demanding than hiking up from the ANAM station above Boquete. The trail begins at the foot of the volcano, at the end of a rough road 7 km (4 mi) east of Volcán. Hire a guide for the hike—the volcano's base has various confusing trails on it. Start before dawn to ensure you return before dark (the hike up and back takes about 12 hours). Pack several liters of water, food for a day, warm, waterproof clothing, sunscreen, and a hat.

Arturo Rivera (☎ *771–5917 or 6690–6632* ⊕ *www.volcantourism.com*) can guide hikers up Volcán Barú, down the Sendero Los Quetzales, or into Parque Internacional La Amistad. He also offers horseback riding and tours of Lagunas de Volcán and Macho del Monte.

Western Wind Ventures (☎ *771–5049 or 6775–0118* ⊕ *naturaltour.tripod. com/index.html*) offers hiking tours up Volcán Barú, on the Sendero Los Quetzales, and into Parque Internacional La Amistad, as well as visits to the Lagunas de Volcán and Macho del Monte.

OFF THE BEATEN PATH

Finca Hartmann. The combination of forest and shaded coffee bushes at this gourmet coffee farm 27 km (16 mi) west of Volcán makes it one of the country's best bird-watching spots. The farm borders Parque Internacional La Amistad, so it's home to an array of wildlife ranging from hummingbirds to collared peccaries. To date, 282 avian species have been identified here, including the brown-hooded parrot, collared trogon, golden-browed chlorophonia, and king vulture. You can take a coffee tour, which is most interesting during the October–April harvest. Six rustic cabins without electricity are available for overnight guests. Getting here is half the fun, since the road winds through amazing scenery. ⊠ *Road to Río Sereno, 27 km (16 mi) west of Volcán, up gravel road on right 300 yards after gas station, Santa Clara* ☎ *6450-1853* ⊕ *www.fincahartmann.com* ▤ *$15* ⊘ *Mon.–Sat. 6–6.*

BAMBITO

★ *7 km (4 mi) north of Volcán, 8 km (4½ mi) south of Cerro Punta.*

Rather than a town, Bambito is a series of farms and houses scattered along the serpentine Río Chiriquí Viejo valley on the western slope of Volcán Barú, between Volcán and Cerro Punta. Since the people who live in the valley do their shopping in nearby Volcán, it has almost no stores or other businesses—just a few hotels—so it lacks the kinds of architectural eyesores that dominate most Panamanian towns.

The valley's scenery seems to grow more impressive with each hairpin turn. As you drive northeast from Volcán, ever closer to the volcano, you suddenly enter the narrow valley and are surrounded by tall trees and sheer rock walls adorned with bromeliads and other foliage. Even if your destination is Cerro Punta, make a few stops to admire the suspension bridges spanning the boulder-strewn river, lush forest clinging to hillsides, wildflowers, and neat wooden farmhouses. Small farms line the road, and several roadside stands sell vegetables, fruit preserves, and fresh fruit *batidos* (smoothies). From December to April, the trade winds whip down the valley, keeping it cool, but it's still warmer than Cerro Punta. Bambito's forests and farms are full of birds, and Volcán's guides can help with bird-watching there.

GETTING HERE AND AROUND

Bambito is reached by turning right at the main intersection in Volcán. The hotels and restaurants are scattered along the road once it enters the valley. Buses head up and down the valley every 30 minutes and will pick you up and drop you off anywhere.

WHERE TO EAT AND STAY

¢–$$

ARGENTINE

✗ **Parrillada Estilo Argentino.** If you're in the mood for beef, this is the place to go. The owners Fernando and Maria serve the best beef in Chiriquí, charcoal-grilled with a baked potato and a salad. The menu also includes *cordero asado* (roast lamb), *corvina, langostinos* (prawns), and chicken cordon bleu. Fresh herbs are from their organic garden, and a good wine selection accompanies each dish. The dining area is furnished with rustic pine tables and chairs but is dark and cramped; you may want to sit out front. ⊠ *Road to Cerro Punta, just south of Hotel Bambito* ☎ 771–5368 ▭ V, MC.

$–$$
★
☾

▦ **Casa Grande.** The setting here is idyllic: massive trees shade the wooden buildings and lawns, the Río Chiriquí Viejo is a stone's toss away, and everything is surrounded by dense forest. Rooms have hardwood floors, flat-screen TVs, iPod docks, big windows, and porches with hammocks or plastic chairs and tables. Suites are bigger and brighter and sleep up to eight people; those up the hill offer more privacy and nicer views. The vast property includes 400 acres of forest, part of which can be explored on a 2-km hiking trail, and the list of activities includes mountain biking, horseback riding, river tubing, fishing, and a zip-line canopy tour. Spa treatments are reasonably priced. The restaurant ($10-$16) serves Italian food, including pizza and fresh trout prepared several ways. Those with children may be interested in the Family Summer Special (offered year-round), which includes room, activities, meals, and drinks for $68 per person. Children nine years and under stay free. **Pros:** surrounded by nature; plenty of activities; children's play area. **Cons:** standard rooms are mediocre; can be swarming with flies during the month of May. ⊠ *Road to Cerro Punta, on left after Hotel Bambito* ☎ 771–5126 ⊕ *www.casagrandebambito.com* ⌨ *10 rooms, 10 suites* ⌂ *In-room: no a/c. In-hotel: restaurant, bar, spa, pool, laundry service, no-smoking rooms* ▭ *AE, MC, V.* ❏❘

$$
☾

▦ **Hotel Bambito.** This alpine-style resort overlooks sheer rock faces and lush slopes across a wide lawn with fountains. Built in the early 1980s, it's a bit timeworn, and they have a hard time keeping the windows clean, but rooms are spacious and the ample facilities are family-friendly. Just beyond a forest of towering eucalyptus trees are tennis courts, an indoor-outdoor pool, a Jacuzzi, and a sauna. You can hike a forest trail, go horseback riding, and take day tours, all arranged by the hotel. Rooms have hardwood floors and picture windows that let in the verdant view. Junior suites have balconies, while master suites have bedroom lofts. Las Truchas restaurant ($$–$$$) next door specializes in fresh trout and offers everything from pastas to chateaubriand. **Pros:** lovely setting; big rooms; covered pool; good restaurant; activities. **Cons:** dated decor; close to road. ⊠ *Road to Cerro Punta on right, beginning of valley* ☎ 771–4265 ⊕ *www.hotelbambito.com* ⌨ *33 rooms, 10 suites* ⌂ *In-room: no a/c, refrigerator, Internet. In-hotel: restaurant, room service, bar, tennis courts, pool, gym, laundry service, no-smoking rooms* ▭ *AE, MC, V* ❏❘ *BP.*

5

CERRO PUNTA

★ *75 km (45 mi) northwest of David, 15 km (9 mi) north of Volcán.*

This bowl-shaped highland valley northwest of Volcán Barú offers some splendid bucolic scenery and is bordered by vast expanses of wilderness that invite bird-watchers, hikers, and nature lovers. A patchwork of vegetable farms covers the valley's undulant floor and clings to the steep slopes that surround it, and ridges are topped with dark cloud forest and rocky crags. On the eastern side of the valley is the large Harras Cerro Punta ranch, where thoroughbred racehorses graze. East of the ranch, a steep slope rises up into a wedge of granite for which the valley was named—*cerro punta* means "pointy hill." That eastern ridge, part of the country's continental divide, is often enveloped in clouds pushed there by the trade winds. That mist, which locals call *bajareque,* often engulfs the valley, then retreats back to the mountaintops. The results are frequent, fleeting rain showers that keep the valley green year-round and produce an inordinate number of rainbows.

The road that winds up through Bambito bursts into the expansive Cerro Punta just west of a few shops, restaurants, and a gas station next to an intersection that marks the beginning of a loop through the valley. If you head straight at that intersection, you will soon pass the road and El Respingo, where the Sendero Los Quetzales begins. Shortly after that is Guadelupe, a small collection of farms including Los Quetzales Lodge and Spa and the orchid farm of Finca Drácula. If you turn left at the intersection, you reach the road to Las Nubes—the entrance to Parque Internacional La Amistad—more quickly, but the whole loop takes only 15 minutes to drive either way. If you take any of the side roads that head into the mountains from the loop, you quickly come upon patches of forest with plenty of birds.

Cerro Punta is the highest inhabited area in Panama, nearly 6,000 feet above sea level. It can get chilly when the sun goes down or behind the clouds, though it is usually warm enough for shorts and T-shirts by day. From December to March the temperature sometimes drops down to almost 4°C (40°F) at night, so you'll want to bring warm clothes and a waterproof jacket, as well as sturdy boots for the slippery mountain trails. Insects aren't a problem here, but the sun is intense, so use sunblock or wear a hat when you aren't in the woods.

★ The most popular hike in Cerro Punta is the **Sendero Los Quetzales,** a footpath through Parque Nacional Volcán Barú that ends in the mountains above Boquete (you can hike it in reverse, but it's entirely uphill). The trail begins at the ANAM station in El Respingo, east of town, where you pay the $5 park admission fee. From there it's a 9-km (5-mi) downhill hike to Alto Chiquero, a short drive from Boquete. The trail winds through the cloud forest and follows the Río Caldera, crossing it several times en route. You might see quetzals, emerald toucanets, collared redstarts, coatis, and other wildlife on the hike, which takes most people three to four hours. ■TIP➜ **Because the trail is not well marked, hire a guide or join an organized tour; the area's bird-watching guides regularly use the trail.** Pack a lunch, lots of water, and rain gear, and wear sturdy waterproof boots. It's possible to hike first thing in the morning and return to Cerro Punta (via bus or taxi) by evening, but the bus from Boquete to Cerro Punta takes four to five hours. The best option is to have your bags transferred to a Boquete hotel and end there for the night. Hire a taxi in Cerro Punta to drop you off at El Respingo, which should cost $15, and arrange for a Boquete taxi to pick you up in Alto Chiquero. Otherwise, walk 90 minutes from the end of the trail through farmland to Bajo Mono, where you can catch public transportation to Boquete.

Los Quetzales Lodge and Spa has a 400-hectare (988-acre) private reserve inside Parque Nacional Volcán Barú, a 20-minute drive, or 30-minute hike from the lodge. The reserve has well-maintained trails through the cloud forest, one of which leads to a small waterfall, and all of which pass moss-laden scenery. It is home to more than 100 bird species, including the resplendent quetzal and 12 kinds of hummingbirds. You must be accompanied by one of the reserve's (non-English-speaking) guides. Guests of the lodge are transported to the reserve every morning (at a mutually agreed-upon time) for $5. Non-guests pay a $20 shared fee for transport, but it's an easy 30-minute hike. ⊠ *3 km (2 mi) east of Guadelupe* ☎ *771–2291* ⊕ *www.losquetzales.com* 🔛 *Free for guests, nonguests $5; guide $10 per hour* ☺ *Daily 6–6.*

★ Anyone with the slightest interest in orchids should visit **Finca Drácula**, which has one of Latin America's largest orchid collections. The farm's name is taken from a local orchid, which has a dark red flower. The main focus here is reproducing orchids for export, but workers also give 40-minute tours, though in limited English. The farm has 2,700 orchid species from Panama and around the world, as well as a laboratory where plants are reproduced using micropropagation methods. The best time to visit is between March and May, when flowers are in bloom. If you don't have a 4WD vehicle, walk 20 minutes from Guadelupe to get here. ⊠ *Road to Los Quetzales reserve, 1 km east of Guadelupe* ☎ *771–2070* 🔛 *$10* ☺ *Tues–Sun 8–noon and 1–5.*

Fodor's Choice **Parque Internacional La Amistad** *(PILA)* stretches from the peaks above
★ Cerro Punta down to the remote hills of Bocas del Toro Province, comprising more than 200,000 hectares (more than 500,000 acres) of remote wilderness. It protects a succession of forest types that together hold most of the country's endangered animals, including jaguars and tapirs, and some 400 bird species, from the rare umbrella bird to the harpy eagle. The name *La Amistad*—Spanish for "friendship"—refers to the park's binational status; Panama's park is contiguous with Costa Rica's Parque Internacional La Amistad, which is slightly smaller than its Panamanian twin and harder to reach. UNESCO has declared it a World Heritage site, and it forms the core of La Amistad Biosphere Reserve, a vast array of parks and indigenous reserves that stretch over much of the Cordillera de Talamanca in Panama and Costa Rica to cover 1.1 million hectares (2.7 million acres) of wilderness.

Cerro Punta provides the most convenient access to the park entrance and ANAM ranger station at Las Nubes, a 15-minute drive from town up a dirt road, where several trails start. You might see any of more than 150 bird species and mammals such as the coati and olingo. If you

5

don't go with a guide, one of the (non-English-speaking) rangers may accompany you on the trails. An excellent bird-watching trail is the **Sendero el Retonio,** a 2-km (1-mi) loop over easy terrain that includes cloud forest and a stand of bamboo. If you have a few hours, hike the **Sendero La Cascada,** a 4-km (2-mi) trail to a ridge with views of the valley and a spectacular waterfall. To reach the park, drive around the loop to the intersection near Entre Ríos, on the northern end of the valley, and follow the road all the way to the park, veering left after you drive through the gate. The last stretch is fit for 4WD vehicles only; a Cerro Punta taxi will drop you there for $10. ⊠ *Las Nubes, 5 km (3 mi) north of Cerro Punta* ☎ *775–2055* ☒ *$5* ☉ *Daily 8–5.*

GETTING HERE AND AROUND
Reach Cerro Punta by turning right at Volcán's main intersection. Buses come and go every 30 minutes and will let you on and off anywhere.

WHERE TO STAY

$
Fodor's Choice
★

🏨 **Cielito Sur**. The best thing about this B&B is the service provided by its Panamanian-American owners, Janet and Glenn Lee. They rent mountain bikes and canoes, prepare box lunches, and organize tours ranging from bird-watching to a guided hike on the Sendero Los Quetzales with luggage transfer to your hotel in Boquete. Then there's the tranquil location at the forest's edge, where a stream runs through the gardens, and birdsong plays from sunrise to sunset. Spacious, well-equipped rooms are named after Indian tribes and decorated with indigenous Panamanian crafts such as baskets, spears, and clay pots. Brighter end rooms are worth the extra $10 and include a kitchenette. Guests share a cozy lounge with a fireplace, DVD, stereo, and computer, as well as a wide covered terrace with rocking chairs for watching the hummingbirds. You might end up skipping lunch after the magnificent breakfasts of eggs, coffee, and fruit that come directly from the property. **Pros:** quiet; near nature; great breakfasts; helpful owners; nice rooms. **Cons:** no restaurant; property often booked far in advance. ⊠ *4 km (2½ mi) south of Cerro Punta center, Nueva Suiza* ⌂ *Apdo. 0424-00022, Volcán, Chiriquí* ☎ *771–2038 or 6602–3008* ⊕ *www.cielitosur.com* ☞ *4 rooms* ☾ *In-room: no a/c, no phone, refrigerator (some), Wi-Fi. In-hotel: bicycles, laundry service, Internet terminal, no kids under 12, no-smoking rooms* ▤ *AE, MC, V* ⦿ *BP.*

¢–$$
★
☾

🏨 **Los Quetzales Lodge and Spa**. This eco-lodge owned by activist Carlos Alfaro has accommodations ranging from backpacker dorms to private cabins in the cloud forest. Rooms in wooden buildings have polished hardwood, photos of local birds, and original art. Standard rooms are slightly cramped, but junior suites are spacious and bright, with wood stoves and kitchenettes; larger master suites also have balconies. Room 21, by the river, is our favorite. At night guests gather in the lounge with wood stoves, couches, and computers. The restaurant ($–$$) serves good pizza, pastas, soups, fresh trout, and organic salads. Bicycles and horseback riding are available; jeeps transport guests to the reserve each morning for guided hikes. Three cabins in the reserve itself lack electricity but have gas stoves and lanterns. Cabins 2 and 3 are gorgeous, perfect for constant exposure to nature. Fresh trout is available at the lodge; otherwise, you must bring your food if you plan to cook for yourself. Cabin 1, a cement duplex near the edge of the forest, is much less attractive. **Pros:** private forest reserve; good restaurant and lounge; lots of activities. **Cons:** most rooms are far from the reserve; service sometimes deficient. ✉ *Guadelupe* ☎ *771–2291* ⊕ *www.losquetzales. com* ↪ *10 rooms, 2 junior suites, 3 suites, 5 cabins, 2 dormitories, 1 chalet* & *In-room: no a/c, refrigerator (some), no TV, Wi-Fi (some). In-hotel: restaurant, room service, bar, spa, gym, bicycles, laundry service, Internet terminal, no-smoking rooms* ⊟ *AE, MC, V* ⫿⦿⫿ *BP.*

SPORTS AND THE OUTDOORS
BIRD-WATCHING
The valley's feathered creatures are most easily spotted around its edges, especially near streams and along the trails that head into the nearby national parks. A good guide can significantly increase the number of species you see.

Ito Santamaría (☎ *6591–1621*), who lives in Guadelupe, is Cerro Punta's best bird-watching guide and the only one who speaks English.

The private nature reserve of **Los Quetzales Lodge and Spa** (☎ *771–2291* ⊕ *www.losquetzales.com*) has guides who speak little English but are good at spotting birds, especially quetzals.

Western Wind Ventures (☎ *771–5049 or 6775–0118* ⊕ *naturaltour.tripod. com/index.html*), a Volcán-based company, arranges birding hikes on the Sendero Los Quetzales or in Parque Internacional La Amistad.

HIKING
Between La Amistad and Volcán Barú national parks, there are enough trails around Cerro Punta to keep you hiking for several days. The area's bird-watching guides are familiar with all the local trails and are happy to guide hikers. Wherever you hike, be sure to pack plenty of water, sunscreen, a hat, and warm, waterproof clothing, even if it's sunny, since the temperature can plummet when a storm rolls in.

LAGO FORTUNA AREA

60 km (36 mi) northeast of David.

The road over the eastern end of the Cordillera de Talamanca that connects the provinces of Chiriquí and Bocas del Toro passes breathtaking views and a large hydroelectric reservoir called Lago Fortuna. The dense forests around Lago Fortuna hold a wealth of birdlife, including such species as black guans, swallow-tailed kites, barbets, euphonias, and various types of hummingbirds. The peaks to the south of the man-made lake are traversed by trails with gorgeous views. Most people simply drive through this area or bypass it by taking one of the quick flights between Chiriquí and Bocas del Toro, but if you take the time to explore its often misty landscapes, you'll be happy you strayed from the beaten path.

The road to Lago Fortuna and Bocas del Toro begins 12 km (7½ mi) east of David on the Interamericana, at a tiny town called Chiriquí, from where it heads north via Gualaca, after which it becomes increasingly steep.

5

After climbing past amazing views of mountainsides and the Chiriquí plains, you reach the tiny outpost of Los Planes. Continue 3½ km (2 mi) beyond its entrance for **Finca Suiza**, a private reserve with 20 hours worth of hiking trails. The trails are well marked, have benches for resting, and lead to waterfalls, lookout points, and a patch of cloud forest. Children under 12 aren't allowed on the trails. ⊠ *Hornito* 🕾 *6615–3774 www.panama.net.tc* ✉ *$8* ⊗ *Nov.–May and Jul.–Aug., daily 7–9.*

GETTING HERE AND AROUND

To drive from David, head east on the Interamericana 12 km (7½ mi) to Chiriquí, where you turn left and drive through Gualaca, then up the slopes toward Chiriquí Grande and Changuinola. Buses to Changuinola depart from David every 60 minutes and can drop you off at either Finca Suiza or Lago Fortuna.

EN ROUTE After Lago Fortuna, the road begins its descent to the Caribbean lowlands. Even if you visit the area as a day trip, it is worth beginning the descent toward the Caribbean for its exuberant scenery. Keep your eye out for a dirt road on the left marked by a sign that says SUBESTACIÓN— it leads to an electrical tower with a great view of the Bocas del Toro Archipelago on a clear day.

WHERE TO STAY

$ 🏨 **Finca Suiza.** This simple, remote lodge is in a private reserve atop the Cordillera de Talamanca. Swiss expats Herbert Brullmann and Monika Kohler have converted part of their home into three guest rooms and a dining room with a stone fireplace. The rooms are bright and spacious, with big baths, two single beds, and walls decorated with Monika's nature photos. They open onto a terrace with rocking chairs and a small lawn hemmed by bougainvillea. Monika prepares three-course dinners ($16) with ingredients from the organic garden; they also make sandwiches for hikes. **Pros:** quiet; close to nature; good hiking; great views. **Cons:** remote; few amenities; two-night minimum stay; can be cold and windy. ⊠ *Hornito* 🕾 *6615–3774* ⊕ *www.panama.net.tc* ➪ *3 rooms* ⌂ *In-room: no a/c, no phone, no TV. In-hotel: laundry service, no kids under 12, no-smoking rooms* ⊟ *No credit cards* ❙◎❙ *EP.*

Bocas del Toro Archipelago

WORD OF MOUTH

"I think the beaches on Bastimentos are the best, and they have a hilltop restaurant which is supposed to be a cool pavilion hang-out spot. All the hiking trails and water activities are much better on Bastimentos than elsewhere in Bocas in my opinion."

—IslandHop100

"I'd say the snorkeling was better in Roatán, but it was pretty good in Bocas [del Toro] as well. One of the differences was that it seemed easier to snorkel off the shore in Roatán, whereas we went out in a boat in Bocas. But we enjoyed Bocas. There was definitely enough to do for a few days."

—SusanInToronto

By David
Dudenhoefer
Updated by
Marlise Kast

With its turquoise waters, sugar-sand beaches, and funky island towns, the relatively isolated archipelago of Bocas del Toro has the same attractions as major Caribbean destinations with a fraction of the crowds and development. Add to this the flora and fauna of its superlush forests and the culture of the province's indigenous community, and you've got St. Thomas-plus, at half the price.

As you fly over the archipelago, you see brown blotches of coral reefs scattered across the sea between islands. Below the surface is a kaleidoscope of corals, sponges, fish, and invertebrates. The crystalline waters that hold those coral gardens wash against half a dozen beaches ranging from forest-hemmed Red Frog Beach to the ivory sands of the Cayos Zapatillas, where lanky coconut palms stretch out over the tide line. The islands have a dozen surf spots—from fun beach breaks to challenging barrels over coral reefs. It also boasts a myriad of trails leading into the jungle where you might see monkeys, sloths, and colorful poison dart frogs.

The eponymous provincial capital of Bocas del Toro has an ample selection of affordable hotels and good restaurants. On any given morning dozens of boats depart from the port, carrying visitors to nearby beaches, reefs, and rain forests. You can soak up local culture at the colorful little town of Old Bank (also known as "Bastimentos Town"), or at indigenous villages on Isla Bastimentos. The islands' original inhabitants, the Ngöbe, live in villages scattered around the province, but the population in the archipelago's main town is a mix of Afro-Caribbean, Hispanic, and Chinese—all proud *bocatoreños,* as the local people and culture are called. Most townspeople are as comfortable speaking English as Spanish, but prefer to speak the local dialect, called Guari-Guari, which is a patois English with traces of Spanish.

Whether you prefer diving, kayaking, surfing, hiking, bird-watching, partying, or swaying in a hammock cooled by an ocean breeze, the Bocas del Toro archipelago can keep you busy—or lazy—for days on end. The province incorporates a large piece of the Panamanian mainland, which is mostly covered with banana farms and a few farm-worker towns. The Cordillera de Talamanca towers to the south of the archipelago and is covered with largely inaccessible wilderness, but if you travel by land between Bocas del Toro and Chiriquí, you can get a good look at its vast, unexplored jungle. Otherwise, you'll want to stick with the islands, which have plenty of sultry rain forest to complement their sand, sea, and sun.

The only caveat is that those rain forests are the result of copious and frequent downpours, which have ruined more than a few vacations. It rains an average of two out of three days in Bocas del Toro, and while heavy showers are often over in a matter of hours, an entire week of rain

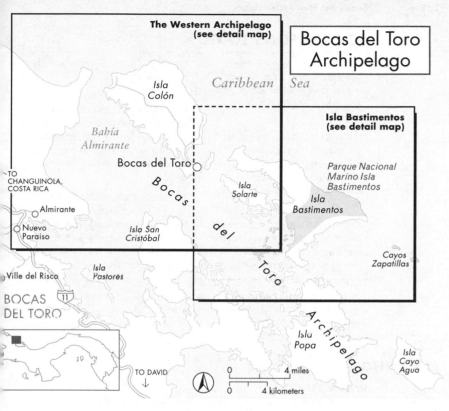

isn't out of the question. Apart from March, September, and October, avoid booking your entire vacation here, since the likelihood of getting sunny days elsewhere in Panama is greater. But don't let the rain scare you away, because when it's sunny, Bocas del Toro is simply amazing.

ORIENTATION AND PLANNING

ORIENTATION

The Bocas del Toro Archipelago represents only a small portion of the large and wild province of the same name, yet it holds virtually all of its attractions. Those islands are scattered across a shallow gulf between banana-dominated lowlands and the rugged Peninsula Valiente. Tourism is centered around Bocas del Toro town, which occupies a spit of land on the southern tip of Isla Colón, the westernmost island. That small town has a tiny airport on its western edge from where most visitors arrive and depart. Water taxis and a ferry ply the waters between the town and the mainland port of Almirante, from which roads lead east to Chiriquí and west to banana farms and the Costa Rican border. To the east of Isla Colón are several other islands with communities and isolated hotels—Islas Carenero, Solarte, and Bastimentos—and by

TOP REASONS TO GO

Idyllic Islands. Jungle-hemmed beaches, coconut palms growing in pale sand, emerald waters...the archipelago has the stuff of tropical fantasies.

Funky Bocas Town. The offbeat, colorful town of Bocas offers a mix of historic architecture, mellow locals, good food, nightlife, and abundant views of the surrounding sea and islands.

Neptune's Gardens. The submarine wonders—from the sponge-studded reef beneath Hospital Point to the seemingly endless coral gardens of

the Cayos Zapatillas—can keep you diving for days.

The Jungle. Though the sea and sand are the big attractions, the rain forests that cover much of the archipelago are home to hundreds of bird species as well as everything from howler monkeys to tiny poison dart frogs.

Caribbean Cultures. Bocas del Toro's cultural mix of Afro-Caribbean, Panamanian, and indigenous Ngöbe tradition adds layers to the islands' personality, making it interesting as well as beautiful.

day, private boats and water taxis travel regularly between the islands. The eastern half of Isla Bastimentos is a wild and beautiful area that is partially protected within Parque Nacional Marino Isla Bastimentos, as are the two idyllic isles of Cayos Zapatillas to the southeast.

PLANNING

WHEN TO GO

The big drawback of Bocas del Toro is the rain. Rain can sometimes fall for days on end, and it can do so at any time of year. Statistically, March is the sunniest month. September and October are the next-driest months, and May and June tend to be nice as well. The locals call the period from mid-August to October their "Second Summer," when waters are calm and ideal for snorkeling and diving. Since May, June, and (especially) September and October are the rainiest months in the rest of Panama, Bocas del Toro is the place to be at those times. December is the wettest month, and July and August are right behind it, though it tends to be sunny only about a third of the time. Despite this, December, July, and August are good months for surfing in the archipelago but the worst months for diving. In January and February the odds of enjoying sunny days are about fifty-fifty. The annual *feria* (fair) in mid-September is party time in Bocas town, as is November, when parades and festivals dominate the streets in honor of Panamanian and Bocaterno independence. Many of the outlying lodges and some restaurants close during May and June.

GETTING HERE AND AROUND
BY AIR
Because it is relatively remote, most people travel to and from Bocas del Toro by air. The Aeropuerto Internacional Bocas del Toro, archipelago's tiny airport, is five blocks from the center of Bocas, at the west end of

A BIT OF HISTORY

The Bocas del Toro archipelago was visited by Christopher Columbus ("Cristobal Colón" in Spanish) in 1502, when he sailed through the area on his fourth voyage to the Americas. Centuries later the islands of Isla Colón and Isla Cristobal were named for the Italian explorer. A few lesser-known conquistadores later ventured into the province but were discouraged by its impenetrable jungles and lack of gold. The Spanish crown virtually ignored the region, leaving it to the indigenous inhabitants and to French and English buccaneers, who rested there between raids. During the early 19th century Afro-Caribbean turtle hunters from the English-speaking islands of San Andrés and Providencia built seasonal camps here. In 1826, some of them brought their families and established the town of Bocas del Toro, which remained a fishing and turtle-hunting village for decades.

In the 1880s the province was transformed when American companies began cultivating bananas on the mainland. Laborers were brought in from Jamaica; Europeans arrived following the collapse of the French canal effort; large, wooden buildings were erected; and the local economy burgeoned. By the time Panama declared independence from Colombia in 1903, Bocas del Toro was a prosperous, cosmopolitan town with several English-language newspapers and U.S., British, German, and French consulates. But a decade later a fungal disease decimated the banana farms, which were abandoned, and new farms were established inland. When the fungal disease returned in the 1930s, the United Fruit Company, the province's main employer, pulled up stakes and moved its Panama operations to Chiriquí, sending the local economy into a tailspin. The company later established its offices on the mainland, and using pesticides to keep the fungi at bay, United Fruit returned to the province in the 1950s with a new name, Chiquita. By this time, the original indigenous people had been wiped out by disease and enforced migrations. It wasn't until the middle of the 20th century that the first Ngöbe settlers returned to the islands.

In the 1990s, a significant number of foreigners began visiting the archipelago, and tourism began to lift the region out of poverty. The 21st century brought a real-estate boom, with foreigners snatching up land and driving prices up by hundreds of percent, while wages hardly rose. Thanks to tourism, Bocas del Toro has become a relatively prosperous community. However, real-estate development has left many locals unable to afford land in their own communities.

Avenida E. Domestic carriers Aeroperlas and Air Panama have three daily flights each between Bocas del Toro and Panama City, and one morning flight between Bocas del Toro and David. Costa Rican airline Nature Air has daily afternoon flights between Bocas and the nearby port of Limón (December–April only), and San José.

Carriers Aeroperlas (☎ 315-7500 or 721-1230 ⊕ www.aeroperlas.com). **Air Panama** (☎ 316-9000 or 721-0841 ⊕ www.flyairpanama.com). **Nature Air** (☎ 506/299-6000 in Costa Rica; 800/235-9272 in the U.S. ⊕ www.natureair. com).

BY BOAT AND FERRY

Boats are the most common means of transportation in Bocas del Toro, and the town of Bocas has several water-taxi companies and dozens of boatmen who provide transportation between Islas Colón, Carenero, and Bastimentos, as well as day tours. The water-taxi companies Bocas Marine Tours, Jam Pan Tours, and Taxi 25 have trips every 30 minutes between Bocas and Almirante ($4), where you can catch a bus to David. It takes 20 minutes to reach Almirante, with departures from 6 AM to 6 PM. Jam Pan also provides transport to the other islands, as do independent boatmen who depart from the dock next to the Farmacia Rosa Blanca, on Calle 3 in Bocas. The fare to Carenero is $1.50, to Old Bank, $2.

If you are heading to Isla Carenero or Bastimentos, it can be less expensive to do as the locals do and travel with boatmen who wait at the dock next to Farmacia Rosa Blanca. Most boat trips cost between $2 and $20, though the farthest lodges are more expensive to reach.

A car is of little use in Bocas del Toro, but there is a car ferry, run by Trasbordadores Marinos, that travels between Almirante and Bocas Monday–Friday (except holidays) and on Sunday, departing from Almirante at 8 AM and Bocas at 4 PM. The trip takes an hour and costs $20–$30, depending on the size of the vehicle.

Contacts Bocas Marine & Tours (✉ *Calle 3, at Av. C* ☎ *757-9033*). **Jam Pan Tours** (✉ *Calle 2, at Av. D* ☎ *757-9619*). **Taxi 25** (✉ *Calle 1, at Av. Central* ☎ *757-9028*). **Trasbordadores Marinos** (✉ *Town port, Almirante* ☎ *6490-7193*).

BY BUS AND TAXI

Transporte Boca del Drago has two shuttle vans that travel the length of Isla Colón, from Bocas del Toro to Bocas del Drago, five times daily on weekdays. The bus departs from Bocas's Parque Bolívar at 7, 10, noon, 3, and 6, and departs from the restaurant at Bocas del Drago 45 minutes later. The cost is $2.50 per person. Share taxis run up and down Bocas's main streets, charging $1 for most trips in town.

Although the trip is long, Bocas del Toro can be reached from Panama City by land. The direct bus from Panama City to Almirante (and vice versa) takes eight hours but is comfortable and costs only $24. If you're in Chiriquí you can bus or taxi from David or Boquete to Almirante (3½ hours), where water taxis depart for Bocas every half-hour. Buses to David depart from Almirante every half-hour from the bus station on the other side of the train tracks from the water-taxi offices and charge $7. Unfortunately, Almirante is a 20-minute walk from the main road that connects David to Changuinola, and buses stop only at a crossroads on the main road. Although it is possible to walk from the water taxi to the crossroads, most travelers find it difficult to locate; it is best to take a taxi to the crossroads for $.50. To catch a bus to Changuinola, head to the bus station in Almirante.

Boquete-based taxi driver Daniel Higgins provides transportation between Boquete and Almirante for $120, though you may get a better price from the taxis that hang out at the bus station in Almirante. Due to storms in 2008, the water-taxi station Finca 60, near the Costa Rica border, is closed indefinitely. Caribe Shuttle offers daily transportation between the Southern Caribbean coast of Costa Rica (Puerto Viejo/ Manzanillo/Cahuita) and Bocas del Toro. The $35 rate includes hotel pickup, border crossing fees, and the 30-minute boat trip to Isla Colon.

Contacts Almirante Bus (☎ 774–0585). **Caribe Shuttle** (☎ 757–9031, 506/ 2750–0626 in Costa Rica ⊕ www. CaribeShuttle.com).**Daniel Higgins** (☎ 6617–0570). **Transporte Boca del Drago** (☎ 6475–4875 or 6743–7969).

RESTAURANTS

The town of Bocas del Toro has an ample restaurant selection, with such surprising options as Thai and Indian cuisine to complement the traditional seafood. Like everything in Bocas, dining is casual and the pace is slow, so be patient for your meal. Local specialties include lobster, whole-fried snapper, octopus, and shrimp served with *patacones* (fried plantain slices) or *yuca frita* (fried cassava strips). Those who do not purchase directly from local fisherman tend to shop at Tropical Markets on the northeast end of Calle 1, where a series of indoor food stalls offers everything from pastries and produce to meats and seafood. At restaurants, opt for bottled water over a glass with ice since tap water is usually unsafe to drink. Although tipping is not obligatory in Bocas, it is greatly appreciated by the locals whose wages generally run $15 per day.

HOTELS

Accommodations here range from rooms in traditional wooden buildings in town to rustic but enchanting bungalows nestled in the wilderness of Isla Bastimentos. All of them have private baths, and all but the eco-lodges have air-conditioning and Internet. Although Bocas del Toro town has an array of budget and moderately priced hotels, the out-of-town lodges tend to be rather expensive, though hardly luxurious. Other advantages of staying in town are the local color and the selection of restaurants, shops, and nightlife. The downside is noise from neighbors and revelers, which is a problem at most in-town hotels. Lodges outside town provide more natural, tranquil settings. You can get information on Bocas lodging on the Bocas Web site (⊕ www.bocas. com). ■ TIP→ A good option is to divide your stay between a hotel in town and one on the outer islands.

WHAT IT COSTS IN U.S. DOLLARS					
	¢	$	$$	$$$	$$$$
Restaurants	under $5	$5–$10	$10–$15	$15–$20	Over $20
Hotels	under $50	$50–$100	$100–$160	$160–$220	Over $220

Restaurant prices are per person for a main course at dinner. Hotel prices are for two people in a standard double room, excluding service and 10% tax.

ESSENTIALS

EMERGENCIES

The clinic in Bocas is good only for first aid. If you have a serious medical problem, you should get on the next flight to Panama City or David.

Emergency Services Fire (☎ 757–9274 *in Bocas del Toro*). **Police** (☎ 757–9217 *in Bocas del Toro*).

INTERNET

Most hotels in Bocas del Toro offer free Internet access to guests and most have Wi-Fi. There are also several Internet cafes on Calle 3.

MONEY MATTERS

There are two ATMs in Bocas: at the Banco Nacional de Panama and on Calle 1, next to the Policía Nacional. They give cash withdrawals from Visa and MasterCard and from Cirrus- and Plus-affiliated debit and credit cards.

SAFETY

Bocas is a safe town, but it has acquired a few sidewalk hustlers and drug dealers in recent years and has a growing drug problem, so don't wander its side streets late at night. The main dangers in the archipelago, however, are sunburn and bug bites. Take a hat, sunscreen, and insect repellent. Drowning is also a real danger, and there are no lifeguards. Don't swim at the beaches if the waves are big, unless you are an experienced surfer, and don't let a boatman take you into rough water in a dugout canoe.

THE WESTERN ARCHIPELAGO

The westernmost island in the archipelago, Isla Colón, is also the most developed, with a road running across it and the provincial capital occupying a peninsula on its southern tip. Across a channel from that urbanized headland is the smaller Isla Carenero. Together with the town of Bocas, this was one of the first places in the archipelago to be settled by people other than Indians. Boats regularly travel between the two communities that are home to the bulk of the archipelago's residents and most of its hotels and restaurants. Isla Solarte, farther to the east, is more sparsely populated, with a few homes near its western extreme. Most travelers stay in Bocas del Toro town and make day trips to the other islands, beaches, and dive spots.

BOCAS DEL TORO

550 km (341 mi) northwest of Panama City, 170 km (105 mi) north of David.

The town of Bocas del Toro, which the locals simply call Bocas, sits on a little headland connected to the island's primary landmass by a narrow isthmus. The western half of that headland is covered by a mangrove swamp, but the eastern half holds a neat grid packed with homes, businesses, and government offices. The town is surrounded by water on three sides, which means it has plenty of ocean views. The nearest

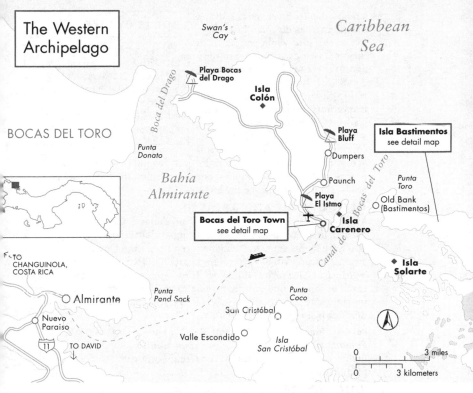

The Western Archipelago

Swan's Cay

Caribbean Sea

Playa Bocas del Drago

Isla Colón

BOCAS DEL TORO

Punta Donato

Bahía Almirante

Boca del Drago

Playa Bluff

Dumpers

Paunch

Playa El Istmo

Bocas del Toro Town
see detail map

Isla Carenero

Isla Bastimentos
see detail map

Punta Toro

Old Bank (Bastimentos)

Canal de Bocas del Toro

Isla Solarte

TO CHANGUINOLA, COSTA RICA

Almirante

Nuevo Paraiso

11 TO DAVID

Punta Pond Sock

San Cristóbal

Valle Escondido

Punta Coco

Isla San Cristóbal

Canal de

0 — 3 miles
0 — 3 kilometers

beach, on the isthmus that connects it to Isla Colón, is not the island's best. In order to play in the surf and sand you either have to boat to Isla Bastimentos or take a bike, taxi, bus, or boat to one of the beaches on Isla Colón. Luckily, Bocas has an abundance of boatmen eager to show you paradise, as well as several dive shops and tour operators offering day trips to beaches and coral reefs.

Although Bocas has little in the way of museums and landmarks, the laid-back town is worth exploring, with its wide streets, weathered Caribbean architecture, and plentiful greenery. It is home to an interesting sampling of humanity, with a majority of Afro-Caribbean or Hispanic extraction, a good number of Chinese, some Ngöbe and Kuna, and a growing number of European and North American expatriates. There are domino-playing fishermen, Rastafarian artisans, and South American surfers. For some islanders, doing nothing seems to be a full-time occupation, and in the heat of the afternoon or the middle of a downpour Bocas has plenty of spots to do just that, with a cool drink and an ocean view.

Most of Bocas's restaurants and other businesses are located along Calle 3, sometimes called Main Street. This is a wide, north–south track stretching from one end of town to the other (seven blocks) and running along the sea for its southern half. Boats to the mainland and other islands depart from docks along that stretch, as do tours bound for fun in the sun, while people from the other islands arrive here to shop and run errands. Halfway up Calle 3, Calle 1 branches off it to the right, passing various hotels and restaurants built over the water. Calle 3 ends at Avenida Norte, which runs west to the isthmus that connects the town to Isla Colón and

> ### BOCAS BY BIKE
>
> Bocas del Toro is a perfect town for biking, which is a good way to get to Bluff Beach. Various businesses rent bikes for about $3 an hour or $15 per day. Among them is **Bocas Bicis** (⊠ *North end of Calle 3, at Av. F* ☎ *6446–0787*).

across the island. If you turn right onto Avenida Norte and walk two blocks to the island's northeast corner, you find the fire station, which holds a couple of antique fire engines.

GETTING HERE AND AROUND

Most people fly to Bocas del Toro from Panama City; Aeroperlas and Air Panama have flights every morning and afternoon. Those airlines also have flights every morning between Bocas and David. Costa Rican airline, Nature Air, has afternoon flights between Bocas and Limón or San José in Costa Rica. Bocas del Toro is too far from Panama City to reach by land in one shot, but if you're in Chiriquí you can bus or taxi to Almirante (3 hours), where water taxis depart to Bocas every 30–60 minutes from 6 AM to 6 PM.

Panama Trails (⊠ *Plaza Morical Piso 11, between Calles 50 and 71, Panama City* ☎ *393–8334* ⊕ *www.panamatrails.com*) organizes local flights, tailor-made itineraries, car rentals, and tours to Bocas del Toro from Panama City.

WHAT TO SEE

❶ Two blocks east of Calle 3 on the right is the local office of the Panamanian Tourism Authority, **ATP (Autoridad de Tourismo Panama)** (⊠ *Calle 1, next to Policía Nacional* ⊕ *www.visitpanama.com* ☎ *757–9642*), housed in a large Caribbean-style building on the water. It has an information desk, a museum on the second floor with information about the area's ecology and history, and a small café in back. It's open weekdays 8:30–3:30.

❷ **Parque Simón Bolívar** (⊠ *Calle 3, at Av. Central*) is a large park shaded by mango trees and royal palms near the north end of Calle 3. Children play here, and locals chat on its cement benches in the evening. North of the park stands the **Palacio Municipal,** a large cement building that houses various government offices.

❸ **Playa Bocas** (⊠ *Av. Norte, 1 km northwest of Calle 3*) stretches along the narrow isthmus that connects the town to Isla Colón, overlooking tranquil Bahia Chitre (Sand Flea Bay). It is a mediocre beach but will do in a pinch. If you have the time and energy, rent a bike and make the rough 40-minute ride out to Bluff Beach *(4 km north of Bocas Town, on Isla Colón),* which is gorgeous. The dozens of simple structures that line Bocas Beach are transformed into exhibits, restaurants, and beer shacks for the annual **Feria del Mar** (Sea Fair), during the second or third week in September. The normally deserted beach becomes packed with locals

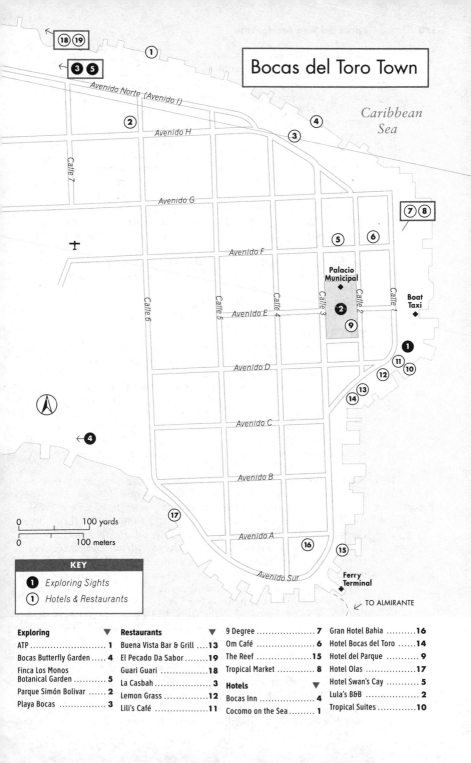

Bocas del Toro Town

Caribbean Sea

Avenido Norte (Avenido I)

Avenido H

Avenido G

Avenido F

Avenido E

Avenido D

Avenido C

Avenido B

Avenido A

Avenido Sur

Calle 7

Calle 6

Calle 5

Calle 4

Calle 3

Calle 2

Calle 1

Palacio Municipal

Boat Taxi

Ferry Terminal

TO ALMIRANTE

0   100 yards
0   100 meters

KEY

- **1** *Exploring Sights*
- (1) *Hotels & Restaurants*

and visitors who enjoy folk dances, a boat race, and a beauty contest.

④ A few minutes west of town by ☺ boat is the **Bocas Butterfly Garden** (✉ *Macca Hill, near Bocas Marina* ☎ *757–9008 or 6671–4724* ⌨ *$5* ☉ *Mon.–Sat. 9–3, Sun. 9–noon*), where a dozen native butterfly species inhabit a screened flyway and a trail leads through a small forest reserve.

⑤ **Finca Los Monos Botanical Garden** (✉ *Idaan Hill, just past the Smithsonian Institute* ☎ *757–9461 or 6729–9943* ⊕ *www.bocasdeltorobotanicalgarden.com* ⌨ *$10* ☉ *Tours Mon at 1 and Fri at 8:30 or by appointment*) has a large collection of heliconia, ginger, palm, and fruit trees in a rain-forest setting with plenty of wildlife.

> ## HURRICANE SEASON?
>
> Bocas del Toro gets plenty of rain, and tropical storms sometimes blow in from the Caribbean. However, Panama is generally considered to be below the hurricane belt, though there's no ironclad guarantee that hurricanes will stick to their assigned area. You can take comfort in the fact that Bocas hasn't been hit by a hurricane in recent history. The most recent natural disasters to affect the area were a 7.2 earthquake in 1991 and tropical storms in 2008 that damaged many buildings.

WHERE TO EAT

$–$$$ ✕ **Buena Vista Bar and Grill.** Perched over the water, the back deck of
AMERICAN   this wooden building is one of the most pleasant places in town to
★   have a meal since it overlooks the sea and nearby Isla Carenero. Boats zip by, and waves wash against the pilings under the floor. The menu ranges from such gringo standards as T-bone steak to the more daring jambalaya, enchiladas, and ginger-orange shrimp. Their selection of salads, burgers, and sandwiches made with imported meats and cheeses makes it a popular lunch spot. Save room for the Bocas Brownie made with organic Cerutti chocolate. ✉ *Calle 1, half a block east of Calle 3* ☎ *757–9035* ⌨ *MC, V* ☉ *Closed Tues.*

$–$$ ✕ **El Pecado Da Sabor.** Nestled under a garden palapa, this eatery—whose
ECLECTIC   name translates as "The Sin Adds Flavor"—is one of Bocas's best. The
Fodor'sChoice   "sin" might refer to gluttony—a temptation when faced with puff pas-
★   tries filled with almond chicken or beef tenderloin with a creamy blue cheese sauce. Certainly, the food is sinfully good, and the colorful decor includes candles and giant devil masks left over from Carnival celebrations. The wait staff is friendly and attentive, and the food presentation makes the meal equally delightful. Avoid Sundays when music from neighboring bars drowns out the pleasantness of the open-air setting. ✉ *At the entrance of Cabana, behind Pizza Libre, Isla Colón* ⌂ *Olga and Stephan, Owners El Pecado Da Sabor, Bocas Special Mail, PTY 18115, P.O. Box 025724, Miami, FL 33102-5724* ☎ *6597–0296* ⌨ *No credit cards* ☉ *Closed Mon. and May–June. No lunch.*

$$$ ✕ **Guari-Guari.** Wooden tables, plastic chairs, and a tin roof hardly do
MEDITERRANEAN   justice to the spectacular six-course, prix-fixe dinner served here. A
Fodor'sChoice   great deal of effort (and love) goes into each dish, prepared by Span-
★   ish chef Monica, who abandoned her law profession to be with German engineer "Ossi" (now serving as the restaurant's charming waiter). Together they have managed to break the barriers of Bocas typical fare

with a tasting menu that includes tuna carpaccio, spinach salad, and pork tenderloin with roasted potatoes and blue cheese sauce. Adding to the experience is the sound of crashing waves near the open-air restaurant. The menu changes daily, and special vegetarian courses can be provided upon request. Since the restaurant is surrounded by lush vegetation, mosquito coils are lit beside each table to keep the bugs away. ✉ *2 km outside Bocas Town, between La Bomba gas station and the Smithsonian* ⌂ *Monica and Ossi, Owners Guari-Guari, Bocas Special Mail, PTY 18115, P.O. Box 025724, Miami, FL 33102-5724* ☎ *6627–1825 or 6575–5513* ⌂ *Reservations essential* ⊟ *No credit cards* ⊙ *Closed Wed.*

$–$$
ECLECTIC
★
✕ **La Casbah.** It would be an understatement to say that this tiny roadside eatery doesn't look like much. With digs like these, you have to stay on top of your kitchen to compete with restaurants on the water, and the Belgian chef does just that. His global menu hops from falafel to gazpacho to shrimp in a Sambuca cream sauce. Daily specials are a good bet, or you can stick with such local favorites as pork loin in a Marsala wine sauce or fish of the day in a coconut sauce. ✉ *Av. Norte, between Calles 3 and 4* ☎ *6477–4727* ⊟ *No credit cards* ⊙ *Closed Sun. and Mon. No lunch.*

$$
ASIAN
✕ **Lemon Grass.** This restaurant's location on the second floor on an old wooden building over the water gives it a great view of the turquoise sea and nearby islands. Tables sit beneath parchment-paper lamps that dangle from a tin roof that roars on rainy days. The English owner, Mike, worked in Southeast Asia before landing in Bocas, where the sea provides the perfect ingredients for his Asian-fusion recipes that include spicy crab cakes, steak teriyaki, various curries, and fish-and-chips. Scribbled on a chalkboard menu are creative cocktails like "Lemon Grass Lips," a punchy blend of rum, lemon juice, and cranberries. The changing dessert selection could include such decadent inventions as Oreo-Baileys cheesecake and a cappuccino tiramisu sundae. ✉ *Calle 2, at the diagonal split* ⌂ *Entrega General, Isla Colón* ☎ *757–9630* ⊟ *No credit cards* ⊙ *Closed Thurs. No lunch Sat.*

¢–$$
ECLECTIC
✕ **Lili's Café.** A fun spot for a light meal with an ocean view, Lili's is at the back of a building over the water at the south end of Calle 1. Seating is limited to a long bar and a few tables on the deck. Order and pay at the window, then wait for Lili and company to deliver one of their creative breakfast items, a sandwich made with home-baked bread, or something along the line of vegetarian quiche. You can get food to go, and there are daily lunch specials. However, unless it's a daily special, this isn't a good place for seafood. You can spice up your vittles with Lili's Killin' Me Man sauce, sold by the bottle. ✉ *Calle 1, next to Tropical Suites* ☎ *6560–8777* ⊟ *No credit cards* ⊙ *No dinner Sat. and Sun.*

$$$
MEDITERRANEAN
★
✕ **9°.** Named for Boca's geographical coordinates on the globe, this waterfront eatery is considered Boca's most upscale restaurant with its white linens and candlelight reflecting off polished wood floors. A blend of Caribbean and French cuisine, the menu features such dishes as filet mignon stuffed with blue cheese and Caribbean vol au vent (pastry filled with octopus and lobster). Try one of the innovative appetizers like a ceviche martini or mushroom cigar. Presentation and service

6

are priorities here, and everything is made in-house including the breads and pastas. The restaurant can be accessed from the water or from the entrance at the end of the Tropical Markets. ✉ *North end of Calle 1* ☎ *757–9400* 🖃 *MC, V* ☉ *Closed Sun.*

$–$$
INDIAN
✕ **Om Café.** You can get authentic Indian cuisine in Bocas del Toro at this cozy café atop a surf shop. Owner Sunanda Mehra is a Canadian of Punjabi descent who raided her aunt's cookbook before running off to Panama. You can savor such improbable delicacies as her prawn vindaloo, *palaak paneer* (fresh cheese in a spinach sauce), chicken tandoori, or any of half-dozen vegetable dishes. In the morning, treat yourself to an Indian breakfast, which includes vindaloo eggs in a roti wrap and *chana bhatura* (garbanzo curry with fried bread), accompanied by a refreshing fruit *lassi* (yogurt smoothie). ✉ *Av. F at Calle 2* ☎ *6624–0898* 🖃 *No credit cards* ☉ *Closed Wed. and May–June. No lunch.*

¢–$$
CARIBBEAN
✕ **The Reef.** Though slightly out of the way, at the southern end of Calle 3, this traditional *bocatoreño* restaurant has a pleasant open-air setting over the water and serves fresh seafood at lower prices than the more centrally located places. It is consequently a popular spot with locals despite the poor service. Fresh delicacies include whole fried red snapper, garlic prawns, a hearty seafood soup, and *parrillada de mariscos* (a seafood mixed grill for two). It has one of the best views in town, and its minimal decoration includes a couple of dugout canoes hanging from the rafters. It occupies a corner of what was once the United Fruit Company dock, where most of the town's able-bodied men once gathered each morning to catch boats to the banana plantations on the mainland. ✉ *Calle 3, across from Hotel Bahia* ✉ *Entrega General, Isla Colón, Bocas del Toro* ☎ *757–9336* 🖃 *No credit cards.*

WHERE TO STAY

$
🏨 **Bocas Inn.** This small lodge in an older wooden building over the water has a great location at the end of Calle 3 and is buffered from the street by a large garden, so it's relatively quiet. It has a lovely second-floor balcony and large, open-air restaurant with plenty of hammocks and chairs from which to contemplate the sea. Most guest rooms are on the second floor of the main building; they have varnished hardwood floors, colorful tile bathrooms, and either one queen or two single beds. The Zapatilla and Escudo rooms, which open onto the common porch with an ocean view, are well worth the extra $10. The rooms over the office, Cristobal and Carenero, are too close to the street. **Pros:** great views; organized tours; good breakfast. **Cons:** no TV; no Internet. ✉ *Av. Norte just west of Calle 3* ✉ *Entrega General, Isla Colón, Bocas del Toro* ☎ *757–9600* ⊕ *www.anconexpeditions.com* ⇘ *7 rooms*

CONSERVING WATER

As unlikely as it may seem in a place where it rains as much as it does in Bocas del Toro, the town suffers periodic water shortages, since it has outgrown its decades-old water system. The best hotels have massive water tanks to ensure they don't run out, but do your part, and conserve water. ■ **TIP→** The tap water in Bocas isn't potable, so drink only bottled or filtered water.

⚘ *In-room: no phone, no TV. In-hotel: restaurant, no-smoking rooms* ▭ *MC, V* ℐ◎ *BP.*

$ 🖫 **Cocomo on the Sea.** This homey waterfront hotel has plenty of com-
★ mon areas for enjoying the ocean views or the small tropical garden.
Rooms are small but cozy, with hardwood floors, white walls decorated
with *molas* (cloth pictures), and colorful Guatemalan bedspreads. They
all have air-conditioning but also ceiling fans and lots of windows to
let in the ocean breeze. The coolest spot is the wide porch over the
water, with a couch and hammocks, where the sumptuous breakfasts
are served. Kayaks are available for paddling to Isla Carenero. The
friendly American owner, Douglas Ruscher, is happy to give travel
advice. **Pros:** great view and common areas; friendly owner; good breakfast. **Cons:** noisy neighbors; no TV; no Internet. ✉ *Av. Norte, at Calle 6*
☏ *757–9259* ⊕ *www.panamainfo.com/cocomo* ⬗ *4 rooms* ⚘ *In-room:
no phone, no TV. In-hotel: water sports, laundry service, no kids under
8, no-smoking rooms* ▭ *MC, V* ℐ◎ *BP.*

$ 🖫 **Gran Hotel Bahia.** This two-story wooden building was the head-
quarters of the United Fruit Company in the 1930s. Today you can
still find the steel money vault beside the hotel lobby. The top floor
served as guest rooms and still has the original veranda overlooking
the bay, where mint juleps were probably the order of the hot tropical days. The spacious rooms have been completely refurbished, with
shiny hardwood floors, double beds, cable TV, air-conditioning, and
small tile bathrooms. Deluxe rooms have queen beds, and two of them
have small balconies. Major construction projects are underway to the
south, and the only decent view is from the veranda, but this could be
the quaintest hotel in town. **Pros:** good value; comfortable. **Cons:** off
water; small windows; nearby construction. ✉ *Southern end of Calle 3*
☏ *757–9626* ⊕ *www.ghbahia.com* ⬗ *18 rooms* ⚘ *In-room: no phone,
safe (some), Wi-Fi. In-hotel: laundry service, no-smoking rooms* ▭
MC, V ℐ◎ *BP.*

$–$$$ 🖫 **Hotel Bocas del Toro.** This attractive hotel on the water was designed
Fodor's Choice by a boat builder, so it's no coincidence that guest rooms look as if they
★ could be on a yacht, with their polished hardwoods and nautical decor.
The bilingual staff is possibly the most helpful in town. Rooms vary in
size and price, but all have flat-screen TVs, orthopedic mattresses, and
a blue and white nautical motif to complement the dark wood. Town-
view rooms can be noisy at night; more expensive ocean-view rooms
are quieter. The open-air restaurant serves a good mix of Panamanian
and international fare, with an ocean view. Day trips and massages
can be arranged. **Pros:** on the water; friendly staff; very clean rooms.
Cons: expensive; street noise at night. ✉ *Calle 2, next to Hotel Limbo*
⌖ *Carla Rankin, Bocas Special Mail, PTY 18115, P.O. Box 025724,
Miami, FL 33102-5724* ☏ *757–9771* ⊕ *www.hotelbocasdeltoro.com*
⬗ *10 rooms, 1 suite* ⚘ *In-room: safe, Wi-Fi (some). In-hotel: restau-
rant, bar, water sports, laundry service, no-smoking rooms* ▭ *AE, MC,
V* ℐ◎ *BP.*

¢ 🖫 **Hotel del Parque.** Hidden behind lush gardens at the southeast corner
of Parque Bolívar, this small, family-run hotel is a short walk from most
restaurants and businesses, yet it's far enough from the main drag to

6

remain tranquil. It's as close as you'll come to staying with a local family since the owners, Luis and Magally Mou, live there. Rooms have big, screened windows, air-conditioning, ceiling fans, cable TV, small bathrooms, and foam mattresses. You can hang out in a hammock on the veranda overlooking the park or on the patio in the back garden. Guests are welcome to use the kitchen, and there's always free fruit and coffee available. **Pros:** inexpensive; central location; communal kitchen. **Cons:** soft beds; street noise. ⊠ *Calle 2, at Parque Bolívar* ☎ *757–9008* ✍ *delparque35@hotmail.com* ➳ *8 rooms* ⚒ *In-room: no phone. In-hotel: Wi-fi, no-smoking rooms* ☰ *MC, V* ⦿| *EP.*

¢   ▦ **Hotel Olas.** Hidden at the south end of town, this large wooden hotel
★   built over the water is one of the best deals in Bocas, comparable to more centrally located inns that charge twice as much. It has an open-air restaurant and bar on a deck in back with a great view of the sea and mainland, where a hearty breakfast is served. Guest rooms are slightly cramped but comfortable enough, with lots of wooden furnishings, a small TV (with cable), and air-conditioning. Request a room with a balcony and ocean view. Affordable boat excursions depart from the floating platform at the back of the restaurant, and Jet Skis are available for rent. **Pros:** inexpensive; on the water; communal computer; quiet. **Cons:** rooms smallish. ⊠ *Av. Sur, at Calle 5* ⟳ *Entrega General, Isla Colón, Bocas del Toro* ☎ *757–9930* ⊕ *www.hotelolas.com* ➳ *24 rooms* ⚒ *In-room: no phone, Wi-fi. In-hotel: restaurant, bar, water sports, laundry service, Internet terminal, no-smoking rooms* ☰ *No credit cards* ⦿| *BP.*

$–$$ ▦ **Hotel Swan's Cay.** This two-story wooden complex behind the Palacio
☾   Municipal fits into Bocas well enough, but inside the lobby feels like Old Europe. The Italian owners seem as out of place as the decor, and if you get one of them to smile, congratulations. Still, their rambling hotel has its selling points, mainly the oceanfront pool, one block behind the hotel, with a small bar beside it. Rooms, with wall-to-wall carpeting, imported furniture, and cable TV, are a mixed bag: some are bright, some are dark, some are musty, and all are in need of a facelift. Ask for one with a balcony. A large restaurant serves good pastas and pizzas. **Pros:** reasonable rates; pool by the sea; restaurant. **Cons:** unfriendly management; musty rooms, incongruous decor. ⊠ *Calle 3, between Avs. F and G* ☎ *757–9090* ⊕ *www.swanscayhotel.com* ➳ *44 rooms, 2 suites* ⚒ *In-room: refrigerator (some). In-hotel: 2 restaurants, bars, pools, laundry service, no-smoking rooms* ☰ *AE, MC, V* ⦿| *EP.*

¢–$ ▦ **Lula's B&B.** Across the street from the water and a short walk from the center of town, this small B&B offers simple accommodations and a hearty breakfast. Run by a friendly couple from Atlanta, who bought the property from Lula in 2006, the lodge has a nice veranda on the second floor with a sea view over rooftops and a self-service bar. Rooms are behind the bar and have wooden floors, air-conditioning, small bathrooms, and a nautical decor. Breakfast is served in a big common area with a computer in one corner. There is an on-site surf school for those who want to hit the waves. **Pros:** inexpensive; nice veranda; good breakfast. **Cons:** rooms pretty basic. ⊠ *Av. Norte, at Calle 6* 🖳 *6629-0836*

⊕ *www.lulabb.com* ↻ *6 rooms* ⚓ *In-room: no phone, no TV, Wi-Fi. In-hotel: Internet terminal, no-smoking rooms* ⊟ *MC, V* ⟨○⟩ *BP.*

$$–$$$ ⊞ **Tropical Suites.** The spacious rooms evoke Florida condos, with their
☽ tropical colors, tile floors, ceiling fans, and sliding glass doors opening
★ onto balconies, half with ocean views. Each room has a queen bed,
cable TV, a kitchenette with breakfast bar, and a large bathroom with
a Jacuzzi tub. The hotel is built over the water, and there's a floating
plastic dock in back with a swimming area and children's slide, though
the water here is not that clean. Pay the extra money for an ocean-
view room—they're nicer and quieter. It is conveniently close to most
restaurants and bars. **Pros:** nice, spacious rooms; great ocean views.
Cons: expensive; can be noisy. ⊠ *South end of Calle 1* ☎ *757–9081*
🖷 *757–9080* ⊕ *www.tropical-suites.com* ↻ *16 suites* ⚓ *In-room: safe,
kitchen, Wi-Fi. In-hotel: laundry facilities, no-smoking rooms* ⊟ *MC,
V* ⟨○⟩ *BP.*

NIGHTLIFE AND THE ARTS

Bocas livens up when the sun goes down, since the temperature
becomes more conducive to movement. The decks of the town's various waterfront restaurants are pleasant spots to enjoy a quiet drink
and conversation.

Aqua Lounge (⊠ *Isla Carenero, across the water from Hotel Bocas del
Toro, Bocas del Toro* ☎ *No phone* ⊕ *www.bocasaqualodge.com*) a one-
minute boat ride from Bocas del Toro, has live DJs on Wednesday and
Saturday, when ladies drink for free. Those who need a break from the
dance floor can sway above the water on the club's wooden swings.

Barco Hundido (*Sunken Ship* ⊠ *Calle 1, at Av. H, Bocas del Toro* ☎ *6512–
9032*) is a funky, open-air affair with tropical gardens and wooden
platforms over the water around a small shipwreck, which is lit at night
so you can watch the fish. Watch your step—more than one partier has
danced into the water here.

El Point (⊠ *Av. F at Calle 2, below Om Cafe, Bocas del Toro* ☎ *No
phone*) is popular with Boca's surf crowd and features a live DJ most
nights.

Iguana (⊠ *Calle 2, next to Lili's Cafe, Bocas del Toro* ☎ *No phone*), in
a wooden building over the water, gets packed with locals on Thursday
nights, when ladies drink for free.

SPORTS AND THE OUTDOORS

SCUBA DIVING AND SNORKELING

Bocas is a fun town, but it is primarily a base for exploring the wonders of the surrounding archipelago, the most impressive of which
are the acres of colorful coral reefs. More than a dozen dive spots are
within five minutes to one hour by boat from Bocas, which has several
good dive centers and dozens of boatmen offering inexpensive excursions that combine snorkeling with beach time. Excursions usually
cost $10–$30, depending on the destination and number of passengers,
and depart at 8 or 9 AM. You can guarantee a lower rate for everyone
if you organize a small group. Two-tank boat dives cost $50–$80,
depending on distance.

Bocas Water Sports (✉ *Calle 3, 1 block south of Parque Bolívar, Bocas del Toro* ☎ *757–9541* ⊕ *www.bocaswatersports.com*) is the town's original dive shop and maintains the best reputation. Diving is offered at a dozen sites, and you can take enriched air nitrox and certification courses. The company also offers daily snorkeling

tours to the Cayos Zapatillas and other spots. Snorkeling equipment and kayaks can be rented.

Boteros Bocatoreños (✉ *Calle 3, across from Hotel Bahia, Bocas del Toro* ☎ *757–9760*) is an association of local boatmen who run inexpensive day trips to the archipelago's most popular spots.

J&J Transparente Boat Tours (✉ *Calle 3, 1 block south of Parque Bolívar, Bocas del Toro* ☎ *757–9915*) has various day trips that combine snorkeling with beach time.

La Buga (✉ *Calle 3, next to Farmacia Rosa Blanca, Bocas del Toro* ☎ *757–9534* ⊕ *www.labugapanama.com*) offers diving and snorkeling trips to outer reefs, ship wrecks, and Tiger Rock.

Starfleet Scuba (✉ *2374 Calle 1, Bocas del Toro* ☎ *757–9630* ⊕ *www.starfleetscuba.com*) offers various two-tank boat dives and snorkeling excursions, and has open water certification courses for $235.

SURFING

Bocas is a short boat ride from the breaks on Islas Colón, Carenero, and Bastimentos, which makes it a great base for surfers.

Azucar Surf (✉ *Av. Norte, at Calle 6, Bocas del Toro* ☎ *6491–2595* ⊕ *www.azucarsurf.com*) is run by Boca's most experienced surfer, Michael Lawson. He offers board rentals, surf lessons, and boat charters to the best spots around the islands.

Mondo Taitu (✉ *Av. G, at Calle 5, Bocas del Toro* ☎ *757–9425*), on the north side of town, rents surfboards.

Tropix (✉ *Calle 3, across from park, Bocas del Toro* ☎ *757–9415*), one of Bocas's two surf shops, is a good place to get advice, wax, or a board.

HORSEBACK RIDING

Hacienda del Toro (⛺ *At Dolphin Bay next to the Indian village of Bocatorito on Isla Cristobal* ☎ *6612–9159* ⊕ *www.haciendadeltoro.com*) has horseback-riding tours ($35) at a ranch and rain-forest reserve on Isla Cristobal, a short boat trip from Bocas. The booking office is located on Calle 3 in Bocas Town.

YOGA

Bocas Yoga (✉ *Calle 4, in the purple building across from La Casbah Restaurant, Bocas del Toro* ☎ *6658–1355* ⊕ *www.bocasyoga.com*) offers several classes daily that specialize in hatha yoga, vinyasa flow, pilates, and meditation. The cost is a very reasonable $5 per session,

UNDER THE SEA

For many a traveler, the submarine wonders of Bocas del Toro's extensive coral reefs are the number-one reason to visit. Though Bocas lacks the spectacular schools of fish you might see at Panama's top Pacific dive sites of Isla de Coiba and Islas Secas, the region has greater coral diversity and hundreds of fish and invertebrate species. You can see dozens of colorful coral and sponge species, and such delicate reef denizens as bristle sea stars, peppermint shrimp, anemones, and sea horses. You may also spot spiny lobsters, moray eels, damselfish, angelfish, spiny puffers, spotted eagle rays, and hundreds of other creatures. Visibility varies, but the water is always warm. The best diving conditions are usually in March and between September and November.

The closest dive spot to town is **Hospital Point**, where an impressive coral and sponge garden extends down a steep wall into the blue depths. This can be appreciated both by snorkelers and scuba divers brave enough to descend the wall. Olas Chicas, on the north shore of Isla

Bastimentos, is a good snorkeling spot, with coral, sponges, and sea fans clinging to volcanic rocks off the beach. Cristobal Light, 5 km (3 mi) southeast of Bocas town, is a good spot for snorkeling and scuba, with a coral garden spread across a platform some 15 feet below the surface. The most popular snorkeling spot in the archipelago is **Crawl Cay** (Coral Cay), an extensive reef on the east side of Isla Bastimentos, which has plenty of coral and invertebrates but fewer fish than nearby Cayos Zapatillas. The most famous snorkeling and scuba spot in the archipelago is **Cayos Zapatillas**, and for good reason; the two idyllic islands are surrounded by more than 1,000 acres of coral reef that is inhabited by an array of marine life. While the area around the islands offers excellent shallow snorkeling, the barrier reef has some good scuba spots, including caves. Unfortunately, the sea is often too rough to dive there. The most spectacular dive site in the archipelago is **Tiger Rock**, east of the Cayos Zapatillas, which offers a deep dive along an impressive wall.

6

and the center is open Monday through Saturday (Friday and Saturday only until 1:15).

SHOPPING

Although souvenir shops are limited in town, several Panamanian vendors sell arts and crafts at the north end of Calle 3 near Las Brisas. Here you'll find a selection of Ngöbe crafts including *chácaras*, colorful hand-woven bags made from natural fibers related to the pineapple. On the first and third Saturday of each month, the Bocas' Farmer's Market (held at Parque Bolivar) is a great place to buy fresh fruits, cacao, baked goods, and indigenous crafts, from 9 AM to 1 PM.

Artesanías Bri Bri (✉ *Calle 3, at Av. B, Bocas del Toro* ☎ 757–9020) sells hammocks, clothing, and indigenous handicrafts, such as the jute bags made by local Ngöbe Indians.

Super Deportes (✆ *Calle C 1, next to Las Brisas, Bocas del Toro* ☎ *757–7007* ⊕ *www.superdeportes.com*) sells surf and skate wear and also rents boards for $20 a day.

ISLA COLÓN

172 km (107 mi) north of David, 2 km (1 mi) north of Bocas.

Though it is the most populated and developed island in the archipelago, Isla Colón is still a wild and beautiful place, with just two dirt roads, two lovely beaches, and significant swaths of tropical forest. The road from Bocas heads north along the isthmus that connects it to Isla Colón, where it soon enters the forest. About 3 km (2 mi) north of town there's a fork in the road where the left branch leads across the island to the beach and community of Bocas del Drago, and the right branch leads to the surf spots of Paunch and Dumpers and beautiful Bluff Beach.

The nicest and biggest beach on Isla Colón is **Bluff Beach** (*Veer right at the* Y *heading out of Bocas Town, continue 4 km north on the coastal road,*), a 7-km (3 ½-mi) stretch of golden sand backed by tropical vegetation and washed by aquamarine waters. It's a great place to spend a day, or even an hour, but it has neither restaurants nor shops nearby, so pack water and snacks. When the waves are big, Playa Bluff has a beach break right on shore, but it can also develop rip currents, so swimmers beware. When the sea is calm it's an excellent swimming beach, and the rocky points at either end have decent snorkeling. Massive leatherback sea turtles nest here from April to September, when a local group runs night tours to look for them. If you're lucky, you may find baby turtles on the beach between June and December.

Boca del Drago (✉ *14 km [9 mi] northwest of Bocas del Toro town*) is a tiny fishing community in the northwest corner of the island that overlooks the mainland across a channel of the same name. It has a narrow beach lined with coconut palms and other foliage that is much smaller than Bluff Beach, but the water there is almost always calm, which makes for good swimming and snorkeling. There are often starfish in the shallows, and the rocks farther out hold coral formations. It's a popular destination for boat tours, but can also be reached by a bus that makes the 40-minute trip from Bocas several times a day. A small restaurant on the beach serves decent seafood and always has plenty of cold beer. Halfway across the island, at the village of Colonia Santeña, is **La Gruta** (*The Grotto* ✉ *7 km [4 mi] north of Bocas, Colonia Santeña*), a bat-filled cave with a stream running out of it, surrounded by ferns and other foliage. Two statues of the Virgin Mary guard its entrance.

Swan's Cay (*Isla de los Pájaros* ✉ *5 km [3 mi] northeast of Boca del Drago*) is a rocky islet off the north coast of Isla Colón that is commonly visited on boat tours to Boca del Drago. The swan it was named for is actually the red-billed tropicbird, an elegant white seabird with a long tail and bright-red bill that nests on the island in significant numbers. Draped with lush foliage, the rugged island has a narrow, natural arch in the middle of it that boatmen can slip through when the seas are calm. The surrounding ocean is a good scuba-diving area.

GETTING HERE AND AROUND

Avenida G leads north from Bocas town over the isthmus to Isla Colón, where the road soon forks. Veer right for Bluff Beach and the surf breaks of Paunch and Dumpers, which can be reached in about 30 minutes on a very rough road by bicycle, or in an hour on foot. A taxi takes about 40 minutes, and costs $20. A boat to Paunch or Dumpers from Bocas town should cost $10. Bocas del Drago is accessible by boat, taxi, or bus. On weekdays buses depart from Parque Bolívar for Bocas del Drago at 6:45, 10, 12, 3, and 6, returning 40 minutes later. The trip costs $2. Taxis charge $20, but the boat trip is the same price, and includes Swan's Cay.

WHERE TO STAY

$$ ⊡ **Playa Mango Resort.** Located on Isla Colón's Big Creek Ranch, this place is far enough from town to be quiet but close enough to allow you to pop in for a meal or shopping. Rooms are just steps from the beach, each with a patio or balcony to admire the ocean view. The array of activities includes scuba diving, kayaking, horseback riding, jungle tours, and ATV tours. The rooms, in two-story cement buildings, won't win any decorating awards, but they're comfortable and have a queen or two single beds, sleeper sofas, a tiny kitchenette, DVD player, air conditioning, and ceiling fans. They surround a pool and grounds shaded by tropical trees with hammocks. **Pros:** on water; quiet; pool; abundant diversions. **Cons:** lousy beach; functional decor; bugs sometimes a problem. ⊠ *4 km (2 mi) north of Bocas del Toro town ☎ 6799–1162 or 843–564–6822 in U.S. ⊕ www.playamango.com ⇨ 15 rooms, 1 suite ⅃ In-room: no phone, kitchen, Wi-Fi. In-hotel: restaurant, room service, bar, pool, beachfront, diving, water sports, bicycles, laundry service, Wi-Fi, no-smoking rooms, airport shuttle ⊟ MC, V ⏇ CP.*

$$$$ ⊡ **Punta Caracol Acqua Lodge.** This collection of spacious bungalows
Fodor'sChoice above the turquoise shallows off Isla Colón's western coast is both
★ gorgeous and innovative. The hotel consists of nine wooden *cabañas* (bungalows) perched atop pilings, all connected to one another, the restaurant, and the mainland by wooden walkways over the ocean. Each cabaña has a living room downstairs that opens onto a wide porch with lounge chairs and a ladder leading down to the crystalline waters. Bedroom lofts hold a king bed or two twins with mosquito nets. The eco-lodge uses only solar energy, has its own sewage-treatment plant, and protects 2 hectares (148 acres) of rain forest and mangrove-forest reserve. Snorkeling, kayaks, breakfast, and dinner by candlelight are included in the rates, and the service is excellent. The isolated property forces guests to relax, which may not be for everyone. It is accessible only by a 15-minute boat trip from town. **Pros:** gorgeous setting; charming rooms; eco-friendly. **Cons:** overpriced; rooms can be hot; sometimes buggy. ⊠ *10 km (6 mi) northwest of Bocas town ☜ Punta Caracol, Isla Colón, Bocas del Toro ☎ 6612–1088 or 6676–7186 ⊕ www. puntacaracol.com ⇨ 8 cabañas, 1 suite ⅃ In-room: no a/c, no phone, safe, no TV. In-hotel: restaurant, bar, diving, water sports, laundry service, no-smoking rooms ⊟ AE, MC, V ⏇ MAP.*

6

SPORTS AND THE OUTDOORS
SCUBA DIVING AND SNORKELING

Isla Colón doesn't have great diving, but it does have good snorkeling, mostly along the west side of the island, which has scattered reefs along the mangrove islets, one of the best of which is in front of the Punta Caracol Acqualodge. Excursions to Boca del Drago and Swan's Cay also include snorkeling.

Barco Hundido (⊠ *Calle 1, at Av. Central, Bocas del Toro* ☎ *6512–9032*) offers snorkeling excursions along the reefs and mangroves west of Isla Colón.

SURFING

There are three good surf breaks on Isla Colón, all of them 5–7 km (3–4 mi) from Bocas. The best months for surfing are November to March, though there are often good swells in July and August. When it pumps, the waves have five- to nine-foot faces, and the reef breaks are hollow. They all require intermediate or expert skills. September and October tend to be the flattest months. There are waves about half the time the rest of the year.

Paunch is a reef break 5 km (3 mi) north of town, around the bend from the Playa Mango Resort, that you have to walk over a coral platform to reach. The best way to get there from town is by boat. It breaks mostly left, and is for intermediate to expert surfers.**Dumpers** is an excellent left reef break on the point north of Paunch, 7 km (4 mi) north of town. It is a quick, hollow wave that gets dangerous when big.**Bluff Beach** has a powerful beach break close to shore when there's a good swell.

TURTLE WATCHING

Playa Bluff (⊠ *Coastal road, 4 km north of Bocas Town*) is a nesting beach for the rare leatherback turtle from April to September, when night tours are led there by members of the Grupo Ecológico Bluff, who are mostly Ngöbe Indians.

Three-hour turtle-watching tours of Playa Bluff start at 9 PM and are arranged by **Suite Hotel Costes** (⊠ *Calle 3, Bocas del Toro* ☎ *757–9848*); they cost $10, plus $40 for transportation, split by the group. Wear long pants and shoes, and bring a flashlight and insect repellent.

ISLA CARENERO

½ km (¼ mi) east of Bocas Town.

Just east of Bocas—practically swimming distance—is a long, forested island called Isla Carenero (Careening Cay), the southern end of which holds a mix of fishermen's shacks, the large homes of foreigners, a few hotels, restaurants, and a small marina. Staying here is a quieter and more natural alternative to sleeping in town, since it has only 450 residents and no roads or automobiles. The island's name comes from the practice of using its narrow beach and shallows to pull ships onto their sides—careening—in order to scrape and repair their hulls. That beach is now dotted with homes and other buildings perched over the water on pilings. Since the island lacks a sewage system, swimming isn't recommended. The eastern side of the island has a rocky coast

PANAMA'S SEA TURTLES

Sea turtles have long been common in the archipelago, where they graze on sea-grass beds by day, and lay their eggs on its beaches by night. Bocas del Toro has a relatively healthy turtle population, which makes it a good place to see those endangered reptiles and an important place for their conservation. Divers may come upon a turtle near one of the reefs, or you can look for them at night on Playa Bluff. Four turtle species feed in the archipelago's waters, but only leatherback and hawksbill turtles nest here in significant numbers.

Hawksbills are the most beautiful marine turtles, thanks to their shiny marbled shells, which have also been their undoing—hawksbills have been hunted for their shells for centuries. Leatherbacks, on the other hand, have smooth, black carapaces that only a mother turtle could love. They are the largest of the sea turtles, and among the largest reptiles in the world, weighing more than half a ton.

From April to September, female turtles crawl slowly onto beaches in the darkness of night to bury their eggs in the sand. Hawksbills lay about 150 eggs the size of Ping-Pong balls, whereas leatherbacks lay fewer, but larger, elongated eggs.

Two months later, eggs hatch and babies dig their way out of the sand, and scurry toward the surf; that is, if nests survive. The area's inhabitants have long eaten turtle eggs, and hunted green turtles for their meat, considered a delicacy. In fact, the town of Bocas was founded by Afro-Caribbean turtle hunters from the island of San Andrés, who were drawn to the area by the abundance of hawksbill turtles. The scenario is common throughout the tropics, which is why sea-turtle species are endangered. Thankfully, the locals stopped hunting hawksbills years ago, and fewer people are now collecting eggs. Other threats to adult turtles include drowning in fishing nets or long lines. Also, leatherbacks sometimes choke on plastic bags, which resemble their favorite food, jellyfish.

The nesting beaches of Playa Larga, on Isla Bastimentos, and the Cayos Zapatillas, are protected within a national park. Members of **Grupo Ecológico Bluff** (☎ *6714–9162*) transplant eggs from nests on Playa Bluff to a hatchery that they guard, to ensure their survival. They also lead tours from May through October to look for nesting turtles at night, and the $10 fee tourists pay them supports their efforts.

but is more forested and sparsely populated, whereas its northern half holds only a handful of foreign-owned homes and a popular surf break known simply as Carenero.

GETTING HERE AND AROUND

Independent boatmen and the water-taxi companies in Bocas provide transportation across the channel between Carenero and town for $2.

WHERE TO STAY

$$ ⬛ **Casa Acuario.** The view from the rooms in this two-story building
★ over the water on the south side of Isla Carenero is of turquoise waters, boats, and the occasional seabird. The building has five spacious, airy

rooms with wooden floors, walls, and ceilings, cane furniture, and several big windows. They open onto wrap-around balconies with memorable views, and are equipped with air-conditioning, ceiling fans, and satellite TV. Rooms sleep up to four, and guests have access to a small beach beside the hotel. Inexpensive breakfasts are served on a deck in back. The owners are proprietors of J&J Boat Tours, so transport to nearby Isla Colón is never more than a phone call away. **Pros:** great views; nice rooms; large discounts for long-term stays. **Cons:** somewhat remote. ⊠ *Southern side of island* ☎ *757–9565* ⊕ *www. bocas.com/casa-acuario.htm* ⬙ *5 rooms* ⚄ *In-room: no phone, Wi-Fi. In-hotel: no-smoking rooms* ⊟ *No credit cards* ❍❘ *EP.*

> ## WORD OF MOUTH
>
> "I highly recommend staying on Carenero Island—there are no cars or roads, only palm trees and sandy grounds and it is 5 minutes by water taxi from Bocas town. There are several great restaurants and tiki bars over the water."
>
> —smgapp

$
Fodor's Choice
★

⛫ **Tierra Verde.** Although it's not directly on the water, this small hotel is tucked into a lush, tropical setting that lends an atmosphere of serenity and seclusion. Owned and operated by brothers Cookie and Ilya, the charming hotel has hardwood floors, French windows, rattan furniture, and a wrap-around balcony with ocean and jungle views. Each room comes with air-conditioning, hot water, a private bathroom, cable TV, and an orthopedic mattress. Two-bedroom suites are double the price but include walk-in closets, a living room, mini-fridge, and private balcony. In front of the property is a small dock with hammocks and chairs from which guests embark for boat trips to the surrounding islands. Since the owners are experienced surfers, they can arrange day-trips to local breaks. A stretch of beach and several restaurants are within walking distance of the hotel. And compared to lodging in Bocas Town, this cozy spot is a real bargain. **Pros:** bilingual owners always on site; in-room massages can be arranged, excellent value. **Cons:** no restaurant; bugs can be a problem. ⊠ *South side of the island, Isla Caranero* ☎ *757–9903* ⊕ *www.hoteltierraverde.com* ⬙ *7 rooms, 2 suites* ⚄ *In-room: no phone, refrigerator (some), Wi-Fi. In-hotel: bar, water sports, Internet terminal, airport shuttle* ⊟ *No credit cards* ❍❘ *CP.*

SPORTS AND THE OUTDOORS
SURFING
The left reef break on the northeast side of Carenero is very popular, since it is the closest break to Bocas and can be reached by an inexpensive, five-minute boat ride. There is also a small beach break on the northern end of the island for less experienced surfers.

ISLA SOLARTE

3 km (2 mi) east of Bocas Town.

Isla Solarte (called "Cayo Nancy" on some maps) is a long, forested island that is home to scattered Ngöbe families and a handful of foreigners. The most visited part of it is Hospital Point on its western tip, which lies just across the deep channel to the east of Isla Carenero.

The ocean around that point is one of the archipelago's most accessible dive sites, appropriate for both scuba and skin diving. It is named for a former hospital that was built to quarantine yellow-fever patients during Bocas del Toro's banana heyday. There are a few homes behind that point, but most of the island is covered with rain forest.

GETTING HERE AND AROUND

Independent boatmen and water-taxi companies in Bocas can take you snorkeling at Hospital Point, a good excursion if you're short of time. The Garden of Eden lodge arranges transportation for guests.

WHERE TO STAY

$$ ★ **Garden of Eden.** Rooms in this small lodge on a knoll in the mangroves of northern Isla Solarte overlook a soothing natural panorama of glassy waters and bright green foliage. The owners, from the Florida Keys, built three wooden rooms next to their home that have plenty of windows to take advantage of the view and breeze (they have fans, too). The "suite," below the poolside rooms, is worth the extra bucks, since it is more private. Breakfast is served beneath a thatch roof next to the pool, as is a succulent selection of lunch and dinner items ranging from barbecued ribs to grilled lobster tail. You can paddle kayaks through the mangroves or cross the bay to Red Frog Beach, a mile away. Tours can be arranged, as can massages and trips to town. **Pros:** great views; spacious rooms; nice pool; friendly. **Cons:** not on the beach; isolated; small grounds. ⊠ *North side of island* ☎ *700–0352 or 6487–4332* ⊕ *www.gardenofedenbocaspanama.com* ⊲ *2 rooms, 1 suite* ₺ *In-room: no a/c, no phone, no TV, Wi-Fi. In-hotel: restaurant, pool, water sports* ⊟ *AE, MC, V.*

LAGUNA BOCATORITO

Sheltered between the islands and the mainland on the southern end of the gulf is Laguna Bocatorito, a large lagoon frequented by schools of bottlenose dolphins. Hidden behind a mess of mangrove islets, it is a lovely area where the cetaceans play in tranquil waters. Independent boatmen and tour operators in Bocas include a quick visit to Bocatorito in day tours to the archipelago's other attractions, often referring to it as "Dolphin Bay." There is no guarantee you'll see dolphins, but most people do; they tend to be more abundant between December and March and June to August.

6

ISLA BASTIMENTOS

Isla Bastimentos covers 52 square km (20 square mi) of varied landscapes, including lush tropical forest, mangrove estuaries, a lake, and several of the archipelago's nicest beaches. It also has several Afro-Caribbean and Ngöbe indigenous communities, and some excellent snorkeling and surfing spots. Old Bank, the archipelago's second-largest town, overlooks a cove on the island's western tip. A 2-km (1-mi) trail leads north from there to a gorgeous swath of sand called Wizard's Beach. The island's northern coast holds four beaches separated by rocky points, the longest of which, (Playa Larga), lies within Parque Nacional Marino Isla Bastimentos. This park also protects a swath of

MANGROVE FORESTS

As you zip across the glassy waters between the islands, you can admire the bright green foliage of mangroves lining the emerald sea. Most of the coastal forest on Bocas del Toro's islands and the bulk of its countless islets are dominated by the red mangrove. This unusual tree with long, red stilt roots that prop it up in the shallows, thrives in saltwater, which is poisonous to most trees. Together with the black and white mangroves and various other plants, the red mangrove forms coastal forests in estuaries and on islets throughout the tropics. Mangrove estuaries are eerily beautiful ecosystems spread between the land and the sea. If you look closely at one you may see barnacles and algae growing on the mangroves' tubular roots, and crabs, shrimp, or small fish around them. Dozens of commercially important fish and seafood species spend the early stages of their lives in the mangroves, which make them a vital component of the ocean's complex web of life. They can also harbor legions of mosquitoes and no-see-ums, so bring your insect repellent if you're going to explore a mangrove estuary.

rain forest and the nearby islands of Cayos Zapatillas. Bastimentos's southern side is lined with mangrove forests and dozens of mangrove islets. There you'll find the indigenous community of Bahia Honda and the beginning of a trail across the island to the second beach, known as Red Frog Beach.

The island's long southeast coast is more distant and remote, taking 40 minutes to reach from Bocas by boat. It lies near the archipelago's best skin-diving spots—Crawl Cay and Cayos Zapatillas—and is backed by thick jungle that is home to an array of wildlife and a small Ngöbe community called Salt Creek. A narrow, forest-lined beach stretches along the coast near Old Point on the island's northeast tip. The coast's southern point, Macca Bite, is hemmed by mangroves, perfect for kayak exploration, and is next to the archipelago's most popular snorkeling spot, Crawl Cay. A short boat ride to the east of either point takes you to the bleached sand and vast coral gardens of the paradisiacal Cayos Zapatillas. There is enough to see and do in the area that you could spend a week boating, swimming, hiking, and paddling through its natural treasures.

OLD BANK (BASTIMENTOS)

4 km (2½ mi) east of Bocas.

Spread along a bay on the island's western tip, between the ocean and forested hills, is a colorful collection of simple wooden buildings known as Old Bank, or Bastimentos town. It is a predominantly Afro-Caribbean community where Guari-Guari—a mix of patois English and traces of Spanish—is the lingua franca. Most people live in elevated wooden houses, some awfully rudimentary, that line sidewalks and dirt paths instead of streets. It's a poor and crowded but friendly place, where children play in the dugout canoes pulled up on shore, families

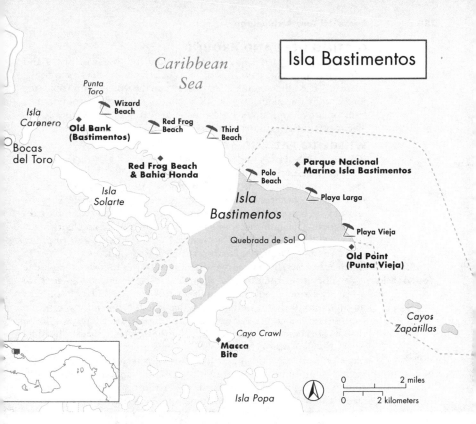

Isla Bastimentos

Caribbean Sea

Punta Toro

Wizard Beach

Isla Carenero

Red Frog Beach

Old Bank (Bastimentos)

Third Beach

Bocas del Toro

Red Frog Beach & Bahia Honda

Polo Beach

Parque Nacional Marino Isla Bastimentos

Isla Solarte

Isla Bastimentos

Playa Larga

Quebrada de Sal

Playa Vieja

Old Point (Punta Vieja)

Cayos Zapatillas

Cayo Crawl

Macca Bite

0 — 2 miles
0 — 2 kilometers

Isla Popa

chat in the shade beneath their homes, and men play dominoes at the local bars. Most of Old Bank's men work in construction or survive off tourism. Old Bank is the home of an authentic calypso band with a not-too-original name—the Beach Boys—who rock the town on Monday nights: Blue Mondays. Old Bank doesn't have a proper sewage system, so swimming in the bay is not recommended, even though the local kids do. Rather, head to one of the nearby beaches instead.

A 20-minute hike north of Old Bank on a trail through cow pastures and forest patches takes you to **Wizard's Beach** *(First Beach)*, a splendid swath of pale sand hemmed by lush vegetation. The wide beige beach extends into turquoise shallows that are perfect for swimming when the sea is calm, and there are large coral reefs around the points on either end of the beach. When the ocean is rough, however, this beach can develop strong rip currents that make swimming dangerous. Surfers enjoy the beach break, but when the swell gets really big, it closes out and is dangerous for surfers, too. The trail to Wizard Beach starts at the east edge of town, just past the soccer field and is sometimes muddy. On the east end of the beach, another footpath leads into the forest to Red Frog Beach, less than 1 km (½ mi) away.

GETTING HERE AND AROUND

Small boats regularly carry people between the towns of Bocas and Old Bank during the day. They depart Bocas from the dock next to the Farmacia Rosa Blanca and Bastimentos from the Muelle Municipal (the long dock in the middle of town). The majority of Bastimentos boatmen hang out at Chow Kai, the hardware store next to Bocas Marine Tours. The trip takes 10 minutes and costs $2 each way.

WHERE TO EAT AND STAY

¢–$$

CARIBBEAN

★

✕**Roots.** Perched over the sea near the center of Old Bank, this rustic, open-air restaurant is known for serving authentic *bocatoreña* food. House specialties include Caribbean chicken (in a mildly spicy sauce), fresh lobster, shrimp, and conch, listed as "snail" on the menu. They are served with a hearty mix of coconut rice, red beans, and a simple cabbage salad. The ambience—a thatch roof with tables and chairs made from tree trunks—is equally authentic. ⊠ *On the water east of police post* ☎ 6473–5111 ▭ *No credit cards* ◷ *Closed Tues.*

$$$–$$$$

Fodor's Choice

★

▦ **Eclypse de Mar.** Built over the water on stilts, this luxurious eco-lodge is the ultimate Caribbean fantasy. Each of its six bungalows comes with a private terrace, ceiling fan, and hot shower. Glass slats have been inserted into the hardwood floors so that guests can admire marine life from inside the bedroom. Adding to the elegance are large windows, thatch roofs, and satin curtains draped over queen-size beds. The hotel runs on solar power, has its own water supply from a spring, and includes a private garden that leads to 6½ acres of rain forest where sloths, birds, butterflies, and red frogs roam. Snorkeling trips to surrounding islands can be arranged, or for those who prefer to paddle closer to the lodge, a glass-bottom kayak is available upon request. Although not as private, there are two standard rooms in the main building for half the price of the bungalows. Built like Punta Caracol, this is half the cost yet still offers pampering and luxury without the feeling you're being quarantined. Additional restaurant options can be found in Bocas, just a 10-minute boat ride away. **Pros:** friendly staff; remote location; innovative design. **Cons:** basic breakfast; loud music can sometimes be heard from Old Bank. ⊠ *Bastimentos Island* ☎ 6430–7576 or 6627–3000 ⊕ *www.eclypsedemar.com* ⇖ *2 rooms, 6 bungalows* ⚴ *In-room: no a/c, no phone, no TV, safe, Wi-Fi. In-hotel: restaurant, room service, bar, beachfront, water sports, Wi-Fi, no kids under 10.* ▭ *AE, MC, V* ◷ *CP.*

SPORTS AND THE OUTDOORS

SCUBA DIVING AND SNORKELING

Old Bank lies closer to Bocas than most of the archipelago's other dive spots, and the local dive operator is less expensive than the dive shops in town, making it an attractive departure point for scuba diving or snorkeling excursions.

Dive Panama (☎ 6567–1812 ⊕ *www.thedutchpirate.com*) is a small, Dutch-owned outfitter in Old Bank that offers inexpensive boat dives, snorkeling excursions, and PADI certification courses. Since the outfit is not located in Bocas Town, you can be picked up at the airport, water taxi stop, or your hotel if you call ahead of time.

SURFING

The north coast of Isla Bastimentos has half a dozen surf breaks, some of which are very hard to reach. **Wizard's Beach** has a fun beach break when the waves are small, but when the swell is big, the beach and nearby point break develop serious currents and require experience. **Silverbacks** is an experts-only reef break in front of the point west of Wizard's Beach that is the only place to surf when a big swell hits. A few times a year it gets over 10 feet high, and it can be surfed when the swell reaches 20 feet, which periodically happens.

RED FROG BEACH AND BAHIA HONDA

8 km (5 mi) east of Bocas, 4 km (2½ mi) east of Old Bank.

A couple of miles east of Old Bank, Isla Bastimentos gets narrow— a mere ½ km (¼ mi) wide—and the sea to the south of it is dotted with mangrove islets. Here you'll find a small dock that marks the entrance to a footpath across the island to Red Frog Beach, one of the loveliest spots in the archipelago, with its golden sand shaded by tropical trees. East of the beach, the island becomes wide again, and is largely covered with lush rain forest that is home to everything from mealy parrots to white-faced capuchin monkeys and countless tiny, bright red poison dart frogs. The scattered homes of local Ngöbe line the bay to the south, known as Bahia Honda, where an indigenous organization has cut a trail through the forest and built a rustic restaurant for tourists. To the east is Parque Nacional Marino Isla Bastimentos and to the south a narrow channel through the mangroves that is the main route to the island's eastern coast and the Cayos Zapatillas.

Remarkable natural beauty and relative accessibility (a five-minute walk from a dock) combine to make **Red Frog Beach** (⊠ *4 km east of Old Bank*) one of the most popular spots in Bocas del Toro. The beach is almost a mile long, with golden sand backed by coconut palms, Indian almond trees, and other tropical greenery. It's the perfect spot for lounging on the sand, playing in the sea, and admiring the amazing scenery. Unfortunately, the area's pristine beauty is threatened by U.S. developers who are bulldozing 70 hectares (173 acres) to build condos, tourist facilities, and a 150-boat marina. A tiny, rustic bar behind the beach sells basic Panamanian lunches and rents snorkeling equipment. When the sea is calm, you can snorkel over the large coral reef off the point on the west end of the beach. ⚠ Red Frog is usually a good swimming beach, but when the surf is up, rip currents can make it dangerous, so don't go beyond waist-deep if the waves are big. To escape the crowd, hike 40 minutes around the point on Red Frog Beach's eastern end to **Polo Beach,** named for a hermit who lived there for years until he sold his land to developers. Finding Polo Beach can be difficult because there are a few places where you have to leave the beach and take a trail, but you are always sticking close to the shoreline. Serious scuba divers should check out the big reef around the island northeast of this beach. The owner of the dock and the land that the trail crosses charges $3 to enter Red Frog Beach.

About 20 Ngöbe homes are scattered around **Bahia Honda** (☎ 6592–5162 *for the restaurant, 6619–5364 for La Loma Jungle Lodge, 6726–0968 for guide Rutilio Milton*), and a group of indigenous families runs a rustic restaurant about five to 10 minutes by boat from the Red Frog dock. Funded by the World Bank in 2002 as part of the Mesoamerican Biological Corridor Project, the restaurant is administered mostly by the women of Bahia Honda. Hiking and boating tours, organized through La Loma Jungle Lodge or directly with local guide Rutilio Milton (call one day in advance to arrange the tour), include exploration of a cave with a stream running out of it and plenty of bats clinging to the stalactite-laden ceiling. The adventure also includes a simple lunch, a weaving demonstration, and a chance to purchase handicrafts such as *chácaras* (colorful woven jute bags).

GETTING HERE AND AROUND

Most day tours to Crawl Cay cost around $20 and include a stop at Dolphin Bay, Hospital Point, and Red Frog Beach before heading back to Bocas. Boat operators will drop you off at Red Frog Beach for $3–$5 from Old Bank and $6–$10 from Bocas, and will pick you up at a specified time. It is possible to hike between Old Bank and Red Frog Beach, a distance of about 4 km (2 mi). Footpaths through the forest connect Red Frog to Wizard Beach, which is a short hike from Old Bank. However, it is recommended to walk only with a guide due to reported robberies that have occurred on the trail.

WHERE TO STAY

$$$ **La Loma Jungle Lodge.** A boat ride through mangroves and a walk
Fodor's Choice across wooden planks will lead you to the tastefully rustic bungalows
★ at this eco-lodge. Perched along a hillside in the rain forest, the wall-less bungalows offer 180-degree views of tropical nature. Oropendolas sing in the treetops, hummingbirds flit about, and sloths cling to the branches overhead. The idealistic owners designed the lodge to limit negative environmental impact and to maximize the benefit to their Ngöbe neighbors using wood from fallen trees and solar power and kerosene lamps. It sits in a 23-hectare (58-acre) private forest reserve with a botanical garden and organic farm, where the owners grow cacao and other food used in sumptuous Panamanian dinners. Spacious bungalows are exposed to jungle life on three sides, though canvas curtains can be drawn when it's rainy or windy. Bungalows have good beds with mosquito nets, handmade furniture, hammocks, and bathrooms inspired by Ngöbe architecture. Although bungalow 1 has electricity and is close to the main lodge, bungalows 2 and 3 offer better views of the secluded bay. Meals, jungle hikes, dugout canoes, and transport to Red Frog Beach are included in the rates, plus you can arrange other inexpensive day tours. **Pros:** in the jungle; friendly; conscientious; good tours of Bastimentos bat caves. **Cons:** very rustic; steep climb to rooms; paths are extremely dark at night. ⊠ *Bahia Honda* ☐ *Entrega General, Isla Colón, Bocas del Toro* ☎ *6619–5364 or 6592–5162* ⊕ *www.thejunglelodge.com* ↪ *3 bungalows* ⬧ *In-room: no a/c, no phone, safe, no TV. In-hotel: restaurant* ☐ *No credit cards* ⦿ *FAP.*

MACCA BITE

20 km (12 mi) southeast of Bocas.

The southernmost point on Isla Bastimento has an odd name, and its origin is as mysterious as Bocas del Toro's, though the theory is that wild macaws once lived there (there are now tame ones at the eponymous lodge). That hilly headland hemmed by mangroves and draped with lush rain forest is a mere 30 minutes from Bocas by boat, yet it feels like the end of the world. Far from the nearest road or streetlight, it is a place where Mother Nature still reigns, where dolphins swim and monkeys roam. The point has two lodges on it that provide constant exposure to nature—one at the edge of the sea, and one at the top of the hill—as well as restaurants that can reward you with a cold beer and fresh seafood after a hard morning of snorkeling.

Just east of Macca Bite is **Crawl Cay** *(Coral Cay)*, a large coral reef that's between five and 35 feet deep. The underwater garden holds an impressive array of coral heads, colorful sponges, large sea fans, and hundreds of small reef fish. It is an excellent spot for snorkelers, who can simply float over the reef and watch the show. The reef also has enough marine life in and around its innumerable crannies to entertain experienced divers. It is sufficiently sheltered that the water there is usually calm and clear, even when the sea is too rough for diving at Cayos Zapatillas. The nearby Crawl Cay Restaurant and its competitors serve cold drinks and fresh seafood on decks built over the water. Order your food before you go snorkeling to avoid a long wait.

GETTING HERE AND AROUND

Tranquilo Bay lodge provides free transportation to and from Bocas on Wednesday and Saturday but charges $100 for the trip on other days. Hotel Macca Bite charges $50 for round-trip transportation. Rates are per trip, not per passenger.

WHERE TO STAY

$$–$$$ ▦ **Hotel Macca Bite.** Perched at the edge of the point, between the mangroves and the sea, this comfortable hotel has inspiring views of crystalline waters dotted with coral heads, the ocean horizon, and nearby Isla Popa. Colorful rooms are in two-story wooden buildings and have varnished wood floors, two queen beds, and nice tile baths. The "suites" are bigger, with high ceilings and more furniture. All rooms open onto wide porches suspended over the water and are perfect for watching needlefish, puffers, and pelicans. What distinguishes this place from comparable lodges is its local ownership and amenities such as air-conditioning and satellite TV. A small, open-air restaurant over the water serves mostly fresh seafood. Behind it are a garden and a patch of forest with tame macaws and monkeys. You can rent snorkeling equipment and kayaks and take tours to nearby Cayos Zapatillas and other spots. **Pros:** on the water; great view; well-equipped rooms; snorkeling; excursions. **Cons:** remote; no transportation at night; occasional no-see-ums. ⊠ *Crawl Cay* ✑ *Apdo 1851-0834, Panama City* ☎ *6673–5155 or 264–5255* ⊕ *www.hotelmaccabite.com* ⬛ *8 room, 3 suites* ⚭ *In-hotel: restaurant, bar, water sports, no-smoking rooms* ▤ *AE, MC, V* ⦿ *MAP.*

$$$$ ⬚ **Popa Paradise Beach Resort.** South of Macca Bite, on the northeastern
☾ tip of Isla Popa, this barefoot luxury resort sits on a white-sand beach
Fodor's Choice backed by 25 acres of tropical rain forest. Winding through the property
★ are freshwater streams, hiking trails, and stone pathways that lead to 10
cottages and a 5,000-square-foot clubhouse. Everything here was built
by hand or transported by a canoe that now rests on the banks of the
hotel's property. Rooms, decorated with silk bedding and Balinese furniture, have air-conditioning, cable TV, DVD players, and large balconies
that face the Zapatillas Cays. Located 200 yards from shore is a shallow
reef where guests can snorkel, kayak, and fish. There are plenty of other
diversions including an infinity pool, volleyball, game room, and boat
trips to Sandubidi (a primitive Ngöbe village). The hotel's restaurant
serves incredibly fresh fish, and everything is prepared with ingredients
from the hotel's own garden. To minimize the resort's environmental
impact, the owners utilize solar panels for power and fresh-water wells.
Pros: family-friendly; excellent food; courteous staff. **Cons:** paths are
dark at night; murky swimming pool; lodge rooms lack character. ⊠ *Isla
Popa* ☎ *832–1498 or 6550–2505* ⊕ *www.popaparadisebeachresort.
com* ⤳ *10 cottages, 5 lodge rooms, 2 suites, 1 penthouse* ⚑ *In-room:
safe, no phone, kitchen (some), refrigerator (some), DVD, Wi-Fi (some).
In-hotel: restaurant, room service, bars, pool, spa, beachfront, diving,
water sports, laundry service, business center, Wi-Fi* ⊟ *MC, V* ⊘ *BP.*

$$$$ ⬚ **Tranquilo Bay.** This all-inclusive jungle lodge is geared toward active
★ travelers—you can kayak, snorkel, hike, surf, or fish, or just stroll the
beach and lounge in a hammock, all amid amazing scenery. The young
American owners offer stays of three, four, or seven-nights in well-
equipped bungalows spread along a forested ridge with panoramic
ocean and island views. Spacious and comfortable, the bungalows have
two queen beds, large bathrooms, air-conditioning, and wrap-around
porches; four view the sea, two the forest. The lodge's 50-hectare (125-
acre) rain-forest reserve borders the national park. Daily tours head to
spots such as the Cayos Zapatillas, Indian villages, various reefs, and
remote isles and beaches. Meals and cocktails are served in a lovely
dining-living room in the main building. **Pros:** varied activities; wild
surroundings; nice rooms; good food. **Cons:** expensive; remote; three-
night minimum stay. ⊠ *Macca Bite, Isla Bastimentos* ⊡ *PTY 12006,
4440 NW 73rd St., Miami, FL 33166* ☎ *380–0721; 713/589-6952 in
U.S.* ⊕ *www.tranquilobay.com* ⤳ *6 bungalows* ⚑ *In-room: no phone,
no TV. In-hotel: restaurant, bar, water sports, laundry service, Internet
terminal* ⊟ *AE, MC, V* ⊘ *Closed June* ⧉ *AI.*

SPORTS AND THE OUTDOORS

The Macca Bite lodges lie near some of the archipelago's best dive sites
and offer daily snorkeling excursions and kayaking. Tranquilo Bay also
offers jungle hiking, sportfishing, and surfing.

COSTA RICA BORDER CROSSING

Bocas del Toro lies geographically close to the Costa Rican beach towns of Puerto Viejo and Cahuita, but traveling between the two isn't as easy as it could be. It usually takes four to five hours to make the trip by land, though it can take longer due to infrequent bus service from the Costa Rican border post of Sixaola. From Bocas, take a water taxi to Almirante, where share taxis frequently leave on the 20-minute trip to Guabito, on the border with Costa Rica. It takes about 30 minutes to cross the border, which includes walking across the Sixaola River on an old railroad bridge. After that, you have to wait for the next bus to Limón, or San José, all of which stop at Puerto Viejo (2 hours) and Cahuita (2½ hours). It is quicker (though considerably more expensive) to take a Nature Air flight to Limón (December–April only) and hire a taxi to take you to Cahuita or Puerto Viejo, a 60- or 80-minute trip south. Year-round, flights are available from San José to Bocas del Toro. Keep in mind that Panama is one hour ahead of Costa Rica.

OLD POINT (PUNTA VIEJA)

8 km (5 mi) northeast of Macca Bite, 28 km (17 mi) southeast of Bocas.

The northeast point of Isla Bastimentos, known as Old Point, is covered with jungle and surrounded by coral reefs. It probably looks about the same as it did when Christopher Columbus sailed through the archipelago five centuries ago, aside from the small hotels nestled in the forest. It's just a 40-minute boat ride from the ATMs and Internet cafés of Bocas. It is thus an easy place to get away from it all and immerse yourself in nature at its finest. A narrow beach lines the coast between Old Point and Salt Creek, and it is backed by exuberant tropical flora where birdsong complements the lapping of the waves against the sand. The ocean bottom here is a bit mucky, but the water is usually calm, and there are coral reefs in the deeper water near the point. A couple of trails lead into the rain forest, one to the nicer, wider beach of Playa Larga, on the island's northern shore.

At the southern end of Punta Vieja that faces Isla Popa, a trail leads to the Ngöbe village of **Salt Creek**, where you can see how the locals live, snap a few photos, or buy indigenous handicrafts such as *chácaras*.

GETTING HERE AND AROUND

Transportation to Al Natural is included in rates. Boatmen in Bocas charge about $60–$80 for a trip to Old Point.

WHERE TO STAY

$$–$$$$
Fodor'sChoice
★

Al Natural. This rustic eco-lodge offers intimate contact with nature by using solar lighting, propane hot-water showers, and ocean breezes in lieu of fans. Bungalows, nestled in the forest behind the beach, are surprisingly exposed, with hardly a wall to them, just mosquito nets, and canvas curtains you can pull shut to protect from wind and rain. The result is a panorama of tropical greenery and turquoise waters visible from your bed. It's Mies van der Rohe—the Bauhaus architect who said "less is more"—meets Robinson Crusoe, with lacquered hardwoods, thatch roofs, and tiny bathrooms. You can stroll the beach, swim in the shallows, or kayak out to the coral reef. All-inclusive packages that include trips to Salt Creek and the Cayos Zapatillas are recommended. Meals are served in a two-story, rustic restaurant, and the dinners are excellent Caribbean-Continental concoctions. The second night is less expensive. Pros: jungle; beach; tranquility; good food; friendly service. Cons: very rustic; few diversions; breakfast and lunch are light. ⊠ *Old Point* ⏚ *Entrega General, Isla Colón, Bocas del Toro* ☎ *757–9004, 6496–0776, or 6576–8605* ⊕ *www.alnaturalresort.com* ⟆ *7 bungalows* ⚲ *In-room: no a/c, no phone, no TV. In-hotel: restaurant, beachfront, water sports* ⊟ *No credit cards* ⊙ *Closed May and June* ⧀ *FAP.*

PARQUE NACIONAL MARINO ISLA BASTIMENTOS

★ About one third of Isla Bastimentos and the two Cayos Zapatillas, to the southeast, lie within **Parque Nacional Marino Isla Bastimentos** *(Bastimentos Island National Marine Park).* The park's 13,226 hectares (32,668 acres) comprise an array of ecosystems ranging from sea-grass beds to rain forest and include some spectacular and ecologically important areas. A few of these are a large lake on Bastimentos, the vast expanses of coral reef to the north and east of the island, and the beaches of Playa Larga and Cayos Zapatillas, which are nesting areas for several sea-turtle species. **Playa Larga** is a long, pristine beach on the northern coast of Isla Bastimentos, so remote that few people make it there. It is nearly impossible to visit it at night, when turtles nest, which makes Playa Bluff a better option for turtle-watching. Playa Larga is most easily visited from Old Point, where a trail leads through the forest to that seemingly endless ribbon of windswept sand. Much of the park is virtually inaccessible, especially the island's forested interior, but you can see most of its flora and fauna in the private reserves of adjacent jungle lodges. That wildlife includes tiny, bright-red poison dart frogs, green iguanas, two-toed sloths, ospreys, parrots, toucans, and collared manakins. The park's coral reefs protect even greater biological diversity, including spiny lobsters, sea stars, barracuda, various snapper species, and countless colorful reef fish.

Most people experience the park's reefs at **Cayos Zapatillas,** two cays southeast of Bastimentos that are the park's crown jewels. Their name translates as "Slipper Cays," which may be due to their shoelike shapes. Those small, elongated isles with ivory sand shaded by coconut palms have the kind of picture-perfect tropical scenery that northern travel companies put in their brochures. The Cayos' most impressive scenery, however, is actually in the surrounding ocean, which holds 500 hectares (1,235 acres) of protected coral reef ranging from a shallow platform around the islands to steep walls pocked with caves. Scuba divers can explore the reef's outer expanses, while snorkelers can enjoy views of the shallow platform adorned with some impressive coral formations. The park tends to have more fish than Crawl Cay and other unprotected dive spots, and divers can expect to see tiny angelfish, parrot fish, squirrelfish, octopi, eels, stingrays, and countless other marine creatures. When seas are rough (as they often are between December and March), scuba diving is limited to the leeward side of the island, making Crawl Cay a more attractive dive spot at that time. There is a ranger station on the island, and a small nature trail through the forest. Bring sunblock, insect repellent, a hat, a towel, water, and snorkeling gear. ☎ *758–6822* ✉ *$10* ☺ *Daily 6–6.*

6

Eastern Panama

WITH KUNA YALA (SAN BLAS
ISLANDS) AND THE DARIÉN

WORD OF MOUTH

"Being on a small, relatively isolated island [in the San Blas Archipelago], was such a wonderfully unique experience, and lazing around on a hammock, outside your overwater cabana, just listening to the water—paradise. (Though for me, longer than three days, would have been too much vegging out)."

—janeq

By David
Dudenhoefer
Updated by
Jeffrey Van
Fleet

The eastern provinces of Kuna Yala and the Darién are Panama at its most pristine, with spectacular scenery, wildlife, and indigenous cultures that have barely changed since the first Spanish explorers arrived here more than five centuries ago.

The region's riveting tropical nature ranges from the colorful diversity of Caribbean coral reefs to amazing birdlife of the rain forest. The traditional Kuna, Emberá, and Wounaan communities that live here offer a fascinating alternative to the modern world. The combination of nature and culture provides the ingredients for unforgettable journeys, on which you might imagine you've traveled back in time or perhaps to the very ends of the Earth. Yet most of the region's lodges lie within a 60-minute flight from Panama City, which is often followed by a dugout canoe trip over aquamarine waters or up a jungle-shaded river. And the flights themselves take you over vast expanses of pure jungle. When it comes to Kuna Yala and the Darién, more than in any other part of Panama, the adventure begins the moment you board your flight.

Nevertheless, true adventure has its price, and it's not for everyone. This region's remarkable but remote attractions lie far from the nearest paved road, convenience store, or ATM, and may require that you put up with conditions you wouldn't stand for at home. Tours and accommodations can be quite expensive; for the cost of a suite in Panama City you may have to settle for a thatched hut with a shared bathroom. You may also have to deal with insects or less-than-fantastic food, but the prize is exposure to extraordinary wildlife, splendid scenery, and unique indigenous cultures. Your adventure may include boat trips to breathtaking islands, jungle hikes, snorkeling over coral reefs, or witnessing ancient rituals. And at night you'll hear only the calls of jungle critters or the slosh of waves against coral.

ORIENTATION AND PLANNING

ORIENTATION

Kuna Yala stretches along Panama's northeast coast from the Central Caribbean eastward to the border with Colombia, comprising everything from forested mountains to the sea beyond the San Blas Islands. The entire province was once called San Blas, but it is known now by its indigenous name, Kuna Yala, which translates as "Land of the Kuna." Only one road penetrates the otherwise isolated province, a dirt track called the Camino Llano-Cartí that traverses its western end. The eastern half of the narrow indigenous territory borders the vast Darién province, the southern half of which holds Parque Nacional Darién, various smaller reserves, and two *comarcas* (indigenous territories). The Carretera Interamericana (Inter-American Highway) is a rutted, muddy

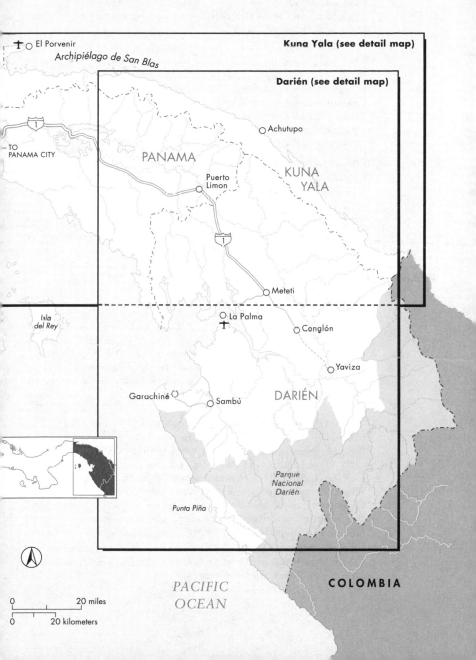

Eastern Panama

Caribbean Sea

El Porvenir
Archipiélago de San Blas

Kuna Yala (see detail map)

Darién (see detail map)

Achutupo

PANAMA

KUNA YALA

TO PANAMA CITY

Puerto Limón

Meteti

Isla del Rey

La Palma

Conglón

Yaviza

Garachiné

Sambú

DARIÉN

Parque Nacional Darién

Punta Piña

COLOMBIA

PACIFIC OCEAN

0   20 miles

0   20 kilometers

TOP REASONS TO GO

Indigenous Cultures. Eastern Panama's indigenous Kuna, Emberá, and Wounaan villages are amazingly traditional, colorful places that provide visitors with unforgettable cross-cultural experiences.

San Blas Islands. The islands of Kuna Yala have ivory beaches shaded by coconut palms and washed by turquoise waters—scenery fit for the covers of travel magazines or the daydreams of snowbound accountants.

Ocean Treasures. Kuna Yala's crystalline sea holds countless coral reefs awash with living rainbows of fish and invertebrates, whereas the white-sand shallows of its islands are idyllic spots for a tranquil swim.

Spectacular Wildlife. The eastern provinces' lush rain forests, mangrove swamps, and cloud forests together hold more than about 500 bird species, and everything from crocodiles to capuchin monkeys.

Fabulous Fishing. More than 250 sport-fishing records have been set in the sea south of the Darién, and you can troll out from one of the world's best fishing lodges.

track in the Darién, where it dead-ends at a frontier town called Yaviza, beyond which there are virtually no roads. Most travelers consequently fly in and out of both regions. There are daily flights to Kuna Yala and twice-weekly flights to the Darién.

PLANNING

WHEN TO GO

It rains almost every afternoon from May to December in the Darién, though the rain lets up a bit in July and August. Most people consequently visit the region from January to May. Kuna Yala has similar seasons, though it gets less rain in September and October, and more in December and January. The sea tends to be rough here from January to April. The best diving months are August to November, when the seas tend to be calm and visibility is better.

BY AIR

The only way to get to most parts of Kuna Yala and the Darién is to fly. The domestic airlines Air Panama and Aeroperlas offer daily flights to several airstrips in Kuna Yala (Achutupo, El Porvenir, Mamitupo, Playón Chico, and Río Sidra) and the Darién (Bahía Piñas and La Palma). ⚠ **Flights often land at several airstrips, so make sure you get off at the correct one!** Charter flights to Santa Cruz de Cana and Bahía Piñas are arranged by lodges based in those locations. There are neither airline offices nor real airports in this region, only simple airstrips, although La Palma has a tiny airport.

Contacts Aeroperlas (☎ *315–7500* ⊕ *www.aeroperlas.com*) **Aeropuerto Ramón Xatruch** (✉ *2 km [1.2 mi] south of La Palma* ☎ *299–6217*) **Air Panama** (☎ *316–9000* ⊕ *www.flyairpanama.com*).

BY BOAT

Motorized dugouts are the most common form of transportation in Kuna Yala and the Darién, where most people travel via jungle rivers. Some of the better lodges in Kuna Yala transport guests in small fiberglass boats, whereas the Tropic Star fishing lodge, in southwest Darién, uses more seaworthy vessels. Most people simply fly in and out of Kuna Yala or the Darién, but you can charter a boat for longer trips in either of them. That can be expensive, and you'll need to speak Spanish or travel with a guide. Most visitors to this region do either the Darién or Kuna Yala. Direct travel between the two provinces means spending a week hiking through the jungle.

Boat transportation is included in the rates of all Kuna Yala hotels and lodges near La Palma. Private boats can be hired at Kuna Yala lodges for special trips, such as to Cayos Holandeses or to nearby areas, but those trips can cost $100 to $200. Boats can also be hired through the Hotel Baquirú Bagará in La Palma for trips to nearby Emberá communities for $100 to $200.

Several cruise lines, including CruiseWest, Holland America, Princess, Seabourn, Silversea, and Windstar make port calls in the San Blas Islands on select Panama Canal and western Caribbean itineraries; CruiseWest also sails to an Emberá village in the Darién. You'll be tendered ashore. The Kuna levy a $5 tax on cruise visitors. It may or may not be included in the price of your shore excursion. The total absence of restaurants means that cruise visits are kept short—usually just under a half-day—with time to be back on ship for the next meal.

BY BUS

Several buses depart from Panama City's Albrook Bus Terminal every morning for Yaviza, where boats can be hired to El Real, but it's a rough 10- to 12-hour trip, and neither town has a decent hotel.

The only part of Kuna Yala that can be reached by road is the western El Porvenir area, via the rough Llano–Cartí road. **Denesio Ramos** (☎ 6695–3229) runs a simple bus service to Cartí, where boats can be hired to lodges near El Porvenir and Río Sidra, departing from Panama City's Plaza Cinco de Mayo daily at 5 AM and returning at 10 AM.

RESTAURANTS

This isn't the part of Panama you head to for epicurean delights. You can count on fresh seafood in Kuna Yala—and little else. If you don't eat seafood, you should mention it when you reserve and again when you arrive. Establishments usually offer lobster, except March through May, when fishing for lobster and all other shellfish is prohibited. Nothing resembling a sit-down restaurant exists in these provinces, so most hotels include three meals in their rates, usually served family-style at fixed times. Purified water, coffee, tea, and fruit juices are free; bottled soft drinks and alcoholic beverages usually cost extra and come with a hefty price tag.

ABOUT THE HOTELS

Most accommodations in this part of Panama range from comfortably rustic to downright primitive. Only Kuna are allowed to own businesses in Kuna Yala; a waga (foreigner) is prohibited from holding property

A BIT OF HISTORY

The first European to visit this part of Panama was Rodrigo de Bastidas, a Spanish explorer who sailed along the San Blas Islands in 1501. The following year Christopher Columbus made it to the coast near El Porvenir on his final voyage to the Americas. In 1510 conquistador Vasco Nuñez de Balboa founded the first Spanish town in Central America, Santa María la Antigua del Darién, in a bay on the eastern end of Kuna Yala. Three years later Balboa departed from Santa María with a group of men to look for a sea that local people had told him lay to the south. After hiking through the Darién jungle for several weeks, Balboa reached the Gulf of San Miguel, where he became the first European to lay eyes on an ocean he dubbed "Pacífico," referring to the gulf's calm waters. Shortly thereafter the Spaniards discovered gold in the mountains of the Darién; mines here became so productive that Spain soon brought in African slaves, as the region's indigenous population succumbed to old-world diseases and inhumane working conditions. Meanwhile, a late 17th-century attempt by Scotland to colonize the Darién failed miserably. Some historians credit the so-called Darién Scheme with so weakening Scotland economically that it had no choice but to agree to a 1707 union with England.

When the conquistadors first arrived in Panama, the Kuna lived in the jungles of northern Colombia, but in the 16th century they began moving up the coast into present-day Panama, where they eventually established their villages in the San Blas Islands. During the 17th and 18th centuries the Kuna allied themselves with French and English pirates, providing them safe harbor and food in exchange for protection from Spain. Kuna warriors often joined the pirates on raids of Spanish gold mines and ports. The Spaniards never subjugated the Kuna, who lived independently until the early 20th century, when the new Republic of Panama government tried to establish a military presence in the San Blas Islands. In 1925 the Kuna rebelled against the Panamanians, killing or capturing all government officials in their territory in what the Kuna call the Revolución de Tule. Subsequent negotiations led to the eventual creation of the Comarca Kuna Yala, an independent territory governed by the Congreso General Kuna, a democratic congress of Kuna chiefs. Decades later the Kuna model was copied by the Emberá and Wounaan, who now share two *comarcas* in the eastern and western lowlands of the Darién, though they gained their autonomy through political pressure rather than revolution.

here. Lodges are pretty basic as a result—most have no hot water, no air-conditioning, and only a few hours of electricity at night—but some of those thatched bungalows have priceless ocean views. There are a few nice Kuna lodges, but the less expensive ones tend to be dirty and serve lamentable food, which is why few are listed in this book. Only three Kuna lodges accept credit cards, and since most lack offices, the owners may meet guests at Albrook Airport the morning they fly to Kuna Yala to collect payment. The alternative is to visit Kuna Yala on a day trip and sleep at Coral Lodge, 26 km (16 mi) away, which has most of the comforts of home *(Santa Isabela in "The Canal and Central Panama")* ⇨. The lodging situation in the Darién ranges from refurbished Emberá huts to the spacious, air-conditioned rooms at Tropic Star. One characteristic all lodges in this region share is that they are quite expensive for what you get—nearly all the accommodations in this chapter fall into the $$$–$$$$ ranges—but rooms come with three meals, guided tours, and transportation, and you can't put a price on an unforgettable adventure. Rates usually drop by 10% for stays of two nights or more. All lodgings in Kuna Yala collect a mandatory per-person, per night visitor tax of $10—it may or may not be included in the price you're quoted—with proceeds going to community development.

WHAT IT COSTS IN U.S. DOLLARS					
	¢	$	$$	$$$	$$$$
Restaurants	under $5	$5–$10	$10–$15	$15–$20	over $20
Hotels	under $50	$50–$100	$100–$160	$160–$220	over $220

Restaurant prices are per person for a main course at dinner. Hotel prices are for two people in a standard double room, excluding service and 10% tax.

ESSENTIALS

EMERGENCIES

The larger islands have police stations with radios to call Panama City for help in an emergency and tiny centros de salud (health centers) that can provide first aid. La Palma has the Darién's only hospital, the small Hospital San José La Palma. Lodges in Santa Cruz de Cana and Bahía Piñas have satellite phones to call Panama City for an air ambulance in case of emergencies.

⚠ **You should fly to Panama City if you have serious health problems in either Kuna Yala or the Darién.**

Emergency Services Ambulance *(La Palma ☎ 299-6219)*. **National police** *(La Palma ☎ 299-6200)*.

MONEY MATTERS

There are no ATMs in this part of Panama, so bring all the money you'll need during your trip. Stock up on small bills in Panama City, since the indigenous vendors, and even some hotels, are usually short on change.

SAFETY

Visiting Parque Nacional Darién without a guide is never advisable. The area near the border of Colombia is dangerous, as armed guerrilla groups have been known to slip into Panamanian territory; some hikers were kidnapped there years ago. When hiking through the forest, be careful where you put your hands and feet because there are plenty of palms with spiny trunks, some stinging insects, and the occasional poisonous snake. The sun is intense at these latitudes, making sunscreen and a brimmed hat musts.

TELEPHONES

Telephone access is difficult in this region. Although Kuna Yala's landline phone numbers have 200-series prefixes just like the capital, this is not Panama City. "Keep trying" should be your mantra when trying to place a call. Hotels near El Porvenir have cell-phone reception, but most areas of Kuna Yala have only pay phones—usually one or two per island.

KUNA YALA (SAN BLAS)

The San Blas Archipelago and surrounding sea are the main attractions in Kuna Yala—an indigenous *comarca* (autonomous territory) stretching more than 200 km (120 mi) along Panama's northeast coast—but the traditional culture of the Kuna is a close second. The comarca is composed of a thin strip of land dominated by a mountain range called the Serranía de San Blas and the more than 350 San Blas Islands that dot the coastal waters. Although much of the world still refers to this region by its former name, San Blas, you'll endear yourself to residents by using the name they give to their home, Kuna Yala. This is a lush and stunning region of forest-cloaked mountains, white-sand beaches, vibrant coral reefs, and timeless villages. Your trip here can consequently combine time on heavenly islands, jungle hiking, handicraft shopping, and exposure to a proud and beautiful indigenous people.

Since coral reefs surround nearly every island, snorkeling is practically obligatory in the archipelago. Most lodges include the use of snorkeling equipment in their rates, and all of them provide daily trips to beaches with reefs nearby. You don't need to swim to appreciate the area's beauty, though, since the scenery topside is just as impressive; coconut groves shade ivory sand, dugout canoes with lateen sails ply turquoise waters, and cane huts with thatch roofs make up island villages. Kuna Yala's greatest beauty, however, may be in the traditional dress of its women, whose striking clothing includes hand-stitched *molas* (appliqué fabric pictures), colorful skirts and scarves, and intricate beadwork on their calves and forearms. Men, however, have gradually abandoned traditional clothing in favor of jeans, polo or tropical cabana shirts, and derby hats (for older men) or baseball caps (for younger men). Times are changing, even in Kuna Yala.

EL PORVENIR

95 km (60 mi) northeast of Panama City. The small island of El Porvenir, on the western end of Kuna Yala, is the most popular gateway into the indigenous territory, as it lies near a dozen other isles scattered around a deep bay. It is the official capital of Kuna Yala, though the indigenous government is decentralized and meets on other islands. El Porvenir is practically uninhabited but has a police station, government offices, and an airstrip (no airport). Daily flights land here around 6:30 AM, when representatives of lodges on nearby islands await guests. The island also has a rudimentary hotel, a decent beach, and a small

museum, but for most travelers it is simply a place to get on and off the plane.

Several islands near El Porvenir have crowded Kuna villages that are interesting places to visit, but the rudimentary hotels on them are the equivalent of backpackers' hostels. Kuna communities have neither sewage systems nor garbage collection, so the water around them is unsafe for swimming. A short boat trip beyond them takes you to uninhabited, white-sand cays shaded by coconut palms that are the area's big attractions. Those idyllic isles hold superb snorkeling, and two of them have rustic lodges that are the area's best options. This part of Kuna Yala has the highest concentration of islands, and receives more visitors than any other area, including seasonal visits by cruise ships. The people on these islands have seen a lot of tourists, and they consequently tend to greet you with the Kuna equivalent of "Come, buy my molas," or by setting their kids up for a $1 photo—the favorite pose is with a parakeet on their head. Don't be offended: it's always good-natured, and they truly need the money. The most popular destinations in Kuna Yala are the uninhabited or sparsely inhabited islands to the east of the bay, which are perfect for snorkeling, swimming, and lounging. Achutupu, or Dog Island, is the most popular and picturesque of these palm-laden paradises, but there are several other islands near Achutupu that cost $1 for a visit, such as Isla Pelícano, with similar bleached beaches and coral reefs offshore but fewer visitors.

> ## ENDS OF THE EARTH
>
> Kuna Yala and the Darién may have pristine nature and traditional cultures, but both provinces lack ATMs and pharmacies, and they have only rudimentary clinics, simple stores, and few phones. While many Darién lodges have bilingual guides, few Kuna lodges have English speakers, though you can hire a guide in Panama City to accompany you. To visit Kuna Yala you must take a flight that leaves around 6 AM—at least they serve you breakfast when you arrive. Guides are essential for the forests and indigenous villages. Bring plenty of sunblock, insect repellent, water bottles, and, in the Darién, hiking boots.

El Porvenir has one of Kuna Yala's two museums, the **Museo de la Nación Kuna** (*Kuna Nation Museum;* ✉ *El Porvenir* ☎ *314–1293 for information in Panama City* ⊕ *www.congresogeneralkuna.org/nacion_kuna.htm* ✉ *$1* ☽ *Daily 8–4*), which is run by the Congreso Kuna. The simple museum housed in a two-story cement building with a thatch roof near the police station has basic exhibits on Kuna basketry, musical instruments, cooking, and fishing.

Just south of El Porvenir is the smaller island of **Wichub Huala**, which is packed with a mix of thatch-roof huts and cement buildings separated by narrow sand paths. As you explore this tiny island you can expect plenty of women to try to sell you handicrafts. We recommend the larger of two Kuna Niskua Lodges in this section of the archipelago, not this one, which occupies a small compound on the south side of the island.

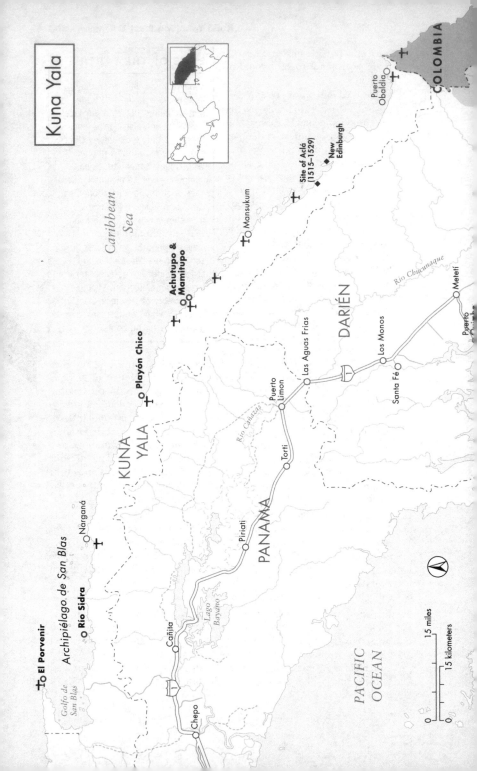

Just to the south of Wichub Huala is the slightly larger island of **Nalunega,** which has a comparable collection of huts and cement structures, including the archipelago's original lodge, the dilapidated 1972 Hotel San Blas.

Deep in the bay to the south of El Porvenir is the adjacent, densely populated island of **Cartí Suitupo** (*Crab Island*). Cruise ships often call here, so it holds a collection of refreshment stands—beverages are occasionally tepid—and plenty of handicraft hawkers. The main attraction here is the small **Museo Kuna** (*Kuna Museum* ⊠ *Cartí Suitupo* ☎ *299–9074* ✉ *$2* ☉ *Daily 8–4*), a family-run museum in a typical Kuna home. The English-speaking guide provides detailed explanations of Kuna life and culture.

★ Most lodges near El Porvenir offer trips to **Achutupu** (*Isla Perro, or Dog Island*), with no dogs but with a palm-lined beach and one resident family. Notice the name: This postcard-perfect Achutupu is not the larger Achutupu to the east (⇨ *Achutupo and Mamitupo, below*). Just off the beach in shallow water lies a sunken metal boat that is home to hundreds of colorful tropical fish. It's a perfect snorkeling spot, with enough marine life to please experienced divers; just beyond it is a large coral reef. The owners of the island charge $2 to visit it, they sell soft drinks, shells, and molas. A less picturesque garbage dump can be seen on the far side of the island (away from the wreck). If you don't want to spoil your moment, don't look behind the house.

GETTING HERE AND AROUND
Air Panama flies daily to El Porvenir (PVE), departing from Panama City's Albrook Airport at 6 AM and returning at 6:35 AM. There are no airline offices in Kuna Yala, so if you arrive by boat, or road, and want to fly out, you can board any flight, if they have empty seats, and then purchase your ticket upon arrival in Panama City. El Porvenir is one part of Kuna Yala that you can reach by land via the Llano-Cartí road; it's a four-hour trip from Panama City to where you catch a boat to the islands; buses make the trip daily. Cartí is an hour from the Burbayar eco-lodge, which drops guests off at the end of the road for a small fee (⇨ *Alto Bayano in "Central Panama"*).

WHERE TO STAY
Hotels here don't match the comfort and service levels offered farther east, but they are worth considering due to their proximity to Achutupu and similar islands. They are expensive for rustic rooms with cold-water showers and nary a fan, but rates include three meals, transfers, daily tours to nearby villages and islands, and snorkeling equipment. Electricity comes from generators that run a few hours each night.

$$$ ▦ **Cabañas Coco Blanco.** Located on a splendid island about the size of a football field, called Ogobsibudup, this small lodge has four thatched *cabañas* on a stretch of lawn next to a sugar-sand beach. Each of those bungalows has cane walls, a wood floor, a tiny bathroom, and double or single beds. It's a gorgeous setting, and the owners do a better job than most of keeping rooms clean and insect-free. An Italian chef helped the Sanchez family improve the food, so you can expect it to be a notch above that of the competition. Hammocks are strung between palms,

coral heads lie submerged off-shore, and a long sandbar connects Ogobsibudup to a nearby island that you can wade to at low tide. The only problem is the staff don't speak English, but a cousin, Nelson Sanchez, does, and he can accompany tourists for about half what tour companies charge. **Pros:** great beach; clean; friendly; good food. **Cons:** rustic; no English spoken. ⊠ *Ogobsibudup* ☎ *6700–9427* 🕾 *Ogobsibudup, Entrega General, El Porvenir* ✉ *cabanascocoblanco@ yahoo.it* 🛏 *4 bungalows* 🜂 *In-room: no a/c, no phone, no TV. In-hotel: restaurant, beachfront, water sports, no-smoking rooms* ▭ *No credit cards* ⎥◯⎥ *FAP.*

> ## BRING SMALL CHANGE
>
> You may want to start stocking up on small bills a couple of days before you head to Kuna Yala or the Darién, because there is plenty to buy in the indigenous villages and an inevitable shortage of change. Even the lodges have trouble breaking big bills when you pay for drinks and other incidentals. Although the region evokes the distant feel of an old National Geographic picture, don't immediately start snapping photos. Many people charge $1 to take their photo, especially in Kuna Yala. This may seem obnoxious, but for most of these people it is one of the only ways they can earn desperately needed cash.

$ 🏨 **Hotel El Porvenir**. This simple hotel next to the runway on El Porvenir is the best option for budget travelers. The rooms, in two cement buildings, are not at all spotless, but they have private bathrooms and tile floors. The advantages of staying here rather than the nearby islands are that the manager speaks some English, there's a beach with relatively clean water, it's quiet, and you can sleep a little later the day you fly out, since the runway is right there. **Pros:** beach; quiet. **Cons:** basic, dark rooms; soft beds. ⊠ *El Porvenir* ☎ *292–4543 or 6653–7766* ⊕ *www. hotelelporvenir.com* 🛏 *14 rooms* 🜂 *In-room: no a/c, no phone, no TV. In-hotel: restaurant, beachfront, water sports, no-smoking rooms* ▭ *No credit cards* ⎥◯⎥ *FAP.*

$$$ 🏨 **Kuna Niskua Isla Waildup**. This tiny solar-powered hotel sits on a sparsely inhabited island 30 minutes east of El Porvenir by boat. The island is lovely, with an ivory beach and healthy coral reefs, and there are several comparable isles nearby. The elevated *cabañas* have cane walls, thatch roofs, rudimentary bathrooms, and small porches with ocean views. Decent meals are served in an open-air restaurant nearby, and the lodge provides snorkeling equipment and electricity for a few hours at night. It belongs to the same owners as the larger Kuna Niskua on Isla Wichub Wala, which has issues with cleanliness and food, but the Walidup installation is better managed. **Pros:** great beach; reef; private bungalows. **Cons:** rustic; no English spoken; rough boat trip Dec.–Apr. ⊠ *Isla Walidup, east of El Porvenir* ☎ *259–9136 or 6709–4484* ⊕ *www.kuna-niskua.com* 🛏 *2 bungalows* 🜂 *In-room: no a/c, no phone, no TV. In-hotel: restaurant, beachfront, water sports, no-smoking rooms* ▭ *No credit cards* ⎥◯⎥ *FAP.*

SPORTS AND THE OUTDOORS

All hotels include snorkeling equipment in their rates, but it isn't always in good shape. (Bring your own if condition and perfect fit matter to you.) Walidup and Coco Blanco have fairly healthy reefs nearby, but the reefs near El Porvenir have been destroyed. The best dive spot in the area is **Achutupu**, which has a shallow wreck surrounded by tropical fish. The healthiest reefs and other marine life in Kuna Yala are in the uninhabited **Cayos Holandeses** (Dutch Keys), 30 km (19 mi) east of El Porvenir. You can hire a boat to take you there for $100–$120.

SHOPPING

Wherever you go in this area, somebody will try to sell you molas, shells, or other handicrafts. Molas usually cost $8 to $20; the Kuna are happy to haggle, but don't bargain too hard; those couple of extra dollars mean a lot more to them than to you.

UNDERWATER KUNA YALA

The Kuna prohibit scuba diving in their territorial waters, but snorkeling is permitted, and the abundance of shallow, protected reefs makes it a world-class experience. Most of the San Blas Islands have coral reefs nearby with massive coral formations, as well as dozens of colorful sponge species, anemones, and sea fans. Hundreds of fish species inhabit the underwater gardens, including damselfish, angelfish, barracudas, eels, cornet fish, puffers, and nurse sharks. Conditions are best between August and November. Don't snorkel close to heavily populated islands; human waste frequently seeps into the sea.

RÍO SIDRA

99 km (62 mi) northeast of Panama City, 19 km (12 mi) southeast of El Porvenir.

The first airstrip to the east of El Porvenir is on the mainland near the islands of Río Sidra, Momarketup, and Isla Ratón. Río Sidra is the largest of those communities, and is a good place to see how the Kuna live, but the real attraction is on and around the sparsely populated islands farther out at sea. Those enchanting isles have immaculate beaches washed by crystalline waters and rustic lodges nestled amid coconut groves. The lodges are alternatives to accommodations near El Porvenir, since they are just as close to Isla Perro and have enough coral reefs nearby to keep you snorkeling for days.

Momarketupo (*Isla Máquina, or Machine Island*), 10 minutes west of Río Sidra by boat, is the best community to visit in this area because it is both more traditional and less cramped than nearby isles. The women here are known for producing quality molas, and the island gets few visitors, so it's a good place to shop.

The **Río Masargandi**, a small river that flows out of the mountains near Río Sidra, provides access to the rain forest and a 30-foot waterfall. Local lodges offer half-day trips to the mainland for an additional charge. ⚠ **Excursions to see wildlife are best done early in the morning, but slather yourself with insect repellent.**

GETTING HERE AND AROUND

Air Panama offers daily flights to Río Sidra's airstrip (RSI) on the mainland, departing from Panama City's Albrook Airport at 6 AM and returning at 6:45 AM. Río Sidra is usually the second stop after El Porvenir, so be sure to get off at the right airstrip. Río Sidra can also be reached by land, via the Llano-Cartí road (⊳ *Getting Here and Around in "El Porvenir")*.

WHERE TO STAY

None of the accommodations near Río Sidra offer private baths, and the bungalows are mini versions of the homes the Kuna have been living in for generations, with sand floors, cane walls, and thatch roofs. Those who can do without comforts are rewarded with phenomenal scenery and great diving.

$$ ⊞ **Cabañas Narasgandup.** Though quite rustic, this lodge has a great setting and is one of the best deals in Kuna Yala. Its *cabañas* are traditional Kuna huts with foam mattresses on hewn-wood beds. Guests share typical Kuna bathrooms, with a barrel of water and a bowl to splash water on yourself instead of a shower, though there are flush toilets and septic tanks. The good news is that the huts are on a beautiful white-sand beach with clean water and coral reefs nearby. The owner, Ausberto, takes guests to Isla Perro and nearby communities and has optional trips to a waterfall or a Kuna burial ground at an additional charge. **Pros:** great beach; friendly service; day trips. **Cons:** very rustic; no English spoken. ⊠ *Ogobsibudup* ☎ *256–6239 or 6537-3071* ✎ *narasgandup@hotmail.com* ⟿ *6 bungalows, none with bath* ⚭ *In-room: no a/c, no phone, no TV. In-hotel: restaurant, beachfront, water sports, no-smoking rooms* ⊟ *No credit cards* ⑩ *FAP.*

$$$ ⊞ **Kuanidup.** This lodge on the charming little private island of Kuanidup
★ has a small beach, hammocks strung between palm trees, and a row of thatched huts. It's a good spot for snorkelers, since it is encircled by a coral reef teaming with life, but the accommodations are super rustic. The tiny huts with sand floors barely offer enough room to walk around the bed, and they are so close to each other that there is little privacy. Everyone shares a few basic bathrooms in a cement building, which can get crowded when the hotel is full. The payoff is the island's beach and reef, not to mention trips to nearby Isla Perro and the Kuna communities. The food is okay, but the rack rate is high for what you get. You may get a discount rate if you book direct or stay more than two nights. **Pros:** lovely island; great snorkeling; pristine area. **Cons:** tiny, rustic rooms; shared bathrooms; can get crowded; no English spoken. ⊠ *Kuanidup, near Río Sidra* ☎ *6635–6737* ⊕ *kuanidup.8k.com* ⟿ *10 huts* ⚭ *In-room: no a/c, no phone, no TV. In-hotel: restaurant, beachfront, water sports, no-smoking rooms* ⊟ *No credit cards* ⑩ *FAP.*

SPORTS AND THE OUTDOORS

The lodges near Río Sidra have good snorkeling nearby and are just as close to Isla Perro as the lodges near El Porvenir. They are considerably closer to the Cayos Holandeses, the best dive spot in the archipelago, though a boat there costs $80 to $100.

PLAYÓN CHICO

150 km (93 mi) northeast of Panama City.

This community of about 3,000 people lies just offshore, with a wooden footbridge connecting it to the mainland, where the town's schools and landing strip are located. Most homes in Playón Chico are traditional thatched buildings, with small gardens shaded by breadfruit, mango, or citrus trees. There are a few cement structures scattered around the island, and the obligatory basketball court near the bridge. It was an important area in the 1925 revolution that led to Kuna autonomy, since it held one of the Panama military outposts that were captured by Kuna warriors.

> ## THE KUNA FLAG
>
> As befits a self-governing region, the flag of Kuna Yala flies proudly here, with Panama's blue-white-red national flag little in evidence. Don't be alarmed at what you see: the local flag contains a black reverse *swastika* on a field of yellow, an ancient Kuna symbol representing an octopus. Like the Sanskrit swastika you'll see almost everywhere in India, it has nothing to do with Nazi Germany.

The lowlands around the landing strip hold the farms of local families, but a nearby hill is topped with the burial ground that resembles a small village. The Kuna bury family members together under thatched shelters complete with the tools and utensils that their spirits require to survive. Forested mountains stand beyond the farmland with trails leading to a waterfall. Insect repellent is essential on the mainland due to sand fleas. There are various uninhabited islands in the area that local lodges take guests to, but they aren't as nice as the cays on the archipelago's western end.

GETTING HERE AND AROUND

Both Air Panama and Aeroperlas fly to Playón Chico airstrip (PYC), departing from Panama City's Albrook Airport at 6 AM and returning at 7 AM. Air Panama flies the route daily; Aeroperlas, daily except Sunday.

WHERE TO STAY

$$$$ **Sapibenega.** With spacious rooms perched over the sea on a private
★ island surrounded by coral reefs, this solar-powered lodge is one of the better hotels in Kuna Yala. The only problem is that rooms are in wooden duplexes divided by cane walls that go only halfway up to the roof, so you can hear everything that happens next door. If you don't have noisy neighbors, the accommodations are nice, with good beds and large balconies over the sea. The hotel's kitchen is one of the best in Kuna Yala, and it's the only place with a real bar. Meals are served in a thatched gazebo over the water with a wonderful view of the mainland, or next to the open-air bar on the island. There's decent snorkeling around the island, and the lodge offers trips to beaches and healthier reefs, as well as tours to Playón Chico, the burial ground, or the waterfall and jungle. The hotel imposes a minimum stay of two nights. **Pros:** big rooms; decent food; roomy island; good tours. **Cons:** rooms lack privacy; no beach on island; little English spoken. ⊠ *Playón*

Chico ☎ *215–1406 or 6676–5548* ⊕ *www.sapibenega.com* ⤳ *6 rooms* ⚇ *In-room: no a/c, no phone, no TV. In-hotel: restaurant, bar, water sports, no-smoking rooms* ▤ *MC, V* ⵏⵓ *FAP.*

$$$ 🖫 **Yandup.** With two kinds of wooden bungalows spread across a grassy island near the coast, Yandup is one of Kuna Yala's better deals. The nicest bungalows are octagonal structures over the water with high thatch roofs, basic bathrooms, and narrow porches. Two smaller bungalows in the middle of the island share a bathroom, and cost $40 less. There's a small beach on a corner of the island with a reef nearby. Yandup offers the best selection of tours to the mainland and has one of the few English-speaking guides in Kuna Yala. Snorkeling equipment is not provided. The hotel occasionally has problems with sand fleas, so bring insect repellent. **Pros:** good rates; friendly guide; small beach. **Cons:** sand fleas a problem April through December. ✉ *Playón Chico* ☎ *394–1408, 6579–2911* ⊕ *www.yandupisland.com* ⤳ *8 bungalows* ⚇ *In-room: no a/c, no phone, no TV. In-hotel: restaurant, beachfront* ▤ *MC, V* ⵏⵓ *FAP.*

SHOPPING

It would be a crime to visit Kuna Yala and not buy a mola. Women usually set up shop outside their homes when tourists arrive in Playón Chico. Bring plenty of small bills, and try to buy from various vendors to benefit as many families as possible.

ACHUTUPO AND MAMITUPO

190 km (118 mi) northeast of Panama City.

Achutupo and Mamitupo are two medium-size communities on islands near the mainland in the eastern half of Kuna Yala. Their claim to fame is the fact that two of the best lodges in the archipelago are on private islands nearby. Since this is the most distant area that you can visit in Kuna Yala, it is the best destination if you're especially interested in Kuna culture or want to buy handicrafts. The people here see fewer tourists and are thus more receptive to visitors. Though there are various uninhabited islands and plenty of coral near Achutupo, the beaches and diving aren't quite as spectacular as what you find around Isla Perro. It's possible to hike into the rain forest to a waterfall on the mainland (bring insect repellent). A tour to the local burial ground is another interesting option, especially early in the morning, when you may see Kuna women leaving gifts of food for their ancestors.

A short trip to the west of Achutupo is the rarely visited island community of **Aligandi**, which played an important role in the Kuna revolt of 1925. You'll see the orange-and-yellow Kuna flag displayed here, as well as a statue of the local revolutionary Simral Colman, one of the architects of the autonomous Kuna state.

GETTING HERE AND AROUND

Both Air Panama and Aeroperlas serve the area from Panama City's Albrook Airport. Air Panama flies to the airstrip at Achutupo (ACU) daily; Aeroperlas flies the same route Tuesday, Thursday, Saturday, and Sunday. Aeroperlas flies to nearby Mamitupo (MPI) Monday,

MOLAS 101

The Kuna are famous for their *molas:* fabric pictures made using a reverse appliqué technique, and Panama's most famous souvenir. Kuna women wear these designs on their blouses, but they are also used to decorate everything from purses to pillows to hot pads to wall hangings. The original molas echoed the geometric designs employed by the Kuna as body paint—Christian missionaries' influence in the 19th century brought modest body covering to the region for the first time, and the word *mola* means "clothing" in Dulegaya, the Kuna language. (And even more utilitarian, *dulegaya* means "people talk.") Over the decades, designs have taken on abstract nature scenes, and, today, even a few TV and cartoon characters show up in the artwork. Regarding the traditional geometric designs, look closely before you buy: some molas feature a reverse swastika, an ancient Kuna symbol. You may not want one of those. Few objects evoke Kuna autonomy like the mola does. The Panamanian government's attempts in the early 20th century to impose Western ways and dress on the people here led to the 1925 Kuna rebellion and subsequent autonomy for Kuna Yala.

Mola production is a major source of income in Kuna Yala, and you'll often see women sewing them as they chat with neighbors. Expect to pay $20 or more for a basic, but well-made mola. Number of layers used increases the price; two is most common, but the premium works incorporate several more layers. Fineness of stitching, up to the point of being nearly invisible, also means a finer mola. Embroidery frequently enhances a mola's design, but a top-notch product creates its design strictly through reverse appliqué technique. Oddly, a bit of wear or fading is not considered to be a flaw. Perhaps a panel had a previous life as a piece of someone's blouse and is now being used in another work. Such a "blemish" adds to the mola's authenticity and means that it wasn't created strictly for tourists.

Bargaining is expected, but don't haggle too hard. Molas are usually already reasonably priced when you consider the labor that went into their production, and those few extra dollars will mean much more to the vendor than to you. If you plan on buying multiple molas, try to buy from a variety of women. You'll benefit more families that way.

7

Wednesday, and Friday. All flights depart from Albrook at 6 AM and return at 7 AM.

WHERE TO STAY

$$$$ ★ **Dad Ibe Lodge.** This hotel occupies a tiny island that's hardly bigger than a basketball court: it must have looked like something from a comic book before locals undertook the construction of three thatched bungalows and an open-air restaurant on either side of it. The island is little more than a swath of pale sand shaded by a dozen coconut palms with hammocks strung between them. The rooms are simple but comfortable, with two queen beds, cane walls, a tiny bathroom, and a balcony. You'll be lulled to sleep by the sound of soft waves washing beneath the floorboards. It's a great place to do nothing, but you can

rent snorkeling equipment and take tours to nearby islands and the community of Aligandi, which few tourists visit. The guide here speaks decent English. Pros: beach; excursions; friendly. Cons: tiny, remote island. ⊠ *Isla Dad Ibe* ☎ *6487–6239* ⊕ *www.dadibelodge.com* ⇆ *3 huts* ♿ *In-room: no a/c, no phone, no TV. In-hotel: restaurant, beachfront, water sports, no-smoking rooms* ⊟ *No credit cards* ⦶ *FAP.*

$$$$
Fodor'sChoice
★

🖭 **Uaguinega** *(Dolphin Island Lodge).* The best bungalows at this friendly lodge on a small island across a channel from Achutupo offer the nicest rooms in Kuna Yala. They have spacious, private bathrooms, high thatch roofs, and roomy back porches with splendid ocean views. Keep in mind when you are booking that the older, standard rooms lack the view and are slightly cramped; ask for a junior suite. Those comfortable bungalows are spread along the shore of the grassy island with hammocks strung between palm trees. The only drawbacks are that the island lacks a beach and snorkeling isn't recommended there because of pollution from nearby Achutupo. However, excursions to nearby islands provide beach and snorkeling time, and the tour of Achutupo in English is excellent. Hikes into the forest and to a waterfall are an additional charge. Pros: spacious bungalows; friendly staff; good food; Internet access. Cons: no beach; several subpar rooms. ⊠ *Achutupo* ☎ *263–7780 in Panama City* ✆ *Apdo. 0823–00287, Panama City* ⊕ *www.uaguinega.com* ⇆ *17 bungalows, 3 rooms* ♿ *In-room: no a/c, no phone, no TV. In-hotel: restaurant, bar, beachfront, water sports, Internet terminal, no-smoking rooms* ⊟ *MC, V* ⦶ *FAP.*

SHOPPING

Shopping is inevitable here, since the streets of Achutupo and Aligandi fill with mola hawkers whenever tourists arrive. You can barter, but try to buy from various vendors so your money benefits more families. In addition to molas, you can often purchase beadwork, wood carvings, or shells.

THE DARIÉN

The easternmost province of the Darién is Panama's wildest, least accessible region, home to extraordinary flora, fauna, and indigenous communities. Its remote eastern and southern extremes are dominated by mountain ranges cloaked with dense jungle, whereas its lowlands are drained by serpentine rivers that flow into the Pacific Ocean at the Golfo de San Miguel. Much of its wilderness is sequestered within Parque Nacional Darién and several nearby protected areas. Those preserves hold imposing, primeval forests dominated by massive tropical trees such as mahogany, strangler fig, and barrel-trunked *cuipos*. They are home to an array of wildlife that includes more than 450 bird species and everything from boa constrictors to strange and wonderful butterflies. While most of that wilderness is inaccessible, there are a half dozen spots that provide easy access to the region's wonders, the best of which are the field stations in Parque Nacional Darién and the Reserva Natural Punta Patiño.

The Darién is a lush and rainy region with muddy rivers lined with the tangled roots of mangroves and thick swaths of elephant grass. Flocks of macaws often pass noisily overhead, and the most popular form of transportation is the dugout canoe. The province's main rivers are dotted with dozens of indigenous Emberá and Wounaan villages that probably look much as the region's towns did when Balboa hiked across the isthmus five centuries ago. Villages such as Mogue and La Marea are set up to receive visitors: a day or two spent in these communities can be an unforgettable experience. The Darién has Panama's best bird-watching and sport fishing, but it is also a good destination for anyone interested in tropical nature and traditional cultures or travelers who simply want to stray from the beaten path.

PARQUE NACIONAL DARIÉN

265 km (164 mi) southeast of Panama City.

Parque Nacional Darién (Darién National Park) stretches along the border of Colombia from Kuna Yala to the Pacific Ocean, covering 579,000 hectares—more than 1.4 million acres—of wilderness that is home to such endangered animals as jaguars, tapirs, and harpy eagles. It is the largest national park in Central America, and the United Nations has designated it a World Heritage site. It comprises a mosaic of ecosystems that includes lowland rain forest, jungle-lined rivers, and several *serranías* (mountain ranges) topped with cloud forests. The park's wildlife consequently ranges from vine snakes to brocket deer, and includes such creatures as the great green macaw and golden-headed quetzal among its nearly 500 bird species.

Despite its ample natural assets, few people make it to Parque Nacional Darién, which is remote and expensive to visit. The easiest and safest way to see the park is by taking a charter flight to **Santa Cruz de Cana,** usually called Cana, a former mining camp on the eastern slope of the Pirre Mountain Range that was converted to a field station by Ancon Expeditions in the 1990s. That rustic lodge is surrounded by pristine forest that is home to such spectacular birds as the crested guan and the blue and gold macaw, plus various species of monkeys and plenty of other jungle denizens. Ancon Expeditions also has a tent camp in the cloud forest a four-hour hike uphill from Cana, where guests usually spend a night.

On the west side of the Pirre Mountain Range, **Estación Pirre** (*Pirre Station*) is one of only two parts of Parque Nacional Darién that accommodates visitors. There's a ranger station 14 km (8 mi) south of the town of El Real. El Real itself can be reached by commercial flights from Panama City, but from there it's a long hike, or a combination of a dugout trip and a hike during the rainy season, to the Pirre Station. The National Environment Authority, ANAM, rents bunks at the ranger station for $10 a night, but you have to bring your own sheets and towels, and you must register in El Real before hiking in. Ancon Expeditions also operates a rugged tent camp near Pirre; an overnight here can be arranged as part of a stay at its Cuna Field Station (⇨ *Cuna Field Station below*). The ecotourism company **Advantage Tours Panama** (⇨ *Chapter 8, Outdoor and Learning Vacations*) can organize four-day hiking tours to Estación Pirre for about $750. ⚠ **Hiring a guide is a necessity**

7

Indigenous Panama

Though the guardians of Panama's earliest cultures represent a mere 6% of the country's population, they are a very visible minority, which is in no small part due to their spectacular dress. Though Panama has seven indigenous ethnicities, most of the country's original peoples belong to three groups—the Kuna, Emberá-Wounaan, and Ngöbe-Buglé—each of which has its distinctive clothing, language, customs, and cultures. In Panama City, you'll notice their varied handicrafts in markets and shops across the city, and photos or murals depict them on many a wall of the capital. Panama celebrates its indigenous cultures more than many nations, and the government has taken care to treat its first citizens better than the regional norm.

An important example of that treatment is the existence of *comarcas*—autonomous indigenous territories—that are administered by each of the major ethnic groups. These isolated territories are for the most part difficult to visit; the exception is the Comarca Kuna Yala, which is served by daily flights from the capital. The comarcas retain much of their forests, which residents conserve, to extract the raw materials for their homes, utensils, tools, medicines, and food. A trip to one of these communities will take you into primeval Panama, past stretches of tropical forest and over crystalline waters that hold coral reefs.

Some 50,000 **Kuna** are Panama's most famous indigenous people, thanks to their tradition of receiving tourists and the colorful traditional dress of Kuna women, which includes beautiful hand-stitched *molas* (patchwork pictures). The Kuna own some of the most spectacular real estate in Central America—a vast entity called Kuna Yala, or Land of the Kuna, from which its people eke out a living fishing, farming coconuts, and tourism. That comarca is governed by a congress of regional sahilas (administrators) who set local laws, distinct from those of Panama, and above all else, work toward the preservation of local culture.

The territory includes the Serranía de San Blas, a long mountain chain covered with jungle that has kept the Kuna isolated for centuries, and approximately 365 San Blas Islands, most of which are paradises in miniature: uninhabited cays of ivory sand and coconut palms. The turquoise sea that surrounds these idyllic isles holds countless acres of coral reef—home to a wealth of marine life—so snorkeling is practically an obligatory part of any trip there. And thanks to daily flights and the existence of more than a dozen rustic lodges that offer tours of the villages, it is the easiest comarca to visit.

Panama's largest indigenous group is the **Ngöbe-Buglé**, consisting of two groups on the Pacific and Atlantic slopes of the Talamanca mountain range, in the western provinces of Chiriquí and Bocas del Toro. Unlike the Kuna and Emberá-Wounaan, who live in relatively compact villages, the Ngöbe-Buglé tend to live on farms, which means their communities lack a town center. They are most easily visited in Bocas del Toro, which has a couple of accessible communities on Isla Bastimentos; Ngöbe families also live in the towns of Bocas and Carenero. Plenty of Ngöbe-Buglé live outside the comarca in agricultural communities such as Cerro Punta, Boquete, and Cerro Azul. You'll find traditional Ngöbe dresses, jute bags,

and bead work for sale at craft markets and stores around the country.

Also look out for the *chaquiras*, decorative beaded necklaces once worn by warriors during celebrations. Originally, these ornaments were made from pebbles, pieces of bone, seashells, and seeds; they are now much more ornamental and created from brightly colored beads and sold to travelers as souvenirs.

Panama's third major indigenous group consists of two related tribes, the **Emberá** and **Wounaan**, who share two comarcas in the eastern Darién province. Collectively known as the Chocó, after the region of northwest Colombia where most of their people live, these two groups have similar languages and live in villages scattered along the larger rivers of eastern Panama, where they make a living farming, fishing, and hunting. The traditional dress of both the Wounaan and Emberá is a loincloth for men and a brightly colored skirt for women, to which they add jewelry and body paint. The influence of Christian missionaries has meant that more and more Emberá and Wounaan are adopting Western dress.

Their beautiful handicrafts include baskets tightly woven from palm and chunga fibers, *cocobolo* wood carvings, sculpted and painted seeds of the *tagua* palm, and lovely rattan baskets dyed with natural colors. Because the government relocated several villages to what is now Parque Nacional Chagres in the 1970s, when their land was inundated by the Bayano hydroelectric project, it is possible to visit an Emberá village on a day trip from Panama City. Those communities, however, have had a lot of contact with modern society, so for a more authentic Emberá experience, you'll want to head to Bayano Lake or the remote jungles of the Darién.

Most Emberá villages in the Darién are not even accessible by plane; rather, you must often travel fairly long distances by boat, but some villages in the Darién do have accommodations for those few tourists who visit. These villages are also visited by small cruise ships that anchor offshore and bring their guests to the villages by inflatable zodiacs or other small craft.

7

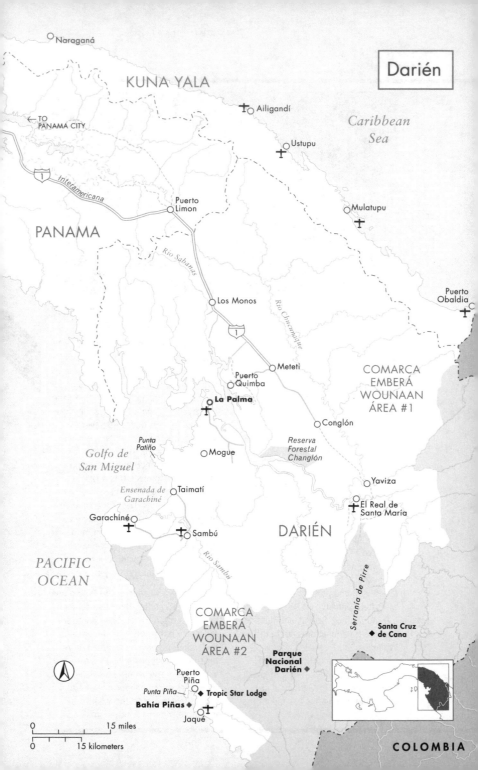

THE DARIÉN GAP

The impenetrable jungle that covers the eastern and southern Darién occupies the only interruption in the Pan-American Highway, which would otherwise run continuously from Alaska to southern Chile. The United States began promoting and underwriting that regional road system in the 1940s, but they asked Panama to leave a so-called "Darién Gap" intact to help prevent foot-and-mouth disease from spreading north from South America. An outbreak of the disease did occur in Colombia in 2009, but there's a more compelling reason to maintain the gap today. Panama is likely in no hurry to complete a road into a neighboring country with numerous armed groups and drug traffickers. This is good news for conservationists, who lament that the highway is flanked by deforested landscapes in the rest of the country. The highway, which is called the *Carretera Interamericana* (Inter-American Highway) in Panama, becomes a muddy track in the Darién, dead-ending about 50 km (31 mi) short of the Colombian border, at the town of Yaviza. To the east and south of that frontier town are dozens of indigenous villages and the biggest remaining expanse of tropical wilderness in Central America, which will hopefully remain intact for generations to come.

for this trip, since trails are not well marked, nobody speaks English, and the forest has plenty of poisonous snakes. Don't hike any deeper into the park than the area around the Pirre, because the border area can be unsafe. ⊠ *14 km (8 mi) south of El Real* ☎ *299–6530* 💲 *$3.50*

GETTING HERE AND AROUND

The only way in and out of Santa Cruz de Cana is on charter flights arranged by Ancon Expeditions that depart twice a week from Panama City's Albrook Airport.

WHERE TO STAY

$$$$
★ 🖽 **Cana Field Station.** Nestled in the forest of Parque Nacional Darién, this rustic field station is Panama's top bird-watching spot operated by the highly regarded Ancon Expeditions. The rooms are pretty basic—it's a refurbished mining camp that was abandoned early in the 20th century—with screened windows, battery-powered lights, and two single beds. Guests share several bathrooms, and the lodge generates electricity for only 90 minutes each morning and at night. The reward for roughing it is constant exposure to nature and access to rare wildlife. The lodge can only be visited on five- or eight-day packages that include charter flights from Panama City, daily tours led by expert birding guides, and hearty meals served family-style. Guests need to be in decent shape. Rates include optional overnights to Ancon's rugged Pirre Tent Camp, a five-hour hike away but located at a refreshing 4,900 feet above sea level. **Pros:** in jungle; great birding; expert guides. **Cons:** rustic; isolated; expensive; limited electricity. ⊠ *Santa Cruz de Cana* ☎ *269–9415 in Panama City* ⊕ *www.anconexpeditions.com* 🛏 *12 rooms, none with bath* ⚇ *In-room: no a/c, no phone, no TV. In-hotel: restaurant, no-smoking rooms* ☰ *MC, V* ⏺ *FAP.*

7

SPORTS AND THE OUTDOORS

Santa Cruz de Cana is Panama's top birding spot, with more than 400 species, many of which are found nowhere else in the country. Those feathered creatures include four kinds of macaw, six parrot species, about two dozen types of hummingbirds, and such rare species as the blue-fronted parrolet, orange-breasted falcon, and golden-headed quetzal. The field station's experienced guides, well-maintained trails, and cloud-forest camp facilitate seeing as many species as possible during your stay.

LA PALMA

176 km (109 mi) southeast of Panama City.

La Palma is the capital of the Darién and is the perfect illustration of just how undeveloped this province is. Situated at the end of a peninsula where the Tuira River flows into the Golfo de San Miguel, La Palma has just one commercial street with a handful of government offices, some basic restaurants, and a couple of rustic hotels. La Palma itself has little to offer visitors, but because it has one of the Darién's few airstrips, it is the point of access for the private nature reserve of Punta Patiño and nearby Emberá villages.

The closest attraction to La Palma is **Fuerte de Boca Chica**, the ruins of a Spanish fortress built in the 18th century to defend the gold mines upriver from pirates. It's a five-minute boat ride from the town dock, where a boat can usually be hired for $15.

★ A fascinating option for adventurous travelers is to spend a few nights in the Emberá village of **La Marea**, a 48-km (30-mi) boat ride southeast of La Palma. Advantage Tours Panama (↦ *Chapter 8, Outdoor and Learning Vacations)* offers four-day tours to La Marea that include nights in rustic accommodations and hiking tours into the nearby rain forest to look for wildlife such as blue-and-gold macaws and harpy eagles.

★ You can get a quick look at Emberá life at the village of **Mogue** (pronounced MOE-gay) on a bank of a river of the same name, about 30 km (19 mi) southwest of La Palma; it can be visited as a day trip. That trip takes you up a winding river through a thick forest to a traditional Emberá community; you can include a hike to the nearby rain forest, which has plenty of wildlife. A boat from La Palma to Mogue costs $100–$200, depending on group size. The tour company **Eco Circuitos** (↦ *Chapter 8, Outdoor and Learning Vacations)* has a three-day tour to Mogue with overnights in traditional Emberá dwellings.

The most comfortable accommodations near La Palma are in the **Reserva Natural Punta Patiño**, a private nature reserve 32 km (20 mi) southwest of town managed by ANCON, the country's biggest conservation group. A former ranch in the midst of ecological restoration, the reserve consists of 26,000 hectares (65,000 acres) of mature forest and former pastureland. It is home to crab-eating raccoons, crocodiles, capybaras (the world's largest rodent), and hundreds of bird species, ranging from the delicate mangrove swallow to the mighty harpy eagle. Ancon Expeditions (↦ *Chapter 8, Outdoor and Learning Vacations)* offers three- and four-day tours at the Punta Patiño Lodge, on the north end of the reserve.

GETTING HERE AND AROUND

Flying is the easiest way to reach La Palma (PLP), and Air Panama flies here on Tuesday and Saturday mornings, departing from Panama City's Albrook Airport at 10:30 AM and returning at 11:20.

WHERE TO STAY

¢ ⊞ **Baiquirú Bagará.** The best accommodations in La Palma, which isn't saying much, are at the back of the long wooden building over the water. The rooms are basic, with ceiling fans; several rooms have large windows and balconies with views of the bay. About half of them share bathrooms; those with private baths also have air-conditioning. **Pros:** nice views; much appreciated air conditioning. **Cons:** some rooms lack private bath and a/c. ⊠ *La Palma, Calle Principal* ☎ *299–6224* ⤵ *13 rooms, 6 with bath* ⚓ *In-room: no a/c (some), no phone, no TV. In-hotel: laundry service* ▭ *No credit cards* ⏏¶ *EP.*

$$$$ ⊞ **Punta Patiño Lodge.** This eco-lodge inside the Reserva Natural Punta
★ Patiño sits on a hill with views of secondary forest and the sea. Its wooden bungalows are the Darién's nicest accommodations, with private (cold-water) showers, air-conditioning, and balconies with hammocks that are good bird-watching platforms. Hearty meals are served family-style in the old ranch house, which has a small bar. Ancon Expeditions (⤳ *Chapter 8, Outdoor and Learning Vacations*) offers three- and four-night packages at the lodge that include transportation, guided hikes, a boat trip to Mogue, access to beaches, and optional horseback riding. **Pros:** nice rooms; air conditioning; expert guides. **Cons:** quite secluded. ⊠ *Punta Patiño* ☎ *269–9415 in Panama City* ⊕ *www.anconexpeditions.com* ⤵ *10 bungalows* ⚓ *In-room: no phone, no TV. In-hotel: restaurant, bar* ▭ *MC, V* ⊘ *Closed Oct. and Nov.* ⏏¶ *FAP*

BAHÍA PIÑAS

230 km (143 mi) southeast of Panama City.

Nestled in the southwest corner of the Darién, just north of the Jaque River, lies remote and beautiful Bahía Piñas, a deep bay with a rocky coastline, where mountains are covered with virgin rain forest and the aquamarine sea teems with an array of marine life. In fact, it's the marine life that draws most people to Piñas Bay, since the quality of its fishing is legendary, with more than 250 world fishing records set in the surrounding waters. Zane Grey fished in the area in the 1950s, and John Wayne and Lee Marvin hooked plenty of billfish here in the '60s. Since then, thousands of anglers have followed in their wake, heading out to Zane Grey Reef in search of sailfish and blue, black, and striped marlin.

Within the bay is the town of Piñas, home to an indigenous community that has traditionally farmed and fished—though most now work at the nearby Tropic Star Lodge. That fishing lodge is not only the local employer but also a benefactor: it makes donations to the local schools and clinic and ensures that the surrounding area will remain wild by

7

protecting a vast expanse of jungle. The lodge's owners also started a conservation organization, Conomar, which successfully lobbied the Panamanian government to ban commercial fishing within 20 mi of the coast near Piñas, which should help to protect the country's best fishing for many years.

GETTING HERE AND AROUND

Air Panama and Aeroperlas fly to Bahía Piñas (BFQ) from Panama City's Albrook Airport. Flights leave at 10:25 AM and return at 11:35 AM. Air Panama does the route Monday, Wednesday and Friday; Aeroperlas, Tuesday and Thursday. Flights are included in the Tropic Star Lodge packages, as is transportation in Panama City.

WHERE TO STAY

$$$$

Fodor's Choice

★

 Tropic Star Lodge. The Tropic Star Lodge, one of the country's most famous accommodations, offers access to world-class sport fishing in a comfortable, friendly atmosphere. Built in the 1960s by a Texas millionaire, Tropic Star has since evolved into one of the world's great fishing lodges. Daily fishing on the lodge's 31-foot Bertrams are included in package rates, as are three meals per day. Hiking, kayaking, and massages are also available. Spacious, air-conditioned guest rooms have two double beds or one king bed, large baths, and a porch with views of Piñas Bay. No TVs or phones disturb the tranquility. Hearty meals, which always include fresh seafood, are served in the air-conditioned restaurant or by the pool. A minimum one-week stay is required during the high season from December to March, but three- and four-night packages are available the rest of the year, when limited nonfishing packages are available for travelers interested in the tropical nature that surrounds the lodge. **Pros:** lots to do; air conditioning. **Cons:** expensive; especially if you're not fishing. ⊠ *Piñas Bay* ☎ *232–8375 in Panama City; 800/682–3424 in the U.S.* ⌖ *635 N. Rio Grande Ave., Orlando FL 32805* ⊕ *www.tropicstar.com* ⇱ *18 rooms* ⚸ *In-room: no phone, safe, no TV. In-hotel: restaurant, room service, bar, pool, beachfront, water sports, laundry service, Internet terminal, no-smoking rooms* ▭ *AE, MC, V* ⊘ *Closed Oct. and Nov.* ⏍ *FAP*

SPORTS AND THE OUTDOORS

The ocean around Piñas Bay has Panama's best fishing, with sailfish and blue and black marlin biting most of the year. Black marlin average 300 to 400 pounds in the area (and sometimes top 1,000 pounds); tuna weighing between 100 and 200 pounds are common. December through February are the best months for black marlin—many people book their weeks at the Tropic Star Lodge years in advance. The marlin fishing drops off in March, improving again from May to September. Sailfish are common in the area from April to September. Fishing at Tropic Star is catch-and-release for billfish, whereas fish for eating, such as tuna and dolphin, are served for dinner. There are plenty of big tuna and dolphin in the area, and smaller fighters such as roosterfish, wahoo, and mackerel inshore, where you can also troll deep for snapper and grouper.

Outdoor and Learning Vacations

WORD OF MOUTH

"Traveling [on a private tour] with Ancon [Expeditions] (or another travel company) means no driving and no buses (definitely would not ride the wild and crazy independent buses). A great way to go with limited time."

—eyemom84

PLANNING YOUR ADVENTURE

CHOOSING A TRIP

With hundreds of choices for special-interest trips to Central America, there are a number of factors to keep in mind when deciding which company and package will be right for you.

How strenuous do you want your trip to be? Adventure vacations are commonly split into "soft" and "hard." Hard adventures, such as strenuous treks (often at high altitudes) or Class IV or V rafting, generally require excellent physical conditioning and previous experience. Most hiking, biking, canoeing/kayaking, and similar soft adventures can be enjoyed by persons of all ages who are in good health and are accustomed to a reasonable amount of exercise. A little honesty goes a long way. Recognize your own level of physical fitness and discuss it with the tour operator before signing on.

How far off the beaten path do you want to go? Depending on your tour operator and itinerary, you'll often have a choice between relatively easy travel with comfortable accommodations or more strenuous activities with overnights spent in basic lodgings or at campsites. Ask yourself if it's the *reality* or the *image* of roughing it that appeals to you. Be honest, and go with a company that can provide what you're looking for.

Is sensitivity to the environment important to you? If so, determine if the environment is equally important to your operator. Does the company protect the fragile environments you'll be visiting? Are some of the company's profits designated for conservation efforts, and are they put back into the communities visited? Does it encourage indigenous people to dress up (or dress down) so that your group can get great photos, or does it respect their cultures? Many of the companies included in this chapter are actively involved in environmental conservation and projects with indigenous communities. Their business's future depends on keeping this fragile ecological and cultural mix alive.

What sort of group is best for you? At its best, group travel attracts curious, like-minded companions with whom to share the day's experiences. Do you enjoy mixing with people from similar backgrounds, or would you prefer to travel with people of different ages and backgrounds? Inquire about group size. Many companies have a maximum of 10 to 16 members, but groups of 30 or more are not unknown. The larger the group, the more time will be spent (or wasted) at rest stops, meals, and hotel arrivals and departures.

Do you want a custom trip? If groups aren't your thing, most companies will customize a trip for you. In fact, this has become a major part of many tour operations. Your itinerary can be as flexible or as rigid as you choose. Such travel offers all the conveniences of a package tour, but the "group" will be composed only of those you've chosen as your travel companions. Responding to a renewed interest in multigenerational travel, many tour operators also offer family trips, with itineraries carefully crafted to appeal to both children and adults.

How much preparatory help do you want? Gorgeous photos and well-written tour descriptions go a long way toward selling a company's trips. Once you've chosen your trip, though, there's a lot of room for your operator to either help you out or leave you out in the cold. For example, does the operator provide useful information about health (suggested or required inoculations, tips for dealing with high altitudes)? Will you get a list of frequently asked questions and their answers? What about recommended readings? Does the company provide equipment needed for sports trips? Can the company provide a list of client referrals? All of these things can make or break a trip, and you should know before you choose an operator whether or not you want help getting answers to all these questions.

Are there hidden costs? Make sure you know what is and what is not included in basic trip costs when comparing tour companies. International airfare is almost always extra. Domestic flights in-country are usually add-ons, but some companies (particularly those offering trips to very distant and isolated regions of Panama) do provide charter air service as a part of their basic trip cost. Is trip insurance required, and if so, is it included? Are airport transfers included? Visa fees? Departure taxes? Gratuities? Although some travelers prefer the option of an excursion or free time, many (especially those visiting a destination for the first time) want to see as much as possible. Paying extra for a number of excursions can significantly increase the total cost of the trip. Many factors affect the price, and the trip that looks cheapest in the brochure could well turn out to be the most expensive. Don't assume that roughing it will save you money, as prices rise with limited access. A lack of essential supplies on-site can require costly special arrangements.

WHAT TYPE OF TRIP

■ **Adventure Tours.** Adrenaline-pumping sports and thrills for the active traveler.

■ **Diving Trips.** Central America's Caribbean coastline is one of the top diving destinations in the world.

■ **Ecotourism.** Spot a resplendent quetzal while staying at a thatched jungle lodge in pristine cloud forests.

■ **Cultural Tourism.** Living and learning with a native culture.

■ **Language Schools.** Learn Spanish while staying with a local family.

■ **Volunteer Vacations.** Get your hands dirty helping save the rain forest or protect the leatherback-turtle breeding grounds.

MONEY MATTERS

Tours in Central America can be found at all price points, but local operators can usually offer the best deal. Tours that are run by local people are generally cheaper and also give the greatest monetary benefit to the local economy. These types of tours are not always listed in guidebooks or on the Internet; often they have to be found in-person or by word of mouth. Safety and date specificity can fluctuate. Few guides speak English and are not always certified. Amenities such as lodging and transportation may be very basic in this category. Some agencies pay attention to the environment while others do not. You really have to do your research on every operator to be sure you are getting exactly what you need. The payoff in terms of price and quality of experience can be considerable if you find the right match for your needs.

On the other end of the spectrum, the large (often international) tour agencies such as Abercrombie & Kent, G.A.P. Adventures, International Expeditions, Panama Trails, and others may be the most expensive, but they provide the greatest range of itinerary choices and highest quality of services. Larger, more well-known companies often use the best transportation, such as private planes, buses, and boats, which rarely break down. First-rate, safe equipment and reliable guides are the norm. Dates and times are set in stone, so you can plan your trip down to the time you step in and out of the airport. Guides are usually English speaking, certified, and well paid. When food and lodging are provided, they are generally of high quality. If you are a traveler who likes to travel in comfort, look for tour operators at this end of the spectrum.

LODGING

The cost of lodging can vary greatly within Panama. Independent travelers tend to favor budget hotels and hostels costing little more than a few dollars a night. Conversely, luxurious five-star hotels geared to package tourists are becoming as common as howler monkeys. Your preference will help determine what type of tour operator is best for you. Most multiday tours include lodging, often at a discounted rate, and they generally offer options that accommodate most budgets through a number of hotels. On the other hand, many hotels have their own tour agencies or sell tours at a discounted rate to particular agencies. You can book either way depending on the specific tours and hotels that interest you. In many instances you don't necessarily have to book accommodation through your tour agency, although you will often save money if you are combining services such as transportation, food, tours, and guides. If you are interested in specific hotels, beach resorts or eco-lodges, your best tour options will be directly through those establishments. Considering the size of many Central American countries, most sights can be seen on one-day tours. This allows you to leave your luggage at the hotel for less hassle.

EQUIPMENT

Good gear is essential: sturdy shoes, a small flashlight or headlamp, rain gear, sunscreen, mosquito protection, and basic medications are all things you should bring with you no matter what kind of tour you're taking. For more technical sports, your choice of tour operator will determine whether you bring your own gear, buy new gear, or rent what they already have. Tour operators can generally provide equipment, but the quality of this equipment can vary. If you're using provided equipment, ask your operator for a written statement concerning the gear to be used. When you arrive, check that your expectations have been met, and complain if they haven't. Many companies do use top-of-the-line equipment; however, the occasional company will cut corners. Prices on equipment purchased in Central America tend to be significantly more expensive (roughly 20% higher) than in North America or Europe. If you prefer or require a specific brand of equipment, bringing your own is a good idea. Airlines accommodate most types of equipment and will likely have packing suggestions if you call ahead. For instance, most bicycle shops can take apart and box up your bike for plane transport. Bringing your own surfboard however, will cost you $175 each way on most airlines, and the boards are seldom handled with care. Airlines may charge additional fees for surpassing size and weight limits. Shipping equipment to Central America tends to be expensive, and if you're not using an agency such as FedEx or DHL (actually, even if you are!) expect the unexpected.

ADVENTURE AND LEARNING VACATIONS

ADVENTURE TOURS

MULTISPORT TOURS

Season: Year-round

Locations: Central Panama, Veraguas, Chiriquí, Bocas del Toro, San Blas, Chagres National Park

Cost: From $1,245 for eight days from Panama City for package tours; from $180 to $700 for daily

Tour Operators: BikeHike Adventures, Boquete Outdoor Adventures, Coral Lodge (⇨ *Lodges and Resorts*), Explorers' Corner, Futura Travel, G.A.P. Adventures, Islas Secas Resort (⇨ *Lodges and Resorts*), Journeys Latin America, Mountain Travel Sobek, Seakunga, Tranquilo Bay (⇨ *Lodges and Resorts*)

Hordes of kayak-toting adventure companies recently made their way to Panama from Costa Rica and have opened up a whole new frontier of Central America touring. Boquete Outdoor Adventures offers a nine-day trip that combines rafting, sea kayaking, island tours, hiking, and tree trekking. Explorers' Corner has 10-day kayaking trips led by two Kuna Yala guides that take you camping in San Blas for a total of 96 to 129 km (60 to 80 mi) of paddling, while Mountain Travel Sobek makes almost the same trip in nine days. G.A.P. Adventures' eight-day Kayak Panama samples the best of the Caribbean coast with five days exploring San Blas and another few days inland hiking and rafting around the Mamoni river basin. Similarly, Seakunga Adventures' eight-day kayaking trip centers on San Blas, but adds rafting and hiking in Chagres National Park. For more of a challenge, Journeys Latin Americas' Camino Real Trek takes you from the Pacific to the Caribbean, an 80 km (50 mi) transcontinental trek in the footsteps of Spanish conquistadors, with time to stop in Chagres National Park, Panama City, and Portobelo.

The companies Bikehike Adventures and Futura Travel run one- to two-week tours that combine biking, hiking, rafting, snorkeling, kayaking, and other sports. The high-end eco-lodges Coral Lodge, Islas Secas, and Tranquilo Bay offer packages that include skin diving, fishing, and other activities in pristine areas.

BIKING

Season: Year-round

Locations: Central Panama, Chiriquí

Cost: $25 for a half-day tour, $265 per day for country tour

Tour Operators: Bikehike Adventures (⇨ *Adventure Tours*)

Panama has mountain-biking potential, but few companies offer biking tours. Bikes can be rented in Panama City, El Valle de Antón, Boquete, and Bocas del Toro. The company Bikehike Adventures runs nine- to 14-day tours that combine mountain biking with kayaking, hiking, rafting, snorkeling, and other outdoor activities.

HORSEBACK RIDING

Season: Year-round

Locations: Central Panama, Azuero Peninsula, Chiriquí, Bocas del Toro

Cost: $20 to $80

Tour Operators: Boquete Outdoor Adventures (⇨ *Adventure Tours*), Coronado Golf & Beach Resort (⇨ *Lodges and Resorts*), Hacienda del Toro (⇨ *Lodges and Resorts*), Los Quetzales Lodge (⇨ *Lodges and Resorts*), Margo Tours

Panama has a cowboy tradition that stretches back to the 17th century, but horseback tours are in short supply. Boquete Outdoor Adventures has half-day trips to Caldera's hot springs. Margo Tours offers a half-day trail ride in the hills outside Panama City, but the best equestrian options are available through hotels in El Valle de Antón, Playa Venao, Boquete, and Cerro Punta. The Coronado Golf & Beach Resort has an equestrian center, but the nicest riding trails are in El Valle de Antón, Boquete, Volcán, and at Hacienda del Toro, in Bocas del Toro, since they lead through the forest.

KAYAKING

Season: Year-round

Locations: Central Panama, Chiriquí, Bocas del Toro, Kuna Yala

Cost: $75 to $185 per day

Tour Operators: Boquete Outdoor Adventures (⇨ *Adventure Tours*), Xtrop

Many coastal hotels have sit-on-top kayaks available for their guests, but serious kayakers should consider taking a tour with the outfitter Xtrop, which offers a sunset paddle on the canal, day trips down the lower Chagres River, and multiday sea-kayak tours of Kuna Yala. Boquete Outdoor Adventures has programs that combine sea kayaking with other outdoor activities; one includes kayaking in both oceans and in the rivers of Chiriquí province.

WHITE-WATER RAFTING

Season: Year-round

Locations: Central Panama, Chiriquí

Cost: $90–$175

Tour Operators: Aventuras Panama, Chiriquí River Rafting, Panama Rafters

Panama has spectacular white-water rafting, with warm-water rivers that flow through stretches of rain forest. Most of the country's rivers are high enough for rafting only between July and December, but the two best ones, the Río Chagres and Río Chiriquí Viejo, can usually be navigated through March. The Chagres is a Class II/III river near Panama City that requires no rafting experience and flows through pristine rain forest. One- and two-day Chagres trips are run by Aventuras Panama. The Chiriquí Viejo is a wilder river that flows through some of the country's most beautiful scenery, with lush forests, canyons, and a waterfall, but it requires prior rafting experience during the rainy months. Panama Rafters and Chiriquí River Rafting run trips on the river. Chiriquí River Rafting also runs trips on the Estí (Class II/III), Gariche (Class II/III), Dolega (Class II/III), and Chiriquí (Class III) rivers between June and November.

BEACHES AND OCEAN SPORTS

BEACHES

Season: Year-round

Locations: Bocas del Toro, San Blas, Veraguas

Cost: from $1,295 for seven days from Panama City

Tour Operators: Adventure Life, G.A.P. Adventures (⇨ *Adventure Tours*), Journeys Latin America (⇨ *Adventure Tours*), Seakunga Adventures (⇨ *Adventure Tours*), Costa Rica Expeditions, Willie's Tours, Wildland Adventures

Escape the crowds on Panama's Caribbean coast where many spots are reachable only by boat or charter jet. The San Blas Islands are some of the cleanest and most serene islands in the world and are home to the Kuna Yala Indians. There are just a few small guesthouses here, but the waters are crystal clear and the marine life is abundant. Every tour operator in the country will be able to arrange kayaking or sailing trips. For something unique, the Punta Caracol resort in the Bocas del Toro archipelago offers affordable overwater bungalows.

DIVING

Season: Year-round (conditions vary by region)

Locations: Central Caribbean, Gulf of Panama, Isla Iguana, Isla Coiba, Gulf of Chiriquí, Bocas del Toro, San Blas Islands

Cost: From $50 for two-tank boat dive to $440 per day for Isla Coiba dive cruise

Tour Operators: Bocas Water Sports, Buzos Boca Brava, Buzos de Azuero, Coral Dreams, Coral Lodge (⇨ *Lodges and Resorts*), Islas Secas Resort (⇨ *Lodges and Resorts*), La Buga, Isla Grande Diver Center, Panama Divers, San Blas Cruises (⇨ *Cruising*), Scuba Coiba, Scuba Panama, Starfleet Scuba

Panama has some of the best diving in the Caribbean and eastern Pacific and is the only country in the world where you can dive both the Pacific and the Atlantic on the same day. The country's most impressive dive destination is remote Isla de Coiba, part of Golfo de Chiriquí National

CLOSE UP

Tour Operators

ADVENTURE TOUR OUTFITTERS
Bikehike Adventures (☎ 888/805–0061 in the U.S.; 0808/234–1403 in the U.K. ⊕ www.bikehike.com).

Boquete Outdoor Adventures (✉ Plaza Los Establos, Av. Central, Boquete ☎ 720–2284 ⊕ www.boqueteoutdooradventures.com).

Explorers' Corner (☎ 877/677–6923 ⊕ www.explorerscorner.com).

Futura Travel (✉ Centro Comercial Camino de Cruces, Panama City ☎ 360–2030 ⊕ www.extremepanama.com).

G.A.P. Adventures (☎ 416/260–0999 in Canada or 800/708–7761 ⊕ www.gapadventures.com).

Journeys Latin America (✉ 020/8747–8315 in the U.K.

⊕ www.journeylatinamerica.co.uk).

Mountain Travel Sobek (☎ 510/594–6000 or 888/831–7526 ⊕ www.mtsobek.com).

Seakunga Adventures (☎ 800/781–2269 or 604/893–8668 in Canada ⊕ www.seakunga.com).

BEACHES
Adventure Life (☎ 800/344–6118 ⊕ www.adventure-life.com).

Costa Rica Expeditions (☎ 506/2257–0766 ⊕ www.costaricaexpeditions.com).

Wildland Adventures (☎ 800/345–4453 or 206/365–0686 ⊕ www.wildland.com).

Willie's Tours ☎ 506/2755–0267 ⊕ www.willies-costarica-tours.com.

BIRD-WATCHING
Exotic Birding (☎ 877/247–3371 in the U.S. ⊕ www.exoticbirding.com).

Field Guides (☎ 800/728–4953 in the U.S. ⊕ www.fieldguides.com).

Nattur Panama (✉ Colón ☎ 442–1340 ⊕ natturpanama.com).

Panama Audubon Society (✉ Altos de Curundú, Panama City ☎ 232–5977 ⊕ www.panamaaudubon.org).

VENT(Victor Emanuel Adventure Tours) (☎ 800/328–8368 in the U.S. ⊕ www.ventbird.com).

DIVING
Bocas Water Sports (✉ Calle 3, Bocas del Toro ☎ 757–9541 ⊕ www.bocaswatersports.com).

Buzos Boca Brava (✉ Marina, Boca Chica ☎ 775–3185 or 6600–6191 ⊕ www.scubadiving-panama.com).

Buzos de Azuero (✉ Calle Principal, Pedasí ☎ 995–2405 ⊕ www.dive-n-fishpanama.com).

Coral Dreams (✉ Aeropuerto, Contadora ☎ 6536–1776 ⊕ www.coraldreams.com).

Isla Grande Dive Center (✉ Isla Grande ☎ 6501–4374 or 232–6994 ⊕ www.buceoenpanama.com).

La Buga (✉ Isla Colon, Bocas del Toro ☎ 757–9534

⊕ www.labugapanama.com).

Panama Divers (✉ Portobelo, Central Panama ☎ 314–0817 or 6613–4405 ⊕ www.panamadivers.com).

Scuba Coiba (✉ Santa Catalina, Veraguas ☎ 6575–0122 ⊕ www.scubacoiba.com).

Scuba Panama (✉ El Dorado, Panama City ☎ 261–3841 ⊕ www.scubapanama.com).

Tour Operators (continued)

Starfleet Scuba (✉ *Bocas del Toro* ☎ *757–9630* ⊕ *www.starfleetscuba. com*).

FISHING
Coiba Adventure Sportfishing (✉ *Pedregal, David* ☎ *636/405–1200; 800/800–0907 in the U.S.* ⊕ *www. coibadventure.com*).

Las Perlas Fishing Charters (✉ *Hotel Contadora, Contadora* ☎ *6689–4916*).

Panama Big Game Fishing Club (✉ *Isla Boca Brava, Chiriquí* ☎ *6674– 4824; 866/281–1225 in the U.S.* ⊕ *www.panamabiggamefishingclub. com*).

Panama Canal Fishing (✉ *Clayton, Panama City* ☎ *315–1905 or 6699– 0507* ⊕ *www.panamacanalfishing. com*).

Panama Fishing and Catching (✉ *Panama City* ☎ *6622–0212* ⊕ *www.panamafishingandcatching. com*).

Pesca Panama (☎ *800/946–3473 in the U.S.* ⊕ *www.pescapanama.com*).

HIKING AND WALKING
Advantage Panama (✉ *Llanos de Curundú, Panama City* ☎ *223–9283 or 6676–2466* ⊕ *www. advantagepanama.com*).

Ancon Expeditions (✉ *Calle Elvira Mendez, Edificio El Dorado No. 3, Panama City* ☎ *269–9415* ⊕ *www. anconexpeditions.com*).

Coffee Adventures (✉ *Entrega General, Boquete Chiriquí* ☎ *720–3852* ⊕ *www.coffeeadventures.net*).

Eco Circuitos Panama (✉ *Calle Amador, Panama City* ☎ *314–0068* ⊕ *www.ecocircuitos.com*).

International Expeditions ☎ *800/633–4734 or 205/428–1700* ⊕ *www.ietravel.com*.

Panoramic Panama (✉ *Quarry Heights, Panama City* ☎ *314–1604* ⊕ *www.panoramicpanama.com*).

Panama Birding (✉ *Clayton, Panama City* ☎ *264–5720; 800/930–3397 in U.S.* ⊕ *www.panamabirding.com*).

Pesantez Tours (✉ *Plaza Balboa, Panama City* ☎ *366–9100* ⊕ *www. pesantez-tours.com*).

HORSEBACK RIDING
Margo Tours (✉ *Calle 50, Panama City* ☎ *264–8888* ⊕ *www.margotours. com*).

INTERNATIONAL TOUR COMPANIES
Abercrombie & Kent (☎ *630/725– 3400 or 800/554–7016* ⊕ *www. abercrombiekent.com*).

Panama Trails (✉ *Calles 50 and 71, Plaza Morical, Panama City* ☎ *393– 8334* ⊕ *www.panamatrails.com*).

KAYAKING
Xtrop (✉ *Balboa, Panama City* ☎ *317–1279* ⊕ *www.xtrop.com*).

LANGUAGE SCHOOLS
AmeriSpan (☎ *215/751–1100* ⊕ *www.amerispan.com*).

Habla Ya (✉ *Boquete* ☎ *720–1294* ⊕ *www.hablayapanama.com*).

Spanish by the River (✉ *Alto Boquete, Entrada a Palmira, 180 mts a mano izquierda, Boquete* ☎ *720–3456* ⊕ *www.spanishatlocations.com*).

8

Tour Operators (continued)

LANGUAGE SCHOOLS (CONT.)
Spanish by the Sea (⊠ *Calle 4, behind Hotel Bahía, Bocas del Toro* ☎ *757–9518* ⊕ *www.spanishatlocations.com*).

Spanish Panama (⊠ *Vía Argentina, above the Greenhouse Restaurant, El Cangrejo,Panama City* ☎ *213–3121* ⊕ *www.spanishpanama.com*) offers inexpensive group classes and one-on-one instruction at your hotel, restaurants, while sightseeing, or at their conveniently located center.

SURFING
Panama Surf (⊠ *El Dorad, Panama City* ☎ *264–1005, 805/617–4612 in U.S.* ⊕ *www.panama-surf.com*).

Panama Surf Tours (⊠ *Panama City* ☎ *6671–7777* ⊕ *www.panamasurftours.com*).

VOLUNTEER VACATIONS
Emerald Planet. (☎ *888/883–0736* ⊕ *www.emeraldplanet.com*).

WHITE-WATER RAFTING
Aventuras Panama (⊠ *El Dorado, Panama City* ☎ *260–0044* ⊕ *www.aventuraspanama.com*).

Chiriquí River Rafting (⊠ *Av. Central, Boquete* ☎ *720–1505* ⊕ *www.panama-rafting.com*).

Panama Rafters (⊠ *Av. Central, Boquete* ☎ *720–2712* ⊕ *www.panamarafters.com*).

LODGES AND RESORTS
Burbayar Lodge (⊠ *Alto Bayano, Central Panama* ☎ *390–6674* ⊕ *www.burbayar.com*).

Coral Lodge (⊠ *Satna Isabell, Central Panama* ☎ *232–0200 or 832–0795* ⊕ *www.corallodge.com*).

Coronado Golf & Beach Resort (⊠ *Coronado, Central Panama* ☎ *264–3164* ⊕ *www.coronadoresort. com*).

Finca Lérida (⊠ *Alto Quiel, Boquete, Chiriquí* ☎ *720–2285* ⊕ *www.fincalerida.com*).

Gone Fishing (⊠ *Boca Chica, Chiriquí* ☎ *851–0104* ⊕ *www.gonefishingpanama.com*)

Hacienda del Mar (☎ *269–6613; 866/433–5627 in U.S.* ⊕ *www.haciendadelmar.net*).

Hacienda del Toro (☎ *6612–9159* ⊕ *www.haciendadeltoro.com*).

Islas Secas Resort (⊠ *Islas Secas, Chiriquí* ☎ *805/729–2737 in the U.S.* ⊕ *www.islassecas.com*)

Los Quetzales Lodge and Spa (⊠ *Cerro Punta, Chriquí* ☎ *771–2182* ⊕ *www.losquetzales.com*).

Morro Negrito Surf Camp (⊠ *Isla Ensenada, Chiriquí* ☎ *832–2831; 760/632–8014 in U.S.* ⊕ *www.panamasurfcamp.com*).

Posada Ecológico Cerro de la Vieja (⊠ *Churuguí Grande, Central Panama* ☎ *983–8900* ⊕ *www.posadalavieja. com*).

Sierra Llorona Panama Lodge (⊠ *Sierra Llorona, Central Panama* ☎ *442–8104* ⊕ *www.sierrallorona. com*).

Tranquilo Bay (⊠ *Isla Bastimentos, Bocas del Toro* ☎ *380–0721; 713/589–6952 in U.S.* ⊕ *www.tranquilobay.com*).

Tropic Star Lodge (⊠ *Piñas Bay, Darién* ☎ *800/682–3424 in the U.S.* ⊕ *www.tropicstar.com*).

Park that protects thousands of acres of reef and more than 700 fish species. Scuba Coiba and Panama Divers offer trips that include nights in rustic rooms on the island. Adding to this impressive dive region are the surrounding areas of Islas Secas, Los Ladrones, Parilla, Isla Boca Brava, Isla Palenque, and Montuoso. Diving around Golfo de Chiriquí is available at the Islas Secas Resort, or on less expensive trips with Buzos Boca Brava, in Boca Chica. Another impressive spot is Isla Iguana, on the east coast of the Azuero Peninsula, where Buzos de Azuero offers inexpensive scuba and skin-diving trips. More accessible sites in the Golfo de Panama can be explored from Isla Contadora with Coral Dreams, or out of Panama City with Scuba Panama, which also offers diving in the Panama Canal and a two-oceans-in-one-day dive trip.

Whereas Panama's Pacific dives offer encounters with schools of big fish, the Caribbean has more coral and sponge diversity and warmer water. Caribbean attractions include vast coral and sponge gardens populated by colorful damselfish, sea stars, and countless other creatures. The most accessible Caribbean diving areas are Portobelo and Isla Grande, about two hours from Panama City, where Panama Divers, Scuba Panama, and the Isla Grande Dive Center provide access to miles of barrier reef, sunken ships, and a plane wreck. The most pristine reefs are found in the Escribano Bank, which you can dive out of Coral Lodge, in Santa Isabel. East of there lie the San Blas Islands of Kuna Yala, where scuba diving is prohibited. Indigenous lodges include snorkeling trips in their rates, but skin divers can visit more pristine reefs and islands on cruises with San Blas Sailing. Panama's other important Caribbean region is Bocas del Toro, which has dozens of dive spots near an array of accommodations. Dive operators such as Bocas Watersports, La Buga, Land and Sea Adventures, and Starfleet Scuba offer dives at impressive spots such as the Cayos Zapatillas and Tiger Rock.

The Caribbean experiences its best diving conditions from September to November and from April to June. Pacific diving tends to be good everywhere from November to January, when seas are calm. Between the Gulf of Panama to Veraguas, high winds make the water progressively colder and cloudier from January to April and can make diving impossible in Contadora and Isla Iguana, though there are more fish around then. Those areas experience better water conditions from July to December. The Gulf of Chiriquí has its best diving conditions between December and July, after which large swells can make dive spots inaccessible and decrease visibility.

FISHING

Season: Year-round (best from January to March)

Locations: The Darién, Gulf of Panama, Azuero Peninsula, Chiriquí, Gatún Lake

Cost: From $300 per day for Gatún Lake to $1,700 per day for fishing cruises or lodge packages

Tour Operators: Buzos de Azuero (⇨ *Diving*), Coiba Adventure Sportfishing, Gone Fishing (⇨ *Lodges and Resorts*), Hacienda del Mar (⇨ *Lodges and Resorts*), Islas Secas Resort (⇨ *Lodges and Resorts*), Las Perlas Fishing Charters, MV *Coral Star* (⇨ *Cruising*), Panama Big Game

Fishing Club, Panama Canal Fishing, Panama Fishing and Catching, Pesca Panama, Tropic Star Lodge (⇨ *Lodges and Resorts*)

Popular legend has it that Panama means "abundance of fish" in a native language. Though the Caribbean fishing is average, Panama's Pacific waters have some of the best fishing in the Western Hemisphere, if not the world, with massive blue and black marlin, Pacific sailfish, tuna, wahoo, dolphin, roosterfish, mackerel, and other fighters in good supply. The country's top fishing spot is remote Bahia Piñas, where the Tropic Star Lodge provides comfortable access to phenomenal fishing. More than 250 world fishing records have been set there, and black marlin average 300 to 600 pounds, whereas tuna between 100 and 200 pounds are regularly hooked. The Golfo de Chiriquí, to the west, is a close second, with lots of marlin, sailfish, and other big fighters near the Hannibal Banks, Isla Montuosa, and Isla de Coiba, where catch-and-release fishing is permitted. Those waters can be fished from the 115-foot MV *Coral Star*, or out of lodges with Gone Fishing, Panama Big Game Fishing Club, Pesca Panama, and Coiba Adventure Fishing. Between those two regions lie the Pearl Islands, where good angling is accessible from Hacienda del Mar, on Isla San José, and Isla Contadora, where Las Perlas Fishing Charters offers affordable trips. Panama Fishing and Catching has charters in the Gulf of Panama and Pacific estuaries out of Panama City. Buzo de Azuero, in Pedasí, has inexpensive charters on the Azuero Peninsula's "Tuna Coast." The best months for marlin are December through March, whereas Pacific sailfish run from April to July. Tuna and other fish are most abundant from December to April. A less expensive alternative to deep-sea fishing is light-tackle angling on Gatún Lake, in the Panama Canal, which has lots of feisty peacock bass, snook, and tarpon. Panama Canal Fishing has family packages and can guarantee you'll catch plenty of fish year-round.

SURFING

Season: Year-round

Locations: Central Pacific, Azuero Peninsula, Veraguas, Chiriquí, Bocas del Toro

Cost: $75–$150 per day

Tour Operators: Morro Negrito Surf Camp (⇨ *Lodges and Resorts*), Panama Surf, Panama Surf Tours

Though it doesn't have as many breaks as nearby Costa Rica, Panama has world-class surf, and several companies offer access to remote breaks. Most of Panama's surf spots are reef breaks, making them better destinations for experienced surfers than for novices, but the country's surf companies offer lessons at its beaches and less treacherous reef breaks. Though there are a few breaks in Central Panama, (most notably at Isla Grande and Playa El Palmar), the country's best surf is at Playa Venao, on the Azuero Peninsula, and Santa Catalina, to the west. The best Pacific surfing is from June to December, when the waves regularly break overhead, whereas the Caribbean tends to get its best surf from November to March and July and August.

Surf tours are an excellent option because most of Panama's breaks are quite remote and are often accessible only by boat. Panama Surf Tours, run by longtime resident Kenny Myers, has a rustic lodge in Santa Catalina and offers guided trips to the country's best spots. Panama Surf, which is run by several Panamanian surfers, provides a comparable selection of surfing package tours. The Morro Negrito Surf Camp, on an island in the Golfo de Chiriquí, provides access to five isolated breaks that are seldom surfed. There are several breaks in Bocas del Toro, some of which are a mere 10-minute boat ride from the town of Bocas.

ECOTOURISM

HIKING AND WALKING

Season: Year-round

Locations: Central Panama, Chiriquí, the Darién

Cost: $30 to $175 per day for expeditions

Tour Operators: Advantage Panama, Ancon Expeditions, Burbayar Lodge (⇨ *Lodges and Resorts*), Coffee Adventures, Eco Circuitos Panama, Finca Lérida (⇨ *Fishing*), Futura Travel (⇨ *Adventure Tour Outfitters*), International Expeditions, Los Quetzales Lodge and Spa (⇨ *Lodges and Resorts*), Panoramic Panama, Panama Birding, Pesantez Tours, Posada Ecológico Cerro de la Vieja (⇨ *Lodges and Resorts*), Sierra Llorona Panama Lodge (⇨ *Lodges and Resorts*)

Hiking and walking are a big part of exploring Panama's forests, and the options for getting into the country's woods range from an early-morning hike through Panama City's Parque Natural Metropolitano to a two-week trek through the jungles of the Darién. All the country's nature-tour operators offer guided hikes and bird-watching trips in parks near Panama City, but only Ancon Expeditions and Eco Circuitos Panama offer multiday trips that include camping in indigenous communities and the rain forest. Ancon Expeditions' Trans-Darién Explorer and Camino Real treks are the most challenging and adventurous expeditions available, but there are plenty of shorter hikes through pristine forest. For forest hikes intermixed with bird-watching, a canal transit and an introduction to the Emberá Indians, try International Expeditions. Various lodges with private reserves and trail systems serve as excellent bases for day hikes, such as Burbayar, Finca Lérida, Los Quetzales Lodge, Posada Ecológica Cerro de la Vieja, Sierra Llorona Panama Lodge, and lodges run by Ancón Expeditions and Panama Birding. Some of the most popular trails are in the mountains, namely in El Valle de Antón and Chiriquí's Volcán Barú and La Amistad national parks, near Boquete and Cerro Punta.

BIRD-WATCHING

Season: Year-round (more species October–March)

Locations: Central Panama, Chiriquí, the Darién

Cost: From $80 for a day tour to $380 per day for package tour

Tour Operators: Advantage Panama (⇨ *Hiking and Walking*), Ancon Expeditions (⇨ *Hiking and Walking*), Coffee Adventures (⇨ *Hiking and Walking*), Eco Circuitos Panama (⇨ *Hiking and Walking*), Exotic Birding, Field Guides, Nattur Panama, Panama Audubon Society, Panama

CRUISING IN PANAMA

Cruise ships regularly transit the Panama Canal, but most provide little exposure to the country's natural and cultural wonders. Exceptions to this rule are companies that offer cruises on smaller ships that include stops at uninhabited islands and indigenous villages. Alternatively, you can take advantage of less expensive cruising options in Panama, such as weekly partial transits of the canal, or monthly full transits, for a fraction of what a day on a cruise ship costs. Cruises run year-round, but there are more options from December through May.

Canal and Bay Tours (⊠ *Bahia Balboa Building, Panama City* ☎ *209–2009* ⊕ *www.canalandbaytours.com*) offers canal cruises every Saturday year-round, with additional cruises on Thursday and Friday from January to April.

Cruise West (☎ *888/851–8133 in the U.S.* ⊕ *www.cruisewest.com*) offers 11- to 14-day cruises that visit parks and villages in Panama and Costa Rica; some of these cruises include a Panama Canal transit.

Linblad Expeditions (☎ *800/397–3348 in the U.S.* ⊕ *www.expeditions. com*) runs eight-day cruises that transit the canal and stop at natural sites such as Isla de Coiba and parks in Costa Rica.

M/V Coral Star (☎ *866/924–2837 in U.S.* ⊕ *www.coralstar.com*) offers one-week cruises to Isla de Coiba and surroundings that can include sport fishing, skin diving, snorkeling, hiking, and sea kayaking. The primary activities on these cruises, however, are fishing and diving.

Pacific Marine Tours (☎ *226–8417* ⊕ *www.pmatours.net*) offers canal cruises as well as expeditions cruises around panama on a 33-foot catamaran motor yacht.

San Blas Sailing (⊠ *Balboa, Panama City* ☎ *314–1800* ⊕ *sanblassailing.com*) offers four-day to three-week sailing cruises to Kuna Yala that visit such remote and pristine areas as the Cayos Holandeses.

Seabourn (☎ *800/929–9391 in the U.S.* ⊕ *www.seabourn.com*) runs two-week luxury cruises that combine Panama with Costa Rica and Belize.

Tauck (☎ *800/788–7885 in the U.S.* ⊕ *www.tauck.com*) offers an 11-day Panama Canal and Costa Rica cruise that combines a canal transit with visits to indigenous villages and Pacific islands.

Birding (⇨ *Hiking and Walking*), Panoramic Panama (⇨ *Hiking and Walking*), Pesantez Tours (⇨ *Hiking and Walking*), VENT

With more than 960 bird species in an area smaller than South Carolina, Panama is a bird-watchers Valhalla. It is not only home to such rare and spectacular species as the blue-and-gold macaw, resplendent quetzal, and harpy eagle, it is a place to witness natural phenomena, such as hawk and vulture migrations or island rookeries where tens of thousands of seabirds gather. The avian diversity is complemented by the fact that there are dozens of world-class birding lodges and the fact that you can visit various bird regions in a week or two. The best months for birding are October to April, when Northern migrants boost the local population, so you might spot an emerald toucanet and a Baltimore oriole in the same tree.

There are birds everywhere in Panama, but the best birding regions are Central Panama, the mountains of western Chiriquí Province, and the jungles of the Darién. The most popular central areas are Parque Nacional Soberanía, where the Panama Audubon Society has held many world-record Christmas bird counts, and Parque Nacional San Lorenzo, which is a good place to see the hawk and vulture migrations in October and March. Central Panama has excellent lodges in the middle of the wilderness, such as Birding Panama's Canopy Tower and Canopy Lodge, the Sierra Llorona Panama Lodge, and the Burbayar. The mountain valleys of Boquete and Cerro Punta, in Chiriquí, have many birds you won't find in other parts of the country, including the resplendent quetzal, which you might see at National Park Baru, La Amistad, Finca Lérida, Finca Hartmann, and Los Quetzales Lodge. Terry van der Vooren of Coffee Adventures is considered Boquete's most knowledgeable bird guide and brings nearly a decade of experience to the area. The easternmost province of the Darién has Panama's most impressive bird diversity, including four macaw species, half a dozen parrot species, and harpy eagles, but it is a most expensive area to visit. The country's best birding is found at Ancon Expeditions' Cana Field Station and the Chiriquí highlands.

Ancon Expeditions have excellent guides and a "Birds of Panama" tour that is comprehensive and affordable. Advantage Panama, Eco Circuitos, and Nattur Panama offer comparable trips. Panama Birding has the country's best birding lodges and good guides. Panoramic Panama and Pesantez Tours specialize in shorter trips. Field Guides and Exotic Birding sell Ancon Expeditions' tours but send an expert guide along, whereas VENT does the same thing using Panama Birding's lodges. The Panama Audubon Society also offers inexpensive weekend excursions that are open to foreigners. In addition, there are a few good, independent birding guides in El Valle de Antón, Boquete, and Cerro Punta.

VOLUNTEER VACATIONS

Season: Year-round

Locations: San Lorenzo National Park

Cost: From $1,499 for seven days from Panama City

Tour Operator: Emerald Planet

Emerald Planet's focus is the Panamanian community of Achiote. You will help the villagers attract ecotourists, who generally stop just short of this village, while also helping villagers to preserve their traditions. The project is in conjunction with the Conway School of Landscape Design and the Massachusetts Audubon Society. Days are divided between volunteering and diverse ecotours in San Lorenzo National Park, where single-day bird counts have exceeded 300 species.

CULTURAL TOURISM

CULTURAL IMMERSION

Season: Year-round

Locations: San Blas Islands

Cost: From $545 for three days from Panama City

Tour Operator: Journeys Latin America (⇨ *Adventure Tours*), Ancon Expeditions (⇨ *Hiking and Walking*)

Journeys Latin America offers a three-day trip to the San Blas Islands, where you'll flit between islands in traditional dugout canoes and stay in thatched huts belonging to the Kuna Yala Indians. If you're lucky, you'll be taken to the communal houses of the *sahilas,* or chief. The local government is completely autonomous. Ancon Expeditions offers similar tours.

LANGUAGE SCHOOLS

Season: Year-round

Locations: Panama City, Boquete, Bocas del Toro

Cost: From $1,600 for four weeks from Panama City

Tour Operators: Amerispan, Habla Ya, Spanish by the River, Spanish by the Sea, Spanish Panama

Amerispan's program in Panama City provides 20 hours of classes per week and a private room with a host family in Altos de Chases, a wealthy suburb of Panama City. It's just a stone's throw from the city's best shopping, dining, and nightlife. Beaches, rain forests, and the canal are all less than an hour's drive away. Amerispan's Spanish course in Bocas del Toro includes 20 hours of classes per week plus lodging in a private cabina. Habla Ya offers group, immersion, and individual classes in Boquete, and also offers some discount lodging for visiting students. Spanish by the Sea offers 20 to 30 hours of classes per week in Bocas del Toro and Boquete. Spanish Panama, right in Panama City, offers inexpensive group classes and one-on-one instruction at your hotel, restaurants, while sightseeing, or at their conveniently located center.

Travel Smart Panama

WORD OF MOUTH

"Taxi rides in Panama City were cheap even though gas was already expensive. I am not sure what the prices are now. Agree on a price BEFORE you start. It is easy to flag down a taxi. Just stand on the curb and wave your hand at the traffic."

—Oldanalyst

GETTING HERE AND AROUND

We're proud of our Web site: Fodors.com is a great place to begin any journey. Scan Travel Wire for suggested itineraries, travel deals, restaurant and hotel openings, and other up-to-the-minute info. Check out Booking to research prices and book plane tickets, hotel rooms, rental cars, and vacation packages. Head to Talk for on-the-ground pointers from travelers who frequent our message boards. You can also link to loads of other travel-related resources.

Panama is the southernmost part of an isthmus that stretches between Colombia and Costa Rica. Although relatively narrow, the country still has hundreds of miles of Pacific and Caribbean coastline. It is bisected by the Panama Canal, which runs north-south across the center of the country. To the east, the Carretera Panamericana heads toward the Darién, home to a vast, near-impenetrable jungle, which creates the only break in the whole highway. The road starts again on the other side of the Colombian border and continues to Patagonia. A coral atoll known as the San Blas Islands lies off this coast and is accessible only by light airplane or boat. The Carretera Panamericana (Panamerican Highway) runs west from Panama City to Costa Rica, passing through Penonomé and Santiago and also offering access to the Azuero Peninsula. Two provinces border Costa Rica: Chiriquí, to the south, and Bocas del Toro, to the north. You can reach Bocas by land from Chiriquí, by light airplane, and by boat.

▋ BY AIR

The country has only one international airport, Aeropuerto Internacional de Tocumen. From New York or Chicago flying time is about five hours; from Miami 2¾ hours; from L.A. 5½ hours; and from Dallas or Houston 4¼ hours. Flights from Toronto via Newark take nine hours, or seven hours via Miami.

Airlines and Airports Airline and Airport Links.com (⊕ *www.airlineandairportlinks.com*) has links to many of the world's airlines and airports.

Airline-Security Issues Transportation Security Administration (⊕ *www.tsa.gov*) has answers for almost every question that might come up.

AIRPORTS

Panama's main air hub is Aeropuerto Internacional de Tocumen (PTY), about 26 km (15 mi) northeast of Panama City. All scheduled international flights land here. The passenger terminal was completely overhauled in 2006 and is now a pleasant glass-walled construction. There's an abundance of shops—most sell luxury clothing and electronics—but only one snack bar and a couple of food carts, so don't plan on much more than a coffee and an expensive sandwich. Tocumen also has a tourist-information booth, ATMs, 24-hour luggage storage, car-rental agencies, and a telephone and Internet center. Arrival and departure formalities are usually efficient. If you arrive two hours prior to departure, you should have ample time to get to the boarding gate. Save time by using online check-in, if your airline offers the service. Likewise, clearing customs and immigration is usually a quick procedure.

Domestic flights operate out of Aeropuerto Marcos A. Gelabert (PAC), more commonly known as Albrook Airport, after the U.S. military base that once stood here. Albrook has a tourist-information stand, an ATM, and some car-rental offices.

Airport Information Aeropuerto Internacional de Tocumen (☎ 238–2761 ⊕ *www.tocumenpanama.aero*). Aeropuerto Marcos A. Gelabert (Albrook Airport) (✉ *Av. Gaillard, Albrook* ☎ 315–0241).

GROUND TRANSPORTATION

Taxis are the quickest way into Panama City from Tocumen Airport. The fare is as much as $40, an expensive ride for Panama, so it's worth finding out if your hotel has a shuttle service. There is no taxi stand at the airport, and only licensed operators are allowed to offer services as you leave the airport doors. Sharing the ride with strangers is commonplace and can reduce the fare you pay; the tourist-information booth often helps travelers band together. The trip can take between 20 and 60 minutes, depending on traffic, and whether the driver takes the Corredor Sur toll road, which is quicker but costs an extra $2.65, which drivers should cover as part of their outrageous fee. Note that taxis are often scarce late at night.

Public buses run frequently between Tocumen and the terminal north of Plaza Cinco de Mayo, but it can be a hassle to hoist your luggage onto them. They cost 70¢ and take 45 to 60 minutes.

The 15-minute taxi ride from Albrook Airport to the city center costs $2 to $3. The bus to Plaza Cinco de Mayo costs 25¢ and takes 25 minutes.

TRANSFERS BETWEEN AIRPORTS

A taxi ride between Tocumen and Albrook airports can top $40, though if you're catching the cab at Albrook you might be able to negotiate a cheaper price. The trip takes about 30 minutes. Alternatively, buses to both airports start and finish at Plaza Cinco de Mayo, but the trip could end up taking a couple of hours.

FLIGHTS

Copa, a Continental partner, is Panama's flagship carrier. It operates direct flights to New York–JFK, Los Angeles, Miami, Washington Dulles, and Orlando. Copa also flies to many Central and South American cities. You can fly to Panama from Houston and Newark on Continental, from Atlanta on Delta, and from Miami on American.

Aeroperlas and Air Panama are Panama's two main domestic carriers and serve destinations all over the country, including San Blas, Bocas del Toro, David, and the Darién. Domestic flights usually cost $100 to $200 round-trip; you can buy tickets directly from the airline or through a travel agent. Sometimes buying your flight at the airport just before you travel is cheaper than planning far in advance.

Airline Contacts American Airlines (☎ 800/433–7300 in North America; 507/269–6022 in Panama ⊕ www.aa.com). **Continental Airlines** (☎ 800/231–0856 in North America; 507/265–0040 in Panama ⊕ www.continental.com). **Copa** (☎ 800/359–2672 in North America; 507/217–2672 in Panama ⊕ www.copaair.com). **Delta Airlines** (☎ 800/241–4141 in North America; 507/214–8118 in Panama ⊕ www.delta.com). **Iberia** (☎ 800/722–4642 in North America; 507/227–3966 in Panama ⊕ www.iberia.com).

Domestic Airlines Aeroperlas (☎ 507/315–7500 in Panama ⊕ www.aeroperlas.com). **Air Panama** (☎ 507/316–9000 in Panama ⊕ www.flyairpanama.com).

CHARTER FLIGHTS

Drop in demand and rising fuel prices have cut back some of the domestic flight services offered by Aeroperlas and Air Panama. Still, they both offer charter flight service, though it can be a bit pricey. A cheaper option might be renting a vehicle and driving. Air Panama does offer a $125 tourist flight over the Panama Canal, which offers, literally, a bird's-eye view of Panama's biggest attraction.

Contacts Aeroperlas (☎ 507/315–7500 in Panama ⊕ www.aeroperlas.com). **Air Panama** (☎ 507/316–9000 in Panama ⊕ www.flyairpanama.com).

∎ BY BOAT AND FERRY

For information about Panama Canal boat trips, see The Canal and Central Panama Essentials in Chapter 3. Arriving in Panama by boat is increasingly popular. Private sailing boats operate between Cartagena in Colombia and San Blas or Portobelo on Panama's Caribbean coast. The few operators cater mainly to backpackers and sometimes expect passengers to help with cooking, cleaning, or sailing. Zuly's and Mamallena, two hostels in Panama City, have ties with reputable sailboat captains and act as booking intermediaries. The trip can take up to five days (you stop at islands in San Blas) and costs $385, including all food.

Within Panama, boats are the only way to get between points in the archipelagos of San Blas and Bocas del Toro and much of the Darién. There are regular, inexpensive water-taxi services connecting the city of Almirante with Bocas del Toro. In the Darién, water taxis run between Puerto Quimba and La Palma. To get farther afield, people wind their way up narrow waterways in dugouts with outboard motors. Rides can be expensive ($60 to $200), especially when traveling alone, so you're often better off going with a tour company.

Contacts Mamallena (☎ 507/6676–6163 ⊕ www.mamallena.com). **Zuly's Independent Backpacker** (☎ 507/269–2665 ⊕ www. geocities.com/zulys_independent_backpacker).

■ BY BUS

INTERNATIONAL BUS SERVICES
You can reach Panama by bus from Costa Rica. Most services cross the border at Paso Canoas. The Darién jungle causes a gap in the Panamerican Highway, meaning bus travel to Colombia is impossible.

Popular with budget travelers, Ticabus is an international bus company connecting all of Central America. A bus leaves Panama City daily at 11 AM and 11 PM and takes 16 hours (direct) to get to San José in Costa Rica. One-way tickets cost $35 for the daytime departure and $25 for the nighttime departure. Ticabus continues to Nicaragua, Honduras, Guatemala, and Mexico. The buses are usually clean, air-conditioned, and comfortable.

Costa Rican company Panaline has daily services between San José and Panama

> **THE MATTER OF METERS**
>
> In directions and addresses in Panama, "100 meters" almost always means one block, regardless of actual measurements. Likewise, 200 meters is two blocks and 50 meters is half a block.

City. The round-trip costs $50; buses leave Panama at midday and take 16 hours.

International Bus Companies Panaline (☎ 507/314–6383 or 507/6764–4540 ⊕ www. panalinecr.com). **Ticabus** (☎ 507/314–6385 ⊕ www.ticabus.com).

DOMESTIC BUS SERVICES
Getting around Panama by bus is comfortable, cheap, and straightforward. Panama City is the main transport hub. Services to towns all over the country (and to the rest of Central America) leave from a huge building in Albrook—half terminal and half mall, it has shops, ATMs, Internet access, and restaurants. To get to smaller cities and beaches, you need to catch minibuses out of regional transit hubs.

Long-distance buses are usually clean and punctual, and the only real annoyance is the occasional blaring radio. The most comfortable buses are those running between Panama City and David. Routes are operated by many different bus companies, and there's no centralized timetable service. The best way to get departure times is to call the bus company or go to the terminal. Similarly, rates are not set in stone, but you can estimate $1 to $2 per hour of travel.

For bus company and terminal information, see the Essentials section in each destination chapter.

■ BY CAR

Panama is probably the best Central American country to drive in, and driving is a great way to see the country. The Panamerican Highway takes you to or near most towns in the country, and with a car you can also visit small villages and explore remote areas more easily. Even secondary roads are usually well sign-posted and in reasonable condition.

True, Panamanian drivers can be a little aggressive, but they're not much worse than New Yorkers or Angelinos. All the same, you're best saving the car for outside Panama City: traffic jams and lack of safe parking can make downtown driving very stressful.

When driving the four-lane section of the Panamerican Highway, don't expect slow drivers in the left lane to get out of the way. It doesn't matter that you can be pulled over and fined for driving in the left lane, which, in theory, is only for passing. You'll just have to floor it and pass, cautiously, on the right.

Panama City is the exception; though pretty staid by Latin American standards, there is a dearth of road signs and, beyond the major avenues, locals don't use—or know—the names of the mostly sign-free streets. Among the biggest hazards are missing manhole covers, flooded streets during downpours, and unmarked inverted circulation streets, which are used as turnarounds between major avenues. Turning down the wrong side street in the wrong part of town is an invitation to get robbed.

GASOLINE

There are plenty of gas stations in and near towns in Panama, and along the Panamerican Highway. Most are open 24 hours. On long trips fill your tank whenever you can, even if you've still got gas left, as the next station could be a long way away. An attendant always pumps the gas and doesn't expect a tip, though a small one is always appreciated. Both cash and credit cards are usually accepted.

Most rental cars run on premium unleaded gas, which is generally a bit more expensive than in the United States.

PARKING

On-street parking generally isn't a good idea in Panama City, as car theft is common. Instead, park in a guarded parking lot—many hotels have them. Many rental agencies insist you follow this rule. Restaurants often have free parking.

RENTAL CARS

Compact cars like a Kia Pinto, Ford Fiesta, VW Fox, or Toyota Yaris start at around $32 a day; for $40–$50 you can rent a Mitsubishi Lancer, a VW Golf, or a Polo. Four-wheel-drive pickups start at $70 a day, though for a 4WD with a full cabin you pay up to $120. International agencies sometimes have cheaper per-day rates, but locals undercut them on longer rentals. Stick shift is the norm in Panama, so check with the rental agency if you only drive an automatic.

Rental-car companies routinely accept driver's licenses from the United States, Canada, and most European countries. Most agencies require a major credit card for a deposit, and some require that you be over 25; they may charge extra insurance if you're not.

A 4WD (*doble tracción* or *cuatro por cuatro*) is only necessary for exploring the Darién, or for other off-road adventures. Many rental agencies prefer—or even stipulate—that you park your car in guarded lots or hotels with private parking, not on the street.

Contacts Avis (☎ 800/331–1084 or 507/238–4056 ⊕ www.avis.com).**Budget** (☎ 800/472–3325 or 507/263–8777 ⊕ www.budget.com). **Dollar** (☎ 866/700–9904 or 507/270–0355 ⊕ www.dollarpanama.com).**Hertz** (☎ 800/654–3001 or 507/260–2111 ⊕ www.hertz.com). **National** (☎ 800/227–7368 or 507/265–3333 ⊕ www.nationalcar.com).**Thrifty** (☎ 800/847–4389 or 507/204–9555 ⊕ www.thrifty.com).

RENTAL CAR INSURANCE

Everyone who rents a car wonders whether the insurance that the rental companies offer is worth the expense. No one—including us—has a simple answer. If you own a car, your personal auto insurance may cover a rental to some degree, though not all policies protect you abroad; always read your policy's fine print. If you don't have auto insurance, then seriously consider buying the collision- or loss-damage waiver (CDW or LDW) from the car-rental company, which eliminates your liability for damage to the car. Some credit cards offer CDW coverage, but it's usually supplemental to your own insurance and rarely covers SUVs, minivans, luxury models, and the like. If your coverage is secondary, you may still be liable for loss-of-use costs from the car-rental company. But no credit-card insurance is valid unless you use that card for *all* transactions, from reserving to paying the final bill. All companies exclude car rental in some countries, so be sure to find out about the destination to which you are traveling. It's sometimes cheaper to buy insurance as part of your general travel insurance policy.

Car rental agencies in Panama require basic third-party liability insurance, and the fee is included in their cheapest quoted rental price. Optional insurance to cover occupants and the deductible if you are in an accident deemed your fault is about $20 extra per day for a compact car.

ROADSIDE EMERGENCIES
Panama has no private roadside assistance clubs—ask rental agencies carefully about what you should do if you break down. If you have an accident, you are legally obliged to stay by your vehicle until the police arrive, which could take a long time. You can also call the transport police or, if you're near Panama City, the tourist police.

Emergency Services **National police** (🕾 *104 [emergencies]* 511–7000 *[information]*). **Tourist police** (🕾 *511–1929*). **Transport police** (🕾 *511–9313*).

ROAD CONDITIONS
The Panamerican Highway is paved along its entire length in Panama, and most secondary roads are paved, too. However, maintenance isn't always a regular process, so worn, pockmarked—or even potholed—surfaces are commonplace. Turnoffs are often sharp, and mountain roads can have terrifying hairpin bends.

In and around Panama City traffic is heavy. The mostly two-lane road from Panama City to the town of Colón is a nightmare between 8 and 9 in the morning and 5 and 6 in the afternoon because of rush-hour traffic. Two highways going north and south out of the city somewhat alleviate the congestion.

Turnoffs and distances are usually clearly signposted. Be especially watchful at traffic lights, as crossing on yellow (or even red) lights is common practice.

FROM PANAMA CITY	TO
Colón	89 km (55 mi)
Penonomé	150 km (93 mi)
Santiago	252 km (157 mi)
David	486 km (302 mi)
Boquete	515 km (320 mi)
Costa Rican Border	592 km (368 mi)

RULES OF THE ROAD
Drivers in Panama stick to the right—most of the time—as in the United States. You cannot turn right on a red light, but you wouldn't tell watching Panamanians drive. Seat belts are required, and the law is now enforced, though locals often still ignore it. Locals take speed-limit signs, the ban on driving with cell phones, and drinking and driving lightly, so drive very defensively. As you approach small towns, watch out for *topes,* the local name for speed bumps, which are often comically referred to as *policías muertos*, or dead cops.

Driving into Panama from Costa Rica is common practice. As well as car ownership papers, ID, and insurance, the only thing you'll need at the border is a lot of patience.

▌BY TAXI

Panamanian taxis range from sleek air-conditioned sedans to stuffy, banged-up rust buckets that seem to run off the sheer will of the driver. Hailing cabs on the street is widely considered safe and is your cheapest option for private (or semi-private) transportation around the city. Short hops are as little as $1; fares within town shouldn't top $3; a trip to an outlying area should run about $5. Unless you're paying for exclusive service (about $8–$10 per hour), drivers will pick up other people, provided they are headed in the same general direction and there is room in the vehicle.

Airport taxis and hotel taxis are nicer but considerably more expensive, so check to see if your hotel has shuttle service. You can also ask cab-hawkers or the tourist information booth at the Tocumen International Airport for a shared cab to the city, which can halve the up-to-$40 fare.

Don't feel obliged to tip, but city cab drivers who strictly adhere to low city fares are genuinely appreciative (and sometimes surprised by) the extra quarter or two. You may want to ask how much the fare is before getting aboard to avoid a tourist premium.

TRAVEL TIMES FROM PANAMA CITY		
To	By Air	By Bus
Bocas del Toro	1 hour	12 hours (to Almirante)
Chitré	½ hour	4 hours
Colón	¼ hour	½ hour
David	1 hour	6 hours
La Palma (Darién)	1½ hours	N/A
Las Tablas	N/A	4½ hours
San Blas	½ hour	N/A

▌BY TRAIN

Panama's only train service is the Panama Canal Railway, which operates between Panama City and Colón on weekdays. Tracks run alongside the canal itself and over causeways in Lago Gatún. The hour-long trip costs $22 each way; trains leave Panama City at 7:15 AM and Colón at 5:15 PM, Monday to Friday. There is no service on weekends and holidays. You can buy tickets at the station before you leave.

Information Panama Canal Railway
(☎ 507/317–6070 ⊕ www.panarail.com).

ESSENTIALS

■ ACCOMMODATIONS

Be it a 300-room behemoth or a bijoux B&B, a five-star chain dripping luxury or a one-off hostel packed with travelers, Panama has plenty of lodging options. "Hotel" isn't the only tag you'll find on accommodation: *hospedaje, pensión, casa de huespedes,* and *posada* also denote somewhere to stay. There are no hard-and-fast rules as to what each name means, though hotels and *posadas* tend to be higher-end places, whereas *hospedajes, pensiones,* and *casas de huespedes* are sometimes smaller and family run. A *residencial* can be a by-the-hour sort of place. Breakfast isn't always included in the room price.

The usual big international chain hotels have rooms and facilities equal to those at home, but usually lack a sense of place. If five-star luxury isn't your top priority, the best deals are undoubtedly with mid-range local hotels. Granted, there's no gym or conference center, but comfortable rooms with private bathrooms, hot water, and much more local character often come at a fraction of the cost of a big chain.

Lodges—both eco- and not-quite-so—are the thing in San Blas and Darién. Some are incredibly luxurious, others more back-to-nature; all are way off the beaten path, so plan on staying a few nights to offset travel time.

During the off-season, hotels will slash rack rates by as much as half.

■ **TIP**➔ Assume that hotels operate on the European Plan (**EP**, no meals) unless we specify that they use the Breakfast Plan (**BP**, with full breakfast), Continental Plan (**CP**, Continental breakfast), Full American Plan (**FAP**, all meals), Modified American Plan (**MAP**, breakfast and dinner) or are all-inclusive (**AI**, all meals and most activities).

For lodging price categories, consult the price charts found near the beginning of each chapter.

> **FODORS.COM CONNECTION**
>
> Before your trip, be sure to check out what other travelers are saying in Talk on www.fodors.com.

APARTMENT AND HOUSE RENTALS

Short-term furnished rentals aren't common in Panama. Ah! Panamá has a reasonable selection of luxurious properties, with prices starting at $2,000 a week. Away.com has rentals in its hotel section. Sublet.com and VRBO deal with more modest apartments, often as cheap as $700 a week.

Contacts Ah! Panamá (⊕ *www.ahpanama. com*). **Away.com** (⊕ *www.away.com*). **Sublet. com** (⊕ *www.sublet.com*).**VRBO** (⊕ *www.vrbo. com*).**Villas International** (☎ *415/499–9490 or 800/221—2260 in U.S.* ⊕ *www.villasintl. com*).

BED-AND-BREAKFASTS

The Panamanian definition of B&B might not coincide with yours: the term is frequently extended to luxury hotels that happen to include breakfast in their price. Indeed, these make up most of the pickings at Bed & Breakfast.com, BnB Finder, and Bed & Breakfast Inns Online. The longer lists at Ah! Panamá and A Thousand Inns include both these and homelier midrange establishments. For cheap, family-run places, try Traveller's Point.

Reservation Services A Thousand Inns (⊕ *www.1000inns.com*). **Ah! Panamá** (⊕ *www.ahpanama.com/travel_and_tourism/ bed_and_breakfast*). **Bed & Breakfast.com** (☎ *512/322–2710 or 800/462–2632* ⊕ *www. bedandbreakfast.com*) also sends out an online newsletter. **Bed & Breakfast Inns Online** (☎ *310/280–7365 or 800/280–4363* ⊕ *www. bbonline.com*). **BnB Finder.com** (☎ *212/432– 7693 or 888/469–6663* ⊕ *www.bnbfinder.com*). **Travellers' Point** (⊕ *www.travellerspoint.com*).

ECO-LODGES

In addition to hotels and hostels, Panama does a brisk trade in so-called eco-lodges, most of which are in the Darién and San Blas. If you are seriously interested in sustainable accommodation, it pays to do your research. The term *eco-lodge* is used freely, sometimes simply to describe a property in a rural or jungle location rather than somewhere that is truly sustainable. The International Ecotourism Society has online resources to help you pick somewhere really green. Responsible Travel is an online travel agency for ethical holidays.

Information International Ecotourism Society (⊕ *www.ecotourism.org*). **Responsible Travel** (⊕ *www.responsibletravel.com*).

HOSTELS

Panama is an established stop along the gringo trail and has a good selection of cheap, shared accommodation in small B&B–style hotels and in hostels. Budget lodging terminology varies: hostel, *hostal* and *la casa de* are commonplace names, and some places are just listed as a hotel or *pensión*. Most establishments have a choice of shared dorms or private rooms. Bathrooms are usually communal.

Staff in most Panamanian hostels are young, enthusiastic, and knowledgeable and can usually inform you about Spanish classes and excursions—many have in-house travel agencies. Hostels do tend to cater to party animals—a family-run hotel might be quieter.

Panama has no HI affiliates, but Traveller's Point and Hostel World have ample listings and booking services. Try to sort out your first nights in advance, then get recommendations from fellow travelers for your next port of call.

Contacts Hostels.com (⊕ *www.hostels.com*). **Hostel World.com** (⊕ *www.hostelworld.com*). **Travellers' Point** (⊕ *www.travellerspoint.com*)

▌COMMUNICATIONS

INTERNET

Internet access is widely available. Most midrange and top-end hotels in big cities have some kind of in-room access (often Wi-Fi) but you need to have a laptop. Computers for guest use are unusual in this kind of establishment, although hostels often have a PC or two for guests.

Panama has a dazzling selection of cyber-cafés. In Panama City it's hard to walk more than a block without tripping over one, and even remote locations usually have at least one. Rates usually range from 50¢ to $1 an hour. Broadband connections are common, and you can expect speeds on par with those in the United States. Many cybercafés also have Internet phone services.

Contacts Cybercafés (⊕ *www.cybercafes.com*) lists over 4,000 Internet cafés worldwide. **ClaroCOM** (☎ *200–0100* ⊕ *www.clarocom.com*) in the heart of El Cangrejo on Vía Veneto, is your best spot for Internet access and also offers 12 hours of Wi-Fi service for $3

PHONES

The country code for Panama is 507. To call Panama from the United States, dial the international access code (011), followed by the country code (507), and the 7-digit phone number, in that order. Note that cell phones have eight digits. Panama does not use area codes. To make collect or calling-card calls, dial 106 from any phone in Panama and an English-speaking operator will connect you.

CALLING WITHIN PANAMA

Panama's telephone system, operated by Cable and Wireless, is cheap and highly efficient. You can make local and long-distance calls from your hotel—usually with a surcharge—and from any public phone box. All local phone numbers have seven digits, except for cell phones, which have eight digits and start with a six.

The bright blue public phone boxes all take phone cards and some also accept coins; you insert coins or your card first, and then dial. You can also use prepaid calling cards from them free of charge. Standard local calls cost 10¢ a minute, less with a prepaid calling card (⇨ *Calling Cards, below)* such as ClaroCOM. For **local directory assistance** (in Spanish), dial 102.

CALLING OUTSIDE PANAMA

To make international calls from Panama, dial 00, then the country code, area code and number. The country code for the United States is 1.

Many cybercafés have Internet phone services: rates are often cheap (they're usually posted outside the shop), but communication quality can vary. You can also make international calls from pay phones using a prepaid card such as ClaroCOM. Dialing the international operator lets you make collect international calls. It's possible to use AT&T, Sprint, and MCI services from Panama, but using a prepaid card is cheaper.

CALLING CARDS

ClaroCOM are by far the best prepaid calling cards, and can be used to make local and international calls from any telephone in Panama. Calls both within Panama and to the United States cost as little as 5¢ a minute; cards come in denominations of $3, $5, $10, and $20. To use them, you dial a free local access number, then enter your PIN number and the number you want to call. You can buy cards from ClaroCOM's Web site, or from

CELL PHONE TIPS

You can purchase a cheap cell phone at numerous outlets and simply "top-up" (pay as you go). Incoming calls are free, and with the cheap cell, you'll have service even in many remote places. Have your family call you to save on roaming charges. Check with your cell-phone provider to see if you have international roaming on your phone.

supermarkets, drugstores, and pharmacies all over the country. Ask for *una tarjeta telefónica de prepago.*

Calling Card Information ClaroCOM
(☎ *200–0100* ⊕ *www.clarocom.com).*

MOBILE PHONES

Mobile phones are immensely popular in Panama. If you have an unlocked tri-band phone and intend to call local numbers, it makes sense to buy a prepaid Panamanian SIM card on arrival—rates will be much better than using your U.S. network. Alternatively, you can buy a cheap handset in Panama for $10–$20.

There are four main mobile-phone companies in Panama: Movistar, owned by Telefónica, Cable and Wireless (whose cellular phone division is called +Móvil), Digicel, and ClaroCOM. Their prices are similar, but Cable and Wireless is said to have better coverage in farther-flung areas of the country. You pay only for outgoing calls, which cost between 5¢ and 50¢ a minute. You can buy a SIM card (*tarjeta SIM*) from any outlet of either company; pay-as-you-go cards (*tarjeta de prepago para celular*) to charge your account are available from supermarkets, drugstores, gas stations, and kiosks.

You can also rent from companies like CellRent or from top-end hotels. A basic phone costs $5 a day, but you have to pay for incoming and outgoing calls, and for theft insurance, so buying a phone might be cheaper.

■ **TIP**➡ **If you travel internationally frequently, save one of your old mobile phones** or buy a cheap one on the Internet; ask your cell phone company to unlock it for you, and take it with you as a travel phone, buying a new SIM card with pay-as-you-go service in each destination.

Contacts Cellular Abroad (☎ 800/287–5072 ⊕ www.cellularabroad.com) rents and sells GMS phones and sells SIM cards that work in many countries. **Mobal** (☎ 888/888–9162 ⊕ www.mobalrental.com) rents mobiles and sells GSM phones (starting at $49) that operate in 140 countries. Per-call rates vary. **Planet Fone** (☎ 888/988–4777 ⊕ www.planetfone.com) rents cell phones, but the per-minute rates are expensive.

▮ CUSTOMS AND DUTIES

You may import 500 cigarettes (or 500 grams of tobacco or 50 cigars) and three bottles of alcohol duty-free. Panamanian customs can be very strict; even if you are only making an airline connection, make sure your papers are in order. You can import duty-free up to $2,000 of various goods; customs is not overly strict on applying duty to things such as personal photography gear that is clearly worth more than $2,000. Prescription drugs should always be accompanied by a doctor's prescription. When departing the country by land, travelers are not allowed to export any duty-free items. Duty-free items, by law, have to be shipped to a foreign address if the buyer is departing from the country by land.

U.S. Information U.S. Customs and Border Protection (⊕ www.cbp.gov).

▮ EATING OUT

Panama's cosmopolitan history is reflected in its food. Panama City has a great range of restaurants serving both local and international fare. Among the latter, Greek, Chinese, Italian, and American eateries are the most common. Fast-food outlets abound—some are names you'll recognize, others are local chains.

Traditional Panamanian food is often referred to as *comida típica*. As you'd expect in a country with so much coastline, seafood plays a big part in local dishes. *Corvina* (sea bass) is a favorite, as are prawns, which are one of the countries top export items. Another standout dish is *ceviche*, chilled, marinated seafood "cooked" using lime juice.

Chicken is the most common meat in Panama. It's the main ingredient, along with yucca, in *sancocho*, robust soup bursting with *culantro*, a powerful local version of cilantro. Rice and beans are as much a staple here as in the rest of Central America but are supplemented by yucca and plantains. Caribbean flavors like lime and coconut milk are common on the northern coast.

Popular snacks include tamales (ground maize stuffed with meat and cooked wrapped inside a banana leaf) and Panama-style tortillas (deep-fried burger-sized patties of corn dough, often topped or filled with cheese). Follow them with Panama's version of flan (akin to crème caramel), the most popular local dessert.

Panama has a fabulous range of tropical fruits, but they're usually sold as a juice, called *chicha*, or shake (either with milk or with water; ask if you don't want extra sugar added). Forget about cutting down your cholesterol while you're in Panama: deep-frying is a way of life here. Goodies to go out of the way for include *patacones* (twice-fried rounds of plantain) and *hojal-dras* (deep-fried flaky dough).

Panamanians might not eat huge quantities of meat, but somehow shredded chicken, ground beef, ham, or meat stock manages to make its way into most dishes, so truly vegetarian options are limited. Remember that in Spanish *carne* (meat) usually refers to red meat, so don't be surprised to get fish or chicken if you ask for something "*sin carne*" (without meat).

Eateries offering traditional Panamanian fare for locals are cheap—you can get a full plate of beans or lentils and rice and fried chicken for as little as $3. Most restaurants, however, charge U.S.-level prices for meals.

MEALS AND MEALTIMES

A typical Panamanian breakfast (*desayuno*) consists of fried tortillas or hojaldras, washed down with coffee. Most hotels catering to foreigners also offer fruit, toast, and cereal, and you can expect breakfast buffets at five-star hotels.

Lunch (*comida* or *almuerzo*) is the main meal and is generally served around midday. Many restaurants do set-price meals of two or three courses at lunch. In Panamanian homes dinner is often merely a light snack eaten around 9 PM. If you're eating out, dinner is just as big a deal as in the United States, but is usually served until 10:30 PM.

Unless otherwise noted, the restaurants listed in this guide are open daily for lunch and dinner.

PAYING

In restaurants with waiter service you pay the check (*la cuenta*) at the end of the meal. You'll usually have to ask for the check; sometimes more than once. In fast-food restaurants and at food stands, you generally pay up-front. Credit cards are accepted in more expensive restaurants, but it's always a good idea to check before you order, especially as some establishments only accept one kind of credit card.

RESERVATIONS AND DRESS

We only mention reservations when they are essential (there's no other way you'll ever get a table) or when they are not accepted. We mention dress only when men are required to wear a jacket or a jacket and tie.

WINES, BEER, AND SPIRITS

Alcohol is available in just about every restaurant in Panama, though cheaper places have limited selections.

For meals and light drinking, beer—usually lager—is the local favorite. Good brands made in Panama include Balboa, Atlas, Panamá, and Soberana, but North American and European brands are also widely available. For more serious drinking, Panamanians reach for a bottle of *seco*, a fierce white rum that gets you under the table in no time. Seco is often mixed with cranberry juice.

Wine still isn't a big thing in Panama, but most decent restaurants have imported bottles from the United States or Chile and Argentina. Imported liquor is also easy to find in supermarkets.

■ ELECTRICITY

You won't need a converter or adapter, as the electrical current in Panama is 110 volts, the same as in the United States. Outlets take either plugs with two flat prongs or two flat prongs with a circular grounded prong.

■ EMERGENCIES

Dial 104 for **police** and 103 for **fire**.

In a medical or dental emergency, ask your hotel staff for information on and directions to the nearest private hospital or clinic. Taxi drivers should also know how to find one, and taking a taxi is often quicker than an ambulance. There is no centralized ambulance service, so if you do need an ambulance, call for one from the hospital you want to go to; alternatively, you can call the Red Cross or SEMM, a private ambulance service. Many private medical insurers provide online lists of hospitals and clinics in different towns. It's a good idea to print out a copy of these before you travel.

For theft, wallet loss, small road accidents, and minor emergencies, contact the nearest police station. Expect all dealings with the police to be a bureaucratic business—it's probably only worth bothering if you need the report for insurance claims.

Most embassies in the capital open at 8:30 and close by noon.

The Hospital Nacional is an excellent private hospital with English-speaking doctors, a 24-hour emergency room, and specialists in many areas. The Centro Médico Paitilla is the country's best, and most expensive, hospital. The Clínica Bella Vista is a private clinic with English-speaking doctors. To take advantage of Panama's state-run health care, head to the public Hospital Santo Tomás.

Pack a basic first-aid kit, especially if you're venturing into more remote areas. If you'll be carrying any medication, bring your doctor's contact information and prescription authorizations. Getting your prescription filled in Panama might be problematic, so bring enough medication for your entire trip.

Two chains of 24-hour supermarket/pharmacies—Arrocha and Rey—have numerous branches.

Foreign Embassies U.S. Embassy (✉ *Avenida Demetrio B. Lakes no. 783Clayton* ☎ *507/207–7000*).

∎ HEALTH

It's safe to drink tap water and have ice in your drinks in urban areas, but stick to bottled water in rural areas.

Two mosquito-borne diseases are prevalent in Panama: dengue fever (especially in Bocas del Toro) and malaria (in the Darién, Bocas del Toro, and San Blas). Prevention is better than a cure: cover up your arms and legs and use a strong insect repellent containing a high concentration

of DEET. Don't hang around outside at sunset, and sleep under a mosquito net in jungle areas. Preventive antimalarial medication may also be necessary: consult your doctor well before you travel. There are no preventive drugs for dengue.

Sunburn and sunstroke are potential health hazards when visiting Panama. Stay out of the sun at midday and use plenty of high-SPF-factor sunscreen when on the beach or hiking. You can buy well-known brands in most Panamanian pharmacies. Protect your eyes with good-quality sunglasses, and bear in mind that you'll burn more easily at higher altitudes and in the water.

OVER-THE-COUNTER REMEDIES

In Panama *farmacias* (drugstores) sell a wide range of medications over the counter, including some, but not all, drugs that would require a prescription in the United States. Familiar brands are easy to find, otherwise ask for what you want with the generic name. Note that acetaminophen—or Tylenol—is called *paracetamol* in Panama (just as in the U.K.). Farmacia Rey and Farmacia Arrocha are two local drugstore chains with branches all over the country, many of which are open 24 hours.

Information Farmacia Arrocha (⊕ *www. arrocha.com*). **Farmacia Rey** (⊕ *www.smrey. com/smr/_farmacia/farmacia.asp*).

SHOTS AND MEDICATIONS

If you're traveling anywhere outside the Canal Zone, you need a yellow fever vaccination. Remember to keep the certificate and carry it with you, as you may be asked to show it when entering another country after leaving Panama.

The CDC recommends mefloquine, proguanil, or doxycycline as preventive antimalarials for adults and infants in Panama if you are going to enter a malaria zone. To be effective, the weekly doses must start a week before you travel and continue four weeks after your return. There is no preventive medication for dengue.

Health Warnings National Centers for Disease Control & Prevention (*CDC* ☏ *877/394-8747 international travelers' health line* ⊕ *www.cdc.gov/travel*). **World Health Organization** (*WHO* ⊕ *www.who.int*).

■ HOURS OF OPERATION

Businesses and government offices typically open weekdays between 8 and 9 AM and close between 4 and 6 PM; many keep these hours on Saturdays, too. Banks open between 8 AM and 3 PM, but ATMs are usually open 24 hours. Standard hours for shops are 9 AM–6 PM, but malls are open a couple of hours longer. Restaurants are generally open until 10:30 PM, as dinner in Panama is eaten later than in the rest of Central America.

HOLIDAYS

Panama's national holidays for 2008 and 2009 are as follows: Año Nuevo (New Year's Day), January 1; Día de los Mártires (Martyrs' Day), January 9; Martes de Carnaval (Carnival Tuesday), Día del Trabajador (Labor Day), May 1; Día de los Difuntos (All Souls' Day), November 2; Día de la Independencia (Independence Day from Colombia), November 3; Primer Grito de la Independencia (First Cry of Independence), November 10; Día de la Emancipación (Emancipation Day from Spain), November 28; Día de la Madre (Mother's Day), December 8; Navidad (Christmas), December 25. Holy Week and the week around Christmas and Carnaval might as well be holidays.

Each region also has its own holidays, and many towns have saint's days.

■ MAIL

Panama's national mail system is called Correo Nacional, or COTEL. There are branches in most cities and towns; standard opening hours are 7 AM to 5 PM. It's best to send mail from big cities—the more remote the origin of your letter, the better the chances of its getting lost. An airmail letter to the United States costs

35¢ and takes a week or two to arrive if posted from Panama City.

You can receive mail by Entrega General (general delivery) at most post offices. Letters should be addressed as follows: [Name on your passport], Entrega General, [city], [province], República de Panamá. There's a Panama City, Florida, so be sure to include the "República de Panamá." Note that for letters to Panama City you also need to include the post office number where you want to receive the correspondence.

Airbox is a private mail company with both incoming and outgoing services to and from the United States. Their standard charge for sending documents is $3.50.

Information Airbox (☏ *269-9774* ⊕ *www. airbox.com.pa*). **Correo Nacional** (☏ *212-7600* ⊕ *www.correos.gob.pa*).

SHIPPING PACKAGES

Sending packages home through COTEL isn't always reliable, so it's worth paying the extra for recorded delivery (*correo registrado*). Most packages take anywhere from a week to a month to arrive in the United States. Many stores—particularly upmarket ones—can ship your purchases for you, for a price. Valuable items are best sent with private express services. International couriers operating in Panama include DHL and Federal Express—overnight delivery for a 1-kg (2.2-pound) package starts at about $100. Sending a 1-kg package to the United States with Airbox costs $8.75 and takes two to three days.

Contacts Airbox (☏ *269-9774* ⊕ *www.airbox. com.pa*). **DHL Worldwide Express** (☏ *271-3510* ⊕ *www.dhl.com*). **Federal Express** (☏ *271-3838* ⊕ *www.fedex.com*).

■ MONEY

Although Panama is more expensive than the rest of Central America, prices sometimes compare favorably to those back home. Midrange hotels and restaurants where locals eat are excellent value. Rooms at first-class hotels and meals at the best restaurants, however, approach those in the United States. Trips into remote parts of the country and adventure travel are also relatively inexpensive.

You can plan your trip around ATMs—cash is king for day-to-day dealings—and credit cards (for bigger spending). U.S. dollars are the local currency; changing any other currency can be problematic. Traveler's checks are useful only as a reserve.

Using large bills is often a problem in Panama, even in big shops or expensive restaurants. Trying to pay for a $3 purchase with a twenty may get you dirty looks, or just a straight "no." Have plenty of ones and fives at hand. Shop owners are wary of forged bills and may record the serial number of $50 or $100 bills, along with your name and passport number; often, they won't even accept bills larger than $20.

Prices throughout this guide are given for adults. Substantially reduced fees are almost always available for children, students, and senior citizens.

ATMS AND BANKS

ATMs—known locally as *cajeros automáticos*—are extremely common in Panama. In big cities even supermarkets and department stores usually have their own ATM. On-screen instructions appear in English; you are usually prompted to select your language. Using large bills can be tricky in Panama; thankfully, most ATMs don't dispense anything larger than a $20. Make withdrawals from ATMs in daylight rather than at night.

To reduce the burden of fees, you may want to make maximum withdrawals of $500.

The main ATM network, which accepts cards with both Cirrus and Plus symbols, is called Sistema Clave. Its Web site lists ATM locations all over the country. Major banks in Panama include Banistmo, Banco General, and Banco Continental. Many international banks also have branches in Panama City.

Information Sistema Clave (⊕ www.sclave. com).

CREDIT CARDS

Throughout this guide, the following abbreviations are used: **AE**, American Express; **DC**, Diners Club; **MC**, Master-Card; and **V**, Visa.

It's a good idea to inform your credit-card company before you travel, especially if you're going abroad and don't travel internationally very often. Otherwise, the credit-card company might put a hold on your card owing to unusual activity—not a good thing halfway through your trip. Record all your credit-card numbers—as well as the phone numbers to call if your cards are lost or stolen—in a safe place, so you're prepared should something go wrong. Both MasterCard and Visa have general numbers you can call (collect if you're abroad) if your card is lost, but you're better off calling the number of your issuing bank, since Master-Card and Visa usually just transfer you to your bank; your bank's number is usually printed on your card.

Credit cards are widely accepted in Panama's urban areas. Visa is the most popular, followed by MasterCard and American Express. Diners Club and Discovery are rarely accepted. If possible, bring more than one credit card, as smaller establishments sometimes accept only one type. In small towns only top-end hotels and restaurants take plastic.

Reporting Lost Cards American Express (☎ 800/528–4800 in U.S., 336/393–1111 collect from abroad ⊕ www.americanexpress. com). **MasterCard** (☎ 800/627–8372 in U.S., 636/722–7111 collect from abroad ⊕ www. mastercard.com).**Visa** (☎ 800/847–2911 in U.S., 410/581–9994 collect from abroad ⊕ www. visa.com).

CURRENCY AND EXCHANGE

Panama's national currency is the U.S. dollar. Don't get confused if you see prices expressed in *balboas*: it's just the local name for the dollar. All bills come in standard American denominations, although Panama also issues its own version of pennies, nickels, dimes, quarters and 50-cent pieces. If you get stuck with these at the end of the trip, you can use them in parking meters, ticket machines, and phones back home. Try to avoid coming to Panama with other currencies, as the exchange rates are generally unfavorable.

■ PACKING

They don't call Panama City "the Miami of the South" for nothing: looks (and being looked at) are important here, and city-slicker locals aren't impressed by sloppy appearances. Think capri pants, skirts, or khakis for urban sightseeing, with something a little dressier for eating out at night. Shorts, T-shirts, tank tops, and bikinis are all acceptable at the beach or farther afield. Leave flashy jewelry behind—it only makes you a target.

"Insect repellent, sunscreen, sunglasses" is your packing mantra; long-sleeve shirts and long pants also help protect your skin from the relentless sun and ferocious mosquitoes. Panama's rainy season lasts from mid-April to December, and rain is common at other times, too, so a foldable umbrella or waterproof jacket is a must. So are sturdy walking boots if you're planning any serious hiking, otherwise sneakers or flats are fine. A handbag-size flashlight is also very useful: blackouts are more common than at home.

In the Darién, a camping mosquito net is invaluable when staying at places with no screens in the windows (or no windows at all). A water purifier and lots of plastic bags are also helpful in the jungle. So much for packing light.

Tissues and antibacterial hand wipes make trips to public toilets a bit pleasanter.

Finding your preferred brands of condoms and tampons in Panama can be hit and miss, so bring necessary supplies of both. All the familiar toiletry brands are widely available.

■ PASSPORTS AND VISAS

Most travelers from Western countries can visit Panama for up to 90 days with the purchase (on arrival) of a $5 tourist visa; you can buy this upon arrival or at the check-in desk of some airlines. The visa may actually say it is valid for only 30 days so ask the usually friendly officer to write "*90 días*" by the stamp on the visa.

Arriving tourists are technically required to show proof that their travels continue beyond Panama. Usually a return ticket will suffice. Airlines are often more demanding than immigration officials on this particular issue: If you don't have a return ticket they might not let you board the plane.

It is not easy to extend your stay in Panama unless you are a retiree investing in property or sponsored by an employer. Immigration offices are inept at best, corrupt at worst, and are more about keeping a huge cadre of lawyers employed. Further, under Panamanian law you can't legally represent yourself at immigration; you are required to have a lawyer do that for you for all but the simplest procedures.

There are immigration offices in Panama City, David, Santiago, Chitré, and at border crossings. Offices are open around 8–3. If you need to extend your stay, grab a cheap round-trip flight to Colombia or Costa Rica (or take the bus to Costa Rica) to qualify for a new entry visa.

Information Consulate of Panama in Washington, D.C. (☎ 202/483–1407 ⊕ *www. embassyofpanama.org*). **Oficina de Migración** (*for visa extension* ⊠ *Av. Cuba and Calle 28, Panama City* ☎ 507/507–1800 ⊕ *www. migracion.gob.pa*).

■ TIP→ **Medical staff at Panamanian public hospitals are well-trained and professional. However, hospitals are underfunded and often lack supplies: as a rule, you're best going to a private clinic, which means medical insurance is a must.**

■ RESTROOMS

Rest rooms in Panama use Western-style toilets. Cleanliness standards vary widely, especially in public facilities such as bus and gas stations. Toilet paper isn't guaranteed, so carry tissues in your day pack. Antibacterial hand wipes—for sanitizing you or the facilities—are also useful.

Find a Loo The Bathroom Diaries (⊕ *www. thebathroomdiaries.com*) is flush with unsanitized info on restrooms the world over—each one located, reviewed, and rated.

■ SAFETY

As Latin American countries go, Panama is relatively safe. In most of the country crime against tourists is usually limited to pickpocketing and bag snatching. Taking a few simple precautions is usually enough to keep you from being a target.

In urban areas attitude is essential. Strive to look aware and purposeful at all times. Look at maps before you go outside, not on a street corner; and keep a firm hold on your purse. At night exercise the same kind of caution you would in any big American city and stay in well-lit areas with plenty of people around. Ask hotel or restaurant staff to call you a taxi at night, rather than flagging one down. If you're driving, park in guarded lots, never on the street; and remove the front of the stereo if that's possible.

In Panama City, the Casco Viejo has a sketchy reputation after dark. It's also best to steer clear of the neighborhoods of El Chorrillo, parts of Caledonia away from the parallel thoroughfares of Peru and Cuba avenues, and El Marañón, where muggings are commonplace. Finally, local drivers are a danger to pedestrians in all the city's neighborhoods, so look twice (or thrice) before crossing the street.

Two places in the country are blots on Panama's safety reputation. The city of Colón is a hot spot for violent crime, and most locals warn against wandering its streets alone. Bordering Colombia, the Darién Province is a largely impenetrable jungle far from the reach of the law. Colombian guerrillas or paramilitary forces have kidnapped tourists crossing the border overland. Drug traffickers ply the region, and the small boats running between the two countries on both the Caribbean and the Pacific are often involved in smuggling. Visiting the Darién on an organized tour is the smart choice.

The most important advice we can give you is that in the unlikely event of being mugged or robbed, do not put up a struggle. Nearly all physical attacks on tourists are the direct result of their resisting would-be pickpockets or muggers. Comply with demands, hand over your stuff, and try to get the situation over with as quickly as possible—then let your travel insurance take care of it.

Report any crimes to the nearest police station. In Panama City you can also ask English-speaking tourist police (identifiable by a white armband) for help. Panamanian police are usually helpful when dealing with foreigners. However, their resources are limited: they'll happily provide you with reports for insurance claims, but tracking down your stolen goods is pretty unlikely.

In Panama you're legally obliged to carry ID—preferably your passport—with you at all times. If you prefer to keep your passport safe, laminate a color copy of the photo page and carry that, together with your driver's license or other photo ID. You may be asked for proof of your identity when dealing with the police, and you can be fined $10 or hauled away if you don't have ID.

■ TIP→ **Distribute your cash, credit cards, IDs, and other valuables between a deep** front pocket, an inside jacket or vest pocket, and a hidden money pouch. Don't reach for the money pouch once you're in public.

Contact **Transportation Security Administration** (*TSA;* ⊕ *www.tsa.gov*).

GOVERNMENT ADVISORIES

Most government advisories warn against independent travel to the Darién region, which borders Colombia. Its dense rain forest has long made it the ideal hideout for Colombian guerrillas and paramilitary forces and drug-smuggling gangs from both countries. Going with an organized tour group that has a good reputation and local contacts is the safe option.

General Information and Warnings Australian Department of Foreign Affairs and Trade (⊕ *www.smartraveller.gov.au*). **Consular Affairs Bureau of Canada** (⊕ *www.voyage. gc.ca*). **U.K. Foreign & Commonwealth Office** (⊕ *www.fco.gov.uk/travel*). **U.S. Department of State** (⊕ *www.travel.state.gov*).

∎ TAXES

Panama has a value-added sales tax (IVA) of 5%–10%, which is usually included in the displayed price. Hotels also have a 10% tax. Visitors departing by air are charged an exit tax of $20, though this is usually included in your ticket.

∎ TIME

Panama is five hours behind GMT, the same as U.S. Eastern Standard Time. Panama does not observe Daylight Savings.

Time Zones Timeanddate.com (⊕ *www. timeanddate.com/worldclock*).

∎ TIPPING

In Panama tipping is a question of rewarding good service rather than an obligation. Restaurant bills don't include gratuities; adding 10% is customary. Bellhops and maids expect tips only in more expensive hotels, and $1–$2 per bag is the norm. You should also give a tip of up to $10 per day to tour guides. Rounding up taxi fares is a way of showing your appreciation to the driver, but it's not expected.

∎ TOURS

Panama has some very professional guides and travel professionals who will take you just about anywhere you want to go or customize a trip for you. Ancon Expeditions has some of the country's best eco-adventure trips, as well as terrific day trips, and educational volunteering opportunities. Eco Circuitos is also one of the country's most reputable tour operators.

∎ TRIP INSURANCE

Comprehensive travel policies typically cover trip cancellation and interruption, letting you cancel or cut your trip short because of a personal emergency, illness, or, in some cases, acts of terrorism in your destination. Such policies also cover evacuation and medical care. Some also cover you for trip delays because of bad weather or mechanical problems as well as for lost or delayed baggage. Another type of coverage to look for is financial default—that is, when your trip is disrupted because a tour operator, airline, or cruise line goes out of business. Generally you must buy this when you book your trip or shortly thereafter, and it's only available to you if your operator isn't on a list of excluded companies.

At the very least, consider buying medical-only coverage. Neither Medicare nor some private insurers cover medical expenses anywhere outside of the United States (including time aboard a cruise ship, even if it leaves from a U.S. port). Medical-only policies typically reimburse you for medical care (excluding that related to pre-existing conditions) and hospitalization abroad and provide for evacuation. You still have to pay the bills and await reimbursement from the insurer, though.

Another option is to sign up with a medical-evacuation assistance company. A membership in one of these companies gets you doctor referrals, emergency evacuation or repatriation, 24-hour hotlines for medical consultation, and other assistance. International SOS Assistance Emergency and AirMed International provide evacuation services and medical referrals. MedjetAssist offers medical evacuation.

Expect comprehensive travel insurance policies to cost about 4% to 7% or 8% of the total price of your trip (it's more like 8%–12% if you're over age 70). A medical-only policy may or may not be cheaper than a comprehensive policy. Always read the fine print of your policy to make sure that you are covered for the risks that are of most concern to you. Compare several policies to make sure you're getting the best price and range of coverage available.

■ TIP→ OK. You know you can save a bundle on trips to warm-weather destinations by traveling in rainy season. But there's also a chance that a severe storm will disrupt your plans. The solution? Look for hotels and resorts that offer storm/hurricane guarantees. Although they rarely allow refunds, most guarantees do let you rebook later if a storm strikes.

Insurance Comparison Sites InsureMyTrip. com (☎ 800/487–4722 ⊕ www.insuremytrip. com). SquareMouth.com (☎ 800/240–0369 or 727/490–5803 ⊕ www.squaremouth.com).

Medical Assistance Companies AirMed International Medical Group (⊕ www. airmed.com) International SOS (⊕ www. internationalsos.com). MedjetAssist (⊕ www.medjetassist.com).

Medical-Only Insurers International Medical Group (☎ 800/628–4664 ⊕ www.imglobal. com). Wallach & Company (☎ 800/237–6615 or 540/687–3166 ⊕ www.wallach.com).

Comprehensive Travel Insurers Access America (☎ 800/284–8300 ⊕ www. accessamerica.com). AIG Travel Guard (☎ 800/826–4919 ⊕ www.travelguard.com).

CSA Travel Protection (☎ 800/711–1197 ⊕ www.csatravelprotection.com). HTH Worldwide (☎ 610/254–8700 ⊕ www.hthworldwide. com). Travelex Insurance (☎ 888/228–9792 ⊕ www.travelex-insurance.com). Travel Insured International (☎ 800/243–3174 ⊕ www.travelinsured.com).

■ VISITOR INFORMATION

The Autoridad de Turismo Panama (Panamanian Tourism Authority, ATP) is Panama's official tourism organization. Its bilingual Web site is an excellent pretrip planning resource: there are overviews of Panama's regions and links to tour operators and hotels

ATP has 15 offices around Panama, open weekdays 8–3:30. The English-speaking staff at ATP offices are friendly and helpful. Their resources—mostly Panama City brochures—tend to plug local tour companies rather than aid independent touring.

Other resources include *The Visitor,* a small, free paper that can be found at most hotels and travel agencies, and *Panama*

Planner an excellent tourism magazine, available at large hotels.

Contacts Autoridad de Turismo Panama (*ATP* ☎ *800/962–1526 in the U.S.; 507/526–7000 in Panama* ⊕ *www.visitpanama.com*).

ONLINE TRAVEL TOOLS

All About Panama Explore Panama (⊕ *www.explorepanama.com*) is one-stop shopping for Panama Tourism 101. **Extreme Panama** (⊕ *www.extremepanama.com*) is a good resource for outdoors and adventure travel in Panama.**Hasta Tarde** (⊕ *www.hastatarde.com*) has comprehensive listings of Panama's cultural goings-on; nightlife features heavily.**Museo de Arte Contemporáneo** (⊕ *www.macpanama.org*) is Panama City's contemporary arts museum. **Panama**

Audubon Society (⊕ *www.panamaaudubon.org*) promotes bird-watching and bird protection in Panama.Packed with maps, listings, and advice, **Panama Info** (⊕ *www.panamainfo.com*) is an excellent resource if you're traveling—or moving—to Panama. **Panama Canal Authority** (⊕ *www.pancanal.com*) has history, photos, and even live Webcasts of Panama's most famous feature. Part online newspaper, part travel guide, **Panama Guide** (⊕ *www.panama-guide.com*) has lots of up-to-date information about what's going on in Panama. **The Panama Report** (⊕ *www.thepanamareport.com*) is full of amusing and helpful articles about travel and life in Panama, as well as lots of investment sales pitches.

INDEX

A

Achiote Road, *134*
Achutupo, *305, 310–312*
Adventure tours, *325–327*
Airports, *338*
Air travel
Azuero Peninsula, 183
Bocas del Toro Archipeligo,
262–263
Central Panama, 110
charter flights, 339
Chiriquí Province, 217–218
Eastern Panama, 298
flights, 338–339
Panama Canal and environs,
110
Panama City, 31
travel times from Panama City,
343
Veraguas, 183
Alberto's✕, *66*
Alcoholic drinks, *348*
Aligandi, *310*
Al Natural⊡, *291–292*
Alto Bayano, *148–149*
Ancon Expeditions, *101*
Apartment rentals, *344*
Aquariums, *52*
ATMs, *351*
ATP (Autoridad de Tourismo
Panama), *268*
Azuero Peninsula, *8, 16,*
182–206
dining, 184, 185, 194, 198, 199
emergencies, 185
history of, 188
lodging, 184, 185, 194, 198,
199, 202, 204–205, 208
orientation, 182
price categories, 185
shopping, 190
sports and the outdoors,
199–201, 203, 205–206
top reasons to go, 184
transportation, 183–184
visitor information, 185
when to go, 183

B

Baha'i House of Worship, *56*
Bahia Honda, *287–288*
Bahía Piñas, *319–320*
Bajo Mono Road, *234*
Balenario Mojagua, *223*
Bambito, *252–253*
Bamboleo (dance club), *96*

Bamboo (bar), *93*
Bananas Village Resort✕ ⊡,
141
Banks, *351*
Barro Colorado, *46*
Bars, *91–93*
Basílica Menor Santiago Após-
tol, *186*
Bastimentos Town, *284–287*
Beaches, *11*
adventure tours, 327, 331
Azuero Peninsula, 200,
201–206
Bocas del Toro Archipeligo,
268, 270, 278, 292
Central Panama, 139, 142, 158,
160, 161–169
Chiriquí Province, 226–227
Panama City, 100
rip currents, 169
Veraguas, 209–211
Bed-and-breakfasts, *344*
Beirut✕, *69*
Biking
adventure tours, 326
Bocas del Toro Archipeligo, 268
Central Panama, 177
Chiriquí Province, 247
Panama Canal and environs,
121–122
Panama City, 100
Bird-watching, *11*
adventure tours, 333–335
Central Panama, 134, 139, 177
Chiriquí Province, 246, 250,
257
Eastern Panama, 318
Panama Canal and environs,
120–121, 125, 127
Panama City, 100–101
quetzal birds, 238–239
Bluff Beach, *278*
Boat and ferry travel, *339–340*
Azuero Peninsula, 184
Bocas del Toro Archipeligo, 264
Central Panama, 110
Eastern Panama, 299
Panama Canal and environs,
110
Veraguas, 184
Boca Chica, *227–230*
Boca del Drago, *278*
Bocas Butterfly Garden, *270*
Bocas del Toro Archipeligo, *8,*
10, 260–293
dining, 265, 286
emergencies, 266

history of, 263
Isla Bastimentos, 283–284
lodging, 265, 279, 281–282,
283, 286, 288, 289–290,
291–292
orientation, 261–262
price categories, 265
sports and the outdoors, 280,
282, 286–287, 290
top reasons to go, 262
transportation, 262–265
Western Archipelago, 266–283
when to go, 262
Bocas del Toro Town, *266–278*
dining, 270–272
exploring, 268–270
lodging, 272–275
nightlife, 275
shopping, 277–278
sports and the outdoors,
275–277
Books on Panama, *355*
Boquete, *233–237, 240–248*
dining, 237, 240–241
exploring, 234–235, 237
lodging, 241–245
nightlife, 245
shopping, 248
sports and the outdoors,
246–248
transportation, 234
Boquete Garden Inn ⊡, *241*
Border crossings, *291*
Breezes Panama ⊡, *166*
Bristol, The✕ ⊡, *78–79*
Buena Vista Bar & Grill✕, *270*
Burbayar Lodge⊡, *149*
Bus travel
Bocas del Toro Archipeligo,
264–265
Central Panama, 110
Chiriquí Province, 218
Eastern Panama, 299
Panama Canal and environs,
110
Panama City, 31, 52
travel times from Panama City,
343
Butterfly gardens, *270*

C

Cabañas Las Veraneras✕ ⊡,
167
Café Barko ✕, *66*
Café René✕, *62–63*
Café Ruiz, *234–235*

NOTES

NOTES

NOTES

NOTES

ABOUT OUR WRITERS

As a freelance journalist and author, **Marlise Elizabeth Kast** has contributed to more than 50 publications, including *Forbes*, *Surfer*, *San Diego Magazine*, and *New York Post*. Her passion for traveling has taken her to 60 countries, including short-term residencies in Switzerland, the Dominican Republic, Spain, and Costa Rica. Following the release of her memoir, *Tabloid Prodigy*, Marlise contributed to the 2009 and 2010 editions of *Fodor's Mexico*, *Fodor's San Diego 2009*, and *Fodor's Puerto Rico 2010*. For *Fodor's Panama*, she updated the Chiriquí Province and Bocas del Toro chapters. She has also written *Day & Overnight Hikes on California's Pacific Crest Trail*, published by Wilderness Press. Marlise recently completed a 13-month surfing and snowboarding expedition through 28 countries. Now based in San Diego, she is currently working on her next full-length manuscript. For more information, visit www.marlisekast.com.

Sean Mattson is a Canadian print journalist and occasional travel writer with more than ten years of experience in Mexico and Central America. He is currently based in Panama City and works primarily for Reuters. For this edition of *Fodor's Panama*, he updated the Panama City, Azuero Peninsula, and Travel Smart chapters.

San José, Costa Rica–based freelance writer **Jeffrey Van Fleet** never passes up the chance to travel to Panama and experience its vibrant, cosmopolitan diversity. He can frequently be seen at the Miraflores Locks admiring the engineering marvel that is the Panama Canal. Jeff updated the Canal and Central Panama, and Eastern Panama chapters for this edition. He has also contributed to Fodor's guides to Costa Rica, Guatemala, Los Cabos and Baja California, Peru, Chile, Argentina, and Central and South America.